# PRAISE FOR
# THE OUTLANDER NOVELS

## OUTLANDER

"Riveting. Gabaldon has a true storyteller's voice."
—*The Globe and Mail*

"Absorbing and heartwarming . . . lavishly evokes the land and lore of Scotland."
—*Publishers Weekly*

"History comes deliciously alive on the page."
—*Daily News* (N.Y.)

## DRAGONFLY IN AMBER

"A triumph! A powerful tale layered in history and myth. I loved every page."—Nora Roberts

"Compulsively readable."—*Publishers Weekly*

"Diana Gabaldon is a born storyteller . . . the pages practically turn themselves."
—*Arizona Republic*

*Please turn the page for more extraordinary acclaim. . . .*

## VOYAGER

"Triumphant . . . Her use of historical detail and a truly adult love story confirm Gabaldon as a superior writer."
—*Publishers Weekly*

"Fine, thrilling writing."
—*The Globe and Mail*

"Memorable storytelling."
—*The Seattle Times*

## DRUMS OF AUTUMN

"Unforgettable characters . . . richly embroidered with historical detail . . . I just can't put it down."
—*The Cincinnati Post*

"Passionate . . . remarkable—a mix of history, fantasy, romance and unabashedly ribald storytelling."
—*The Arizona Republic*

"Wonderful . . . This is escapist historical fiction at its best."
—*San Antonio Express-News*

*Also by Diana Gabaldon*

# DIANA GABALDON

# THE FIERY CROSS

SEAL BOOKS

Seal Books and colophon are trademarks of
Random House of Canada Limited.

THE FIERY CROSS
Seal Books/published by arrangement with Delacorte Press
Delacorte Press edition published 2001
Seal Books edition published March 2004

ISBN 0-7704-2797-9

Cover illustration courtesy of Diana Gabaldon and Running Changes, Inc.

Seal Books are published by Random House of Canada Limited.
"Seal Books" and the portrayal of a seal are the property of
Random House of Canada Limited.

Visit Random House of Canada Limited's website: www.randomhouse.ca

PRINTED AND BOUND IN THE USA

OPM   10  9  8  7  6  5  4  3  2  1

*This book is for my Sister, Theresa Gabaldon,*
*with whom I told the first Stories.*

# ACKNOWLEDGMENTS

The author's profound thanks to . . .

. . . my editor, Jackie Cantor, always the book's champion above all.

. . . my agent, Russ Galen, who's always on my side, with shield and lance.

. . . Stacey Sakal, Tom Leddy, and the other wonderful Production people who have sacrificed their time, talent, and mental health to the production of this book.

. . . Kathy Lord, that rarest and most delightful of creatures, an excellent copy editor.

. . . Virginia Norey, the book's designer *(aka Book Goddess)*, who somehow managed to fit the Whole Thing between two covers and make it look great.

. . . Irwyn Applebaum and Nita Taublib, publisher and deputy publisher, who came to the party, and brought their stuff.

. . . Rob Hunter and Rosemary Tolman, for unpublished information on the War of the Regulation and their very colorful and interesting ancestors, James Hunter and Hermon Husband. *(No, I don't make all these people up; just some of them.)*

. . . Beth and Matthew Shope, and Liz Gaspar, for information on North Carolina Quaker history and beliefs. *(And we do note as a matter of strict accuracy that Hermon Husband was not technically a Quaker at the time of this story, having been put out of the local Meeting for being too inflammatory.)*

. . . Bev LaFlamme, Carol Krenz, and their *(respectively)* French and French-Canadian husbands *(who no doubt wonder just what sort of friends their wives have, anyway),* for expert opinions on the subtleties of French bowel movements, and help with Very Picturesque French idioms.

. . . Julie Giroux, for Roger's music, and the marvelous "Culloden Symphony," Roy Williamson for "The Flower of Scotland" (words and music) copyright © The Corries (music) Ltd.

. . . Roger H.P. Coleman, R.W. Odlin, Ron Parker, Ann Chapman, Dick Lodge, Olan Watkins, and many members of the Compuserve Masonic Forum for information on Freemasonry and Irregular Lodges, circa 1755 *(which was a good bit prior to the establishment of the Scottish Rite, so let's not bother writing me about that, shall we?)*

. . . Karen Watson and Ron Parker, for advice on WWII London Tube Stations—with which I proceeded to take minor technical liberties.

. . . Steven Lopata, Hall Elliott, Arnold Wagner, R.G. Schmidt, and Mike Jones, honorable warriors all, for useful discussions of how men think and behave, before, during, and after battle.

. . . R.G. Schmidt and several other nice persons whose names I unfortunately forgot to write down, who contributed bits and pieces of helpful information regarding Cherokee belief, language, and custom. *(The bear-hunting chant ending with "Yoho!" is a matter of historical record. There are lots of things I couldn't make up if I tried.)*

. . . the Chemodurow family, for generously allowing me to take liberties with their personae, in portraying them as Russian swineherds. *(Russian boars really were imported into North Carolina for hunting in the 18th century. This may have something to do with the popularity of barbecue in the South.)*

. . . Laura Bailey, for invaluable advice and commentary on 18th century costume and customs—most of which I paid careful attention to.

. . . Susan Martin, Beth Shope, and Margaret Campbell, for expert opinions on the flora, fauna, geography, weather, and mental climate of North Carolina *(and all of whom wish to note that only a barbarian would put tomatoes in barbecue sauce)*. Aberrations in these aspects of the story are a result of inadvertence, literary license, and/or pigheadedness on the part of the author.

. . . Janet McConnaughey, Varda Amir-Orrel, Kim Laird, Elise Skidmore, Bill Williams, Arlene McCrea, Lynne Sears Williams, Babs Whelton, Joyce McGowan, and the dozens of other kind and helpful people of the Compuserve Writers Forum, who will answer any silly question at the drop of a hat, especially if it has anything to do with maiming, murder, disease, quilting, or sex.

. . . Dr. Ellen Mandell, for technical advice on how to hang someone, then cut his throat, and not kill him in the process. Any errors in the execution of this advice are mine.

. . . Piper Fahrney, for his excellent descriptions of what it feels like to be taught to fight with a sword.

. . . David Cheifetz, for dragon-slaying.

. . . Iain MacKinnon Taylor, for his invaluable help with Gaelic translations, and his lovely suggestions for Jamie's bonfire speech.

. . . Karl Hagen, for advice on Latin grammar, and to Barbara Schnell, for Latin and German bits, to say nothing of her stunning translations of the novels into German.

. . . Julie Weathers, my late father-in-law, Max Watkins, and Lucas, for help with the horses.

. . . the Ladies of Lallybroch, for their enthusiastic and continuing moral support, including the thoughtful international assortment of toilet paper.

. . . the several hundred people who have kindly and voluntarily sent me interesting information on everything from the development and uses of penicillin to the playing of bodhrans, the distribution of red spruce, and the way possum tastes *(I'm told it's greasy, in case you were wondering)*.

. . . and to my husband, Doug Watkins, for the last line of the book.

—Diana Gabaldon
www.dianagabaldon.com

*I have lived through war, and lost much. I know what's worth the fight, and what is not.*

*Honor and courage are matters of the bone, and what a man will kill for, he will sometimes die for, too.*

*And that, O kinsman, is why a woman has broad hips; that bony basin will harbor a man and his child alike. A man's life springs from his woman's bones, and in her blood is his honor christened.*

*For the sake of love alone, would I walk through fire again.*

# PART ONE

## *In Medias Res*

# HAPPY THE BRIDE
# THE SUN SHINES ON

*Mount Helicon*
*The Royal Colony of North Carolina*
*Late October, 1770*

I WOKE TO THE PATTER OF RAIN on canvas, with the feel of my first husband's kiss on my lips. I blinked, disoriented, and by reflex put my fingers to my mouth. To keep the feeling, or to hide it? I wondered, even as I did so.

Jamie stirred and murmured in his sleep next to me, his movement rousing a fresh wave of scent from the cedar branches under our bottom quilt. Perhaps the ghost's passing had disturbed him. I frowned at the empty air outside our lean-to.

*Go away, Frank,* I thought sternly.

It was still dark outside, but the mist that rose from the damp earth was a pearly gray; dawn wasn't far off. Nothing stirred, inside or out, but I had the distinct sense of an ironic amusement that lay on my skin like the lightest of touches.

*Shouldn't I come to see her married?*

I couldn't tell whether the words had formed themselves in my thoughts, or whether they—and that kiss—were merely the product of my own subconscious. I had fallen asleep with my mind still busy with wedding preparations; little wonder that I should wake from dreams of weddings. And wedding nights.

I smoothed the rumpled muslin of my shift, uneasily aware that it was rucked up around my waist and that my skin was flushed with more than sleep. I didn't remember anything concrete about the dream that had wakened me; only a confused jumble of image and sensation. I thought perhaps that was a good thing.

I turned over on the rustling branches, nudging close to Jamie. He was warm and smelled pleasantly of woodsmoke and whisky, with a faint tang of sleepy maleness under it, like the deep note of a lingering chord. I stretched myself, very slowly, arching my back so that my pelvis nudged his hip. If he were sound asleep or disinclined, the gesture was slight enough to pass unnoticed; if he were not . . .

He wasn't. He smiled faintly, eyes still closed, and a big hand ran slowly down my back, settling with a firm grip on my bottom.

"Mmm?" he said. "Hmmmm." He sighed, and relaxed back into sleep, holding on.

I nestled close, reassured. The immediate physicality of Jamie was more than enough to banish the touch of lingering dreams. And Frank—if that *was* Frank—was right, so far as that went. I was sure that if such a thing were possible, Bree would want both her fathers at her wedding.

I was wide awake now, but much too comfortable to move. It was raining outside; a light rain, but the air was cold and damp enough to make the cozy nest of quilts more inviting than the distant prospect of hot coffee. Particularly since the getting of coffee would involve a trip to the stream for water, making up the campfire—oh, God, the wood would be damp, even if the fire hadn't gone completely out—grinding the coffee in a stone quern and brewing it, while wet leaves blew round my ankles and drips from overhanging tree branches slithered down my neck.

Shivering at the thought, I pulled the top quilt up over my bare shoulder and instead resumed the mental catalogue of preparations with which I had fallen asleep.

Food, drink . . . luckily I needn't trouble about that. Jamie's aunt Jocasta would deal with the arrangements; or rather, her black butler, Ulysses, would. Wedding guests—no difficulties there. We were in the middle of the largest Gathering of Scottish Highlanders in the Colonies, and food and drink were being provided. Engraved invitations would not be necessary.

Bree would have a new dress, at least; Jocasta's gift as well. Dark blue wool—silk was both too expensive and too impractical for life in the backwoods. It was a far cry from the white satin and orange blossom I had once envisioned her wearing to be married in—but then, this was scarcely the marriage anyone might have imagined in the 1960s.

I wondered what Frank might have thought of Brianna's husband. He likely would have approved; Roger was a historian—or once had been—like Frank himself. He was intelligent and humorous, a talented musician and a gentle man, thoroughly devoted to Brianna and little Jemmy.

*Which is very admirable indeed,* I thought in the direction of the mist, *under the circumstances.*

*You admit that, do you?* The words formed in my inner ear as though he had spoken them, ironic, mocking both himself and me.

Jamie frowned and tightened his grasp on my buttock, making small whuffling noises in his sleep.

*You know I do,* I said silently. *I always did, and you know it, so just bugger off, will you?!*

I turned my back firmly on the outer air and laid my head on Jamie's shoulder, seeking refuge in the feel of the soft, crumpled linen of his shirt.

I rather thought Jamie was less inclined than I—or perhaps Frank—to give Roger credit for accepting Jemmy as his own. To Jamie, it was a simple matter of obligation; an honorable man could not do otherwise. And I knew he had his doubts as to Roger's ability to support and protect a family in the Carolina wilderness. Roger was tall, well-built, and capable—but "bonnet, belt, and swordie" were the stuff of songs to Roger; to Jamie, they were the tools of his trade.

The hand on my bottom squeezed suddenly, and I started.

"Sassenach," Jamie said drowsily, "you're squirming like a toadling in a wee lad's fist. D'ye need to get up and go to the privy?"

"Oh, you're awake," I said, feeling mildly foolish.

"I am *now*," he said. The hand fell away, and he stretched, groaning. His bare feet popped out at the far end of the quilt, long toes spread wide.

"Sorry. I didn't mean to wake you."

"Och, dinna fash yourself," he assured me. He cleared his throat and rubbed a hand through the ruddy waves of his loosened hair, blinking. "I was dreaming like a fiend; I always do when I sleep cold." He lifted his head and peered down across the quilt, wiggling his exposed toes with disfavor. "Why did I not sleep wi' my stockings on?"

"Really? What were you dreaming about?" I asked, with a small stab of uneasiness. I rather hoped he hadn't been dreaming the same sort of thing I had.

"Horses," he said, to my immediate relief. I laughed.

"What sort of fiendish dreams could you be having about horses?"

"Oh, God, it was terrible." He rubbed his eyes with both fists and shook his head, trying to clear the dream from his mind. "All to do wi' the Irish kings. Ye ken what MacKenzie was sayin' about it, at the fire last night?"

"Irish ki—oh!" I remembered, and laughed again at the recollection. "Yes, I do."

Roger, flushed with the triumph of his new engagement, had regaled the company around the fireside the night before with songs, poems, and entertaining historical anecdotes— one of which concerned the rites with which the ancient Irish kings were said to have been crowned. One of these involved the successful candidate copulating with a white mare before the assembled multitudes, presumably to prove his virility— though I thought it would be a better proof of the gentleman's *sangfroid*, myself.

"I was in charge o' the horse," Jamie informed me. "And *everything* went wrong. The man was too short, and I had to find something for him to stand on. I found a rock, but I couldna lift it. Then a stool, but the leg came off in my hand. Then I tried to pile up bricks to make a platform, but they crumbled to sand. Finally they said it was all right, they would just cut the legs off the mare, and I was trying to stop them doing that, and the man who would be king was jerkin' at his breeks and complaining that his fly buttons wouldna come loose, and then someone noticed that it was a *black* mare, and that wouldna do at all."

I snorted, muffling my laughter in a fold of his shirt for fear of wakening someone camped near us.

"Is that when you woke up?"

"No. For some reason, I was verra much affronted at that. I said it *would* do, in fact the black was a much better horse, for everyone knows that white horses have weak een, and I said the offspring would be blind. And they said no, no, the black was ill luck, and I was insisting it was not, and . . ." He stopped, clearing his throat.

"And?"

He shrugged and glanced sideways at me, a faint flush creeping up his neck.

"Aye, well. I said it would do fine, I'd show them. And I had just grasped the mare's rump to stop her moving, and was getting ready to . . . ah . . . make myself king of Ireland. *That's* when I woke."

I snorted and wheezed, and felt his side vibrate with his own suppressed laughter.

"Oh, now I'm *really* sorry to have wakened you!" I wiped my eyes on the corner of the quilt. "I'm sure it was a great loss to the Irish. Though I do wonder how the queens of Ireland felt about that particular ceremony," I added as an afterthought.

"I canna think the ladies would suffer even slightly by comparison," Jamie assured me. "Though I have heard of men who prefer—"

"I wasn't thinking of *that*," I said. "It was more the hygienic implications, if you see what I mean. Putting the cart before the horse is one thing, but putting the horse before the queen . . ."

"The—oh, aye." He was flushed with amusement, but his skin darkened further at that. "Say what ye may about the Irish, Sassenach, but I do believe they wash now and then. And under the circumstances, the king might possibly even have found a bit of soap useful, in . . . in . . ."

"*In medias res*?" I suggested. "Surely not. I mean, after all, a horse is quite large, relatively speaking . . ."

"It's a matter of readiness, Sassenach, as much as room," he said, with a repressive glance in my direction. "And I can see that a man might require a bit of encouragement, under the circumstances. Though it's *in medias res*, in any case," he added. "Have ye never read Horace? Or Aristotle?"

"No. We can't all be educated. And I've never had much time for Aristotle, after hearing that he ranked women somewhere below worms in his classification of the natural world."

"The man can't have been married." Jamie's hand moved slowly up my back, fingering the knobs of my spine through my shift. "Surely he would ha' noticed the bones, else."

I smiled and lifted a hand to his own cheekbone, rising stark and clean above a tide of auburn stubble.

As I did so, I saw that the sky outside had lightened into dawn; his head was silhouetted by the pale canvas of our shelter, but I could see his face clearly. The expression on it reminded me exactly why he had taken off his stockings the night before. Unfortunately, we had both been so tired after the prolonged festivities that we had fallen asleep in mid-embrace.

I found that belated memory rather reassuring, offering as it did some explanation both for the state of my shift and for the dreams from which I had awakened. At the same time, I felt a chilly draft slide its fingers under the quilt, and shivered. Frank and Jamie were very different men, and there was no doubt in my mind as to who had kissed me, just before waking.

"Kiss me," I said suddenly to Jamie. Neither of us had yet brushed our teeth, but he obligingly skimmed my lips with his, then, when I caught the back of his head and pressed him closer, shifted his weight to one hand, the better to adjust the tangle of bedclothes round our lower limbs.

"Oh?" he said, when I released him. He smiled, blue eyes creasing into dark triangles in the dimness. "Well, to be sure, Sassenach. I must just step outside for a moment first, though."

He flung back the quilt and rose. From my position on the ground, I had a rather unorthodox view which provided me with engaging glimpses under the hem of his long linen shirt.

I did hope that what I was looking at was not the lingering result of his nightmare, but thought it better not to ask.

"You'd better hurry," I said. "It's getting light; people will be up and about soon."

He nodded and ducked outside. I lay still, listening. A few birds cheeped faintly in the distance, but this was autumn; not even full light would provoke the raucous choruses of spring and summer. The mountain and its many camps still lay slumbering, but I could feel small stirrings all around, just below the edge of hearing.

I ran my fingers through my hair, fluffing it out round my shoulders, and rolled over, looking for the water bottle. Feeling cool air on my back, I glanced over my shoulder, but dawn had come and the mist had fled; the air outside was gray but still.

I touched the gold ring on my left hand, restored to me the night before, and still unfamiliar after its long absence. Perhaps it was his ring that had summoned Frank to my dreams. Perhaps tonight at the wedding ceremony, I would touch it again, deliberately, and hope that he could see his daughter's happiness somehow through my eyes. For now, though, he was gone, and I was glad.

A small sound, no louder than the distant birdcalls, drifted through the air. The brief cry of a baby waking.

I had once thought that no matter the circumstances, there ought really to be no more than two people in a marriage bed. I still thought so. However, a baby was more difficult to banish than the ghost of a former love; Brianna and Roger's bed must perforce accommodate three.

The edge of the canvas lifted, and Jamie's face appeared, looking excited and alarmed.

"Ye'd best get up and dress, Claire," he said. "The soldiers are drawn up by the creek. Where are my stockings?"

I sat bolt upright, and far down the mountainside the drums began to roll.

COLD FOG LAY like smoke in the hollows all round; a cloud had settled on Mount Helicon like a broody hen on a single egg, and the air was thick with damp. I blinked blearily across a stretch of rough grass, to where a detachment of the 67th Highland regiment was drawn up in full splendor by the creek, drums rumbling and the company piper tootling away, grandly impervious to the rain.

I was very cold, and more than slightly cross. I'd gone to bed in the expectation of waking to hot coffee and a nourishing breakfast, this to be followed by two weddings, three christenings, two tooth extractions, the removal of an infected toenail, and other entertaining forms of wholesome social intercourse requiring whisky.

Instead, I'd been wakened by unsettling dreams, led into amorous dalliance, and then dragged out into a cold drizzle *in medias* bloody *res*, apparently to hear a proclamation of some sort. No coffee yet, either.

It had taken some time for the Highlanders in their camps to rouse themselves and stagger down the hillside, and the piper had gone quite purple in the face before he at last blew the final blast and left off with a discordant wheeze. The echoes were still ringing off the mountainside, as Lieutenant Archibald Hayes stepped out before his men.

Lieutenant Hayes's nasal Fife accent carried well, and the wind was with him. Still, I was sure the people farther up the mountain could hear very little. Standing as we did at the foot of the slope, though, we were no more than twenty yards from the Lieutenant and I could hear every word, in spite of the chattering of my teeth.

*"By his EXCELLENCY, WILLIAM TRYON, Esquire, His Majesty's Captain-General, Governor, and Commander-in-Chief, in and over the said Province,"* Hayes read, lifting his voice in a bellow to carry above the noises of wind and water, and the premonitory murmurs of the crowd.

The moisture shrouded trees and rocks with dripping mist, the clouds spat intermittent sleet and freezing rain, and erratic winds had lowered the temperature by some thirty degrees. My left shin, sensitive to cold, throbbed at the spot where I had broken the bone two years before. A person given to portents and metaphors might have been tempted to draw comparisons between the nasty weather and the reading of the Governor's Proclamation, I thought—the prospects were similarly chill and foreboding.

"*Whereas*," Hayes boomed, glowering at the crowd over his paper, "*I have received information that a great Number of outrageous and disorderly Persons did tumultuously assemble themselves together in the Town of Hillsborough, on the 24th and 25th of last Month, during the sitting of the Superior Court of Justice of that District to oppose the Just Measures of Government and in open Violation of the Laws of their Country, audaciously attacking his Majesty's Associate Justice in the Execution of his Office, and barbarously beating and wounding several Persons in and during the sitting of said Court, and offering other enormous Indignities and Insults to his Majesty's Government, committing the most violent Outrages on the Persons and properties of the Inhabitants of the said Town, drinking Damnation to their lawful Sovereign King George and Success to the Pretender—*"

Hayes paused, gulping air with which to accomplish the next clause. Inflating his chest with an audible whoosh, he read on:

"*To the End therefore, that the Persons concerned in the said outrageous Acts may be brought to Justice, I do, by the Advice and Consent of his Majesty's Council, issue this my Proclamation, hereby requiring and strictly enjoining all his Majesty's Justices of the Peace in this Government to make diligent Inquiry into the above recited Crimes, and to receive the Deposition of such Person or Persons as shall appear before them to make Information of and concerning the same; which Depositions are to be transmitted to me, in Order to be laid before the General Assembly, at New Bern, on the 30th day of November next, to which time it stands Prorogued for the immediate Dispatch of Public Business.*"

A final inhalation; Hayes's face was nearly as purple as the piper's by now.

"*Given under my Hand, and the Great Seal of the Province, at New Bern, the 18th Day of October, in the 10th Year of his Majesty's Reign, Anno Domini 1770.*

*"Signed, William Tryon,"* Hayes concluded, with a final puff of steamy breath.

"Do you know," I remarked to Jamie, "I believe that was all one single sentence, bar the closing. Amazing, even for a politician."

"Hush, Sassenach," he said, his eyes still fixed on Archie Hayes. There was a subdued rumble from the crowd behind me, of interest and consternation—touched with a certain amount of amusement at the phrases regarding treasonous toasts.

This was a Gathering of Highlanders, many of them exiled to the Colonies in the wake of the Stuart Rising, and had Archie Hayes chosen to take official notice of what was said over the cups of ale and whisky passed round the fires the night before . . . but then, he had but forty soldiers with him, and whatever his own opinions of King George and that monarch's possible damnation, he kept them wisely to himself.

Some four hundred Highlanders surrounded Hayes's small beachhead on the creekbank, summoned by the tattoo of drums. Men and women sheltered among the trees above the clearing, plaids and arisaids pulled tight against the rising wind. They too were keeping their own counsel, judging from the array of stony faces visible under the flutter of scarves and bonnets. Of course, their expressions might derive from cold as much as from natural caution; my own cheeks were stiff, the end of my nose had gone numb, and I hadn't felt my feet anytime since daybreak.

"Any person wishing to make declaration concerning these most serious matters may entrust such statements safely to my care," Hayes announced, his round face an official blank. "I will remain in my tent with my clerk for the rest of the day. God save the King!"

He handed the Proclamation to his corporal, bowed to the crowd in dismissal, and turned smartly toward a large canvas tent that had been erected near the trees, regimental banners flapping wildly from a standard next to it.

Shivering, I slid a hand into the slit of Jamie's cloak and over the crook of his arm, my cold fingers comforted by the warmth of his body. Jamie pressed his elbow briefly to his side in acknowledgment of my frozen grasp, but didn't look down at me; he was studying Archie Hayes's retreating back, eyes narrowed against the sting of the wind.

A compact and solid man, of inconsequent height but considerable presence, the Lieutenant moved with great deliberation, as though oblivious of the crowd on the hillside above. He vanished into his tent, leaving the flap invitingly tied up.

Not for the first time, I reluctantly admired Governor Tryon's political instincts. This Proclamation was clearly being read in towns and villages throughout the colony; he could have relied on a local magistrate or sheriff to carry his message of official fury to this Gathering. Instead, he had taken the trouble to send Hayes.

Archibald Hayes had taken the field at Culloden by his father's side, at the age of twelve. Wounded in the fight, he had been captured and sent south. Presented with a choice of transportation or joining the army, he had taken the King's shilling and made the best of it. The fact that he had risen to be an officer in his mid-thirties, in a time when most commissions were bought rather than earned, was sufficient testimony to his abilities.

He was as personable as he was professional; invited to share our food and fire the day before, he had spent half the night talking with Jamie—and the other half moving from fire to fire under the aegis of Jamie's presence, being introduced to the heads of all the important families present.

And whose notion had that been? I wondered, looking up at Jamie. His long, straight nose was reddened by the cold, his eyes hooded from the wind, but his face gave no inkling of what he was thinking. And that, I thought, was a bloody good indication that he was thinking something rather dangerous. Had he known about this Proclamation?

No English officer, with an English troop, could have brought such news into a Gathering like this, with any hope of cooperation. But Hayes and his Highlanders, stalwart in their tartan . . . I didn't miss the fact that Hayes had had his tent erected with its back to a thick grove of pines; anyone who wished to speak to the Lieutenant in secret could approach through the woods, unseen.

"Does Hayes expect someone to pop out of the crowd, rush into his tent, and surrender on the spot?" I murmured to Jamie. I personally knew of at least a dozen men among those present who had taken part in the Hillsborough riots; three of them were standing within arm's length of us.

Jamie saw the direction of my glance and put his hand over mine, squeezing it in a silent adjuration of discretion. I lowered my brows at him; surely he didn't think I would give anyone away by inadvertence? He gave me a faint smile and one of those annoying marital looks that said, more plainly than words, *You know how ye are, Sassenach. Anyone who sees your face kens just what ye think.*

I sidled in a little closer, and kicked him discreetly in the ankle. I might have a glass face, but it certainly wouldn't arouse comment in a crowd like this! He didn't wince, but the smile spread a little wider. He slid one arm inside my cloak, and drew me closer, his hand on my back.

Hobson, MacLennan, and Fowles stood together just in front of us, talking quietly among themselves. All three came from a tiny settlement called Drunkard's Creek, some fifteen miles from our own place on Fraser's Ridge. Hugh Fowles was Joe Hobson's son-in-law, and very young, no more than twenty. He was doing his best to keep his composure, but his face had gone white and clammy as the Proclamation was read.

I didn't know what Tryon intended to do to anyone who could be proved to have had a part in the riot, but I could feel the currents of unrest created by the Governor's Proclamation passing through the crowd like the eddies of water rushing over rocks in the nearby creek.

Several buildings had been destroyed in Hillsborough, and a number of public officials dragged out and assaulted in the street. Gossip had it that one ironically titled justice of the peace had lost an eye to a vicious blow aimed with a horsewhip. No doubt taking this demonstration of civil disobedience to heart, Chief Justice Henderson had escaped out of a window and fled the town, thus effectively preventing the Court from sitting. It was clear that the Governor was *very* annoyed about what had happened in Hillsborough.

Joe Hobson glanced back at Jamie, then away. Lieutenant Hayes's presence at our fire the previous evening had not gone unremarked.

If Jamie saw the glance, he didn't return it. He lifted one shoulder in a shrug, tilting his head down to speak to me.

"I shouldna think Hayes expects anyone to give themselves up, no. It may be his duty to ask for information; I thank God it isna mine to answer." He hadn't spoken loudly, but loudly enough to reach the ears of Joe Hobson.

Hobson turned his head and gave Jamie a small nod of wry acknowledgment. He touched his son-in-law's arm, and they turned away, scrambling up the slope toward the scattered campsites above, where their womenfolk were tending the fires and the younger children.

This was the last day of the Gathering; tonight there would be marryings and christenings, the formal blessing of love and its riotous fruits, sprung from the loins of the unchurched multitude during the year before. Then the last songs would be sung, the last stories told, and dancing done amid the leaping flames of many fires—rain or no rain. Come morning, the Scots and their households would all disperse back to their homes, scattered from the settled banks of the Cape Fear River to the wild mountains of the west—carrying news of the Governor's Proclamation and the doings at Hillsborough.

I wiggled my toes inside my damp shoes and wondered uneasily who among the crowd might think it their duty to answer Hayes's invitation to confession or incrimination. Not Jamie, no. But others might. There had been a good deal of boasting about the riots in Hillsborough during the week of the Gathering, but not all the listeners were disposed to view the rioters as heroes, by any means.

I could feel as well as hear the mutter of conversation breaking out in the wake of the Proclamation; heads turning, families drawing close together, men moving from group to group, as the content of Hayes's speech was relayed up the hill, repeated to those who stood too far away to have heard it.

"Shall we go? There's a lot to do yet before the weddings."

"Aye?" Jamie glanced down at me. "I thought Jocasta's slaves were managing the food and drink. I gave Ulysses the barrels of whisky—he'll be *soghan*."

"Ulysses? Did he bring his wig?" I smiled at the thought. The *soghan* was the man who managed the dispensing of drink and refreshment at a Highland wedding; the term actually meant something like "hearty, jovial fellow." Ulysses was possibly the most dignified person I had ever seen— even without his livery and powdered horsehair wig.

"If he did, it's like to be stuck to his head by the evening." Jamie glanced up at the lowering sky and shook his head. "Happy the bride the sun shines on," he quoted. "Happy the corpse the rain falls on."

"That's what I like about Scots," I said dryly. "An appropriate proverb for all occasions. Don't you dare say that in front of Bree."

"What d'ye take me for, Sassenach?" he demanded, with a half-smile down at me. "I'm her father, no?"

"Definitely yes." I suppressed the sudden thought of Brianna's other father, and glanced over my shoulder, to be sure she wasn't in hearing.

There was no sign of her blazing head among those nearby. Certainly her father's daughter, she stood six feet tall in her stocking feet; nearly as easy as Jamie himself to pick out of a crowd.

"It's not the wedding feast I need to deal with, anyway," I said, turning back to Jamie. "I've got to manage breakfast, then do the morning clinic with Murray MacLeod."

"Oh, aye? I thought ye said wee Murray was a charlatan."

"I said he was ignorant, stubborn, and a menace to the public health," I corrected. "That's not the same thing— quite."

"Quite," said Jamie, grinning. "Ye mean to educate him, then—or poison him?"

"Whichever seems most effective. If nothing else, I might accidentally step on his fleam and break it; that's probably the only way I'll stop him bleeding people. Let's go, though, I'm freezing!"

"Aye, we'll away, then," Jamie agreed, with a glance at the soldiers, still drawn up along the creekbank at parade rest.

"No doubt wee Archie means to keep his lads there 'til the crowd's gone; they're going a wee bit blue round the edges."

Though fully armed and uniformed, the row of Highlanders was relaxed; imposing, to be sure, but no longer threatening. Small boys—and not a few wee girls—scampered to and fro among them, impudently flicking the hems of the soldiers' kilts or dashing in, greatly daring, to touch the gleaming muskets, dangling canteens, and the hilts of dirks and swords.

"Abel, *a charaid*!" Jamie had paused to greet the last of the men from Drunkard's Creek. "Will ye ha' eaten yet the day?"

MacLennan had not brought his wife to the Gathering, and thus ate where luck took him. The crowd was dispersing around us, but he stood stolidly in place, holding the ends of a red flannel handkerchief pulled over his balding head against the spatter of rain. Probably hoping to cadge an invitation to breakfast, I thought cynically.

I eyed his stocky form, mentally estimating his possible consumption of eggs, parritch, and toasted bread against the dwindling supplies in our hampers. Not that simple shortage of food would stop any Highlander from offering hospitality—certainly not Jamie, who was inviting MacLennan to join us, even as I mentally divided eighteen eggs by nine people instead of eight. Not fried, then; made into fritters with grated potatoes, and I'd best borrow more coffee from Jocasta's campsite on the way up the mountain.

We turned to go, and Jamie's hand slid suddenly downward over my backside. I made an undignified sound, and Abel MacLennan turned round to gawk at me. I smiled brightly at him, resisting the urge to kick Jamie again, less discreetly.

MacLennan turned away, and scrambled up the slope in front of us with alacrity, coattails bouncing in anticipation over worn breeks. Jamie put a hand under my elbow to help me over the rocks, bending down as he did so to mutter in my ear.

"Why the devil are ye not wearing a petticoat, Sassenach?" he hissed. "Ye've nothing at all on under your skirt—you'll catch your death of cold!"

"You're not wrong there," I said, shivering in spite of my cloak. I did in fact have on a linen shift under my gown, but it was a thin, ragged thing, suitable for rough camping-out in summertime, but quite insufficient to stem the wintry blasts that blew through my skirt as though it were cheesecloth.

"Ye had a fine woolen petticoat yesterday. What's become of it?"

"You don't want to know," I assured him.

His eyebrows went up at this, but before he could ask further questions, a scream rang out behind us.

"Germain!"

I turned to see a small blond head, hair flying as the owner streaked down the slope below the rocks. Two-year-old Germain had taken advantage of his mother's preoccupation with his newborn sister to escape custody and make a dash for the row of soldiers. Eluding capture, he charged headlong down the slope, picking up speed like a rolling stone.

"Fergus!" Marsali screamed. Germain's father, hearing his name, turned round from his conversation, just in time to see his son trip over a rock and fly headlong. A born acrobat, the little boy made no move to save himself, but collapsed gracefully, rolling into a ball like a hedgehog as he struck the grassy slope on one shoulder. He rolled like a cannonball through the ranks of soldiers, shot off the edge of a rocky shelf, and plopped with a splash into the creek.

There was a general gasp of consternation, and a number of people ran down the hill to help, but one of the soldiers had already hurried to the bank. Kneeling, he thrust the tip of his bayonet through the child's floating clothes and towed the soggy bundle to the shore.

Fergus charged into the icy shallows, reaching out to clasp his waterlogged son.

*"Merci, mon ami, merci beaucoup,"* he said to the young soldier. *"Et toi, garnement,"* he said, addressing his spluttering offspring with a small shake. *"Comment vas-tu,* ye wee chowderheid?"

The soldier looked startled, but I couldn't tell whether the cause was Fergus's unique patois, or the sight of the gleaming hook he wore in place of his missing left hand.

"That's all right then, sir," he said, with a shy smile. "He'll no be damaged, I think."

Brianna appeared suddenly from behind a chinkapin tree, six-month-old Jemmy on one shoulder, and scooped baby Joan neatly out of Marsali's arms.

"Here, give Joanie to me," she said. "You go take care of Germain."

Jamie swung the heavy cloak from his shoulders and laid it in Marsali's arms in place of the baby.

"Aye, and tell the soldier laddie who saved him to come and share our fire," he told her. "We can feed another, Sassenach?"

"Of course," I said, swiftly readjusting my mental calculations. Eighteen eggs, four loaves of stale bread for toast—no, I should keep back one for the trip home tomorrow—three dozen oatcakes if Jamie and Roger hadn't eaten them already, half a jar of honey . . .

Marsali's thin face lighted with a rueful smile, shared among the three of us, then she was gone, hastening to the aid of her drenched and shivering menfolk.

Jamie looked after her with a sigh of resignation, as the wind caught the full sleeves of his shirt and belled them out with a muffled *whoomp*. He crossed his arms across his chest, hunching his shoulders against the wind, and smiled down at me, sidelong.

"Ah, well. I suppose we shall both freeze together, Sassenach. That's all right, though. I wouldna want to live without ye, anyway."

"Ha," I said amiably. "You could live naked on an ice floe, Jamie Fraser, and melt it. What have you done with your coat and plaid?" He wore nothing besides his kilt and sark save shoes and stockings, and his high cheekbones were reddened with cold, like the tips of his ears. When I slipped a hand back inside the crook of his arm, though, he was warm as ever.

"Ye dinna want to know," he said, grinning. He covered my hand with one large, callused palm. "Let's go; I'm starved for my breakfast."

"Wait," I said, detaching myself. Jemmy was indisposed

to share his mother's embrace with the newcomer, and howled and squirmed in protest, his small round face going red with annoyance under a blue knitted cap. I reached out and took him from Brianna, as he wriggled and fussed in his wrappings.

"Thanks, Mama." Brianna smiled briefly, boosting tiny Joan into a more secure position against her shoulder. "Are you sure you want that one, though? This one's quieter—and weighs half as much."

"No, he's all right. Hush, sweetie, come see Grannie." I smiled as I said it, with the still-new feeling of mingled surprise and delight that I could actually be someone's grandmother. Recognizing me, Jemmy abandoned his fuss and went promptly into his mussel-clinging-to-a-rock routine, chubby fists gripped tight in my hair. Disentangling his fingers, I peered over his head, but things below seemed under control.

Fergus, breeches and stockings soaking wet, Jamie's cloak draped round his shoulders, was wringing out his shirtfront one-handed, saying something to the soldier who had rescued Germain. Marsali had whipped off her arisaid and wrapped the little boy in it, her loosened blond hair flying out from under her kerch like cobwebs in the wind.

Lieutenant Hayes, attracted by the noise, was peering out from the flap of his tent like a whelk from its shell. He looked up, and caught my eye; I waved briefly, then turned to follow my own family back to our campsite.

Jamie was saying something to Brianna in Gaelic, as he helped her over a rocky patch in the trail ahead of me.

"Yes, I'm ready," she said, replying in English. "Where's your coat, Da?"

"I lent it to your husband," he said. "We dinna want him to look a beggar at your wedding, aye?"

Bree laughed, wiping a flying strand of red hair out of her mouth with her free hand.

"Better a beggar than an attempted suicide."

"A what?" I caught up with them as we emerged from the shelter of the rocks. The wind barreled across the open space, pelting us with sleet and bits of stinging gravel, and I pulled the knitted cap further down over Jemmy's ears, then pulled the blanket up over his head.

"Whoof!" Brianna hunched over the swaddled baby girl she carried, sheltering her from the blast. "Roger was shaving when the drums started up; he nearly cut his throat. The front of his coat is covered with bloodstains." She glanced at Jamie, eyes watering with the wind. "So you've seen him this morning. Where is he now, do you know?"

"The lad's in one piece," he assured her. "I told him to go and talk wi' Father Donahue, while Hayes was about his business." He gave her a sharp look. "Ye might have told me the lad was no a Catholic."

"I might," she said, unperturbed. "But I didn't. It's no big deal to me."

"If ye mean by that peculiar expression, that it's of no consequence—" Jamie began with a distinct edge in his voice, but was interrupted by the appearance of Roger himself, resplendent in a kilt of green-and-white MacKenzie tartan, with the matching plaid draped over Jamie's good coat and waistcoat. The coat fit decently—both men were of a size, long-limbed and broad-shouldered, though Jamie was an inch or two the taller—and the gray wool was quite as becoming to Roger's dark hair and olive skin as it was to Jamie's burnished auburn coloring.

"You look very nice, Roger," I said. "Where did you cut yourself?" His face was pink, with the raw look common to just-shaved skin, but otherwise unmarked.

Roger was carrying Jamie's plaid under his arm, a bundle of red and black tartan. He handed it over and tilted his head to one side, showing me the deep gash just under his jawbone.

"Just there. Not so bad, but it bled like the dickens. They don't call them cutthroat razors for nothing, aye?"

The gash had already crusted into a neat dark line, a cut some three inches long, angled down from the corner of his jaw across the side of his throat. I touched the skin near it briefly. Not bad; the blade of the razor had cut straight in, no flap of skin needing suture. No wonder it had bled a lot, though; it did look as though he had tried to cut his throat.

"A bit nervous this morning?" I teased. "Not having second thoughts, are you?"

"A little late for that," Brianna said dryly, coming up beside me. "Got a kid who needs a name, after all."

"He'll have more names than he knows what to do with," Roger assured her. "So will you—Mrs. MacKenzie."

A small flush lit Brianna's face at the name, and she smiled at him. He leaned over and kissed her on the forehead, taking the cocooned baby from her as he did so. A look of sudden shock crossed his face as he felt the weight of the bundle in his arms, and he gawked down at it.

"That's not ours," Bree said, grinning at his look of consternation. "It's Marsali's Joan. Mama has Jemmy."

"Thank God," he said, holding the bundle with a good deal more caution. "I thought he'd evaporated or something." He lifted the blanket slightly, exposing tiny Joan's sleeping face, and smiled—as people always did—at sight of her comical quiff of brown hair, which came to a point like a Kewpie doll's.

"Not a chance," I said, grunting as I hoisted a well-nourished Jemmy, now peacefully comatose in his own wrappings, into a more comfortable position. "I think he's gained a pound or two on the way uphill." I was flushed from exertion, and held the baby a little away from myself, as a sudden wave of heat flushed my cheeks and perspiration broke out under the waves of my disheveled hair.

Jamie took Jemmy from me, and tucked him expertly under one arm like a football, one hand cupping the baby's head.

"Ye've spoken wi' the priest, then?" he said, eyeing Roger skeptically.

"I have," Roger said dryly, answering the look as much as the question. "He's satisfied I'm no the Anti-Christ. So long as I'm willing the lad should be baptized Catholic, there's no bar to the wedding. I've said I'm willing."

Jamie grunted in reply, and I repressed a smile. While Jamie had no great religious prejudices—he had dealt with, fought with, and commanded far too many men, of every possible background—the revelation that his son-in-law was a Presbyterian—and had no intention of converting—had occasioned some small comment.

Bree caught my eye and gave me a sidelong smile, her own eyes creasing into blue triangles of catlike amusement.

"Very wise of you not to mention religion ahead of time," I murmured, careful not to speak loudly enough for Jamie to hear me. Both men were walking ahead of us, still rather stiff in their attitudes, though the formality of their demeanor was rather impaired by the trailing draperies of the babies they carried.

Jemmy let out a sudden squawk, but his grandfather swung him up without breaking stride, and he subsided, round eyes fixed on us over Jamie's shoulder, sheltered under the hooding of his blanket. I made a face at him, and he broke into a huge, gummy smile.

"Roger wanted to say something, but I told him to keep quiet." Bree stuck out her tongue and wiggled it at Jemmy, then fixed a wifely look on Roger's back. "I knew Da wouldn't make a stramash about it, if we waited 'til just before the wedding."

I noted both her astute evaluation of her father's behavior, and her easy use of Scots. She resembled Jamie in a good deal more than the obvious matter of looks and coloring; she had his talent for human judgment and his glibness with language. Still, there was something niggling at my mind, something to do with Roger and religion . . .

We had come up close enough behind the men to hear their conversation.

". . . about Hillsborough," Jamie was saying, leaning toward Roger so as to be heard over the wind. "Calling for information about the rioters."

"Oh, aye?" Roger sounded both interested and wary. "Duncan Innes will be interested to hear that. He was in Hillsborough during the troubles, did you know?"

"No." Jamie sounded more than interested. "I've barely seen Duncan to speak to this week. I'll ask him, maybe, after the wedding—if he lives through it." Duncan was to marry Jamie's aunt, Jocasta Cameron, in the evening, and was nervous to the point of prostration over the prospect.

Roger turned, shielding Joan from the wind with his body as he spoke to Brianna.

"Your aunt's told Father Donahue he can hold the weddings in her tent. That'll be a help."

"Brrrr!" Bree hunched her shoulders, shivering. "Thank goodness. It's no day to be getting married under the greenwood tree."

A huge chestnut overhead sent down a damp shower of yellow leaves, as though in agreement. Roger looked a little uneasy.

"I don't imagine it's quite the wedding you maybe thought of," he said. "When ye were a wee girl."

Brianna looked up at Roger and a slow, wide smile spread across her face. "Neither was the first one," she said. "But I liked it fine."

Roger's complexion wasn't given to blushing, and his ears were red with cold in any case. He opened his mouth as though to reply, caught Jamie's gimlet eye, and shut it again, looking embarrassed but undeniably pleased.

"Mr. Fraser!"

I turned to see one of the soldiers making his way up the hill toward us, his eyes fixed on Jamie.

"Corporal MacNair, your servant, sir," he said, breathing hard as he reached us. He gave a sharp inclination of the head. "The Lieutenant's compliments, and would ye be so good as to attend him in his tent?" He caught sight of me, and bowed again, less abruptly. "Mrs. Fraser. My compliments, ma'am."

"Your servant, sir." Jamie returned the Corporal's bow. "My apologies to the Lieutenant, but I have duties that require my attendance elsewhere." He spoke politely, but the Corporal glanced sharply up at him. MacNair was young, but not callow; a quick look of understanding crossed his lean, dark face. The last thing any man would want was to be seen going into Hayes's tent by himself, immediately following that Proclamation.

"The Lieutenant bids me request the attendance upon him of Mr. Farquard Campbell, Mr. Andrew MacNeill, Mr. Gerald Forbes, Mr. Duncan Innes, and Mr. Randall Lillywhite, as well as yourself, sir."

A certain amount of tension left Jamie's shoulders.

"Does he," he said dryly. So Hayes meant to consult the powerful men of the area: Farquard Campbell and Andrew MacNeill were large landowners and local magistrates; Gerald Forbes a prominent solicitor from Cross Creek, and a justice of the peace; Lillywhite a magistrate of the circuit court. And Duncan Innes was about to become the largest plantation owner in the western half of the colony, by virtue of his impending marriage to Jamie's widowed aunt. Jamie himself was neither rich nor an official of the Crown—but he *was* the proprietor of a large, if still largely vacant, land grant in the backcountry.

He gave a slight shrug and shifted the baby to his other shoulder, settling himself.

"Aye. Well, then. Tell the Lieutenant I shall attend him as soon as may be convenient."

Nothing daunted, MacNair bowed and went off, presumably in search of the other gentlemen on his list.

"And what's all that about?" I asked Jamie. "Oops." I reached up and skimmed a glistening strand of saliva from Jemmy's chin before it could reach Jamie's shirt. "Starting a new tooth, are we?"

"I've plenty of teeth," Jamie assured me, "and so have you, so far as I can see. As to what Hayes may want with me, I canna say for sure. And I dinna mean to find out before I must, either." He cocked one ruddy eyebrow at me, and I laughed.

"Oh, a certain flexibility in that word 'convenient,' is there?"

"I didna say it would be convenient for *him*," Jamie pointed out. "Now, about your petticoat, Sassenach, and why you're scampering about the forest bare-arsed—Duncan, *a charaid*!" The wry look on his face melted into genuine pleasure at sight of Duncan Innes, making his way toward us through a small growth of bare-limbed dogwood.

Duncan clambered over a fallen log, the process made rather awkward by his missing left arm, and arrived on the path beside us, shaking water droplets from his hair. He was already dressed for his wedding, in a clean ruffled shirt and starched linen stock above his kilt, and a coat of scarlet broadcloth trimmed in gold lace, the empty sleeve pinned up with a brooch. I had never seen Duncan look so elegant, and said so.

"Och, well," he said diffidently. "Miss Jo did wish it." He shrugged off the compliment along with the rain, carefully brushing away dead needles and bits of bark that had adhered to his coat in the passage through the pines.

"Brrr! A gruesome day, *Mac Dubh*, and no mistake." He looked up at the sky and shook his head. "Happy the bride the sun shines on; happy the corpse the rain falls on."

"I do wonder just how delighted you can expect the average corpse to be," I said, "whatever the meteorological conditions. But I'm sure Jocasta will be quite happy regardless," I added hastily, seeing a look of bewilderment spread itself across Duncan's features. "And you too, of course!"

"Oh . . . aye," he said, a little uncertainly. "Aye, of course. I thank ye, ma'am."

"When I saw ye coming through the wood, I thought perhaps Corporal MacNair was nippin' at your heels," Jamie said. "You're no on your way to see Archie Hayes, are you?"

Duncan looked quite startled.

"Hayes? No, what would the Lieutenant want wi' me?"

"You were in Hillsborough in September, aye? Here, Sassenach, take this wee squirrel away." Jamie interrupted himself to hand me Jemmy, who had decided to take a more active interest in the proceedings and was attempting to climb his grandfather's torso, digging in his toes and making loud grunting noises. The sudden activity, however, was not Jamie's chief motive for relieving himself of the burden, as I discovered when I accepted Jemmy.

"Thanks a lot," I said, wrinkling my nose. Jamie grinned at me, and turned Duncan up the path, resuming their conversation.

"Hmm," I said, sniffing cautiously. "Finished, are you? No, I thought not." Jemmy closed his eyes, went bright red, and emitted a popping noise like muffled machine-gun fire. I undid his wrappings sufficiently to peek down his back.

"Whoops," I said, and hastily unwound the blanket, just in time. "*What* has your mother been feeding you?"

Thrilled to have escaped his swaddling bands, Jemmy

churned his legs like a windmill, causing a noxious yellowish substance to ooze from the baggy legs of his diaper.

"Pew," I said succinctly, and holding him at arm's length, headed off the path toward one of the tiny rivulets that meandered down the mountainside, thinking that while I could perhaps do without such amenities as indoor plumbing and motorcars, there were times when I sincerely missed things like rubber pants with elasticated legs. To say nothing of toilet rolls.

I found a good spot on the edge of the little stream, with a thick coating of dead leaves. I knelt, laid out a fold of my cloak, and parked Jemmy on it on his hands and knees, pulling the soggy clout off without bothering to unpin it.

"Weee!" he said, sounding surprised as the cold air struck him. He clenched his fat little buttocks and hunched like a small pink toad.

"Ha," I told him. "If you think a cold wind up the bum is bad, just wait." I scooped up a handful of damp yellow-brown leaves, and cleaned him off briskly. A fairly stoic child, he wiggled and squirmed, but didn't screech, instead making high-pitched "Eeeeee" noises as I excavated his crevices.

I flipped him over, and with a hand held prophylactically over the danger zone, administered a similar treatment to his private parts, this eliciting a wide, gummy grin.

"Oh, you *are* a Hieland man, aren't you?" I said, smiling back.

"And just what d'ye mean by that remark, Sassenach?" I looked up to find Jamie leaning against a tree on the other side of the streamlet. The bold colors of his dress tartan and white linen sark stood out bright against the faded autumn foliage; face and hair, though, made him look like some denizen of the wood, all bronze and auburn, with the wind stirring his hair so the free ends danced like the scarlet maple leaves above.

"Well, he's apparently impervious to cold and damp," I said, concluding my labors and discarding the final handful of soiled leaves. "Beyond that . . . well, I've not had much to do with male infants before, but isn't this rather precocious?"

One corner of Jamie's mouth curled up, as he peered at

the prospect revealed under my hand. The tiny appendage stood up stiff as my thumb, and roughly the same size.

"Ah, no," he said. "I've seen a many wee lads in the raw. They all do that now and again." He shrugged, and the smile grew wider. "Now, whether it's only *Scottish* lads, I couldna be saying . . ."

"A talent that improves with age, I daresay," I said dryly. I tossed the dirty clout across the streamlet, where it landed at his feet with a splat. "Get the pins and rinse that out, will you?"

His long, straight nose wrinkled slightly, but he knelt without demur and picked the filthy thing up gingerly between two fingers.

"Oh, so *that's* what ye've done wi' your petticoat," he said. I had opened the large pocket I wore slung at my waist and extracted a clean, folded rectangle of cloth. Not the unbleached linen of the clout he held, but a thick, soft, often-washed wool flannel, dyed a pale red with the juice of currants.

I shrugged, checked Jemmy for the prospect of fresh explosions, and popped him onto the new diaper.

"With three babies all in clouts, and the weather too damp to dry anything properly, we were rather short of clean bits." The bushes around the clearing where we had made our family camp were all festooned with flapping laundry, most of it still wet, owing to the inopportune weather.

"Here." Jamie stretched across the foot-wide span of rock-strewn water to hand me the pins extracted from the old diaper. I took them, careful not to drop them in the stream. My fingers were stiff and chilly, but the pins were valuable; Bree had made them of heated wire, and Roger had carved the capped heads from wood, in accordance with her drawings. Honest-to-goodness safety pins, if a bit larger and cruder than the modern version. The only real defect was the glue used to hold the wooden heads to the wire; made from boiled milk and hoof parings, it was not entirely waterproof, and the heads had to be reglued periodically.

I folded the diaper snugly about Jemmy's loins and thrust a pin through the cloth, smiling at sight of the wooden cap.

Bree had taken one set and carved a small, comical frog—each with a wide, toothless grin—onto each one.

"All right, Froggie, here you go, then." Diaper securely fastened, I sat down and boosted him into my lap, smoothing down his smock and attempting to rewrap his blanket.

"Where did Duncan go?" I asked. "Down to see the Lieutenant?"

Jamie shook his head, bent over his task.

"I told him not to go yet. He *was* in Hillsborough during the troubles there. Best he should wait a bit; then if Hayes should ask, he can swear honestly there's no man here who took part in the riots." He looked up and smiled, without humor. "There won't be, come nightfall."

I watched his hands, large and capable, wringing out the rinsed clout. The scars on his right hand were usually almost invisible, but they stood out now, ragged white lines against his cold-reddened skin. The whole business made me mildly uneasy, though there seemed no direct connection with us.

For the most part, I could think of Governor Tryon with no more than a faint sense of edginess; he was, after all, safely tucked away in his nice new palace in New Bern, separated from our tiny settlement on Fraser's Ridge by three hundred miles of coastal towns, inland plantations, pine forest, piedmont, trackless mountains, and sheer howling wilderness. With all the other things he had to worry about, such as the self-styled "Regulators" who had terrorized Hillsborough, and the corrupt sheriffs and judges who had provoked the terror, I hardly thought he would have time to spare a thought for us. I hoped not.

The uncomfortable fact remained that Jamie held title to a large grant of land in the North Carolina mountains as the gift of Governor Tryon—and Tryon in turn held one small but important fact tucked away in his vest pocket: Jamie was a Catholic. And Royal grants of land could be made only to Protestants, by law.

Given the tiny number of Catholics in the colony, and the lack of organization among them, the question of religion was rarely an issue. There were no Catholic churches, no resident Catholic priests; Father Donahue had made the arduous journey down from Baltimore, at Jocasta's request. Jamie's aunt Jocasta and her late husband, Hector Cameron, had been influential among the Scottish community here for so long that no one would have thought of questioning their religious background, and I thought it likely that few of the Scots with whom we had been celebrating all week knew that we were Papists.

They were, however, likely to notice quite soon. Bree and Roger, who had been handfasted for a year, were to be married by the priest this evening, along with two other Catholic couples from Bremerton—and with Jocasta and Duncan Innes.

"Archie Hayes," I said suddenly. "Is he a Catholic?"

Jamie hung the wet clout from a nearby branch and shook water from his hands.

"I havena asked him," he said, "but I shouldna think so. That is, his father was not; I should be surprised if he was— and him an officer."

"True." The disadvantages of Scottish birth, poverty, and being an ex-Jacobite were sufficiently staggering; amazing enough that Hayes had overcome these to rise to his present position, without the additional burden of the taint of Papistry.

What was troubling me, though, was not the thought of Lieutenant Hayes and his men; it was Jamie. Outwardly, he was calm and assured as ever, with that faint smile always hiding in the corner of his mouth. But I knew him very well; I had seen the two stiff fingers of his right hand—maimed in an English prison—twitch against the side of his leg as he traded jokes and stories with Hayes the night before. Even now, I could see the thin line that formed between his brows when he was troubled, and it wasn't concern over what he was doing.

Was it simply worry over the Proclamation? I couldn't see why that should be, given that none of our folk had been involved in the Hillsborough riots.

". . . a Presbyterian," he was saying. He glanced over at me with a wry smile. "Like wee Roger."

The memory that had niggled at me earlier dropped suddenly into place.

"You knew that," I said. "You *knew* Roger wasn't a Catholic. You saw him baptize that child in Snaketown, when we . . . took him from the Indians." Too late, I saw the shadow cross his face, and bit my tongue. When we took Roger—and left in his place Jamie's dearly loved nephew Ian.

A shadow crossed his face momentarily, but he smiled, pushing away the thought of Ian.

"Aye, I did," he said.

"But Bree—"

"She'd marry the lad if he were a Hottentot," Jamie interrupted. "Anyone can see that. And I canna say I'd object overmuch to wee Roger if he *were* a Hottentot," he added, rather to my surprise.

"You wouldn't?"

Jamie shrugged, and stepped over the tiny creek to my side, wiping wet hands on the end of his plaid.

"He's a braw lad, and he's kind. He's taken the wean as his own and said no word to the lass about it. It's no more than a man should do—but not every man would."

I glanced down involuntarily at Jemmy, curled up cozily in my arms. I tried not to think of it myself, but could not help now and then searching his bluntly amiable features for any trace that might reveal his true paternity.

Brianna had been handfast with Roger, lain with him for one night—and then been raped two days later, by Stephen Bonnet. There was no way to tell for sure who the father had been, and so far Jemmy gave no indication of resembling either man in the slightest. He was gnawing his fist at the moment, with a ferocious scowl of concentration, and with his soft fuzz of red-gold plush, he looked like no one so much as Jamie himself.

"Mm. So why all the insistence on having Roger vetted by a priest?"

"Well, they'll be married in any case," he said logically. "I want the wee lad baptized a Catholic, though." He laid a large hand gently on Jemmy's head, thumb smoothing the tiny red brows. "So if I made a bit of a fuss about MacKenzie, I thought they'd be pleased to agree about *an gille ruaidh* here, aye?"

I laughed, and pulled a fold of blanket up around Jemmy's ears.

"And I thought Brianna had *you* figured out!"

"So does she," he said, with a grin. He bent suddenly and kissed me.

His mouth was soft and very warm. He tasted of bread and butter, and he smelled strongly of fresh leaves and unwashed male, with just the faintest trace of effluvium of diaper.

"Oh, that's nice," I said with approval. "Do it again."

The wood around us was still, in the way of woods. No bird, no beast, just the sough of leaves above and the rush of water underfoot. Constant movement, constant sound—and at the center of it all, a perfect peace. There were a good many people on the mountain, and most of them not that far away—yet just here, just now, we might have been alone on Jupiter.

I opened my eyes and sighed, tasting honey. Jamie smiled at me, and brushed a fallen yellow leaf from my hair. The baby lay in my arms, a heavy, warm weight, the center of the universe.

Neither of us spoke, not wishing to disturb the stillness. It was like being at the tip of a spinning top, I thought—a whirl of events and people going on all round, and a step in one direction or another would plunge us back into that spinning frenzy, but here at the very center—there was peace.

I reached up and brushed a scatter of maple seeds from his shoulder. He seized my hand, and brought it to his mouth with a sudden fierceness that startled me. And yet his lips were tender, the tip of his tongue warm on the fleshy mound at the base of my thumb—the mount of Venus, it's called, love's seat.

He raised his head, and I felt the sudden chill on my hand, where the ancient scar showed white as bone. A letter "J," cut in the skin, his mark on me.

He laid his hand against my face, and I pressed it there with my own, as though I could feel the faded "C" he bore on his own palm, against the cold skin of my cheek. Neither of us spoke, but the pledge was made, as we had made it once before, in a place of sanctuary, our feet on a scrap of bedrock in the shifting sands of threatened war.

It was not near; not yet. But I heard it coming, in the sound of drums and proclamation, saw it in the glint of steel, knew the fear of it in heart and bone when I looked in Jamie's eyes.

The chill had gone, and hot blood throbbed in my hand as though to split the ancient scar and spill my heart's blood for him once again. It would come, and I could not stop it.

But this time, I wouldn't leave him.

I FOLLOWED JAMIE out of the trees, across a scrabble of rocks and sand and tufted grass, to the well-trampled trail that led upward to our campsite. I was counting in my head, readjusting the breakfast requirements yet again, in light of Jamie's revelation that he had invited two more families to join us for the meal.

"Robin McGillivray and Geordie Chisholm," he said, holding back a branch for me to pass. "I thought we should make them welcome; they mean to come and settle on the Ridge."

"Do they," I said, ducking as the branch slapped back behind me. "When? And how many of them are there?"

These were loaded questions. It was close to winter—much too close to count on building even the crudest cabin for shelter. Anyone who came to the mountains now would likely have to live in the big house with us, or crowd into one of the small settlers' cabins that dotted the Ridge. Highlanders could, did, and would live ten to a room when necessary. With my less strongly developed sense of English hospitality, I rather hoped it wouldn't be necessary.

"Six McGillivrays and eight Chisholms," Jamie said, smiling. "The McGillivrays will come in the spring, though. Robin's a gunsmith—he'll have work in Cross Creek for the winter—and his family will bide with kin in Salem—his wife's German—until the weather warms."

"Oh, that's good." Fourteen more for breakfast, then, plus

me and Jamie, Roger and Bree, Marsali and Fergus, Lizzie and her father—Abel MacLennan, mustn't forget him—oh, and the soldier lad who'd rescued Germain, that made twenty-four . . .

"I'll go and borrow some coffee and rice from my aunt, shall I?" Jamie had been reading the growing look of dismay on my features. He grinned, and held out his arms for the baby. "Give me the laddie; we'll go visiting, and leave your hands free for the cooking."

I watched them go with a small sense of relief. Alone, if only for a few moments. I drew a long, deep breath of damp air, becoming aware of the soft patter of the rain on my hood.

I loved Gatherings and social occasions, but was obliged to admit to myself that the strain of unrelieved company for days on end rather got on my nerves. After a week of visiting, gossip, daily medical clinics, and the small but constant crises that attend living rough with a large family group, I was ready to dig a small hole under a log and climb in, just for the sake of a quarter hour's solitude.

Just at the moment, though, it looked as though I might be saved the effort. There were shouts, calls, and snatches of pipe music from higher up the mountain; disturbed by the Governor's Proclamation, the Gathering was reestablishing its normal rhythm, and everyone was going back to their family hearths, to the clearing where the competitions were held, to the livestock pens beyond the creek, or to the wagons set up to sell everything from ribbons and churns to powdered mortar and fresh—well, relatively fresh—lemons. No one needed me for the moment.

It was going to be a very busy day, and this might be my only chance of solitude for a week or more—the trip back would take at least that long, moving slowly with a large party, including babies and wagons. Most of the new tenants had neither horses nor mules, and would make the journey on foot.

I needed a moment to myself, to gather my strength and focus my mind. What focus I had, though, was not on the logistics of breakfast or weddings, nor even on the impending surgery I was contemplating. I was looking farther forward, past the journey, longing for home.

Fraser's Ridge was high in the western mountains, far beyond any town—or even any established roads. Remote and isolated, we had few visitors. Few inhabitants, too, though the population of the Ridge was growing; more than thirty families had come to take up homesteads on Jamie's granted land, under his sponsorship. Most of these were men he had known in prison, at Ardsmuir. I thought Chisholm and McGillivray must be ex-prisoners, too; Jamie had put out a standing invitation for such men, and would hold to it, no matter the expense involved in helping them—or whether we could afford it.

A raven flew silently past, slow and heavy, its feathers burdened by the rain. Ravens were birds of omen; I wondered whether this one meant us good or ill. Rare for any bird to fly in such weather—that must mean it was a special omen.

I knocked the heel of my hand against my head, trying to smack the superstition out of it. Live with Highlanders long enough, and every damn rock and tree meant something!

Perhaps it did, though. There were people all round me on the mountain—I knew that—and yet I felt quite alone, shielded by the rain and fog. The weather was still cold, but I was not. The blood thrummed near the surface of my skin, and I felt heat rise in my palms. I reached a hand out to the pine that stood by me, drops of water trembling on each needle, its bark black with wet. I breathed its scent and let the water touch my skin, cool as vapor. The rain fell in shushing stillness all around me, dampening my clothes 'til they clung to me softly, like clouds upon the mountain.

Jamie had told me once that he must live on a mountain, and I knew now why this was so—though I could in no wise have put the notion into words. All my scattered thoughts receded, as I listened for the voice of rocks and trees—and heard the bell of the mountain strike once, somewhere deep beneath my feet.

I might have stood thus enchanted for some time, all thought of breakfast forgotten, but the voices of rocks and trees hushed and vanished with the clatter of feet on the nearby path.

"Mrs. Fraser."

It was Archie Hayes himself, resplendent in bonnet and sword despite the wet. If he was surprised to see me standing by the path alone, he didn't show it, but inclined his head in courteous greeting.

"Lieutenant." I bowed back, feeling my cheeks flush as though he had caught me in the midst of bathing.

"Will your husband be about, ma'am?" he asked, voice casual. Despite my discomfiture, I felt a stab of wariness. Young Corporal MacNair had come to fetch Jamie, and failed. If the mountain had come to Mohammed now, the matter wasn't casual. Was Hayes intending to drag Jamie into some sort of witch-hunt for Regulators?

"I suppose so. I don't really know *where* he is," I said, consciously not looking up the hill to the spot where Jocasta's big tent showed its canvas peak among a stand of chestnut trees.

"Ah, I expect he'll be that busy," Hayes said comfortably. "A great deal to do for a man like himself, and this the last day of the Gathering."

"Yes. I expect . . . er . . . yes."

The conversation died, and I was left in a state of increasing discomfort, wondering how on earth I was to escape without inviting the Lieutenant to breakfast. Even an Englishwoman couldn't get away with the rudeness of not offering food without exciting remark.

"Er . . . Corporal MacNair said you wanted to see Farquard Campbell as well," I said, seizing the bull by the horns. "Perhaps Jamie's gone to talk with him. Mr. Campbell, I mean." I waved helpfully toward the Campbells' family campsite, which lay on the far side of the slope, nearly a quarter mile from Jocasta's.

Hayes blinked, drops running from his lashes down his cheeks.

"Aye," he said. "Perhaps that's so." He stood a moment longer, then tipped his cap to me. "Good day to ye, mum." He turned away up the path—toward Jocasta's tent. I stood watching him go, all sense of peace destroyed.

"Damn," I said under my breath, and set off to see about breakfast.

## LOAVES AND FISHES

W E HAD CHOSEN A SITE well off the main path, but situated in a small, rocky clearing with a good view of the wide creekbank below. Glancing downward through a scrim of holly bushes, I could see the flash of green-and-black tartans as the last of the soldiers dispersed; Archie Hayes encouraged his men to mingle with the people at the Gathering, and most were only too glad to obey.

I wasn't sure whether this policy of Archie's was dictated by guile, penury, or simply humanitarianism. Many of his soldiers were young, separated from home and family; they were glad of the chance to hear Scottish voices again, to be welcomed at a homely fireside, offered brose and parritch, and to bask in the momentary warmth of familiarity.

As I came out of the trees, I saw that Marsali and Lizzie were making a small fuss of the bashful young soldier who had fished Germain out of the creek. Fergus stood close to the fire, wisps of steam rising from his wet garments, muttering in French as he rubbed Germain's head briskly with a towel, one-handed. His hook was braced against the little boy's shoulder to keep him steady, and the blond head wobbled back and forth, Germain's face quite tranquil, in complete disregard of his father's scolding.

Neither Roger nor Brianna were anywhere in sight, but I was rather alarmed to see Abel MacLennan sitting on the far side of the clearing, nibbling a bit of toasted bread on a stick. Jamie was already back with the borrowed supplies, which he was unpacking on the ground next to the fire. He was frowning to himself, but the frown melted into a smile at sight of me.

"There ye are, Sassenach!" he said, rising to his feet. "What kept ye?"

"Oh . . . I met an acquaintance on the trail," I said, with a significant look toward the young soldier. It was evidently not significant enough, since Jamie knitted his brows in puzzlement.

"The Lieutenant is looking for you," I hissed, leaning close to him.

"Well, I kent *that*, Sassenach," he said, in a normal tone of voice. "He'll find me soon enough."

"Yes, but . . . ahem." I cleared my throat and raised my brows, glancing pointedly from Abel MacLennan to the young soldier. Jamie's notions of hospitality wouldn't countenance having his guests dragged away from under his rooftree, and I would have supposed that the same principle applied to his campfire as well. The young soldier might find it awkward to arrest MacLennan, but I was sure the Lieutenant would have no such hesitation.

Jamie looked rather amused. Raising his own brows, he took my arm, and led me over to the young man.

"My dear," he said formally, "may I present Private Andrew Ogilvie, late of the village of Kilburnie? Private Ogilvie, my wife."

Private Ogilvie, a ruddy-faced boy with dark curly hair, blushed and bowed.

"Your servant, mum!"

Jamie squeezed my arm lightly.

"Private Ogilvie was just telling me that the regiment is bound for Portsmouth, in Virginia—there to take ship for Scotland. Ye'll be glad to see home, I expect, lad?"

"Oh, aye, sir!" the lad said fervently. "The regiment will disband in Aberdeen, and then I'm off home, so fast as my legs will carry me!"

"The regiment is disbanding?" Fergus asked, coming to join the conversation, a towel draped round his neck and Germain in his arms.

"Aye, sir. With the Frenchies settled—er, beggin' your

pardon, sir—and the Indians safe, there's naught for us to do here, and the Crown willna pay us to sit at home," the lad said ruefully. "Peace may be a guid thing, all in all, and I'm glad of it, surely. But there's no denying as it's hard on a soldier."

"Almost as hard as war, aye?" Jamie said dryly. The boy flushed darkly; young as he was, he couldn't have seen much in the way of actual fighting. The Seven Years War had been over for nearly ten years—at which time Private Ogilvie would likely still have been a barefoot lad in Kilburnie.

Ignoring the boy's embarrassment, Jamie turned to me.

"The lad tells me," he added, "that the Sixty-seventh is the last regiment left in the Colonies."

"The last Highland regiment?" I asked.

"No, mum, the last of the Crown's regular troops. There are the garrisons here and there, I suppose, but all of the standing regiments have been recalled to England or Scotland. We're the last—and behind our time, too. We meant to sail from Charleston, but things went agley there, and so we're bound for Portsmouth now, so fast as we can make speed. It's late in the year, but the Lieutenant's had word of a ship that may risk passage to take us. If not—" He shrugged, glumly philosophic. "Then we shall winter in Portsmouth, I suppose, and make shift as we can."

"So England means to leave us unprotected?" Marsali looked rather shocked at the thought.

"Oh, I shouldna think there's any great danger, mum," Private Ogilvie assured her. "We've dealt wi' the Frenchies for good and all, and the Indians willna be up to much without the frogs to stir them up. Everything's been quite peaceful for a good time now, and doubtless it'll stay so." I made a small noise in the back of my throat, and Jamie squeezed my elbow lightly.

"Have ye not thought perhaps to stay, then?" Lizzie had been peeling and grating potatoes while listening to this; she put down the bowl of glistening white shreds by the fire and began to smear grease on the griddle. "Stay in the Colonies, I mean. There's plenty of land still to be had, to the west."

"Oh." Private Ogilvie glanced down at her, her white

kerch modestly bent over her work, and his color deepened again. "Well, I will say I've heard worse prospects, miss. But I am bound to go wi' my regiment, I'm afraid."

Lizzie picked up two eggs and cracked them neatly against the side of the bowl. Her own face, usually pale as whey, bore a faint pink echo of the Private's rich blush.

"Ah. Well, it's a great pity that ye should go awa so soon," she said. Her pale blond lashes swept down against her cheeks. "Still, we'll not send ye away on an empty stomach."

Private Ogilvie went slightly pinker round the ears.

"That's . . . verra kind of ye, miss. Verra kind indeed."

Lizzie glanced up shyly, and blushed more deeply.

Jamie coughed gently and excused himself, leading me away from the fire.

"Christ," he said in an undertone, bending down so I could hear him. "And she's been a woman less than a full day, too! Have ye been givin' her lessons, Sassenach, or are women just born wi' it?"

"Natural talent, I expect," I said circumspectly.

The unexpected advent of Lizzie's menarche after supper last night had in fact been the straw that broke the camel's back, with regard to clean clouts, and the precipitating event that had caused me to sacrifice my petticoat. Lizzie naturally had no menstrual cloths with her, and I didn't want to oblige her to share the children's diapers.

"Mmphm. I suppose I'd best begin looking for a husband for her, then," Jamie said in resignation.

"A husband! Why, she's scarcely fifteen!"

"Aye, so?" He glanced at Marsali, who was rubbing Fergus's dark hair dry with the towel, and then back at Lizzie and her soldier, and raised a cynical brow at me.

"Aye, so, yourself," I said, a little crossly. All right, Marsali *had* been only fifteen when she married Fergus. That didn't mean—

"The point being," Jamie went on, dismissing Lizzie for the moment, "that the regiment leaves for Portsmouth tomorrow; they havena got either time nor disposition to trouble with this business in Hillsborough—that's Tryon's concern."

"But what Hayes said—"

"Oh, if anyone tells him anything, I'm sure he'll send the

depositions along to New Bern—but as for himself, I imagine he'd not much care if the Regulators set fire to the Governor's Palace, so long as it doesna delay his sailing."

I heaved a deep sigh, reassured. If Jamie was right, the last thing Hayes would do was take prisoners, no matter what the evidence to hand. MacLennan was safe, then.

"But what do you suppose Hayes wants with you and the others, then?" I asked, bending to rummage in one of the wicker hampers for another loaf of bread. "He *is* hunting you—in person."

Jamie glanced back over his shoulder, as though expecting the Lieutenant to appear at any moment through the holly bushes. As the screen of prickly green remained intact, he turned back to me, frowning slightly.

"I dinna ken," he said, shaking his head, "but it's naught to do with this business of Tryon's. If it was that, he might have told me last night—for that matter, if he cared himself about the matter, he *would* have told me last night," he added. "No, Sassenach, depend upon it, the rioters are no more than a matter of duty to wee Archie Hayes.

"As for what he wants wi' me—" He leaned over my shoulder to swipe a finger round the top of the honey pot. "I dinna mean to trouble about it until I must. I've three kegs of whisky left, and I mean to turn them into a plowshare, a scythe blade, three ax-heids, ten pound of sugar, a horse, and an astrolabe before this evening. Which is a conjuring trick that might take some attention, aye?" He drew the sticky tip of his finger gently across my lips, then turned my head toward him and bent to kiss me.

"An astrolabe?" I said, tasting honey. I kissed him back. "Whatever for?"

"And then I want to go home," he whispered, ignoring the question. His forehead was pressed against mine, and his eyes very blue.

"I want to take ye to bed—*in* my bed. And I mean to spend the rest of the day thinking what to do to ye once I've got ye there. So wee Archie can just go and play at marbles with his ballocks, aye?"

"An excellent thought," I whispered back. "Care to tell him that yourself?"

My eye had caught the flash of a green-and-black tartan on the other side of the clearing, but when Jamie straightened up and whirled round, I saw that the visitor was in fact not Lieutenant Hayes but rather John Quincy Myers, who was sporting a soldier's plaid wrapped round his waist, the ends fluttering gaily in the breeze.

This added a further touch of color to Myers's already striking sartorial splendor. Extremely tall, and decorated from the top down with a slouch hat stuck through with several needles and a turkey quill, two ragged pheasant feathers knotted into his long black hair, a vest of dyed porcupine quills worn over a beaded shirt, his usual breechclout, and leggings wrapped with strings of small bells, the mountain man was hard to miss.

"Friend James!" John Quincy smiled broadly at sight of Jamie, and hastened forward, hand extended and bells chiming. "Thought I should find you at your breakfast!"

Jamie blinked slightly at this vision, but gamely returned the mountain man's encompassing handshake.

"Aye, John. Will ye join us?"

"Er . . . yes," I chimed in, with a surreptitious look into the food hamper. "Please do!"

John Quincy bowed ceremoniously to me, sweeping off his hat.

"Your servant, ma'am, and I'm much obliged. Maybe later. Right now, I come to fetch away Mr. Fraser, though. He's wanted, urgent-like."

"By whom?" Jamie asked warily.

"Robbie McGillivray, he says his name is. You know the man?"

"Aye, I do." Whatever Jamie knew about McGillivray, it was causing him to delve into the small chest where he kept his pistols. "What's the trouble?"

"Well." John Quincy scratched meditatively at his bushy black beard. " 'Twas his wife as asked me to come find you, and she don't speak what you'd call right good English, so may be as I've muddled the account of it a bit. But what I *think* she said to me was as how there was a thief-taker who'd grabbed holt of her son, sayin' as how the boy was one o' the ruffians who broke up Hillsborough, and meanin' to take him to the gaol in New Bern. Only Robbie, he says no one's takin' a son of his anywhere, and—well, after that, the poor woman got right flustered and I couldn't make out but one word to the dozen. But I do believe Robbie would 'preciate it if you'd come by and lend a hand with the proceedings."

Jamie grabbed Roger's bloodstained green coat, which was hung on a bush waiting to be cleaned. Shrugging into it, he thrust the newly loaded pistol through his belt.

"Where?" he said.

Myers gestured economically with one large thumb, and pushed off into the holly bushes, Jamie at his heels.

Fergus, who had been listening to this exchange, Germain in his arms, set the boy down at Marsali's feet.

"I must go help *Grand-père*," he told Germain. He picked up a stick of firewood and put it into the little boy's hands. "You stay; protect *Maman* and little Joan from bad people."

*"Oui, Papa."* Germain scowled fiercely under his blond fringe and took a firm grip on his stick, settling himself to defend the camp.

Marsali, MacLennan, Lizzie, and Private Ogilvie had been watching the byplay with rather glazed looks. As Fergus picked up another length of firewood and plunged purposefully into the holly bushes, Private Ogilvie came to life, stirring uneasily.

"Er . . ." he said. "Perhaps I . . . should I go for my sergeant, do ye think, ma'am? If there's like to be any trouble . . ."

"No, no," I said hurriedly. The last thing we needed was for Archie Hayes and his regiment to show up en masse. This struck me as the sort of situation which would benefit strongly from being kept unofficial.

"I'm sure everything will be quite all right. It's sure to be nothing but a misunderstanding. Mr. Fraser will sort it directly, never fear." Even as I spoke, I was sidling round the fire toward the spot where my medical supplies lay, sheltered from the drizzle under a sheet of canvas. Reaching under the edge, I grabbed my small emergency kit.

"Lizzie, why don't you give Private Ogilvie some of the strawberry preserves for his toast? And Mr. MacLennan would like a bit of honey in his coffee, I'm sure. Do excuse me, won't you, Mr. MacLennan, I must just go and . . . er . . ." Smiling inanely, I sidled through the holly leaves. As the branches swished and crackled behind me, I paused to take my bearings. A faint chime of bells reached me on the rainy wind; I turned toward the sound, and broke into a run.

IT WAS SOME WAY; I was out of breath and sweating from the exercise by the time I caught them up near the competition field. Things were just getting under way; I could hear the buzz of talk from the crowd of men gathering, but no shouts of encouragement or howls of disappointment as yet. A few brawny specimens stamped to and fro, stripped to the waist and swinging their arms to limber up; the local "strongmen" of various settlements.

The drizzle had started up again; the wetness gleamed on curving shoulders and plastered swirls of dark body hair flat against the pale skins of chests and forearms. I had no time to appreciate the spectacle, though; John Quincy threaded his way adroitly through the knots of spectators and competitors, waving cordially to this and that acquaintance as we passed. On the far side of the crowd, a small man detached himself from the mass and came hurrying to meet us.

"*Mac Dubh!* Ye've come, then—that's good."

"Nay bother, Robbie," Jamie assured him. "What's to do, then?"

McGillivray, who looked distinctly harried, glanced at the strongmen and their supporters, then jerked his head toward the nearby trees. We followed him, unnoticed by the crowd gathering round two large stones wrapped with rope, which I assumed some of the strongmen present were about to prove their prowess by lifting.

"It's your son, is it, Rob?" Jamie asked, dodging a water-filled pine branch.

"Aye," Robbie answered, "or it was."

That sounded sinister. I saw Jamie's hand brush the butt of his pistol; mine went to my medical kit.

"What's happened?" I asked. "Is he hurt?"

"Not him," McGillivray replied cryptically, and ducked ahead, beneath a drooping chestnut bough hung with scarlet creeper.

Just beyond was a small open space, not really big enough to be called a clearing, tufted with dead grass and studded with pine saplings. As Fergus and I ducked under the creeper after Jamie, a large woman in homespun whirled toward us, shoulders hunching as she raised the broken tree limb she clutched in one hand. She saw McGillivray, though, and relaxed fractionally.

*"Wer ist das?"* she asked suspiciously, eyeing us. Then John Quincy appeared from under the creeper, and she lowered the club, her solidly handsome features relaxing further.

"Ha, Myers! You brung me den Jamie, *oder?*" She cast me a curious look, but was too busy glancing between Fergus and Jamie to inspect me closely.

"Aye, love, this is Jamie Roy—*Sheumais Mac Dubh.*" McGillivray hastened to take credit for Jamie's appearance, putting a respectful hand on his sleeve. "My wife, Ute, *Mac Dubh.* And *Mac Dubh*'s son," he added, waving vaguely at Fergus.

Ute McGillivray looked like a Valkyrie on a starchy diet; tall, very blond, and broadly powerful.

"Your servant, ma'am," Jamie said, bowing.

*"Madame,"* Fergus echoed, making her a courtly leg.

Mrs. McGillivray dropped them a low curtsy in return, eyes fixed on the prominent bloodstains streaking the front of Jamie's—or rather, Roger's—coat.

*"Mein Herr,"* she murmured, looking impressed. She turned and beckoned to a young man of seventeen or eighteen, who had been lurking in the background. He bore such a marked resemblance to his small, wiry, dark-haired father that his identity could scarcely be in doubt.

"Manfred," his mother announced proudly. *"Mein* laddie."

Jamie inclined his head in grave acknowledgment.

"Mr. McGillivray."

"Ah . . . your s-servant, sir?" The boy sounded rather dubious about it, but put out his hand to be shaken.

"A pleasure to make your acquaintance, sir," Jamie

assured him, shaking it. The courtesies duly observed, he looked briefly round at the quiet surroundings, raising one eyebrow.

"I had heard that you were suffering some inconvenience wi' regard to a thief-taker. Do I take it that the matter has been resolved?" He glanced in question from McGillivray Junior to McGillivray Senior.

The three McGillivrays exchanged assorted glances among themselves. Robin McGillivray gave an apologetic cough.

"Well, not to say *resolved*, quite, *Mac Dubh*. That is to say . . ." He trailed off, the harried look returning to his eyes.

Mrs. McGillivray gave him a stern look, then turned to Jamie.

"*Ist kein* bother," she told him. "*Ich haf den* wee ball of shite safe put. But only we want to know, how we best *den Korpus* hide?"

"The . . . body?" I said, rather faintly.

Even Jamie looked a bit disturbed at that.

"Ye've killed him, Rob?"

"Me?" McGillivray looked shocked. "Christ's sake, *Mac Dubh*, what d'ye take me for?"

Jamie raised the eyebrow again; evidently the thought of McGillivray committing violence was scarcely far-fetched. McGillivray had the grace to look abashed.

"Aye, well. I suppose I might have—and I did—well, but, *Mac Dubh*! That business at Ardsmuir was all long ago and done wi', aye?"

"Aye," Jamie said. "It was. What about this business wi' the thief-taker, though? Where is he?"

I heard a muffled giggle behind me, and swung round to see that the rest of the family McGillivray, silent 'til now, was nonetheless present. Three teenaged girls sat in a row on a dead log behind a screen of saplings, all immaculately attired in clean white caps and aprons, only slightly wilted with the rain.

"*Meine* lassies," Mrs. McGillivray announced, with a wave in their direction—unnecessarily, since all three of the girls looked like smaller versions of herself. "Hilda, Inga, *und* Senga."

Fergus bowed elegantly to the three.

*"Enchanté, Mesdemoiselles."*

The girls giggled and bobbed their heads in response, but without rising, which struck me as odd. Then I noticed some disturbance taking place under the skirt of the oldest girl; a sort of heaving flutter, accompanied by a muffled grunt. Hilda swung her heel sharply into whatever it was, all the time smiling brightly at me.

There was another grunt—much louder this time—from under the skirt, which caused Jamie to start and turn in her direction.

Still smiling brightly, Hilda bent and delicately picked up the edge of her skirt, under which I could see a frantic face, bisected by a dark strip of cloth tied round his mouth.

"That's him," said Robbie, sharing his wife's talent for stating the obvious.

"I see." Jamie's fingers twitched slightly against the side of his kilt. "Ah . . . perhaps we could have him out, then?"

Robbie motioned to the girls, who all stood up together and stepped aside, revealing a small man who lay against the base of the dead log, bound hand and foot with an assortment of what looked like women's stockings, and gagged with someone's kerchief. He was wet, muddy, and slightly battered round the edges.

Myers bent and hoisted the man to his feet, holding him by the collar.

"Well, he ain't much to look at," the mountain man said critically, squinting at the man as though evaluating a substandard beaver skin. "I guess thief-takin' don't pay so well as ye might think."

The man was in fact skinny and rather ragged, as well as disheveled, furious—and frightened. Ute sniffed contemptuously.

*"Saukerl!"* she said, and spat neatly on the thief-taker's boots. Then she turned to Jamie, full of charm.

"So, *mein Herr*. How we are to kill him best?"

The thief-taker's eyes bulged, and he writhed in Myers's

grip. He bucked and twisted, making frantic gargling noises behind the gag. Jamie looked him over, rubbing a knuckle across his mouth, then glanced at Robbie, who gave a slight shrug, with an apologetic glance at his wife.

Jamie cleared his throat.

"Mmphm. Ye had something in mind, perhaps, ma'am?"

Ute beamed at this evidence of sympathy with her intentions, and drew a long dagger from her belt.

"I thought maybe to butcher, *wie ein Schwein, ja?* But see . . ." She poked the thief-taker gingerly between the ribs; he yelped behind the gag, and a small spot of blood bloomed on his ragged shirt.

"Too much *Blut*," she explained, with a moue of disappointment. She waved at the screen of trees, behind which the stone-lifting seemed to be proceeding well. "*Die Leute* will schmell."

"Schmell?" I glanced at Jamie, thinking this some unfamiliar German expression. He coughed, and brushed a hand under his nose. "Oh, *smell*!" I said, enlightened. "Er, yes, I think they might."

"I dinna suppose we'd better shoot him, then," Jamie said thoughtfully. "If ye're wanting to avoid attention, I mean."

"I say we break his neck," Robbie McGillivray said, squinting judiciously at the trussed thief-taker. "That's easy enough."

"You think?" Fergus squinted in concentration. "I say a knife. If you stab in the right spot, the blood is not so much. The kidney, just beneath the ribs in back . . . eh?"

The captive appeared to take exception to these suggestions, judging from the urgent sounds proceeding from behind the gag, and Jamie rubbed his chin dubiously.

"Well, that's no verra difficult," he agreed. "Or strangle him. But he *will* lose his bowels. If it were to be a question of the smell, even crushing his skull . . . but tell me, Robbie, how does the man come to be here?"

"Eh?" Robbie looked blank.

"You're no camped nearby?" Jamie waved a hand briefly at the tiny clearing, making his meaning clear. There was no trace of hearthfire; in fact, no one had camped on this side of the creek. And yet all the McGillivrays were here.

"Oh, no," Robbie said, comprehension blossoming on his spare features. "Nay, we're camped some distance up. Only, we came to have a wee keek at the heavies"—he jerked his head toward the competition field—"and the friggin' vulture spied our Freddie and took hold of him, so as to drag him off." He cast an unfriendly look at the thief-taker, and I saw that a coil of rope dangled snakelike from the man's belt. A pair of iron manacles lay on the ground nearby, the dark metal already laced with orange rust from the damp.

"We saw him grab aholt of Brother," Hilda put in at this point. "So we grabbed aholt of *him* and pushed him through here, where nobody could see. When he said he meant to take Brother away to the sheriff, me and my sisters knocked him down and sat on him, and Mama kicked him a few times."

Ute patted her daughter fondly on one sturdy shoulder.

"They are *gut*, strong *Mädchen, meine* lasses," she told Jamie. "Ve *komm* see *hier die Wettkämpfer*, maybe choose husband for Inga or Senga. Hilda *hat einen Mann* already promised," she added, with an air of satisfaction.

She looked Jamie over frankly, her eye dwelling approvingly on his height, the breadth of his shoulders, and the general prosperity of his appearance.

"He is fine, big, your *Mann*," she said to me. "You haf sons, maybe?"

"No, I'm afraid not," I said apologetically. "Er . . . Fergus is married to my husband's daughter," I added, seeing her gaze shift appraisingly to Fergus.

The thief-taker appeared to feel that the subject was drifting somewhat afield, and summoned attention back to himself with an indignant squeal behind his gag. His face, which had gone pale at the discussion of his theoretical demise, had grown quite red again, and his hair was matted down across his forehead in spikes.

"Oh, aye," Jamie said, noticing. "Perhaps we should let the gentleman have a word?"

Robbie narrowed his eyes at this, but reluctantly nodded. The competitions had got well under way by now, and there was a considerable racket emanating from the field; no one would notice the odd shout over here.

"Don't let 'em kill me, sir! You know it ain't right!" Hoarse from his ordeal, the man fixed his appeal on Jamie as soon as the gag was removed. "I'm only doin' as I ought, delivering a criminal to justice!"

"Ha!" all the McGillivrays said at once. Unanimous as their sentiment appeared to be, the expression of it immediately disintegrated into a confusion of expletives, opinions, and a random volley of kicks aimed at the gentleman's shins by Inga and Senga.

"Stop that!" Jamie said, raising his voice enough to be heard over the uproar. As this had no result, he grabbed McGillivray Junior by the scruff of the neck and roared, *"Ruhe!"* at the top of his lungs, which startled them into momentary silence, with guilty looks over their shoulders in the direction of the competition field.

"Now, then," Jamie said firmly. "Myers, bring the gentleman, if ye will. Rob, Fergus, come along with ye. *Bitte*, Madame?" He bowed to Mrs. McGillivray, who blinked at him, but then nodded in slow acquiescence. Jamie rolled an eye at me, then, still holding Manfred by the neck, he marched the male contingent off toward the creek, leaving me in charge of the ladies.

"Your *Mann*—he will save my son?" Ute turned to me, fair brows knitted in concern.

"He'll try." I glanced at the girls, who were huddled together behind their mother. "Do you know whether your brother *was* at Hillsborough?"

The girls looked at one another, and silently elected Inga to speak.

"Well, *ja*, he was, then," she said, a little defiantly. "But he wasna riotin', not a bit of it. He'd only gone for to have a bit of harness mended, and was caught up in the mob."

I caught a quick glance exchanged between Hilda and Senga, and deduced that this was perhaps not the entire story. Still, it wasn't my place to judge, thank goodness.

Mrs. McGillivray's eyes were fixed on the men, who stood murmuring together some distance away. The thief-taker had been untied, save for his hands, which remained bound. He stood with his back against a tree, looking like a cornered rat, eyeteeth showing in a snarl of defiance. Jamie and Myers were both looming over him, while Fergus stood by, frowning attentively, his chin propped on his hook. Rob McGillivray had taken out a knife, with which he was contemplatively flicking small chips of wood from a pine twig, glancing now and then at the thief-taker with an air of dark intent.

"I'm sure Jamie will be able to . . . er . . . do something," I said, privately hoping that the something wouldn't involve too much violence. The unwelcome thought occurred to me that the diminutive thief-taker would probably fit tidily in one of the empty food hampers.

*"Gut."* Ute McGillivray nodded slowly, still watching. "Better that I do not kill him." Her eyes turned suddenly back to me, light blue and very bright. "But I vill do it, if I must."

I believed her.

"I see," I said carefully. "But—I do beg your pardon—but even if that man took your son, could you not go to the sheriff too, and explain . . ."

More glances among the girls. This time it was Hilda who spoke.

*"Nein,* ma'am. See, it wouldna have been sae bad, had the thief-taker come on us at the camp. But down here—" She widened her eyes, nodding toward the competition field, where a muffled thud and a roar of approval marked some successful effort.

The difficulty, apparently, was Hilda's fiancé, one Davey Morrison, from Hunter's Point. Mr. Morrison was a farmer of some substance, and a man of worth, as well as an athlete skilled in the arcana of stone-throwing and caber-tossing. He had family, too—parents, uncles, aunts, cousins—all of the most upright character and—I gathered—rather judgmental attitudes.

Had Manfred been taken by a thief-taker in front of such a crowd, filled with Davey Morrison's relations, word would have spread at the speed of light, and the scandal would result in the prompt rupture of Hilda's engagement—a prospect that clearly perturbed Ute McGillivray much more than the notion of cutting the thief-taker's throat.

"Bad, too, I kill him and someone see," she said frankly, waving at the thin scrim of trees shielding us from the competition field. *"Die* Morrisons would not like."

"I suppose they might not," I murmured, wondering whether Davey Morrison had any idea what he was getting into. "But you—"

"I vill haf *meine* lassies well wed," she said firmly, nodding several times in reinforcement. "I find *gut* men *für Sie*, fine big men, *mit* land, *mit* money." She put an arm round Senga's shoulders and hugged her tight. *"Nicht wahr, Liebchen?"*

*"Ja,* Mama," Senga murmured, and laid her neat capped head affectionately on Mrs. McGillivray's broad bosom.

Something was happening on the men's side of things; the thief-taker's hands had been untied, and he stood rubbing his wrists, no longer scowling, but listening to whatever Jamie was saying with an expression of wariness. He glanced at us, then at Robin McGillivray, who said something to him and nodded emphatically. The thief-taker's jaw worked, as though he were chewing over an idea.

"So you all came down to watch the competitions this morning and look for suitable prospects? Yes, I see."

Jamie reached into his sporran and drew out something, which he held under the thief-taker's nose, as though inviting him to smell it. I couldn't make out what it was at this distance, but the thief-taker's face suddenly changed, going from wariness to alarmed disgust.

*"Ja,* only to look." Mrs. McGillivray was not watching; she patted Senga and let her go. "Ve go now to Salem, where *ist meine Familie.* Maybe ve find there a good *Mann,* too."

Myers had stepped back from the confrontation now, his shoulders drooping in relaxation. He inserted a finger under the edge of his breechclout, scratched his buttocks comfortably, and glanced around, evidently no longer interested in the proceedings. Seeing me looking in his direction, he ambled back through the sapling grove.

"No need to worry more, ma'am," he assured Mrs. McGillivray. "I knew Jamie Roy would take care of it, and so he has. Your lad's safe."

*"Ja?"* she said. She looked doubtfully toward the sapling grove, but it was true; the attitudes of all the men had relaxed now, and Jamie was handing the thief-taker back his set of

manacles. I saw the way he handled them, with brusque distaste. He had worn irons, at Ardsmuir.

*"Gott sei dank,"* Mrs. McGillivray said, with an explosive sigh. Her massive form seemed suddenly to diminish as the breath went out of her.

The little man was leaving, making his way away from us, toward the creek. The sound of the swinging irons at his belt reached us in a faint chime of metal, heard between the shouts of the crowd behind us. Jamie and Rob McGillivray stood close together, talking, while Fergus watched the thief-taker's departure, frowning slightly.

"Exactly what did Jamie tell him?" I asked Myers.

"Oh. Well." The mountain man gave me a broad, gap-toothed grin. "Jamie Roy told him serious-like that it was surely luck for the thief-taker—his name's Boble, by the way, Harley Boble—that we done come upon y'all when we did. He give him to understand that if we hadn't, then this lady here"—he bowed toward Ute—"would likely have taken him home in her wagon, and slaughtered him like a hog, safe out of sight."

Myers rubbed a knuckle under his red-veined nose and chortled softly in his beard.

"Boble said as how he didn't believe it, he thought she was only a-tryin' to scare him with that knife. But then Jamie Roy leaned down close, confidential-like, and said he mighta thought the same—only that he'd heard so much about Frau McGillivray's reputation as a famous sausage-maker, and had had the privilege of bein' served some of it to his breakfast this morning. Right about then, Boble started to lose the color in his face, and when Jamie Roy pulled out a bit of sausage to show him—"

"Oh, dear," I said, with a vivid memory of exactly what that sausage smelled like. I had bought it the day before from a vendor on the mountain, only to discover that it had been improperly cured, and once sliced, smelled so strongly of rotting blood that no one had been able to stomach it at supper. Jamie had wrapped the offending remainder in his handkerchief and put it in his sporran, intending either to procure a refund or to shove it down the vendor's throat. "I see."

Myers nodded, turning to Ute.

"And your husband, ma'am—bless his soul, Rob McGillivray's a real born liar—chimes in solemn-like, agreeing to it all, shakin' his head and sayin' as how he's got his work cut out to shoot enough meat for you."

The girls tittered.

"Da can't kill anything," Inga said softly to me. "He willna even wring a chicken's neck."

Myers raised his shoulders in a good-humored shrug, as Jamie and Rob made their way toward us through the wet grass.

"So Jamie promised on his word as a gentleman to protect Boble from you, and Boble promised on *his* word as a . . . well, he said as he'd keep clear of young Manfred."

"Hmp," said Ute, looking rather disconcerted. She didn't mind at all being considered an habitual murderess, and was quite pleased that Manfred was out of danger—but was rather put out at having her reputation as a sausage-maker maligned.

"As though I vould effer make such shite," she said, wrinkling her nose in disdain at the odorous lump of meat Jamie offered for her inspection. "Pfaugh. *Ratzfleisch*." She waved it away with a fastidious gesture, then turned to her husband and said something softly in German.

Then she took a deep breath and expanded once more, gathering all her children like a hen clucking after chicks, urging them to thank Jamie properly for his help. He flushed slightly at the chorus of thanks, bowing to her.

"*Gern geschehen,*" he said. "*Euer ergebener Diener, Frau Ute.*"

She beamed at him, composure restored, as he turned to say something in parting to Rob.

"Such a fine, big *Mann*," she murmured, shaking her head slightly as she looked him up and down. Then she turned, and caught my glance from Jamie to Rob—for while the gunsmith was a handsome man, with close-clipped, dark curly hair and a chiseled face, he was also fine-boned as a sparrow, and some inches shorter than his wife, reaching approximately to the level of her brawny shoulder. I couldn't help wondering, given her apparent admiration for large men . . .

"Oh, vell," she said, and shrugged apologetically. "Luff, you know." She sounded as though love were an unfortunate but unavoidable condition.

I glanced at Jamie, who was carefully swaddling his sausage before tucking it back into his sporran. "Well, yes," I said. "I do."

BY THE TIME we returned to our own campsite, the Chisholms were just departing, having been capably fed by the girls. Fortunately, Jamie had brought plenty of food from Jocasta's camp, and I sat down at last to a pleasant meal of potato fritters, buttered bannocks, fried ham, and—at last!—coffee, wondering just what *else* might happen today. There was plenty of time; the sun was barely above the trees, almost invisible behind the drifting rain clouds.

A little later, pleasantly full of breakfast, and with a third cup of coffee to hand, I went and threw back the canvas covering what I thought of as my medical supply dump. It was time to begin the business of organizing for the morning's surgery; looking at jars of sutures, restocking the herb jars in my chest, refilling the large alcohol bottle, and brewing up the medicines that must be made fresh.

Somewhat depleted of the commoner herbs I had brought with me, my stock had been augmented by the good offices of Myers, who had brought me several rare and useful things from the Indian villages to the north, and by judicious trading with Murray MacLeod, an ambitious young apothecary who had made his way inland and set up shop in Cross Creek.

I bit the inside of my cheek, considering young Murray. He harbored the usual sort of nasty notions that passed for medical wisdom nowadays—and was not shy about asserting the superiority of such scientific methods as bleeding and blistering over the old-fashioned herbcraft that such ignorant crones as myself were prone to practice!

Still, he was a Scot, and thus possessed of a strong streak of pragmatism. He had given Jamie's powerful frame one look and hastily swallowed the more insulting of his opinions. I had six ounces of wormwood and a jar of wild ginger root, and he wanted them. He was also shrewd enough to have observed that many more of the folk on the mountain who ailed with anything came to me than to him—and that most who accepted my cures were improved. If I had secrets, he wanted those, too—and I was more than happy to oblige.

Good, I had plenty of willow bark still left. I hesitated over the small rank of bottles in the upper right tray of the chest. I had several very strong emmenagogues—blue cohosh, ergot, and pennyroyal—but picked instead the gentler tansy and rue, setting a handful into a bowl and pouring boiling water on them to steep. Beyond its effects in easing menstruation, tansy had a reputation for calming nerves—and a more naturally nervous person than Lizzie Wemyss it would be difficult to imagine.

I glanced back at the fire, where Lizzie was shoveling the last of the strawberry preserves into Private Ogilvie, who appeared to be dividing his attention among Lizzie, Jamie, and his slice of toast—the greater proportion going to the toast.

Rue was quite a good anthelmintic, to boot. I didn't *know* that Lizzie suffered from worms, but a good many people in the mountains did, and a dose would certainly do her no harm.

I eyed Abel MacLennan covertly, wondering whether to slip a quick slug of hellbrew into his coffee as well—he had the pinched, anemic look of one with intestinal parasites, in spite of his stocky build. Perhaps, though, the look of pale disquiet on his features was due more to his knowledge of thief-takers in the vicinity.

Baby Joan was wailing with hunger again. Marsali sat down, reached under her arisaid to unfasten her bodice, and set the baby to her breast, her lip clenched between her teeth with trepidation. She winced, gasped in pain, then relaxed a little, as the milk began to flow.

Cracked nipples. I frowned and returned to a perusal of the medicine chest. Had I brought any sheep's-wool ointment? Drat, no. I didn't want to use bear grease, with Joan suckling; perhaps sunflower oil . . .

"A bit of coffee, my dear?" Mr. MacLennan, who had been watching Marsali with troubled sympathy, extended his fresh cup toward her. "My own wife did say as hot coffee eased the pangs of nursing a wean. Whisky in it's better"— his mournful jowls lifted a bit—"but all the same . . ."

*"Taing."* Marsali took the cup with a grateful smile. "I'm chilled right through this morning." She sipped the steaming liquid cautiously, and a small flush crept into her cheeks.

"Will you be going back to Drunkard's Creek tomorrow, Mr. MacLennan?" she asked politely, handing back the empty cup. "Or are ye traveling to New Bern wi' Mr. Hobson?"

Jamie looked up sharply, breaking off his conversation with Private Ogilvie.

"Hobson is going to New Bern? How d'ye ken that?"

"Mrs. Fowles says so," Marsali replied promptly. "She told me when I went to borrow a dry shirt for Germain— she's got a lad his size. She's worrit for Hugh—that's her husband—because her father—that's Mr. Hobson—wishes him to go along, but he's scairt."

"Why is Joe Hobson going to New Bern?" I asked, peering over the top of my medicine chest.

"To present a petition to the Governor," Abel MacLennan said. "Much good it will do." He smiled at Marsali, a little sadly. "No, lassie. I dinna ken where I'm bound, tell ye the truth. 'Twon't be to New Bern, though."

"Nor back to your wife at Drunkard's Creek?" Marsali looked at him in concern.

"My wife's dead, lass," MacLennan said softly. He smoothed the red kerchief across his knee, easing out the wrinkles. "Dead two months past."

"Oh, Mr. Abel." Marsali leaned forward and clasped his hand, her blue eyes full of pain. "I'm that sorry!"

He patted her hand, not looking up. Tiny drops of rain gleamed in the sparse strands of his hair, and a trickle of moisture ran down behind one large red ear, but he made no move to wipe it away.

Jamie had stood up while questioning Marsali. Now he sat down on the log beside MacLennan, and laid a hand gently on the smaller man's back.

"I hadna heard, *a charaid,*" he said quietly.

"No." MacLennan looked blindly into the transparent flames. "I—well, the truth of it is, I'd not told anyone. Not 'til now."

Jamie and I exchanged looks across the fire. Drunkard's Creek couldn't possibly harbor more than two dozen souls, in a scatter of cabins spread along the banks. Yet neither the Hobsons nor the Fowleses had mentioned Abel's loss—evidently he really hadn't told anyone.

"What was it happened, Mr. Abel?" Marsali still clasped his hand, though it lay quite limp, palm-down on the red kerchief.

MacLennan looked up then, blinking.

"Oh," he said vaguely. "So much happened. And yet . . . not really very much, after all. Abby—Abigail, my wife—she died of a fever. She got cold, and . . . she died." He sounded faintly surprised.

Jamie poured a bit of whisky into an empty cup, picked up one of MacLennan's unresisting hands, and folded it around the cup, holding the fingers in place with his own, until MacLennan's hand tightened its grasp.

"Drink it, man," he said.

Everyone was silent, watching as MacLennan obediently tasted the whisky, sipped, sipped again. Young Private Ogilvie shifted uneasily on his stone, looking as though he should like to return to his regiment, but he too stayed put, as though fearing an abrupt departure might somehow injure MacLennan further.

MacLennan's very stillness drew every eye, froze all talk. My hand hovered uneasily over the bottles in my chest, but I had no remedy for this.

"I had enough," he said suddenly. "I did." He looked up from his cup and glanced round the fire, as though challenging anyone to dispute him. "For the taxes, aye? It was no so good a year as it might have been, but I was careful. I'd ten bushels of corn put aside, and four good deer hides. It was worth more than the six shillings of the tax."

But the taxes must be paid in hard currency; not in corn and hides and blocks of indigo, as the farmers did their business. Barter was the common means of trade—I knew that well enough, I thought, glancing down at the bag of odd things folk had brought me in payment for my herbs and simples. No one ever paid for anything in money—save the taxes.

"Well, that's only reasonable," said MacLennan, blinking earnestly at Private Ogilvie, as though the young man had protested. "His Majesty canna well be doing wi' a herd of pigs, or a brace of turkeys, now can he? No, I see quite well why it must be hard money, anyone could. And I had the corn; it would ha' brought six shillings, easy."

The only difficulty, of course, lay in turning ten bushels of corn into six shillings of tax. There were those in Drunkard's Creek who might have bought Abel's corn, and were willing—but no one in Drunkard's Creek had money, either. No, the corn must be taken to market in Salem; that was the closest place where hard coin might be obtained. But Salem lay nearly forty miles from Drunkard's Creek—a week's journey, there and back.

"I'd five acres in late barley," Abel explained. "Ripe and yellochtie, achin' for the scythe. I couldna leave it to be spoilt, and my Abby—she was a wee, slight woman, she couldna be scything and threshing."

Unable to spare a week from his harvest, Abel had instead sought help from his neighbors.

"They're guid folk," he insisted. "One or two could spare me the odd penny—but they'd their ain taxes to pay, hadn't they?" Still hoping somehow to scrape up the necessary coin without undertaking the arduous trip to Salem, Abel had delayed—and delayed too long.

"Howard Travers is Sheriff," he said, and wiped unconsciously at the drop of moisture that formed at the end of his nose. "He came with a paper, and said he mun' put us oot, and the taxes not paid."

Faced with necessity, Abel had left his wife in their cabin, and gone posthaste to Salem. But by the time he returned, six shillings in hand, his property had been seized and sold—to Howard Travers's father-in-law—and his cabin was inhabited by strangers, his wife gone.

"I kent she'd no go far," he explained. "She'd not leave the bairns."

And that in fact was where he found her, wrapped in a threadbare quilt and shivering under the big spruce tree on the hill that sheltered the graves of the four MacLennan children, all dead in their first year of life. In spite of his entreaties, Abigail would not go down to the cabin that had been theirs, would seek no aid from those who had dispossessed her. If it was madness from the fever that gripped her, or only stubbornness, he could not tell; she had clung to the branches of the tree with demented strength, crying out the names of her children—and there had died in the night.

His whisky cup was empty. He set it carefully on the ground by his feet, ignoring Jamie's gesture toward the bottle.

"They'd given her leave to carry awa what she could. She'd a bundle with her, and her grave-claes in it. I ken weel her sitting down the day after we were wed, to spin her winding-sheet. It had wee flowers all along one edge, that she'd made; she was a good hand wi' a needle."

He had wrapped Abigail in her embroidered shroud, buried her by the side ˙of their youngest child, and then walked two miles down the road, intending, he thought, to tell the Hobsons what had happened.

"But I came to the house, and found them all abuzzing like hornets—Hugh Fowles had had a visit from Travers, come for the tax, and no money to pay. Travers grinned like an ape and said it was all one to him—and sure enough, ten days later he came along wi' a paper and three men, and put them oot."

Hobson had scraped up the money to pay his own taxes, and the Fowleses were crowded in safely enough with the rest of the family—but Joe Hobson was foaming with wrath over the treatment of his son-in-law.

"He was a-rantin', Joe, bleezin' mad wi' fury. Janet Hobson bid me come and sit, and offered me supper, and there was Joe shoutin' that he'd take the price of the land out of Howard Travers's hide, and Hugh slumped down like a trampled dog, and his wife greetin', and the weans all squealin' for their dinners like a brood o' piglets, and . . . well, I thought of telling them, but then . . ." He shook his head, as though confused anew.

Sitting half-forgotten in the chimney-corner, he had been overcome by a strange sort of fatigue, one that made him so tired that his head nodded on his neck, lethargy stealing over him. It was warm, and he was overcome with a sense of unreality. If the crowded confines of the Hobsons' one-roomed cabin were not real, neither was the quiet hillside and its fresh grave beneath the spruce tree.

He slept under the table, and woke before dawn, to find that the sense of unreality persisted. Everything around him seemed no more than a waking dream. MacLennan himself seemed to have ceased to exist; his body rose, washed itself, and ate, nodded and spoke without his cognizance. None of the outer world existed any longer. And so it was that when Joe Hobson had risen and announced that he and Hugh would go to Hillsborough, there to seek redress from the Court, that Abel MacLennan had found himself marching down the road along with them, nodding and speaking when spoken to, with no more will than a dead man.

"It did come to me, walkin' doon the road, as we were all dead," he said dreamily. "Me and Joe and Hugh and the rest. I might sae well be one place as anither; it was only moving 'til the time came to lay my bones beside Abby. I didna mind it."

When they reached Hillsborough, he had paid no great mind to what Joe intended; only followed, obedient and un-thinking. Followed, and walked the muddy streets sparkling with broken glass from shattered windows, seen the torch-light and mobs, heard the shouts and screams—all quite un-moved.

"It was no but dead men, a-rattling their bones against one anither," he said with a shrug. He was still for a moment, then turned his face to Jamie, and looked long and earnestly up into his face.

"Is it so? Are ye dead, too?" One limp, callused hand floated up from the red kerchief, and rested lightly against the bone of Jamie's cheek.

Jamie didn't recoil from the touch, but took MacLennan's hand and brought it down again, held tight between his own.

"No, *a charaid*," he said softly. "Not yet."

MacLennan nodded slowly.

"Aye. Give it time," he said. He pulled his hands free and sat for a moment, smoothing his kerchief. His head kept bobbing, nodding slightly, as though the spring of his neck had stretched too far.

"Give it time," he repeated. "It's none sae bad." He stood up then, and put the square of red cloth on his head. He turned to me and nodded politely, his eyes vague and troubled.

"I thank ye for the breakfast, ma'am," he said, and walked away.

# 3

# BILIOUS HUMOURS

ABEL MacLENNAN'S DEPARTURE put an abrupt end to breakfast. Private Ogilvie excused himself with thanks, Jamie and Fergus went off in search of scythes and astrolabes, and Lizzie, wilting in the absence of Private Ogilvie, declared that she felt unwell and subsided palely into one of the lean-to shelters, fortified with a large cup of tansy and rue decoction.

Fortunately, Brianna chose to reappear just then, sans Jemmy. She and Roger had breakfasted with Jocasta, she assured me. Jemmy had fallen asleep in Jocasta's arms, and since both parties appeared content with that arrangement, she had left him there, and come back to help me with the morning's clinic.

"Are you sure you want to help me this morning?" I eyed Bree dubiously. "It's your wedding day, after all. I'm sure Lizzie or maybe Mrs. Martin could—"

"No, I'll do it," she assured me, swiping a cloth across the seat of the tall stool I used for my morning surgery. "Lizzie's feeling better, but I don't think she's up to festering feet and putrid stomachs." She gave a small shudder, closing her eyes at the memory of the elderly gentleman whose ulcerated heel I had debrided the day before. The pain had caused him to vomit copiously on his tattered breeches, which in turn had caused several of the people waiting for my attention to throw up too, in sympathetic reflex.

I felt a trifle queasy at the memory myself, but drowned it with a final gulp of bitter coffee.

"No, I suppose not," I agreed reluctantly. "Still, your gown isn't quite finished, is it? Perhaps you should go—"

"It's fine," she assured me. "Phaedre's hemming my dress, and Ulysses is ordering all the servants around up there like a drill sergeant. I'd just be in the way."

I gave way without further demur, though I wondered a little at her alacrity. While Bree wasn't squeamish about the exigencies of normal life, like skinning animals and cleaning fish, I knew the proximity of people with disfiguring conditions or obvious illness bothered her, though she did her best to disguise it. It wasn't distaste, I thought, but rather a crippling empathy.

I lifted the kettle and poured freshly boiled water into a large, half-full jar of distilled alcohol, narrowing my eyes against hot clouds of alcoholic steam.

It *was* difficult to see so many people suffering from things that could have been easily treated in a time of antiseptics, antibiotics, and anesthesia—but I had learned detachment in the field hospitals of a time when such medical innovations were not only new but rare, and I knew both the necessity and the value of it.

I could not help anyone, if my own feelings got in the way. And I must help. It was as simple as that. But Brianna had no such knowledge to use as a shield. Not yet.

She had finished wiping down the stools, boxes, and other impedimenta for the morning surgery, and straightened up, a small frown between her brows.

"Do you remember the woman you saw yesterday? The one with the retarded little boy?"

"Not something you'd forget," I said, as lightly as possible.

"Why? Here, can you deal with this?" I gestured at the folding table I used, which was stubbornly declining to fold up properly, its joints having swollen with the damp.

Brianna frowned slightly, studying it, then struck the offending joint sharply with the side of her hand. It gave way and collapsed obediently at once, recognizing superior force.

"There." She rubbed the side of her hand absently, still frowning. "You were making a big thing of telling her to try not to have any more children. The little boy—was it an inheritable condition, then?"

"You might say that," I replied dryly. "Congenital syphilis."

She looked up, blanching.

"Syphilis? You're sure?"

I nodded, rolling up a length of boiled linen for bandaging. It was still very damp, but no help for it.

"The mother wasn't showing overt signs of the late stages—yet—but it's quite unmistakable in a child."

The mother had come simply to have a gumboil lanced, the little boy clinging to her skirts. He'd had the characteristic "saddle nose," with its pushed-in bridge, as well as a jaw so malformed that I wasn't surprised at his poor nutrition; he could barely chew. I couldn't tell how much of his evident backwardness was due to brain damage and how much to deafness; he appeared to have both, but I hadn't tested their extent—there being exactly nothing I could do to remedy either condition. I had advised the mother to give him pot liquor, which might help with the malnutrition, but there was little else to be done for him, poor mite.

"I don't see it so often here as I did in Paris or Edinburgh, where there were a lot of prostitutes," I told Bree, tossing the ball of bandages into the canvas bag she held open. "Now and then, though. Why? You don't think Roger has syphilis, do you?"

She looked at me, openmouthed. Her look of shock was obliterated by an instant flood of angry red.

"I do *not*!" she said. "Mother!"

"Well, I didn't really think so," I said mildly. "Happens in the best of families, though—and you *were* asking."

She snorted heavily.

"I was *asking* about contraception," she said, through her teeth. "Or at least I meant to, before you started in with the *Physician's Guide to Venereal Disease.*"

"Oh, that." I eyed her thoughtfully, taking in the dried milk stains on her bodice. "Well, breast-feeding is reasonably effective. Not absolute, by any means, but fairly effective. Less so, after the first six months"—Jemmy was now six months old—"but still effective."

"Mmphm," she said, sounding so like Jamie that I had to bite my lower lip in order not to laugh. "And exactly what *else* is effective?"

I hadn't really discussed contraception—eighteenth-century style—with her. It hadn't seemed necessary when she first appeared at Fraser's Ridge, and then it *really* wasn't necessary, she being already pregnant. So she thought it was now?

I frowned, slowly putting rolls of bandage and bundles of herbs into my bag.

"The most common thing is some sort of barrier. A piece of silk or a sponge, soaked with anything from vinegar to brandy—though if you have it, tansy oil or oil of cedar is supposed to work the best. I *have* heard of women in the Indies using half a lemon, but that's obviously not a suitable alternative here."

She uttered a short laugh.

"No, I wouldn't think so. I don't think the tansy oil works all that well, either—that's what Marsali was using when she got pregnant with Joan."

"Oh, she *was* using it? I thought perhaps she'd just not bothered once—and once is enough."

I felt, rather than saw her stiffen, and bit my lip again, this time in chagrin. Once *had* been enough—we just didn't know *which* once. She hunched her shoulders, though, then let them fall, deliberately dismissing whatever memories my thoughtless remark had conjured.

"She said she'd been using it—but she might have forgotten. It doesn't work all the time, though, does it?"

I slung the bag of surgical linens and dried herbs over my shoulder and picked up the medical chest by the leather strap Jamie had made for it.

"The only thing that always works is celibacy," I said. "I suppose that isn't a satisfactory option in the present case?"

She shook her head, her eyes fixed broodingly on a cluster of young men visible through the trees below, taking turns at pitching stones across the creek.

"That's what I was afraid of," she said, and bent to pick up the folding table and a pair of stools.

I looked round the clearing, considering. Anything else? No worry about leaving the campfire, even if Lizzie fell asleep; nothing on the mountainside would burn in this weather; even the kindling and firewood we had stored at the end of our lean-to the day before were damp. Something was missing, though . . . what? Oh, yes. I put down the box for a moment and knelt to crawl into the lean-to. I dug about in the jumble of quilts, coming out finally with my tiny leather medicine pouch.

I said a brief prayer to St. Bride and slipped it round my neck and down inside the bodice of my dress. I was so much in the habit of wearing the amulet when I set out to practice medicine that I had almost ceased to feel ridiculous about this small ritual—almost. Bree was watching me, a rather odd look on her face, but she said nothing.

I didn't, either; merely picked up my things and followed her across the clearing, stepping carefully round the boggiest spots. It wasn't raining now, but the clouds sat on the tops of the trees, promising more at any moment, and wisps of mist rose from fallen logs and dripping bushes.

Why was Bree worrying about contraception? I wondered. Not that I didn't think it sensible—but why now? Perhaps it was to do with the imminence of her wedding to Roger. Even if they had been living as man and wife for the last several months—and they had—the formality of vows spoken before God and man was enough to bring a new sobriety to even the giddiest of young people. And neither Bree nor Roger was giddy.

"There is another possibility," I said to the back of her neck, as she led the way down the slippery trail. "I haven't tried it on anyone yet, so I can't say how reliable it may be. Nayawenne—the old Tuscaroran lady who gave me my medicine bag—she said there were 'women's herbs.' Different mixtures for different things—but one plant in particular for that; she said the seeds of it would keep a man's spirit from overwhelming a woman's."

Bree paused, half-turning as I came up beside her.

"Is that how the Indians see pregnancy?" One corner of her mouth curled wryly. "The man wins?"

I laughed.

"Well, in a way. If the woman's spirit is too strong for the man's, or won't yield to it, she can't conceive. So if a woman wants a child and can't have one, most often the shaman will treat her husband, or both of them, rather than just her."

She made a small throaty noise, partly amusement—but only partly.

"What's the plant—the women's herb?" she asked. "Do you know it?"

"I'm not positive," I admitted. "Or not sure of the name, I should say. She did show it to me, both the growing plant and the dried seeds, and I'm sure I'd know it again—but it wasn't a plant I knew by an English name. One of the Umbelliferae, though," I added helpfully.

She gave me an austere look that reminded me once more of Jamie, then turned to the side to let a small stream of Campbell women go by, clattering with empty kettles and pails, each one bobbing or bowing politely to us as they passed on their way down to the creek.

"Good day to ye, Mistress Fraser," said one, a neat young woman that I recognized as one of Farquard Campbell's younger daughters. "Is your man about? My faither would be glad of a word, he says."

"No, he's gone off, I'm afraid." I gestured vaguely; Jamie could be anywhere. "I'll tell him if I see him, though."

She nodded and went on, each of the women behind her pausing to wish Brianna happiness on her wedding day, their woolen skirts and cloaks brushing small showers of rainwater from the bayberry bushes that lined the path here.

Brianna accepted their good wishes with gracious politeness, but I saw the small line that formed between her thick red brows. Something was definitely bothering her.

"What?" I said bluntly, as soon as the Campbells were out of earshot.

"What's what?" she said, startled.

"What's troubling you?" I asked. "And don't say 'nothing,' because I see there is. Is it to do with Roger? Are you having second thoughts about the wedding?"

"Not exactly," she replied, looking wary. "I want to marry Roger, I mean—*that's* all right. It's just . . . I just . . . thought of something . . ." She trailed off, and a slow flush rose in her cheeks.

"Oh?" I asked, feeling rather alarmed. "What's that?"

"Venereal disease," she blurted. "What if I have it? Not Roger, not him, but—from Stephen Bonnet?"

Her face was flaming so hotly that I was surprised not to see the raindrops sizzle into steam when they struck her skin. My own face felt cold, my heart tight in my chest. The possibility had occurred to me—vividly—at the time, but I hadn't wanted even to suggest such a thing, if she hadn't thought of it herself. I remembered the weeks of watching her covertly for any hint of malaise—but women often showed no symptoms of early infection. Jemmy's healthy birth had been a relief in more ways than one.

"Oh," I said softly. I reached out and squeezed her arm. "Don't worry, lovey. You haven't."

She took a deep breath, and let it out in a pale misty cloud, some of the tension leaving her shoulders.

"You're sure?" she said. "You can tell? I feel all right, but I thought—women don't always have symptoms."

"They don't," I said, "but men most certainly do. And if Roger had contracted anything nasty from *you*, I'd have heard about it long since."

Her face had faded somewhat, but the pinkness came back at that. She coughed, mist rising from her breath.

"Well, that's a relief. So Jemmy's all right? You're sure?"

"Absolutely," I assured her. I had put drops of silver nitrate—procured at considerable cost and difficulty—in his eyes at birth, just in case, but I was indeed sure. Aside from the lack of any specific signs of illness, Jemmy had an air of robust health about him that made the mere thought of infection incredible. He radiated well-being like a potful of stew.

"Is that why you asked about contraception?" I asked,

waving a greeting as we passed the MacRaes' campsite. "You were worried about having more children, in case . . ."

"Oh. No. I mean—I hadn't even thought about venereal disease until you mentioned syphilis, and then it just struck me as a horrible realization—that he might have—" She stopped and cleared her throat. "Er, no. I just wanted to know."

A slippery patch of trail put paid to the conversation at that point, but not to my speculations.

It wasn't that a young bride's mind might not turn lightly to thoughts of contraception—but under the circumstances . . . what was it? I wondered. Fear for herself, or for a new baby? Childbirth could be dangerous, of course—and anyone who had seen the attendees at my surgery or heard the women's conversations round the campfires in the evening could be in no doubt as to the dangers to infants and children; it was the rare family that had not lost at least one infant to fever, morbid sore throat, or "the squitters"—uncontrolled diarrhea. Many women had lost three, four, or more babies. I remembered Abel MacLennan's story, and a small shiver ran down my spine.

Still, Brianna was very healthy, and while we did lack important things like antibiotics and sophisticated medical facilities, I had told her not to underestimate the power of simple hygiene and good nutrition.

No, I thought, watching the strong curve of her back as she lifted the heavy equipment over an entangling root that hunched across the trail. It wasn't that. She might have reason to be concerned, but she wasn't basically a fearful person.

Roger? On the face of it, it would seem that the best thing to do was to become pregnant again quickly, with a child that was definitely Roger's. That would certainly help to cement their new marriage. On the other hand . . . what if she did? Roger would be more than pleased—but what about Jemmy?

Roger had sworn a blood oath, taking Jemmy as his own. But human nature was human nature, and while I was sure that Roger would never abandon or neglect Jemmy, it was quite possible that he would feel differently—and obviously differently—for a child he knew was his. Would Bree risk that?

On due consideration, I rather thought she was wise to wait—if she could. Give Roger time to feel a close bond with Jemmy, before complicating the family situation with another child. Yes, very sensible—and Bree *was* an eminently sensible person.

It wasn't until we had arrived, finally, at the clearing where the morning surgeries were held that another possibility occurred to me.

"Can we be helpin' ye at all, Missus Fraser?"

Two of the younger Chisholm boys hurried forward to help, relieving me and Brianna of our heavy loads, and without being told, started in at once to unfold tables, fetch clean water, kindle a fire, and generally make themselves useful. They were no more than eight and ten, and watching them work, I realized afresh that in this time, a lad of twelve or fourteen could be essentially a grown man.

Brianna knew that, too. She would never leave Jemmy, I knew—not while he needed her. But . . . later? What might happen when he left *her*?

I opened my chest and began slowly to lay out the necessary supplies for the morning's work: scissors, probe, forceps, alcohol, scalpel, bandages, tooth pliers, suture needles, ointments, salves, washes, purges . . .

Brianna was twenty-three. She might be no more than in her mid-thirties by the time Jem was fully independent. And if he no longer needed her care—she and Roger might possibly go back. Back to her own time, to safety—to the interrupted life that had been hers by birth.

But only if she had no further children, whose helplessness would keep her here.

"Good morn to ye, ma'am." A short, middle-aged gentleman stood before me, the morning's first patient. He was bristling with a week's worth of whiskers, but noticeably pallid round the gills, with a clammy look and bloodshot eyes so raw with smoke and whisky that his malady was instantly discernible. Hangover was endemic at the morning surgery.

"I've a wee gripin' in my guts, ma'am," he said, swallowing unhappily. "Would ye have anything like to settle 'em, maybe?"

"Just the thing," I assured him, reaching for a cup. "Raw egg and a bit of ipecac. Have you a good vomit, and you'll be a new man."

THE SURGERY was held at the edge of the big clearing at the foot of the hill, where the great fire of the Gathering burned at night. The damp air smelled of soot and the acrid scent of wet ashes, but the blackened patch of earth—some ten feet across, at least—was already disappearing under a crisscross of fresh branches and kindling. They'd have a time starting it tonight, I thought, if the drizzle kept up.

The gentleman with the hangover disposed of, there was a short lull, and I was able to give my attention to Murray MacLeod, who had set up shop a short distance away.

Murray had gotten an early start, I saw; the ground by his feet was dark, the scattered ashes sodden and squishy with blood. He had an early patient in hand, too—a stout gentleman whose red, spongy nose and flabby jowls gave testimony to a life of alcoholic excess. He had the man stripped to his shirt despite the rain and cold, sleeve turned up and tourniquet in place, the bleeding bowl held across the patient's knees.

I was a good ten feet from the stool where Murray plied his trade, but could see the man's eyes, yellow as mustard even in the dim morning light.

"Liver disease," I said to Brianna, taking no particular pains to lower my voice. "You can see the jaundice from here, can't you?"

"Bilious humors," MacLeod said loudly, snapping open his fleam. "An excess of the humors, clear as day." Small, dark, and neat in his dress, Murray was not personally impressive, but he *was* opinionated.

"Cirrhosis due to drink, I daresay," I said, coming closer and looking the patient over dispassionately.

"An impaction of the bile, owing to an imbalance of the

phlegm!" Murray glowered at me, clearly thinking I intended to steal his thunder, if not his patient.

I ignored him and bent down to examine the patient, who looked alarmed at my scrutiny.

"You have a hard mass just under the ribs on the right, don't you?" I said, kindly. "Your piss is dark, and when you shit, it's black and bloody, am I right?"

The man nodded, mouth hanging open. We were beginning to attract attention.

"Mo-therr." Brianna was standing behind me. She gave Murray a nod and bent to mutter in my ear. "What can you do for cirrhosis, Mother? Nothing!"

I stopped, biting my lip. She was right. In my urge to show off by making the diagnosis—and keep Murray from using his stained, rusty-looking fleam on the man—I had overlooked the minor point that I had no alternative treatment to offer.

The patient was glancing back and forth between us, plainly uneasy. With an effort, I smiled at him, and nodded to Murray.

"Mr. MacLeod has the right of it," I said, forcing the words past my teeth. "Liver disease, surely—caused by an excess of humors." I supposed one could consider alcohol a humor, after all; the folk drinking Jamie's whisky last night had evidently found it hilarious.

Murray's face had been tense with suspicion; at my capitulation, it went quite comically blank with astonishment. Stepping in front of me, Brianna seized advantage of the moment.

"There's a charm," she said, smiling charmingly at him. "It . . . er . . . sharpens the blade, and eases the flow of the humors. Let me show you." Before he could tighten his grip, she snatched the fleam from his hand and turned to our small surgery fire, where a pot of water hung steaming from a tripod.

"In the name of Michael, wielder of swords, defender of souls," she intoned. I trusted that taking the name of St. Michael in vain was not actual blasphemy—or if it was, that Michael would not object in a good cause. The men laying the fire had stopped to watch, as had a few people coming to the surgery.

She raised the fleam and made a large, slow sign of the cross with it, looking from side to side, to be sure she had the attention of all the onlookers. She did; they were agog. Towering over most of the gawkers, blue eyes narrowed in concentration, she reminded me strongly of Jamie in some of his more bravura performances. I could only hope she was as good at it as he was.

"Bless this blade, for the healing of your servant," she said, casting her eyes up to heaven, and holding the fleam above the fire in the manner of a priest offering the Eucharist. Bubbles were rising through the water, but it hadn't quite reached the boil.

"Bless its edge, for the drawing of blood, for the spilling of blood, for the ... er ... the letting of poison from the body of your most humble petitioner. Bless the blade ... bless the blade ... bless the blade in the hand of your humble servant. ... Thanks be to God for the brightness of the metal." Thanks be to God for the repetitious nature of Gaelic prayers, I thought cynically.

Thanks be to God, the water was boiling. She lowered the short, curved blade to the surface of the water, glowered significantly at the crowd, and declaimed, "Let the cleansing of the waters from the side of our Lord Jesus be upon this blade!"

She plunged the metal into the water and held it until the steam rising over the wooden casing reddened her fingers. She lifted the fleam and transferred it hastily to her other hand, raising it into the air as she surreptitiously waggled the scalded hand behind her.

"May the blessing of Michael, defender from demons, be on this blade and on the hand of its wielder, to the health of the body, to the health of the soul. Amen!"

She stepped forward and presented the fleam ceremoniously to Murray, handle first. Murray, no fool, gave me a look in which keen suspicion was mingled with a reluctant appreciation for my daughter's theatrical abilities.

"Don't touch the blade," I said, smiling graciously. "It will break the charm. Oh—and you repeat the charm, each time you use the blade. It has to be done with the water *boiling*, mind."

"Mmphm," he said, but took the fleam carefully by the handle. With a short nod to Brianna, he turned away to his patient, and I to mine—a young girl with nettle rash. Brianna followed, wiping her hands on her skirt and looking pleased with herself. I heard the patient's soft grunt behind me, and the ringing patter of blood running into the metal bowl.

I felt rather guilty about MacLeod's patient, but Brianna had been quite right; there was absolutely nothing I could do for him under the circumstances. Careful long-term nursing, coupled with excellent nutrition and a complete abstinence from alcohol, might prolong his life; the chances of the first two were low, the third, nonexistent.

Brianna had brilliantly saved him from a potentially nasty blood infection—and seized the opportunity to provide a similar protection for all MacLeod's future patients—but I couldn't help a nagging sense of guilt that I could not do more myself. Still, the first medical principle I had learned as a nurse on the battlefields of France still held: treat the patient in front of you.

"Use this ointment," I said sternly to the girl with nettle rash, "and *don't scratch*."

4

# WEDDING GIFTS

THE DAY HADN'T CLEARED, but the rain had ceased for the moment. Fires smoked like smudge pots, as people hastened to take advantage of the momentary cessation to feed their carefully hoarded coals, pushing damp wood into the kindling blazes in a hasty effort to dry damp clothes and blankets. The air was still restless, though, and clouds of woodsmoke billowed ghostlike through the trees.

One such plume surged across the trail before him, and Roger turned to skirt it, making his way through tussocks of wet grass that soaked his stockings, and hanging boughs of pine that left dark patches of wetness on the shoulders of his coat as he passed. He paid the damp no mind, intent on his mental list of errands for the day.

To the tinkers' wagons first, to buy some small token as a wedding present for Brianna. What would she like? he wondered. A bit of jewelry, a ribbon? He had very little money, but felt the need to mark the occasion with a gift of some sort.

He would have liked to put his own ring on her finger when they made their vows, but she had insisted that the cabochon ruby that had belonged to her grandfather would do fine; it fit her hand perfectly, and there was no need to spend money on another ring. She was a pragmatic person, Bree was—sometimes dismayingly so, in contrast to his own romantic streak.

Something practical but ornamental, then—like a painted chamber pot? He smiled to himself at the idea, but the notion of practicality lingered, tinged with doubt.

He had a vivid memory of Mrs. Abercrombie, a staid and practical matron of Reverend Wakefield's congregation, who had arrived at the manse in hysterics one evening in the midst of supper, saying that she had killed her husband, and whatever should she do? The Reverend had left Mrs. Abercrombie in the temporary care of his housekeeper, while he and Roger, then a teenager, had hastened to the Abercrombie residence to see what had happened.

They had found Mr. Abercrombie on the floor of his kitchen, fortunately still alive, though groggy and bleeding profusely from a minor scalp wound occasioned by his having been struck by the new electric steam iron which he had presented to his wife on the occasion of their twenty-third wedding anniversary.

"But she said the old one scorched the tea towels!" Mr.

Abercrombie had repeated at plaintive intervals, as the Reverend skillfully taped up his head with Elastoplast, and Roger mopped up the kitchen.

It was the vivid memory of the gory splotches on the worn lino of the Abercrombies' kitchen that decided him. Pragmatic Bree might be, but this was their wedding. Better, worse, death do us part. He'd go for romantic—or as romantic as could be managed on one shilling, threepence.

There was a flash of red among the spruce needles nearby, like the glimpse of a cardinal. Bigger than the average bird, though; he stopped, bending to peer through an opening in the branches.

"Duncan?" he said. "Is that you?"

Duncan Innes came out of the trees, nodding shyly. He still wore the scarlet Cameron tartan, but had left off his splendid coat, instead wrapping the end of his plaid shawl-like round his shoulders in the cozy old style of the Highlands.

"A word, *a Smeòraich?*" he said.

"Aye, sure. I'm just off to the tinkers'—walk with me." He turned back to the trail—now clear of smoke—and they made their way companionably across the mountain, side by side.

Roger said nothing, waiting courteously for Duncan to choose his way into the conversation. Duncan was diffident and retiring by temperament, but observant, perceptive, and stubborn in a very quiet way. If he had something to say, he'd say it—given time. At last he drew breath and started in.

"*Mac Dubh* did say to me as how your Da was a minister—that's true, is it?"

"Aye," Roger said, rather startled at the subject. "Or at least—my real father was killed, and my mother's uncle adopted me; it was him was the minister." Even as he spoke, Roger wondered why he should feel it necessary to explain. For most of his life, he had thought and spoken of the Reverend as his father; and surely it made no difference to Duncan.

Duncan nodded, clicking his tongue in sympathy.

"But ye will have been Presbyterian yourself, then? I did hear *Mac Dubh* speak of it." Despite Duncan's normal good manners, a brief grin showed beneath the edge of his ragged mustache.

"I expect ye did, aye," Roger replied dryly. He'd be surprised if the whole Gathering hadn't heard *Mac Dubh* speak of it.

"Well, the thing about it is, so am I," Duncan said, sounding rather apologetic.

Roger looked at him in astonishment.

"You? I thought you were Catholic!"

Duncan made a small embarrassed noise, lifting the shoulder of his amputated arm in a shrug.

"No. My great-grandda on my mother's side was a Covenanter—verra fierce in his beliefs, aye?" He smiled, a little shyly. "That was watered down a good bit before it came to me; my Mam was godly, but Da wasna much of a one for the kirk, nor was I. And when I met up wi' *Mac Dubh* . . . well, it wasna as though he'd asked me to go to Mass with him of a Sunday, was it?"

Roger nodded, with a brief grunt of comprehension. Duncan had met with Jamie in Ardsmuir Prison, after the Rising. While most of the Jacobite troops had been Catholic, he knew there had been Protestants of different stripes among them, too—and most would likely have kept quiet about it, outnumbered by the Catholics in close quarters. And it was true enough that Jamie's and Duncan's later career in smuggling would have offered few occasions for religious discourse.

"Aye, so. And your wedding to Mrs. Cameron tonight . . ."

Duncan nodded, and sucked in a corner of his mouth, gnawing contemplatively at the edge of his mustache.

"That's it. Am I bound, d'ye think, to say anything?"

"Mrs. Cameron doesn't know? Nor Jamie?"

Duncan shook his head silently, eyes on the trampled mud of the trail.

Roger realized that it was, of course, Jamie whose opinion was important here, rather than Jocasta Cameron's. The issue of differing religion had evidently not seemed important to Duncan—and Roger had never heard that Jocasta was in any way devout—but hearing about Jamie's response to Roger's Presbyterianism, Duncan had now taken alarm.

"Ye went to see the priest, *Mac Dubh* said." Duncan glanced at him sidelong. "Did he—" He cleared his throat, flushing. "I mean, did he oblige ye to be . . . baptized Romish?"

An atrocious prospect to a devout Protestant, and plainly an uncomfortable one to Duncan. It was, Roger realized, an uncomfortable thought to him, too. Would he have done it, if he had to, to wed Bree? He supposed he would have, in the end, but he admitted to having felt a deep relief that the priest hadn't insisted on any sort of formal conversion.

"Ah . . . no," Roger said, and coughed as another fan of smoke washed suddenly over them. "No," he repeated, wiping streaming eyes. "But they don't baptize you, ye know, if ye've been christened already. You have been, aye?"

"Oh, aye." Duncan seemed heartened by that. "Aye, when I—that is—" A faint shadow crossed his face, but whatever thought had caused it was dismissed with another shrug. "Yes."

"Well, then. Let me think a bit, aye?"

The tinkers' wagons were already in sight, huddled like oxen, their merchandise shrouded in canvas and blankets against the rain, but Duncan stopped, clearly wanting the matter settled before going on to anything else.

Roger rubbed a hand over the back of his neck, thinking.

"No," he said finally. "No, I think ye needna say anything. See, it'll not be a Mass, only the marriage service—and that's just the same. Do ye take this woman, do ye take this man, richer, poorer, all that."

Duncan nodded, attentive.

"I can say that, aye," he said. "Though it did take a bit of coming to, the richer, poorer bit. Ye'll ken that, though, yourself."

He spoke quite without any sense of irony, merely as one stating an obvious fact, and was plainly taken aback at his glimpse of Roger's face in response to the remark.

"I didna mean anything amiss," Duncan said hastily. "That is, I only meant—"

Roger waved a hand, trying to brush it off.

"No harm done," he said, his voice as dry as Duncan's had been. "Speak the truth and shame auld Hornie, aye?"

It *was* the truth, too, though he had somehow managed to overlook it until this moment. In fact, he realized with a sinking sensation, his situation was a precise parallel with Duncan's: a penniless man without property, marrying a rich—or potentially rich—woman.

He had never thought of Jamie Fraser as being rich, perhaps because of the man's natural modesty, perhaps simply because he wasn't—yet. The fact remained that Fraser was the proprietor of ten thousand acres of land. If a good bit of that land was still wilderness, it didn't mean it would stay that way. There were tenants on that property now; there would be more soon. And when those tenancies began to pay rents, when there were sawmills and gristmills on the streams, when there were settlements and stores and taverns, when the handful of cows and pigs and horses had multiplied into fat herds of thriving stock under Jamie's careful stewardship . . . Jamie Fraser might be a very rich man indeed. And Brianna was Jamie's only natural child.

Then there was Jocasta Cameron, demonstrably already a very rich woman, who had stated her intention to make Brianna her heiress. Bree had exigently refused to countenance the notion—but Jocasta was as naturally stubborn as her niece, and had had more practice at it. Besides, no matter what Brianna said or did, folk would suppose . . .

And that was what was truly sitting in the bottom of his stomach like a curling stone. Not just the realization that he was in fact marrying well above his means and position—but the realization that everyone in the entire colony had realized it long ago, and had probably been viewing him cynically— and gossiping about him—as a rare chancer, if not an outright adventurer.

The smoke had left a bitter taste of ashes at the back of his mouth. He swallowed it down, and gave Duncan a crooked smile.

"Aye," he said. "Well. Better or worse. I suppose they must see *something* in us, eh? The women?"

Duncan smiled, a little ruefully.

"Aye, something. So, ye think it will be all right, then, about the religion? I wouldna have either Miss Jo or *Mac*

*Dubh* think I meant aught amiss by not speaking. But I didna like to make a fizz about it, and it's no needed."

"No, of course not," Roger agreed. He took a deep breath and brushed damp hair off his face. "Nay, I think it's all right. When I spoke to the—the Father, the only condition he made was that I should let any children be baptized as Catholics. But since that's not a consideration for you and Mrs. Cameron, I suppose . . ." He trailed off delicately, but Duncan seemed relieved at the thought.

"Och, no," he said, and laughed, a little nervously. "No, I think I'm no bothered about that."

"Well, then." Roger forced a smile, and clapped Duncan on the back. "Here's luck to you."

Duncan brushed a finger beneath his mustache, nodding. "And you, *a Smeòraich*."

He had expected Duncan to go off about his business, once his question was answered, but the man instead came with him, wandering slowly along the row of wagons in Roger's wake, peering at the wares on display with a slight frown.

After a week's haggling and bartering, the wagons were as full as they had been to start with—or more so, heaped with sacks of grain and wool, casks of cider, bags of apples, stacks of hides and other sundries taken in trade. The stock of fancies had dwindled considerably, but there were still things to be bought, as evidenced by the crowd of folk clustering round the wagons, thick as aphids on a rosebush.

Roger was tall enough to peer over the heads of most customers, and made his way slowly along the rank of wagons, squinting at this or that, trying to envision Brianna's response to it.

She was a beautiful woman, but not inclined to fuss over her looks. In fact, he had narrowly stopped her cutting off most of her glorious red mane out of impatience at it dangling in the gravy and Jemmy yanking on it. Maybe a ribbon *was* practical. Or a decorated comb? More likely a pair of handcuffs for the wean.

He paused by a vendor of cloth goods, though, and bent to peer under the canvas, where caps and bright ribbons hung safely suspended out of the wet, stirring in the cool dimness like the tentacles of brilliant jellyfish. Duncan, plaid hitched up about his ears against the gusting breeze, came closer, to see what he was looking at.

"Looking for something in particular, are ye, sirs?" A peddler-woman leaned forward over her goods, bosom resting on her folded arms, and divided a professional smile between them.

"Aye," Duncan said, unexpectedly. "A yard of velvet. Would ye be having such a thing? Good quality, mind, but the color's not important."

The woman's eyebrows lifted—even in his best clothes, Duncan would strike no one as a dandy—but she turned without comment and began to rootle through her diminished stock.

"D'ye think Mrs. Claire would have some lavender left?" Duncan asked, turning to Roger.

"Aye, I know she has," Roger replied. His puzzlement must have shown on his face, for Duncan smiled and ducked his head diffidently.

" 'Twas a thought I had," he said. "Miss Jo suffers from the megrims, and doesna sleep sae well as she might. I mind, my mither had a lavender pillow, and said she fell asleep like a babe the moment she laid her head upon it. So I thought, perhaps a bit o' velvet—so as she could feel it against her cheek, aye?—and perhaps Mrs. Lizzie would stitch it up for me. . . ."

*In sickness and in health . . .*

Roger nodded his approval, feeling touched—and slightly shamed—by Duncan's thoughtfulness. He had had the impression that the marriage between Duncan and Jocasta Cameron was principally a matter of convenience and good business—and perhaps it was. But mad passion wasn't a necessary prerequisite for tenderness or consideration, was it?

Duncan, purchase concluded, took his leave and went off with the velvet safely sheltered under his plaid, leaving Roger to make a slow circuit of the remaining vendors, mentally selecting, weighing, and discarding, as he wracked his brain to think what item of this myriad would best please his bride. Earrings? No, the kid would pull them. Same for a necklace—*or* a hair ribbon, now he thought.

Still, his mind dwelled on jewelry. Normally, she wore very little. But she *had* worn her father's ruby ring—the one Jamie had given him, the one he had given her when she accepted him for good—all through the Gathering. Jem slobbered on it now and then, but couldn't really damage it.

He stopped suddenly, letting the crowd flow round him. He could see the gold in his mind's eye, and the deep pink-red of the cabochon ruby, vivid on her long pale finger. *Her father's ring.* Of course; why had he not seen that before?

True, Jamie had given him the ring, but that didn't make it his to give in turn. And he wanted, very suddenly and very badly, to give Brianna something truly of his own.

He turned with decision, and made his way back to a wagon whose metal wares gleamed and glinted, even in the rain. He knew from experiment that his little finger was just the size of her ring finger.

"This one," he said, holding up a ring. It was cheap; made of braided strands of copper and brass, it would undoubtedly turn her finger green in minutes. *So much the better*, he thought, handing over his money. Whether she wore it all the time or not, she would be marked as his.

*For this reason shall a woman leave her father's house, and cleave unto her husband, and the two shall be one flesh.*

5

## RIOTOUS UNREST

B Y THE END OF THE FIRST HOUR, I had a substantial crowd of patients waiting, despite the intermittent drizzle. It was the final day of the Gathering, and people who had stood the pain of a toothache or the doubt of a rash had suddenly decided that they must seize the chance of having it seen to.

I dismissed a young woman with incipient goiter, admonishing her to procure a quantity of dried fish, as she lived too far inland to be sure of getting fresh each day, and eat some daily for its iodine content.

"Next!" I called, brushing damp hair out of my eyes.

The crowd parted like the Red Sea, revealing a small, elderly man, so thin he might be a walking skeleton, clad in rags and carrying a bundle of fur in his arms. As he shambled toward me through the ranks of recoiling people, I discovered the reason for the crowd's deference; he stank like a dead raccoon.

For a moment, I thought the pile of grayish fur might *be* a dead raccoon—there was already a small pile of furs and hides near my feet, though my patients usually went to the trouble of separating these from their original possessors before presenting them to me—but then the fur stirred, and a pair of bright eyes peered out of the tangled mass.

"My dog's hurt," the man announced brusquely. He set the dog on my table, shoving the jumble of instruments aside, and pointed to a jagged tear in the animal's flank. "You'll tend him."

This wasn't phrased as a request, but it was, after all, the dog who was my patient, and *he* seemed fairly civil. Medium-sized and short-legged, with a bristly, mottled coat and ragged ears, he sat placidly panting, making no effort to get away.

"What happened to him?" I moved the tottering basin out of danger, and bent to rummage for my jar of sterile sutures. The dog licked my hand in passing.

"Fightin' with a she-coon."

"Hmm," I said, surveying the animal dubiously. Given its improbable parentage and evident friendliness, I thought any overtures made to a female raccoon were probably inspired by lust, rather than ferocity. As though to confirm this impression, the animal extruded a few inches of moist pink reproductive equipment in my direction.

"He likes you, Mama," Bree said, keeping a straight face.

"How flattering," I muttered, hoping that the dog's owner would not be moved to any similar demonstration of regard. Fortunately, the old man appeared not to like me in the slightest; he ignored me completely, sunken eyes fixed broodingly on the clearing below, where the soldiers were going through some drill.

"Scissors," I said, resigned, holding out my palm.

I clipped away the matted fur near the wound, and was pleased to find no great swelling or other signs of infection. The gash had clotted well; evidently it had been some time since the injury. I wondered whether the dog had met its nemesis on the mountain. I didn't recognize the old man, nor did he have the speech of a Scot. Had he been at the Gathering at all? I wondered.

"Er . . . would you hold his head, please?" The dog might be friendly; that didn't mean his good nature would remain unimpaired as I jabbed a needle through his hide. His owner stayed sunk in gloom, though, and made no move to oblige. I glanced around for Bree, looking for help, but she had suddenly disappeared.

"Here, *a bhalaich*, here, then," said a soothing voice beside me, and I turned in surprise to find the dog sniffing interestedly at the proffered knuckles of Murray MacLeod. Seeing my look of surprise, he shrugged, smiled, and leaned over the table, grabbing the astonished dog by scruff and muzzle.

"I should advise ye to be quick about it, Mrs. Fraser," he said.

I took a firm grip of the leg nearest me and started in. The dog responded exactly as most humans did in similar circumstances, wriggling madly and trying to escape, its claws scrabbling on the rough wood of the table. At one point, it succeeded in breaking free of Murray, whereupon it leaped off the table altogether and made for the wide-open spaces, sutures trailing. I flung myself bodily upon it, and rolled through leaves and mud, scattering onlookers in all directions until one or two of the bolder souls came to my assistance, pinning the mangy beast to the ground so that I might finish the job.

I tied the last knot, clipped the waxed thread with Murray's fleam—which had in fact been trampled underfoot in the struggle, though unfortunately not broken—and took my knee off the hound's side, panting nearly as heavily as the dog was.

The spectators applauded.

I bowed, a little dazed, and shoved masses of disheveled curls out of my face with both hands. Murray was in no better case, his queue come undone and a jagged rent in his coat, which was covered with mud. He bent, seized the dog under the belly, and swung it off its feet, heaving it up on the table beside its owner.

"Your dog, sir," he said, and stood wheezing gently.

The old man turned, laid a hand on the dog's head, and frowned, glancing back and forth between me and Murray, as though unsure what to make of this tag-team approach to surgery. He looked back over his shoulder toward the soldiers below, then turned toward me, his sparse brows knotted over a beak of a nose.

"Who're *they*?" he said, in tones of deep puzzlement. Not waiting for an answer, he shrugged, turned, and walked off. The dog, tongue lolling, hopped off the table and trotted off at its owner's side, in search of more adventure.

I took a deep breath, brushed mud off my apron, smiled thanks to Murray, and turned to wash my hands before dealing with the next patient.

"Ha," said Brianna, under her breath. "Got him!" She lifted her chin slightly, indicating something over my shoulder, and I turned to look.

The next patient was a gentleman. A real gentleman, that is, judging by his dress and bearing, both of which were a good deal superior to the general run. I had noticed him hovering near the edge of the clearing for some time, glancing back and forth between my center of operations and that of Murray, obviously in doubt as to which medico should have the privilege of his custom. Evidently the incident of the trapper's dog had tipped the balance in my favor.

I glanced at Murray, who was looking distinctly po-faced. A gentleman would likely pay in cash. I gave Murray a slight shrug of apology, then put on a pleasant professional smile, and gestured the new patient onto my stool.

"Do sit down, sir," I said, "and tell me where it hurts."

The gentleman was a Mr. Goodwin of Hillsborough, whose chief complaint, it seemed, was a pain in his arm. This was not his only trouble, I saw; a freshly healed scar zigzagged down the side of his face, the livid weal drawing down the corner of his eye and giving him a most ferocious squint. A faint discoloration over the cheek showed where some heavy object had hit him square above the jaw, as well, and his features had the blunt and swollen look of someone who had been badly beaten in the not-so-distant past.

Gentlemen were as likely to engage in brawls as anyone, given sufficient provocation, but this one seemed of rather advanced years for such entertainments, looking to be in his middle fifties, with a prosperous paunch pressing against the silver-buttoned waistcoat. Perhaps he had been set upon somewhere and robbed, I thought. Not on his way to the Gathering, though; these injuries were weeks old.

I felt my way carefully over his arm and shoulder, making him lift and move the arm slightly, asking brief questions as I palpated the limb. The trouble was obvious enough; he had dislocated the elbow, and while the dislocation had fortunately reduced itself, I thought he had torn a tendon, which was now caught between the olecranon process and the head of the ulna, the injury being thus aggravated by movement of the arm.

Not that that was all; palpating my way carefully down his arm, I discovered no fewer than three half-healed simple fractures to the bones of his forearm. The damage was not all internal; I could see the fading remnants of two large bruises on the forearm above the sites of fracture, each an irregular blotch of yellow-green with the darker red-black of deep hemorrhage at the center. Self-defense injuries, I thought, or I was a Chinaman.

"Bree, find me a decent splint, will you?" I asked. Bree nodded silently and vanished, leaving me to anoint Mr. Goodwin's lesser contusions with cajeput ointment.

"How did you come by these injuries, Mr. Goodwin?" I asked casually, sorting out a length of linen bandage. "You look as though you've been in quite a fight. I hope at least the other fellow looks worse!"

Mr. Goodwin smiled faintly at my attempted witticism.

" 'Twas a battle, indeed, Mrs. Fraser," he replied, "and yet no fight of my own. A matter of misfortune, rather—being in the wrong place at the wrong time, as you might say. Still . . ." He closed the squinting eye in reflex as I touched the scar. An artless job by whoever had stitched it, but cleanly healed.

"Really?" I said. "Whatever happened?"

He grunted, but seemed not displeased at the necessity of telling me.

"You heard the officer this morning, surely, ma'am—reading out the Governor's words regarding the atrocious behavior of the rioters?"

"I shouldn't think the Governor's words escaped anyone's attention," I murmured, pulling gently on the skin with my fingertips. "So you were at Hillsborough, is that what you're telling me?"

"Indeed it is." He sighed, but relaxed a little, finding that I wasn't hurting him with my probings. "I live within the town of Hillsborough, in point of fact. And if I had remained quietly at home—as my good wife begged me to do"—he gave a rueful half-smile—"doubtless I should have escaped."

"They do say that curiosity killed the cat." I had spotted something when he smiled, and pressed gently with my thumb over the discolored area on his cheek. "Someone struck you across the face here, with some force. Did they break any teeth?"

He looked mildly startled.

"Aye, ma'am. But it's nothing you can mend." He pulled up his upper lip, revealing a gap where two teeth were missing. One premolar had been knocked out clean, but the other had broken off at the root; I could see a jagged line of yellowed enamel, gleaming against the dark red of his gum.

Brianna, arriving at this juncture with the splint, made a slight gagging noise. Mr. Goodwin's other teeth, while essentially whole, were heavily crusted with yellow calculus, and quite brown with the stains of tobacco chewing.

"Oh, I think I can help a bit there," I assured him, ignoring Bree. "It's painful to bite there, isn't it? I can't mend it, but I can draw the remnants of the broken tooth, and treat the gum to prevent infection. Who hit you, though?"

He shrugged slightly, watching with a slightly apprehensive interest as I laid out the shiny pliers and straight-bladed scalpel for dentistry.

"To tell the truth, ma'am, I scarcely know. I had but ventured into the town to visit the courthouse. I am bringing suit against a party in Edenton," he explained, a frown forming on his face at the thought of it, "and I am required to file documents in support of this action. However, I was unable to transact my business, as I found the street before the courthouse quite choked with men, many armed with cudgels, whips, and rough implements of that sort."

Seeing the mob, he had thought to leave, but just then, someone threw a rock through a window of the courthouse. The crash of glass acted on the mob like a signal, and they had surged forward, breaking down the doors and shouting threats.

"I became concerned for my friend, Mr. Fanning, whom I knew to be within."

"Fanning . . . that would be Edmund Fanning?" I was only listening with half an ear, as I decided how best to approach the extraction, but I did recognize that name. Farquard Campbell had mentioned Fanning, while telling Jamie the gory details of the riots following in the wake of the Stamp Act a few years previous. Fanning had been appointed postmaster for the colony, a lucrative position that had likely cost him a pretty penny to acquire, and had cost him still more dearly when he had been obliged to resign it under force. Evidently, his unpopularity had escalated in the five years since.

Mr. Goodwin compressed his lips, tightening them to a seam of disapproval.

"Yes, ma'am, that is the gentleman. And whatever scandal folk do spread about him, he has ever been a friend to me and mine—so when I heard such grievous sentiments expressed, to the threat of his life, I determined that I must go to his aid."

In this gallant endeavor, Mr. Goodwin had been less than successful.

"I tried to force a path through the crowd," he said, his

eyes fixed on my hands as I laid his arm along the splint and arranged the linen bandage beneath it. "I could not make much way, though, and had barely gained the foot of the steps, when there came a great shout from within, and the crowd fell back, carrying me with it."

Struggling to keep his feet, Mr. Goodwin had been horrified to see Edmund Fanning dragged bodily through the courthouse door, knocked down, and then pulled feet first down the steps, his head striking each one in turn.

"Such a noise as it made," he said, shuddering. "I could hear it above the shouting, thumping like a melon being rolled downstairs."

"Dear me," I murmured. "But he wasn't killed, was he? I hadn't heard of any deaths at Hillsborough. Relax your arm, please, and take a deep breath."

Mr. Goodwin took a deep breath, but only in order to utter a loud snort. This was succeeded by a much deeper gasp, as I turned the arm, freeing the trapped tendon and bringing the joint into good alignment. He went quite pale, and a sheen of sweat broke out on his pendulous cheeks, but he blinked a few times, and recovered nobly.

"And if he wasn't, it was by no mercy of the rioters," he said. "'Twas only that they thought to have better sport with the Chief Justice, and so left Fanning insensible in the dust, as they rushed inside the courthouse. Another friend and I made shift to raise the poor man, and sought to make off with him to a place of shelter nearby, when comes the halloo in our rear, and we were beset all at once by the mob. That was how I came by this"—he raised his freshly splinted arm—"and these." He touched the weal by his eye, and the shattered tooth.

He frowned at me, heavy brows drawn down.

"Believe me, ma'am, I hope some folk here are moved to give up the names of the rioters, that they may be justly punished for such barbarous work—but were I to see here the fellow who struck me, I shouldn't be inclined to surrender him to the Governor's justice. Indeed I should not!"

His fists closed slowly, and he glowered at me as though suspecting that I had the miscreant in question hidden under my table. Brianna shifted uneasily behind me. No doubt she was thinking, as I was, of Hobson and Fowles. Abel MacLennan I was inclined to consider an innocent bystander, no matter what he might have done in Hillsborough.

I murmured something sympathetically noncommittal, and brought out the bottle of raw whisky I used for disinfection and crude anesthesia. The sight of it seemed to hearten Mr. Goodwin considerably.

"Just a bit of this to . . . er . . . fortify your spirits," I suggested, pouring him out a healthy cupful. And disinfect the nasty environs of his mouth, too. "Hold it in your mouth for a moment before you swallow—it will help to numb your tooth."

I turned to Bree, as Mr. Goodwin obediently took a large gulp of the liquor and sat with his mouth full, cheeks puffed like a frog about to burst into song. She seemed a little pale, though I wasn't sure whether it was Mr. Goodwin's story or the view of his teeth that had affected her.

"I don't think I'll need you any longer this morning, darling," I said, patting her arm in reassurance. "Why don't you go and see whether Jocasta is ready for the weddings tonight?"

"You're sure, Mama?" Even as she asked, she was untying her blood-spotted apron and rolling it into a ball. Seeing her glance toward the trailhead, I looked in that direction and saw Roger lurking behind a bush, his eyes fixed on her. I saw his face light when she turned toward him, and felt a small warm glow at sight of it. Yes, they would be all right.

"Now then, Mr. Goodwin. Just you take a drop more of that, and we'll finish dealing with this little matter." I turned back to my patient, smiling, and picked up the pliers.

# 6

# FOR AULD LANG SYNE

ROGER WAITED AT THE EDGE of the clearing, watching Brianna as she stood by Claire's side, pounding herbs, measuring off liquids into small bottles, and tearing bandages. She had rolled up her sleeves, in spite of the chill, and the effort of ripping the tough linen made the muscles of her bare arms flex and swell beneath the freckled skin.

Strong in the wrists, he thought, with a faintly disturbing memory of Estella in Dickens's *Great Expectations*. Noticeably strong all over; the wind flattened her skirt against the solid slope of hips and a long thigh pressed briefly against the fabric as she turned, smooth and round as an alder trunk.

He wasn't the only one noticing. Half the people waiting for the attention of the two physicians were watching Brianna; some—mostly women—with faint and puzzled frowns, some—all men—with a covert admiration tinged with earthy speculation that gave Roger an urge to step into the clearing and assert his rights to her on the spot.

*Well, let them look*, he thought, quelling the urge. *It only matters if she's looking back, aye?*

He moved out of the trees, just a little, and her head turned at once as she caught sight of him. The slight frown on her face melted at once, her face lighting. He smiled back, then jerked his head in invitation, and turned away down the path, not waiting.

Was he sufficiently petty to want to demonstrate to that gang of gawpers that his woman would drop everything and come at his beck? Well . . . yes, he was. Embarrassment at that realization was tempered by a pleasantly fierce sense of possession at the sound of her step on the path above; yes, she *would* come to him.

She had left her work behind, but carried something in her hand; a small packet, wrapped in paper and tied with thread. He put out a hand and led her off the path, down toward a small copse where a scrim of tattered red and yellow maple leaves offered a decent semblance of privacy.

"Sorry to take you from your work," he said, though he wasn't.

"It's okay. I was glad to get away. I'm afraid I'm not all that good at blood and guts." She made a rueful face at the admission.

"That's all right," he assured her. "It's not one of the things I was looking for in a wife."

"Maybe you should have been," she said, shooting him a brooding sort of glance. "Here in *this* place, you might need a wife who can pull your teeth when they go bad, and sew your fingers back on when you cut them off chopping wood."

The grayness of the day seemed to have affected her spirits—or perhaps it was the job she had been doing. A brief glance at the run of Claire's patients was enough to depress anyone—anyone but Claire—with their parade of deformities, mutilations, wounds, and ghastly illnesses.

At least what he meant to tell Brianna might take her mind off the more gruesome details of eighteenth-century life for a bit. He cupped her cheek, and smoothed one thick red brow with a chilly thumb. Her face was cold, too, but the flesh behind her ear, beneath her hair, was warm—like her other hidden places.

"I've got what I wanted," he said firmly. "What about you, though? You're sure ye don't want a man who can scalp Indians and put dinner on the table with his gun? Blood's not my main thing, either, aye?"

A spark of humor reappeared in her eyes, and her air of preoccupation lightened.

"No, I don't think I want a bloody man," she said. "That's what Mama calls Da—but only when she's mad at him."

He laughed.

"And what will you call me, when you're mad at me?" he teased. She looked at him speculatively, and the spark grew brighter.

"Oh, don't worry; Da won't teach me any bad words in Gaelic, but Marsali taught me a lot of really evil things to say in French. Do you know what *un soûlard* is? *Une grande gueule*?"

"*Oui, mon petit chou*—not that I've ever seen a cabbage with quite such a red nose." He flicked a finger at her nose, and she ducked, laughing.

*"Maudit chien!"*

"Save something for after the wedding," he advised. "Ye might need it." He took her hand, to draw her toward a convenient boulder, then noticed again the small package she held.

"What's that?"

"A wedding present," she said, and held it out to him with two fingers, distasteful as though it had been a dead mouse.

He took it gingerly, but felt no sinister shapes through the paper. He bounced it on his palm; it was light, almost weightless.

"Embroidery silk," she said, in answer to his questioning look. "From Mrs. Buchanan." The frown was back between her brows, and that look of . . . worry? No, something else, but damned if he could put a name to it.

"What's wrong with embroidery silk?"

"Nothing. It's what it's for." She took the package from him, and tucked it into the pocket she wore tied under her petticoat. She was looking down, rearranging her skirts, but he could see the tightness of her lips. "She said it's for our winding claes."

Spoken in Brianna's odd version of a Bostonian Scots accent, it took a moment for Roger to decipher this.

"Winding cl—oh, you mean shrouds?"

"Yes. Evidently, it's my wifely duty to sit down the morning after the wedding and start spinning cloth for my shroud." She bit the words off through clenched teeth. "That way, I'll have it woven and embroidered by the time I die in childbirth. And if I'm a fast worker, I'll have time to make

one for you, too—otherwise, your *next* wife will have to finish it!"

He would have laughed, had it not been clear that she was
really upset.

"Mrs. Buchanan is a great fool," he said, taking her hands.
"You should not be letting her worry you with her nonsense."
Brianna glanced at him under lowered brows.

"Mrs. Buchanan," she said precisely, "is ignorant, stupid,
and tactless. The one thing she *isn't* is wrong."

"Of course she is," he said, with assumed certainty, feeling nonetheless a stab of apprehension.

"How many wives has Farquard Campbell buried?" she
demanded. "Gideon Oliver? Andrew MacNeill?"

Nine, among the three of them. MacNeill would take a
fourth wife this evening—an eighteen-year-old girl from
Weaver's Gorge. The stab came again, deeper, but he ignored it.

"And Jenny ban Campbell's borne eight children and deviled two husbands into the ground," he countered firmly. "For
that matter, Mrs. Buchanan herself has five bairns, and she's
certainly still kicking. I've seen them; turnip-headed to a
man, but all healthy."

That got him a reluctant twitch of the mouth, and he
pressed on, encouraged.

"You've no need to fear, hen. You had no trouble with
Jemmy, aye?"

"Yeah? Well, if you think it's no trouble, next time *you* can
do it!" she snapped, but the corner of her mouth curled
slightly up. She tugged at his hand, but he held on, and she
didn't resist.

"So you're willing there should be a next time, are you?
Mrs. Buchanan notwithstanding?" His tone was deliberately
light, but he drew her close and held her, his face hidden in
her hair, for fear she should see how much the question
meant to him.

She wasn't fooled. She drew back a little, and her eyes,
blue as water, searched his.

"You'd marry me, but live celibate?" she asked. "That's
the only sure way. The tansy oil doesn't always work—look
at Marsali!" The existence of baby Joan was eloquent testi-

mony to the ineffectiveness of that particular method of birth control. Still . . .

"There are other ways, I expect," he said. "But if you want celibacy—then yes, you'll have it."

She laughed, because his hand had tightened possessively on her arse, even as his lips renounced it. Then the laughter faded, and the blue of her eyes grew darker, clouded.

"You mean it, don't you?"

"Yes," he said, and did, though the thought of it lay heavy in his chest, like a swallowed stone.

She sighed, and drew her hand down the side of his face, tracing the line of his neck, the hollow of his throat. Her thumb pressed against his hammering pulse, so he felt the beat of it, magnified in his blood.

He meant it, but he bent his head to hers and took her mouth, so short of breath he must have hers, needing so urgently to join with her that he would do it in whatever way he might—hands, breath, mouth, arms; his thigh pressed between hers, opening her legs. Her hand lay flat against his chest, as though to push him off—then tightened convulsively, grasping shirt and flesh together. Her fingers dug deep in the muscle of his breast, and then they were glued together, openmouthed and gasping, front teeth scraping painfully in the flurry of their wanting.

"I don't . . . we're not . . ." He broke free for a moment, his mind grasping dimly for the fragments of words. Then her hand found its way under his kilt, a cold, sure touch on his heated flesh, and he lost all power of speech.

"Once more before we quit," she said, and her breath wreathed him in heat and mist. "For old times' sake." She sank to her knees in the wet yellow leaves, pulling him down to her.

IT HAD STARTED raining again; her hair lay tumbled round her, streaked with damp. Her eyes were closed, her face upturned to the drizzling heavens, and raindrops struck her face, rolling down like tears. She wasn't sure whether to laugh or cry, in fact.

Roger lay with her, half on her, his weight a warm and solid comfort, his kilt spread over their tangled bare legs, protection from the rain. Her hand cupped the back of his head and stroked his hair, wet and sleek as a black seal's fur.

He stirred then, with a groan like a wounded bear, and lifted himself. A draft of cold air struck her newly exposed body, damp and heated where they had touched.

"I'm sorry," he muttered. "God, I'm sorry. I shouldn't have done that." She opened one eye to a slit; he rose to his knees above her, swaying, and bent to pull her crumpled skirt down into decency. He'd lost his stock, and the cut under his jaw had reopened. She'd torn his shirt, and his waistcoat hung open, half its buttons gone. He was streaked with mud and blood and there were dead leaves and acorn fragments in the waves of his loose black hair.

"It's all right," she said, and sat up. She was in no better case; her breasts were heavy with milk, and huge wet spots had soaked through the fabric of shift and bodice, chilling her skin. Roger saw, and picked up her fallen cloak, draping it gently around her shoulders.

"Sorry," he said again, and reached to brush the tangled hair from her face; his hand was cold against her cheek.

"It's okay," she said, trying to gather all the stray fragments of herself that seemed to be rolling round the tiny clearing like beads of mercury. "It's only six months, and I'm still nursing Jemmy. It's—I mean, I think it's still safe." But for how much longer? she wondered. Little jolts of desire still shot through her, mingled with spurts of dread.

She had to touch him. She picked up one corner of her cloak and pressed it to the seeping wound beneath his jaw. Celibacy? When the feel of him, the smell of him, the memory of the last few minutes, made her want to knock him flat in the leaves and do it all again? When tenderness for him welled up in her like the milk that rushed unbidden to her breasts?

Her breasts ached with unsatisfied desire, and she felt dribbles of milk run tickling down her ribs beneath the cloth. She touched one breast, heavy and swollen, her guarantee of safety—for a while.

Roger put away her hand, reaching up to touch the cut.

"It's all right," he said. "It's stopped bleeding." He wore the oddest expression—or expressions. Normally his face was pleasantly reserved, even a little stern. Now his features seemed unable to settle themselves, shifting from moment to moment between a look of undeniable satisfaction and one of just as undeniable dismay.

"What's the matter, Roger?"

He shot her a quick glance, then looked away, a slight flush rising in his cheeks.

"Oh," he said. "Well. It's only that we . . . er . . . we aren't actually married at the moment."

"Well, of course not. The wedding's not 'til tonight. Speaking of which . . ." She looked at Roger, and a bubble of laughter rose from the pit of her stomach. "Oh, dear," she said, fighting back a fit of giggles. "You look like somebody's had their will of you in the woods, Mr. MacKenzie."

"Very funny, Mrs. Mac," he said, eyeing her own bedraggled state. "Ye've been in a rare fight, too, by the looks of you. But what I meant was that we've been handfast for the last year—and that's legally binding, in Scotland at least. But the year and a day have been up for a bit—and we're not formally married 'til this evening."

She squinted at him, wiping rain out of her eyes with the back of one hand, and once more gave way to the urge to laugh.

"My God, you think it *matters*?"

He grinned back, a little reluctantly.

"Well, no. It's only I'm a preacher's lad; I know it's fine—but somewhere inside is an old Scotch Calvinist, muttering that it's just a wee bit wicked, to be carrying on so with a woman not really my wife."

"Ha," she said, and settled her arms comfortably on her drawn-up knees. She leaned to one side and nudged him gently.

"Old Scotch Calvinist, my ass. What is it, really?"

He wouldn't look directly at her, but kept his eyes down, looking at the ground. Droplets glittered on his strongly marked dark brows and lashes, gilding the skin of his cheekbones with silver. He drew a deep breath, and let it out slowly.

"I can't say you're not right to be afraid," he said quietly. "I hadn't realized—not really thought about it before today—just how dangerous marriage is for a woman." He looked up and smiled at her, though the look of worry stayed in his moss-green eyes.

"I want you, Bree—more than I can say. It's only that I was thinking of what we just did and how fine it was—and realizing that I'll maybe—no, I *will*—be risking your life if I keep on doing it. But damned if I want to stop!"

The small strands of dread had coalesced into a cold snake that ran down her backbone and coiled deep in her belly, twisting around her womb. She knew what he wanted, and it wasn't only the thing they'd just shared—powerful as that was. Knowing what he wanted, though—and why—how could she hesitate to give it to him?

"Yeah." She took a breath to match his, and blew it out in a plume of white. "Well, it's too late to worry about that, I think." She looked at him and touched his arm. "I want you, Roger." She pulled down his head and kissed him, taking comfort from her fears in the strength of his arm around her, the warmth of his body beside her.

"Oh, God, Bree," he murmured into her hair. "I want to tell you that I'll keep you safe, save you and Jemmy from anything that might threaten you—ever. It's a terrible thing, to think it might be me that would be the threat, that I could kill you with my love—but it's true."

His heart was beating under her ear, solid and steady. She felt the warmth return to her hands, clasped tight on the bones of his back, and the thaw reached deeper, uncoiling some of the frozen strands of fear inside her.

"It's all right," she said at last, wanting to offer him the comfort he could not quite give her. "I'm sure it'll be okay. I've got the hips for it, everybody says so. Jugbutt, that's me." She ran a hand ruefully down the lush swell of one hip, and he smiled, following her hand with his own.

"You know what Ronnie Sinclair said to me last night? He was watching you bend down to pick up a stick of wood for the fire, and he sighed and said, 'Ye ken how to pick a good lass, MacKenzie? Start at the bottom and work your way up!' Oof!" He recoiled, laughing, as she slugged him.

Then he bent and kissed her, very gently. The rain was still falling, pattering on the layer of dead leaves. Her fingers were sticky with the blood from his wound.

"You want a baby, don't you?" she asked softly. "One you know is yours?"

He kept his head bent for a moment, but at last looked up at her, letting her see the answer in his face; a great yearning, mingled with anxious concern.

"I don't mean—" he began, but she put a hand across his mouth to stop him.

"I know," she said. "I understand." She did—almost. She was an only child, as he was; she knew the yearning for connection and closeness—but hers had been gratified. She had had not one loving father but two. A mother who had loved her beyond the bounds of space and time. The Murrays of Lallybroch, that unexpected gift of family. And most of all, her son, her flesh, her blood, a small and trusting weight that anchored her firmly to the universe.

But Roger was an orphan, alone in the world for such a long time. His parents gone before he knew them, his old uncle dead—he had no one to claim him, no one to love him for the sake only of his flesh and bone—no one save her. Little wonder if he hungered for the certainty she held in her arms when she nursed her child.

He cleared his throat suddenly.

"I—ah—I was going to give ye this tonight. But maybe . . . well." He reached into the inner pocket of his coat and handed her a soft bundle, wrapped in cloth.

"Sort of a wedding present, aye?" He was smiling, but she could see the uncertainty in his eyes.

She opened the cloth, and a pair of black button eyes looked up at her. The doll wore a shapeless smock of green calico, and red-yarn hair exploded from its head. Her heart beat heavily in her chest, and her throat tightened.

"I thought the wean might like it—to chew on, perhaps."

She moved, and the pressure of the sodden fabric on her breasts made them tingle. She was afraid, all right; but there were things stronger than fear.

"There'll be a next time," she said, and laid a hand on his arm. "I can't say when—but there will."

He laid his hand on hers and squeezed it tight, not looking at her.

"Thanks, Jugbutt," he said at last, very softly.

THE RAIN WAS HEAVIER; it was pissing down now. Roger thumbed the wet hair out of his eyes and shook himself like a dog, scattering drops from the tight-woven wool of coat and plaid. There was a smear of mud down the front of the gray wool; he brushed at it, to no effect.

"Christ, I can't be getting married like this," he said, trying to lighten the mood between them. "I look like a beggar."

"It's not too late, you know," she said. She smiled, teasing a little tremulously. "You could still back out."

"It's been too late for me since the day I saw you," he said gruffly. "Besides," he added, lifting one brow, "your father would gut me like a hog if I said I'd had second thoughts on the matter."

"Ha," she said, but the hidden smile popped out, dimpling one cheek.

"Bloody woman! You like the idea!"

"Yes. No, I mean." She was laughing again now; that's what he'd wanted. "I don't want him to gut you. It's just nice to know he *would*. A father ought to be protective."

She smiled at him, touched him lightly. "Like you, Mr. MacKenzie."

That gave him an odd, tight feeling in the chest, as though his waistcoat had shrunk. Then a tinge of cold, as he recalled what he had to tell her. Fathers and their notions of protection varied, after all, and he wasn't sure how she would see this one.

He took her arm and drew her away, out of the rain and into the shelter of a clump of hemlocks, where the layers of needles lay dry and fragrant underfoot, protected by the wide-spreading branches overhead.

"Well, come and sit with me a moment, Mrs. Mac. It's not important, but there's a small thing I wanted to tell you about before the wedding." He drew her down to sit beside him on a rotting log, rusted with lichen. He cleared his throat, gathering the thread of his story.

"When I was in Inverness, before I followed you through the stones, I spent some time trolling through the Reverend's bumf, and I came across a letter to him, written by your father. By Frank Randall, I mean. It's no great matter—not now—but I thought . . . well, I thought perhaps there should be no secrets between us, before we marry. I told your father about it last night. So let me tell you now."

Her hand lay warm in his, but the fingers tightened as he talked, and a deep line grew between her brows as she listened.

"Again," she said, when he'd finished. "Tell me that again."

Obligingly, he repeated the letter—as he'd memorized it, word for word. As he'd told it the night before, to Jamie Fraser.

"That gravestone in Scotland with Da's name on it is a *fake*?" Her voice rose slightly with astonishment. "Dad—Frank—had the Reverend make it, and put it there, in the kirkyard at St. Kilda, but Da isn't—won't be, I mean—won't be under it?"

"Yes, he did, and no, he won't," Roger said, keeping careful track of the "he's" involved. "He—Frank Randall, that is—meant the stone as a sort of acknowledgment, I think; a debt owed to your father—your other father, I mean; Jamie."

Brianna's face was blotched with chill, the ends of nose and ears nipped red as the heat of their lovemaking faded.

"But he couldn't know we'd ever find it, Mama and me!"

"I don't know that he *wanted* you to find it," Roger said. "Perhaps he didn't know, either. But he felt he had to make the gesture. Besides," he added, struck by a memory, "didn't Claire say that he'd meant to bring you to England, just before he was killed? Perhaps he meant to take you there, make sure you found it—then leave it to you and Claire what to do."

She sat still, chewing that one over.

"He knew, then," she said slowly. "That he—that Jamie Fraser survived Culloden. He *knew* . . . but he didn't say?"

"I don't think you can blame him for not saying," Roger said gently. "It wasn't only selfish, you know."

"Wasn't it?" She was still shocked, but not yet angry. He could see her turning it over, trying to see it all before making up her mind what to think, how to feel.

"No. Think of it, hen," he urged. The spruce was cold at his back, the bark of the fallen log damp under his hand. "He loved your mother, aye, and didn't want to risk losing her again. That's maybe selfish, but she was his wife first, after all; no one could blame him for not wanting to give her up to another man. But that's not all of it."

"What's the rest, then?" Her voice was calm, blue eyes straight and level.

"Well—what if he *had* told her? There she was, with you, a young child—and remember, neither of them would have thought that you might cross through the stones as well."

The eyes were still straight, but clouded once more with trouble.

"She would have had to choose," she said softly, her gaze fixed on him. "To stay with us—or go to him. To Jamie."

"To leave you behind," Roger said, nodding, "or to stay, and live her life, knowing her Jamie was alive, maybe reachable—but out of reach. Break her vows—on purpose, this time—and abandon her child . . . or live with yearning. I can't think *that* would have done your family life much good."

"I see." She sighed, the steam of her exhaled breath disappearing like a ghost in cold air.

"Perhaps Frank was afraid to give her the choice," Roger said, "but he did save her—and you—from the pain of having to make it. At least then."

Her lips drew in, pushed out, relaxed.

"I wonder what her choice would have been, if he *had* told her," she said, a little bleakly. He laid his hand on hers, squeezed lightly.

"She would have stayed," he said, with certainty. "She made the choice once, did she not? Jamie sent her back, to keep you safe, and she went. She would have known he wanted that, and she would have stayed—so long as you needed her. She wouldn't have gone back, even when she did, save that you insisted. Ye ken that well enough, surely?"

Her face eased a bit, accepting this.

"I guess you're right. But still . . . to know he was alive, and not try to reach him . . ."

He bit the inside of his cheek, to keep from asking. *If it were your choice, Brianna? If it was the bairn or me?* For how could any man force a choice like that on a woman whom he loved, even hypothetically? Whether for her sake or his own . . . he would not ask.

"But he did put that gravestone there. Why did he do that?" The line between her brows was still deep, but no longer straight; it twisted with a growing perturbation.

He hadn't known Frank Randall, but he felt a certain empathy for the man—and not only a disinterested sympathy, either. He hadn't fully realized why he'd felt he must tell her about the letter now, before the wedding, but his own motives were becoming clearer—and more disturbing to him—by the moment.

"I think it was obligation, as I said. Not just to Jamie or your mother—to you. If it—" he started, then stopped and squeezed her hand, hard. "Look. Take wee Jemmy. He's mine, as much as you are—he always will be." He took a deep breath. "But if I were the other man . . ."

"If you were Stephen Bonnet," she said, and her lips were tight, gone white with chill.

"If I were Bonnet," he agreed, with a qualm of distaste at the notion, "if I knew the child was mine, and yet he was being raised by a stranger—would I not want the child to know the truth, sometime?"

Her fingers convulsed in his, and her eyes went dark.

"You mustn't tell him! Roger, for God's sake, promise me you won't tell him, ever!"

He stared at her in astonishment. Her nails were digging painfully into his hand, but he made no move to free himself.

"Bonnet? Christ, no! If I ever see the man again, I'll not waste time talking!"

"Not Bonnet." She shuddered, whether from cold or emotion, he couldn't tell. "God, keep away from that man! No, it's Jemmy I mean." She swallowed hard, and gripped both his hands. "Promise me, Roger. If you love me, promise that you'll never tell Jemmy about Bonnet, never. Even if something happens to me—"

"Nothing will happen to you!"

She looked at him, and a small, wry smile formed on her lips.

"Celibacy's not my thing, either. It might." She swallowed. "And if it does . . . promise me, Roger."

"Aye, I promise," he said, reluctantly. "If you're sure."

"I'm sure!"

"Would you not have wanted ever to know, then—about Jamie?"

She bit her lip at that, her teeth sinking deep enough to leave a purple mark in the soft pink flesh.

"Jamie Fraser is not Stephen Bonnet!"

"Agreed," he said dryly. "But I wasna speaking of Jemmy to start with. All I meant was that if I were Bonnet, I should want to know, and—"

"He does know." She pulled her hand from his, abruptly, and stood up, turning away.

"He *what*?" He caught up with her in two strides, and grabbed her by the shoulder, turning her back to face him. She flinched slightly, and he loosened his grip. He took a deep breath, fighting to keep his voice calm. "Bonnet knows about Jemmy?"

"Worse than that." Her lips were trembling; she pressed them tightly together to stop it, then opened them just enough to let the truth escape. "He thinks Jemmy is his."

She wouldn't sit down with him again, but he drew her arm tightly through his and made her walk with him, walk through the falling rain and tumbled stones, past the rush of the creek and the swaying trees, until the movement calmed her enough to talk, to tell him about her days left alone at River Run, a prisoner of her pregnancy. About Lord John Grey, her father's friend, and hers; how she had confided to Lord John her fears and struggles.

"I was afraid you were dead. All of you—Mama, Da, you." Her hood had fallen back and she made no effort to reclaim it. Her red hair hung in dripping rattails on her shoulders, and droplets clung to her thick red brows.

"The last thing Da said to me—he didn't say it, even, he wrote it—he had to write it, I wouldn't talk to him. . . ." She swallowed and ran a hand beneath her nose, wiping away a pendant drop. "He said—I had to find a way to . . . to forgive him. B-Bonnet."

"To do *what*?" She pulled her arm away slightly, and he realized how hard his fingers were digging into her flesh. He loosened his grip, with a small grunt of apology, and she tilted her head briefly toward him in acknowledgment.

"He knew," she said, and stopped. She turned to face him, her feelings now in hand. "You know what happened to him—at Wentworth."

Roger gave a short, awkward nod. In actuality, he had no clear notion what had been done to Jamie Fraser—and had no wish to know more than he did. He knew about the scars on Fraser's back, though, and knew from the few things Claire had said that these were but a faint reminder.

"He knew," she said steadily. "And he knew what had to be done. He told me—if I wanted to be . . . whole . . . again, I had to find a way to forgive Stephen Bonnet. So I did."

He had Brianna's hand in his, held so tight that he felt the small shift of her bones. She had not told him, he had not asked. The name of Stephen Bonnet had never been mentioned between them, not until now.

"You did." He spoke gruffly, and had to stop to clear his throat. "You found him, then? You spoke to him?"

She brushed wet hair back from her face, nodding. Grey had come to her, told her that Bonnet had been taken, condemned. Awaiting transport to Wilmington and execution, he was being held in the cellar beneath the Crown warehouse in Cross Creek. It was there that she had gone to him, bearing what she hoped was absolution—for Bonnet, for herself.

"I was huge." Her hand sketched the bulge of advanced pregnancy before her. "I told him the baby was his; he was going to die, maybe it would be some comfort to him, to think that there'd be . . . something left."

Roger felt jealousy grip his heart, so abrupt in its attack

that for a moment, he thought the pain was physical. *Something left*, he thought. *Something of him. And what of me? If I die tomorrow—and I might, girl! Life's chancy here for me as well as you—what will be left of me, tell me that?*

He oughtn't ask, he knew that. He'd vowed never to voice the thought that Jemmy was not his, ever. If there was a true marriage between them, then Jem was the child of it, no matter the circumstances of his birth. And yet he felt the words spill out, burning like acid.

"So you were sure the child was his?"

She stopped dead and turned to look at him, eyes wide with shock.

"No. No, of course not! If I knew that, I would have told you!"

The burning in his chest eased, just a little.

"Oh. But you told him it was—you didn't say to him that there was doubt about it?"

"He was going to die! I wanted to give him some comfort, not tell him my life story! It wasn't any of his goddamn business to hear about you, or our wedding night, or—damn you, Roger!" She kicked him in the shin.

He staggered with the force of it, but grabbed her arm, preventing her from running off.

"I'm sorry!" he said, before she could kick him again, or bite him, which she looked prepared to do. "I'm sorry. You're right, it wasn't his business—and it's not my business, either, to be making you think of it all again."

She drew in a deep breath through her nose, like a dragon preparing to sear him into ash. The spark of fury in her eyes lessened slightly, though her cheeks still blazed with it. She shook off his hand, but didn't run away.

"Yes, it is," she said. She gave him a dark, flat look. "You said there shouldn't be secrets between us, and you were right. But when you tell a secret, sometimes there's another one behind it, isn't there?"

"Yeah. But it's not— I don't mean—"

Before he could say more, the sound of feet and conversation interrupted him. Four men came out of the mist, speaking casually in Gaelic. They carried sharpened sticks and nets, and all were barefoot, wet to the knees. Strings of fresh-caught fish gleamed dully in the rain-light.

*"A Smeòraich!"* One man, peering out from under the sodden brim of his slouch hat, caught sight of them and broke into a broad grin, as shrewd eyes passed over their dishevelment. "It is yourself, Thrush! And the daughter of the Red One, too? What, can you not restrain yourselves until the darkness?"

"No doubt it is sweeter to taste stolen fruit than to wait on a blessing from a shriveled priest." Another man thrust back his bonnet on his head, and clasped himself briefly, making clear just what he meant by "shriveled."

"Ah, no," said the third, wiping drops from the end of his nose as he eyed Brianna, her cloak pulled tight around her. "He's no but after singing her a wee wedding song, is he not?"

"I know the words to that song, too," said his companion, his grin broadening enough to show a missing molar. "But I sing it still more sweetly!"

Brianna's cheeks had begun to blaze again; her Gaelic was less fluent than Roger's, but she was certainly able to gather the sense of crude teasing. Roger stepped in front of her, shielding her with his body. The men meant no harm, though; they winked and grinned appreciatively, but made no further comment. The first man pulled off his hat and beat it against his thigh, shedding water, then set to business.

"It's glad I am to be meeting you thus, *a Òranaiche*. My mother did hear your music at the fire last night, and told it to my aunts and my cousins, how your music was making the blood dance in her feet. So now they will hear nothing but that you must come and sing for the ceilidh at Spring Creek. It is my youngest cousin will be wed, and her the only child of my uncle, who owns the flour mill."

"It will be a great affair, surely!" put in one of the younger men, the son of the first speaker, by his resemblance to the former.

"Oh, it's a wedding?" said Roger, in slow, formal Gaelic. "We'll have an extra herring, then!"

The two older men burst into laughter at the joke, but their sons merely looked bewildered.

"Ah, the lads would not be knowing a herring, was it slapped wet against their cheeks," said the bonneted man, shaking his head. "Born here, the two of them."

"And where was your home in Scotland, sir?" The man jerked, surprised at the question, put in clear-voiced Gaelic. He stared at Brianna for a moment, then his face changed as he answered her.

"Skye," he said softly. "Skeabost, near the foot of the Cuillins. I am Angus MacLeod, and Skye is the land of my sires and my grandsires. But my sons were born here."

He spoke quietly, but there was a tone in his voice that quelled the hilarity in the younger men as though a damp blanket had been thrown over them. The man in the slouch hat looked at Brianna with interest.

"And were you born in Scotland, *a nighean*?"

She shook her head mutely, drawing the cloak higher on her shoulders.

"I was," said Roger, answering a look of inquiry. "In Kyle of Lochalsh."

"Ah," said MacLeod, satisfaction spreading itself across his weathered features. "It is so, then, that you know all the songs of the Highlands and the Isles?"

"Not all," said Roger, smiling. "But many—and I will learn more."

"Do that," said MacLeod, nodding slowly. "Do that, Singer—and teach them to your sons." His eye lighted on Brianna, and a faint smile curled on his lips. "Let them sing to my sons, that they will know the place they came from—though they will never see it."

One of the younger men stepped forward, bashfully holding out a string of fish, which he presented to Brianna.

"For you," he said. "A gift for your wedding."

Roger could see one corner of her mouth twitch slightly—with humor or incipient hysteria? he wondered—but she stretched out a hand and took the dripping string with grave dignity. She picked up the edge of her cloak with one hand, and swept them all a deep curtsy.

*"Chaneil facal agam dhuibh ach taing,"* she said, in her slow, strangely accented Gaelic. I have no words to say to you but thanks.

The young men went pink, and the older men looked deeply pleased.

"It is good, *a nighean*," said MacLeod. "Let your husband teach you, then—and teach the *Gaidhlig* to your sons. May you have many!" He swept off his bonnet and bowed extravagantly to her, bare toes squelching in the mud to keep his balance.

"Many sons, strong and healthy!" chimed in his companion, and the two lads smiled and nodded, murmuring shyly. "Many sons to you, mistress!"

Roger made the arrangements for the ceilidh automatically, not daring to look at Brianna. They stood in silence, a foot or two apart, as the men left, casting curious looks behind them. Brianna stared down into the mud and grass where they stood, arms crossed in front of her. The burning feeling was still in Roger's chest, but now it was different. He wanted to touch her, to apologize again, but he thought that would only make things worse.

In the end, she moved first. She came to him and laid her head on his chest, the coolness of her wet hair brushing the wound in his throat. Her breasts were huge, hard as rocks against his chest, pushing against him, pushing him away.

"I need Jemmy," she said softly. "I need my baby."

The words jammed in his throat, caught between apology and anger. He had not realized how much it would hurt to think of Jemmy as belonging to someone else—not his, but Bonnet's.

"I need him, too," he whispered at last, and kissed her briefly on the forehead before taking her hand to cross the meadow once again. The mountain above lay shrouded in mist, invisible, though shouts and murmurs, scraps of speech and music drifted down, like echoes from Olympus.

# 7

# SHRAPNEL

THE DRIZZLE HAD STOPPED by mid-morning, and brief glimpses of pale blue sky showed through the clouds, giving me some hope that it might clear by evening. Proverbs and omens quite aside, I didn't want the wedding ceremonies dampened for Brianna's sake. It wouldn't be St. James's with rice and white satin, but it could at least be *dry*.

I rubbed my right hand, working out the cramp from the tooth-pulling pliers; Mr. Goodwin's broken tooth had been more troublesome to extract than I expected, but I had managed to get it out, roots and all, sending him away with a small bottle of raw whisky, and instructions to swish it round his mouth once an hour to prevent infection. Swallowing was optional.

I stretched, feeling the pocket under my skirt swing against my leg with a small but gratifying *chink*. Mr. Goodwin had indeed paid cash; I wondered whether it was enough for an astrolabe, and what on earth Jamie wanted with one. My speculations were disturbed, though, by a small but official-sounding cough behind me.

I turned around to find Archie Hayes, looking mildly quizzical.

"Oh!" I said. "Ah—can I help you, Lieutenant?"

"Weel, that's as may be, Mistress Fraser," he said, looking me over with a slight smile. "Farquard Campbell said his slaves are convinced that ye can raise the dead, so it might be as a bit of stray metal would pose no great trial to your skills as a surgeon?"

Murray MacLeod, overhearing, uttered a loud snort at this, and turned away to his own waiting patients.

"Oh," I said again, and rubbed a finger under my nose, embarrassed. One of Campbell's slaves had suffered an epileptic seizure four days before, happening to recover abruptly from it just as I laid an exploratory hand on his chest. In vain had I tried to explain what had happened; my fame had spread like wildfire over the mountain.

Even now, a small group of slaves squatted near the edge of the clearing, playing at knucklebones and waiting 'til the other patients should be attended to. I gave them a narrow eye, just in case; if one of them were dying or dangerously ill, I knew they would make no effort to tell me—both from deference to my white patients, and from their confident conviction that if anything drastic should happen while they were waiting, I would simply resurrect the corpse at my own convenience and deal with the problem then.

All of them seemed safely vertical at the moment, though, and likely to remain so for the immediate future. I turned back to Hayes, wiping muddy hands on my apron.

"Well . . . let me see the bit of metal, why don't you, and I'll see what can be done."

Nothing loath, Hayes stripped off bonnet, coat, waistcoat, stock, and shirt, together with the silver gorget of his office. He handed his garments to the aide who accompanied him, and sat down on my stool, his placid dignity quite unimpaired by partial nakedness, by the gooseflesh that stippled his back and shoulders, or by the murmur of awed surprise that went up from the waiting slaves at sight of him.

His torso was nearly hairless, with the pale, suety color of skin that had gone years with no exposure to sunlight, in sharp contrast to the weathered brown of his hands, face, and knees. The contrasts went further than that, though.

Over the milky skin of his left breast was a huge patch of bluish-black that covered him from ribs to clavicle. And while the nipple on the right was a normal brownish-pink, the one on the left was a startling white. I blinked at the sight, and heard a soft *"A Dhia!"* behind me.

*"A Dhia, tha e 'tionndadh dubh!"* said another voice, somewhat louder. By God, he is turning black!

Hayes appeared not to hear any of this, but sat back to let me make my examination. Close inspection revealed that the dark coloration was not natural pigmentation but a mottling caused by the presence of innumerable small dark granules embedded in the skin. The nipple was gone altogether, replaced by a patch of shiny white scar tissue the size of a sixpence.

"Gunpowder," I said, running my fingertips lightly over the darkened area. I'd seen such things before; caused by a misfire or shot at close range, which drove particles of powder—and often bits of wadding and cloth—into the deeper layers of the skin. Sure enough, there were small bumps beneath the skin, evident to my fingertips, dark fragments of whatever garment he had been wearing when shot.

"Is the ball still in you?" I could see where it had entered; I touched the white patch, trying to envision the path the bullet might have taken thereafter.

"Half of it is," he replied tranquilly. "It shattered. When the surgeon went to dig it out, he gave me the bits of it. When I fitted them together after, I couldna make but half a ball, so the rest of it must have stayed."

"Shattered? A wonder the pieces didn't go through your heart or your lung," I said, squatting down in order to squint more closely at the injury.

"Oh, it did," he informed me. "At least, I suppose that it must, for it came in at my breast as ye see—but it's keekin' out from my back just now."

To the astonishment of the multitudes—as well as my own—he was right. I could not only feel a small lump, just under the outer border of his left scapula, I could actually *see* it; a darkish swelling pressing against the soft white skin.

"I will be damned," I said, and he gave a small grunt of amusement, whether at my surprise or my language, I couldn't tell.

Odd as it was, the bit of shrapnel presented no surgical difficulty. I dipped a cloth into my bowl of distilled alcohol, wiped the area carefully, sterilized a scalpel, and cut quickly into the skin. Hayes sat quite still as I did it; he was a soldier and a Scot, and as the markings on his breast bore witness, he had endured much worse than this.

I spread two fingers and pressed them on either side of the incision; the lips of the small slit pouted, then a dark, jagged bit of metal suddenly protruded like a stuck-out tongue—far enough for me to grasp it with forceps and pull it free. I dropped the discolored lump into Hayes's hand, with a small exclamation of triumph, then clapped a pad soaked with alcohol against his back.

He expelled a long breath between pursed lips, and smiled over his shoulder at me.

"I thank ye, Mrs. Fraser. This wee fellow has been wi' me for some time now, but I canna say as I'm grieved to part company with him." He cupped his blood-smeared palm, peering at the bit of fractured metal in it with great interest.

"How long ago did it happen?" I asked curiously. I didn't think the bit of shrapnel had actually passed completely through his body, though it certainly gave the illusion of having done so. More likely, I thought, it had remained near the surface of the original wound, and traveled slowly round the torso, propelled between skin and muscle by Hayes's movements, until reaching its present location.

"Oh, twenty year and more, mistress," he said. He touched the patch of tough, numbed white that had once been one of the most sensitive spots on his body. "That happened at Culloden."

He spoke casually, but I felt gooseflesh ripple over my arms at the name. Twenty years and more . . . twenty-five, more like. At which point . . .

"You can't have been more than twelve!" I said.

"No," he replied, one eyebrow lifted. "Eleven. My birthday was the next day, though."

I choked back whatever I might have said in reply. I had thought I had lost my capacity to be shocked by the realities of the past, but evidently not. Someone had shot him—an eleven-year-old boy—at point-blank range. No chance of mistake, no shot gone awry in the heat of battle. The man who had shot him had known it was a child he meant to kill—and had fired, anyway.

My lips pressed tight as I examined my incision. No more than an inch long, and not deep; the fractured ball had lain just below the surface. Good, it wouldn't need stitching. I pressed a clean pad to the wound and moved in front of him, to fasten the linen strip that bound it in place.

"A miracle you survived," I said.

"It was that," he agreed. "I was lyin' on the ground, and Murchison's face over me, and I—"

"Murchison!" The exclamation popped out of me, and I saw a flicker of satisfaction cross Hayes's face. I had a brief premonitory qualm, remembering what Jamie had said about Hayes the night before. *He thinks more than he says, does wee Archie—and he talks quite a lot. Be careful of him, Sassenach.* Well, a little late for caution—but I doubted it could matter; even if it *had* been the same Murchison—

"You'll ken the name, I see," Hayes observed pleasantly. "I had heard in England that a Sergeant Murchison of the 26th was sent to North Carolina. But the garrison at Cross Creek was gone when we reached the town—a fire, was it?"

"Er, yes," I said, rather edgy at this reference. I was glad that Bree had left; only two people knew the whole truth of what had happened when the Crown's warehouse on Cross Creek burned, and she was one of them. As for the other— well, Stephen Bonnet was not likely to cross paths with the Lieutenant anytime soon—if Bonnet himself was still alive.

"And the men of the garrison," Hayes pursued, "Murchison and the rest—where have they gone, d'ye know?"

"Sergeant Murchison is dead," said a deep, soft voice behind me. "Alas."

Hayes looked beyond me and smiled.

*"A Sheumais ruaidh,"* he said. "I did think ye might come to your wife, sooner or later. I've been seekin' ye the morn."

I was startled at the name, and so was Jamie; a look of surprise flashed across his features, then disappeared, replaced by wariness. No one had called him "Red Jamie" since the days of the Rising.

"I heard," he said dryly. He sat down on my extra stool, facing Hayes. "Let's have it, then. What is it?"

Hayes pulled up the sporran that dangled between his knees, rummaged for a moment, and pulled out a square of folded paper, secured with a red wax seal, marked with a crest I recognized. My heart skipped a beat at the sight; I somehow doubted that Governor Tryon was sending me a belated birthday wish.

Hayes turned it over, checked carefully to see that the name inscribed on the front was Jamie's, and handed it across. To my surprise, Jamie didn't open it at once, but sat holding it, eyes fixed on Hayes's face.

"What brought ye here?" he asked abruptly.

"Ah, duty, to be sure," Hayes answered, thin brows arched in innocent astonishment. "Does a soldier do aught for any other reason?"

"Duty," Jamie repeated. He tapped the missive idly against his leg. "Aye, well. Duty might take ye from Charleston to Virginia, but there are quicker ways to get there."

Hayes started to shrug, but desisted at once, as the movement jarred the shoulder I was bandaging.

"I had the Proclamation to bring, from Governor Tryon."

"The Governor's no authority over you or your men."

"True," Hayes agreed, "but why should I not do the man a service, and I could?"

"Aye, and did he ask ye to do him the service, or was it your own notion?" Jamie said, a distinct tone of cynicism in his voice.

"Ye've grown a bit suspicious in your auld age, *a Sheumais ruaidh*," Hayes said, shaking his head reprovingly.

"That's how I've lived to grow as auld as I have," Jamie replied, smiling slightly. He paused, eyeing Hayes. "Ye say it was a man named Murchison who shot ye on the field at Drumossie?"

I had finished the bandaging; Hayes moved his shoulder experimentally, testing for pain.

"Why, ye kent that, surely, *a Sheumais ruaidh*. D'ye not recall the day, man?"

Jamie's face changed subtly, and I felt a small tremor of unease. The fact was that Jamie had almost no memory of the last day of the clans, of the slaughter that had left so many bleeding in the rain—him among them. I knew that small scenes from that day came back to him now and again in his sleep, fragments of nightmare—but whether it was from trauma, injury, or simple force of will, the Battle of Culloden was lost to him—or had been, until now. I didn't think he wanted it back.

"A great deal happened then," he said. "I dinna remember everything, no." He bent his head abruptly, and thrust a thumb beneath the fold of the letter, opening it so roughly that the wax seal shattered into fragments.

"Your husband's a modest man, Mistress Fraser." Hayes nodded to me as he summoned his aide with a flip of the hand. "Has he never told ye what he did that day?"

"There was a good bit of gallantry on that field," Jamie muttered, head bent over the letter. "And quite a bit of the reverse." I didn't think he was reading; his eyes were fixed, as though he were seeing something else, beyond the paper that he held.

"Aye, there was," Hayes agreed. "But it does seem worth remark, when a man's saved your life, no?"

Jamie's head jerked up at that, startled. I moved across to stand behind him, a hand laid lightly on his shoulder. Hayes took the shirt from his aide and put it slowly on, smiling in an odd, half-watchful way.

"Ye dinna recall how ye struck Murchison across the head, just as he was set to bayonet me on the ground? And then ye picked me up and carried me from the field, awa to a bittie well nearby? One of the chiefs lay on the grass there, and his men were bathin' his heid in the water, but I could see he was deid, he lay so still. There was someone there to tend me; they wished ye to stay, too, for ye were wounded and bleeding, but ye would not. Ye wished me well, in the name of St. Michael—and went back then, to the field."

Hayes settled the chain of his gorget, adjusting the small silver crescent beneath his chin. Without his stock, his throat looked bare, defenseless.

"Ye looked fair wild, man, for there was blood runnin' doon your face and your hair was loose on the wind. Ye'd sheathed your sword to carry me, but ye pulled it again as ye turned away. I didna think I should see ye again, for if ever I saw a man set to meet his death . . ."

He shook his head, his eyes half-closed, as though he saw not the sober, stalwart man before him, not the Fraser of

Fraser's Ridge—but Red Jamie, the young warrior who had not gone back from gallantry, but because he sought to throw his life away, feeling it a burden—because he had lost me.

"Did I?" Jamie muttered. "I had . . . forgotten." I could feel the tension in him, singing like a stretched wire under my hand. A pulse beat quick in the artery beneath his ear. There were things he had forgotten, but not that. Neither had I.

Hayes bent his head, as his aide fastened the stock around his neck, then straightened and nodded to me.

"I thank ye, ma'am, 'twas most gracious of ye."

"Think nothing of it," I said, dry-mouthed. "My pleasure." It had come on to rain again; the cold drops struck my hands and face, and moisture glimmered on the strong bones of Jamie's face, caught trembling in his hair and thick lashes.

Hayes shrugged himself into his coat, and fastened the loop of his plaid with a small gilt brooch—the brooch his father had given him, before Culloden.

"So Murchison is dead," he said, as though to himself. "I did hear"—his fingers fumbled for a moment with the clasp of the brooch—"as how there were two brothers of that name, alike as peas in the pod."

"There were," Jamie said. He looked up then, and met Hayes's eyes. The Lieutenant's face showed no more than mild interest.

"Ah. And would ye know, then, which it was? . . ."

"No. But it is no matter; both are dead."

"Ah," Hayes said again. He stood a moment, as though thinking, then bowed to Jamie, formally, bonnet held against his chest.

"*Buidheachas dhut, a Sheumais mac Brian*. And may Blessed Michael defend you." He lifted the bonnet briefly to me, clapped it on his head, and turned to go, his aide following in silence.

A gust of wind blew through the clearing, with a chilly burst of rain upon it, so like the freezing April rain of Culloden. Jamie shivered suddenly beside me, with a deep, convulsive shudder that crumpled the letter he still held in his hand.

"How much do you remember?" I asked, looking after Hayes, as he picked his way across the blood-soaked ground.

"Almost nothing," he replied. He stood up and turned to look down at me, his eyes as dark as the clouded skies above. "And that is still too much."

He handed me the crumpled letter. The rain had blotted and smeared the ink here and there, but it was still quite readable. By contrast to the Proclamation, it contained *two* sentences—but the additional period didn't dilute its impact.

*New Bern, 20 October*

*Colonel James Fraser*

*Whereas the Peace and good Order of this Government has been lately violated and much Injury done to the Persons and Properties of many Inhabitants of this Province by a Body of People who Stile themselves Regulators, I do by the Advice of his Majesty's Council Order and direct you forthwith to call a General Muster of so many Men as you Judge suitable to serve in a Regiment of Militia, and make Report to me as soon as possible of the Number of Volunteers that are willing to turn out in the Service of their King and Country, when called upon, and also what Number of effective Men belong to your Regiment who can be ordered out in case of an Emergency, and in case any further Violence should be attempted to be committed by the Insurgents. Your Diligent and punctual Obedience to these Orders will be well received by*

*Your Obed't. Servant,*
*William Tryon*

I folded the rain-spotted letter neatly up, noticing remotely that my hands were shaking. Jamie took it from me, and held it between thumb and forefinger, as though it were some disagreeable object—as indeed it was. His mouth quirked wryly as he met my eyes.

"I had hoped for a little more time," he said.

8

# THE FACTOR

AFTER BRIANNA LEFT TO RETRIEVE
Jemmy from Jocasta's tent, Roger made his way
slowly up the hill toward their own campsite. He exchanged greetings and accepted congratulations from people
he passed, but scarcely heard what was said to him.

*There'll be a next time*, she'd said. He held the words
close, turning them over in his mind like a handful of coins
in his pocket. She hadn't been just saying it. She meant it,
and it was a promise that at the moment meant even more to
him than the ones she'd made on their first wedding night.

The thought of weddings reminded him, finally, that there
was in fact another coming. He glanced down at himself, and
saw that Bree hadn't been exaggerating about his appearance. Damn, and it was Jamie's coat, too.

He began to brush off the pine needles and streaks of
mud, but was interrupted by a halloo from the path above. He
looked up, to see Duncan Innes making his way carefully
down the steep slope, body canted to compensate for his
missing arm. Duncan had put on his splendid coat, scarlet
with blue facings and gold buttons, and his hair was plaited
tight under a stylish new black hat. The transformation from
Highland fisherman to prosperous landowner was startling;
even Duncan's attitude seemed changed, more confident by
half.

Duncan was accompanied by a tall, thin, elderly gentleman, very neat but threadbare in appearance, his scanty
white locks tied back from a high and balding brow. His
mouth had collapsed from lack of teeth, but retained its

humorous curve, and his eyes were blue and bright, set in a long face whose skin was stretched so tight across the bone as scarce to leave enough to wrinkle round the eyes, though deep lines carved the mouth and brow. With a long-beaked nose, and clad in rusty, tattered black, he looked like a genial vulture.

*"A Smeòraich,"* Duncan hailed Roger, looking pleased. "The very man I hoped to find! And I trust you're weel-fettled against your marriage?" he added, his eyes falling quizzically on Roger's stained coat and leaf-strewn hair.

"Oh, aye." Roger cleared his throat, converting his coat-brushing to a brief thump of his chest, as though to loosen phlegm. "Damp weather for a wedding, though, eh?"

"Happy the corpse the rain falls on," Duncan agreed, and laughed, a little nervously. "Still, we'll hope not to die o' the pleurisy before we're wed, eh, lad?" He settled the fine crimson coat more snugly on his shoulders, flicking an imaginary speck of dust from the cuff.

"You're very fine, Duncan," Roger said, hoping to distract attention from his own disreputable state with a bit of raillery. "Quite like a bridegroom!"

Duncan flushed a little behind his drooping mustache, and his one hand twiddled with the crested buttons on his coat.

"Ah, well," he said, seeming mildly embarrassed. "Miss Jo did say as she didna wish to stand up wi' a scarecrow." He coughed, and turned abruptly to his companion, as though the word had suddenly reminded him of the man's presence.

"Mr. Bug, here's Himself's good-son, Roger Mac, him I tellt ye of." He turned back toward Roger, waving vaguely at his companion, who stepped forward, extending his hand with a stiff but cordial bow. "This will be Arch Bug, *a Smeòraich."*

"Your servant, Mr. Bug," Roger said politely, slightly startled to observe that the large bony hand gripping his was missing its first two fingers.

"Ump," Mr. Bug replied, his manner indicating that he reciprocated the sentiment sincerely. He might have intended to expand on the subject, but when he opened his mouth, a high-pitched feminine voice, a little cracked with age, seemed to emerge from it.

"It's that kind, sir, of Mr. Fraser, and I'm sure as he'll have nay reason to regret it, indeed he'll not, as I said to him myself. I canna tell ye what a blessing it is, and us not sure where our next bite was comin' from or how to keep a roof above our heads! I said to Arch, I said, now we must just trust in Christ and Our Lady, and if we mun starve, we shall do it in a state of grace, and Arch, he says to me . . ."

A small, round woman, threadbare and elderly as her husband, but likewise neatly mended, emerged into view, still talking. Short as she was, Roger hadn't seen her, hidden behind the voluminous skirts of her husband's ancient coat.

"Mistress Bug," Duncan whispered to him, unnecessarily.

". . . and no but a silver ha'penny to bless ourselves with, and me a-wondering whatever was to become of us, and then that Sally McBride was sayin' as how she'd heard that Jamie Fraser had need of a good—"

Mr. Bug smiled above his wife's head. She halted in midsentence, eyes widening in shock at the state of Roger's coat.

"Why, look at that! Whatever have ye been up to, lad? Have ye had an accident? It looks as though someone's knocked ye down and dragged ye by your heels through the dung heap!"

Not waiting for answers, she whipped a clean kerchief from the bulging pocket tied at her waist, spat liberally on it, and began industriously cleaning the muddy smears from the breast of his coat.

"Oh, you needn't . . . I mean . . . er . . . thanks." Roger felt as though he'd been caught in some kind of machinery. He glanced at Duncan, hoping for rescue.

"Jamie Roy's asked Mr. Bug to come and be factor at the Ridge." Duncan seized the momentary lull afforded by Mrs. Bug's preoccupation to give a word of explanation.

"Factor?" Roger felt a small jolt at the word, as though someone had punched him just beneath the breastbone.

"Aye, for times when Himself must be abroad or occupied with other business. For it's true enough—fields and tenants dinna tend themselves."

Duncan spoke with a certain note of ruefulness; once a simple fisherman from Coigach, he frequently found the responsibilities of running a large plantation onerous, and he glanced now at Mr. Bug with a small gleam of covetousness, as though he thought momentarily of tucking this useful person into his pocket and taking him home to River Run. Of course, Roger reflected, that would have meant taking Mrs. Bug, too.

"And just the thing it is, too, *such* good fortune, and me telling Arch just yesterday that the best we might hope for was to find work in Edenton or Cross Creek, with Arch maybe takin' to the boats, but that's such a perilous living, is it no? Wet to the skin half the time and deadly agues risin' up from the swamps like ghoulies and the air sae thick wi' the miasma as it's not fit to breathe, and me perhaps to be takin' in laundry in the toon whilst he was gone abroad on the water, though I'm sure I should hate that, for we havena been apart one night since we married, have we, my dearie?"

She cast a glance of devotion upward at her tall husband, who smiled gently down at her. Perhaps Mr. Bug was deaf, Roger thought. Or perhaps they had only been married a week?

Without his needing to inquire, though, he was informed that the Bugs had been husband and wife for more than forty years. Arch Bug had been a minor tacksman to Malcolm Grant of Glenmoriston, but the years after the Rising had been hard. The estate he had held for Grant having been confiscated by the English Crown, Bug had made do for some years as a crofter, but then had been obliged by hardship and starvation to take his wife and their little remaining money and seek a new life in America.

"We had thought to try in Edinburgh—" the old gentleman said, his speech slow and courtly, with a soft Highland lilt. So he *wasn't* deaf, Roger thought. Yet.

"—for I had a cousin there as was to do wi' one of the banking houses, and we thought that perhaps it would be that he could speak a word in someone's ear—"

"But I was far too ancient and lacked sufficient skill—"

"—and lucky they would have been to have him, too! But nay, such fools as they were, they wouldna think of it, and so we had to come awa and try if we might . . ."

Duncan met Roger's eye and hid a smile beneath his

drooping mustache as the tale of the Bugs' adventures poured out in this syncopated fashion. Roger returned the smile, trying privately to dismiss a niggling sense of discomfort.

Factor. Someone to oversee matters on the Ridge, to mind the planting, tend the harvest, deal with the concerns of tenants when Jamie Fraser was away or busy. An obvious necessity, with the recent influx of new tenants and the knowledge of what the next few years would bring.

It wasn't until this moment, though, that Roger realized that he had subconsciously assumed that *he* would be Jamie's right hand in such affairs. Or the left, at least.

Fergus assisted Jamie to some extent, riding on errands and fetching back information. Fergus's lack of a hand limited what he could do physically, though, and he couldn't be dealing with the paperwork or accounts; Jenny Murray had taught the French orphan her brother had adopted to read—after a fashion—but had failed utterly to give him a grasp of numbers.

Roger stole a glance at Mr. Bug's hand, resting now in affection on his wife's plump shoulder. It was broad, workworn, and strong-looking despite the mutilation, but the remaining fingers were badly twisted with arthritis, the joints knobby and painful in appearance.

So Jamie thought that even an elderly, half-crippled man would be better equipped than Roger to handle the affairs of Fraser's Ridge? That was an unexpectedly bitter thought.

He knew his father-in-law had doubts of his ability, beyond any father's natural mistrust of the man bedding his daughter. Totally tone-deaf himself, Jamie would naturally not value Roger's musical gift. And while Roger was decently sized and hardworking, it was unfortunately true that he had little practical knowledge of animal husbandry, hunting, or the use of deadly weapons. And granted, he had no great experience in farming or in running a large estate— which Mr. Bug plainly did. Roger would be the first to admit these things.

But he was Jamie's son-in-law, or about to be. Damn it, Duncan had just introduced him that way! He might have been raised in another time—but he was a Highland Scot, for all that, and he was well aware that blood and kinship counted for more than anything.

The husband of an only daughter would normally be considered as the son of the house, coming only second to the head of the household in authority and respect. Unless there was something drastically wrong with him. If he were commonly known to be a drunkard, for instance—or criminally dissolute. Or feeble-minded . . . Christ, was that what Jamie thought of him? A hopeless numpty?

"Sit ye doon, young man, and I'll attend to *this* fine boorachie," Mrs. Bug interrupted these dark musings. She pulled on his sleeve, making clicking noises of disapproval as she viewed the leaves and twigs in his hair.

"Look at ye, all gluthered and blashed about! Fightin', was it? Och, weel, I hope the other fellow looks worse, that's all I can say."

Before he could protest, she had him seated on a rock, had whipped a wooden comb from her pocket and the thong from his hair, and was dealing with his disordered locks in a brisk manner that felt calculated to rip several strands from his scalp.

"Thrush, is it, they call ye?" Mrs. Bug paused in her tonsorial activity, holding up a strand of glossy black and squinting suspiciously at it, as though in search of vermin.

"Oh, aye, but it's no for the color of his bonnie black locks," Duncan put in, grinning at Roger's obvious discomfiture. "It's for the singin'. Honey-throated as a wee nightingale, is Roger Mac."

"Singing?" cried Mrs. Bug. She dropped the lock of hair, enchanted. "Was it you we heard last night, then? Singin' 'Ceann-ràra,' and 'Loch Ruadhainn'? And playin' on the bodhran with it?"

"Well, it might have been," Roger murmured modestly. The lady's unbounded admiration—expressed at great length—flattered him, and made him ashamed of his momentary resentment of her husband. After all, he thought, seeing the shabbiness of her much-mended apron, and the lines in her face, the old people had clearly had a hard time of it. Perhaps Jamie had hired them as much from charity as from his own need of help.

That made him feel somewhat better, and he thanked Mrs. Bug very graciously for her assistance.

"Will ye come along to our fire now?" he asked, with an inquiring glance at Mr. Bug. "Ye'll not have met Mrs. Fraser yet, I suppose, or—"

He was interrupted by a noise like a fire engine's siren, distant but obviously coming closer. Quite familiar with this particular racket, he was not surprised to see his father-in-law emerge from one of the trails that crisscrossed the mountain, Jem squirming and squalling like a scalded cat in his arms.

Jamie, looking mildly harried, handed the child across to Roger. Roger took him and—for lack of any other inspiration—stuck his thumb in the wide-open mouth. The noise ceased abruptly, and everyone relaxed.

"What a sweet laddie!" Mrs. Bug stood a-tiptoe to coo over Jem, while Jamie, looking highly relieved, turned to greet Mr. Bug and Duncan.

"Sweet" was not the adjective Roger himself would have chosen. "Berserk" seemed more like it. The baby was bright red in the face, the tracks of tears staining his cheeks, and he sucked furiously on the sustaining thumb, eyes squashed shut in an effort to escape a patently unsatisfactory world. What hair he had was sticking up in sweaty spikes and whorls, and he had come out of his wrappings, which hung in disreputable folds and draggles. He also smelled like a neglected privy, for reasons which were all too obvious.

An experienced father, Roger at once instituted emergency measures.

"Where's Bree?"

"God knows, and He's no telling," Jamie said briefly. "I've been searchin' the mountainside for her since the wean woke in my arms and decided he wasna satisfied wi' my company." He sniffed suspiciously at the hand which had been holding his grandson, then wiped it on the skirts of his coat.

"He's not so very pleased with mine, either, seems like." Jem was champing on the thumb, drool running down his chin and over Roger's wrist, uttering squeals of frustration. "Have ye seen Marsali, then?" He knew Brianna didn't like anyone to feed Jemmy but herself, but this was plainly an emergency. He cast an eye about, hoping to spot a nursing mother somewhere nearby who might take pity on the child, if not on him.

"Let me have the poor wee bairnie," said Mrs. Bug, reaching for the baby and immediately altering her status from chattering busybody to angel of light, so far as Roger was concerned.

"There, now, *a leannan,* there, there." Recognizing a higher authority when he saw it, Jemmy promptly shut up, his eyes rounded with awe as he regarded Mrs. Bug. She sat down with the little boy on her lap and began to deal with him in the same firm and efficient manner with which she had just dealt with his father. Roger thought that perhaps Jamie had hired the wrong Bug to be factor.

Arch, though, was exhibiting both intelligence and competence, asking sensible questions of Jamie regarding stock, crops, tenants, and so forth. *But I could do that,* Roger thought, following the conversation closely. *Some of it,* he amended honestly, as the talk suddenly veered into a discussion of bag-rot. Perhaps Jamie was right to seek someone more knowledgeable . . . but Roger could learn, after all. . . .

"And who's the bonnie laddie, noo?" Mrs. Bug had risen to her feet, cooing over Jemmy, now respectably transformed into a tightly swaddled cocoon. She traced the line of a round cheek with one stubby finger, then glanced at Roger. "Aye, aye, he's eyes just like his father, then, hasn't he?"

Roger flushed, forgetting about bag-rot.

"Oh? I should say he favors his mother, mostly."

Mrs. Bug pursed her lips, narrowing her eyes at Roger, then shook her head decidedly, and patted Jem on the top of his head.

"Not the hair, maybe, but the shape of him, aye, that's yours, lad. Those fine broad shoulders!" She gave Roger a brief nod of approval, and kissed Jem on the brow. "Why, I shouldna be surprised but what his een will turn green as he ages, either. Mark me, lad, he'll be the spit of you by the time he's grown! Won't ye, wee mannie?" She nuzzled Jemmy. "Ye'll be a big, braw lad like your Da, won't ye, then?"

*It's the usual thing folk say*, he reminded himself, trying to quell the absurd rush of pleasure he felt at her words. *The old wifies, they always say how a bairn resembles this one or that one.* He discovered suddenly that he was afraid even to admit the possibility that Jemmy could really be his—he wanted it so badly. He told himself firmly that it didn't matter; whether the boy was his by blood or not, he would love and care for him as his son. He would, of course. But it did matter, he found—oh, it did.

Before he could say anything further to Mrs. Bug, though, Mr. Bug turned toward him, to include him courteously in the men's conversation.

"MacKenzie, is it?" he asked. "And will ye be one of the MacKenzies of Torridon, then, or maybe from Kilmarnock?"

Roger had been fielding similar questions all through the Gathering; exploring a person's antecedents was the normal beginning of any Scottish conversation—something that wouldn't change a bit in the next two hundred years, he thought, wariness tempered by the comfortable familiarity of the process. Before he could answer, though, Jamie's hand squeezed his shoulder.

"Roger Mac's kin to me on my mother's side," he said casually. "It will be MacKenzie of Leoch, aye?"

"Oh, aye?" Arch Bug looked impressed. "You're far afield, then, lad!"

"Och, no more than yourself, sir, surely—or anyone here, for that matter." Roger waved briefly at the mountainside above, from which the sounds of Gaelic shouts and the music of bagpipes drifted on the damp air.

"No, no, lad!" Mrs. Bug, Jemmy propped against her shoulder, rejoined the conversation. "That's no what Arch is meanin'," she explained. "It's that you're a good long way from the others."

"Others?" Roger exchanged a look with Jamie, who shrugged, equally puzzled.

"From Leoch," Arch got in, before his wife seized the thread of talk between her teeth.

"We did hear it on the ship, aye? There were a gaggle of them, all MacKenzies, all from the lands south of the auld castle. They'd stayed on after the laird left, him and the first lot, but now they meant to go and join what was left o' the clan, and see could they mend their fortunes, because—"

"The laird?" Jamie interrupted her sharply. "That would be Hamish mac Callum?" Hamish, son of Colum, Roger translated to himself, and paused. Or rather, Hamish mac Dougal—but there were only five people in the world who knew that. Perhaps only four, now.

Mrs. Bug was nodding emphatically. "Aye, aye, it is himself they were calling so. Hamish mac Callum MacKenzie, laird of Leoch. The third laird. They said it, just so. And—"

Jamie had evidently caught the knack of dealing with Mrs. Bug; by dint of ruthless interruption, he succeeded in extracting the story in less time than Roger would have thought possible. Castle Leoch had been destroyed by the English, in the purge of the Highlands following Culloden. So much Jamie had known, but, imprisoned himself, had had no word of the fate of those who lived there.

"And no great heart to ask," he added, with a rueful tilt of the head. The Bugs glanced at each other and sighed in unison, the same hint of melancholy shadowing their eyes that shaded Jamie's voice. It was a look Roger was well accustomed to by now.

"But if Hamish mac Callum still lives . . ." Jamie had not taken his hand from Roger's shoulder, and at this it squeezed tight. "That's news to gladden the heart, no?" He smiled at Roger, with such obvious joy that Roger felt an unexpected grin break out on his own face in answer.

"Aye," he said, the weight on his heart lightening. "Aye, it is!" The fact that he would not know Hamish mac Callum MacKenzie from a hole in the ground was unimportant; the man was indeed kin to him—blood kin—and that *was* a glad thought.

"Where have they gone, then?" Jamie demanded, dropping his hand. "Hamish and his followers?"

To Acadia—to Canada, the Bugs agreed. To Nova Scotia? To Maine? No—to an island, they decided, after a convoluted conference. Or was it perhaps—

Jemmy interrupted the proceedings with a yowl indicating imminent starvation, and Mrs. Bug started as though poked with a stick.

"We mun be takin' this puir lad to his Mam," she said rebukingly, dividing a glare impartially among the four men, as though accusing them collectively of conspiracy to murder the child. "Where does your camp lie, Mr. Fraser?"

"I'll guide ye, ma'am," Duncan said hastily. "Come wi' me."

Roger started after the Bugs, but Jamie kept him with a hand on his arm.

"Nay, let Duncan take them," he said, dismissing the Bugs with a nod. "I'll speak wi' Arch later. I've a thing I must say to you, *a chliamhuinn.*"

Roger felt himself tense a bit at the formal term of address. So, was this where Jamie told him just what defects of character and background made him unsuitable to take responsibility for things at Fraser's Ridge?

But no, Jamie was bringing out a crumpled paper from his sporran. He handed it to Roger with a slight grimace, as though the paper burned his hand. Roger scanned it quickly, then glanced up from the Governor's brief message.

"Militia. How soon?"

Jamie lifted one shoulder.

"No one can say, but sooner than any of us should like, I think." He gave Roger a faint, unhappy smile. "Ye'll have heard the talk round the fires?"

Roger nodded soberly. He had heard the talk in the intervals of the singing, around the edges of the stone-throwing contests, among the men drinking in small groups under the trees the day before. There had been a fistfight at the caber-tossing—quickly stopped, and with no damage done—but anger hung in the air of the Gathering, like a bad smell.

Jamie rubbed a hand over his face and through his hair, and shrugged, sighing.

" 'Twas luck I should have come across auld Arch Bug and his wife today. If it comes to the fighting—and it will, I suppose, later, if not now—then Claire will ride with us. I shouldna like to leave Brianna to manage on her own, and it can be helped."

Roger felt the small nagging weight of doubt drop away, as all became suddenly clear.

"On her own. You mean—ye want me to come? To help raise men for the militia?"

Jamie gave him a puzzled look.

"Aye, who else?"

He pulled the edges of his plaid higher about his shoulders, hunched against the rising wind. "Come along, then, Captain MacKenzie," he said, a wry note in his voice. "We've work to do before you're wed."

9

# GERM OF DISSENT

I PEERED UP THE NOSE of one of Farquard Campbell's slaves, half my mind on the nasal polyp obstructing the nostril, the other half on Governor Tryon. Of the two, I felt more charitably toward the polyp, and I intended to cauterize *that* out of existence with a hot iron.

It seemed so bloody unfair, I thought, frowning as I sterilized my scalpel and set the smallest cauterizing iron in a dish of hot coals.

Was this the beginning? Or one of them? It was the end of 1770; in five years more, all of the thirteen Colonies would be at war. But each colony would come to that point by a different process. Having lived in Boston for so long, I knew from Bree's school lessons what the process had been—or would be—for Massachusetts. Tax, Boston Massacre, Harbor, Hancock, Adams, Tea Party, all that. But North Carolina? How had it happened—how *would* it happen— here?

It could be happening now. Dissension had been simmering for several years between the planters of the eastern seaboard and the hardscrabble homesteaders of the western backcountry. The Regulators were mostly drawn from the latter class; the former were wholeheartedly in Tryon's camp—on the side of the Crown, that was to say.

"All right now?" I had given the slave a good slug of medicinal whisky, by way of fortification. I smiled encouragingly, and he nodded, looking uncertain but resigned.

I had never heard of Regulators, but here they were, nonetheless—and I had seen enough by now to know just how much the history books left out. Were the seeds of revolution being sown directly under my own nose?

Murmuring soothingly, I wrapped a linen napkin round my left hand, took firm hold of the slave's chin with it, poked the scalpel up his nostril and severed the polyp with a deft flick of the blade. It bled profusely, of course, the blood gushing warmly through the cloth round my hand, but evidently was not very painful. The slave looked surprised, but not distressed.

The cautery iron was shaped like a tiny spade, a bit of square, flattened metal on the end of a slender rod with a wooden handle. The flat bit was smoking in the fire, the edges glowing red. I pressed the cloth hard against the man's nose to blot the blood, took it away, and in the split second before the blood spurted out again, pressed the hot iron up his nose against the septum, hoping against hope that I'd got the proper spot.

The slave made a strangled noise in his throat, but didn't move, though tears poured down his cheeks, wet and warm on my fingers. The smell of searing blood and flesh was just the same as the scent that rose from the barbecue pits. My stomach growled loudly; the slave's bulging, bloodshot eye met mine, astonished. My mouth twitched, and he giggled faintly through the tears and snot.

I took the iron away, cloth poised. No fresh blood flowed. I tilted the man's head far back, squinting to see, and was pleased to find the small, clean mark, high on the mucosa. The burn would be a vivid red, I knew, but without the light of a scope, it looked black, a small scab hidden like a tick in the hairy shadows of the nostril.

The man spoke no English; I smiled at him, but addressed his companion, a young woman who had clutched his hand throughout the ordeal.

"He'll be quite all right. Tell him, please, not to pick at the scab. If there should be swelling, pus or fever"—I paused, for the next line should be—"go to your doctor at once," and that was not an option.

"Go to your mistress," I said, instead, reluctantly. "Or find an herb-woman." The present Mrs. Campbell was young, and rather muddleheaded, from the little I knew of her. Still, any plantation mistress should have the knowledge and where-withal to treat a fever. And if it should go past simple infection and into septicemia . . . well, there was not much anyone could do, in that case.

I patted the slave's shoulder and sent him off, beckoning to the next in line.

Infection. That was what was brewing. Things seemed quiet overall—after all, the Crown was withdrawing all its troops! But dozens, hundreds, thousands of tiny germs of dissent must linger, forming pockets of conflict throughout the Colonies. The Regulation was only one.

A small bucket of distilled alcohol stood by my feet, for disinfecting instruments. I dipped the cautery iron in this, then thrust it back in the fire; the alcohol ignited with a brief, lightless *piff!*

I had the unpleasant feeling that the note presently burning a hole in Jamie's sporran was a similar flame, touched to one of a million small fuses. Some might be stamped out, some would fizzle on their own—but enough would burn, and go on burning, searing their destructive way through homes and families. The end of it would be a clean excision, but a great deal of blood would flow before the hot iron of guns should sear the open wound.

Were we never to have a little peace, Jamie and I?

"THERE'S DUNCAN MACLEOD, he's got three hundred acres near the Yadkin River, but no one on it save himself and his brother." Jamie rubbed a sleeve over his face, wiping off the sheen of moisture that clung to his bones. He blinked to clear his vision, and shook himself like a dog, spattering drops that had condensed in his hair.

"But," he went on, gesturing toward the plume of smoke that marked MacLeod's fire, "he's kin to auld Rabbie Cochrane. Rabbie's not come to the Gathering—ill wi' the dropsy, I hear—but he's got eleven grown bairns, scattered over the mountains like seed corn. So, take your time wi' MacLeod, make sure he's pleased to come, then tell him to send word to Rabbie. We'll muster at Fraser's Ridge in a fortnight, tell him."

He hesitated, one hand on Roger's arm to prevent an abrupt departure. He squinted into the haze, reckoning up the possibilities. They'd visited three campsites together, and got the pledges of four men. How many more could be found at the Gathering?

"After Duncan, go across to the sheep pens. Angus Og will be there, surely—ye ken Angus Og?"

Roger nodded, hoping he recalled the correct Angus Og. He'd met at least four men of that name in the last week, but one of them had had a dog at heel, and reeked of raw wool.

"Campbell, aye? Bent like a fishhook, and a cast in one eye?"

"Aye, that's him." Jamie gave a nod of approbation, relaxing his grip. "He's too crabbit to fight himself, but he'll see his nephews come, and spread the word amongst the settlements near High Point. So, Duncan, Angus . . . oh, aye, Joanie Findlay."

"Joanie?"

Fraser grinned.

"Aye, auld Joan, they call her. Her camp's near my aunt, her and her brother, Iain Mhor."

Roger nodded, dubious.

"Aye. It's her I speak to, though, is it?"

"Ye'll have to," Fraser said. "Iain Mhor's got nay speech. She's two more brothers who have, though, and two sons old enough to fight. She'll see they come."

Jamie cast an eye upward; the day had warmed slightly

and it wasn't raining so much as misting—a mizzle, they'd call it in Scotland. The clouds had thinned enough to show the disk of the sun, a pale blurry wafer still high in the sky, but sinking lower. Another two hours of good light, maybe.

"That'll do," he decided, wiping his nose on his sleeve. "Come back to the fire when ye've done wi' auld Joan, and we'll have a bit of supper before your wedding, aye?" He gave Roger an up-cocked brow and a slight smile, then turned away. Before Roger could move off, he turned back.

"Say straight off as you're Captain MacKenzie," he advised. "They'll mind ye better." He turned again and strode off in search of the more recalcitrant prospects on his list.

MacLeod's fire burned like a smudge pot in the mist. Roger turned toward it, repeating the names under his breath like a mantra. "Duncan MacLeod, Rabbie Cochrane, Angus Og Campbell, Joanie Findlay . . . Duncan MacLeod, Rabbie Cochrane . . ." No bother; three times and he'd have it cold, no matter whether it was the words of a new song to be learned, facts in a textbook, or directions to the psychology of potential militia recruits.

He could see the sense of finding as many of the back-country Scots as possible now, before they scattered away to their farms and cabins. And he was heartened by the fact that the men Fraser had approached so far had accepted the militia summons with no more than a mild glower and throat-clearings of resignation.

Captain MacKenzie. He felt a small sense of embarrassed pride at the title Fraser had casually bestowed on him. "Instant Soldier," he muttered derisively to himself, straightening the shoulders of his sodden coat. "Just add water."

At the same time, he'd admit to a faint tingle of excitement. It might amount to no more than playing soldiers, now, indeed—but the thought of marching with a militia regiment, muskets shouldered and the smell of gunpowder on their hands . . .

It was less than four years from now, he thought, and militiamen would stand on the green at Lexington. Men who were no more soldiers to start with than these men he spoke to in the rain—no more than him. Awareness shivered over his skin, settled in his belly with an odd weight of significance.

It was coming. Christ, it was really coming.

MacLEOD WAS NO TROUBLE, but it took longer than he'd thought to find Angus Og Campbell, up to his arse in sheep, and irascible at the distraction. "Captain MacKenzie" had had little effect on the old bastard; the invocation of "Colonel Fraser"—spoken with a degree of menace—had had more. Angus Og had chewed his long upper lip with moody concentration, nodded reluctantly, and gone back to his bargaining with a gruff, "Aye, I'll send word."

The mizzle had stopped and the clouds were beginning to break up by the time he climbed back up the slope to Joan Findlay's camp.

"Auld Joan," to his surprise, was an attractive woman in her mid-thirties, with sharp hazel eyes that regarded him with interest under the folds of her damp arisaid.

"So it's come to that, has it?" she said, in answer to his brief explanation of his presence. "I did wonder, when I heard what the soldier-laddie had to say this morning."

She tapped her lip thoughtfully with the handle of her wooden pudding-spoon.

"I've an aunt who lives in Hillsborough, ken. She's a room in the King's House, straight across the street from Edmund Fanning's house—or where it used to be." She gave a short laugh, though it held no real humor.

"She wrote to me. The mob came a-boilin' down the street, wavin' pitchforks like a flock o' demons, she said. They cut Fanning's house from its sills, and dragged the whole of it down wi' ropes, right before her eyes. So now we're meant to send our men to pull Fanning's chestnuts from the fire, are we?"

Roger was cautious; he'd heard a good deal of talk about Edmund Fanning, who was less than popular.

"I couldna say as to that, Mrs. Findlay," he said. "But the Governor—"

Joan Findlay snorted expressively.

"Governor," she said, and spat into the fire. "Pah. The Governor's friends, more like. But there—poor men mun bleed for the rich man's gold, and always will, eh?"

She turned to two small girls who had materialized behind her, silent as small shawled ghosts.

"Annie, fetch your brothers. Wee Joanie, you stir the pot. Mind ye scrape the bottom well so it doesna burn." Handing the spoon to the smallest girl, she turned away, beckoning Roger to follow.

It was a poor camp, with no more than a woolen blanket stretched between two bushes to provide a shelter of sorts. Joan Findlay squatted down before the cavelike recess so provided, and Roger followed, bending down to peer over her shoulder.

"*A bhràthair*, here's Captain MacKenzie," she said, reaching out a hand to the man that lay on a pallet of dry grass under the blanket's shelter. Roger felt a sudden shock at the man's appearance, but suppressed it.

A spastic, they would have called him in the Scotland of Roger's own time; what did they call such a condition now? Perhaps nothing in particular; Fraser had said only, *He has nay speech.*

No, nor proper movement, either. His limbs were bony and wasted, his body twisted into impossible angles. A tattered quilt had been laid over him, but his jerking movements had pulled it awry, so that the cloth was bunched, wrenched hard between his legs, and his upper body was left exposed, the worn shirt also rumpled and pulled half off by his struggles. The pale skin over shoulder and ribs gleamed cold and blue-toned in the shadows.

Joan Findlay cupped a hand about the man's cheek and turned his head so that he could look at Roger.

"This will be my brother Iain, Mr. MacKenzie," she said, her voice firm, daring him to react.

The face too was distorted, the mouth pulled askew and drooling, but a pair of beautiful—and intelligent—hazel eyes looked back at Roger from the ruin. He took firm grip of his feelings and his own features, and reached out, taking the man's clawed hand in his own. It felt terrible, the bones sharp and fragile under skin so cold it might have been a corpse's.

"Iain Mhor," he said softly. "I have heard your name. Jamie Fraser sends ye his regards."

The eyelids lowered in a graceful sweep of acknowledgment, and came up again, regarding Roger with calm brightness.

"The Captain's come to call for militiamen," Joan said from behind Roger's shoulder. "The Governor's sent orders, aye? Seems he's had enough o' riot and disorder, so he says; he'll put it down by force." Her voice held a strong tone of irony.

Iain Mhor's eyes shifted to his sister's face. His mouth moved, struggling for shape, and his narrow chest strained with effort. A few croaking syllables emerged, thick with spittle, and he fell back, breathing hard, eyes intent on Roger.

"Will there be bounty money paid, he says, Captain?" Joan translated.

Roger hesitated. Jamie had addressed that question, but there was no definite answer. He could feel the subdued eagerness, though, both in the woman behind him and the man who lay before him. The Findlays were grinding poor; that much was plain from the little girls' ragged frocks and bare feet, from the threadbare clothes and bedding that gave Iain Mhor scant shelter from the cold. But honesty compelled him to answer.

"I don't know. There is none advertised as yet—but there may be." The payment of bounty money depended on the response to the Governor's call; if a simple order produced insufficient troops, the Governor might see fit to provide further inducement for militiamen to answer the summons.

An expression of disappointment flickered in Iain Mhor's eyes, replaced almost at once by resignation. Any income would have been welcome, but it was not really expected.

"Well, then." Joan's voice held the same resignation. Roger felt her draw back and turn aside, but he was still held by the long-lashed hazel eyes. They met his, unflinching and curious. Roger hesitated, unsure whether to simply take his leave. He wanted to offer help—but God, what help was there?

He stretched out a hand toward the gaping shirt, the rumpled quilt. Little enough, but something.

"May I?"

The hazel eyes closed for a moment, opened in acquiescence, and he set about the chore of putting things straight. Iain Mhor's body was emaciated, but surprisingly heavy, and awkward to lift from such an angle.

Still, it took no more than a few moments, and the man lay decently covered, and warmer at least. Roger met the hazel eyes again, smiled, nodded awkwardly, and backed away from the grass-lined nest, wordless as Iain Mhor himself.

Joan Findlay's two sons had come; they stood by their mother, sturdy lads of sixteen and seventeen, regarding Roger with cautious curiosity.

"This will be Hugh," she said, reaching up to put a hand on one shoulder, then the other, "and Iain Og."

Roger inclined his head courteously.

"Your servant, gentlemen."

The boys exchanged glances with each other, then looked at their feet, smothering grins.

"So, *Captain* MacKenzie." Joan Findlay's voice came down hard on the word. "If I lend ye my sons, will ye promise me, then, to send them safe home?"

The woman's hazel eyes were as bright and intelligent as her brother's—and as unflinching. He braced himself not to look away.

"So far as it lies in my power, ma'am—I will see them safe."

The edge of her mouth lifted slightly; she knew quite well what was in his power and what was not. She nodded, though, and her hands dropped to her sides.

"They'll come."

He took his leave then, and walked away, the weight of her trust heavy on his shoulders.

# 10

# GRANNIE BACON'S GIFTS

THE LAST OF MY PATIENTS seen to, I stood on my toes and stretched luxuriously, feeling a pleasant glow of accomplishment. For all the conditions that I couldn't really treat, all the illnesses I couldn't cure . . . still, I had done what I could, and had done it well.

I closed the lid of my medical chest and picked it up in my arms; Murray had graciously volunteered to bring back the rest of my impedimenta—in return for a bag of dried senna leaves and my spare pill-rolling tile. Murray himself was still attending his last patient, frowning as he prodded the abdomen of a little old lady in bonnet and shawl. I waved in farewell at him, and he gave me an abstracted nod, turning to pick up his fleam. At least he did remember to dip it into the boiling water; I saw his lips move as he spoke Brianna's charm under his breath.

My feet were numb from standing on the cold ground, and my back and shoulders ached, but I wasn't really tired. There were people who would sleep tonight, their pain relieved. Others who would heal well now, wounds dressed cleanly and limbs set straight. A few whom I could truthfully say I had saved from the possibility of serious infection or even death.

And I had given yet another version of my own Sermon on the Mount, preaching the gospel of nutrition and hygiene to the assembled multitudes.

"Blessed are those who eat greens, for they shall keep their teeth," I murmured to a red-cedar tree. I paused to pull off a few of the fragrant berries, and crushed one with my thumbnail, enjoying the sharp, clean scent.

"Blessed are those who wash their hands after wiping their arses," I added, pointing a monitory finger at a blue jay who had settled on a nearby branch. "For they shall not sicken."

The camp was in sight now, and with it, the delightful prospect of a cup of hot tea.

"Blessed are those who boil water," I said to the jay, seeing a plume of steam rising from the small kettle hung over our fire. "For they shall be called saviors of mankind."

"Mrs. Fraser, mum?" A small voice piped up beside me, breaking my reverie, and I looked down to see Eglantine Bacon, aged seven, and her younger sister, Pansy, a pair of round-faced, towheaded little girls, liberally sprinkled with freckles.

"Oh, hallo, dear. And how are you?" I asked, smiling down at them. Quite well, from the looks of them; illness in a child is generally visible at a glance, and both the small Bacons were obviously blooming.

"Very well, mum, thank ye kindly." Eglantine gave a short bob, then reached over and pushed on Pansy's head to make her curtsy, too. The courtesies observed—the Bacons were townspeople, from Edenton, and the girls had been raised to have nice manners—Eglantine reached into her pocket and handed me a large wad of fabric.

"Grannie Bacon's sent ye a present," she explained proudly, as I unfolded the material, which proved to be an enormous mobcap, liberally embellished with lace and trimmed with lavender ribbons. "She couldna come to the Gathering this year, but she said as we must bring ye this, and give ye her thanks for the medicine ye sent for her . . . roo-mah-tics." She pronounced the word carefully, her face screwed up in concentration, then relaxed, beaming in pride at having gotten it out properly.

"Why, thank you. How lovely!" I held the cap up to admire, privately thinking a few choice things about Grannie Bacon.

I had encountered that redoubtable lady a few months earlier, at Farquard Campbell's plantation, where she was visiting Farquard's aged and obnoxious mother. Mrs. Bacon was almost as old as the ancient Mrs. Campbell, and quite as capable of annoying her descendants, but also possessed of a lively sense of humor.

She had disapproved, audibly, repeatedly, and eventually to my face, of my habit of going about with my head uncovered, it being her opinion that it was unseemly for a woman of my age not to wear either cap or kerch, reprehensible for the wife of a man of my husband's position—and furthermore, that only "backcountry sluts and women of low character" wore their hair loose upon their shoulders. I had laughed, ignored her, and given her a bottle of Jamie's second-best whisky, with instructions to have a wee nip with her breakfast and another after supper.

A woman to acknowledge a debt, she had chosen to repay it in characteristic fashion.

"Will ye not put it on?" Eglantine and Pansy were looking trustfully up at me. "Grannie told us to be sure ye put it on, so as we could tell her how it suited ye."

"Did she, indeed." No help for it, I supposed. I shook the object out, twisted up my hair with one hand, and pulled the mobcap on. It drooped over my brow, almost reaching the bridge of my nose, and draped my cheeks in ribboned swathes, so that I felt like a chipmunk peering out from its burrow.

Eglantine and Patsy clapped their hands in paroxysms of delight. I thought I heard muffled sounds of amusement from somewhere behind me, but didn't turn to see.

"Do tell your grannie I said thank you for the lovely present, won't you?" I patted the girls gravely on their blond heads, offered them each a molasses toffee from my pocket, and sent them off to their mother. I was just reaching up to pull off the excrescence on my head, when I realized that their mother was present—had probably been there all along, in fact, lurking behind a persimmon tree.

"Oh!" I said, converting my reach into an adjustment of the floppy chapeau. I held the overhanging flap up with one finger, the better to peer out. "Mrs. Bacon! I didn't see you there."

"Mrs. Fraser." Polly Bacon's face was flushed a delicate rose color—no doubt from the chill of the day. She had her lips pressed tight together, but her eyes danced under the ruffle of her own very proper cap.

"The girls wanted to give ye the cap," she said, tactfully averting her gaze from it, "but my mother-in-law did send ye another wee gift. I thought perhaps I'd best bring that myself, though."

I wasn't sure I wanted anything to do with any more of Grannie Bacon's gifts, but took the proffered parcel with as much grace as I could manage. It was a small bag of oiled silk, plumply stuffed with something, with a faintly sweet, slightly oily botanical scent about it. A crude picture of a plant had been drawn on the front in brownish ink; something with an upright stalk and what looked like umbels. It looked faintly familiar, but I could put no name to it. I undid the string, and poured a small quantity of tiny dark-brown seeds out into my palm.

"What are these?" I asked, looking up at Polly in puzzlement.

"I don't know what they're called in English," she said. "The Indians call them *dauco*. Grannie Bacon's own grannie was a Catawba medicine woman, aye? That's where she learnt the use of them."

"Was she really?" I was more than interested now. No wonder the drawing seemed familiar; this must be the plant that Nayawenne had once shown me—the women's plant. To be sure of it, though, I asked.

"What is the use of them?"

The color rose higher in Polly's cheeks, and she glanced round the clearing to be sure no one was close enough to hear before leaning forward to whisper to me.

"They stop a woman from getting wi' child. Ye take a teaspoonful each day, in a glass of water. Each day, mind, and a man's seed canna take hold in the womb." Her eyes met mine, and while the light of amusement still lingered at the backs of them, something more serious was there as well.

"Grannie said ye were a conjure-woman, she could tell. And that bein' so, ye'd have cause often to help women. And when it is a matter of miscarriage, stillbirth, or childbed fever, let alone the misery of losing a live babe—she said I must tell ye that an ounce o' prevention is worth a pound o' cure."

"Tell your mother-in-law thank you," I said sincerely. The

average woman of Polly's age might have five or six children; she had the two girls, and lacked the drained look of a woman worn with ill-timed bearing. Evidently, the seeds worked.

Polly nodded, the smile breaking out on her face.

"Aye, I'll tell her. Oh—she said as how her grannie told her it was women's magic; ye dinna mention it to men."

I glanced thoughtfully across the clearing, to where Jamie stood in conversation with Archie Hayes, Jemmy blinking sleepily in the crook of his arm. Yes, I could well see that some men might take exception to old Grannie Bacon's medicine. Was Roger one of them?

Bidding farewell to Polly Bacon, I took my chest across to our lean-to, and tucked the bag of seeds carefully away in it. A very useful addition to my pharmacopeia, if Nayawenne and Mrs. Bacon's grannie were correct. It was also a singularly well-timed gift, considering my earlier conversation with Bree.

Even more valuable than the small heap of rabbit skins I had accumulated, though those were more than welcome. Where had I put them? I looked round the scattered rubble of the campsite, half-listening to the men's conversation behind me. There they were, just under the edge of the canvas. I lifted the lid of one of the empty food hampers to put them away for the journey home.

". . . Stephen Bonnet."

The name stung my ear like a spider's bite, and I dropped the lid with a bang. I glanced quickly round the campsite, but neither Brianna nor Roger was within hearing distance. Jamie's back was turned to me, but it was he who had spoken.

I pulled the mobcap off my head, hung it carefully from a dogwood branch, and went purposefully to join him.

WHATEVER THE MEN had been talking about, they stopped when they saw me. Lieutenant Hayes thanked me gracefully once more for my surgical assistance, and took his leave, his bland round face revealing nothing.

"What *about* Stephen Bonnet?" I said, as soon as the Lieutenant was out of earshot.

"That's what I was inquiring about, Sassenach. Is the tea brewed yet?" Jamie made a move toward the fire, but I stopped him with a hand on his arm.

"Why?" I demanded. I didn't let go my grip, and he reluctantly turned to face me.

"Because I wish to know where he is," he said evenly. He made no pretense of not understanding me, and a small, cold feeling flickered through my chest.

"Did Hayes know where he is? Has he heard anything of Bonnet?"

He shook his head, silent. He was telling me the truth. My fingers loosened with relief, and he moved his arm out of my grasp—not angrily, but with a sense of quiet and definite detachment.

"It *is* my business!" I said, answering the gesture. I kept my voice low, glancing round to be sure that neither Bree nor Roger was within hearing. I didn't see Roger; Bree was standing by the fire, absorbed in conversation with the Bugs, the elderly couple Jamie had engaged to help care for the farm. I turned back to Jamie.

"Why are you looking for that man?"

"Is it not sense to know where danger may lie?" He wasn't looking at me but over my shoulder, smiling and nodding at someone. I glanced back to see Fergus heading for the fire, rubbing a cold-reddened hand beneath his arm. He waved cheerfully with his hook, and Jamie lifted a hand halfway in acknowledgment, but turned away a little, still facing me, effectively preventing Fergus from coming to join us.

The cold feeling returned, sharp as though someone had pierced my lung with a sliver of ice.

"Oh, of course," I said, as coolly as I could. "You want to know where he is, so that you can take pains not to go there, is that it?"

Something that might have been a smile flickered across his face.

"Oh, aye," he said. "To be sure." Given the scarcity of

population in North Carolina in general, and the remoteness of Fraser's Ridge in particular, the chances of our stumbling over Stephen Bonnet by accident were roughly equivalent to walking out of the front door and stepping on a jellyfish—and Jamie bloody knew it.

I narrowed my eyes at him. The corner of his wide mouth drew in for a moment, then relaxed, his eyes gone back to seriousness. There was precisely one good reason for his wanting to locate Stephen Bonnet—and *I* bloody knew *that*.

"Jamie," I said, and put a hand on his arm again. "Leave him alone. Please."

He put his own hand over mine, squeezing, but I felt no reassurance from the gesture.

"Dinna fash yourself, Sassenach. I've asked throughout the Gathering, all through the week, inquiring of men from Halifax to Charleston. There's nay report of the man anywhere in the colony."

"Good," I said. It was, but the fact did not escape me that he had been hunting Bonnet with assiduity—and had told me nothing of it. Nor did it escape me that he had not promised to stop looking.

"Leave him alone," I repeated softly, my eyes holding his. "There's enough trouble coming; we don't need more." He had drawn close to me, the better to forestall interruption, and I could feel the power of him where he touched me, his arm beneath my hand, his thigh brushing mine. Strength of bone and fire of mind, all wrapped round a core of steel-hard purpose that would make him a deadly projectile, once set on any course.

"Ye say it is your business." His eyes were steady, the blue of them bleached pale with autumn light. "I know it is mine. Are ye with me, then?"

The ice blossomed in my blood, spicules of cold panic. Damn him! He meant it. There was one reason to seek out Stephen Bonnet, and one reason only.

I swung round on my heel, pulling him with me, so we stood pressed close together, arms linked, looking toward the fire. Brianna, Marsali, and the Bugs were now listening raptly to Fergus, who was recounting something, his face alight with cold and laughter. Jemmy's face was turned toward us over his mother's shoulder, round-eyed and curious.

"*They* are your business," I said, my voice pitched low and trembling with intensity. "And mine. Hasn't Stephen Bonnet done enough damage to them, to us?"

"Aye, more than enough."

He pulled me closer to him; I could feel the heat of him through his clothes, but his voice was cold as the rain. Fergus's glance flicked toward us; he smiled warmly at me and went on with his story. To him, no doubt we looked like a couple sharing a brief moment of affection, heads bent together in closeness.

"I let him go," Jamie said quietly. "And evil came of it. Can I let him wander free, knowing what he is, and that I have loosed him to spread ruin? It is like loosing a rabid dog, Sassenach—ye wouldna have me do that, surely."

His hand was hard, his fingers cold on mine.

"You let him go once; the Crown caught him again—if he's free now, it's not your fault!"

"Perhaps not my fault that he is free," he agreed, "but surely it is my duty to see he doesna stay so—if I can."

"You have a duty to your family!"

He took my chin in his hand and bent his head, his eyes boring into mine.

"Ye think I would risk them? Ever?"

I held myself stiff, resisting for a long moment, then let my shoulders slump, my eyelids drop in capitulation. I took a long, trembling breath. I wasn't giving in altogether.

"There's risk in hunting, Jamie," I said softly. "You know it."

His grip relaxed, but his hand still cupped my face, his thumb tracing the outline of my lips.

"I know it," he whispered. The mist of his breath touched my cheek. "But I have been a hunter for a verra long time, Claire. I willna bring danger to them—I swear it."

"Only to yourself? And just what do you think will happen to us, if you—"

I caught a glimpse of Brianna from the corner of my eye. She had half-turned, seeing us, and was now beaming tender approval on this scene of what she supposed to be parental fondness. Jamie saw her, too; I heard a faint snort of amusement.

"Nothing will happen to me," he said definitely, and gathering me firmly to him, stifled further argument with an encompassing kiss. A faint spatter of applause rose from the direction of the fire.

*"Encore!"* shouted Fergus.

*"No,"* I said to him as he released me. I whispered, but spoke vehemently for all that. "Not *encore*. I don't want to hear the name of Stephen Bonnet ever bloody again!"

"It will be all right," he whispered back, and squeezed my hand. "Trust me, Sassenach."

# 11

# PRIDE

ROGER DIDN'T LOOK BACK, but thoughts of the Findlays went with him as he made his way downhill from their camp, through clumps of brush and trodden grass.

The two boys were sandy-haired and fair, short—though taller than their mother—but broad-shouldered. The two younger children were dark, tall, and slender, with their mother's hazel eyes. Given the gap of years between the older boys and their younger siblings, Roger concluded from the evidence that Mrs. Findlay had likely had two husbands. And from the look of things now was a widow again.

Perhaps he should mention Joan Findlay to Brianna, he thought, as further evidence that marriage and childbirth were not necessarily mortal to women. Or perhaps it was better just to leave that subject lie quiet for a bit.

Beyond thoughts of Joan and her children, though, he was haunted by the soft, bright eyes of Iain Mhor. How old was he? Roger wondered, grasping the springy branch of a pine to keep from sliding down a patch of loose gravel. Impossible to tell from looking; the pale, twisted face was lined and worn—but with pain and struggle, not age. He was no larger than a boy of twelve or so, but Iain Mhor was older than his namesake, clearly—and Iain Og was sixteen.

He was likely younger than Joan; but perhaps not. She had treated him with deference, bringing Roger to him as a woman would naturally bring a visitor to the head of the family. Not greatly younger, then—say thirty or more?

Christ, he thought, how did a man like that survive so long in times like these? But as he had backed awkwardly away from Iain Mhor, one of the little girls had crawled into the crude shelter from the back, pushing a bowl of milk pudding before her, and had sat down matter-of-factly by her uncle's head, spoon in hand. Iain Mhor had limbs and fingers enough—he had a family.

That thought gave Roger a tight feeling in his chest, somewhere between pain and gladness—and a sinking feeling lower down, as he recalled Joan Findlay's words.

*Send them safe home.* Aye, and if he didn't, then Joan was left with two young girls and a helpless brother. Had she any property? he wondered.

He had heard a good deal of talk on the mountain about the Regulation since the morning's Proclamation. Given that the matter had plainly not been sufficiently important to make it into the history books, he thought this militia business was unlikely to come to anything. If it did, though, he vowed to himself that he would find some way of keeping Iain Og and Hugh Findlay well away from any danger. And if there was bounty money, they should have their share.

In the meantime . . . he hesitated. He had just passed Jocasta Cameron's camp, bustling like a small village, with its cluster of tents, wagons, and lean-tos. In anticipation of her wedding—now a double wedding—Jocasta had brought almost all of her house slaves, and not a few of the field hands as well. Beyond the livestock, tobacco, and goods brought for trade, there were trunks of clothes and bedding and dishes, trestles, tables, hogsheads of ale, and mountains of food intended for the celebration afterward. He and Bree had breakfasted with Mrs. Cameron in her tent this morning off china painted with roses: slices of succulent fried ham, studded with cloves, oatmeal porridge with cream and sugar, a compote of preserved fruit, fresh corn dodgers with honey, Jamaican coffee . . . his stomach contracted with a pleasant growl of recollection.

The contrasts between that lavishness and the recent poverty of the Findlay encampment were too much to be borne with complacence. He turned upon his heel with sudden decision, and began the short climb back to Jocasta's tent.

Jocasta Cameron was at home, so to speak; he saw her mud-soaked boots outside the tent. Sightless as she was, she still ventured out to call upon friends, escorted by Duncan or her black butler, Ulysses. More often, though, she allowed the Gathering to come to her, and her own tent seethed with company throughout the day, all the Scottish society of the Cape Fear and the colony coming to enjoy her renowned hospitality.

For the moment, though, she seemed fortunately alone. Roger caught a glimpse of her through the lifted flap, reclining in her cane-bottomed chair, feet in slippers, and her head fallen back in apparent repose. Her body servant, Phaedre, sat on a stool near the open tent flap, needle in hand, squinting in the hazy light over a spill of blue fabric that filled her lap.

Jocasta sensed him first; she sat up in her armchair, and her head turned sharply as he touched the tent flap. Phaedre glanced up belatedly, reacting to her mistress's movement rather than his presence.

"Mr. MacKenzie. It *is* the Thrush, is it no?" Mrs. Cameron said, smiling in his direction.

He laughed, and ducked his head to enter the tent, obeying her gesture.

"It is. And how did ye ken that, Mrs. Cameron? I've said not a word, let alone sung one. Have I a tuneful manner of breathing?" Brianna had told him of her aunt's uncanny ability to compensate for her blindness by means of other senses, but he was still surprised at her acuity.

"I heard your step, and then I smelt the blood on you," she said matter-of-factly. "The wound's come open again, has it not? Come, lad, sit. Will we fetch ye a dish of tea, or a dram? Phaedre—a cloth, if ye please."

His fingers went involuntarily to the gash in his throat. He'd forgotten it entirely in the rush of the day's events, but she was right; it had bled again, leaving a crusty stain down the side of his neck and over the collar of his shirt.

Phaedre was already up, assembling a tray from the array of cakes and biscuits on a small table by Jocasta's chair. Were it not for the earth and grass underfoot, Roger thought, he would scarcely know they were not in Mrs. Cameron's drawing room at River Run. She was wrapped in a woolen arisaid, but even that was fastened by a handsome cairngorm brooch.

"It's nothing," he said, self-conscious, but Jocasta took the cloth from her maid's hand and insisted on cleaning the cut herself. Her long fingers were cool on his skin, and surprisingly deft.

She smelled of woodsmoke, as everybody on the mountain did, and the tea she had been drinking, but there was none of the faintly camphorated musty odor he normally associated with elderly ladies.

"Tch, ye've got it on your shirt," she informed him, fingering the stiff fabric disapprovingly. "Will we launder it for ye? Though I dinna ken d'ye want to wear it sopping; it'll never dry by nightfall."

"Ah, no, ma'am. I thank ye, I've another. For the wedding, I mean."

"Well, then." Phaedre had produced a small pot of medicinal grease; he recognized it as one of Claire's, by the smell of lavender and goldenseal. Jocasta scooped up a thumbnail of the ointment and spread it carefully over his wound, her fingers steady on his jawbone.

Her skin was well-kept and soft, but it showed the effects not only of age but weather. There were ruddy patches in her cheeks, nets of tiny broken veins that from a slight distance lent her an air of health and vitality. Her hands showed no liver spots—of course, she was of a wealthy family; she would have worn gloves out-of-doors all her life—but the joints were knobbed and the palms slightly callused from the tug of reins. Not a hothouse flower, this daughter of Leoch, despite her surroundings.

Finished, she passed her hand lightly over his face and head, picked a dried leaf from his hair, then wiped his face with the damp cloth, surprising him. She dropped the cloth, then took his hand, wrapping her own fingers around his.

"There, now. Presentable once more! And now that ye're fit for company, Mr. MacKenzie—did ye come to speak to me, or were ye only passing by?"

Phaedre put down a dish of tea and a saucer of cake by his side, but Jocasta continued to hold his left hand. He found that odd, but the unexpected atmosphere of intimacy made it slightly easier to begin his request.

He put it simply; he had heard the Reverend make such requests for charity before, and knew it was best to let the situation speak for itself, leaving ultimate decision to the conscience of the hearer.

Jocasta listened carefully, a small furrow between her brows. He'd expected her to pause for thought when he'd finished, but instead she replied at once.

"Aye," she said, "I ken Joanie Findlay, and her brother, too. Ye're right, her husband was carried off by the consumption, two year gone. Jamie Roy spoke to me of her yesterday."

"Oh, he did?" Roger felt mildly foolish.

Jocasta nodded. She leaned back a little, pursing her lips in thought.

"It's no just a matter of offering help, ye ken," she explained. "I'm glad of the chance. But she's a proud woman, Joan Findlay—she willna take charity." Her voice held a slight note of reproval, as though Roger ought to have realized that.

Perhaps he should, he thought. But he had acted on the impulse of the moment, moved by the Findlays' poverty. It hadn't occurred to him that if she had little else, it would be that much more important to Joan Findlay to cling to her one valuable possession—her pride.

"I see," he said slowly. "But surely—there must be a way to help that wouldn't offer offense?"

Jocasta tilted her head slightly to one side, then the other, in a small mannerism that he found peculiarly familiar. Of course—Bree did that now and then, when she was considering something.

"There may be," she said. "The feast tonight—for the wedding, aye?—the Findlays will be there, of course, and well-fed. It wouldna be amiss for Ulysses to make up a wee parcel of food for them to take for the journey home—'twould save it spoiling, after all." She smiled briefly, then the look of concentration returned to her features.

"The priest," she said, with a sudden air of satisfaction.

"Priest? Ye mean Father Donahue?"

One thick, burnished brow lifted at him.

"Ye ken another priest on the mountain? Aye, of course I do." She lifted her free hand, and Phaedre, ever alert, came to her mistress's side.

"Miss Jo?"

"Look out some bits from the trunks, lass," Jocasta said, touching the maid's arm. "Blankets, caps, an apron or two; breeks and plain shirts—the grooms can spare them."

"Stockings," Roger put in quickly, thinking of the little girls' dirty bare feet.

"Stockings." Jocasta nodded. "Plain stuff, but good wool and well-mended. Ulysses has my purse. Tell him to give ye ten shillings—sterling—and wrap it in one o' the aprons. Then make a bundle of the things and take them to Father Donahue. Tell him they're for Joan Findlay, but he's no to say where they've come from. He'll know what to say." She nodded again, satisfied, and dropped her hand from the maid's arm, making a little shooing gesture.

"Off wi' ye, then—see to it now."

Phaedre murmured assent and left the tent, pausing only to shake out the blue thing she had been sewing and fold it carefully over her stool. It was a decorated stomacher for Brianna's wedding dress, he saw, done with an elegant lacing of ribbons. He had a sudden vision of Brianna's white breasts, swelling above a low neckline of dark indigo, and returned to the conversation at hand with some difficulty.

"I beg your pardon, ma'am?"

"I said—will that do?" Jocasta was smiling at him, with a slightly knowing expression, as though she had been able to read his thoughts. Her eyes were blue, like Jamie's and Bree's, but not so dark. They were fixed on him—or at least pointed at him. He knew she could not see his face, but she did give the eerie impression of being able to see *through* him.

"Yes, Mrs. Cameron. That's—it's most kind of ye." He brought his feet under him, to stand and take his leave. He expected her to let go of his hand at once, but instead, she tightened her grip, restraining him.

"None so fast. I've a thing or two to say to ye, young man."

He settled back on his chair, composing himself.

"Of course, Mrs. Cameron."

"I wasna sure whether to speak now or wait until it was done—but as ye're here alone now . . ." She bent toward him, intent.

"Did my niece tell ye, lad, that I meant to make her heiress to my property?"

"Aye, she did."

He was at once on guard. Brianna had told him, all right—making it clear in no uncertain terms what she thought of that particular proposal. He steeled himself to repeat her objections now, hoping to do it more tactfully than she might have done herself. He cleared his throat.

"I'm sure my wife is most conscious of the honor, Mrs. Cameron," he began cautiously, "but—"

"Is she?" Jocasta asked dryly. "I shouldna have thought so, to hear her talk. But doubtless ye ken her mind better than I do. Be that as it may, though, I mean to tell her that I've changed my own mind."

"Oh? Well, I'm sure she'll—"

"I've told Gerald Forbes to be drawing up a will, leaving River Run and all its contents to Jeremiah."

"To—" It took a moment for his brain to make the connection. "What, to wee Jemmy?"

She was still leaning forward a little, as though peering at his face. Now she sat back, nodding, still holding firmly to his hand. It came to him, finally, that, unable to see his face, she thought to read him by means of this physical connection.

She was welcome to anything his fingers might tell her, he thought. He was too stunned at this news to have any notion how to respond to it. Christ, what would Bree say about it?

"Aye," she said, and smiled pleasantly. "It came to me, ye see, as how a woman's property becomes her husband's when she weds. Not that there are no means of settling it upon her, but it's difficult, and I wouldna involve lawyers more than I must—I think it always a mistake to go to the law, do ye not agree, Mr. MacKenzie?"

With a sense of complete astonishment, he realized that he was being deliberately insulted. Not only insulted, but warned. She thought—she did! She thought he was after Brianna's presumed inheritance, and was warning him not to resort to any legal contortions to get it. Mingled shock and outrage sealed his tongue for a moment, but then he found words.

"Why, that is the most—so ye take thought for Joan Findlay's pride, but ye think I have none? Mrs. Cameron, how dare ye suggest that—"

"Ye're a handsome lad, Thrush," she said, holding tight to his hand. "I've felt your face. And you've the name of MacKenzie, which is a good one, to be sure. But there are MacKenzies aplenty in the Highlands, aren't there? Men of honor, and men without it. Jamie Rôy calls ye kinsman—but perhaps that's because ye're handfast to his daughter. I dinna think *I* ken your family."

Shock was giving way to a nervous impulse to laugh. Ken his family? Not likely; and how should he explain that he was the grandson—six times over—of her own brother, Dougal? That he was, in fact, not only Jamie's nephew, but her own as well, if a bit further down the family tree than one might expect?

"Nor does anyone I've spoken to this week at the Gathering," she added, head tilted to one side like a hawk watching prey.

So that was it. She'd been asking about him among her company—and had failed to turn up anyone who knew anything of his antecedents, for obvious reasons. A suspicious circumstance, to be sure.

He wondered whether she supposed he was a confidence trickster who had taken Jamie in, or whether perhaps he was meant to be involved in some scheme *with* Jamie? No, hardly that; Bree had told him that Jocasta had originally wanted to leave her property to Jamie—who had refused, wary of close involvement with the old leg-trap. His opinion of Jamie's intelligence was reaffirmed.

Before he could think of some dignified retort, she patted his hand, still smiling.

"So, I thought to leave it all to the wee lad. That will be a tidy way of managing, won't it? Brianna will have the use of the money, of course, until wee Jeremiah should come of age—unless anything should happen to the child, that is."

Her voice held a definite note of warning, though her mouth continued to smile, her blank eyes still fixed wide on his face.

"What? What in the name of God d'ye mean by that?" He pushed his stool back, but she held tight to his hand. She was very strong, despite her age.

"Gerald Forbes will be executor of my will, and there are three trustees to manage the property," she explained. "If Jeremiah should come to any mischief, though, then everything will go to my nephew Hamish." Her face was quite serious now. "You'd not see a penny."

He twisted his fingers in hers and squeezed, hard enough that he felt her bony knuckles press together. Let her read what she liked in that, then! She gasped, but he didn't let go.

"Are ye saying to me that ye think I would harm that child?" His voice sounded hoarse to his own ears.

She had gone pale, but kept her dignity, teeth clenched and chin upraised.

"Have I said so?"

"Ye've said a great deal—and what ye've not said speaks louder than what ye have. How dare you imply such things to me?" He released her hand, all but flinging it back in her lap.

She rubbed her reddened fingers slowly with her other hand, lips pursed in thought. The canvas sides of the tent breathed in the wind with a crackling sound.

"Well, then," she said at last. "I'll offer ye my apology, Mr. MacKenzie, if I've wronged ye in any way. I thought it would be as well, though, for ye to know what was in my mind."

"As well? As well for whom?" He was on his feet, and turned toward the flap. With great difficulty, he kept himself from seizing the china plates of cakes and biscuits and smashing them on the ground as a parting gesture.

"For Jeremiah," she said levelly, behind him. "And Brianna. Perhaps, lad, even for you."

He swung round, staring at her.

"Me? What d'ye mean by that?"

She gave the ghost of a shrug.

"If ye canna love the lad for himself, I thought ye might treat him well for the sake of his prospects."

He stared at her, words jamming in his throat. His face felt hot, and the blood throbbed dully in his ears.

"Oh, I ken how it is," she assured him. "It's only to be understood that a man might not feel just so kindly toward a bairn his wife's borne to another. But if—"

He stepped forward then and gripped her hard by the shoulder, startling her. She jerked, blinking, and the candle flames flashed from the cairngorm brooch.

"Madam," he said, speaking very softly into her face. "I do not want your money. My wife does not want it. And *my son* will not have it. Cram it up your hole, aye?"

He let her go, turned, and strode out of the tent, brushing past Ulysses, who looked after him in puzzlement.

# 12

# VIRTUE

**P**EOPLE MOVED THROUGH the gathering shadows of late afternoon, visiting from one fireside to another, as they had each day, but there was a different feeling on the mountain today.

In part it was the sweet sadness of leavetaking; the parting of friends, the severing of newfound loves, the knowledge that some faces would be seen tonight for the last time on earth. In part it was anticipation; the longing for home, the pleasures and dangers of the journey to come. In part, sheer weariness; cranky children, men harried by responsibility, women exhausted by the labor of cooking over open fires, maintaining a family's clothes and health and appetites from the sustenance of saddlebags and mule packs.

I could sympathize with all three attitudes myself. Beyond the sheer excitement of meeting new people and hearing new talk, I had had the pleasure—for pleasure it definitely was, despite its grimmer aspects—of new patients, seeing novel ailments and curing what could be cured, grappling with the need to find a way to treat what could not.

But the longing for home was strong: my spacious hearth, with its huge cauldron and its roasting jack, the light-filled peace of my surgery, with the fragrant bunches of nettle and dried lavender overhead, dusty gold in the afternoon sun. My feather bed, soft and clean, linen sheets smelling of rosemary and yarrow.

I closed my eyes for a moment, summoning up a wistful vision of this haven of delight, then opened them to reality: a crusted griddle, black with the remnants of scorched oatcake;

soggy shoes and frozen feet; damp clothes that chafed with grit and sand; hampers whose abundance had dwindled to a single loaf of bread—well-nibbled by mice—ten apples, and a heel of cheese; three screeching babies; one frazzled young mother with sore breasts and cracked nipples; one expectant bride with a case of incipient nerves; one white-faced serving-maid with menstrual cramps; four slightly inebriated Scotsmen—and one Frenchman in similar condition—who wandered in and out of camp like bears and were not going to be any help whatever in packing up this evening . . . and a deep, clenching ache in my lower belly that gave me the unwelcome news that my own monthly—which had grown thankfully much less frequent than monthly of late—had decided to keep Lizzie's company.

I gritted my teeth, plucked a cold, damp clout off a clump of brush, and made my way duck-footed down the trail toward the women's privy trench, thighs pressed together.

The first thing to greet me on my return was the hot stink of scorching metal. I said something very expressive in French—a useful bit of phraseology acquired at L'Hôpital des Anges, where strong language was often the best medical tool available.

Marsali's mouth fell open. Germain looked at me in admiration and repeated the expression, correctly and with a beautiful Parisian accent.

"Sorry," I said, looking to Marsali in apology. "Someone's let the teakettle boil dry."

"Nay matter, Mother Claire," she said with a sigh, juggling little Joanie, who'd started to scream again. "It's no worse than the things his father teaches him a-purpose. Is there a dry cloth?"

I was already hunting urgently for a dry cloth or a pot-lifter with which to grasp the wire handle, but nothing came to hand save soggy diapers and damp stockings. Kettles were hard to come by, though, and I wasn't sacrificing this one. I wrapped my hand in a fold of my skirt, seized the handle, and jerked the kettle away from the flames. The heat shot through the damp cloth like a bolt of lightning, and I dropped it.

"*Merde!*" said Germain, in happy echo.

"Yes, quite," I said, sucking a blistered thumb. The kettle hissed and smoked in the wet leaves, and I kicked at it, rolling it off onto a patch of mud.

*"Merde, merde, merde, merde,"* sang Germain, with a fair approximation of the tune of "Rose, Rose"—a manifestation of precocious musical feeling that went lamentably unappreciated in the circumstances.

"Do hush, child," I said.

He didn't. Jemmy began to screech in unison with Joan, Lizzie—who had had a relapse owing to the reluctant departure of Private Ogilvie—began to moan under her bush, and it started in to hail, small white pellets of ice dancing on the ground and pinging sharply off my scalp. I pulled the soggy mobcap off a branch and clapped it on my head, feeling like an extremely put-upon toad beneath a particularly homely mushroom. All it wanted was warts, I thought.

The hail was short-lived. As the rush and clattering lessened, though, the crunching noise of muddy boots came up the path. Jamie, with Father Kenneth Donahue in tow, crusted hail on their hair and shoulders.

"I've brought the good Father for tea," he said, beaming round the clearing.

"No, you haven't," I said, rather ominously. And if he thought I'd forgotten about Stephen Bonnet, he was wrong about that, too.

Turning at the sound of my voice, he jerked in an exaggeration of startled shock at sight of me in my mobcap.

"Is that you, Sassenach?" he asked in mock alarm, pretending to lean forward and peek under the drooping frill of my cap. Owing to the presence of the priest, I refrained from kneeing Jamie in some sensitive spot, and contented myself instead with an attempt to turn him into stone with my eyes, à la Medusa.

He appeared not to notice, distracted by Germain, who was now dancing in little circles while singing theme and variations on my initial French expression, to the tune of "Row, Row, Row Your Boat." Father Donahue was going bright pink with the effort of pretending that he didn't understand any French.

*"Tais toi, petit sot,"* Jamie said, reaching into his sporran.

He said it amiably enough, but with the tone of one whose expectation of being obeyed is so absolute as not to admit question. Germain stopped abruptly, mouth open, and Jamie promptly thumbed a sweetie into it. Germain shut his mouth and began concentrating on the matter at hand, songs forgotten.

I reached for the kettle, using a handful of my hem again as pot holder. Jamie bent, picked up a sturdy twig, and hooked the handle of the kettle neatly from my hand with it.

*"Voilà!"* he said, presenting it.

*"Merci,"* I said, with a distinct lack of gratitude. Nonetheless, I accepted the stick and set off toward the nearest rivulet, smoking kettle borne before me like a lance.

Reaching a rock-studded pool, I dropped the kettle with a clang, ripped off the mobcap, flung it into a clump of sedge, and stamped on it, leaving a large, muddy footprint on the linen.

"I didna mean to say it wasna flattering, Sassenach," said an amused voice behind me.

I raised a cold brow in his direction.

"You didn't mean to say it *was* flattering, did you?"

"No. It makes ye look like a poisonous toadstool. Much better without," he assured me.

He pulled me toward him and bent to kiss me.

"It's not that I don't appreciate the thought," I said, and the tone of my voice stopped him, a fraction of an inch from my mouth. "But one inch farther and I think I might just bite a small piece out of your lip."

Moving like a man who has just realized that the stone he has casually picked up is in actuality a wasp's nest, he straightened up and very, very slowly took his hands off my waist.

"Oh," he said, and tilted his head to one side, lips pursed as he surveyed me.

"Ye do look a bit frazzled, at that, Sassenach."

No doubt this was true, but it made me feel like bursting into tears to hear it. Evidently the urge showed, because he took me—very gently—by the hand, and led me to a large rock.

"Sit," he said. "Close your eyes, *a nighean donn*. Rest yourself a moment."

I sat, eyes closed and shoulders slumped. Sloshing noises and a muted clang announced that he was cleaning and filling the kettle.

He set the filled kettle at my feet with a soft clunk, then eased himself down on the leaves beside it, where he sat quietly. I could hear the faint sigh of his breath, and the occasional sniff and rustle as he wiped a dripping nose on his sleeve.

"I'm sorry," I said at last, opening my eyes.

He turned, half-smiling, to look up at me.

"For what, Sassenach? It's not as though ye've refused my bed—or at least I hope it's not come to that yet."

The thought of making love just at the moment was absolutely at the bottom of my list, but I returned the half-smile.

"No," I said ruefully. "After two weeks of sleeping on the ground, I wouldn't refuse *anyone's* bed." His eyebrows went up at that, and I laughed, taken off-guard.

"No," I said again. "I'm just . . . frazzled." Something griped low in my belly, and proceeded to twist. I grimaced, and pressed my hands over the pain.

"Oh!" he said again, in sudden understanding. "That kind of frazzled."

"That kind of frazzled," I agreed. I poked at the kettle with one toe. "I'd better take that back; I need to boil water so I can steep some willow bark. It takes a long time." It did; it would take an hour or more, by which time the cramps would be considerably worse.

"The hell with willow bark," he said, producing a silver flask from the recesses of his shirt. "Try this. At least ye dinna need to boil it first."

I unscrewed the stopper and inhaled. Whisky, and very good whisky, too.

"I love you," I said sincerely, and he laughed.

"I love ye too, Sassenach," he said, and gently touched my foot.

I took a mouthful and let it trickle down the back of my

throat. It seeped pleasantly through my mucous membranes, hit bottom, and rose up in a puff of soothing, amber-colored smoke that filled all my crevices and began to extend warm, soothing tendrils round the source of my discomfort.

"Oooooo," I said, sighing, and taking another sip. I closed my eyes, the better to appreciate it. An Irishman of my acquaintance had once assured me that very good whisky could raise the dead. I wasn't disposed to argue the point.

"That's wonderful," I said, when I opened my eyes again. "Where did you get it?" This was twenty-year-old Scotch, if I knew anything about it—a far cry from the raw spirit that Jamie had been distilling on the ridge behind the house.

"Jocasta," he said. "It was meant to be a wedding gift for Brianna and her young man, but I thought ye needed it more."

"You're right about that."

We sat in a companionable silence, and I sipped slowly, the urge to run amok and slaughter everyone in sight gradually subsiding, along with the level of whisky in the flask.

The rain had moved off again, and the foliage dripped peacefully around us. There was a stand of fir trees near; I could smell the cool scent of their resin, pungent and clean above the heavier smell of wet, dead leaves, smoldering fires, and soggy fabrics.

"It's been three months since the last of your courses," Jamie observed casually. "I thought they'd maybe stopped."

I was always a trifle taken aback to realize how acutely he observed such things—but he was a farmer and a husbandman, after all. He was intimately acquainted with the gynecological history and estrus cycle of every female animal he owned; I supposed there was no reason to think he'd make an exception simply because I was not likely either to farrow or come in heat.

"It's not like a tap that just switches off, you know," I said, rather crossly. "Unfortunately. It just gets rather erratic and eventually it stops, but you haven't any idea when."

"Ah."

He leaned forward, arms folded across the tops of his knees, idly watching twigs and bits of leaf bobbing through the riffles of the stream.

"I'd think it would maybe be a relief to have done wi' it all. Less mess, aye?"

I repressed the urge to draw invidious sexual comparisons regarding bodily fluids.

"Maybe it will," I said. "I'll let you know, shall I?"

He smiled faintly, but was wise enough not to pursue the matter; he could hear the edge in my voice.

I sipped a bit more whisky. The sharp cry of a wood-pecker—the kind Jamie called a yaffle—echoed deep in the woods and then fell silent. Few birds were out in this weather; most simply huddled under what shelter they could find, though I could hear the conversational quacking of a small flock of migratory ducks somewhere downstream. *They* weren't bothered by the rain.

Jamie stretched himself suddenly.

"Ah . . . Sassenach?" he said.

"What is it?" I asked, surprised.

He ducked his head, uncharacteristically shy.

"I dinna ken whether I've done wrong or no, Sassenach, but if I have, I must ask your forgiveness."

"Of course," I said, a little uncertainly. What was I forgiving him for? Probably not adultery, but it could be just about anything else, up to and including assault, arson, highway robbery, and blasphemy. God, I hoped it wasn't anything to do with Bonnet.

"What have you done?"

"Well, as to myself, nothing," he said, a little sheepishly. "It's only what I've said *you'd* do."

"Oh?" I said, with minor suspicion. "And what's that? If you told Farquard Campbell that I'd visit his horrible old mother again . . ."

"Oh, no," he assured me. "Nothing like that. I promised Josiah Beardsley that ye'd maybe take out his tonsils today, though."

"That I'd *what*?" I goggled at him. I'd met Josiah Beards-ley, a youth with the worst-looking set of abscessed tonsils I'd ever seen, the day before. I'd been sufficiently impressed by the pustulated state of his adenoids, in fact, to have de-scribed them in detail to all and sundry over dinner—causing Lizzie to go green round the gills and give her second potato to Germain—and had mentioned at the time that surgery was really the only possible effective cure. I hadn't expected Jamie to go drumming up business, though.

"Why?" I asked.

Jamie rocked back a little, looking up at me.

"I want him, Sassenach."

"You do? What for?" Josiah was barely fourteen—or at least he thought he was fourteen; he wasn't really sure when he'd been born and his parents had died too long ago to say. He was undersized even for fourteen, and badly nourished, with legs slightly bowed from rickets. He also showed evidence of assorted parasitic infections, and wheezed with what might be tuberculosis, or merely a bad case of bronchitis.

"A tenant, of course."

"Oh? I'd have thought you had more applicants than you can handle, as it is."

I didn't just think so; I knew so. We had absolutely no money, though the trade Jamie had done at the Gathering had just about—not quite—cleared our indebtedness to several of the Cross Creek merchants for ironmongery, rice, tools, salt, and other small items. We had land in plenty—most of it forest—but no means to assist people to settle on it or farm it. The Chisholms and McGillivrays were stretching well past our limits, in terms of acquiring new tenantry.

Jamie merely nodded, dismissing these complications.

"Aye. Josiah's a likely lad, though."

"Hmm," I said dubiously. It was true that the boy seemed tough—which was likely what Jamie meant by "likely"; simply to have survived this long by himself was evidence of that. "Maybe so. So are lots of others. What's he got that makes you want him specially?"

"He's fourteen."

I looked at him, one brow raised in question, and his mouth twisted in a wry smile.

"Any man between sixteen and sixty must serve in the militia, Sassenach."

I felt a small, unpleasant contraction in the pit of my stomach. I hadn't forgotten the Governor's unwelcome summons, but what with one thing and another, I hadn't had the leisure to reflect on exactly what the practical consequences of it were likely to be.

Jamie sighed and stretched out his arms, flexing his knuckles until they cracked.

"So you'll do it?" I asked. "Form a militia company and go?"

"I must," he said simply. "Tryon's got my ballocks in his hand, and I'm no inclined to see whether he'll squeeze, aye?"

"I was afraid of that."

Jamie's picturesque assessment of the situation was unfortunately accurate. Looking for a loyal and competent man willing to undertake the settlement of a large section of wild backcountry, Governor Tryon had offered Jamie a Royal grant of land just east of the Treaty Line, with no requirement of quitrent for a period of ten years. A fair offer, though given the difficulties of settlement in the mountains, not quite so generous as it might have looked.

The catch was that holders of such grants were legally required to be white Protestant males of good character, above the age of thirty. And while Jamie met the other requirements, Tryon was well aware of his Catholicism.

Do as the Governor required, and . . . well, the Governor was a successful politician; he knew how to keep his mouth shut about inconvenient matters. Defy him, though, and it would take no more than a simple letter from New Bern to deprive Fraser's Ridge of its resident Frasers.

"Hmm. So you're thinking that if you take the available men from the Ridge—can't you leave out a few?"

"I havena got so many to start with, Sassenach," he pointed out. "I can leave Fergus, because of his hand, and Mr. Wemyss to look after our place. He's a bond servant, so far as anyone knows, and only freemen are obliged to join the militia."

"And only able-bodied men. That lets out Joanna Grant's husband; he's got a wooden foot."

He nodded.

"Aye, and old Arch Bug, who's seventy if he's a day. That's four men—and maybe eight boys under sixteen—to look after thirty homesteads and more than a hundred and fifty people."

"The women can probably manage fairly well by themselves," I said. "It's winter, after all; no crops to deal with. And there shouldn't be any difficulties with the Indians, not these days." My ribbon had come loose when I pulled off the cap. Hair was escaping from its undone plaits in every direction, straggling down my neck in damp, curly strands. I pulled the ribbon off and tried to comb my hair out with my fingers.

"What's so important about Josiah Beardsley, anyway?" I asked. "Surely one fourteen-year-old boy can't make so much difference."

"Beardsley's a hunter," Jamie answered, "and a good one. He brought in nearly two hundred weight of wolf, deer, and beaver skins to the Gathering—all taken by himself alone, he said. I couldna do better, myself."

That was a true encomium, and I pursed my lips in silent appreciation. Hides were the main—in fact, the only—winter crop of any value in the mountains. We had no money now—not even the paper Proclamation money, worth only a fraction of sterling—and without hides to sell in the spring, we were going to have difficulty getting the seed corn and wheat we needed. And if all the men were required to spend a good part of the winter tramping round the colony subduing Regulators instead of hunting . . .

Most women on the Ridge could handle a gun, but almost none could hunt effectively, as they were tethered to their homes by the needs of their children. Even Bree, who was a very good hunter, could venture no more than half a day's travel away from Jemmy—not nearly far enough for wolf and beaver.

I rubbed a hand through my damp locks, fluffing out the loosened strands.

"All right, I understand that part. Where do the tonsils come in, though?"

Jamie looked up at me and smiled. Without answering at once, he got to his feet and circled behind me. With a firm hand, he gathered in the fugitive strands, captured the flying bits, and braided it into a tight, thick plait at the base of my neck. He bent over my shoulder, plucked the ribbon from my lap, and tied it neatly in a bow.

"There." He sat down by my feet again. "Now, as to the tonsils. Ye told the lad he must have them out, or his throat would go from bad to worse."

"It will."

Josiah Beardsley had believed me. And, having come near death the winter before when an abscess in his throat had nearly suffocated him before bursting, he was not eager to risk another such occurrence.

"You're the only surgeon north of Cross Creek," Jamie pointed out. "Who else could do it?"

"Well, yes," I said uncertainly. "But—"

"So, I've made the lad an offer," Jamie interrupted. "One section of land—wee Roger and myself will help him to put up a cabin on it when the time comes—and he'll go halves with me in whatever he takes in the way of skins for the next three winters. He's willing—provided you'll take out his tonsils as part o' the bargain."

"But why today? I can't take someone's tonsils out here!" I gestured at the dripping forest.

"Why not?" Jamie raised one eyebrow. "Did ye not say last night it was a small matter—only a few wee cuts wi' your smallest knife?"

I rubbed a knuckle under my nose, sniffing with exasperation. "Look, just because it isn't a massive bloody job like amputating a leg doesn't mean it's a simple matter!" It was, in fact, a relatively simple operation—surgically speaking. It was the possibility of infection following the procedure, and the need for careful nursing—a poor substitute for antibiotics, but much better than neglect—that raised complications.

"I can't just whack out his tonsils and turn him loose," I said. "When we get back to the Ridge, though—"

"He doesna mean to come back with us directly," Jamie interrupted.

"Why not?" I demanded.

"He didna say; only that he had a bit of business to do, and would come to the Ridge by the first week of December. He can sleep in the loft above the herb shed," he added.

"So you—and he—expect me just to slash out his tonsils, put in a few stitches, and see him on his merry way?" I asked sardonically.

"Ye did nicely wi' the dog," he said, grinning.

"Oh, you heard about that."

"Oh, aye. And the lad who chopped his foot with an ax, and the bairns wi' milk rash, and Mrs. Buchanan's toothache, and your battle wi' Murray MacLeod over the gentleman's bile ducts . . ."

"It *was* rather a busy morning." I shuddered briefly in remembrance, and took another sip of whisky.

"The whole Gathering is talking of ye, Sassenach. I did think of the Bible, in fact, seeing all the crowd clamoring round ye this morning."

"The Bible?" I must have looked blank at the reference, because the grin got wider.

"And the whole multitude sought to touch him," Jamie quoted. "For there went virtue out of him, and healed them all."

I laughed ruefully, interrupting myself with a small hiccup. "Fresh out of virtue at the moment, I'm afraid."

"Dinna fash. There's plenty in the flask."

Thus reminded, I offered him the whisky, but he waved it away, brows drawn down in thought. Melting hail had left wet streaks in his hair, and it lay like ribbons of melted bronze across his shoulders—like the statue of some military hero, weathered and glistening in a public park.

"So ye'll do the lad's tonsils, once he comes to the Ridge?"

I thought a moment, then nodded, swallowing. There would still be dangers in it, and normally I wouldn't do purely elective surgery. But Josiah's condition was truly dreadful, and the continued infections might well kill him eventually, if I didn't take some steps to remedy it.

Jamie nodded, satisfied.

"I'll see to it, then."

My feet had thawed, even wet as they were, and I was beginning to feel warm and pliable. My belly still felt as though I'd swallowed a large volcanic rock, but I wasn't minding all that much.

"I was wondering something, Sassenach," he said.

"Yes?"

"Speakin' of the Bible, ye ken."

"Got Scripture on the brain today, have you?"

One corner of his mouth curled up as he glanced at me.

"Aye, well. It's only I was thinking. When the Angel of the Lord comes along to Sarah and tells her she'll have a bairn the next year, she laughs and says that's a rare jest, as it's ceased to be wi' her after the manner of women."

"Most women in that situation likely wouldn't think it at all a funny idea," I assured him. "I often think God's got a very peculiar sense of humor, though."

He looked down at the large maple leaf he was shredding between thumb and forefinger, but I caught the faint twitch of his mouth.

"I've thought that now and again myself, Sassenach," he said, rather dryly. "Be that as it may, she did have the bairn, aye?"

"The Bible says she did. *I'm* not going to call the book of Genesis a liar." I debated the wisdom of drinking more, but decided to save it for a rainy—well, a rainier—day, and put the stopper back in the flask. I could hear a certain amount of stirring in the direction of the campsite, and my ears caught a word of inquiry, borne on the chilly breeze.

"Someone's looking for Himself," I said. "Again."

Himself glanced over his shoulder and grimaced slightly, but made no immediate move to answer the call. He cleared his throat, and I saw a faint flush move up the side of his neck.

"Well, the point is," he said, carefully not looking at me, "that so far as I ken, if your name's not Mary and the Holy Ghost isna involved in the matter, there's only the one way of getting wi' child. Am I right?"

"So far as I know, yes." I put a hand over my mouth to stifle a rising hiccup.

"Aye. And if so . . . well, that must mean that Sarah was still bedding wi' Abraham at the time, no?"

He still wasn't looking at me, but his ears had gone pink, and I belatedly realized the point of this religious discussion. I reached out a toe and prodded him gently in the side.

"You were thinking perhaps I wouldn't want you anymore?"

"Ye dinna want me *now*," he pointed out logically, eyes on the crumbled remains of his leaf.

"I feel as though my belly is full of broken glass, I'm half-soaked and mud to the knees, and whoever's looking for you is about to burst through the shrubbery with a pack of blood-hounds at any moment," I said, with a certain amount of as-perity. "Are you actually inviting me to participate in carnal revelry with you in that mound of soggy leaves? Because if you are—"

"No, no," he said hastily. "I didna mean now. I only meant—I was only wondering if—" The tips of his ears had gone a dull red. He stood up abruptly, brushing dead leaves from his kilt with exaggerated force.

"If," I said in measured tones, "you were to get me with child at this point in the proceedings, Jamie Fraser, I would have your balls *en brochette*." I rocked back, looking up at him. "As for bedding with you, though . . ."

He stopped what he was doing and looked at me. I smiled at him, letting what I thought show plainly on my face.

"Once you have a bed again," I said, "I promise I won't re-fuse it."

"Oh," he said. He drew a deep breath, looking suddenly quite happy. "Well, that's all right, then. It's only—I won-dered, ye ken."

A sudden loud rustling in the shrubbery was followed by the appearance of Mr. Wemyss, whose thin, anxious face poked out of a nannyberry bush.

"Oh, it's yourself, sir," he said, in evident relief.

"I suppose it must be," Jamie said, in resignation. "Is there a difficulty, Mr. Wemyss?"

Mr. Wemyss was delayed in answering, having become in-extricably entangled with the nannyberry bush, and I was obliged to go and help release him. A onetime bookkeeper who had been obliged to sell himself as an indentured servant, Mr. Wemyss was highly unsuited to life in the wilderness.

"I do apologize for troubling ye, sir," he said, rather red in the face. He picked nervously at a spiny twig that had caught in his fair, flyaway hair.

"It's only—well, she did say as she meant to cleave him from crown to crutch wi' her ax if he didna leave off, and he said no woman would speak to him in that manner, and she does *have* an ax . . ."

Accustomed to Mr. Wemyss's methods of communication, Jamie sighed, reached out for the whisky flask, uncorked it, and took a deep, sustaining swig. He lowered the flask and fixed Mr. Wemyss with a gimlet eye.

"Who?" he demanded.

"Oh! Er . . . did I not say? Rosamund Lindsay and Ronnie Sinclair."

"Mmphm."

Not good news; Rosamund Lindsay *did* have an ax; she was roasting several pigs in a pit near the creek, over hickory embers. She also weighed nearly two hundred pounds and, while normally good-humored, was possessed of a notable temper when roused. For his part, Ronnie Sinclair was entirely capable of irritating the Angel Gabriel, let alone a woman trying to cook in the rain.

Jamie sighed and handed the flask back to me. He squared his shoulders, shaking droplets from his plaid as he settled it.

"Go and tell them I'm coming, Mr. Wemyss," he said.

Mr. Wemyss's thin face expressed the liveliest apprehension at the thought of coming within speaking range of Rosamund Lindsay's ax, but his awe of Jamie was even greater. He bobbed a quick, neat bow, turned, and blundered straight into the nannyberry bush again.

A wail like an approaching ambulance betokened the appearance of Marsali, Joan in her arms. She plucked a clinging branch from Mr. Wemyss's coat sleeve, nodding to him as she stepped carefully round him.

"Da," she said, without preamble. "Ye've got to come. Father Kenneth's been arrested."

Jamie's eyebrows shot up.

"Arrested? Just now? By whom?"

"Aye, this minute! A nasty fat man who said he was sheriff o' the county. He came up wi' two men and they asked who was the priest, and when Father Kenneth said it was him, they seized him by the arms and marched him straight off, with none so much as a by your leave!"

The blood was rising in Jamie's face, and his two stiff fingers tapped briefly against his thigh.

"They've taken him from my hearth?" he said. *"A Dhia!"*

This was plainly a rhetorical question, and before Marsali could answer it, a crunching of footsteps came from the other direction, and Brianna popped into sight from behind a pine tree.

"What?" he barked at her. She blinked, taken aback.

"Ah . . . Geordie Chisholm says one of the soldiers stole a ham from his fire, and will you go and see Lieutenant Hayes about it?"

"Yes," he said promptly. "Later. Meanwhile, do you go back wi' Marsali and find out where they've taken Father Kenneth. And Mr. Wemyss—" But Mr. Wemyss had at last escaped the clinging embrace of the nannyberry bush. A distant crashing signaled his rush to fulfill his orders.

A quick look at Jamie's face convinced both girls that a swift retreat was the order of the day, and within seconds, we were alone again. He took a deep breath, and let it slowly out through his teeth.

I wanted to laugh, but didn't. Instead I moved closer; cold and damp as it was, I could feel the heat of his skin through his plaid.

"At least it's only the sick ones who want to touch me," I said. I held out the flask to him. "What do *you* do when all the virtue's gone out of you?"

He glanced down at me, and a slow smile spread across his face. Ignoring the flask, he stooped, cupped my face in his hands, and kissed me, very gently.

"That," he said.

Then he turned and strode downhill, presumably full of virtue once more.

# BEANS AND BARBECUE

I TOOK THE KETTLE BACK to our camp, only to find the place momentarily deserted. Voices and laughter in the distance indicated that Lizzie, Marsali, and Mrs. Bug—presumably with children in tow—were on their way to the women's privy, a latrine trench dug behind a convenient screen of juniper, some way from the campsites. I hung the full kettle over the fire to boil, then stood still for a moment, wondering in which direction my efforts might be best directed.

While Father Kenneth's situation might be the most serious in the long run, it wasn't one where my presence would be likely to make a difference. But I *was* a doctor—and Rosamund Lindsay *did* have an ax. I patted my damp hair and garments into some sort of order, and started downhill toward the creek, abandoning the mobcap to its fate.

Jamie had evidently been of the same mind regarding the relative importance of the emergencies in progress. When I fought my way through the thicket of willow saplings edging the creek, I found him standing by the barbecue pit, in peaceful conversation with Ronnie Sinclair—meanwhile leaning casually on the handle of the ax, of which he had somehow managed to possess himself.

I relaxed a bit when I saw that, and took my time in joining the party. Unless Rosamund decided to strangle Ronnie with her bare hands or beat him to death with a ham—neither of these contingencies being at all unthinkable—my medical services might not be needed after all.

The pit was a broad one, a natural declivity bored out of

the clay creekbank by some distant flood and then deepened by judicious spadework in the years succeeding. Judging by the blackened rocks and drifts of scattered charcoal, it had been in use for some time. In fact, several different people were using it now; the mingled scents of fowl, pork, mutton, and possum rose up in a cloud of apple-wood and hickory smoke, a savory incense that made my mouth water.

The sight of the pit was somewhat less appetizing. Clouds of white smoke billowed up from the damp wood, half-obscuring a number of shapes that lay upon their smoldering pyres—many of these looking faintly and hair-raisingly human through the haze. It reminded me all too vividly of the charnel pits on Jamaica, where the bodies of slaves who had not survived the rigors of the Middle Passage were burned, and I swallowed heavily, trying not to recall the macabre roasting-meat smell of those funeral fires.

Rosamund was working down in the pit at the moment, her skirt kirtled well above plump knees and sleeves rolled back to bare her massive arms as she ladled a reddish sauce onto the exposed ribs of a huge hog's carcass. Around her lay five more gigantic shapes, shrouded in damp burlap, with the wisps of fragrant smoke curling up around them, vanishing into the soft drizzle.

"It's poison, is what it is!" Ronnie Sinclair was saying hotly, as I came up behind him. "She'll ruin it—it'll no be fit for pigs when she's done!"

"It *is* pigs, Ronnie," Jamie said, with considerable patience. He rolled an eye at me, then glanced at the pit, where sizzling fat dripped onto the biers of hickory coals below. "Myself, I shouldna think ye could do anything to a pig—in the way of cooking, that is—that would make it not worth the eating."

"Quite true," I put in helpfully, smiling at Ronnie. "Smoked bacon, grilled chops, roasted loin, baked ham, headcheese, sausage, sweetbreads, black pudding . . . somebody once said you could make use of everything in a pig but the squeal."

"Aye, well, but this is the barbecue, isn't it?" Ronnie said stubbornly, ignoring my feeble attempt at humor. "Anyone kens that ye sass a barbecued hog wi' vinegar—that's the proper way of it! After all, ye wouldna put gravel into your sausage meat, would ye? Or boil your bacon wi' sweepings from the henhouse? Tcha!" He jerked his chin toward the white pottery basin under Rosamund's arm, making it clear that its contents fell into the same class of inedible adulterants, in his opinion.

I caught a savory whiff as the wind changed. So far as I could tell from smell alone, Rosamund's sauce seemed to include tomatoes, onions, red pepper, and enough sugar to leave a thick blackish crust on the meat and a tantalizing caramel aroma in the air.

"I expect the meat will be very juicy, cooked like that," I said, feeling my stomach begin to knot and growl beneath my laced bodice.

"Aye, a wonderful fat lot of pigs they are, too," Jamie said ingratiatingly, as Rosamund glanced up, glowering. She was black to the knees and her square-jowled face was streaked with rain, sweat, and soot. "Will they have been wild hogs, ma'am, or gently reared?"

"Wild," she said, with a certain amount of pride, straightening up and wiping a strand of wet, graying hair off her brow. "Fattened on chestnut mast—nothin' like it to give a flavor to the meat!"

Ronnie Sinclair made a Scottish noise indicative of derision and contempt.

"Aye, the flavor's so good ye must hide it under a larding o' yon grisly sauce that makes it look as though the meat's no even cooked yet, but bleeding raw!"

Rosamund made a rather earthy comment regarding the supposed manhood of persons who felt themselves squeamish at the thought of blood, which Ronnie seemed disposed to take personally. Jamie skillfully maneuvered himself between the two, keeping the ax well out of reach.

"Oh, I'm sure it's verra well cooked indeed," he replied soothingly. "Why, Mistress Lindsay has been hard at work since dawn, at least."

"Long before that, Mr. Fraser," the lady replied, with a certain grim satisfaction. "You want decent barbecue, you start at least a day before, and tend it all through the night. I been a-minding of these hogs since yesterday afternoon."

She drew in a great sniff of the rising smoke, wearing a be-atific expression.

"Ah, that's the stuff! Not but what a savory sass like this 'un is wasted on you bastardly Scots," Rosamund said, re-placing the burlap and patting it tenderly into place. "You've pickled your tongues with that everlastin' vinegar you slop on your victuals. It's all I can do to stop Kenny a-puttin' it on his corn bread and porridge of a mornin'."

Jamie raised his voice, drowning out Ronnie's incensed response to this calumny.

"And was it Kenny that hunted the hogs for ye, mistress? Wild hogs have a chancy nature; surely it's a dangerous busi-ness to be stalking beasts of that size. Like the wild boar that we hunted in Scotland, aye?"

"Ha." Rosamund cast a look of good-natured scorn toward the slope above, where her husband—roughly half her size—presumably was engaged in less strenuous pur-suits. "No, indeed, Mr. Fraser, I kilt this lot myself. With that ax," she added pointedly, nodding toward the instrument in question and narrowing her eyes in a sinister fashion at Ron-nie. "Caved in their skulls with one blow, I did."

Ronnie, not the most perceptive of men, declined to take the hint.

"It's the tomato fruits she's using, *Mac Dubh*," he hissed, tugging at Jamie's sleeve and pointing at the red-crusted bowl. "Devil's apples! She'll poison us all!"

"Oh, I shouldna think so, Ronnie." Jamie took a firm grip on Ronnie's arm, and smiled engagingly at Rosamund. "Ye mean to sell the meat, I suppose, Mrs. Lindsay? It's a poor merchant that would kill her customers, aye?"

"I ain't yet lost a one, Mr. Fraser," Rosamund agreed, turning back another sheet of burlap and leaning over to dribble sauce from a wooden ladle over a steaming haunch. "Ain't never had but good words about the taste, neither," she said, "though a-course that would be in Boston, where I come from."

*Where folk have sense,* her tone clearly implied.

"I met a man from Boston, last time I went to Char-lottesville," Ronnie said, his foxy brows drawn down in disapproval. He tugged, trying to free his arm from Jamie's grip, but to no avail. "He said to me as it was his custom to have beans at his breakfast, and oysters to his supper, and so he'd done every day since he was a wean. A wonder he hadna blown up like a pig's bladder, filled wi' such wretched stuff as that!"

"Beans, beans, they're good for your heart," I said cheerily, seizing the opening. "The more you eat, the more you fart. The more you fart, the better you feel—so let's have beans for every meal!"

Ronnie's mouth dropped open, as did Mrs. Lindsay's. Jamie whooped with laughter, and Mrs. Lindsay's look of astonishment dissolved into a booming laugh. After a moment, Ronnie rather reluctantly joined in, a small grin twisting up the corner of his mouth.

"I lived in Boston for a time," I said mildly, as the hilarity died down a bit. "Mrs. Lindsay, that smells wonderful!"

Rosamund nodded with dignity, gratified.

"Why, so it does, ma'am, and I say so." She leaned toward me, lowering her voice—slightly—from its normal stentorian range. "It's my private receipt what does it," she said, with a proprietorial pat of the pottery bowl. "Brings out the flavor, see?"

Ronnie's mouth opened, but only a small yelp emerged, the evident result of Jamie's hand tightening about his biceps. Rosamund ignored this, engaging in an amiable discussion with Jamie that terminated in her agreeing to reserve an entire carcass for use at the wedding feast.

I glanced at Jamie, hearing this. Given that Father Kenneth was probably at present en route either back to Baltimore or to the gaol in Edenton, I had my doubts as to whether any marriages would in fact take place tonight.

On the other hand, I had learned never to underestimate Jamie, either. With a final word of compliment to Mrs. Lindsay, he dragged Ronnie bodily away from the pit, pausing just long enough to thrust the ax into my hands.

"See that safe, aye, Sassenach?" he said, and kissed me briefly. He grinned down at me. "And where did ye learn so much about the natural history of beans, tell me?"

"Brianna brought it home from school when she was about six," I said, smiling back. "It's really a little song."

"Tell her to sing it to her man," Jamie advised. The grin widened. "He can write it down in his wee book."

He turned away, putting a companionable arm firmly about the shoulders of Ronnie Sinclair, who showed signs of trying to escape back in the direction of the barbecue pit.

"Come along wi' me, Ronnie," he said. "I must just have a wee word wi' the Lieutenant. He wishes to buy a ham of Mistress Lindsay, I think," he added, blinking at me in the owllike fashion that passed with him for winking. He turned back to Ronnie. "But I ken he'll want to hear whatever ye can tell him, about his Da. Ye were a great friend of Gavin Hayes, no?"

"Oh," said Ronnie, his scowl lightening somewhat. "Aye. Aye, Gavin was a proper man. A shame about it." He shook his head, obviously referring to Gavin's death a few years before. He glanced up at Jamie, lips pursed. "Does his lad ken what happened?"

A tender question, that. Gavin had in fact been hanged in Charleston, for theft—a shameful death, by anyone's standards.

"Aye," Jamie said quietly. "I had to tell him. But it will help, I think, if ye can tell him a bit about his Da earlier—tell him how it was for us, there in Ardsmuir." Something—not quite a smile—touched his face as he looked at Ronnie, and I saw an answering softness on Sinclair's face.

Jamie's hand tightened on Ronnie's shoulder, then dropped away, and they set off up the hill, side by side, the subtleties of barbecue forgotten.

*How it was for us* . . . I watched them go, linked by the conjuration of that one simple phrase. Five words that recalled the closeness forged by days and months and years of shared hardship; a kinship closed to anyone who had not likewise lived through it. Jamie seldom spoke of Ardsmuir; neither did any of the other men who had come out of it and lived to see the New World here.

Mist was rising from the hollows on the mountain now; within moments, they had disappeared from view. From the hazy forest above, the sound of Scottish male voices drifted down toward the smoking pit, chanting in amiable unison:

*"Beans, beans, they're good for your heart . . ."*

RETURNING TO THE CAMPSITE, I found that Roger had returned from his errands. He stood near the fire, talking with Brianna, a troubled look on his face.

"Don't worry," I told him, reaching past his hip to retrieve the rumbling teakettle. "I'm sure Jamie will sort it somehow. He's gone to deal with it."

"He has?" He looked slightly startled. "He knows already?"

"Yes, as soon as he finds the sheriff, I imagine it will all come right." I upended the chipped teapot I used in camp with one hand, shook the old leaves out onto the ground, and putting it on the table, tipped a little boiling water in from the kettle to warm the pot. It had been a long day, and likely to be a long evening as well. I was looking forward to the sustenance of a properly brewed cup of tea, accompanied by a slice of the fruitcake one of my patients had given me during the morning clinic.

"The sheriff?" Roger gave Brianna a baffled look, faintly tinged with alarm. "She hasn't set a sheriff on me, has she?"

"Set a sheriff on you? Who?" I said, joining in the chorus of bafflement. I hung the kettle back on its tripod, and reached for the tin of tea leaves. "Whatever have you been doing, Roger?"

A faint flush showed over his high cheekbones, but before he could answer, Brianna snorted briefly.

"Telling Auntie Jocasta where she gets off." She glanced at Roger, and her eyes narrowed into triangles of mildly malicious amusement as she envisioned the scene. "Boy, I wish I'd been there!"

"Whatever did you say to her, Roger?" I inquired, interested.

The flush deepened, and he looked away.

"I don't wish to repeat it," he said shortly. "It wasna the sort of thing one ought to say to a woman, let alone an elderly one, and particularly one about to be related to me by marriage. I was just asking Bree whether I maybe ought to go and apologize to Mrs. Cameron before the wedding."

"No," Bree said promptly. "The nerve of her! You had every right to say what you did."

"Well, I don't regret the substance of my remarks," Roger said to her, with a wry hint of a smile. "Only the form.

"See," he said, turning to me, "I'm only thinking that perhaps I should apologize, to keep it from being awkward tonight—I don't want Bree's wedding to be spoiled."

"Bree's wedding? You think I'm getting married by myself?" she asked, lowering thick red brows at him.

"Oh, well, no," he admitted, smiling a little. He touched her cheek, gently. "I'll stand up next ye, to be sure. But so long as we end up married, I'm not so much bothered about the ceremony. Ye'll want it to be nice, though, won't ye? Put a damper on the occasion, and your auntie crowns me with a stick of firewood before I can say 'I will.' "

I was by now consumed by curiosity to know just what he *had* said to Jocasta, but thought I had better address the more immediate issue, which was that at the moment of going to press, it appeared that there might be no wedding to be spoiled.

"And so Jamie's out looking for Father Kenneth now," I finished. "Marsali didn't recognize the sheriff who took him, though, which makes it difficult."

Roger's dark brows lifted, then drew together in concern.

"I wonder . . ." he said, and turned to me. "Do ye know, I think perhaps I saw him, just a few moments ago."

"Father Kenneth?" I asked, knife suspended over the fruitcake.

"No, the sheriff."

"What? Where?" Bree half-turned on one heel, glaring round. Her hand curled up into a fist, and I thought it rather fortunate that the sheriff wasn't in sight. Having Brianna arrested for assault really *would* have a dampening effect on the wedding.

"He went that way." Roger gestured downhill, toward the

creek—and Lieutenant Hayes's tent. As he did so, we heard the sound of footsteps squelching through mud, and a moment later, Jamie appeared, looking tired, worried, and highly annoyed. Obviously, he hadn't yet found the priest.

"Da!" Bree greeted him with excitement. "Roger thinks he's seen the sheriff who took Father Kenneth!"

"Oh, aye?" Jamie at once perked up. "Where?" His left hand curled up in anticipation, and I couldn't help smiling. "What's funny?" he demanded, seeing it.

"Nothing," I assured him. "Here, have some fruitcake." I handed him a slice, which he promptly crammed into his mouth, returning his attention to Roger.

"Where?" he demanded, indistinctly.

"I don't know that it was the man you're looking for," Roger told him. "He was a raggedy wee man. But he had got a prisoner; he was taking one of the fellows from Drunkard's Creek off in handcuffs. MacLennan, I think."

Jamie choked and coughed, spewing small bits of masticated fruitcake into the fire.

"He arrested Mr. MacLennan? And you *let* him?" Bree was staring at Roger in consternation. Neither she nor Roger had been present when Abel MacLennan had told his story over breakfast, but both of them knew him.

"I couldna very well prevent him," Roger pointed out mildly. "I did call out to MacLennan to ask if he wanted help—I thought I'd fetch your Da or Farquard Campbell, if he did. But he just looked through me, as though I might have been a ghost, and then when I called again, he gave me an odd sort of smile and shook his head. I didna think I ought to go and beat up a sheriff, just on general principle. But if you—"

"Not a sheriff," Jamie said hoarsely. His eyes were watering, and he paused to cough explosively again.

"A thief-taker," I told Roger. "Something like a bounty hunter, I gather." The tea wasn't nearly brewed yet; I found a half-full stone bottle of ale and handed that to Jamie.

"Where will he be taking Abel?" I asked. "You said Hayes didn't want prisoners."

Jamie shook his head, swallowed, and lowered the bottle, breathing a little easier.

"He doesna. No, Mr. Boble—it must be him, aye?—will take Abel to the nearest magistrate. And if wee Roger saw him just the now . . ." He turned, thinking, brows furrowed as he surveyed the mountainside around us.

"It will be Farquard, most likely," he concluded, his shoulders relaxing a little. "I ken four justices of the peace and three magistrates here at the Gathering, and of the lot, Campbell's the only one camped on this side."

"Oh, that's good." I sighed in relief. Farquard Campbell was a fair man; a stickler for the law, but not without compassion—and more importantly, perhaps, a very old friend of Jocasta Cameron.

"Aye, we'll ask my aunt to have a word—perhaps we'd best do it before the weddings." He turned to Roger. "Will ye go, MacKenzie? I must be finding Father Kenneth, if there are to *be* any weddings."

Roger looked as though he, too, had just choked on a bit of fruitcake.

"Er . . . well," he said, awkwardly. "Perhaps I'm no the best man to be saying anything to Mrs. Cameron just now."

Jamie was staring at him in mingled interest and exasperation.

"Why not?"

Blushing fiercely, Roger recounted the substance of his conversation with Jocasta—lowering his voice nearly to the point of inaudibility at the conclusion.

We heard it clearly enough, nonetheless. Jamie looked at me. His mouth twitched. Then his shoulders began to shake. I felt the laughter bubble up under my ribs, but it was nothing to Jamie's hilarity. He laughed almost silently, but so hard that tears came to his eyes.

"Oh, Christ!" he gasped at last. He clutched his side, still wheezing faintly. "God, I've sprung a rib, I think." He reached out and took one of the half-dried clean clouts from a bush, carelessly wiping his face with it.

"All right," he said, recovering himself somewhat. "Go and see Farquard, then. If Abel's there, tell Campbell I'll stand surety for him. Bring him back with ye." He made a brief shooing gesture, and Roger—puce with mortification but stiff with dignity—departed at once. Bree followed him, casting a glance of reproof at her father, which merely had the effect of causing him to wheeze some more.

I drowned my own mirth with a gulp of steaming tea, blissfully fragrant. I offered the cup to Jamie, but he waved it away, content with the rest of the ale.

"My aunt," he observed, lowering the bottle at last, "kens verra well indeed what money will buy and what it will not."

"And she's just bought herself—and everyone else in the county—a good opinion of poor Roger, hasn't she?" I replied, rather dryly.

Jocasta Cameron was a MacKenzie of Leoch; a family Jamie had once described as "charming as the larks in the field—and sly as foxes, with it." Whether Jocasta had truly had any doubt herself of Roger's motives in marrying Bree, or merely thought to forestall idle gossip along the Cape Fear, her methods had been undeniably successful. She was probably up in her tent chortling over her cleverness, looking forward to spreading the story of her offer and Roger's response to it.

"Poor Roger," Jamie agreed, his mouth still twitching. "Poor but virtuous." He tipped up the bottle of ale, drained it, and set it down with a brief sigh of satisfaction. "Though come to that," he added, glancing at me, "she's bought the lad something of value as well, hasn't she?"

*"My son,"* I quoted softly, nodding. "Do you think he realized it himself before he said it? That he really feels Jemmy is his son?"

Jamie made an indeterminate movement with his shoulders, not quite a shrug.

"I canna say. It's as well he should have that fixed in his mind, though, before the next bairn comes along—one he kens for sure is his."

I thought of my conversation that morning with Brianna, but decided it was wiser to say nothing—at least for now. It was, after all, a matter between Roger and Bree. I only nodded, and turned to tidy away the tea things.

I felt a small glow in the pit of my stomach that was only partly the result of the tea. Roger had sworn an oath to take Jemmy as his own, no matter what the little boy's true paternity might be; he was an honorable man, Roger, and he meant it. But the speech of the heart is louder than the words of any oath spoken by lips alone.

When I had gone back, pregnant, through the stones, Frank had sworn to me that he would keep me as his wife, would treat the coming child as his own—would love me as he had before. All three of those vows his lips and mind had done his best to keep, but his heart, in the end, had sworn only one. From the moment that he took Brianna in his arms, she was his daughter.

But what if there had been another child? I wondered suddenly. It had never been a possibility—but if it had? Slowly, I wiped the teapot dry and wrapped it in a towel, contemplating the vision of that mythical child; the one Frank and I might have had, but never did, and never would. I laid the wrapped teapot in the chest, gently, as though it were a sleeping baby.

When I turned back, Jamie was still standing there, looking at me with a rather odd expression—tender, yet somehow rueful.

"Did I ever think to thank ye, Sassenach?" he said, his voice a little husky.

"For what?" I said, puzzled. He took my hand, and drew me gently toward him. He smelled of ale and damp wool, and very faintly of the brandied sweetness of fruitcake.

"For my bairns," he said softly. "For the children that ye bore me."

"Oh," I said. I leaned slowly forward, and rested my forehead against the solid warmth of his chest. I cupped my hands at the small of his back beneath his coat, and sighed. "It was . . . my pleasure."

"MR. FRASER, MR. FRASER!" I lifted my head and turned to see a small boy churning down the steep slope behind us, arms waving to keep his balance and face bright red with cold and exertion.

"Oof!" Jamie got his hands up just in time to catch the boy as he hurtled down the last few feet, quite out of control. He boosted the little boy, whom I recognized as Farquard

Campbell's youngest, up in his arms and smiled at him. "Aye, Rabbie, what is it? Does your Da want me to come for Mr. MacLennan?"

Rabbie shook his head, shaggy hair flying like a sheep-dog's coat.

"No, sir," he panted, gasping for breath. He gulped air and the small throat swelled like a frog's with the effort to breathe and speak at once. "No, sir. My Da says he's heard where the priest is and I should show ye the way, sir. Will ye come?"

Jamie's brows flicked up in momentary surprise. He glanced at me, then smiled at Rabbie, and nodded, bending down to set him on his feet.

"Aye, lad, I will. Lead on, then!"

"Delicate of Farquard," I said to Jamie under my breath, with a nod at Rabbie, who scampered ahead, looking back over his shoulder now and then, to be sure we were managing to keep up with him. No one would notice a small boy, among the swarms of children on the mountain. Everyone would most assuredly have noticed had Farquard Campbell come himself or sent one of his adult sons.

Jamie huffed a little, the mist of his breath a wisp of steam in the gathering chill.

"Well, it's no Farquard's concern, after all, even if he has got a great regard for my aunt. And I expect if he's sent the lad to tell me, it means he kens the man who's responsible, and doesna mean to choose up sides wi' me against him." He glanced at the setting sun, and gave me a rueful look.

"I did say I should find Father Kenneth by sunset, but still—I dinna think we shall see a wedding tonight, Sassenach."

Rabbie led us onward and upward, tracing the maze of footpaths and trampled dead grass without hesitation. The sun had finally broken through the clouds; it had sunk deep in the notch of the mountains, but was still high enough to wash the slope with a warm, ruddy light that momentarily belied the chill of the day. People were gathering to their family fires now, hungry for their suppers, and no one spared a glance for us among the bustle.

At last, Rabbie came to a stop, at the foot of a well-marked path that led up and to the right. I had crisscrossed the mountain's face several times during the week of the Gathering, but had never ventured up this high. Who was in custody of Father Kenneth, I wondered—and what did Jamie propose to do about it?

"Up there," Rabbie said unnecessarily, pointing to the peak of a large tent, just visible through a screen of longleaf pine.

Jamie made a Scottish noise in the back of his throat at sight of the tent.

"Oh," he said softly, "so that's how it is?"

"Is it? Never mind how it is; *whose* is it?" I looked dubiously at the tent, which was a large affair of waxed brown canvas, pale in the gloaming. It obviously belonged to someone fairly wealthy, but wasn't one I was familiar with myself.

"Mr. Lillywhite, of Hillsborough," Jamie said, and his brows drew down in thought. He patted Rabbie Campbell on the head, and handed him a penny from his sporran. "Thank ye, laddie. Run away to your Mam now; it'll be time for your supper." Rabbie took the coin and vanished without comment, pleased to be finished with his errand.

"Oh, really." I cocked a wary eye at the tent. That explained a few things, I supposed—though not everything. Mr. Lillywhite was a magistrate from Hillsborough, though I knew nothing else about him, save what he looked like. I had glimpsed him once or twice during the Gathering, a tall, rather drooping man, his figure made distinctive by a bottle-green coat with silver buttons, but had never formally met him.

Magistrates were responsible for appointing sheriffs, which explained the connection with the "nasty fat man" Marsali had described, and why Father Kenneth was incarcerated here—but that left open the question of whether it was the sheriff or Mr. Lillywhite who had wanted the priest removed from circulation in the first place.

Jamie put a hand on my arm, and drew me off the path, into the shelter of a small pine tree.

"Ye dinna ken Mr. Lillywhite, do you, Sassenach?"

"Only by sight. What do you want me to do?"

He smiled at me, a hint of mischief in his eyes, despite his worry for Father Kenneth.

"Game for it, are ye?"

"Unless you're proposing that I bat Mr. Lillywhite over the head and liberate Father Kenneth by force, I suppose so. That sort of thing is much more your line of country than mine."

He laughed at that, and gave the tent what appeared to be a wistful look.

"I should like nothing better," he said, confirming this impression. "It wouldna be difficult in the least," he went on, eyeing the tan canvas sides of the tent appraisingly as they flexed in the wind. "Look at the size of it; there canna be more than two or three men in there, besides the priest. I could wait until the full dark, and then take a lad or two and—"

"Yes, but what do you want me to do now?" I interrupted, thinking I had best put a stop to what sounded a distinctly criminal train of thought.

"Ah." He abandoned his machinations—for the moment—and squinted at me, appraising my appearance. I had taken off the bloodstained canvas apron I wore for surgery, had put up my hair neatly with pins, and was reasonably respectable in appearance, if a trifle mud-draggled round the hems.

"Ye dinna have any of your physician's kit about ye?" he asked, frowning dubiously. "A bottle of swill, a bittie knife?"

"Bottle of swill, indeed. No, I—oh, wait a moment. Yes, there are these; will they do?" Digging about in the pocket tied at my waist, I had come up with the small ivory box in which I kept my gold-tipped acupuncture needles.

Evidently satisfied, Jamie nodded, and pulled out the silver whisky flask from his sporran.

"Aye, they'll do," he said, handing me the flask. "Take this too, though, for looks. Go up to the tent, Sassenach, and tell whoever's guarding the priest that he's ailing."

"The guard?"

"The priest," he said, giving me a look of mild exasperation. "I daresay everyone will ken ye as a healer by now, and know ye on sight. Say that Father Kenneth has an illness that you've been treating, and he must have a dose of his medicine at once, lest he sicken and die on them. I dinna suppose they want that—and they'll not be afraid of you."

"I shouldn't imagine they need be," I agreed, a trifle caustically. "You don't mean me to stab the sheriff through the heart with my needles, then?"

He grinned at the thought, but shook his head.

"Nay, I only want ye to learn why they've taken the priest and what they mean to do with him. If I were to go and demand answers myself, it might put them on guard."

Meaning that he had not completely abandoned the notion of a later commando raid on Mr. Lillywhite's stronghold, should the answers prove unsatisfactory. I glanced at the tent and took a deep breath, settling my shawl about my shoulders.

"All right," I said. "And what are you intending to do while I'm about it?"

"I'm going to go and fetch the bairns," he said, and with a quick squeeze of my hand for luck, he was off down the trail.

I WAS STILL WONDERING exactly what he meant by *that* cryptic statement—which "bairns"? Why?—as I came within sight of the open tent flap, but all speculation was driven from my mind by the appearance of a gentleman therein who met Marsali's description of "a nasty, fat man" so exactly that I had no doubt of his identity. He was short and toadlike, with a receding hairline, a belly that strained the buttons of a food-stained linen vest, and small, beady eyes that watched me as though assessing my immediate prospects as a food item.

"Good day to you, ma'am," he said. He viewed me without enthusiasm, no doubt finding me less than toothsome, but inclined his head with formal respect.

"Good day," I replied cheerily, dropping him a brief curtsy. Never hurt to be polite—at least not to start with. "You'll be the sheriff, won't you? I'm afraid I haven't had the pleasure of a formal introduction. I'm Mrs. Fraser—Mrs. James Fraser, of Fraser's Ridge."

"David Anstruther, Sheriff of Orange County—your servant, ma'am," he said, bowing again, though with no real evidence of delight. He didn't show any surprise at hearing Jamie's name, either. Either he simply wasn't familiar with it—rather unlikely—or he had been expecting such an ambassage.

That being so, I saw no point in beating round the bush.

"I understand that you're entertaining Father Donahue," I said pleasantly. "I've come to see him; I'm his physician."

Whatever he'd been expecting, it wasn't that; his jaw dropped slightly, exposing a severe case of malocclusion, well-advanced gingivitis, and a missing bicuspid. Before he could close it, a tall gentleman in a bottle-green coat stepped out of the tent behind him.

"Mrs. Fraser?" he said, one eyebrow raised. He bowed punctiliously. "You say you wish to speak with the clerical gentleman under arrest?"

"Under arrest?" I affected great surprise at that. "A priest? Why, whatever can he have done?"

The Sheriff and the magistrate exchanged glances. Then the magistrate coughed.

"Perhaps you are unaware, madam, that it is illegal for anyone other than the clergy of the established Church—the Church of England, that is—to undertake his office within the colony of North Carolina?"

I was not unaware of that, though I also knew that the law was seldom put into effect, there being relatively few of any kind of clergy in the colony to start with, and no one bothering to take any official notice of the itinerant preachers—many of them free lances in the most basic sense of the word—who did appear from time to time.

"Gracious!" I said, affecting shocked surprise to the best of my ability. "No, I had no idea. Goodness me! How very strange!" Mr. Lillywhite blinked slightly, which I took as an indication that that would just about do, in terms of my creating an impression of well-bred shock. I cleared my throat, and brought out the silver flask and case of needles.

"Well. I do hope any difficulties will be soon resolved. However, I should very much like to see Father Donahue for a moment. As I said, I am his physician. He has an . . . indisposition"—I slid back the cover of the case, and delicately displayed the needles, letting them imagine something suitably virulent—"that requires regular treatment. Might I see him for a moment, to administer his medicine? I . . . ah . . . should not like to see any mischief result from a lack of care on my part, you know." I smiled, as charmingly as possible.

The Sheriff pulled his neck down into the collar of his coat and looked malevolently amphibious, but Mr. Lillywhite seemed better affected by the smile. He hesitated, looking me over.

"Well, I am not sure that . . ." he began, when the sound of footsteps came squelching up the path behind me. I turned, half-expecting to see Jamie, but instead beheld my recent patient, Mr. Goodwin, one cheek still puffed from my attentions, but sling intact.

He was quite as surprised to see me, but greeted me with great cordiality, and a cloud of alcoholic fumes. Evidently Mr. Goodwin had been taking my advice regarding disinfection very seriously.

"Mrs. Fraser! You have not come to minister to my friend Lillywhite, I trust? I expect Mr. Anstruther would benefit from a good purge, though—clear the bilious humors, eh, David? Haha!" He clapped the Sheriff on the back in affectionate camaraderie; a gesture Anstruther suffered with no more than a small grimace, giving me some idea of Mr. Goodwin's importance in the social scheme of Orange County.

"George, my dear," Mr. Lillywhite greeted him warmly. "You are acquainted with this charming lady, then?"

"Oh, indeed, indeed I am, sir!" Mr. Goodwin turned a beaming countenance upon me. "Why, Mrs. Fraser did me great service this morning, great service indeed! See here!" He brandished his bound and splinted arm, which, I was pleased to see, was evidently giving him no pain whatever at the moment, though that probably had more to do with his self-administered anesthesia than with my workmanship.

"She quite cured my arm, with no more than a touch here, a touch there—and drew a broken tooth so clean that I scarce felt a thing! 'Ook!" He stuck a finger into the side of his mouth and pulled back his cheek, exposing a tuft of bloodstained wadding protruding from the tooth socket and a neat line of black stitching on the gum.

"Really, I am most impressed, Mrs. Fraser." Lillywhite sniffed at the waft of cloves and whisky from Mr. Goodwin's mouth, looking interested, and I saw the bulge of his cheek as his own tongue tenderly probed a back tooth.

"But what brings you up here, Mrs. Fraser?" Mr. Goodwin turned the beam of his joviality on me. "So late in the day—perhaps you will do me the honor of taking a bit of supper at my fire?"

"Oh, thank you, but I can't, really," I said, smiling as charmingly as possible. "I've just come to see another patient—that is—"

"She wants to see the priest," Anstruther interrupted.

Goodwin blinked at that, taken only slightly aback.

"Priest. There is a priest here?"

"A Papist," Mr. Lillywhite amplified, lips curling back a bit from the unclean word. "It came to my attention that there was a Catholic priest concealed in the assembly, who proposed to celebrate a Mass during the festivities this evening. I sent Mr. Anstruther to arrest him, of course."

"Father Donahue is a friend of mine," I put in, as forcefully as possible. "And he was not concealed; he was invited quite openly, as the guest of Mrs. Cameron. He is also a patient, and requires treatment. I've come to see that he gets it."

"A friend of yours? Are you Catholic, Mrs. Fraser?" Mr. Goodwin looked startled; it obviously hadn't occurred to him that he was being treated by a Popish dentist, and his hand went to his swollen cheek in bemusement.

"I am," I said, hoping that merely being a Catholic wasn't also against Mr. Lillywhite's conception of the law.

Evidently not. Mr. Goodwin gave Mr. Lillywhite a nudge.

"Oh, come, Randall. Let Mrs. Fraser see the fellow, what harm can it do? And if he's truly Jocasta Cameron's guest . . ."

Mr. Lillywhite pursed his lips in thought for a moment, then stood aside, holding back the flap of canvas for me.

"I suppose there can be no harm in your seeing your . . . friend," he said slowly. "Come in, then, madam."

Sundown was at hand, and the tent was dark inside, though one canvas wall still glowed brightly with the sinking sun behind it. I shut my eyes for a moment, to accustom them to the change of light, then blinked and looked about to get my bearings.

The tent seemed cluttered but relatively luxurious, being equipped with a camp bed and other furniture, the air within scented not only by damp canvas and wool but with the perfume of Ceylon tea, expensive wine, and almond biscuits.

Father Donahue was silhouetted in front of the glowing canvas, sitting on a stool behind a small folding table, on which were arrayed a few sheets of paper, an inkstand, and a quill. They might as well have been thumbscrews, pincers, and a red-hot poker, judging from his militantly upright attitude, evocative of expectant martyrdom.

The clinking of flint and tinderbox came from behind me, and then the faint glow of a light. This swelled, and a black boy—Mr. Lillywhite's servant, I supposed—came forward and silently set a small oil lamp on the table.

Now that I got a clear look at the priest, the impression of martyrdom grew more pronounced. He looked like Saint Stephen after the first volley of stones, with a bruise on his chin and a first-rate black eye, empurpled from browridge to cheekbone and swollen quite shut.

The nonblackened eye widened at sight of me, and he started up with an exclamation of surprise.

"Father Kenneth." I gripped him by the hand and squeezed, smiling broadly for the benefit of whatever audience might be peeking through the flap. "I've brought your medicine. How are you feeling?" I raised my eyebrows and waggled them, indicating that he should play along with the deception. He stared at me in fascination for a moment, but then appeared to catch on. He coughed, then, encouraged by my nod, coughed again, with more enthusiasm.

"It's . . . very kind of ye to . . . think of me, Mrs. Fraser," he wheezed, between hacks.

I pulled off the top of the flask, and poured out a generous measure of whisky.

"Are you quite all right, Father?" I asked, low-voiced, as I leaned across to hand it to him. "Your face . . ."

"Oh, it's nothing, Mrs. Fraser dear, not at all," he assured me, his faint Irish accent coming out under the stress of the occasion. " 'Twas only that I made the mistake of resistin' when the Sheriff arrested me. Not but what in the shock of it all, I didn't do a small bit of damage to the poor man's ballocks, and him only doing of his duty, may God forgive me." Father Kenneth rolled his undamaged eye upward in a pious expression—quite spoiled by the unregenerate grin underneath.

Father Kenneth was no more than middle height, and looked older than his years by virtue of the hard wear imposed by long seasons spent in the saddle. Still, he was no more than thirty-five, and lean and tough as whipcord under his worn black coat and frayed linen. I began to understand the Sheriff's belligerence.

"Besides," he added, touching his black eye gingerly, "Mr. Lillywhite did tender me a most gracious apology for the hurt." He nodded toward the table, and I saw that an opened bottle of wine and a pewter cup stood among the writing materials—the cup still full, and the level of wine in the bottle not down by much.

The priest picked up the whisky I had poured and drained it, closing his eyes in dreamy benediction.

"And a finer medicine I hope never to benefit from," he said, opening them. "I do thank ye, Mistress Fraser. I'm that restored, I might walk on water meself." He remembered to cough, this one a delicate hack, fist held over his mouth.

"What's wrong with the wine?" I asked, with a glance toward the door.

"Oh, not a thing," he said, taking his hand away. "Only that I did not think it quite right to accept the magistrate's refreshments, under the circumstances. Call it conscience." He smiled at me again, but this time with a note of wryness in the grin.

"Why have they arrested you?" I asked, my voice low. I looked again at the tent's door, but it was empty, and I caught the murmur of voices outside. Evidently, Jamie had been right; they weren't suspicious of me.

"For sayin' of the Holy Mass," he replied, lowering his voice to match mine. "Or so they said. It's a wicked lie, though. I've not said Mass since last Sunday, and that was in Virginia." He was looking wistfully at the flask. I picked it up and poured another generous tot.

I frowned a bit, thinking, while he drank it, more slowly this time. Whatever were Mr. Lillywhite and company up to? They couldn't, surely, be meaning to bring the priest to trial on the charge of saying Mass. It would be no great matter to find false witnesses to say he had, of course—but what would be the point of it?

While Catholicism was certainly not popular in North Carolina, I could see no great purpose in the arrest of a priest who would be leaving in the morning in any case. Father Kenneth came from Baltimore and meant to return there; he had come to the Gathering only as a favor to Jocasta Cameron.

"Oh!" I said, and Father Kenneth looked at me inquiringly over the rim of his cup.

"Just a thought," I said, gesturing to him to continue. "Do you happen to know whether Mr. Lillywhite is personally acquainted with Mrs. Cameron?" Jocasta Cameron was a prominent and wealthy woman—and one of strong character, therefore not without enemies. I couldn't see why Mr. Lillywhite would go out of his way to disoblige her in such a peculiar fashion, even so, but . . .

"I am acquainted with Mrs. Cameron," said Mr. Lillywhite, speaking behind me. "Though alas, I can claim no intimate friendship with the lady." I whirled to find him standing just within the tent's entrance, followed by Sheriff Anstruther and Mr. Goodwin, with Jamie bringing up the rear. The latter flicked an eyebrow at me, but otherwise maintained an expression of solemn interest.

Mr. Lillywhite bowed to me in acknowledgment.

"I have just been explaining to your husband, Madame, that it is my regard for Mrs. Cameron's interests that led me to attempt to regularize Mr. Donahue's position, so as to allow his continued presence in the colony." Mr. Lillywhite nodded coldly at the priest. "However, I am afraid my suggestion was summarily rejected."

Father Kenneth put down his cup and straightened up, his working eye bright in the lamplight.

"They wish me to sign an oath, sir," he said to Jamie, with

a gesture at the paper and quill on the table before him. "To the effect that I do not subscribe to a belief in transubstantiation."

"Do they, indeed." Jamie's voice betrayed no more than polite interest, but I understood at once what the priest had meant by his remark regarding conscience.

"Well, he can't do that, can he?" I said, looking round the circle of men. "Catholics—I mean—*we*"—I spoke with some emphasis, looking at Mr. Goodwin—"*do* believe in transubstantiation. Don't we?" I asked, turning to the priest, who smiled slightly in response, and nodded.

Mr. Goodwin looked unhappy, but resigned, his alcoholic joviality substantially reduced by the social awkwardness.

"I'm sorry, Mrs. Fraser, but that is the law. The only circumstance under which a clergyman who does not belong to the established Church may remain in the colony—legally—is upon the signing of such an oath. Many do sign it. You know the Reverend Urmstone, the Methodist circuit rider? He has signed the oath, as has Mr. Calvert, the New Light minister who lives near Wadesboro."

The Sheriff looked smug. Repressing an urge to stamp on his foot, I turned to Mr. Lillywhite.

"Well, but Father Donahue can't sign it. So what do you propose to do with him? Throw the poor man in gaol? You can't do that—he's ill!" On cue, Father Kenneth coughed obligingly.

Mr. Lillywhite eyed me dubiously, but chose instead to address Jamie.

"I could by rights imprison the man, but out of regard for you, Mr. Fraser, and for your aunt, I shall not do so. He must, however, leave the colony tomorrow. I shall have him escorted into Virginia, where he will be released from custody. You may rest assured that all care will be taken to assure his welfare on the journey." He turned a cold gray eye on the Sheriff, who straightened up and tried to look reliable, with indifferent results.

"I see." Jamie spoke lightly, looking from one man to another, his eyes coming to rest on the Sheriff. "I trust that is true, sir—for if I should hear of any harm coming to the good Father, I should be . . . most distressed."

The Sheriff met his gaze, stone-faced, and held it until Mr. Lillywhite cleared his throat, frowning at the Sheriff.

"You have my word upon it, Mr. Fraser."

Jamie turned to him, bowing slightly.

"I could ask no more, sir. And yet if I may presume— might the Father not spend tonight in comfort among his friends, that they might take their leave of him? And that my wife might attend his injuries? I would stand surety for his safe delivery into your hand come morning."

Mr. Lillywhite pursed his lips and affected to consider this suggestion, but the magistrate was a poor actor. I realized with some interest that he had foreseen this request, and had his mind made up already to deny it.

"No, sir," he said, trying for a tone of reluctance. "I regret that I cannot grant your request. Though if the priest wishes to write letters to various of his acquaintance"—he gestured at the sheaf of papers—"I will undertake to see them promptly delivered."

Jamie cleared his own throat and drew himself up a bit.

"Well, then," he said. "I wonder whether I might make so bold as to ask . . ." He paused, seeming slightly embarrassed.

"Yes, sir?" Lillywhite looked at him curiously.

"I wonder whether the good Father might be allowed to hear my confession." Jamie's eyes were fixed on the tent pole, sedulously avoiding mine.

"Your confession?"

Lillywhite looked astonished at this, though the Sheriff made a noise that might charitably be called a snigger.

"Got something pressing on your conscience?" Anstruther asked rudely. "Or p'r'aps you have some premonition of impending death, eh?" He gave an evil smile at this, and Mr. Goodwin, looking shocked, rumbled a protest at him. Jamie ignored both of them, focusing his regard on Mr. Lillywhite.

"Yes, sir. It has been some time since I last had the opportunity of being shriven, ye see, and it may well be some time before such a chance occurs again. As it is—" At this point, he caught my eye, and made a slight but emphatic motion with his head toward the tent flap. "If ye will excuse us for a moment, gentlemen?"

Not waiting for a response, he seized me by the elbow and propelled me swiftly outside.

"Brianna and Marsali are up the path wi' the weans," he hissed in my ear, the moment we were clear of the tent. "Make sure Lillywhite and yon bastard of a sheriff are well away, then fetch them in."

Leaving me standing on the path, astonished, he ducked back into the tent.

"Your pardon, gentlemen," I heard him say. "I thought perhaps . . . there are some things a man shouldna quite like to be saying before his wife . . . you understand?"

There were male murmurs of understanding, and I caught the word "confession" repeated in dubious tones by Mr. Lillywhite. Jamie lowered his voice to a confidential rumble in response, interrupted by a rather loud, "You *what*?" from the Sheriff, and a peremptory shushing by Mr. Goodwin.

There was a bit of confused conversation, then a shuffle of movement, and I barely made it off the path and into the shelter of the pines before the tent flap lifted and the three Protestants emerged from the tent. The day had all but faded now, leaving burning embers of sunlit cloud in the sky, but close as they were, there was enough light for me to see the air of vague embarrassment that beset them.

They moved a few steps down the path, stopping no more than a few feet from my own hiding place. They stood in a cluster to confer, looking back at the tent, from which I could now hear Father Kenneth's voice, raised in a formal Latin blessing. The lamp in the tent went out, and the forms of Jamie and the priest, dim shadows on the canvas, disappeared into a confessional darkness.

Anstruther's bulk sidled closer to Mr. Goodwin.

"What in fuck's name is transubstantiation?" he muttered.

I saw Mr. Goodwin's shoulders straighten as he drew himself up, then hunch toward his ears in a shrug.

"In all honesty, sir, I am not positive of the meaning of the term," he said, rather primly, "though I perceive it to be some form of pernicious Papist doctrine. Perhaps Mr. Lillywhite could supply you with a more complete definition—Randall?"

"Indeed," the magistrate said. "It is the notion that by the priest's speaking particular words in the course of offering his Mass, bread and wine are transformed into the very substance of Our Savior's body and blood."

"What?" Anstruther sounded confused. "How can anyone do that?"

"Change bread and wine into flesh and blood?" Mr. Goodwin sounded quite taken aback. "But that is witchcraft, surely!"

"Well, it would be, if it happened," Mr. Lillywhite said, sounding a bit more human. "The Church very rightly holds that it does not."

"Are we sure of that?" Anstruther sounded suspicious. "Have you seen them do it?"

"Have I attended a Catholic Mass? Assuredly not!" Lillywhite's tall form drew up, austere in the gathering dusk. "What do you take me for, sir!"

"Now, Randall, I am sure the Sheriff means no offense." Goodwin put a placatory hand on his friend's arm. "His office deals with more earthly matters, after all."

"No, no, no offense meant, sir, none at all," Anstruther said hurriedly. "I was meaning more, like, has *anybody* seen this kind of goings-on, so as to be a decent witness, for the prosecution of it, I mean."

Mr. Lillywhite appeared still to be somewhat offended; his voice was cold in reply.

"It is scarcely necessary to have witnesses to the heresy, Sheriff, as the priests themselves willingly admit to it."

"No, no. Of course not." The Sheriff's squat form seemed to flatten obsequiously. "But if I'm right, sir, Papists do . . . er . . . *partake* of this—this transubwhatnot, aye?"

"Yes, so I am told."

"Well, then. That's frigging cannibalism, isn't it?" Anstruther's bulk popped up again, enthused. "I know *that's* against the law! Why not let this bugger do his bit of hocus-pocus, and we'll arrest the whole boiling lot of 'em, eh? Get shut of any number of the bastards at one blow, I daresay."

Mr. Goodwin emitted a low moan. He appeared to be massaging his face, no doubt to ease a recurrent ache from his tooth.

Mr. Lillywhite exhaled strongly through his nose.

"No," he said evenly. "I am afraid not, Sheriff. My instructions are that the priest is not to be allowed to perform any ceremonial, and shall be prevented from receiving visitors."

"Oh, aye? And what's he doing now, then?" Anstruther demanded, gesturing toward the darkened tent, where Jamie's voice had begun to speak, hesitant and barely audible. I thought perhaps he was speaking in Latin.

"That is quite different," Lillywhite said testily. "Mr. Fraser is a gentleman. And the prohibition against visitors is to insure that the priest shall perform no secret marriages; hardly a concern at present."

"Bless me, Father, for I have sinned." Jamie's voice spoke in English, suddenly louder, and Mr. Lillywhite started. Father Kenneth murmured interrogatively.

"I have been guilty of the sins of lust and impurity, both in thought and in my flesh," Jamie announced—with what I thought rather more volume than was quite discreet.

"Oh, to be sure," said Father Kenneth, suddenly louder too. He sounded interested. "Now, these sins of impurity—what form, precisely, did they take, my son, and upon how many occasions?"

"Aye, well. I've looked upon women with lust, to be starting with. How many occasions—oh, make it a hundred, at least, it's been a time since I was last to confession. Did ye need to know which women, Father, or only what it was I thought of doing to them?"

Mr. Lillywhite stiffened markedly.

"I think we'll not have time for the lot, Jamie dear," said the priest. "But if ye were to tell me about one or two of these occasions, just so as I could be formin' a notion as to the . . . er . . . severity of the offense . . . ?"

"Och, aye. Well, the worst was likely the time wi' the butter churn."

"Butter churn? Ah . . . the sort with the handle pokin' up?" Father Kenneth's tone encompassed a sad compassion for the lewd possibilities suggested by this.

"Oh, no, Father; it was a barrel churn. The sort that lies on its side, aye, with a wee handle to turn it? Well, it's only that she was workin' the churn with great vigor, and the laces of her bodice undone, so that her breasts wobbled to and fro, and the cloth clinging to her with the sweat of her work. Now, the churn was just the right height—and curved, aye?—so as make me think of bendin' her across it and lifting her skirts, and—"

My mouth opened involuntarily in shock. That was my bodice he was describing, my breasts, and my butter churn! To say nothing of my skirts. I remembered that particular occasion quite vividly, and if it had started with an impure thought, it certainly hadn't stopped there.

A rustling and murmuring drew my attention back to the men on the path. Mr. Lillywhite had grasped the Sheriff—still leaning avidly toward the tent, ears flapping—by the arm and was hissing at him as he forced him hastily down the path. Mr. Goodwin followed, though with an air of reluctance.

The noise of their departure had unfortunately drowned out the rest of Jamie's description of that particular occasion of sin, but had luckily also covered the leaf-rustling and twig-snapping behind me that announced the appearance of Brianna and Marsali, Jemmy and Joan swaddled in their arms and Germain clinging monkeylike to his mother's back.

"I thought they'd never go," Brianna whispered, peering over my shoulder toward the spot where Mr. Lillywhite and his companions had disappeared. "Is the coast clear?"

"Yes, come along." I reached for Germain, who leaned willingly into my arms.

*"Ou qu'on va, Grand-mère?"* he inquired in a sleepy voice, blond head nuzzling affectionately into my neck.

"Shh. To see *Grand-père* and Father Kenneth," I whispered to him. "We have to be very quiet, though."

"Oh. Like this?" he hissed, in a loud whisper, and began to sing a very vulgar French song, chanting half under his breath.

"Shh!" I clapped a hand across his mouth, moist and sticky with whatever he'd been eating. "Don't sing, sweetheart, we don't want to wake the babies."

I heard a small, stifled noise from Marsali, a strangled snort from Bree, and realized that Jamie was still confessing. He appeared to have hit his stride, and was now inventing freely—or at least I hoped so. He certainly hadn't been doing any of that with *me*.

I poked my head out, looking up and down the trail, but no one was near. I motioned to the girls, and we scuttled across the path and into the darkened tent.

Jamie stopped abruptly as we fumbled our way inside. Then I heard him say quickly, "And sins of anger, pride, and jealousy—oh, and the odd wee bit of lying as well, Father. Amen." He dropped to his knees, raced through an Act of Contrition in French, and was on his feet and taking Germain from me before Father Kenneth had finished saying the *"Ego te absolvo."*

My eyes were becoming adapted to the dark; I could make out the voluminous shapes of the girls, and Jamie's tall outline. He stood Germain on the table before the priest, saying, "Quickly, then, Father; we havena much time."

"We haven't any water, either," the priest observed. "Unless you ladies thought to bring any?" He had picked up the flint and tinderbox, and was attempting to relight the lamp.

Bree and Marsali exchanged appalled glances, then shook their heads in unison.

"Dinna fash, Father." Jamie spoke soothingly, and I saw him reach out a hand for something on the table. There was the brief squeak of a cork being drawn, and the hot, sweet smell of fine whisky filled the tent, as the light caught and grew from the wick, the wavering flame steadying to a small, clear light.

"Under the circumstances . . ." Jamie said, holding out the open flask to the priest.

Father Kenneth's lips pressed together, though I thought with suppressed amusement, rather than irritation.

"Under the circumstances, aye," he repeated. "And what should be more appropriate than the water of life, after all?" He reached up, undid his stock, and pulled up a leather string fastened round his neck, from which dangled a wooden cross and a small glass bottle, stoppered with a cork.

"The holy chrism," he explained, undoing the bottle and setting it on the table. "Thank the Virgin Mother that I had it on my person. The Sheriff took the box with my Mass things." He made a quick inventory of the objects on the table, counting them off on his fingers. "Fire, chrism, water—of a sort—and a child. Very well, then. You and your husband will stand as godparents to him, I suppose, ma'am?"

This was addressed to me, Jamie having gone to take up a station by the tent flap.

"For all of them, Father," I said, and took a firm grip on Germain, who seemed disposed to leap off the table. "Hold still, darling, just for a moment."

I heard a small *whish* behind me; metal drawn from oiled leather. I glanced back to see Jamie, dim in the shadows, standing guard by the door with his dirk in his hand. A qualm of apprehension curled through my belly, and I heard Bree draw in her breath beside me.

"Jamie, my son," said Father Kenneth, in a tone of mild reproval.

"Be going on with it, if ye please, Father," Jamie replied, very calmly. "I mean to have my grandchildren baptized this night, and no one shall prevent it."

The priest drew in his breath with a slight hiss, then shook his head.

"Aye. And if you kill someone, I hope there'll be time for me to shrive you again before they hang us both," he muttered, reaching for the oil. "If there's a choice about it, try for the Sheriff, will you, man dear?"

Switching abruptly to Latin, he pushed back Germain's heavy mop of blond hair and his thumb flicked deftly over forehead, lips, and then—diving under the boy's gown in a gesture that made Germain double up in giggles—heart, in the sign of the Cross.

"On-behalf-of-this-child-do-you-renounce-Satan-and-all-his-works?" he asked, speaking so fast that I scarcely realized he was speaking English again, and barely caught up in time to join with Jamie in the godparents' response, dutifully reciting, "I do renounce them."

I was on edge, keeping an ear out for any noises that might portend the return of Mr. Lillywhite and the Sheriff, envisioning just what sort of brouhaha might ensue if they did come back to discover Father Kenneth in the midst of what would surely be considered an illicit "ceremonial."

I glanced back at Jamie; he was looking at me, and gave

me a faint smile that I thought was likely meant for reassurance. If so, it failed utterly; I knew him too well. He wanted his grandchildren baptized, and he would see their souls safely given into God's care, if he died for it—or if we all went to gaol, Brianna, Marsali, and the children included. Of such stuff are martyrs made, and their families are obliged to lump it.

"Do-you-believe-in-one-God-the-Father-the-Son-and-the-Holy-Ghost?"

"Stubborn man," I mouthed at Jamie. His smile widened, and I turned back, hastily chiming in with his firm, "I do believe." Was that a footfall on the path outside, or only the evening wind, making the tree branches crack as it passed?

The questions and responses finished, and the priest grinned at me, looking like a gargoyle in the flickering lamplight. His good eye closed briefly in a wink.

"We'll take it that your answers will be the same for the others, shall we, ma'am? And what will be this sweet lad's baptismal name?"

Not breaking his rhythm, the priest took up the whisky flask, and dribbled a careful stream of spirit onto the little boy's head, repeating, "I baptize thee, Germain Alexander Claudel MacKenzie Fraser, in the Name of the Father, the Son, and the Holy Ghost, Amen."

Germain watched this operation with profound interest, round blue eyes crossing as the amber liquid ran down the shallow bridge of his nose and dripped from its stubby tip. He put out a tongue to catch the drops, then made a face at the taste.

"Ick," he said clearly. "Horse piss."

Marsali made a brief, shocked "Tst!" at him, but the priest merely chuckled, swung Germain off the table, and beckoned to Bree.

She held Jemmy over the table, cradled in her arms like a sacrifice. She was intent on the baby's face, but I saw her head twitch slightly, her attention drawn by something outside. There *were* sounds on the path below; I could hear voices. A group of men, I thought, talking together, voices genial but not drunken.

I tensed, trying not to look at Jamie. If they came in, I

decided, I had better grab Germain, scramble under the far edge of the tent, and run for it. I took a preparatory grip on the collar of his gown, just in case. Then I felt a gentle nudge as Bree shifted her weight against me.

"It's all right, Mama," she whispered. "It's Roger and Fergus." She nodded toward the dark, then returned her attention to Jemmy.

It was, I realized, and the skin of my temples prickled with relief. Now that I knew, I could make out the imperious, slightly nasal sound of Fergus's voice, raised in a lengthy oration of some kind, and a low Scottish rumble that I thought must be Roger's. A higher-pitched titter that I recognized as Mr. Goodwin's drifted through the night, followed by some remark in Mr. Lillywhite's aristocratic drawl.

I did glance at Jamie this time. He still held the dirk, but his hand had fallen to his side, and his shoulders had lost a little of their tension. He smiled at me again, and this time I returned it.

Jemmy was awake, but drowsy. He made no objection to the oil, but startled at the cold touch of the whisky on his forehead, eyes popping open and arms flinging wide. He uttered a high-pitched "Yeep!" of protest, then, as Bree gathered him hastily up into his blanket against her shoulder, screwed up his face and tried to decide whether he was sufficiently disturbed to cry about it.

Bree patted his back like a bongo drum and made little hooting noises in his ear, distracting him. He settled for plugging his mouth with a thumb and glowering suspiciously at the assemblage, but by that time, Father Kenneth was already pouring whisky on the sleeping Joan, held low in Marsali's arms.

"I baptize thee, Joan Laoghaire Claire Fraser," he said, following Marsali's lead, and I glanced at Marsali, startled. I knew she was called Joan for Marsali's younger sister, but I hadn't known what the baby's other names would be. I felt a small lump in my throat, watching Marsali's shawled head bent over the child. Both her sister and her mother, Laoghaire, were in Scotland; the chances of either ever seeing this tiny namesake were vanishingly small.

Suddenly, Joan's slanted eyes popped wide open and so

did her mouth. She let out a piercing shriek, and everyone started as though a bomb had exploded in our midst.

"Go in peace, to serve the Lord! And go fast!" Father Kenneth said, his fingers already nimbly corking up bottle and flask, frantically whisking away all traces of the ceremony. Down the path, I could hear voices raised in puzzled question.

Marsali was out the tent flap in a flash, the squalling Joan against her breast, a protesting Germain clutched by the hand. Bree paused just long enough to put a hand behind Father Kenneth's head and kiss him on the forehead.

"Thank you, Father," she whispered, and was gone in a flurry of skirts and petticoats.

Jamie had me by the arm and was hustling me out of the tent as well, but stopped for a half-second at the door, turning back.

"Father?" he called in a whisper. *"Pax vobiscum!"*

Father Kenneth had already seated himself behind the table, hands folded, the accusing sheets of blank paper spread out once more before him. He looked up, smiling slightly, and his face was perfectly at peace in the lamplight, black eye and all.

*"Et cum spiritu tuo,* man," he said, and raised three fingers in parting benediction.

"WHAT ON EARTH did you do that for?" Brianna's whisper floated back to me, loud with annoyance. She and Marsali were only a few feet in front of us, going slowly because of the children, but close as they were, the girls' shawled and bunchy shapes were scarcely distinguishable from the bushes overgrowing the path.

"Do what? Leave that, Germain; let's find Papa, shall we? No, don't put it in your mouth!"

"You pinched Joanie—I saw you! You could have got us all caught!"

"But I had to!" Marsali sounded surprised at the accusation. "And it wouldna have mattered, really—the christening was done by then. They couldna make Father Kenneth take it back, now, could they?" She giggled slightly at the thought, then broke off. "Germain, I said drop it!"

"What do you mean, you had to? Let go, Jem, that's my hair! Ow! Let go, I said!"

Jemmy was evidently now wide awake, interested in the novel surroundings, and wanting to explore them, judging from his repeated exclamations of "Argl!" punctuated by the occasional curious "Gleb?"

"Why, she was asleep!" Marsali said, sounding scandalized. "She didna wake when Father Kenneth poured the water—I mean the whisky—on her head—Germain, come back here! *Thig air ais a seo!*—and ye ken it's ill luck for a child not to make a wee skelloch when it's baptized; that's how ye ken as the original sin is leaving it! I couldna let the *diabhol* stay in my wee lassie. Could I, *mo mhaorine*?" There were small kissing noises, and a faint coo from Joanie, promptly drowned by Germain, who had started to sing again.

Bree gave a small snort of amusement, her irritation fading.

"Oh, I see. Well, as long as you had a good reason. Though I'm not so sure it worked on Jemmy and Germain. Look at the way they're acting—I'd swear they were possessed. Ow! Don't bite me, you little fiend, I'll feed you in a minute!"

"Och, well, they're boys, after all," Marsali said tolerantly, raising her voice slightly to be heard above the racket. "Everyone kens that boys are full o' the devil; I suppose it would take more than a bit of holy water to drown it all, even if it *was* ninety-proof. Germain! *Where* did ye hear such a filthy song, ye wee ratten?"

I smiled, and next to me, Jamie laughed quietly, listening to the girls' conversation. We were far enough from the scene of the crime by now not to worry about being heard, among the snatches of song, fiddle music, and laughter that flickered through the trees with the light of the campfires, bright against the growing dark.

The business of the day was largely done, and folk were settling down to the evening meal, before the calling, the singing, and the last round of visits started. The scents of smoke and supper trailed tantalizing fingers through the cold, dark air, and my stomach rumbled gently in answer to their summons. I hoped Lizzie was sufficiently restored as to have begun cooking.

"What's *mo mhaorine*?" I asked Jamie. "I haven't heard that one before."

"It means 'my wee potato,' I think," he said. "It's Irish, aye? She learnt it from the priest."

He sighed, sounding deeply satisfied with the evening's work so far.

"May Bride bless Father Kenneth for a nimble-fingered man; for a moment, I thought we wouldna manage it. Is that Roger and wee Fergus?"

A couple of dark shadows had come out of the wood to join the girls, and the sound of muffled laughter and murmured voices—punctuated by raucous shrieks from both little boys at sight of their daddies—drifted back to us from the little knot of young families.

"It is. And speaking of that, my little sweet potato," I said, taking a firm grip of his arm to slow him, "what do you mean by telling Father Kenneth all that about me and the butter churn?"

"Ye dinna mean to say ye minded, Sassenach?" he said, in tones of surprise.

"Of course I minded!" I said. The blood rose warm in my cheeks, though I wasn't sure whether this was due to the memory of his confession—or to the memory of the original occasion. My innards warmed slightly at that thought as well, and the last remnants of cramp began to subside as my womb clenched and relaxed, eased by the pleasant inward glow. It was scarcely a suitable time or place, but perhaps later in the evening, we might manage sufficient privacy—I pushed the thought hastily aside.

"Privacy quite aside, it wasn't a sin at all," I said primly. "We're married, for goodness' sake!"

"Well, I did confess to telling lies, Sassenach," he said. I couldn't see the smile on his face, but I could hear it well enough in his voice. I supposed he could hear mine, too.

"I had to think of a sin frightful enough to drive Lillywhite away—and I couldna confess to theft or buggery; I may have to do business with the man one day."

"Oh, so you think he'd be put off by sodomy, but he'd consider your attitude toward women in wet chemises just a minor flaw of character?" His arm was warm under the cloth of his shirt. I touched the underside of his wrist, that vulnerable place where the skin lay bare, and stroked the line of the vein that pulsed there, disappearing under the linen toward his heart.

"Keep your voice down, Sassenach," he murmured, touching my hand. "Ye dinna want the bairns to hear ye. Besides," he added, his voice dropping low enough that he was obliged to lean down and whisper in my ear, "it's not all women. Only the ones with lovely round arses." He let go my hand and patted my backside familiarly, showing remarkable accuracy in the darkness.

"I wouldna cross the road to see a scrawny woman, if she were stark naked and dripping wet. As for Lillywhite," he resumed, in a more normal tone of voice, but without removing his hand, which was molding the cloth of my skirt thoughtfully round one buttock, "he may be a Protestant, Sassenach, but he's still a man."

"I didn't realize the two states were incompatible," Roger's voice said dryly, coming out of the darkness nearby.

Jamie snatched his hand away as though my bottom were on fire. It wasn't—quite—but there was no denying that his flint had struck a spark or two among the kindling, damp as it was. It was a long time before bedtime, though.

Pausing just long enough to administer a brief, private squeeze to Jamie's anatomy that made him gasp sharply, I turned to find Roger clasping a large wriggling object in his arms, its nature obscured by the dark. Not a piglet, I surmised, despite the loud grunting noises it was making, but rather Jemmy, who seemed to be gnawing fiercely on his father's knuckles. A small pink fist shot out into a random patch of light, clenched in concentration, then disappeared, meeting Roger's ribs with a solid thump.

Jamie gave a small grunt of amusement himself, but wasn't discomposed in the slightest by having his opinion of Protestants overheard.

" 'All are gude lasses,' " he quoted in broad Scots, " 'but where do the ill wives come frae?' "

"Eh?" Roger said, sounding a bit bewildered.

"Protestants are *born* wi' pricks," Jamie explained, "the men, at least—but some let them wither from disuse. A man who spends his time pokin' his . . . nose into others' sinfulness has nay time to tend his own."

I converted a laugh into a more tactful cough.

"And some just become bigger pricks, what with the practice," Roger said, more dryly still. "Aye, well. I came to thank you . . . for managing about the baptism, I mean."

I noticed the slight hesitation; he still had not settled on any comfortable name by which to call Jamie to his face. Jamie addressed *him* impartially as "Wee Roger," "Roger Mac," or "MacKenzie"—more rarely, by the Gaelic nickname Ronnie Sinclair had given Roger, *a Smeòraich*, in honor of his voice. *Singing Thrush*, it meant.

"It's me should be thanking you, *a charaid*. We shouldna have managed there at the last, save for you and Fergus," Jamie said, laughter warming his own voice.

Roger was clearly visible in outline, tall and lean, with the glow of someone's fire behind him. One shoulder rose as he shrugged, and he shifted Jemmy to his other arm, wiping residual drool from his hand against the side of his breeches.

"No trouble," he said, a little gruffly. "Will the—the Father be all right, d'ye think? Brianna said he'd been roughly handled. I hope they'll not mistreat him, once he's away."

Jamie sobered at that. He shrugged a little as he straightened the coat on his shoulders.

"I think he'll be safe enough, aye—I had a word with the Sheriff." There was a certain grim emphasis on "word" that made his meaning clear. A substantial bribe might have been more effective, but I was well aware that we had exactly two shillings, threepence, and nine farthings in cash to our names at the moment. Better to save the money and rely on threats, I thought. Evidently Jamie was of the same mind.

"I shall speak to my aunt," he said, "and have her send a note tonight to Mr. Lillywhite, wi' her own opinion on the subject. That will be a better safeguard for Father Kenneth than anything I can say myself."

"I don't suppose she'll be at all pleased to hear that her

wedding is postponed," I observed. She wouldn't be. Daughter of a Highland laird and widow of a very rich planter, Jocasta Cameron was used to having her own way.

"No, she won't," Jamie agreed wryly, "though I suppose Duncan may be a bit relieved."

Roger laughed, not without sympathy, and fell in beside us as we started down the path. He shifted Jemmy, still grunting ferociously, under his arm like a football.

"Aye, he will. Poor Duncan. So the weddings are definitely off, are they?"

I couldn't see Jamie's frown, but I felt the movement as he shook his head doubtfully.

"Aye, I'm afraid so. They wouldna give the priest to me, even with my word to hand him over in the morning. We could maybe take him by force, but even so—"

"I doubt that would help," I interrupted, and told them what I had overheard while waiting outside the tent.

"So I can't see them standing round and letting Father Kenneth perform marriages," I finished. "Even if you got him away, they'd be combing the mountain for him, turning out tents and causing riots."

Sheriff Anstruther wouldn't be without aid; Jamie and his aunt might be held in good esteem among the Scottish community, but Catholics in general and priests in particular weren't.

"Instructions?" Jamie repeated, sounding astonished. "You're sure of it, Sassenach? It was Lillywhite who said he had 'instructions'?"

"It was," I said, realizing for the first time how peculiar that was. The Sheriff was plainly taking instructions from Mr. Lillywhite, that being his duty. But who could be giving instructions to the magistrate?

"There's another magistrate here, and a couple of justices of the peace, but surely . . ." Roger said slowly, shaking his head as he thought. A loud squawk interrupted his thoughts, and he glanced down, the light from a nearby fire shining off the bridge of his nose, outlining a faint smile as he spoke to his offspring. "What? You're hungry, laddie? Don't fret yourself, Mummy will be back soon."

"Where *is* Mummy?" I said, peering into the shifting mass of shadows ahead. A light wind had risen, and the bare branches of oak and hickory rattled like sabers overhead. Still, Jemmy was more than loud enough for Brianna to hear him. I caught Marsali's voice faintly up ahead, engaged in what appeared to be amiable conversation with Germain and Fergus regarding supper, but there was no sound of Bree's lower, huskier Boston-bred tones.

"Why?" Jamie said to Roger, raising his voice to be heard over the wind.

"Why what? Here, Jem, see that? Want it? Aye, of course ye do. Yes, good lad, gnaw on that for a bit." A spark of light caught something shiny in Roger's free hand; then the object disappeared, and Jemmy's cries ceased abruptly, succeeded by loud sucking and slurping noises.

"What is that? It isn't small enough for him to swallow, is it?" I asked anxiously.

"Ah, no. It's a watch chain. Not to worry," Roger assured me, "I've a good grip on the end of it. If he swallows it, I can pull it back out."

"Why would someone not want you to be married?" Jamie said patiently, ignoring the imminent danger to his grandson's digestive system.

"Me?" Roger sounded surprised. "I shouldn't think anyone cares whether I'm married or not, save myself—and you, perhaps," he added, a touch of humor in his voice. "I expect ye'd like the boy to have a name. Speaking of that"—he turned to me, the wind pulling long streamers of his hair loose and turning him into a wild black fiend in silhouette—"what *did* he end up being named? At the christening, I mean."

"Jeremiah Alexander Ian Fraser MacKenzie," I said, hoping I recalled it correctly. "Is that what you wanted?"

"Oh, I didn't mind so much what he was called," Roger said, edging gingerly round a large puddle that spread across the path. It had begun to sprinkle again; I could feel small chilly drops on my face, and see the dimpling of the water in the puddle where the firelight shone across it.

"I wanted Jeremiah, but I told Bree the other names were

up to her. She couldn't quite decide between John for John Grey, and—and Ian, for her cousin, but of course they're the same name in any case."

Again I noticed the faint hesitation, and I felt Jamie's arm stiffen slightly under my hand. Jamie's nephew Ian was a sore point—and fresh in everyone's mind, thanks to the note we had received from him the day before. That must be what had decided Brianna at last.

"Well, if it isna you and my daughter," Jamie pursued doggedly, "then who is it? Jocasta and Duncan? Or the folk from Bremerton?"

"You think someone's out specially to prevent the marriages tonight?" Roger seized the opportunity to talk about something other than Ian Murray. "You don't think it's just general dislike of Romish practices, then?"

"It might be, but it's not. If it were, why wait 'til now to arrest the priest? Wait a bit, Sassenach, I'll fetch ye over."

Jamie let go of my hand and stepped round the puddle, then reached back, grabbed me by the waist, and lifted me bodily across in a swish of skirts. The wet leaves slipped and squelched under my boots as he set me down, but I seized his arm for balance, righting myself.

"No," Jamie continued the conversation, turning back toward Roger. "Lillywhite and Anstruther have no great love of Catholics, I expect, but why stir up a stramash now, when the priest would be gone in the morning, anyway? Do they maybe think he'll corrupt all the God-fearing folk on the mountain before dawn if they dinna keep him in ward?"

Roger gave a short laugh at that.

"No, I suppose not. Is there anything else the priest was meant to do tonight, beyond performing marriages and baptisms?"

"Perhaps a few confessions," I said, pinching Jamie's arm. "Nothing else that I know of." I squeezed my thighs together, feeling an alarming shift in my intimate arrangements. Damn, one of the pins holding the cloth between my legs had come loose when Jamie lifted me. Had I lost it?

"I don't suppose they'd be trying to keep him from hearing someone's confession? Someone in particular, I mean?"

Roger sounded doubtful, but Jamie took the idea and turned it round in his hands, considering.

"They'd no objection to his hearing mine. And I shouldna think they'd care if a Catholic was in mortal sin or not, as by their lights, we're all damned anyway. But if they kent someone desperately needed confession, and they thought there was something to be gained by it . . ."

"That whoever it was might pay for access to the priest?" I asked skeptically. "Really, Jamie, these are Scots. I should imagine that if it were a question of paying out hard money for a priest, your Scottish Catholic murderer or adulterer would just say an Act of Contrition and hope for the best."

Jamie snorted slightly, and I saw the white mist of his breath purl round his head like candle smoke; it was getting colder.

"I daresay," he said dryly. "And if Lillywhite had any thought of setting up in the confession business, he's left it a bit late in the day to make much profit. But what if it wasna a matter of stopping someone's confession—but rather only of making sure that they overheard it?"

Roger uttered a pleased grunt, evidently thinking this a promising supposition.

"Blackmail? Aye, that's a thought," he said, with approval. Blood will out, I thought; Oxford-educated or not, there was little doubt that Roger was a Scot. There was a violent upheaval under his arm, followed by a wail from Jemmy. Roger glanced down.

"Oh, did ye drop your bawbee? Where's it gone, then?" He hoicked Jemmy up onto his shoulder like a bundle of laundry and squatted down, poking at the ground in search of the watch chain, which Jemmy had evidently hurled into the darkness.

"Blackmail? I think that's a trifle far-fetched," I objected, rubbing a hand under my nose, which had begun to drip. "You mean they might suspect that Farquard Campbell, for instance, had committed some dreadful crime, and if they knew about it for sure, they could hold him up about it? Isn't that awfully devious thinking? If you find a pin down there, Roger, it's mine."

"Well, Lillywhite and Anstruther are Englishmen, are they not?" Jamie said, with a delicate sarcasm that made Roger laugh. "Deviousness and double-dealing come naturally to that race, no, Sassenach?"

"Oh, rubbish," I said tolerantly. "Pot calling the kettle black isn't in it. Besides, they didn't try to overhear *your* confession."

"I havena got anything to be blackmailed for," Jamie pointed out, though it was perfectly obvious that he was only arguing for the fun of it.

"Even so," I began, but was interrupted by Jemmy, who was becoming increasingly restive, flinging himself to and fro with intermittent steam-whistle shrieks. Roger grunted, pinched something gingerly between his fingers, and stood up.

"Found your pin," he said. "No sign of the chain, though."

"Someone will find it in the morning," I said, raising my voice to be heard over the increasing racket. "Perhaps you'd better let me take him." I reached for the baby, and Roger surrendered his burden with a distinct air of relief—explained when I got a whiff of Jemmy's diaper.

"Not *again*?" I said. Apparently taking this as a personal reproach, he shut his eyes and started to howl like an air-raid siren.

"Where *is* Bree?" I asked, trying simultaneously to cradle him reassuringly and to keep him at a sanitary distance. "Ouch!" He seemed to have taken advantage of the darkness to grow a number of extra limbs, all of which were flailing or grabbing.

"Oh, she's just gone to run a wee errand," Roger said, with an air of vagueness that made Jamie turn his head sharply. The light caught him in profile, and I saw the thick red brows drawn down in suspicion. Fire gleamed off the long, straight bridge of his nose as he lifted it, questioning. Obviously, he smelled a rat. He turned toward me, one eyebrow lifted. Was I in on it?

"I haven't any idea," I assured him. "Here, I'm going across to McAllister's fire to borrow a clean clout. I'll see you at our camp in a bit."

Not waiting for an answer, I took a firm grasp on the baby and shuffled into the bushes, heading for the nearest campsite. Georgiana McAllister had newborn twins—I'd delivered them four days before—and was happy to provide me with both a clean diaper and a private bush behind which to effect my personal repairs. These accomplished, I chatted with her and admired the twins, all the while wondering about the recent revelations. Between Lieutenant Hayes and his proclamation, the machinations of Lillywhite and company, and whatever Bree and Roger were up to, the mountain seemed a perfect hotbed of conspiracy tonight.

I was pleased that we had managed the christening—in fact, I was surprised to find just how gratified I did feel about it—but I had to admit to a pang of distress over Brianna's canceled wedding. She hadn't said much about it, but I knew that both she and Roger had been looking forward very much to the blessing of their union. The firelight winked briefly, accusingly, off the gold ring on my left hand, and I mentally threw up my hands in Frank's direction.

*And just what do you expect me to do about it?* I demanded silently, while externally agreeing with Georgiana's opinion on the treatment of pinworms.

"Ma'am?" One of the older McAllister girls, who had volunteered to change Jemmy, interrupted the conversation, dangling a long, slimy object delicately between two fingers. "I found this gaud in the wean's cloot; is it maybe your man's?"

"Good grief!" I was shocked by the watch chain's reappearance, but a moment's rationality corrected my first alarmed impression that Jemmy had in fact swallowed the thing. It would take several hours for a solid object to make its way through even the most active infant's digestive tract; evidently he had merely dropped his toy down the front of his gown and it had come to rest in his diaper.

"Gie it here, lass." Mr. McAllister, catching sight of the watch chain, reached out and took it with a slight grimace. He pulled a large handkerchief from the waist of his breeks and wiped the object carefully, bringing to light the gleam of silver links and a small round fob, bearing some kind of seal.

I noted the fob with some grimness, and made a mental resolve to give Roger a proper bollocking about what he let Jemmy put in his mouth. Thank goodness it hadn't come off.

"Why, that's Mr. Caldwell's wee gaud, surely!" Georgiana leaned forward, peering over the heads of the twins she was nursing.

"Is it?" Her husband squinted at the object, and fumbled in his shirt for his spectacles.

"Aye, I'm sure it is! I saw it when he preached Sunday. The first of my pains was just comin' on," she explained, turning to me, "and I had to come away before he'd finished. He saw me turn to go, and must ha' thought he'd outstayed his welcome, for he pulled the watch from his pocket to have a wee keek, and I saw the glint from that bittie round thing on the chain."

"That's called a seal, *a nighean*," her husband informed her, having now settled a pair of half-moon spectacles firmly atop his nose, and turning the little metal emblem over between his fingers. "You're right, though, it's Mr. Caldwell's, for see?" A horny finger traced the outline of the figure on the seal: a mace, an open book, a bell, and a tree, standing on top of a fish with a ring in its mouth.

"That's from the University of Glasgow, that is. Mr. Caldwell's a scholar," he told me, blue eyes wide with awe. "Been to learn the preachin', and a fine job he makes of it.

"You did miss a fine finish, Georgie," he added, turning to his wife. "He went sae red in the face, talkin' of the Abomination of Desolation and the wrath at world's end, that I thought surely he'd have an apoplexy, and then what should we do? For he wouldna have Murray MacLeod to him, Murray bein' in the way of a heretic to Mr. Caldwell—he's New Light, Murray"—Mr. McAllister explained in an aside to me—"and Mrs. Fraser here a Papist, as well as bein' otherwise engaged wi' you and the bairns."

He leaned over and patted one of the twins gently on its bonneted head, but it paid no attention, blissfully absorbed in its suckling.

"Hmp. Well, Mr. Caldwell could ha' burst himself, for all I cared at the time," his wife said frankly. She hitched up her double armload and settled herself more comfortably. "And for mysel', I shouldna much mind if the midwife was a red Indian or English—oh, I do beg your pardon, Mrs. Fraser—so long as she kent how to catch a babe and stop the bleedin'."

I murmured something modest, brushing away Georgiana's apologies, in favor of finding out more about the watch chain's origins.

"Mr. Caldwell. He's a preacher, you say?" A certain suspicion was stirring in the back of my mind.

"Oh, aye, the best I've heard," Mr. McAllister assured me. "And I've heard 'em all. Now, Mr. Urmstone, he's a grand one for the sins, but he's on in years, and gone a bit hoarse now, so as ye need to be right up front to hear him—and that's a bit dangerous, ye ken, as it's the folk in front whose sins he's likely to start in upon. The New Light fella, though, he's nay much; no voice to him."

He dismissed the unfortunate preacher with the scorn of a connoisseur.

"Mr. Woodmason's all right; a bit stiff in his manner—an Englishman, aye?—but verra faithful about turning up for services, for all he's well stricken in years. Now, young Mr. Campbell from the Barbecue Church—"

"This wean's fair starved, ma'am," the girl holding Jemmy put in. Evidently so; he was red in the face and keening. "Will I give him a bit o' parritch, maybe?"

I gave a quick glance at the pot over the fire; it was bubbling, so likely well-cooked enough to kill most germs. I pulled out the horn spoon I carried in my pocket, which I could be sure was reasonably clean, and handed it to the girl.

"Thank you so much. Now, this Mr. Caldwell—he wouldn't by chance be a Presbyterian, would he?"

Mr. McAllister looked surprised, then beamed at my perceptivity.

"Why, so he is, indeed! Ye'll have heard of him, then, Mrs. Fraser?"

"I think perhaps my son-in-law is acquainted with him," I said, with a tinge of irony.

Georgiana laughed.

"I should say your grandson kens him, at least." She nodded at the chain, draped across her husband's broad palm.

"Bairns that size are just like magpies; they'll seize upon any shiny bawbee they see."

"So they do," I said slowly, staring at the silver links and their dangling fob. That put something of a different complexion on the matter. If Jemmy had picked Mr. Caldwell's pocket, it had obviously been done sometime before Jamie had arranged the impromptu christening.

But Bree and Roger had known about Father Kenneth's arrest and the possible cancelation of their wedding well before that; there would have been plenty of time for them to make other plans while Jamie and I were dealing with Rosamund, Ronnie, and the other assorted crises. Plenty of time for Roger to go and talk to Mr. Caldwell, the Presbyterian minister—with Jemmy along for the ride.

And as soon as Roger had confirmed the unlikelihood of the priest's performing any marriages tonight, Brianna had disappeared on a vague "errand." Well, if Father Kenneth had wanted to interview a Presbyterian groom before marrying him, I supposed Mr. Caldwell might be allowed the same privilege with a prospective Papist bride.

Jemmy was devouring porridge with the single-mindedness of a starving piranha; we couldn't leave quite yet. That was just as well, I thought; let Brianna break the news to her father that she would have her wedding after all—priest or no priest.

I spread out my skirt to dry the damp hem, and the firelight glowed from both my rings. A strong disposition to laugh bubbled up inside me, at the thought of what Jamie would say when he found out, but I suppressed it, not wanting to explain my amusement to the McAllisters.

"Shall I take that?" I said instead to Mr. McAllister, with a nod toward the watch chain. "I think perhaps I shall be seeing Mr. Caldwell a little later."

# HAPPY THE BRIDE
# THE MOON SHINES ON

W E WERE LUCKY. The rain held off, and shredding clouds revealed a silver moon, rising lopsided but luminous over the slope of Black Mountain; suitable illumination for an intimate family wedding.

I had met David Caldwell, though I hadn't recalled it until I saw him; a small but immensely personable gentleman, very tidy in his dress, despite camping in the open for a week. Jamie knew him, too, and respected him. That didn't prevent a certain tightness of expression as the minister came into the firelight, his worn prayer book clasped in his hands, but I nudged Jamie warningly, and he at once altered his expression to one of inscrutability.

I saw Roger glance once in our direction, then turn back to Bree. There might have been a slight smile at the corner of his mouth, or it could have been only the effect of the shadows. Jamie exhaled strongly through his nose, and I nudged him again.

"You had your way over the baptism," I whispered. He lifted his chin slightly. Brianna glanced in our direction, looking slightly anxious.

"I havena said a word, have I?"

"It's a perfectly respectable Christian marriage."

"Did I say it was not?"

"Then look *happy*, damn you!" I hissed. He exhaled once more, and assumed an expression of benevolence one degree short of outright imbecility.

"Better?" he asked, teeth clenched in a genial smile. I saw

Duncan Innes turn casually toward us, start, and turn hastily away, murmuring something to Jocasta, who stood near the fire, white hair shining, and a blindfold over her damaged eyes to shield them from the light. Ulysses, standing behind her, had in fact put on his wig in honor of the ceremony; it was all I could see of him in the darkness, hanging apparently disembodied in the air above her shoulder. As I watched, it turned sideways, toward us, and I caught the faint shine of eyes beneath it.

"Who that, *Grand-mère*?"

Germain, escaped as usual from parental custody, popped up near my feet, pointing curiously at the Reverend Caldwell.

"That's a minister, darling. Auntie Bree and Uncle Roger are getting married."

*"C'est quoĩ minster?"*

I drew a deep breath, but Jamie beat me to it.

"It's a sort of priest, but not a proper priest."

"Bad priest?" Germain viewed the Reverend Caldwell with substantially more interest.

"No, no," I said. "He's not a bad priest at all. It's only that . . . well, you see, we're Catholics, and Catholics have priests, but Uncle Roger is a Presbyterian—"

"That's a heretic," Jamie put in helpfully.

"It is *not* a heretic, darling, *Grand-père* is being funny— or thinks he is. Presbyterians are . . ."

Germain was paying no attention to my explanation, but instead had tilted his head back, viewing Jamie with fascination.

"Why *Grand-père* is making faces?"

"We're verra happy," Jamie explained, expression still fixed in a rictus of amiability.

"Oh." Germain at once stretched his own extraordinarily mobile face into a crude facsimile of the same expression—a jack-o'-lantern grin, teeth clenched and eyes popping. "Like this?"

"Yes, darling," I said, in a marked tone. "*Just* like that."

Marsali looked at us, blinked, and tugged at Fergus's sleeve. He turned, squinting at us.

"Look happy, Papa!" Germain pointed to his gigantic smile. "See?"

Fergus's mouth twitched, as he glanced from his offspring to Jamie. His face went blank for a moment, then adjusted itself into an enormous smile of white-toothed insincerity. Marsali kicked him in the ankle. He winced, but the smile didn't waver.

Brianna and Roger were having a last-minute conference with Reverend Caldwell, on the other side of the fire. Brianna turned from this, brushing back her loose hair, saw the phalanx of grinning faces, and stared, her mouth slightly open. Her eyes went to me; I shrugged helplessly.

Her lips pressed tight together, but curved upward irrepressibly. Her shoulders shook with suppressed laughter. I felt Jamie quiver next to me.

Reverend Caldwell stepped forward, a finger in his book at the proper place, put his spectacles on his nose, and smiled genially at the assemblage, blinking only slightly when he encountered the row of leering countenances.

He coughed, and opened his Book of Common Worship.

"Dearly beloved, we are assembled here in the presence of God . . ."

I felt Jamie relax slightly, as the words went on, evidencing unfamiliarity, perhaps, but no great peculiarities. I supposed that he had in fact never taken part in a Protestant ceremony before—unless one counted the impromptu baptism Roger himself had conducted among the Mohawk. I closed my eyes and sent a brief prayer upward for Young Ian, as I did whenever I thought of him.

"Let us therefore reverently remember that God has established and sanctified marriage, for the welfare and happiness of mankind . . ."

Opening them, I saw that all eyes now were focused on Roger and Brianna, who stood facing each other, hands entwined. They were a handsome pair, nearly of a height, she bright and he dark, like a photograph and its negative. Their faces were nothing alike, and yet both had the bold bones and clean curves that were their joint legacy from the clan MacKenzie.

I glanced across the fire to see the same echo of bone and flesh in Jocasta, tall and handsome, her blind face turned in absorption toward the sound of the minister's voice. As I watched, I saw her hand reach out and rest on Duncan's arm, the long white fingers gently squeeze. The Reverend Caldwell had kindly offered to perform their marriage as well, but Jocasta had refused, wishing to wait instead for a Catholic ceremony.

"We are in no great hurry, after all, are we, my dear?" she had asked Duncan, turning toward him with an outward exhibition of deference that fooled no one. Still, I thought that Duncan had seemed relieved, rather than disappointed, by the postponement of his own wedding.

"By His apostles, He has instructed those who enter into this relation to cherish a mutual esteem and love . . ."

Duncan had put a hand over Jocasta's, with a surprising air of tenderness. That marriage would not be one of love, I thought, but mutual esteem—yes, I thought there was that.

"I charge you both, before the great God, the Searcher of all hearts, that if either of you know any reason why ye may not lawfully be joined together in marriage, ye do now confess it. For be ye well assured that if any persons are joined together otherwise than as God's Word allows, their union is not blessed by Him."

Reverend Caldwell paused, glancing warningly back and forth between Roger and Brianna. Roger shook his head slightly, his eyes fixed on Bree's face. She smiled faintly in response, and the Reverend cleared his throat and continued.

The air of muted hilarity around the fire had subsided; there was no sound but the Reverend's quiet voice and the crackle of the flames.

"Roger Jeremiah, wilt thou have this Woman to be thy wife, and wilt thou pledge thy troth to her, in all love and honor, in all duty and service, in all faith and tenderness, to live with her, and cherish her, according to the ordinance of God, in the holy bond of marriage?"

"I will," Roger said, his voice deep and husky.

I heard a deep sigh to my right, and saw Marsali lean her head on Fergus's shoulder, a dreamy look on her face. He turned his head and kissed her brow, then leaned his own dark head against the whiteness of her kerch.

"I will," Brianna said clearly, lifting her chin and looking up into Roger's face, in response to the minister's question.

Mr. Caldwell looked benevolently round the circle, firelight glinting on his spectacles.

"Who giveth this Woman to be married to this Man?"

There was the briefest of pauses, and I felt Jamie jerk slightly, taken by surprise. I squeezed his arm, and saw the firelight gleam on the gold ring on my hand.

"Oh. I do, to be sure!" he said. Brianna turned her head and smiled at him, her eyes dark with love. He gave her back the smile, then blinked, clearing his throat, and squeezed my hand hard.

I felt a slight tightening of the throat myself, as they spoke their vows, remembering both of my own weddings. And Jocasta? I wondered. She had been married three times; what echoes of the past did she hear in these words?

"I, Roger Jeremiah, take thee, Brianna Ellen, to be my wedded wife . . ."

The light of memory shone on most of the faces around the fire. The Bugs stood close together, looking at each other with identical gazes of soft devotion. Mr. Wemyss, standing by his daughter, bowed his head and closed his eyes, a look of mingled joy and sadness on his face, no doubt thinking of his own wife, dead these many years.

"In plenty and in want . . ."

"In joy and in sorrow . . ."

"In sickness and in health . . ."

Lizzie's face was rapt, eyes wide at the mystery being carried out before her. How soon might it be her turn, to stand before witnesses and make such awesome promises?

Jamie reached across and took my right hand in his, his fingers linking with mine, and the silver of my ring shone red in the glow of the flames. I looked up into his face and saw the promise spoken in his eyes, as it was in mine.

"As long as we both shall live."

# THE FLAMES OF
# DECLARATION

THE GREAT FIRE BELOW was blazing, damp
wood snapping with cracks that rang like pistol shots
against the mountainside—a distant gunfire, though,
and little noticed through the noise of merrymaking.

While she had elected not to be married by the Reverend
Caldwell, Jocasta had nonetheless generously provided a lavish wedding feast in honor of Roger and Brianna's nuptials.
Wine, ale, and whisky flowed like water under the aegis of
Ulysses, whose white wig bobbed through the mob round
our family campfire, ubiquitous as a moth round a candle
flame.

Despite the chill damp and the clouds that had regathered
overhead, at least half the Gathering was here, dancing to the
music of fiddle and mouth organ, descending locustlike on
the groaning tables of delicacies, and drinking the health of
the newlyweds—and the eventually-to-be-wed—with so
much enthusiasm that if all such wishes were to take effect,
Roger, Bree, Jocasta, and Duncan would each live to be a
thousand, at least.

I thought I might be good for a hundred years or so, myself. I was feeling no pain; nothing but an encompassing
sense of giddy well-being, and a pleasant sense of impending
dissolution.

At one side of the fire, Roger was playing a borrowed guitar, serenading Bree before a rapt circle of listeners. Closer,
Jamie sat on a log with Duncan and his aunt, talking with
friends.

"Madam?" Ulysses materialized at my elbow, tray in

hand and resplendent in livery, behaving as though he were in the parlor at River Run, rather than on a soggy mountainside.

"Thank you." I accepted a pewter cup full of something, and discovered it to be brandy. Fairly good brandy, too. I took a small sip and let it percolate through my sinuses. Before I could absorb much more of it, though, I became conscious of a sudden lull in the surrounding gaiety.

Jamie glanced around the circle, gathering eyes, then stood and held out his arm to me. I was a little surprised, but hastily replaced the cup on Ulysses's tray, smoothed back my hair, tucked in my kerchief, and went to take my place at his side.

*"Thig a seo, a bhean uasa,"* he said, smiling at me. Come, lady. He turned and raised his chin, summoning the others. Roger put down his guitar at once, covering it carefully with a canvas, then held out a hand to Bree.

*"Thig a seo, a bhean,"* he said, grinning. With a look of surprise, she got to her feet, Jemmy in her arms.

Jamie stood still, waiting, and little by little, the others rose, brushing away pine needles and sand from hems and seats, laughing and murmuring in puzzlement. The dancers, too, paused in their whirling, and came to see what was to do, the fiddle music dying away in the rustle of curiosity.

Jamie led me down the dark trail toward the leaping flames of the great bonfire below, the others following in a murmur of speculation. At the end of the main clearing he stopped and waited. Dark figures flitted through the shadows; a man's shape stood in silhouette before the fire, arm raised.

"The Menzies are here!" the man called, and flung the branch that he carried into the fire. Faint cheers went up, from those of his clan and sept within hearing.

Another took his place—MacBean—and another—Ogilvie. Then it was our turn.

Jamie walked forward alone, into the light of the leaping flames. The fire was built of oak and pinewood, and it burned higher than a tall man, tongues of transparent yellow so pure and ardent as almost to burn white against the blackened sky. The light of it shone on his upturned face, on his head and shoulders, and threw a long shadow that stretched halfway across the open ground behind him.

"We are gathered here to welcome old friends," he said in Gaelic. "And meet new ones—in hopes that they may join us in forging a new life in this new country."

His voice was deep and carrying; the last scraps of conversation ceased as the folk pushing and crowding around the fire hushed and craned to listen.

"We have all suffered much hardship on the road here." He turned slowly, looking from face to face around the fire. Many of the men of Ardsmuir were here: I saw the Lindsay brothers, homely as a trio of toads; Ronnie Sinclair's fox-eyed face, ginger hair slicked up in horns; the Roman-coin features of Robin McGillivray. All looked out from the shadows, ridge of brow and bridge of nose shining in the glow, each face crossed by fire.

Under the influence of brandy and emotion, I could easily see too the ranks of ghosts who stood behind them; the families and friends who remained still in Scotland, whether on the earth . . . or under it.

Jamie's own face was lined with shadow, the firelight showing the mark of time and struggle on his flesh as wind and rain mark stone.

"Many of us died in battle," he said, his voice scarcely audible above the rustle of the fire. "Many died of burning. Many of us starved. Many died at sea, many died of wounds and illness." He paused. "Many died of sorrow."

His eyes looked beyond the firelit circle for a moment, and I thought perhaps he was searching for the face of Abel MacLennan. He lifted his cup then, and held it high in salute for a moment.

*"Slàinte!"* murmured a dozen voices, rising like the wind.

*"Slàinte!"* he echoed them—then tipped the cup, so that a little of the brandy fell into the flames, where it hissed and burned blue for an instant's time.

He lowered the cup, and paused for a moment, head bent. He lifted his head then, and raised the cup toward Archie Hayes, who stood across the fire from him, round face unreadable, fire sparking from his silver gorget and his father's brooch.

"While we mourn the loss of those who died, we must also pay tribute to you who fought and suffered with equal valor—and survived."

*"Slàinte!"* came the salute, louder this time with the rumble of male voices.

Jamie closed his eyes for an instant, then opened them, looking toward Brianna, who stood with Lizzie and Marsali, Jemmy in her arms. The rawness and strength of his features stood out by contrast with the round-faced innocence of the children, the gentleness of the young mothers—though even in their delicacy, I thought, the firelight showed the seams of Scottish granite in their bones.

"We pay tribute to our women," he said, lifting the cup in turn to Brianna, to Marsali, and then, turning, to me. A brief smile touched his lips. "For they are our strength. And our revenge upon our enemies will be at the last the revenge of the cradle. *Slàinte!*"

Amid the shouts of the crowd, he drained the wooden cup, and threw it into the fire, where it lay dark and round for a moment, then burst all at once into brilliant flame.

*"Thig a seo!"* he called, putting out his right hand to me. *"Thig a seo, a Shorcha, nighean Eanruig, neart mo chridhe."* Come to me, he said. *Come to me, Claire, daughter of Henry, strength of my heart.* Scarcely feeling my feet or those I stumbled over, I made my way to him, and clasped his hand, his grip cold but strong on my fingers.

I saw him turn his head; was he looking for Bree? But no—he stretched out his other hand toward Roger.

*"Seas ri mo làmh, Roger an t'òranaiche, mac Jeremiah MacChoinneich!"* *Stand by my hand, Roger the singer, son of Jeremiah MacKenzie.* Roger stood stock-still for a moment, eyes dark on Jamie, then moved toward him, like one sleepwalking. The crowd was still excited, but the shouting had died down, and people craned to hear what was said.

"Stand by me in battle," he said in Gaelic, his eyes fixed on Roger, left hand extended. He spoke slowly and clearly, to be sure of understanding. "Be a shield for my family—and for yours, son of my house."

Roger's expression seemed suddenly to dissolve, like a

face seen in water when a stone is tossed into it. Then it solidified once more, and he clasped Jamie's hand, squeezing hard.

Jamie turned to the crowd then, and began the calling. This was something I had seen him do before, many years before, in Scotland. A formal invitation and identification of tenants by a laird, it was a small ceremony often done on a quarter-day or after the harvest. Faces lighted here and there with recognition; many of the Highland Scots knew the custom, though they would not have seen it in this land before tonight.

"Come to me, Geordie Chisholm, son of Walter, son of Connaught the Red!"

"Stand with me, *a Choinnich*, Evan, Murdo, you sons of Alexander Lindsay of the Glen!"

"Come to my side, Joseph Wemyss, son of Donald, son of Robert!" I smiled to see Mr. Wemyss, flustered but terribly pleased at this public inclusion, make his way toward us, head proudly raised, fair hair flying wild in the wind of the great fire.

"Stand by me, Josiah the hunter!"

Was Josiah Beardsley here? Yes, he was; a slight, dark form slid out of the shadows, to take up a shy place in the group near Jamie. I caught his eye and smiled at him; he looked hastily away, but a small, embarrassed smile clung to his lips, as though he had forgotten it was there.

It was an impressive group by the time he had finished— nearly forty men, gathered shoulder-close and flushed as much with pride as with whisky. I saw Roger exchange a long look with Brianna, who was beaming across the fire at him. She bènt her head to whisper something to Jemmy, who was submerged in his blankets, half-asleep in her arms. She picked up one of his wee paws and waved it limply toward Roger, who laughed.

"... *Air mo mhionnan...*" Distracted, I had missed Jamie's final statement, catching only the last few words. Whatever he had said met with approval, though; there was a low rumble of solemn assent from the men around us, and a moment's silence.

Then he let go my hand, stooped, and picked up a branch from the ground. Lighting this, he held it aloft, then threw the blazing brand high into the air. It tumbled end over end as it fell straight down, into the heart of the fire.

"The Frasers of the Ridge are here!" he bellowed, and the clearing erupted in a massive cheer.

As we made our way back up the slope to resume the interrupted festivities, I found myself next to Roger, who was humming something cheerful under his breath. I put a hand on his sleeve, and he looked down at me, smiling.

"Congratulations," I said, smiling back. "Welcome to the family—son of the house."

He grinned enormously.

"Thanks," he said. "Mum."

We came to a level spot, and walked side by side for a moment, not speaking. Then he said, in a quite different tone, "That was . . . something quite special, wasn't it?"

I didn't know whether he meant historically special, or special in personal terms. In either case, he was right, and I nodded.

"I didn't catch all of the last bit, though," I said. "And I don't know what *earbsachd* means—do you?"

"Oh . . . aye. I know." It was quite dark here between the fires; I could see no more of him than a darker smudge against the black of shrub and tree. There was an odd note in his voice, though. He cleared his throat.

"It's an oath—of a sort. He—Jamie—he swore an oath to us, to his family and tenants. Support, protection, that kind of thing."

"Oh, yes?" I said, mildly puzzled. "What do you mean, 'of a sort'?"

"Ah, well." He was silent for a moment, evidently marshaling his words. "It means a word of honor, rather than just an oath," he said carefully. *"Earbsachd"*—he pronounced it YARB-sochk—"was once said to be the distinguishing characteristic of the MacCrimmons of Skye, and meant basically that their word once given must unfailingly be acted upon at no matter what cost. If a MacCrimmon said he would do something"—he paused and drew breath—"he would do it, though he should burn to death in the doing."

His hand came up under my elbow, surprisingly firm.

"Here," he said quietly. "Let me help; it's slippery under-foot."

# ON THE NIGHT THAT OUR
# WEDDING IS ON US

**W**ILL YOU SING FOR ME, Roger?"

She stood in the opening of the borrowed tent, facing outward. From the back, he could see no more than her silhouette against the gray of the clouded sky, her long hair drifting in the rainy wind. She had worn it unbound to be married—maiden's hair, though she had a child.

It was cold tonight, quite different from that first night together, that hot, gorgeous night that had ended in anger and betrayal. Months of other nights lay between that one and this—months of loneliness, months of joy. And yet his heart beat as fast now as it had on their first wedding night.

"I always sing for you, hen." He came behind her, drew her back against him, so that her head rested on his shoulder, her hair cool and live against his face. His arm curled round her waist, holding her secure. He bent his head, nuzzling for the curve of her ear.

"No matter what," he whispered, "no matter where. No matter whether you're there to hear or not—I'll always sing for you."

She turned into his arms then, with a small hum of content in her throat, and her mouth found his, tasting of barbecued meat and spiced wine.

The rain pattered on the canvas above, and the cold of late autumn curled up from the ground around their feet. The first time, the air had smelled of hops and mudflats; their bower had had the earthy tang of hay and donkeys. Now the air was live with pine and juniper, spiced with the smoke of smoldering fires—and the faint, sweet note of baby shit.

And yet she was once more dark and light in his arms, her face hidden, her body gleaming. Then she had been moist and molten, humid with the summer. Now her flesh was cool as marble, save where he touched it—and yet the summer lived still in the palm of his hand where he touched her, sweet and slick, ripe with the secrets of a hot, dark night. It was right, he thought, that these vows should have been spoken as the first ones had, out of doors, part of wind and earth, fire and water.

"I love you," she murmured against his mouth, and he seized her lip between his teeth, too moved to speak the words in reply just yet.

There had been words between them then, as there had been words tonight. The words were the same, and he had meant them the first time no less than he did now. Yet it *was* different.

The first time he had spoken them to her alone, and while he had done so in the sight of God, God had been discreet, hovering well in the background, face turned away from their nakedness.

Tonight he said them in the blaze of firelight, before the face of God and the world, her people and his. His heart had been hers, and whatever else he had—but now there was no question of him and her, his and hers. The vows were given, his ring put on her finger, the bond both made and witnessed. They were one body.

One hand of their joint organism crushed a breast a little too hard, and one throat made a small sound of discomfort. She drew back from him a little, and he felt rather than saw her grimace. The air came cold between them and his own skin felt suddenly raw, exposed, as though he had been severed from her with a knife.

"I need—" she said, and touched her breast, not finishing. "Just a minute, okay?"

Claire had fed the child while Brianna went to make her overtures to Reverend Caldwell. Bursting with porridge and stewed peaches, Jemmy could scarcely be roused to suckle briefly before relapsing into somnolence and being taken away by Lizzie, his wee round belly tight as a drum. That was as well for their privacy—drugged into such a gluttonous stupor, it was unlikely the bairn would wake before dawn. The price of it, though, was the unused milk.

No one living in the same house with a nursing mother was likely to be unaware of her breasts, let alone her husband. They had a life of their own, those breasts. They changed size from hour to hour, for the one thing, swelling from their normal soft globes into great round hard bubbles that gave him the eerie feeling that if he touched one it would burst.

Now and then, one *did* burst, or at least gave that impression. The ridge of soft flesh would rise like kneaded bread, slowly but surely pushing above the edge of Brianna's bodice. Then suddenly there would be a big, wet circle on the cloth, appearing magically, as though some invisible person had thrown a snowball at her. Or two snowballs—for what one breast did, its fellow rushed at once to follow suit.

Sometimes the Heavenly Twins were foiled, though; Jemmy drained one side, but inconsiderately fell asleep before performing the same service for the other. This left his mother gritting her teeth, gingerly taking the swollen orb in the palm of her hand, pressing the edge of a pewter cup just under the nipple to catch the spray and dribble as she eased the aching fullness, enough to sleep herself.

She was doing it now; modestly turned away from him, an arisaid gathered round her shoulders against the chill. He could hear the hiss of the milk, a tiny chime against the metal.

He was reluctant to drown the sound, which he found erotic, but nonetheless picked up the guitar, and put his thumb to the strings, his hand on the frets. He didn't strum or strike chords, but plucked single notes, small voices to echo his own, the thrum of one string ringing through the chanted line.

A love song, to be sure. One of the very old ones, in the

Gaelic. Even if she didn't know all the words, he thought she'd take the sense of it.

> *"On the night that our wedding is on us,*
> *I will come leaping to thee with gifts,*
> *On the night that our wedding is on us . . ."*

He closed his eyes, seeing in memory what the night now hid. Her nipples were the color of ripe plums and the size of ripe cherries, and Roger had a vivid mental picture of how one would feel in his mouth. He had suckled them once, long before—before the coming of Jemmy—but no more.

> *"You will get a hundred silver salmon . . .*
> *A hundred badger skins . . ."*

She never asked him not to, never turned away—and yet he could tell by the faint intake of her breath that, often, she was bracing herself not to flinch when he touched her breasts.

Was it only tenderness? he wondered. Did she not trust him to be gentle?

He shied away from the thought, drowning it in a small cascade of notes, liquid as a waterfall.

*It might not be you*, whispered the voice, stubbornly refusing to be distracted. *Perhaps it was* him—*something that he did to her.*

*Fuck. Off*, he thought succinctly to the voice, marking each word with a sharp-plucked string. Stephen Bonnet would have no place in their wedding bed. None.

He laid a hand on the strings to silence them briefly, and as she slid the arisaid from her shoulders, began again, this time in English. A special song, too—one for the two of them alone. He didn't know whether anyone else might hear, but it made no difference if they did. She stood and slid the shift from her shoulders as his fingers touched the quiet opening of the Beatles' "Yesterday."

He heard her laugh, once, then sigh, and the linen whispered against her skin as it fell.

She came naked behind him as the soft melancholy

yearning of the song filled the dark. Her hand stroked his hair, gathered it tight at the nape of his neck. She swayed, and he felt her press against his back, her breasts soft now, yielding and warm through his shirt, her breath tickling his ear. Her hand rested on his shoulder briefly, then slid down inside his shirt, fingers cool on his chest. He could feel the warm hard metal of her ring on his skin, and felt a surge of possession that pulsed through him like a gulp of whisky, a heat suffusing his flesh.

He ached to turn and take hold of her, but pushed the urge down, heightening anticipation. He bent his head closer to the strings, and sang until all thought left him and there was nothing left but his body and hers. He could not have said when her hand closed over his on the frets, and he rose and turned to her, still filled with the music and his love, soft and strong and pure in the dark.

SHE LAY QUIET in the dark, feeling the thunder of her heart boom slowly in her ears. The throb of it echoed in the pulse of her neck, her wrists, her breasts, her womb. She had lost track of her boundaries; slowly the sense of limbs and digits, head and trunk, of space occupied, returned. She moved the single finger glued between her legs, and felt the last of the tingling shocks run down her thighs as it slid free.

She drew breath slowly, listening.

His breath still came in long, regular exhalations; thank God, he hadn't wakened. She had been careful, moving no more than a fingertip, but the final jolt of climax had struck her so hard that her hips jerked as her belly quivered and convulsed, her heels digging into the pallet with a loud rustling of straw.

He'd had a very long day—they all had. Even so, she could still hear faint sounds of festivity on the mountainside around them. The chance to celebrate like this came so rarely that no one would let something so inconsequential as rain, cold, or tiredness keep them from the revels.

She herself felt like a puddle of liquid mercury; soft and

heavy, shimmering with each heartbeat. The effort of moving was unthinkable; but her final convulsion had pulled the quilt off his shoulders, and the skin of his back lay smooth and bare, dark by contrast with the pale cloth. The pocket of warmth around her was snug and perfect, but she couldn't luxuriate while he lay exposed to the chilly midnight air like that. Tendrils of fog had crept under the tent flap and hung ghostlike and clammy all around them; she could see the faint gleam of moisture on the high curve of his cheekbone.

She summoned back the notion of bones and muscles, found a motor neuron in working order, and sternly ordered it to fire. Embodied once more, she rolled onto her side, facing him, and gently pulled the quilt up around his ears. He stirred and murmured something; she stroked his tumbled black hair and he smiled faintly, eyelids half-opening in the blank stare of one who sees dreams. They dropped again and he took a long, sighing breath and fell back asleep.

"I love you," she whispered, filled with tenderness.

She stroked his back lightly, loving the feel of his flat shoulder blades through the quilt, the solid knob of bone at the nape of his neck, and the long, smooth groove that ran down the center of his spine to arch into the swell of his buttocks. A cold breeze rippled the tiny hairs of her arm, and she pulled it back under the covers, letting her hand rest lightly on Roger's bottom.

The feel of it was no novelty, but thrilled her just the same, with its perfect warm roundness, its coarse curly hair. A faint echo of her solitary joy encouraged her to do it again, and her free hand crept between her legs, but sheer exhaustion stayed her, limp fingers cupped on the swollen flesh, one languid finger tracing the slickness.

She'd hoped it would be different tonight. Without the ever-present danger of waking Jemmy, free to take as much time as they wanted, and riding the waves of emotion from their exchange of vows, she'd thought . . . but it was the same.

It wasn't that she wasn't aroused; quite the contrary. Every movement, each touch, imprinted itself in the nerves of her skin, the crevices of mouth and memory, drowning her with scent, branding her with sensation. But no matter how wonderful the lovemaking, there remained some odd sense of distance, some barrier that she couldn't penetrate.

And so once more she found herself lying beside him as he slept, reliving in memory each moment of the passion they had just shared—and able in memory at last to yield to it.

Perhaps it was that she loved him too much, she thought, was too mindful of his pleasure to take her own. The satisfaction she felt when he lost himself, gasping and moaning in her arms, was far greater than the simple physical pleasure of climax. And yet, there was something darker under that; a peculiar sense of triumph, as though she had won some undeclared and unacknowledged contest between them.

She sighed and butted her forehead against the curve of his shoulder, enjoying the reek of him—a smell of strong and bitter musk, like pennyroyal.

The thought of herbs reminded her, and she reached down again, cautiously so as not to waken him, and slid one slippery finger deep inside to check. No, it was all right; the slip of sponge soaked with tansy oil was still in place, its fragile, pungent presence safeguarding the entrance to her womb.

She moved closer, and he moved unconsciously, his body half-turning to accommodate her, his warmth at once enclosing her, comforting her. His hand groped like a bird flying blind, skimming her hip, her soft belly, in search of a resting place. She seized it in both hands and folded it, secure beneath her chin. His hand curled over hers; she kissed one large, rough knuckle and he sighed deeply, his hand relaxing.

The sounds of revelry on the mountain had faded, as the dancers tired, and the musicians grew hoarse and weary. The rain began again, pattering on the canvas overhead, and gray mist touched her face with cool damp fingers. The smell of wet canvas made her think of camping trips as a child with her father, with their mingled sensations of excitement and safety, and she nestled deeper into the curve of Roger's body, feeling a similar sense of comfort and anticipation.

It was early days, she thought. They had all their lives before them. The time of surrender would surely come.

# 17

# WATCH FIRE

FROM WHERE THEY LAY, he could see down through a gap in the rocks, all the way to the watch fire that burned before Hayes's tent. The great fire of the Gathering had burned itself to embers, the glow of it faint memory of the towering flames of declaration, but the smaller fire burned steady as a star against the cold night. Now and then a dark, kilted figure rose to tend it, stood stark for a moment against the brightness, then faded back again into the night.

He was faintly conscious of the racing clouds that dimmed the moon, the heavy flutter of the canvas overhead, and the rock-black shadows of the mountain slope, but he had no eyes for anything save the fire below, and the white patch of the tent behind it, shapeless as a ghost.

He had slowed his breath, relaxed the muscles of arms and chest, back, buttocks, legs. Not in an attempt to sleep; sleep was far from him, and he had no mind to seek it.

Nor was it an attempt to fool Claire into thinking he slept. So close against his body, so close to his mind as she was, she would know him wakeful. No, it was only a signal to her; an acknowledged pretense that freed her from any need to pay heed to him. She might sleep, knowing him occupied within the walnut shell of his mind, having no immediate demand to make of her.

Few slept on the mountain tonight, he thought. The sound of the wind masked the murmur of voices, the shuffle of movement, but his hunter's senses registered a dozen small stirrings, identifying things half-heard, putting names to moving shadows. A scrape of shoe leather on rock, the flap of a blanket shaken out. That would be Hobson and Fowles, making a quiet departure alone in the dark, fearful of waiting for the morning, lest they be betrayed in the night.

A few notes of music came down on a gust of wind from above; concertina and fiddle. Jocasta's slaves, unwilling to surrender this rare celebration to the needs of sleep or the imperatives of weather.

An infant's thin wail. Wee Jemmy? No, from behind. Tiny Joan, then, and Marsali's voice, low and sweet, singing in French.

"*. . . Alouette, gentille alouette . . .*"

There, a sound he had expected; footsteps passing on the far side of the rocks that bordered his family's sanctuary. Quick and light, headed downhill. He waited, eyes open, and in a few moments heard the faint hail of a sentry near the tent. No figure showed in the firelight below, but the tent flap beyond it stirred, gaped open, then fell unbroken.

As he had thought, then; sentiment lay strong against the rioters. It was not held a betrayal of friends, but rather the necessary giving up of criminals for the protection of those who chose to live by law. It might be reluctant—the witnesses had waited for the dark—but not secretive.

"*. . . je te plumerai la tête . . .*"

It occurred to him to wonder why the songs sung to bairns were so often gruesome, and no thought given to the words they took in with their mothers' milk. The music of the songs was no more to him than tuneless chanting—perhaps that was why he paid more mind than most to the words.

Even Brianna, who came from what was presumably a more peaceable time, sang songs of fearsome death and tragic loss to wee Jem, all with a look on her face as tender as the Virgin nursing the Christ Child. That verse about the miner's daughter who drowned amidst her ducklings . . .

It occurred to him perversely to wonder what awful things the Blessed Mother might have counted in her own repertoire of cradle songs; judging from the Bible, the Holy Land had been no more peaceful than France or Scotland.

He would have crossed himself in penance for the notion, but Claire was lying on his right arm.

"Were they wrong?" Claire's voice came softly from beneath his chin, startling him.

"Who?" He bent his head to hers, and kissed the thick softness of her curls. Her hair smelt of woodsmoke and the sharp, clear tang of juniper berries.

"The men in Hillsborough."

"Aye, I think so."

"What would you have done?"

He sighed, moved one shoulder in a shrug.

"Can I say? Aye, if it was me that was cheated, and no hope of redress, I might have laid hands on the man who'd done it. But what was done there—ye heard it. Houses torn down and set afire, men dragged out and beaten senseless only for cause of the office they held . . . no, Sassenach. I canna say what I might have done—but not that."

She turned her head a little, so he saw the high curve of her cheekbone, rimmed in light, and the flexing of the muscle that ran in front of her ear as she smiled.

"I didn't think you would. Can't see you as part of a mob."

He kissed her ear, not to reply directly. *He* could see himself as part of a mob, all too easily. That was what frightened him. He knew much too well the strength of it.

One Highlander was a warrior, but the mightiest man was only a man. It was the madness that took men together that had ruled the glens for a thousand years; that thrill of the blood, when you heard the shrieks of your companions, felt the strength of the whole bear you up like wings, and knew immortality—for if you should fall of yourself, still you would be carried on, your spirit shrieking in the mouths of those who ran beside you. It was only later, when the blood lay cold in limp veins, and deaf ears heard the women weeping . . .

"And if it wasn't a man who cheated you? If it was the Crown, or the Court? No one person, I mean, but an institution."

He knew where she meant to lead him. He tightened his arm around her, her breath warm on the knuckles of his hand, curled just under her chin.

"It isna that. Not here. Not now." The rioters had lashed out in response to the crimes of men, of individuals; the price of those crimes might be paid in blood, but not requited by war—not yet.

"It isn't," she said quietly. "But it will be."

"Not now," he said again.

The piece of paper was safely hidden in his saddlebag, its damnable summons concealed. He must deal with it, and soon, but for tonight he would pretend it wasn't there. One final night of peace, with his wife in his arms, his family around him.

Another shadow by the fire. Another hail by the sentry, one more to pass through the traitor's gate.

"And are *they* wrong?" A slight tilt of her head toward the tent below. "The ones going to turn in their acquaintances?"

"Aye," he said, after a moment. "They're wrong as well."

A mob might rule, but it was single men would pay the price for what was done. Part of the price was the breaking of trust, the turning of neighbor against neighbor, fear a noose squeezing tight until there was no longer any breath of mercy or forgiveness.

It had come on to rain; the light spatter of drops on the canvas overhead turned to a regular thrum, and the air grew live with the rush of water. It was a winter storm; no lightning lit the sky, and the looming mountains were invisible.

He held Claire close, curving his free hand low over her belly. She sighed, a small sound of pain in it, and settled herself, her arse nesting round as an egg in the cup of his thighs. He could feel the melting begin as she relaxed, that odd merging of his flesh with hers.

At first it had happened only when he took her, and only at the last. Then sooner and sooner, until her hand upon him was both invitation and completion, a surrender inevitable, offered and accepted. He had resisted now and then, only to be sure he could, suddenly fearful of the loss of himself. He had thought it a treacherous passion, like the one that swept a mob of men, linking them in mindless fury.

Now he trusted it was right, though. The Bible did say it, *Thou shalt be one flesh*, and *What God has joined together, let no man put asunder*.

He had survived such a sundering once; he could not stand it twice, and live. The sentries had put up a canvas lean-to near their fire to shelter them from the rain. The flames sputtered as the rain blew in, though, and lit the pale cloth with a flicker that pulsed like a heartbeat. He was not afraid to die with her, by fire or any other way—only to live without her.

The wind changed, carrying with it the faint sound of laughter from the tiny tent where the newlyweds slept—or didn't. He smiled to himself, hearing it. He could only hope that his daughter would find such joy in her marriage as he had—but so far, so good. The lad's face lit when he looked at her.

"What will you do?" Claire said quietly, her words almost lost in the pattering of the rain.

"What I must."

It was no answer, but the only one.

There was no world outside this small confine, he told himself. Scotland was gone, the Colonies were going—what lay ahead he could only dimly imagine from the things Brianna told him. The only reality was the woman held fast in his arms; his children and grandchildren, his tenants and servants—these were the gifts that God had given to him; his to harbor, his to protect.

The mountainside lay dark and quiet, but he could feel them there all round him, trusting him to see them safe. If God had given him this trust, surely He would also grant the strength to keep it.

He was becoming aroused by the habit of close contact, his rising cock uncomfortably trapped. He wanted her, had been wanting for days, the urge pushed aside in the bustle of the Gathering. The dull ache in his balls echoed what he thought must be the ache in her womb.

He had taken her in the midst of her courses now and then, when the two of them had wanted too urgently for waiting. He had found it messy and disturbing, but exciting too, leaving him with a faint sense of shame that was not entirely unpleasant. Now was not the time or place for it, of course, but the memory of other times and other places made him shift, twisting away from her, not to trouble her with the bodily evidence of his thoughts.

Yet what he felt now was not lust—not quite. Nor was it

even the need of her, the wanting of soul's company. He wished to cover her with his body, possess her—for if he could do that, he could pretend to himself that she was safe. Covering her so, joined in one body, he might protect her. Or so he felt, even knowing how senseless the feeling was.

He had stiffened, his body tensing involuntarily with his thoughts. Claire stirred, and reached back with one hand. She laid it on his leg, let it lie for a moment, then reached gently farther up, in drowsy question.

He bent his head, put his lips behind her ear. Said what he was thinking, without thought.

"Nothing will harm ye while there is breath in my body, *a nighean donn*. Nothing."

"I know," she said. Her limbs went slowly slack, her breathing eased, and the soft round of her belly swelled under his palm as she melted into sleep. Her hand stayed on him, covering him. He lay stiff and wide awake, long after the watch fire had been quenched by the rain.

# PART TWO

*The Chieftain's Call*

# 18

## NO PLACE LIKE HOME

GIDEON DARTED OUT his head like a snake, aiming for the leg of the rider just ahead.

*"Seas!"* Jamie wrenched the big bay's head around before he could take a bite. "Evil-minded whoreson," he muttered under his breath. Geordie Chisholm, unaware of his narrow escape from Gideon's teeth, caught the remark, and looked back over his shoulder, startled. Jamie smiled and touched his slouch hat apologetically, nudging the horse past Chisholm's long-legged mule.

Jamie kicked Gideon ungently in the ribs, urging him past the rest of the slow-moving travelers at a speed fast enough to keep the brute from biting, kicking, trampling stray bairns, or otherwise causing trouble. After a week's journey, he was all too well acquainted with the stallion's proclivities. He passed Brianna and Marsali, halfway up the column, at a slow trot; by the time he passed Claire and Roger, riding at the head, he was moving too fast to do more than flourish his hat at them in salute.

*"A mhic an dhiobhail,"* he said, clapping the hat back on and leaning low over the horse's neck. "Ye're a deal too lively for your own good, let alone mine. See how long ye last in the rough, eh?"

He pulled hard left, off the trail, and down the slope, trampling dry grass and brushing leafless dogwood out of the way with a gunshot snapping of twigs. What the seven-sided son of a bitch needed was flat country, where Jamie could gallop the bejesus out of him and bring him back blowing. Given that there wasn't a flat spot in twenty miles, he'd have to do the next best thing.

He gathered up the reins, clicked his tongue, jabbed both heels into the horse's ribs, and they charged up the shrubby hillside as though they had been fired from a cannon.

Gideon was large-boned, well-nourished, and sound of wind, which was why Jamie had bought him. He was also a hard-mouthed, bad-tempered reester of a horse, which was why he hadn't cost much. More than Jamie could easily afford, even so.

As they sailed over a small creek, jumped a fallen log, and hared up an almost vertical hillside littered with scrub oak and persimmon, Jamie found himself wondering whether he'd got a bargain or committed suicide. That was the last coherent thought he had before Gideon veered sideways, crushing Jamie's leg against a tree, then gathered his hindquarters and charged down the other side of the hill into a thicket of brush, sending coveys of quail exploding from under his huge flat hooves.

Half an hour of dodging low branches, lurching through streams, and galloping straight up as many hillsides as Jamie could point them at, and Gideon was, if not precisely tractable, at least exhausted enough to be manageable. Jamie was soaked to the thighs, bruised, bleeding from half a dozen scratches, and breathing nearly as hard as the horse. He was, however, still in the saddle, and still in charge.

He turned the horse's head toward the sinking sun and clicked his tongue again.

"Come on, then," he said. "Let's go home."

They had exerted themselves mightily, but given the rugged shape of the land, had not covered so much ground as to lose themselves entirely. He turned Gideon's head upward, and within a quarter hour, had come out onto a small ridge he recognized.

They picked their way along the ridge, searching for a safe way down through the tangles of chinkapin, poplar, and spruce. The party was not far away, he knew, but it could take some time to cross to them, and he would as soon rejoin them before they reached the Ridge. Not that Claire or MacKenzie could not guide them—but he admitted to himself that he wished very much to return to Fraser's Ridge at the head of the party, leading his people home.

"Christ, man, ye'd think ye were Moses," he muttered, shaking his head in mock dismay at his own pretensions.

The horse was lathered, and when the trees opened out for a space, Jamie halted for a moment's rest—relaxing the reins, but keeping a sufficient grip as to discourage any notions the outheidie creature might still be entertaining. They stood among a grove of silver birch, at the lip of a small rocky outcrop above a forty-foot drop; he thought the horse held much too high an opinion of himself to contemplate self-destruction, but best to be careful, in case he had any thought of flinging his rider off into the laurels below.

The breeze was from the west. Jamie lifted his chin, enjoying the cold touch of it on his heated skin. The land fell away in undulating waves of brown and green, kindled here and there with patches of color, lighting the mist in the hollows like the glow of campfire smoke. He felt a peace come over him at the sight, and breathed deep, his body relaxing.

Gideon relaxed, too, all the feistiness draining slowly out of him like water from a leaky bucket. Slowly, Jamie let his hands drop lightly on the horse's neck, and the horse stayed still, ears forward. Ah, he thought, and the realization stole over him that this was a Place.

He thought of such places in a way that had no words, only recognizing one when he came to it. He might have called it holy, save that the feel of such a place had nothing to do with church or saint. It was simply a place he belonged to be, and that was sufficient, though he preferred to be alone when he found one. He let the reins go slack across the horse's neck. Not even a thrawn-minded creature like Gideon would give trouble here, he felt.

Sure enough, the horse stood quiet, massive dark withers steaming in the chill. They could not tarry long, but he was deeply glad of the momentary respite—not from the battle with Gideon, but from the press of people.

He had learned early on the trick of living separately in a crowd, private in his mind when his body could not be. But he was born a mountain-dweller, and had learned early, too, the enchantment of solitude, and the healing of quiet places.

Quite suddenly, he had a vision of his mother, one of the small vivid portraits that his mind hoarded, producing them unexpectedly in response to God knew what—a sound, a smell, some passing freak of memory.

He had been snaring for rabbits on a hillside then, hot and sweaty, his fingers pricked with gorse and his shirt stuck to him with mud and damp. He had seen a small grove of trees and gone to them for shade. His mother was there, sitting in the greenish shadow, on the ground beside a tiny spring. She sat quite motionless—which was unlike her—long hands folded in her lap.

She had not spoken, but smiled at him, and he had gone to her, not speaking either, but filled with a great sense of peace and contentment, resting his head against her shoulder, feeling her arm go about him and knowing he stood at the center of the world. He had been five, maybe, or six.

As suddenly as it had come, the vision disappeared, like a bright trout vanishing into dark water. It left behind it the same deep sense of peace, though—as though someone had briefly embraced him, a soft hand touched his hair.

He swung himself down from the saddle, needing the feel of the pine needles under his boots, some physical connection with this place. Caution made him tie the reins to a stout pine, though Gideon seemed calm enough; the stallion had dropped his head and was nuzzling for tufts of dried grass. Jamie stood still for a moment, then turned himself carefully to the right, facing the north.

He no longer recalled who had taught him this—whether it was Mother, Father, or Auld John, Ian's father. He spoke the words, though, as he turned himself sunwise, murmuring the brief prayer to each of the four airts in turn, and ended facing west, into the setting sun. He cupped his empty hands and the light filled them, spilling from his palms.

> *"May God make safe to me each step,*
> *May God make open to me each pass,*
> *May God make clear to me each road,*
> *And may He take me in the clasp of His own two*
> *hands."*

With an instinct older than the prayer, he took the flask from his belt and poured a few drops on the ground.

Scraps of sound reached him on the breeze; laughter and calling, the sound of animals making their way through brush. The caravan was not far away, only across a small hollow, coming slowly round the curve of the hillside opposite. He should go now, to join them on the last push upward to the Ridge.

Still he hesitated for a moment, loath to break the spell of the Place. Some tiny movement caught the corner of his eye, and he bent down, squinting as he peered into the deepening shadows beneath a holly bush.

It sat frozen, blending perfectly with its dusky background. He would never have seen it had his hunter's eye not caught its movement. A tiny kitten, its gray fur puffed out like a ripe milkweed head, enormous eyes wide open and unblinking, almost colorless in the gloom beneath the bush.

"*A Chait,*" he whispered, putting out a slow finger toward it. "Whatever are ye doing here?"

A feral cat, no doubt; born of a wild mother, fled from some settlers' cabin, and long free of the trap of domesticity. He brushed the wispy fur of its breast, and it sank its tiny teeth suddenly into his thumb.

"Ow!" He jerked away, and examined the drop of blood welling from a small puncture wound. He glowered at the cat for a moment, but it merely stared back at him, and made no move to run. He paused, then made up his mind. He shook the blood drop from his finger onto the leaves, an offering to join the dram he had spilled, a gift to the spirits of this Place—who had evidently made up their minds to offer him a gift, themselves.

"All right, then," he said under his breath. He knelt, and stretched out his hand, palm up. Very slowly, he moved one finger, then the next, and the next and the next, then again, in the undulant motion of seaweed in the water. The big pale eyes fixed on the movement, watching as though hypnotized. He could see the tip of the miniature tail twitch, very slightly, and smiled at the sight.

If he could guddle a trout—and he could—why not a cat?

He made a small noise through his teeth, a whistling hiss, like the distant chittering of birds. The kitten stared, mesmerized, as the gently swaying fingers moved invisibly closer. When at last he touched its fur again, it made no move to escape. One finger edged beneath the fur, another slid under the cold wee pads of one paw, and it let him scoop it gently into his hand and lift it from the ground.

He held it for a moment against his chest, stroking it with one finger, tracing the silken jawline, the delicate ears. The tiny cat closed its eyes and began to purr in ecstasy, rumbling in his palm like distant thunder.

"Oh, so ye'll come away wi' me, will you?" Receiving no demur from the cat, he opened the neck of his shirt and tucked the tiny thing inside, where it poked and prodded at his ribs for a bit before curling up against his skin, purr reduced to a silent but pleasant vibration.

Gideon seemed pleased by the rest; he set off willingly enough, and within a quarter hour, they had caught up with the others. The stallion's momentary docility evaporated, though, under the strain of the final upward climb.

Not that the horse could not master the steep trail; what he couldn't abide was following another horse. It didn't matter whether Jamie wished to lead them home or not—if Gideon had anything to do with the matter, they would be not only in the lead, but several furlongs ahead.

The column of travelers was strung out over half a mile, each family party traveling at its own speed: Frasers, MacKenzies, Chisholms, MacLeods, and Aberfeldys. At every space and widening of the trail, Gideon shouldered his way rudely ahead, shoving past pack mules, sheep, foot-travelers, and mares; he even scattered the three pigs trudging slowly behind Grannie Chisholm. The pigs bolted into the brush in a chorus of panicked oinks as Gideon bore down upon them.

Jamie found himself more in sympathy with the horse than not; eager to be home and working hard to get there, irritated by anything that threatened to hold him back. At the moment, the main impediment to progress was Claire, who had—blast the woman—halted her mare in front of him and slid off in order to gather yet another bit of herbage from the trailside. As though the entire house was not filled from doorstep to rooftree with plants already, and her saddlebags a-bulge with more!

Gideon, picking up his rider's mood with alacrity, stretched out his neck and nipped the mare's rump. The mare bucked, squealed, and shot off up the trail, loose reins dangling. Gideon made a deep rumbling noise of satisfaction and started off after her, only to be jerked unceremoniously to a halt.

Claire had whirled round at the noise, eyes wide. She looked up at Jamie, up the trail after her vanished horse, then back at him. She shrugged apologetically, hands full of tattered leaves and mangy roots.

"Sorry," she said, but he saw the corner of her mouth tuck in and the flush rise in her skin, the smile glimmering in her eyes like morning light on trout water. Quite against his will, he felt the tension in his shoulders ease. He had had it in mind to rebuke her; in fact, he still did, but the words wouldn't quite come to his tongue.

"Get up, then, woman," he said instead, gruffly, with a nod behind him. "I want my supper."

She laughed at him and scrambled up, kilting her skirts out of the way. Gideon, irascible at this additional burden, whipped round to take a nip of anything he could reach. Jamie was ready for that; he snapped the end of the rein sharply off the stallion's nose, making him jerk back and snort in surprise.

"That'll teach ye, ye wee bastard." He pulled his hat over his brow and settled his errant wife securely, fluttering skirts tucked in beneath her thighs, arms round his waist. She rode without shoes or stockings, and her long calves were white and bare against the dark bay hide. He gathered up the reins and kicked the horse, a trifle harder than strictly necessary.

Gideon promptly reared, backed, twisted, and tried to scrape them both off under a hanging poplar bough. The kitten, rudely roused from its nap, sank all its claws into Jamie's midsection and yowled in alarm, though its noise was quite lost in Jamie's much louder screech. He yanked the horse's head halfway round, swearing, and shoved at the hindquarters with his left leg.

No easy conquest, Gideon executed a hop like a

corkscrew. There was a small "eek!" and a sudden feeling of emptiness behind him, as Claire was slung off into the brush like a bag of flour. The horse suddenly yielded to the pull on his mouth, and shot down the path in the wrong direction, hurtling through a screen of brambles and skidding to a halt that nearly threw him onto his hindquarters in a shower of mud and dead leaves. Then he straightened out like a snake, shook his head, and trotted nonchalantly over to exchange nuzzles with Roger's horse, which was standing at the edge of the spring clearing, watching them with the same bemusement exhibited by its dismounted rider.

"All right there?" asked Roger, raising one eyebrow.

"Certainly," Jamie replied, trying to gasp for breath while keeping his dignity. "And you?"

"Fine."

"Good." He was already swinging down from the saddle as he spoke. He flung the reins toward MacKenzie, not waiting to see whether he caught them, and ran back toward the trail, shouting, "Claire! Where are ye?"

"Just here!" she called cheerfully. She emerged from the shadow of the poplars, with leaves in her hair and limping slightly, but looking otherwise undamaged. "Are you all right?" she asked, cocking one eyebrow at him.

"Aye, fine. I'm going to shoot that horse." He gathered her in briefly, wanting to assure himself that she was in fact whole. She was breathing heavily, but felt reassuringly solid, and kissed him on the nose.

"Well, don't shoot him until we get home. I don't want to walk the last mile or so in my bare feet."

"Hey! Let that alone, ye bugger!"

He let go of Claire and turned to find Roger snatching a fistful of ragged-looking plants away from Gideon's questing Roman nose. More plants—what was this mania for gathering? Claire was still panting from the accident, but leaned forward to see them, looking interested.

"What's that you've got, Roger?"

"For Bree," he said, holding them up for her inspection. "Are they the right kind?" To Jamie's jaundiced eye, they looked like the yellowed tops of carrots gone to seed and left too long in the ground, but Claire fingered the mangy foliage, and nodded approval.

"Oh, yes," she said. "*Very* romantic!"

Jamie made a small tactful noise, indicating that they ought perhaps to be making their way, since Bree and the slower-moving tribe of Chisholms would be catching them up soon.

"Yes, all right," Claire said, patting his shoulder in what he assumed she meant to be a soothing gesture. "Don't snort; we're going."

"Mmphm," he said, and bent to put a hand under her foot. Tossing her up into the saddle, he gave Gideon a "Don't try it on, you bastard" look and swung up behind her.

"You'll wait for the others, then, and bring them up?" Without waiting for Roger's nod, Jamie reined around and set Gideon upon the trail again.

Mollified at being far in the lead, Gideon settled down to the job at hand, climbing steadily through the thickets of hornbeam and poplar, chestnut and spruce. Even so late in the year, some leaves still clung to the trees, and small bits of brown and yellow floated down upon them like a gentle rain, catching in the horse's mane, resting in the loose, thick waves of Claire's hair. It had come down in her precipitous descent, and she hadn't bothered to put it up again.

Jamie's own equanimity returned with the sense of progress, and was quite restored by the fortuitous finding of the hat he had lost, hanging from a white oak by the trail, as though placed there by some kindly hand. Still, he remained uneasy in his mind, and could not quite grasp tranquillity, though the mountain lay at peace all round him, the air hazed with blue and smelling of wood-damp and evergreens.

Then he realized, with a sudden jolt in the pit of his stomach, that the kitten was gone. There were itching furrows in the skin of his chest and abdomen, where it had climbed him in a frantic effort to escape, but it must have popped out the neck of his shirt and been flung off his shoulder in the mad career down the slope. He glanced from side to side, searching in the shadows under bushes and trees, but it was a vain hope. The shadows were lengthening, and they were on the main trail now, where he and Gideon had torn through the wood.

"Go with God," he murmured, and crossed himself briefly.

"What's that?" Claire asked, half-turning in the saddle.

"Nothing," he said. After all, it was a wild cat, though a small one. Doubtless it would manage.

Gideon worked the bit, pecking and bobbing. Jamie realized that the tension in his hands was running through the reins once more, and consciously slackened his grip. He loosened his grip on Claire, too, and she took a sudden deep breath.

His heart was beating fast.

It was impossible for him ever to come home after an absence without a certain sense of apprehension. For years after the Rising, he had lived in a cave, approaching his own house only rarely, after dark and with great caution, never knowing what he might find there. More than one Highland man had come home to his place to find it burned and black, his family gone. Or worse, still there.

Well enough to tell himself not to imagine horrors; the difficulty was that he had no need of imagination—memory sufficed.

The horse dug with his haunches, pushing hard. No use to tell himself this was a new place; it was, with its own dangers. If there were no English soldiers in these mountains, there were still marauders. Those too shiftless to take root and fend for themselves, but who wandered the backcountry, robbing and plundering. Raiding Indians. Wild animals. And fire. Always fire.

He had sent the Bugs on ahead, with Fergus to guide them, to save Claire dealing with the simultaneous chores of arrival and hospitality. The Chisholms, the MacLeods, and Billy Aberfeldy, with his wife and wee daughter, would all bide with them at the big house for a time; he had told Mrs. Bug to begin cooking at once. Decently mounted and not hindered by children or livestock, the Bugs should have reached the Ridge two days before. No one had come back to say aught was amiss, so perhaps all was well. But still . . .

He hadn't realized that Claire was tensed, too, until she suddenly relaxed against him, a hand on his leg.

"It's all right," she said. "I smell chimney smoke."

He lifted his head to catch the air. She was right; the tang of burning hickory floated on the breeze. Not the stink of remembered conflagration, but a homely whiff redolent with the promise of warmth and food. Mrs. Bug had presumably taken him at his word.

They rounded the last turn of the trail and saw it, then, the high fieldstone chimney rising above the trees on the ridge, its fat plume of smoke curling over the rooftree.

The house stood.

He breathed deep in relief, noticing now the other smells of home; the faint rich scent of manure from the stable, of meat smoked and hanging in the shed, and the breath of the forest nearby—damp wood and leaf-rot, rock and rushing water, the touch of it cold and loving on his cheek.

They came out of the chestnut grove and into the large clearing where the house stood, solid and neat, its windows glazed gold with the last of the sun.

It was a modest frame house, whitewashed and shingle-roofed, clean in its lines and soundly built, but impressive only by comparison with the crude cabins of most settlers. His own first cabin still stood, dark and sturdy, a little way down the hill. Smoke was curling from that chimney, too.

"Someone's made a fire for Bree and Roger," Claire said, nodding at it.

"That's good," he said. He tightened his arm about her waist, and she made a small, contented noise in her throat, wriggling her bottom into his lap.

Gideon was happy, too; he stretched out his neck and whinnied to the two horses in the penfold, who trotted to and fro in the enclosure, calling greetings. Claire's mare was standing by the fence, reins dangling; she curled her lip in what looked like derision, the wee besom. From somewhere far down the trail behind them came a deep, joyous bray; Clarence the mule, hearing the racket and delighted to be coming home.

The door flew open, and Mrs. Bug popped out, round and flustered as a tumble-turd. Jamie smiled at sight of her, and gave Claire an arm to slide down before dismounting himself.

"All's well, all's well, and how's yourself, sir?" Mrs. Bug was reassuring him before his boots struck ground. She had a pewter cup in one hand, a polishing cloth in the other, and didn't cease her polishing for an instant, even as she turned up her face to accept his kiss on her withered round cheek.

She didn't wait for an answer, but turned at once and stood a-tiptoe to kiss Claire, beaming.

"Oh, it's grand that you're home, ma'am, you and Himself, and I've the supper all made, so you'll not be worrit a bit with it, ma'am, but come inside, come inside, and be takin' off those dusty cloots, and I'll send old Arch along to the mash-hoose for a bit of the lively, and we'll . . ." She had Claire by one hand, towing her into the house, talking and talking, the other hand still polishing briskly away, her stubby fingers dexterously rubbing the cloth inside the cup. Claire gave him a helpless glance over one shoulder, and he grinned at her as she disappeared inside the house.

Gideon shoved an impatient nose under his arm and bumped his elbow.

"Oh, aye," he said, recalled to his chores. "Come along, then, ye prickly wee bastard."

By the time he had the big horse and Claire's mare unsaddled, wiped down, and turned out to their feed, Claire had escaped from Mrs. Bug; coming back from the paddock, he saw the door of the house swing open and Claire slip out, looking guiltily over her shoulder as though fearing pursuit.

Where was she bound? She didn't see him; she turned and hurried toward the far corner of the house, disappearing in a swish of homespun. He followed, curious.

Ah. She had seen to her surgery; now she was going to her garden before it got completely dark; he caught a glimpse of her against the sky on the upward path behind the house, the last of the daylight caught like cobwebs in her hair. There would be little growing now, only a few sturdy herbs and the overwintering things like carrots and onions and turnips, but it made no difference; she always went to see how things were, no matter how short a time she had been gone.

He understood the urge; he would not feel entirely home

himself until he had checked all the stock and buildings, and made sure of matters up at the still.

The evening breeze brought him an acrid hint from the distant privy, suggesting that matters there were shortly going to require his attention, speaking of buildings. Then he bethought him of the new tenants coming, and relaxed; digging a new privy would be just the thing for Chisholm's eldest two boys.

He and Ian had dug this one, when they first came to the Ridge. God, he missed the lad.

"*A Mhicheal bheanaichte,*" he murmured. *Blessed Michael, protect him.* He liked MacKenzie well enough, but had it been his choice, he would not have exchanged Ian for the man. It had been Ian's choice, though, not his, and no more to be said about it.

Pushing away the ache of Ian's loss, he stepped behind a tree, loosened his breeks, and relieved himself. If she saw him, Claire would doubtless make what she considered witty remarks about dogs and wolves marking their home ground as they returned to it. Nothing of the sort, he replied to her mentally; why walk up the hill, only to make matters worse in the privy? Still, if you came down to it, it *was* his place, and if he chose to piss on it . . . He tidied his clothes, feeling more settled.

He raised his head and saw her coming down the path from the garden, her apron bulging with carrots and turnips. A gust of wind sent the last of the leaves from the chestnut grove swirling round her in a yellow dance, sparked with light.

Moved by sudden impulse, he stepped deeper into the trees and began to look about.

Normally, he paid attention only to such vegetation as was immediately comestible by horse or man, sufficiently straight-grained to serve for planks and timbers, or so obstructive as to pose difficulty in passage. Once he began looking with an eye to aesthetics, though, he found himself surprised at the variety to hand.

Stalks of half-ripe barley, the seeds laid in rows like a woman's plait. A dry, fragile weed that looked like the lace

edging on a fine handkerchief. A branch of spruce, unearthly
green and cool among the dry bits, leaving its fragrant sap on
his hand as he tore it from the tree. A twig of glossy dried
oak leaves that reminded him of her hair, in shades of gold
and brown and gray. And a bit of scarlet creeper, snatched for
color.

Just in time; she was coming round the corner of the
house. Lost in thought, she passed within a foot or two of
him, not seeing him.

*"Sorcha,"* he called softly, and she turned, eyes narrowed
against the rays of the sinking sun, then wide and gold with
surprise at the sight of him.

"Welcome home," he said, and held out the small bouquet
of leaves and twigs.

"Oh," she said. She looked at the bits of leaf and stick
again, and then at him, and the corners of her mouth trembled, as though she might laugh or cry, but wasn't sure
which. She reached then, and took the plants from him, her
fingers small and cold as they brushed his hand.

"Oh, Jamie—they're *wonderful.*" She came up on her toes
and kissed him, warm and salty, and he wanted more, but she
was hurrying away into the house, the silly wee things
clasped to her breast as though they were gold.

He felt pleasantly foolish, and foolishly pleased with himself. The taste of her was still on his mouth.

*"Sorcha,"* he whispered, and realized that he had called
her so a moment before. Now, that was odd; no wonder she
had been surprised. It was her name in the Gaelic, but he
never called her by it. He liked the strangeness of her, the
Englishness. She was his Claire, his Sassenach.

And yet in the moment when she passed him, she was
*Sorcha.* Not only "Claire," it meant—but light.

He breathed deep, contented.

He was suddenly ravenous, both for food and for her, but
he made no move to hasten inside. Some kinds of hunger
were sweet in themselves, the anticipation of satisfaction as
keen a pleasure as the slaking.

Hoofsteps and voices; the others were finally here. He had
a sudden urge to keep his peaceful solitude a moment longer,
but too late—in seconds, he was surrounded by confusion,

the shrill cries of excited children and calls of distracted mothers, the welcoming of the newcomers, the bustle and rush of unloading, turning out the horses and mules, fetching feed and water . . . and yet in the midst of this Babel, he moved as though he were still alone, peaceful and quiet in the setting sun. He had come home.

IT WAS FULL DARK before everything was sorted, the smallest of the wild Chisholm bairns rounded up and sent inside for his supper, all the stock cared for and settled for the night. He followed Geoff Chisholm toward the house, but then held back, lingering for a moment in the dark dooryard.

He stood for a moment, idly chafing his hands against the chill as he admired the look of the place. Snug barn and sound sheds, a penfold and paddock in good repair, a tidy fence of palisades around Claire's scraggly garden, to keep out the deer. The house loomed white in the early dark, a benevolent spirit guarding the ridge. Light spilled from every door and window, and the sound of laughter came from inside.

He sensed a movement in the darkness, and turned to see his daughter coming from the spring house, a pail of fresh milk in her hand. She stopped by him, looking at the house.

"Nice to be home, isn't it?" she said softly.

"Aye," he said. "It is." They looked at each other, smiling. Then she leaned forward, peering closely at him. She turned him, so the light from the window fell on him, and a small frown puckered the skin between her brows.

"What's that?" she said, and flicked at his coat. A glossy scarlet leaf fell free and floated to the ground. Her brows went up at sight of it. "You'd better go and wash, Da," she said. "You've been in the poison ivy."

"YE MIGHT HAVE TOLD ME, Sassenach." Jamie glowered at the table near the bedroom window, where I'd set his bouquet in a cup of water. The bright, blotchy red of the poison ivy glowed, even in the dimness of the firelight. "And ye might get rid of it, too. D'ye mean to mock me?"

"No, I don't," I said, smiling as I hung my apron from the peg and reached for the laces of my gown. "But if I'd told you when you gave it to me, you'd have snatched it back. That's the only posy you've ever given me, and I don't imagine I'll get another; I mean to keep it."

He snorted, and sat down on the bed to take off his stockings. He'd already stripped off coat, stock, and shirt, and the firelight gleamed on the slope of his shoulders. He scratched at the underside of one wrist, though I'd told him it was psychosomatic; he hadn't any signs of rash.

"You've never come home with poison ivy rash," I remarked. "And you're bound to have run into it now and again, so much time as you spend in the woods and the fields. I think you must be immune to it. Some people are, you know."

"Oh, aye?" He looked interested at that, though he went on scratching. "Is that like you and Brianna not catching illness?"

"Something like, but for different reasons." I peeled off the gown of pale green homespun—more than a little grubby, after a week's travel—and stripped off my stays with a sigh of relief.

I got up to check the pan of water I had set to heat in the embers. Some of the newcomers had been sent off to spend the night with Fergus and Marsali, or with Roger and Bree, but the kitchen, the surgery, and Jamie's study below were full of guests, all sleeping on the floor. I wasn't going to bed without washing off the stains of travel, but I didn't care to provide a public spectacle while doing it, either.

The water shimmered with heat, tiny bubbles clinging to the sides of the pot. I put a finger in, just to check—lovely and hot. I poured some into the basin and put the rest back to keep warm.

"We aren't completely immune, you know," I warned him. "Some things—like smallpox—we can't ever catch, Roger and Bree and I, because we've been vaccinated against them, and it's permanent. Other things, like cholera and typhoid, we aren't *likely* to catch, but the injections don't give permanent immunity; it wears off after a time."

I bent to rummage in the saddlebags he had brought up and dumped by the door. Someone at the Gathering had given me a sponge—a real one, imported from the Indies—in payment for my extracting an abscessed tooth. Just the thing for a quick bath.

"Things like malaria—what Lizzie has—"

"I thought ye'd cured her of that," Jamie interrupted, frowning.

I shook my head, regretful.

"No, she'll always have it, poor thing. All I can do is try to lessen the severity of the attacks, and keep them from coming too often. It's in her blood, you see."

He pulled off the thong that bound back his hair, and shook out the ruddy locks, leaving them ruffled round his head like a mane.

"That doesna make any sense," he objected, rising to unfasten his breeks. "Ye told me that when a person had the measles, if he lived, he'd not get it again, because it stayed in the blood. And so I couldna catch pox or measles now, because I'd had them both as a child—they're in my blood."

"Well, it's not quite the same thing," I said, rather lamely. The thought of trying to explain the differences among active immunity, passive immunity, acquired immunity, antibodies, and parasitic infection was more of a challenge than I felt up to, after a long day's ride.

I dipped the sponge into the basin, let it take up water, then squeezed it out, enjoying the oddly silky, fibrous texture. A fine mist of sand floated out of the pores and settled to the bottom of the china basin. The sponge was softening as it took up water, but I could still feel a hard spot at one edge.

"Speaking of riding—"

Jamie looked mildly startled.

"Were we speaking of riding?"

"Well, no, but I was thinking of it." I waved a hand, dismissing the inconsequent distinction. "In any case, what do you mean to do about Gideon?"

"Oh." Jamie dropped his breeks in a puddle on the floor and stretched himself, considering. "Well, I canna afford just to shoot him, I suppose. And he's a braw enough fellow. I'll cut him, to start. That may settle his mind a bit."

"Cut him? Oh, castrate him, you mean. Yes, I suppose that would get his attention, though it seems a bit drastic." I hesitated a moment, reluctant. "Do you want me to do it?"

He stared at me in amazement, then burst out laughing.

"Nay, Sassenach, I dinna think cutting an eighteen-hand stallion is a job for a woman, surgeon or no. It doesna really require the delicate touch, aye?"

I was just as pleased to hear this. I had been working at the sponge with my thumb; it loosened a bit, and a tiny shell popped suddenly out of a large pore. It floated down through the water, a perfect miniature spiral, tinted pink and purple.

"Oh, look," I said, delighted.

"What a bonnie wee thing." Jamie leaned over my shoulder, a big forefinger gently touching the shell at the bottom of the basin. "How did it get into your sponge, I wonder?"

"I expect the sponge ate it by mistake."

"Ate it?" One ruddy eyebrow shot up at that.

"Sponges are animals," I explained. "Or to be more exact, stomachs. They suck in water, and just absorb everything edible as it passes through."

"Ah, so that's why Bree called the bairn a wee sponge. They do that." He smiled at the thought of Jemmy.

"Indeed they do." I sat down and slipped the shift off my shoulders, letting the garment fall to my waist. The fire had taken the chill off the room, but it was still cold enough that the skin of my breasts and arms bloomed into gooseflesh.

Jamie picked up his belt and carefully removed the assorted impedimenta it held, laying out pistol, cartridge box, dirk, and pewter flask on top of the small bureau. He lifted the flask and raised an inquiring eyebrow in my direction.

I nodded enthusiastically, and he turned to find a cup amid the rubble of oddments. With so many people and their belongings stuffed into the house, all of our own saddlebags, plus the bundles and bits acquired at the Gathering, had been carried up and dumped in our room; the humped shadows of the luggage flickering on the wall gave the chamber the odd look of a grotto, lined with lumpy boulders.

Jamie was as much a sponge as his grandson, I reflected, watching him rootle about, completely naked and totally unconcerned about it. He took in everything, and seemed able to deal with whatever came his way, no matter how familiar or foreign to his experience. Maniac stallions, kidnapped priests, marriageable maidservants, headstrong daughters, and heathen sons-in-law . . . Anything he could not defeat, outwit, or alter, he simply accepted—rather like the sponge and its embedded shell.

Pursuing the analogy further, I supposed I was the shell. Snatched out of my own small niche by an unexpected strong current, taken in and surrounded by Jamie and his life. Caught forever among the strange currents that pulsed through this outlandish environment.

The thought gave me a sudden queer feeling. The shell lay still at the bottom of the basin—delicate, beautiful . . . but empty. Rather slowly, I raised the sponge to the back of my neck and squeezed, feeling the tickle of warm water down my back.

For the most part, I felt no regrets. I had chosen to be here; I *wanted* to be here. And yet now and then small things like our conversation about immunity made me realize just how much had been lost—of what I had had, of what I had been. It was undeniable that some of my soft parts had been digested away, and the thought did make me feel a trifle hollow now and then.

Jamie bent to dig in one of the saddlebags, and the sight of his bare buttocks, turned toward me in all innocence, did much to dispel the momentary sense of disquiet. They were gracefully shaped, rounded with muscle—and pleasingly dusted with a red-gold fuzz that caught the light of fire and candle. The long, pale columns of his thighs framed the shadow of his scrotum, dark and barely visible between them.

He had found a cup at last, and poured it half full. He turned and handed it to me, lifting his eyes from the surface of the dark liquid, startled to find me staring at him.

"What is it?" he said. "Is there something the matter, Sassenach?"

"No," I said, but I must have sounded rather doubtful, for his brows drew momentarily together.

"No," I said, more positively. I took the cup from him and smiled, lifting it slightly in acknowledgment. "Only thinking."

An answering smile touched his lips.

"Aye? Well, ye dinna want to do too much of that late at night, Sassenach. It will give ye the nightmare."

"Daresay you're right about that." I sipped from the cup; rather to my surprise, it was wine—and very good wine. "Where did you get this?"

"From Father Kenneth. It's sacramental wine—but not consecrated, aye? He said the Sheriff's men would take it; he would as soon it went with me."

A slight shadow crossed his face at mention of the priest.

"Do you think he'll be all right?" I asked. The Sheriff's men had not struck me as civilized enforcers of an abstruse regulation, but rather as thugs whose prejudice was momentarily constrained by fear—of Jamie.

"I hope so." Jamie turned aside, restless. "I told the Sheriff that if the Father were misused, he and his men would answer for it."

I nodded silently, sipping. If Jamie learned of any harm done to Father Donahue, he would indeed make the Sheriff answer for it. The thought made me a trifle uneasy; this wasn't a good time to make enemies, and the Sheriff of Orange County wasn't a good enemy to have.

I looked up to find Jamie's eyes still fixed on me, though now with a look of deep appreciation.

"You're in good flesh these days, Sassenach," he observed, tilting his head to one side.

"Flatterer," I said, giving him a cold look as I picked up the sponge again.

"Ye must have gained a stone, at least, since the spring," he said with approval, disregarding the look and circling round me to inspect. "It's been a good fat summer, aye?"

I turned round and flung the wet sponge at his head.

He caught it neatly, grinning.

"I didna realize how well ye'd filled out, Sassenach, so bundled as ye've been these last weeks. I havena seen ye naked in a month, at least." He was still eyeing me with an air of appraisal, as though I were a prime entrant in the Silver Medalist Round at the Shropshire Fat Pigs Show.

"Enjoy it," I advised him, my cheeks flushed with annoyance. "You may not see it again for quite some time!" I snatched the top of the chemise up again, covering my—undeniably rather full—breasts.

His eyebrows rose in surprise at my tone.

"You're never angry wi' me, Sassenach?"

"Certainly not," I said. "Whatever gives you an idea like *that*?"

He smiled, rubbing the sponge absently over his chest as his eyes traveled over me. His nipples puckered at the chill, dark and stiff among the ruddy, curling hairs, and the damp gleamed on his skin.

"I like ye fat, Sassenach," he said softly. "Fat and juicy as a plump wee hen. I like it fine."

I might have considered this a simple attempt to remove his foot from his mouth, were it not for the fact that naked men are conveniently equipped with sexual lie detectors. He *did* like it fine.

"Oh," I said. Rather slowly, I lowered the chemise. "Well, then."

He lifted his chin, gesturing. I hesitated for a moment, then stood up and let the chemise fall on the floor, joining his breeks. I reached across and took the sponge from his hand.

"I'll . . . um . . . just finish washing, shall I?" I murmured. I turned my back, put a foot on the stool to wash, and heard an encouraging rumble of appreciation behind me. I smiled to myself, and took my time. The room was getting warmer; by the time I had finished my ablutions, my skin was pink and smooth, with only a slight chill in fingers and toes.

I turned round at last, to see Jamie still watching me, though he still rubbed at his wrist, frowning slightly.

"Did *you* wash?" I asked. "Even if it doesn't trouble you, if you have oil from the poison ivy on your skin, it can get on things you touch—and *I'm* not immune to the stuff."

"I scrubbed my hands with lye soap," he assured me,

putting them on my shoulders in illustration. Sure enough, he smelled strongly of the acrid soft soap we made from suet and wood-ash—it wasn't perfumed toilet soap, but it did get things clean. Things like floorboards and iron pots. No wonder he'd been scratching; it wasn't easy on the skin, and his hands were rough and cracked.

I bent my head and kissed his knuckles, then reached across to the small box where I kept my personal bits and pieces, and took out the jar of skin balm. Made of walnut oil, beeswax, and purified lanolin from boiled sheep's wool, it was pleasantly soothing, green-scented with the essences of chamomile, comfrey, yarrow, and elderflowers.

I scooped out a bit with my thumbnail, and rubbed it between my hands; it was nearly solid to begin with, but liquefied nicely when warmed.

"Here," I said, and took one of his hands between my own, rubbing the ointment into the creases of his knuckles, massaging his callused palms. Slowly, he relaxed, letting me stretch each finger as I worked my way down the joints and rubbed more ointment into the tiny scrapes and cuts. There were still marks on his hands where he had kept the leather reins wrapped tightly.

"The posy's lovely, Jamie," I said, nodding at the little bouquet in its cup. "Whatever made you do it, though?" While in his own way quite romantic, Jamie was thoroughly practical as well; I didn't think he had ever given me a completely frivolous present, and he was not a man to see value in any vegetation that could not be eaten, taken medicinally, or brewed into beer.

He shifted a bit, clearly uncomfortable.

"Aye, well," he said, looking away. "I just—I mean—well, I had a wee thing I meant to give ye, only I lost it, but then you seemed to think it a sweet thing that wee Roger had plucked a few gowans for Brianna, and I—" He broke off, muttering something that sounded like *"Ifrinn!"* under his breath.

I wanted very much to laugh. Instead, I lifted his hand and kissed his knuckles, lightly. He looked embarrassed, but pleased. His thumb traced the edge of a half-healed blister on my palm, left by a hot kettle.

"Here, Sassenach, ye need a bit of this, too. Let me," he said, and leaned to take a dab of the green ointment. He engulfed my hand in his, warm and still slippery with the oil and beeswax mixture.

I resisted for a moment, but then let him take my hand, making deep slow circles on my palm that made me want to close my eyes and melt quietly. I gave a small sigh of pleasure, and must have closed my eyes after all, because I didn't see him move in close to kiss me; just felt the brief soft touch of his mouth.

I raised my other hand, lazily, and he took it, too, his fingers smoothing mine. I let my fingers twine with his, thumbs jousting gently, the heels of our hands lightly rubbing. He stood close enough that I felt the warmth of him, and the delicate brush of the sun-bleached hairs on his arm as he reached past my hip for more of the ointment.

He paused, kissing me lightly once more in passing. Flames hissed on the hearth like shifting tides, and the firelight flickered dimly on the whitewashed walls, like light dancing on the surface of water far above. We might have been alone together at the bottom of the sea.

"Roger wasn't being strictly romantic, you know," I said. "Or maybe he was—depending how one wants to look at it."

Jamie looked quizzical, as he took my hand again. Our fingers locked and twined, moving slowly, and I sighed with pleasure.

"Aye?"

"Bree asked me about birth control, and I told her what methods there are now—which are frankly not all that good, though better than nothing. But old Grannie Bacon gave me some seeds that she says the Indians use for contraception; supposed to be very effective."

Jamie's face underwent the most comical change, from drowsy pleasure to wide-eyed astonishment.

"Birth con—what? She—ye mean he—those clatty weeds—"

"Well, yes. Or at least I think they may help prevent pregnancy."

"Mmphm." The movement of his fingers slowed, and his brows drew together—more in concern than disapproval, I thought. Then he returned to the job of massaging my hands, enveloping them in his much larger grasp with a decided movement that obliged me to yield to him.

He was quiet for a few moments, working the ointment into my fingers more in the businesslike way of a man rubbing saddle soap into harness than one making tender love to his wife's devoted hands. I shifted slightly, and he seemed to realize what he was doing, for he stopped, frowning, then squeezed my hands lightly and let his face relax. He lifted my hand to his lips, kissed it, then resumed his massage, much more slowly.

"Do ye think——" he began, and stopped.

"What?"

"Mmphm. It's only—does it not seem a bit strange to ye, Sassenach? That a young woman newly wed should be thinking of such a thing?"

"No, it doesn't," I said, rather sharply. "It seems entirely sensible to me. And they aren't all that newly wed—they've been . . . I mean, they *have* got a child already."

His nostrils flared in soundless disagreement.

"*She* has a child," he said. "That's what I mean, Sassenach. It seems to me that a young woman well-suited with her man wouldna be thinking first thing how *not* to bear his child. Are ye sure all is well between them?"

I paused, frowning as I considered the notion.

"I think so," I said at last, slowly. "Remember, Jamie—Bree comes from a time where women *can* decide whether or when to have babies, with a fair amount of certainty. She'd feel that such a thing was her right."

The wide mouth moved, pursed in thought; I could see him struggling with the notion—one entirely contrary to his own experience.

"That's the way of it, then?" he asked, finally. "A woman can say, I will, or I won't—and the man has no say in it?" His voice was filled with astonishment—and disapproval.

I laughed a little.

"Well, it's not *exactly* like that. Or not all the time. I mean, there are accidents. And ignorance and foolishness; a lot of women just let things happen. And most women would certainly *care* what their men thought about it. But yes . . . I suppose if you come right down to it, that's right."

He grunted slightly.

"But MacKenzie's from that time, too. So he'll think nothing odd of it?"

"He picked the weeds for her," I pointed out.

"So he did." The line stayed between his brows, but the frown eased somewhat.

It was growing late, and the muffled rumble of talk and laughter was dying down in the house below. The growing quiet of the house was pierced suddenly by a baby's wail. Both of us stood still, listening—then relaxed as the murmur of the mother's voice reached us through the closed door.

"Besides, it's not so unusual for a young woman to think of such a thing—Marsali came and asked me about it, before she married Fergus."

"Oh, did she?" One eyebrow went up. "Did ye not tell her, then?"

"Of course I did!"

"Whatever ye told her didna work all that well, did it?" One corner of his mouth curled up in a cynic smile; Germain had been born approximately ten months following his parents' marriage, and Marsali had become pregnant with Joan within days of weaning him.

I felt a flush rising in my cheeks.

"Nothing works all the time—not even modern methods. And for that matter—nothing works at all if you don't use it." In fact, Marsali had wanted contraception not because she didn't want a baby—but only because she had feared that pregnancy would interfere with the intimacy of her relationship with Fergus. *When we get to the prick part, I want to like it* had been her words on that memorable occasion, and my own mouth curled at the memory.

My equally cynical guess was that she had liked it fine, and had decided that pregnancy was unlikely to diminish her appreciation of Fergus's finer points. But that rather came back to Jamie's fears about Brianna—for surely her intimacy with Roger was well established. Still, that was hardly . . .

One of Jamie's hands remained entwined with mine; the other left my fingers and reached elsewhere—very lightly.

"Oh," I said, beginning to lose my train of thought.

"Pills, ye said." His face was quite close, eyes hooded in thought as he worked. "That's how it's done—then?"

"Um . . . oh. Yes."

"Ye didna bring any with you," he said. "When ye came back."

I breathed deep and let it out, feeling as though I were beginning to dissolve.

"No," I said, a little faintly.

He paused a moment, hand cupped lightly.

"Why not?" he asked quietly.

"I . . . well, I . . . I actually—I thought—you have to keep taking them. I couldn't have brought enough. There's a permanent way, a small operation. It's fairly simple, and it makes one permanently . . . barren." I swallowed. Viewing the prospect of coming back to the past, I had in fact thought seriously about the possibilities of pregnancy—and the risks. I thought the possibility very low indeed, given both my age and previous history, but the risk . . .

Jamie stood stock-still, looking down.

"For God's sake, Claire," he said at last, low-voiced. "Tell me that ye did it."

I took a deep breath, and squeezed his hand, my fingers slipping a little.

"Jamie," I said softly, "if I'd done it, I would have told you." I swallowed again. "You . . . would have wanted me to?"

He was still holding my hand. His other hand left me, touched my back, pressed me—very gently—to him. His skin was warm on mine.

We stood close together, touching, not moving, for several minutes. He sighed then, chest rising under my ear.

"I've bairns enough," he said quietly. "I've only the one life—and that's you, *mo chridhe*."

I reached up and touched his face. It was furrowed with tiredness, rough with whiskers; he hadn't shaved in days.

I *had* thought about it. And had come very close indeed to asking a surgeon friend to perform the sterilization for me.

Cold blood and clear head had argued for it; no sense in taking chances. And yet . . . there was no guarantee that I would survive the journey, would reach the right time or place, would find him again. Still less, a chance that I might conceive again at my age.

And yet, gone from him for so long, not knowing if I might find him—I could not bring myself to destroy any possibility between us. I did not want another child. But if I found him, and *he* should want it . . . then I would risk it for him.

I touched him, lightly, and he made a small sound in his throat and laid his face against my hair, holding me tight. Our lovemaking was always risk and promise—for if he held my life in his hands when he lay with me, I held his soul, and knew it.

"I thought . . . I thought you'd never see Brianna. And I didn't know about Willie. It wasn't right for me to take away any chance of your having another child—not without telling you."

*You are Blood of my blood*, I had said to him, *Bone of my bone*. That was true, and always would be, whether children came of it or not.

"I dinna want another child," he whispered. "I want you."

His hand rose, as though by itself, touched my breast with a fingertip, left a shimmer of the scented ointment on my skin. I wrapped my hand, slippery and green-scented, round him, and stepped backward, bringing him with me toward the bed. I had just enough presence of mind left to extinguish the candle.

"Don't worry for Bree," I said, reaching up to touch him as he rose over me, looming black against the firelight. "Roger picked the weeds for her. He knows what she wants."

He gave a deep sigh, the breath of a laugh, that caught in his throat as he came to me, and ended in a small groan of pleasure and completion as he slid between my legs, well-oiled and ready.

"I ken what I want, too," he said, voice muffled in my hair. "I shall pick ye another posy, tomorrow."

DRUGGED WITH FATIGUE, languid with love, and lulled by the comforts of a soft, clean bed, I slept like the dead.

Somewhere toward dawn, I began to dream—pleasant dreams of touch and color, without form. Small hands touched my hair, patted my face; I turned on my side, half-conscious, dreaming of nursing a child in my sleep. Tiny soft fingers kneaded my breast, and my hand came up to cup the child's head. It bit me.

I shrieked, shot bolt upright in bed, and saw a gray form race across the quilt and disappear over the end of the bed. I shrieked again, louder.

Jamie shot sideways out of bed, rolled on the floor, and came up standing, shoulders braced and fists half-clenched.

"What?" he demanded, glaring wildly round in search of marauders. "Who? What?"

"A rat!" I said, pointing a trembling finger at the spot where the gray shape had vanished into the crevice between bed-foot and wall.

"Oh." His shoulders relaxed. He scrubbed his hands over his face and through his hair, blinking. "A rat, aye?"

"A rat in our *bed*," I said, not disposed to view the event with any degree of calm. "It bit me!" I peered closely at my injured breast. No blood to speak of; only a couple of tiny puncture marks that stung slightly. I thought of rabies, though, and my blood ran cold.

"Dinna fash yourself, Sassenach. I'll deal with it." Squaring his shoulders once more, Jamie picked up the poker from the hearth and advanced purposefully on the bed-foot. The footboard was solid; there was a space of only a few inches between it and the wall. The rat must be trapped, unless it had managed to escape in the scant seconds between my scream and Jamie's eruption from the quilts.

I got up onto my knees, ready to leap off the bed if necessary. Scowling in concentration, Jamie raised the poker, reached out with his free hand, and flipped the hanging coverlid out of the way.

He whipped the poker down with great force—and jerked it aside, smashing into the wall.

"What?" I said.

"What?" he echoed, in a disbelieving tone. He bent closer, squinting in the dim light, then started to laugh. He dropped the poker, squatted on the floor, and reached slowly into the space between the bed-foot and wall, making a small chirping noise through his teeth. It sounded like birds feeding in a distant bush.

"Are you *talking* to the rat?" I began to crawl toward the foot of the bed, but he motioned me back, shaking his head, while still making the chirping sound.

I waited, with some impatience. Within a minute, he made a grab, evidently catching whatever it was, for he gave a small exclamation of satisfaction. He stood up, smiling, a gray, furry shape clutched by the nape, dangling like a tiny purse from his fingers.

"Here's your wee ratten, Sassenach," he said, and gently deposited a ball of gray fur on the coverlet. Huge eyes of a pale celadon green stared up at me, unblinking.

"Well, goodness," I said. "Wherever did *you* come from?" I extended a finger, very slowly. The kitten didn't move. I touched the edge of a tiny gray-silk jaw, and the big green eyes disappeared, going to slits as it rubbed against my finger. A surprisingly deep purr rumbled through its miniature frame.

*"That,"* Jamie said, with immense satisfaction, "is the present I *meant* to give ye, Sassenach. He'll keep the vermin from your surgery."

"Well, possibly very *small* vermin," I said, examining my new present dubiously. "I think a large cockroach could carry him—is it a him?—off to its lair, let alone a mouse."

"He'll grow," Jamie assured me. "Look at his feet."

He—yes, it was a he—had rolled onto his back and was doing an imitation of a dead bug, paws in the air. Each paw was roughly the size of a broad copper penny, small enough by themselves, but enormous by contrast with the tiny body. I touched the minuscule pads, an immaculate pink in their thicket of soft gray fur, and the kitten writhed in ecstasy.

A discreet knock came at the door, and I snatched the sheet up over my bosom as the door opened and Mr. Wemyss's head poked in, his hair sticking up like a pile of wheat straw.

"Er . . . I hope all is well, sir?" he asked, blinking short-sightedly. "My lass woke me, sayin' as she thought there was a skelloch, like, and then we heard a bit of a bang, like—" His eyes, hastily averted from me, went to the scar of raw wood in the whitewashed wall, left by Jamie's poker.

"Aye, it's fine, Joseph," Jamie assured him. "Only a wee cat."

"Oh, aye?" Mr. Wemyss squinted toward the bed, his thin face breaking into a smile as he made out the blot of gray fur. "A cheetie, is it? Well, and he'll be a fine help i' the kitchen, I've nae doubt."

"Aye. Speakin' of kitchens, Joseph—d'ye think your lassie might bring up a dish of cream for the baudrons here?"

Mr. Wemyss nodded and disappeared, with a final avuncular smile at the kitten.

Jamie stretched, yawned, and scrubbed both hands vigorously through his hair, which was behaving with even more reckless abandon than usual. I eyed him, with a certain amount of purely aesthetic appreciation.

"You look like a woolly mammoth," I said.

"Oh? And what is a mammoth, besides big?"

"A sort of prehistoric elephant—you know, the animals with the long trunks?"

He squinted down the length of his body, then looked at me quizzically.

"Well, I thank ye for the compliment, Sassenach," he said. "Mammoth, is it?" He thrust his arms upward and stretched again, casually arching his back, which—quite inadvertently, I didn't think—enhanced any incidental resemblances that one might note between the half-engorged morning anatomy of a man, and the facial adornments of a pachyderm.

I laughed.

"That's not *precisely* what I meant," I said. "Stop waggling; Lizzie's coming in any minute. You'd better put your shirt on or get back in bed."

The sound of footsteps on the landing sent him diving under the quilts, and sent the little cat scampering up the sheet in fright. In the event, it was Mr. Wemyss himself who had brought the dish of cream, sparing his daughter a possible sight of Himself in the altogether.

The weather being fine, we had left the shutters open the night before. The sky outside was the color of fresh oysters, moist and pearly gray. Mr. Wemyss glanced at it, blinked and nodded at Jamie's thanks, and toddled back to his bed, thankful for a last half hour's sleep before the dawn.

I disentangled the kitten, who had taken refuge in my hair, and set him down by the bowl of cream. I didn't suppose he could ever have seen a bowl of cream in his life, but the smell was enough—in moments, he was whisker-deep, lapping for all he was worth.

"He's a fine thrum to him," Jamie remarked approvingly. "I can hear him from here."

"He's lovely; wherever did you get him?" I nestled into the curve of Jamie's body, enjoying his warmth; the fire had burned far down during the night, and the air in the room was chilly, sour with ash.

"Found him in the wood." Jamie yawned widely, and relaxed, propping his head on my shoulder to watch the tiny cat, who had abandoned himself to an ecstasy of gluttony. "I thought I'd lost him when Gideon bolted—I suppose he'd crept into one of the saddlebags, and came up wi' the other things."

We lapsed into a peaceful stupor, drowsily cuddled in the warm nest of our bed, as the sky lightened, moment by moment, and the air came alive with the voices of waking birds. The house was waking, too—a baby's wail came from below, followed by the stir and shuffle of rising, the murmur of voices. We should rise, too—there was so much to be done—and yet neither of us moved, each reluctant to surrender the sense of quiet sanctuary. Jamie sighed, his breath warm on my bare shoulder.

"A week, I think," he said quietly.

"Before you must go?"

"Aye. I can take that long to settle things here, and speak to the men from the Ridge. A week then, to pass through the country between the Treaty Line and Drunkard's Creek and call a muster—then I'll bring them here to drill. If Tryon should call up the militia, then . . ."

I lay quiet for a moment, my hand wrapped round Jamie's, his loose fist curled against my breast.

"If he calls, I'll go with you."

He kissed the back of my neck.

"D'ye wish it?" he said. "I dinna think there will be need. Neither you nor Bree know of any fighting will be done here now."

"That only means that if anything *will* happen, it won't be a huge battle," I said. "This—the Colonies—it's a big place, Jamie. And two hundred years of things happening—we wouldn't know about the smaller conflicts, especially ones that happened in a different place. Now, in Boston—" I sighed, squeezing his hand.

I wouldn't know a great deal about events in Boston myself, but Bree would; growing up there, she had been exposed in school to a good bit of local and state history. I had heard her telling Roger things about the Boston Massacre—a small confrontation between citizens and British troops that had taken place the past March.

"Aye, I suppose that's true," he said. "Still, it doesna seem as though it will come to anything. I think Tryon only means to frighten the Regulators into good behavior."

This was in fact likely. However, I was quite aware of the old adage—"Man proposes and God disposes"—and whether it was God or William Tryon in charge, heaven only knew what might happen in the event.

"Do you think so?" I asked. "Or only hope so?"

He sighed, and stretched his legs, his arm tightening about my waist.

"Both," he admitted. "Mostly I hope. And I pray. But I do think so, too."

The kitten had completely emptied the dish of cream. He sat down with an audible thump on his tiny backside, rubbed the last of the delicious white stuff from his whiskers, then ambled slowly toward the bed, sides bulging visibly. He sprang up onto the coverlet, burrowed close to me, and fell promptly asleep.

Perhaps not quite asleep; I could feel the small vibration of his purring through the quilt.

"What do you think I should call him?" I mused aloud, touching the tip of the soft, wispy tail. "Spot? Puff? Cloudy?"

"Foolish names," Jamie said, with a lazy tolerance. "Is that what ye were wont to call your pussie-baudrons in Boston, then? Or England?"

"No. I've never had a cat before," I admitted. "Frank was allergic to them—they made him sneeze. And what's a good Scottish cat name, then—Diarmuid? McGillivray?"

He snorted, then laughed.

"Adso," he said, positively. "Call him Adso."

"What sort of name is that?" I demanded, twisting to look back at him in amazement. "I've heard a good many peculiar Scottish names, but that's a new one."

He rested his chin comfortably on my shoulder, watching the kitten sleep.

"My mother had a wee cat named Adso," he said, surprisingly. "A gray cheetie, verra much like this one."

"Did she?" I laid a hand on his leg. He rarely spoke of his mother, who had died when he was eight.

"Aye, she did. A rare mouser, and that fönd of my mother; he didna have much use for us bairns." He smiled in memory. "Possibly because Jenny dressed him in baby-gowns and fed him rusks, and I dropped him into the millpond, to see could he swim. He could, by the way," he informed me, "but he didna like to."

"I can't say I blame him," I said, amused. "Why was he called Adso, though? Is it a saint's name?" I was used to the peculiar names of Celtic saints, from Aodh—pronounced OOH—to Dervorgilla, but hadn't heard of Saint Adso before. Probably the patron saint of mice.

"Not a saint," he corrected. "A monk. My mother was verra learned—she was educated at Leoch, ye ken, along with Colum and Dougal, and could read Greek and Latin, and a bit of the Hebrew as well as French and German. She didna have so much opportunity for reading at Lallybroch, of course, but my father would take pains to have books fetched for her, from Edinburgh and Paris."

He reached across my body to touch a silky, translucent ear, and the kitten twitched its whiskers, screwing up its face as though about to sneeze, but didn't open its eyes. The purr continued unabated.

"One of the books she liked was written by an Austrian,

from the city of Melk, and so she thought it a verra suitable name for the kit."

"Suitable . . . ?"

"Aye," he said, nodding toward the empty dish, without the slightest twitch of lip or eyelid. "Adso of Milk."

A slit of green showed as one eye opened, as though in response to the name. Then it closed again, and the purring resumed.

"Well, if he doesn't mind, I suppose I don't," I said, resigned. "Adso it is."

# THE DEVIL YE KEN

A WEEK LATER, we—that is, the women—were engaged in the backbreaking business of laundry when Clarence the mule let out his clarion announcement that company was coming. Little Mrs. Aberfeldy leaped as though she'd been stung by a bee, and dropped an armload of wet shirts in the dirt of the yard. I could see Mrs. Bug and Mrs. Chisholm opening their mouths in reproach, and took the opportunity to wipe my hands on my apron and hurry round to the front, to greet whatever visitor might be approaching.

Sure enough; a bay mule was coming out of the trees at the head of the trail, followed by a fat brown mare on a leading rein. The mule's ears flicked forward and he brayed enthusiastically in reply to Clarence's greeting. I stuck my fingers in my ears to block the ungodly racket, and squinted against the dazzle of the afternoon sun to make out the mule's rider.

"Mr. Husband!" Pulling my fingers out of my ears, I hurried forward to greet him.

"Mrs. Fraser—good day to thee!"

Hermon Husband pulled off his black slouch hat and gave me a brief nod of greeting, then slid off the mule with a groan that spoke of a good many hours in the saddle. His lips moved soundlessly in the framework of his beard as he straightened stiffly; he was a Quaker, and didn't use strong language. Not out loud, at least.

"Is thy husband at home, Mrs. Fraser?"

"I just saw him heading for the stable; I'll go and find him!" I shouted, above the continued braying of the mules. I took the hat from him, and gestured toward the house. "I'll see to your animals!"

He nodded thanks and limped slowly round the house, toward the kitchen door. From the back, I could see how painfully he moved; he could barely put weight on his left foot. The hat in my hand was covered with dust and mud stains, and I had smelled the odor of unwashed clothes and body when he stood near me. He'd been a long time riding, and not just today—for a week or more, I thought, and sleeping rough for the most of it.

I unsaddled the mule, removing in the process two worn saddlebags half-filled with printed pamphlets, badly printed and crudely illustrated. I studied the illustration with some interest; it was a woodcut of several indignant and righteous-looking Regulators defying a group of officials, among whom was a squat figure I had no trouble identifying as David Anstruther; the caption didn't mention him by name, but the artist had captured the Sheriff's resemblance to a poisonous toad with remarkable facility. Had Husband taken to delivering the bloody things door-to-door? I wondered.

I turned the animals out into the paddock, dumped the hat and saddlebags by the porch, then trekked up the hill to the stable, a shallow cave that Jamie had walled with thick palisades. Brianna referred to it as the maternity ward, since the usual occupants were imminently expectant mares, cows, or sows.

I wondered what brought Hermon Husband here—and

whether he was being followed. He owned a farm and a small mill, both at least two days' ride from the Ridge; not a journey he would undertake simply for the pleasure of our company.

Husband was one of the leaders of the Regulation, and had been jailed more than once for the rabble-rousing pamphlets he printed and distributed. The most recent news I had heard of him was that he had been read out of the local Quaker meeting, the Friends taking a dim view of his activities, which they regarded as incitement to violence. I rather thought they had a point, judging from the pamphlets I'd read.

The door of the stable stood open, allowing the pleasantly fecund scents of straw, warm animals, and manure to drift out, along with a stream of similarly fecund words. Jamie, no Quaker, did believe in strong language, and was using rather a lot of it, albeit in Gaelic, which tends toward the poetic, rather than the vulgar.

I translated the current effusion roughly as, "May your guts twine upon themselves like serpents and your bowels explode through the walls of your belly! May the curse of the crows be upon you, misbegotten spawn of a lineage of dung flies!" Or words to that effect.

"Who are you talking to?" I inquired, putting my head round the stable door. "And what's the curse of the crows?"

I blinked against the sudden dimness, seeing him only as a tall shadow against the piles of pale hay stacked by the wall. He turned, hearing me, and strode into the light from the door. He'd been running his hands through his hair; several strands were pulled from their binding, standing on end, and there were straws sticking out of it.

*"Tha nighean na galladh torrach!"* he said, with a ferocious scowl and a brief gesture behind him.

"White daughter of a bi—oh! You mean that blasted sow has done it again?"

The big white sow, while possessed of superior fatness and amazing reproductive capacity, was also a creature of low cunning, and impatient of captivity. She had escaped her brood pen twice before, once by the expedient of charging Lizzie, who had—wisely—screamed and dived out of the way as the pig barged past, and again by assiduously rooting up one side of the pen, lying in wait until the stable door was opened, and knocking me flat as she made for the wide-open spaces.

This time, she hadn't bothered with strategy, but merely smashed out a board from her pen, then rooted and dug under the palisades, making an escape tunnel worthy of British prisoners-of-war in a Nazi camp.

"Aye, she has," Jamie said, reverting to English now that his initial fury had subsided somewhat. "As for the curse o' the crows, it depends. It might mean ye want the corbies to come down on a man's fields and eat his corn. In this case, I had in mind the birds pecking out the evil creature's eyes."

"I suppose that would make her easier to catch," I said, sighing. "How near is she to farrowing, do you think?"

He shrugged and shoved a hand through his hair.

"A day, two days, three, maybe. Serve the creature right if she farrows in the wood and is eaten by wolves, her and her piglets together." He kicked moodily at the heap of raw earth left by the sow's tunneling, sending a cascade of dirt down into the hole. "Who's come? I heard Clarence yammering."

"Hermon Husband."

He turned sharply toward me, instantly forgetting the pig.

"Has he, then?" he said softly, as though to himself. "Why, I wonder?"

"So did I. He's been riding for some time—distributing pamphlets, evidently."

I had to scamper after Jamie as I added this; he was already striding down the hill toward the house, tidying his hair as he went. I caught up just in time to brush bits of straw from his shoulders before he reached the yard.

Jamie nodded casually to Mrs. Chisholm and Mrs. MacLeod, who were hoicking steaming bales of wet clothes from the big kettle with paddles and spreading them on bushes to dry. I scuttled along with Jamie, ignoring the women's accusing stares and trying to look as though I had much more important concerns to deal with than laundry.

Someone had found Husband refreshment; a plate of partially eaten bread and butter and a half-full mug of buttermilk lay on the table. So did Husband, who had put his head on his folded arms and fallen asleep. Adso crouched on the table beside him, fascinated by the bushy gray whiskers that quivered like antennae with the Quaker's reverberating snores. The kitten was just reaching an experimental paw toward Husband's open mouth when Jamie nabbed him by the scruff of the neck and dropped him neatly into my hands.

"Mr. Husband?" he said quietly, leaning over the table. "Your servant, sir."

Husband snorted, blinked, then sat up suddenly, nearly upsetting the buttermilk. He goggled briefly at me and Adso, then seemed to recollect where he was, for he shook himself, and half-rose, nodding to Jamie.

"Friend Fraser," he said thickly. "I am—I beg pardon—I have been—"

Jamie brushed away his apologies and sat down opposite him, casually picking up a slice of bread and butter from the plate.

"May I be of service to ye, Mr. Husband?"

Husband scrubbed a hand over his face, which did nothing to improve his looks, but did seem to rouse him more fully. Seen clearly in the soft afternoon light of the kitchen, he looked even worse than he had outside, his eyes pouched and bloodshot and his grizzled hair and beard tangled in knots. He was only in his mid-fifties, I knew, but looked at least ten years older. He made an attempt to straighten his coat, and nodded to me, then Jamie.

"I thank thee for the hospitality of thy welcome, Mrs. Fraser. And thee also, Mr. Fraser. I have come indeed to ask a service of thee, if I may."

"Ye may ask, of course," Jamie said courteously. He took a bite of bread and butter, raising his eyebrows in question.

"Will thee buy my horse?"

Jamie's eyebrows stayed raised. He chewed slowly, considering, then swallowed.

"Why?"

Why, indeed. It would have been a great deal easier for Husband to sell a horse in Salem or High Point, if he didn't want to ride as far as Cross Creek. No one in his right mind would venture to a remote place like the Ridge, simply to sell a horse. I set Adso on the floor and sat down beside Jamie, waiting for the answer.

Husband gave him a look, clear and direct for all its bloodshot quality.

"Thee is appointed a colonel of militia, I'm told."

"For my sins," Jamie said, bread poised in the air. "Do ye suppose the Governor has given me money to provide mounts for my regiment?" He took a bite, half-smiling.

The corner of Husband's mouth lifted briefly in acknowledgment of the joke. A colonel of militia supplied his regiment himself, counting upon eventual reimbursement from the Assembly; one reason why only men of property were so appointed—and a major reason why the appointment was not considered an unalloyed honor.

"If he had, I should be pleased to take some of it." At Jamie's gesture of invitation, Husband reached out and selected another slice of bread and butter, which he munched gravely, looking at Jamie under thick salt-and-pepper brows. Finally, he shook his head.

"Nay, friend James. I must sell my stock to pay the fines levied upon me by the Court. If I do not sell what I can, it may be seized. And if I will not, then I have no choice save to quit the colony and remove my family elsewhere—and if I remove, then I must dispose of what I cannot take—for what price I may get."

A small line formed between Jamie's brows.

"Aye, I see," he said slowly. "I would help ye, Hermon, in any way I might. Ye ken that, I hope. But I have scarce two shillings in cash money—not even proclamation money, let alone sterling. If there is anything I have that would be of use to ye, though . . ."

Husband smiled slightly, his harsh features softening.

"Aye, friend James. Thy friendship and thy honor are of great use to me, indeed. For the rest . . ." He sat back from the table, groping in the small shoulder bag he had set down beside him. He came up with a thin letter, bearing a red wax seal. I recognized the seal, and my chest tightened.

"I met the messenger at Pumpkin Town," Husband said, watching as Jamie took the letter and put his thumb beneath the flap. "I offered to carry the letter to thee, as I was bound here in any case."

Jamie's brows lifted, but his attention was focused on the sheet of paper in his hand. I came close, to see over his shoulder.

*November 22, 1770*

*Colonel James Fraser*

> *Whereas I am informed that those who stile themselves Regulators have gathered together in some force near Salisbury, I have sent word to General Waddell to proceed thither at once with the militia troops at his disposal in hopes of dispersing this unlawful assemblage. You are requested and commanded to gather such men as you judge fit to serve in a Regiment of Militia, and proceed with them to Salisbury with as much despatch as may be managed so as to join the General's troops on or before 15 December, at which point he will march upon Salisbury. So far as possible, bring with you flour and other provision sufficient to supply your men for a space of two weeks.*

> *Your ob't. servant,*
> *William Tryon*

The room was quiet, save for the soft rumbling of the cauldron over the coals in the hearth. Outside, I could hear the women talking in short bursts, interspersed with grunts of effort, and the smell of lye soap drifted through the open window, mingling with the scents of stew and rising bread.

Jamie looked up at Husband.

"Ye ken what this says?"

The Quaker nodded, the lines of his face sagging in sudden fatigue.

"The messenger told me. The Governor has no wish to keep his intent secret, after all."

Jamie gave a small grunt of agreement, and glanced at me. No, the Governor wouldn't want to keep it secret. So far as

Tryon was concerned, the more people who knew that Waddell was heading for Salisbury with a large militia troop, the better. Hence also the setting of a specific date. Any wise soldier would prefer to intimidate an enemy rather than fight him—and given that Tryon had no official troops, discretion was certainly the better part of valor.

"What about the Regulators?" I asked Husband. "What are they planning to do?"

He looked mildly startled.

"Do?"

"If your people are assembling, it is presumably to some purpose," Jamie pointed out, a slightly sardonic tone to his voice. Husband heard it, but didn't take exception.

"Certainly there is purpose," he said, drawing himself up with some dignity. "Though thee is mistaken to say these men are mine, in any way save that of brethren, as are all men. But as to purpose, it is only to protest the abuses of power as are all too common these days—the imposition of illegal taxes, the unwarranted seizure of—"

Jamie made an impatient gesture, cutting him off.

"Aye, Hermon, I've heard it. Worse, I've read your writings about it. And if that is the Regulators' purpose, what is yours?"

The Quaker stared at him, thick brows raised and mouth half open in question.

"Tryon has no wish to keep his intentions secret," Jamie elaborated, "but you might. It doesna serve the Regulators' interest that those intentions be carried out, after all." He stared at Husband, rubbing a finger slowly up and down the long, straight bridge of his nose.

Husband raised a hand and scratched at his chin.

"Thee mean why did I bring that"—he nodded toward the letter, which lay open on the table—"when I might have suppressed it?"

Jamie nodded patiently.

"I do."

Husband heaved a deep sigh, and stretched himself, joints cracking audibly. Small white puffs of dust rose from his coat, dissipating like smoke. He settled back into himself then, blinking and looking more comfortable.

"Putting aside any consideration of the honesty of such conduct, friend James . . . I did say that it was thy friendship that would be of most use to me."

"So ye did." The hint of a smile touched the corner of Jamie's mouth.

"Say for the sake of argument that General Waddell does march upon a group of Regulators," Husband suggested. "Is it to the benefit of the Regulators to face men who do not know them, and are inimical to them—or to face neighbors, who know them and are perhaps in some sympathy with their cause?"

"Better the Devil ye ken than the Devil ye don't, eh?" Jamie suggested. "And I'm the Devil ye ken. I see."

A slow smile blossomed on Husband's face, matching the one on Jamie's.

"One of them, friend James. I have been a-horse these ten days past, selling my stock and visiting in one house and another, across the western part of the colony. The Regulation makes no threat, seeks no destruction of property; we wish only that our complaints be heard, and addressed; it is to draw attention to the widespread nature and the justness of these complaints that those most offended are assembling at Salisbury. But I cannot well expect sympathy from those who lack information of the offense, after all."

The smile faded from Jamie's face.

"Ye may have my sympathy, Hermon, and welcome. But if it comes to it . . . I am Colonel of militia. I will have a duty to be carried out, whether that duty is to my liking or no."

Husband flapped a hand, dismissing this.

"I would not ask thee to forsake duty—if it comes. I pray it does not." He leaned forward a little, across the table. "I would ask something of thee, though. My wife, my children . . . if I must leave hurriedly . . ."

"Send them here. They will be safe."

Husband sat back then, shoulders slumping. He closed his eyes and breathed once, deeply, then opened them and set his hands on the table, as though to rise.

"I thank thee. As to the mare—keep her. If my family should have need of her, someone will come. If not—I should greatly prefer that thee have the use of her, rather than some corrupt sheriff."

I felt Jamie move, wanting to protest, and laid a hand on his leg to stop him. Hermon Husband needed reassurance, much more than he needed a horse he could not keep.

"We'll take good care of her," I said, smiling into his eyes. "And of your family, if the need comes. Tell me, what is her name?"

"The mare?" Hermon rose to his feet, and a sudden smile split his face, lightening it amazingly. "Her name is Jerusha, but my wife calls her Mistress Piggy; I am afraid she does possess a great appetite," he added apologetically to Jamie, who had stiffened perceptibly at the word "pig."

"No matter," Jamie said, dismissing pigs from his mind with an obvious effort. He rose, glancing at the window, where the rays of the afternoon sun were turning the polished pinewood of the sills and floors to molten gold. "It grows late, Hermon. Will ye not sup with us, and stop the night?"

Husband shook his head, and stooped to retrieve his shoulder bag.

"Nay, friend James, I thank thee. I have many places still to go."

I insisted that he wait, though, while I made up a parcel of food for him, and he went with Jamie to saddle his mule while I did so. I heard them talking quietly together as they came back from the paddock, voices so low-pitched that I couldn't make out the words. As I came out onto the back porch with the package of sandwiches and beer, though, I heard Jamie say to him, with a sort of urgency, "Are ye sure, Hermon, that what ye do is wise—or necessary?"

Husband didn't answer immediately, but took the parcel from me with a nod of thanks. Then he turned to Jamie, the mule's bridle in his other hand.

"I am minded," he said, glancing from Jamie to me, "of James Nayler. Thee will have heard of him?"

Jamie looked as blank as I did, and Hermon smiled in his beard.

"He was an early member of the Society of Friends, one of those who joined George Fox, who began the Society in

England. James Nayler was a man of forceful conviction, though he was ... individual in his expression of it. Upon one famous occasion, he walked naked through the snow, whilst shouting doom to the city of Bristol. George Fox inquired of him then, 'Is thee *sure* the Lord told thee to do this?' "

The smile widened, and he put his hat carefully back on his head.

"He said that he was. And so am I, friend James. God keep thee and thy family."

# 20

# SHOOTING LESSONS

B RIANNA GLANCED BACK over her shoulder, feeling guilty. The house below had disappeared beneath a yellow sea of chestnut leaves, but the cries of her child still rang in her ears.

Roger saw her look back down the mountainside, and frowned a little, though his voice was light when he spoke.

"He'll be fine, hen. You know your mother and Lizzie will take good care of him."

"Lizzie will spoil him rotten," she agreed, but with a queer tug at her heart at the admission. She could easily see Lizzie carrying Jemmy to and fro all day, playing with him, making faces at him, feeding him rice pudding with molasses ... Jemmy would love the attention, once he got over the distress of her leaving. She felt a sudden surge of territorial feeling regarding Jemmy's small pink toes; she hated the very idea of Lizzie playing Ten Wee Piggies with him.

She hated leaving him, period. His shrieks of panic as she pried his grip from her shirt and handed him over to her mother echoed in her mind, magnified by imagination, and his tearstained look of outraged betrayal lingered in her mind.

At the same time, her need to escape was urgent. She couldn't wait to peel Jem's sticky, clutching hands off her skin and speed away into the morning, free as one of the homing geese that honked their way south through the mountain passes.

She supposed, reluctantly, that she wouldn't feel nearly so guilty about leaving Jemmy, had she not secretly been so eager to do it.

"I'm sure he'll be fine," she reassured herself, more than Roger. "It's just . . . I've never really left him for very long before."

"Mmphm." Roger made a noncommittal noise that might have been interpreted as sympathy. His expression, however, made it clear that he personally thought it well past time that she *had* left the baby.

A momentary spurt of anger warmed her face, but she bit her tongue. He hadn't said anything, after all—had clearly made an effort not to say anything, in fact. She could make an effort, too—and she supposed that it was perhaps not fair to quarrel with someone on the basis of what you thought they were thinking.

She choked off the acrimonious remark she'd had in mind, and instead smiled at him.

"Nice day, isn't it?"

The wary look faded from his face, and he smiled, too, his eyes warming to a green as deep and fresh as the moss that lay in thick beds at the shaded feet of the trees they passed.

"Great day," he said. "Feels good to be out of the house, aye?"

She shot a quick look at him, but it seemed to be a simple statement of fact, with no ulterior motives behind it.

She didn't answer, but nodded in agreement, lifting her face to the errant breeze that wandered through the spruce and fir around them. A swirl of rusty aspen leaves blew down, clinging momentarily to the homespun of their breeches and the light wool of their stockings.

"Wait a minute."

On impulse, she stopped and pulled off her leather buskins and stockings, pushing them carelessly into the rucksack on her shoulder. She stood still, eyes closed in ecstasy, wiggling long bare toes in a patch of damp moss.

"Oh, Roger, try it! This is wonderful!"

He lifted one eyebrow, but obligingly set down the gun—he had taken it, when they left the house, and she had let him, despite a proprietorial urge to carry it herself—undid his own footgear, and cautiously slid one long-boned foot into the moss beside hers. His eyes closed involuntarily, and his mouth rounded into a soundless "ooh."

Moved by impulse, she leaned over and kissed him. His eyes flew open in startlement, but he had fast reflexes. He wrapped a long arm around her waist and kissed her back, thoroughly. It was an unusually warm day for late autumn, and he wore no coat, only a hunting shirt. His chest felt startlingly immediate through the woolen cloth of his shirt; she could feel the tiny bump of his nipple rising under the palm of her hand.

God knew what might have happened next, but the wind changed. A faint cry drifted up from the sea of tossing yellow below. It might have been a baby's cry, or perhaps only a distant crow, but her head swiveled toward it, like a compass needle pointing to true north.

It broke the mood, and he let go, stepping back.

"D'ye want to go back?" he asked, sounding resigned.

She pressed her lips together and shook her head.

"No. Let's get a little farther away from the house, though. We don't want to bother them with the noise. Of—of shooting, I mean."

He grinned, and she felt the blood rise hot in her face. No, she couldn't pretend she hadn't realized there was more than one motive for this private expedition.

"No, not that, either," he said. He stooped for his shoes and stockings. "Come on, then."

She declined to put on her own footwear, but took the opportunity to reappropriate the gun. It wasn't that she didn't trust him with it, though he admitted he hadn't fired such a gun before. She just liked the feel of it, and felt secure with its weight balanced on her shoulder, even unloaded. A Land pattern musket, it was more than five feet long, and weighed a good ten pounds or so, but the butt of the polished walnut stock fitted snugly into her hand and the weight of the steel barrel felt right, laid in the hollow of her shoulder, muzzle to the sky.

"You're going to go barefoot?" Roger cast a quizzical glance at her feet, then ahead, up the mountainside, where a faint path wove through blackberry brambles and fallen branches.

"Just for a while," she assured him. "I used to go barefoot all the time when I was little. Daddy—Frank—took us to the mountains every summer, to the White Mountains or the Adirondacks. After a week, the bottoms of my feet were like leather; I could have walked on hot coals and not felt a thing."

"Aye, I did, too," he said, smiling, and tucked his shoes away as well. "Granted," he said, with a nod toward the faint path that wove its way through brush and half-buried granite outcrops, "the walking along the riverbank of the Ness or the shingle by the Firth was a bit easier going than this, stones notwithstanding."

"That's a point," she said, frowning slightly at his feet. "Have you had a tetanus shot recently? In case you step on something sharp and get punctured?"

He was already climbing ahead of her, choosing his footing cautiously.

"I had injections for everything one could possibly have injections for, before I came through the stones," he assured her, over one shoulder. "Typhoid, cholera, dengue fever, the lot. I'm sure tetanus was in there."

"Dengue fever? I thought I'd had shots for everything, too, but not that one." Digging her toes into the cool mats of dead grass, she took a few long strides to catch him up.

"Shouldn't need it up here." The path ambled round the curve of a steep bank overgrown with yellowing pawpaw and vanished under the overhang of a clump of black-green hemlock. He held the heavy branches back for her and she ducked under them into the pungent gloom, gun held carefully crosswise.

"I wasn't sure where I might have to go, see." His voice

came from behind her, casual, damped by the darkened air under the trees. "If it was the coastal towns, or the West Indies . . . there were . . . there *are*," he corrected himself, automatically, "any number of entertaining African diseases, brought in by the slave ships. Thought I'd best be prepared."

She took advantage of the rough terrain not to answer, but was dismayed—and at the same time, rather shamefully pleased—to discover the lengths to which he'd been prepared to go in order to follow and find her.

The ground was covered with the mottled brown of shed needles, but so damp that there was neither crackle nor prick beneath her feet. It felt spongy, cool, and pleasant under her bare soles, with a give to it that made her think the mass of dead needles must be a foot thick, at least.

"Ow!" Roger, not so lucky in his passage, had set his foot on a rotten persimmon and slid, barely catching himself by grabbing hold of a holly bush, which promptly stabbed him with its prickly leaves.

"Shit," he said, sucking the wounded thumb. "Good thing about the tetanus, aye?"

She laughed in agreement, but found herself worrying as they climbed. What about Jemmy, when he began to walk, and clamber over mountains barefoot? She'd seen enough of the small MacLeods and Chisholms—to say nothing of Germain—to realize that small boys punctured, scraped, lacerated, and fractured themselves on a weekly basis, at least. She and Roger were protected against things like diphtheria and typhoid—Jemmy would have no such protection.

She swallowed, remembering the night before. That murderous horse of her father's had bitten him in the arm, and Claire had made Jamie sit down shirtless before the fire while she cleaned and dressed the bite. Jemmy had poked a curious head up from his cradle, and his grandfather, smiling, had scooped him out and taken him upon his knee.

"Gallopy trot, gallopy trot," he'd chanted, bouncing a delighted Jemmy gently up and down. " 'Tis a wicked horse that I have got!/Gallopy trot, gallopy trot/Let's send him to hell and then he'll be hot!"

It wasn't the charming scene of the two redheads giggling at each other that stuck in her mind, though; it was the firelight glowing in her son's translucent, perfect, untouched skin—and shining silver on the webbed scars across her father's back, black-red on the bloody gash in his arm. It was a dangerous time for men.

She couldn't keep Jem safe from harm; she knew that. But the thought of him—or Roger—being injured or ill made her stomach knot and cold sweat come out on the sides of her face.

"Is your thumb all right?" She turned back toward Roger, who looked surprised, having forgotten all about his thumb.

"What?" He looked at it, puzzled. "Aye, of course."

Nonetheless, she took his hand, and kissed the wounded thumb.

"You be *careful*," she said fiercely.

He laughed, and looked surprised when she glared at him.

"I will," he said, sobering a little. He nodded at the gun she carried. "Don't worry; I may not have fired one, but I know a wee bit about them. I won't blow my fingers off. Does this look all right for a bit of practice?"

They had come out into a heath bald, a high meadow thick with grass and rhododendron. There was a stand of aspen at the far side, their pale branches aflutter with a few late tatters of gold and crimson leaves, vivid against the deep blue sky. A stream gurgled downhill, somewhere out of sight, and a red-tailed hawk circled high overhead. The sun was well up now, warm on her shoulders, and there was a pleasant, grassy bank nearby.

"Just right," she said, and swung the gun down from her shoulder.

IT WAS A beautiful gun, more than five feet long, but so perfectly balanced you could rest it across your outstretched arm without a wobble—which Brianna was doing, by way of demonstration.

"See?" she said, pulling her arm in and sweeping the stock up to her shoulder in one fluid movement. "That's the balance point; you want to put your left hand right there, grab the stock by the trigger with your right, and butt it back into your shoulder. Snug it in, really solidly. There's some kick to it." She bumped the burled walnut stock gently into the socket of her buckskinned shoulder in illustration, then lowered the gun and handed it to Roger, with a somewhat more tender caution than she showed when handing him her infant child, he noted wryly. On the other hand, so far as he could tell, Jemmy was much more indestructible than the gun.

She showed him, hesitant at first, reluctant to correct him. He bit his own tongue, though, and imitated her carefully, following the smooth flow of the steps from ripping the cartridge open with his teeth to priming, loading, ramming, and checking, annoyed at his own novice awkwardness, but secretly fascinated—and more than slightly aroused—by the casual ferocity of her movements.

Her hands were nearly as large as his own, though finely boned; she handled the long gun with the familiarity other women showed with needle and broom. She wore breeks of homespun, and the long muscle of her thigh rose up tight and round against the cloth when she squatted beside him, head bent as she groped in her leather bag.

"What, you packed a lunch?" he joked. "I thought we'd just shoot something and eat it."

She ignored him. She pulled out a ragged white kerchief to use as a target, and shook it out, frowning critically. Once he had thought of her scent as jasmine and grass; now she smelled of gunpowder, leather, and sweat. He breathed it, his fingers unobtrusively stroking the wood of the gunstock.

"Ready?" she said, glancing at him with a smile.

"Oh, aye," he said.

"Check your flint and priming," she said, rising. "I'll pin up the target."

Seen from the back, her ruddy hair clubbed tightly back, and clad in a loose buckskin hunting shirt that covered her from shoulder to thigh, her resemblance to her father was intensified to a startling degree. No mistaking the two, though, he thought. Breeks or no, Jamie Fraser had never in life had an arse like *that*. He watched her walk, congratulating himself on his choice of instructor.

His father-in-law would have given him a lesson, will-

ingly. Jamie was a fine shot, and a patient teacher; Roger had
seen him taking the Chisholm boys out after supper, to practice blasting away at rocks and trees in the empty cornfield. It
was one thing for Jamie to know that Roger was inexperienced with guns; it was another to suffer the humiliation of
demonstrating just *how* inexperienced, under that dispassionate blue gaze.

Beyond the matter of pride, though, he had an ulterior
motive in asking Brianna to come out shooting with him. Not
that he thought said motive was in any way hidden; Claire
had glanced from him to her daughter when he had suggested it, and looked amused in a particularly knowing way
that had made Brianna frown and say, "Mother!" in an accu-
satory tone of voice.

Beyond the all-too-brief hours of their wedding night at
the Gathering, this was the first—and only—time he'd had
Brianna to himself, free from the insatiable demands of her
offspring.

He caught the gleam of sun off metal as she lowered her
arm. She was wearing his bracelet, he realized with a deep
feeling of pleasure. He had given it to her when he'd asked
her to marry him—a lifetime ago, in the freezing mists of a
winter night in Inverness. It was a simple circlet of silver, engraved with a series of phrases in French. *Je t'aime*, it said: *I
love you. Un peu, beaucoup, passionnément, pas du tout: A
little, a lot, passionately—not at all*.

"*Passionnément*," he murmured, envisioning her wearing
nothing *but* his bracelet and her wedding ring.

First things first, though, he told himself, and picked up a
fresh cartridge. After all, they had time.

SATISFIED THAT HIS loading habits were on the way
to being well established, if not yet rapid, Brianna finally allowed him to practice sighting, and at last, to shoot.

It took a dozen tries before he could hit the white square
of the kerchief, but the sense of exultation he felt when a
dark spot appeared suddenly near the edge of it had him
reaching for a fresh cartridge before the smoke of the shot

had dissipated. The sense of excited accomplishment took him through another dozen cartridges, scarcely noticing anything beyond the jerk and boom of the gun, the flash of powder, and the breathless instant of realization when he saw an occasional shot go home.

The kerchief hung in tatters by this time, and small clouds of whitish smoke floated over the meadow. The hawk had decamped at the sound of the first shot, along with all the other birds of the neighborhood, though the ringing in his ears sounded like a whole chorus of distant titmice.

He lowered the gun and looked at Brianna, grinning, whereupon she burst into laughter.

"You look like the end man in a minstrel show," she said, the end of her nose going pink with amusement. "Here, clean up a little, and we'll try shooting from farther away."

She took the gun and handed him a clean handkerchief in exchange. He wiped black soot from his face, watching as she swiftly swabbed the barrel and reloaded. She straightened, then heard something; her head rose suddenly, eyes fixing on an oak across the meadow.

Ears still ringing from the roar of the gun, Roger had heard nothing. Swinging round, though, he caught a flicker of movement; a dark gray squirrel, poised on a pine branch at least thirty feet above the ground.

Without the slightest hesitation, Brianna raised the gun to her shoulder and seemed to fire in the same motion. The branch directly under the squirrel exploded in a shower of wood chips, and the squirrel, blown off its feet, plunged to the ground, bouncing off the springy evergreen branches as it went.

Roger ran across to the foot of the tree, but there was no need to hurry; the squirrel lay dead, limp as a furry rag.

"Good shot," he said in congratulation, holding up the corpse as Brianna came to see. "But there's not a mark on him—you must have scared him to death."

Brianna gave him a level look from beneath her brows.

"If I'd meant to hit him, Roger, I'd have hit him," she said, with a slight edge of reproof. "And if I *had* hit him, you'd be holding a handful of squirrel mush. You don't aim right at something that size; you aim to hit just under them and knock them down. It's called barking," she explained, like a kindly kindergarten teacher correcting a slow pupil.

"Oh, aye?" He repressed a small sense of irritation. "Your father teach you that?"

She gave him a slightly odd look before replying.

"No, Ian did."

He made a noncommittal noise in response to that. Ian was a point of awkwardness in the family. Brianna's cousin had been well-loved, and he knew the whole family missed him. Still, they hesitated to speak of Young Ian before Roger, out of delicacy.

It hadn't exactly been Roger's *fault* that Ian Murray had remained with the Mohawk—but there was no denying that he had had a part in the matter. If he hadn't killed that Indian . . .

Not for the first time, he pushed aside the confused memories of that night in Snaketown, but felt nonetheless the physical echoes; the quicksilver rush of terror through his belly and the judder of impact through the muscles of his forearms, as he drove the broken end of a wooden pole with all his strength into a shadow that had sprung up before him out of the shrieking dark. A very solid shadow.

Brianna had crossed the meadow, and set up another target; three irregular chunks of wood set on a stump the size of a dinner table. Without comment, he wiped his sweating hands on his breeks, and concentrated on the new challenge, but Ian Murray refused to leave his mind. He'd barely seen the man, but remembered him clearly; hardly more than a youth, tall and gangly, with a homely but appealing face.

He couldn't think of Murray's face without seeing it as he last had, scabbed with a line of freshly tattooed dots that looped across the cheeks and over the bridge of his nose. His face was brown from the sun, but the skin of his freshly plucked scalp had been a fresh and startling pink, naked as a baby's bum and blotched red from the irritation of the plucking.

"What's the matter?"

Brianna's voice startled him, and the barrel jerked up as he fired, the shot going wild. Or wilder, rather. He hadn't managed to hit any of the wooden blocks in a dozen shots.

He lowered the gun and turned to her. She was frowning, but didn't look angry, only puzzled and concerned.

"What's wrong?" she asked again.

He took a deep breath and rubbed his sleeve across his face, careless of the smears of black soot.

"Your cousin," he said abruptly. "I'm sorry about him, Bree."

Her face softened, and the worried frown eased a little.

"Oh," she said. She laid a hand on his arm and drew near, so he felt the warmth of her closeness. She sighed deeply and laid her forehead against his shoulder.

"Well," she said at last, "I'm sorry, too—but it isn't any more your fault than mine or Da's—or Ian's, for that matter." She gave a small snort that might have been intended for a laugh. "If it's anyone's fault, it's Lizzie's—and nobody blames *her*."

He smiled at that, a little wryly.

"Aye, I see," he answered, and cupped a hand over the cool smoothness of her plait. "You're right. And yet—I killed a man, Bree."

She didn't startle or jerk away, but somehow went completely still. So did he; it was the last thing he'd meant to say.

"You never told me that before," she said at last, raising her head to look at him. She sounded tentative, unsure whether to pursue the matter. The breeze lifted a strand of hair across her face, but she didn't move to brush it away.

"I—well, to tell ye the truth, I've scarcely thought of it." He dropped his hand, and the stasis was broken. She shook herself a little and stood back.

"That sounds terrible, doesn't it? But—" He struggled for words. He'd not meant to say anything, but now he'd started, it seemed urgently necessary to explain, to put it into proper words.

"It was at night, during a fight in the village. I escaped—I'd a bit of broken pole in my hand, and when someone loomed up out of the darkness, I . . ."

His shoulders slumped suddenly, as he realized that there was no possible way to explain, not really. He looked down at the gun he still held.

"I didn't know I'd killed him," he said quietly, eyes on the flint. "I didn't even see his face. I still don't know who it was—though it had to be someone I knew; Snaketown was a small village, I knew all *ne rononkwe*." Why, he wondered suddenly, had he never once thought of asking who the dead man was? Plain enough; he hadn't asked because he didn't want to know.

*"Ne rononkwe?"* She repeated the words uncertainly.

"The men . . . the warriors . . . braves. It's what they call themselves, the Kahnyen'kehaka." The Mohawk words felt strange on his tongue; alien and familiar at once. He could see wariness on her face, and knew his speaking of it had sounded odd to her; not the way one uses a foreign term, handling it gingerly, but the way her father sometimes casually mingled Gaelic and Scots, mind seizing on the most available word in either language.

He stared down at the gun in his hand, as though he'd never seen one before. He wasn't looking at her, but felt her draw near again, still tentative, but not repulsed.

"Are you . . . sorry about it?"

"No," he said at once, and looked up at her. "I mean . . . aye, I'm sorry it happened. But sorry I did it—no." He had spoken without pausing to weigh his words, and was surprised—and relieved—to find them true. He felt regret, as he'd told her, but what guilt there was had nothing to do with the shadow's death, whoever it had been. He had been a slave in Snaketown, and had no great love for any of the Mohawk, though some were decent enough. He'd not intended killing, but had defended himself. He'd do it again, in the same circumstance.

Yet there was a small canker of guilt—the realization of just how easily he had dismissed that death. The Kahnyen'kehaka sang and told stories of their dead, and kept their memory alive around the fires of the longhouses, naming them for generations and recounting their deeds. Just as the Highlanders did. He thought suddenly of Jamie Fraser, face ablaze at the great fire of the Gathering, calling his people by name and by lineage. *Stand by my hand, Roger the singer, son of Jeremiah MacKenzie.* Perhaps Ian Murray found the Mohawk not so strange, after all.

Still, he felt obscurely as though he had deprived the unknown dead man of name, as well as life, seeking to blot him out by forgetting, to behave as though that death had never happened, only to save himself from the knowledge of it. And that, he thought, was wrong.

Her face was still, but not frozen; her eyes rested on his with something like compassion. Still, he looked away, back at the gun whose barrel he gripped. His fingers, soot-stained, had left greasy black ovals on the metal; she reached out and took it from him, rubbing the marks away with the hem of her shirt.

He let her take it, and watched, rubbing his dirty fingers against the side of his breeches.

"It's just . . . does it not seem that if ye must kill a man, it should be on purpose? Meaning it?"

She didn't answer, but her lips pursed slightly, then relaxed.

"If you shoot someone with this, Roger, it will be on purpose," she said quietly. She looked up at him, then, blue eyes intent, and he saw that what he had taken for compassion was in fact a fierce stillness, like the small blue flames in a burned-out log.

"And if you have to shoot someone, Roger, I want you to mean it."

TWO DOZEN ROUNDS later, he could hit the wooden blocks at least once in six tries. He would have kept it up, doggedly, but she could see the muscles in his forearms beginning to tremble as he lifted the gun, stilled by effort of will. He would begin to miss more often now, out of fatigue, and that would do him no good.

Or her. Her breasts were beginning to ache, engorged with milk. She'd have to do something about it soon.

"Let's go and eat," she said, smiling as she took the musket from him after the last shot. "I'm starving."

The exertion of shooting, reloading, putting up targets, had kept them both warm, but it was nearly winter, and the air was cold; much too cold, she thought regretfully, to lie naked in the dry ferns. But the sun was warm, and with forethought, she had packed two ratty quilts in her rucksack, along with the lunch.

He was quiet, but it was a comfortable quiet. She watched him cut slivers from the chunk of hard cheese, dark lashes lowered, and admired the long-limbed, competent look of him, fingers neat and quick, gentle mouth compressed slightly as he concentrated on his work, a drop of sweat rolling down the high brown curve of his cheekbone, in front of his ear.

She wasn't sure what to make of what he had told her. Still, she knew enough to realize that it was a good thing that he had told her, even though she didn't like to hear or think of his time with the Mohawk. It had been a bad time for her—alone, pregnant, doubting whether he or her parents would ever return—as well as for him. She reached to accept a bit of cheese, brushed his fingers with her own, and leaned forward, to make him kiss her.

He did, then sat back, his eyes gone soft green and clear, free of the shadow that had haunted them.

"Pizza," he said.

She blinked, then laughed. It was one of their games; taking turns to think of things they missed from the other time, the time before—or after, depending how you looked at it.

"Coke," she said promptly. "I think I could maybe do pizza—but what good is pizza without Coca-Cola?"

"Pizza with beer is perfectly fine," he assured her. "And we can have beer—not that Lizzie's homemade hell-brew is quite on a par with MacEwan's Lager, yet. But you really think you could make pizza?"

"Don't see why not." She nibbled at the cheese, frowning. "This wouldn't do"—she brandished the yellowish remnant, then popped it in her mouth—"too strong-flavored. But I think . . ." She paused to chew and swallow, then washed it down with a long drink of rough cider.

"Come to think of it, this would go pretty well with pizza." She lowered the leather bottle and licked the last sweet, semi-alcoholic drops from her lips. "But the cheese—I think maybe sheep's cheese would do. Da brought some from Salem last time he went there. I'll ask him to get some more and see how it melts."

She squinted against the bright, pale sun, calculating.

"Mama's got plenty of dried tomatoes, and tons of garlic. I know she has basil—don't know about the oregano, but I could do without that. And crust—" She waved a dismissive hand. "Flour, water, and lard, nothing to it."

He laughed, handing her a biscuit filled with ham and Mrs. Bug's piccalilli.

"How Pizza Came to the Colonies," he said, and lifted the cider bottle in brief salute. "Folk always wonder where humanity's great inventions come from; now we know!"

He spoke lightly, but there was an odd tone in his voice, and his glance held hers.

"Maybe we do know," she said softly, after a moment. "You ever think about it—why? Why we're here?"

"Of course." The green of his eyes was darker now, but still clear. "So do you, aye?"

She nodded, and took a bite of biscuit and ham, the piccalilli sweet with onion and pungent in her mouth. Of course they thought of it. She and Roger and her mother. For surely it had meaning, that passage through the stones. It must. And yet . . . her parents seldom spoke of war and battle, but from the little they said—and the much greater quantity she had read—she knew just how random and how pointless such things could sometimes be. Sometimes a shadow rises, and death lies nameless in the dark.

Roger crumbled the last of his bread between his fingers, and tossed the crumbs a few feet away. A chickadee flew down, pecked once, and was joined within seconds by a flock that swooped down out of the trees, vacuuming up the crumbs with chattering efficiency. He stretched, sighing, and lay back on the quilt.

"Well," he said, "if you ever figure it out, ye'll be sure to tell me, won't you?"

Her heartbeat was tingling in her breasts; no longer safely contained behind the rampart of her breastbone, but set loose to crackle through her flesh, small jolts of electricity tweaking her nipples. She didn't dare to think of Jem; the barest hint of him and her milk would let down in a gush.

Before she could let herself think too much about it, she pulled the hunting shirt over her head.

Roger's eyes were open, fixed on her, soft and brilliant as the moss beneath the trees. She undid the knot of the linen strip, and felt the cool touch of the wind on her bare breasts. She cupped them in her hands, feeling the heaviness rise, begin to tingle and crest.

"Come here," she said softly, eyes on his. "Hurry. I need you."

THEY LAY HALF-CLOTHED and comfortably tangled beneath the tattered quilt, sleepy and sticky with half-dried milk, the heat of their joining still warm around them.

The sun through the empty branches overhead made black ripples behind the lids of her closed eyes, as though she looked down through a dark red sea, wading in the blood-warm water, seeing black volcanic sand change and ripple round her feet.

Was he awake? She didn't turn her head or open her eyes to see, but tried to send a message to him, a slow, lazy pulse of a heartbeat, a question surging from blood to blood. *Are you there?* she asked silently. She felt the question move up through her chest and out along her arm; she imagined the pale underside of her arm and the blue vein along it, as though she might see some telltale subterranean flash as the impulse threaded through her blood and down her forearm, reached her palm, her finger, and delivered the faintest throb of its pressure against his skin.

Nothing happened at once. She could hear his breathing, slow and regular, a counterpoint to the sough of breeze through trees and grass, like surf coming in upon a sandy shore.

She imagined herself as a jellyfish, he another. She could see them clearly; two transparent bodies, lucent as the moon, veils pulsing in and out in hypnotic rhythm, borne on the tide toward one another, tendrils trailing, slowly touching . . .

His finger crossed her palm, so lightly it might have been the brush of fin or feather.

*I'm here*, it said. *And you?*

Her hand closed over it, and he rolled toward her.

LATE IN THE YEAR as it was, the light died early. It was still a month 'til the winter solstice, but by mid-afternoon, the sun was already brushing the slope of Black Mountain, and their shadows stretched to impossible lengths before them as they turned eastward, toward home.

She carried the gun; instruction was over for the day, and while they weren't hunting, if the opportunity of game offered, she would take it. The squirrel she had killed earlier was already cleaned and tucked in her sack, but that was barely flavoring for a vegetable stew. A few more would be nice. Or a possum, she thought dreamily.

She wasn't sure of the habits of possum, though; perhaps they hibernated over winter, and if so, they might already be gone. The bears were still active; she'd seen half-dried scat on the trail, and scratches on the bark of a pine, still oozing yellow sap. A bear was good game, but she didn't mean either to look for one, or to risk shooting at one unless it attacked them—and that wasn't likely. Leave bears alone, and they'll generally leave you alone; both her fathers had told her that, and she thought it excellent advice.

A covey of bobwhite blasted out of a nearby bush like exploding shrapnel, and she jerked, heart in her mouth.

"Those are good to eat, aren't they?" Roger nodded at the last of the disappearing gray-white blobs. He had been startled, too, but less than she had, she noticed with annoyance.

"Yeah," she said, disgruntled at being taken unawares. "But you don't shoot them with a musket, unless all you want is feathers for a pillow. You use a fowling piece, with bird shot. It's like a shotgun."

"I know," he said, shortly.

She felt disinclined to talk, jarred out of their peaceful mood. Her breasts were beginning to swell again; it was time to go home, to find Jemmy.

Her step quickened a little at the thought, even as her mind reluctantly surrendered the memory of the pungent smell of crushed dry fern, the glow of sunlight on Roger's bare brown shoulders above her, the hiss of her milk, gilding his chest in a spray of fine droplets, slick and warm and cool by turns between their writhing bodies.

She sighed deeply, and heard him laugh, low in his throat.

"Mmm?" She turned her head, and he motioned to the ground before them. They had begun to move together as they walked, neither noticing the unconscious pull of the gravitational force that bound them. Now their shadows had merged at the top, so an odd, four-legged beast paced spider-like before them, its two heads tilted toward each other.

He put an arm around her waist, and one shadow-head dipped, joining the other in a single bulbous shape.

"It's been a good day, aye?" he said softly.

"Aye, it has," she said, and smiled. She might have spoken further, but a sound came to her above the rattle of tree branches, and she pulled suddenly away.

"What—" he began, but she put a finger to her lips to shush him, beckoning as she crept toward a growth of red oak.

It was a flock of turkeys, scratching companionably in the earth beneath a large oak tree, turning up winter grubs from the mat of fallen leaves and acorns. The late sun shone low, lighting the iridescence in their breast feathers, so the birds' drab black glimmered with tiny rainbows as they moved.

She had the gun already loaded, but not primed. She groped for the powder flask at her belt and filled the pan, scarcely looking away from the birds. Roger crouched beside her, intent as a hound dog on the scent. She nudged him, and held the gun toward him in invitation, one eyebrow up. The turkeys were no more than twenty yards away, and even the smaller ones were the size of footballs.

He hesitated, but she could see the desire to try it in his eyes. She thrust the gun firmly into his hands and nodded toward a gap in the brush.

He shifted carefully, trying for a clear line of sight. She hadn't taught him to fire from a crouch as yet, and he wisely didn't try, instead standing, though it meant firing downward. He hesitated, the long barrel wavering as he shifted his aim from one bird to another, trying to choose the best shot. Her fingers curled and clenched, aching to correct his aim, to pull the trigger.

She felt him draw breath and hold it. Then three things happened, so quickly as to seem simultaneous. The gun went off with a huge *phwoom!*, a spray of dried oak leaves fountained up from the earth under the tree, and fifteen turkeys lost their minds, running like a demented football squad straight at them, gobbling hysterically.

The turkeys reached the brush, saw Roger, and took to the air like flying soccer balls, wings frantically clapping the air. Roger ducked to avoid one that soared an inch above his head, only to be struck in the chest by another. He reeled backward, and the turkey, clinging to his shirt, seized the opportunity to run nimbly up his shoulder and push off, raking the side of his neck with its claws.

The gun flew through the air. Brianna caught it, flipped a cartridge from the box on her belt, and was grimly reloading and ramming as the last turkey ran toward Roger, zigged away, saw her, zagged in the other direction, and finally zoomed between them, gobbling alarms and imprecations.

She swung around, sighted on it as it left the ground, caught the black blob outlined for a split second against the brilliant sky, and blasted it in the tail feathers. It dropped like a sack of coal, and hit the ground forty yards away with an audible thud.

She stood still for a moment, then slowly lowered the gun. Roger was staring at her, openmouthed, pressing the cloth of his shirt against the bloody scratches on his neck. She smiled at him, a little weakly, feeling her hands sweaty on the wooden stock and her heart pounding with delayed reaction.

"Holy God," Roger said, deeply impressed. "That wasn't just luck, was it?"

"Well . . . some," she said, trying for modesty. She failed, and felt a grin blossom across her face. "Maybe half."

Roger went to retrieve her prize while she cleaned the gun again, coming back with a ten-pound bird, limp-necked and leaking blood like a punctured waterskin.

"What a thing," he said. He held it at arm's length to drain, admiring the vivid reds and blues of the bare, warty head and dangling wattle. "I don't think I've ever seen one, save roasted on a platter, with chestnut dressing and roast potatoes."

He looked from the turkey to her with great respect, and nodded at the gun.

"That's great shooting, Bree."

She felt her cheeks flush with pleasure, and restrained the urge to say, "Aw, shucks, it warn't nothin'," settling instead for a simple, "Thanks."

They turned again toward home, Roger still carrying the dripping carcass, held slightly out from his body.

"You haven't been shooting all that long, either," Roger was saying, still impressed. "What's it been, six months?"

She didn't want to lower his estimation of her prowess, but laughed, shrugged, and told the truth anyway.

"More like six years. Really more like ten."

"Eh?"

"Daddy—Frank—taught me to shoot when I was eleven or twelve. He gave me a twenty-two when I was thirteen, and by the time I was fifteen, he was taking me to shoot clay pigeons at ranges, or to hunt doves and quail on weekends in the fall."

Roger glanced at her in interest.

"I thought Jamie'd taught you; I'd no idea Frank Randall was such a sportsman."

"Well," she said slowly. "I don't know that he was."

One black brow went up in inquiry.

"Oh, he knew how to shoot," she assured him. "He'd been in the Army during World War Two. But he never shot much himself; he'd just show me, and then watch. In fact, he never even owned a gun."

"That's odd."

"Isn't it?" She moved deliberately closer to him, nudging his shoulder so that their shadows merged again; now it looked like a two-headed ogre, carrying a gun over one shoulder, and a third head held bloodily in its hand. "I wondered about that," she said, with attempted casualness. "After you told me—about his letter and all that, at the Gathering."

He shot her a sharp look.

"Wondered what?"

She took a deep breath, feeling the linen strips bite into her breasts.

"I wondered why a man who didn't ride or shoot should take such pains to see that his daughter could do both those things. I mean, it wasn't like it was common for girls to do that." She tried to laugh. "Not in Boston, anyway."

There was no sound for a moment but the shuffling of their feet through dry leaves.

"Christ," Roger said softly, at last. "He looked for Jamie Fraser. He said so, in his letter."

"And he found a Jamie Fraser. He said that, too. We just don't know whether it was the right one or not." She kept her eyes on her boots, wary of snakes. There were copperheads in the wood, and timber rattlers; she saw them now and then, basking on rocks or sunny logs.

Roger took a deep breath, lifting his head.

"Aye. And so you're wondering now—what else might he have found?"

She nodded, not looking up.

"Maybe he found me," she said softly. Her throat felt tight. "Maybe he knew I'd go back, through the stones. But if he did—he didn't tell me."

He stopped walking, and put a hand on her arm to turn her toward him.

"And perhaps he didn't know that at all," he said firmly. "He may only have thought ye *might* try it, if you ever found out about Fraser. And if you did find out, and did go . . . then he wanted you to be safe. I'd say no matter what he knew, that's what he wanted; you to be safe." He smiled, a little crookedly. "Like you want me to be safe. Aye?"

She heaved a deep sigh, feeling comfort descend on her with his words. She'd never doubted that Frank Randall had loved her, all the years of her growing up. She didn't want to doubt it now.

"Aye," she said, and tilted up an inch on her toes to kiss him.

"Fine, then," he said, and gently touched her breast, where the buckskin of her shirt showed a small wet patch. "Jem'll be hungry. Come on; it's time we were home."

They turned again and went down the mountain, into the golden sea of chestnut leaves, watching their shadows go before them as they walked, embracing.

"Do you think—" she began, and hesitated. One shadow head dipped toward the other, listening.

"Do you think Ian's happy?"

"I hope so," he replied, and his arm tightened round her. "If he has a wife like mine—then I'm sure he is."

# TWENTY-TWENTY

N OW, HOLD THIS over your left eye, and read the smallest line you can see clearly."

With a long-suffering air, Roger held the wooden spoon over his right eye and narrowed his left, concentrating on the sheet of paper I had pinned to the kitchen door. He was standing in the front hall, just inside the door, as the length of the corridor was the only stretch of floor within the house approaching twenty feet.

"*Et tu Brute?*" he read. He lowered the spoon and looked at me, one dark eyebrow raised. "I've never seen a literate eye chart before."

"Well, I always did think the 'f, e, 5, z, t, d' things on the regular charts rather boring," I said, unpinning the paper and flipping it over. "Other eye, please. What's the smallest line you can read easily?"

He reversed the spoon, squinted at the five lines of hand-printing—done in such even decrements of size as I could manage—and read the third one, slowly.

"*Eat no onions.* What's that from?"

"Shakespeare, of course," I said, making a note. "*Eat no*

*onions nor garlic, for we are to utter sweet breath.* That's the smallest you can read, is it?"

I saw Jamie's expression alter subtly. He and Brianna were standing just behind Roger, out on the porch, watching the proceedings with great interest. Brianna was leaning slightly toward Roger, a faintly anxious expression on her face, as though willing him to see the letters.

Jamie's expression, though, showed slight surprise, faint pity—and an undeniable glint of satisfaction. *He*, evidently, could read the fifth line without trouble. *I honor him.* One from *Julius Caesar: As he was valiant, I honor him; as he was ambitious, I slew him.*

He felt my gaze on him, and the expression vanished, his face instantly resuming its usual look of good-humored inscrutability. I narrowed my eyes at him, with a "You're not fooling *me*" sort of look, and he looked away, the corner of his mouth twitching slightly.

"You can't make out any of the next line?" Bree had moved close to Roger, as though drawn by osmosis. She stared intently at the paper, then at him, with an encouraging look. Obviously she could see the last two lines without difficulty, too.

"No," Roger said, rather shortly. He'd agreed to let me check his eyes at her request, but he obviously wasn't happy about it. He slapped the palm of his hand lightly with the spoon, impatient to be done with this. "Anything else?"

"Just a few small exercises," I said, as soothingly as possible. "Come in here, where the light is better." I put a hand on his arm and drew him toward my surgery, giving Jamie and Bree a hard look as I did so. "Brianna, why don't you go and lay the table for supper? We won't be long."

She hesitated for a moment, but Jamie touched her arm and said something to her in a low voice. She nodded, glanced once more at Roger with a small, anxious frown, and went. Jamie gave me an apologetic shrug, and followed her.

Roger was standing among the litter in my surgery, looking like a bear that hears barking hounds in the distance—simultaneously annoyed and wary.

"There's no need for this," he said, as I closed the door. "I see fine. I just don't shoot very well yet. There's nothing the matter with my eyes." Still, he made no move to escape, and I picked up the hint of doubt in his voice.

"Shouldn't think there is," I said lightly. "Let me have just a quick look, though . . . just curiosity on my part, really. . . ." I got him sat down, however reluctantly, and for lack of the standard small flashlight, lit a candle.

I brought it close to check the dilation of his pupils. His eyes were the most lovely color, I thought; not hazel at all, but a very clear dark green. Dark enough to look almost black in shadow, but a startling color—almost emerald— when seen directly in bright light. A disconcerting sight, to one who had known Geilie Duncan and seen her mad humor laugh out of those clear green depths. I did hope Roger hadn't inherited anything *but* the eyes from her.

He blinked once, involuntarily, long black lashes sweeping down over them, and the memory disappeared. These eyes were beautiful—but calm, and above all, sane. I smiled at him, and he smiled back in reflex, not understanding.

I passed the candle before his face, up, down, right, left, asking him to keep looking at the flame, watching the changes as his eyes moved to and fro. Since no answers were required in this exercise, he began to relax a bit, his fists gradually uncurling on his thighs.

"Very nice," I said, keeping my voice low and soothing. "Yes, that's good . . . can you look up, please? Yes, now look down, toward the corner by the window. Mm-hm, yes . . . Now, look at me again. You see my finger? Good, now close your left eye and tell me if the finger moves. Mm-hmmm . . ."

Finally, I blew out the candle, and straightened up, stretching my back with a small groan.

"So," Roger said lightly, "what's the verdict, Doctor? Shall I go and be making myself a white cane?" He waved away the drifting wisps of smoke from the blown-out candle, making a good-attempt at casualness—belied only by the slight tension in his shoulders.

I laughed.

"No, you won't need a Seeing Eye dog for some time yet, nor even spectacles. Though speaking of that—you said you'd never seen a literate eye chart before. But you have seen eye charts, I take it. Did you ever wear glasses as a child?"

He frowned, casting his mind back.

"Aye, I did," he said slowly. "Or rather"—a faint grin showed on his face—"I *had* a pair of specs. Or two or three. When I was seven or eight, I think. They were a nuisance, and gave me a headache. So I was inclined to leave them on the public bus, or at school, or on the rocks by the river . . . I can't recall actually *wearing* them for more than an hour at a time, and after I'd lost the third pair, my father gave up." He shrugged.

"I've never felt as though I needed spectacles, to be honest."

"Well, you don't—now."

He caught the tone of my voice and looked down at me, puzzled.

"What?"

"You're a bit shortsighted in the left eye, but not by enough to cause you any real difficulty." I rubbed the bridge of my nose, as though feeling the pinch of spectacles myself. "Let me guess—you were good at hockey and football when you were at school, but not at tennis."

He laughed at that, eyes crinkling at the corners.

"Tennis? At an Inverness grammar school? Soft Southron sport, we'd have called it; game for poofters. But I take your point—no, you're right, I was fine at the football, but not much at rounders. Why?"

"You don't have any binocular vision," I said. "Chances are that someone noticed it when you were a child, and made an effort to correct it with prismatic lenses—but it's likely that it would have been too late by the time you were seven or eight," I added hastily, seeing his face go blank. "If that's going to work, it needs to be done very young—before the age of five."

"I don't . . . binocular vision? But doesn't everyone? . . . I mean, both my eyes do work, don't they?" He looked mildly bewildered. He looked down into the palm of his hand, closing one eye, then the other, as though some answer might be found among the lines there.

"Your eyes are fine," I assured him. "It's just that they

don't work *together*. It's really a fairly common condition—and many people who have it don't realize it. It's just that in some people, for one reason or another, the brain never learns to merge the images coming in from both eyes in order to make a three-dimensional image."

"I don't see in three dimensions?" He looked at me, now, squinting hard, as though expecting me suddenly to flatten out against the wall.

"Well, I haven't quite got a trained oculist's kit"—I waved a hand at the burned-out candle, the wooden spoon, the drawn figures, and a couple of sticks I had been using—"nor yet an oculist's training. But I'm reasonably sure, yes."

He listened quietly as I explained what I could. His vision seemed fairly normal, in terms of acuity. But since his brain was not fusing the information from his eyes, he must be estimating the distance and relative location of objects simply by unconscious comparison of their sizes, rather than by forming a real 3-D image. Which meant . . .

"You can see perfectly well for almost anything you want to do," I assured him. "And you very likely can learn to shoot all right; most of the men I see shooting close one eye when they fire, anyway. But you might have trouble hitting moving targets. You can see what you're aiming at, all right—but without binocular vision, you may not be able to tell *precisely* where it is in order to hit it."

"I see," he said. "So, if it comes to a fight, I'd best rely on straightforward bashing, is that it?"

"In my humble experience of Scottish conflicts," I said, "most fights amount to no more than bashing, anyway. You only use a gun or arrow if your goal is murder—and in that case, a blade is usually the weapon of preference. So much surer, Jamie tells me."

He gave a small grunt of amusement at that, but said nothing else. He sat quietly, considering what I'd told him, while I tidied up the disorder left by the day's surgery. I could hear thumping and clanging from the kitchen, and the pop and sizzle of fat that went with the tantalizing aroma of frying onions and bacon that floated down the corridor.

It was going to be a hasty meal; Mrs. Bug had been busy all day with the preparations for the militia expedition. Still, even Mrs. Bug's least elaborate spreads were well worth the eating.

Muffled voices came through the wall—Jemmy's sudden wail, a brief exclamation from Brianna, another from Lizzie, then Jamie's deep voice, evidently comforting the baby while Bree and Lizzie dealt with dinner.

Roger heard them, too; I saw his head turn toward the sound.

"Quite a woman," he said, with a slow smile. "She can kill it *and* cook it. Which looks like being a good thing, under the circumstances," he added ruefully. "Evidently I won't be putting much meat on the table."

"Pah," I said briskly, wishing to forestall any attempt on his part to feel sorry for himself. "I've never shot a thing in my life, and I put food on this table every day. If you really feel you must kill things, you know, there are plenty of chickens and geese and pigs. And if you can catch that damnable white sow before she undermines the foundation entirely, you'll be a local hero."

That made him smile, though with a wry twist to it nonetheless.

"I expect my self-respect will recover, with or without the pigs," he said. "The worst of it will be telling the sharpshooters"—he jerked his head toward the wall, where Brianna's voice mingled with Jamie's in muffled conversation—"what the problem is. They'll be very kind—like one is to somebody who's missing a foot."

I laughed, finished swabbing out my mortar, and reached up to put it away in the cupboard.

"Bree's only worrying about you, because of this Regulation trouble. But Jamie thinks it won't amount to anything; the chances of you needing to shoot someone are very small. Besides, birds of prey haven't got binocular vision, either," I added, as an afterthought. "Except for owls. Hawks and eagles can't have; their eyes are on either side of their heads. Just tell Bree and Jamie I said you have eyes like a hawk."

He laughed outright at that, and stood up, dusting off the skirts of his coat.

"Right, I will." He waited for me, opening the door to the

hall for me. As I reached it, though, he put a hand on my arm, stopping me.

"This binocular thing," he said, gesturing vaguely toward his eyes. "I was born with it, I suppose?"

I nodded.

"Yes, almost certainly."

He hesitated, clearly not knowing quite how to put what he wanted to say.

"Is it . . . inherited, then? My father was in the RAF; he can't have had it, surely—but my mother wore spectacles. She kept them on a chain round her neck; I remember playing with it. I might have gotten the eye thing from her, I mean."

I pursed my lips, trying to recall what—if anything—I had ever read on the subject of inherited eye disorders, but nothing concrete came to mind.

"I don't know," I said at last. "It might be. But it might not, too. I really don't know. Are you worried about Jemmy?"

"Oh." A faint look of disappointment crossed his features, though he blotted it out almost at once. He gave me an awkward smile, and opened the door, holding it for me to pass through.

"No, not worried. I was just thinking—if it was inherited, and if the little fella should have it, too . . . then I'd know."

The corridor was full of the savory scents of squirrel stew and fresh bread, and I was starving, but I stood still, staring up at him.

"I wouldn't wish it on him," Roger said hastily, seeing my expression. "Not at all! Just, if it should be that way—" He broke off and looked away, swallowing. "Look, don't tell Bree I thought of it, please."

I touched his arm lightly.

"I think she'd understand. Your wanting to know—for sure."

He glanced at the kitchen door, from which Bree's voice rose, singing "Clementine," to Jemmy's raucous pleasure.

"She might understand," he said. "That doesn't mean she wants to hear it."

# THE FIERY CROSS

THE MEN WERE GONE. Jamie, Roger, Mr.
Chisholm and his sons, the MacLeod brothers ...
they had all disappeared before daybreak, leaving no
trace behind save the jumbled remains of a hasty breakfast,
and a collection of muddy bootprints on the doorsill.

Jamie moved so quietly that he seldom woke me when he
left our bed to dress in the dark predawn. He did usually
bend to kiss me goodbye, though, murmuring a quick en-
dearment in my ear and leaving me to carry the touch and
scent of him back into dreams.

He hadn't wakened me this morning.

That job had been left to the tender offices of the junior
Chisholms and MacLeods, several of whom had held a
pitched battle directly under my window, just after dawn.

I had sprung into wakefulness, momentarily confused by
the shouts and screams, my hands reaching automatically for
sponge and oxygen, syringe and alcohol, visions of a hospital emergency room vivid around me. Then I drew breath,
and smelled woodsmoke, not ethanol. I shook my head,
blinking at the sight of a rumpled blue and yellow quilt, the
peaceful row of clothes on their pegs, and the wash of pure,
pale light streaming through half-opened shutters. Home. I
was home, on the Ridge.

A door banged open below, and the racket died abruptly,
succeeded by a scuffle of flight, accompanied by muffled
giggling.

"Mmmphm!" said Mrs. Bug's voice, grimly satisfied at
having routed the rioters. The door closed, and the clank of

wood and clang of metal from below announced the commencement of the day's activities.

When I went down a few moments later, I found that good lady engaged simultaneously in toasting bread, boiling coffee, making parritch, and complaining as she tidied up the men's leavings. Not about the untidiness—what else could be expected of men?—but rather that Jamie had not waked her to provide a proper breakfast for them.

"And how's Himself to manage, then?" she demanded, brandishing the toasting-fork at me in reproach. "A fine, big man like that, and him out and doing wi' no more to line his wame than a wee sup of milk and a stale bannock?"

Casting a bleary eye over the assorted crumbs and dirty crockery, it appeared to me that Himself and his companions had probably accounted for at least two dozen corn muffins and an entire loaf of salt-rising bread, accompanied by a pound or so of fresh butter, a jar of honey, a bowl of raisins, and all of the first milking.

"I don't think he'll starve," I murmured, dabbing up a crumb with a moistened forefinger. "Is the coffee ready?"

The older Chisholm and MacLeod children had mostly been sleeping by the kitchen hearth at night, rolled in rags or blankets. They were up and out now, their coverings heaped behind the settle. As the smell of food began to permeate the house, murmurous sounds of rising began to come through the walls and down the stairs, as the women dressed and tended the babies and toddlers. Small faces began to reappear from outside, peeking hungrily round the edge of the door.

"Have ye washed your filthy paws, wee heathens?" Mrs. Bug demanded, seeing them. She waved a porridge spoon at the benches along the table. "If ye have, come in and set yourselves doon. Mind ye wipe your muddy feet!"

Within moments, the benches and stools were filled, Mrs. Chisholm, Mrs. MacLeod, and Mrs. Aberfeldy yawning and blinking among their offspring, nodding and murmuring "Good morn" to me and each other, straightening a kerchief here and a shirttail there, using a thumb wet with spittle to plaster down the spiked hair on a little boy's head or wipe a smudge from a little girl's cheek.

Faced with a dozen gaping mouths to feed, Mrs. Bug was in her element, hopping back and forth between hearth and table. Watching her bustle to and fro, I thought she must have been a chickadee in a former life.

"Did you see Jamie when he left?" I asked, as she paused momentarily to refill all the coffee cups, a large uncooked sausage in her other hand.

"No, indeed." She shook her head, neat white in its kerch. "I didna ken a thing about it. I heard my auld lad up and stirring before dawn, but I thought it was only him out to the privy, he not liking to trouble me with the noise o' the pot. He didna come back, though, and by the time I waked myself, they'd all gone off. Ah! None of that, now!"

Catching a movement from the corner of her eye, she dotted a six-year-old MacLeod smartly on the head with her sausage, causing him to snatch his fingers back from the jam jar.

"Perhaps they've gone hunting," Mrs. Aberfeldy suggested timidly, spooning porridge into the little girl she held on her knee. Barely nineteen, she seldom said much, shy of the older women.

"Better they be hunting homesteads, and timber for houses," Mrs. MacLeod said, hoisting a baby onto her shoulder and patting its back. She pushed a strand of graying hair out of her face and gave me a wry smile. "It's nay reflection upon your hospitality, Mrs. Fraser, but I'd as soon not spend the winter under your feet. Geordie! Leave your sister's plaits alone, or ye'll wish ye had!"

Not at my best so early in the day, I smiled and murmured something politely incomprehensible. I would as soon not have five or ten extra people in my house for the winter, either, but I wasn't sure it could be avoided.

The Governor's letter had been quite specific; all able-bodied men in the backcountry were to be mustered as militia troops and to report to Salisbury by mid-December. That left very little time for house-building. Still, I hoped Jamie had some plan for relieving the congestion; Adso the kitten had taken up semipermanent residence in a cupboard in my surgery, and the scene in the kitchen was quickly assuming its usual daily resemblance to one of the paintings of Hieronymus Bosch.

At least the kitchen had lost its early morning chill with so many bodies crowded into it, and was now comfortably warm and noisy. What with the mob scene, though, it was several moments before I noticed that there were four young mothers present, rather than three.

"Where did you come from?" I asked, startled at sight of my daughter, huddled frowsily under a rug in a corner of the settle.

Bree blinked sleepily and shifted Jemmy, who was nursing with single-minded concentration, oblivious of the crowd.

"The Muellers showed up in the middle of the night and pounded on our door," she said, yawning. "Eight of them. They didn't speak much English, but I *think* they said Da sent for them."

"Really?" I reached for a slice of raisin cake, narrowly beating a young Chisholm to it. "Are they still there?"

"Uh-huh. Thanks, Mama." She stretched out a hand for the bit of cake I offered her. "Yes. Da came and hauled Roger out of bed while it was still dark, but he didn't seem to think he needed the Muellers yet. When Roger left, a big old Mueller got up off the floor, said, *'Bitte, Maedle,'* and lay down next to me." A delicate pink flushed her cheeks. "So I thought maybe I'd get up and come up here."

"Oh," I said, suppressing a smile. "That would be Gerhard." Eminently practical, the old farmer would see no reason why he should lay his old bones on a hard plank floor, if there was bed space available.

"I suppose so," she said indistinctly, through a mouthful of cake. "I guess he's harmless, but even so . . ."

"Well, he'd be no danger to *you*," I agreed. Gerhard Mueller was the patriarch of a large German family who lived between the Ridge and the Moravian settlement at Salem. He was somewhere in his late seventies, but by no means harmless.

I chewed slowly, remembering how Jamie had described to me the scalps nailed to the door of Gerhard's barn.

Women's scalps, long hair dark and silken, ends lifting in the wind. *Like live things*, he'd said, his face troubled at the memory, *like birds, pinned to the wood*. And the white one Gerhard had brought to me, wrapped in linen and flecked with blood. No, not harmless. I swallowed, the cake feeling dry in my throat.

"Harmless or not, they'll be hungry," said Mrs. Chisholm practically. She bent and gathered up a corn-dolly, a soggy diaper, and a squirming toddler, contriving somehow to leave a hand free for her coffee. "Best we clear this lot awa, before the Germans smell food and come hammering at the door."

"Is there anything left to feed them?" I said, uneasily trying to remember how many hams were left in the smokeshed. After two weeks of hospitality, our stores were dwindling at an alarming rate.

"Of course there is," Mrs. Bug said briskly, slicing sausage and flipping the slices onto the sizzling griddle. "Let me just ha' done with this lot, and ye can send them along for their breakfasts. You, *a muirninn*—" She tapped a girl of eight or so on the head with her spatula. "Run ye doon the root cellar and fetch me up an apronful of potatoes. Germans like potatoes."

By the time I had finished my porridge and begun to collect up bowls to wash, Mrs. Bug, broom in hand, was sweeping children and debris out of the back door with ruthless efficiency, while issuing a stream of orders to Lizzie and Mrs. Aberfeldy—Ruth, that was her name—who seemed to have been dragooned as assistant cooks.

"Shall I help . . ." I began, rather feebly, but Mrs. Bug shook her head and made small shooing motions with the broom.

"Dinna think of it, Mrs. Fraser!" she said. "You'll have enough to do, I'm sure, and—here now, ye'll no be comin' intae my nice, clean kitchen wi' those mucky boots! Out, out and wipe them off before ye think of setting foot in here!"

Gerhard Mueller, followed by his sons and nephews, stood in the doorway, nonplussed. Mrs. Bug, undeterred either by the fact that he towered over her by more than a foot, or that he spoke no English, screwed up her face and poked fiercely at his boots with her broom.

I waved welcomingly to the Muellers, then seized the chance of escape, and fled.

SEEKING TO AVOID the crowd in the house, I washed at the well outside, then went to the sheds and occupied myself in taking inventory. The situation was not as bad as I'd feared; we had enough, with careful management, to last out the winter, though I could see that Mrs. Bug's lavish hand might have to be constrained a bit.

Besides six hams in the smokeshed, there were four sides of bacon and half another, plus a rack of dried venison and half of a relatively recent carcass. Looking up, I could see the low roof beams, black with soot and thick with clusters of smoked, dried fish, split and bound stiffly in bunches, like the petals of large ugly flowers. There were ten casks of salt fish, as well, and four of salt pork. A stone crock of lard, a smaller one of the fine leaf lard, another of headcheese . . . I had my doubts about that.

I had made it according to the instructions of one of the Mueller women, as translated by Jamie, but I had never seen headcheese myself, and was not quite sure it was meant to look like *that*. I lifted the lid and sniffed cautiously, but it smelled all right; mildly spiced with garlic and peppercorn, and no scent at all of putrefaction. Perhaps we wouldn't die of ptomaine poisoning, though I had it in mind to invite Gerhard Mueller to try it first.

"How can ye bide the auld fiend in your house?" Marsali had demanded, when Gerhard and one of his sons had ridden up to the Ridge a few months earlier. She had heard the story of the Indian women from Fergus, and viewed the Germans with horrified revulsion.

"And what would ye have me do?" Jamie had demanded in return, spoon lifted halfway from his bowl. "Kill the Muellers—all of them, for if I did for Gerhard, I'd have to do for the lot—and nail their hair to *my* barn?" His mouth quirked slightly. "I should think it would put the cow off her milk. It would put me off the milkin', to be sure."

Marsali's brow puckered, but she wasn't one to be joked out of an argument.

"Not that, maybe," she said. "But ye let them into your house, and treat them as friends!" She glanced from Jamie to me, frowning. "The women he killed—*they* were your friends, no?"

I exchanged a look with Jamie, and gave a slight shrug. He paused for a moment, gathering his thoughts, as he slowly stirred his soup. Then he laid down the spoon and looked at her.

"It was a fearful thing that Gerhard did," he said simply. "But it was a matter of vengeance to him; thinking as he did, he couldna have done otherwise. Would it make matters better for me to take vengeance on him?"

"*Non,*" Fergus said positively. He laid a hand on Marsali's arm, putting a stop to whatever she might have said next. He grinned up at her. "Of course, Frenchmen do not believe in vengeance."

"Well, perhaps some Frenchmen," I murmured, thinking of the Comte St. Germain.

Marsali wasn't to be put off so easily, though.

"Hmph," she said. "What ye mean is, they weren't *yours*, isn't it?" Seeing Jamie's brow flick up in startlement, she pressed the point. "The women who were murdered. But if it were your family? If it had been me and Lizzie and Brianna, say?"

"That," said Jamie evenly, "is my point. It *was* Gerhard's family." He pushed back from the table and stood up, leaving half his soup unfinished. "Are ye done, Fergus?"

Fergus cocked a sleek brow at him, picked up his bowl, and drank it down, Adam's apple bobbing in his long brown throat.

"*Oui,*" he said, wiping his mouth on his sleeve. He stood and patted Marsali on the head, then plucked a strand of her straw-pale hair free of her kerch. "Do not worry yourself, *ma douce*—even though I do not believe in vengeance, if anyone should hunt your hair, I promise I will make a tobacco pouch of his scrotum. And your papa will tie up his stockings with the malefactor's entrails, surely."

Marsali gave a small *pfft!* of irritated amusement and slapped at his hand, and no more was said about Gerhard Mueller.

I lifted the heavy crock of headcheese and set it down by the door of the smokeshed, so as not to forget it when I went back to the house. I wondered whether Gerhard's son Frederick had come with him—likely so; the boy was less than twenty, not an age willing to be left out of anything that promised excitement. It was Frederick's young wife Petronella and her baby who had died—of measles, though Gerhard had thought the infection a deliberate curse put on his family by the Tuscarora.

Had Frederick found a new wife yet? I wondered. Very likely. Though if not . . . there were two teenaged girls among the new tenants. Perhaps Jamie's plans involved finding them fast husbands? And then there was Lizzie . . .

The corncrib was more than three-quarters full, though there were worrying quantities of mouse droppings on the ground outside. Adso was growing rapidly, but perhaps not fast enough; he was just about the size of an average rat. Flour—that was a little low, only eight sacks. There might be more at the mill, though; I must ask Jamie.

Sacks of rice and dried beans, bushels of hickory nuts, butternuts, and black walnuts. Heaps of dried squash, burlap bags of oatmeal and cornmeal, and gallon upon gallon of apple cider and cider vinegar. A crock of salted butter, another of fresh, and a basket of spherical goat cheeses, for which I had traded a bushel of blackberries and another of wild currants. The rest of the berries had been carefully dried, along with the wild grapes, or made up into jam or preserve, and were presently hidden in the pantry, safe—I hoped—from childish depredations.

The honey. I stopped, pursing my lips. I had nearly twenty gallons of purified honey, and four large stone jars of honeycomb, gleaned from my hives and waiting to be rendered and made into beeswax candles. It was all kept in the walled cave that served as stable, in order to keep safe from bears. It wasn't safe from the children who had been deputed to feed the cows and pigs in the stable, though. I hadn't seen any tell-tale sticky fingers or faces yet, but it might be as well to take some preventative steps.

Between meat, grain, and the small dairy, it looked as though no one would starve this winter. My concern now was the lesser but still important threat of vitamin deficiency. I glanced at the chestnut grove, its branches now completely bare. It would be a good four months before we saw much of fresh greenery, though I did have plenty of turnips and cab-bage still in the ground.

The root cellar was reassuringly well-stocked, heady with the earthy smell of potatoes, the tang of onions and garlic, and the wholesome, bland scent of turnips. Two large barrels of apples stood at the back—with the prints of several sets of childish feet leading up to them, I saw.

I glanced up. Enormous clusters of wild scuppernong grapes had been hung from the rafters, drying slowly into raisins. They were still there, but the lower, more reachable bunches had been reduced to sprays of bare stems. Perhaps I needn't worry about outbreaks of scurvy, then.

I wandered back toward the house, trying to calculate how many provisions should be sent with Jamie and his militia, how much left for the consumption of the wives and chil-dren. Impossible to say; that would depend in part on how many men he raised, and on what they might bring with them. He was appointed Colonel, though; the responsibility of feeding the men of his regiment would be primarily his, with reimbursement—if it ever came—to be paid later by ap-propriation of the Assembly.

Not for the first time, I wished heartily that I knew more. How long might the Assembly be a functional body?

Brianna was out by the well, walking round and round it with a meditative look furrowing her brows.

"Pipe," she said, without preliminaries. "Do people make metal piping now? The Romans did, but—"

"I've seen it in Paris and Edinburgh, being used to carry rain off roofs," I offered. "So it exists. I'm not sure I've seen any in the Colonies, though. If there is any, it will be terribly expensive." Beyond the simplest of things, like horseshoes, all ironmongery had to be imported from Britain, as did all other metal goods like copper, brass, and lead.

"Hmm. At least they'll know what it is." She narrowed her eyes, calculating the slope of land between well and house, then shook her head and sighed. "I can make a pump, I think. Getting water into the house is something else." She yawned suddenly, and blinked, eyes watering slightly in the sunlight. "God, I'm so tired, I can't think. Jemmy squawked all night and just when he finally conked out, the Muellers showed up—I don't think I slept at all."

"I recall the feeling," I said, with sympathy—and grinned.

"Was I a very cranky baby?" Brianna asked, grinning back.

"Very," I assured her, turning toward the house. "And where is yours?"

"He's with—"

Brianna stopped dead, clutching my arm.

"What—" she said. "What in the name of God is *that*?"

I turned to look, and felt a spasm of shock, deep in the pit of my stomach.

"It's quite evident *what* it is," I said, walking slowly toward it. "The question is—why?"

It was a cross. Rather a big cross, made of dried pine boughs, stripped of their twigs and bound together with rope. It was planted firmly at the edge of the dooryard, near the big red spruce that guarded the house.

It stood some seven feet in height, the branches slender, but solid. It was not bulky or obtrusive—and yet its quiet presence seemed to dominate the dooryard, much as a tabernacle dominates a church. At the same time, the effect of the thing seemed neither reverent nor protective. In fact, it was bloody sinister.

"Are we having a revival meeting?" Brianna's mouth twitched, trying to make a joke of it. The cross made her as uneasy as it did me.

"Not that I've heard of." I walked slowly round it, looking up and down. Jamie had made it—I could tell that by the quality of the workmanship. The branches had been chosen for straightness and symmetry, carefully trimmed, the ends tapered. The cross piece had been neatly notched to fit the upright, the rope binding crisscrossed with a sailor's neatness.

"Maybe Da's starting his own religion." Brianna lifted a brow; she recognized the workmanship, too.

Mrs. Bug appeared suddenly round the corner of the house, a bowl of chicken feed in her hands. She stopped dead at sight of us, her mouth opening immediately. I braced myself instinctively for the onslaught, and heard Brianna snicker under her breath.

"Och, there ye are, ma'am! I was just sayin' to Lizzie as how it was a shame, a mortal shame it is, that those spawn should be riotin' upstairs and doon, and their nasty leavings scattered all about the hoose, and even in Herself's own stillroom, and she said to me, did Lizzie, she said—"

"In my surgery? What? Where? What have they done?" Forgetting the cross, I was already hastening toward the house, Mrs. Bug hard on my heels, still talking.

"I did catch twa o' them wee de'ils a-playin' at bowls in there with your nice blue bottles and an apple, and be sure I boxed their ears sae hard for it I'm sure they're ringin' still, the wicked creeturs, and them a-leavin' bits of good food to rot and go bad, and—"

"My bread!" I had reached the front hall, and now flung open the door of the surgery to find everything within spick-and-span—including the countertop where I had laid out my most recent penicillin experiments. It now lay completely bare, its oaken surface scoured to rawness.

"Nasty it was," Mrs. Bug said from the hall behind me. She pressed her lips together with prim virtue. "Nasty! Covered wi' mold, just covered, all blue, and—"

I took a deep breath, hands clenched at my sides to avoid throttling her. I shut the surgery door, blotting out the sight of the empty counter, and turned to the tiny Scotswoman.

"Mrs. Bug," I said, keeping my voice level with great effort, "you know how much I appreciate your help, but I *did* ask you not to—"

The front door swung open and crashed into the wall beside me.

"Ye wretched auld besom! How dare ye to lay hands on my weans!"

I swung round to find myself nose-to-nose with Mrs. Chisholm, face flushed with fury and armed with a broom, two red-faced toddlers clinging to her skirts, their cheeks smeared with recent tears. She ignored me completely, her attention focused on Mrs. Bug, who stood in the hallway on my other side, bristling like a diminutive hedgehog.

"You and your precious weans!" Mrs. Bug cried indignantly. "Why, if ye cared a stitch for them, ye'd be raisin' them proper and teachin' them right from wrong, not leavin' them to carouse about the hoose like Barbary apes, strewin' wreck and ruin from attic to doorstep, and layin' their sticky fingers on anything as isna nailed to the floor!"

"Now, Mrs. Bug, really, I'm sure they didn't mean—" My attempt at peacemaking was drowned out by steam-whistle shrieks from all three Chisholms, Mrs. Chisholm's being by far the loudest.

"Who are you, to be callin' my bairns thieves, ye maundering auld nettercap!" The aggrieved mother waved the broom menacingly, moving from side to side as she tried to get at Mrs. Bug. I moved with her, hopping back and forth in an effort to stay between the two combatants.

"Mrs. Chisholm," I said, raising a placating hand. "Margaret. Really, I'm sure that—"

"Who am I?" Mrs. Bug seemed to expand visibly, like rising dough. "Who am I? Why, I'm a God-fearin' woman and a Christian soul! Who are *you* to be speakin' to your elders and betters in such a way, you and your evil tribe a-traipsin' the hills in rags and tatters, wi'out sae much as a pot to piss in?"

"Mrs. Bug!" I exclaimed, whirling round to her. "You mustn't—"

Mrs. Chisholm didn't bother trying to find a rejoinder to this, but instead lunged forward, broom at the ready. I flung my arms out to prevent her shoving past me; finding herself foiled in her attempt to swat Mrs. Bug, she instead began poking at her over my shoulder, jabbing wildly with the broom as she tried to skewer the older woman.

Mrs. Bug, obviously feeling herself safe behind the barricade of my person, was hopping up and down like a Ping-Pong ball, her small round face bright red with triumph and fury.

"Beggars!" she shouted, at the top of her lungs. "Tinkers! Gypsies!"

"Mrs. Chisholm! Mrs. Bug!" I pleaded, but neither paid the least attention.

*"Kittock! Mislearnit pilsh!"* bellowed Mrs. Chisholm, jabbing madly with her broom. The children shrieked and yowled, and Mrs. Chisholm—who was a rather buxom woman—trod heavily on my toe.

This came under the heading of more than enough, and I rounded on Mrs. Chisholm with fire in my eye. She shrank back, dropping the broom.

"Ha! Ye pert trull! You and—"

Mrs. Bug's shrill cries behind me were suddenly silenced, and I whirled round again to see Brianna, who had evidently run round the house and come in through the kitchen, holding the diminutive Mrs. Bug well off the floor, one arm round her middle, the other hand firmly pressed across her mouth. Mrs. Bug's tiny feet kicked wildly, her eyes bulging above the muffling hand. Bree rolled her eyes at me, and retreated through the kitchen door, carrying her captive.

I turned round to deal with Mrs. Chisholm, only to see the flick of her homespun gray skirt, disappearing hastily round the corner of the doorstep, a child's wail receding like a distant siren. The broom lay at my feet. I picked it up, went into the surgery, and shut the door behind me.

I closed my eyes, hands braced on the empty counter. I felt a sudden, irrational urge to hit something—and did. I slammed my fist on the counter, pounded it again and again with the meaty side of my hand, but it was built so solidly that my blows made scarcely any sound, and I stopped, panting.

What on earth was the matter with me? Annoying as Mrs. Bug's interference was, it was not critical. Neither was Mrs. Chisholm's maternal pugnacity—she and her little fiends would be gone from the house sooner or later. Sooner, I hoped.

My heart had begun to slow a little, but prickles of irritation still ran over my skin like nettle rash. I tried to shake it off, opening the big cupboard to assure myself that neither

Mrs. Bug's nor the children's depredations had harmed anything truly important.

No, it was all right. Each glass bottle had been polished to a jewellike gleam—the sunlight caught them in a blaze of blue and green and crystal—but each had been put back exactly in its place, each neatly written label turned forward. The gauzy bundles of dried herbs had been shaken free of dust, but carefully hung back on their nails.

The sight of the assembled medicines was calming. I touched a jar of anti-louse ointment, feeling a miser's sense of gratification at the number and variety of bags and jars and bottles.

Alcohol lamp, alcohol bottle, microscope, large amputation saw, jar of sutures, box of plasters, packet of cobweb— all were arrayed with military precision, drawn up in ranks like ill-assorted recruits under the eye of a drill sergeant. Mrs. Bug might have the flaws of her greatness, but I couldn't help but admit her virtue as a housekeeper.

The only thing in the cabinet that plainly hadn't been touched was a tiny leather bag, the amulet given to me by the Tuscaroran shaman Nayawenne; that lay askew in a corner by itself. Interesting that Mrs. Bug wouldn't touch that, I thought; I had never told her what it was, though it did look Indian, with the feathers—from raven and woodpecker— thrust through the knot. Less than a year in the Colonies, and less than a month in the wilderness, Mrs. Bug regarded all things Indian with acute suspicion.

The odor of lye soap hung in the air, reproachful as a housekeeper's ghost. I supposed I couldn't really blame her; moldy bread, rotted melon, and mushy apple slices might be research to me; to Mrs. Bug, they could be nothing but a calculated offense to the god of cleanliness.

I sighed and closed the cupboard, adding the faint perfume of dried lavender and the skunk scent of pennyroyal to the ghosts of lye and rotted apples. I had lost experimental preparations many times before, and this one had not been either complex or in a greatly advanced state. It would take no more than half an hour to replace it, setting out fresh bits of bread and other samples. I wouldn't do it, though; there wasn't enough time. Jamie was clearly beginning to gather his militiamen; it could be no more than a few days before they would depart for Salisbury, to report to Governor Tryon. Before *we* would depart—for I certainly meant to accompany them.

It occurred to me, quite suddenly, that there hadn't been enough time to finish the experiment when I had set it up to begin with. I had known we would leave soon; even if I got immediate good growth, I would not have had time to collect, dry, purify . . . I'd known that, consciously—and yet I had done it anyway, gone right on with my plans, pursuing my routines, as though life were still settled and predictable, as though nothing whatever might threaten the tenor of my days. As though acting might make it true.

"You really are a fool, Beauchamp," I murmured, pushing a curl of hair tiredly behind one ear. I went out, shutting the door of the surgery firmly behind me, and went to negotiate peace between Mrs. Bug and Mrs. Chisholm.

SUPERFICIALLY, peace in the house was restored, but an atmosphere of uneasiness remained. The women went about their work tense and tight-lipped; even Lizzie, the soul of patience, was heard to say "Tcha!" when one of the children spilled a pan of buttermilk across the steps.

Even outside, the air seemed to crackle, as though a lightning storm were near. As I went to and fro from sheds to house, I kept glancing over my shoulder at the sky above Roan Mountain, half-expecting to see the loom of thunderheads—and yet the sky was still the pale slate-blue of late autumn, clouded with nothing more than the wisps of mare's tails.

I found myself distracted, unable to settle to anything. I drifted from one task to another, leaving a pile of onions half-braided in the pantry, a bowl of beans half-shelled on the stoop, a pair of torn breeks lying on the settle, needle dangling from its thread. Again and again, I found myself crossing the yard, coming from nowhere in particular, bound upon no specific errand.

I glanced up each time I passed the cross, as though expecting it either to have disappeared since my last trip, or to have acquired some explanatory notice, neatly pinned to the wood. If not *Iesus Nazarenus Rex Iudaeorum*, then *something*. But no. The cross remained, two simple sticks of pinewood, bound together by a rope. Nothing more. Except, of course, that a cross is *always* something more. I just didn't know what it might be, this time.

Everyone else seemed to share my distraction. Mrs. Bug, disedified by the conflict with Mrs. Chisholm, declined to make any lunch, and retired to her room, ostensibly suffering from headache, though she refused to let me treat it. Lizzie, normally a fine hand with food, burned the stew, and billows of black smoke stained the oak beams above the hearth.

At least the Muellers were safely out of the way. They had brought a large cask of beer with them, and had retired after breakfast back to Brianna's cabin, where they appeared to be entertaining themselves very nicely.

The bread refused to rise. Jemmy had begun a new tooth, a hard one, and screamed and screamed and screamed. The incessant screeching twisted everyone's nerves to the snapping point, including mine. I should have liked to suggest that Bree take him away somewhere out of earshot, but I saw the deep smudges of fatigue under her eyes and the strain on her face, and hadn't the heart. Mrs. Chisholm, tried by the constant battles of her own offspring, had no such compunction.

"For God's sake, why do ye no tak' that bairn awa to your own cabin, lass?" she snapped. "If he mun greet so, there's no need for us all to hear it!"

Bree's eyes narrowed dangerously.

"Because," she hissed, "your two oldest sons are sitting in my cabin, drinking with the Germans. I wouldn't want to disturb them!"

Mrs. Chisholm's face went bright red. Before she could speak, I quickly stepped forward and snatched the baby away from Bree.

"I'll take him out for a bit of a walk, shall I?" I said, hoisting him onto my shoulder. "I could use some fresh air. Why don't you go up and lie down on my bed for a bit, darling?" I said to Bree. "You look just a little tired."

"Uh-huh," she said. One corner of her mouth twitched. "And the Pope's a little bit Catholic, too. Thanks, Mama." She kissed Jemmy's hot, wet cheek, and vanished toward the stairwell.

Mrs. Chisholm scowled horridly after her, but caught my eye, coughed, and called to her three-year-old twins, who were busily demolishing my sewing basket.

The cold air outside was a relief, after the hot, smoky confines of the kitchen, and Jemmy quieted a little, though he continued to squirm and whine. He rubbed his hot, damp face against my neck, and gnawed ferociously on the cloth of my shawl, fussing and drooling.

I paced slowly to and fro, patting him gently and humming "Lilibuleero" under my breath. I found the exercise soothing, in spite of Jemmy's crankiness. There was only one of him, after all, and he couldn't talk.

"You're a male, too," I said to him, pulling his woolen cap over the soft bright down that feathered his skull. "As a sex, you have your defects, but I will say that catfighting isn't one of them."

Fond as I was of individual women—Bree, Marsali, Lizzie, and even Mrs. Bug—I had to admit that taken en masse, I found men much easier to deal with. Whether this was the fault of my rather unorthodox upbringing—I had been raised largely by my Uncle Lamb and his Persian manservant, Firouz—my experiences in the War, or simply an aspect of my own unconventional personality, I found men soothingly logical and—with a few striking exceptions—pleasingly direct.

I turned to look at the house. It stood serene amid the spruce and chestnut trees, elegantly proportioned, soundly built. A face showed at one of the windows. The face stuck out its tongue and pressed flat against the pane, crossing its eyes above squashed nose and cheeks. High-pitched feminine voices and the sound of banging came to me faintly through the cold, clean air.

"Hmm," I said.

Reluctant as I was to leave home again so soon, and little as I liked the idea of Jamie being involved in armed conflicts of any kind, the thought of going off to live in the company of twenty or thirty unshaven, reeking men for a week or two had developed a certain undeniable attraction. If it meant sleeping on the ground . . .

"Into each life some rain must fall," I told Jemmy with a sigh. "But I suppose you're just learning that now, aren't you, poor thing?"

"Gnnnh!" he said, and drew himself up into a ball to escape the pain of his emergent teeth, his knees digging painfully into my side. I settled him more comfortably on my hip, and gave him an index finger to chew on. His gums were hard and knobbly; I could feel the tender spot where the new tooth was coming in, swollen and hot under the skin. A piercing shriek came from the house, followed by the sound of shouts and running feet.

"You know," I said conversationally, "I think a bit of whisky would be just the thing for that, don't you?" and withdrawing the finger, I tucked Jemmy up against my shoulder. I ducked past the cross and into the shelter of the big red spruce—just in time, as the door of the house burst open and Mrs. Bug's penetrating voice rose like a trumpet on the chilly air.

IT WAS A LONG WAY to the whisky clearing, but I didn't mind. It was blessedly quiet in the forest, and Jemmy, lulled by the movement, finally relaxed into a doze, limp and heavy as a little sandbag in my arms.

So late in the year, all the deciduous trees had lost their leaves; the trail was ankle-deep in a crackling carpet of brown and gold, and maple seeds whirled past on the wind, brushing my skirt with a whisper of wings. A raven flew past, high above. It gave an urgent, raucous cry, and the baby jerked in my arms.

"Hush," I said, hugging him close. "It's nothing, lovey; just a bird."

Still, I looked after the raven, and listened for another. They were birds of portent—or so said Highland superstition. One raven was an omen of change; two were good fortune; three were ill. I tried to dismiss such notions from my mind—but Nayawenne had told me the raven was my guide, my spirit animal—and I never saw the big, black shadows pass overhead without a certain shiver up the spine.

Jemmy stirred, gave a brief squawk, and fell back into silence. I patted him and resumed my climb, wondering as I made my way slowly up the mountain, what animal might be his guide?

The animal spirit chose you, Nayawenne told me, not the other way around. You must pay careful attention to signs and portents, and wait for your animal to manifest itself to you. Ian's animal was the wolf; Jamie's the bear—or so the Tuscarora said. I had wondered at the time what one was supposed to do if chosen by something ignominious like a shrew or a dung beetle, but was too polite to ask.

Only one raven. I could still hear it, though it was out of sight, but no echoing cry came from the firs behind me. An omen of change.

"You could have saved yourself the trouble," I said to it, under my breath so as not to wake the baby. "Hardly as though I needed telling, is it?"

I climbed slowly, listening to the sigh of the wind and the deeper sound of my own breath. At this season, change was in the air itself, the scents of ripeness and death borne on the breeze, and the breath of winter in its chill. Still, the rhythms of the turning earth brought change that was expected, ordained; body and mind met it with knowledge and—on the whole—with peace. The changes coming were of a different order, and one calculated to disturb the soul.

I glanced back at the house; from this height, I could see only the corner of the roof, and the drifting smoke from the chimney.

"What do you think?" I said softly, Jemmy's head beneath my chin, round and warm in its knitted cap. "Will it be yours? Will you live here, and your children after you?"

It would be a very different life, I thought, from the one he might have led. If Brianna had risked the stones to take him back—but she had not, and so the little boy's fate lay here. Had she thought of that? I wondered. That by staying, she chose not only for herself, but him? Chose war and igno-

rance, disease and danger, but had risked all that, for the sake
of his father—for Roger. I was not entirely sure it had been
the right choice—but it hadn't been my choice to make.

Still, I reflected, there was no way of imagining before-
hand what having a child was like—no power of the mind
was equal to the knowledge of just what the birth of a child
could do, wresting lives and wrenching hearts.

"And a good thing, too," I said to Jemmy. "No one in their
right mind would do it, otherwise."

My sense of agitation had faded by now, soothed by the
wind and the peace of the leafless wood. The whisky clearing, as we called it, was hidden from the trail. Jamie had
spent days searching the slopes above the Ridge, before finding a spot that met his requirements.

Or spots, rather. The malting floor was built in a small
clearing at the foot of a hollow; the still was farther up the
mountain in a clearing of its own, near a small spring that
provided fresh, clear water. The malting floor was out of direct sight of the trail, but not difficult to get to.

"No point in hiding it," Jamie had said, explaining his
choice to me, "when anyone wi' a nose could walk to it
blindfolded."

True enough; even now, when there was no grain actively
fermenting in the shed or toasting on the floor, a faintly
fecund, smoky scent lingered in the air. When grain was
"working," the musty, pungent scent of fermentation was
perceptible at a distance, but when the sprouting barley
was spread on the floor above a slow fire, a thin haze of
smoke hung over the clearing, and the smell was strong
enough to reach Fergus's cabin, when the wind was right.

No one was at the malting floor now, of course. When a
new batch was working, either Marsali or Fergus would be
here to tend it, but for the moment, the roofed floor lay
empty, smooth boards darkened to gray by use and weather.
There was a neat stack of firewood piled nearby, though,
ready for use.

I went close enough to see what sort of wood it was; Fergus liked hickory, both because it split more easily, and
for the sweet taste it gave the malted grain. Jamie, deeply

traditional in his approach to whisky, would use nothing but oak. I touched a chunk of split wood; wide grain, light wood, thin bark. I smiled. Jamie had been here recently, then.

Normally, a small keg of whisky was kept at the malting floor, both for the sake of hospitality and caution. "If someone should come upon the lass alone there, best she have something to give them," Jamie had said. "It's known what we do there; best no one should try to make Marsali tell them where the brew is." It wasn't the best whisky—generally a very young, raw spirit—but certainly good enough either for uninvited visitors or a teething child.

"You haven't got any taste buds yet, anyway, so what's the odds?" I murmured to Jemmy, who stirred and smacked his lips in his sleep, screwing up his tiny face in a scowl.

I hunted about, but there was no sign of the small whisky keg either in its usual place behind the bags of barley or inside the pile of firewood. Perhaps taken away for refilling, perhaps stolen. No great matter, in either case.

I turned to the north, past the malting floor, took ten steps and turned right. The stone of the mountain jutted out here, a solid block of granite thrusting upward from the growth of tupelo and buttonbush. Only it wasn't solid. Two slabs of stone leaned together, the open crack below them masked by holly bushes. I pulled my shawl over Jemmy's face to protect him from the sharp-edged leaves, and squeezed carefully behind them, ducking down to go through the cleft.

The stone face fell away in a crumple of huge boulders on the far side of the cleft, with saplings and undergrowth sprouting willy-nilly in the crevices between the rocks. From below, it looked impassable, but from above, a faint trail was visible, threading down to another small clearing. Hardly a clearing; no more than a gap in the trees, where a clear spring bubbled from the rock and disappeared again into the earth. In summer, it was invisible even from above, shielded by the leafy growth of the trees around it.

Now, on the verge of winter, the white glimmer of the rock by the spring was easily visible through the leafless scrim of alder and mountain ash. Jamie had found a large, pale boulder, and rolled it to the head of the spring, where he had scratched the form of a cross upon it, and said a prayer, consecrating the spring to our use. I had thought at the time of making a joke equating whisky with holy water—thinking of Father Kenneth and the baptisms—but had on second thoughts refrained; I wasn't so sure Jamie would think it a joke.

I made my way cautiously down the slope, the faint trail leading through the boulders, and finally round an outcrop of rock, before debouching into the spring clearing. I was warm from the walking, but it was cold enough to numb my fingers where I gripped the edges of my shawl. And Jamie was standing at the edge of the spring in nothing but his shirt.

I stopped dead, hidden by a scrubby growth of evergreens.

It wasn't his state of undress that halted me, but rather something in the look of him. He looked tired, but that was only reasonable, since he had been up and gone so early.

The ragged breeks he wore for riding lay puddled on the ground nearby, his belt and its impedimenta neatly coiled beside them. My eye caught a dark blotch of color, half-hidden in the grass beyond; the blue and brown cloth of his hunting kilt. As I watched, he pulled the shirt over his head and dropped it, then knelt down naked by the spring and splashed water over his arms and face.

His clothes were mud-streaked from riding, but he wasn't filthy, by any means. A simple hand-and-face wash would have sufficed, I thought—and could have been accomplished in much greater comfort by the kitchen hearth.

He stood up, though, and taking the small bucket from the edge of the spring, scooped up cold water and poured it deliberately over himself, closing his eyes and gritting his teeth as it streamed down his chest and legs. I could see his balls draw up tight against his body, looking for shelter as the icy water sluiced through the auburn bush of his pubic hair and dripped off his cock.

"Your grandfather has lost his bloody mind," I whispered to Jemmy, who stirred and grimaced in his sleep, but took no note of ancestral idiosyncrasies.

I knew Jamie wasn't totally impervious to cold; I could see him gasp and shudder from where I stood in the shelter of the rock, and I shivered in sympathy. A Highlander born and bred, he simply didn't regard cold, hunger, or general discomfort as anything to take account of. Even so, this seemed to be taking cleanliness to an extreme.

He took a deep, gasping breath, and poured water over himself a second time. When he bent to scoop up the third bucketful, it began to dawn on me what he was doing.

A surgeon scrubs before operating for the sake of cleanliness, of course, but that isn't all there is to it. The ritual of soaping the hands, scrubbing the nails, rinsing the skin, repeated and repeated to the point of pain, is as much a mental activity as a physical one. The act of washing oneself in this obsessive way serves to focus the mind and prepare the spirit; one is washing away external preoccupation, sloughing petty distraction, just as surely as one scrubs away germs and dead skin.

I had done it often enough to recognize this particular ritual when I saw it. Jamie was not merely washing; he was cleansing himself, using the cold water not only as solvent but as mortification. He was preparing himself for something, and the notion made a small, cold trickle run down my own spine, chilly as the spring water.

Sure enough, after the third bucketful, he set it down and shook himself, droplets flying from the wet ends of his hair into the dry grass like a spatter of rain. No more than half-dry, he pulled the shirt back over his head, and turned to the west, where the sun lay low between the mountains. He stood still for a moment—very still.

The light streamed through the leafless trees, bright enough that from where I stood, I could see him now only in silhouette, light glowing through the damp linen of his shirt, the darkness of his body a shadow within. He stood with his head lifted, shoulders up, a man listening.

For what? I tried to still my own breathing, and pressed the baby's capped head gently into my shoulder, to keep him from waking. I listened, too.

I could hear the sound of the woods, a constant soft sigh of needle and branch. There was little wind, and I could hear the water of the spring nearby, a muted rush past stone and root. I heard quite clearly the beating of my own heart, and Jemmy's breath against my neck, and suddenly I felt afraid, as though the sounds were too loud, as though they might draw the attention of something dangerous to us.

I froze, not moving at all, trying not to breathe, and like a rabbit under a bush, to become part of the wood around me. Jemmy's pulse beat blue, a tender vein across his temple, and I bent my head over him, to hide it.

Jamie said something aloud in Gaelic. It sounded like a challenge—or perhaps a greeting. The words seemed vaguely familiar—but there was no one there; the clearing was empty. The air felt suddenly colder, as though the light had dimmed; a cloud crossing the face of the sun, I thought, and looked up—but there were no clouds; the sky was clear. Jemmy moved suddenly in my arms, startled, and I clutched him tighter, willing him to make no sound.

Then the air stirred, the cold faded, and my sense of apprehension passed. Jamie hadn't moved. Now the tension went out of him, and his shoulders relaxed. He moved just a little, and the setting sun lit his shirt in a nimbus of gold, and caught his hair in a blaze of sudden fire.

He took his dirk from its discarded sheath, and with no hesitation, drew the edge across the fingers of his right hand. I could see the thin dark line across his fingertips, and bit my lips. He waited a moment for the blood to well up, then shook his hand with a sudden hard flick of the wrist, so that droplets of blood flew from his fingers and struck the standing stone at the head of the pool.

He laid the dirk beneath the stone, and crossed himself with the blood-streaked fingers of his right hand. He knelt then, very slowly, and bowed his head over folded hands.

I'd seen him pray now and then, of course, but always in public, or at least with the knowledge that I was there. Now he plainly thought himself alone, and to watch him kneeling so, stained with blood and his soul given over, made me feel that I spied on an act more private than any intimacy of the body. I would have moved or spoken, and yet to interrupt seemed a sort of desecration. I kept silent, but found I was no longer a spectator; my own mind had turned to prayer unintended.

*Oh, Lord*, the words formed themselves in my mind,

without conscious thought, *I commend to you the soul of your servant James. Help him, please.* And dimly thought, but help him with what?

Then he crossed himself, and rose, and time started again, without my having noticed it had stopped. I was moving down the hillside toward him, grass brushing my skirt, with no memory of having taken the first step. I didn't recall his rising, but Jamie was walking toward me, not looking surprised, but his face filled with light at sight of us.

*"Mo chridhe,"* he said softly, smiling, and bent to kiss me. His beard stubble was rough and his skin still chilled, fresh with water.

"You'd better put your trousers on," I said. "You'll freeze."

"I'll do. *Ciamar a tha thu, an gille ruaidh?*"

To my surprise, Jemmy was awake and drooling, eyes wide blue in a rose-leaf face, all hint of temper gone without a trace. He leaned, twisting to reach for Jamie, who lifted him gently from my arms and cradled him against a shoulder, pulling the woolly cap down snugly over his ears.

"We're starting a tooth," I told Jamie. "He wasn't very comfortable, so I thought perhaps a bit of whisky on his gums . . . there wasn't any in the house."

"Oh, aye. We can manage that, I think. There's a bit in my flask." Carrying the baby to the spot where his clothes lay, he bent and rummaged one-handed, coming up with the dented pewter flask he carried on his belt.

He sat on a rock, balancing Jemmy on his knee, and handed me the flask to open.

"I went to the mash house," I said, pulling the cork with a soft *pop*, "but the cask was gone."

"Aye, Fergus has it. Here, I'll do it; my hands are clean." He held out his left index finger, and I dribbled a bit of the spirit onto it.

"What's Fergus doing with it?" I asked, settling myself on the rock beside him.

"Keeping it," he said, uninformatively. He stuck the finger in Jemmy's mouth, gently rubbing at the swollen gum. "Oh, there it is. Aye, that hurts a bit, doesn't it? Ouch!" He reached down and gingerly disentangled Jemmy's fingers from their grip on the hairs of his chest.

"Speaking of that . . ." I said, and reached out to take his right hand. Shifting his other arm to keep hold of Jemmy, he let me take the hand and turn his fingers upward.

It was a very shallow cut, just across the tips of the first three fingers—the fingers with which he had crossed himself. The blood had already clotted, but I dribbled a bit more of the whisky over the cuts and cleaned the smears of blood from his palm with my handkerchief.

He let me tend him in silence, but when I finished and looked up at him, he met my eyes with a faint smile.

"It's all right, Sassenach," he said.

"Is it?" I said. I searched his face; he looked tired, but tranquil. The slight frown I had seen between his brows for the last few days was gone. Whatever he was about, he had begun it.

"Ye saw, then?" he asked quietly, reading my own face.

"Yes. Is it—it's to do with the cross in the dooryard, is it?"

"Oh, in a way, I suppose."

"What is it for?" I asked bluntly.

He pursed his lips, rubbing gently at Jemmy's sore gum. At last he said, "Ye never saw Dougal MacKenzie call the clan, did you?"

I was more than startled at this, but answered cautiously.

"No. I saw Colum do it once—at the oath-taking at Leoch."

He nodded, the memory of that long-ago night of torches deep in his eyes.

"Aye," he said softly. "I mind that. Colum was chief, and the men would come when he summoned them, surely. But it was Dougal who led them to war."

He paused a moment, gathering his thoughts.

"There were raids, now and again. That was a different thing, and often no more than a fancy that took Dougal or Rupert, maybe an urge born of drink or boredom—a small band out for the fun of it, as much as for cattle or grain. But to gather the clan for war, all the fighting men—that was a rarer thing. I only saw it the once, myself, but it's no a sight ye would forget."

The cross of pinewood had been there when he woke one morning at the castle, surprising him as he crossed the courtyard. The inhabitants of Leoch were up and about their business as usual, but no one glanced at the cross or referred to it in any way. Even so, there were undercurrents of excitement running through the castle.

The men stood here and there in knots, talking in undertones, but when he joined a group, the talk shifted at once to desultory conversation.

"I was Colum's nephew, aye, but newly come to the castle, and they kent my sire and grandsire." Jamie's paternal grandfather had been Simon, Lord Lovat—chief of the Frasers of Lovat, and no great friend of the MacKenzies of Leoch.

"I couldna tell what was afoot, but something was; the hair on my arms prickled whenever I caught someone's eye." At last, he had made his way to the stable, and found Old Alec, Colum's Master of Horse. The old man had been fond of Ellen MacKenzie, and was kind to the son for his mother's sake, as well as his own.

"'Tis the fiery cross, lad," he'd told Jamie, tossing him a currycomb and jerking his head toward the stalls. "Ye'll not ha' seen it before?"

It was auld, he'd said, one of the ways that had been followed for hundreds of years, no one quite knowing where it had started, who had done it first or why.

"When a Hielan' chief will call his men to war," the old man had said, deftly running his gnarled hand through a knotted mane, "he has a cross made, and sets it afire. It's put out at once, ken, wi' blood or wi' water—but still it's called the fiery cross, and it will be carried through the glens and corries, a sign to the men of the clan to fetch their weapons and come to the gathering place, prepared for battle."

"Aye?" Jamie had said, feeling excitement hollow his belly. "And who do we fight, then? Where do we ride?"

The old man's grizzled brow had crinkled in amused approval at that "we."

"Ye follow where your chieftain leads ye, lad. But tonight, it will be the Grants we go against."

"It was, too," Jamie said. "Though not that night. When darkness came, Dougal lit the cross and called the clan. He doused the burnin' wood wi' sheep's blood—and two men rode out of the courtyard wi' the fiery cross, to take it through the mountains. Four days later, there were three hundred men in that courtyard, armed wi' swords, pistols, and dirks—and at dawn on the fifth day, we rode to make war on the Grants."

His finger was still in the baby's mouth, his eyes distant as he remembered.

"That was the first time I used my sword against another man," he said. "I mind it well."

"I expect you do," I murmured. Jemmy was beginning to squirm and fuss again; I reached across and lifted him into my own lap to check—sure enough, his clout was wet. Luckily, I had another, tucked into my belt for convenience. I laid him out across my knee to change.

"And so this cross in our dooryard . . ." I said delicately, eyes on my work. "To do with the militia, is it?"

Jamie sighed, and I could see the shadows of memory moving behind his eyes.

"Aye," he said. "Once, I could have called, and the men would come without question—because they were mine. Men of my blood, men of my land."

His eyes were hooded, looking out over the mountainside that rose up before us. I thought he did not see the wooded heights of the Carolina wilderness, though; rather, the scoured mountains and rocky crofts of Lallybroch. I laid my free hand on his wrist; the skin was cold, but I could feel the heat of him, just below the surface, like a fever rising.

"They came for you—but you came for them, Jamie. You came for them at Culloden. You took them there—and you brought them back."

Ironic, I thought, that the men who had come then to serve at his summons were for the most part still safe at home in Scotland. No part of the Highlands had been untouched by war—but Lallybroch and its people were for the most part still whole—because of Jamie.

"Aye, that's so." He turned to look at me, and a rueful smile touched his face. His hand tightened on mine for a moment, then relaxed, and the line deepened again between his brows. He waved a hand toward the mountains around us.

"But these men—there is no debt of blood between them and me. They are not Frasers; I am not born either laird or chief to them. If they come to fight at my call, it will be of their own will."

"Well, that," I said dryly, "and Governor Tryon's."

He shook his head at that.

"Nay, not that. Will the Governor ken which men are here, or which ones come to meet his summons?" He grimaced slightly. "He kens me—and that will do nicely."

I had to admit the truth of this. Tryon would neither know nor care whom Jamie brought—only that he appeared, with a satisfactory number of men behind him, ready to do the Governor's dirty work.

I pondered that for a moment, patting Jemmy's bottom dry with the hem of my skirt. All I knew of the American Revolution were the things I had heard at second hand from Brianna's schoolbooks—and I, of all people, knew just how great the gap could be between written history and the reality.

Also, we had lived in Boston, and the schoolbooks naturally reflected local history. The general impression one got from reading about Lexington and Concord and the like was that the militia involved every able-bodied man in the community, all of whom sprang into action at the first hint of alarm, eager to perform their civic duty. Perhaps they did, perhaps not—but the Carolina backcountry wasn't Boston, not by a long chalk.

"*. . . ready to ride and spread the alarm,*" I said, half under my breath, "*to every Middlesex village and farm.*"

"What?" Jamie's brows shot up. "Where's Middlesex?"

"Well, you'd think it was halfway between male and female," I said, "but it's really just the area round Boston. Though of course that's named after the one in England."

"Yes?" he said, looking bewildered. "Aye, if ye say so, Sassenach. But—"

"Militia." I lifted Jemmy, who was bucking and squirming like a landed fish, making noises of extreme protest at being forcibly diapered. He kicked me in the stomach. "Oh, give over, child, do."

Jamie reached over and took the baby under the arms, hoisting him from my lap.

"Here, I'll have him. Does he need more whisky?"

"I don't know, but at least he can't squawk if your finger's in his mouth." I relinquished Jemmy with some relief, returning to my train of thought.

"Boston's been settled for more than a hundred years, even now," I said. "It *has* villages and farms—and the farms aren't all that far from the villages. People have been living there for a long time; everyone knows each other."

Jamie was nodding patiently at each of these startling revelations, trusting that I would eventually come to some point. Which I did, only to discover that it was the same point he'd been making to me.

"So when someone musters militia there," I said, suddenly seeing what he'd been telling me all along, "they come, because they're accustomed to fighting together to defend their towns and because no man would want to be thought a coward by his neighbors. But here . . ." I bit my lip, contemplating the soaring mountains all around us.

"Aye," he said, nodding, seeing the realization dawn in my face. "It's different here."

There was no settlement large enough to be called a town within a hundred miles, save the German Lutherans at Salem. Bar that, there was nothing in the backcountry but scattered homesteads; sometimes a place where a family had settled and spread, brothers or cousins building houses within sight of one another. Small settlements and distant cabins, some hidden in the mountain hollows, screened by laurels, where the residents might not see another white face for months—or years—at a time.

The sun had sunk below the angled slope of the mountain, but the light still lingered, a brief wash of color that stained the trees and rocks gold around us and flushed the distant peaks with blue and violet. There were living creatures in that cold, brilliant landscape, I knew, habitations nearby and warm bodies stirring; but so far as the eye could see, nothing moved.

Mountain settlers would go without question to help a neighbor—because they might as easily require such help themselves at any moment. There was, after all, no one else to turn to.

But they had never fought for a common purpose, had

nothing in common to defend. And to abandon their homesteads and leave their families without defense, in order to
serve the whim of a distant governor? A vague notion of duty
might compel a few; a few would go from curiosity, from
restlessness, or in the vague hope of gain. But most would go
only if they were called by a man they respected; a man that
they trusted.

*I am not born either laird or chief to them,* he'd said. Not
born to them, no—but born to it, nonetheless. He could, if he
wished, make himself chief.

"Why?" I asked softly. "Why will you do it?" The shadows were rising from the rocks, slowly drowning the light.

"Do you not see?" One eyebrow lifted as he turned his
head to me. "Ye told me what would happen at Culloden—
and I believed ye, Sassenach, fearful as it was. The men of
Lallybroch came home safe as much because of you as because of me."

That was not entirely true; any man who had marched to
Nairn with the Highland army would have known that disaster lay somewhere ahead. Still . . . I *had* been able to help in
some small way, to make sure that Lallybroch was prepared,
not only for the battle, but its aftermath. The small weight of
guilt that I always felt when I thought of the Rising lifted
slightly, easing my heart.

"Well, perhaps. But what—"

"Ye've told me what will happen here, Sassenach. You and
Brianna and MacKenzie, all three. Rebellion, and war—and
this time . . . victory."

Victory. I nodded numbly, remembering what I knew of
wars and the cost of victory. It was, however, better than defeat.

"Well, then." He stooped to pick up his dirk, and gestured
with it to the mountains around us. "I have sworn an oath to
the Crown; if I break it in time of war, I am a traitor. My land
is forfeit—and my life—and those who follow me will share
my fate. True?"

"True." I swallowed, hugging my arms tight around me,
wishing I still held Jemmy. Jamie turned to face me, his eyes
hard and bright.

"But the Crown willna prevail, this time. Ye've told me. And if the King is overthrown—what then of my oath? If I have kept it, then I am traitor to the rebel cause."

"Oh," I said, rather faintly.

"Ye see? At some point, Tryon and the King will lose their power over me—but I dinna ken when that may be. At some point, the rebels will hold power—but I dinna ken when *that* may be. And in between . . ." He tilted the point of his dirk downward.

"I do see. A very tidy little cleft stick," I said, feeling somewhat hollow as I realized just how precarious our situation was.

To follow Tryon's orders now was plainly the only choice. Later, however . . . for Jamie to continue as the Governor's man into the early stages of the Revolution was to declare himself a Loyalist—which would be fatal, in the long run. In the short run, though, to break with Tryon, forswear his oath to the King, and declare for the rebels . . . that would cost him his land, and quite possibly his life.

He shrugged, with a wry twist of the mouth, and sat back a little, easing Jemmy on his lap.

"Well, it's no as though I've never found myself walking between two fires before, Sassenach. I may come out of it a bit scorched round the edges, but I dinna think I'll fry." He gave a faint snort of what might be amusement. "It's in my blood, no?"

I managed a short laugh.

"If you're thinking of your grandfather," I said, "I admit he was good at it. Caught up with him in the end, though, didn't it?"

He tilted his head from one side to the other, equivocating.

"Aye, maybe so. But do ye not think things perhaps fell out as he wished?"

The late Lord Lovat had been notorious for the deviousness of his mind, but I couldn't quite see the benefit in planning to have his head chopped off, and said so.

Jamie smiled, despite the seriousness of the discussion.

"Well, perhaps beheading wasna quite what he'd planned,

but still—ye saw what he did; he sent Young Simon to battle, and he stayed home. But which of them was it who paid the price on Tower Hill?"

I nodded slowly, beginning to see his point. Young Simon, who was in fact close to Jamie's own age, had not suffered physically for his part in the Rising, overt though it had been. He had not been imprisoned or exiled, like many of the Jacobites, and while he had lost most of his lands, he had in fact regained quite a bit of his property since, by means of repeated and tenacious lawsuits brought against the Crown.

"And Old Simon *could* have blamed his son, and Young Simon would have ended up on the scaffold—but he didn't. Well, I suppose even an old viper like that might hesitate to put his own son and heir under the ax."

Jamie nodded.

"Would ye let someone chop off your head, Sassenach, if it was a choice betwixt you and Brianna?"

"Yes," I said, without hesitation. I was reluctant to admit that Old Simon might have possessed such a virtue as family feeling, but I supposed even vipers had some concern for their children's welfare.

Jemmy had abandoned the proffered finger in favor of his grandfather's dirk, and was gnawing fiercely on the hilt. Jamie wrapped his hand around the blade, holding it safely away from the child, but made no effort to take the knife away.

"So would I," Jamie said, smiling slightly. "Though I do hope it willna come to that."

"I don't think either army was—will be—inclined to behead people," I said. That did, of course, leave a number of other unpleasant options available—but Jamie knew that as well as I did.

I had a sudden, passionate wish to urge him to throw it all up, turn away from it. Tell Tryon to stuff his land, tell the tenants they must make their own way—abandon the Ridge and flee. War was coming, but it need not engulf us; not this time. We could go south, to Florida, or to the Indies. To the west, to take refuge with the Cherokee. Or even back to Scotland. The Colonies would rise, but there were places one could run to.

He was watching my face.

"This," he said, a gesture dismissing Tryon, the militia, the Regulators, "this is a verra little thing, Sassenach, perhaps nothing in itself. But it is the beginning, I think."

The light was beginning to fail now; the shadow covered his feet and legs, but the last of the sun threw his own face into strong relief. There was a smudge of blood on his forehead, where he had touched it, crossing himself. I should have wiped it away, I thought, but made no move to do so.

"If I will save these men—if they will walk wi' me between the fires—then they must follow me without question, Sassenach. Best it begins now, while not so much is at stake."

"I know," I said, and shivered.

"Are ye cold, Sassenach? Here, take the wean and go home. I'll come in a bit, so soon as I'm dressed."

He handed me Jemmy and the dirk, since the two seemed momentarily inseparable, and rose. He picked up his kilt and shook out the tartan folds, but I didn't move. The blade of the knife was warm where I gripped it, warm from his hand.

He looked at me in question, but I shook my head.

"We'll wait for you."

He dressed quickly, but carefully. Despite my apprehensions, I had to admire the delicacy of his instincts. Not his dress kilt, the one in crimson and black, but the hunting kilt. No effort to impress the mountain men with richness; but an oddity of dress, enough to make the point to the other Highlanders that he was one of them, to draw the eye and interest of the Germans. Plaid pinned up with the running-stag brooch, his belt and scabbard, clean wool stockings. He was quiet, absorbed in what he was doing, dressing with a calm precision that was unnervingly reminiscent of the robing of a priest.

It would be tonight, then. Roger and the rest had clearly gone to summon the men who lived within a day's ride; tonight he would light his cross and call the first of his men—and seal the bargain with whisky.

"So Bree was right," I said, to break the silence in the clearing. "She said perhaps you were starting your own religion. When she saw the cross, I mean."

He glanced at me, startled. He looked in the direction where the house lay, then his mouth curled wryly.

"I suppose I am," he said. "God help me."

He took the knife gently away from Jemmy, wiped it on a fold of his plaid, and slid it away into its scabbard. He was finished.

I stood to follow him. The words I couldn't speak—wouldn't speak—were a ball of eels in my throat. Afraid one would slither free and slip out of my mouth, I said instead, "Was it God you were calling on to help you? When I saw you earlier?"

"Och, no," he said. He looked away for a second, then met my eyes with a sudden queer glance. "I was calling Dougal MacKenzie."

I felt a deep and sudden qualm go through me. Dougal was long dead; he had died in Jamie's arms on the eve of Culloden—died with Jamie's dirk in his throat. I swallowed, and my eyes flicked involuntarily to the knife at his belt.

"I made my peace wi' Dougal long ago," he said softly, seeing the direction of my glance. He touched the hilt of the knife, with its knurl of gold, that had once been Hector Cameron's. "He was a chieftain, Dougal. He will know that I did then as I must—for my men, for you—and that I will do it now again."

I realized now what it was he had said, standing tall, facing the west—the direction to which the souls of the dead fly home. It had been neither prayer nor plea. I knew the words—though it was many years since I had heard them. He had shouted *"Tulach Ard!"*—the war cry of clan MacKenzie.

I swallowed hard.

"And will he . . . help you, do you think?"

He nodded, serious.

"If he can," he said. "We will ha' fought together many times, Dougal and I; hand to hand—and back to back. And after all, Sassenach—blood is blood."

I nodded back, mechanically, and lifted Jemmy up against my shoulder. The sky had bleached to a winter white, and shadow filled the clearing. The stone at the head of the spring stood out, a pale and ghostly shape above black water.

"Let's go," I said. "It's nearly night."

# THE BARD

IT WAS FULL DARK when Roger finally reached his own door, but the windows glowed welcomingly, and sparks showered from the chimney, promising warmth and food. He was tired, chilled, and very hungry, and he felt a deep and thankful appreciation for his home—substantially sharpened by the knowledge that he would leave it on the morrow.

"Brianna?" He stepped inside, squinting in the dim glow, looking for his wife.

"There you are! You're so late! Where have you been?" She popped out of the small back room, the baby balanced on her hip and a heap of tartan cloth clutched to her chest. She leaned over it to kiss him briefly, leaving him with a tantalizing taste of plum jam.

"I've been riding up hill and down dale for the last ten hours," he said, taking the cloth from her and tossing it onto the bed. "Looking for a mythical family of Dutchmen. Come here and kiss me properly, aye?"

She obligingly wrapped her free arm round his waist and gave him a lingering, plum-scented kiss that made him think that hungry as he was, dinner could perhaps wait for a bit. The baby, however, had other ideas, and set up a loud wail that made Brianna hastily detach herself, grimacing at the racket.

"Still teething?" Roger said, observing his offspring's red and swollen countenance, covered with a shiny coating of snot, saliva, and tears.

"How did you guess?" she said caustically. "Here, can

you take him, just for a minute?" She thrust Jemmy, writhing, into his father's arms, and tugged at her bodice, the green linen damply creased and stained with pale splotches of spit-up milk. One of her breasts bobbed into view, and she reached out for Jemmy, sitting down with him in the nursing chair by the fire.

"He's been fussing all day," she said, shaking her head as the baby squirmed and whined, batting at the proffered nourishment with a fretful hand. "He won't nurse for more than a few minutes, and when he does, he spits it up again. He whines when you pick him up, but he screams if you set him down." She shoved a hand tiredly through her hair. "I feel like I've been wrestling alligators all day."

"Oh, mm. That's too bad." Roger rubbed his aching lower back, trying not to be ostentatious about it. He pointed toward the bed with his chin. "Ah . . . what's the tartan for?"

"Oh, I forgot—that's yours." Attention momentarily distracted from the struggling child, she glanced up at Roger, taking in for the first time his disheveled appearance. "Da brought it down for you to wear tonight. You have a big smudge of mud on your face, by the way—did you fall off?"

"Several times." He moved to the washstand, limping only slightly. One sleeve of his coat and the knee of his breeches were plastered with mud, and he rubbed at his chest, trying to dislodge bits of dry leaf that had got down the neck of his shirt.

"Oh? That's too bad. Shh, shh, shh," she crooned to the child, rocking him to and fro. "Did you hurt yourself?"

"Ah, no. It's fine." He shed the coat and turned his back, pouring water from the pitcher into the bowl. He splashed cold water over his face, listening to Jemmy's squeals and privately calculating the odds of being able to make love to Brianna sometime before having to leave next morning. Between Jemmy's teeth and his grandfather's plans, the chances seemed slight, but hope sprang eternal.

He blotted his face with the towel, glancing covertly around in hopes of food. Both table and hearth were empty, though there was a strong vinegar scent in the air.

"Sauerkraut?" he guessed, sniffing audibly. "The Muellers?"

"They brought two big jars of it," Brianna said, gesturing toward the corner where a stone crock stood in the shadows. "That one's ours. Did you get anything to eat while you were out?"

"No." His belly rumbled loudly, evidently willing to consider cold sauerkraut, if that was all that was on offer. Presumably there would be food at the big house, though. Cheered by this thought, he pulled off his breeches and began the awkward business of pleating up the tartan cloth to make a belted plaid.

Jemmy had quieted a little, now making no more than intermittent yips of discomfort as his mother rocked him to and fro.

"What was that about mythical Dutchmen?" Brianna asked, still rocking, but now with a moment's attention to spare.

"Jamie sent me up to the northeast to look for a family of Dutchmen he'd heard had settled near Boiling Creek—to tell the men about the militia summons and have them come back with me, if they would." He frowned at the cloth laid out on the bed. He'd worn a plaid like this only twice before, and both times, had had help to put the thing on. "Is it important for me to wear this, do you think?"

Brianna snorted behind him with brief amusement.

"I think you'd better wear *something*. You can't go up to the big house in nothing but your shirt. You couldn't find the Dutchmen, then?"

"Not so much as a wooden shoe." He had found what he *thought* was Boiling Creek, and had ridden up the bank for miles, dodging—or not—overhanging branches, bramble patches, and thickets of witch hazel, but hadn't found a sign of anything larger than a fox that had slipped across his path, disappearing into the brush like a flame suddenly extinguished.

"Maybe they moved on. Went up to Virginia, or Pennsylvania." Brianna spoke with sympathy. It had been a long, exhausting day, with failure at the end of it. Not a terrible failure; Jamie had said only, "Find them if ye can"—and if he *had* found them, they might not have understood his rudimentary Dutch, gained on brief holidays to the Amsterdam of the 1960s. Or might not have come, in any case. Still, the small failure nagged at him, like a stone in his shoe.

He glanced at Brianna, who grinned widely at him in anticipation.

"All right," he said with resignation. "Laugh if ye must." Getting into a belted plaid wasn't the most dignified thing a man could do, given that the most efficient method was to lie down on the pleated fabric and roll like a sausage on a girdle. Jamie could do it standing up, but then, the man had had practice.

His struggles—rather deliberately exaggerated—were rewarded by Brianna's giggling, which in turn seemed to have a calming effect on the baby. By the time Roger made the final adjustments to his pleats and drapes, mother and child were both flushed, but happy.

Roger made a leg to them, flourishing, and Bree patted her own leg in one-handed applause.

"Terrific," she said, her eyes traveling appreciatively over him. "See Daddy? Pretty Daddy!" She turned Jemmy, who stared openmouthed at the vision of male glory before him and blossomed into a wide, slow smile, a trickle of drool hanging from the pouting curve of his lip.

Roger was still hungry, sore, and tired, but it didn't seem so important. He grinned, and held out his arms toward the baby.

"Do you need to change? If he's full and dry, I'll take him up to the house—give you a bit of time to fix up."

"You think I need fixing up, do you?" Brianna gave him an austere look down her long, straight nose. Her hair had come down in wisps and straggles, her dress looked as though she'd been sleeping in it for weeks, and there was a dark smear of jam on the upper curve of one breast.

"You look great," he said, bending and swinging Jemmy deftly up. "Hush, *a bhalaich*. You've had enough of Mummy, and she's definitely had enough of you for a bit. Come along with me."

"Don't forget your bodhran!" Bree called after him as he headed for the door. He glanced back at her, surprised.

"What?"

"Da wants you to sing. Wait, he gave me a list."

"A list? Of *what*?" To the best of Roger's knowledge, Jamie Fraser paid no attention whatever to music. It rankled him a bit, in fact, though he seldom admitted it—that his own greatest skill was one that Fraser didn't value.

"Songs, of course." She furrowed her brow, conjuring up the memorized list. "He wants you to do 'Ho Ro!' and 'Birniebouzle,' and 'The Great Silkie'—you can do other stuff in between, he said, but he wants those—and then get into the warmongering stuff. That's not what *he* called it, but you know what I mean—'Killiecrankie' and 'The Haughs of Cromdale,' and 'The Sherrifsmuir Fight.' Just the older stuff, though; he says don't do the songs from the '45, except for 'Johnnie Cope'—he wants that one for sure, but toward the end. And—"

Roger stared at her, disentangling Jemmy's foot from the folds of his plaid.

"I wouldn't have thought your father so much as knew the names of songs, let alone had preferences."

Brianna had stood up and was reaching for the long wooden pin that held her hair in place. She pulled it out and let the thick red shimmer cascade over shoulders and face. She ran both hands through the ruddy mass and pushed it back, shaking her head.

"He doesn't. Have preferences, I mean. Da's completely tone-deaf. Mama says he has a good sense of rhythm, but he can't tell one note from another."

"That's what I thought. But why—"

"He may not listen to music, Roger, but he *listens*." She glanced at him, snigging the comb through the tangles of her hair. "And he watches. He knows how people act—and how they feel—when they hear you do those songs."

"Does he?" Roger murmured. He felt an odd spark of pleasure at the thought that Fraser had indeed noticed the effect of his music, even if he didn't appreciate it personally. "So—he means me to soften them up, is that it? Get them in the mood before he goes on for his own bit?"

"That's it." She nodded, busy untying the laces of her bodice. Escaped from confinement, her breasts bobbed suddenly free, round and loose under the thin muslin shift.

Roger shifted his weight, easing the fit of his plaid. She

caught the slight movement and looked at him. Slowly, she drew her hands up, cupping her breasts and lifting them, her eyes on his and a slight smile on her lips. Just for a moment, he felt as though he had stopped breathing, though his chest continued to rise and fall.

She was the first to break the moment, dropping her hands and turning to delve into the chest where she kept her linen.

"Do you know exactly what he's up to?" she asked, her voice muffled in the depths of the chest. "Did he have that cross up when you left?"

"Aye, I know about it." Jemmy was making small huffing noises, like a toy engine struggling up a hill. Roger tucked him under one arm, his hand cradling the fat little belly. "It's a fiery cross. D'ye ken what that is?"

She emerged from the chest, a fresh shift in her hands, looking mildly disturbed.

"A fiery cross? You mean he's going to *burn* a cross in the yard?"

"Well, not burn it all the way, no." Taking down his bodhran with his free hand and flicking a finger against the drum head to check the tautness, he explained briefly the tradition of the fiery cross. "It's a rare thing," he concluded, moving the drum out of Jemmy's grasping reach. "I don't think it was ever done in the Highlands again, after the Rising. Your father told me he'd seen it once, though—it's something really special, to see it done here."

Flushed with historical enthusiasm, he didn't notice at once that Brianna seemed slightly less eager.

"Maybe so," she said uneasily. "I don't know . . . it sort of gives me the creeps."

"Eh?" Roger glanced at her in surprise. "Why?"

She shrugged, pulling the crumpled shift off over her head.

"I don't know. Maybe it's just that I *have* seen burning crosses—on the evening news on TV. You know, the KKK—or do you know? Maybe they don't—didn't—report things like that on television in Britain?"

"The Ku Klux Klan?" Roger was less interested in fanatical bigots than in the sight of Brianna's bare breasts, but made an effort to focus on the conversation. "Oh, ayè, heard of them. Where d'you think they got the notion?"

"What? You mean—"

"Sure," he said cheerfully. "They got it from the Highland immigrants—from whom they were descended, by the byè. That's why they called it 'Klan,' aye? Come to think," he added, interested, "it could be this—tonight—that's the link. The occasion that brings the custom from the Old World to the New, I mean. Wouldn't that be something?"

"Something," Brianna echoed faintly. She'd pulled on a fresh shift, and now shook out a clean dress of blue linen, looking uneasy.

"Everything starts somewhere, Bree," he said, more gently. "Most often, we don't know where or how; does it matter if this time we do? And the Ku Klux Klan won't get started for a hundred years from now, at least." He hoisted Jemmy slightly, bouncing him on one hip. "It won't be us who sees it, or even wee Jeremiah here—maybe not even his son."

"Great," she said dryly, pulling on her stays and reaching for the laces. "So our *great*-grandson can end up being the Grand Dragon."

Roger laughed.

"Aye, maybe so. But for tonight, it's your father."

## PLAYING WITH FIRE

H E WASN'T SURE what he had expected. Something like the spectacle of the great fire at the Gathering, perhaps. The preparation was the same, involving large quantities of food and drink. A huge keg of beer and a smaller one of whisky stood on planks at the edge of the dooryard, and a huge roast pig on a spit of green hickory turned slowly over a bed of coals, sending whiffs of smoke and mouthwatering aromas through the cold evening air.

He grinned at the fire-washed faces in front of him, slicked with grease and flushed with booze, and struck his bodhran. His stomach rumbled loudly, but the noise was drowned beneath the raucous chorus of "Killiecrankie."

> *"O, I met the De-ev-il and Dundeeee . . .*
> *On the brae-aes o' Killiecrankie-O!"*

He would have earned his own supper by the time he got it. He had been playing and singing for more than an hour, and the moon was rising over Black Mountain now. He paused under cover of the refrain, just long enough to grab the cup of ale set under his stool and wet his throat, then hit the new verse fresh and solid.

> *"I fought on land, I fought on sea,*
> *At hame I fought my auntie, Oh!*
> *I met the Devil and Dundee . . .*
> *On the braes o' Killiecrankie-O!"*

He smiled professionally as he sang, meeting an eye here, focusing on a face there, and calculated progress in the back of his mind. He'd got them going now—with a bit of help from the drink on offer, admittedly—and well stuck into what Bree had called "the warmongering stuff."

He could feel the cross standing at his back, almost hidden by the darkness. Everyone had had a chance to see it, though; he'd heard the murmurs of interest and speculation.

Jamie Fraser was away to one side, out of the ring of firelight. Roger could just make out his tall form, dark in the shadow of the big red spruce that stood near the house. Fraser had been working his way methodically through the group all evening, stopping here and there to exchange cordialities, tell a joke, pause to listen to a problem or a story. Now he stood alone, waiting. Nearly time, then—for whatever he meant to do.

Roger gave them a moment for applause and his own refreshment, then launched into "Johnnie Cope," fast, fierce,
and funny.

He'd done that one at the Gathering, several times, and
knew pretty much how they'd take it. A moment's pause, uncertainty, then the voices beginning to join in—by the end of
the second verse, they'd be whooping and shouting ribald remarks in the background.

Some of the men here had fought at Prestonpans; if they'd
been defeated at Culloden, they'd still routed Johnnie Cope's
troops first, and loved the chance to relive that famous victory. And those Highlanders who hadn't fought had heard
about it. The Muellers, who had likely never heard of Charles
Stuart and probably understood one word in a dozen, seemed
to be improvising their own sort of yodeling chorus round
the back, waving their cups in sloshing salute to each verse.
Aye, well, so long as they were having a good time.

The crowd was half-shouting the final chorus, nearly
drowning him out.

> *"Hey, Johnnie Cope, are ye walking yet?*
> *And are your drums a-beatin' yet?*
> *If ye were walkin', I wad wait,*
> *Tae gang tae the coals in the mornin'!"*

He hit a final thump, and bowed to huge applause. That
was the warm-up done; time for the main act to come on-
stage. Bowing and smiling, he rose from his stool and faded
off, fetching up in the shadows near the hacked remains of
the huge pork carcass.

Bree was there waiting for him, Jemmy wide-awake and
owl-eyed in her arms. She leaned across and kissed him,
handing him the kid as she did so, and taking his bodhran in
exchange.

"You were great!" she said. "Hold him; I'll get you some
food and beer."

Jem usually wanted to stay with his mother, but was too
stupefied by the noise and the leaping flames to protest the
handover. He snuggled against Roger's chest, gravely sucking his thumb.

Roger was sweating from the exertion, his heart beating fast from the adrenaline of performance, and the air away from the fire and the crowd was cold on his flushed face. The baby's swaddled weight felt good against him, warm and solid in the crook of his arm. He'd done well, and knew it. Let's hope it was what Fraser wanted.

By the time Bree reappeared with a drink and a pewter plate heaped with sliced pork, apple fritters, and roast potatoes, Jamie had come into the circle of firelight, taking Roger's place before the standing cross.

He stood tall and broad-shouldered in his best gray gentleman's coat, kilted below in soft blue tartan, his hair loose and blazing on his shoulders, with a small warrior's plait down one side, adorned with a single feather. Firelight glinted from the knurled gold hilt of his dirk and the brooch that held his looped plaid. He looked pleasant enough, but his manner overall was serious, intent. He made a good show—and knew it.

The crowd quieted within seconds, men elbowing their more garrulous neighbors to silence.

"Ye ken well enough what we're about here, aye?" he asked without preamble. He raised his hand, in which he held the Governor's crumpled summons, the red smear of its official seal visible in the leaping firelight. There was a rumble of agreement; the crowd was still cheerful, blood and whisky coursing freely through their veins.

"We are called in duty, and we come in honor to serve the cause of law—and the Governor."

Roger saw old Gerhard Mueller, leaning to one side to hear the translation that one of his sons-in-law was murmuring in his ear. He nodded his approval, and shouted, *"Ja! Lang lebe Governor!"* There was a ripple of laughter, and echoing shouts in English and Gaelic.

Jamie smiled, waiting for the noise to die down. As it did, he turned slowly, nodding as he looked from one face to the next, acknowledging each man. Then he turned to the side and lifted a hand to the cross that stood stark and black behind him.

"In the Highlands of Scotland, when a chieftain would set himself for war," he said, his tone casually conversational, but pitched to be heard throughout the dooryard, "he would burn the fiery cross, and send it for a sign through the lands of his clan. It was a signal to the men of his name, to gather their weapons and come to the gathering place, prepared for battle."

There was a stir in the midst of the crowd, a brief nudging and more cries of approval, though these were more subdued. A few men had seen this, or at least knew what he was talking about. The rest raised their chins and craned their necks, mouths half-open in interest.

"But this is a new land, and while we are friends"—he smiled at Gerhard Mueller—"*Ja, Freunde*, neighbors, and countrymen"—a look at the Lindsay brothers—"and we will be companions in arms, we are not clan. While I am given command, I am not your chief."

*The hell you aren't*, Roger thought. *Or well on your way to it, anyroad*. He took a last deep swallow of cold beer and put down cup and plate. The food could wait a bit longer. Bree had taken back the baby and had his bodhran tucked under her arm; he reached for it, and she gave him a glancing smile, but most of her attention was fixed on her father.

Jamie bent and pulled a torch from the fire, stood with it in his hand, lighting the broad planes and sharp angles of his face.

"Let God witness here our willingness, and may God strengthen our arms—" He paused, to let the Germans catch up. "But let this fiery cross stand as testament to our honor, to invoke God's protection for our families—until we come safe home again."

He turned and touched the torch to the upright of the cross, holding it until the dry bark caught and a small flame grew and glimmered from the dark wood.

Everyone stood silent, watching. There was no sound but the shift and sigh of the crowd, echoing the sough of the wind in the wilderness around them. It was no more than a tiny tongue of fire, flickering in the breeze, on the verge of going out altogether. No petrol-soaked roar, no devouring conflagration. Roger felt Brianna sigh beside him, some of the tension leaving her.

The flame steadied and caught. The edges of the jigsaw-pieces of pine bark glowed crimson, then white, and vanished into ash as the flame began to spread upward. It was big and solid, and would burn slowly, this cross, halfway through the night, lighting the dooryard as the men gathered beneath it, talking, eating, drinking, beginning the process of becoming what Jamie Fraser meant them to be: friends, neighbors, companions in arms. Under his command.

Fraser stood for a moment, watching, to be sure the flame had caught. Then he turned back to the crowd of men and dropped his torch back into the fire.

"We cannot say what may befall us. God grant us courage," he said, very simply. "God grant us wisdom. If it be His will, may He grant us peace. We ride in the morning."

He turned then and left the fire, glancing to find Roger as he did so. Roger nodded back, swallowed to clear his throat, and began to sing softly from the darkness, the opening to the song Jamie had wanted to finish the proceedings—"The Flower of Scotland."

> *"Oh flower of Scotland,*
> *When will we see your like again?*
> *That fought and died for*
> *Your wee bit hill and glen . . ."*

Not one of the songs Bree called the warmongering ones. It was a solemn song, that one, and melancholy. But not a song of grief, for all that; one of remembrance, of pride and determination. It wasn't even a legitimately ancient song—Roger knew the man who'd written it, in his own time—but Jamie had heard it, and knowing the history of Stirling and Bannockburn, strongly approved the sentiment.

> *"And stood against him,*
> *Proud Edward's army,*
> *And sent him homeward*
> *Tae think again."*

The Scottish members of the crowd let him sing alone through the verse, but voices lifted softly, then louder, in the refrain.

*"And sent him ho-omeward . . .
Tae think again!"*

He remembered something Bree had told him, lying in bed the night before, during the few moments when both of them were still conscious. They had been talking of the people of the times, speculating as to whether they might one day meet people like Jefferson or Washington face to face; it was an exciting—and not at all impossible—prospect. She had mentioned John Adams, quoting something she had read that he had said—or would say, rather—during the Revolution:

*"I am a warrior, that my son may be a merchant—and his son may be a poet."*

*"The hills are bare now,
And autumn leaves lie thick and still,
O'er land that is lost now,
Which those so dearly held.*

*And stood against him,
Proud Edward's army,
And sent him homeward
Tae think again."*

No longer Edward's army, but George's. And yet the same proud army. He caught a glimpse of Claire, standing with the other women, apart, at the very edge of the circle of light. Her face was remote and she stood very still, hair floating loose around her face, the gold eyes dark with inner shadow—fixed on Jamie, who stood quiet by her side.

The same proud army with which she had once fought; the proud army with which his father had died. He felt a catch at his throat, and forced air from down deep, singing through it fiercely. *I will be a warrior, that my son may be a merchant—and his son may be a poet.* Neither Adams nor Jefferson had fought; Jefferson had no son. He had been the poet, whose words had echoed through the years, raised armies, burned in the hearts of those who would die for them, and for the country founded on them.

*Perhaps it's the hair*, Roger thought ironically, seeing the gleam of ruddy light as Jamie moved, watching silently over the thing he had started. Some Viking tinge in the blood, that gave those tall fiery men the gift of rousing men to war.

> *"That fought and died for*
> *Your wee bit hill and glen . . ."*

So they had; so they would again. For that was what men always fought for, wasn't it? Home and family. Another glint of red hair, loose in firelight, by the bones of the pig. Bree, holding Jemmy. And if Roger found himself now bard to a displaced Highland chieftain, still he must try also to be a warrior when the time came, for the sake of his son, and those who would come after.

> *"And sent him homeward*
> *Tae think again.*
>
> *Tae think . . . again."*

# THE ANGELING OF MY REST

LATE AS IT WAS, we made love by unspoken consent, each wanting the refuge and reassurance of the other's flesh. Alone in our bedroom, with the shutters closed tight against the sounds of the voices in the dooryard—poor Roger was still singing, by popular demand—we could shed the urgencies and fatigues of the day—at least for a little while.

He held me tightly afterward, his face buried in my hair, clinging to me like a talisman.

"It will be all right," I said softly, and stroked his damp hair, dug my fingers deep into the place where neck and shoulder met, the muscle there hard as wood beneath the skin.

"Aye, I know." He lay still for a moment, letting me work, and the tension of his neck and shoulders gradually relaxed, his body growing heavier on mine. He felt me draw breath under him, and moved, rolling onto his side.

His stomach rumbled loudly, and we both laughed.

"No time for dinner?" I asked.

"I canna eat, just before," he answered. "It gives me cramp. And there wasna time, after. I dinna suppose there's anything edible up here?"

"No," I said regretfully. "I had a few apples, but the Chisholms got them. I'm sorry, I should have thought to bring something up for you." I did know that he seldom ate "before"—before any fight, confrontation, or other socially stressful situation, that is—but hadn't thought that he might not have a chance to eat afterward, what with everyone and his brother wanting to "have just a wee word, sir."

"It's not as though ye didna have other things to think of, Sassenach," he answered dryly. "Dinna fash yourself; I'll do 'til breakfast."

"Are you sure?" I put a foot out of bed, making to rise. "There's plenty left; or if you don't want to go down, I could go and—"

He stopped me with a hand on my arm, then dragged me firmly back under the covers, tucking me spoon-fashion into the curve of his body and wrapping an arm over me to insure that I stayed there.

"No," he said definitely. "This may be the last night I spend in a bed for some time. I mean to stay in it—with you."

"All right." I snuggled obediently under his chin, and relaxed against him, just as pleased to stay. I understood; while no one would come to fetch us unless there was some emergency, the mere sight of either of us downstairs would cause an immediate rush of people needing this or that, wanting to ask a question, offer advice, require something ... much better to stay here, snug and peaceful with each other.

I had put out the candle, and the fire was burning low. I wondered briefly whether to get up and add more wood, but decided against it. Let it burn itself to embers if it liked; we would be gone at daybreak.

Despite my tiredness and the serious nature of the journey, I was looking forward to it. Beyond the lure of novelty and the possibility of adventure, there was the delightful prospect of escape from laundry, cookery, and female warfare. Still, Jamie was right; tonight was likely the last we would have of privacy and comfort for some little time.

I stretched, consciously enjoying the soft embrace of the feather bed, the smooth, clean sheets with their faint scent of rosemary and elderflower. Had I packed sufficient bedding?

Roger's voice reached through the shutters, still strong but beginning to sound a bit ragged with fatigue.

"The Thrush had best get to his bed," Jamie said, with mild disapproval, "if he means to bid his wife a proper farewell."

"Goodness, Bree and Jemmy went to bed hours ago!" I said.

"The wean, perhaps; the lass is still there. I heard her voice, a moment ago."

"Is she?" I strained to listen, but made out no more than a rumble of muted applause as Roger brought his song to a close. "I suppose she wants to stay with him as long as she can. Those men are going to be exhausted in the morning— to say nothing of hung over."

"So long as they can sit a horse, I dinna mind if they slip off to have a vomit in the weeds now and again," Jamie assured me.

I nestled down, covers drawn up warm around my shoulders. I could hear the deep rumble of Roger's voice, laughing, but declining firmly to sing anymore. Little by little, the noises in the dooryard ceased, though I could still hear bumpings and rattlings as the beer keg was picked up and shaken empty of the last few drops. Then a hollow thud as someone dropped it on the ground.

There were noises in the house; the sudden yowl of a wakening baby, footsteps in the kitchen, the sleepy whine of toddlers disturbed by the men, a woman's voice raised in remonstrance, then reassurance.

My neck and shoulders ached, and my feet were sore from the long walk to the whisky spring, carrying Jemmy. Still, I found myself annoyingly wakeful, unable to shut out the noises of the external world as completely as the shutters blocked it from view.

"Can you remember everything you did today?" This was a small game we played sometimes at night, each trying to recall in detail everything done, seen, heard, or eaten during the day, from getting up to going to bed. Like writing in a journal, the effort of recall seemed to purge the mind of the day's exertions, and we found great entertainment in each other's experiences. I loved to hear Jamie's daily accounts, whether pedestrian or exciting, but he wasn't in the mood tonight.

"I canna remember a thing that happened before we closed the chamber door," he said, squeezing my buttock in a companionable way. "After that, though, I expect I could recall a detail or two."

"It's reasonably fresh in my mind, too," I assured him. I curled my toes, caressing the tops of his feet.

We stopped speaking, then, and began to shift and settle toward sleep, as the sounds below ceased, replaced by the buzz and rasp of miscellaneous snores. Or at least I tried to. Late as it was, and exhausted as my body undoubtedly was, my mind appeared determined to stay up and carouse. Fragments of the day appeared behind my eyelids the moment I shut my eyes—Mrs. Bug and her broom, Gerhard Mueller's muddy boots, bare-stemmed grape clusters, blanched tangles of sauerkraut, the round halves of Jemmy's miniature pink bottom, dozens of young Chisholms running amok . . . I resolutely strove to discipline my fugitive mind by turning instead to a mental checklist of my preparations for leaving.

This was most unhelpful, as within moments I was wide awake with suppressed anxiety, imagining the complete destruction of my surgery; Brianna, Marsali, or the children succumbing to some sudden hideous epidemic; and Mrs.

Bug inciting riot and bloodshed from one end of the Ridge to the other.

I rolled onto my side, looking at Jamie. He had rolled onto his back as usual, arms neatly folded across his abdomen like a tomb figure, profile pure and stern against the dying glow of the hearth, tidily composed for sleep. His eyes were closed, but there was a slight frown on his face, and his lips twitched now and then, as though he were conducting some kind of interior argument.

"You're thinking so loudly, I can hear you from over here," I said, in conversational tones. "Or are you only counting sheep?"

His eyes opened at once, and he turned over to smile ruefully at me.

"I was counting pigs," he informed me. "And doing nicely, too. Only I kept catchin' sight of that white creature from the corner of my eye, skippin' to and fro just out of reach, taunting me."

I laughed with him, and scooted toward him. I laid my forehead against his shoulder and heaved a deep sigh.

"We really must sleep, Jamie. I'm so tired, my bones feel as though they're melting, and you've been up even longer than I have."

"Mmm." He put an arm around me, pulling me into the curve of his shoulder.

"That cross—it isn't going to catch the house afire, is it?" I asked after a moment, having thought of something else to worry about.

"No." He sounded slightly drowsy. "It's burnt out long since."

The fire in the hearth had burned down to a bed of glowing embers. I rolled over again and lay watching them for a few minutes, trying to empty my mind of everything.

"When Frank and I were married," I said, "we went to be counseled by a priest. He advised us to begin our married life by saying the rosary together in bed each night. Frank said he wasn't sure whether this was meant to be devotion, an aid to sleep, or only a Church-sanctioned method of birth control."

Jamie's chest vibrated with silent laughter behind me.

"Well, we could try if ye like, Sassenach," he said. "Though ye'll have to keep count of the Hail Marys; you're lyin' on my left hand and my fingers have gone numb."

I shifted slightly to allow him to pull his hand out from under my hip.

"Not that, I don't think," I said. "But perhaps a prayer. Do you know any good going-to-bed prayers?"

"Aye, lots," he said, holding up his hand and flexing his fingers slowly as the blood returned to them. Dark in the dimness of the room, the slow movement reminded me of the way in which he lured trout from under rocks. "Let me think a bit."

The house below was silent now, save for the usual creaks and groans of settling timbers. I thought I heard a voice outside, raised in distant argument, but it might have been no more than the rattle of tree branches in the wind.

"Here's one," Jamie said at last. "I'd nearly forgotten it. My father taught it to me, not so long before he died. He said he thought I might one day find it useful."

He settled himself comfortably, head bent so his chin rested on my shoulder, and began to speak, low and warm-voiced, in my ear.

> *"Bless to me, O God, the moon that is above me,*
> *Bless to me, O God, the earth that is beneath me,*
> *Bless to me, O God, my wife and my children,*
> *And bless, O God, myself who have care of them;*
> *Bless to me my wife and my children,*
> *And bless, O God, myself who have care of them."*

He had begun with a certain self-consciousness, hesitating now and then to find a word, but that had faded with the speaking. Now he spoke soft and sure, and no longer to me, though his hand lay warm on the curve of my waist.

> *"Bless, O God, the thing on which mine eye doth rest,*
> *Bless, O God, the thing on which my hope doth rest,*
> *Bless, O God, my reason and my purpose,*
> *Bless, O bless Thou them, Thou God of life;*
> *Bless, O God, my reason and my purpose,*
> *Bless, O bless Thou them, Thou God of life."*

His hand smoothed the curve of my hip, lifted to stroke my hair.

> *"Bless to me the bed companion of my love,*
> *Bless to me the handling of my hands,*
> *Bless, O bless Thou to me, O God, the fencing of my*
> *defense,*
> *And bless, O bless to me the angeling of my rest;*
> *Bless, O bless Thou to me, O God, the fencing of my*
> *defense,*
> *And bless, O bless to me the angeling of my rest."*

His hand lay still, curled under my chin. I wrapped my own hand round his, and sighed deeply.

"Oh, I like that. Especially 'the angeling of my rest.' When Bree was small, we'd put her to bed with an angel prayer—'May Michael be at my right, Gabriel at my left, Uriel behind me, Rafael before me—and above my head, the Presence of the Lord.' "

He didn't answer, but squeezed my fingers in reply. An ember in the hearth fell apart with a soft *whuff*, and sparks floated for an instant in the dimness of the room.

Sometime later, I returned briefly to consciousness, feeling him slide out of bed.

"Wha—?" I said sleepily.

"Nothing," he whispered. "Just a wee note I'd meant to write. Sleep, *a nighean donn*. I'll wake beside ye."

*Fraser's Ridge, 1 December, 1770*
*James Fraser, Esq., to Lord John Grey,*
*Mount Josiah Plantation*

*My Lord,*

*I write in hopes that all continues well with your*
*Establishment and its Inhabitants; my particular*
*Regard to your Son.*

*All are well in my House and—so far as I am aware—at River Run, as well. The Nuptials planned for my Daughter and my Aunt, of which I wrote you, were unexpectedly interfered with by Circumstance (principally a Circumstance by the name of Mr. Randall Lillywhite, whose Name I mention in case it may one Day pass your Cognizance), but my Grandchildren were fortunately christened, and while my Aunt's Wedding has been postponed to a later Season, my Daughter's Union with Mr. MacKenzie was solemnized by the Courtesy of the Reverend Mr. Caldwell, a worthy Gentleman, though Presbyterian.*

*Young Jeremiah Alexander Ian Fraser MacKenzie (the name "Ian" is of course the Scottish variant of "John"—my Daughter's Compliment to a Friend, as well as her Cousin) survived both the Occasion of his Baptism and the Journey home in good Spirit. His Mother bids me tell you that your Namesake now possesses no fewer than four Teeth, a fearsome Accomplishment which renders him exceeding dangerous to those unwary Souls charmed by his apparent Innocence, who surrender their Digits all unknowing to his pernicious Grasp. The Child bites like a Crocodile.*

*Our Population here exhibits a gratifying Growth of late, with the addition of some twenty Families since last I wrote. God has prospered our Efforts during the Summer, blessing us with an Abundance of Corn and wild Hay, and an Abundance of Beasts to consume them. I estimate the Hogs running at large in my Wood to number no fewer than forty at present, two Cows have borne Calves, and I have bought a new Horse. This Animal's Character lies in grave Doubt, but his Wind does not.*

*Thus, my good News.*

*And so to the bad. I am made Colonel of Militia, ordered to muster and deliver so many Men as I can to the Service of the Governor, by mid-month, this Service to be of Aid in the Suppression of local Hostilities.*

*You may have heard, during your visit to North*

Carolina, of a Group of Men who style themselves
"Regulators"—or you may not, as other Matters compelled your Attention on that Occasion (my Wife is
pleased to hear good Report of your own Health, and
sends with this a Parcel of Medicines, with Instructions for their Administration should you still be
plagued with Headache).

These Regulators are no more than Rabble, less
disciplined in their Actions even than the Rioters
whom we hear have hanged Gov. Richardson in Effigy
in Boston. I do not say there is no Substance to their
Complaint, but the Means of its Expression seems
unlikely to result in Redress by the Crown—rather, to
provoke both Sides to further Excess, which cannot
fail to end in Injury.

There was a serious outbreak of Violence in Hillsborough on 24 September, in which much Property
was wantonly destroyed and Violence done—some
justly, some not—to officials of the Crown. One Man,
a Justice, was grievously Wounded; many of the Regulation were arrested. Since then, we have heard little
more than Murmurs; Winter damps down Discontent,
which smolders by the Hearths of Cottages and Pot-
houses, but once let out with the Spring Airing, it will
flee abroad like the foul Odors from a sealed House,
staining the Air.

Tryon is an able Man, but not a Farmer. If he were,
he would scarce think of seeking to make War in Winter. Still, it may be that he hopes by making Show of
Force now—when he is likely sure it will not be
needed—so to intimidate the Rapscallions as to obvi-
ate its Necessity later. He is a Soldier.

Such remarks bring me to the true Point of this
Missive. I expect no evil Outcome of the present
Enterprise, and yet—you are a Soldier, too, even as I
am. You know the Unpredictability of Evil, and what
Catastrophe may spring from trivial Beginnings.

No man can know the Particulars of his own End—
save that he will have one. Thus, I have made such
Provision as I can, for the Welfare of my Family.

*I enumerate them here, as you will not know them all: Claire Fraser, my beloved Wife; my Daughter Brianna and her Husband, Roger MacKenzie, and their Child, Jeremiah MacKenzie. Also my Daughter Marsali and her Husband, Fergus Fraser (who is my adopted Son)—they have now two young ones, Germain and Joan by Name. Wee Joan is named for Marsali's sister, known as Joan MacKenzie, presently abiding still in Scotland. I have not the leisure to acquaint you with the History of the Situation, but I am disposed for good Reason to regard this young Woman likewise as a Daughter, and I hold myself similarly obligated for her Welfare, and that of her Mother, one Laoghaire MacKenzie.*

*I pray you for the Sake of our long Friendship and for the Sake of your Regard for my Wife and Daughter, that if Mischance should befall me in this Enterprise, you will do what you can to see them safe.*

*I depart upon the Morrow's Dawn, which is now not far off.*

> *Your most humble and obedient Servant,*
> *James Alexander Malcolm MacKenzie Fraser*

*Postscriptum: My Thanks for the Intelligence you provide in answer to my earlier Query regarding Stephen Bonnet. I note your accompanying Advice with the greatest Appreciation and Gratitude for its kind Intent—though as you suspect, it will not sway me.*

*Post-Postscriptum: Copies of my Will and Testament, and of the Papers pertaining to my Property and Affairs here and in Scotland, will be found with Farquard Campbell, of Greenoaks, near Cross Creek.*

# PART THREE

*Alarms and
Excursions*

# 26

# THE MILITIA RISES

HE WEATHER FAVORED US, keeping cold but clear. With the Muellers and the men from the nearby homesteads, we set out from Fraser's Ridge with a party of nearly forty men—and me.

Fergus would not serve with the militia, but had come with us to raise men, he being the most familiar with the nearby settlements and homesteads. As we approached the Treaty Line, and the farthest point of our peripatetic muster, we formed a respectable company in number, if not in expertise. Some of the men had been soldiers once, if not trained infantrymen; either in Scotland, or in the French and Indian Wars. Many had not, and each evening saw Jamie conducting military drills and practice, though of a most unorthodox sort.

"We havena got time to drill them properly," he'd told Roger over the first evening's fire. "It takes weeks, ken, to shape men so they willna run under fire."

Roger merely nodded at that, though I thought a faint look of uneasiness flickered across his face. I supposed he might be having doubts regarding his own lack of experience, and exactly how he himself would respond under fire. I'd known a lot of young soldiers in my time.

I was kneeling by the fire, cooking corn dodgers on an iron griddle set in the ashes. I glanced up at Jamie, to find him looking at me, a slight smile hidden in the corner of his mouth. He'd not only known young soldiers; he'd been one. He coughed, and bent forward to stir the coals with a stick, looking for more of the quails I'd set to bake, wrapped in clay.

"It's the natural thing, to run from danger, aye? The point of drilling troops is to accustom them to an officer's voice, so they'll hear, even over the roar of guns, and obey without thinkin' of the danger."

"Aye, like ye train a horse not to bolt at noises," Roger interrupted, sardonically.

"Aye, like that," Jamie agreed, quite seriously. "The difference being that ye need to make a horse believe ye ken better than he does; an officer only needs to be louder." Roger laughed, and Jamie went on, half-smiling.

"When I went for a soldier in France, I was marched to and fro and up and down, and wore a pair of boots clear through before they gave me powder for my gun. I was sae weary at the end of a day of drilling that they could have shot off cannon by my pallet and I wouldna have turned a hair."

He shook his head a little, the half-smile fading from his face. "But we havena got the time for that. Half our men will have had a bit of soldiering; we must depend on them to stand if it comes to fighting, and keep heart in the others." He glanced past the fire, and gestured toward the fading vista of trees and mountains.

"It's no much like a battlefield, is it? I canna say where the battle may be—if there is one—but I think we must plan for a fight where there's cover to be had. We'll teach them to fight as Highlanders do; to gather or to scatter at my word, and otherwise, to make shift as they can. Only half the men were soldiers, but all of them can hunt." He raised his chin, gesturing toward the recruits, several of whom had bagged small game during the day's ride. The Lindsay brothers had shot the quail we were eating.

Roger nodded, and bent down, scooping a blackened ball of clay out of the fire with his own stick, keeping his face hidden. Almost all. He had gone out shooting every day since our return to the Ridge, and had still to bag even a possum. Jamie, who had gone with him once, had privately expressed the opinion to me that Roger would do better to hit the game on the head with his musket, rather than shoot at it.

I lowered my brows at Jamie; he raised his at me, returning my stare. Roger's feelings could take care of themselves, was the blunt message there. I widened my own eyes, and rose.

"But it isn't really like hunting, is it?" I sat down beside Jamie, and handed him one of the hot corn dodgers. "Especially now."

"What d'ye mean by that, Sassenach?" Jamie broke the corn dodger open, half-closing his eyes in bliss as he inhaled the hot, fragrant steam.

"For one, you don't know that it will come to a fight at all," I pointed out. "For another, if it does, you won't be facing trained troops—the Regulators aren't soldiers, any more than your men are. For a third, you won't really be trying to kill the Regulators; only frighten them into retreat or surrender. And for a fourth"—I smiled at Roger—"the point of hunting is to kill something. The point of going to war is to come back alive."

Jamie choked on a bite of corn dodger. I thumped him helpfully on the back, and he rounded on me, glaring. He coughed crumbs, swallowed, and stood up, plaid swinging.

"Listen to me," he said, a little hoarsely. "Ye're right, Sassenach—and ye're wrong. It's no like hunting, aye. Because the game isna usually trying to kill *you*. Mind me—" He turned to Roger, his face grim. "She's wrong about the rest of it. War is killing, and that's all. Think of anything less—think of half-measures, think of frightening—above all, think of your own skin—and by God, man, ye will be dead by nightfall of the first day."

He flung the remains of his corn dodger into the fire, and stalked away.

I SAT FROZEN for a moment, until heat from the fresh corn dodger I was holding seeped through the cloth round it and burned my fingers. I set it down on the log with a muffled "ouch," and Roger shifted a little on his log.

"All right?" he said, though he wasn't looking at me. His eyes were fixed on the direction in which Jamie had vanished, toward the horses.

"Fine." I soothed my scorched fingertips against the cold, damp bark of the log. With the awkward silence eased by this little exchange, I found it possible to address the matter at hand.

"Granted," I said, "that Jamie has a certain amount of experience from which to speak . . . I do think what he said was rather an overreaction."

"Do you?" Roger didn't seem upset or taken aback by Jamie's remarks.

"Of course I do. Whatever happens with the Regulators, we know perfectly well that it isn't going to be an all-out war. It's likely to be nothing at all!"

"Oh, aye." Roger was still looking into the darkness, lips pursed in thoughtfulness. "Only—I think that's not what he was talking about."

I lifted one eyebrow at him, and he shifted his gaze to me, with a wry half-smile.

"When he went out hunting with me, he asked me what I knew about what was coming. I told him. Bree said he'd asked her, and she told him, too."

"What was coming—you mean, the Revolution?"

He nodded, eyes on the fragment of corn dodger he was crumbling between long, callused fingers.

"I told him what I knew. About the battles, the politics. Not all the detail, of course, but the chief battles I remembered; what a long, drawn-out, bloody business it will be." He was quiet for a moment, then looked up at me, a slight glint of green in his eye.

"I suppose ye'd call it fair exchange. It's hard to tell with him, but I *think* I maybe scared him. He's just returned the favor."

I gave a small snort of amusement, and stood up, brushing crumbs and ashes off my skirt.

"The day you scare Jamie Fraser by telling him war stories, my lad," I said, "will be the day hell freezes over."

He laughed, not discomposed in the slightest.

"Maybe I didn't scare him, then—though he got very quiet. But I tell you what"—he sobered somewhat, though the glint stayed in his eye—"he did scare me, just now."

I glanced off in the direction of the horses. The moon hadn't yet risen, and I couldn't see anything but a vague jumble of big, restless shadows, with an occasional gleam of firelight off a rounded rump or the brief shine of an eye. Jamie wasn't visible, but I knew he was there; there was a subtle shift and mill of movement among the horses, with faint whickers or snorts, that told me someone familiar was among them.

"He wasn't just a soldier," I said at last, speaking quietly, though I was fairly sure Jamie was too far away to hear me. "He was an officer."

I sat down on the log again, and put a hand on the corn dodger. It was barely warm now. I picked it up, but didn't bite into it.

"I was a combat nurse, you know. In a field hospital in France."

He nodded, dark head cocked in interest. The fire threw deep shadows on his face, emphasizing the contrast of heavy brow and strong bones with the gentle curve of his mouth.

"I nursed soldiers. They were *all* scared." I smiled a little, sadly. "The ones who'd been under fire remembered, and the ones who hadn't, imagined. But it was the officers who couldn't sleep at night."

I ran a thumb absently over the bumpy surface of the corn dodger. It felt faintly greasy, from the lard.

"I sat with Jamie once, after Preston, while he held one of his men in his arms as he died. And wept. He remembers that. He doesn't remember Culloden—because he can't bear to." I looked down at the lump of fried dough in my hand, picking at the burned bits with my thumbnail.

"Yes, you scared him. He doesn't want to weep for you. Neither do I," I added softly. "It may not be now, but when the time does come—take care, will you?"

There was a long silence. Then, "I will," he said quietly. He stood up and left, his footsteps fading quickly into silence on the damp earth.

The other campfires burned brightly, as the night deepened. The men still kept to the company of relative and friend, each small group around its own fire. As we went on, they would begin to join together, I knew. Within a few days, there would be one large fire, everyone gathered together in a single circle of light.

Jamie wasn't scared by what Roger had told him, I thought—but by what he himself knew. There were two choices for a good officer: let concern for his responsibilities tear him apart—or let necessity harden him to stone. He knew that.

And as for me . . . I knew a few things, too. I had been married to two soldiers—officers, both; for Frank had been one, too. I had been nurse and healer, on the fields of two wars.

I knew the names and dates of battles; I knew the smell of blood. And of vomit, and voided bowels. A field hospital sees the shattered limbs, the spilled guts, and bone ends . . . but it also sees the men who never raised a gun, but died there anyway, of fever and dirt and sickness and despair.

I knew that thousands died of wounds and killing on the battlefields of two World Wars; I knew that hundreds upon hundreds of thousands died there of infection and disease. It would be no different now—nor in four years.

And that scared me very much indeed.

THE NEXT NIGHT, we made camp in the woods on Balsam Mountain, a mile or so above the settlement of Lucklow. Several of the men wanted to push on, to reach the hamlet of Brownsville. Brownsville was the outer point of our journey, before turning back toward Salisbury, and it held the possibility of a pothouse—or at least a hospitable shed to sleep in—but Jamie thought better to wait.

"I dinna want to scare the folk there," he had explained to Roger, "riding in with a troop of armed men after dark. Better to announce our business by daylight, then give the men a day—and a night—to make ready to leave." He had stopped then, and coughed heavily, shoulders racked with the spasm.

I didn't like either the looks of Jamie or the sound of him. He had the patchy look of a mildewed quilt, and when he came to the fire to fill his dinner bowl, I could hear a faint wheezing sigh in every breath. Most of the men were in similar condition; red noses and coughing were endemic, and the fire popped and sizzled every few moments, as someone hawked and spat into it.

I should have liked to tuck Jamie up in bed with a hot stone to his feet, a mustard plaster on his chest, and a hot tisane of aromatic peppermint and ephedra leaves to drink. Since it would have taken a brace of cannon, leg irons, and several armed men to get him there, I contented myself with fishing up a particularly meaty ladle of stew and plopping it into his bowl.

"Ewald," Jamie called hoarsely to one of the Muellers. He stopped and cleared his throat, with a sound like tearing flannel. "Ewald—d'ye take Paul and fetch along more wood for the fire. It'll be a cold night."

It already was. Men were standing so close to the fire that the fringes of their shawls and coats were singed, and the toes of their boots—those who had boots—stank of hot leather. My own knees and thighs were close to blistering, as I stood perforce near the blaze in order to serve out the stew. My backside was like ice, though, in spite of the old pair of breeks I wore under shift and petticoat—both for insulation and for the avoidance of excessive friction while on horseback. The Carolina backwoods were no place for a sidesaddle.

The last bowl served, I turned round to eat my own stew, with the fire at my back, a grateful bloom of warmth embracing my frozen bottom.

"All right, is it, ma'am?" Jimmy Robertson, who had made the stew, peered over my shoulder in search of compliment.

"Lovely," I assured him. "Delicious!" In fact, it was hot and I was hungry. That, plus the fact that I hadn't had to cook it myself, lent a sufficient tone of sincerity to my words that he retired, satisfied.

I ate slowly, enjoying the heat of the wooden bowl in my chilly hands, as well as the soothing warmth of food in my stomach. The cacophony of sneezing and hacking behind me did nothing to impair the momentary sense of well-being engendered by food and the prospect of rest after a long day in the saddle. Even the sight of the woods around us, bone-cold and black under growing starlight, failed to disturb me.

My own nose had begun to run rather freely, but I hoped it was merely the result of eating hot food. I swallowed experimentally, but there was no sign of sore throat, nor rattling of congestion in my chest. Jamie rattled; he had finished eating and come to stand beside me, warming his backside at the blaze.

"All right, Sassenach?" he asked hoarsely.

"Just vasomotor rhinitis," I replied, dabbing at my nose with a handkerchief.

"Where?" He cast a suspicious look at the forest. "Here? I thought ye said they lived in Africa."

"What—oh, rhinoceroses. Yes, they do. I just meant my nose is running, but I haven't got *la grippe*."

"Oh, aye? That's good. I have," he added unnecessarily, and sneezed three times in succession. He handed me his emptied bowl, in order to use both hands to blow his nose, which he did with a series of vicious honks. I winced slightly, seeing the reddened, raw look of his nostrils. I had a bit of camphorated bear grease in my saddlebag, but I was sure he wouldn't let me anoint him in public.

"Are you sure we oughtn't to push on?" I asked, watching him. "Geordie says the village isn't far, and there is a road—of sorts."

I knew the answer to that; he wasn't one to alter strategy for the sake of personal comfort. Besides, camp was already made and a good fire going. Still, beyond my own longing for a warm, clean bed—well, any bed, I wasn't fussy—I was worried for Jamie. Close to, the sigh in his breath had a deeper, wheezing note to it that troubled me.

He knew what I meant. He smiled, tucking away the sodden kerchief in his sleeve.

"I'll do, Sassenach," he said. "It's no but a wee cold in the neb. I've been a deal worse than this, many times."

Paul Mueller heaved another log onto the fire; a big ember broke and roared up with a flare that made us step away in order to avoid the spray of sparks. Well baked in the rear by this time, I turned to face the fire. Jamie, though, stayed facing outward, a slight frown on his face as he surveyed the shadows of the looming wood.

The frown relaxed, and I turned to see two men emerging from the woods, shaking needles and bits of bark from their clothes. Jack Parker, and a new man—I didn't yet know his name, but he was plainly a recent immigrant from somewhere near Glasgow, judging from his speech.

"All quiet, sir," said Parker, touching his hat in brief salute. "Cold as charity, though."

"Aye, Ah hivny felt ma privates anytime since dinner," the Glaswegian chimed in, grimacing and rubbing himself as he headed for the fire. "Might as well be gone aetegither!"

"I take your meaning, man," Jamie said, grinning. "Went for a piss a moment ago, but I couldna find it." He turned amid the laughter and went to check the horses, a half-finished second bowl of stew in one hand.

The other men were already making ready their bedrolls, debating the wisdom of sleeping with feet or head near the fire.

"It'll scorch the soles o' your boots, and ye get too close," argued Evan Lindsay. "See? Charred the pegs right out, and now look!" He lifted one large foot, exhibiting a battered shoe with a wrapping of rough twine tied round it to hold it together. The leather soles and heels were sometimes stitched, but more often fastened with tiny whittled pegs of wood or leather, glued with pine gum or some other adhesive. The pine gum in particular was flammable; I'd seen occasional sparks burst from the feet of men who slept with their feet too near the fire, when a shoe peg suddenly ignited from the heat.

"Better than settin' your hair on fire," Ronnie Sinclair argued.

"I dinna think the Lindsays need worry about that owermuch." Kenny grinned at his elder brother, and tugged down the knit cap he wore—like his two brothers—over a balding head.

"Aye, headfirst every time," Murdo agreed. "Ye dinna want to chill your scalp; it'll go right to your liver, and then you're a dead man." Murdo was tenderly solicitous of his

exposed scalp, being seldom seen without either his knitted
nightcap or a peculiar hat made from the hairy skin of a possum, lined and rakishly trimmed with skunk fur. He glanced
enviously at Roger, who was tying back his own thick black
hair with a bit of leather string.

"MacKenzie needna worry; he's furred like a bear!"

Roger grinned in response. Like the others, he had
stopped shaving when we left the Ridge; now, eight days
later, a thick scurf of dark stubble did give him a fiercely ur-
sine look. It occurred to me that beyond convenience, a
heavy beard undoubtedly kept the face warm on nights like
this; I tucked my own bare and vulnerable chin down into the
sheltering folds of my shawl.

Returning from the horses in time to hear this, Jamie
laughed, too, but it ended in a spasm of coughing. Evan
waited 'til it ended.

"How say ye, *Mac Dubh*? Heads or tails?"

Jamie wiped his mouth on his sleeve and smiled. Hairy
as the rest, he looked a proper Viking, with the fire glinting
red, gold, and silver from his sprouting beard and loosened
hair.

"Nay bother, lads," he said. "I'll sleep warm enough nay
matter *how* I'm laid." He tilted his head in my direction, and
there was a general rumble of laughter, with a spattering of
mildly crude remarks in Scots and Gaelic from the Ridge
men.

One or two of the new recruits eyed me with a brief, instinctive speculation, quickly abandoned after a glance at
Jamie's height, breadth, and air of genial ferocity. I met one
man's eyes and smiled; he looked startled, but then smiled
back, ducking his head in shyness.

How the hell did Jamie do that? One brief, crude joke,
and he'd laid public claim to me, removed me from any
threat of unwanted advances, and reasserted his position as
leader.

"Just like a bloody baboon troop," I muttered under my
breath. "And I'm sleeping with the head baboon!"

"Baboons are the monkeys with no tails?" Fergus asked,
turning from an exchange with Ewald about the horses.

"You know quite well they are." I caught Jamie's eye, and

his mouth curled up on one side. I knew what he was thinking, and he knew I did; the smile widened.

Louis of France kept a private zoo at Versailles, among the inhabitants of which were a small troop of mandrill baboons. One of the most popular Court activities on spring afternoons was to visit the baboon quarters, there to admire both the sexual prowess of the male, and his splendidly multicolored bottom.

One M. de Ruvel had offered—in my hearing—to have his posterior similarly tattooed, if it would result in such a favorable reception by the ladies of the Court. He had, however, been firmly informed by Madame de la Tourelle that his physique was in every way inferior to that of the mandrill, and coloring it was unlikely to improve matters.

The firelight made it difficult to tell, but I was reasonably sure that Jamie's own rich color owed as much to suppressed amusement as to heat.

"Speakin' of tails," he murmured in my ear. "Have ye got those infernal breeks on?"

"Yes."

"Take them off."

"What, here?" I gave him a wide-eyed look of mock innocence. "You want me to freeze my arse off?"

His eyes narrowed slightly, with a blue cat-gleam in the depths.

"Oh, it wilna freeze," he said softly. "I'll warrant ye that."

He moved behind me, and the fierce shimmer of the blaze on my flesh was replaced by the cool solidness of his body. No less fierce, though, as I discovered when he put his arms round my waist and drew me back against him.

"Oh, you found it," I said. "How nice."

"Found what? Had you lost something?" Roger paused, coming from the horses with a lumpy roll of blankets under one arm, his bodhran under the other.

"Oh, just a pair of auld breeks," Jamie said blandly. Under cover of my shawl, one hand slid inside the waistband of my skirt. "D'ye mean to give us a song, then?"

"If anyone likes, sure." Roger smiled, the firelight ruddy on his features. "Actually, I'm meaning to learn one; Evan's promised to sing me a silkie-song his grannie knew."

Jamie laughed.

"Oh, I ken that one, I think."

One of Roger's eyebrows shot up, and I twisted slightly round, to look up at Jamie in surprise.

"Well, I couldna *sing* it," he said mildly, seeing our amazement. "I ken the words, though. Evan sang it often and again, in the prison at Ardsmuir. It's a bit bawdy," he added, with that faintly prim tone that Highlanders often adopt, just before telling you something truly shocking.

Roger recognized it, and laughed.

"I'll maybe write it down, then," he said. "For the benefit of future generations."

Jamie's fingers had been working skillfully away, and at this point, the breeks—which were his, and thus about six sizes too large for me—came loose and dropped silently to the ground. A cold draft whooshed up under my skirt and struck my newly bared nether portions. I drew in my breath with a faint gasp.

"Cold, isn't it?" Roger hunched his shoulders, smiling as he shivered exaggeratedly in sympathy.

"Yes, indeed," I said. "Freeze the balls off a brass monkey, wouldn't it?"

Jamie and Roger burst into simultaneous coughing fits.

SENTRY IN PLACE and horses bedded down, we retired to our own resting place, a discreet distance from the circle by the fire. I had dug the largest rocks and twigs out of the leaf mold, cut spruce branches, and spread our blankets over them by the time Jamie finished his last round of the camp. The warmth of food and fire had faded, but I didn't begin to shiver in earnest until he touched me.

I would have moved at once to get under the blankets, but Jamie still held me. His original intent appeared intact—to say the least—but his attention was momentarily distracted. His arms were still clasped round me, but he was standing quite still, head up as though listening, looking into the murk of the wood. It was full dark; no more showed of the trees than the glow of fire reflected from the few trunks that stood nearest the camp—the last shadow of twilight had faded, and everything beyond was a depthless black.

"What is it?" I drew back a little, pressing instinctively against him, and his arms tightened round me.

"I dinna ken. But I do feel something, Sassenach." He moved a little, lifting his head in restless query, like a wolf scenting the wind, but no message reached us save a distant rattling of leafless branches.

"If it's no rhinoceroses, it's something," he said softly, and a whisper of unease raised the hairs on the back of my neck. "A moment, lass."

He left me, the wind blowing suddenly cold about me with the loss of his presence, and went to speak quietly with a couple of the men.

And what might he feel, out there in the dark? I had the greatest respect for Jamie's sense of danger. He had lived too long as hunter and as hunted, not to sense the edgy awareness that lay between the two—invisible or not.

He returned a moment later, and squatted beside me as I burrowed shivering into the blankets.

"It's all right," he said. "I've said we'll have two guards tonight, and each man to keep his piece loaded and to hand. But I think it's all right." He looked beyond me, into the wood, but his face now was merely thoughtful.

"It's all right," he repeated again, more certainly.

"Is it gone?"

He turned his head, his lips curling slightly. His mouth looked soft, tender and vulnerable amid the stiff, ruddy wires of his starting beard.

"I dinna ken if it was ever there, Sassenach," he said. "I thought I felt eyes upon me, but it could have been a passing wolf, an owl—or nay more than a restless *spiorad*, a-roaming in the wood. But aye, it's gone now."

He smiled at me; I saw the flicker of the light that rimmed his head and shoulders as he turned, silhouetted by the fire. Beyond, the sound of Roger's voice drifted to me above the crackle of the fire, as he learned the melody of the silkie-song, following Evan's voice, hoarse but confident. Jamie slid into the blankets beside me and I turned to him, cold hands fumbling to return the favor he had done me earlier.

We shivered convulsively, urgent for each other's warmth. I found him, and he turned me, ruffling up the layers of fabric between us, so that he lay behind me, his arm secure around me, the small secret patches of our nakedness joined in warmth beneath the blankets. I lay facing the darkness of the wood, watching the firelight dance among the trees, as Jamie moved behind me—behind, between, within—warm and big, and so slowly as scarcely to rustle the branches beneath us. Roger's voice rose strong and sweet above the murmur of the men, and the shivering slowly stopped.

I WOKE MUCH LATER beneath a blue-black sky, dry-mouthed, the rasping sigh of Jamie's breath in my ear. I had been dreaming; one of those pointless dreams of uneasy repetition, that fades at once with the waking but leaves a nasty taste in mouth and mind. Needing both water and relief of my bladder, I squirmed carefully out from under Jamie's arm, and slid out from between the blankets. He stirred and groaned slightly, snuffling in his sleep, but didn't wake.

I paused to lay a hand lightly on his forehead. Cool, no fever. Perhaps he was right, then—just a bad cold. I stood up, reluctant to leave the warm sanctuary of our nest, but knowing I couldn't wait until morning.

The songs were stilled, the fire smaller now, but still burning, kept up by the sentry on duty. It was Murdo Lindsay; I could see the white fur of his possum-skin cap, perched atop what looked like a huddled pile of clothing and blankets. The anonymous Glaswegian crouched on the other side of the clearing, musket on his knees; he nodded to me, face shadowed by the brim of his slouch hat. The white cap turned in my direction too, at the sound of my step. I sketched a wave, and Murdo nodded toward me, then turned back toward the wood.

The men lay in a shrouded circle, buried in their blankets. I felt a sudden qualm as I walked between them. With the spell of night and dreams still on me, I shivered at sight of the silent forms, lying so still, side by side. Just so had they laid the bodies at Amiens. At Preston. Still and shrouded, side by side, faces covered and anonymous. War seldom looks on the faces of its dead.

And why should I wake from love's embrace, thinking of war and the sleeping ranks of dead men? I wondered, stepping lightly past the shrouded line of bodies. Well, that was simple enough, given our errand. We were headed for battle—if not now, then soon enough.

One blanket-wrapped form grunted, coughed, and turned over, face invisible, indistinguishable from the others. The movement startled me, but then one big foot thrust free of the blanket, revealing Evan Lindsay's twine-wrapped shoe. I felt the anxious burden of imagination ease, with this evidence of life, of individuality.

It's the anonymity of war that makes the killing possible. When the nameless dead are named again on tombstone and on cenotaph, then they regain the identity they lost as soldiers, and take their place in grief and memory, the ghosts of sons and lovers. Perhaps this journey would end in peace. The conflict that was coming, though . . . the world would hear of that, and I stepped past the last of the sleeping men, as though walking through an evil dream not fully waked from.

I picked up a canteen from the ground near the saddlebags and drank deep. The water was piercingly cold, and my somber thoughts began to dissipate, washed away by the sweet, clean taste of it. I paused, gasping from the coldness, and wiped my mouth.

Best take some back to Jamie; if he wasn't wakened by my absence, he would be by my return, and I knew his mouth would be dry as well, since he was completely unable to breathe through his nose at the moment. I slung the strap of the canteen over my shoulder and stepped into the shelter of the wood.

It was cold under the trees, but the air was still and crystal clear. The shadows that had seemed sinister viewed from the fireside were oddly reassuring, seen from the shelter of the wood. Turned away from the fire's glow and crackle, my eyes and ears began to adapt to the dark. I heard the rustle of something small in the dried grass nearby, and the unexpected distant hooting of an owl.

Finished, I stood still for a few minutes, enjoying the momentary solitude. It was very cold, but very peaceful. Jamie had been right, I thought; whatever might or might not have been here earlier, the wood held nothing inimical now.

As though my thought of him had summoned him, I heard a cautious footfall, and the slow, wheezing rasp of his breath. He coughed, a muffled, strangled noise that I didn't like at all.

"Here I am," I said softly. "How's the chest?"

The cough choked off in a sudden wheeze of panic, and there was a crunch and flurry among the leaves. I saw Murdo start up by the fire, musket in hand, and then a dark shape darted past me.

"Hoy!" I said, startled rather than frightened. The shape stumbled, and by reflex, I swung the canteen off my shoulder and whirled it by the strap. It struck the figure in the back with a hollow *thunk!* and whoever it was—certainly not Jamie—fell to his knees, coughing.

There followed a short period of chaos, with men exploding out of their blankets like startled jack-in-the-boxes, incoherent shouting, and general mayhem. The Glaswegian leaped over several struggling bodies and charged into the wood, musket over his head, bellowing. Barreling into the darkness, he charged the first shape he saw, which happened to be me. I went flying headlong into the leaves, where I ended inelegantly sprawled and windless, the Glaswegian kneeling on my stomach.

I must have given a sufficiently feminine grunt as I fell, for he paused, narrowly checking himself as he was about to club me in the head.

"Eh?" He put down his free hand and felt cautiously. Feeling what was unmistakably a breast, he jerked back as though burned, and slowly edged off me.

"Err . . . hmm!" he said.

"Whoof," I replied, as cordially as possible. The stars were spinning overhead, shining brightly through the leafless branches. The Glaswegian disappeared, with a small Scottish noise of embarrassment. There was a lot of shouting and crashing, off to my left, but I hadn't attention for anything at the moment bar getting my wind back.

By the time I made it back onto my feet, the intruder had been captured and dragged into the light of the fire.

Had he not been coughing when I hit him, he likely would have gotten away. As it was, though, he was hacking and wheezing so badly that he could barely stand upright, and his face was dark with the effort to snatch a breath in passing. The veins on his forehead stood out like worms, and he made an eerie whistling noise as he breathed—or tried to.

"What the hell are *you* doing here?" Jamie demanded hoarsely, then paused to cough in sympathy.

This was a purely rhetorical question, since the boy plainly couldn't talk. It was Josiah Beardsley, my potential tonsillectomy patient, and whatever he'd been doing since the Gathering, it hadn't improved his health to any marked extent.

I hurried to the fire, where the coffeepot sat in the embers. I seized it in a fold of my shawl and shook it. Good, there was some left, and since it had been brewing since supper, it would be strong as Hades.

"Sit him down, loosen his clothes, bring me cold water!" I shoved my way into the circle of men around the captive, forcing them aside with the hot coffeepot.

Within a moment or two, I had a mug of strong coffee at his lips, black and tarry, diluted with no more than a splash of cold water to keep it from burning his mouth.

"Breathe out slowly to the count of four, breathe in to the count of two, breathe out and take a drink," I said. The whites of his eyes showed all round the iris, and spittle had collected at the corners of his mouth. I put a firm hand on his shoulder though, urging him to breathe, to count, to breathe—and the desperate straining eased a little.

One sip, one breath, one sip, one breath, and by the time the coffee was all inside him, his face had faded from its alarming crimson hue to something more approximating fish belly, with a couple of faint reddish marks where the men had hit him. The air still whistled in his lungs, but he *was* breathing, which was a substantial improvement.

The men stood about murmuring and watching with interest, but it was cold, it was late, and as the excitement of the capture faded, they began to droop and yawn. It was, after all, only a lad, and a scrawny, ill-favored one at that. They departed willingly enough to their blankets when Jamie dispatched them, leaving Jamie and me to attend to our unexpected guest.

I had him swaddled in spare blankets, larded with camphorated bear grease, and provided with another cup of coffee in his hands, before I would let Jamie question him. The boy seemed deeply embarrassed at my attentions, shoulders hunched and eyes on the ground, but I didn't know whether he was simply unused to being fussed over, or whether it was the looming presence of Jamie, arms crossed, that discomfited him.

He was small for fourteen, and thin to the point of emaciation; I could have counted his ribs when I opened his shirt to listen to his heart. No beauty otherwise; his black hair had been chopped short, and stood on his head in matted spikes, thick with dirt, grease, and sweat, and his general aspect was that of a flea-ridden monkey, eyes large and black in a face pinched with worry and suspicion.

At last having done all I could, I was satisfied with the look of him. At my nod, Jamie lowered himself to the ground beside the boy.

"So, Mr. Beardsley," he said pleasantly. "Have ye come to join our troop of militia, then?"

"Ah . . . no." Josiah rolled the wooden cup between his hands, not looking up. "I . . . uh . . . my business chanced to take me this way, that's all." He spoke so hoarsely that I winced in sympathy, imagining the soreness of his inflamed throat.

"I see." Jamie's voice was low and friendly. "So ye saw our fire by chance, and thought to come and seek shelter and a meal?"

"I did, aye." He swallowed, with evident difficulty.

"Mmphm. But ye came earlier, no? You were in the wood just after sundown. Why wait 'til past moonrise to make yourself known?"

"I didn't . . . I wasn't . . ."

"Oh, indeed ye were." Jamie's voice was still friendly, but firm. He put out a hand and grasped Josiah's shirtfront, forcing the boy to look at him.

"Look ye, man. There's a bargain between us. You're my tenant; it's agreed. That means you've a right to my protection. It means also that I've a right to hear the truth."

Josiah looked back, and while there was fear and wariness in the look, there was also a sense of self-possession that seemed far older than fourteen. He made no effort to look away, and there was a look of deep calculation in the clever black eyes.

This child—if one could regard him as a child; plainly Jamie didn't—was used to relying on himself alone.

"I said to you, sir, that I would come to your place by the New Year, and so I mean to. What I do in the meantime is my own affair."

Jamie's brows shot up, but he nodded slowly, and released his grip.

"True enough. You'll admit, though, that one might be curious."

The boy opened his mouth as though to speak, but changed his mind and buried his nose instead in his cup of coffee.

Jamie tried again.

"May we offer you help in your business? Will ye travel a ways with us, at least?"

Josiah shook his head.

"No. I am obliged to you, sir, but the business is best managed by myself alone."

Roger had not gone to sleep, but sat a little behind Jamie, watching silently. He leaned forward now, green eyes intent on the boy.

"This business of yours," he said. "It's not by any means connected with that mark on your thumb?"

The cup hit the ground and coffee splashed up, spattering my face and bodice. The boy was out of his blankets and halfway across the clearing before I could blink my eyes to see what was happening—and by then, Jamie was up and after him. The boy had circled the fire; Jamie leaped over it. They disappeared into the wood like fox and hound, leaving Roger and me gaping after them.

For the second time that night, men erupted from their bedrolls, grabbing for their guns. I began to think the

Governor would be pleased with his militia; they were certainly ready to spring into action at a moment's notice.

"What in hell . . . ?" I said to Roger, wiping coffee from my eyebrows.

"Maybe I shouldn't have mentioned it so suddenly," he said.

"Wha? Wha? What's amiss, then?" bellowed Murdo Lindsay, glaring round as he swept his musket barrel past the shadowed trees.

"Are we attacked? Where's the bastards?" Kenny popped up on hands and knees beside me, peering out from under the band of his knitted cap like a toad beneath a watering pot.

"Nobody. Nothing's happened. I mean—it's really quite all right!"

My efforts to calm and explain went largely unnoticed in the racket. Roger, however, being much larger and much louder, succeeded at last in quelling the disturbance and explaining matters—so far as they could be explained. What did a lad more or less matter? With considerable grumbling, the men settled down once more, leaving Roger and me staring at each other over the coffeepot.

"What was it, then?" I asked, a little testily.

"The mark? I'm pretty sure it was the letter 'T'—I saw it when you made him take the coffee and he wrapped his hand round the cup."

My stomach tightened. I knew what that meant; I'd seen it before.

"Thief," Roger said, eyes on my face. "He's been branded."

"Yes," I said unhappily. "Oh, dear."

"Would the folk on the Ridge not accept him, if they knew?" Roger asked.

"I doubt most of them would be much bothered," I said. "It's not that; it's that he ran when you mentioned it. He isn't just a convicted thief—I'm afraid he may be a fugitive. And Jamie called him, at the Gathering."

"Ah." Roger scratched absently at his whiskers. "*Earb-sachd*. Jamie will feel obliged to him in some way, then?"

"Something like that."

Roger was a Scot, and—technically, at least—a Highlander. But he had been born long after the death of the clans, and neither history nor heritage could ever have taught him the strength of the ancient bonds between laird and tenant, between chief and clansman. Most likely, Josiah himself had no idea of the importance of the *earbsachd*—of what had been promised and accepted on both sides. Jamie had.

"Do you think Jamie will catch him?" Roger asked.

"I expect he already has. He can't be tracking the boy in the dark, and if he'd lost him, he would have come back already."

There were other possibilities—that Jamie had fallen over a precipice in the dark, tripped on a stone and broken his leg, or met with a catamount or a bear, for instance—but I preferred not to dwell on those.

I stood up, stretching my cramped limbs, and looked into the woods, where Jamie and his prey had disappeared. Josiah might be a good woodsman and hunter; Jamie had been one much longer. Josiah was small, quick, and impelled by fear; Jamie had a considerable advantage in size, strength, and sheer bloody-mindedness.

Roger stood up beside me. His lean face was slightly troubled, as he peered into the encircling trees.

"It's taking a long time. If he's caught the lad, what's he doing with him?"

"Extracting the truth from him, I imagine," I said. I bit my lip at the thought. "Jamie doesn't like being lied to."

Roger looked down at me, mildly startled.

"How?"

I shrugged.

"However he can." I'd seen him do it by reason, by guile, with charm, with threats—and on occasion, by means of brute force. I hoped he hadn't had to use force—though more for his sake than Josiah's.

"I see," Roger said quietly. "Well, then."

The coffeepot was empty; I bundled my cloak round me and went down to the stream to rinse and fill it, hung it to brew once more above the fire, and sat down to wait.

"You should go to sleep," I said to Roger, after a few minutes. He merely smiled at me, wiped his nose, and hunched deeper into his cloak.

"So should you," he said.

There was no wind, but it was very late, and the cold had settled well into the hollow, lying damp and heavy on the ground. The men's blankets had grown limp with condensation, and I could feel the dense chill of the ground seeping through the folds of my skirt. I thought about retrieving my breeches, but couldn't muster the energy to search for them. The excitement of Josiah's appearance and escape had faded, and the lethargy of cold and fatigue was setting in.

Roger poked up the fire a bit, and added a few small chunks of wood. I tucked another fold of skirt beneath my thighs and pulled cloak and shawl close around me, burying my hands in the folds of fabric. The coffeepot hung steaming, the hiss of occasional droplets falling into the fire punctuating the phlegm-filled snores of the sleeping men.

I wasn't seeing the blanket-rolled shapes, though, or hearing the sough of dark pines. I heard the crackle of dried leaves in a Scottish oak wood, in the hills above Carryarrick. We had camped there, two days before Prestonpans, with thirty men from Lallybroch—on our way to join Charles Stuart's army. And a young boy had come suddenly out of the dark; a knife had glinted in the light of a fire.

A different place, a different time. I shook myself, trying to dispel the sudden memories: a thin white face and a boy's eyes huge with shock and pain. The blade of a dirk, darkening and glowing in the embers of the fire. The smell of gunpowder, sweat, and burning flesh.

*"I mean to shoot you,"* he had told John Grey. *"Head, or heart?"* By threat, by guile—by brute force.

That was then; this was now, I told myself. But Jamie would do what he thought he must.

Roger sat quietly, watching the dancing flames and the wood beyond. His eyes were hooded, and I wondered what he was thinking.

"D'you worry for him?" he asked softly, not looking at me.

"What, now? Or ever?" I smiled, though without much humor. "If I did, I'd never rest."

He turned his head toward me, and a faint smile touched his lips.

"You're resting now, are you?"

I smiled again, a real one in spite of myself.

"I'm not pacing to and fro," I answered. "Nor yet wringing my hands."

One dark eyebrow flicked up.

"Might help keep them warm."

One of the men stirred, muttering in his wrappings, and we ceased talking for a moment. The coffeepot was boiling; I could hear the soft rumble of the liquid inside.

Whatever could be keeping him? He couldn't be taking all this time to question Josiah Beardsley—he would either have gotten what answers he required in short order, or he would have let the boy go. No matter what the boy had stolen, it was no concern of Jamie's—save for the promise of the *earbsachd*.

The flames were mildly hypnotic; I could look into the wavering glow and see in memory the great fire of the Gathering, the figures dark around it, and the sound of distant fiddles. . . .

"Should I go to look for him?" Roger asked suddenly, low-voiced.

I jerked, startled out of sleepy hypnosis. I rubbed a hand over my face and shook my head to clear it.

"No. It's dangerous to go into strange woods in the dark, and you couldn't find him anyway. If he isn't back by the morning—that will be time enough."

As the moments wore slowly on, I began to think that the dawn *might* come before Jamie did. I was worried for Jamie—but there was in fact nothing that could be done before the morning. Disquieting thoughts tried to push their way in; did Josiah have a knife? Surely he did. But even if the boy was desperate enough to use it, could he possibly take Jamie by surprise? I pushed aside these anxious speculations, trying to occupy my mind instead with counting the number of coughs from the men around the fire.

Number eight was Roger; a deep, loose cough that shook his shoulders. Was he worried for Bree and Jemmy? I wondered. Or did he wonder whether Bree worried about *him*? I could have told him that, but it wouldn't have helped him to know. Men fighting—or preparing to fight—needed the idea of home as a place of utter safety; the conviction that all was well there kept them in good heart and on their feet, marching, enduring. Other things would make them fight, but fighting is such a small part of warfare. . . .

*A damned important part, Sassenach*, said Jamie's voice in the back of my head.

I began at last to nod off, waking repeatedly as my head jerked sharply on my neck. The last time, it was the feel of hands on my shoulders that wakened me, but only briefly. Roger eased me to the ground, wadding half my shawl beneath my head for a pillow, tucking the rest of it snug about my shoulders. I caught a brief glimpse of him in silhouette against the fire, black and bearlike in his cloak, and then I knew no more.

I DON'T KNOW how long I slept; I woke quite suddenly, at the sound of an explosive sneeze nearby. Jamie was sitting a few feet away, holding Josiah Beardsley's wrist in one hand, his dirk in the other. He paused long enough to sneeze twice more, wiped his nose impatiently on his sleeve, then thrust the dirk into the embers of the fire.

I caught the stink of hot metal, and raised myself abruptly on one elbow. Before I could say or do anything, something twitched and moved against me. I looked down in astonishment, then up, then down again, convinced in my muddled state that I was still dreaming.

A young boy lay under my cloak, curled against my body, sound asleep. I saw black hair and a scrawny frame, a pallid skin smeared with grime and grazed with scratches. Then there was a sudden loud hiss from the fire and I jerked my gaze back to see Jamie press Josiah's thumb against the searing metal of his blackened dirk.

Jamie glimpsed my convulsive movement from the corner of his eye and scowled in my direction, lips pursed in a silent adjuration to stillness. Josiah's face was contorted, lips drawn back from his teeth in agony—but he made no noise. On the far side of the fire, Kenny Lindsay sat watching, silent as a rock.

Still convinced that I was dreaming—or hoping that I was—I put a hand on the boy curled against me. He moved again, and the feel of solid flesh under my fingers woke me completely. My hand closed on his shoulder, and his eyes sprang open, wide with alarm.

He jerked away, scrambling awkwardly to get to his feet. Then he saw his brother—for plainly Josiah *was* his brother—and stopped abruptly, glancing wildly around the clearing, at the scattered men, at Jamie, Roger, and me.

Ignoring what must have been the frightful pain of a burned hand, Josiah rose from his seat and stepped quick and soft to his brother's side, taking him by the arm.

I got to my feet, moving slowly so as not to frighten them. They watched me, identical looks of wariness on the thin, white faces. Identical. Yes, just the same pinched faces— though the other boy's hair was worn long. He was dressed in nothing but a ragged shirt, and he was barefoot. I saw Josiah squeeze his brother's arm in reassurance, and began to suspect just what it was he had stolen. I summoned a smile for the two of them, then stretched out my hand to Josiah.

"Let me see your hand," I whispered.

He hesitated a moment, then gave me his right hand. It was a nice, neat job; so neat that it made me slightly faint for a moment. The ball of the thumb had been sliced cleanly off, the open wound cauterized with searing metal. A red-black, crusted oval had replaced the incriminating brand.

There was a soft movement behind me; Roger had fetched my medicine box and set it down by my feet.

There wasn't a great deal to do for the injury, save apply a little gentian ointment and bandage the thumb with a clean, dry cloth. I was conscious of Jamie as I worked; he had sheathed his dirk and risen quietly, to go and rummage among the packs and saddlebags. By the time I had finished my brief job, he was back, with a small bundle of food wrapped in a kerchief, and a spare blanket tied in a roll. Over his arm were my discarded breeches.

He handed these to the new boy, gave the food and blanket to Josiah, then clapped a hand on the boy's shoulder, and squeezed hard. He touched the other boy gently, turning him toward the wood with a hand on his back. Then he jerked his head toward the trees, and Josiah nodded. He touched his forehead to me, the bandage glinting white on his thumb, and whispered, "Thank'ee, ma'am."

The two boys disappeared silently into the forest, the twin's bare feet winking pale below the flapping hem of the breeks as he followed his brother.

Jamie nodded to Kenny, then sat down again by the fire, shoulders slumping in sudden exhaustion. I poured him coffee and he took it, his mouth twitching in an attempted smile of acknowledgment that dissipated in a fit of heavy coughing.

I reached for the cup before it could spill, and caught Roger's eye over Jamie's shoulder. He nodded toward the east, and laid a finger across his lips, then shrugged with a grimace of resignation. He wanted as much as I did to know what had just happened—and why. He was right, though; the night was fading. Dawn would be here soon, and the men— all accustomed to wake at first light—would be floating toward the surface of consciousness.

Jamie had stopped coughing, but was making horrible gurgling noises in an attempt to clear his throat—he sounded rather like a pig drowning in mud.

"Here," I whispered, giving him back the cup. "Drink it, and lie down. You should sleep a little."

He shook his head and lifted the cup to his lips. He swallowed, grimacing at the bitterness.

"Not worth it," he croaked. He nodded toward the east, where the tufted pines were now inked black on a graying sky. "And besides, I've got to think what the hell to do now."

# 27

# DEATH COMES CALLING

I COULD SCARCELY CONTAIN my impatience until the men had roused and eaten, broken camp—in an irritatingly leisurely fashion—and mounted. At last, though, I found myself once more on horseback, riding through a morning so crisp and cold, I thought the air might shatter as I breathed it.

"Right," I said without preamble, as my mount nosed her way up next to Jamie's. "Talk."

He glanced back at me and smiled. His face was creased with tiredness, but the brisk air—and a lot of very strong coffee—had revived him. Despite the troubled night, I felt quick and lively myself, blood coursing near the surface of my skin and blooming in my cheeks.

"Ye dinna mean to wait for wee Roger?"

"I'll tell him later—or you can." There was no way of riding three abreast; it was only owing to a washout that had left a fan of gravel down the mountainside that we were able to pick our way side by side for the moment, out of hearing of the others. I nudged my mount closer to Jamie's, my knees wreathed in steam from the horse's nostrils.

Jamie rubbed a hand over his face, and shook himself, as though to throw off fatigue.

"Aye, well," he said. "You'll have seen they were brothers?"

"I did notice that, yes. Where the hell did the other one come from?"

"From there." He lifted his chin, pointing toward the west. Thanks to the washout, there was an unimpeded view of a small cove in the hollow below—one of those natural breaks in the wilderness, where the trees gave way to meadow and stream. From the trees at the edge of the cove, a thin plume of smoke rose upward, pointing like a finger in the still, cold air.

Squinting, I could make out what looked like a small farmhouse, with a couple of rickety outbuildings. As I watched, a tiny figure emerged from the house and headed toward one of the sheds.

"They're just about to discover that he's gone," Jamie said, a trifle grimly. "Though with luck, they'll think he's only gone to the privy, or to milk the goats."

I didn't bother asking how he knew they had goats.

"Is that their home? Josiah and his brother?"

"In a manner of speaking, Sassenach. They were bond servants."

*"Were?"* I said skeptically. Somehow I doubted that the brothers' terms of indenture had just happened to expire the night before.

Jamie lifted one shoulder in a shrug, and wiped a dripping nose on his sleeve.

"Unless someone catches them, aye."

"You caught Josiah," I pointed out. "What did he tell you?"

"The truth," he said, with a slight twist of the mouth. "Or at least I think so."

He had hunted Josiah through the dark, guided by the sound of the boy's frantic wheezing, and trapped him at last in a rocky hollow, seizing him in the dark. He had wrapped the freezing boy in his plaid, sat him down, and with judicious application of patience and firmness—augmented with sips of whisky from his flask—had succeeded at last in extracting the story.

"The family were immigrants—father, mother, and six bairns. Only the twins survived the passage; the rest perished of illness at sea. There were no relatives here—or none that met the boat, at any rate—and so the ship's master sold them. The price wouldna cover the cost of the family's passage, so the lads were indentured for thirty years, their wages to be put toward the debt."

His voice in the telling was matter-of-fact; these things happened. I knew they did, but was much less inclined to accept them without comment.

"Thirty years! Why, that's—how old were they at the time?"

"Two or three," he said.

I was taken aback at that. Overlooking the basic tragedy, that was some mitigation, I supposed; if the boys' purchaser had been providing for their welfare as children . . . but I remembered Josiah's scrawny ribs, and the bowing of his legs. They hadn't been all that well provided for. But then, neither were a good many children who came from loving homes.

"Josiah's no idea who his parents were, where they came from, nor what their names were," Jamie explained. He coughed briefly, and cleared his throat.

"He kent his own name, and that of his brother—the brother's name is Keziah—but nothing else. Beardsley is the name o' the man who took them, but as for the lads, they dinna ken if they're Scots, English, Irish—with names like that, they likely aren't German or Polish, but even that's not impossible."

"Hmm." I puffed a cloud of thoughtful steam, temporarily obscuring the farmhouse below. "So Josiah ran away. I imagine that had something to do with the brand on his thumb?"

Jamie nodded, eyes on the ground as his horse picked its way down the slope. The ground to either side of the gravel was soft, and clumps of black dirt showed like creeping fungus through the scree.

"He stole a cheese—he was honest enough about that." His mouth widened in momentary amusement. "Took it from a dairy shed in Brownsville, but the dairymaid saw him. In fact, the maid said 'twas the other—the brother—who took it, but . . ." Jamie's ruddy brows drew together for a moment.

"Perhaps Josiah wasna so honest about it as I thought. At any rate, one of the boys took the cheese; Beardsley caught the two of them with it and summoned the sheriff, and Josiah took the blame—and the punishment."

The boy had run away from the farm following this incident, which took place two years before. Josiah had—he told Jamie—always intended to return and rescue his brother, so soon as he could contrive a place for them to live. Jamie's offer had seemed a godsend to him, and he had left the Gathering to make his way back on foot.

"Imagine his surprise to find us perched there on the hillside," Jamie said, and sneezed. He wiped his nose, eyes watering slightly. "He was lurking close by, trying to make up his mind whether to wait until we'd gone, or find out whether we were headed for the farm—thinking if so, we might make a fine distraction for him to slip in and steal away his brother."

"So you decided to slip in with him instead, and help with the stealing." My own nose was dripping from the cold. I groped for my handkerchief with one hand, trusting to the horse, Mrs. Piggy, not to catapult us head over heels down the mountain while I blew my nose. I eyed Jamie over the hanky. He still had the clammy, red-nosed look of illness, but his high cheekbones were flushed with the morning sun and he looked remarkably cheerful for a man who'd been out in a cold wood all night. "Fun, was it?"

"Oh, aye, it was. I've not done anything like that in years." Jamie's eyes creased into blue triangles with his grin. "It reminded me o' raiding into the Grants' lands with Dougal and his men, when I was a lad. Creepin' through the dark, stealing into the barn without a sound—Christ, I had to stop myself in time before I took the cow. Or I would have, if they'd had one."

I sniffed, and laughed indulgently.

"You are the most complete bandit, Jamie," I said.

"Bandit?" he said, mildly affronted. "I'm a verra honest man, Sassenach. Or at least I am when I can afford to be," he amended, with a quick glance behind, to be sure we were not overheard.

"Oh, you're entirely honest," I assured him. "Too honest for your own good, in fact. You're just not very law-abiding."

This observation appeared to disconcert him slightly, for he frowned and made a gruff sound in his throat that might have been either a Scottish noise of disagreement or merely an attempt to dislodge phlegm. He coughed, then reined in, and standing up in his stirrups, waved his hat to Roger, who was some distance up the slope. Roger waved back, and turned his horse's nose in our direction.

I pulled my horse in beside Jamie, and dropped the reins on its neck.

"I'll have wee Roger take the men on to Brownsville," Jamie explained, sitting back in his saddle, "while I go and call upon the Beardsleys alone. Will ye come with me, Sassenach, or go on wi' Roger?"

"Oh, I'll come with you," I said, without hesitation. "I want to see what these Beardsleys are like."

He smiled and brushed back his hair with one hand before replacing his hat. He wore his hair loose to cover his neck and ears against the cold, and it shone like molten copper in the morning sun.

"I thought ye might. Mind your face, though," he said, in half-mocking warning. "Dinna go gape-jawed or gooseberry, and they mention their missing servant lad."

"Mind your own face," I said, rather crossly. "Gooseberry, indeed. Did Josiah say that he and his brother were badly treated?" I wondered whether there had been more to Josiah's leaving than the cheese incident.

Jamie shook his head.

"I didna ask, and he didna say—but ask yourself, Sassenach: would ye leave a decent home to go and live in the woods alone, to make your bed in cold leaves and eat grubs and crickets 'til ye learned to hunt meat?"

He nudged his horse into motion, and rode up the slope to meet Roger, leaving me pondering that conjecture. He returned a few moments later, and I turned my mount in beside him, another question in my mind.

"But if things were bad enough here as to force him to leave—why didn't his brother go with him?"

Jamie glanced at me, surprised, but then smiled, a little grimly.

"Keziah's deaf, Sassenach."

Not born deaf, from what Josiah had told him; his twin had lost his hearing as the result of an injury, occurring at the age of five or so. Keziah could therefore speak, but not hear any but the loudest of noises; and unable to perceive the sound of rustling leaves or shuffling feet, could neither hunt nor avoid pursuit.

"He says Keziah understands him, and doubtless he does. When we crept into the barn, I kept watch below while the lad went up the ladder to the loft. I didna hear a sound, but within a minute, both lads were down on the floor beside me, Keziah rubbing the sleep from his eyes. I hadna realized they were twins; gave me a turn to see the two of them, so like."

"I wonder why Keziah didn't bring away his breeches," I said, touching on one thing that had been puzzling me.

Jamie laughed.

"I asked. Seems he'd taken them off the night before, left them in the hay, and one o' the barn cats had kittens on them. He didna want to disturb her."

I laughed too, though with an uneasy memory of pale bare feet, blue-tinged skin showing purple in the firelight.

"Kind lad. And his shoes?"

"He hadn't any."

By now we had reached the bottom of the slope. The horses milled for a moment, turning in a slow gyre round Jamie as directions were decided, rendezvous appointed, farewells taken. Then Roger—with only slight evidence of self-consciousness—whistled through his teeth and waved his hat in the air in summons. I watched him ride away, and noticed him half-turn in the saddle, then turn back, looking straight ahead.

"He's no sure they'll really follow him," Jamie said, watching. He shook his head critically, then shrugged, dismissing it. "Aye, well. He'll manage, or not."

"He'll manage," I said, thinking of the night before.

"I'm glad ye think so, Sassenach. Come on, then." He clicked his tongue and reined his horse's head around.

"If you're not sure Roger can manage, why are you sending him on his own?" I inquired of his back, swaying in the saddle as we turned into the thin copse that lay between us and the now-invisible farm. "Why not keep the men together, and take them into Brownsville yourself?"

"For one thing, he'll no learn, and I dinna give him the chance. For another . . ." He paused, turning to look back at me. "For another, I didna want the whole boiling coming along to the Beardsleys' and maybe hearing of their missing servant. The whole camp saw Josiah last night, aye? If you've a lad missing, and hear of a lad popping up and causing a stir in the forest nearby, conclusions might be drawn, d'ye not think?"

He turned back, and I followed him through a narrow defile between the pine trees. Dew gleamed like diamonds on bark and needle, and small icy drops fell from the boughs above, startling my skin where they fell.

"Unless this Beardsley is old or infirm, though, won't he be joining you?" I objected. "Someone's bound to mention Josiah in his hearing sooner or later."

He shook his head, not turning round.

"And tell him what, if they do? They saw the lad when we dragged him in, and they saw him run away again. For all they ken, he got clear away."

"Kenny Lindsay saw them both when you brought them back."

He shrugged.

"Aye, I had a word wi' Kenny, while we were saddling the horses. He'll say nothing." He was right, I knew. Kenny was one of his Ardsmuir men; he would follow Jamie's orders without question.

"No," Jamie went on, skillfully reining round a large boulder, "Beardsley's not infirm; Josiah told me he's an Indian trader—taking goods across the Treaty Line to the Cherokee villages. What I don't know is if he's to home just now. If he is, though—" He drew breath and paused to cough as the cold air tickled his lungs.

"That's the other reason for sending the men ahead," he continued, wheezing slightly. "We'll not join them again until tomorrow, I think. By that time, they'll have had a night to drink and be sociable in Brownsville; they'll scarce recall the lad, and be the less likely to speak of him in Beardsley's hearing. With luck, we'll be well away before anything's said—no chance of Beardsley leaving us to pursue the lad then."

So he was counting on the Beardsleys being sufficiently hospitable as to put us up for the night. A reasonable expectation, in this neck of the woods. Listening to him cough again, I resolved to sit on his chest this evening, if necessary, and oblige him to be well-greased with camphor, whether he liked it or not.

We emerged from the trees, and I glanced dubiously at the farmhouse ahead. It was smaller than I had thought, and rather shabby, with a cracked step, a sagging porch, and a wide patch of shingles missing from the weathered roof. Well, I had slept in worse places, and likely would again.

The door to a stunted barn gaped open, but there was no sign of life. The whole place seemed deserted, save for the plume of smoke from the chimney.

I had meant what I said to Jamie, though I hadn't been entirely accurate. He *was* honest, and also law-abiding—provided that the laws were those he chose to respect. The mere fact that a law had been established by the Crown was not, I knew, sufficient to make it law in his eyes. Other laws, unwritten, he would likely die for.

Still, while the law of property meant somewhat less to an erstwhile Highland raider than it might to others, it hadn't escaped my attention—and therefore certainly hadn't escaped his—that he was about to claim both hospitality and duty from a man whose property he had just helped to abscond. Jamie had no deep-seated objection to indenture as such, I knew; ordinarily, he would respect such a claim. That he hadn't meant that he perceived some higher law in operation—though whether that was friendship, pity, the claim of his *earbsachd*, or something else, I didn't know. He had paused, waiting for me.

"Why did you decide to help Josiah?" I asked bluntly, as we made our way across the ragged cornfield that lay before the house. Dry stalks snapped beneath the horses' feet, and ice crystals glittered on the litter of dead leaves.

Jamie took off his hat, and set it on the saddle before him, as he tied back his hair in preparation for meeting company.

"Well, I said to him that if he was set on this course, so be it. But if he chose to come to the Ridge—alone or with his brother—then we must rid him of the mark on his thumb, for it would cause talk, and word might get back to yon Beardsley, wi' the devil to pay and a' that."

He took a deep breath and let it out, the smoke of it wisping white around his head, then turned to look at me, his face serious.

"The lad didna hesitate for a moment, though he'd been branded; he knew. And I'll tell ye, Sassenach—while a man may do a desperate thing once from love or courage . . . it takes something more than that, if ye've done it once already, and ye know damn well what it's going to feel like to have to do it again."

He turned away without waiting for my response, and rode into the dooryard, scattering a flock of foraging doves. He sat his horse upright, his shoulders broad and square. There was no hint of the deep-webbed scars that lined his back beneath the homespun cloak, but I knew them well.

So that was it, I thought. *As in water face answereth to face, so the heart of man to man.* And the law of courage was the one he had lived by for the longest.

SEVERAL CHICKENS HUDDLED on the porch, fluffed into balls of yellow-eyed resentment. They muttered balefully among themselves as we dismounted, but were too cold to do more than shuffle away from us, reluctant to abandon their patch of sunshine. Several boards of the porch itself were broken, and the yard nearby was littered with scraps of half-hewn lumber and scattered nails, as though someone had meant to mend it, but had not yet found a moment to attend to the job. The procrastination had lasted for some time, I thought; the nails were rusty, and the newly cut boards had warped and split with damp.

"Ho! The house!" Jamie shouted, stopping in the center of the dooryard. This was accepted etiquette for approaching a strange house; while most people in the mountains were hospitable, there were not a few who viewed strangers warily— and were inclined to make introductions at gunpoint, until the callers' bona fides should be established.

With this in mind, I kept a cautious distance behind Jamie, but made sure I was visible, ostentatiously spreading my skirts and brushing them down, displaying my gender as evidence of our peaceable intent.

Damn, there was a small hole burnt through the brown wool, no doubt from a flying campfire spark. I concealed the burned spot in a fold of skirt, thinking how odd it was that everyone regarded women as inherently harmless. Had I been so inclined, I could easily have burgled houses and murdered hapless families from one end of the Ridge to the other.

Fortunately the impulse to do so hadn't struck me, though it *had* dawned on me now and then that the Hippocratic Oath and its injunction to "Do no harm" might not have strictly to do with medical procedure. I'd had the impulse to dot one of my more recalcitrant patients over the head with a stick of firewood more than once, but had so far managed to keep the urge in check.

Of course, most people hadn't the advantage of a doctor's jaundiced view of humanity. And it was true that women didn't go in so much for the recreational sorts of mayhem that men enjoyed—I rarely found women beating each other into pulp for fun. Give them a good motive, though, and . . .

Jamie was walking toward the barn, shouting at intervals, to no apparent effect. I glanced round, but there were no fresh tracks in the dooryard save our own. A scatter of dung balls lay near the half-hewn log, but those had plainly been left days ago; they were moist with dew, but not fresh—most had crumbled to powder.

No one had come, no one had gone, save on foot. The Beardsleys, whoever and however many of them there were, were likely still within.

Lying low, though. It was early, but not so early that farm people would not already be about their chores; I had seen someone earlier, after all. I stepped back and shaded my eyes against the rising sun, looking for any sign of life. I was more than curious about these Beardsleys—and more than slightly apprehensive about the prospects of having one or more male Beardsleys riding with us, given recent events.

I turned back to the door, and noticed an odd series of notches cut into the wood of the jamb. Each one was small, but there were a great many, running the complete length of one doorpost, and halfway down the other. I looked closer;

they were arranged in groups of seven, a scant width of un-scarred wood between the groups, as a prisoner might count, keeping track of the weeks.

Jamie emerged from the barn, followed by a faint bleat-ing. The goats he'd mentioned, of course; I wondered whether it had been Keziah's job to milk them—if it was, his absence was going to become rapidly apparent, if it wasn't already.

Jamie took a few paces toward the house, cupped his hands round his mouth, and shouted again. No answer. He waited a few moments, then shrugged and strode up onto the porch, where he hammered on the door with the hilt of his dirk. It made enough noise to wake the dead, had there been any in the vicinity, and sent the chickens squawking away in a feather-scattering panic, but no one appeared in answer to the thunderous summons.

Jamie glanced back at me, one eyebrow raised. People didn't normally go off and leave their farms untended, not if they had livestock.

"Someone's here," he said, in answer to the unvoiced thought. "The goats are fresh-milked; there are drops still on their teats."

"Do you think they could all be out searching for . . . er . . . you know who?" I murmured, moving closer to him.

"Perhaps." He moved to the side, bending to peer into a window. It had once been glassed, but most of the panes were cracked or missing, and a sheet of ratty muslin had been tacked over the opening. I saw Jamie frown at it, with the craftsman's disdain for a shoddy repair.

He turned his head suddenly, then looked at me.

"D'ye hear something, Sassenach?"

"Yes. I thought it was the goats, but . . ."

The bleat came again—this time unmistakably from the house. Jamie set his hand to the door, but it didn't budge.

"Bolted," he said briefly, and moved back to the window, where he reached carefully into the frame and pulled loose a corner of the muslin cloth.

"Phew," I said, wrinkling my nose at the air that wafted out. I was used to the odors of a winter-sealed cabin, where the scents of sweat, dirty clothes, wet feet, greasy hair, and slop jars mingled with baking bread, stewing meat, and the subtler notes of fungus and mold, but the aroma within the Beardsley residence went well beyond the norm.

"Either they're keeping the pigs in the house," I said, with a glance at the barn, "or there are ten people living in there who haven't come out since last spring."

"It's a bit ripe," Jamie agreed. He put his face into the window, grimacing at the stink, and bellowed, "*Thig a mach!* Come out, Beardsley, or I'm comin' in!"

I peered over his shoulder, to see whether this invitation might produce results. The room within was large, but so crowded that scarcely any of the stained wooden floor was visible through the rubble. Sniffing cautiously, I deduced that the barrels I saw contained—among other things—salt fish, tar, apples, beer, and sauerkraut, while bundles of woolen blankets dyed with cochineal and indigo, kegs of black powder, and half-tanned hides reeking of dog turds lent their own peculiar fragrances to the unique mephitis within. Beardsley's trade goods, I supposed.

The other window had been covered as well, with a tattered wolf hide, so that the interior was dim and shadowy; with all the boxes, bundles, barrels, and bits of furniture lying in heaps, it looked like a poverty-stricken version of Ali Baba's cave.

The sound came again from the back of the house, somewhat louder; a noise midway between a squeal and a growl. I took a step back, sound and acrid smell together vividly recalling an image of dark fur and sudden violence.

"Bears," I suggested, half-seriously. "The people are gone and there's a bear inside."

"Aye, Goldilocks," Jamie said, very dryly. "Nay doubt. Bears or not, there's something wrong. Fetch the pistols and cartridge box from my saddlebag."

I nodded and turned to go, but before I could step off the porch, a shuffling noise came from inside, and I turned back sharply. Jamie had grasped his dirk, but as he saw whatever was inside, his hand relaxed on the hilt. His eyebrows also rose in surprise, and I leaned over his arm to see.

A woman peered out from between two hillocks of goods, looking round suspiciously, like a rat peering out of a garbage dump. She was not particularly ratlike in appearance, being wavy-haired and quite stout, but she blinked at us in the calculating way of vermin, reckoning the threat.

"Go away," she said, evidently concluding that we were not the vanguard of an invading army.

"Good morning to ye, ma'am," Jamie began, "I am James Fraser, of—"

"I don't care who you are," she replied. "Go away."

"Indeed I will not," he said firmly. "I must speak with the man o' the house."

An extraordinary expression crossed her plump face; concern, calculation, and what might have been amusement.

"Must you?" she said. She had a slight lisp; it came out as *mutht you?* "And who says that you must?"

Jamie's ears were beginning to redden slightly, but he answered calmly enough.

"The Governor, madam. I am *Colonel* James Fraser," he said, with emphasis, "charged with the raising of militia. All able-bodied men between the ages of sixteen and sixty are called to muster. Will ye fetch Mr. Beardsley, please?"

"Mili-ish-ia, is it?" she said, handling the word with care. "Why, who will you be fighting, then?"

"With luck, no one. But the call to muster is sent out; I must answer, and so must all able-bodied men within the Treaty Line." Jamie's hand tightened on the crosspiece of the inner frame and rattled it experimentally. It was made of flimsy pine sticks, the wood shrunken and badly weathered; he could plainly rip it out of the wall and step through the opening, if he chose to do so. He met her eyes straight on, and smiled pleasantly.

She narrowed her eyes and pursed her lips, thinking.

"Able-bodied men," she said at last. "Hmp. Well, we've none of those. The bond lad's run off again, but even if he were here, he's not able; deaf as that doorpotht, and quite as dumb." She nodded toward the door in illustration. "If you care to hunt him down, you're welcome to keep him, though."

It didn't look as though there would be any hue and cry after Keziah, then. I took a deep breath, in a sigh of relief, but let it out again, swiftly.

Jamie wasn't giving up easily.

"Is Mr. Beardsley in the house?" he asked. "I wish to see him." He gave an experimental tug on the frame, and the dry wood cracked with a sound like a pistol shot.

"He's thcarce fit for company," she said, and the odd note was back in her voice; wary, but at the same time, filled with something like excitement.

"Is he ill?" I asked, leaning over Jamie's shoulder. "I might be able to help; I'm a doctor."

She shuffled forward a step or two, and peered at me, frowning under a heavy mass of wavy brown hair. She was younger than I'd thought; seen in better light, the heavy face showed no cobweb of age or slackening of flesh.

"A doctor?"

"My wife's well-kent as a healer," Jamie said. "The Indian folk call her White Raven."

"The conjure woman?" Her eyes flew wide in alarm, and she took a step back.

Something struck me odd about the woman, and looking at her, I realized what it was. Despite the reek in the house, both the woman's person and her dress were clean, and her hair was soft and fluffy—not at all the norm at this time of year, when people generally didn't bathe for several months in the cold weather.

"Who are you?" I asked bluntly. "Are you Mrs. Beardsley? Or perhaps Miss Beardsley?"

No more than twenty-five, I thought, in spite of the bulk of her swaddled figure. Her shoulders swelled fatly under her shawl, and the width of her hips brushed the barrels she stood between. Evidently trade with the Cherokee was sufficiently profitable to keep Beardsley's family in adequate food, if not his bond servants. I eyed her with some dislike, but she met my gaze coolly enough.

"I am Mrs. Beardthley."

The alarm had faded; she pursed her lips, and pushed them in and out, regarding me with an air of calculation. Jamie flexed his arm, and the window frame cracked loudly.

"Come you in, then."

The odd tone was still in her voice; half defiance, half eagerness. Jamie caught it and frowned, but released his grip on the frame.

She moved out from between the boxes and turned toward the door. I caught no more than a glimpse of her in motion, but that was enough to see that she was lame; one leg dragged, her shoe scraping on the wooden floor.

There was a bumping and grunting as she fumbled with the bolt; a grating noise, and then a *thunk* as she dropped it on the floor. The door was warped, stuck in its frame; Jamie put his shoulder to it and it sprang loose and swung in, boards quivering with the shock. How long since it had been opened? I wondered.

A good long time, evidently. I heard Jamie snort and cough as he went in, and did my best to breathe through my mouth as I followed. Even so, the smell was enough to knock a ferret over. Beyond the reek of the goods, there was an outhouse smell from somewhere; stale urine and a ripe fecal stench. Rotting food, too, but something else besides. My nostrils twitched cautiously as I tried to inhale no more than a few molecules of air for analysis.

"How long has Mr. Beardsley been ill?" I asked.

I had picked out a distinct stench of sickness amid the general fetor. Not only the ghost of long-dried vomit, but the sweet smell of purulent discharge and that indefinable musty, yeast-rising odor that seems to be simply the smell of illness itself.

"Oh . . . thome time."

She shut the door behind us, and I felt a sudden surge of claustrophobia. Inside, the air seemed thick, both from the stench and from the lack of light. I had a great impulse to rip down the coverings from both windows and let in a little air, and clenched my hands in the fabric of my cloak to keep from doing it.

Mrs. Beardsley turned sideways and scuttled crablike through a narrow passage left between the stacks of goods. Jamie glanced at me, made a Scottish noise of disgust in his throat, and ducked under a jutting bundle of tent poles to follow her. I made my way cautiously after, trying not to notice that my foot fell now and then on objects of an unpleasant squashiness. Rotten apples? Dead rats? I pinched my nose and didn't look down.

The farmhouse was simple in construction; one big room across the front, one behind.

The rear room was a striking contrast to the squalid clutter of the front. There was no ornament or decoration; the room was plain and orderly as a Quaker meeting hall. Everything was bare and spotless, the wooden table and stone hearth scrubbed to rawness, a few pewter utensils gleaming dully on a shelf. One window here had been left uncovered, glass intact, and the morning sun fell across the room in pure white radiance. The room was quiet and the air still, increasing the odd feeling that we had entered a sanctuary of some sort from the chaos of the front room.

The impression of peace was dispelled at once by a loud noise from above. It was the sound we had heard earlier, but close at hand, a loud squeal filled with desperation, like a tortured hog. Jamie started at the sound, and turned at once toward a ladder at the far side of the room, which led upward to a loft.

"He'th up there," Mrs. Beardsley said—unnecessarily, as Jamie was already halfway up the ladder. The squealing noise came again, more urgently, and I decided not to fetch my medicine box before investigating.

Jamie's head appeared at the top of the ladder as I grasped it.

"Bring a light, Sassenach," he said briefly, and his head vanished.

Mrs. Beardsley stood motionless, hands buried in her shawl, making no effort to find a light. Her lips were pressed tight together, her plump cheeks mottled with red. I pushed past her, seized a candlestick from the shelf, and knelt to light it at the hearth before hastening upward.

"Jamie?" I poked my head above the edge of the loft, holding my candle cautiously above my head.

"Here, Sassenach." He was standing at the far end of the loft, where the shadows lay thickest. I scrambled over the top of the ladder and made my way toward him, stepping gingerly.

The stench was much stronger here. I caught the gleam of something in the dark, and brought the candle forward to see.

Jamie drew in his breath, as shocked as I was, but quickly mastered his emotion.

"Mr. Beardsley, I presume," he said.

The man was enormous—or had been. The great curve of his belly still rose whalelike out of the shadows, and the hand that lay slack on the floorboards near my foot could have cupped a cannonball with ease. But the flesh of the upper arm hung slack, white and flabby, the massive chest sunken in the center. What must once have been the neck of a bull had wasted to stringiness, and a single eye gleamed, frantic behind strands of matted hair.

The eye widened, and he made the noise again, his head straining upward urgently. I felt a shudder go through Jamie. It was enough to raise the hair on the back of my own neck, but I disregarded it, pushing the candlestick into Jamie's hands.

"Hold the light for me."

I sank to my knees, too late feeling the liquid ooze through the fabric of my skirt. The man lay in his own filth, and had been lying so for quite some time; the floor was thick with slime and wet. He was naked, covered by no more than a linen blanket, and as I turned it back, I glimpsed ulcerated sores amid the smears of ordure.

It was clear enough what ailed Mr. Beardsley; one side of his face sagged grotesquely, the eyelid drooping, and both the arm and the leg on the near side of his body splayed limp and dead, the joints left knobby and weirdly distorted by the falling away of the muscle around them. He snuffled and bleated, tongue poking and slobbering from the corner of his mouth in his vain but urgent attempts at speech.

"Hush," I said to him. "Don't talk; it's all right now."

I took the wrist to check his pulse; the flesh moved loosely on the bones of his arm, with not the slightest twitch of response to my touch.

"A stroke," I said softly to Jamie. "An apoplexy, you call it." I put my hand on Beardsley's chest, to offer the comfort of touch.

"Don't worry," I said to him. "We've come to help." I

spoke reassuringly, though even as I said the words, I wondered what help was possible. Well, cleanliness and warmth at least; it was nearly as cold in the loft as it was outside, and his chest was chilly and pebbled with gooseflesh among the bushy hair.

The ladder creaked heavily, and I turned to see the outline of Mrs. Beardsley's fluffy head and heavy shoulders, silhouetted by the light from the kitchen below.

"How long has he been like this?" I asked sharply.

"Perhapth . . . a month," she said, after a pause. "I could not move him," she said, defensive. "He ith too heavy."

That was plainly true. However . . .

"Why is he up here?" Jamie demanded. "If ye didna move him, how did he get here?" He turned, shedding the light of the candle over the loft. There was little here that would draw a man; an old straw mattress, a few scattered tools, and bits of household rubbish. The light shone on Mrs. Beardsley's face, turning her pale blue eyes to ice.

"He wath . . . chathing me," she said faintly.

"What?" Jamie strode over to the ladder, and bending down, seized her by the arm, helping her—rather against her will, it seemed—to clamber up the rest of the way into the loft.

"What d'ye mean, chasing you?" he demanded. She hunched her shoulders, looking round and homely as a cookie jar in her bundled shawls.

"He thtruck me," she said simply. "I came up the ladder to get away from him, but he followed. I tried to hide back here in the thadows, and he came, but then . . . he fell. And . . . he could not get up." She shrugged again.

Jamie held the candlestick near her face. She gave a small nervous smile, eyes darting from me to Jamie, and I saw that the lisp was caused by the fact that her front teeth were broken—snapped off at an angle, just beyond the gums. A small scar ran through her upper lip; another showed white in the hairs of one eyebrow.

A horrible noise came from the man on the floor—a furious squeal of what sounded like protest—and she flinched, eyes shut tight in reflexive dread.

"Mmphm," Jamie said, glancing from her to her husband.

"Aye. Well. Fetch up some water, ma'am, and ye will. Another candle and some fresh rags as well," he called after her departing back as she hastened toward the ladder, only too glad to be given an excuse to leave.

"Jamie—bring back the light, will you?"

He came and stood beside me, holding the candle so it shed its glow on the ruined body. He gave Beardsley a dark look of mingled pity and dislike, and shook his head slowly.

"God's judgment, d'ye think, Sassenach?"

"Not entirely God's, I don't think," I said, my voice lowered so as not to carry to the kitchen below. I reached up and took the candlestick from him. "Look."

A flask of water and a plate of bread, hard and tinged with blue mold, stood in the shadows near Beardsley's head; orts and bits of gluey, half-chewed bread covered the floor nearby. She had fed him—enough to keep him alive. Yet I had seen great quantities of food in that front room as we passed— hanging hams, barrels of dried fruit and salt fish and sauerkraut.

There were bundles of furs, jugs of oil, piles of woolen blankets—and yet the master of those goods lay here in the dark, starved and shivering beneath a single sheet of linen.

"Why did she not just let him die, I wonder?" Jamie asked softly, eyes fixed on the moldy bread. Beardsley gargled and growled at this; his open eye rolled angrily, tears running down his face and snot bubbling from his nose. He flailed and grunted, arching his body in frustration, collapsing with a meaty thud that shook the boards of the loft.

"He can understand you, I think. Can you?" I addressed this remark to the sick man, who gobbled and drooled in a manner that made it clear that he understood at least that he was being spoken to.

"As to why . . ."

I gestured toward Beardsley's legs, moving the candle slowly above them. Some of the sores were indeed compression sores, caused by lying helpless for a long time. Others were not. Parallel slashes, clearly made by a knife, showed black and clotted on one massive thigh. The shin was decorated with a regular line of ulcerations, angry red wounds rimmed with black and oozing. Burns, left to fester.

Jamie gave a small grunt at the sight, and glanced over his shoulder, toward the ladder. The sound of a door opening came from below, and a cold draft blew up into the loft, making the candle flame dance wildly. The door shut, and the flame steadied.

"I can make shift to lower him, I think." Jamie lifted the candle, assessing the beams overhead. "A sling, perhaps, with a rope put over yon beam there. Is it all right to move him?"

"Yes," I said, but I wasn't paying attention. Bending over the sick man's legs, I had caught a whiff of something that I hadn't smelled in a long, long time—a very bad and sinister stink.

I hadn't encountered it often, but even once would have been enough; the pungent smell of gas gangrene is strikingly memorable. I didn't want to say anything that might alarm Beardsley—if he was capable of understanding—so instead, I patted him reassuringly and stood up to go and fetch the candle from Jamie for a better look.

He gave it to me, leaning close to murmur in my ear as he did so.

"Can ye do aught for him, Sassenach?"

"No," I said, equally low-voiced. "Not for the apoplexy, that is. I can treat the sores and give him herbs against fever—that's all."

He stood for a moment, looking at the humped figure in the shadows, now quiescent. Then he shook his head, crossed himself, and went quickly down the ladder to hunt a rope.

I went slowly back to the sick man, who greeted me with a thick "Haughhh" and a restless thumping of one leg, like a rabbit's warning. I knelt by his feet, talking soothingly of nothing in particular, while I held the light close to examine them. The toes. All the toes on his dead foot had been burned, some only blistered, others burned nearly to the bone. The first two toes had gone quite black, and a greenish tinge spread over the upper aspect of the foot nearby.

I was appalled—as much by the thought of what might have led to this as by the action itself. The candle wavered; my hands were shaking, and not only with cold. I was not only horrified by what had happened here; I was also worried by the immediate prospects. What on earth were we to do about these wretched people?

Plainly we couldn't take Beardsley with us—just as plainly, he could not be left here, under the care of his wife. There were no near neighbors to look in, no one else on the farm to safeguard him. I supposed we might manage to transport him to Brownsville; there might be a wagon in the barn. But even if so, what then?

There was no hospital to care for him. If one of the homes in Brownsville might take him in for the sake of charity . . . well and good, but seeing Beardsley's state after a month, I thought it unlikely that his condition—in terms either of paralysis or speech—would improve much. Who would keep him, if it meant caring for him day and night for the rest of his life?

The rest of his life, of course, could be rather short, depending on my success in dealing with the gangrene. Worry retreated as my mind turned to the immediate problem. I would have to amputate; it was the only possibility. The toes were easy—but the toes might not be enough. If I had to take off the foot or part of it, we ran a greater risk from shock and infection.

Could he feel it? Sometimes stroke victims retained feeling in an affected limb, but not movement, sometimes movement without feeling—sometimes neither. Cautiously, I touched the gangrenous toe, eyes on his face.

His working eye was open, focused on the beams overhead. He didn't glance at me or make a noise, which answered that question. No, he couldn't feel the foot. That was a relief, in a way—at least he wouldn't suffer pain from the amputation. Nor, it occurred to me, had he felt the damage inflicted on his limb. Had she been aware of that? Or had she chosen to attack his dead side only because he retained some strength on the other, and might still defend himself?

There was a soft rustle behind me. Mrs. Beardsley was back. She set down a bucket of water and a pile of rags, then stood behind me, watching in silence as I began to sponge away the filth.

"Can you cure him?" she asked. Her voice was calm, remote, as though she spoke of a stranger.

The patient's head lolled suddenly back, so his open eye fixed on me.

"I think I can help a bit," I said carefully. I wished Jamie would return. Aside from need of my medical box, I was finding the company of the Beardsleys rather unnerving.

The more so when Mr. Beardsley inadvertently released a small quantity of urine. Mrs. Beardsley laughed, and he made a sound in reply that made the goose bumps rise on my arms. I wiped the liquid off his thigh and went on with my work, trying to ignore it.

"Have you or Mr. Beardsley any kin nearby?" I asked, as conversationally as possible. "Someone who might come to lend you a hand?"

"No one," she said. "He took me from my father's house in Maryland. To thith place." *This place* was spoken as though it were the fifth circle of hell; so far as I could see, there was certainly some resemblance at the present moment.

The door opened below, and a welcome draft of cold air announced Jamie's return. There was a clunking noise as he set my box on the table, and I hastily rose, eager to escape them, if only for a moment.

"There's my husband with my medicines. I'll just . . . er . . . go and fetch . . . um . . ." I edged past Mrs. Beardsley's bulk, and fled down the ladder, sweating in spite of the chill in the house.

Jamie stood by the table, frowning as he turned a length of rope in his hands. He glanced up as he heard me, and his face relaxed a little.

"How is it, Sassenach?" he asked, low-voiced, with a jerk of the chin toward the loft.

"Very bad," I whispered, coming to stand beside him. "Two of his toes are gangrenous; I'll have to take them off. And she says they've no family near to help."

"Mmphm." His lips tightened, and he bent his attention to the sling he was improvising.

I reached for my medical chest, to check my instruments, but stopped when I saw Jamie's pistols lying on the table beside it, along with his powder horn and shot case. I touched his arm and jerked my head at them, mouthing, "What?" at him.

The line between his brows deepened, but before he could answer, a dreadful racket came from the loft above, a great thrashing and thumping, accompanied by a gargling noise like an elephant drowning in a mud bog.

Jamie dropped the rope and shot for the ladder, with me at his heels. He let out a shout as his head topped the ladder, and dived forward. As I scrambled into the loft behind him, I saw him in the shadows, grappling with Mrs. Beardsley.

She smashed an elbow at his face, hitting him in the nose. This removed any inhibitions he might have had about man-handling a woman, and he jerked her round to face him and struck her with a short, sharp uppercut to the chin that clicked her jaws and made her stagger, eyes glazing. I dashed forward to save the candle, as she collapsed on her rump in a pouf of skirts and petticoats.

"God . . . dab . . . that . . . womad." Jamie's voice was muffled, his sleeve pressed across his face to stanch the flow of blood from his nose, but the sincerity in it was unmistakable.

Mr. Beardsley was flopping like a landed fish, wheezing and gurgling. I lifted the candle and found him flailing at his neck with one splayed hand. A linen kerchief had been twisted into a rope and wrapped round his neck, and his face was black, his one eye popping. I hastily seized the kerchief and undid it, and his breathing eased with a great whoosh of fetid air.

"If she'd been faster, she'd have had him." Jamie lowered his blood-streaked arm and felt his nose tenderly. "Christ, I think she broke my dose."

"Why? Why did you thtop me?" Mrs. Beardsley was still conscious, though swaying and glassy-eyed. "He thould die, I want him to die, he mutht die."

"*A nighean na galladh,* ye could ha' killed him at your leisure any time this month past, if ye wanted him dead," Jamie said impatiently. "Why in God's name wait until ye had witnesses?"

She looked up at him, eyes suddenly sharp and clear.

"I did not want him dead," she said. "I wanted him to *die*." She smiled, showing the stubs of her broken teeth. "Thlowly."

"Oh, Christ," I said, and wiped a hand across my face. It was only mid-morning, but I felt as though the day had lasted several weeks already. "It's my fault. I told her I thought I could help; she thought I'd save him, maybe cure him altogether." The curse of a reputation for magic healing! I might have laughed, had I been in the mood for irony.

There was a sharp, fresh stink in the air, and Mrs. Beardsley turned on her husband with a cry of outrage.

"Filthy beast!" She scrambled to her knees, snatched up a hard roll from the plate, and threw it at him. It bounced off his head. "Filthy, thtinking, dirty, wicked . . ." Jamie seized her by the hair as she hurled herself at the prone body, grabbed her arm, and jerked her away, sobbing and shrieking abuse.

"Bloody hell," he said, over the uproar. "Fetch me that rope, Sassenach, before I kill them both myself."

The job of getting Mr. Beardsley down from the loft was enough to leave both Jamie and me sweat-soaked and streaked with filth, reeking and weak in the knees with effort. Mrs. Beardsley squatted on a stool in the corner, quiet and malevolent as a toad, making no effort to help.

She gave a gasp of outrage when we laid the big, lolling body on the clean table, but Jamie glared at her, and she sank back on her stool, mouth clamped to a thin, straight line.

Jamie wiped his bloodstained sleeve across his brow, and shook his head as he looked at Beardsley. I didn't blame him; even cleaned up, warmly covered, and with a little warm gruel spooned into him, the man was in a dreadful state. I examined him once more, carefully, in the light from the window. No doubt about the toes; the stink of gangrene was distinct, and the greenish tinge covered the outer dorsal aspect of the foot.

I'd have to take more than the toes—I frowned, feeling my way carefully around the putrefying area, wondering whether it was better to try for a partial amputation between the metacarpals, or simply to take the foot off at the ankle. The ankle dissection would be faster, and while I would normally try for the more conservative partial amputation, there was really no point to it in this case; Beardsley was plainly never going to walk again.

I gnawed my lower lip dubiously. For that matter, the whole business might be moot; he burned with intermittent fever, and the sores on legs and buttocks oozed with suppuration. What were the chances of his recovering from the amputation without dying of infection?

I hadn't heard Mrs. Beardsley come up behind me; for a heavyset woman, she moved with remarkable silence.

"What do you mean to do?" she asked, her voice sounding neutral and remote.

"Your husband's toes are gangrenous," I said. No point in trying not to alarm Beardsley now. "I'll have to amputate his foot." There was really no choice, though my heart sank at the notion of spending the next several days—or weeks— here, nursing Beardsley. I could hardly leave him to the tender care of his wife!

She circled the table slowly, coming to a stop near his feet. Her face was blank, but a tiny smile appeared at the corners of her mouth, winking on and off, as though quite without her willing it. She looked at the blackened toes for a long minute, then shook her head.

"No," she said softly. "Let him rot."

The question of Beardsley's understanding was resolved, at least; his open eye bulged, and he let out a shriek of rage, thrashing and flailing in an effort to get at her, so that he came perilously near to falling onto the floor in his struggles. Jamie seized him, shoving and heaving to keep his ponderous bulk on the table. As Beardsley at last subsided, gasping and making mewling noises, Jamie straightened up, gasping himself, and gave Mrs. Beardsley a look of extreme dislike.

She hunched her shoulders, pulling her shawl tight around them, but didn't retreat or look away. She raised her chin defiantly.

"I am hith wife," she said. "I thall not let you cut him. It ith a rithk to hith life."

"It's certain death if I don't," I said shortly. "And a nasty one, too. You—" I didn't get to finish; Jamie put a hand on my shoulder, squeezing hard.

"Take her outside, Claire," he said quietly.

"But—"

"Outside." His hand tightened on my shoulder, almost painful in its pressure. "Dinna come back until I call for ye."

His face was grim, but there was something in his eyes that made me go hollow and watery inside. I glanced at the sideboard, where his pistols lay beside my medicine chest, then back at his face, appalled.

"You can't," I said.

He looked at Beardsley, his face bleak.

"I would put down a dog in such case without a second's thought," he said softly. "Can I do less for him?"

"He is not a dog!"

"No, he is not." His hand dropped from my shoulder, and he circled the table, until he stood by Beardsley's side.

"If ye understand me, man—close your eye," he said quietly. There was a moment's silence, and Beardsley's bloodshot eye fixed on Jamie's face—with undeniable intelligence. The lid closed slowly, then rose again.

Jamie turned to me.

"Go," he said. "Let it be his choice. If—or if not—I will call for ye."

My knees were trembling, and I knotted my hands in the folds of my skirt.

"No," I said. I looked at Beardsley, then swallowed hard and shook my head. "No," I said again. "I—if you . . . you must have a witness."

He hesitated a moment, but then nodded.

"Aye, you're right." He glanced at Mrs. Beardsley. She stood stock-still, hands knotted under her apron, eyes darting from me to Jamie to her husband and back. Jamie shook his head briefly, then turned back to the stricken man, squaring his shoulders.

"Blink once for yes, twice for nay," he said. "You understand?"

The eyelid lowered without hesitation.

"Listen, then." Jamie drew a deep breath and began to speak, in a flat, unemotional tone of voice, his eyes steady on the ruined face and the fierce gaze of its open eye.

"Ye ken what has happened to you?"

Blink.

"Ye ken that my wife is a physician, a healer?"

The eye rolled in my direction, then back to Jamie. Blink.

"She says that you have suffered an apoplexy, that the damage canna be mended. You understand?"

A huffing sound came from the lopsided mouth. This was not news. Blink.

"Your foot is putrid. If it is not taken off, you will rot and die. You understand?"

No response. The nostrils flared suddenly, moist, questing; then the air was expelled with a snort. He had smelled the rot; had suspected, perhaps, but not known for sure that it came from his own flesh. Not 'til now. Slowly, a blink.

The quiet litany went on, statements and questions, each a shovelful of dirt, taken from a deepening grave. Each ending with the inexorable words, "You understand?"

My hands and feet and face felt numb. The odd sense of sanctuary in the room had altered; it felt like a church, but no longer a place of refuge. A place now in which some ritual took place, leading to a solemn, predestined end.

And it was predestined, I understood. Beardsley had made his choice long since—perhaps even before we arrived. He had had a month in that purgatory, after all, suspended in the cold dark between heaven and earth, in which to think, to come to grips with his prospects and make his peace with death.

Did he understand?

Oh, yes, very well.

Jamie bent over the table, one hand on Beardsley's arm, a priest in stained linen, offering absolution and salvation. Mrs. Beardsley stood frozen in the fall of light from the window, a stolid angel of denunciation.

The statements and the questions came to an end.

"Will ye have my wife take your foot and tend your wounds?"

One blink, then two, exaggerated, deliberate.

Jamie's breathing was audible, the heaviness in his chest making a sigh of each word.

"Do ye ask me to take your life?"

Though one half of his face sagged lifeless and the other was drawn and haggard, there was enough of Beardsley left to show expression. The workable corner of the mouth turned up in a cynical leer. *What there is left of it*, said his silence. The eyelid fell—and stayed shut.

Jamie closed his own eyes. A small shudder passed over him. Then he shook himself briefly, like a man shaking off cold water, and turned to the sideboard where his pistols lay.

I crossed swiftly to him, laying a hand on his arm. He didn't look at me, but kept his eyes on the pistol he was priming. His face was white, but his hands were steady.

"Go," he said. "Take her out."

I looked back at Beardsley, but he was my patient no longer; his flesh beyond my healing or my comfort. I went to the woman and took her by the arm, turning her toward the door. She came with me, walking mechanically, and did not turn to look back.

THE OUTDOORS SEEMED unreal, the sunlit yard unconvincingly ordinary. Mrs. Beardsley pulled free of my grip and headed toward the barn, walking fast. She glanced back over her shoulder at the house, then broke into a heavy run, disappearing through the open barn door as though fiends were after her.

I caught her sense of panic and nearly ran after her. I didn't, though; I stopped at the edge of the yard and waited. I could feel my heart beating, slowly, thumping in my ears. That seemed unreal, too.

The shot came, finally, a small flat sound, inconsequent amid the soft bleating of goats from the barn and the rustle of chickens scratching in the dirt nearby. Head, I wondered suddenly, or heart, and shuddered.

It was long past noon; the cold, still air of the morning had risen and a chilly breeze moved through the dooryard, stirring dust and wisps of hay. I stood and waited. He would have paused, I thought, to say a brief prayer for Beardsley's soul. A moment passed, two, then the back door opened. Jamie came out, took a few steps, then stopped, bent over, and vomited.

I started forward, in case he needed me, but no. He

straightened and wiped his mouth, then turned and walked across the yard away from me, heading for the wood.

I felt suddenly superfluous, and rather oddly affronted. I had been at work no more than moments before, deeply absorbed in the practice of medicine. Connected to flesh, to mind and body; attentive to symptoms, aware of pulse and breath, the vital signs. I hadn't liked Beardsley in the least, and yet I had been totally engaged in the struggle to preserve his life, to ease his suffering. I could still feel the odd touch of his slack, warm flesh on my hands.

Now my patient was abruptly dead, and I felt as though some small part of my body had been amputated. I thought I was perhaps a trifle shocked.

I glanced at the house, my original sense of caution superseded by distaste—and something deeper. The body must be washed, of course, and decently laid out for burial. I had done such things before—with no great qualms, if without enthusiasm—and yet I found myself now with a great reluctance to go back into the place.

I'd seen death by violence—and many much more distasteful than this was likely to have been. Death was death. Whether it came as passage, as parting, or in some cases, as dearly desired release . . . Jamie had freed Beardsley very suddenly from the prison of his stricken body; did his spirit perhaps still linger in the house, having not yet realized its freedom?

"You are being superstitious, Beauchamp," I said severely to myself. "Stop it at once." And yet I didn't take a step toward the house, but hovered in the yard, keyed up like an indecisive hummingbird.

If Beardsley was beyond my help, and Jamie in no need of it, there was still one who might require it. I turned my back on the house and went toward the barn.

This was no more than a large open shed with a loft, fragrantly dark and filled with hay and moving shapes. I stood in the doorway until my eyes adjusted. There was a stall in one corner, but no horse. A rickety fence with a milking stanchion made a goat pen in the other corner; she was crouched inside it, on a pile of fresh straw. Half a dozen goats crowded and bumped around her, jostling and nibbling at the fringes of her shawl. She was little more than a hunched shape, but I caught the brief shine of a wary eye in the shadows.

"Ith it over?" The question was asked softly, barely audible above the quiet grunting and bleating.

"Yes." I hesitated, but she seemed in no need of my support; I could see better now—she had a small kid curled in her lap, her fingers stroking the small, silky head. "Are you quite all right, Mrs. Beardsley?"

Silence, then the heavy figure shrugged and settled, some tension seeming to leave her.

"I thcarthely know," she said softly. I waited, but she neither moved nor spoke further. The peaceful company of the goats seemed as likely as mine to be a comfort to her, so I turned and left them, rather envying her the warm refuge of the barn and her cheerful companions.

We had left the horses in the dooryard, still saddled, tethered to an alder sapling. Jamie had loosened their girths and removed their saddlebags when he went to fetch my medicine box, but had not taken the time to unsaddle them. I did that now; plainly it would be some time yet before we could leave. I took off the bridles as well, and hobbled them, turning them loose to graze on the winter-brown grass that still grew thickly at the edge of the pines.

There was a hollowed half-log on the western side of the house, plainly meant to serve as a horse trough, but it was empty. Welcoming the chore for the delay it allowed me, I raised water from the well and emptied bucket after bucket into the trough.

Wiping my wet hands on my skirt, I looked round for further useful occupation, but there wasn't any. No choice, then. I braced myself, poured more water into the bucket, dropped in the hollow drinking gourd that stood on the edge of the well, and carried it back around the house, concentrating fiercely on not spilling any, in order to avoid thinking about the prospects within.

When I raised my eyes, I was startled to see that the back door stood open. I was sure it had been closed before. Was Jamie inside? Or Mrs. Beardsley?

Keeping a wary distance, I craned my neck to peep into

the kitchen, but as I sidled closer, I heard the steady *chuff* of a spade shifting dirt. I went around the far corner to find Jamie digging near a mountain-ash tree that stood by itself in the yard, a short distance from the house. He was still in shirtsleeves, and the wind blew the stained white linen against his body, ruffling the red hair over his face.

He brushed it back with one wrist, and I saw with a small sense of shock that he was crying. He wept silently and somehow savagely, attacking the soil as though it were an enemy. He caught my movement from a corner of his eye, and stopped, swiping a blood-smeared shirtsleeve quickly across his face, as though to wipe away sweat from his brow.

He was breathing hoarsely, loud enough to hear from a distance. I came silently and offered him the gourd of water, along with a clean handkerchief. He didn't meet my eyes, but drank, coughed, drank again, handed back the gourd, and blew his nose, gingerly. It was swollen, but no longer bleeding.

"We won't sleep here tonight, will we?" I ventured to ask, seating myself on the chopping block that stood under the ash tree.

He shook his head.

"God, no," he said hoarsely. His face was blotched and his eyes bloodshot, but he had firm hold of himself. "We'll see him decently buried and go. I dinna mind if we sleep cold in the wood again—but not here." I agreed wholeheartedly with that notion, but there was one thing more to be considered.

"And . . . her?" I asked delicately. "Is she in the house? The back door is open."

He grunted, and thrust in his shovel.

"No, that was me. I'd forgot to leave it open when I came out before—to let the soul go free," he explained, seeing my upraised eyebrow.

It was the complete matter-of-factness with which he offered this explanation, rather than the fact that it echoed my own earlier notion, that made the hairs prickle along my neck.

"I see," I said, a little faintly.

Jamie dug steadily for a bit, the shovel biting deep into the dirt. It was loamy soil and leaf mold here; the digging was easy. At last, without breaking the swing of the blade, he said, "Brianna told me a story she'd read once. I dinna recall all about it, quite, but there was a murder done, only the person killed was a wicked man, who had driven someone to it. And at the end, when the teller of the tale was asked what should be done, he said, 'Let pass the justice of God.'"

I nodded. I was in agreement, though it seemed a trifle hard on the person who found himself required to be the instrument of such justice.

"Do you suppose that's what it was, in this case? Justice?"

He shook his head; not in negation, but in puzzlement, and went on digging. I watched him for a bit, soothed by his nearness and by the hypnotic rhythm of his movements. After a bit, though, I stirred, steeling myself to face the task awaiting me.

"I suppose I'd best go and lay out the body and clear up the loft," I said reluctantly, drawing my feet under me to rise. "We can't leave that poor woman alone with such a mess, no matter what she did."

"No, wait, Sassenach," Jamie said, pausing in his digging. He glanced at the house, a little warily. "I'll go in with ye, in a bit. For now"—he nodded toward the edge of the wood—"d'ye think ye could fetch a few stones for the cairn?"

A cairn? I was more than slightly surprised at this; it seemed an unnecessary elaboration for the late Mr. Beardsley. Still, there were undoubtedly wolves in the wood; I'd seen scats on the trail two days before. It also occurred to me that Jamie might be contriving an honorable excuse for me to postpone entering the house again—in which case, hauling rocks seemed a thoroughly desirable alternative.

Fortunately, there was no shortage of suitable rocks. I fetched the heavy canvas apron that I wore for surgery from my saddlebag, and began to trundle to and fro, an ant collecting laborious crumbs. After half an hour or so of this, the thought of entering the house had begun to seem much less objectionable. Jamie was still hard at it, though, so I kept on.

I stopped finally, gasping, and dumped yet another load out of my apron onto the ground by the deepening grave. The shadows were falling long across the dooryard, and the air was cold enough that my fingers had gone numb—a good thing, in view of the various scrapes and nicks on them.

"You look a right mess," I observed, shoving a disheveled mass of hair off my own face. "Has Mrs. Beardsley come out yet?"

He shook his head, but took a moment to get his breath back before replying.

"No," he said, in a voice so hoarse I could scarcely hear him. "She's still wi' the goats. I daresay it's warm in there."

I eyed him uneasily. Grave-digging is hard work; his shirt was clinging to his body, soaked through in spite of the coldness of the day, and his face was flushed—with labor, I hoped, rather than fever. His fingers were white and as stiff as mine, though; it took a visible effort for him to uncurl them from the handle of the shovel.

"Surely that's deep enough," I said, surveying his work. I would myself have settled for the shallowest of gouges in the soft earth, but slipshod work was never Jamie's way. "Do stop, Jamie, and change your shirt at once. You're wringing wet; you'll catch a terrible chill."

He didn't bother arguing, but took up the spade and carefully neatened the corners of the hole, shaping the sides to keep them from crumbling inward.

The shadows under the pine trees were growing thick, and the chickens had all gone to roost, feathery blobs perched in the trees like bunches of brown mistletoe. The forest birds had fallen silent, too, and the shadow of the house fell long and cold across the new grave. I hugged my elbows, and shivered at the quiet.

Jamie tossed the shovel onto the ground with a clunk, startling me. He climbed up out of the hole, and stood still for a minute, eyes closed, swaying with weariness. Then he opened his eyes and smiled tiredly at me.

"Let's finish, then," he said.

WHETHER THE OPEN DOOR had indeed allowed the deceased's spirit to flee, or whether it was only that Jamie was with me, I felt no hesitation in entering the house now. The fire had gone out, and the kitchen was cold and dim, yet there was no sense of anything evil within. It was simply . . . empty.

Mr. Beardsley's mortal remains rested peacefully under one of his own trade blankets, mute and still. Empty, too.

Mrs. Beardsley had declined to assist with the formalities—or even to enter the house, so long as her husband's body remained inside—so I swept the hearth, kindled a new fire, and coaxed it into reluctant life, while Jamie took care of the mess in the loft. By the time he came down again, I had turned to the main business at hand.

Dead, Beardsley seemed much less grotesque than he had in life; the twisted limbs were relaxed, the air of frantic struggle gone. Jamie had placed a linen towel over the head, though when I peeked beneath it, I could see that there was no gory mess to deal with; Jamie had shot him cleanly through the blind eye, and the ball had not burst the skull. The good eye was closed now, the blackened wound left staring. I laid the towel gently back over the face, its symmetry restored in death.

Jamie climbed down the ladder, and came quietly to stand behind me, touching my shoulder briefly.

"Go and wash," I said, gesturing behind me to the small kettle of water I had hung over the fire to heat. "I'll manage here."

He nodded, stripped off his sodden, filthy shirt, and dropped it on the hearth. I listened to the small, homely noises he made as he washed. He coughed now and then, but his breathing sounded somewhat easier than it had outside in the cold.

"I didna ken it might be that way," he said from behind me. "I thought an apoplexy would kill a man outright."

"Sometimes that's so," I said, a little absently, frowning as I concentrated on the job at hand. "Most often that's the way of it, in fact."

"Aye? I never thought to ask Dougal, or Rupert. Or Jenny. Whether my father—" The sentence stopped abruptly, as though he had swallowed it.

Ah. I felt a small jolt of realization in my solar plexus. So that was it. I hadn't remembered, but he had told me of it, years before, soon after we were married. His father had seen Jamie flogged at Fort William, and under the shock of it, had suffered an apoplexy and died. Jamie, wounded and ill, had been spirited away from the Fort and gone into exile. He had not been told of his father's death until weeks later—had no chance of farewell, had been able neither to bury his father nor honor his grave.

"Jenny would have known," I said gently. "She would have told you, if . . ." If Brian Fraser had suffered a death of such lingering ignominy as this, dwindled and shrunken, powerless before the eyes of the family he had striven to protect.

Would she? If she had nursed her father through incontinence and helplessness? If she had waited days or weeks, suddenly bereft of both father and brother, left alone to stare death in the face as it approached, moment by slow moment . . . and yet Jenny Fraser was a very strong woman, who had loved her brother dearly. Perhaps she would have sought to shield him, both from guilt and from knowledge.

I turned to face him. He was half-naked, but clean now, with a fresh shirt from his saddlebag in his hands. He was looking at me, but I saw his eyes slip beyond me, to fasten on the corpse with a troubled fascination.

"She would have told you," I repeated, striving to infuse my voice with certainty.

Jamie drew a deep, painful breath.

"Perhaps."

"She would," I said more firmly.

He nodded, drew another deep breath, and let it out, more easily. I realized that the house was not the only thing haunted by Beardsley's death. Jenny held the key of the only door that could be opened for Jamie, though.

I understood now why he had wept, and had taken such care with the digging of the grave. Not from either shock or charity, let alone from regard for the dead man—but for the sake of Brian Fraser; the father he had neither buried nor mourned.

I turned back and drew the edges of the blanket up, folded them snugly over the cleaned and decent remains, and tied it with twine at head and feet, making a tidy, anonymous package. Jamie was forty-nine; the same age at which his father had died. I stole a quick glance at him, as he finished dressing. If his father had been such a one as he was . . . I felt a sudden pang of sorrow, for the loss of so much. For strength cut off and love snuffed out, for the loss of a man I knew had been great, only from the reflection I saw of him in his son.

Dressed, Jamie circled round the table to help me lift the body. Instead of putting his hands under it, though, he reached across and took my hands in both of his.

"Swear to me, Claire," he said. His voice was nearly gone with hoarseness; I had to lean close to hear it. "If it should one day fall to my lot as it did to my father . . . then swear ye will give me the same mercy I gave this wretched bugger here."

There were fresh blisters on his palms from the digging; I felt the strange softness of them, fluid-filled and shifting as he gripped my hands.

"I'll do what must be done," I whispered back, at last. "Just as you did." I squeezed his hands and let them go. "Come now and help me bury him. It's over."

## 28

## BROWNSVILLE

IT WAS MID-AFTERNOON before Roger, Fergus, and the militia reached Brownsville, having missed their road and wandered in the hills for several hours before meeting two Cherokee who pointed the way.

Brownsville was half a dozen ramshackle huts, strewn among the dying brush of a hillside like a handful of rubbish tossed into the weeds. Near the road—if the narrow rut of churned black mud could be dignified by such a word—two cabins leaned tipsily on either side of a slightly larger and more solid-looking building, like drunkards leaning cozily on a sober companion. Rather ironically, this larger building seemed to operate as Brownsville's general store and tap-room, judging from the barrels of beer and powder and the stacks of drenched hides that stood in the muddy yard beside it—though to apply either term to it was granting that more dignity than it deserved, too, Roger thought.

Still, it was plainly the place to start—if only for the sake of the men with him, who had begun to vibrate like iron filings near a magnet at sight of the barrels; the yeasty scent of beer floated out like a welcome. He wouldn't say no to a pint, either, he thought, waving a hand to signal a halt. It was a numbingly cold day, and a long time since this morning's breakfast. They weren't likely to get anything beyond bread or stew here, but as long as it was hot and washed down with some sort of alcohol, no one would complain.

He slid off his horse, and had just turned to call to the others when a hand clutched his arm.

*"Attendez."* Fergus spoke softly, barely moving his lips. He was standing beside Roger, looking at something beyond him. "Do not move."

Roger didn't, nor did any of the men still on their horses. Whatever Fergus saw, so did they.

"What is it?" Roger asked, keeping his voice low, too.

"Someone—two someones—are pointing guns at us, through the window."

"Ah." Roger noted Jamie's good sense in not riding into Brownsville after dark the night before. Evidently, he knew something about the suspicious nature of remote places.

Moving very slowly, he raised both his hands into the air, and jerked his chin at Fergus, who reluctantly did the same, his hook gleaming in the afternoon sun. Still keeping his hands up, Roger turned very slowly. Even knowing what to expect, he felt his stomach contract at sight of the two long, gleaming barrels protruding from behind the oiled deerskin that covered the window.

"Hallo the house!" he shouted, with as much authority as could be managed with his hands over his head. "I am

Captain Roger MacKenzie, in command of a militia company under Colonel James Fraser, of Fraser's Ridge!"

The only effect of this intelligence was to cause one gun barrel to swivel, centering on Roger, so that he could look straight down the small, dark circle of its muzzle. The unwelcome prospect did, though, cause him to realize that the other gun had not been trained on him to start with. It had been, and remained, pointing steadily over his right shoulder, toward the cluster of men who still sat their horses behind him, shifting in their saddles and murmuring uneasily.

Great. Now what? The men were waiting for him to do *something*. Moving slowly, he lowered his hands. He was drawing breath to shout again, but before he could speak, a hoarse voice rang out from behind the deerskin.

"I see you, Morton, you bastard!"

This imprecation was accompanied by a significant jerk of the first gun barrel, which turned abruptly from Roger to focus on the same target as the second—presumably Isaiah Morton, one of the militiamen from Granite Falls.

There was a scuffling noise among the mounted men, startled shouts, and then all hell broke loose as both guns went off. Horses reared and bolted, men bellowed and swore, and drifts of acrid white smoke fumed from the window.

Roger had thrown himself flat at the first explosion. As the echoes died away, though, he scrambled up as though by reflex, flung mud out of his eyes, and charged the door, headfirst. To his detached surprise, his mind was working very clearly. Brianna took twenty seconds to load and prime a gun, and he doubted that these buggers were much faster. He thought he had just about ten seconds' grace left, and he meant to use them.

He hit the door with his shoulder, and it flew inward, smashing against the wall inside and causing Roger to rush staggering into the room and crash into the wall on the opposite side. He struck his shoulder a numbing blow on the chimney piece, bounced off, and managed somehow to keep his feet, stumbling like a drunkard.

Several people in the room had turned to gape at him. His vision cleared enough to see that only two of them were in fact holding guns. He took a deep breath, lunged for the nearest of these, a scrawny man with a straggling beard, and seized him by the shirtfront, in imitation of a particularly fearsome third-form master at Roger's grammar school.

"What do you think you are doing, you *wee* man, you!?" he roared, jerking the man up onto his toes. Mr. Sanderson would have been pleased, he supposed, at the thought that his example had been so memorable. Effective, too; while the scrawny man in Roger's grip did not either wet himself or snivel, as the first-form students occasionally had under such treatment, he did make small gobbling sounds, pawing ineffectually at Roger's hand clutching his shirt.

"You, sir! Leave hold of my brother!" Roger's victim had dropped both his gun and powder horn when seized, spilling black powder all over the floor. The other gunman had succeeded in reloading his weapon, though, and was now endeavoring to bring it to bear on Roger. He was somewhat impeded in this attempt by the three women in the room, two of whom were blethering and pulling at his gun, getting in his way. The third had flung her apron over her head and was uttering loud, rhythmic shrieks of hysteria.

At this point, Fergus strolled into the house, an enormous horse pistol in his hand. He pointed this negligently at the man with the gun.

"Be so kind as to put that down, if you will," he said, raising his voice to be heard above the racket. "And perhaps, Madame, you could pour some water upon this young woman? Or slap her briskly?" He gestured toward the screaming woman with his hook, wincing slightly at the noise.

Moving as though hypnotized, one of the women went slowly toward the screeching girl, shook her roughly by the shoulder, and began to murmur in the girl's ear, not taking her eyes off Fergus. The shrieking stopped, replaced by irregular gulps and sobs.

Roger felt an immense relief. Sheer rage, simple panic, and the absolute necessity of doing *something* had got him this far, but he would freely admit that he had not the slightest idea what to do next. He took a deep breath, feeling his legs begin to tremble, and slowly lowered his victim, releasing his grip with an awkward nod. The man took several fast steps backward, then stood brushing at the creases in his shirt, narrowed eyes fixed on Roger in resentment.

"And who in blazes are *you*?" The second man, who had indeed put his weapon down, looked at Fergus in confusion.

The Frenchman waved his hook—which, Roger noticed, seemed to fascinate the women—in a gesture of dismissal.

"That is of no importance," he said grandly, lifting his aristocratically prominent nose another inch. "I require—that is, *we* require"—he amended, with a polite nod toward Roger—"to know who *you* are."

The inhabitants of the cabin all exchanged confused looks, as though wondering who they might in fact be. After a moment's hesitation, though, the larger of the two men thrust out his chin pugnaciously.

"My name is Brown, sir. Richard Brown. This is my brother, Lionel, my wife, Meg, my brother's daughter, Alicia"—that appeared to be the girl in the apron, who had now removed the garment from her head and stood tearstained and gulping—"and my sister, Thomasina."

"Your servant, Madame, Mesdemoiselles." Fergus made the ladies an extremely elegant bow, though taking good care to keep his pistol aimed at Richard Brown's forehead. "My apologies for the disturbance."

Mrs. Brown nodded back, looking a little glazed. Miss Thomasina Brown, a tall, severe-looking person, looked from Roger to Fergus and back with the expression of one comparing a cockroach and a centipede, deciding which to step on first.

Fergus, having managed to transform the atmosphere from an armed confrontation to that of a Parisian *salon*, looked pleased. He glanced at Roger and inclined his head, clearly handing management of the situation over to him.

"Right." Roger was wearing a loose woolen hunting shirt, but he felt as though it were a straitjacket. He took another deep breath, trying to force air into his chest. "Well. As I said, I am . . . ah . . . Captain MacKenzie. We are charged by Governor Tryon with raising a militia company, and have come to notify you of your obligation to provide men and supplies."

Richard Brown looked surprised at this; his brother glowered. Before they could offer objections, though, Fergus moved closer to Roger, murmuring, "Perhaps we should discover whether they have killed Mr. Morton, *mon capitaine*, before we accept them into our company?"

"Oh, mphm." Roger fixed the Browns with as stern an expression as possible. "Mr. Fraser. Will you see about Mr. Morton? I will remain here." Keeping the Browns in his gaze, he held out a hand for Fergus's pistol.

"Oh, yon Morton's still canty, Captain. He isny wae us, forbye, 'cause he's ta'en to the broosh like a bit' moggie wae a scorchit tail, but he wiz movin' a' his limbs when I saw um last." A nasal Glaswegian voice spoke from the doorway, and Roger glanced over to see a cluster of interested heads peering into the cabin, Henry Gallegher's bristly nob among them. A number of drawn guns were also in evidence, and Roger's breath came a little easier.

The Browns had lost interest in Roger, and were staring at Gallegher in sheer bewilderment.

"What did he say?" Mrs. Brown whispered to her sister-in-law. The older lady shook her head, lips drawn in like a pursestring.

"Mr. Morton is alive and well," Roger translated for them. He coughed. "Fortunately for you," he said to the male Browns, with as much menace as he could contrive to put into his voice. He turned to Gallegher, who had now come into the room and was leaning against the doorjamb, musket in hand and looking distinctly entertained.

"Is everyone else all right, then, Henry?"

Gallegher shrugged.

"They crap-bags hivny holed anyone, but they gie'd your saddlebag rare laldy wae a load o' bird shot. Sir," he added as an afterthought, teeth showing in a brief flash through his beard.

"The bag with the whisky?" Roger demanded.

"Get awa!" Gallegher bugged his eyes in horror, then grinned in reassurance. "Nah, t'other."

"Och, well." Roger waved a hand dismissively. "That's only my spare breeks, isn't it?"

This philosophical response drew laughter and hoots of support from the men crammed in the doorway, which heartened Roger enough to round on the smaller Brown.

"And what d'ye have against Isaiah Morton?" he demanded.

"He's dishonored my daughter," Mr. Brown replied promptly, having recovered his composure. He glared at Roger, beard twitching with anger. "I told him I'd see him dead at her feet, if ever he dared show his wretched countenance within ten miles of Brownsville—and damn my eyes if the grass-livered spittle-snake hasn't the face to ride right up to my door!"

Mr. Richard Brown turned to Gallegher.

"You mean to tell me we both *missed* the bastard?"

Gallegher shrugged apologetically.

"Aye. Sorry."

The younger Miss Brown had been following this exchange, mouth hanging slightly open.

"They missed?" she asked, hope lighting her reddened eyes. "Isaiah's still alive?"

"Not for long," her uncle assured her grimly. He reached down to pick up his fowling piece, and all the female Browns burst out in a chorus of renewed screeches, as the guns of the militia at the door all raised simultaneously, trained on Brown. He very slowly put the gun back down.

Roger glanced at Fergus, who lifted one brow and gave the slightest of shrugs. Up to him.

The Browns had drawn together, the two brothers glaring at him, the women huddled behind them, sniffling and murmuring. Militiamen poked their heads curiously through the windows, all staring at Roger, waiting for direction.

And just what was he to tell them? Morton was a member of the militia, and therefore—he assumed—entitled to its protection. Roger couldn't very well turn him over to the Browns, no matter what he'd done—always assuming he could be caught. On the other hand, Roger was charged with enlisting the Browns and the rest of the able-bodied men in Brownsville, and extracting at least a week's supplies from them as well; they didn't look as though such a suggestion would be well received at this point.

He had the galling conviction that Jamie Fraser would have known immediately how best to resolve this diplomatic crisis. He personally hadn't a clue.

He did, at least, have a delaying tactic. Sighing, he lowered the pistol, and reached for the pouch at his waist.

"Henry, fetch in the saddlebag with the whisky, aye? And Mr. Brown, perhaps ye will allow me to purchase some food, and a barrel of your beer, for my men's refreshment."

And with luck, by the time it was all drunk, Jamie Fraser would be here.

# ONE-THIRD OF A GOAT

IT WASN'T QUITE OVER, after all. It was well past dark by the time we had finished everything at the Beardsley farm, tidied up, repacked the bags, and resaddled the horses. I thought of suggesting that we eat before leaving—we had had nothing since breakfast—but the atmosphere of the place was so disturbing that neither Jamie nor I had any appetite.

"We'll wait," he said, heaving the saddlebags over the mare's back. He glanced over his shoulder at the house. "I'm hollow as a gourd, but I couldna stomach a bite within sight o' this place."

"I know what you mean." I glanced back, too, uneasily, though there was nothing to see; the house stood still and empty. "I can't wait to get away from here."

The sun had sunk below the trees, and a chill blue shadow spread across the hollow where the farmhouse stood. The raw earth of Beardsley's grave showed dark with moisture, a humped mound beneath the bare branches of the mountain ash. It was impossible to look at it without thinking of the weight of wet earth and immobility, of corruption and decay.

*You will rot and die*, Jamie had said to him. I hoped the reversal of those two events had been of some benefit to Beardsley—it had not, to me. I hugged my shawl tight around my shoulders and breathed out hard, then deeply in, hoping the cold, clean scent of the pines would eradicate the phantom reek of dead flesh that seemed to cling to hands and clothes and nose.

The horses were shifting, stamping, and shaking their manes, eager to be off. I didn't blame them. Unable to stop myself, I looked back once more. A more desolate sight would be hard to imagine. Even harder to imagine was the thought of staying here, alone.

Evidently, Mrs. Beardsley *had* imagined it, and come to similar conclusions. At this point, she emerged from the barn, the kid in her arms, and announced that she was coming with us. So, evidently, were the goats. She handed me the kid, and disappeared back into the barn.

The kid was heavy and half-asleep, flexible little joints folded up into a cozy bundle. It huffed warm air over my hand, nibbling gently to see what I was made of, then made a small "meh" of contentment and relaxed into peaceful inertness against my ribs. A louder "meh!" and a nudge at my thigh announced the presence of the kid's mother, keeping a watchful eye on her offspring.

"Well, she can't very well leave them here," I muttered to Jamie, who was making disgruntled noises in the dusk behind me. "They have to be milked. Besides, it's not a terribly long way, is it?"

"D'ye ken how fast a goat walks, Sassenach?"

"I've never had occasion to time one," I said, rather testily, shifting my small hairy burden. "But I shouldn't think they'd be a lot slower than the horses, in the dark."

He made a guttural Scottish noise at that, rendered more expressive even than usual by the phlegm in his throat. He coughed.

"You sound awful," I said. "When we get where we're going, I'm taking the mentholated goose grease to you, my lad."

He made no objection to this proposal, which rather alarmed me, as indicating a serious depression of his vitality. Before I could inquire further into his state of health, though, I was interrupted by the emergence from the barn of Mrs. Beardsley, leading six goats, roped together like a gang of jovially inebriate convicts.

Jamie viewed the procession dubiously, sighed in resignation, and turned to a consideration of the logistical problems at hand. There was no question of mounting Mrs. Beardsley on Gideon the Man-Eater. Jamie glanced from me to Mrs. Beardsley's substantial figure, then at the small form of my mare, little bigger than a pony, and coughed.

After a bit of contemplation, he had Mrs. Beardsley mounted on Mrs. Piggy, the sleepy kid balanced before her. I would ride with him, on Gideon's withers, theoretically preventing any attempt on that animal's part to fling me off his hindquarters into the underbrush. He tied a rope round the billy goat's neck, and affixed this loosely to the mare's saddle, but left the nannies loose.

"The mother will stay wi' the kid, and the others will follow the billy here," he told me. "Goats are sociable creatures; they'll no be wanting to stray awa by themselves. Especially not at night. Shoo," he muttered, pushing an inquisitive nose out of his face as he squatted to check the saddle girth. "I suppose pigs would be worse. They *will* gang their own way." He stood up, absently patting a hairy head.

"If anything should come amiss, pull it loose at once," he told Mrs. Beardsley, showing her the half-bow loop tied to the saddle near her hand. "If the horse should run away wi' ye all, your wee fellow there will be hangit."

She nodded, a hunched mound atop the horse, then lifted her head and looked toward the house.

"We should go before moonrithe," she said softly. "She cometh out then."

An icy ripple ran straight up my spine, and Jamie jerked, head snapping round to look at the darkened house. The fire had gone out, and no one had thought to close the open door; it gaped like an empty eye socket.

"She *who*?" Jamie asked, a noticeable edge in his voice.

"Mary Ann," Mrs. Beardsley answered. "She was the latht

one." There was no emphasis whatever in her voice; she sounded like a sleepwalker.

"The last *what*?" I asked.

The latht wife," she replied, and picked up her reins. "She thtands under the rowan tree at moonrithe."

Jamie's head turned toward me. It was too dark to see his expression, but I didn't need to. I cleared my throat.

"Ought we . . . to close the door?" I suggested. Mr. Beardsley's spirit had presumably got the idea by now, and whether or not Mrs. Beardsley had any interest in the house and its contents, it didn't seem right to leave it at the mercy of marauding raccoons and squirrels, to say nothing of anything larger that might be attracted by the scent of Mr. Beardsley's final exit. On the other hand, I really had no desire at all to approach the empty house.

"Get on the horse, Sassenach."

Jamie strode across the yard, slammed the door somewhat harder than necessary, then came back—walking briskly—and swung into the saddle behind me.

"Hup!" he said sharply, and we were off, the glow of a rising half-moon just visible above the trees.

It was perhaps a quarter mile to the head of the trail, the ground rising from the hollow in which the Beardsleys' farmhouse stood. We were moving slowly, because of the goats, and I watched the grass and shrubs as we brushed through them, wondering whether they seemed more visible only because my eyes were adapting to the dark—or because the moon had risen.

I felt quite safe, with the powerful bulk of the horse under me, the sociable natter of the goats around us, and Jamie's equally reassuring presence behind me, one arm clasped about my waist. I wasn't sure that I felt quite safe enough to turn and look back again, though. At the same time, the urge to look was so compelling as almost to counter the sense of dread I felt about the place. Almost.

"It's no really a rowan tree, is it?" Jamie's voice came softly from behind me.

"No," I said, taking heart from the solid arm around me. "It's a mountain ash. Very like, though." I'd seen mountain ash many times before; the Highlanders often planted them near cabins or houses because the clusters of deep orange berries and the pinnate leaves did indeed look like the rowan tree of Scotland—a close botanical relative. I gathered that Jamie's comment stemmed not from taxonomic hairsplitting, though, but rather from doubt as to whether the ash possessed the same repellent qualities, in terms of protection from evil and enchantment. He hadn't chosen to bury Beardsley under that tree from a sense either of aesthetics or convenience.

I squeezed his blistered hand, and he kissed me gently on top of the head.

At the head of the trail, I did glance back, but I could see nothing but a faint gleam from the weathered shingles of the farmhouse. The mountain ash and whatever might—or might not—be under it were hidden in darkness.

Gideon was unusually well-behaved, having made no more than a token protest at being double-mounted. I rather thought he was happy to leave the farm behind, too. I said as much, but Jamie sneezed and expressed the opinion that the wicked sod was merely biding his time while planning some future outrage.

The goats seemed inclined to view this nocturnal excursion as a lark, and ambled along with the liveliest interest, snatching mouthfuls of dry grass, bumping into one another and the horses, and generally sounding like a herd of elephants in the crackling underbrush.

I felt great relief at leaving the Beardsley place at last. As the pines blotted out the last sight of the hollow, I resolutely turned my mind from the disturbing events of the day, and began to think what might await us in Brownsville.

"I hope Roger's managed all right," I said, leaning back against Jamie's chest with a small sigh.

"Mmphm." From long experience, I diagnosed this particular catarrhal noise as indicating a polite general agreement with my sentiment, this overlaying complete personal indifference to the actuality. Either he saw no reason for concern, or he thought Roger could sink or swim.

"I hope he's found an inn of sorts," I offered, thinking this prospect might meet with a trifle more enthusiasm. "Hot food and a clean bed would be lovely."

"Mmphm." That one held a touch of humor, mingled with an inborn skepticism—fostered by long experience—regarding the possible existence of such items as hot food and clean beds in the Carolina backcountry.

"The goats seem to be going along very well," I offered, and waited in anticipation.

"Mmphm." Grudging agreement, mingled with a deep suspicion as to the continuance of good behavior on the part of the goats.

I was carefully formulating another observation, in hopes of getting him to do it again—three times was the record so far—when Gideon suddenly bore out Jamie's original mistrust by flinging up his head with a loud snort and rearing.

I crashed back into Jamie's chest, hitting my head on his collarbone with a thump that made me see stars. His arm crushed the air out of me as he dragged at the reins one-handed, shouting.

I had no idea what he was saying, or even whether he was shouting in English or Gaelic. The horse was screaming, rearing and pawing with his hooves, and I was scrabbling for a grip on anything at all, mane, saddle, reins. . . . A branch whipped my face and blinded me. Pandemonium reigned; there was screeching and bleating and a noise like tearing fabric and then something hit me hard and sent me flying into the darkness.

I wasn't knocked out, but it didn't make much difference. I was sprawled in a tangle of brush, struggling for breath, unable to move, and unable to see anything whatever beyond a few scattered stars in the sky overhead.

There was an ungodly racket going on some little distance away, in which a chorus of panicked goats figured largely, punctuated by what I took to be a woman's screams. Two women's screams.

I shook my head, confused. Then I flung myself over and started crawling, having belatedly recognized what was making that noise. I had heard panthers scream often enough—but always safely far in the distance. This one wasn't far away at all. The tearing-fabric noise I'd heard had been the cough of a big cat, very close at hand.

I bumped into a large fallen log and promptly rolled under

it, wedging myself as far into the small crevice there as possible. It wasn't the best hiding place I'd ever seen, but might at least prevent anything leaping out of a tree onto me.

I could still hear Jamie shouting, though the tenor of his remarks had changed to a sort of hoarse fury. The goats had mostly quit yammering—surely the cat couldn't have killed all of them? I couldn't hear anything of Mrs. Beardsley, either, but the horses were making a dreadful fuss, squealing and stamping.

My heart was hammering against the leafy ground, and a cold sweat tingled along my jaw. There isn't much for invoking raw terror like the primitive fear of being eaten, and my sympathies were entirely with the animals. There was a crashing in the brush near at hand, and Jamie shouting my name.

"Here," I croaked, unwilling to move out of my refuge until I knew for certain where the panther was—or at least knew for certain that it wasn't anywhere near me. The horses had stopped squealing, though they were still snorting and stamping, making enough noise to indicate that neither of them had either fallen prey to our visitor or run away.

"Here!" I called, a little louder.

More crashing, close at hand. Jamie stumbled through the darkness, crouched, and felt under the log until his hand encountered my arm, which he seized.

"Are ye all right, Sassenach?"

"I hadn't thought to notice, but I think so," I replied. I slid cautiously out from under my log, taking stock. Bruises here and there, abraded elbows, and a stinging sensation where the branch had slapped my cheek. Basically all right, then.

"Good. Come quick, he's hurt." He hauled me to my feet and started propelling me through the dark with a hand in the small of my back.

"Who?"

"The goat, of course."

My eyes were well-adapted to the dark by now, and I made out the large shapes of Gideon and the mare, standing under a leafless poplar, manes and tails swishing with agitation. A smaller shape that I took to be Mrs. Beardsley was crouched nearby, over something on the ground.

I could smell blood, and a powerful reek of goat. I squatted and reached out, touching rough, warm hair. The goat
jerked at my touch, with a loud "MEHeheh!" that reassured
me somewhat. He might be hurt, but he wasn't dying—at
least not yet; the body under my hands was solid and vital,
muscles tense.

"Where's the cat?" I asked, locating the ridged hardness
of the horns and feeling my way hastily backward along the
spine, then down the ribs and flanks. The goat had objections, and heaved wildly under my hands.

"Gone," Jamie said. He crouched down, too, and put a
hand on the goat's head. "There, now, *a bhalaich*. It's all
right, then. *Seas, mo charaid.*"

I could feel no open wound on the goat's body, but I could
certainly smell blood; a hot, metallic scent that disturbed the
clean night air of the wood. The horses did, too; they whick-
ered and moved uneasily in the dark.

"Are we fairly *sure* it's gone?" I asked, trying to ignore the
sensation of eyes fastened on the back of my neck. "I smell
blood."

"Aye. The cat took one of the nannies," Jamie informed
me. He knelt next to me, laying a big hand on the goat's
neck.

"Mrs. Beardsley loosed this brave laddie, and he went for
the cat, bald-heided. I couldna see it all, but I think the creature maybe slapped at him; I heard it screech and spit, and
the billy gave a skelloch just then, too. I think his leg is
maybe broken."

It was. With that guidance, I found the break easily, low
on the radius of the right front leg. The skin wasn't broken,
but the bone was cracked through; I could feel the slight dis-
placement of the raw ends. The goat heaved and thrust his
horns at my arm when I touched the leg. His eyes were wild
and rolling, the odd square pupils visible but colorless in the
faint moonlight.

"Can ye mend him, Sassenach?" Jamie asked.

"I don't know." The goat was still struggling, but the flurries of movement were growing perceptibly weaker, as shock
set in. I bit my lip, groping for a pulse in the fold between leg
and body. The injury itself was likely repairable, but shock

was a great danger; I had seen plenty of animals—and a few people, for that matter—die quickly following a traumatic incident, of injuries that were not fatal in themselves.

"I don't know," I said again. My fingers had found a pulse at last; it was trip-hammer fast, and thready. I was trying to envision the possibilities for treatment, all of them crude. "He may well die, Jamie, even if I can set the leg. Do you think perhaps we ought to slaughter him? He'd be a lot easier to carry, as meat."

Jamie stroked the goat's neck, gently.

"It would be a great shame, and him such a gallant creature."

Mrs. Beardsley laughed at that, a nervous small giggle, like a girl's, coming out of the dark beyond Jamie's bulk.

"Hith name ith Hiram," she said. "He'th a good boy."

"Hiram," Jamie repeated, still stroking. "Well, then, Hiram. *Courage, mon brave.* You'll do. You've balls as big as melons."

"Well, persimmons, maybe," I said, having inadvertently encountered the testicles in question while making my examination. "Perfectly respectable, though, I'm sure," I added, taking shallow breaths. Hiram's musk glands were working overtime. Even the harsh iron smell of blood took second place.

"I was speaking figuratively," Jamie informed me, rather dryly. "What will ye be needing, Sassenach?"

Evidently, the decision had been made; he was already rising to his feet.

"Right, then," I said, brushing back my hair with the back of a wrist. "Find me a couple of straight branches, about a foot long, no twigs, and a bit of rope from the saddlebags. Then you can help here," I added, trying to achieve a good grip on my struggling patient. "Hiram seems to like you. Recognizes a kindred spirit, no doubt."

Jamie laughed at that, a low, comforting sound at my elbow. He stood up with a final scratch of Hiram's ears, and rustled off, coming back within moments with the requested items.

"Right," I said, loosing one hand from Hiram's neck in order to locate the sticks. "I'm going to splint it. We'll have to carry him, but the splint will keep the leg from flexing and doing any more damage. Help me get him onto his side." Hiram, whether from male pride or goat stubbornness—always assuming these to be different things—kept trying to stand up, broken leg notwithstanding. His head was bobbing alarmingly, though, as the muscles in his neck weakened, and his body lurched from side to side. He scrabbled feebly at the ground, then stopped, panting heavily.

Mrs. Beardsley hovered over my shoulder, the kid still clutched in her arms. It gave a faint bleat, as though it had awakened suddenly from a nightmare, and Hiram gave a loud, echoing "Mehh" in reply.

"There's a thought," Jamie murmured. He stood up suddenly, and took the kid from Mrs. Beardsley. Then he knelt down again, pushing the little creature up close to Hiram's side. The goat at once ceased struggling, bending his head around to sniff at his offspring. The kid cried, pushing its nose against the big goat's side, and a long, slimy tongue snaked out, slobbering over my hand as it sought the kid's head.

"Work fast, Sassenach," Jamie suggested.

I needed no prompting, and within minutes, had the leg stabilized, the splinting padded with one of the multiple shawls Mrs. Beardsley appeared to be wearing. Hiram had settled, making only occasional grunts and exclamations, but the kid was still bleating loudly.

"Where is its mother?" I asked, though I didn't need to hear the answer. I didn't know a great deal about goats, but I knew enough about mothers and babies to realize that nothing but death would keep a mother from a child making that sort of racket. The other goats had come back, drawn by curiosity, fear of the dark, or a simple desire for company, but the mother didn't push forward.

"Poor Beckie," said Mrs. Beardsley sadly. "Thuch a thweet goat."

Dark forms bumped and jostled; there was a whuff of hot air in my ear as one nibbled at my hair, and another stepped on my calf, making me yelp as the sharp little hooves scraped the skin. I made no effort to shoo them away, though; the presence of his harem seemed to be doing Hiram the world of good.

I had the leg bones back in place and the splint bandaged firmly round them. I had found a good pulse point at the base of his ear, and was monitoring it, Hiram's head resting in my lap. As the other goats pressed in, nuzzling at him and making plaintive noises, he suddenly lifted his head and rolled up onto his chest, the broken leg awkwardly stuck out before him in its bindings.

He swayed to and fro like a drunken man for a moment, then uttered a loud, belligerent "MEEEEEHHH" and lurched onto three feet. He promptly fell down again, but the action cheered everyone. Even Mrs. Beardsley emitted a faint trill of pleasure at the sight.

"All right." Jamie stood up, and ran his fingers through his hair with a deep sigh. "Now, then."

"Now, then *what*?" I asked.

"Now I shall decide what to do," he said, with a certain edge to his voice.

"Aren't we going on to Brownsville?"

"We might," he said. "If Mrs. Beardsley happens to ken the way well enough to find the trail again by starlight?" He turned expectantly toward her, but I could see the negative motion of her head, even in the shadows.

It dawned on me that we were, in fact, no longer on the trail—which was in any case no more than a narrow deer track, winding through the forest.

"We can't be terribly far off it, surely?" I looked round, peering vainly into the dark, as though some lighted sign might indicate the position of the trail. In fact, I had no idea even in which direction it might lie.

"No," Jamie agreed. "And by myself, I daresay I could pick it up sooner or later. But I dinna mean to go floundering through the forest in the dark with this lot." He glanced round, evidently counting noses. Two very skittish horses, two women—one distinctly odd and possibly homicidal— and six goats, two of them incapable of walking. I rather saw his point.

He drew his shoulders back, shrugging a little, as though to ease a tight shirt.

"I'll go and have a keek round. If I find the way at once, well and good. If I don't, we'll camp for the night," he said.

"It will be a deal easier to look for the trail by daylight. Be careful, Sassenach."

And with a final sneeze, he vanished into the woods, leaving me in charge of the camp followers and wounded.

The orphaned goat was becoming louder and more anguished in its cries; it hurt my ears, as well as my heart. Mrs. Beardsley, though, had become somewhat more animated in Jamie's absence; I thought she was rather afraid of him. Now she brought up one of the other nannies, persuading her to stand still for the orphan to suckle. The kid was reluctant for a moment, but hunger and the need for warmth and reassurance were overwhelming, and within a few minutes, it was feeding busily, its small tail wagging in a dark flicker of movement.

I was happy to see it, but conscious of a small feeling of envy; I was all at once aware that I had eaten nothing all day, that I was very cold, desperately tired, sore in a number of places—and that without the complications of Mrs. Beardsley and her companions, I would long since have been safely in Brownsville, fed, warm, and tucked up by some friendly fireside. I put a hand on the kid's stomach, growing round and firm with milk, and thought rather wistfully that I should like someone simply to take care of *me*. Still, for the moment, I seemed to be the Good Shepherd, and no help for it.

"Do you think it might come back?" Mrs. Beardsley crouched next to me, shawl pulled tight around her broad shoulders. She spoke in a low tone, as though afraid someone might overhear.

"What, the panther? No, I don't think so. Why should it?" Nonetheless, a small shiver ran over me, as I thought of Jamie, alone somewhere in the dark. Hiram, his shoulder firmly jammed against my thigh, snorted, then laid his head on my knee with a long sigh.

"Thome folk thay the catth hunt in pairth."

"Really?" I stifled a yawn—not of boredom, simply fatigue. I blinked into the darkness, a chilled lethargy stealing over me. "Oh. Well, I should think a good-sized goat would do for two. Besides"—I yawned again, a jaw-cracking stretch—"besides, the horses would let us know."

Gideon and Mrs. Piggy were companionably nose-and-tailing it under the poplar tree, showing no signs now of agitation. This seemed to comfort Mrs. Beardsley, who sat down on the ground quite suddenly, her shoulders sagging as though the air had gone out of her.

"And how are you feeling?" I inquired, more from an urge to maintain conversation than from any real desire to know.

"I am glad to be gone from that place," she said simply.

I definitely shared that sentiment; our present situation was at least an improvement on the Beardsley homestead, even with the odd panther thrown in. Still, that didn't mean I was anxious to spend very long here.

"Do you know anyone in Brownsville?" I asked. I wasn't sure how large a settlement it was, though from the conversation of some of the men we had picked up, it sounded like a fair-sized village.

"No." She was silent for a moment, and I felt rather than saw her tilt back her head, looking up at the stars and the peaceful moon.

"I . . . have never been to Brownsville," she added, almost shyly.

Or anywhere else, it seemed. She told the story hesitantly, but almost eagerly, with no more than slight prodding on my part.

Beardsley had—in essence—bought her from her father, and brought her, with other goods acquired in Baltimore, down to his house, where he had essentially kept her prisoner, forbidding her to leave the homestead, or to show herself to anyone who might come to the house. Left to do the work of the homestead while Beardsley traveled into the Cherokee lands with his trade goods, she had had no society but a bond lad—who was little company, being deaf and speechless.

"Really," I said. In the events of the day, I had quite forgotten Josiah and his twin. I wondered whether she had known both of them, or only Keziah.

"How long is it since you came to North Carolina?" I asked.

"Two yearth," she said softly. "Two yearth, three month, and five dayth." I remembered the marks on the doorpost, and wondered when she had begun to keep count. From the very beginning? I stretched my back, disturbing Hiram, who grumbled.

"I see. By the way, what is your Christian name?" I asked, belatedly aware that I had no idea.

"Frantheth," she said, then tried again, not liking the mumbled sound of it. "Fran-*cess*," the end of it a hiss through her broken teeth. She gave a shrug, then, and laughed—a small, shy sound. "Fanny," she said. "My mother called me Fanny."

"Fanny," I said, encouragingly. "That's a very nice name. May I call you so?"

"I . . . would be pleathed," she said. She drew breath again, but stopped without speaking, evidently too shy to say whatever she'd had in mind. With her husband dead, she seemed entirely passive, quite deprived of the force that had animated her earlier.

"Oh," I said, belatedly realizing. "Claire. Do call me Claire, please."

"Claire—how pretty."

"Well, it hasn't any esses, at least," I said, not thinking. "Oh—I do beg your pardon!"

She made a small *pff* sound of dismissal. Encouraged by the dark, the faint sense of intimacy engendered by the exchange of names—or simply from a need to talk, after so long—she told me about her mother, who had died when she was twelve, her father, a crabber, and her life in Baltimore, wading out along the shore at low tide to rake oysters and gather mussels, watching the fishing craft and the warships come in past Fort Howard to sail up the Patapsco.

"It wath . . . peatheful," she said, rather wistfully. "It wath tho open—nothing but the thky and the water." She tilted back her head again, as though yearning for the small bit of night sky visible through the interlacing branches overhead. I supposed that while the forested mountains of North Carolina were refuge and embrace to a Highlander like Jamie, they might well seem claustrophobic and alien to someone accustomed to the watery Chesapeake shore.

"Will you go back there, do you think?" I asked.

"Back?" She sounded slightly startled. "Oh. I . . . I hadn't thought . . ."

"No?" I had found a tree trunk to lean against, and stretched slightly, to ease my back. "You must have seen that your—that Mr. Beardsley was dying. Didn't you have some plan?" Beyond the fun of torturing him slowly to death, that is. It occurred to me that I had been getting altogether too comfortable with this woman, alone in the dark with the goats. She might truly have been Beardsley's victim—or she might only be saying so now, to enlist our aid. It would behoove me to remember the burned toes on Beardsley's foot, and the appalling state of that loft. I straightened up a little, and felt for the small knife I carried at my belt—just in case.

"No." She sounded a little dazed—and no wonder, I supposed. I felt more than a little dazed myself, simply from emotion and fatigue. Enough so that I almost missed what she said next.

"What did you say?"

"I thaid . . . Mary Ann didn't tell me what I wath to do . . . after."

"Mary Ann," I said cautiously. "Yes, and that would be . . . the first Mrs. Beardsley, would it?"

She laughed, and the hair on my neck rippled unpleasantly.

"Oh, no. Mary Ann wath the fourth one."

"The . . . fourth one," I said, a little faintly.

"Thye'th the only one he buried under the rowan tree," she informed me. "That wath a mithtake. The otherth are in the woodth. He got lazy, I think; he did not want to walk tho far."

"Oh," I said, for lack of any better response.

"I told you—sshe thtands under the rowan tree at moonrithe. When I thaw her there at firtht, I thought sshe wath a living woman. I wath afraid of what *he* might do, if he thaw her there alone—tho I sstole from the houthe to warn her."

"I see." Something in my voice must have sounded less than credulous, for her head turned sharply toward me. I took a firmer grip on the knife.

"You do not believe me?"

"Of course I do!" I assured her, trying to edge Hiram's head off my lap. My left leg had gone to sleep from the pressure of his weight, and I had no feeling in my foot.

"I can thow you," she said, and her voice was calm and

certain. "Mary Ann told me where they were—the otherth—and I found them. I can thow you their graveth."

"I'm sure that won't be necessary," I said, flexing my toes to restore circulation. If she came toward me, I decided, I would shove the goat into her path, roll to the side, and make off as fast as possible on all fours, shouting for Jamie. And where in bloody hell *was* Jamie, anyway?

"So . . . um . . . Fanny. You're saying that Mr. Beardsley"—it occurred to me that I didn't know his name either, but I thought I would just as soon keep my relations with his memory formal, under the circumstances—"that your husband *murdered* four wives? And no one knew?" Not that anyone necessarily *would* know, I realized. The Beardsley homestead was very isolated, and it wasn't at all unusual for women to die—of accident, childbirth, or simple overwork. Someone might have known that Beardsley had lost four wives—but it was entirely possible that no one cared how.

"Yeth." She sounded calm, I thought; not incipiently dangerous, at least. "He would have killed me, too—but Mary Ann thtopped him."

"How did she do that?"

She drew a deep breath and sighed, settling herself on the ground. There was a faint, sleepy bleat from her lap, and I realized that she was holding the kid again. I relaxed my grip on the knife; she could hardly attack me with a lapful of goat.

She had, she said, gone out to speak to Mary Ann whenever the moon was high; the ghostly woman appeared under the rowan tree only between half-moon wax and half-moon wane—not in the dark of the moon, or at creseent.

"Very particular," I murmured, but she didn't notice, being too absorbed in the story.

This had gone on for some months. Mary Ann had told Fanny Beardsley who she was, informed her of the fate of her predecessors, and the manner of her own death.

"He choked her," Fanny confided. "I could see the markth of his handth on her throat. Sshe warned me that he would do the thame to me, one day."

One night a few weeks later, Fanny was sure that the time had come.

"He wath far gone with the rum, you thee," she explained. "It wath alwayth worth when he drank, and thith time . . ."

Trembling with nerves, she had dropped the trencher with his supper, splattering food on him. He had sprung to his feet with a roar, lunging for her, and she had turned and fled.

"He wath between me and the door," she said. "I ran for the loft. I hoped he would be too drunk to manage the ladder, and he wath."

Beardsley had stumbled, lurching, and dragged the ladder down with a crash. As he struggled, mumbling and cursing, to put it into place again, there came a knock on the door.

Beardsley shouted to know who it was, but no answer came; only another knock at the door. Fanny had crept to the edge of the loft, to see his red face glaring up at her. The knock sounded for a third time. His tongue was too thick with drink to speak coherently; he only growled in his throat and held up a finger in warning to her, then turned and staggered toward the door. He wrenched it open, looked out—and screamed.

"I have never heard thuch a thound," she said, very softly. "Never."

Beardsley turned and ran, tripping over a stool and sprawling full-length, scrabbling to his feet, stumbling to the foot of the ladder and scrambling up it, missing rungs and clawing for purchase, crying out and shouting.

"He kept thouting to me to help him, help him." Her voice held an odd note; perhaps only astonishment that such a man should have called to her for help—but with a disquieting note that I thought betrayed a deep and secret pleasure in the memory.

Beardsley had reached the top of the ladder, but could not take the final step into the loft. Instead, his face had gone suddenly from red to white, his eyes rolled back, and then he fell senseless onto his face on the boards, his legs dangling absurdly from the edge of the loft.

"I could not get him down; it wath all I could do to pull him up into the loft." She sighed. "And the retht . . . you know."

"Not quite." Jamie spoke from the dark near my shoulder, making me jump. Hiram grunted indignantly, shaken awake.

"How the hell long have *you* been there?" I demanded.

"Long enough." He moved to my side and knelt beside me, a hand on my arm. "And what was it at the door, then?" he asked Mrs. Beardsley. His voice held no more than light interest, but his hand was tight on my arm. A slight shudder went over me. *What*, indeed.

"Nothing," she said simply. "There wath no one there at all, that I could thee. But—you can thee the rowan tree from that door, and there *wath* a half-moon rithing."

There was a marked period of silence at this. Finally, Jamie rubbed a hand hard over his face, sighed, and got to his feet.

"Aye. Well. I've found a spot where we can shelter for the night. Help me wi' the goat, Sassenach."

We were on hilly ground, spiked with rocky outcrops and small tangles of sweet shrub and greenbrier, making the footing between the trees so uncertain in the dark that I fell twice, catching myself only by luck before breaking my neck. It would have been difficult going in broad daylight; by night, it was nearly impossible. Fortunately, it was no more than a short distance to the spot Jamie had found.

This was a sort of shallow gash in the side of a crumbling clay bank, overhung with a tattered grapevine and thatched with matted grasses. At one time, there had been a stream here, and the water had carved away a good-sized chunk of earth from the bank, leaving an overhanging shelf. Something had diverted the flow of water some years ago, though, and the rounded stones of what had been the streambed were scattered and half-sunk in mossy soil; one rolled under my foot and I fell to one knee, striking it painfully on another of the beastly stones.

"All right, Sassenach?" Jamie heard my rude exclamation and stopped, turning toward me. He stood on the hillside just above me, Hiram on his shoulders. From below, silhouetted against the sky, he looked grotesque and rather frightening; a tall, horned figure with hunched and monstrous shoulders.

"Fine," I said, rather breathless. "Just here, is it?"

"Aye. Help me . . . will ye?" He sounded a lot more breathless than I did. He sank carefully to his knees, and I hurried to help him lower Hiram to the ground. Jamie stayed kneeling, one hand on the ground to brace himself.

"I hope it won't be too hard to find the trail in the morning," I said, watching him anxiously. His head was bent with exhaustion, air rattling wetly in his chest with each breath. I wanted him in a place with fire and food, as fast as possible.

He shook his head, and coughed, clearing his throat.

"I ken where it is," he said, and coughed again. "It's only—" The coughing shook him hard; I could see his shoulders braced against it. When he stopped, I put a hand gently on his back, and could feel a fine, constant tremor running through him; not a chill, just the trembling of muscles forced beyond the limits of their strength.

"I canna go any further, Claire," he said softly, as though ashamed of the admission. "I'm done."

"Lie down," I said, just as softly. "I'll see to things."

There was a certain amount of bustle and confusion, but within a half hour or so, everyone was more or less settled, the horses hobbled, and a small fire going.

I knelt to check my chief patient, who was sitting on his chest, splinted leg stuck out in front. Hiram, with his ladies safely gathered behind him in the shelter of the bank, emitted a belligerent "Meh!" and threatened me with his horns.

"Ungrateful sod," I said, pulling back.

Jamie laughed, then broke off to cough, his shoulders shaking with the spasm. He was curled at one side of the depression in the bank, head pillowed on his folded coat.

"And as for you," I said, eyeing him, "I wasn't joking about that goose grease. Open your cloak, lift your shirt, and do it now."

He narrowed his eyes at me, and shot a quick glance in Mrs. Beardsley's direction. I hid a smile at his modesty, but gave Mrs. Beardsley the small kettle from my saddlebag and sent her off to fetch water and more firewood, then dug out the gourd of mentholated ointment.

Jamie's appearance alarmed me slightly, now that I had a good look at him. He was pale and white-lipped, red-rimmed round the nostrils, and his eyes were bruised with fatigue. He looked very sick, and sounded worse, the breath wheezing in his chest with each respiration.

"Well, I suppose if Hiram wouldn't die in front of his nannies, you won't die in front of me, either," I said dubiously, scooping out a thumbful of the fragrant grease.

"I am not dying in the least degree," he said, rather crossly. "I'm only a wee bit tired. I shall be entirely myself in the morn—oh, Christ, I hate this!"

His chest was quite warm, but I thought he wasn't fevered; it was hard to tell, my own fingers being very cold.

He jerked, made a high-pitched "eee" noise, and tried to squirm away. I seized him firmly by the neck, put a knee in his belly, and proceeded to have my way with him, all protests notwithstanding. At length, he gave up struggling and submitted, only giggling intermittently, sneezing, and uttering an occasional small yelp when I reached a particularly ticklish spot. The goats found it all very entertaining.

In a few minutes, I had him well-greased and gasping on the ground, the skin of his chest and throat red from rubbing and shiny with grease, a strong aroma of peppermint and camphor in the air. I patted a thick flannel into place on his chest, pulled down his shirt, drew the folds of his cloak around him, and tucked a blanket up snugly under his chin.

"Now, then," I said with satisfaction, wiping my hands on a cloth. "As soon as I have hot water, we'll have a nice cup of horehound tea."

He opened one eye suspiciously.

"We will?"

"Well, you will. I'd rather drink hot horse piss, myself."

"So would I."

"Too bad; it hasn't any medicinal effects that I know of."

He groaned and shut the eye. He breathed heavily for a moment, sounding like a diseased bellows. Then he raised his head a few inches, opening his eyes.

"Is yon woman back yet?"

"No, I imagine it will take her a little time to find the stream in the dark." I hesitated. "Did you . . . hear everything she was telling me?"

He shook his head.

"Not all—but enough. Mary Ann and that?"

"Yes, that."

He grunted.

"Did ye believe her, Sassenach?"

I didn't reply immediately, but took my time in cleaning the goose grease out from under my fingernails.

"I did at the time," I finally said. "Just now—I'm not sure."

He grunted again, this time with approval.

"I shouldna think she's dangerous," he said. "But keep your wee knife about ye, Sassenach—and dinna turn your back on her. We'll take watch and watch about; wake me in an hour."

He shut his eyes, coughed, and without further ado, fell fast asleep.

CLOUDS WERE BEGINNING to drift across the moon, and a cold wind stirred the grass on the bank above us.

"Wake him in an hour," I muttered, shifting myself in an effort to achieve some minimal level of comfort on the rocky ground. "Ha, bloody ha." I leaned over and hoisted Jamie's head into my lap. He groaned slightly, but didn't twitch.

"Sniffles," I said accusingly to him. "Ha!"

I wriggled my shoulders and leaned back, finding some support against the sloping wall of our shelter. Despite Jamie's warning, it seemed unnecessary to keep an eye on Mrs. Beardsley; she had obligingly built up the fire, then curled up among the goats and—being merely flesh and blood, and therefore exhausted by the day's events—had gone immediately to sleep. I could hear her on the far side of the fire, snoring peacefully among the assorted wheezings and grunts of her companions.

"And what do you think you are, anyway?" I demanded of the heavy head resting on my thigh. "Vulcanized rubber?" My fingers touched his hair, quite without intent, and smoothed it gently. One corner of his mouth lifted suddenly, in a smile of startling sweetness.

It was gone as quickly as it had come, and I stared at him

in astonishment. No, he was sound asleep; his breath came hoarse but even, and the long parti-colored lashes rested dark against his cheeks. Very softly, I stroked his head again.

Sure enough; the smile flickered like the touch of a flame, and disappeared. He sighed, very deeply, bent his neck to nuzzle closer, then relaxed completely, his body going limp.

"Oh, Christ, Jamie," I said softly, and felt tears sting my eyes.

It had been years since I'd seen him smile in his sleep like that. Not since the early days of our marriage, in fact—at Lallybroch.

*He'd always do it as a wee lad*, his sister Jenny had told me then. *I think it means he's happy.*

My fingers curled into the soft, thick hair at the nape of his neck, feeling the solid curve of his skull, the warm scalp and the hair-thin line of the ancient scar across it.

"Me, too," I whispered to him.

## 30

## SPAWN OF SATAN

MRS. MacLEOD and her two children had gone to stay with Evan Lindsay's wife, and with the leaving of the MacLeod brothers with the militia, plus Geordie Chisholm and his two eldest sons, the congestion in the big house was eased substantially. Not nearly enough, though, Brianna reflected, considering that Mrs. Chisholm remained.

The problem was not Mrs. Chisholm as such; the problem was Mrs. Chisholm's five younger children, all boys, and referred to collectively—by Mrs. Bug—as "the spawn of Satan." Mrs. Chisholm, perhaps understandably, objected to this terminology. While the other inhabitants of the house were less forthright than Mrs. Bug in stating their opinions, there was a remarkable unanimity among them. Three-year-old twin boys *would* have that effect, Brianna thought, eyeing Jemmy with some trepidation as she envisioned the future.

He was at the moment giving no indication of a potential for future rampage, being half-asleep on the rag rug of Jamie's study, where Brianna had retired in the faint hope of fifteen minutes' semi-solitude in which to write. Residual awe of Jamie was sufficient to keep the little warts out of this room, for the most part.

Mrs. Bug had informed eight-year-old Thomas, six-year-old Anthony, and five-year-old Toby Chisholm that Mrs. Fraser was a notable witch; a White Lady, who would undoubtedly turn them into toads on the spot—and no great loss to society, she gave them to understand—should any harm come to the contents of her surgery. That didn't keep them out—quite the opposite; they were fascinated—but it had so far prevented them breaking much.

Jamie's inkstand stood to hand on the table; a hollow gourd, neatly corked with a large acorn, with a pottery jar of neatly sharpened turkey quills beside it. Motherhood had taught Brianna to seize random moments; she seized this one, and a quill, flipping open the cover of the small journal in which she kept what she thought of as her private accounts.

> *Last night I dreamed about making soap. I haven't made soap yet, myself, but I'd been scrubbing the floor yesterday, and the smell of the soap was still on my hands when I went to bed. It's a nasty smell, some-thing between acid and ashes, with a horrible faint stink from the hog fat, like something that's been dead for a long time.*
>
> *I was pouring water into a kettle of wood ash, to make lye, and it was turning to lye even as I poured. Big clouds of poisonous smoke were coming up from the kettle; it was yellow, the smoke.*
>
> *Da brought me a big bowl of suet, to mix with the lye, and there were babies' fingers in it. I don't*

*remember thinking there was anything strange about this—at the time.*

Brianna had been trying to ignore a series of crashing noises from upstairs, which sounded like several persons jumping up and down on a bedstead. These ceased abruptly, succeeded by a piercing scream, which in turn was followed by the sound of flesh meeting flesh in a loud slap, and several more screams of assorted pitches.

She flinched and shut her eyes tight, recoiling as the sounds of conflict escalated. A moment more, and they were thundering down the stairs. With a glance at Jemmy, who had been startled awake, but didn't seem frightened—my God, he was getting used to it, she thought—she put down the quill and stood up, sighing.

Mr. Bug was there to tend the farm and livestock and re-pel physical threats; Mr. Wemyss was there to chop firewood, haul water, and generally maintain the fabric of the house. But Mr. Bug was silent, Mr. Wemyss timid; Jamie had left Brianna formally in charge. She was, therefore, the court of appeal, and judge in all conflicts. Herself, if you would.

Herself flung open the study door and glowered at the mob. Mrs. Bug, red in the face—as usual—and brimming with accusation. Mrs. Chisholm, ditto, overflowing with ma-ternal outrage. Little Mrs. Aberfeldy, the color of an egg-plant, clutching her two-year-old daughter, Ruth, protectively to her bosom. Tony and Toby Chisholm, both in tears and covered with snot. Toby had a red handprint on the side of his face; little Ruthie's wispy hair appeared to be oddly shorter on one side than the other. They all began to talk at once.

". . . Red savages!"

". . . My baby's beautiful hair!"

"She started it!"

". . . Dare to strike my son!"

"We was just playin' at scalpin', ma'am . . ."

". . . EEEEEEEEEEE!"

". . . and torn a great hole in my feather bed, the wee spawn!"

"*Look* what she's done, the wicked auld besom!"

"*Look* what they've done!"

"Look ye, ma'am, it's only . . ."

"AAAAAAAAAAA!"

Brianna stepped out into the corridor and slammed the door behind her. It was a solid door, and the resultant boom temporarily halted the outcry. On the other side, Jemmy began to cry, but she ignored him for the moment.

She drew a deep breath, prepared to wade into the melee, but then thought better of it. She couldn't face the thought of the interminable wrangling that would come of dealing with them as a group. Divide and conquer was the only way.

"I am *writing*," she declared instead, and looked narrow-eyed from face to face. "Something important." Mrs. Aberfeldy looked impressed; Mrs. Chisholm affronted; Mrs. Bug astonished.

She nodded coolly to each one in turn.

"I'll talk to each of you about it later. Aye?"

She opened the door, stepped inside, and shut it very gently on the three pop-eyed faces, then pressed her back against it, closed her eyes, and let out the breath she had been holding.

There was silence outside the door, then a distinct "Hmp!" in Mrs. Chisholm's voice, and the noise of footsteps going away—one set up the stairs, another toward the kitchen, and a heavier tread into the surgery across the hall. A rush of small footsteps out the front door announced Tony and Toby making their escape.

Jemmy ceased wailing when he saw her, and started sucking his thumb instead.

"I hope Mrs. Chisholm doesn't know anything about herbs," she told him, whispering. "I'm sure Grandma keeps poisons in there." A good thing her mother had taken the box of saws and scalpels with her, at least.

She stood still a moment, listening. No sounds of breaking glass. Perhaps Mrs. Chisholm had merely stepped into the surgery in order to avoid Mrs. Aberfeldy and Mrs. Bug. Brianna sank down in the straight chair by the small table her father used as a desk. Or maybe Mrs. Chisholm was lying in wait, hoping to snare Brianna to listen to her own grievances, as soon as the others were safely out of the way.

Jemmy was now lying on his back with his feet in the air,

happily mangling a bit of rusk he had found somewhere. Her journal had fallen to the floor. Hearing Mrs. Chisholm come out of the surgery, she hastily seized the quill, and snatched one of the ledger books from the stack on the desk with the other.

The door opened an inch or two. There was a moment's silence, during which she bent her head, frowning in exaggerated concentration at the page before her, scratching with an empty quill. The door closed again.

"Bitch," she said, under her breath. Jemmy made an interrogative noise, and she looked down at him. "You didn't hear that, all right?"

Jemmy made an agreeable noise and crammed the soggy remnant of his toast into his left nostril. She made an instinctive movement to take it away from him, then stopped herself. She wasn't in the mood for any more conflict this morning. Or this afternoon, either.

She tapped the black quill thoughtfully on the ledger page. She'd have to do something, and fast. Mrs. Chisholm might have found the deadly nightshade—and she *knew* Mrs. Bug had a cleaver.

Mrs. Chisholm had the advantage in weight, height, and reach, but Brianna personally would put her money on Mrs. Bug, in terms of guile and treachery. As for poor little Mrs. Aberfeldy, she'd be caught in the crossfire, riddled with verbal bullets. And little Ruthie would likely be bald as an egg before another week was out.

Her father would have sorted them out in nothing flat by the joint exercise of charm and male authority. She gave a small snort of amusement at the thought. Come, he sayeth to one, and she curleth up at his feet, purring like Adso the cat. Go, he sayeth to another, and she goeth promptly out into the kitchen and baketh him a plate of buttered muffins.

Her mother would have seized the first excuse to escape the house—to tend a distant patient or gather medicinal herbs—and left them to fight it out among themselves, returning only when a state of armed neutrality had been restored. Brianna hadn't missed the look of relief on her mother's face as she swung up into her mare's saddle—or the faintly apologetic glance she sent her daughter. Still, neither strategy was going to work for her—though the urge to seize Jemmy and run for the hills was pretty strong.

For the hundredth time since the men had left, she wished passionately that she could have gone with them. She could imagine the bulk of a horse moving under her, the clean, cold air in her lungs, and Roger riding by her side, the sun glowing off his dark hair, and unseen adventure to be faced together, somewhere ahead.

She missed him with a deep ache, like a bruise to the bone. How long might he be gone, if it really came to fighting? She pushed that thought aside, not wanting to look at the thought that came after it; the thought that if it came to fighting, there was a possibility—however faint—that he would come back ill or injured—or wouldn't come back at all.

"It's *not* going to come to that," she said firmly, aloud. "They'll be back in a week or two."

There was a rattling sound as a blast of icy rain struck the window. The weather was turning cold; it would be snowing by nightfall. She shivered, drawing the shawl around her shoulders, and glanced at Jem to see that he was warm enough. His smock was puddled up around his middle, his diaper was plainly damp, and one stocking had fallen off, leaving his small pink foot bare. He appeared not to notice, being absorbed in babbling a song to the bare toes idly flexing overhead.

She looked dubiously at him, but he seemed happy enough—and the brazier in the corner *was* putting out some heat.

"Okay," she said, and sighed. She had Jem, and that was that. That *being* that, the problem was to find some means of dealing with the Three Furies before they drove her crazy or assassinated each other with rolling pin or knitting needle.

"Logic," she said to Jemmy, sitting up straight in the chair and pointing the quill at him. "There must be a logical way. It's like that problem where you have to get a cannibal, a missionary, and a goat across a river in a canoe. Let me think about this."

Jem began trying to get his foot into his crumb-encrusted mouth, despite the clear illogic of the procedure.

"You must take after Daddy," she told him, tolerantly. She put the quill back in its jar, and started to close the ledger, then stopped, attracted by the sprawling entries. The sight of Jamie's characteristically messy writing still gave her a faint thrill, remembering her first sight of it—on an ancient deed of sasine, its ink gone pale brown with age.

This ink had been pale brown to start with, but had now darkened, the iron-gall mixture achieving its typical blue-black with exposure to air over a day or so.

It was not so much a ledger, she saw, as a logbook, recording the daily activities of the farm.

> *16 July—Rec'd six weaned piglets of Pastor Gottfried, in trade for two bottles muscat wine and a goosewing axhead. Have put them in the stable 'til they be grown enough to forage conveniently.*
>
> *17 July—One of the hives commenced to swarm in the afternoon, and came into the stable. My wife fortunately recaptured the swarm, which she housed in an empty churn. She says Ronnie Sinclair must make her a new one.*
>
> *18 July—Letter from my aunt, asking advice re sawmill on Grinder's Creek. Replied, saying I will ride to inspect the situation within the month. Letter sent with R. Sinclair, who goes to Cross Creek with a load of 22 barrels, from which I am to receive half his profit toward payment of debt on cobbler's tools. Have arranged to deduct cost of new churn from this amount.*

The flow of entries was soothing, as peaceful as the summer days they recorded. She felt the knot of tension between her shoulder blades beginning to relax, and her mind began to loosen and stretch, ready to seek a way out of her difficulties.

> *20 July—Barley in the lower field as high as my stocking-tops. A healthy heifer calf born to red cow soon after midnight. All well. An excellent day.*
>
> *21 July—Rode to Muellers'. Exchanged one jar*

*honeycomb for leather bridle in poor repair (but can
be mended). Home well after dark, in consequence of
seeing a twilight hatch rising upon the pond near Hol-
lis's Gap. Stopped to fish, and caught a string of ten
fine trout. Six eaten for supper; the rest will do for
breakfast.*

*22 July—My grandson has a rash, though my wife
declares it of no moment. The white sow has broken
through her pen again and escaped into the forest. I
am in two minds whether I shall pursue her or only
express sympathy for the unfortunate predator that
first encounters her. Her temper is similar to that of
my daughter at the moment, the latter having slept little these past few nights . . .*

Brianna leaned forward, frowning at the page.

*. . . in consequence of the infant's screaming,
which my wife says is the colic and will pass. I trust
she is right. Meanwhile, I have settled Brianna and
the child in the old cabin, which is some relief to us in
the house, if not to my poor daughter. The white sow
ate four of her last litter before I could prevent her.*

"Why, you bloody *bastard*!" she said. She was familiar
with the white sow in question, and not flattered by the comparison. Jemmy, alarmed by her tone, stopped crooning and
dropped his toast, his mouth beginning to quiver.

"No, no, it's all right, sweetie." She got up and scooped
him into her arms, swaying gently to soothe him. "Shh, it's
all right. Mummy is just talking to Grandpa, that's all. You
didn't hear that word either, okay? Shh, shh."

Jemmy was reassured, but leaned out from her arms,
reaching after his discarded meal with small grunts of anxiety. She stooped and picked it up, eyeing the half-dissolved
object with distaste. The crust was not only stale and wet, but
had acquired a light coating of what seemed to be cat hair.

"Ick. You don't really want that, do you?"

Evidently he did, and was persuaded only with difficulty
to accept a large iron bull's ring—used for leading male

animals by the nose, she noted with some irony—from the shelf in lieu of it. A brief nibble confirmed the desirability of the nose ring, though, and he settled down in her lap to single-minded gnawing, allowing her to reread the conclusion of the offensive entry.

"Hmm." She leaned back, shifting Jemmy's weight more comfortably. He could sit up easily now, though it still seemed incredible that his noodle-neck could support the round dome of his head. She regarded the ledger broodingly.

"It's a thought," she said to Jemmy. "If I shift the old bi— I mean, Mrs. Chisholm—to our cabin, it will get her and her horrible little monsters out of everyone's hair. Then . . . hmm. Mrs. Aberfeldy and Ruthie could go in with Lizzie and her father, if we move the trundle from Mama and Da's room in there. The Bugs get their privacy back, and Mrs. Bug stops being an evil-minded old . . . er . . . anyway, then I suppose you and I could sleep in Mama and Da's room, at least 'til they come back."

She hated to think of moving from the cabin. It was her home, her private place, her family's place. She could go there and close the door, leaving the furor here behind. Her things were there; the half-built loom, the pewter plates, the pottery jug she had painted—all the small, homely objects with which she had made the space her own.

Beyond the sense of possession and peace, she had an uncomfortable sense of something like superstition about leaving it. The cabin was the home Roger had shared with her; to leave it, however temporarily, seemed somehow an admission that he might not return to share it again.

She tightened her grip on Jemmy, who ignored her in favor of concentration on his toy, his fat little fists shiny with drool where he grasped the ring.

No, she didn't want to give up her cabin at all. But it *was* an answer, and a logical one. Would Mrs. Chisholm agree? The cabin was much more crudely built than the big house, and lacking its amenities.

Still, she was pretty sure Mrs. Chisholm would accept the suggestion. If ever she'd seen someone whose motto was, "Better to reign in hell than serve in heaven . . ." Despite her trouble, she felt a small bubble of laughter rise beneath her stays.

She reached out and flipped the ledger closed, then tried to replace it on the stack from which she'd taken it. One-handed, though, and encumbered by Jemmy, she couldn't quite reach, and the book slipped off, falling back onto the table.

"Rats," she muttered, and scooted forward on her chair, reaching to pick it up again. Several loose sheets had fallen out, and she stuffed these back as tidily as she could with her free hand.

One, plainly a letter, had the remnants of its wax seal still attached. Her eye caught the impression of a smiling half-moon, and she paused. That was Lord John Grey's seal. It must be the letter he had sent in September, in which he described his adventures hunting deer in the Dismal Swamp; her father had read it to the family several times—Lord John was a humorous correspondent, and the deer hunt had been beset by the sort of misfortunes that were no doubt uncomfortable to live through, but which made picturesque recounting afterward.

Smiling in memory, she flipped the letter open with her thumb, looking forward to seeing the story again, only to find that she was looking at something quite different.

*13 October, Anno Domini 1770*

*Mr. James Fraser*
*Fraser's Ridge, North Carolina*

*My dear Jamie,*

> *I woke this Morning to the sound of the Rain which has beat upon us for the last Week, and to the gentle clucking of several Chickens, who had come to roost upon my Bedstead. Rising under the Stare of numerous beady Eyes, I went to make Inquiry as to this Circumstance, and was informed that the River has risen so far under the Impetus of the recent Rain as to have*

*undermined both the Necessary House and the
Chicken Coop. The contents of the latter were rescued
by William (my Son, whom you will recall), and two of
the Slaves, who swept the dispossessed Fowl out of the
passing Floodwaters with Brooms. I cannot say whose
was the Notion to sequester the hapless feathered
Flood Victims in my Sleeping Chamber, but I hold certain Suspicions in this regard.*

*Resorting to use of my Chamber Pot (I could wish
that the Chickens shared this Facility, they are dis-
tressing incontinent Fowl), I dressed and ventured
forth to see what might be salvaged. Some few Boards
and the shingled Roof of the Chicken Coop remain,
but my Privy, alas, has become the Property of King
Neptune—or whatever minor water Deity presides
over so modest a Tributary as our River.*

*I pray you will suffer no Concern for us, though;
the House is at some distance from the River, and
safely placed upon a Rise of Ground, such as to render
us quite safe from even the most incommodious flooding. (The Necessary had been dug by the old homestead, and we had not yet attempted a new structure
more convenient; this minor disaster, by affording us
the* Necessary *opportunity for rebuilding, thus may
prove a blessing in disguise.)*

Brianna rolled her eyes at the pun, but smiled nonetheless.
Jemmy dropped his ring and began at once to whine for it.
She stooped to pick it up, but stopped halfway down, riveted
by the words at the beginning of the next paragraph.

*Your letter mentions Mr. Stephen Bonnet, and
inquires whether I have news or knowledge of him. I
have met with him, you will collect, but have unfortunately no Memory whatever of the Encounter, not even
to Recalling of his Appearance, though as you know, I
carry a small Hole in my Head, as a singular
Memento of the occasion. (You may inform your Lady
Wife that I am healed well, with no further Symptoms*

_of Discomfort than the occasional Headache. Beyond
this, the Silver Plate with which the Opening is covered is subject to sudden chill when the Weather is
cold, which tends to make my left Eye water, and to
cause a great Discharge of Snot, but this is of no consequence.)_

_As I thus share your Interest in Mr. Bonnet and his
Movements, I have long since had Inquiries dispersed
among such Acquaintance as I have near the Coast,
since the Descriptions of his Machinations cause me
to believe the man is most like to be found there (this
is a comforting Notion, given the Great Distance
between the Coast and your remote Eyrie). The River
being navigable to the Sea, however, I had some
Thought that the River Captains and Water Scallywags
who now and again grace my Dinner Table might at
some Point bear me Word of the man._

_I am not pleased by the Obligation to report that
Bonnet still resides among the Living, but both Duty
and Friendship compel me to impart such Particulars
of him as I have obtained. These are sparse; the
Wretch appears sensible of his criminal Situation, so
far as to render him subtle in his Movements until
now._

Jemmy was kicking and squawking. As though in a
trance, she stooped, holding him, and picked up the ring, her
eyes still fixed on the letter.

_I had heard little of him, save a Report at one Point
that he had repaired to France—good News. However,
two Weeks past I had a Guest, one Captain Liston
("Captain" being no more than a title of courtesy; he
claims service with the Royal Navy, but I will stake a
Hogshead of my best Tobacco [a sample of which you
will find accompanying this Missive—and if you do
not, I would be obliged to hear of it, since I do not
altogether trust the Slave by whom I send it] that
he has never so much as smelled the Ink on a_

*Commission, let alone the Reek of the Bilges) who
gave me a more recent—and highly disagreeable—
History of the man Bonnet.*

*Finding himself at large in the Port of Charleston,
Liston said that he fell in with some Companions of
low Aspect, who invited him to accompany them to a
Cockfight, held in the Innyard of an Establishment
called the Devil's Glass. Among the Rabble there was
a Man notable for the fineness of his Dress, and the
Freedom with which he spent his Coin—Liston heard
this man referred to as Bonnet, and was told by the
Landlord that this Bonnet had the name of a Smuggler
upon the Outer Banks, being Popular with the Merchants of the coastal Towns in North Carolina, though
much less so with the Authorities, who were Helpless
to deal with the Man by reason of his Business and the
dependence of the Towns of Wilmington, Edenton, and
New Bern upon his Trade.*

*Liston took little further Note of Bonnet (he said)
until an Altercation rose over a Wager upon the Fighting. Hot Words were exchanged, and nothing would do
save Honor be satisfied by the drawing of Blood.
Nothing loath, the Spectators at once began to wager
upon the Outcome of the human Contest, in the same
manner as that of the fighting Fowl.*

*One combatant was the man Bonnet, the other a
Captain Marsden, a half-pay Army Captain known to
my Guest as a good Swordsman. This Marsden, feeling
himself the injured Party, damned Bonnet's eyes, and
invited the Smuggler to accommodate him upon the
Spot, an Offer at once accepted. Wagers ran heavy
upon Marsden, his Reputation being known, but it was
soon clear that he had met his Match and more in
Bonnet. Within no more than a few moments, Bonnet
succeeded in disarming his Opponent, and in Wounding him so grievously in the Thigh that Marsden sank
down upon his Knees and yielded to his Opponent—
having no Choice in the Matter at that Point, to be
sure.*

*Bonnet did not accept of this Surrender, though, but*

instead performed an Act of such Cruelty as made the
deepest Impression upon all who saw it. Remarking
with great coolness that it was not his own Eyes that
would be damned, he drew the Tip of his Weapon
across Marsden's Eyes, twisting it in such Fashion as
not only to blind the Captain, but to inflict such Mutilation as would make him an Object of the greatest
Horror and Pity to all who might behold him.

Leaving his Foe thus mangled and fainting upon
the bloody Sand of the Innyard, Bonnet cleansed his
Blade by wiping it upon Marsden's Shirtfront,
sheathed it, and left—though not before removing
Marsden's Purse, which he claimed in payment of his
original Wager. None present had any Stomach to prevent him, having so cogent an Example of his Skill
before them.

I recount this History both to acquaint you with
Bonnet's last known whereabouts, and as warning to
his Nature and Abilities. I know you are already well
acquainted with the Former, but I draw your Attention
to the Latter, out of due Regard for your Well-being.
Not that I expect a word of my well-meant Advice will
find lodging in your Breast, so filled must it be with
animadverse Sentiment toward the Man, but I would
beg that you take Notice at least of Liston's Mention of
Bonnet's Connexions.

Upon the occasion of my own Meeting with the
man, he was a Condemned Felon, and I cannot think
he has since performed such Service toward the
Crown as would gain him official Pardon. If he is content to flaunt himself thus openly in Charleston—
where scant Years ago he escaped the Hangman's
Noose—it would seem he is in no great Fears for his
Safety—and this can only mean that he now enjoys the
Protection and Patronage of powerful Friends. You
must discover and beware of these, if you seek to
destroy Bonnet.

I will continue my Inquiries in this regard, and
notify you at once of any further Particulars. In the
meantime, keep you well, and spare a thought now

*and again to your drenched and shivering Acquaintance in Virginia. I remain, sir, with all good Wishes toward your Wife, Daughter, and Family,*

> *Your ob't. servant,*
> *John William Grey, Esq.*
> *Mount Josiah Plantation*
> *Virginia*

*Postscriptum: I have been in search of an Astrolabe, per your Request, but so far have heard of nothing that would suit your Purpose. I am sending to London this month for assorted Furnishings, though, and will be pleased to order one from Halliburton's in Green Street, their Instruments are of the highest Quality.*

Very slowly, Brianna sat back down on the chair. She placed her hands gently but firmly over her son's ears, and said a very bad word.

# 31

# ORPHAN OF THE STORM

I FELL ASLEEP, leaning against the bank, with Jamie's head on my lap. I dreamed luridly, as one does when cold and uncomfortable. I dreamed of trees; endless, monotonous forests of them, with each trunk and leaf and needle etched like scrimshaw on the inside of my eyelids, each one crystal-sharp, all just alike. Yellow goat-eyes floated in the air between the tree trunks, and the wood of my mind rang with the screams of she-panthers and the crying of motherless children.

I woke suddenly, with the echoes of their cries still ringing in my ears. I was lying in a tangle of cloaks and blankets, Jamie's limbs heavily entwined with my own, and a fine, cold snow was falling through the pines.

Granules of ice crusted my brows and lashes, and my face was cold and wet with melted snow. Momentarily disoriented, I reached out by reflex to touch Jamie; he stirred and coughed thickly, his shoulder shaking under my hand. The sound of it brought back the events of the day before—Josiah and his twin, the Beardsley farm, Fanny's ghosts; the smell of ordure and gangrene and the cleaner reek of gunpowder and wet earth. The bleating of goats, still echoing from my dreams.

A thin cry came through the whisper of snow, and I sat up abruptly, flinging back the blankets in a spray of icy powder. Not a goat. Not at all.

Startled awake, Jamie jerked and rolled instinctively away from the mess of cloaks and blankets, coming up in a crouch, hair in a wild tangle and eyes darting round in search of threat.

"What?" he whispered hoarsely. He reached for his knife, lying nearby in its sheath on the ground, but I lifted a hand to stop him moving.

"I don't know. A noise. Listen!"

He lifted his head, listening, and I saw his throat move painfully as he swallowed. I could hear nothing but the chisping of the snow, and saw nothing but dripping pines. Jamie heard something, though—or saw it; his face changed suddenly.

"There," he said softly, nodding at something behind me. I scrambled round on my knees, to see what looked like a small heap of rags, lying some ten feet away, next to the ashes of the burned-out fire. The cry came again, unmistakable this time.

"Jesus H. Roosevelt Christ." I was scarcely aware of having spoken, as I scrambled toward the bundle. I snatched it up and began to root through the layers of swaddling cloth. It was plainly alive—I had heard it cry—and yet it lay inert, almost weightless in the curve of my arm.

The tiny face and hairless skull were blue-white, the

features closed and sere as the husk of a winter fruit. I laid my palm over nose and mouth and felt a faint, moist warmth against my skin. Startled by my touch, the mouth opened in a mewling cry, and the slanted eyes crimped tighter shut, sealing out the threatening world.

"Holy God." Jamie crossed himself briefly. His voice was little more than a phlegmy crackle; he cleared his throat and tried again, glancing around. "Where's the woman?"

Shocked by the child's appearance, I had not paused to consider its origin, nor was there time to do so now. The baby twitched a little in its wrappings, but the tiny hands were cold as ice, the skin mottled blue and purple with chill.

"Never mind her now—get my shawl, will you, Jamie? The poor thing's nearly frozen." I fumbled one-handed with the lacing of my bodice; it was an old one that opened down the front, worn for ease of dressing on the trail. I pulled loose my stays and the drawstring of my shift and pressed the small icy creature against my bare breasts, my skin still warm from sleep. A blast of wind drove stinging snow across the exposed skin of my neck and shoulders. I pulled my shift hastily up over the child and hunched myself, shivering. Jamie flung the shawl round my shoulders, then wrapped his arms round us both, hugging fiercely as though to force the heat of his own body into the child.

The heat of him was considerable; he was burning with fever.

"My God, are you all right?" I spared a glance up at him; white-faced and red-eyed, but steady enough.

"Aye, fine. Where is she?" he asked again, hoarsely. "The woman."

Gone, evidently. The goats were huddled close together under the shelter of the bank; I saw Hiram's horns bobbing among the nannies' brindled backs. Half a dozen pairs of yellow eyes watched us with interest, reminding me of my dreams.

The place where Mrs. Beardsley had lain was empty, with no more than a patch of flattened grass to testify that she had ever been there. She must have gone some distance away in order to give birth; there was no trace of it near the fire.

"It is hers?" Jamie asked. I could still hear the congestion in his voice, but the small wheezing sound in his chest had eased; that was a relief.

"I suppose it must be. Where else could it have come from?"

My attention was divided between Jamie and the child—it had begun to stir, with little crablike movements against my belly—but I spared a glance around our makeshift camp. The pines stood black and silent under the whispering snow; if Fanny Beardsley had gone into the forest, no trace remained on the matted needles to mark her passage. Snow crystals rimed the trunks of the trees, but not enough had fallen to stick to the ground; no chance of footprints.

"She can't have gone far," I said, craning to peer round Jamie's shoulder. "She hasn't taken either of the horses." Gideon and Mrs. Piggy stood close together under a spruce tree, ears morosely flattened by the weather, their breath making clouds of steam around them. Seeing us up and moving, Gideon stamped and whinnied, big yellow teeth showing in an impatient demand for sustenance.

"Aye, ye auld bugger, I'm coming." Jamie dropped his arms and stepped back, wiping his knuckles beneath his nose.

"She couldna have taken a horse, if she meant to be secret. If she had, the other would have made a fuss and roused me." He laid a gentle hand on the bulge under my shawl. "I'll need to go and feed them. Is he all right, Sassenach?"

"He's thawing out," I assured him. "But he—or she, for that matter—will be hungry, too." The baby was beginning to move more, squirming sluggishly, like a chilled worm, its mouth blindly groping. The feeling was shocking in its familiarity; my nipple sprang up by reflex, the flesh of my breast tingling with electricity as the tiny mouth groped, rooted, found the nipple, and clamped on.

I gave a small yelp of surprise, and Jamie raised one eyebrow.

"It . . . um . . . *is* hungry," I said, readjusting my burden.

"I see that, Sassenach," he said. He glanced at the goats, still snug in their sheltered spot by the bank, but beginning to shift and stir with drowsy grumbles. "He's no the only one starving. A moment, aye?"

We had brought large forage nets of dry hay from the Beardsley farm; he opened one of these and scattered feed for the horses and goats, then returned to me. He stooped to disentangle one of the cloaks from the damp heap of coverings, and put it round my shoulders, then rootled through the pack for a wooden cup, with which he purposefully approached the grazing goats.

The baby was suckling strongly, my nipple pulled deep into its mouth. I found this reassuring so far as the health of the child was concerned, but the sensation was rather unsettling.

"It's not that I mind at all, really," I said to the child, trying to distract both of us. "But I'm afraid I'm *not* your mother, you see? Sorry."

And where in bloody hell *was* its mother, anyway? I turned slowly round in a circle, searching the landscape more carefully, but still discerned no trace of Fanny Beardsley, let alone any reason for her disappearance—or her silence.

What on earth could have happened? Mrs. Beardsley could have—and quite obviously *had*—hidden an advanced pregnancy under that mound of fat and wrappings—but why should she have done so?

"Why not tell us? I wonder," I murmured to the top of the baby's head. It was growing restless, and I rocked from foot to foot to soothe it. Well, perhaps she had feared that Jamie wouldn't take her with us, if he knew she was so far gone with child. I didn't blame her for not wanting to remain in that farmhouse, whatever the circumstance.

But still, why had she now abandoned the child? *Had* she abandoned it? I considered for a moment the possibility that someone, or something—my spine prickled momentarily at the thought of panthers—had come and stolen the woman from the fireside, but my common sense dismissed the notion.

A cat or bear might conceivably have entered the camp without waking Jamie or me, exhausted as we were, but there wasn't a chance that it could have come near without raising alarms from the goats and horses, who had all had quite enough to do with wild beasts by this time. And a wild animal looking for prey would clearly prefer a tender tidbit like this child, to a tough item like Mrs. Beardsley.

But if a human agency had been responsible for Fanny Beardsley's disappearance—why had they left the child?

Or, perhaps, brought it back?

I sniffed deeply to clear my nose, then turned my head, breathing in and out, testing the air from different quarters. Birth is a messy business, and I was thoroughly familiar with the ripe scents of it. The child in my arms smelled strongly of such things, but I could detect no trace at all of blood or birth waters on the chilly wind. Goat dung, horse manure, cut hay, the bitter smell of wood ash, and a good whiff of camphorated goose grease from Jamie's clothes—but nothing else.

"Right, then," I said aloud, gently jiggling my burden, who was growing restless. "She went away from the fire to give birth. Either she went by herself—or someone made her go. But if someone took her and saw that she was about to deliver, why would they have bothered bringing you back? Surely they'd either have kept you, killed you, or simply left you to die. Oh—sorry. Didn't mean to upset you. Shh, darling. Hush, hush."

The baby, beginning to thaw from its stupor, had had time to consider what else was lacking in its world. It had relinquished my breast in frustration, and was wriggling and wailing with encouraging strength by the time Jamie returned with a steaming cup of goat's milk and a moderately clean handkerchief. Twisting this into a makeshift teat, he dipped it in the milk and carefully inserted the dripping cloth into the open maw. The mewling ceased at once, and we both sighed with relief as the noise stopped.

"Ah, that's better, is it? *Seas, a bhalaich, seas,*" Jamie was murmuring to the child, dipping more milk. I peered down at the tiny face, still pale and waxy with vernix, but no longer chalky, as it suckled with deep concentration.

"How could she have left it?" I wondered aloud. "And why?"

That was the best argument for kidnapping; what else could have made a new mother abandon her child? To say nothing of making off on foot into a darkened wood immediately after giving birth, heavy-footed and sore, her own flesh still torn and oozing . . . I grimaced at the thought, my womb tightening in sympathy.

Jamie shook his head, his eyes still intent on his task.

"She had some reason, but Christ and the saints only ken what it is. She didna hate the child, though—she might have left it in the wood, and us none the wiser."

That was true; she—or someone—had wrapped the baby carefully, and left it as close to the fire as she could. She wished it to survive, then—but without her.

"You think she left willingly, then?"

He nodded, glancing at me.

"We're no far from the Treaty Line here. It *could* be Indians—but if it was, if someone took her, why should they not capture us as well? Or kill us all?" he asked logically. "And Indians would have taken the horses. Nay, I think she went on her own. But as to why . . ." He shook his head, and dipped the handkerchief again.

The snow was falling faster now, still a dry, light snow, but beginning to stick in random patches. We should leave soon, I thought, before the storm grew worse. It seemed somehow wrong, though, simply to go, with no attempt to determine the fate of Fanny Beardsley.

The whole situation seemed unreal. It was as though the woman had suddenly vanished through some sorcery, leaving this small substitute in exchange. It reminded me bizarrely of the Scottish tales of changelings; fairy offspring left in the place of human babies. I couldn't fathom what the fairies could possibly want with Fanny Beardsley, though.

I knew it was futile, but turned slowly round once more, surveying our surroundings. Nothing. The clay bank loomed over us, fringed with dry, snow-dusted grass. The trickle of a tiny stream ran past a little distance away, and the trees rustled and sighed in the wind. There was no mark of hoof or foot on the layer of damp, spongy needles, and no hint of any trail. The woods were not at all silent, what with the wind, but dark and deep, all right.

"And miles to go before we sleep," I remarked, turning back to Jamie with a sigh.

"Eh? Ah, no, it's no more than an hour's ride to Brownsville," he assured me. "Or maybe two," he amended, glancing up at the white-muslin sky, from which the snow was falling faster. "I ken where we are, now it's light."

He coughed again, a sudden spasm racking his body, then straightened, and handed me the cup and dummy.

"Here, Sassenach. Feed the poor wee *sgaogan* while I tend the beasts, aye?"

*Sgaogan*. A changeling. So the air of supernatural strangeness about the whole affair had struck him, too. Well, the woman had claimed to see ghosts; perhaps one of them had come for her? I shivered, and cradled the baby closer.

"Is there any settlement near here, besides Brownsville? Anywhere Mrs. Beardsley might have decided to go?"

Jamie shook his head, a line between his brows. The snow melted where it touched his heated skin, and ran down his face in tiny streams.

"Naught that I ken," he said. "Is the wean takin' to the goat's milk?"

"Like a kid," I assured him, and laughed. He looked puzzled, but one side of his mouth turned up nonetheless—he wanted humor just now, whether he understood the joke or not.

"That's what the Americans call—will call—children," I told him. "Kids."

The smile broadened across his face.

"Oh, aye? So that's why Brianna and MacKenzie call wee Jem so, is it? I thought it was only a bit of private fun between them."

He milked the rest of the goats quickly while I dribbled more nourishment into the child, bringing back a brimming bucket of warm milk for our own breakfast. I should have liked a nice hot cup of tea—my fingers were chilled and numb from dipping the false teat over and over—but the creamy white stuff was delicious, and as much comfort to our chilled and empty stomachs as to the little one's.

The child had stopped suckling, and had wet itself copiously; a good sign of health, by and large, but rather inconvenient just at the moment, as both its swaddling cloth and the front of my bodice were now soaked.

Jamie rootled hastily through the packs once again, this

time in search of diapering and dry clothes. Fortunately, Mrs. Piggy had been carrying the bag in which I kept lengths of linen and wads of cotton lint for cleansing and bandaging. He took a handful of these and the child, while I went about the awkward and drafty business of changing my shift and bodice without removing skirt, petticoat, or cloak.

"P-put on your own cloak," I said, through chattering teeth. "You'll die of f-frigging pneumonia."

He smiled at that, eyes focused on his job, though the tip of his nose glowed redly in contrast to his pale face.

"I'm fine," he croaked, then cleared his throat with a noise like ripping cloth, impatient. "Fine," he repeated, more strongly, then stopped, eyes widening in surprise.

"Oh," he said, more softly. "Look. It's a wee lassie."

"Is it?" I dropped to my knees beside him to look.

"Rather plain," he said, critically surveying the little creature. "A good thing she'll have a decent dowry."

"I don't suppose you were any great beauty when you were born, either," I said rebukingly. "She hasn't even been properly cleaned, poor thing. What do you mean about her dowry, though?"

He shrugged, contriving to keep the child covered with a shawl, meanwhile sliding a folded sheet of linen dexterously beneath her miniature bottom.

"Her father's dead and her mother's gone. She's no brothers or sisters to share, and I didna find any will in the house saying that anyone else was to have Beardsley's property. There's a decent farm left, though, and a good bit in trade goods there—to say nothing of the goats." He glanced at Hiram and his family, and smiled. "So they'll all be hers, I expect."

"I suppose so," I said slowly. "So she'll be a rather well-to-do little girl, won't she?"

"Aye, and she's just shit herself. Could ye not have done that before I'd put ye on a fresh clout?" he demanded of the child. Unfazed by the scolding, the little girl blinked sleepily at him and gave a soft belch.

"Oh, well," he said, resigned. He shifted himself to better shelter her from the wind, lifted the coverings briefly, and wiped a smear of blackish slime deftly off the budlike privates.

The child seemed healthy, though rather undersized; she was no bigger than a large doll, her stomach bulging slightly with milk. That was the immediate difficulty; small as she was, and with no body fat for insulation, she would die of hypothermia within a very short time, unless we could keep her warm as well as fed.

"Don't let her get chilled." I put my hands in my armpits to warm them, in preparation for picking up the child.

"Dinna fash yourself, Sassenach. I must just wipe her wee bum and then—" He stopped, frowning.

"What's this, Sassenach? Is she damaged, d'ye think? Perhaps yon silly woman dropped her?"

I leaned close to look. He held the baby's feet up in one hand, a wad of soiled cotton lint in the other. Just above the tiny buttocks was a dark bluish discoloration, rather like a bruise.

It wasn't a bruise. It was, though, an explanation of sorts.

"She isn't hurt," I assured him, pulling another of Mrs. Beardsley's discarded shawls up to shelter her daughter's bald head. "It's a Mongol spot."

"A what?"

"It means the child is black," I explained. "African, I mean, or partly so." Jamie blinked, startled, then bent to peer into the shawl, frowning.

"No, she isn't. She's as pale as ye are yourself, Sassenach."

That was quite true; the child was so white as to seem devoid of blood.

"Black children don't usually look black at birth," I explained to him. "In fact, they're often quite pale. The pigmentation of the skin begins to develop some weeks later. But they're often born with this faint discoloration of the skin at the base of the spine—it's called a Mongol spot."

He rubbed a hand over his face, blinking away snowflakes that tried to settle on his lashes.

"I see," he said slowly. "Aye, well, that explains a bit, does it not?"

It did. The late Mr. Beardsley, whatever else he might have been, had assuredly not been black. The child's father had been. And Fanny Beardsley, knowing—or fearing—that the child she was about to bear would reveal her as an adulteress, had thought it better to abandon the child and flee before the truth was revealed. I wondered whether the mysterious father had had anything to do with what had happened to Mr. Beardsley, for that matter.

"Did she know for sure that the father was a Negro, I wonder?" Jamie touched the small underlip, now showing a tinge of pink, gently with one finger. "Or did she never see the child at all? For after all, she must have given birth in the dark. If she had seen it looked white, perhaps she would ha' chosen to brazen it out."

"Perhaps. But she didn't. Who do you suppose the father can have been?" Isolated as the Beardsleys' farm had been, I couldn't imagine Fanny having the opportunity to meet very many men, other than the Indians who came to trade. Did Indian babies perhaps have Mongol spots? I wondered.

Jamie glanced bleakly around at the desolate surroundings, and scooped the child up into his arms.

"I dinna ken, but I shouldna think he'll be hard to spot, once we've reached Brownsville. Let's go, Sassenach."

JAMIE RELUCTANTLY DECIDED to leave the goats behind, in the interest of reaching shelter and sustenance for the child as quickly as possible.

"They'll be fine here for a bit," he said, scattering the rest of the hay for them. "The nannies willna leave the auld fellow—and ye're no going anywhere for the present, are ye, *a bhalaich*?" He scratched Hiram between the horns in farewell, and we left to a chorus of protesting *mehs*, the goats having grown used to our company.

The weather was worsening by the moment; as the temperature rose, the snow changed from dry powder to large, wet flakes that stuck to everything, dusting ground and trees with icing sugar, and melting down through the horses' manes.

Well-muffled in my thick hooded cloak, with multiple shawls beneath and the child snuggled in a makeshift sling against my stomach, I was quite warm, in spite of the flakes that brushed my face and stuck in my lashes. Jamie coughed now and then, but on the whole, looked much healthier than he had; the need to take charge of an emergency had energized him.

He rode just behind me, keeping an eye out in case of marauding panthers or other menaces. I thought myself that any self-respecting cat—particularly one with a bellyful of goat—would spend a day like this curled up in some cozy den, not out tramping through the snow. Still, it was very reassuring to have him there; I was vulnerable, riding with one hand on the reins, the other wrapped protectively over the bulge under my cloak.

The child was sleeping, I thought, but not quiet; it stretched and squirmed with the slow, languid movements of the water world, not yet accustomed to the freedom of life outside the womb.

"Ye look as though you're wi' child, Sassenach." I glanced back over my shoulder, to see Jamie looking amused under the brim of his slouch hat, though I thought there was something else in his expression; perhaps a slight wistfulness.

"Probably because I *am* with child," I replied, shifting slightly in the saddle to accommodate the movements of my companion. "It's just somebody else's child I'm with." The pressure of small knees and head and elbows shifting against my belly were in fact unsettlingly like the sensations of pregnancy; the fact that they were outside rather than inside made remarkably little difference.

As though drawn to the swelling under my cloak, Jamie nudged Gideon up beside me. The horse snorted and tossed his head, wanting to push ahead, but Jamie held him back with a soft *"Seas!"* of rebuke, and he subsided, huffing steam.

"Ye're troubled for her?" Jamie asked, with a nod toward the surrounding forest.

No need to ask whom he meant. I nodded, my hand on the curled tiny backbone, arched still to fit the curve of the vanished womb. Where was she, Fanny Beardsley, alone in the wood? Crawled off to die like a wounded beast—or making, perhaps, for some imagined haven, floundering blindly through frozen leaf mold and deepening snow, heading back, maybe, toward the Chesapeake Bay and some memory of open sky, of broad waters and happiness?

Jamie leaned over and laid a hand on mine where it curled over the sleeping child; I could feel the chill of his ungloved fingers through the layer of cloth between us.

"She's made her choice, Sassenach," he said. "And she's trusted us wi' the bairn. We'll see the wee lass safe; that's all we can do for the woman."

I couldn't turn my hand to take his, but nodded. He let my hand go with a squeeze and dropped back, and I turned my face toward our destination, my lashes wet and spiky as I blinked away the melting drops.

By the time we came in sight of Brownsville, though, most of my concern for Fanny Beardsley had been subsumed by anxiety for her daughter. The child was awake and bawling, pummeling my liver with tiny fists in search of food.

I lifted myself in the saddle, peering through the curtain of falling snow. How big a place was Brownsville? I could see no more than the roofline of a single cabin peeping through the evergreen of pine and laurel. One of the men from Granite Falls had said it was sizable, though—what was "sizable," here in the backcountry? What were the odds that at least one of the residents of Brownsville might be a woman with a nursing child?

Jamie had emptied out the canteen and filled it with goat's milk, but it was better, I thought, to reach shelter before trying to feed the baby again. If there was a mother who might offer her milk to the child, that would be best—but if not, the goat's milk would need to be heated; cold as it was outside, to give the baby cold milk might lower her body temperature dangerously.

Mrs. Piggy snorted out a great gout of steam, and suddenly picked up her pace. She knew civilization when she smelled it—and other horses. She threw up her head and whinnied piercingly. Gideon joined her, and when the racket stopped, I could hear the encouraging replies of a number of horses in the distance.

"They're here!" I exhaled in a steamy burst of relief. "The militia—they made it!"

"Well, I should hope so, Sassenach," Jamie replied, taking a firm grip to prevent Gideon's bolting. "If wee Roger couldna find a village at the end of a straight trail, I'd have my doubts of his wits as well as his eyesight." But he was smiling, too.

As we came round a curve in the trail, I could see that Brownsville really *was* a village. Chimney smoke drifted up in soft gray plumes from a dozen cabins, scattered over the hillside that rose to our right, and a cluster of buildings stood together by the road, clearly placed for custom, judging from the rubble of discarded kegs, bottles, and other rubbish strewn in the dead weeds of the roadside.

Across the road from this pothouse, the men had erected a crude shelter for the horses, roofed with pine boughs and walled on one side with more branches to break the wind. The militiamen's horses were gathered under this in a cozy knot, hobbled and snorting, wreathed in clouds of their mingled breath.

Spotting this refuge, our own horses were moving at a good clip; I had to pull heavily on the reins one-handed in order to keep Mrs. Piggy from breaking into a trot, which would have seriously jostled my passenger. As I hauled her back to a reluctant walk, a slight figure detached itself from the shelter of a pine tree and stepped into the road before us, waving.

"Milord," Fergus greeted Jamie, as Gideon slewed to a reluctant halt. He peered up at Jamie from beneath the band of an indigo-dyed knitted cap, which he wore pulled down over his brows. It made his head look rather like the top of a torpedo, dark and dangerous. "You are well? I thought perhaps you had encountered some difficulty."

"Och." Jamie waved vaguely at me, indicating the bulge beneath my cloak. "No really a difficulty; it's only—"

Fergus was staring over Gideon's shoulder at the bulge with some bemusement.

"*Quelle virilité, Monsieur,*" he said to Jamie, in tones of deep respect. "My congratulations."

Jamie gave him a scathing look and a Scottish noise that

sounded like boulders rolling underwater. The baby began to cry again.

"First things first," I said. "Are there any women here with babies? This child needs milk, and she needs it now."

Fergus nodded, eyes wide with curiosity.

"*Oui*, milady. Two, at least, that I have seen."

"Good. Lead me to them."

He nodded again, and taking hold of Piggy's halter, turned toward the settlement.

"What's amiss, then?" Jamie inquired, and cleared his throat. In my anxiety for the baby, I hadn't paused to consider what Fergus's presence meant. Jamie was right, though; simple concern for our well-being wouldn't have brought him out on the road in this weather.

"Ah. We appear to have a small difficulty, milord." He described the events of the previous afternoon, concluding with a Gallic shrug and a huff of breath. ". . . and so Monsieur Morton has taken refuge with the horses"—he nodded ahead, toward the makeshift shelter—"while the rest of us enjoy the *hospitalité* of Brownsville."

Jamie looked a trifle grim at this; no doubt from a contemplation of what the *hospitalité* for forty-odd men might cost.

"Mmphm. I take it that the Browns dinna ken Morton is there?"

Fergus shook his head.

"Why *is* Morton there?" I asked, having temporarily stifled the baby by putting it to my own breast. "I should have thought he'd be off away, back to Granite Falls, and pleased to be alive."

"He will not go, milady. He says he cannot forgo the bounty." Word had come just before our departure from the Ridge; the Governor was offering forty shillings per man as an inducement to serve in the militia; a substantial sum, particularly to a new homesteader such as Morton, facing a bleak winter.

Jamie rubbed a hand slowly over his face. This was a dilemma, all right; the militia company needed the men and supplies from Brownsville, but Jamie could scarcely conscript several Browns who would immediately attempt to assassinate Morton. Nor could he afford to pay Morton's bounty himself. Jamie looked as though he were tempted to assassinate Morton personally, but I supposed this wasn't a reasonable alternative.

"Perhaps Morton could be induced to marry the girl?" I suggested delicately.

"I thought of that," Fergus said. "Regretfully, Monsieur Morton is already possessed of a wife in Granite Falls." He shook his head, which was beginning to look like a small snowcapped hillock in his cap.

"Why did the Browns not follow yon Morton?" Jamie asked, apparently following his own train of thought. "If an enemy comes upon your land, and you wi' your kin, ye dinna just let him flee; ye hunt him down and kill him."

Fergus nodded, clearly familiar with this brand of Highland logic.

"I believe that was the intent," he said. "They were distracted, however, by *le petit Roger*."

I could hear a distinct note of amusement in his voice; so could Jamie.

"What did he do?" he asked warily.

"Sang to them," Fergus said, the amusement becoming more pronounced. "He has been singing most of the night, and playing upon his drum. The entire village came to hear—there are six men of suitable age for the militia, and," he added practically, "the two women *avec lait*, as I said, milady."

Jamie coughed, wiped a hand under his nose, and nodded to Fergus, with a wave at me.

"Aye. Well, the wee lass must eat, and I canna stay back or the Browns will tumble to it that Morton's here. Go and say to him that I shall come and speak to him as soon as may be."

He reined his horse's head toward the tavern, and I nudged Mrs. Piggy to follow.

"What are you going to do about the Browns?" I asked.

"Christ," Jamie said, more to himself than to me. "How in hell should I know?" And coughed again.

# 32

# MISSION ACCOMPLISHED

OUR ARRIVAL, with the baby created a sufficient sensation to distract everyone in Brownsville from their private concerns, be these practical or homicidal. A look of intense relief crossed Roger's face at sight of Jamie, though this was instantly suppressed, replaced by a bland attitude of square-shouldered self-assurance. I ducked my head to hide a smile, and glanced at Jamie, wondering if he had noted this rapid transformation. He sedulously avoided my eye, indicating that he had.

"Ye've done well," he said in a casual undertone, clapping Roger's shoulder in greeting before turning to receive the salutations of the other men and introductions to our involuntary hosts.

Roger merely nodded in an offhand sort of way, but his face took on a muted glow, as though someone had lit a candle inside him.

Young Miss Beardsley caused a great stir; one of the nursing mothers was fetched and at once put the screeching baby to her breast, hastily handing me her own child in exchange. A three-month-old boy of placid temperament, he looked up at me with mild bewilderment, but seemed not to object to the substitution, merely blowing a few thoughtful spit bubbles in my direction.

A certain amount of confusion ensued, with everyone asking questions and offering speculations at once, but Jamie's story—edited to terseness—of events at the Beardsley farm put a stop to the hubbub. Even the red-eyed young woman whom I recognized from Fergus's story as

Isaiah Morton's inamorata forgot her grief, listening open-mouthed.

"Poor little creature," she said, peering at the baby as it suckled fiercely at her cousin's breast. "So you have no parents at all, it seems." Miss Brown cast a dark look at her own father, apparently thinking orphanhood had its advantages.

"What will become of her?" Mrs. Brown asked, with more practicality.

"Oh, we'll see she's taken good care of, my dear. She'll find a secure place with us." Her husband put a reassuring hand on her arm, at the same time exchanging a glance with his brother. Jamie saw it, too; I saw his mouth twitch as though he might say something, but he shrugged slightly and turned instead to confer with Henry Gallegher and Fergus, his two stiff fingers tapping gently on his leg.

The elder Miss Brown leaned toward me, preparing to ask another question, but was prevented by a sudden blast of arctic wind that blew through the big room, lifting the loose hides over the windows and peppering the room with a spray of snow like frozen bird shot. Miss Brown gave a small whoop, abandoned her curiosity, and ran to fasten down the window coverings; everyone else stopped discussing the Beardsleys and began hastily to batten down hatches.

I caught a quick glimpse outside, as Miss Brown struggled with the unwieldy hides. The storm had arrived now in good earnest. Snow was coming down thick and fast; the black ruts of the road had all but disappeared under a coating of white, and it was obvious that Fraser's Company was going nowhere for the time being. Mr. Richard Brown, looking mildly disgruntled, nonetheless graciously offered us a second night's shelter, and the militiamen settled in for supper among the houses and barns of the village.

Jamie went out to bring in our bedding and provisions from the horses, and see them fed and sheltered. Presumably he would also take the opportunity to speak privately with Isaiah Morton, if the latter was still lurking out there in the blizzard.

I did wonder what Jamie meant to do with his mountain Romeo, but I hadn't time for much speculation. It was getting on now for twilight, and I was sucked into the swirl of activity around the hearth, as the women rose to the fresh challenge of providing supper for forty unexpected guests.

Juliet—that is, the younger Miss Brown—moped sullenly in the corner, refusing to help. She did, though, take over care of the Beardsley baby, rocking the little girl and crooning to her long after it was plain that the child was asleep.

Fergus and Gallegher had been sent off to retrieve the goats, and returned with them just before suppertime, wet and muddy to the knees, their beards and eyebrows frosted with snow. The nannies were wet and snow-caked, too, their chilled udders red with cold, milk-swollen and swinging painfully against their legs. They were enchanted to be back in the bosom of civilization, though, and nattered to each other in cheerful excitement.

Mrs. Brown and her sister-in-law took the goats off to the tiny barn to be milked, leaving me in charge of the stewpot and Hiram, who was installed in solitary majesty near the hearth, contained in a makeshift pen composed of an overturned table, two stools, and a blanket chest.

The cabin was essentially one large, drafty room, with a walled loft above and a small lean-to at the back for storage. Crowded as it was with tables, benches, stools, kegs of beer, bundles of hides, a small handloom in one corner, a chiffonier—with a most incongruous chiming clock, adorned with cupids—in another, a bed against the wall, two settles by the hearth, a musket and two fowling pieces hung above the chimney breast, and various aprons and cloaks on pegs by the door, the presence of a sick goat was surprisingly inconsequential.

I had a look at my erstwhile patient, who *mehed* ungratefully at me, long blue tongue protruding in derision. Snow was melting from the deep spirals of his horns, leaving them black and shiny, and his coat was soaked into brindled spikes round his shoulders.

"There's gratitude for you," I said rebukingly. "If it weren't for Jamie, you'd be cooking *over* that fire, instead of beside it, and good enough for you, too, you wicked old sod."

*"Meh!"* he said shortly.

Still, he was cold, tired, and hungry, and his harem wasn't

there to be impressed, so he suffered me to rub his head and scratch his ears, feed him wisps of hay, and—eventually—to step into his pen and run a light hand down his injured leg to check the splinting. I was more than a little tired and hungry, too, having had nothing to eat since a little goat's milk at dawn. Between the smell of the simmering stew and the flickering light and shadows in the room, I felt light-headed, and very slightly disembodied, as though I were floating a foot or two above the floor.

"You're a nice old lad, aren't you?" I murmured. After an afternoon spent in close contact with babies, all in varying stages of moistness and shrieking, the company of the irascible old goat was rather soothing.

"Is he going to die?"

I looked up in surprise, having quite forgotten the younger Miss Brown, who had been overlooked in the shadows of the settle. She was standing by the hearth now, still holding the Beardsley baby and frowning down at Hiram, who was trying to nibble the edge of my apron.

"No," I said, twitching the cloth out of his mouth. "I shouldn't think so." What *was* her name? I groped blearily through my memory, matching up faces and names from the earlier flurry of introductions. Alicia, that was it, though I couldn't help still thinking of her as Juliet.

She wasn't much older than Juliet; barely fifteen, if that. She was a plain child, though, round-jawed and pasty. Narrow in the shoulder and broad through the hip; not much of the jewel in the Ethiop's ear about her. She said nothing more, and to keep the conversation going, I nodded at the baby, still in her arms. "How's the little one?"

"All right," she said listlessly. She stood staring at the goat a moment longer. Then tears suddenly welled in her eyes.

"I wish *I* was dead," she said.

"Oh, really?" I said, taken aback. "Er . . . well . . ." I rubbed a hand over my face, trying to summon enough presence of mind to deal with this. Where was the beastly girl's mother? I cast a quick look at the door, but heard no one coming. We were momentarily alone, the women milking or minding supper, the men all caring for the stock.

I stepped out of Hiram's pen and laid a hand on her arm.

"Look," I said in a low voice. "Isaiah Morton's not worth it. He's married; did you know that?"

Her eyes went wide, then squinted nearly shut, spurting sudden tears. No, evidently she hadn't known.

Tears were pouring down her cheeks and dripping on the baby's oblivious head. I reached out and took the swaddled child gently from her, steering her toward the settle with my free hand.

"H-how did you . . . ? Wh-who . . . ?" She was gurgling and sniffling, trying to ask questions and get control of herself at the same time. A man's voice shouted something outside, and she scrubbed frantically at her cheeks with her sleeve.

The gesture reminded me that while the situation seemed rather melodramatic—not to say slightly comic—in my currently muzzy frame of mind, it was a matter of great seriousness to the principals involved in it. After all, her male relations *had* tried to kill Morton, and would certainly try again, if they found him. I tensed at the sound of approaching feet, and the baby stirred and whined a little in my arms. But the footsteps crunched past in the road, and the sound vanished in the wind.

I sat down beside Alicia Brown, sighing with the sheer pleasure of taking weight off my feet. Every muscle and joint in my body ached from the aftereffects of the previous day and night, though I hadn't had time until now to think about it much. Jamie and I would undoubtedly spend the night wrapped in blankets on someone's floor; I eyed the grimy, firelit boards with an emotion approaching lust.

It was incongruously peaceful in the large room, with the snow whispering down outside, and the stewpot burbling away in the hearth, filling the air with the enticing scents of onion, venison, and turnips. The baby slept on my breast, emanating peaceful trust. I would have liked just to sit and hold her, thinking of nothing, but duty called.

"How do I know? Morton told one of my husband's men," I said. "I don't know who his wife is, though; only that she lives in Granite Falls." I patted the tiny back, and the baby burped faintly and relaxed again, her breath warm beneath my ear. The women had washed and oiled her, and she smelled rather like a fresh pancake. I kept one eye on the door, and the other warily on Alicia Brown, in case of further hysterics.

She sniffed and sobbed, hiccuped once, and then relapsed into silence, staring at the floor.

"I wish I was *dead*," she whispered again, in tones of such fierce despair that I set both eyes on her, startled. She sat hunched, hair hanging limply beneath her cap, her hands fisted and crossed protectively over her belly.

"Oh, dear," I said. Given her pallor, the circumstances, and her behavior toward the Beardsley baby, that particular gesture made it no great leap to the obvious conclusion. "Do your parents know?"

She gave me a quick look, but didn't bother asking how *I* knew.

"Mama and Aunt do."

She was breathing through her mouth, with intermittent wet snuffles.

"I thought—I thought Papa would have to let me wed him, if—"

I never had thought blackmail a very successful basis for marriage, but this seemed the wrong time to say so.

"Mmm," I said instead. "And does Mr. Morton know about it?"

She shook her head, disconsolate.

"Does he—does his wife have children, do you know?"

"I've no idea." I turned my head, listening. I could hear men's voices in the distance, carried on the wind. So could she; she gripped my arm with surprising strength, wet brown eyes spike-lashed and urgent.

"I heard Mr. MacKenzie and the men talking last night. They said you were a healer, Mrs. Fraser—one said you were a conjure woman. About babies. Do you know how—"

"Someone's coming." I pulled away from her, interrupting before she could finish. "Here, take care of the baby. I need to—to stir the stew."

I thrust the child unceremoniously into her arms and rose. When the door opened to admit a blast of wind and snow along with a large number of men, I was standing at the hearth, spoon in hand, eyes fixed on the pot and my mind bubbling as vigorously as the stew.

She hadn't had time to ask explicitly, but I knew what she'd been about tò say. *Conjure woman,* she'd called me. She wanted my help to get rid of the child, almost certainly. How? I wondered. How could a woman think of such a thing, with a living child in her arms, less than a day out of the womb?

But she was very young. Very young, and suffering from the shock of hearing that her lover was untrue. Not yet far enough advanced in pregnancy to show, either; if she hadn't yet felt her own child move, no doubt it seemed quite unreal to her. She'd seen it only as a means of forcing her father's consent; now it likely seemed a trap that had closed suddenly upon her.

No wonder if she was distraught, looking frantically for escape. Give her a little time to recover, I thought, glancing at the settle, where the shadows hid her. I should talk to her mother, to her aunt. . . .

Jamie appeared suddenly beside me, rubbing reddened hands over the fire, snow melting from the folds of his clothes. He looked extremely cheerful, in spite of his cold, the complications of Isaiah Morton's love life, and the storm going on outside.

"How is it, Sassenach?" he asked hoarsely, and without waiting for me to reply, took the spoon from my hand, put one hard, cold arm around me, and pulled me off my feet and up into a hearty kiss, made the more startling by the fact that his half-sprouted beard was thickly encrusted with snow.

Emerging slightly dazed from this stimulating embrace, I realized that the general attitude of the men in the room was similarly jolly. Backs were being slapped, boots stamped, and coats shaken to the accompaniment of the sort of hoots and roaring noises men make when feeling particularly exuberant.

"What is it?" I asked, looking round in surprise. To my astonishment, Joseph Wemyss stood in the center of the crowd. The tip of his nose was red with cold, and he was being knocked half off his feet by men smacking him on the back in congratulations. "What's happened?"

Jamie gave me a brilliant smile, teeth gleaming in the frozen wilderness of his face, and thrust a limp crumple of wet paper into my hand, fragments of red wax still clinging to it.

The ink had run with the wet, but I could make out the relevant words. Hearing of General Waddell's intended approach, the Regulators had decided that discretion was the better part of valor. They had dispersed. And as per this order from Governor Tryon—the militia was stood down.

"Oh, *good*!" I said. And flinging my arms round Jamie, kissed him back, snow and ice notwithstanding.

THRILLED WITH THE NEWS of the stand-down, the militia took advantage of the bad weather to celebrate. Equally thrilled not to be obliged to join the militia, the Browns instead joined heartily in the celebration, contributing three large kegs of Thomasina Brown's best home-brewed beer and six gallons of hard cider to the cause—at half-cost.

By the time supper was over, I sat in the corner of a settle with the Beardsley baby in my arms, half-dissolved with weariness, and kept vertical only by the fact that there was no place as yet to lie down. The air shimmered with smoke and conversation, I had drunk strong cider with my supper, and both faces and voices tended to swim in and out of focus, in a way that was not at all disagreeable, though mildly disconcerting.

Alicia Brown had had no further chance to speak with me—but I had had no chance to speak with her mother or her aunt. The girl had taken up a seat by Hiram's pen, and was methodically feeding the goat crusts of corn bread left from supper, her face set in lines of sullen misery.

Roger was singing French ballads, by popular request, in a soft, true voice. A young woman's face floated into view in front of me, eyebrows raised in question. She said something, lost in the babble of voices, then reached gently to take the baby from me.

Of course. Jemima, that was her name. The young mother

who had offered to nurse the child. I stood up to give her room on the settle, and she put the baby at once to her breast.

I leaned against the chimney piece, watching with dim approval as she cupped the child's head, guiding it and murmuring. She was both tender and businesslike; a good combination. Her own baby—little Christopher, that was his name—snored peacefully in his grandmother's arms, as the old lady bent to light her clay pipe from the fire.

I glanced back at Jemima, and had the oddest sense of déjà vu. I blinked, trying to catch the fleeting vision, and succeeded in capturing a sense of overwhelming closeness, of warmth and utter peace. For an instant, I thought it was the sense of nursing a child, and then, odder still, realized that it was not the mother's sense I felt . . . but the child's. I had the very distinct memory—if that's what it was—of being held against a warm body, mindless and replete in the sure conviction of absolute love.

I closed my eyes, and took a firmer grip on the chimney breast, feeling the room begin a slow and lazy spin about me.

"Beauchamp," I murmured, "you are *quite* drunk."

If so, I wasn't the only one. Delighted at the prospect of imminent return to their homes, the militiamen had absorbed most of the drinkables in Brownsville, and were working assiduously on the remainder. The party was beginning to break up now, though, with men stumbling off to cold beds in barns and sheds, others thankfully rolling up in blankets by the fire.

I opened my eyes to see Jamie throw back his head and yawn enormously, gape-jawed as a baboon. He blinked and stood up, shaking off the stupor of food and beer, then glanced toward the hearth and saw me standing there. He was plainly as tired as I was, if not quite as giddy, but he had a sense of deep content about him, apparent in the long-limbed ease with which he stretched and settled himself.

"I'm going to see to the horses," he said to me, voice husky from grippe and much talking. "Fancy a walk in the moonlight, Sassenach?"

THE SNOW HAD STOPPED, and there *was* moonlight, glowing through a haze of vanishing cloud. The air was lung-chillingly cold, still fresh and restless with the ghost of the passing storm, and did much to clear my spinning head.

I felt a childish delight in being the first to mark the virgin snow, and stepped high and carefully, making neat bootprints and looking back to admire them. The line of footprints wasn't very straight, but fortunately no one was testing my sobriety.

"Can you recite the alphabet backward?" I asked Jamie, whose footsteps were wavering companionably along with my own.

"I expect so," he replied. "Which one? English, Greek, or Hebrew?"

"Never mind." I took a firmer grip of his arm. "If you remember all three forward, you're in better condition than I am."

He laughed softly, then coughed.

"You're never drunk, Sassenach. Not on three cups of cider."

"Must be fatigue, then," I said dreamily. "I feel as though my head's bobbing about on a string like a balloon. How do you know how much I drank? Do you notice *everything*?"

He laughed again, and folded a hand round mine where it clutched his arm.

"I like to watch ye, Sassenach. Especially in company. You've the loveliest shine to your teeth when ye laugh."

"Flatterer," I said, feeling nonetheless flattered. Given that I hadn't so much as washed my face in several days, let alone bathed or changed my clothes, my teeth were likely the only things about me that could be honestly admired. Still, the knowledge of his attention was singularly warming.

It was a dry snow, and the white crust compressed beneath our feet with a low crunching noise. I could hear Jamie's breathing, hoarse and labored still, but the rattle in his chest had gone, and his skin was cool.

"It will be fair by morning," he said, looking up at the hazy moon. "D'ye see the ring?"

It was hard to miss; an immense circle of diffuse light that ringed the moon, covering the whole of the eastern sky. Faint stars were showing through the haze; it would be bright and clear within the hour.

"Yes. We can go home tomorrow, then?"

"Aye. It will be muddy going, I expect. Ye can feel the air changing; it's cold enough now, but the snow will melt as soon as the sun's full on it."

Perhaps it would, but it *was* cold enough now. The horses' brushy shelter had been reinforced with more cut branches of pine and hemlock, and it looked like a small, lumpy hillock rising from the ground, thickly covered over with snow. Dark patches had melted clear, though, warmed by the horses' breath, and wisps of steam rose from them, scarcely visible. Everything was quiet, with a palpable sense of drowsy content.

"Morton will be cozy, if he's in there," I observed.

"I shouldna think so. I sent Fergus out to tell him the militia was disbanded, so soon as Wemyss came wi' the note."

"Yes, but if I were Isaiah Morton, I don't know that I would have set straight out on the road home in a blinding snowstorm," I said dubiously.

"Likely ye would, if ye had all the Browns in Brownsville after ye wi' guns," he said. Nonetheless, he paused in his step, raised his voice a little, and called "Isaiah!" in a croaking rasp.

There was no answer from the makeshift stable, and taking my arm again, he turned back toward the house. The snow was virgin no longer, trampled and muddied by the prints of many feet, as the militia dispersed to their beds. Roger had stopped singing, but there were still voices from inside the house; not everyone was ready to retire.

Reluctant to go back at once to the atmosphere of smoke and noise, we walked by unspoken mutual consent round the house and barn, enjoying the silence of the snowy wood and the nearness of each other. Coming back, I saw that the door of the lean-to at the rear of the house stood ajar, creaking in the wind, and pointed it out to Jamie.

He poked his head inside, to see that all was in order, but then, instead of closing the door, he reached back and took my arm, pulling me into the lean-to after him.

"I'd a question to ask ye, Sassenach, before we go in," he said. He set the door open, so the moonlight streamed in, shining dimly on the hanging hams, the hogsheads and burlap bags that inhabited the lean-to with us.

It was cold inside, but out of the wind I at once felt warmer, and put back the hood of my cloak.

"What is it?" I said, mildly curious. The fresh air had cleared my head, at least, and while I knew I would be as good as dead the instant I lay down, for the moment I had that sense of pleasant lightness that comes with the feeling of effort completed, honor satisfied. It had been a terrible day and night, and a long day after, but now it was done, and we were free.

"Do ye want her, Sassenach?" he asked softly. His face was a pale oval, blurred by the mist of his breath.

"Who?" I asked, startled. He gave a small grunt of amusement.

"The child. Who else?"

Who else, indeed.

"Do I want her—to keep her, you mean?" I asked cautiously. "Adopt her?" The notion hadn't crossed my mind consciously, but must have been lurking somewhere in my subconscious, for I was not startled at his question, and at the speaking, the idea sprang into full flower.

My breasts had been tender since the morning, feeling full and engorged, and I felt the demanding tug of the little girl's mouth in memory. I could not feed the baby myself—but Brianna could, or Marsali. Or she could live on cow's milk, goat's milk.

I realized suddenly that I had unconsciously cupped one breast, and was gently massaging it. I stopped at once, but Jamie had seen it; he moved closer and put an arm around me. I leaned my head against him, the rough weave of his hunting shirt cold against my cheek.

"Do *you* want her?" I asked. I wasn't sure whether I was hopeful of his answer, or fearful of it. The answer was a slight shrug.

"It's a big house, Sassenach," he said. "Big enough."

"Hmm," I said. Not a resounding declaration—and yet I knew it was commitment, no matter how casually expressed.

He had acquired Fergus in a Paris brothel, on the basis of three minutes' acquaintance, as a hired pickpocket. If he took this child, he would treat her as a daughter. Love her? No one could guarantee love—not he . . . and not I.

He had picked up my dubious tone of voice.

"I saw ye with the wean, Sassenach, riding. Ye've a great tenderness about ye always—but when I saw ye so, wi' the bairn tumbling about beneath your cloak, it—I remembered, how it was, how ye looked, when ye carried Faith."

I caught my breath. To hear him speak the name of our first daughter like that, so matter-of-factly, was startling. We spoke of her seldom; her death was so long in the past that sometimes it seemed unreal, and yet the wound of her loss had scarred both of us badly.

Faith herself was not unreal at all, though.

She was near me, whenever I touched a baby. And this child, this nameless orphan, so small and frail, with skin so translucent that the blue threads of her veins showed clear beneath—yes, the echoes of Faith were strong. Still, she wasn't *my* child. Though she could be; that was what Jamie was saying.

Was she perhaps a gift to us? Or at least our responsibility?

"Do you think we ought to take her?" I asked cautiously. "I mean—what might happen to her if we don't?"

Jamie snorted faintly, dropping his arm, and leaned back against the wall of the house. He wiped his nose, and tilted his head toward the faint rumble of voices that came through the chinked logs.

"She'd be well cared for, Sassenach. She's in the way of being an heiress, ken."

That aspect of the matter hadn't occurred to me at all.

"Are you sure?" I said dubiously. "I mean, the Beardsleys are both gone, but as she's illegitimate—"

He shook his head, interrupting me.

"Nay, she's legitimate."

"But she can't be. No one realizes it yet except you and me, but her father—"

"Her father was Aaron Beardsley, so far as the law is concerned," he informed me. "By English law, a child born in wedlock is the legal child—*and* heir—of the husband—even if it's known for a fact that the mother committed adultery. And yon woman did say that Beardsley married her, no?"

It struck me that he was remarkably positive about this particular provision of English law. It also struck me—in time, thank God, before I said anything—exactly *why* he was positive.

William. His son, conceived in England, and so far as anyone in England knew—with the exception of Lord John Grey—presumably the ninth Earl of Ellesmere. Evidently, he legally *was* the ninth Earl, according to what Jamie was telling me, whether the eighth Earl had been his father or not. The law really was an ass, I thought.

"I see," I said slowly. "So little Nameless will inherit all Beardsley's property, even after they discover that he can't have been her father. That's . . . reassuring."

His eyes met mine for a moment, then dropped.

"Aye," he said quietly. "Reassuring." There might have been a hint of bitterness in his voice, but if there was, it vanished without trace as he coughed and cleared his throat.

"So ye see," he went on, matter-of-factly, "she's in no danger of neglect. An Orphan Court would give Beardsley's property—goats and all"—he added, with a faint grin—"to whomever is her guardian, to be used for her welfare."

"And her guardians'," I said, suddenly recalling the look Richard Brown had exchanged with his brother, when telling his wife the child would be "well cared for." I rubbed my nose, which had gone numb at the tip.

"So the Browns would take her willingly, then."

"Oh, aye," he agreed. "They kent Beardsley; they'll ken well enough how valuable she is. It would be a delicate matter to get her away from them, in fact—but if ye want the child, Sassenach, then ye'll have her. I promise ye that."

The whole discussion was giving me a very queer feeling. Something almost like panic, as though I were being pushed by some unseen hand toward the edge of a precipice. Whether that was a dangerous cliff or merely a foothold for a larger view remained to be seen.

I saw in memory the gentle curve of the baby's skull, and the tissue-paper ears, small and perfect as shells, their soft pink whorls fading into an otherworldly tinge of blue.

To give myself a little time to organize my thoughts, I asked, "What did you mean, it would be a delicate matter to get her away from the Browns? They've no claim on her, have they?"

He shook his head.

"Nay, but none of them shot her father, either."

"What—oh." That was a potential trap that I hadn't seen; the possibility that Jamie might be accused of killing Beardsley in order to get his hands on the trader's farm and goods, by then adopting the orphan. I swallowed, the back of my throat tasting faintly of bile.

"But no one knows how Aaron Beardsley died, except us," I pointed out. Jamie had told them only that the trader had had an apoplexy and died, leaving out his own role as the angel of deliverance.

"Us and Mrs. Beardsley," he said, a faint tone of irony in his voice. "And if she should come back, and accuse me of murdering her husband? It would be hard to deny, and I'd taken the child."

I forbore from asking why she might do such a thing; in light of what she had already done, it was clear enough that Fanny Beardsley might do anything.

"She won't come back," I said. Whatever my own uncertainties about the rest of it, I was sure that in this respect at least, I spoke the truth. Wherever Fanny Beardsley had gone—or why—I was sure she had gone for good.

"Even if she did," I went on, pushing aside my vision of snow drifting through an empty wood, and a wrapped bundle lying by the burned-out fire, "I was there. I could say what happened."

"If they'd let ye," Jamie agreed. "Which they wouldna. You're a marrit woman, Sassenach; ye couldna testify in a court, even if ye weren't my own wife."

That brought me up short. Living as we did in the wilderness, I seldom encountered the more outrageous legal injustices of the times in a personal way, but I was aware of some of them. He was right. In fact, as a married woman, I had no legal rights at all. Ironically enough, Fanny Beardsley *did*, being now a widow. *She* could testify in a court of law—if she wished.

"Well, bloody hell!" I said, with feeling. Jamie laughed, though quietly, then coughed.

I snorted, with a satisfactory explosion of white vapor. I wished momentarily that I was a dragon; it would have been extremely enjoyable to huff flame and brimstone on a number of people, starting with Fanny Beardsley. Instead, I sighed, my harmless white breath vanishing in the dimness of the lean-to.

"I see what you mean by 'delicate,' then," I said.

"Aye—but not impossible." He cupped a large, cold hand along my cheek, turning my face up to his. His eyes searched my own, dark and intent.

"If ye want the child, Claire, I will take her, and manage whatever comes."

If I wanted her. I could feel the soft weight of the child, sleeping on my breast. I had forgotten the intoxication of motherhood for years; pushed aside the memory of the feelings of exaltation, exhaustion, panic, delight. Having Germain and Jemmy and Joan nearby, though, had reminded me vividly.

"One last question," I said. I took his hand and brought it down, fingers linked with mine. "The baby's father wasn't white. What might that mean to her?"

I knew what it would have meant in Boston of the 1960s, but this was a very different place, and while in some ways society here was more rigid and less officially enlightened than the time I had come from, in others it was oddly much more tolerant.

Jamie considered carefully, the stiff fingers of his right hand tapping out a silent rhythm of contemplation on the head of a barrel of salt pork.

"I think it will be all right," he said at last. "There's no question of her being taken into slavery. Even if it could be proved that her father was a slave—and there's no proof at all—a child takes the mother's status. A child born to a free woman is free; a child born to a slave woman is a slave. And whatever yon dreadful woman might be, she wasna a slave."

"Not in name, at least," I said, thinking of the marks on the doorpost. "But beyond the question of slavery . . . ?"

He sighed and straightened.

"I think not," he said. "Not here. In Charleston, aye, it would likely matter; at least if she were in society. But in the backcountry?"

He shrugged. True enough; so close as we were to the Treaty Line, there were any number of mixed-breed children. It was in no way unusual for settlers to take wives among the Cherokee. It was a good deal rarer to see children born of a black and white liaison in the backcountry, but they were plentiful in the coastal areas. Most of them slaves—but there, nonetheless.

And wee Miss Beardsley would not be "in society," at least, not if we left her with the Browns. Here, her potential wealth would matter a great deal more than the color of her skin. With us, it might be different, for Jamie was—and always would be, despite his income or lack of it—a gentleman.

"That wasn't the last question, after all," I said. I laid a hand over his, cold on my cheek. "The last one is—why are you suggesting the notion?"

"Ah. Well, I only thought . . ." He dropped his hand, and looked away. "What ye said when we came home from the Gathering. That ye could have chosen the safety of barrenness—but did not, for my sake. I thought—" He stopped again, and rubbed the knuckle of his free hand hard along the bridge of his nose. He took a deep breath and tried again.

"For my sake," he said firmly, addressing the air in front of him as though it were a tribunal, "I dinna want ye to bear another child. I wouldna risk your loss, Sassenach," he said, his voice suddenly husky. "Not for a dozen bairns. I've daughters and sons, nieces and nephews, grandchildren—weans enough."

He looked at me directly then, and spoke softly.

"But I've no life but you, Claire."

He swallowed audibly, and went on, eyes fixed on mine.

"I did think, though . . . if ye do want another child . . . perhaps I could still give ye one."

Brief tears blurred my eyes. It was cold in the lean-to, and our fingers were stiff. I fumbled my hand into his, squeezing tight.

Even as we had spoken, my mind had been busy, envisioning possibilities, difficulties, blessings. I did not need to think further, for I knew the decision had made itself. A child was a temptation of the flesh, as well as of the spirit; I knew the bliss of that unbounded oneness, as I knew the bittersweet joy of seeing that oneness fade as the child learned itself and stood alone.

But I had crossed some subtle line. Whether it was that I was born myself with some secret quota embodied in my flesh, or only that I knew my sole allegiance must be given elsewhere now . . . I knew. As a mother, I had the lightness now of effort complete, honor satisfied. Mission accomplished.

I leaned my forehead against his chest and spoke into the shadowed cloth above his heart.

"No," I said softly. "But, Jamie . . . I so love you."

WE STOOD WRAPPED in each other's arms for a time, hearing the rumble of voices from the other side of the wall that separated the house from the lean-to, but silent ourselves, and content with the peace of it. We were at once too exhausted to make the effort to go in, and reluctant to abandon the tranquillity of our rude retreat.

"We'll have to go in soon," I murmured at last. "If we don't, we'll fall down right here, and be found in the morning, along with the hams."

A faint wheeze of laughter ran through his chest, but before he could answer, a shadow fell over us. Someone stood in the open door, blocking the moonlight.

Jamie lifted his head sharply, hands tight on my shoulders, but then he let his breath out, and his grip relaxed, allowing me to step back and turn round.

"Morton," Jamie said, in a long-suffering sort of voice. "What in Christ's name are ye doing here?"

Isaiah Morton didn't much look like a rakish seducer, but then, I supposed tastes must differ. He was slightly shorter than I, but broad through the shoulder, with a barrel-shaped torso and slightly bowed legs. He did have rather pleasant-looking eyes and a nice mop of wavy hair, though I was unable to tell the color of either, in the dim light of the lean-to. I estimated his age at somewhere in the early twenties.

"Colonel, sir," he said in a whisper. "Ma'am." He gave me a quick, brief bow. "Didn't mean to give you fright, ma'am. Only I heard the Colonel's voice and thought I best seize the day, so to speak."

Jamie regarded Morton narrowly.

"So to speak," he repeated.

"Yes, sir. I couldn't make out how I was to get Ally to come forth, and was just a-circling of the house again, when I caught heed of you and your lady talking."

He bowed to me again, as though by reflex.

"Morton," Jamie said, softly, but with a certain amount of steel in his voice, "why have ye not gone? Did Fergus not tell ye that the militia is stood down?"

"Oh, aye, sir, he did, sir." He bowed to Jamie this time, looking faintly anxious. "But I couldn't go, sir, not without seeing Ally."

I cleared my throat and glanced at Jamie, who sighed and nodded to me.

"Er . . . I'm afraid that Miss Brown has heard about your prior entanglement," I said delicately.

"Eh?" Isaiah looked blank, and Jamie made an irritable noise.

"She means the lass kens ye've a wife already," he said brutally, "and if her father doesna shoot ye on sight, she may stab ye to the heart. And if neither of them succeeds," he went on, drawing himself up to his fully menacing height, "I'm inclined to do the job myself, wi' my bare hands. What sort of man would slip round a lass and get her with child, and him with no right to give it his name?"

Isaiah Morton paled noticeably, even in the dim light.

"With child?"

"She is," I said, quite coldly.

"She is," Jamie repeated, "and now, ye wee bigamist, ye'd best leave, before—"

He stopped speaking abruptly, as Isaiah's hand came out

from under his cloak, holding a pistol. Close as he was, I could see that it was both loaded and cocked.

"I'm that sorry, sir," he said apologetically. He licked his lips, glancing from Jamie to me, and back. "I wouldn't do you harm, sir, nor certain sure your lady. But you see, I just got to see Ally." His rather pudgy features firmed a little, though his lips seemed inclined to tremble. Still, he pointed the pistol at Jamie with decision.

"Ma'am," he said to me, "if might be as you'd be so kind, would you go on into the house and fetch Ally out? We'll . . . just wait here, the Colonel and me."

I hadn't had time to feel afraid. I wasn't really afraid now, though I was speechless with astonishment.

Jamie closed his eyes briefly, as though praying for strength. Then he opened them and sighed, his breath a white cloud in the cold air.

"Put it down, idiot," he said, almost kindly. "Ye ken fine ye willna shoot me, and so do I."

Isaiah tightened both his lips and his trigger finger, and I held my breath. Jamie continued to look at him, his gaze a mixture of censure and pity. At last, the finger relaxed, and the pistol barrel sank, along with Isaiah's eyes.

"I just got to see Ally, Colonel," he said softly, looking at the ground.

I drew a deep breath, and looked up at Jamie. He hesitated, then nodded.

"All right, Sassenach. Go canny, aye?"

I nodded, and turned to slip into the house, hearing Jamie mutter something under his breath in Gaelic behind me, to the general effect that he must have lost his mind.

I wasn't sure he hadn't, though I had also felt the strength of Morton's appeal. If any of the Browns happened to discover this rendezvous, though, there would be hell to pay—and it wouldn't be only Morton who paid.

The floor inside was littered with sleeping bodies wrapped in blankets, though a few men still huddled round the hearth, gossiping and passing a jug of something spirituous among themselves. I looked carefully, but fortunately Richard Brown was not among them.

I made my way across the room, carefully stepping

through and over the bodies on the floor, and peered into the bed that stood against the wall as I passed. Richard Brown and his wife were both curled up in it, sound asleep, nightcaps pulled well down over their respective ears, though the house was warm enough, what with all the trapped body heat.

There was only one place that Alicia Brown could be, and I pushed open the door to the loft stair, as quietly as I could. It made little difference; no one by the fire paid the slightest attention. One of the men appeared to be trying to get Hiram to drink from the jug, with some success.

By contrast to the room below, the loft was quite cold. This was because the small window was uncovered, and quite a lot of snow had drifted in, together with a freezing wind. Alicia Brown was lying in the little snowdrift under the window, stark naked.

I walked over and stood looking down at her. She lay stiffly on her back, arms folded over her chest. She was shivering, and her eyes were squinched shut with ferocious concentration. Obviously, she hadn't heard my footsteps, over the noises from below.

"What in God's name are you doing?" I inquired politely.

Her eyes popped open and she gave a small shriek. Then she clapped a hand over her mouth and sat up abruptly, staring at me.

"I've heard of a number of novel ways of inducing miscarriage," I told her, picking up a quilt from the cot and dropping it over her shoulders, "but freezing to death isn't one of them."

"If I'm d-dead, I won't need to m-m-miscarry," she said, with a certain amount of logic. Nonetheless, she drew the quilt around her, teeth chattering.

"Scarcely the best means of committing suicide, either, I shouldn't think," I said. "Though I don't mean to sound critical. Still, you can't do it now; Mr. Morton is out in the lean-to and won't go away until you come down to speak to him, so you'd better get up and put something on."

Her eyes flew wide and she scrambled to her feet, her muscles so stiff with cold that she stumbled awkwardly and would have fallen, had I not grabbed her arm. She said nothing more, but dressed as quickly as her chilled fingers would allow, wrapping a thick cloak around herself.

Bearing in mind Jamie's adjuration to "Go canny," I sent her down the narrow stair alone. Alone, she would be merely assumed to be going to the privy—if anyone even noticed her departure. Both of us together might cause comment.

Left by myself in the darkened loft, I drew my own cloak around me and went to the narrow window to wait for the few minutes necessary before I could leave, too. I heard the soft thump of the door closing below, but couldn't see Alicia from this high angle. Judging from her response to my summons, she didn't intend to stab Isaiah to the heart, but heaven knew what either of them *did* intend.

The clouds were gone now, and the frozen landscape stretched before me, brilliant and ghostly under a setting moon. Across the road, the horses' brushy shelter stood dark, dappled with clumps of snow. The air had changed, as Jamie had said, and warmed by the horses' breath, chunks of melting snow slid free and plopped to the ground.

In spite of my annoyance with the young lovers, and the undertones of comic absurdity attending the whole situation, I couldn't help but feel some sympathy for them. They were so in earnest, so intent on nothing but each other.

And Isaiah's unknown wife?

I hunched my shoulders, shivering slightly inside my cloak. I should disapprove—I did, in fact—but no one knew the true nature of a marriage, save those who made it. And I was too aware of living in a glass house, to think of throwing stones myself. Almost absently, I stroked the smooth metal of my gold wedding ring.

Adultery. Fornication. Betrayal. Dishonor. The words dropped softly in my mind, like the clumps of falling snow, leaving small dark pits, shadows in moonlight.

Excuses could be made, of course. I had not sought what had happened to me, had fought against it, had had no choice. Except that, in the end, one always has a choice. I had made mine, and everything had followed from it.

Bree, Roger, Jemmy. Any children that might be born to

them in the future. All of them were here, in one way or another, because of what I had chosen to do, that far-off day on Craigh na Dun.

*You take too much upon yourself.* Frank had said that to me, many times. Generally in tones of disapproval, meaning that I did things he would have preferred I did not. But now and then in kindness, meaning to relieve me of some burden.

It was in kindness that the thought came to me now, whether it was truly spoken, or only called forth from my exhausted memory for what comfort the words might hold. Everyone makes choices, and no one knows what may be the end of any of them. If my own was to blame for many things, it was not to blame for everything. Nor was harm all that had come of it.

*'Til death us do part.* There were a great many people who had spoken those vows, only to abandon or betray them. And yet it came to me that neither death nor conscious choice dissolved some bonds. For better or for worse, I had loved two men, and some part of them both would be always with me.

The dreadful thing, I supposed, was that while I had often felt a deep and searing regret for what I had done, I had never felt guilt. With the choice so far behind me, now, perhaps, I did.

I had apologized to Frank a thousand times, and never once had I asked him for forgiveness. It occurred to me suddenly that he had given it, nonetheless—to the best of his ability. The loft was dark, save for faint lines of light that seeped through the chinks of the floor, but it no longer seemed empty.

I stirred abruptly, pulled from my abstraction by sudden movement below. Silent as flying reindeer, two dark figures darted hand-in-hand across the field of snow, cloaks like clouds around them. They hesitated for a moment outside the horses' shelter, then disappeared inside.

I leaned on the sill, heedless of the snow crystals under my palms. I could hear the noise of the horses rousing; whickers and stamping came clearly to me across the clear air. The sounds in the house below had grown fainter; now a clear, loud *"Meh-eh-eh!"* came up through the floorboards, as Hiram sensed the horses' uneasiness.

There was renewed laughter from below, temporarily drowning the sounds across the road. Where was Jamie? I leaned out, the wind billowing the hood of my cloak, brushing a spray of ice across my cheek.

There he was. A tall dark figure, walking across the snow toward the shelter, but going slowly, kicking up white clouds of dusty ice. What . . . but then I realized that he was following in the lovers' tracks, stamping and floundering deliberately to obliterate a trail that must tell its story clearly to any of the trackers in the house below.

A hole appeared suddenly in the brushy shelter, as a section of the branched wall fell away. Clouds of steam roiled out into the air, and then a horse emerged, carrying two riders, and set off to the west, urged from a walk to a trot and then a canter. The snow was not deep; no more than three or four inches. The horse's hooves left a clear dark trail, leading down the road.

A piercing whinny rose from the shelter, followed by another. Sounds of alarm came from below, scuffling and thuds as men rolled from their blankets or lunged for their weapons. Jamie had disappeared.

All at once, horses burst from the shelter, knocking down the wall and trampling the fallen branches. Snorting, whinnying, kicking, and jostling, they spilled out over the road in a chaos of flying manes and rolling eyes. The last of them sprang from the shelter and joined the runaway, tail whisking away from the switch that landed on its rump.

Jamie flung away the switch and ducked back into the shelter, just as the door below flung open, spilling pale gold light over the scene.

I seized the opportunity of the commotion to run downstairs without being seen. Everyone was outside; even Mrs. Brown had rushed out, nightcap and all, leaving the quilts pulled half off the bed. Hiram, smelling strongly of beer, swayed and *meh*ed tipsily at me as I passed, yellow eyes moist and protuberant with conviviality.

Outside, the roadway was full of half-dressed men,

surging to and fro and waving their arms in agitation. I caught sight of Jamie in the midst of the crowd, gesticulating with the best of them. Among the excited bits of question and comment, I heard scraps of speech—"spooked" ... "panther?" ... "goddamn!" and the like.

After a bit of milling around and incoherent argument, it was unanimously decided that the horses would likely come back by themselves. Snow was blowing off the trees in veils of whirling ice; the wind stuck freezing fingers through every crevice of clothing.

"Would *you* stay out on a night like this?" Roger demanded, reasonably enough. It being generally decided that no sane man would—and horses being, if not quite sane, certainly sensible creatures—the party began to trickle back into the house, shivering and grumbling as the heat of excitement began to die down.

Among the last stragglers, Jamie turned toward the house and saw me, still standing on the porch. His hair was loose and the light from the open door lit him like a torch. He caught my eye, rolled his own toward heaven, and raised his shoulders in the faintest of shrugs.

I put cold fingers to my lips and blew him a small frozen kiss.

# PART FOUR

*I Hear No Music*

*But the Sound of Drums*

# HOME FOR CHRISTMAS

W**HAT WOULD YOU HAVE DONE?"** Brianna asked. She turned over, moving carefully in the narrow confines of Mr. Wemyss's bed, and parked her chin comfortably in the hollow of Roger's shoulder.

"What would I have done about what?" Warm through for the first time in weeks, filled to bursting with one of Mrs. Bug's dinners, and having finally achieved the nirvana of an hour's privacy with his wife, Roger felt pleasantly drowsy and detached.

"About Isaiah Morton and Alicia Brown."

Roger gave a jaw-cracking yawn and settled himself deeper, the corn-shuck mattress rustling loudly under them. He supposed the whole house had heard them at it earlier, and he didn't really care. She'd washed her hair in honor of his homecoming; waves of it spread over his chest, a silky rich gleam in the dim glow of the hearth. It was only late afternoon, but the shutters were closed, giving the pleasant illusion that they were inside a small private cave.

"I don't know. What your Da did, I suppose; what else? Your hair smells great." He smoothed a lock of it around his finger, admiring the shimmer.

"Thanks. I used some of that stuff Mama makes with walnut oil and marigolds. What about Isaiah's poor wife in Granite Falls, though?"

"What about her? Jamie couldn't force Morton to go home to her—assuming that she wants him back," he added logically. "And the girl—Alicia—was evidently more than willing; your father couldn't very well have made a kerfuffle about Morton leaving with her, unless he wanted the man dead. If the Browns had found Morton there, they would have killed him on the spot and nailed his hide to their barn door."

He spoke with conviction, remembering the pointed guns that had greeted him in Brownsville. He smoothed the hair behind her ear, and lifted his head far enough to kiss her between the eyebrows. He'd been imagining that for days, that smooth pale space between the heavy brows. It seemed like a tiny oasis among the vivid danger of her features; the flash of eyes and blade of nose were more than attractive, to say nothing of a mobile brow and a wide mouth that spoke its mind as much by its shape as by its words—but not peaceful. After the last three weeks, he was in a mood for peace.

He sank back on the pillow, tracing the stern arch of one ruddy brow with a finger.

"I think the best he could do under the circumstances was to give the young lovers a bit of room to get safe away," he said. "And they did. By the morning, the snow was already melting to mud, and with all the trampling, you couldn't have told whether a regiment of bears had marched through, let alone which way they were going."

He spoke with feeling; the weather had turned suddenly to a warm thaw, and the militia had returned to their homes in good spirits, but muddy to the eyebrows.

Brianna sighed, her breath raising a pleasant gooseflesh across his chest. She lifted her own head a little, peering in interest.

"What? Have I got filth stuck to me still?" He had washed, but in haste, eager to eat, more eager to get to bed.

"No. I just like it when you get goose bumps. All the hairs on your chest stand up, and so do your nipples." She flicked one of the objects in question lightly with a fingernail, and a fresh wave of gooseflesh raced across his chest for her entertainment. He arched his back a little, then relaxed. No, he'd have to go downstairs soon, to deal with the evening chores; he'd heard Jamie go out already.

Time for a change of subject. He breathed deep, then

lifted his head from the pillow, sniffing with interest at the rich aroma seeping through the floor from the kitchen below.

"What's that cooking?"

"A goose. Or geese—a dozen of them." He thought he caught an odd undertone in her voice, a faint tinge of regret.

"Well, that's a treat," he said, running a lingering hand down the length of her back. A pale gold down covered her back and shoulders, invisible save when there was candle-light behind her, as there was now. "What's the occasion? For our homecoming?"

She lifted her head from his chest and gave him what he privately classified as A Look.

"For Christmas," she said.

"What?" He groped blankly, trying to count the days, but the events of the last three weeks had completely erased his mental calendar. "When?"

"Tomorrow, idiot," she said with exaggerated patience. She leaned over and did something unspeakably erotic to his nipple, then heaved herself up in a rustle of bedclothes, leaving him bereft of blissful warmth and exposed to chilly drafts.

"Didn't you see all the greenery downstairs when you came in? Lizzie and I made the little Chisholm monsters go out with us to cut evergreens; we've been making wreaths and garlands for the last three days." The words were some-what muffled, as she wormed her way into her shift, but he thought she sounded only incredulous, rather than angry. He could hope.

He sat up and swung his feet down, toes curling as they came in contact with the cold boards of the floor. His own cabin had a braided rug by the bed—but his cabin was full of Chisholms at the moment, or so he was informed. He rubbed a hand through his hair, groping for inspiration, and found it.

"I didn't see anything when I came in but you."

That was the simple truth, and evidently honesty was the best policy. Her head popped through the neckhole of her shift and she gave him a narrow look, which faded into a slow smile as she saw the evident sincerity stamped on his features.

She came over to the bed and put her arms around him, enveloping his head in a smother of marigolds, butter-soft linen, and . . . milk. Oh, aye. The kid would be needing to eat again soon. Resigned, he put his arms round the swell of her hips and rested his head between her breasts for the few moments that were his own meager share of that abundance.

"Sorry," he said, words muffled in her warmth. "I'd forgotten it entirely. I'd have brought you and Jem something, if I'd thought."

"Like what? A piece of Isaiah Morton's hide?" She laughed and let go, straightening up to smooth her hair. She was wearing the bracelet he'd given her on an earlier Christmas Eve; the hearthlight glinted off the silver as she lifted her arm.

"Aye, ye could cover a book in it, I suppose. Or make a pair of wee boots for Jem." It had been a long ride, men and horses pushing past tiredness, eager for home. He felt boneless, and would have asked no better present himself than to go back to bed with her, pressed tight together in warmth, to drift toward the inviting depths of deep black sleep and amorous dreams. Duty called, though; he yawned, blinked, and heaved himself up.

"Are the geese for our supper tonight, then?" he asked, squatting to poke through the discarded pile of mud-caked garments he'd shucked earlier. He might have a clean shirt somewhere, but with the Chisholms in his cabin, and Bree and Jem temporarily lodged here in the Wemysses' room, he had no idea where his own things were. No sense to put on something clean only to go and muck out a byre and feed horses, anyway. He'd shave and change before supper.

"Uh-huh. Mrs. Bug has half a hog barbecuing in a pit outside for tomorrow's Christmas dinner. I shot the geese yesterday, though, and she wanted to use them fresh. We were hoping you guys would be home in time."

He glanced at her, picking up the same undertone in her voice.

"Ye don't care for goose?" he asked. She looked down at him, with an odd expression.

"I've never eaten one," she answered. "Roger?"

"Aye?"

"I was just wondering. I wanted to ask if you knew . . ."

"If I know what?"

He was moving slowly, still wrapped in a pleasant fog of exhaustion and lovemaking. She had put her gown on, brushed her hair, and put it up neatly in a thick coil on her neck, all in the time it had taken him to disentangle his stockings and breeches. He shook the breeks absentmindedly, sending a shower of dried mud fragments pattering over the floor.

"Don't do that! What's the matter with you?" Flushed with sudden annoyance, she snatched the breeks away from him. She thrust open the shutters and leaned out, flapping the garment violently over the sill. She jerked the shaken breeks back in and threw them in his general direction; he dived to catch them.

"Hey. What's the matter with *you*?"

"Matter? You shower dirt all over the floor and you think there's something wrong with *me*?"

"Sorry. I didn't think—"

She made a noise deep in her throat. It wasn't very loud, but it was threatening. Obeying a deep-seated masculine reflex, he shoved a leg into his breeches. Whatever might be happening, he'd rather meet it with his trousers on. He jerked them up, talking fast.

"Look, I'm sorry I didn't think of it being Christmas. It was—there were important things to deal with; I lost track. I'll make it up to ye. Perhaps when we go to Cross Creek for your aunt's wedding. I could—"

"The hell with Christmas!"

"What?" He stopped, breeks half-buttoned. It was winter dusk, and dark in the room, but even by candlelight, he could see the color rising in her face.

"The hell with Christmas, the hell with Cross Creek—and the fucking hell with you, too!" She punctuated this last with a wooden soap dish from the washstand, which whizzed past his left ear and smacked into the wall behind him.

"Now just a fucking minute!"

"Don't you use language like that to me!"

"But you—"

"You and your 'important things'!" Her hand tightened on

the big china ewer and he tensed, ready to duck, but she thought better of it and her hand relaxed.

"I've spent the last *month* here, up to my eyeballs in laundry and baby shit and screeching women and horrible children while you're out doing 'important things' and you come marching in here covered in mud and tromp all over the clean floors without even noticing they *were* clean in the first place! Do you have any idea what a pain it is to scrub pine floors on your hands and knees? With lye soap!" She waved her hands at him in accusation, but too quickly for him to see whether they were covered with gaping sores, rotted off at the wrist, or merely reddened.

". . . And you don't even want to look at your son or hear anything about him—he's learned to *crawl*, and I wanted to show you, but all *you* wanted was to go to bed, and you didn't even bother to shave first . . ."

Roger felt as though he'd walked into the blades of a large, rapidly whirling fan. He scratched at his short beard, feeling guilty.

"I . . . ah . . . thought you wanted to—"

"I did!" She stamped her foot, raising a small cloud of dust from the disintegrated mud. "That hasn't got anything to do with it!"

"All right." He bent to get his shirt, keeping one eye warily on her. "So—you're mad because I didn't notice you'd washed the floor, is that it?"

"No!"

"No," he repeated. He took a deep breath and tried again. "So, it *is* that I forgot it's Christmas?"

"No!"

"You're angry that I wanted to make love to you, even though you wanted to do it, too?"

"NO! Would you just shut up?"

Roger was strongly tempted to accede to this request, but a dogged urge to get to the bottom of things made him push on.

"But I don't understand why—"

"I know you don't! *That's* the problem!"

She spun on her bare heel and stomped over to the chest that stood by the window. She flung back the lid with a bang, and began rummaging, with a series of small snorts and growls.

He opened his mouth, shut it again, and jerked the dirty shirt on over his head. He felt simultaneously irritated and guilty, a bad combination. He finished dressing in an atmosphere of charged silence, considering—and rejecting—possible remarks and questions, all of which seemed likely to inflame the situation further.

She had found her stockings, yanked them on, and gartered them with small savage movements, then thrust her feet into a pair of battered clogs. Now she stood at the open window, drawing deep breaths of air as though she were about to perform a set of RAF exercises.

His inclination was to escape while she wasn't looking, but he couldn't bring himself simply to leave, with something wrong—whatever in God's name it was—between them. He could still feel the sense of closeness that they had shared, less than a quarter of an hour before, and couldn't bring himself to believe that it had simply evaporated into thin air.

He walked up behind her, slowly, and put his hands on her shoulders. She didn't whirl round and try either to stamp on his foot or to knee him in the stones, so he took the risk of kissing her lightly on the back of the neck.

"You were going to ask me something about geese."

She took a deep breath and let it out in a sigh, relaxing just a little against him. Her anger seemed to have vanished as quickly as it had appeared, leaving him baffled but grateful. He put his arms round her waist, and pulled her back against him.

"Yesterday," she said, "Mrs. Aberfeldy burnt the biscuits for breakfast."

"Oh. Aye?"

"Mrs. Bug accused her of being too taken up with her daughter's hair ribbons to pay attention to what she was doing. And what was she doing—Mrs. Bug said—putting blueberries into buttermilk biscuits in the first place?"

"Why shouldn't one put blueberries into buttermilk biscuits?"

"I have no idea. But Mrs. Bug doesn't think you should.

And then Billy MacLeod fell down the stairs, and his mother was nowhere to be found—she went to the privy and got stuck—and—"

"She *what*?" Mrs. MacLeod was short and rather stout, but had a well-defined rear aspect, with an arse like two cannonballs in a sack. It was all too easy to envision such an accident befalling her, and Roger felt laughter gurgle up through his chest. He tried manfully to stifle it, but it emerged through his nose in a painful snort.

"We shouldn't laugh. She had splinters." Despite this rebuke, Brianna herself was quivering against him, tremors of mirth fracturing her voice.

"Christ. What then?"

"Well, Billy was screaming—he didn't break anything, but he banged his head pretty hard—and Mrs. Bug shot out of the kitchen with her broom, hollering because she thought we were being attacked by Indians, and Mrs. Chisholm went to find Mrs. MacLeod and started yelling from the privy, and . . . well, anyway, the geese came over in the middle of all of it, and Mrs. Bug looked up at the ceiling with her eyes popping, then said 'Geese!' so loud that everybody stopped yelling, and she ran into Da's study and came back with the fowling piece and shoved it at me."

She had relaxed a little with the telling. She snorted, and settled back against him.

"I was so mad, I just really *wanted* to kill something. And there·were a lot of them—the geese—you could hear them calling all across the sky."

He had seen the geese, too. Black V-shapes, flexing in the winds of the upper air, arrowing their way through the winter sky. Heard them calling, with a strange feeling of loneliness at the heart, and wished she were beside him there.

Everyone had rushed out to watch; the wild Chisholm children and a couple of the half-wild Chisholm dogs went scampering through the trees with whoops and barks of excitement, to retrieve the fallen birds, while Brianna shot and reloaded, as quickly as she could.

"One of the dogs got one, and Toby tried to wrestle it away, and the dog bit him, and he was running around and around the yard screaming that his finger was bitten off, and there was blood all over him, and nobody could make him stop so we could see whether it was, and Mama wasn't here, and Mrs. Chisholm was down by the creek with the twins . . ."

She was stiffening again, and he could see the hot blood rising once more, flushing the back of her neck. He tightened his hold on her waist.

"Was his finger bitten off, then?"

She stopped and took a deep breath, then looked round at him over her shoulder, the color fading slightly from her face.

"No. The skin wasn't even broken; it was goose blood."

"Well, so. Ye did well, didn't you? The larder full, not a finger lost—and the house still standing."

He'd meant it as a joke, and was surprised to feel her heave a deep sigh, a little of the tension going out of her.

"Yes," she said, and her voice held a note of undeniable satisfaction. "I did. All present and accounted for—and everybody fed. With minimal bloodshed," she added.

"Well, it's true what they say about omelettes and eggs, aye?" He laughed and bent to kiss her, then remembered his beard. "Oh—sorry. I'll go and shave, shall I?"

"No, don't." She turned as he released her, and brushed a fingertip across his jaw. "I sort of like it. Besides, you can do that later, can't you?"

"Aye, I can." He bent his head and kissed her gently, but thoroughly. Was that it, then? She'd only wanted him to say that she'd done well, left on her own to run the place? He was thinking she deserved it, if so. He'd known she hadn't been only sitting by the hearth singing cradle songs to Jemmy in his absence—but he hadn't envisioned the gory details.

The smell of her hair and the musk of her body was all round him, but breathing deep to get more of it, he realized that the room was fragrant with juniper and balsam, too, and the mellow scent of beeswax candles. Not just one; there were three of them, set in candlesticks about the room. Normally, she would have lit a rush dip, saving the valuable candles, but the small room glowed now with soft gold light, and he realized that the bloom of it had lit them through their lovemaking, leaving him with memories of russet and ivory and the gold down that covered her like a lion's pelt, the shadowed crimson and purple of her secret places, the dark of his skin on the paleness of hers—memories that glowed vivid against white sheets in his mind.

The floor *was* clean—or had been—its white-pine boards scrubbed, and the corners strewn with dried rosemary. He could see the tumbled bed past her ear, and realized that she'd made it up with fresh linen and a new quilt. She'd taken trouble for his homecoming. And he'd come barging in, brimming with his adventures, expecting praise for the feat of coming back alive, and seeing none of it—blind to everything in his urgent need to get his hands on her and feel her body under his.

"Hey," he said softly in her ear. "I may be a fool, but I love you, aye?"

She sighed deeply, her breasts pushing against his bare chest, warm even through the cloth of shift and gown. They were firm; filling with milk, but not yet hard.

"Yeah, you are," she said frankly, "but I love you too. And I'm glad you're home."

He laughed and let go. There was a branch of juniper tacked above the window, heavy with its clouded blue-green berries. He reached up and broke off a sprig, kissed it, and tucked it into the neck of her gown, between her breasts, as a token of truce—and apology.

"Merry Christmas. Now, what was it about the geese?"

She put a hand to the juniper sprig, a half-smile growing, then fading.

"Oh. Well. It's not important. It's just . . ." He followed the direction of her eyes, turned, and saw the sheet of paper, propped up behind the basin on the washstand.

It was a drawing, done in charcoal; wild geese against a stormy sky, striving through the air above a lash of wind-tossed trees. It was a wonderful drawing, and looking at it gave him the same odd feeling at the heart that hearing the geese themselves had done—half joy, half pain.

"Merry Christmas," Brianna said softly, behind him. She came to stand beside him, wrapping a hand around his arm.

"Thanks. It's . . . God, Bree, you're good." She was. He bent and kissed her, hard, needing to do something to lessen the sense of yearning that haunted the paper in his hand.

"Look at the other one." She pulled a little away from him, still holding his arm, and nodded at the washstand.

He hadn't realized there were two. The other drawing had been behind the first.

She *was* good. Good enough to chill the blood at his heart. The second drawing was in charcoal, too, the same stark blacks and whites and grays. In the first, she had seen the wildness of the sky, and put it down: yearning and courage, effort enduring in faith amid the emptiness of air and storm. In this, she had seen stillness.

It was a dead goose, hung by the feet, its wings half-spread. Neck limp and beak half-open, as though even in death it sought flight and the loud-calling company of its companions. The lines of it were grace, the details of feather, beak, and empty eyes exquisite. He had never seen anything so beautiful, nor so desolate, in his life.

"I drew that last night," she said quietly. "Everybody was in bed, but I couldn't sleep."

She had taken a candlestick and prowled the crowded house, restless, going outside at last in spite of the cold, seeking solitude, if not rest, in the chill dark of the outbuildings. And in the smokeshed, by the light of the embers there, had been struck by the beauty of the hanging geese, their clear plumage black and white against the sooty wall.

"I checked to be sure Jemmy was sound asleep, then brought my sketch box down and drew, until my fingers were too cold to hold the charcoal anymore. That was the best one." She nodded at the picture, her eyes remote.

For the first time, he saw the blue shadows in her face, and imagined her by candlelight, up late at night and all alone, drawing dead geese. He would have taken her in his arms then, but she turned away, going to the window, where the shutters had begun to bang.

The thaw had faded, to be followed by a freezing wind that stripped the last sere leaves from the trees and sent acorns and chestnut hulls sailing through the air to rattle on the roof like buckshot. He followed her, reached past her to draw in the shutters and fasten them against the bitter wind.

"Da told me stories, while I was—while I was waiting for Jemmy to be born. I wasn't paying close attention"—the corner of her mouth quirked with wryness—"but a bit here and there stuck with me."

She turned around then, and leaned against the shutters, hands gripping the sill behind her.

"He said when a hunter kills a greylag goose, he must wait by the body, because the greylag mate for life, and if you kill only one, the other will mourn itself to death. So you wait, and when the mate comes, you kill it, too."

Her eyes were dark on his, but the candle flames struck glints of blue in their depths.

"What I wondered is—are all geese like that? Not only greylags?" She nodded at the pictures.

He touched her, and cleared his throat. He wanted to comfort her, but not at the price of an easy lie.

"Maybe so. I don't know for sure, though. You're worried, then, about the mates of the birds you shot?"

The soft pale lips pressed tight together, then relaxed.

"Not worried. Just . . . I couldn't help thinking about it, afterward. About them, flying on . . . alone. You were gone— I couldn't help thinking—I mean, I *knew* you were all right, this time, but next time, you might not come—well, never mind. It's just silly. Don't worry about it."

She stood up, and would have pushed past him into the room, but he put his arms around her and held her, close so she couldn't see his face.

He knew that she didn't absolutely require him—not to make hay, to plow, to hunt for her. If needs must, she could do those things herself—or find another man. And yet . . . the wild geese said she needed *him*—would mourn his loss if it came. Perhaps forever. In his present vulnerable mood, that knowledge seemed a great gift.

"Geese," he said at last, his voice half-muffled in her hair. "The next-door neighbors kept geese, when I was a wee lad. Big white buggers. Six of them; they went round in a gang, all high-nosed and honking. Terrorized dogs and children and folk that passed by on the street."

"Did they terrorize you?" Her breath tickled warm on his collarbone.

"Oh, aye. All the time. When we played in the street,

they'd rush out honking and peck at us and beat us with their wings. When I wanted to go out into the back garden to play with a mate, Mrs. Graham would have to come, too, to drive the bastards off to their own yard with a broomstick.

"Then the milkman came by one morning while the geese were in their front garden. They went for him, and he ran for his float—and his horse took fright at all the honking and screeching, and stamped two of the geese flatter than bannocks. The kids on the street were all thrilled."

She was laughing against his shoulder, half-shocked but amused.

"What happened then?"

"Mrs. Graham took them and plucked them, and we had goose pie for a week," he said matter-of-factly. He straightened up and smiled at her. She was flushed and rosy. "That's what I ken about geese—they're wicked buggers, but they taste great."

He turned and plucked his mud-stained coat from the floor.

"So, then. Let me help your Da with the chores, and then I want to see how ye've taught my son to crawl."

## CHARMS

I TOUCHED A FINGER to the gleaming white surface, then rubbed my fingers together appraisingly.

"There is absolutely nothing greasier than goose grease," I said with approval. I wiped my fingers on my apron and took up a large spoon.

"Nothing better for a nice pastry crust," Mrs. Bug agreed.

She stood on her tiptoes, watching jealously as I divided the soft white fat, ladling it from the kettle into two large stone crocks; one for the kitchen, one for my surgery.

"A nice venison pie we'll have for Hogmanay," she said, eyes narrowing as she envisioned the prospect. "And the haggis to follow, wi' cullen skink, and a bit o' corn crowdie . . . and a great raisin tart wi' jam and clotted cream for sweeties!"

"Wonderful," I murmured. My own immediate plans for the goose grease involved a salve of wild sarsaparilla and bittersweet for burns and abrasions, a mentholated ointment for stuffy noses and chest congestion, and something soothing and pleasantly scented for diaper rash—perhaps a lavender infusion, with the juice of crushed jewelweed leaves.

I glanced down in search of Jemmy; he had learned to crawl only a few days before, but was already capable of an astonishing rate of speed, particularly when no one was looking. He was sitting peaceably enough in the corner, though, gnawing intently at the wooden horse Jamie had carved for him as a Christmas present.

Catholic as many of them were—and nominally Christian as they *all* were—Highland Scots regarded Christmas primarily as a religious observance, rather than a major festive occasion. Lacking priest or minister, the day was spent much like a Sunday, though with a particularly lavish meal to mark the occasion, and the exchange of small gifts. My own gift from Jamie had been the wooden ladle I was presently using, its handle carved with the image of a mint leaf; I had given him a new shirt with a ruffle at the throat for ceremonial occasions, his old one having worn quite away at the seams.

With a certain amount of forethought, Mrs. Bug, Brianna, Marsali, Lizzie, and I had made up an enormous quantity of molasses toffee, which we had distributed as a Christmas treat to all the children within earshot. Whatever it might do to their teeth, it had the beneficial effect of gluing their mouths shut for long periods, and in consequence, the adults had enjoyed a peaceful Christmas. Even Germain had been reduced to a sort of tuneful gargle.

Hogmanay was a different kettle of fish, though. God knew what feverish pagan roots the Scottish New Year's celebration sprang from, but there was a reason why I wanted to have a good lot of medicinal preparations made up in advance—the same reason Jamie was now up at the whisky spring, deciding which barrels were sufficiently aged as not to poison anyone.

The goose grease disposed of, there was a good bit of dark broth left in the bottom of the kettle, aswirl with bits of crackled skin and shreds of meat. I saw Mrs. Bug eyeing it, visions of gravy dancing in her brain.

"Half," I said sternly, reaching for a large bottle.

She didn't argue; merely shrugged her rounded shoulders and settled back on her stool in resignation.

"Whatever will ye do with that, though?" she asked curiously, watching as I put a square of muslin over the neck of the bottle, in order to strain the broth. "Grease, aye, it's a wonder for the salves. And broth's good for a body wi' the ague or a wabbly wame, to be sure—but it willna keep, ye know." One sketchy eyebrow lifted at me in warning, in case I hadn't actually known that. "Leave it more than a day or two, and it'll be blue with the mold."

"Well, I do hope so," I told her, ladling broth into the muslin square. "I've just set out a batch of bread to mold, and I want to see if it will grow on the broth, too."

I could see assorted questions and responses flickering through her mind, all based on a growing fear that this mania of mine for rotten food was expanding, and would soon engulf the entire output of the kitchen. Her eyes darted toward the pie safe, then back at me, dark with suspicion.

I turned my head to hide a smile, and found Adso the kitten balanced on his hind legs on the bench, foreclaws anchored in the tabletop, his big green eyes watching the movements of the ladle with fascination.

"Oh, you want some, too?" I reached for a saucer from the shelf and filled it with a dark puddle of broth, savory with bits of goose meat and floating fat globules.

"This is from my half," I assured Mrs. Bug, but she shook her head vigorously.

"Not a bit of it, Mrs. Fraser," she said. "The bonnie wee laddie's caught *six* mice in here in the past two days." She beamed fondly at Adso, who had leaped down and was lapping broth as fast as his tiny pink tongue could move. "Yon cheetie's welcome to anything he likes from my hearth."

"Oh, has he? Splendid. He can come and have a go at the ones in my surgery, then." We were presently entertaining a plague of mice; driven indoors by cold weather, they skittered along the baseboards like shadows after nightfall, and even in broad daylight, shot suddenly across floors and leaped out of opened cupboards, causing minor heart failure and broken dishes.

"Well, ye can scarcely blame the mice," Mrs. Bug observed, darting a quick glance at me. "They go where the food is, after all."

The pool of broth had nearly drained through the muslin, leaving a thick coating of flotsam behind. I scraped this off and dropped it on Adso's saucer, then scooped up a fresh ladle of broth.

"Yes, they do," I said, evenly. "And I'm sorry about it, but the mold is important. It's medicine, and I—"

"Oh, aye! Of course it is," she assured me hurriedly. "I ken that." There was no tinge of sarcasm in her voice, which rather surprised me. She hesitated, then reached through the slit in her skirt, into the capacious pocket that she wore beneath.

"There was a man, as lived in Auchterlonie—where we had our hoose, Arch and me, in the village there. He was a carline, was Johnnie Howlat, and folk went wary near him— but they went. Some went by day, for grass cures and graiths, and some went by night, for to buy charms. Ye'll ken the sort?" She darted another glance at me, and I nodded, a little uncertainly.

I knew the sort of person she meant; some Highland charmers dealt not only in remedies—the "graiths" she'd mentioned—but also in minor magic, selling lovephilters, fertility potions . . . ill wishes. Something cold slid down my back and vanished, leaving in its wake a faint feeling of unease, like the slime trail of a snail.

I swallowed, seeing in memory the small bunch of thorny plants, so carefully bound with red thread and with black. Placed beneath my pillow by a jealous girl named

Laoghaire—purchased from a witch named Geillis Duncan. A witch like me.

Was that what Mrs. Bug was getting at? "Carline" was not a word I was certain of, though I thought it meant "witch," or something like it. She was regarding me thoughtfully, her normal animation quite subdued.

"He was a filthy wee mannie, Johnnie Howlat was. He'd no woman to do for him, and his cot smelt of dreadful things. So did he." She shivered suddenly, in spite of the fire at her back.

"Ye'd see him, sometimes, in the wood or on the moor, pokin' at the ground. He'd find creatures that had died, maybe, and bring back their skins and their feet, bones and teeth for to make his charms. He wore a wretched auld smock, like a farmer, and sometimes ye'd see him comin' doon the path wi' something pooched up under his smock, and stains of blood—and other things—seepin' through the cloth."

"Sounds most unpleasant," I said, eyes fixed on the bottle as I scraped the cloth again and ladled more broth. "But people went to him anyway?"

"There was no one else," she said simply, and I looked up. Her dark eyes fixed unblinkingly on mine, and her hand moved slowly, fingering something inside her pocket.

"I didna ken at first," she said. "For Johnnie kept mool from the graveyard and bone dust and hen's blood and all manner of such things, but you"—she nodded thoughtfully at me, white kerch immaculate in the fire-glow—"ye're a cleanly sort."

"Thank you," I said, both amused and touched. That was a high compliment from Mrs. Bug.

"Bar the moldy bread," she added, the corners of her mouth primming slightly. "And that heathen wee pooch ye keep in your cabinet. But it's true, no? Ye're a charmer, like Johnnie was?"

I hesitated, not knowing what to say. The memory of Cranesmuir was vivid in my mind, as it had not been for many years. The last thing I wanted was for Mrs. Bug to be spreading the rumor that I was a carline—some already called me a conjure-woman. I was not worried about legal prosecution as a witch—not here, not now. But to have a reputation for healing was one thing; to have people come to me for help with the other things that charmers dealt in . . .

"Not exactly," I said, guardedly. "It's only that I know a bit about plants. And surgery. But I really don't know anything at all about charms or . . . spells."

She nodded in satisfaction, as though I had confirmed her suspicions instead of denying them.

Before I could respond, there was a sound from the floor like water hitting a hot pan, followed by a loud screech. Jemmy, tiring of his toy, had cast it aside and crawled over to investigate Adso's saucer. The cat, disinclined to share, had hissed at the baby and frightened him. Jemmy's shriek in turn had frightened Adso under the settle; only the tip of a small pink nose and a flicker of agitated whiskers showed from the shadows.

I picked Jem up and soothed his tears, while Mrs. Bug took over the broth-straining. She looked over the goose debris on the platter and picked out a leg bone, the white cartilage at the end smooth and gleaming.

"Here, laddie." She waved it enticingly under Jemmy's nose. He at once stopped crying, grabbed the bone, and put it in his mouth. Mrs. Bug selected a smaller wing bone, with shreds of meat still clinging to it, and put that down on the saucer.

"And that's for you, lad," she said to the darkness under the settle. "Dinna fill your wame too full, though—stay hungry for the wee moosies, aye?"

She turned back to the table, and began to scoop the bones into a shallow pan.

"I'll roast these; they'll do for soup," she said, eyes on her work. Then without changing tone or looking up, she said, "I went to him once, Johnnie Howlat."

"Did you?" I sat down, Jemmy on my knee. "Were you ill?"

"I wanted a child."

I had no idea what to say; I sat still, listening to the drip of the broth through the muslin cloth, as she scraped the last bit of gristle neatly into the roasting pan, and carried it to the hearth.

"I'd slippit four, in the course of a year," she said, back turned to me. "Ye'd not think it, to look at me now, but I was nay more than skin and bane, the color o' whey, and my paps shrunk awa to nothing."

She settled the pan firmly into the coals and covered it.

"So I took what money we had, and I went to Johnnie Howlat. He took the money, and put water in a pan. He sat me doon on the one side of it and him on the other, and there we sat for a verra long time, him starin' into the water and me starin' at him.

"At last, he shook himself a bit and got up, and went awa to the back of his cot. 'Twas dark, and I couldna see what he did, but he rummaged and poked, and said things beneath his breath, and finally he came back to me, and handed me a charm."

Mrs. Bug straightened up and turned round. She came close, and laid her hand on Jemmy's silky head, very gently.

"He said to me, Johnnie did, that here was a charm that would close up the mouth of my womb, and keep a babe safe inside, until it should be born. But there was a thing he'd seen, lookin' in the water, and he must tell me. If I bore a live babe, then my husband would die, he said. So he would give me the charm, and the prayer that went with it—and then it was my choice, and who could say fairer than that?"

Her stubby, work-worn finger traced the curve of Jemmy's cheek. Engaged with his new toy, he paid no attention.

"I carried that charm in my pocket for a month—and then I put it away."

I reached up and put my hand over hers, squeezing. There was no sound but the baby's slobbering and the hiss and pop of the bones in the coals. She stayed still for a moment, then drew her hand away, and put it back in her pocket. She drew out a small object, and put it on the table beside me.

"I couldna quite bring myself to throw it away," she said, gazing down at it dispassionately. "It cost me three silver pennies, after all. And it's a wee thing; easy enough to carry along when we left Scotland."

It was a small chunk of stone, pale pink in color, and veined with gray, badly weathered. It had been crudely carved into the shape of a pregnant woman, little more than a huge belly, with swollen breasts and buttocks above a pair of stubby legs that tapered to nothing. I had seen such figures before—in museums. Had Johnnie Howlat made it himself? Or perhaps found it in his pokings through wood and moor, a remnant of much more ancient times?

I touched it gently, thinking that whatever Johnnie Howlat might have been, or might have seen in his pan of water, he had no doubt been astute enough to have seen the love between Arch and Murdina Bug. Was it easier for a woman, then, to forswear the hope of children, thinking it a noble sacrifice for the sake of a much-loved husband, than to suffer bitterness and self-blame for constant failure? Carline he may have been, Johnnie Howlat—but a charmer, indeed.

"So," Mrs. Bug said, matter-of-factly, "it may be as ye'll find some lass who's a use for it. Shame to let it go to waste, aye?"

# HOGMANAY

THE YEAR ENDED clear and cold, with a small, brilliant moon that rose high in the violet-black vault of the sky, and flooded the coves and trails of the mountainside with light. A good thing, as people came from all over the Ridge—and some, even farther—to keep Hogmanay at "the Big House."

The men had cleared the new barn and raked the floor clean for the dancing. Jigs and reels and strathspeys—and a number of other dances for which I didn't know the names, but they looked like fun—were executed under the light of bear-oil lanterns, accompanied by the music of Evan Lindsay's scratchy fiddle and the squeal of his brother Murdo's wooden flute, punctuated by the heartbeat thump of Kenny's bodhran.

Thurlo Guthrie's ancient father had brought his pipes, too—a set of small uilleann pipes that looked nearly as decrepit as did Mr. Guthrie, but produced a sweet drone. The melody of his chanter sometimes agreed with the Lindsays' notion of a particular tune, and sometimes didn't, but the overall effect was cheerful, and sufficient whisky and beer had been taken by this point in the festivities that no one minded in the least.

After an hour or two of the dancing, I privately decided that I understood why the word "reel" had come to indicate drunkenness; even performed without preliminary lubrication, the dance was enough to make one dizzy. Done under the influence of whisky, it made all the blood in my head whirl round like the water in a washing machine. I staggered off at the end of one such dance, leaned against one of the barn's uprights, and closed one eye, in hopes of stopping the spinning sensation.

A nudge on my blind side caused me to open that eye, revealing Jamie, holding two brimming cups of something. Hot and thirsty as I was, I didn't mind what it was, so long as it was wet. Fortunately it was cider, and I gulped it.

"Drink it like that, and ye'll founder, Sassenach," he said, disposing of his own cider in precisely similar fashion. He was flushed and sweating from the dancing, but his eyes sparkled as he grinned at me.

"Piffle," I said. With a bit of cider as ballast, the room had quit spinning, and I felt cheerful, if hot. "How many people are in here, do you think?"

"Sixty-eight, last time I counted." He leaned back beside me, viewing the milling throng with an expression of deep content. "They come in and out, though, so I canna be quite sure. And I didna count the weans," he added, moving slightly to avoid collision as a trio of small boys caromed through the crowd and shot past us, giggling.

Heaps of fresh hay were stacked in the shadows at the sides of the barn; the small bodies of children too wee to stay awake were draped and curled among them like so many barn kittens. The flicker of lantern light caught a gleam of silky red-gold; Jemmy was sound asleep in his blanket, happily lulled by the racket. I saw Bree come out of the dancing and lay her hand briefly on him to check, then turn back. Roger put out a hand to her, dark and smiling, and she took it, laughing as they whirled back into the stamping mass.

People did come in and out—particularly small groups of young people, and courting couples. It was freezing and frost-crisp outside, but the cold made cuddling with a warm body that much more appealing. One of the older MacLeod boys passed near us, his arm round a much younger girl—one of old Mr. Guthrie's granddaughters, I thought; he had three of them, all much alike to look at—and Jamie said something genial to him in Gaelic that made his ears go red. The girl was already pink with dancing, but went crimson in the face.

"What did you say to them?"

"It doesna bear translation," he said, putting a hand in the small of my back. He was pulsing with heat and whisky, alight with a flame of joy; looking at him was enough to kindle my own heart. He saw that, and smiled down at me, the heat of his hand burning through the cloth of my gown.

"D'ye want to go outside for a moment, Sassenach?" he said, his voice pitched low and rich with suggestion.

"Well, since you mention it . . . yes," I said. "Maybe not just yet, though." I nodded past him, and he turned to see a cluster of elderly ladies sitting on a bench against the wall, all viewing us with the bright-eyed curiosity of a flock of crows. Jamie waved and smiled at them, making them all burst into pink-faced giggles, and turned back to me with a sigh.

"Aye, well. In a bit, then—after the first-footing, maybe."

The latest spate of dancing came to an end, and there was a general surge in the direction of the tub of cider, presided over by Mr. Wemyss at the far end of the barn. The dancers clustered round it like a horde of thirsty wasps, so that all that was visible of Mr. Wemyss was the top of his head, fair hair almost white under the glow of the lanterns.

Seeing it, I looked round for Lizzie, to see whether she was enjoying the party. Evidently so; she was holding court on a hay bale, surrounded by four or five gawky boys, who were all behaving very much like the dancers round the cider tub.

"Who's the big one?" I asked Jamie, calling his attention to the small gathering with a nod of my head. "I don't recognize him." He glanced over, squinting slightly.

"Oh," he said, relaxing, "that will be Jacob Schnell. He's ridden over from Salem with a friend; they came with the Muellers."

"Really." Salem was a good long ride; nearly thirty miles. I wondered whether the attraction had been the festivities alone. I looked for Tommy Mueller, whom I had privately marked out as a possible match for Lizzie, but didn't see him in the crowd.

"Do you know anything about this Schnell lad?" I asked, giving the boy in question a critical look. He was a year or two older than the other boys dancing attendance on Lizzie, and quite tall. Plain-featured but good-natured-looking, I thought; heavy-boned, and with a thickness through the middle that foretold the development of a prosperous paunch in middle age.

"I dinna ken the lad himself, but I've met his uncle. It's a decent family; I think his father's a cobbler." We both looked automatically at the young man's shoes; not new, but very good quality, and with pewter buckles, large and square in the German fashion.

Young Schnell appeared to have gained an advantage; he was leaning close, saying something to Lizzie, whose eyes were fixed on his face, a slight frown of concentration wrinkling the skin between her fair brows as she tried to make out what he was saying. Then she worked it out, and her face relaxed in laughter.

"I dinna think so." Jamie shook his head, a slight frown on his face as he watched them. "The family's Lutheran; they wouldna let the lad marry a Catholic—and it would break Joseph's heart to send the lass to live so far away."

Lizzie's father *was* deeply attached to her; and having lost her once, he was unlikely to give her so far away in marriage as to lose sight of her again. Still, I thought that Joseph Wemyss would do almost anything to insure his daughter's happiness.

"He might go with her, you know."

Jamie's expression grew bleak at the thought, but he nodded in reluctant acknowledgment.

"I suppose so. I should hate to lose him; though I suppose Arch Bug might—"

Shouts of *"Mac Dubh!"* interrupted him.

"Come on, *a Sheumais ruaidh*, show him how!" Evan called from the far end of the barn, and jerked his bow authoritatively.

There had been a break in the dancing, to give the musicians time to breathe and have a drink, and in the interim, some of the men had been trying their hand at sword dancing, which could be done with only the accompaniment of pipes or to a single drum.

I had been paying little attention to this, only hearing the shouts of encouragement or derision from that end of the barn. Evidently, most of those present were no great hand at the sport—the latest gentleman to try it had tripped over one of the swords and fallen flat; he was being helped to his feet, red-faced and laughing, returning genial insults with his friends as they beat the hay and dirt from his clothes.

*"Mac Dubh, Mac Dubh!"* Kenny and Murdo shouted in invitation, beckoning, but Jamie waved them off, laughing.

"Nay, I havena done that in more time than I—"

*"Mac Dubh! Mac Dubh! Mac Dubh!"* Kenny was thumping his bodhran, chanting in rhythm, and the group of men around him were joining in. *"Mac Dubh! Mac Dubh! Mac Dubh!"*

Jamie cast me a brief look of helpless appeal, but Ronnie Sinclair and Bobby Sutherland were already heading purposefully toward us. I stepped away, laughing, and they seized him each by an arm, smothering his protests with raucous shouts as they hustled him into the center of the floor.

Applause and shouts of approval broke out as they deposited him in a clear space, where the straw had been trampled into the damp earth far enough to make a hard-packed surface. Seeing that he had no choice, Jamie drew himself up and straightened his kilt. He caught my eye, rolled an eye in mock resignation, and began to take off his coat, waistcoat, and boots, as Ronnie scrambled to lay out the two crossed broadswords at his feet.

Kenny Lindsay began to tap gently on his bodhran, hesitating between the beats, a sound of soft suspense. The crowd murmured and shifted in anticipation. Clad in shirt, kilt, and stockinged feet, Jamie bowed elaborately, turning sunwise to dip four times, to each of the "airts" in turn. Then he stood upright, and moved to take his place, standing just above the crossed swords. His hands lifted, fingers pointing stiff above his head.

There was an outburst of clapping nearby, and I saw Brianna put two fingers in her mouth and give an earsplitting whistle of approbation—to the marked shock of the people standing next to her.

I saw Jamie glance at Bree, with a faint smile, and then his eyes found mine again. The smile stayed on his lips, but there was something different in his expression; something rueful. The beat of the bodhran began to quicken.

A Highland sword dance was done for one of three reasons. For exhibition and entertainment, as he was about to do it now. For competition, as it was done among the young men at a Gathering. And as it first was done, as an omen. Danced on the eve of a battle, the skill of the dancer foretold success or failure. The young men had danced between crossed swords, the night before Prestonpans, before Falkirk. But not before Culloden. There had been no campfires the night before that final fight, no time for bards and battle songs. It didn't matter; no one had needed an omen, then.

Jamie closed his eyes for a moment, bent his head, and the beat of the drum began to patter, quick and fast.

I knew, because he had told me, that he had first done the sword dance in competition, and then—more than once—on the eve of battles, first in the Highlands, then in France. The old soldiers had asked him to dance, had valued his skill as reassurance that they would live and triumph. For the Lindsays to know his skill, he must also have danced in Ardsmuir. But that was in the Old World, and in his old life.

He knew—and had not needed Roger to tell him—that the old ways had changed, were changing. This was a new world, and the sword dance would never again be danced in earnest, seeking omen and favor from the ancient gods of war and blood.

His eyes opened, and his head snapped up. The tipper struck the drum with a sudden *thunk!* and it began with a shout from the crowd. His feet struck down on the pounded earth, to the north and the south, to the east and the west, flashing swift between the swords.

His feet struck soundless, sure on the ground, and his shadow danced on the wall behind him, looming tall, long arms upraised. His face was still toward me, but he didn't see me any longer, I was sure.

The muscles of his legs were strong as a leaping stag's beneath the hem of his kilt, and he danced with all the skill of the warrior he had been and still was. But I thought he danced now only for the sake of memory, that those watching might not forget; danced, with the sweat flying from his brow as he worked, and a look of unutterable distance in his eyes.

PEOPLE WERE STILL TALKING of it when we adjourned to the house, just before midnight, for stovies, beer, and cider, before the first-footing.

Mrs. Bug brought out a basket of apples, and gathered all the young unmarried girls together in a corner of the kitchen, where—with much giggling and glancing over shoulders toward the young men—each peeled a fruit, keeping the peeling in one piece. Each girl tossed her peel behind her, and the group all whirled round to cluster and exclaim over the fallen strip and see what was the shape of the letter it made.

Apple peelings being by their nature fairly circular, there were a good many "C"s, "G"s, and "O"s discovered—good news for Charley Chisholm, and Young Geordie Sutherland—and much speculation as to whether "Angus Og" might be the meaning of an "O" or not, for Angus Og MacLeod was a canty lad, and much liked, while the only "Owen" was an elderly widower, about five feet tall, and with a large wen on his face.

I had taken Jemmy up to put him to bed, and after depositing him limp and snoring in his cradle, came down in time to see Lizzie cast her peeling.

"'C'!" chorused two of the Guthrie girls, almost knocking heads as they bent to look.

"No, no, it's a 'J'!"

Appealed to as the resident expert, Mrs. Bug bent down, eyeing the strip of red peel with her head on one side, like a robin sizing up a likely worm.

"A 'J' it is, to be sure," she ruled, straightening up, and the group burst out in giggles, turning as one to stare at John Lowry, a young farmer from Woolam's Mill, who peered over his shoulder at them in total bewilderment.

I caught a flash of red from the corner of my eye, and turned to see Brianna in the doorway to the hall. She tilted her head, beckoning me, and I hurried to join her.

"Roger's ready to go out, but we couldn't find the ground salt; it wasn't in the pantry. Do you have it in your surgery?"

"Oh! Yes, I have," I said guiltily. "I'd been using it to dry snakeroot, and forgot to put it back."

Guests packed the porches and lined the wide hallway, spilling out of the kitchen and Jamie's study, all talking, drinking, and eating, and I threaded my way through the crush after her toward my surgery, exchanging greetings as I ducked brandished cups of cider, stovie crumbs crunching under my feet.

The surgery itself was nearly empty, though; people tended to avoid it, through superstition, painful associations, or simple wariness, and I had not encouraged them to go in, leaving the room dark, with no fire burning. Only one candle was burning in the room now, and the only person present was Roger, who was poking among the bits and pieces I'd left on the counter.

He looked up as we entered, smiling. Still faintly flushed from the dancing, he had put his coat back on and draped a woolen scarf round his neck; his cloak lay over the stool beside him. Custom held that the most fortunate "firstfoot" on a Hogmanay was a tall and handsome dark-haired man; to welcome one as the first visitor across the threshold after midnight brought good fortune to the house for the coming year.

Roger being beyond argument the tallest—and quite the best-looking—dark man available, he had been elected to be firstfoot, not only for the Big House, as folk called it, but for those homes nearby. Fergus and Marsali and the others who lived near had already rushed off to their houses, to be ready to greet their firstfoot when he should come.

A red-haired man, though, was frightful ill luck as a first-foot, and Jamie had been consigned to his study, under the riotous guard of the Lindsay brothers, who were to keep him safely bottled up 'til after midnight. There were no clocks nearer than Cross Creek, but old Mr. Guthrie had a pocket watch, even older than himself; this instrument would declare the mystic moment when one year yielded to the next. Given the watch's propensity for stopping, I doubted that this would be more than a symbolic pronouncement, but that was quite enough, after all.

"Eleven-fifty," Brianna declared, popping into the surgery after me, her own cloak over her arm. "I just checked Mr. Guthrie's watch."

"Plenty of time. Are ye coming with me, then?" Roger grinned at Bree, seeing her cloak.

"Are you kidding? I haven't been out after midnight in years." She grinned back at him, swirling the cloak around her shoulders. "Got everything?"

"All but the salt." Roger nodded toward a canvas bag on the counter. A firstfoot was to bring gifts to the house: an egg, a faggot of wood, a bit of salt—and a bit of whisky, thus insuring that the household would not lack for necessities during the coming year.

"Right. Where did I—oh, Christ!" Swinging open the cupboard door to search for the salt, I was confronted by a pair of glowing eyes, glaring out of the darkness at me.

"Good grief." I put a hand over my chest, to keep my heart from leaping out, waving the other hand weakly at Roger, who had sprung up at my cry, ready to defend me. "Not to worry—it's just the cat."

Adso had taken refuge from the party, bringing along the remains of a freshly killed mouse for company. He growled at me, evidently thinking I meant to snatch this treat for myself, but I pushed him crossly aside, digging the small bag of ground salt out from behind his furry hindquarters.

I closed the cupboard door, leaving Adso to his feast, and handed Roger the salt. He took it, laying down the object he had had in his hand.

"Where did ye get that wee auld wifie?" he asked, nodding toward the object as he put the salt away in his bag. I glanced at the counter, and saw that he had been examining the little pink stone figure that Mrs. Bug had given me.

"Mrs. Bug," I replied. "She says it's a fertility charm—which is certainly what it looks like. It *is* very old, then?" I'd thought it must be, and seeing Roger's interest confirmed the impression.

He nodded, still looking at the thing.

"Very old. The ones I've seen in museums are dated at thousands of years." He traced the bulbous outlines of the stone with a reverent forefinger.

Brianna moved closer to see, and without thinking, I set a hand on her arm.

"What?" she said, turning her head to smile at me. "I shouldn't touch it? Do they work *that* well?"

"No, of course not."

I took my hand away, laughing, but feeling rather self-conscious. At the same time, I became aware that I would really rather she *didn't* touch it, and was relieved when she merely bent down to examine it, leaving it on the counter. Roger was looking at it, too—or rather, he was looking at Brianna, his eyes fixed on the back of her head with an odd intensity. I could almost imagine that he was willing her to touch the thing, as strongly as I was willing her not to.

*Beauchamp*, I said silently to myself, *you have had much too much to drink tonight.* All the same, I reached out by impulse and scooped the figure up, dropping it into my pocket.

"Come on! We have to go!" The odd mood of the moment abruptly broken, Brianna straightened up and turned to Roger, urging him.

"Aye, right. Let's go, then." He slung the bag over his shoulder and smiled at me, then took her arm and they disappeared, letting the surgery door close behind them.

I put out the candle, ready to follow them, and then stopped, suddenly reluctant to go back at once to the chaos of the celebration.

I could feel the whole house in movement, throbbing around me, and light flowed under the door from the hall. Just here, though, it was quiet. In the silence, I felt the weight of the little idol in my pocket, and pressed it, hard and lumpy against my leg.

There is nothing special about January the first, save the meaning we give to it. The ancients celebrated a new year at Imbolc, at the beginning of February, when the winter slackens and the light begins to come back—or the date of the spring equinox, when the world lies in balance between the powers of dark and light. And yet I stood there in the dark, listening to the sound of the cat chewing and slobbering in the cupboard, and felt the power of the earth shift and stir beneath my feet as the year—or something—prepared to change. There was noise and the sense of a crowd nearby, and yet I stood alone, while the feeling rose through me, hummed in my blood.

The odd thing was that it was not strange in the slightest. It was nothing that came from outside me, but only the acknowledgment of something I already possessed, and recognized, though I had no notion what to call it. But midnight was fast approaching. Still wondering, I opened the door, and stepped into the light and clamor of the hall.

A shout from across the hall betokened the arrival of the magic hour, as announced by Mr. Guthrie's timepiece, and the men came jostling out of Jamie's office, joking and pushing, faces turned expectantly toward the door.

Nothing happened. Had Roger decided to go to the back door, given the crowd in the kitchen? I turned to look down the hall, but no, the kitchen doorway was crowded with faces, all looking back at me in expectation.

Still no knock at the door, and there was a small stir of restiveness in the hallway, and a lull in conversation, one of those awkward silences when no one wants to talk for fear of sudden interruption.

Then I heard the sound of footsteps on the porch, and a

rapid knock, one-two-three. Jamie, as householder, stepped forward to fling the door open and bid the firstfoot welcome. I was near enough to see the look of astonishment on his face, and looked quickly to see what had caused it.

Instead of Roger and Brianna, two smaller figures stood on the porch. Skinny and bedraggled, but definitely dark-haired, the two Beardsley twins stepped shyly in together, at Jamie's gesture.

"A happy New Year to you, Mr. Fraser," said Josiah, in a bullfrog croak. He bowed politely to me, still holding his brother by the arm. "We've come."

THE GENERAL AGREEMENT was that dark-haired twins were a most fortunate omen, obviously bringing twice the luck of a single firstfoot. Nonetheless, Roger and Bree—who had met the twins hesitating in the yard, and sent them up to the door—went off to do their best for the other houses on the Ridge, Bree being severely warned not to enter any house until Roger had crossed the threshold.

Fortunate or not, the appearance of the Beardsleys caused a good deal of talk. Everyone had heard of the death of Aaron Beardsley—the official version, that is, which was that he had perished of an apoplexy—and the mysterious disappearance of his wife, but the advent of the twins caused the whole affair to be raked up and talked over again. No one knew what the boys had been doing between the militia's expedition and New Year's; Josiah said only "wanderin'" in his raspy croak, when asked—and his brother Keziah said nothing at all, obliging everyone to talk about the Indian trader and his wife until exhaustion caused a change of subject.

Mrs. Bug took the Beardsleys at once under her wing, taking them off to the kitchen to be washed, warmed, and fed. Half the partygoers had gone home to be firstfooted; those who would not leave 'til morning split into several groups. The younger people returned to the barn to dance—or to seek a bit of privacy among the hay bales—the older ones sat to talk of memories by the hearth, and those who had overindulged in dance or whisky curled up in any convenient corner—and quite a few inconvenient ones—to sleep.

I found Jamie in his study, leaning back in his chair with his eyes closed, a drawing of some kind on the table before him. He wasn't asleep, and opened his eyes when he heard my step.

"Happy New Year," I said softly, and bent to kiss him.

"A guid New Year to you, *a nighean donn*." He was warm and smelled faintly of beer and dried sweat.

"Still want to go outside?" I asked, with a glance at the window. The moon had set long since, and the stars burned faint and cold in the sky. The yard outside was bleak and black.

"No," he said frankly, rubbing a hand over his face. "I want to go to bed." He yawned and blinked, trying to smooth down the disheveled bits of hair sticking up on the top of his head. "I want you to come, too, though," he added, generously.

"I'd like nothing better," I assured him. "What's that?" I circled round behind him, looking over his shoulder at the drawing, which seemed to be some sort of floor plan, with mathematical calculations scribbled in the margins.

He sat up, looking a trifle more alert.

"Ah. Well, this is wee Roger's gift to Brianna, for Hogmanay."

"He's building her a house? But they—"

"Not her." He grinned up at me, hands flat on either side of the drawing. "The Chisholms."

Roger, with a guile that would have become Jamie himself, had scouted round among the settlers on the Ridge, and engineered an agreement between Ronnie Sinclair and Geordie Chisholm.

Ronnie had a large and commodious cabin next to his cooperage. So the agreement was that Ronnie, who was unmarried, would move into the cooper's shop, where he could easily sleep. The Chisholms would then move into Ronnie's cabin, to which they would at once—weather allowing—add two rooms, as per the plan on Jamie's table. In return, Mrs. Chisholm would undertake to make Ronnie's meals and do his washing. In the spring, when the Chisholms took possession of their own homestead and built a house there, Ronnie would take back his newly enlarged cabin—when the grandness of his improved accommodation might prove sufficient inducement for some young woman to accept his proposal of marriage, he hoped.

"And in the meantime, Roger and Bree get back their cabin, Lizzie and her father stop sleeping in the surgery, and everything is beer and skittles!" I squeezed his shoulders, delighted. "That's a wonderful arrangement!"

"What's a skittle?" he inquired, frowning back at me in puzzlement.

"One of a set of ninepins," I said. "I believe the expression is meant to exemplify a state of general delight with prevailing conditions. Did you do the plan?"

"Aye. Geordie's no carpenter, and I dinna want the place to fall down about his ears." He squinted at the drawings, then took a quill from the jar, flipped open the inkwell, and made a small correction to one of the figures.

"There," he said, dropping the quill. "That'll do. Wee Roger wants to show it to Bree when they come back tonight; I said I'd leave it out for him."

"She'll be thrilled." I leaned against the back of his chair, massaging his shoulders with my hands. He leaned back, the weight of his head warm against my stomach, and closed his eyes, sighing in pleasure.

"Headache?" I asked softly, seeing the vertical line between his eyes.

"Aye, just a bit. Oh, aye, that's nice." I had moved my hands to his head, gently rubbing his temples.

The house had quieted, though I could still hear the rumble of voices in the kitchen. Beyond them, the high sweet sound of Evan's fiddle drifted through the cold, still air.

" 'My Brown-Haired Maid,' " I said, sighing reminiscently. "I do love that song." I pulled loose the ribbon binding his plait, and unbraided the hair, enjoying the soft, warm feel of it as I spread it with my fingers.

"It's rather odd that you don't have an ear for music," I said, making small talk to distract him, as I smoothed the ruddy arcs of his brows, pressing just within the edge of the orbit. "I don't know why, but an aptitude for mathematics often goes along with one for music. Bree has both."

"I used to," he said absently.

"Used to what?"

"Have both." He sighed and bent forward to stretch his neck, his elbows resting on the table. "Oh, Christ. Please. Oh, aye. Ah!"

"Really?" I massaged his neck and shoulders, kneading the tight muscles hard through the cloth. "You mean you used to be able to *sing*?" It was a family joke; while possessed of a fine speaking voice, Jamie's sense of pitch was so erratic that any song in his voice was a chant so tuneless that babies were stunned, rather than lulled, to sleep.

"Well, perhaps not that, so much." I could hear the smile in his voice, muffled by the fall of hair that hid his face. "I could tell one tune from another, though—or say if a song was sung badly or well. Now it's no but noise or screeching." He shrugged, dismissing it.

"What happened?" I asked. "And when?"

"Oh, it was before I kent ye, Sassenach. In fact, quite soon before." He lifted a hand, reaching toward the back of his head. "Do ye recall, I'd been in France? It was on my way back wi' Dougal MacKenzie and his men, when Murtagh came across ye, wanderin' the Highlands in your shift. . . ."

He spoke lightly, but my fingers had found the old scar under his hair. It was no more now than a thread, the welted gash healed to a hairbreadth line. Still, it had been an eight-inch wound, laid open with an ax. It had nearly killed him at the time, I knew; he had lain near death in a French abbey for four months, and suffered from crippling headaches for years.

"It was that? You mean that you . . . couldn't hear music anymore, after you were hurt?"

His shoulders lifted briefly in a shrug.

"I hear no music but the sound of drums," he said simply. "I've the rhythm of it still, but the tune is gone."

I stopped, my hands on his shoulders, and he turned to look back at me, smiling, trying to make a joke of it.

"Dinna be troubled for it, Sassenach; it's no great matter. I didna sing well even when I *could* hear it. And Dougal didna kill me, after all."

"Dougal? You do think it was Dougal, then?" I was surprised at the certainty in his voice. He had thought at the time that it might perhaps have been his uncle Dougal who had made the murderous attack upon him—and then, surprised by his own men before being able to finish the job, had pretended instead to have found him wounded. But there had been no evidence to say for sure.

"Oh, aye." He looked surprised, too, but then his face changed, realizing.

"Oh, aye," he said again, more slowly. "I hadna thought—you couldna tell what he said, could you? When he died, I mean—Dougal." My hands were still resting on his shoulders, and I felt an involuntary shiver run through him. It spread through my hands and up my arms, raising the hairs all the way to the back of my neck.

As clearly as though the scene took place before me now, I could see that attic room in Culloden House. The bits and pieces of discarded furniture, things toppled and rolling from the struggle—and on the floor at my feet, Jamie crouching, grappling with Dougal's body as it bucked and strained, blood and air bubbling from the wound where Jamie's dirk had pierced the hollow of his throat. Dougal's face, blanched and mottled as his lifeblood drained away, eyes fierce black and fixed on Jamie as his mouth moved in Gaelic silence, saying . . . something. And Jamie's face, as white as Dougal's, eyes locked on the dying man's lips, reading that last message.

"What did he say?" My hands were tight on his shoulders, and his face was turned away as my thumbs rose up under his hair to seek the ancient scar again.

*"Sister's son or no—I would that I had killed you, that day on the hill. For I knew from the beginning that it would be you or me."* He spoke calm and low-voiced, and the very emotionlessness of the words made the shudder pass again, this time from me to him.

It was quiet in the study. The sound of voices in the kitchen had died to a murmur, as though the ghosts of the past gathered there to drink and reminisce, laughing softly among themselves.

"So that was what you meant," I said quietly. "When you said you'd made your peace with Dougal."

"Aye." He leaned back in his chair and reached up, his hands wrapping warmly round my wrists. "He was right, ken. It *was* him or me, and would have been, one way or the other."

I sighed, and a small burden of guilt dropped away. Jamie had been fighting to defend me, when he killed Dougal, and I had always felt that death to be laid at my door. But he was right, Dougal; too much lay between them, and if that final conflict had not come then, on the eve of Culloden, it would have been another time.

Jamie squeezed my wrists, and turned in his chair, still holding my hands.

"Let the dead bury the dead, Sassenach," he said softly. "The past is gone—the future is not come. And we are here together, you and I."

## WORLDS UNSEEN

THE HOUSEHOLD WAS QUIET; it was the perfect opportunity for my experiments. Mr. Bug had gone to Woolam's Mill, taking the Beardsley twins; Lizzie and Mr. Wemyss had gone to help Marsali with the new mash; and Mrs. Bug, having left a pot of porridge and a platter of toast in the kitchen, was out, too, combing the woods for the half-wild hens, catching them one by one and dragging them in by the feet to be installed in the handsome new chicken coop her husband had built. Bree and Roger sometimes came up to the big house for their breakfast, but more often chose to eat by their own hearth, as was the case this morning.

Enjoying the peace of the empty house, I made up a tray with cup, teapot, cream, and sugar, and took it with me to my surgery, along with my samples. The early morning light was perfect, pouring through the window in a brilliant bar of gold. Leaving the tea to steep, I took a couple of small glass bottles from the cupboard and went outside.

The day was chilly but beautiful, with a clear pale sky that promised a little warmth later in the morning. At the moment, though, it was cold enough that I was glad of my warm shawl, and the water in the horses' trough was frigid, rimmed with sheets of fragile ice. Not cold enough to kill the microbes, I supposed; I could see long strands of algae coating the boards of the trough, swaying gently as I buckled the thin crust of ice and disturbed the water, scraping one of my bottles along the slimy edge of the trough.

I scooped up further samples of liquid from the spring-house and from a puddle of muddy standing water near the privy, then hurried back to the house to make my trials while the light was still good.

The microscope stood by the window where I had set it up the day before, all gleaming brass and bright mirrors. A few seconds' work to place droplets on the glass slides I'd laid ready, and I bent to peer through the eyepiece with rapt anticipation.

The ovoid of light bulged, diminished, went out altogether. I squinted, turning the screw as slowly as I could, and . . . there it was. The mirror steadied and the light resolved itself into a perfect pale circle, window to another world.

I watched, enchanted, as the madly beating cilia of a paramecium bore it in hot pursuit of invisible prey. Then a quiet drifting, the field of view itself in constant movement as the drop of water on my slide shifted in its microscopic tides. I waited a moment more, in hopes of spotting one of the swift and elegant Euglena, or even a hydra, but no such luck; only bits of mysterious black-green, daubs of cellular debris and burst algal cells.

I shifted the slide to and fro, but found nothing else of

interest. That was all right; I had plenty of other things to look at. I rinsed the glass rectangle in a cup of alcohol, let it dry for a moment, then dipped a glass rod into one of the small beakers I had lined up before my microscope, dabbing a drop of liquid onto the clean slide.

It had taken some experimentation to put the microscope together properly; it wasn't much like a modern version, particularly when reduced to its component parts for storage in Dr. Rawlings's handsome box. Still, the lenses were recognizable, and with that as a starting point, I had managed to fit the optical bits into the stand without much trouble. Obtaining sufficient light, though, had been more difficult, and I was thrilled finally to have got it working.

"What are ye doing, Sassenach?" Jamie, with a piece of toast in one hand, paused in the doorway.

"Seeing things," I said, adjusting the focus.

"Oh, aye? What sorts of things?" He came into the room, smiling. "Not ghosties, I trust. I will have had enough o' those."

"Come look," I said, stepping back from the microscope. Mildly puzzled, he bent and peered through the eyepiece, screwing up his other eye in concentration.

He squinted for a moment, then gave an exclamation of pleased surprise.

"I see them! Wee things with tails, swimming all about!" He straightened up, smiling at me with a look of delight, then bent at once to look again.

I felt a warm glow of pride in my new toy.

"Isn't it marvelous?"

"Aye, marvelous," he said, absorbed. "Look at them. Such busy wee strivers as they are, all pushing and writhing against one another—and such a mass of them!"

He watched for a few moments more, exclaiming under his breath, then straightened up, shaking his head in amazement.

"I've never seen such a thing, Sassenach. Ye'd told me about the germs, aye, but I never in life imagined them so! I thought they might have wee teeth, and they don't—but I never kent they would have such handsome, lashing wee tails, or swim about in such numbers."

"Well, some microorganisms do," I said, moving to peer into the eyepiece again myself. "These particular little beasts aren't germs, though—they're sperms."

"They're what?"

He looked quite blank.

"Sperms," I said patiently. "Male reproductive cells. You know, what makes babies?"

I thought he might just possibly choke. His mouth opened, and a very pretty shade of rose suffused his countenance.

"Ye mean seed?" he croaked. "Spunk?"

"Well . . . yes." Watching him narrowly, I poured steaming tea into a clean beaker and handed it to him as a restorative. He ignored it, though, his eyes fixed on the microscope as though something might spring out of the eyepiece at any moment and go writhing across the floor at our feet.

"Sperms," he muttered to himself. "Sperms." He shook his head vigorously, then turned to me, a frightful thought having just occurred to him.

"Whose are they?" he asked, his tone one of darkest suspicion.

"Er . . . well, yours, of course." I cleared my throat, mildly embarrassed. "Who else's would they be?"

His hand darted reflexively between his legs, and he clutched himself protectively.

"How the hell did ye get them?"

"How do you think?" I said, rather coldly. "I woke up in custody of them this morning."

His hand relaxed, but a deep blush of mortification stained his cheeks dark crimson. He picked up the beaker of tea and drained it at a gulp, temperature notwithstanding.

"I see," he said, and coughed.

There was a moment of deep silence.

"I . . . um . . . didna ken they could stay alive," he said at last. "Errrrm . . . outside, I mean."

"Well, if you leave them in a splotch on the sheet to dry out, they don't," I said, matter-of-factly. "Keep them from drying out, though"—I gestured at the small, covered beaker, with its small puddle of whitish fluid—"and they'll do for a few hours. In their proper habitat, though, they can live for up to a week after . . . er . . . release."

"Proper habitat," he repeated, looking pensive. He darted a quick glance at me. "Ye do mean—"

"I do," I said, with some asperity.

"Mmphm." At this point, he recalled the piece of toast he still held, and took a bite, chewing meditatively.

"Do folk know about this? Now, I mean?"

"Know what? What sperm look like? Almost certainly. Microscopes have been around for well over a hundred years, and the first thing anyone with a working microscope does is to look at everything within reach. Given that the inventor of the microscope was a man, I should certainly think that . . . Don't you?"

He gave me a look, and took another bite of toast, chewing in a marked manner.

"I shouldna quite like to refer to it as 'within reach,' Sassenach," he said, through a mouthful of crumbs, and swallowed. "But I do take your meaning."

As though compelled by some irresistible force, he drifted toward the microscope, bending to peer into it once more.

"They seem verra fierce," he ventured, after a few moments' inspection.

"Well, they do need to be," I said, suppressing a smile at his faintly abashed air of pride in his gametes' prowess. "It's a long slog, after all, and a terrific fight at the end of it. Only one gets the honor, you know."

He looked up, blank-faced. It dawned on me that he *didn't* know. He'd studied languages, mathematics, and Greek and Latin philosophy in Paris, not medicine. And even if natural scientists of the time were aware of sperm as separate entities, rather than a homogenous substance, it occurred to me that they probably didn't have any idea what sperm actually did.

"Wherever did you *think* babies came from?" I demanded, after a certain amount of enlightenment regarding eggs, sperms, zygotes, and the like, which left Jamie distinctly squiggle-eyed. He gave me a rather cold look.

"And me a farmer all my life? I ken precisely where they come from," he informed me. "I just didna ken that . . . er . . . that all of this daffery was going on. I thought . . . well, I thought a man plants his seed into a woman's belly, and it . . .

well . . . grows." He waved vaguely in the direction of my stomach. "You know—like . . . seed. Neeps, corn, melons, and the like. I didna ken they swim about like tadpoles."

"I see." I rubbed a finger beneath my nose, trying not to laugh. "Hence the agricultural designation of women as being either fertile or barren!"

"Mmphm." Dismissing this with a wave of his hand, he frowned thoughtfully at the teeming slide. "A week, ye said. So it's possible that the wee lad really *is* the Thrush's get?"

Early in the day as it was, it took half a second or so for me to make the leap from theory to practical application.

"Oh—Jemmy, you mean? Yes, it's quite possible that he's Roger's child." Roger and Bonnet had lain with Brianna within two days of each other. "I told you—and Bree—so."

He nodded, looking abstracted, then remembered the toast and pushed the rest of it into his mouth. Chewing, he bent for another look through the eyepiece.

"Are they different, then? One man's from another, I mean?"

"Er . . . not to look at, no." I picked up my cup of tea and had a sip, enjoying the delicate flavor. "They *are* different, of course—they carry the characteristics a man passes to his offspring. . . ." That was about as far as I thought it prudent to go; he was sufficiently staggered by my description of fertilization; an explanation of genes and chromosomes might be rather excessive at the moment. "But you can't see the differences, even with a microscope."

He grunted at that, swallowed the mouthful of toast, and straightened up.

"Why are ye looking, then?"

"Just curiosity." I gestured at the collection of bottles and beakers on the countertop. "I wanted to see how fine the resolution of the microscope was, what sorts of things I might be able to see."

"Oh, aye? And what then? What's the purpose of it, I mean?"

"Well, to help me diagnose things. If I can take a sample of a person's stool, for instance, and see that he has internal parasites, then I'd know better what medicine to give him."

Jamie looked as though he would have preferred not to

hear about such things right after breakfast, but nodded. He drained his beaker and set it down on the counter.

"Aye, that's sensible. I'll leave ye to get on with it, then."

He bent and kissed me briefly, then headed for the door. Just short of it, though, he turned back.

"The, um, sperms . . ." he said, a little awkwardly.

"Yes?"

"Can ye not take them out and give them decent burial or something?"

I hid a smile in my teacup.

"I'll take good care of them," I promised. "I always do, don't I?"

THERE THEY WERE. Dark stalks, topped with clublike spores, dense against the pale bright ground of the microscope's field of view. Confirmation.

"Got them." I straightened up, slowly rubbing the small of my back as I looked over my preparations.

A series of slides lay in a neat fan beside the microscope, each bearing a dark smear in the middle, a code written on the end of each slide with a bit of wax from a candle stub. Samples of mold, taken from damp corn bread, from spoiled biscuit, and a bit of discarded pastry crust from the Hogmanay venison pie. The crust had yielded the best growth by far; no doubt it was the goose grease.

Of the various test substrates I had tried, those were the three resultant batches of mold that had contained the highest proportion of *Penicillium*—or what I could be fairly sure was *Penicillium*. There were a dismaying number of molds that would grow on damp bread, in addition to several dozen different strains of *Penicillium*, but the samples I had chosen contained the best matches for the textbook pictures of *Penicillium* sporophytes that I had committed to memory, years ago, in another life.

I could only hope that my memory wasn't faulty—and that the strains of mold I had here were among those species that produced a large quantity of penicillin, that I had not inadvertently introduced any virulent bacteria into the meat-broth mixture, and that—well, I could hope for a lot of things, but there came a point when one abandoned hope for faith, and trusted fate for charity.

A line of broth-filled bowls sat at the back of the counter-top, each covered with a square of muslin to prevent things—insects, airborne particles, and mouse droppings, to say nothing of mice—from falling in. I had strained the broth and boiled it, then rinsed each bowl with boiling water before fill-ing it with the steaming brown liquid. That was as close as I could come to a sterile medium.

I had then taken scrapings from each of my best mold samples, and swished the knife blade gently through the cooled broth, dissipating the clumps of soft blue as best I could before covering the bowl with its cloth and leaving it to incubate for several days.

Some of the cultures had thrived; others had died. A cou-ple of bowls showed hairy dark green clumps that floated be-neath the surface like submerged sea beasts, dark and sinister. Some intruder—mold, bacterium, or perhaps a colo-nial alga—but not the precious *Penicillium*.

Some anonymous child had spilled one bowl; Adso had knocked another onto the floor, maddened by the scent of goose broth, and had lapped up the contents, mold and all, with every evidence of enjoyment. There obviously hadn't been anything toxic in *that* one; I glanced down at the little cat, curled up in a pool of sunshine on the floor, the picture of somnolent well-being.

In three of the remaining bowls, though, spongy velvet mats of mottled blue covered the surface, and my examina-tion of a sample taken from one of them had just confirmed that I did indeed have what I sought. It wasn't the mold itself that was antibiotic—it was a clear substance secreted *by* the mold, as a means of protecting itself from attack by bacteria. That substance was penicillin, and that was what I wanted.

I had explained as much to Jamie, who sat on a stool watching me as I poured the broth from each live culture through another bit of gauze to strain it.

"So what ye've got there is broth that the mold has pissed in, is that right?"

"Well, if you insist on putting it that way, yes." I gave him an austere glance, then took up the strained solution and began distributing it into several small stoneware jars.

He nodded, pleased to have got it right.

"And the mold piss is what cures sickness, aye? That's sensible."

"It is?"

"Well, ye use other sorts of piss for medicine, so why not that?"

He lifted the big black casebook in illustration. I had left it open on the counter after recording the latest batch of experiments, and he had been amusing himself by reading some of the earlier pages, those recorded by the book's previous owner, Dr. Daniel Rawlings.

"Possibly Daniel Rawlings did—*I* don't." Hands busy, I lifted my chin at the entry on the open page. "What was he using it for?"

*"Electuary for the Treatment of Scurvy,"* he read, finger following the neat small lines of Rawlings's script. *"Two Heads of Garlic, crushed with six Radishes, to which are added Peru Balsam and ten drops of Myrrh, this Compound mixed with the Water of a Man-child so as to be conveniently drunk."*

"Bar the last, it sounds like a rather exotic condiment," I said, amused. "What would it go with best, do you think? Jugged hare? Ragout of veal?"

"Nay, veal's too mild-flavored for radish. Hodgepodge of mutton, maybe," he replied. "Mutton will stand anything." His tongue flicked absentmindedly across his upper lip in contemplation.

"Why a man-child, d'ye think, Sassenach? I've seen the mention of it in such receipts before—Aristotle has it so, and so have some of the other ancient philosophers."

I gave him a look, as I began tidying up my slides.

"Well, it's certainly easier to collect urine from a male child than from a little girl; just try it, sometime. Oddly enough, though, urine from baby boys *is* very clean, if not entirely sterile; it may be that the ancient philosophers noticed they had better results with it in their formulae, because it was cleaner than the usual drinking water, if they were getting that from public aqueducts and wells and the like."

"Sterile meaning that it hasna got the germs in it, not that it doesna breed?" He gave my microscope a rather wary glance.

"Yes. Or rather—it doesn't breed germs, because there aren't any there."

With the countertop cleared, save for the microscope and the jars of penicillin-containing broth—or at least I hoped that's what they were—I began the preparations for surgery, taking down my small case of surgical instruments, and fetching a large bottle of grain alcohol out of the cupboard.

I handed this to Jamie, along with the small alcohol burner I had contrived—an empty ink bottle, with a twisted wick of waxed flax drawn up through a cork stuck into the neck.

"Fill that up for me, will you? Where are the boys?"

"In the kitchen, getting drunk." He frowned in concentration, carefully pouring the alcohol. "Is the urine of wee lassies not clean, then? Or is it only harder to get?"

"No, actually, it isn't as clean as that of boys." I unfolded a clean cloth on the countertop and laid out two scalpels, a pair of long-nosed forceps, and a bunch of small cautery irons. I dug about in the cupboard, unearthing a handful of cotton pledgets. Cotton cloth was hideously expensive, but I had had the good fortune to cajole a sack of raw cotton bolls from Farquard Campbell's wife, in return for a jar of honey.

"The . . . um . . . route to the outside isn't quite so direct, you might say. So the urine tends to pick up bacteria and bits of debris from the skin folds." I looked over my shoulder at him and smiled. "Not that you ought to go feeling superior on that account."

"I shouldna dream of it," he assured me. "Are ye ready, then, Sassenach?"

"Yes, fetch them in. Oh, and bring the basin!"

He went out, and I turned to face the east window. It had snowed heavily the day before, but today was a fine, bright day, clear and cold, with the sun reflecting off the snow-covered trees with the light of a million diamonds. I couldn't have asked for better; I should need all the light I could get.

I set the cautery irons in the small brazier to heat. Then I fetched my amulet from the cabinet, put it round my neck so it hung beneath the bodice of my gown, and took down the heavy canvas apron from its hook behind the door. I put that on, too, then went to the window and looked out at the cold icing-sugar landscape, emptying my mind, steadying my spirit for what I was about to do. It was not a difficult operation, and I had done it many times before. I had not, however, done it on someone who was sitting upright and conscious, and that always made a difference.

I hadn't done it in several years, either, and I closed my eyes in recollection, visualizing the steps to take, feeling the muscles of my hand twitch slightly in echo of my thoughts, anticipating the movements I would make.

"God help me," I whispered, and crossed myself.

Stumbling footsteps, nervous giggles, and the rumble of Jamie's voice came from the hallway, and I turned round smiling to greet my patients.

A month of good food, clean clothes, and warm beds had improved the Beardsleys immensely, in terms of both health and appearance. They were both still small, skinny, and slightly bowlegged, but the hollows of their faces had filled out a bit, their dark hair lay soft against their skulls, and the look of hunted wariness had faded a little from their eyes.

In fact, both pairs of dark eyes were presently a little glazed, and Lizzie was obliged to grab Keziah by the arm in order to prevent his stumbling over a stool. Jamie had Josiah gripped firmly by the shoulder; he steered the boy over to me, then set down the pudding basin he carried under his other arm.

"All right, are you?" I smiled at Josiah, looking deep into his eyes, and squeezed his arm in reassurance. He swallowed hard, and gave me a rather ghastly grin; he wasn't drunk enough not to be scared.

I sat him down, chatting soothingly, wrapped a towel round his neck, and set the basin on his knees. I hoped he wouldn't drop it; it was china, and the only large pudding basin we had. To my surprise, Lizzie came to stand behind him, putting her small hands on his shoulders.

"Are you sure you want to stay, Lizzie?" I asked dubiously. "We can manage all right, I think." Jamie was thoroughly accustomed to blood and general carnage; I didn't think Lizzie could ever have seen anything beyond the common sorts of illness and perhaps a childbirth or two.

"Oh, no, ma'am; I'll stay." She swallowed, too, but set her small jaw bravely. "I promised Jo and Kezzie as I'd stay with them, all through."

I glanced at Jamie, who lifted one shoulder in the hint of a shrug.

"All right, then." I took one of the stoneware jars of penicillin broth, poured it into two cups, and gave one to each of the twins to drink.

Stomach acid would likely inactivate most of the penicillin, but it would—I hoped—kill the bacteria in their throats. Following surgery, another dose washed over the raw surfaces might prevent infection.

There was no way of knowing exactly how much penicillin there might be in the broth; I might be giving them massive doses—or too little to matter. At least I was reasonably sure that whatever penicillin was in the broth was presently active. I had no means of stabilizing the antibiotic, and no notion how long it might be potent—but fresh as it was, the solution was bound to be medicinally active, and there was a good chance that the rest of the broth would remain usable for at least the next few days.

I would make new cultures, as soon as the surgery was complete; with luck, I could dose the twins regularly for three or four days, and—with greater luck—thus prevent any infections.

"Oh, so ye can drink the stuff, can ye?" Jamie was eyeing me cynically over Josiah's head. I had injected him with penicillin following a gunshot injury a few years before, and he obviously now considered that I done so with purely sadistic intent.

I eyed him back.

"You can. Injectable penicillin is much more effective, particularly in the case of an active infection. However, I haven't any means of injecting it just at present, and this is meant to prevent them getting an infection, not to cure one. Now, if we're *quite* ready . . ."

I had thought that Jamie would restrain the patient, but both Lizzie and Josiah insisted that this was not necessary;

Josiah would sit quite still, no matter what. Lizzie still gripped his shoulders, her face paler than his, and her small knuckles sharp and white.

I had examined both boys at length the day before, but had another quick look before starting, using a tongue depressor made of a slip of ash wood. I showed Jamie how to use this to keep the tongue pressed out of my way, then took up forceps and scalpel and drew a long breath.

I looked deep into Josiah's dark eyes, and smiled; I could see two tiny reflections of my face there, both looking pleasantly competent.

"All right, then?" I asked.

He couldn't speak, with the tongue depressor in his mouth, but made a good-natured sort of grunt that I took for assent.

I needed to be quick, and I was. The preparations had taken hours; the operation, no more than a few seconds. I seized one spongy red tonsil with the forceps, stretched it toward me, and made several small, quick cuts, deftly separating the layers of tissue. A trickle of blood was running out of the boy's mouth and down his chin, but nothing serious.

I pulled the gobbet of flesh free, dropped it into the basin, and shifted my grip to the other tonsil, where I repeated the process, only a trifle more slowly in consequence of working backhanded.

The whole thing couldn't have taken more than thirty seconds per side. I drew the instruments out of Josiah's mouth, and he goggled at me, astonished. Then he coughed, gagged, leaned forward, and another small chunk of flesh bounced into the basin with a small *splat*, together with a quantity of bright red blood.

I seized him by the nose and thrust his head back, stuffed pledgets into his mouth to absorb sufficient blood that I could see what I was doing, then snatched a small cautery iron and took care of the largest vessels; the smaller ones could clot and seal on their own.

His eyes were watering ferociously, and his hands were clamped in a death grip on the basin, but he had neither moved nor made a sound. I hadn't expected that he would, after what I had seen when Jamie removed the brand from his thumb. Lizzie was still gripping his shoulders, her eyes tight shut. Jamie reached up and tapped her on the elbow, and her eyes sprang open.

"Here, *a muirninn*, he's done. Take him and put him to his bed, aye?"

Josiah declined to go, though. Mute as his brother, he shook his head violently, and sat down upon a stool, where he sat swaying and white-faced. He gave his brother a ghastly grin, his teeth outlined in blood.

Lizzie hovered between the two boys, looking back and forth between them. Jo caught her eye, and pointed firmly at Keziah, who had assumed the patient's stool with an outward show of fortitude, chin upraised. She patted Jo gently on the head, and went at once to take hold of Keziah's shoulders. He turned his head and gave her a smile of remarkable sweetness, then bent his head and kissed her hand. Then he turned to me, shutting his eyes and opening his mouth; he looked just like a nestling begging for worms.

This operation was somewhat more complicated; his tonsils and adenoids were terribly enlarged, and badly scarred from chronic infection. It was a bloody business; both the towel and my apron were heavily splattered before I had done. I finished the cautery and looked closely at my patient, who was white as the snow outside, and completely glassy-eyed.

"Are you all right?" I asked. He couldn't hear me, but my concerned expression was clear enough. His mouth twitched in what I thought was a gallant effort to smile. He began to nod; then his eyes rolled up and he slid off the stool, ending with a crash at my feet. Jamie caught the basin, rather neatly.

I thought Lizzie might faint as well; there was blood everywhere. She did totter a little, but went obediently to sit down beside Josiah when I told her to. Josiah sat looking on, squeezing Lizzie's hand fiercely while Jamie and I picked up the pieces.

Jamie gathered Keziah up in his arms; the boy lay limp and bloodstained, looking like a murdered child. Josiah rose to his feet, his eyes resting anxiously on his brother's unconscious body.

"It will be all right," Jamie said to him, in tones of

complete confidence. "I told ye, my wife is a great healer." They all turned then, and looked at me, smiling: Jamie, Lizzie, and Josiah. I felt as though I ought to take a bow, but contented myself with smiling, too.

"It will be all right," I said, echoing Jamie. "Go and rest now."

The small procession left the room, more quietly than they had come in, leaving me to put away my instruments and tidy up.

I felt very happy, glowing with the calm sort of satisfaction that attends successful work. I had not done this sort of thing for a long time; the exigencies and limitations of the eighteenth century precluded most surgeries save those done in emergency. Without anesthesia and antibiotic, elective surgery was simply too difficult and too dangerous.

But now I had penicillin, at least. And it *would* be all right, I thought, humming to myself as I extinguished the flame of my alcohol lamp. I had felt it in their flesh, touching the boys as I worked. No germ would threaten them, no infection mar the cleanliness of my work. There was always luck in the practice of medicine—but the odds had shifted today, in my favor.

"All shall be well," I quoted to Adso, who had silently materialized on the counter, where he was industriously licking one of the empty bowls, "and all shall be well, and all manner of thing shall be well."

The big black casebook lay open on the counter where Jamie had left it. I turned to the back pages, where I had been recording the progress of my experiments, and took up my quill. Later, after supper, I would write down the details of the surgery. For the moment . . . I paused, then wrote *Eureka!* at the bottom of the page.

# MAIL CALL

FERGUS UNDERTOOK his bimonthly trip to Cross Creek in mid-February, returning with salt, needles, indigo, a few more miscellaneous necessities, and a bag full of mail. He arrived in mid-afternoon, so anxious to get back to Marsali that he stayed only long enough for a quick mug of beer, leaving Brianna and me to sort through the parcels, gloating over the bounty.

There was a thick stack of newspapers from Wilmington and New Bern; a few from Philadelphia and Boston as well, sent by friends in the north to Jocasta Cameron, and thence forwarded on to us. I flipped through these; the most recent was dated three months prior. No matter; newspapers were as good as novels, in a place where reading material was almost literally scarcer than gold.

Jocasta had also sent two issues of *Brigham's Lady's Book* for Brianna, this being a periodical featuring drawings of fashionable London costumes, and articles of interest to women of such tastes.

*"How to Clean Gold Lace,"* Brianna read, arching one eyebrow as she opened one of these at random. "That's something everybody ought to know how to do, for sure."

"Look in the back," I advised her. "That's where they publish the articles about how to avoid catching gonorrhea and what to do about your husband's piles."

The other brow went up, making her look just like Jamie, presented with some highly questionable proposition.

"If my husband gave me gonorrhea, I think he could just worry about his own piles." She turned several pages, and the eyebrows arched higher. *"A Spur to Venus. This being a List of infallible Remedys for Fatigue of the Male Member."*

I peered over her arm, my own eyebrows rising.

"Goodness. *A Dozen of Oysters, soaked overnight in a Mixture of Wine and Milk, to be baked in a Tart with Crushed Almonds and Lobstermeat, and served with Spiced Peppers.* I don't know what it would do for the male member, but it would probably give the gentleman attached to it violent indigestion. Of course, we haven't got any oysters here anyway."

"No loss," she assured me, frowning at the page in concentration. "Oysters remind me of big plugs of snot."

"That's only the raw ones; they're more or less edible when cooked. Speaking of snot, though—where's Jemmy?"

"Asleep, or at least I hope so." She cast a suspicious eye toward the ceiling, but no untoward noises manifested themselves, and she returned to the page.

"Here's one we could do. *The Testicles of a Male Animal*—like you'd get them from a female animal—*taken with six large Mushrooms and boyled in Sour Ale until tender, then both Testicles and Mushrooms to be sliced thin, well-pepper'd and seasoned with Salt, then sprinkl'd with Vinegar and brown'd before the Fire until crusty.* Da hasn't gotten around to castrating Gideon yet, has he?"

"No. I'm sure he'd be happy to give you the objects in question, if you want to try."

She went very pink in the face, and cleared her throat with a noise that reminded me even more of her father. "I—um—don't think we need that *just* yet."

I laughed and left her to her fascinated perusal, turning back to the mail.

There was a wrapped object addressed to Jamie that I knew must be a book, sent from a bookseller in Philadelphia, but with Lord John Grey's seal affixed—a daub of blue wax whimsically marked with a smiling half-moon and a single star. Half our library came from John Grey, who insisted that he sent us books primarily for his own satisfaction, as he knew no one in the Colonies other than Jamie who was capable of carrying on a decent discussion of literature.

There were several letters addressed to Jamie, too; I looked these over carefully, in hopes of seeing his sister's characteristic spiky script, but no such luck. There was a letter from Ian, who wrote faithfully once a month, but nothing from Jenny; there had been no word from her in the past six months; not since Jamie had written reluctantly to tell her of the fate of her youngest son.

I frowned, setting the letters in a small stack at the edge of the desk for Jamie's later attention. I could scarcely blame Jenny, under the circumstances—but I'd been there, after all. It hadn't been Jamie's fault, even though he'd accepted the blame for it. Young Ian had chosen to stay with the Mohawk. He was a man, if a young one, and the decision was his to make. But then, I reflected, he had been still a lad when he left his parents, and likely still was, so far as Jenny was concerned.

I knew that her silence hurt Jamie deeply, though. He continued to write to her, as he always had, stubbornly putting down a few paragraphs most evenings, putting by the pages until someone should be going down from the mountain, to Cross Creek or Wilmington. He was never obvious about it, but I saw the way his eyes flicked across each batch of letters, looking for her writing, and the almost-invisible tightening at the corner of his mouth when he didn't find it.

"Drat you, Jenny Murray," I murmured under my breath. "Forgive him and have done with it!"

"Hmm?" Brianna had put down the periodical and was examining a square letter, frowning as she did so.

"Nothing. What's that you have there?" I put down the letters I had been sorting and came to look.

"It's from Lieutenant Hayes. What do you think he's writing about?"

A tiny spurt of adrenaline tightened my belly. It must also have shown on my unwary face, for Brianna put down the letter and looked at me, brow furrowed.

"What?" she demanded.

"Nothing," I said, but it was too late. She stood looking at me, a fist doubled on her hip, and raised one brow.

"You are the most terrible liar, Mama," she said tolerantly. Without hesitation, she broke the seal.

"That's addressed to your father," I said, though my protest lacked strength.

"Um-hm. So was the other one," she said, head bent over the unfolded sheet of paper.

"What?" But I had come to her side, and was reading over her arm, even as I spoke.

> *Lieutenant Archibald Hayes*
> *Portsmouth, Virginia*

*Mr. James Fraser*
*Fraser's Ridge, North Carolina*

*January 18, 1771*

*Sir—*

> *I write to inform you that we are at present in Portsmouth, and like to remain here until Spring. If you are acquainted with any Sea Captains willing to grant Passage to Perth for forty Men, on promise of Recompense from the Army once Port is reached, I should be glad to hear of it at your earliest Convenience.*

> *In the Meantime, we have put our Hands to various Labors, that we might sustain ourselves through the Winter Months. Several of my Men have obtained Work in the Repair of Boats, which are plentiful here. I myself am employed as Cook in a local Tavern, but make shift to visit my Men regularly in the assorted Quarters where they are lodged, to make myself acquainted with their State.*

> *I called upon one such Lodging two Evenings ago. In course of Conversation, one of the Men—a Private Ogilvie, whom I think you will know—mentioned to me a Conversation which he had overheard in the Shipyard. As this pertained to one Stephen Bonnet, who I recollect is of Interest to you, I pass on herewith the Intelligence of the Matter.*

> *Bonnet appears by Report to be a Smuggler, scarce an uncommon Occupation in the Area. Howsoever, he seems to deal in a higher Quality—and Quantity—of*

*Contraband than is the usual, and in Consequence,
the Nature of his Connexions appears also unusual.
Which is to say that certain Warehouses on the Carolina Coast periodically contain Goods of a Nature
not generally to be found therein, and that such Visita-
tions coincide with Sightings of Stephen Bonnet in the
Taverns and "Holes" nearby.*

*Private Ogilvie has little Recollection of specific
Names overheard, as he had no Knowledge that Bonnet was of Interest, and mentioned the Matter to me
only as a curious Piece of Information. One Name
mentioned was "Butler," he says, but he is uncertain
whether this Name had aught to do with Bonnet.
Another name was "Karen," but Ogilvie does not
know whether this pertained to a Woman or perhaps to
a Ship.*

*A Warehouse which he supposed to be a particular
Building indicated in the Conversation—though he
freely admits that he is uncertain of this—happened to
be at no great Distance from the Shipyard, and when
he told me of his Intelligence, I took it upon myself to
pass by this Building and make Enquiries concerning
its Ownership. The Building is owned jointly by two
Partners: one Ronald Priestly and one Phillip Wylie. I
have no Information concerning either Man at Present, but will continue my Enquiries as my Time
permits.*

*Having learned the Above, I have made an Effort to
solicit Conversation concerning Bonnet in the local
Taprooms, but to little Effect. I should say that the
Name is known, but few wish to speak of him.*

> *You most obedient servant,*
> *Archibald Hayes, Lieutenant*
> *67th Highland Regiment*

All the normal noises of the house were still around us,
but Bree and I seemed suddenly to be together in a small,
clear bubble of silence, where time had abruptly stopped.

I felt reluctant to put down the letter, for that would mean that time would go on, and something must at that point be done. At the same time, I wanted not merely to put it down but to throw it into the fire, and pretend neither of us had seen it.

Then Jemmy began to cry upstairs, Brianna jerked in response and turned toward the door, and things began to move normally again.

I set the letter down in a space by itself, and returned to the rest of the mail, setting things tidily aside for Jamie's later attention, putting the newspapers and periodicals into a neat stack, untying the string round the parcel; as I had supposed, it was a book—Tobias Smollett's *The Expedition of Humphrey Clinker.* I wound up the string and tucked it into my pocket, while all the time a small "Now-what, now-what" beat in the back of my mind like a metronome.

Brianna came back, carrying Jemmy, who was red and creased from his nap, and obviously in that state of mind where one rouses from sleep to a dazed irritation at the intrusive demands of consciousness. I sympathized.

She sat down, pulled down the neck of her shift, and put the baby to her breast. His cries ceased like magic, and I had a moment of intense wishfulness that I could do something that immediately effective for her. As it was, she looked pale, but composed.

I had to say something.

"I am sorry, sweetheart," I said. "I tried to stop him—Jamie, I mean. I know he didn't mean you to know about it. To worry about it."

"That's okay. I already knew." Reaching across one-handed, she slid one of the ledgers out of the stack Jamie kept on his desk, and holding it by the spine, shook out a folded letter. She nodded over Jemmy's head at it.

"Look at that. I found it while you were gone with the militia."

I read Lord John's account of the duel between Bonnet and Captain Marsden, feeling a coldness gather beneath my breastbone. I hadn't been under any illusions regarding Bonnet's character, but I hadn't known that he had that much skill. I greatly preferred dangerous criminals to be incompetent.

"I thought maybe Lord John was just answering a casual question for Da—but I guess not. What do you think?" Bree asked. Her tone was cool, almost detached, as though she were inquiring my opinion of a hair-ribbon or a shoe-buckle. I looked up at her sharply.

"What do *you* think?" It was Brianna who was important in this—or that was *my* opinion.

"About what?" Her eyes slid away from mine, glancing off the letter, then fastening themselves on the curve of Jemmy's head.

"Oh, the price of tea in China, for starters," I said, with some irritation. "Going on promptly to the topic of Stephen Bonnet, if you like." It felt oddly shocking to say the name out loud; we had all avoided it for months, by unspoken consent.

Her teeth were fastened in her lower lip. She kept her eyes fixed on the floor for a moment, then shook her head, very slightly.

"I don't want to hear about him, or think about him," she said, very evenly. "And if I ever see him again, I might just . . . just . . ." She shuddered violently, then looked up at me, eyes fierce and sudden.

"What's *wrong* with him?" she cried. "How could he do this?" Her clenched fist struck her thigh, and Jemmy, startled, lost his grip and began to wail.

"Your father, you mean—not Bonnet."

She nodded, pressing Jemmy back toward her breast, but he had picked up her agitation, and was squirming and howling. I reached down and took him, hoisting him to my shoulder and patting his back in automatic comfort. Bree's hands, left empty, fastened on her knees, crumpled the cloth of her skirt.

"Why couldn't he leave Bonnet alone?" She had to raise her voice to be heard above the baby's wailing, and the bones of her face seemed to have shifted, so that the skin looked tight-drawn over them.

"Because he's a man—and a bloody Highlander," I said. " 'Live and let live' is not in their vocabulary." Milk was dripping slowly from her nipple onto the fabric of her shift; I reached out one-handed and tweaked the cloth up to cover her. She put a hand over her breast and pressed hard to stop the milk.

"What does he mean to do, though? If he finds him."

"*When* he finds him, I'm afraid," I said reluctantly. "Because I don't believe he's going to stop looking until he does. As to what he'll do then . . . well . . . then he'll kill him, I suppose." It sounded oddly offhand, put that way, and yet I didn't see any other way of putting it, really.

"You mean he'll *try* to kill him." She glanced at the letter from Lord John, then away, swallowing. "What if he . . ."

"Your father has a great deal of experience in killing people," I said bleakly. "In fact, he's awfully good at it—though he hasn't done it for some time."

This didn't seem to reassure her to any great extent. It hadn't reassured me, either.

"It's such a big place," she murmured, shaking her head. "America, I mean. Why couldn't he just—go away? Far away?" An excellent question. Jemmy was snorting, rubbing his face furiously in my shoulder, but no longer screaming.

"I was rather hoping that Stephen Bonnet would have the good sense to go and pursue his smuggling in China or the West Indies, but I suppose he has local connections that he didn't want to abandon." I shrugged, patting Jemmy.

Brianna let go of her skirt and reached for the baby, who was still twisting like an eel.

"Well, he doesn't know he has Sherlock Fraser and his sidekick Lord John Watson on his trail, after all." It was a brave try, but her lip trembled as she said it, and she bit the lower one again. I hated to cause her more worry, but there was no point now in avoiding things.

"No, but he very likely will, before too long," I said reluctantly. "Lord John is very discreet—Private Ogilvie isn't. If Jamie goes on asking questions—and he will, I'm afraid—his interest is going to be rather widely known before long." I wasn't sure whether Jamie had hoped to discover Bonnet quickly and take him unawares—or whether his plan was to smoke Bonnet out into the open by means of his inquiries. Or whether he meant in fact to draw Bonnet's attention deliberately, and cause him to come to *us*. The last possibility made me a little weak in the knees, and I sat down heavily on the stool.

Brianna drew a slow, deep breath and let it out through her nose, settling the baby back at her breast.

"Does Roger know? I mean, is he in on this—this— bloody *vendetta*?"

I shook my head.

"I don't think so. I mean, I'm sure not. He would have told you—wouldn't he?"

Her expression eased a little, though a shadow of doubt still darkened her eyes.

"I'd hate to think he'd keep something like that from me. On the other hand," she added, voice sharpening a little in accusation, "*you* did."

I felt the sting of it, and pressed my lips tight together.

"You said that you didn't want to think of Stephen Bonnet," I said, looking away from the turbulence of feeling in her face. "Naturally not. I—we—didn't want you to have to." With a certain feeling of inevitability, I realized that I was being drawn into the vortex of Jamie's intentions, through no consent of my own.

"Now, look," I said briskly, sitting up straight and giving Brianna a sharp look. "*I* don't think it's a good idea to look for Bonnet, and I've done all I could to discourage Jamie from doing it. In fact," I added ruefully, with a nod toward Lord John's letter, "I thought I *had* discouraged him. But apparently not."

A look of determination was hardening Brianna's mouth, and she settled herself more solidly in the chair.

"*I'll* bloody discourage him," she said.

I gave her a look, considering. If anyone had the necessary stubbornness and force of character to sway Jamie from his chosen path, it would be his daughter. That was, however, a very large "if."

"You can try," I said, a little dubiously.

"Don't I have the right?" Her initial shock had vanished, and her features were back under control, her expression cold and hard. "Isn't it for me to say whether I want . . . what I want?"

"Yes," I agreed, a twinge of uneasiness rippling down my back. Fathers were inclined to think they had rights, too. So were husbands. But perhaps that was better left unsaid.

A momentary silence fell between us, broken only by Jemmy's noises, and the calling of crows outside. Almost by impulse, I asked the question that had risen to the surface of my mind.

"Brianna. What do you want? Do you want Stephen Bonnet dead?"

She glanced at me, then away, looking out the window while she patted Jemmy's back. She didn't blink. Finally, her eyes closed briefly, then opened to meet mine.

"I can't," she said, low-voiced. "I'm afraid if I ever let that thought in my mind . . . I'd never be able to think about anything else, I'd want it so much. And I will be *damned* if I'll let . . . him . . . ruin my life that way."

Jemmy gave a resounding belch, and spit up a little milk. Bree had an old linen towel across her shoulder, and deftly wiped his chin with it. Calmer now, he had lost his look of vexed incomprehension, and was concentrating intently on something over his mother's shoulder. Following the direction of his clear blue gaze, I saw the shadow of a spiderweb, high up in the corner of the window. A gust of wind shook the window frame, and a tiny spot moved in the center of the web, very slightly.

"Yeah," Brianna said, very softly. "I do want him dead. But I want Da and Roger alive, more."

# THE DREAMTIME

ROGER HAD GONE to sing for Joel MacLeod's
nephew's wedding, as arranged at the Gathering, and
come home with a new prize, which he was anxious
to commit to paper before it should escape.

He left his muddy boots in the kitchen, accepted a cup of
tea and a raisin tart from Mrs. Bug, and went directly to the
study. Jamie was there, writing letters; he glanced up with an
absent murmur of acknowledgment, but then returned to his
composition, a slight frown between his heavy brows as he
formed the letters, hand cramped and awkward on the quill.

There was a small, three-shelf bookcase in Jamie's study,
which held the entire library of Fraser's Ridge. The serious
works occupied the top shelf: a volume of Latin poetry, Caesar's *Commentaries*, the *Meditations* of Marcus Aurelius, a
few other classic works, Dr. Brickell's *Natural History of
North Carolina*, lent by the Governor and never returned, and
a schoolbook on mathematics, much abused, with *Ian Murray the Younger* written on the flyleaf in a staggering hand.

The middle shelf was given over to more light-minded
reading: a small selection of romances, slightly ragged with
much reading, featuring *Robinson Crusoe*; *Tom Jones*, in a
set of seven small, leather-covered volumes; *Roderick Random*, in four volumes; and Sir Henry Richardson's monstrous
*Pamela*, done in two gigantic octavo bindings—the first of
these decorated with multiple bookmarks, ranging from a
ragged dried maple leaf to a folded penwiper, these indicating the points which various readers had reached before giving up, either temporarily or permanently. A copy of *Don*

*Quixote* in Spanish, ratty, but much less worn, since only Jamie could read it.

The bottom shelf held a copy of *Dr. Sam. Johnson's Dictionary*, Jamie's ledgers and account books, several of Brianna's sketchbooks, and the slender buckram-bound journal in which Roger recorded the words of unfamiliar songs and poems acquired at ceilidhs and hearthsides.

He took a stool on the other side of the table Jamie used as a desk, and cut a new quill for the job, taking care with it; he wanted these records to be readable. He didn't know precisely what use the collection might be put to, but he had been ingrained with the scholar's instinctive value for the written word. Perhaps this was only for his own pleasure and use—but he liked the feeling that he might be leaving something to posterity as well, and took pains both to write clearly and to document the circumstances under which he had acquired each song.

The study was peaceful, with no more than Jamie's occasional sigh as he stopped to rub the kinks from his cramped hand. After a while, Mr. Bug came to the door, and after a brief colloquy, Jamie put away his quill and went out with the factor. Roger nodded vaguely as they bade him farewell, mind occupied with the effort of recall and recording.

When he finished, a quarter of an hour later, his mind was pleasantly empty, and he sat back, stretching the ache from his shoulders. He waited a few moments for the ink to be thoroughly dry before he put the book away, and while waiting, went to pull out one of Brianna's sketchbooks from the bottom shelf.

She wouldn't mind if he looked; she had told him he was welcome to look at them. At the same time, she showed him only the occasional drawing, those she was pleased with, or had done especially for him.

He turned over the pages of the notebook, feeling the sense of curiosity and respect that attends the prying into mystery, searching for small glimpses of the workings of her mind.

There were lots of portrait sketches of the baby in this one, a study in circles.

He paused at one small sketch, caught by memory. It was a sketch of Jemmy sleeping, back turned, his small sturdy body curled up in a comma. Adso the cat was curled up beside him, in precisely similar fashion, his chin perched on Jemmy's fat little foot, eyes slits of comatose bliss. He remembered that one.

She drew Jemmy often—nearly every day, in fact—but seldom fullface.

"Babies don't really have faces," she had told him, frowning critically at her offspring, who was industriously gnawing on the leather strap of Jamie's powder horn.

"Oh, aye? And what's that on the front of his head, then?" He had lain flat on the floor with the baby and the cat, grinning up at her, which made it easier for her to look down her nose at him.

"I mean, strictly speaking. Naturally they have faces, but they all look alike."

"It's a wise father that kens his own child, eh?" he joked, regretting it instantly, as he saw the shadow cloud her eyes. It passed, quick as a summer cloud, but it had been there, nonetheless.

"Well, not from an artist's point of view." She drew the blade of her penknife at an angle across the tip of the charcoal stick, sharpening the point. "They don't have any bones—that you can see, I mean. And it's the bones that you use to show the shape of a face; without bones, there isn't much there."

Bones or not, she had a remarkable knack for capturing the nuances of expression. He smiled at one sketch; Jemmy's face wore the aloof and unmistakable expression of one concentrating hard on the production of a truly terrible diaper.

Beyond the pictures of Jemmy, there were several pages of what looked like engineering diagrams. Finding these of no great interest, he bent and replaced the book, then drew out another.

He realized at once that it was not a sketchbook. The pages were dense with Brianna's tidy, angular writing. He flipped curiously through the pages; it wasn't really a diary, but appeared to be a sort of record of her dreams.

*Last night I dreamed that I shaved my legs.* Roger smiled at the inconsequence, but a vision of Brianna's shins, long-boned and glimmering, kept him reading.

*I was using Daddy's razor and his shaving cream, and I was thinking that he'd complain when he found out, but I wasn't worried. The shaving cream came in a white can with red letters, and it said Old Spice on the label. I don't know if there ever was shaving cream like that, but that's what Daddy always smelled of, Old Spice aftershave and cigarette smoke. He didn't smoke, but the people he worked with did, and his jackets always smelled like the air in the living room after a party.*

Roger breathed in, half-conscious of the remembered scents of fresh baking and tea, furniture polish and ammonia. No cigarettes at the decorous gatherings held in the manse's parlor—and yet his father's jackets too had smelled of smoke.

*Once Gayle told me that she'd gone out with Chris and hadn't had time to shave her legs, and she spent the whole evening trying to keep him from putting his hand on her knee, for fear he'd feel the stubble. After-ward, I never shaved my legs without thinking of that, and I'd run my fingers up my thigh, to see whether I could feel anything there, or if it was okay to stop shaving at my kneecaps.*

The hair on Brianna's thighs was so fine it could not be felt; and only seen when she rose up naked over him, with the sun behind her gilding her body, gleaming through that delicate nimbus of secrecy. The thought that no one would ever see it but himself gave him a small glow of satisfaction, like a miser counting each hair of gold and copper, enjoying his secret fortune undisturbed by any fear of theft.

He turned the page, feeling unspeakably guilty at this intrusion, yet drawn irresistibly by the urge to penetrate the intimacy of her dreams, to know the images that filled her sleeping mind.

The entries were undated, but each entry began with the same words: *Last night, I dreamed.*

*Last night I dreamed that it was raining. Hardly surprising, since it was raining, and has been for two days. When I went out to the privy this morning, I had to jump over a huge puddle by the door, and sank up to the ankles in the soft spot by the blackberries.*

*We went to bed last night with the rain pounding on the roof. It was so nice to curl up with Roger and be warm in our bed, after a wet, chilly day. Raindrops fell down the chimney and hissed in the fire. We told each other stories from our youths—maybe that's where the dream came from, thinking about the past.*

*There wasn't much to the dream, just that I was looking out a window in Boston, watching the cars go past, throwing up big sheets of water from their wheels, and hearing the swoosh and rush of their tires on the wet streets. I woke up still hearing that sound; it was so clear in my mind that I actually went to the window and peeked out, half expecting to see a busy street, full of cars rushing through the rain. It was a shock to see spruce trees and chestnuts and wild grass and creepers, and hear nothing but the soft patter of raindrops bouncing and trembling on the burdock leaves.*

*Everything was so vivid a green, so lush and over-grown, that it seemed like a jungle, or an alien planet—a place I'd never been, with nothing I recognized, though in fact I see it every day.*

*All day, I've heard the secret rush of tires in the rain, somewhere behind me.*

Feeling guilty, but fascinated, Roger turned the page.

*Last night I dreamed of driving my car. It was my own blue Mustang, and I was driving fast down a*

*winding road, through the mountains—these moun-
tains. I never have driven through these mountains,
though I have been through the mountain woodlands
in upstate New York. It was definitely here, though; I
knew it was the Ridge.*

*It was so real. I can still feel my hair snapping in
the wind, the wheel in my hands, the vibration of the
motor and the rumble of tires on the pavement. But
that sensation—as well as the car—is impossible. It
can't happen now, anywhere but in my head. And yet
there it is, embedded in the cells of my memory, as
real as the privy outside, waiting to be called back to
life at the flick of a synapse.*

*That's another oddness. Nobody knows what a
synapse is, except me and Mama and Roger. What a
strange feeling; as though we three share all kinds of
secrets.*

*Anyway, that particular bit—the driving—is trace-
able to a known memory. But what about the dreams,
equally vivid, equally real, of things I do not know of
my waking self. Are some dreams the memories of
things that haven't happened yet?*

*Last night I dreamed that I made love with Roger.*

He had been about to close the book, feeling a sense of
guilt at his intrusion. The guilt was still there—in spades—
but totally insufficient to overcome his curiosity. He glanced
at the door, but the house was quiet; women were moving
about in the kitchen, but no one was near the study.

*Last night I dreamed that I made love with Roger.*
*It was great; for once I wasn't thinking, wasn't
watching from the outside, like I always do. In fact, I
wasn't even aware of myself for a long time. There was
just this . . . very wild, exciting stuff, and I was part of
it and Roger was part of it, but there wasn't any him
or me, just us.*

*The funny thing is that it was Roger, but I didn't*

*think of him like that. Not by his name—not that name.
It was like he had another name, a secret, real one—
but I knew what it was.*

*(I've always thought everybody has that kind of
name, the kind that isn't a word. I know who I am—
and whoever it is, her name isn't "Brianna." It's me,
that's all. "Me" works fine as a substitute for what I
mean—but how do you write down someone else's
secret name?)*

*I knew Roger's real name, though, and that seemed
to be why it was working. And it really was working,
too; I didn't think about it or worry about it, and I
only thought toward the very end, Hey, it's happening!*

*And then it did happen and everything dissolved
and shook and throbbed—*

Here she had blacked out the rest of the line, with a small,
cross note in the margin, that said,

*Well, none of the books I've ever read could describe
it, either!*

Despite his shocked fascination, Roger laughed aloud,
then choked it off, glancing round hastily to see that he was
still alone. There were noises in the kitchen, but no sound of
footsteps in the hall, and his eyes went back to the page like
iron filings drawn to a magnet.

*I had my eyes closed—in the dream, that is—and I
was lying there with little electric shocks still going
off, and I opened my eyes and it was Stephen Bonnet
inside me.*

*It was such a shock it woke me up. I felt like I'd
been screaming—my throat was all raw—but I
couldn't have been, because Roger and the baby were
sound asleep. I was hot all over, so hot I was sweating,
but I was cold, too, and my heart was pounding. It
took a long time before things settled down enough for
me to go back to sleep; all the birds were carrying on.
That's what finally let me go back to sleep, in fact—*

*the birds. Da—and Daddy, too, come to think of it—
told me that the jays and crows give alarm calls, but
songbirds stop singing when someone comes near, so
when you're in a forest, you listen for that. With so
much racket in the trees by the house, I knew it was
safe—nobody was there.*

There was a small blank space at the foot of the page. He
turned it, feeling his palms sweat and his heartbeat heavy in
his ears. The writing resumed at the top of the page. Before,
the writing had been fluid, almost hasty, the letters flattened
as they raced across the page. Here, they were formed with
more care, rounded and upright, as though the first shock of
the experience were spent, and she had returned, with a stubborn caution, to think further about it.

*I tried to forget it, but that didn't work. It kept com-
ing back and coming back into my mind, so I finally
went out by myself to work in the herb shed. Mama
keeps Jemmy when I'm there because he gets in
things, so I knew I could be alone. So I sat down in the
middle of all the hanging bunches and closed my eyes
and tried to remember every single thing about it, and
think to myself about the different parts, "That's okay,"
or "That's just a dream." Because Stephen Bonnet
scared me, and I felt sick when I thought of the end—
but I really wanted to remember how. How it felt, and
how I did it, so maybe I can do it again, with Roger.
But I keep having this feeling that I can't, unless I
can remember Roger's secret name.*

There the entry stopped. The dreams continued on the
next page, but Roger didn't read further. He closed the book
very carefully and slid it back behind the others on the shelf.
He rose to his feet and stood looking out the window for
some time, unconsciously rubbing his sweating palms over
the seams of his breeches.

# PART FIVE

*'Tis Better to Marry Than Burn*

# 39

# IN CUPID'S GROVE

DO YE THINK they'll share a bed?"

Jamie didn't raise his voice, but he'd made no effort to lower it, either. Luckily, we were standing at the far end of the terrace, too far away for the bridal couple to hear. A number of heads turned in our direction, though.

Ninian Bell Hamilton was openly staring at us. I smiled brightly and fluttered my closed fan at the elderly Scotsman in greeting, meanwhile giving Jamie a swift nudge in the ribs.

"A nice, respectable sort of thing for a nephew to be wondering about his aunt," I said under my breath.

Jamie shifted out of elbow range and lifted an eyebrow at me.

"What's respectable to do with it? They'll be married. And well above the age of consent, both o' them," he added, with a grin at Ninian, who went bright pink with smothered mirth. I didn't know how old Duncan Innes was, but my best guess put him in his mid-fifties. Jamie's aunt Jocasta had to be at least a decade older.

I could just see Jocasta over the heads of the intervening crowd, graciously accepting the greetings of friends and neighbors at the far end of the terrace. A tall woman gowned in russet wool, she was flanked by huge stone vases holding sprays of dried goldenrod, and her black butler Ulysses stood at her shoulder, dignified in wig and green livery. With an elegant white lace cap crowning her bold MacKenzie bones, she was undeniably the queen of River Run Plantation. I stood on tiptoe, searching for her consort.

Duncan was slightly shorter than Jocasta, but he should still have been visible. I'd seen him earlier in the morning, dressed in an absolute blaze of Highland finery, in which he looked dashing, if terribly self-conscious. I craned my neck, putting a hand on Jamie's arm to keep my balance. He grabbed my elbow to steady me.

"What are ye looking for, Sassenach?"

"Duncan. Shouldn't he be with your aunt?"

No one could tell by looking that Jocasta was blind—that she stood between the big vases to keep her bearings, or that Ulysses was there to whisper in her ear the names of approaching guests. I saw her left hand drift outward from her side, touch empty air, and drift back. Her face didn't change, though; she smiled and nodded, saying something to Judge Henderson.

"Run away before the wedding night?" suggested Ninian, lifting his chin and both eyebrows in an effort to see over the crowd without standing on his toes. "I'd maybe feel a bit nervous at the prospect myself. Your aunt's a handsome woman, Fraser, but she could freeze the ballocks off the King o' Japan, and she wanted to."

Jamie's mouth twitched.

"Duncan's maybe caught short," he said. "Whatever the reason. He's been to the necessary house four times this morning."

My own brows went up at this. Duncan suffered from chronic constipation; in fact, I had brought a packet of senna leaves and coffee-plant roots for him, in spite of Jamie's rude remarks about what constituted a suitable wedding present. Duncan must be more nervous than I'd thought.

"Well, it's no going to be any great surprise to my aunt, and her wi' three husbands before him," Jamie said, in reply to a murmured remark of Hamilton's. "It'll be the first time Duncan's been married, though. That's a shock to any man. I remember my own wedding night, aye?" He grinned at me, and I felt the heat rise in my cheeks. I remembered it, too—vividly.

"Don't you think it's rather warm out here?" I flicked my fan into an arc of ivory lace, and fluttered it over my cheeks.

"Really?" he said, still grinning at me. "I hadna taken notice of it."

"Duncan has," Ninian put in. His wrinkled lips pursed closed, holding in the laughter. "Sweating like a steamed pudding when I saw him last."

It was in fact a little chilly out, in spite of the cast-iron tubs full of hot embers that sent the sweet smell of apple-wood smoke wisping up from the corners of the stone terrace. Spring had sprung, and the lawns were fresh and green, as were the trees along the river, but the morning air still held a sharp nip of winter's bite. It *was* still winter in the mountains, and we had encountered snow as far south as Guildford on our journey toward River Run, though daffodils and crocuses poked bravely through it.

It was a clear, bright March day now, though, and house, terrace, lawn, and garden were thronged with wedding guests, glowing in their finery like an unseasonable flight of butterflies. Jocasta's wedding was clearly going to be the social event of the year, so far as Cape Fear society was concerned; there must be nearly two hundred people here, from places as far distant as Halifax and Edenton.

Ninian said something to Jamie in low-voiced Gaelic, with a sidelong glance at me. Jamie replied with a remark elegant in phraseology and extremely crude in content, blandly meeting my eye as the older man choked with laughter.

I did in fact understand Gaelic fairly well by now, but there were moments when discretion was the better part of valor. I spread my fan wide, concealing my expression. True, it took some practice to achieve grace with a fan, but it was a useful social tool to someone cursed, as I was, with a glass face. Even fans had their limits, though.

I turned away from the conversation, which gave every promise of degenerating further, and surveyed the party for signs of the absent bridegroom. Perhaps Duncan was truly ill, and not with nerves. If so, I should have a look at him.

"Phaedre! Have you seen Mr. Innes this morning?" Jocasta's body servant was flying past, her arms full of tablecloths, but came abruptly to a halt at my call.

"Ain't seen Mister Duncan since breakfast, ma'am," she said, with a shake of her neatly capped head.

"How did he seem then? Did he eat well?" Breakfast was an ongoing affair of several hours, the resident guests serving themselves from the sideboard and eating as they chose. It was more likely nerves than food poisoning that was troubling Duncan's bowels, but some of the sausage I had seen on the sideboard struck me as highly suspect.

"No, ma'am, nary a bite." Phaedre's smooth brow puckered; she was fond of Duncan. "Cook tried to tempt him with a nice coddled egg, but he just shook his head and looked peaked. He did take a cup of rum punch, though," she said, seeming somewhat cheered at the thought.

"Aye, that'll settle him," Ninian remarked, overhearing. "Dinna trouble yourself, Mrs. Claire; Duncan will be well enough."

Phaedre curtsied and made off toward the tables being set up under the trees, starched apron flapping in the breeze. The succulent aroma of barbecuing pork wafted through the chill spring air, and fragrant clouds of hickory smoke rose from the fires near the smithy, where haunches of venison, sides of mutton, and broiled fowl in their dozens turned on spits. My stomach gurgled loudly in anticipation, despite the tight lacing of my stays.

Neither Jamie nor Ninian appeared to notice, but I took a discreet step away, turning to survey the lawn that stretched from the terrace to the river landing. I wasn't so positive of the virtues of rum, particularly taken on an empty stomach. Granted, Duncan wouldn't be the first groom to go to the altar in an advanced state of intoxication, but still . . .

Brianna, brilliant in blue wool the color of the spring sky, was standing near one of the marble statues that graced the lawn, Jemmy balanced on her hip, deep in conversation with Gerald Forbes, the lawyer. She also had a fan, but at the moment, it was being put to better use than usual—Jemmy had got hold of it and was munching on the ivory handle, a look of fierce concentration on his small pink face.

Of course, Brianna had less need of good fan technique than I did, she having inherited Jamie's ability to hide all thoughts behind a mask of pleasant blandness. She had the mask in place now, which gave me a good idea of her opinion of Mr. Forbes. Where was Roger? I wondered. He'd been with her earlier.

I turned to ask Jamie what he thought of this epidemic of disappearing husbands, only to discover that he had joined it. Ninian Hamilton had turned away to talk to someone else, and the space at my side was now occupied by a pair of slaves, staggering under the weight of a fresh demijohn of brandywine as they headed for the refreshment tables. I stepped hastily out of their way, and turned to look for Jamie.

He had vanished into the crowd like a grouse into heather. I turned slowly, surveying the terrace and lawns, but there wasn't a sign of him among the milling crowd. I frowned against the bright sunlight, shading my eyes with my hand.

It wasn't as though he were inconspicuous, after all; a Highlander with the blood of Viking giants in his veins, he stood head and shoulders above most men, and his hair caught the sun like polished bronze. To add icing to the cake, he was dressed today in his best to celebrate Jocasta's wedding—a belted plaid in crimson and black tartan, with his good gray coat and weskit, and the gaudiest pair of red-and-black Argyle stockings ever to grace a Scotsman's shins. He should have stood out like a splotch of blood on fresh linen.

I didn't find him, but did see a familiar face. I stepped off the terrace and eeled my way through the knots of party-goers.

"Mr. MacLennan!" He turned toward my call, looking surprised, but then a cordial smile spread across his blunt features.

"Mrs. Fraser!"

"How lovely to see you," I said, giving him my hand. "How are you?" He looked much better than when last seen, clean and decent in a dark suit and plain laced hat. There were hollows in his cheeks, though, and a shadow behind his eyes that remained even as he smiled at me.

"Oh . . . I'm well enough, ma'am. Quite well."

"Are you—where are you living, these days?" That seemed a more delicate question than "Why aren't you in jail?" No fool, he answered both questions.

"Och, well, your husband was sae kind as to write to Mr.

Ninian there"—he nodded across the lawn toward the lean figure of Ninian Bell Hamilton, who was in the middle of a heated discussion of some kind—"and to tell him of my trouble. Mr. Ninian's a great friend to the Regulation, ken— and a great friend of Judge Henderson's, forbye." He shook his head, mouth pursed in puzzlement.

"I couldna say quite how it fell out, but Mr. Ninian came and fetched me out of the gaol, and took me into his own household. So I am there, for the present. 'Twas kind—verra kind." He spoke with evident sincerity, and yet with a certain air of abstraction. He fell silent then. He was still looking at me, but his eyes were blank. I groped for something to say, hoping to bring him back to the present, but a shout from Ninian brought him out of his trance, saving me the trouble. Abel excused himself politely to me and went to assist in the argument.

I strolled down the lawn, nodding to acquaintances over my fan. I was glad to see Abel again, and know he was physically well, at least—but I couldn't deny that the sight of him cast a chill over my heart. I had the feeling that in fact, it made little difference to Abel MacLennan where his body resided; his heart still lay in the grave with his wife.

Why had Ninian brought him today? I wondered. Surely a wedding could not but recall his own marriage to him; weddings did that to everyone.

The sun had risen high enough to warm the air, but I shivered. The sight of MacLennan's grief reminded me too much of the days after Culloden, when I had gone back to my own time, knowing Jamie dead. I knew too well that deadness of heart; the sense of sleepwalking through days and lying open-eyed at night, finding no rest, knowing only emptiness that was not peace.

Jocasta's voice floated down from the terrace, calling to Ulysses. She had lost three husbands, and now was fixed to take a fourth. Blind she might be, but there was no deadness in her eyes. Did that mean she had not cared deeply for any of her husbands? I wondered. Or only that she was a woman of great strength, capable of overcoming grief, not once, but over and again?

I had done it once, myself—for Brianna's sake. But Jocasta had no children; not now, at least. Had she once had them, and put aside the pain of a sundered heart, to live for a child?

I shook myself, trying to dispel such melancholy thoughts. It was, after all, a festive occasion, and a day to match. The dogwoods in the grove were in bloom, and courting bluebirds and cardinals shot in and out of the greening trees like bits of confetti, crazed with lust.

"But of course they have," a woman was saying, in an authoritative tone of voice. "My God, they've shared a house for months now!"

"Aye, that's so," one of her companions agreed, sounding doubtful. "But ye wouldna think it from the looks of them. Why, they scarcely glance at each other! Ah . . . I mean— well, of course, she canna be looking at him, blind as she is, but ye'd think . . ."

It wasn't only the birds, I thought, amused. A certain sense of rising sap suffused the whole gathering. Glancing up at the terrace, I could see young women clustered, tittering and gossiping in small groups like hens, while the men strode oh-so-casually up and down in front of them, gaudy as peacocks in their party clothes. I wouldn't be surprised if at least a few engagements resulted from this celebration—and a few pregnancies as well. Sex was in the air; I could smell it, under the heady fragrances of spring flowers and cooking food.

The sense of melancholy had quite left me, though I still had a strong urge to find Jamie.

I had gone down one side of the lawn and up the other, but saw no sign of him anywhere between the big plantation house and the dock, where slaves in livery were still greeting latecomers arriving by water. Among those still expected— and very late indeed—was the priest who was to perform the wedding.

Father LeClerc was a Jesuit, bound from New Orleans to a mission near Quebec, but seduced from the strict path of duty by a substantial donation made by Jocasta to the Society of Jesus. Money might not buy happiness, I reflected, but it was a useful commodity, nonetheless.

I glanced in the other direction and stopped dead. At one

side, Ronnie Campbell caught my eye and bowed; I lifted my fan in acknowledgment, but was too distracted to speak to him. I hadn't found Jamie, but I had just spotted the likely reason for his abrupt disappearance. Ronnie's father, Farquard Campbell, was coming up the lawn from the landing, accompanied by a gentleman in the red and fawn of His Majesty's army, and another in naval uniform—Lieutenant Wolff.

The sight gave me an unpleasant shock. Lieutenant Wolff was not my favorite person. He wasn't all that popular with anyone else who knew him, either.

I supposed it was reasonable for him to have been invited, as His Majesty's navy was the principal buyer of River Run's production of timber, tar, and turpentine, and Lieutenant Wolff was the navy's representative in such matters. And it was possible that Jocasta had invited him for more personal reasons as well—the Lieutenant had at one point asked her to marry him. Not, as she had dryly noted, from any desire for her person, but rather to get his hands on River Run.

Yes, I could see her enjoying the Lieutenant's presence here today. Duncan, less naturally given to ulterior motives and manipulations, might not.

Farquard Campbell had spotted me, and was making for me through the crowd, the armed forces in tow. I got my fan up and made the necessary facial adjustments for polite conversation, but—much to my relief—the Lieutenant spotted a servant carrying a tray of glasses across the terrace and sheared off in pursuit, abandoning his escort in favor of refreshment.

The other military gentleman glanced after him, but dutifully followed Farquard. I squinted at him, but he was no one I'd met before, I was sure. Since the removal of the last Highland regiment in the autumn, the sight of a red coat was unusual anywhere in the colony. Who could this be?

My features fixed in what I hoped was a pleasant smile, I sank into a formal curtsy, spreading my embroidered skirts to best advantage.

"Mr. Campbell." I glanced covertly behind him, but Lieutenant Wolff had fortunately vanished in the pursuit of alcoholic sustenance.

"Mrs. Fraser. Your servant, ma'am." Farquard made me a graceful leg in reply. An elderly, desiccated-looking man, Mr. Campbell was sedate as usual in black broadcloth, a small burst of ruffles at the throat being his only concession to the festivities.

He looked over my shoulder, frowning slightly in puzzlement. "I had seen—I *thought* I had seen your husband with you?"

"Oh. Well, I think he's ... er ... gone ..." I twiddled my fan delicately toward the trees where the necessary facilities lurked, separated from the main house by an aesthetic distance and a screen of small white pines.

"Ah, I see. Just so." Campbell cleared his throat, and gestured to the man who accompanied him. "Mrs. Fraser, may I present Major Donald MacDonald?"

Major MacDonald was a rather hawk-nosed but handsome gentleman in his late thirties, with the weathered face and erect bearing of a career soldier, and a pleasant smile belied by a pair of sharp blue eyes, the same pale, vivid shade as Brianna's dress.

"Your servant, ma'am." He bowed, very gracefully. "May I say, ma'am, how particularly that color becomes you?"

"You may," I said, relaxing a little. "Thank you."

"The Major is but recently arrived in Cross Creek. I assured him he would find no greater opportunity to pursue acquaintance with his countrymen and familiarize himself with his surroundings." Farquard swept a hand around the terrace, encompassing the party—which did indeed comprise a Who's Who of Scottish society along the Cape Fear.

"Indeed," the Major said politely. "I have not heard so many Scottish names since last I was in Edinburgh. Mr. Campbell gives me to understand that your husband is the nephew of Mrs. Cameron—or Mrs. Innes, perhaps I should say?"

"Yes. Have you met Mrs. .... er ... Innes yet?" I glanced toward the far end of the terrace. Still no sign of Duncan, let alone Roger or Jamie. Blast it, where *was* everybody? Holding summit conferences in the necessary house?

"No, but I shall look forward to presenting my compliments. The late Mr. Cameron was by way of being an acquaintance of my father, Robert MacDonald of Stornoway." He inclined his wigged head a respectful inch in the direction of the small white marble building at the side of the lawn—the mausoleum that presently sheltered the fleshly remnants of Hector Cameron. "Has your husband any connection with the Frasers of Lovat, by chance?"

With an internal groan, I recognized a Scottish spiderweb in the making. The meeting of any two Scots invariably began with the casting out of skeins of inquiry until enough strands of relation and acquaintanceship had stuck to form a useful network. I tended to become entangled in the sticky strands of sept and clan, myself, ending up like a fat, juicy fly, thoroughly trapped and at the mercy of my questioner.

Jamie had survived the intrigues of French and Scottish politics for years by means of such knowledge, though— skating precariously along the secret strands of such webs, keeping away from the sticky snares of loyalty and betrayal that had doomed so many others. I settled myself to pay attention, struggling to place this MacDonald among the thousand others of his ilk.

MacDonald of Keppoch, MacDonald of the Isles, MacDonald of Clanranald, MacDonald of Sleat. How many kinds of MacDonald were there, anyway? I wondered, a little crossly. Surely one or two should be sufficient to most purposes.

MacDonald of the Isles, evidently; the Major's family hailed from the Isle of Harris. I kept one eye out during the interrogation, but Jamie had safely gone to earth.

Farquard Campbell—no mean player himself—seemed to be enjoying the verbal game of battledore and shuttlecock, his dark eyes flicking back and forth between me and the Major with a look of amusement. The amusement faded into a look of surprise as I finished a rather confused analysis of Jamie's paternal lineage, in response to the Major's expert catechism.

"Your husband's grandfather was Simon, Lord Lovat?" Campbell said. "The Old Fox?" His voice rose slightly with incredulity.

"Well . . . yes," I said, a little uneasily. "I thought you knew that."

"Indeed," said Farquard. He looked as though he had swallowed a brandied plum, noticing too late that the stone was still in it. He'd known Jamie was a pardoned Jacobite, all right, but plainly Jocasta hadn't mentioned his close connection with the Old Fox—executed as a traitor for his role in the Stuart Rising. Most of the Campbells had fought on the Government side of that particular brouhaha.

"Yes," MacDonald said, ignoring Campbell's reaction. He frowned slightly in concentration. "I have the honor to be slightly acquainted with the present Lord Lovat—the title has been restored, I collect?"

He went on, turning to Campbell in explanation. "That would be Young Simon, who raised a regiment to fight the French in . . . '58? No, '57. Yes, '57. A gallant soldier, excellent fighting man. And he would be your husband's . . . nephew? No, uncle."

"Half-uncle," I clarified. Old Simon had been married three times, and made no secret of his extramarital by-blows—of which Jamie's father had been one. No need to point that out, though.

MacDonald nodded, lean face clearing in satisfaction at having got it all neatly sorted. Farquard's face relaxed a little, hearing that the family reputation had gone so far toward rehabilitation.

"Papist, of course," MacDonald added, "but an excellent soldier, nonetheless."

"Speaking of soldiers," Campbell interrupted, "do you know . . ."

I breathed a sigh of relief that made my corset strings creak, as Mr. Campbell smoothly led the Major into an analysis of some past military event. The Major, it seemed, was not on active duty, but like many, presently retired on half-pay. Unless and until the Crown found some further use for his services, he was thus left to mooch round the Colonies in search of occupation. Peace was hard on professional soldiers.

*Just wait*, I thought, with a small premonitory shiver. Four years, or less, and the Major would be busy enough.

I caught a flash of tartan from the corner of my eye and turned to look, but it was neither Jamie nor Duncan. One less mystery, though; it was Roger, dark-haired and handsome in his kilt. His face lit as he spotted Brianna, and his stride lengthened. She turned her head, as though feeling his presence, and her own face brightened in answer.

He reached her side, and without the least acknowledgment of the gentleman with her, embraced her and kissed her soundly on the mouth. As they drew apart, he held out his arms for Jemmy, and dropped another kiss on the silky red head.

I returned to the conversation at hand, belatedly realizing that Farquard Campbell had been talking for some time without my having any notion what he had said. Seeing my bemusement, he smiled, a little wryly.

"I must go and pay my respects elsewhere, Mrs. Fraser," he said. "If you will pardon me? I shall leave you to the Major's excellent company." He touched his hat courteously, and eeled off toward the house, perhaps intending to track down Lieutenant Wolff and stop him pocketing the silver.

Thus marooned with me, the Major cast about for suitable conversation, and fell back upon the most commonly asked question between new acquaintances.

"Are you and your husband long arrived in the colony, ma'am?"

"Not long," I said, rather wary. "Three years or so. We live in a small settlement in the backcountry—" I waved my closed fan toward the invisible mountains to the west. "A place called Fraser's Ridge."

"Ah, yes. I have heard of it." A muscle twitched near the corner of his mouth, and I wondered uneasily just what he had heard. Jamie's still was an open secret in the backcountry, and among the Scottish settlers of the Cape Fear—in fact, several kegs of raw whisky from the still were sitting in plain sight by the stables, Jamie's wedding present to his aunt and Duncan—but I hoped the secret wasn't quite so open that an army officer newly arrived in the colony would already have heard about it.

"Tell me, Mrs. Fraser . . ." He hesitated, then plunged ahead. "Do you encounter a great deal of . . . factionalism in your area of the colony?"

"Factionalism? Oh, er . . . no, not a great deal." I cast a wary eye toward Hector Cameron's mausoleum, where Hermon Husband's dark Quaker gray showed up like a blot against the pure white marble. Factionalism was a code word for the activities of men like Husband and James Hunter—Regulators.

The Governor's militia action in December had quashed the violent demonstrations, but the Regulation was still a simmering pot under a very tight lid. Husband had been arrested and imprisoned for a short time in February on the strength of his pamphlets, but the experience had in no way softened either his disposition or his language. A boilover could happen at any time.

"I am pleased to hear it, ma'am," Major MacDonald said. "Do you hear much news, remotely situated as you are?"

"Not a great deal. Er . . . nice day, isn't it? We've been so fortunate in the weather this year. Was it an easy journey from Charleston? So early in the year—the mud . . ."

"Indeed, ma'am. We had some small difficulties, but no more than . . ."

The Major was assessing me quite openly as he chatted, taking in the cut and quality of my gown, the pearls at my throat and ears—borrowed from Jocasta—and the rings on my fingers. I was familiar with such a look; there was no hint of lechery or flirtation in it. He was simply judging my social standing and my husband's level of prosperity and influence.

I took no offense. I was busy doing the same thing to him, after all. Well-educated and of good family; that much was plain from his rank alone, though the heavy gold signet on his right hand clinched the matter. Not personally well-off, though; his uniform was worn at the seams, and his boots were deeply scarred, though well-polished.

A light Scots accent with a hint of French gutturality—experience in Continental campaigns. And very newly arrived in the colony, I thought; his face was drawn from recent illness, and the whites of his eyes bore the slight tinge of jaundice common to new arrivals, who tended to contract everything from malaria to dengue fever, when exposed to the seething germ pools of the coastal towns.

"Tell me, Mrs. Fraser—" the Major began.

"You insult not only me, sir, but every man of honor here present!"

Ninian Bell Hamilton's rather high-pitched voice rang out through a lull in the general conversation, and heads turned all over the lawn.

He was face-to-face with Robert Barlow, a man I had been introduced to earlier in the morning. A merchant of some kind, I vaguely recalled—from Edenton? Or possibly New Bern. A heavyset man with the look of one unused to contradiction, he was sneering openly at Hamilton.

"Regulators, you call them? Gaolbirds and rioters! You suggest that such men possess a sense of honor, do you?"

"I do not suggest it—I state it as fact, and will defend it as such!" The old gentleman drew himself upright, hand groping for a sword-hilt. Fortunately for the occasion, he wasn't wearing a sword; none of the gentlemen present were, given the congeniality of the gathering.

Whether this fact affected Barlow's behavior, I couldn't have said, but he laughed contemptuously, and turned his back on Hamilton, to walk away. The elderly Scot, inflamed, promptly kicked Barlow in the buttocks.

Taken unaware and off balance, Barlow pitched forward, landing on hands and knees, his coattails ludicrously up over his ears. Whatever their respective political opinions, all the onlookers burst into laughter. Thus encouraged, Ninian puffed up like a bantam rooster and strutted round his fallen opponent to address him from the front.

I could have told him that this was a tactical error, but then, I had the benefit of seeing Barlow's face, which was crimson with mortified rage. Eyes bulging, he scrambled awkwardly to his feet and launched himself with a roar, knocking the smaller man flat.

The two of them rolled in the grass, fists and coattails flying, to whoops of encouragement from the spectators. Wedding guests came rushing from lawn and terrace to see what was going on. Abel MacLennan pushed his way through the mob, obviously intent on offering support to his patron. Richard Caswell seized his arm to prevent him, and he swung round, pushing Caswell off balance.

James Hunter, lean face alight with glee, tripped Caswell, who sat down hard on the grass, looking surprised. Caswell's son George let out a howl of outrage and punched Hunter in the kidney. Hunter whirled round and slapped George on the nose.

A number of ladies were shrieking—not all with shock. One or two appeared to be cheering on Ninian Hamilton, who had got temporarily atop his victim's chest and was endeavoring to throttle him, though with little success, owing to Barlow's thick neck and heavy stock.

I looked frantically round for Jamie—or Roger, or Duncan. Goddamn it, where were they all?

George Caswell had fallen back in surprise, hands to his nose, which was dribbling blood down his shirtfront. De-Wayne Buchanan, one of Hamilton's sons-in-law, was shoving his way purposefully through the gathering crowd. I didn't know whether he meant to get his father-in-law off Barlow, or assist him in his attempt to murder the man.

"Oh, bloody hell," I muttered to myself. "Here, hold this." I thrust my fan at Major MacDonald, and hitched up my skirts, preparing to wade into the melee, and deciding whom to kick first—and where—for best effect.

"Do you want me to stop it?"

The Major, who had been enjoying the spectacle, looked disappointed at the thought, but resigned to duty. At my rather startled nod, he reached for his pistol, pointed it skyward, and discharged it into the air.

The bang was loud enough to temporarily silence everyone. The combatants froze, and in the momentary lull, Hermon Husband shoved his way into the scene.

"Friend Ninian," he said, nodding cordially round. "Friend Buchanan. Allow me." He grabbed the elderly Scot by both arms and lifted him bodily off Barlow. He gave James Hunter a warning look; Hunter gave an audible "Humph!" but retired a few steps.

The younger Mrs. Caswell, a woman of sense, had got her husband off the field of battle already, and was applying a handkerchief to his nose. DeWayne Buchanan and Abel MacLennan had each got hold of one of Ninian Hamilton's arms, and were making a great show of restraining him as they marched him off toward the house—though it was reasonably apparent that either one of them could simply have picked him up and carried him.

Richard Caswell had got up by himself, and while looking rather affronted, was evidently not disposed to hit anyone. He stood brushing dried grass from the back of his coat, lips pressed together in disapproval.

"Your fan, Mrs. Fraser?" Jerked from my appraisal of the conflict, I found Major MacDonald politely offering me back my fan. He looked quite pleased with himself.

"Thank you," I said, taking it and eyeing him with some respect. "Tell me, Major, do you always go about with a loaded pistol?"

"An oversight, ma'am," he replied blandly. "Though perhaps a fortunate one, aye? I had been in the town of Cross Creek yesterday, and as I was returning alone to Mr. Farquard Campbell's plantation after dark, I thought it would be as well to go canny on the road."

He nodded over my shoulder.

"Tell me, Mrs. Fraser, who is the ill-shaven individual? He seems a man of guts, despite his lack of address. Will he take up the cudgels in his own behalf now, do ye think?"

I swung round, to see Hermon Husband nose-to-nose with the risen Barlow, his round black hat thrust down on his head and his beard bristling with pugnacity. Barlow stood his ground, red-faced and thunder-browed, but had his arms folded tightly across his chest as he listened to Husband.

"Hermon Husband is a Quaker," I said, with a slight tone of reproof. "No, he won't resort to violence. Just words."

Quite a lot of words. Barlow kept trying to interject his own opinions, but Husband ignored these, pressing his argument with such enthusiasm that drops of spittle flew from the corners of his mouth.

". . . an heinous miscarriage of justice! Sheriffs, or so they call themselves, who have not been appointed by any legal writ, but rather appoint themselves for the purposes of corruptly enriching themselves and scorn all legitimate . . ."

Barlow dropped his arms, and began to edge backward, in an effort to escape the barrage. When Husband paused momentarily to draw breath, though, Barlow seized the opportunity to lean forward and jab a threatening finger into Husband's chest.

"You speak of justice, sir? What have riot and destruction to do with justice? If you advocate the ruin of property as means to redress your grievances—"

"I do not! But is the poor man to fall a spoil to the unscrupulous, and his plight pass unregarded? I say to you, sir, God will unmercifully requite those who oppress the poor, and—"

"What are they arguing about?" MacDonald asked, viewing the exchange with interest. "Religion?"

Seeing Husband involved, and realizing that no further punch-ups were to be expected, most of the crowd had lost interest, wandering away toward the buffet tables and the braziers on the terrace. Hunter and a few other Regulators hung about to give Husband moral support, but most of the guests were planters and merchants. While they might side with Barlow in theory, in practice most were disinclined to waste a rare festive occasion in controversy with Hermon Husband over the rights of the tax-paying poor.

I wasn't all that eager to examine the rhetoric of the Regulation in detail, either, but did my best to give Major MacDonald a crude overview of the situation.

". . . and so Governor Tryon felt obliged to raise the militia to deal with it, but the Regulators backed down," I concluded. "But they haven't abandoned their demands, by any means."

Husband hadn't abandoned his argument, either—he never did—but Barlow had at last succeeded in extricating himself, and was restoring his tissues at the refreshment tables under the elm trees in company with some sympathetic friends, who all cast periodic glances of disapproval in Husband's direction.

"I see," MacDonald said, interested. "Farquard Campbell did tell me something of this disruptive movement. And the Governor has raised a militia on occasion to deal with it, you say, and may again. Who commands his troops, do you know?"

"Um . . . I believe General Waddell—that's Hugh Waddell—has command of several companies. But the

Governor himself was in command of the main body; he's been a soldier himself."

"Has he indeed?" MacDonald seemed to find this very interesting; he hadn't put away his pistol, but was fondling it in an absentminded sort of way. "Campbell tells me that your husband is the holder of a large grant of land in the backcountry. He is by way of being an intimate of the Governor?"

"I wouldn't put it that strongly," I said dryly. "But he does *know* the Governor, yes."

I felt a trifle uneasy at this line of conversation. It was— strictly speaking—illegal for Catholics to hold Royal land grants in the Colonies. I didn't know whether Major Mac-Donald was aware of that fact, but he did plainly realize that Jamie was likely a Catholic, given his family background.

"Do you suppose your husband might be prevailed upon for an introduction, dear lady?" The pale blue eyes were bright with speculation, and I realized suddenly what he was after.

A career soldier with no war was at a distinct disadvantage in terms of occupation and income. The Regulation might be a tempest in a teapot, but on the other hand, if there was any prospect of military action . . . After all, Tryon had no regular troops; he might well be inclined to welcome— and to pay—an experienced officer, if the militia were called out again.

I cast a wary eye toward the lawn. Husband and his friends had withdrawn a bit, and were in close conversation in a little knot near one of Jocasta's new statues. If the recent near-brawl was any indication, the Regulation was still dangerously on the boil.

"That might be done," I said cautiously. I couldn't see any reason why Jamie would object to providing a letter of introduction to Tryon—and I did owe the Major something, after all, for having averted a full-scale riot. "You'd have to ask my husband, of course, but I'd be happy to put in a word for you."

"You shall have my utmost gratitude, ma'am." He put away his pistol, and bowed low over my hand. Straightening up, he glanced over my shoulder. "I think I must take my leave now, Mrs. Fraser, but I shall hope to make your husband's acquaintance soon."

The Major marched off toward the terrace, and I turned, to see Hermon Husband stumping toward me, Hunter and a few other men in his wake.

"Mrs. Fraser, I must ask thee to give my good wishes and my regrets to Mrs. Innes, if thee will," he said without preamble. "I must go."

"Oh, must you leave so soon?" I hesitated. On the one hand, I wanted to urge him to stay; on the other, I could foresee further trouble if he did. Barlow's friends had not taken their eyes off him since the near-brawl.

He saw the thought cross my face, and nodded soberly. The flush of debate had faded from his face, leaving it set in grim lines.

"It will be better so. Jocasta Cameron has been a good friend to me and mine; it would ill repay her kindness for me to bring discord to her wedding celebrations. I would not choose that—and yet, I cannot in conscience remain silent, hearing such pernicious opinions as I have received here." He gave Barlow's group a look of cold contempt, which was met in kind.

"Besides," he added, turning his back on the Barlowites in dismissal, "we have business that compels our attention elsewhere." He hesitated, clearly wondering whether to tell me more, but then decided against it. "Thee will tell her?"

"Yes, of course. Mr. Husband—I'm sorry."

He gave me a faint smile, tinged with melancholy, and shook his head, but said no more. As he left, though, trailed by his companions, James Hunter paused to speak to me, low-voiced.

"The Regulators are a-gathering. There's a big camp, up near Salisbury," he said. "You might see fit to tell your husband that."

He nodded, put his hand to his hat-brim, and without waiting for acknowledgment, strode off, his dark coat disappearing in the crowd like a sparrow swallowed by a flock of peacocks.

FROM MY VANTAGE POINT at the edge of the terrace, I could see the whole sweep of the party, which flowed in a stream of festivity from house to river, its eddy-pools obvious to the knowledgeable eye.

Jocasta formed the eye of the largest social swirl—but smaller pools swirled ominously around Ninian Bell Hamilton and Richard Caswell, and a restless current meandered through the party, leaving deposits of conversation along its edges, rich in the fertile silt of speculation. From the things I overheard, the question of our hosts' putative sex life was the predominant subject of conversation—but politics ran a close second.

I still saw no sign either of Jamie or of Duncan. There was the Major again, though. He stopped, a glass of cider in each hand; he had caught sight of Brianna. I smiled, watching.

Brianna often stopped men in their tracks, though not always entirely from admiration. She had inherited a number of things from Jamie; slanted blue eyes and flaming hair, a long straight nose and a wide, firm mouth; the bold facial bones that came from some ancient Norseman. In addition to these striking attributes, though, she had also inherited his height. In a time when the average woman stood a hair less than five feet tall, Brianna reached six. People were inclined to stare.

Major MacDonald was doing so, cider forgotten in his hands. Roger noticed; he smiled and nodded, but took that one step closer to Brianna that said unmistakably, *She's mine, mate.*

Watching the Major in conversation, I noticed how pale and spindly he looked by comparison with Roger, who stood nearly as tall as Jamie. He was broad-shouldered and olive-skinned, and his hair shone black as a crow's wing in the spring sun, perhaps the legacy of some ancient Spanish invader. I had to admit that there was no noticeable resemblance between him and little Jem, ruddy as a fresh-forged brass candlestick. I could see the flash of white as Roger smiled; the Major kept his lips pulled down when smiling, as most people over the age of thirty did, to hide the gaps and decay that were endemic. Perhaps it was the stress of the Major's occupation, I thought; perhaps merely the effects of poor nourishment. Being of good family didn't mean a child in this time ate very well.

I ran my tongue lightly over my own teeth, testing the biting edge of my incisors. Straight and sound, and I took considerable pains to see they would stay that way, given the current state of the art of dentistry.

"Why, Mrs. Fraser." A light voice broke in on my thoughts, and I looked round to find Phillip Wylie at my elbow. "Whatever can you be thinking, my dear? You look positively . . . feral." He took my hand and lowered his voice, baring his own fairly decent teeth in a suggestive smile.

"I am not your dear," I said with some acerbity, jerking my hand out of his. "And as for feral, I'm surprised no one has bitten you in the backside yet."

"Oh, I have hopes," he assured me, eyes twinkling. He bowed, managing in the process to get hold of my hand again. "Might I have the honor to claim a dance later, Mrs. Fraser?"

"Indeed you may not," I said, tugging. "Let go."

"Your wish is my command." He let go, but not before planting a light kiss on the back of my hand. I suppressed the urge to wipe the moist spot on my skirt.

"Go away, child," I said. I flicked my fan at him. "Shoo."

Phillip Wylie was a dandy. I had met him twice before, and on both occasions, he had been got up regardless: satin breeches, silk stockings, and all the trappings that went with them, including powdered wig, powdered face, and a small black crescent beauty mark, stuck dashingly beside one eye.

Now, however, the rot had spread. The powdered wig was mauve, the satin waistcoat was embroidered with—I blinked. Yes, with lions and unicorns, done in gold and silver thread. The satin breeches were fitted to him like a bifurcated glove, and the crescent had given way to a star at the corner of his mouth. Mr. Wylie had become a macaroni—with cheese.

"Oh, I have no intention of deserting you, Mrs. Fraser," he assured me. "I have been searching everywhere for you."

"Oh. Well, you've found me," I said, eyeing his coat, which was velvet, rose in color, and had six-inch cuffs of palest pink silk and button-covers embroidered with scarlet peonies. "Though it's no wonder you had trouble. I expect you were blinded by the glare from your waistcoat."

Lloyd Stanhope was with him, as usual, quite as prosperous, but much more plainly dressed than his friend. Stanhope guffawed, but Wylie ignored him, and bowed low, making me a graceful leg.

"Ah, well, Fortuna has smiled upon me this year. The trade with England has quite recovered, may the gods be thanked—and I have had my share of it, and more besides. You must come with me to see—"

I was saved at this point by the sudden appearance of Adlai Osborn, a well-to-do merchant from somewhere up the coast, who tapped Wylie on the shoulder. Seizing the opportunity afforded by the distraction, I put up my fan and sidled away through a gap in the crowd.

Left momentarily to my own devices, I strolled nonchalantly off the terrace and down the lawn. I still had an eye out for Jamie or Duncan, but this was my first opportunity to examine Jocasta's latest acquisitions, which were causing considerable comment among the wedding guests. These were two statues, carved from white marble, one standing squarely in the center of each lawn.

The one closest to me was a life-size replica of a Greek warrior—Spartan, I assumed, from the fact that the more frivolous items of attire had been omitted, leaving the gentleman clad in a sturdy-looking plumed helmet, with a sword in one hand. A large shield was planted at his feet, strategically placed so as to cover the more glaring deficiencies of his wardrobe.

There was a matching statue on the right lawn, this one of Diana the Huntress. While the lady was rather skimpily draped, and her shapely white marble breasts and buttocks were attracting a certain amount of sidelong appreciation from the gentlemen present, she was no match for her companion, in terms of public fascination. I smiled behind my fan, seeing Mr. and Mrs. Sherston swan past the statue without so much as a glance. After all, their raised noses and bored looks at each other said, such artworks were commonplace in Europe. Only rude Colonials, lacking both experience and breeding, would consider it a *spectacle*, my dear.

Examining the statue myself, I discovered that it was not an anonymous Greek after all, but rather Perseus. From this new angle, I could see that what I had assumed to be a rock resting beside the shield was in fact the severed head of a Gorgon, half its snakes standing on end in shocked dismay.

The evident artistry of these reptiles was affording an excuse for close examination of the statue by a number of ladies, who were brazening it out, pursing their lips knowingly and making sounds of admiration about the sculptor's skillfulness in rendering every scale, just so. Every so often one would allow her eyes to dart upward for a split second, before jerking her gaze back to the Gorgon, cheeks reddened—by the morning air and the mulled wine being served, no doubt.

My attention was distracted from Perseus by a steaming mug of this beverage, thrust beneath my nose in invitation.

"Do have some, Mrs. Fraser." It was Lloyd Stanhope, roundly amiable. "You wouldn't want to take a chill, dear lady."

There was no danger of that, given the increasing warmth of the day, but I accepted the cup, enjoying the scent of cinnamon and honey that wafted from it.

I leaned to one side, looking for Jamie, but he was still nowhere to be seen. A group of gentlemen arguing the merits of Virginia tobacco versus indigo as a crop were clustered round one side of Perseus, while the statue's rear aspect now sheltered three young girls, who were glancing at it from behind their fans, red-faced and giggling.

". . . unique," Phillip Wylie was saying to someone. The eddies of conversation had brought him back to my side. "Absolutely unique! Black pearls, they're called. Never seen anything like them, I'll wager." He glanced round and, seeing me, reached out to touch my elbow lightly. "I collect you have spent some time in France, Mrs. Fraser. Have you seen them there, perhaps?"

"Black pearls?" I said, scrambling to catch hold of the threads of the conversation. "Well, yes, a few. I recall the

Archbishop of Rouen had a small Moorish page boy who wore a very large one in his nose."

Stanhope's jaw sagged ludicrously. Wylie stared at me for a split second, then uttered a whoop of laughter so loud that both the tobacco lobby and the giggling girls stopped dead and stared at us.

"You will be the death of me, my dear lady," Wylie wheezed, as Stanhope declined into choked snorts of mirth. Wylie drew out a lacy kerchief and dabbed delicately at the corners of his eyes, lest tears of merriment blotch his powder.

"Really, Mrs. Fraser, have you not seen my treasures?" He grasped my elbow and propelled me out of the crowd with surprising skill. "Come, let me show you."

He guided me smoothly through the gathering throng and past the side of the house, where a flagged path led toward the stables. Another crowd—mostly men—was clustered round the paddock, where Jocasta's groom was throwing down hay for several horses.

There were five of them—two mares, a couple of two-year-olds, and a stallion. All five black as coal, with coats that gleamed in the pale spring sun, even shaggy as they were with winter hair. I was no expert in horse conformation, but knew enough by now to notice the deep chests, barreled vaults, and sculpted quarters, which gave them a peculiar but deeply appealing look of elegant sturdiness. Beyond the beauties of conformation and coat, though, what was most striking about these horses was their hair.

These black horses had great floating masses of silky hair—almost like women's hair—that rose and fluttered with their movements, matching the graceful fall of their long, full tails. In addition, each horse had delicate black feathers decorating hoof and fetlock, that lifted like floating milkweed seed with each step. By contrast to the usual rawboned riding horses and rough draft animals used for haulage, these horses seemed almost magical—and from the awed comment they were occasioning among the spectators, might as well have come from Fairyland as from Phillip Wylie's plantation in Edenton.

"They're yours?" I spoke to Wylie without looking at him,

unwilling to take my eyes away from the enchanting sight. "Wherever did you get them?"

"Yes," he said, his usual affectations erased by simple pride. "They are mine. They are Friesians. The oldest breed of warm-bloods—their lineage can be traced back for centuries.

"As to where I got them"—he leaned over the fence, extending a hand palm-up and wiggling his fingers toward the horses in invitation—"I have been breeding them for several years. I brought these at Mrs. Cameron's invitation; she has it in mind perhaps to purchase one of my mares, and suggested that one or two of her neighbors might also be interested. As for Lucas, here, though"—the stallion had come over, recognizing his owner, and was submitting gracefully to having his forehead rubbed—"he is not for sale."

Both mares were heavily in foal; Lucas was the sire, and so had been brought, Wylie said, as proof of the bloodlines. That, I thought, privately amused, and for purposes of showing him off. Wylie's "black pearls" were exciting keen interest, and a number of the horse-breeding gentlemen from the neighborhood had gone visibly green with envy at sight of Lucas. Phillip Wylie preened like a cock grouse.

"Oh, there ye are, Sassenach." Jamie's voice came suddenly in my ear. "I was looking for you."

"Were you, indeed?" I said, turning away from the paddock. I felt a sudden warmth under my breastbone at sight of him "And where have *you* been?"

"Oh, here and there," Jamie said, undisturbed by my tone of accusation. "A verra fine horse indeed, Mr. Wylie." A polite nod, and he had me by the arm and headed back toward the lawn before Wylie's murmured "Your servant, sir" had been quite voiced.

"What are ye doing out here wi' wee Phillip Wylie?" Jamie asked, picking his way through a flock of house slaves, who streamed past from the cookhouse with platters of food steaming alluringly under white napkins.

"Looking at his horses," I said, putting a hand over my stomach in hopes of suppressing the resounding borborygmi occasioned by the sight of food. "And what have you been doing?"

"Looking for Duncan," he said, guiding me round a puddle. "He wasna in the necessary, nor yet the smithy, the stables, the kitchen, the cookhouse. I took a horse and rode out to the tobacco-barns, but not a smell of the man."

"Perhaps Lieutenant Wolff has assassinated him," I suggested. "Disappointed rival, and all that."

"Wolff?" He stopped, frowning at me in consternation. "Is yon gobshite here?"

"In the flesh," I replied, waving my fan toward the lawn. Wolff had taken up a station next the refreshment tables, his short, stout figure unmistakable in its blue and white naval uniform. "Do you suppose your aunt invited him?"

"Aye, I do," he said, sounding grim but resigned. "She couldna resist rubbing his nose in it, I expect."

"That's what I thought. He's only been here for half an hour or so, though—and if he goes on mopping it up at that rate," I added, looking disapprovingly at the bottle clutched in the Lieutenant's hand, "he'll be out cold before the wedding takes place."

Jamie dismissed the Lieutenant with a contemptuous gesture.

"Well, then, let him pickle himself and welcome, so long as he only opens his mouth to pour drink in. Where's Duncan hidden himself, though?"

"Perhaps he's thrown himself in the river?" It was meant as a joke, but I glanced toward the river nonetheless, and saw a boat headed for the landing, the oarsman standing in the prow to throw his mooring rope to a waiting slave. "Look—is that the priest at last?"

It was; a short, tubby figure, black soutane hiked up over hairy knees as he scrambled ignominiously onto the dock, with the help of a push from the boatmen below. Ulysses was already hurrying down to the landing, to greet him.

"Good," Jamie said, in tones of satisfaction. "We've a priest, then, and a bride. Two of three—that's progress. Here, Sassenach, wait a bit—your hair's coming down." He traced the line of a fallen curl slowly down my back, and I obligingly let the shawl fall back from my shoulders.

Jamie put up the curl again, with a skill born of long practice, then kissed me gently on the nape of the neck, making me shiver. He wasn't immune to the prevailing airs of spring, either.

"I suppose I must go on looking for Duncan," he said, with a tinge of regret. His fingers lingered on my back, thumb delicately tracing the groove of my spine. "Once I've found him, though . . . there must be some place here with a bit of privacy to it."

The word "privacy" made me lean back against Jamie, and glance toward the riverbank, where a clump of weeping willows sheltered a stone bench—quite a private and romantic spot, especially at night. The willows were thick with green, but I caught a flash of scarlet through the drooping branches.

"Got him!" I exclaimed, straightening up so abruptly that I trod on Jamie's toe. "Oh—sorry!"

"Nay matter," he assured me. He had followed the direction of my glance, and now drew himself up purposefully. "I'll go and fetch him out. Do ye go up to the house, Sassenach, and keep an eye on my aunt and the priest. Dinna let them escape until this marriage is made."

JAMIE MADE HIS WAY down the lawn toward the willows, absently acknowledging the greetings of friends and acquaintances as he went. In truth, his mind was less on Duncan's approaching nuptials than on thoughts of his own wife.

He was generally aware that he had been blessed in her beauty; even in her usual homespun, knee-deep in mud from her garden, or stained and fierce with the blood of her calling, the curve of her bones spoke to his own marrow, and those whisky eyes could make him drunk with a glance. Besides, the mad collieshangie of her hair made him laugh.

Smiling to himself even at the thought, it occurred to him that he *was* slightly drunk. Liquor flowed like water at the party, and there were already men leaning on old Hector's mausoleum, glaze-eyed and slack-jawed; he caught a glimpse of someone behind the thing, too, having a piss in the shrubbery. He shook his head. There'd be a body under every bush by nightfall.

Christ. One thought of bodies under bushes, and his mind had presented him with a blindingly indecent vision of Claire, lying sprawled and laughing under one, breasts falling out of her gown and the dead leaves and dry grass the same colors as her rumpled skirts and the curly brown hair between her— He choked the thought off abruptly, bowing cordially to old Mrs. Alderdyce, the Judge's mother.

"Your servant, ma'am."

"Good day to ye, young man, good day." The old lady nodded magisterially and passed by, leaning on the arm of her companion, a long-suffering young woman who gave Jamie a faint smile in response to his salute.

"Master Jamie?" One of the maids hovered beside him, holding out a tray of cups. He took one, smiling his thanks, and drank half its contents in a gulp.

He couldn't help it. He had to turn and look after Claire. He caught no more than a glimpse of the top of her head among the crowd on the terrace—she wouldn't wear a proper cap, of course, the stubborn wee besom, but had some foolishness pinned on instead, a scrap of lace caught up with a cluster of ribbons and rose hips. That made him want to laugh, too, and he turned back toward the willows, smiling to himself.

It was seeing her in the new gown that did it. It had been months since he'd seen her dressed like a lady, narrow-waisted in silk, and her white breasts round and sweet as winter pears in the low neck of her gown. It was as though she were suddenly a different woman; one intimately familiar and yet still excitingly strange.

His fingers twitched, remembering that one rebel lock, spiraling free down her neck, and the feel of her slender nape—and the feel of her plump warm arse through her skirts, pressed against his leg. He had not had her in more than a week, what with the press of people round them, and was feeling the lack acutely.

Ever since she had shown him the sperms, he had been uncomfortably aware of the crowded conditions that must now and then obtain in his balls, an impression made forcibly stronger in situations such as this. He kent well enough that there was no danger of rupture or explosion—and yet he couldn't help but think of all the shoving going on.

Being trapped in a seething mass of others, with no hope of escape, was one of his own personal visions of Hell, and he paused for a moment outside the screen of willow trees, to administer a brief squeeze of reassurance, which he hoped might calm the riot for a bit.

He'd see Duncan safely married, he decided, and then the man must see to his own affairs. Come nightfall, and if he could do no better than a bush, then a bush it would have to be. He pushed aside a swath of willow branches, ducking to go through.

"Duncan," he began, and then stopped, the swirl of carnal thoughts disappearing like water down a sewer. The scarlet coat belonged not to Duncan Innes but to a stranger who turned toward him, with surprise equal to his own. A man in the uniform of His Majesty's army.

THE LOOK OF MOMENTARY startlement faded from the man's face, almost as quickly as Jamie's own surprise. This must be MacDonald, the half-pay soldier Farquard Campbell had mentioned to him. Evidently Farquard had described him to MacDonald, as well; he could see the man had put a name to him.

MacDonald held a cup of punch, as well; the slaves had been busy. He drained the cup deliberately, then set it down on the stone bench, wiping his lips on the back of his hand.

"Colonel Fraser, I presume?"

"Major MacDonald," he replied, with a nod that mingled courtesy with wariness. "Your servant, sir."

MacDonald bowed, punctilious:

"Colonel. If I might command a moment of your time?" He glanced over Jamie's shoulder; there were giggles on the riverbank behind them, and the excited small screams of very young women pursued by very young men. "In private?"

Jamie noted the usage of his militia title with a sour amusement, but nodded briefly, and discarded his own cup, still half-full, alongside the Major's.

He tilted his head toward the house in inquiry; MacDonald nodded and followed him out of the willows, as loud rustlings and squealings announced that the bench and its sheltering trees had now become the province of the younger element. He wished them good luck with it, privately noting the location for his own possible use, after dark.

The day was cold but still and bright, and a number of guests, mostly men who found the civilized atmosphere within too suffocating for their tastes, were clustered in argumentative groups in the corners of the terrace, or strolling round the paths of the newly-sprouting garden, where their tobacco pipes might fume in peace. Assessing the latter venue as the best means of avoiding interruption, Jamie led the Major toward the brick-lined path that curved toward the stables.

"Have you seen Wylie's Friesians?" the Major asked as they rounded the house, making casual conversation 'til they should be safely out of earshot.

"Aye, I have. The stallion's a fine animal, is he not?" By reflex, Jamie's eyes turned toward the paddock by the barn. The stallion was browsing, nibbling at the weeds by the trough, while the two mares head-and-tailed it companionably near the stable, broad backs shining in the pale sun.

"Aye? Well, perhaps." The Major squinted toward the paddock, one eye half-shut in dubious agreement. "Sound enough, I daresay. Good chest. All that hair, though— wouldn't do in a cavalry horse, though I suppose if it were proper shaved and dressed . . ."

Jamie suppressed the urge to ask whether MacDonald liked his women shaved as well. The image of the loosened curl spiraling down that bare white neck was still in his mind. Perhaps the stables might afford a better opportunity. . . . He pushed that thought aside, for later reference.

"You had some matter with which ye were concerned, Major?" he asked, more abruptly than he'd meant to.

"Not so much my own concern," MacDonald replied equably. "I had been told that you have some interest in the whereabouts of a gentleman named Stephen Bonnet. Am I reliably informed, sir?"

He felt the name like a blow to the chest; it took his wind for a moment. Without conscious thought, his left hand curled over the hilt of his dirk.

"I—yes. You know his whereabouts?"

"Unfortunately, no." MacDonald's brow lifted, seeing his response. "I ken where he *has* been, though. A wicked lad, our Stephen, or so I gather?" he inquired, with a hint of jocularity.

"Ye might say so. He has killed men, robbed me—and raped my daughter," Jamie said bluntly.

The Major drew breath, face darkening in sudden understanding.

"Ah, I see," he said softly. He lifted his hand briefly, as though to touch Jamie's arm, but let it fall to his side. He walked a few steps further, brows puckered in concentration.

"I see," he said again, all hint of amusement gone from his voice. "I hadn't realized . . . yes. I see." He lapsed into silence once again, his steps slowing as they neared the paddock.

"I trust you do intend to tell me what ye know of the man?" Jamie said politely. MacDonald glanced up at him, and appeared to recognize that regardless of his intentions, Jamie's own intent was to gain what knowledge he had, whether by conversation or more direct methods.

"I have not met the man myself," MacDonald said mildly. "What I know, I learnt in the course of a social evening in New Bern last month."

It was an evening of whist tables hosted by Davis Howell, a wealthy shipowner and a member of the Governor's Royal Council. The party, small but select, had begun with an excellent supper, then moved on to cards and conversation, well marinated with rum punch and brandy.

As the hour grew late and the smoke of cigarillos heavy in the air, the conversation grew unguarded, and there were jocular references to the recent improvement in one Mr. Butler's fortunes, with much half-veiled speculation as to the source of his new riches. One gentleman, expressing envy, was heard to say, "If one could but have a Stephen Bonnet in one's pocket . . ." before being elbowed into silence by a friend whose discretion was not quite so much dissolved in rum.

"Was Mr. Butler among those present at this soiree?" Jamie asked sharply. The name was unfamiliar, but if Butler was known to members of the Royal Council . . . well, the circles of power in the colony were small; someone in them would be known to his aunt, or to Farquard Campbell.

"No, he wasn't." They had reached the paddock; Mac-Donald rested his folded arms atop the rail, eyes fixed on the stallion. "He resides, I believe, in Edenton."

As did Phillip Wylie. The stallion—Lucas, that was his name—sidled toward them, soft black nostrils flaring in curiosity. Jamie stretched out his knuckles mechanically and, the horse proving amiable, rubbed the sleek jawline. Beautiful as the Friesian was, he scarcely noticed it, his thoughts spinning like a whirligig.

Edenton lay on the Albemarle Sound, easily accessible by boat. Likely, then, that Bonnet had returned to his sailor's trade—and with it, piracy and smuggling.

"Ye called Bonnet 'a wicked lad,' " he said, turning to MacDonald. "Why?"

"Much of a hand at whist, Colonel Fraser?" MacDonald glanced at him inquiringly. "I recommend it particularly. It shares some advantage with chess, in terms of discovering the mind of one's opponent, and the greater advantage, in that it can be played against a greater number." The hard-bitten lines of his face relaxed momentarily in a faint smile. "And the still greater advantage that it is possible to earn a living by it, which is seldom the case with chess."

"I am familiar with the game, sir," Jamie returned, with extreme dryness.

MacDonald was a half-pay officer, with neither official duties nor an active regiment. It was by no means unusual for such men to eke out their meager salary by the acquisition of small bits of intelligence, which might be sold or traded. No price was being asked—now—but that didn't mean that the debt would not be called in later. Jamie gave a brief nod in acknowledgment of the situation, and MacDonald nodded in turn, satisfied. He would say what he wanted, in good time.

"Well, sir. I was, as ye might suppose, intrigued to learn who this Bonnet might be—and if he were indeed a golden egg, which goose's arse he'd dropped out of."

MacDonald's companions had regained their caution, though, and he could learn nothing further of the mysterious Bonnet—save the effect he had on those who had met him.

"You'll ken that often enough, ye learn as much from what men don't say, as what they do? Or from *how* they say it?" Without waiting for Jamie's nod, he went on.

"There were eight of us at play. Three were making free with their speculations, but I could see they kent nay more of Mr. Bonnet than I did myself. Two more seemed neither to know nor to care, but the last two—" He shook his head. "They became very quiet, sir. Like those who will not speak of the devil, for fear of summoning him."

MacDonald's eyes were bright with speculation.

"You are familiar with the fellow Bonnet yourself?"

"I am. The two gentlemen who knew him?"

"Walter Priestly and Hosea Wright," MacDonald responded promptly. "Both particular friends of the Governor."

"Merchants?"

"Among other things. Both have warehouses; Wright in Edenton and Plymouth, Priestly in Charleston, Savannah, Wilmington, and Edenton. Priestly has business concerns in Boston, as well," MacDonald added as an afterthought. "Though I know little of their nature. Oh—and Wright's a banker."

Jamie nodded. His hands were folded together beneath the tails of his coat as he walked; no one could see how tightly his fingers clenched.

"I believe I have heard of Mr. Wright," he said. "Phillip Wylie mentioned that a gentleman of that name owns a plantation near his own."

MacDonald nodded in affirmation. The end of his nose had gone quite red, and small broken blood vessels stood out in his cheeks, mementoes of years spent campaigning.

"Aye, that would be Four Chimneys." He glanced sidewise at Jamie, tongue probing a back tooth as he thought.

"Ye mean to kill him, then?"

"Of course not," Jamie replied evenly. "A man so well-connected wi' those in high places?"

MacDonald looked at him sharply, then away with a brief snort.

"Aye. Just so."

They paced side by side for several moments without speech, each occupied with his private calculations—and each aware of the other's.

The news of Bonnet's associations cut both ways; on the one hand, it would likely make the man easier to find. On the other, those associations would complicate matters quite a bit, when it came to the killing. It wouldn't stop Jamie—and MacDonald clearly perceived that—but it was a matter for thought, to be sure.

MacDonald himself was a considerable complication. Bonnet's business associates would be interested to hear that someone meant to cut off their source of profit—and would be more than likely to take action to prevent it. They would also pay well for the news that their golden goose was threatened; a prospect MacDonald would naturally appreciate.

There was no immediate way of corking up MacDonald, though; Jamie lacked the means for bribery, and that was a poor recourse in any case, as a man who could be bought once was always for sale.

He glanced at MacDonald, who met his eye, smiled slightly, then turned his head away. No, intimidation wouldn't serve, even had he a mind to threaten one who'd done him a service. What, then? He could scarcely knock MacDonald on the head, only to prevent his spilling to Wright, Priestly, or Butler.

Well, and if it could not be bribery or force, the only thing left to stop the man's mouth was blackmail. Which presented its own complications, insofar as he knew nothing—for the moment—to MacDonald's discredit. A man who lived as the Major did almost certainly had weak spots, but finding them . . . how much time might he have?

That thought triggered another.

"How did ye hear that I sought news of Stephen Bonnet?"

he demanded abruptly, breaking in on MacDonald's own contemplations.

MacDonald shrugged, and settled his hat and wig more firmly.

"I heard it from a half dozen different sources, sir, in places from taverns to magistrates' courts. Your interest is well known, I fear. But not," he added delicately, with a sideways glance, "its reason."

Jamie grunted, deep in his throat. It seemed he had no knife with but a single edge. Casting a wide net had brought him his fish—but without doubt, it had also caused ripples that might warn away the whale. If the whole coast knew he sought Bonnet—then so did Bonnet.

Perhaps this was a bad thing; or perhaps it was not. If Brianna were to hear of it—she had been outspoken in her desire that he leave Bonnet to his own fate. That was nonsense, of course, but he hadn't argued with her; only listened with every appearance of consideration. She need know nothing until the man was safely dead, after all. If an unwary word were to reach her before that, though . . . He had only begun to turn the possibilities over in his mind when MacDonald spoke again.

"Your daughter . . . that would be Mrs. MacKenzie, would it?"

"Does it matter?" He spoke coldly, and MacDonald's lips tightened briefly.

"No. To be sure. 'Twas only—I had some conversation of Mrs. MacKenzie, and found her most . . . charming. The thought of—" He broke off, clearing his throat. "I have a daughter, myself," he said abruptly, stopping and turning to face Jamie.

"Aye?" Jamie had not heard that MacDonald was married. Quite possibly he wasn't. "That would be in Scotland?"

"In England. Her mother's English." The chill had painted streaks of color on the soldier's weathered skin. They deepened, but MacDonald's pale blue eyes stayed steady on Jamie's, the same color as the hazy sky behind him.

Jamie felt the tightness down his backbone ease. He lifted his shoulders in a shrug, and let them fall. MacDonald nodded infinitesimally. The two men turned, without discussion, and started back toward the house, conversing casually of the price of indigo, the latest news from Massachusetts, and the surprising clemency of the weather for the season.

"I had spoken with your wife, a little earlier," MacDonald remarked. "A charming woman, and most amiable—you are a fortunate man, sir."

"I am inclined to think so," Jamie replied, darting a glance at MacDonald.

The soldier coughed, delicately.

"Mrs. Fraser was so kind as to suggest that you might consider providing me with a letter of introduction to his Excellency, the Governor. In light of the recent threat of conflict, she thought that perhaps a man of my experience might be able to provide something in the way of . . . you see?"

Jamie saw fine. And while he doubted that Claire had suggested any such thing, he was relieved to find the price asked so cheap.

"It shall be done at once," he assured MacDonald. "See me after the wedding this afternoon, and I shall have it in hand for ye."

MacDonald inclined his head, looking gratified.

As they reached the path that led to the necessary houses, MacDonald nodded farewell and took his leave with a raised hand, passing by Duncan Innes, who was coming from that direction, looking drawn and haggard as a man will whose bowels are tied in sheepshank knots.

"Are ye well, Duncan?" Jamie asked, eyeing his friend with some concern. Despite the coolness of the day, a faint sheen of sweat shone on Innes's brow, and his cheeks were pale. Jamie hoped that if it were an ague, it wasn't catching.

"No," Innes said, in answer to his question. "No, I am . . . *Mac Dubh*, I must speak to ye."

"Of course, *a charaid*." Alarmed by the man's appearance, he took hold of Duncan's arm, to support him. "Shall I fetch my wife to ye? D'ye need a wee dram?" From the smell of him, he'd had several already, but nothing out of the ordinary for a bridegroom. He didn't appear to be the worse for drink, but was plainly the worse for something. Perhaps a bad mussel at last night's supper. . . .

Innes shook his head. He swallowed, and grimaced, as though something hard was stuck in his throat. He drew air through his nose then, and set his shoulders, steeling himself to something.

"No, *Mac Dubh*, it's yourself I am needing. A bit of counsel, if ye might be so kind . . ."

"Aye, Duncan, surely." More curious than alarmed now, he let go of Duncan's arm. "What is it, man?"

"About—about the wedding night," Duncan blurted. "I— that is, I have—" He broke off abruptly, seeing someone turning into the path before them, heading for the necessary.

"This way." Jamie turned toward the kitchen gardens, which were safely enclosed in sheltering brick walls. Wedding night? he thought, both reassured and curious. Duncan had not been married before, he knew, and when they were in Ardsmuir together, Duncan had never spoken of women as some men did. He had thought it only a modest constraint at the time, but perhaps . . . but no, Duncan was well past fifty; surely the opportunity had occurred.

That left buggery or the clap, he thought, and he'd swear Duncan had no taste for boys. A bit awkward, to be sure, but he had full faith that Claire could deal with it. He did hope it was only drip, and not the French disease, though; that was a cruel plague.

"Here, *a charaid*," he said, drawing Duncan after him into the shelter of the onion beds. "We'll be quite private here. Now, then, what's your trouble?"

# 40

## DUNCAN'S SECRET

FATHER LeCLERC SPOKE NO ENGLISH, with the exception of a jolly "Tally-ho!" which he used alternately as a greeting, an interjection of amazement, and an exclamation of approbation. Jocasta was still at her toilette, so I introduced the priest to Ulysses, then escorted him to the main parlor, saw him provided with suitable refreshment, and sat him down to make conversation with the Sherstons, who were Protestant and rather bug-eyed at meeting a Jesuit, but so eager to show off their French that they were willing to overlook Father LeClerc's unfortunate profession.

Mentally wiping my brow after this bit of delicate social rapprochement, I made my excuses and went out to the terrace, to see whether Jamie had succeeded in retrieving Duncan. Neither man was in sight, but I met Brianna, coming up from the lawn with Jemmy.

"Hallo, darling, how are you?" I reached for Jemmy, who seemed restless, squirming and smacking his lips like someone sitting down to a six-course meal after a trek through the Sahara. "Hungry, are we?"

"Hak!" he said, then feeling this perhaps an insufficient explanation, repeated the syllable several times, with increasing volume, bouncing up and down by way of emphasis.

"*He's* hungry; *I'm* about to explode," Brianna said, lowering her voice and plucking gingerly at her bosom. "I'm just going to take him upstairs and feed him. Auntie Jocasta said we could use her room."

"Oh? That's good. Jocasta's just gone up herself—to rest a bit and change, she said. The wedding's set for four o'clock, now the priest is here." I had just heard the case clock in the hall chime noon; I did hope Jamie had got Duncan safely in hand. Perhaps he should be shut up somewhere, to prevent his wandering away again.

Bree reached to take Jemmy back, sticking a prophylactic knuckle in his mouth to muffle his remarks.

"Do you know the Sherstons?" she asked.

"Yes," I replied warily. "Why, what have they done?"

She raised one eyebrow at me.

"They've asked me to paint a portrait of Mrs. Sherston. A commission, I mean. Evidently Auntie Jocasta sang my praises to them, and showed them some of the things I did when I stayed here last spring, and now they want a picture."

"Really? Oh, darling, that's marvelous!"

"Well, it will be if they have any money," she said practically. "What do you think?"

It was a good question; fine clothes and appointments didn't always reflect actual worth, and I didn't know much about the Sherstons' circumstances; they were from Hillsborough, not Cross Creek.

"Well, they're rather vulgar," I said dubiously, "and dreadful snobs, but I think he's legitimately rich. He owns a brewery, I think. But ask Jocasta; she'll know for sure."

"Rah-tha vul-gah," she drawled, mocking my own accent, and grinned. "Who's a snob, then?"

"I am not a snob," I said with dignity. "I am a keen observer of social nuance. Have you seen your father and Duncan anywhere?"

"Not Duncan, but Da's down there by the trees with Mr. Campbell." She pointed helpfully, and I spotted Jamie's bright hair and crimson tartan, a fiery gleam at the bottom of the lawn. Not a sign of Duncan's scarlet coat, though.

"Damn the man," I said. "Where *has* he got to?"

"Went to the necessary, and fell in," Bree suggested. "All right, hold your horses, we're going!" Addressing this last to Jemmy, who was uttering plaintive cries suggestive of imminent starvation, she disappeared into the house.

I settled my shawl and strolled down the lawn to join

Jamie. A picnic lunch was being served to accommodate the guests, and I snatched a biscuit and a slice of ham as I passed the refreshment tables, improvising a hasty snack in order to stave off my own hunger pangs.

The air was still cool, but the sun was high and hot on my shoulders; it was a relief to join the men in the shade of a small grove of oaks that stood near the bottom of the lawn. They were pin oaks, and had begun to leaf out already, the unfolding leaves peeping out like a baby's fingers. What had Nayawenne told me about oaks? Oh, yes; one planted corn when the oak leaves were the size of a squirrel's ear.

Judging by that, the slaves could be planting corn in the River Run kitchen garden any day now. It would be weeks before the oak leaves were out on the Ridge, though.

Jamie had evidently just said something humorous, for Campbell made the low, creaking noise that passed with him for laughter, nodding to me in greeting.

"I shall leave ye to the practice of your own affairs, then," he said to Jamie, recovering his composure. "Call upon me, though, at need." He shaded his eyes, looking up toward the terrace.

"Ah, the prodigal returns. In shillings, sir, or bottles of brandy?"

I turned to look as well, in time to see Duncan crossing the terrace, nodding and smiling shyly to well-wishers as he passed. I must have looked bewildered, for Mr. Campbell bowed to me, dry mouth crooked with amusement.

"I'd laid your husband a small wager, ma'am."

"Five to one on Duncan, the night," Jamie explained. "That he and my aunt will share a bed, I mean."

"Goodness," I said, rather crossly. "Is anyone here talking of anything else? Minds like sewers, the lot of you."

Campbell laughed, then turned aside, distracted by the urgencies of a small grandson.

"Don't tell me ye werena wondering the same thing." Jamie nudged me gently.

"Indeed I was not," I said primly. I wasn't—but only because I already knew.

"Oh, indeed," he said, one corner of his mouth curling up.

"And you wi' lechery as plain on your face as whiskers on a cat."

"Whatever do you mean by that?" I demanded. Just in case he was right, I flicked the fan open and covered the lower half of my face. I peered over its ivory lacework, batting my eyelashes in mock innocence.

He made a derisive Scottish noise in his throat. Then, with a quick glance round, he bent low and whispered in my ear.

"It means ye look as ye do when ye want me to come to your bed." A warm breath stirred the hair over my ear. "Do you?"

I smiled brilliantly at Mr. Campbell, who was viewing us with interest over his grandson's head, snapped the fan open, and using it as a shield, stood on tiptoe to whisper in Jamie's ear. I dropped back on my heels and smiled demurely at him, fanning away for all I was worth.

Jamie looked mildly shocked, but definitely pleased. He glanced at Mr. Campbell, who had fortunately turned away, drawn into conversation elsewhere. Jamie rubbed his nose and regarded me with intense speculation, his dark blue gaze lingering on the scalloped neckline of my new gown. I fluttered the fan delicately over my décolletage.

"Ah . . . we could . . ." His eyes flicked up, assessing our surroundings for possible prospects of seclusion, then down again, ineluctably drawn to the fan as though it were a magnet.

"No we couldn't," I informed him, smiling and bowing to the elderly Misses MacNeil, who were strolling past behind him. "Every nook and cranny in the house is filled with people. So are the barns and stables and outbuildings. And if you had in mind a rendezvous under a bush on the riverbank, think again. This dress cost a bloody fortune." A fortune in illegal whisky, but a fortune nonetheless.

"Oh, I ken that well enough."

His eyes traveled slowly over me, from the coils of upswept hair to the tips of my new calf-leather shoes. The dress was pale amber silk, bodice and hem embroidered with silk leaves in shades of brown and gold, and if I did say so myself, it fit me like a glove.

"Worth it," he said softly, and leaned down to kiss me. A chilly breeze stirred the oak branches overhead, and I moved closer to him, seeking his warmth.

What with the long journey from the Ridge and the crush of guests caused by the impending celebration, we hadn't shared a bed ourselves in more than a week.

It wasn't so much an amorous encounter I wanted—though I would certainly not say no, if the opportunity offered. What I missed was simply the feel of his body next to mine; being able to reach out a hand in the dark and rest it on the long swell of his thigh; to roll toward him in the morning and cup his round, neat buttocks in the curve of thigh and belly; to press my cheek against his back and breathe the scent of his skin as I slipped into sleep.

"Damn," I said, resting my forehead briefly in the folds of his shirt ruffle, and inhaling the mingled scents of starch and man with longing. "You know, if your aunt and Duncan *don't* need the bed, perhaps . . ."

"Oh, so ye *were* wondering."

"No, I wasn't," I said. "Besides, what business is it of yours?"

"Oh, none at all," he said, unperturbed. "Only I've been asked by four men this morning if I think they will—or have done already. Which is rather a compliment to my aunt, no?"

It was true; Jocasta MacKenzie must be well into her sixties, and yet the thought of her sharing a man's bed was by no means unthinkable. I had met any number of women who had gratefully abandoned all notion of sex, directly the cessation of childbearing made it possible—but Jocasta wasn't one of them. At the same time—

"They haven't," I said. "Phaedre told me yesterday."

"I know. Duncan told me, just now." He was frowning slightly, but not at me. Toward the terrace, where the bright splotch of Duncan's tartan showed between the huge stone vases.

"Did he?" I was more than a little surprised at that. A sudden suspicion struck me. "You didn't *ask* him, did you?"

He gave me a slightly reproachful look.

"I did not," he said. "What d'ye take me for, Sassenach?"

"A Scot," I said. "Sex fiends, the lot of you. Or so one

would think, listening to all the talk around here." I gave Far-quard Campbell a hard look, but he had turned his back, en-grossed in conversation.

Jamie regarded me thoughtfully, scratching the corner of his jaw.

"Sex fiends?"

"You know what I mean."

"Oh, aye, I do. I'm only wondering—is that an insult, would ye say, or a compliment?"

I opened my mouth, then paused. I gave him back the thoughtful look.

"If the shoe fits," I said, "wear it."

He burst out laughing, which made a number of those nearby turn and look at us. Taking my arm, he steered me across the lawn and into the patchy shade of the elms.

"I did mean to ask ye something, Sassenach," he said, checking over his shoulder to be sure we were out of earshot. "Can ye find occasion to speak wi' my aunt, alone?"

"In this madhouse?" I glanced toward the terrace; a swarm of well-wishers surrounded Duncan like bees round a flower patch. "Yes, I suppose I could catch her in her room, before she comes down for the wedding. She's gone up to rest." I wouldn't mind a lie-down, either; my legs ached with hours of standing, and my shoes were new and slightly too tight.

"That'll do." He nodded pleasantly to an approaching ac-quaintance, then turned his back, shielding us from interrup-tion.

"All right," I said. "Why?"

"Well, it's to do wi' Duncan." He looked at once amused and slightly worried. "There's a wee difficulty, and he canna bring himself to speak to her about it."

"Don't tell me," I said. "He was married before, and he thought his first wife was dead, but he's just seen her here, eating cullen skink."

"Well, no," he said, smiling. "Not so bad as that. And per-haps it's nay so troublesome as Duncan fears. But he's worrit in his mind about it, and yet he canna bring himself to speak to my aunt; he's a bit shy of her, aye?"

Duncan was a shy and modest man altogether; an ex-fisherman pressed into service during the Rising, he had been captured after Culloden, and spent years in prison. He had been released, rather than transported, only because he had contracted blood poisoning from a scratch, and had lost one arm, making him unfit for labor and unsalable as an indenture. I didn't have to wonder whose idea this marriage had been; such lofty aspirations would never have occurred to Duncan in a million years.

"I can see that. What's he worried about, though?"

"Well," he said slowly, "it's true that Duncan hasna been wed before. Did ye not wonder why?"

"No," I said. "I'd just assumed that the Rising had—oh, dear." I stopped, catching a notion of what this might be about. "It's not—goodness. You mean . . . he likes men?" My voice rose involuntarily.

"No!" he said, scandalized. "Christ, ye dinna think I'd let him marry my aunt, and him a sodomite? Christ." He glanced around, to be sure no one had heard this calumny, and shepherded me into the shelter of the trees, just in case.

"Well, you wouldn't necessarily know, would you?" I asked, amused.

"I'd know," he said grimly. "Come along." He lifted an overhanging bough and ushered me beneath it, a hand in the small of my back. The grove was a large one, and it was easy enough to get out of sight of the party.

"No," he said again, reaching a small open space well in among the trunks. "The filthy mind of you, Sassenach! No, it's nothing o' the sort." He glanced behind him, but we were a good distance from the lawn, and reasonably shielded from view. "It's only that he's . . . incapable." He lifted one shoulder slightly, looking profoundly uncomfortable at the thought.

"What—impotent?" I felt my mouth hanging open, and closed it.

"Aye. He was betrothed, as a young man, but there was a dreadful accident; a cart horse knocked him into the street and kicked him in the scrotum." He made a slight motion, as though to touch himself for reassurance, but checked it. "He healed, but it—well, he wasna fit for nuptial rites any longer, so he released the young woman and she marrit elsewhere."

"The poor man!" I said, with a pang of sympathy. "Gracious, poor Duncan's had nothing but bad luck."

"Well, he's alive," Jamie observed. "A good many others aren't. Besides"—he gestured over one shoulder, at the spread of River Run behind him—"I shouldna be inclined to call his present situation precisely unlucky. Bar the one small difficulty, that is," he added.

I frowned, running through the medical possibilities. If the accident had resulted in severe vascular damage, there wasn't much I could do; I was in no way equipped for fine reconstructive surgery. If it were only a hemocoel, though, then perhaps . . .

"When he was a young man, you said? Hmm. Well, it's not promising, after so long, but I can certainly have a look and see whether—"

Jamie stared at me, incredulous.

"A look? Sassenach, the man goes puce when ye inquire after the health of his bowels, and he nearly died o' shame, telling me. He'll have an apoplexy, and ye go pokin' his privates."

A strand of hair had been pulled loose by an oak twig; I pushed it irritably behind my ear.

"Well, what did you expect me to do, then? I can't heal him with spell-casting!"

"Of course not," he said, a little impatiently. "I dinna want ye to do anything to Duncan—only to speak to my aunt."

"What—you mean she doesn't know? But they've been engaged to be married for months, and living together for most of it!"

"Aye, but . . ." Jamie made the odd half-shrugging gesture he used when feeling embarrassed or uncomfortable, as though his shirt were too tight. "D'ye see—when the question of marriage rose, it never occurred to Duncan that it was a matter of . . . mmphm."

"Mmphm," I said, raising one eyebrow. "Doesn't marriage usually involve at least the possibility of mmphm?"

"Well, he didna think my aunt was wanting him for his manly beauty, aye?" Jamie said, raising his own brows back at me. "It seemed only a matter of business and convenience—there are things he could manage as owner of River

Run that he couldna do as overseer. At that, he wouldna have agreed, save she persuaded him."

"And he never thought to mention this . . . this impediment?"

"Oh, he thought. But there wasna any indication that my aunt regarded marriage in any but the sense of business. *She* didna mention the matter of bed; he was too shy to say. And the question didna really arise, ken."

"I gather that it now *has* arisen? What happened? Did your aunt slip her hand under his kilt this morning and make a bawdy remark about the wedding night?"

"He didna happen to say," he replied dryly. "But it wasna until this morning, when he began to hear the jests among the guests, that it occurred to Duncan that perhaps my aunt was expecting him to . . . well."

He lifted one shoulder, and let it fall. "He couldna think what to do, and was in a panic, listening to everyone."

"I see." I rubbed a knuckle across my upper lip, thinking. "Poor Duncan; no wonder he's been nervous."

"Aye." Jamie straightened up, with the air of one having settled something. "So, if ye'll be so kind as to speak wi' Jocasta, and see it's all straight—"

"Me? You want *me* to tell her?"

"Well, I shouldna think she'll mind greatly," he said, looking quizzically down at me. "After all, at her age, I shouldna think—"

I made a rude noise.

"Her age? Your grandfather Simon was well into his seventies and still putting it about, when last seen."

"My aunt is a woman," he said, rather austerely. "If ye hadna noticed it."

"And you think that makes a difference?"

"You don't?"

"Oh, it makes a difference, all right," I said. I leaned back against a tree, arms crossed under my bosom, and gave him a look from under my lashes. "When I am a hundred and one, and you're ninety-six, I'll invite you to my bed—and we'll see which one of us rises to the occasion, hmm?"

He looked at me thoughtfully, a glint in the dark blue of his eyes.

"I've a mind to take ye where ye stand, Sassenach," he said. "Payment on account, hmm?"

"I've a mind to take you up on it," I said. "However . . ." I glanced through the screen of branches toward the house, which was clearly visible. The trees were beginning to leaf out, but the tiny sprays of tender green were by no means sufficient camouflage. I turned back, just as Jamie's hands descended on the swell of my hips.

Events after that were somewhat confused, with the predominant impressions being an urgent rustling of fabric, the sharp scent of trodden onion grass, and the crackling of last year's oak leaves, dry underfoot.

My eyes popped open a few moments later.

"Don't stop!" I said, disbelieving. "Not *now*, for God's sake!"

He grinned down at me, stepping back and letting his kilt fall into place. His face was flushed a ruddy bronze with effort, and his chest heaved under his shirt ruffles.

He grinned maliciously, and wiped a sleeve across his forehead.

"I'll gie ye the rest when I'm ninety-six, aye?"

"You won't live that long! Come here!"

"Oh," he said. "So ye'll speak to my aunt."

"Effing blackmailer," I panted, fumbling at the folds of his kilt. "I'll get you for this, I swear I will."

"Oh, aye. You will."

He put an arm round my waist and swung me off my feet, turning round so that his back was to the house, screening me with his body. His long fingers deftly ruffled up the skirt of my gown, then the two petticoats beneath, and even more deftly, slid between my bare legs.

"Hush," he murmured in my ear. "Ye dinna want folk to hear, do ye?" He set his teeth gently in the curve of my ear, and proceeded about his business in a workmanlike way, ignoring my intermittent—and admittedly rather feeble—struggles.

I was more than ready and he knew what he was doing. It didn't take long. I dug my fingers into his arm, hard as an iron bar across my middle, arched backward for a moment of dizzying infinity, and then collapsed against him, twitching like a worm on the end of a hook. He made a deep chuckling sound, and let go of my ear.

A cold breeze had sprung up, and was wafting the folds of my skirts about my legs. The scent of smoke and food drifted through the cool spring air, along with the rumble of talk and laughter from the lawn. I could dimly hear it, under the slow, loud thumping of my heart.

"Come to think of it," Jamie remarked, releasing me, "Duncan has still got the one good hand." He set me gently on my feet, keeping hold of my elbow, lest my knees give way. "Ye might mention that to my aunt, if ye think it will help."

41

## MUSIC HATH CHARMS

ROGER MacKENZIE MADE HIS WAY through the crowd, nodding here and there to a familiar face, but pushing on purposefully, preventing any attempt at conversation. He was not in a talkative mood.

Brianna had gone off to feed the kid, and while he missed her, he was just as pleased that she was out of sight for the moment. He didn't care at all for the sort of looks she'd been getting. Those directed at her face were admiring, but respectful enough; he'd caught that wee bastard Forbes staring at her rear view with an expression similar to the one the gentlemen were using on the undraped marble goddess on the lawn, though.

At the same time, he was more than proud of her. She was gorgeous in her new dress, and he felt a pleasant sense of possession when he looked at her. Still, his pleasure was slightly spoiled by the uneasy thought that she looked as though she belonged here, mistress of all this . . . this . . .

Yet another slave trotted past him, skirts hooped up over one arm as she made for the house, a basin of fresh rolls balanced on her head and another under her arm. How many slaves did Jocasta Cameron keep? he wondered.

Of course, that alone put the notion of Brianna's inheriting River Run out of the question. She wouldn't countenance the notion of slaves, not ever. Nor would he himself; still, it was comforting to think that it wasn't merely his own pride keeping Bree from her rightful inheritance.

He caught the thin wail of a fiddle coming from the house, and felt his ears prick up at the sound. Of course there would be music for the party. And with luck, a few new songs that he didn't know.

He turned across the terrace toward the house. He hadn't a notebook with him, but doubtless Ulysses could provide him with something. He bowed to Mrs. Farquard Campbell, who looked like a particularly horrible but expensive lampshade in pink silk. He paused to let her precede him into the house, biting the inside of his cheek as the four-foot spread of her skirt stuck momentarily in the three-foot doorway. She twitched adroitly sideways, though, and sidled crabwise into the hall, Roger following at a respectful distance.

The fiddle had ceased, but he could hear the twang and throb of instruments being handled and tuned nearby. They were in the big drawing room, whose double doors could be thrown open to allow dancers to spill out across the foyer, when the time came. At the moment, there were only a few guests in the drawing room, engaged in casual conversation.

Roger made his way past Ulysses, who was standing at the hearth, immaculate in wig and green livery, a poker held at the ready as he supervised two maidservants in the making of a gigantic vat of fresh rum punch. His eyes flicked automatically to the door, registered Roger's presence and identity, then returned to his business.

The musicians were huddled at the far end of the room, casting occasional thirsty glances at the hearth as they readied their instruments.

"What will you be giving us the day?" Roger inquired, pausing beside the fiddler. He smiled as the man turned round to him. " 'Ewie wi' the Crooked Horn,' perhaps, or 'Shawn Bwee'?"

"Oh, God love ye, sir, nothin' fancy." The conductor of the small ensemble, a cricketlike Irishman whose bent back was belied by the brightness of his eyes, waved a hand in cordial scorn at his motley crew of musicians.

"They ain't up to more than jigs and reels. No more are the folk as will be dancin', though," he added, practically. " 'Tisn't the Assembly Rooms in Dublin, after all, nor even Edenton; a good fiddler can keep 'em up to snuff."

"And that would be you, I expect?" Roger said with a smile, nodding at the cracked fiddle case the conductor had set on a whatnot, carefully out of the way of being stepped or sat on.

"That would be me," the gentleman agreed, with a graceful bow of acknowledgment. "Seamus Hanlon, sir—your servant."

"I am obliged, sir. Roger MacKenzie, of Fraser's Ridge." He returned the bow, taking pleasure in the old-fashioned formality, and clasped Hanlon's hand briefly, careful of the twisted fingers and knobby joints. Hanlon saw his care of the arthritic hand and gave a brief grimace of deprecation.

"Ah, they'll be fine with a drop of lubrication, so they will." Hanlon flexed one hand experimentally, then flipped the fingers in dismissal, fixing Roger with a bright glance.

"And yourself, sir; I felt the calluses on your fingertips. Not a fiddler, perhaps, but would ye be after playin' some stringed instrument?"

"Only to pass the time of an evening; nothing like you gentlemen." Roger nodded politely toward the ensemble, which, now unpacked, boasted a battered cello, two viols, a trumpet, a flute, and something which he thought might have started life as a hunting horn, though it appeared to have been amended since by the addition of several odd loops of tubing that stuck out in different directions.

Hanlon eyed him shrewdly, taking in his breadth of chest.

"And hark at the voice in him! Sure, and you're a singer, Mr. MacKenzie?"

Roger's reply was interrupted by a loud thump and a dolorous twang behind him. He whirled to see the cello player inflating himself over his instrument in the manner of a hen with a very large chick, to protect it from further injury by the gentleman who had evidently kicked it carelessly in passing.

"Watch yourself, then!" the cellist snapped. "Clumsy sot!"

"Oh?" The intruder, a stocky man in naval uniform, glowered menacingly at the cellist. "You dare . . . dare shpeak to me . . ." His face was flushed an unhealthy red, and he swayed slightly as he stood; Roger could smell the fumes of alcohol from a distance of six feet.

The officer raised a forefinger to the cellist, and appeared to be on the point of speech. A tongue tip showed pinkly between his teeth, but no words emerged. His empurpled jowls quivered for a moment, then he abandoned the attempt, turned on his heel, and made off, swerving narrowly to avoid an incoming footman with a tray of drinks, and caroming off the doorjamb as he passed into the corridor.

"'Ware, then, Mr. O'Reilly." Seamus Hanlon spoke dryly to the cellist. "Were we near the sea, I should reckon there'd be a press-gang waitin' for ye, the instant ye set foot outside. As it is, I'd put no odds on him layin' for ye with a marlinspike or something of the kind."

O'Reilly spat eloquently on the floor.

"I know him," he said contemptuously. "Wolff, he's called. Dog, more like, and a poor dog at that. He's tight as a tick—he'll not remember me, an hour hence."

Hanlon squinted thoughtfully at the doorway through which the Lieutenant had vanished.

"Well, that's as may be," he allowed. "But I know the gentleman, too, and I do believe his mind may be somewhat sharper than his behavior might suggest." He stood for a moment, tapping the bow of his fiddle thoughtfully against the palm of his hand, then turned his head toward Roger.

"Fraser's Ridge, ye said? Will ye be a kinsman of Mrs. Cameron's—or Mrs. Innes, I should say?" he corrected himself.

"I'm married to Jamie Fraser's daughter," Roger said patiently, having discovered that this was the most efficient description, as most of the county appeared to know who Jamie Fraser was, and it prevented further questions regarding Roger's own family connections.

"Ho-ho," Seamus said, looking visibly impressed. "Well, then. Hum!"

"What's that bladder doing here, anyway?" the cellist demanded, still glaring after the departed officer. He patted his instrument soothingly. "Everyone knows he meant to wed Mrs. Cameron and have River Run for himself. I wonder he's the tripes to show his face today!"

"Perhaps he's come to show there are no hard feelings," Roger suggested. "A civil gesture—best man won and all that, aye?"

The musicians emitted a medley of sniggers and guffaws at this suggestion.

"Maybe," said the flutist, shaking his head over his instrument. "But if you're any friend to Duncan Innes, tell him to watch his back in the dançin'."

"Aye, do that," Seamus Hanlon concurred. "Be off with ye, young man, and speak to him—but see ye come back."

He crooked a finger at the waiting footman, and scooped a cup neatly from the proffered tray. He lifted this in salute, grinning at Roger over its rim. "It may be you'll know a tune or two that's new to me."

# THE DEASIL CHARM

**B**RIANNA SAT BACK in the leather wing chair before the hearth, nursing Jemmy as she watched her great-aunt ready herself for the wedding.

"What you think, then?" Phaedre asked, dipping the silver

comb into a small pot of pomade. "Dress it up high, with the curls over the top?" Her voice was hopeful, but wary. She disapproved overtly of her mistress's refusal to wear a wig, and would do her level best to create a similarly fashionable effect with Jocasta's own hair, if allowed.

"Tosh," said Jocasta. "This isn't Edinburgh, child, let alone London." She leaned back, head lifted and eyes closed, basking. Bright spring sunshine poured through the panes, sparking off the silver comb, and making dark shadows of the slave's hands against the nimbus of shining white hair.

"Maybe not, but 'taint the wild Caribee nor the back-country, neither," Phaedre countered. "You the mistress here; this your weddin'. Everybody be lookin' at you—you want-in' to shame me, wear your hair down your shoulders like a squaw, and everybody be thinkin' I don't know my busi-ness?"

"Oh, heaven forbid." Jocasta's wide mouth twisted with an irritable humor. "Dress it simply, if you please, swept back and put up with combs. Perhaps my niece will let you show off your skill on her locks."

Phaedre cast a narrow glance over her shoulder at Bri-anna, who simply smiled and shook her head. She'd worn a lace-edged cap for the sake of public decency, and wasn't disposed to fuss with her hair. The slave snorted, and re-sumed her attempt to cajole Jocasta. Brianna closed her eyes, letting the amicable bickering recede into the background. Warm sun fell through the casement over her feet, and the fire purred and crackled at her back, embracing her like the old woolen shawl she had wrapped about herself and little Jem.

Beyond the voices of Jocasta and Phaedre, she could hear the thrum of the house below. Every room in the house was bursting with guests. Some were staying at nearby planta-tions, and had ridden in for the festivities, but enough were staying at River Run overnight that all the bedchambers were full, with guests sleeping five and six to a bed, and more on pallets in the tents by the river landing.

Brianna eyed the expanse of Jocasta's big tester bed envi-ously. Between the exigencies of travel, Jemmy, and the crowded conditions at River Run, she and Roger hadn't slept together in more than a week, and weren't likely to, until they returned to the Ridge.

Not that sleeping together was the major concern, nice as it was. The tug of the baby's mouth on her breast aroused a number of nonmaternal urges elsewhere, which required both Roger and a little privacy for satisfaction. They had started something promising the night before, in the pantry, but had been interrupted by one of the kitchen slaves, coming in to fetch a cheese. Perhaps the stable? She stretched her legs out, toes curling, and wondered whether the grooms slept in the stable or not.

"Well, I shall wear the brilliants, then, but only to please you, *a nighean*." Jocasta's humorous voice pulled her out of the alluring vision of a dark, hay-lined stall, and Roger's body, naked limbs half-seen in the gloom.

She glanced up from Jemmy's blissful suckling, to where Jocasta sat upon the window seat, the spring light through the casement falling across her face. She looked abstracted, Bree thought, as though she were listening to something faint and far-off, that only she could hear. Maybe the hum of the wedding guests below.

The murmur in the house below reminded her of her mother's summer hives; a thrum that you could hear if you put your ear against one of the bee gums, a distant sound of busy content. The product of this particular swarm was talk, rather than honey, though the intent was similar—the laying up of reserves to see them through bleak and nectarless days of deprivation.

"That will do, that will do." Jocasta waved Phaedre away, getting to her feet. She shooed the maid out of the room, then stood tapping her fingers restlessly on the dressing table, clearly thinking of further details that should be attended to. Jocasta's brows drew together, and she pressed two fingers against the skin above her eyes.

"Have you got a headache, Auntie?" Brianna kept her voice low, so as not to disturb Jemmy, who was nearly asleep. Jocasta dropped her hand and turned toward her niece with a small, wry smile.

"Och, it's nothing. Whenever the weather turns, my poor head turns with it!"

In spite of the smile, Brianna could see small lines of pain tugging at the corners of Jocasta's eyes.

"Jem's nearly finished. I'll go and fetch Mama, shall I? She could make you a tisane."

Jocasta flapped a hand in dismissal, pushing away the pain with an obvious effort.

"No need, *a muirninn*. It's none so bad as that." She rubbed at her temple, careful of the hairdressing, the gesture belying her words.

Jemmy's mouth released its hold with a small, milky *pop!* and his head lolled back. The crook of Brianna's elbow was hot and sweaty, where his head had rested; his tiny ear was crumpled and crimson. She lifted his inert body and sighed with relief as the cool air struck her skin. A soft belch bubbled out of him with a dribble of excess milk, and he subsided against her shoulder like a half-filled water balloon.

"Full, is he?" Jocasta smiled, blind eyes turned toward them at the faint sound.

"As a drum," Brianna assured her. She patted his small back, to be sure, but heard no more than the soft sigh of sleep-filled breathing. She rose, wiped the milk from his chin, and laid the baby on his stomach in his makeshift cradle, a drawer from Jocasta's mahogany chiffonier, laid on the floor and thickly padded with pillows and quilts.

Brianna hung the shawl over the back of the chair, shivering slightly in a draft that leaked around the window frame. Not wanting to risk her new dress being stained with spit-up milk, she'd been nursing Jemmy in shift and stockings, and her bare forearms were pebbled with gooseflesh.

Jocasta turned her head in answer to the creak of wood and rustle of fabric, as Brianna opened the big armoire and took out two linen petticoats and her dress, smoothing the panels of soft, pale blue wool with satisfaction. She had woven the cloth and engineered the design of the gown herself—though Mrs. Bug had spun the thread, Claire had dyed it with indigo and saxifrage, and Marsali had helped with the sewing.

"Shall I call Phaedre back to dress ye, lass?"

"No, that's all right, I can manage—if you'll help me with

the laces?" She didn't like to call on the services of the slaves, any more than could be helped. The petticoats were no problem; she simply stepped into them, one at a time, and fastened the drawstrings round her waist. The stays needed to be laced up the back, though, and so did the gown itself.

Jocasta's brows were still dark, bronze against the pale apricot hue of her skin. They rose a little at the suggestion that she help to dress her niece, but she nodded, with no more than a brief hesitation. She turned her blind eyes toward the hearth, frowning a little.

"I suppose I can. The laddie's not too near the fire, is he? Sparks can jump, aye?"

Brianna wriggled into the stays, scooping her breasts up into the scalloped hollows that supported them, then pulled the gown on over them.

"No, he's not too near the fire," she said patiently. She'd made the bodice with light boning in the front and sides. Brianna turned slightly to and fro, admiring the effect in Jocasta's looking glass. Catching sight in the mirror of her aunt's slight frown behind her, she rolled her eyes at herself, then bent and pulled the drawer a little farther from the hearth, just in case.

"Thanks to ye for humoring an auld woman," Jocasta said dryly, hearing the scrape of wood.

"You're welcome, Aunt," Brianna replied, letting both warmth and apology show in her voice. She laid a hand on her great-aunt's shoulder, and Jocasta put her own long hand over it, squeezing gently.

"It's no that I think ye're a neglectful mother, aye?" Jocasta said. "But when ye've lived so long as I have, ye may be cautious, too, lass. I have seen dreadful things happen to bairns, ye ken?" she said, more softly. "And I should rather be set afire myself, than see harm come to our bonnie lad."

She moved behind Brianna and ran her hands lightly down her niece's back, finding the lacings without trouble.

"Ye've regained your figure, I see," the old woman said with approval, her hands skimming the sides of Brianna's waist. "What is this—crewelwork? What color is it?"

"Dark indigo blue. Flowering vines done in heavy cotton, to contrast with the pale blue wool." She took one of Jocasta's hands and guided the fingertips lightly over the vines that covered each bone in the bodice, running from the scalloped neck to the V of the waist, dropped sharply in front to show off the trim figure Jocasta had remarked upon.

Brianna drew in her breath as the laces tightened, glancing from her reflection to her son's small head, round as a cantaloupe and heartbreakingly perfect. Not for the first time, she wondered about her great-aunt's life. Jocasta had had children, or at least Jamie thought so—but she never spoke of them, and Brianna hesitated to ask. Perhaps lost in infancy; so many were. Her chest tightened at the thought.

"Dinna fash yourself," her aunt said. Jocasta's face readjusted itself into determined cheerfulness in the mirror. "Yon laddie's born for great things; nay harm will come to him, I'm sure."

She turned, the green silk of her dressing gown rustling over her petticoats, leaving Bree freshly startled at her aunt's ability to divine people's feelings, even without seeing their faces.

"Phaedre!" Jocasta called. "Phaedre! Bring my case—the black one."

Phaedre was nearby, as always, and a brief rustling in the drawers of the armoire produced the black case. Jocasta sat down with it at her secretary.

The black leather case was old and worn, a narrow box covered in weathered hide, unadorned save for its silver hasp. Jocasta kept her best jewels in a much grander case of velvet-lined cedarwood, Brianna knew. What could be in this one?

She moved to stand beside her aunt as Jocasta put back the lid. Inside the case was a short length of turned wood, the thickness of a finger, and on it were ranged three rings: a plain band of gold set with a beryl, another with a large cabochon emerald, and the last with three diamonds, surrounded by smaller stones that caught the light and threw it back in rainbows that danced across the walls and beams.

"What a lovely ring!" Bree exclaimed involuntarily.

"Oh, the diamond one? Well, Hector Cameron was aye a rich man," said Jocasta, absently touching the biggest ring. Her long fingers—unadorned—sorted deftly through a small

*652   Diana   Gabaldon*

heap of trinkets that lay in the box beside the rings, and came out with something small and dull.

She handed the tiny object to Brianna, who discovered it to be a small pierced-work tin brooch, rather tarnished, made in the shape of a heart.

"That's a *deasil* charm, *a muirninn*," Jocasta said, with a satisfied nod. "Put it on the wean's skirts, behind."

"A charm?" Brianna glanced at Jemmy's huddled form. "What kind of charm?"

"Against the fairies," Jocasta said. "Keep it pinned to the lad's smock—always to the back, mind—and naught born of the Auld Folk will trouble him."

The hair on Brianna's forearms prickled slightly at the matter-of-factness in the old woman's voice.

"Your mother should ha' told ye," Jocasta went on, with a hint of reproval in her voice. "But I ken as she's a Sassenach, and your father likely wouldna think of it. Men don't," she added, with a hint of bitterness. "It's a woman's job to see to the weans, to keep them from harm."

Jocasta stooped to the kindling basket and groped among the bits of debris, coming up with a long pine twig in her hand, the bark still on it.

"Take that," she commanded, holding it out toward Brianna. "Light the end of it from the hearth, and walk ye round the bairn three times. Sunwise, mind!"

Mystified, Brianna took the stick and thrust it into the fire, then did as she was bid, holding the flaming twig well away from both the makeshift cradle and her blue wool skirts. Jocasta tapped her foot rhythmically on the floor, and chanted, half under her breath.

She spoke in Gaelic, but slowly enough that Brianna could make out most of the words.

> *"Wisdom of serpent be thine,*
> *Wisdom of raven be thine,*
> *Wisdom of valiant eagle.*
>
> *Voice of swan be thine,*
> *Voice of honey be thine,*
> *Voice of the Son of the stars.*

> *Sain of the fairy-woman be thine,*
> *Sain of the elf-dart be thine,*
> *Sain of the red dog be thine.*
>
> *Bounty of sea be thine,*
> *Bounty of land be thine,*
> *Bounty of the Father of Heaven.*
>
> *Be each day glad for thee,*
> *No day ill for thee,*
> *A life joyful, satisfied."*

Jocasta paused for a moment, a slight frown on her face, as though listening for any backtalk from Fairyland. Evidently satisfied, she motioned toward the hearth.

"Throw it into the fire. Then the wean will be safe from burning."

Brianna obeyed, finding to her fascination that she did not find any of this even faintly ridiculous. Odd, but very satisfying to think that she was protecting Jem from harm—even harm from fairies, which she didn't personally believe in. Or she hadn't, before this.

A thread of music drifted up from below; the screek of a fiddle, and the sound of a voice, deep and mellow. She couldn't make out any words, but knew the sound of the song.

Jocasta cocked her head, listening, and smiled.

"He's a good voice, your young man."

Brianna listened, too. Very faintly, she heard the familiar rise and fall of "My Love Is in America," somewhere below. *When I sing, it's always for you.* Her breasts were soft now, drained of milk, but they tingled slightly at the memory.

"You have good ears, Auntie," she said, tucking the thought away with a smile.

"Are ye pleased in your marriage?" Jocasta asked abruptly. "D'ye find yourself well-suited wi' the lad?"

"Yes," Brianna said, a little startled. "Yes—very much."

"That's good." Her great-aunt stood still, head tilted to the side, still listening. "Aye, that's good," she repeated, softly.

Seized by impulse, Brianna laid a hand on the older woman's wrist.

"And you, Auntie?" she asked. "Are you . . . pleased?"

"Happy" seemed not quite the word, in view of that row of rings in the case. "Well-suited" seemed not quite right, either, with her memory of Duncan, skulking in the corner of the drawing room the night before, shy and wordless whenever anyone but Jamie spoke to him, sweating and nervous this morning.

"Pleased?" Jocasta sounded puzzled. "Oh—to be married, ye mean!" To Brianna's relief, her aunt laughed, the lines of her face drawing up in genuine amusement.

"Oh, aye, surely," she said. "Why, it's the first time I shall ha' changed my name in fifty years!"

With a small snort of amusement, the old lady turned toward the window and pressed her palm against the glass.

"It's a fine day out, lass," she said. "Why not take your cloak and have a bit of air and company?"

She was right; the distant river gleamed silver through a lacework of green branches, and the air inside, so cozy a few moments ago, seemed now suddenly stale and frowsty.

"I think I will." Brianna glanced toward the makeshift cradle. "Shall I call Phaedre to watch the baby?"

Jocasta waved a hand at her, shooing.

"Och, away wi' ye. I'll mind the bairnie. I dinna mean to go down yet a while."

"Thanks, Auntie." She kissed the old woman's cheek, and turned to go—then, with a glance at her aunt, took a step back toward the hearth, and unobtrusively slid the cradle a little farther from the fire.

THE AIR OUTSIDE was fresh, and smelled of new grass and barbecue smoke. It made her want to skip down the brick paths, blood humming in her veins. She could hear the strains of music from the house, and the sound of Roger's voice. A quick turn in the fresh air, and then she'd go in; perhaps Roger would be ready for a break by then, and they could—

"Brianna!" She heard her name, hissed from behind the wall of the kitchen garden, and turned, startled, to find her father's head poking cautiously round the corner, like a ruddy snail. He jerked his chin at her and disappeared.

She cast a quick look over her shoulder to be sure no one was watching, and hastily whisked round the wall into the shelter of a sprouting carrot bed, to find her father crouched over the recumbent body of one of the black maids, who was sprawled atop a pile of aging manure with her cap over her face.

"What on earth—" Brianna began. Then she caught a whiff of alcohol, pungent among the garden scents of carrot tops and sun-ripened manure. "Oh." She squatted next to her father, skirts ballooning over the brick path.

"It was my fault," he explained. "Or some of it, at least. I left a cup under the willows, still half-full." He nodded toward the brick path, where one of Jocasta's punch cups lay on its side, a sticky drop of liquid still clinging to its rim. "She must have found it."

Brianna leaned over and sniffed at the edge of the maid's rumpled cap, now fluttering with heavy snores. Rum punch was the prevailing odor, but she also detected the richly sour scent of ale and the smooth tang of brandy. Evidently the slave had been thriftily disposing of any dregs left in the cups she collected for washing.

She lifted the ruffled edge of the cap with a cautious finger. It was Betty, one of the older maids, her face slack-lipped and drop-jawed in alcoholic stupor.

"Aye, it wasna the first half-cup she'd had," Jamie said, seeing her. "She must have been reeling. I canna think how she walked so far from the house, in such condition."

Brianna glanced back, frowning. The brick-walled kitchen garden was near to the cookhouse, but a good three hundred yards from the main house, and separated from it by a rhododendron hedge, and several flower beds.

"Not just how," Brianna said, and tapped a finger against her lip in puzzlement. "Why?"

"What?" He had been frowning at the maid, but glanced up at her tone. She rose, and tilted her head at the snoring woman.

"Why *did* she walk out here? It looks like she's been tip-pling all day—she can't have been dashing out here with every cup; somebody would have noticed. And why bother? It's not like it would be hard to do without being noticed. If I were drinking leftovers, I'd just stay there under the willows and gulp it."

Her father gave her a startled look, replaced at once with one of wry amusement.

"Would ye, then? Aye, that's a thought. But perhaps there was enough in the cup that she thought to enjoy it in peace."

"Maybe so. But there are surely hiding places nearer the river than this." She reached down and scooped up the empty cup. "What was it you were drinking, rum punch?"

"No, brandy."

"Then it wasn't yours that pushed her over the edge." She held out the cup, tilting it so he could see the dark dregs at the bottom. Jocasta's rum punch was made not only with the usual rum, sugar, and butter but also with dried currants, the whole concoction being mulled with a hot poker. The result not only was dark brown in color but always left a heavy sed-iment in the cups, composed of tiny grains of soot from the poker and the charred remnants of incinerated currants.

Jamie took the cup from her, frowning. He inserted his nose into the cup and took a deep sniff, then stuck a finger into the liquid and put it in his mouth.

"What is it?" she asked, seeing his face change.

"Punch," he said, but ran the tip of his tongue back and forth over his teeth, as though to cleanse it. "With laudanum, I think."

"Laudanum! Are you sure?"

"No," he said frankly. "But there's something in it beyond dried currants, or I'm a Dutchman." He held the cup out to her, and she took it, sniffing furiously. She couldn't make out much beyond the sweet, burned smell of rum punch. Perhaps there was a sharper tang, something oily and aromatic . . . perhaps not.

"I'll take your word for it," she said, wiping the tip of her nose on the back of her hand. She glanced at the supine maid. "Shall I go look for Mama?"

Jamie squatted beside the maid and inspected her carefully. He lifted a limp hand and felt it, listened to her breathing, then shook his head.

"I canna say whether she's drugged, or only drunk—but I dinna think she's dying."

"What shall we do with her? We can't leave her lie."

He looked down at the slave, frowning.

"No, of course not." He stooped and—quite gently—gathered the woman into his arms. One worn shoe fell off, and Brianna retrieved it from the brick walk.

"D'ye ken where she sleeps?" Jamie asked, gingerly negotiating his stertorous burden round the edge of a cucumber frame.

"She's a house slave; she must sleep in the attics."

He nodded, tossing his head to dislodge a strand of red hair that had blown into his mouth.

"Verra well, then, we'll go round the stables and see can we get up the back stair without bein' seen. Go across, will ye, lass, and signal me when it's clear."

She tucked shoe and cup under her cloak to hide them, then ducked quickly out onto the narrow walk that led past the kitchen garden, branching to cookhouse and necessary. She glanced to and fro, feigning casualness. There were a few people within sight, near the paddock, but that was some distance away—and all of them had their backs to her, engrossed with Mr. Wylie's black Dutch horses.

As she turned to signal to her father, she caught sight of Mr. Wylie himself, escorting a lady into the stable block. A gleam of gold silk—wait, it was her mother! Claire's pale face turned momentarily in her direction, but her attention was fixed on something Wylie was saying, and she didn't notice her daughter on the path.

Bree hesitated, wanting to call to her mother, but couldn't do so without attracting unwanted attention. Well, at least she knew where Claire was. She could come and fetch her mother to help—once they had Betty safely tucked away.

WITH A FEW CLOSE alarms and near-misses, they managed to get Betty up to the long attic room she shared with the other female house servants. Jamie, panting, dumped her unceremoniously on one of the narrow beds, then wiped his sweating brow on his coat sleeve, and, long nose wrinkled, began fastidiously to dust manure crumbs from the skirts of his coat.

"So, then," he said, a little grumpily. "She's safe, aye? If ye tell one of the other slaves she's taken ill, I suppose no one who matters will find out."

"Thanks, Da." She leaned close and kissed his cheek. "You're a sweet man."

"Oh, aye," he said, sounding resigned. "My bones are filled wi' honey, to be sure." Still, he didn't look displeased. "Have ye got that shoe, still?" He took off the maid's remaining shoe, and placed it neatly beside its fellow beneath the bed, then drew the coarse woolen blanket gently over the woman's feet, grimy white in their thick stockings.

Brianna checked the maid's condition; so far as she could tell, everything seemed all right; the woman was still snoring wetly, but in a reassuringly regular manner. As they tiptoed cautiously back down the rear stairs, she gave Jamie the silver cup.

"Here. Did you know this was one of Duncan's cups?"

"No." He arched one brow, frowning. "What d'ye mean, 'Duncan's cups'?"

"Aunt Jocasta had a set of six cups made for Duncan, for a wedding present. She showed them to me yesterday. See?" She turned the cup in her hand, to show him the engraved monogram—"I," for "Innes," with a tiny fish, its scales beautifully detailed, swimming round the letter.

"Does that help?" she asked, seeing his brow crease in interest.

"It may." He pulled out a clean cambric handkerchief and wrapped the cup carefully before putting it in the pocket of his coat. "I'll go and find out. Meanwhile, can ye find Roger Mac?"

"Of course. Why?"

"Well, it does occur to me that if yon Betty drank part of a cup of rum punch and was laid out like a fish on a slab, then I should like to find whoever drank the first part of it, and see if they're in a similar condition." He raised one brow at her.

"If the punch was drugged, then likely it was meant for someone, aye? I thought perhaps you and Roger Mac might look round discreetly for bodies in the shrubbery."

That aspect of the matter hadn't struck her in the rush to get Betty upstairs.

"All right. I should find Phaedre or Ulysses first, though, and tell one of them that Betty's sick."

"Aye. If ye speak with Phaedre, ye might inquire whether yon Betty is an opium-eater as well as a bibber. Though I will say I think it unlikely," he added dryly.

"So do I," she said, matching his tone. She took his point, though; perhaps the punch had not been drugged, but Betty had taken the laudanum herself, on purpose. It was possible; she knew Jocasta kept some in the stillroom. If she had taken it herself, though, was it for recreational use—or had the maid perhaps intended to commit suicide?

She frowned at Jamie's back, as he paused at the foot of the stair, listening before stepping onto the landing. It was easy enough to think that the misery of slavery might dispose one to suicide. At the same time, honesty compelled her to admit that Jocasta's house servants lived reasonably well; better than any number of free individuals—black *or* white—that she'd seen in Wilmington and Cross Creek.

The servants' room was clean, the beds rough but comfortable. The house servants had decent clothes, even to shoes and stockings, and more than enough to eat. As for the sorts of emotional complications that could lead one to contemplate suicide—well, those weren't limited to slaves.

Much more likely that Betty was merely a toper, of the sort who would drink anything even vaguely alcoholic—the reek of her garments certainly suggested as much. But in that case, why take the risk of stealing laudanum, on a day when the wedding party insured there would be an abundance of every kind of drink?

She was reluctantly forced to the same conclusion that she was sure her father had already reached. Betty had taken the laudanum—if that's what it was, she reminded herself—by accident. And if that was so . . . whose cup had she drunk from?

Jamie turned, lips pursed to enjoin silence, and beckoned

to her that the coast was clear. She followed him quickly across the landing and outside, letting out her breath in relief as they arrived on the path unobserved.

"What were you doing there in the first place, Da?" she asked. He looked blank.

"In the kitchen garden," she elaborated. "How did you find Betty?"

"Oh." He took her arm, fetching her away from the house. They walked casually toward the paddock; innocent guests bent on viewing the horses. "I was just havin' a word wi' your mother, over by the grove. I came back through the kitchen garden, and there the woman was, flat on her back on the shit heap."

"That's a point, isn't it?" she asked. "Did she lie down in the garden on purpose, or was it only an accident that you found her there?"

He shook his head.

"I dinna ken," he said. "But I mean to speak to Betty, once she's sober. D'ye ken where your mother is now?"

"Yes, she's with Phillip Wylie. They were headed for the stables, I think." Her father's nostrils flared slightly at mention of Wylie, and she suppressed a smile.

"I'll find her," he said. "Meanwhile, lass, do you go and speak to Phaedre—and, lass—"

She had already turned to go; at this, she looked back, surprised.

"I think perhaps ye should tell Phaedre to say nothing unless someone asks her where Betty is, and if they do, to tell you—or me." He straightened abruptly, clearing his throat. "Go find your husband then, lass—and, lass? Make sure no one kens what you're about, aye?"

He lifted one brow, and she nodded in reply. He turned on his heel then, and strode off toward the stables, the fingers of his right hand tapping gently against his coat as though he were deep in thought.

The chilly wind nipped under her skirts and petticoats, belling them out and sending a deep shiver through her flesh. She understood his implication well enough.

If it was neither attempted suicide nor accident—then it might be intended murder. But of whom?

# 43

## FLIRTATIONS

JAMIE HAD GIVEN ME a lingering kiss for encouragement after our interlude, and crashed off through
the underbrush, intending to hunt down Ninian Bell
Hamilton and find out just what the Regulators were up to at
the camp Hunter had mentioned. I followed, after a moment's
interval for decency, but paused at the edge of the grove
before emerging back into public view, to be sure I was
seemly.

I had a rather light-headed sense of well-being, and my
cheeks were very flushed, but I thought that wasn't incriminating in and of itself. Neither would coming out of the wood
be inculpatory; women and men alike often simply stepped
into the shelter of the trees along the lawn in order to relieve
themselves, rather than making their way to the overcrowded
and smelly necessaries. Coming out of the wood flushed and
breathing heavily, with leaves in my hair and sap stains on
my skirt, though, would cause a certain amount of comment
behind the fans.

There were a few sandburs and an empty cicada shell
clinging to my skirt, a ghostly excrescence that I picked off
with a shudder of distaste. There were dogwood petals on my
shoulder; I brushed them off and felt carefully over my hair,
dislodging a few more that fluttered away like scraps of fragrant paper.

Just as I stepped out from under the trees, it occurred to
me to check the back of my skirt for stains or bits of bark,
and I was craning my neck to see over my shoulder when I
walked slap into Phillip Wylie.

"Mrs. Fraser!" He caught me by the shoulders, to prevent my falling backward. "Are you quite all right, my dear?"

"Yes, certainly." My cheeks were flaming legitimately at this point, and I stepped back, shaking myself back into order. Why did I keep bumping into Phillip Wylie? Was the little pest following me? "I do apologize."

"Nonsense, nonsense," he said heartily. "It was my fault entirely. Deuced clumsy of me. May I get you something to restore your spirits, my dear? A glass of cider? Wine? Rum punch? A syllabub? Applejack? Or—no, brandy. Yes, allow me to bring you a bit of brandy to recover from the shock!"

"No, nothing, thank you!" I couldn't help laughing at his absurdities, and he grinned back, obviously thinking himself very witty.

"Well, if you are quite recovered, then, dear lady, you must come with me. I insist."

He had my hand tucked into the crook of his arm, and was towing me determinedly off in the direction of the stable, despite my protests.

"It will take no more than a moment," he assured me. "I have been looking forward all day to showing you my surprise. You will be utterly entranced, I give you my word!"

I subsided feebly; it seemed less trouble to go and look at the damned horses again than to argue with him—and there was plenty of time to speak with Jocasta before the wedding, in any case. This time, though, we skirted the paddock where Lucas and his companions were submitting tolerantly to inspection by a couple of bold gentlemen who had climbed the fence for a closer look.

"That *is* an amazingly good-tempered stallion," I said with approval, mentally contrasting Lucas's kindly manners with Gideon's rapacious personality. Jamie still had not found time to castrate the horse, who had consequently bitten almost everyone, horse and man alike, on the journey to River Run.

"A mark of the breed," Wylie replied, pushing open the door that led to the main stable. "They are the most amiable of horses, though a gentle disposition does not impair their intelligence, I do assure you. This way, Mrs. Fraser."

By contrast with the brilliant day outside, it was pitch-dark in the stable; so dark that I stumbled over an uneven brick in the floor, and Mr. Wylie seized my arm as I lurched forward with a startled cry.

"Are you all right, Mrs. Fraser?" he asked, setting me upright again.

"Yes," I said, a little breathless. In fact I had both stubbed my toe viciously and turned my ankle; my new morocco-heeled shoes were lovely, but I wasn't used to them yet. "Just let me stand a moment—'til my eyes adjust."

He did, but he didn't let go of my arm. Instead, he pulled my hand through the crook of his elbow and set it solidly, to give me more support.

"Lean on me," he said, simply.

I did, and we stood quietly for a moment, me with my injured foot drawn up like a heron's, waiting for my toes to stop throbbing. For once, Mr. Wylie seemed bereft of quips and sallies; perhaps because of the peaceful atmosphere.

Stables on the whole *are* peaceful, horses and the people who tend them being generally kindly sorts of creatures. This one, though, had a special air, both quiet and vibrant. I could hear small rustlings and stampings, and the contented noise of a horse champing hay close at hand.

So close to Phillip Wylie, I was aware of his perfume, but even the expensive whiff of musk and bergamot was overcome by the stable smells. It smelled of fresh straw and grain, of brick and wood, but there was a faint scent as well of more elemental things—manure and blood and milk; the basic elements of motherhood.

"It's rather womblike in here, isn't it?" I said softly. "So warm and dark, I mean. I can almost feel the heartbeat."

Wylie laughed, but quietly.

"That's mine," he said. He touched a hand briefly to his waistcoat, a dark shadow against the pale satin.

My eyes adapted quickly to the dark, but even so, the place was very dim. The lithe shadow-shape of a stable cat glided past, making me wobble and set down my injured foot. It wouldn't yet bear weight, but I could at least put it to the floor.

"Can you stand for a moment alone?" Wylie asked. Without waiting for my reply, he detached himself and went to light a lantern that stood on a nearby stool. There were a few faint chinks of flint and steel, then the wick caught and a soft globe of yellow light ballooned around us. Taking my arm again with his free hand, he led me toward the far end of the stable.

They were in the loose-box at the end. Phillip raised the lantern high, turning to smile at me as he did so. The lantern light gleamed on hide that shone and rippled like midnight water, and glowed in the huge brown eyes of the mare as she turned toward us.

"Oh," I said softly, "how beautiful," and then, a little louder, "Oh!" The mare had moved a little, and her foal peered out from behind her mother's legs. She was long-legged and knob-kneed, her tiny rump and sloping shoulders rounded echoes of her mother's muscular perfection. She had the same large, kind eyes, fringed with long, long lashes—but instead of the sleek hide of rippling black, she was a dark reddish-brown and fuzzy as a rabbit, with an absurd little whisk broom of a tail.

Her dam had the same glorious profusion of flowing mane I had noted on the Friesians in the paddock; the baby had a ridiculous crest of stiff hair, about an inch long, that stuck straight up like a toothbrush.

The foal blinked once, dazzled by the light, then ducked swiftly behind the shelter of her mother's body. A moment later, a small nose protruded cautiously into sight, nostrils twitching. A big eye followed, blinked—and the nose vanished, only to reappear almost instantly, a little further this time.

"Why, you little flirt!" I said, delighted.

Wylie laughed.

"She is indeed," he said, voice filled with pride of ownership. "Are they not magnificent?"

"Well, yes," I said, considering. "They are. Still, I'm not sure that's quite it. 'Magnificent' seems more like what you'd say of a stallion, or a warhorse of some kind. These horses are . . . well, they're *sweet*!"

Wylie gave a small, amused sort of snort.

"Sweet?" he said. *"Sweet?"*

"Well, you know," I said, laughing. "Charming. Good-natured. Delightful."

"All those things," he said, turning to me. "And beautiful, as well." He wasn't looking at the horses, but rather at me, a faint smile on his face.

"Yes," I said, feeling a small, obscure twinge of unease. "Yes, they are very beautiful."

He was standing very close; I took a step to the side and turned away, under the pretext of looking at the horses again. The foal was nuzzling at the mare's swollen udder, scraggy tail waggling with enthusiasm.

"What are their names?" I asked.

Wylie moved to the bar of the loose-box, casually, but in such a way that his arm brushed my sleeve as he reached above me to hang the lantern from a hook on the wall.

"The mare's name is Tessa," he said. "You saw the sire, Lucas. As for the filly . . ." He reached for my hand, and lifted it, smiling. "I thought I might name her La Belle Claire."

I didn't move for a second, stunned by sheer disbelief at the expression that showed quite clearly on Phillip Wylie's face.

"What?" I said blankly. Surely I was wrong, I thought. I tried to snatch my hand away, but I had hesitated one second too long, and his fingers tightened on mine. Surely he wasn't really meaning to . . .

He was.

"Charming," he said softly, and moved closer. "Good-natured. Delightful. And . . . beautiful." He kissed me.

I was so shocked that I didn't move for a moment. His mouth was soft, the kiss brief and chaste. That hardly mattered, though; it was the fact that he had done it.

"Mr. Wylie!" I said. I took a hasty step back, but was brought up short by the rail.

"Mrs. Fraser," he said softly, and took the same step forward. "My dear."

"I am *not* your—" I began, and he kissed me again. Without the least hint of chasteness. Still shocked, but no longer stunned, I shoved him, hard. He wobbled, and lost his grip on my hand, but recovered instantly, seizing me by the arm and slipping his other hand behind me.

"Flirt," he whispered, and lowered his face toward mine. I kicked him. Unfortunately, I kicked him with my injured foot, which deprived the blow of much force, and he ignored it.

I began to struggle in good earnest, as the sense of stunned disbelief faded into the awareness that the young man had one hand firmly on my backside. At the same time, I was aware that there were a good many people in the vicinity of the stable; the last thing I wanted was to attract attention.

"Stop that!" I hissed. "Stop it at once!"

"You madden me," he breathed, pressing me to his bosom and attempting to stick his tongue in my ear.

I certainly thought he was mad, but I declined absolutely to accept any responsibility for the condition. I jerked back as far as I could—not far, with the railing at my back—and fought to get one hand between us. Shock quite gone by now, I was thinking with surprising clarity. I couldn't knee him in the balls; he had one leg thrust between my own, trapping a wodge of skirt in my way. If I could get my hand round his throat and get a sound hold of his carotids, though, he'd drop like a rock.

I did get hold of his throat, but his blasted stock was in the way; my fingers scrabbled at it, and he jerked to the side, grabbing at my hand.

"Please," he said. "I want—"

"I don't give a damn *what* you want!" I said. "Let go of me this instant, you—you—" I groped wildly for some suitable insult. "You—*puppy*!"

Rather to my surprise, he stopped. His face couldn't go pale, being already covered in rice flour—I could taste it on my lips—but his mouth was set, and his expression was . . . rather wounded.

"Is that really what you think of me?" he asked in a low voice.

"Yes, it bloody is!" I said. "What else am I to think? Have you lost your mind, behaving in this—this despicable fashion? What is the matter with you?"

"Despicable?" He seemed quite taken aback to hear his

advances described in this fashion. "But I—that is, you—I thought you were . . . I mean, might be not averse—"

"You can't," I said, positively. "You can't possibly have thought anything of the sort. I've never given you the *slightest* reason to think such a thing!" Nor had I—intentionally. The uneasy thought came to me, though, that perhaps my perceptions of my own behavior were not quite the same as Phillip Wylie's.

"Oh, haven't you?" His face was changing, clouding with anger. "I beg to differ with you, madam!"

I had told him I was old enough to be his mother; it had never for a moment occurred to me that he didn't believe it.

"Flirt," he said again, though in quite a different tone than the first time. "No reason? You have given me every reason, since the first occasion of our meeting."

"What?" My voice went up a tone, in incredulity. "I've never done anything but engage you in civil conversation. If that constitutes flirtation in *your* book, my lad, then—"

"Don't call me that!"

Oh, so he *had* noticed that there was a difference of age. He simply hadn't appreciated the magnitude, I thought. It came to me, with a certain feeling of apprehension, that at Phillip's level of society, most flirtation was indeed conducted under the guise of banter. What in the name of God had I said to him?

I had some dim recollection of having discussed the Stamp Act with him and his friend Stanhope. Yes, taxes, and, I thought, horses—but surely that couldn't have been sufficient to inflame his misapprehensions?

*"Thine eyes are like the fishpools in Heshbon,"* he said, low-voiced and bitter. "Do you not recall the evening when I said that to you? The Song of Solomon is merely 'civil conversation' to you, is it?"

"Good grief." I was, despite myself, beginning to feel slightly guilty; we *had* had a brief exchange along those lines, at Jocasta's party, two or three years ago. And he remembered it? The Song of Solomon was reasonably heady stuff; perhaps the simple reference . . . Then I shook myself mentally, and drew myself up straight.

"Nonsense," I declared. "You were teasing me, and I simply answered you in kind. Now, I really must—"

"You came in here with me today. Alone." He took another step toward me, eyes determined. He was talking himself back into it, the fatheaded popinjay!

"Mr. Wylie," I said firmly, sliding sideways. "I am terribly sorry if you have somehow misunderstood the situation, but I am very happily married, and I have no romantic interest in you whatsoever. And now, if you will excuse me . . ." I ducked past him, and hurried out of the stable, as fast as my shoes would allow. He made no effort to follow me, though, and I reached the outdoors unmolested, my heart beating fast.

There were people near the paddock; I turned in the other direction, going round the end of the stable block before anyone should see me. Once out of sight, I made a swift inventory, checking to be sure that I didn't look too disheveled. I didn't know whether anyone had seen me going into the stable with Wylie; I could only hope no one had seen my hasty exit.

Only one lock of hair had come down in the recent contretemps; I pinned it carefully back, and dusted a few bits of straw from my skirts. Fortunately, he hadn't torn my clothes; a retucked kerchief and I was quite decent again.

"Are ye all right, Sassenach?"

I leaped like a gaffed salmon, and so did my heart. I whirled, adrenaline jolting through my chest like an electic current, to find Jamie standing beside me, frowning slightly as he surveyed me.

"What have ye been doing, Sassenach?"

My heart was still stuck in my throat, choking me, but I forced out what I hoped were a few nonchalant words.

"Nothing. I mean, looking at the horses—horse. The mare. She has a new foal."

"Aye, I know," he said, looking at me oddly.

"Did you find Ninian? What did he have to say?" I groped behind my head, tidying my hair and taking the opportunity to turn away a little, to avoid his eye.

"He says it's true—though I hadna doubted it. There are more than a thousand men, camped near Salisbury. And more joining them each day, he says. The auld mumper is pleased about it!" He frowned, drumming the two stiff fingers of his right hand lightly against his leg, and I realized that he was rather worried.

Not without cause. Putting aside the threat of conflict itself, it was spring. Only the fact that River Run was in the piedmont had allowed us to come to Jocasta's wedding; down here, the woods were cloudy with blossom and crocuses popped through the earth like orange and purple dragon's-teeth, but the mountains were still cloaked in snow, the tree branches sporting swollen buds. In two weeks or so, those buds would burst, and it would be time for the spring planting on Fraser's Ridge.

True, Jamie had provided for such an emergency by finding old Arch Bug, but Arch could manage only so much by himself. And as for the tenants and homesteaders . . . if the militia were raised again, the women would be left to do the planting alone.

"The men in this camp—they're men who've left their land, then?" Salisbury was in the piedmont, as well. It wasn't thinkable for working farmers to abandon their land at this time of year for the sake of protest against the government, no matter how annoyed they were.

"Left it, or lost it," he said briefly. The frown deepened as he looked at me. "Have ye spoken wi' my aunt?"

"Ah . . . no," I said, feeling guilty. "Not yet. I was just going . . . oh—you said there was another problem. What else has happened?"

He made a sound like a hissing teakettle, which for him betokened rare impatience.

"Christ, I'd nearly forgot her. One of the slave women's been poisoned, I think."

"What? Who? How?" My hands dropped from my hair as I stared at him. "Why didn't you tell me?"

"I *am* telling ye, am I not? Dinna fash yourself, she's in no danger. Only stinking drunk." He twitched his shoulders irritably. "The only difficulty is that perhaps it wasna her that was meant to be poisoned. I've sent Roger Mac and Brianna to look, and they've not come back to say anyone's dead, so maybe not."

"*Maybe* not?" I rubbed the bridge of my nose, distracted from the extant worries by this new development. "I grant you, alcohol is poisonous, not that anyone seems ever to realize it, but there's a difference between being drunk and being deliberately poisoned. What do you mean—"

"Sassenach," he interrupted.

"What?"

"What in the name o' God have ye been doing?" he burst out.

I stared at him in bewilderment. His face had been growing redder as we talked, though I had supposed it to be only frustration and worry over Ninian, and the Regulators. It dawned on me, catching a dangerous blue glint in his eye, that there was something rather more personal about his attitude. I tilted my head to one side, giving him a wary look.

"What do you mean, what have I been doing?"

His lips pressed tight together, and he didn't answer. Instead, he extended a forefinger and touched it, very delicately, beside my mouth. He turned his hand over then, and presented me with a small dark object clinging to the tip of his finger—Phillip Wylie's star-shaped black beauty mark.

"Oh." I felt a distinct buzzing in my ears. "That. Er . . ." My head felt light, and small spots—all shaped like black stars—danced before my eyes.

"Yes, that," he snapped. "Christ, woman! I'm deviled to death wi' Duncan's havers and Ninian's pranks—and why did ye not tell me he'd been fighting wi' Barlow?"

"I'd scarcely describe it as a fight," I said, struggling to regain a sense of coolness. "Besides, Major MacDonald put a stop to it since *you* were nowhere to be found. And if you want to be told things, the Major wants—"

"I ken what he wants." He dismissed the Major with a curt flick of his hand. "Aye, I'm up to my ears in Majors and Regulators and drunken maid servants, and *you're* out in the stable, canoodling wi' that fop!"

I felt the blood rising behind my eyes, and curled my fists, in order to control the impulse to slap him.

"I was *not* 'canoodling' in the slightest degree, and you know it! The beastly little twerp made a pass at me, that's all."

"A pass? Made love to ye, ye mean? Aye, I can see that!"

"He did not!"

"Oh, aye? Ye asked him to let ye try his bawbee on for luck, then?" He waggled the finger with the black patch under my nose, and I slapped it away, recalling a moment too late that "make love to" merely meant to engage in amorous flirtation, rather than fornication.

"I *mean*," I said, through clenched teeth, "that he kissed me. Probably for a joke. I'm old enough to be his mother, for God's sake!"

"More like his grandmother," Jamie said brutally. "Kissed ye, forbye—why in hell did ye encourage him, Sassenach?"

My mouth dropped open in outrage—insulted as much at being called Phillip Wylie's grandmother as at the accusation of having encouraged him.

"Encourage him? Why, you bloody idiot! You know perfectly well I didn't encourage him!"

"Your own daughter saw ye go in there with him! Have ye no shame? With all else there is to deal with here, am I to be forced to call the man out, as well?"

I felt a slight qualm at the thought of Brianna, and a larger one at the thought of Jamie challenging Wylie to a duel. He wasn't wearing his sword, but he'd brought it with him. I stoutly dismissed both thoughts.

"*My* daughter is neither a fool nor an evil-minded gossip," I said, with immense dignity. "She wouldn't think a thing of my going to look at a horse, and why ought she? Why ought anyone, for that matter?"

He blew out a long breath through pursed lips, and glared at me.

"Why, indeed? Perhaps because everyone saw ye flirt with him on the lawn? Because they saw him follow ye about like a dog after a bitch in heat?" He must have seen my expression alter dangerously at that, for he coughed briefly and hurried on.

"More than one person's seen fit to mention it to me. D'ye think I like bein' made a public laughingstock, Sassenach?"

"You—you—" Fury choked me. I wanted to hit him, but I could see interested heads turning toward us. "'Bitch in heat'? How dare you say such a thing to me, you bloody bastard?"

He had the decency to look slightly abashed at that, though he was still glowering.

"Aye, well. I shouldna have said it quite that way. I didna mean—but ye *did* go off with him, Sassenach. As though I hadna enough to contend with, my own wife . . . and if ye'd gone to see my aunt, as I asked ye, then it wouldna have happened in the first place. Now see what ye've done!"

I had changed my mind about the desirability of a duel. I wanted Jamie and Phillip Wylie to kill each other, promptly, publicly, and with the maximum amount of blood. I also didn't care who was looking. I made a very serious effort to castrate him with my bare hands, and he grabbed my wrists, pulling them up sharply.

"Christ! Folk are watching, Sassenach!"

"I . . . don't . . . bloody . . . care!" I hissed, struggling to get free. "Let go of me, and I'll fucking give them something to watch!"

I didn't take my eyes off his face, but I was aware of a good many other faces turning toward us in the crowd on the lawn. So was he. His brows drew together for a moment, then his face set in sudden decision.

"All right, then," he said. "Let them watch."

He wrapped his arms around me, pressed me tight against himself, and kissed me. Unable to get loose, I quit fighting, and went stiff and furious instead. In the distance, I could hear laughter and raucous whoops of encouragement. Ninian Hamilton shouted something in Gaelic that I was pleased not to understand.

He finally moved his lips off mine, still holding me tightly against him, and very slowly bent his head, his cheek lying cool and firm next to mine. His body was firm, too, and not at all cool. The heat of him was leaching through at least six layers of cloth to reach my own skin: shirt, waistcoat, coat, gown, shift, and stays. Whether it was anger, arousal, or both, he was fully stoked and blazing like a furnace.

"I'm sorry," he said quietly, his breath hot and tickling in my ear. "I didna mean to insult ye. Truly. Shall I kill him, and then myself?"

I relaxed, very slightly. My hips were pressed solidly against him, and with only five layers of fabric between us there, the effect was reassuring.

"Perhaps not quite yet," I said. I felt light-headed from the rush of adrenaline, and took a deep breath to steady myself. Then I drew back a little, recoiling from the pungent reek that wafted off his clothes. Had I not been so upset, I would have noticed immediately that he was the source of the vile aroma I had been smelling.

"What on earth have you been doing?" I sniffed at the breast of his coat, frowning. "You smell terrible! Like—"

"Manure," he said, sounding resigned. "Aye, I know." His arms relaxed.

"Yes, manure," I said, sniffing further. "And rum punch"—he hadn't been drinking rum punch himself, though; I had tasted nothing but brandy when he kissed me—"and something awful, like old sweat, and—"

"Boiled turnips," he said, sounding more resigned. "Aye, the maid servant I was telling ye about, Sassenach. Betty, she's called." He tucked my hand into the crook of his arm, and with a deep bow of acknowledgment toward the crowd—who all applauded, damn them—turned to steer me toward the house.

"It would be as well if ye can get anything sensible out of her," he said, with a glance toward the sun, which hung in mid-sky above the tops of the willows along the river. "But it's growing late; I think perhaps ye'd best go up and speak to my aunt first, if there's to be a wedding at four o'clock."

I took a deep breath, trying to settle myself. A good deal of unexpended emotion was still sloshing round inside me, but there was plainly work to do.

"Right, then," I said. "I'll see Jocasta, and then have a look at Betty. As for Phillip Wylie . . ."

"As for Phillip Wylie," he interrupted, "dinna give him another thought, Sassenach." A certain look of inward intentness grew in his eyes. "I'll take care of him, later."

# 44

## PRIVATE PARTS

I LEFT JAMIE in the parlor, and made my way up the stairs and along the hall toward Jocasta's room, nodding distractedly to friends and acquaintances encountered along the way. I was disconcerted, annoyed—and at the same time, reluctantly amused. I hadn't spent so much time in bemused contemplation of a penis since I was sixteen or so, and here I was, preoccupied with three of the things.

Finding myself alone in the hall, I opened my fan, peering thoughtfully into the tiny round looking glass that served as a lake in the pastoral scene painted on it. Meant as an aid to intrigue rather than grooming, the glass showed me no more than a few square inches of my face at once—one eye and its arched brow regarded me quizzically.

It was quite a pretty eye, I admitted. There were lines around it, true, but it was nicely shaped, gracefully lidded, and equipped with long, curving lashes whose dark sable complemented the black pupil and contrasted very strikingly with the gold-flecked amber of the iris.

I moved the fan a bit, to get a view of my mouth. Full-lipped, and rather fuller than usual at present, to say nothing of a dark, moist pink. The lips looked as though someone had been kissing them rather roughly. They also looked as though they'd liked it.

"Hm!" I said, and snapped shut the fan.

With my blood no longer boiling, I could admit that Jamie might perhaps be right about Phillip Wylie's intent in making objectionable advances to me. He might not be, too. But regardless of the young man's underlying motives, I did have incontrovertible proof that he had found me physically appealing, grandmother or not. I rather thought I wouldn't mention that to Jamie, though; Phillip Wylie was a very annoying young man, but upon cooler reflection, I had decided that I would prefer not to have him disemboweled on the front lawn, after all.

Still, maturity did alter one's perspective somewhat. For all the personal implications of those male members in an excited state, it was the flaccid one that most interested me at the moment. My fingers itched to get hold of Duncan Innes's private parts—figuratively, at least.

There were not so many kinds of trauma, short of outright castration, that would cause physical impotence. Surgery nowadays being the primitive affair it was, I supposed that it was possible that whatever doctor had attended the original injury—if one did—had in fact simply removed both testicles. If that were the case, though, would Duncan not have said so?

Well, perhaps not. Duncan was an intensely shy and modest man, and even a more extroverted personality might hesitate to confide a misfortune of that extent, even to an intimate friend. Could he have concealed such an injury in the close confines of a prison, though? I drummed my fingers on the inlaid marquetry of the table outside Jocasta's door, considering.

It was certainly possible for men to go for several years without bathing; I'd seen a few who obviously had. On the other hand, the prisoners at Ardsmuir had been forced to work outdoors, cutting peat and quarrying stone; they would have had regular access to open water, and presumably would at least have washed periodically, if only to keep the itching of vermin at bay. I supposed one could wash without necessarily stripping naked, though.

I suspected that Duncan was still more or less intact. It was much more likely, I thought, that his impotence was psychological in origin; having one's testes badly bruised or crushed was bound to give a man pause, after all, and an early experiment might easily have convinced Duncan that all was up with him—or rather, down.

I paused before knocking, but not for long. I had had

some experience of giving people bad news, after all, and the one thing that experience had taught me was that there was no point in preparation, or worry over what to say. Eloquence didn't help, and bluntness was no bar to sympathy.

I rapped sharply on the door, and entered at Jocasta's invitation.

Father LeClerc was present, seated at a small table in the corner, dealing in a workmanlike manner with a large assortment of edibles. Two bottles of wine—one empty—stood on the table as well, and the priest looked up at my entrance with a greasily beaming smile that appeared to go round his face and tie together behind his ears.

"Tally-ho, Madame!" he said cheerfully, and brandished a turkey leg at me in greeting. "Tally-ho, Tally-ho!"

*"Bonjour"* seemed almost repressive by contrast, so I contented myself with a curtsy and a brief "Cheerio, then!" in reply.

There was clearly no way of dislodging the priest, and nowhere else to take Jocasta, as Phaedre was in the dressing room, making a great to-do with a pair of clothes brushes. Still, given the limits of Father LeClerc's English, I supposed absolute privacy was not a requirement.

I touched Jocasta's elbow, therefore, and murmured discreetly that perhaps we might sit down in the window seat, as I had something of importance to discuss with her. She looked surprised, but nodded, and with a bow of excuse toward Father LeClerc—who didn't notice, being occupied with a stubborn bit of gristle—came to sit down beside me.

"Aye, niece?" she said, having adjusted her skirts over her knees. "What is it, then?"

"Well," I said, taking a deep breath, "it's to do with Duncan. You see . . ."

And she did. Her face grew quite blank with astonishment as I began to talk, but I was conscious of a growing sense of something else in her attitude as she listened—almost . . . relief, I thought, surprised.

Her lips pursed in absorption, the blind blue eyes fixed in her usual unsettling way, a little over my right shoulder. There was concern in her manner, but no great distress. Her expression was altering, in fact, changing from startlement to the look of one who suddenly finds an explanation for a previously troubling circumstance—and is both relieved and satisfied to have discovered it.

It occurred to me that she and Duncan *had* been living under the same roof for more than a year, and had been engaged to be married for months. Duncan's attitude toward her in public was always respectful—even deferential—and thoughtful, but he made no physical gestures of tenderness or possession toward her. That was not unusual in the least, for the times; though some gentlemen were demonstrative toward their wives, others were not. But perhaps he hadn't made such gestures in private, either, and she had expected them.

She had been beautiful, was handsome still, and quite accustomed to the admiration of men; sightless or not, I had seen her flirt skillfully with Andrew MacNeill, Ninian Bell Hamilton, Richard Caswell—even with Farquard Campbell. Perhaps she had been surprised, and even mildly discomfited, to provoke no apparent show of physical interest from Duncan.

Now she knew why, though, and drew in a deep breath, shaking her head slowly.

"My God, the poor man," she said. "To suffer such a thing, and come to terms with it and then, all at once, to have it be dragged up afresh to worry him. Dear Bride, why cannot the past leave us be in what peace we have made with it?" She looked down, blinking, and I was both surprised and touched to see that her eyes were moist.

A large presence loomed up suddenly beyond her, and I glanced up to see Father LeClerc hovering over us, like a sympathetic thundercloud in his black habit.

"Is there trouble?" he said to me, in French. "Monsieur Duncan, he has suffered some injury?"

Jocasta didn't speak more than *"Comment allez-vous?"* French, but was clearly able to understand the tone of the question, as well as to pick out Duncan's name.

"Don't tell him," she said to me, with some urgency, putting her hand on my knee.

"No, no," I assured her. I looked up at the priest, flicking my fingers in indication that there was nothing to worry about.

*"Non, non,"* I said in turn to him. *"Ce n'est rien."* It's nothing.

He frowned at me, uncertain, then glanced at Jocasta.

"A difficulty of the marriage bed, is it?" he asked bluntly, in French. My face must have betrayed dismay at this, for he gestured discreetly downward, toward the front of his habit. "I heard the word 'scrotum,' Madame, and think you do not speak of animals."

I realized—a good bit too late—that while Father LeClerc spoke no English, he most certainly spoke Latin.

*"Merde,"* I said under my breath, causing Jocasta, who had glanced up sharply at the word "scrotum" herself, to turn back toward me. I patted her hand reassuringly, trying to make up my mind what to do. Father LeClerc was regarding us with curiosity, but also with great kindness in his soft brown eyes.

"I'm afraid he's guessed the general shape of things," I said apologetically to Jocasta. "I think perhaps I had better explain."

Her upper teeth fastened over her lower lip, but she made no demur, and I explained matters in French, as briefly as I could. The priest's eyebrows rose, and he clutched automatically for the wooden rosary that hung from his belt.

*"Oui, merde, Madame,"* he said. *"Quelle tragédie."* He crossed himself briefly with the crucifix, then quite unselfconsciously wiped the grease from his beard onto his sleeve, and sat down beside Jocasta.

"Ask her, please, Madame, what is her desire in this matter," he said to me. The tone was polite, but it was an order.

"Her desire?"

*"Oui.* Does she wish still to be married to Monsieur Duncan, even knowing this? For see you, Madame, by the laws of Holy Mother Church, such an impediment to consummation is a bar to true marriage. I ought not to administer the sacrament of matrimony, knowing this. However—" he hesitated, pursing his lips in thought as he glanced at Jocasta. "However, the purpose of such provision is the intent that marriage

shall be a fruitful union, if God so wills. In this case, there is no question of God willing such a thing. So, you see . . ." He raised one shoulder in a Gallic shrug.

I translated this question to Jocasta, who had been squinting toward the priest, as though she could divine his meaning by sheer force of will. Enlightened, her face grew blank, and she sat back a little. Her face had assumed a MacKenzie look; that characteristic calm, still mask that meant a great deal of furious thinking was going on behind it.

I was slightly disturbed, and not only on Duncan's behalf. It hadn't occurred to me that this revelation could prevent the wedding. Jamie wanted his aunt protected, and Duncan provided for. The marriage had seemed the perfect answer; he would be perturbed if things should come unstuck at this late date.

After only a moment, though, Jocasta stirred, letting out her breath in a deep sigh.

"Well, thank Christ I'd the luck to get a Jesuit," she said dryly. "One of them could argue the Pope out of his drawers, let alone deal wi' a small matter of reading the Lord's mind. Aye, tell him I do desire to be married, still."

I conveyed this to Father LeClerc, who frowned slightly, examining Jocasta with great attention. Unaware of this scrutiny, she raised one brow, waiting for his reply.

He cleared his throat, and spoke, his eyes still on her, though he was speaking to me.

"Tell her this, Madame, if you please. While it is true that procreation is the basis of this law of the Church, that is not the only matter to consider. For marriage—true marriage of a man and woman—this . . . union of the flesh, it is important of itself. The language of the rite—the two shall become one flesh, it says, and there is reason for that. Much happens between two people who share a bed, and joy in each other. That is not all a marriage is, but it is something, truly."

He spoke with great seriousness, and I must have looked surprised, for he smiled slightly, now looking directly at me.

"I have not always been a priest, Madame," he said. "I was married once. I know what that is, as I know what it is to put aside forever that . . . fleshly . . . part of life." The wooden beads of his rosary clicked softly together as he shifted.

I nodded, took a deep breath, and translated this directly as he had said it. Jocasta listened, but took no time for thought this time; her mind was made up.

"Tell him I thank him for his advice," she said, with only the slightest edge in her voice. "I too have been married before—more than once. And with his help, I shall be married once again. Today."

I translated, but he had already taken her meaning from her upright posture and the tone of her voice. He sat for a moment, rubbing his beads between his fingers, then nodded.

*"Oui, Madame,"* he said. He reached over and squeezed her hand in gentle encouragement. "Tally-ho, Madame!"

# 45

# IF IT QUACKS . . .

WELL, THAT WAS ONE DOWN, I thought, mounting the stairs to the attic. Next on the agenda of pressing affairs, the slave Betty. Had she really been drugged? It had been more than two hours since Jamie had discovered her in the kitchen garden, but I thought I might still be able to discern symptoms, if she had been as badly affected as he had described her. I heard the muffled chime of the grandfather clock far below. One, two, three. An hour left before the wedding—though it could easily be postponed a bit, if Betty required more attention than I expected.

Given the undesirable position of Catholics in the colony, Jocasta would not offend her guests—mostly Protestants of one stripe or another—by obliging them to witness the Popish ceremony itself. The marriage would be performed discreetly, in her boudoir, and then the newlywed couple would descend the stairs arm-in-arm, to celebrate with their friends, all of whom could then diplomatically pretend that Father LeClerc was merely an eccentrically dressed wedding guest.

As I neared the attic, I was surprised to hear a murmur of voices above. The door to the female slaves' dormitory stood ajar; I pushed it open, to discover Ulysses standing at the head of one narrow bed, arms folded, looking like an avenging angel carved in ebony. Obviously, he considered this unfortunate occurrence to be a grave dereliction of duty on Betty's part. A small, dapper man in a frock coat and a large wig stooped by her side, some small object in his hand.

Before I could speak, he pressed this against the maid's limp arm. There was a small, sharp *click!* and he removed the object, leaving a rectangle of welling blood, a rich dark red against the slave's brown skin. The drops bloomed, merged, and began to trickle down her arm and into a bleeding bowl at her elbow.

"A scarificator," the little man explained to Ulysses, with some pride, displaying his object. "A great improvement over such crudities as lancets and fleams. Got it from Philadelphia!"

The butler bent his head courteously, either in acceptance of the invitation to examine the instrument, or acknowledgment of its distinguished provenance.

"I am sure Mistress Cameron is most obliged for your kind condescension, Dr. Fentiman," he murmured.

Fentiman. So, this was the medical establishment of Cross Creek. I cleared my throat and Ulysses lifted his head, eyes alert.

"Mistress Fraser," he said, with a small bow. "Dr. Fentiman has just been—"

"Mistress Fraser?" Doctor Fentiman had swung round, and was eyeing me with the same sort of suspicious interest with which I was viewing him. Evidently he'd been hearing things, too. Manners triumphed, though, and he made me a leg, one hand to the bosom of his satin waistcoat.

"Your servant, ma'am," he said, wobbling slightly as he came upright again. I smelled gin on his breath, and saw it in the blossoms of burst blood vessels in his nose and cheeks.

"Enchanted, I'm sure," I said, giving him my hand to kiss. He looked at first surprised, but then bent over it with a deep flourish. I looked over his powdered head, trying to make out as much as I could in the dim light of the attic.

Betty might as well have been dead for a week, judging from the ashy cast of her skin, but such light as there was in the attic came through thick oiled paper nailed across the tiny gables. Ulysses himself looked gray, like charcoal frosted with ash.

The blood from the slave's arm had already begun to clot; that was good—though I shuddered to think how many people Fentiman might have used his nasty little implement on since acquiring it. His case was open on the floor beside the bed, and I saw no indication that he thought of cleaning his instruments between usages.

"Your kindness does you great credit, Mrs. Fraser," the doctor pronounced, straightening up, but keeping hold of my hand—to steady himself, I thought. "There is no need of your troubling yourself, however. Mrs. Cameron is an old and valued acquaintance; I am quite content to attend her slave." He smiled benignly, blinking in an attempt to bring me into focus.

I could hear the maid's breathing, deep and stertorous, but quite regular. I itched to get my hands on her pulse. I inhaled deeply, as unobtrusively as possible. Above the pungent scent of Dr. Fentiman's wig, which had evidently been treated with nettle powder and hyssop against lice, and a strong fog of ancient sweat and tobacco from the doctor's body, I caught the sharp copper scent of fresh blood, and the older reek of caked, decayed blood from the inside of his case. No, Fentiman didn't clean his blades.

Beyond that, I could easily smell the alcoholic miasma that Jamie and Brianna had described, but I couldn't tell how much of it came from Betty, and how much from Fentiman. If there was any hint of laudanum in the mix, I would have to get closer to detect it, and do it fast, before the volatile aromatic oils could completely evanesce.

"How exceedingly kind of you, Doctor," I said, smiling insincerely. "I'm sure my husband's aunt is most grateful for your efforts. But surely a gentleman such as yourself—I mean, you must have many more important demands upon your attention. I'm sure that Ulysses and I can see to the woman's nursing; you'll surely be missed by your companions." Especially those eager to win a few pounds off you at cards, I thought. They'll want a chance before you sober up!

Rather to my surprise, the doctor did not at once succumb to the flattery of this speech. Releasing my hand, he smiled at me with an insincerity equal to my own.

"Oh, no, not at all, my dear. I assure you, no nursing is required here. It is no more than a simple case of overindulgence, after all. I have administered a strong emetic; as soon as it shall have its effect, the woman may safely be left. Do return to your pleasures, my dear lady; there is no need for you to risk soiling such a lovely gown, no need at all."

Before I could remonstrate, there came a heavy gagging noise from the bed, and Doctor Fentiman turned at once, snatching up the chamber pot from beneath the bed.

In spite of his own impairment, he was commendably attentive to the patient. I would myself have hesitated to administer an emetic to a comatose patient, but I had to admit that it wasn't an unreasonable thing to do in a case of suspected poisoning, even if the poison was something as commonly accepted as alcohol—and if Dr. Fentiman had perhaps detected the same thing Jamie had . . .

The slave had eaten heavily; no surprise, with so much food available for the festivities. That in itself might have saved her life, I thought, slowing the absorption of alcohol—and anything else—into her bloodstream. The vomitus reeked of mingled rum and brandy, but I did think I smelled the ghost of opium as well, faint and sickly sweet, among the other odors.

"What sort of emetic did you use?" I asked, bending over the woman and thumbing open one eye. The iris stared upward, brown and glassy as an agate marble, the pupil shrunk to a pinpoint. Ha, definitely opium.

"Mrs. Fraser!" Dr. Fentiman glared at me in irritation, his wig fallen half askew over one ear. "Do you go, please, and cease interfering! I am greatly occupied, and have no time to indulge your fancies. You, sir—remove her!" He waved a hand at Ulysses and turned back to the bed, shoving his wig into place as he did so.

"Why, you little—" I choked off the intended epithet, seeing Ulysses take an uncertain step toward me. He clearly hesitated to remove me bodily, but it was just as clear that he would obey the Doctor's orders in preference to mine.

Trembling with fury, I swept around and left the room.

Jamie was waiting for me at the foot of the stair. Seeing my face as I descended, he took my arm at once and led me out into the yard.

"That—that—" Words failed me.

"Officious worm?" he supplied helpfully. "Unsonsie sharg?"

"Yes! Did you hear him?! The gall of him, that jumped-up butcher, that bloody little . . . squirt! No time to indulge my fancies! How dare he?"

Jamie made a guttural noise, indicating sympathetic outrage.

"Shall I go up and knivvle him?" he inquired, hand on his dirk. "I could gut him for ye—or just beat his face in, if ye'd rather."

Attractive as this prospect sounded, I was forced to decline.

"Well . . . no," I said, bringing my choler under control with some difficulty. "No, I don't think you'd better do that."

The echo of our similar conversation regarding Phillip Wylie struck me. It struck Jamie, too; I saw one corner of his long mouth curl with wry humor.

"Damn," I said ruefully.

"Aye," he agreed, reluctantly taking his hand off his dirk. "It doesna look as though I shall be allowed to spill anyone's blood today, does it?"

"You want to, do you?"

"Verra much," he said, dryly. "So do you, Sassenach, from the looks of it."

I couldn't argue with that; I should have liked nothing better than to disembowel Dr. Fentiman with a blunt spoon. Instead, I rubbed a hand over my face, and took a deep breath, bringing my feelings back into some semblance of order.

"Is he likely to kill the woman?" Jamie asked, jerking his chin back toward the house.

"Not immediately." Bleeding and purging were highly objectionable and possibly dangerous, but not likely to be instantly fatal. "Oh—you were probably right about the laudanum."

Jamie nodded, pursing his lips thoughtfully.

"Well, then. The important thing is to speak wi' Betty, once she's in a condition to make sense. Ye dinna think Fentiman's the sort to stand watch over a sick slave's bed?"

Now it was my turn to think, but finally I shook my head.

"No. He *was* doing his best for her," I admitted reluctantly. "But so far as I could tell, she's in no great danger. She should be watched, but only in case she should vomit and choke in her sleep, and I doubt he'd hang about to do that, even if he thinks of it."

"Well, then." He stood in thought for a moment, the breeze lifting strands of red hair from the crown of his head. "I've sent Brianna and her man to poke about and see whether any of the guests is snoring in a corner. I'll go and do the same for the slaves. Can ye maybe steal up to the attic when Fentiman's gone, and talk to Betty as soon as she wakes?"

"I imagine so." I would have gone up in any case, if only to assure myself of Betty's welfare. "Don't take too long, though; they're almost ready for the wedding."

We stood for a moment, looking at each other.

"Dinna fash yourself, Sassenach," he said softly, and tucked a wisp of hair behind my ear. "The doctor's a wee fool; dinna mind him."

I touched his arm, thankful for his comfort and wishing to offer him the same solace for bruised feelings.

"I am sorry about Phillip Wylie," I said. I realized at once that no matter what my intentions, the effect of this reminder had not been soothing. The soft curve of his mouth tightened, and he moved back, his shoulders stiffening.

"Dinna fash yourself about him, either, Sassenach," he said. His voice was still soft, but there was nothing even slightly reassuring in it. "I shall settle wi' Mr. Wylie, by and by."

"But—" I broke off, helpless. Evidently there was nothing I could say or do that would make matters right again. If Jamie felt his honor offended—and he plainly did, regardless of what I said—then Wylie would pay for it, and that was all about it.

"You are the most pigheaded man I have ever met," I said crossly.

"Thank you," he said, with a small bow.

"That was not a compliment!"

"Aye, it was." And with another bow, he turned on his heel and strode off on his errand.

46

## QUICKSILVER

TO JAMIE'S RELIEF, the wedding went off with no further difficulties. The ceremony—conducted in French—took place in Jocasta's small sitting room upstairs, attended only by the bridal pair, the priest, himself and Claire as witnesses, and Brianna and her young man. Jemmy had been present, too, but scarcely counted, as he had slept through the service.

Duncan had been pale, but composed, and Jamie's aunt had spoken her vows in a firm voice, with no evidence of hesitation. Brianna, recently wed herself and sentimental in consequence, had looked on with misty approbation, squeezing her lad's arm tight, and Roger Mac looking down at her tender-eyed. Even knowing what he did regarding the nature of this particular marriage, Jamie had felt moved himself by the sacrament, and had lifted Claire's fingers to his lips, brushing a brief kiss across them as the fat little priest intoned the blessing.

Then, the formalities concluded and the wedding contracts signed, they had all come down to join the guests at a lavish wedding supper, under the light of torches that lined the terrace, their long flames streaming over tables that groaned with the abundance of River Run.

He took a glass of wine from one of the tables, and leaned back against the low terrace wall, feeling the tension of the day drain away down his spine. One down, then.

The maid Betty was still out like a brained ox, but safe enough for the present. No one else had been found poisoned, so it was likely she'd taken the stuff herself. Auld Ninian and Barlow were both nearly as legless as the maid, and no threat to each other or anyone else. And whatever Husband and his Regulators were up to, they were doing it at a safe distance. Jamie felt pleasantly light, relieved of responsibility, and ready to turn his mind to recreation.

He raised his glass in automatic salute to Caswell and Osborn, who wandered by, heads together in earnest discourse. He had no wish for political conversation, though; he got up and turned aside, making his way through the crowds near the refreshment tables.

What he really wanted was his wife. Early as it was, the sky was already dark, and a sense of reckless festivity was spreading over the house and terrace as the torches flamed high. The air was cold, and with good wine pulsing through his blood, his hands recalled the warm touch of her under her skirt in the grove, soft and succulent as a split peach in his palm, sun-ripe and juicy.

He wanted her badly.

There. At the end of the terrace, torchlight shining on the waves of her hair, where it swooped up under that ridiculous bit of lace. His fingers twitched; once he got her alone, he'd take out her pins, one by one, and pile up her hair on her head with his hands, for the pleasure of letting it fall again, loose down her back.

She was laughing at something Lloyd Stanhope had said, a glass in her hand. Her face was slightly flushed with wine and the sight of it gave him a pleasurable itch of anticipation.

Bedding her could be anything from tenderness to riot,

but to take her when she was a bit the worse for drink was always a particular delight.

Intoxicated, she took less care for him than usual; abandoned and oblivious to all but her own pleasure, she would rake him, bite him—and beg him to serve her so, as well. He loved the feeling of power in it, the tantalizing choice between joining her at once in animal lust, or of holding himself—for a time—in check, so as to drive her at his whim.

He sipped his own wine, savoring the rare pleasure of a decent vintage, and watched her covertly. She was the center of a small knot of gentlemen, with whom she seemed to be enjoying a clash of wits. A glass or two loosened her tongue and limbered her mind, as it did his. A few glasses more, and her glow would turn to a molten heat. It was early yet, and the real feasting not yet started.

He caught her eye briefly on him, and smiled. He held the goblet by its bowl and his fingers curved round the smooth glass as though it were her breast. She saw, and understood. She lowered her lashes in coquetry to him, and turned back to her conversation, color heightened.

The delightful paradox of having her in drink was that, having abandoned consciousness of him as anything save the agent of her own sensation, she would also cease to guard herself in any way, and thus lay entirely open to him. He might tease and caress, or churn her like butter, leading her through frenzy to gasping limpness beneath him, lying at his mercy.

She was using her fan to good effect, opening her eyes wide over the edge of it, in feigned shock at something that sodomite Forbes had said. He ran the tip of his tongue thoughtfully within the tender margin of his lower lip, tasting sweet silver blood in memory. Mercy? No, he would have none.

That decision made, he was turning his mind to the more practical problem of finding a spot sufficiently secluded to carry out this engaging agenda, but was interrupted by the advent of Milford Lyon, looking sleek and full of himself. He had been introduced, but knew little of the man.

"Mr. Fraser. A word with you, sir?"

"Your servant, sir."

He turned aside for a moment to set down his glass, a slight shift of his weight enough to effect discreet adjustment of his plaid, glad that he wasn't wearing tight satin breeks like that fop, Wylie. Indecent, he thought them, and grossly uncomfortable, forbye. Why, a man would be risking slow emasculation in female company, if he were not a natural eunuch—and Wylie clearly wasn't that, for all his powder and patches. A belted plaid, though, could hide a multitude of sins—or at the least, a dirk and pistol—let alone a random cockstand.

"Shall we walk a bit, Mr. Lyon?" he suggested, turning back. If the man had such private business as his manner implied, they had best not stand here, where they might be interrupted at any moment by one of the wedding guests.

They strolled slowly to the end of the terrace, exchanging commonplaces with each other, and pleasantries with passersby, until they had gained the freedom of the yard, where they hesitated for a moment.

"The paddock, perhaps?" Not waiting for Lyon's nod of assent, Jamie turned toward the distant stable yard. He wanted to see the Friesians again, in any case.

"I have heard much of you, Mr. Fraser," Lyon began pleasantly, as they ambled toward the tall clock tower of the stable block.

"Have you, sir? Well, and I trust not a great deal of it was to my discredit, then." He had heard a bit about Lyon; a dealer in what anyone would buy or sell—and maybe not just that bit too scrupulous regarding the provenance of his goods. Rumor had it that he dealt in things less tangible than iron and paper on occasion, too, but that was only rumor.

Lyon laughed, showing teeth that were even enough, but badly stained with tobacco.

"Indeed not, Mr. Fraser. Bar the slight impediment of your familial connections—which can scarcely be held to be your fault, though folk *will* make assumptions—I have heard none but the most glowing encomiums, both of your character and your accomplishments."

*A Dhia*, Jamie thought, blackmail and butter, all in the first sentence. Was it only that North Carolina was a backwater, and not worth the time of a more competent intriguer?

He smiled politely, with a murmur of modest dismissal, and waited to see what the blockheid wanted.

Not so much, at least to start. The strength of Fraser's militia regiment, and the names of the men. That was interesting, he thought. Lyon was not the Governor's man, then, or he would have such information to hand. Who was behind him, if anyone? Not the Regulation surely; the only one of them with a spare shilling to his name was Ninian Bell Hamilton, and if auld Ninian had wanted to know a thing, he would have come and asked himself. One of the rich planters from the coast, then? Most aristocrats had an interest in the colony that went no further than their pockets.

Which led to the logical conclusion that whoever Lyon's intended market was thought there'd be something either to gain or to lose from the potential disaffections in the colony. Who might that be?

"Chisholm, McGillivray, Lindsay . . ." Lyon was saying reflectively. "So the majority of your men are Scottish Highlanders. The sons of earlier settlers, are they, or perhaps retired soldiers, like yourself, sir?"

"Oh, I should doubt that a soldier is ever truly retired, sir," Jamie said, stooping to let one of the stable dogs smell his knuckles. "Once a man has lived under arms, I suspect he is marked for life. In fact I have heard it remarked that old soldiers never die; they just fade away."

Lyon laughed immoderately at that, declaring it a fine epigram, was it his own? Without stopping to hear the answer, he went on, clearly paddling into well-charted waters.

"I am pleased to hear such a sentiment expressed, Mr. Fraser. His Majesty has always relied upon the stoutness of the Highlanders, and their abilities as fighting men. Did you or your neighbors perhaps serve with your cousin's regiment? The Seventy-eighth Frasers acquitted themselves with great distinction during the recent conflict; I daresay the art of warfare runs in the blood, eh?"

That was a bald enough swipe. Young Simon Fraser was not in fact his cousin, but his half-uncle, son of his grandfather. It was as expiation of the old man's treason and in an effort to retrieve the family fortunes and estates that Young Simon had raised two regiments for the Seven Years' War—

what Brianna persisted in calling the French and Indian Wars, as though Britain had had nothing to do with it.

Lyon was asking now whether Jamie had also sought to establish his credentials as a loyal soldier of the Crown, by taking commission with one of the Highland regiments? He could scarcely believe the flat-footedness of the man.

"Ah, no. I regret that I was unable to serve in such a capacity," Jamie said. "An indisposition from an earlier campaign, you understand?" The minor indisposition of having been a prisoner of the Crown for several years after the Rising, though he did not mention that. If Lyon didn't know it already, there was no sense in telling him.

They had reached the paddock by now, and leaned comfortably upon the split-rail fence. The horses had not yet been put away for the night; the big black creatures moved like shadows, their coats glossy in the torchlight.

"What strange horses, are they not?" He interrupted Lyon's disquisition on the evils of factionalism, watching them move in fascination.

It wasn't just the enormously long, silky manes, rippling like water as they tossed their heads, nor yet the coal-black coats nor the springy arch of the neck, thicker and more muscular than Jocasta's thoroughbreds. Their bodies were thick as well, broad through chest, withers, and barrel so that each one seemed almost blocky—and yet they moved as gracefully as any horse he had ever seen, adroit and light-footed, with a sense of playfulness and intelligence.

"Yes, it is a very old breed," Lyon said, putting aside his inquisitiveness for the moment in order to watch. "I've seen them before—in Holland."

"Holland. Ye will have traveled there a great deal?"

"Not so much. I was there some years ago, though, and chanced to meet a kinsman of yours. A wine merchant named Jared Fraser?"

Jamie felt a jolt of surprise, succeeded by a warm sense of pleasure at the mention of his cousin.

"Did ye indeed? Aye, Jared is my father's cousin. I trust ye found him well."

"Very well indeed." Lyon moved fractionally closer, settling himself on the fence, and Jamie realized that they had now reached the point of the man's business, whatever that might be. He drained the rest of the wine in his glass and set it down, prepared to listen.

"I understand that a . . . talent for liquor runs in the family as well, Mr. Fraser."

He laughed, though he felt no great humor.

"A taste, perhaps, sir. I couldna say, as to talent."

"Couldn't you? Ah, well. I am sure you are too modest, Mr. Fraser. The quality of your whisky is well known."

"Ye flatter me, sir." He knew what was coming now, and settled himself to pretend attention. It wouldn't be the first time someone had suggested a partnership; he to provide the whisky, they to manage the distribution of it to Cross Creek, to Wilmington, even as far as Charleston. Lyon, it seemed, had grander schemes in mind.

The best aged stuff would go by boat up the coast to Boston and Philadelphia, he suggested. The raw whisky, though, could go across the Treaty Line, there to be delivered to the Cherokee villages, in return for hides and furs. He had partners, who would provide . . .

Jamie listened in growing disapproval, then cut Lyon off abruptly.

"Aye. I thank ye for your interest, sir, but I fear I havena anything like sufficient product for what ye suggest. I make whisky only for my family's use, and a few barrels beyond that, now and then, for local trade. No more."

Lyon grunted amiably.

"I am sure you could increase your production, Mr. Fraser, given your knowledge and skill. If it were to be a matter of the materials . . . some arrangement could be made, I am sure . . . I can speak with the gentlemen who would be our partners in the enterprise, and—"

"No, sir. I fear not. If ye will excuse me . . . ?" He bowed abruptly, turned on his heel, and headed back toward the terrace, leaving Lyon in the dark.

He must ask Farquard Campbell about Lyon. The man would bear watching. It was not that Jamie had any great objection to smuggling. He did, however, have a great objection to being caught at it, and could think of few things more dangerous than a large-scale operation of the sort Lyon was suggesting, where he himself would be involved up to the neck, but have no control over the more dangerous parts of the process.

Aye, the thought of the money was attractive, but not so much as to blind him to the risks. If he were to engage in such a trade, he would do it himself, perhaps with the aid of Fergus or Roger Mac—maybe old Arch Bug and Joe Wemyss—but no one else. A great deal safer to keep it small, keep it private . . . though since Lyon had suggested the notion, perhaps it was worth a bit of thought. Fergus was no farmer, that was sure; something must be found for him to do, and the Frenchman was well acquainted with the risky business, as they called it, from their time in Edinburgh. . . .

He strolled back to the terrace, pondering, but the sight of his wife erased all thought of whisky from his mind.

Claire had left Stanhope and his cronies, and stood by the buffet table, looking over the delicacies on display with a faint frown upon her broad clear brow, as though puzzled by such surfeit.

He saw Gerald Forbes's eyes rest on her, alight with speculation, and he moved at once by reflex, interposing himself neatly between his wife and the lawyer. He felt the man's eyes slap against his back, and smiled grimly to himself. *Mine, corbie*, he thought to himself.

"Can ye not decide where to begin, Sassenach?" He reached down and took the empty wineglass from her hand, taking advantage of the movement to come close against her back, feeling the warmth of her through his clothes.

She laughed, and swayed back against him, leaning on his arm. She smelled faintly of rice powder and warm skin, with the scent of rose hips in her hair.

"I'm not even terribly hungry. I was just counting the jellies and preserves. There are thirty-seven different ones—unless I've missed my count."

He spared a glance for the table, which did indeed hold a bewildering array of silver dishes, porcelain bowls, and wooden platters, groaning with more food than would feed a Highland village for a month. He wasn't hungry, either, though. At least not for puddings and savories.

"Well, Ulysses will have seen to that; he wouldna have my aunt's hospitality put to shame."

"No fear of that," she assured him. "Did you see the barbecue pit out back? There are no fewer than three whole oxen roasting on spits out there, and at least a dozen pigs. I didn't even try to count the chickens and ducks. Do you think it's just hospitality, or is your aunt meaning to make a show of what a good job Duncan's done—showing off how profitable River Run is under his management, I mean?"

"I suppose she might," he said, though privately he thought it unlikely that Jocasta's motives were either so thoughtful or so generous in nature. He considered that the lavishness of the present celebration was much more likely owing to her desire to wipe Farquard Campbell's eye, overshadowing the fete he had held at Greenoaks in December, to celebrate his most recent marriage.

And speaking of marriage . . .

"Here, Sassenach." He deposited her empty glass on a passing tray borne by a servant, and took a full one in return, which he set in her hand.

"Oh, I'm not—" she began; but he forestalled her, taking another glass from the proffered tray and lifting it to her in salute. Her cheeks flushed deeper, and her eyes glowed amber.

"To beauty," he said softly, smiling.

I FELT PLEASANTLY liquid inside, as though belly and limbs were filled with quicksilver. It wasn't all to do with the wine, though that was very good. More the release of tension, after all the worries and conflicts of the day.

It had been a quiet, tender wedding, and while the evening's celebration was likely to be noisy in the extreme—I had heard a number of the younger men plotting vulgar hilarities for the later festivities—I needn't worry about any of that. My own intent had been to enjoy the delightful supper that had been laid on, perhaps take a glass or two more of the excellent wine . . . and then find Jamie and go to investigate the romantic potential of the stone bench beneath the willows.

Jamie had appeared a trifle prematurely in the program, insofar as I had not yet eaten anything, but I had no objection to rearranging my priorities. There would be plenty of leftovers, after all.

The torchlight burnished him, making hair and brows and skin glow like copper. The evening breeze had come up, flapping tablecloths and pulling the torch flames into fiery tongues, and it nipped strands of hair from his queue and lashed them across his face. He raised his glass, smiling at me across the rim.

"To beauty," he said softly, then drank, not taking his eyes off me.

The quicksilver shifted, quivering through my hips and down the backs of my legs.

"To . . . ah . . . privacy," I replied, with a slight lift of my own glass. Feeling pleasantly reckless, I reached slowly up, and deliberately pulled the ornamented lace from my hair. Half-unpinned, curls fell loose down my back, and I heard someone draw in his breath in shock behind me.

In front of me, Jamie's face went suddenly blank, his eyes fixed on me like a hawk's on a rabbit. I lifted my glass, holding his eyes with mine, and drank, swallowing slowly as I drained it. The scent of black grapes perfumed the inside of my head and the heat of the wine warmed my face, my throat, my breasts, my skin. Jamie moved abruptly to take the empty glass from my hand, his fingers cold and hard on mine.

And then a voice spoke from the candlelit French doors behind him.

"Mr. Fraser."

We both started, and the glass fell between us, exploding into shards on the flags of the terrace. Jamie whirled round, his left hand going by reflex to the hilt of his dirk. Then it relaxed, as he saw the silhouetted figure, and he stepped back, mouth twisting in a wry grimace.

Phillip Wylie stepped out into the torchlight. His color was high enough to show through the powder, burning in hectic spots across his cheekbones.

"My friend Stanhope has proposed a table or two of whist this evening," he said. "Will you not join us, Mr. Fraser?"

Jamie gave him a long, cool look, and I saw the damaged fingers of his right hand twitch, very slightly. The pulse was throbbing at the side of his neck, but his voice was calm.

"At whist?"

"Yes." Wylie gave a thin smile, sedulously avoiding looking at me. "I hear you are a good hand at the cards, sir." He pursed his lips. "Though of course, we do play for rather high stakes. Perhaps you do not feel that you—"

"I shall be delighted," Jamie said, in a tone of voice that made it perfectly clear that the only thing that would truly have delighted him was the prospect of cramming Phillip Wylie's teeth down his throat.

The teeth in question gleamed briefly.

"Ah. Splendid. I shall . . . look forward to the occasion."

"Your servant, sir." Jamie bowed abruptly, then spun on his heel, seized my elbow, and marched off down the terrace, me decorously in tow.

I marched along, keeping step and keeping silence, until we were safely out of earshot. The quicksilver had shot up out of my lower regions, and was rolling nervously up and down my spine, making me feel dangerously unstable.

"Are you quite out of your mind?" I inquired politely. Receiving nothing but a brief snort in reply, I dug in my heels and pulled on his arm to make him stop.

"That was not a rhetorical question," I said, rather more loudly. "High-stakes whist?"

Jamie was indeed an excellent card player. He also knew most of the possible ways of cheating at cards. However, whist was difficult if not impossible to cheat at, and Phillip Wylie also had the reputation of an excellent player—as did Stanhope. Beyond this, there remained the fact that Jamie didn't happen to possess *any* stakes, let alone high ones.

"Ye expect me to allow yon popinjay to trample my honor, and then insult me to my face?" He swung round to face me, glaring.

"I'm sure he didn't mean—" I began, but broke off. It was quite apparent that if Wylie had not intended outright insult, he had meant it as a challenge—and to a Scot, the two were likely indistinguishable.

"But you don't *have* to do it!"

I would have had a much greater effect had I been arguing with the brick wall of the kitchen garden.

"I do," he said stiffly. "I have my pride."

I rubbed a hand over my face in exasperation.

"Yes, and Phillip Wylie plainly knows it! Heard the one about pride going before a fall, have you?"

"I havena the slightest intention of falling," he assured me. "Will ye give me your gold ring?"

My mouth fell open in shock.

"Will I . . . my ring?" My fingers went involuntarily to my left hand, and the smooth gold of Frank's wedding band.

He was watching me intently, eyes steady on mine. The torches along the terrace had been lit; the dancing light caught him from the side, throwing the stubborn set of his bones into sharp relief, lighting one eye with burning blue.

"I shall need a stake," he said quietly.

"Bloody hell." I swung away from him, and stood staring off the edge of the terrace. The torches on the lawn had been lit, too, and Perseus's white marble buttocks glimmered through the dark.

"I willna lose it," Jamie said behind me. His hand rested on my shoulder, heavy through my shawl. "Or if I do—I shall redeem it. I know ye . . . value it."

I twitched my shoulder out from under his hand, and moved a few steps away. My heart was pounding, and my face felt at once clammy and hot, as though I were about to faint.

He didn't speak, or touch me; only stood there, waiting.

"The gold one," I said at last, flatly. "Not the silver?" Not *his* ring; not *his* mark of ownership.

"The gold is worth more," he said, and then, after the briefest hesitation, added, "in terms of money."

"I know that." I turned round to face him. The torch flames fluttered in the wind and cast a moving light across his features that made them hard to read.

"I meant—hadn't you better take both of them?" My hands were cold and slippery with sweat; the gold ring came off easily; the silver was tighter, but I twisted it past my knuckle. I took his hand and dropped the two rings clinking into it.

Then I turned and walked away.

47

## THE LISTS OF VENUS

ROGER MADE HIS WAY from the drawing room out onto the terrace, threading through the gathering crowd that clustered thick as lice round the supper tables. He was hot and sweating and the night air struck coldly refreshing on his face. He paused in the shadows at the end of the terrace, where he could unbutton his waistcoat inconspicuously and flap his shirtfront a bit, letting the cold air inside.

The pine torches that lined the edge of the terrace and the brick paths were flickering in the wind, casting wildly shifting shadows over the mass of celebrants, from which limbs and faces emerged and disappeared in bewildering succession. Fire gleamed off silver and crystal, gold lace and shoe-buckles, earrings and coat buttons. From a distance, it looked as though the assembly were lit by fireflies, winking in and out among the dark mass of rustling fabric. Brianna was not wearing anything reflective, he thought, but she should be easy enough to spot, nonetheless, on account of her height.

He had caught no more than tantalizing glimpses of her during the day; she had been dancing attendance on her aunt, or caring for Jemmy, or engaged in conversation with the—apparently—dozens of people she knew from her earlier sojourn at River Run. He didn't begrudge her the opportunity in the least; there was precious little society to be had on

Fraser's Ridge, and he was pleased to see her enjoying herself.

He'd been having a great time himself; his throat had an agreeably raspy feeling now, from the exertion of prolonged singing, and he had learned three new songs from Seamus Hanlon, safely committed to memory. He'd bowed out at last, and left the little orchestra playing in the drawing room, throbbing away in a steamy haze of effort, sweat, and alcohol.

There she was; he caught the glint of her hair as she came out of the parlor doors, turning back to say something to the woman behind her.

She caught sight of him as she turned back, and her face lit up, touching off a complementary warm glow beneath his rebuttoned waistcoat.

"There you are! I've barely seen you all day. Heard you now and then, though," she added, with a nod toward the open drawing-room doors.

"Oh, aye? Sound all right, did it?" he asked casually, shamelessly fishing for compliments. She grinned and tapped his chest with her closed fan, mimicking the gesture of an accomplished coquette—which she wasn't.

"Oh, Mrs. MacKenzie," she said, pitching her voice high and through her nose, "your husband's voice is divinity itself! Were I so fortunate, I am sure I should spend hours just *drrrinking* in the sound of it!"

He laughed, recognizing Miss Martin, old Miss Bledsoe's young and rather plain companion, who had hung about wide-eyed and sighing while he sang ballads in the afternoon.

"You know you're good," she said, dropping back into her own voice. "You don't need me to tell you."

"Maybe not," he admitted. "Doesn't mean I don't like to hear it, though."

"Really? The adulation of the multitudes isn't enough?" She was laughing at him, eyes gone to triangles of amusement.

He didn't know how to answer that, and laughed instead, taking her hand.

"D'ye want to dance?" He cocked his head toward the end

of the terrace where the French doors to the drawing room stood open, letting out the cheerful strains of "Duke of Perth," then back toward the tables. "Or to eat?"

"Neither. I want to get away from here for a minute; I can hardly breathe." A drop of sweat ran down her neck, glinting red in the torchlight before she swiped it away.

"Great." He took her hand and drew it through his arm, turning toward the herbaceous border that lay beyond the terrace. "I know just the place."

"Great. Oh—wait. Maybe I do want something to eat." She lifted a hand and stopped a slave boy, coming up to the terrace from the cookhouse with a small covered tray from which an appetizing steam wafted into the air. "What's that, Tommy? Can I have some?"

"You have all you want, Miss Bree." He smiled, whipping the napkin away to display a selection of savories. She inhaled beatifically.

"I want them all," she said, taking the tray, to Tommy's amusement. Roger, seizing the chance, murmured his own request to the slave, who nodded, disappeared, and returned within moments with an open bottle of wine and two goblets. Roger took these, and together they wandered down the path that led from the house to the dock, sharing tidbits of news along with the pigeon pies.

"Did you find any of the guests passed out in the shrubbery?" she asked, her words muffled by a mouthful of mushroom pasty. She swallowed, and became more distinct. "When Da asked you to go and look this afternoon, I mean."

He snorted briefly, selecting a dumpling made of sausage and dried pumpkin.

"Ken the difference between a Scottish wedding and a Scottish funeral, do ye?"

"No, what?"

"The funeral has one less drunk."

She laughed, scattering crumbs, and took a Scotch egg.

"No," he said, steering her skillfully to the right of the dock, and toward the willows. "Ye'll see a few feet sticking out of the bushes now, but this afternoon, they hadn't had the time to get rat-legged yet."

"You have *such* a way with words," she said appreciatively. "I went and talked to the slaves; all present and accounted for, and mostly sober, too. A couple of the women admitted that Betty does tipple at parties, though."

"To say the least, from what your Da said. Stinking, he described her as, and I gather he didn't mean only drunk." Something small and dark leaped out of his path. Frog; he could hear them piping away in the grove.

"Mmm. Mama said she seemed to be okay later on, in spite of Dr. Fentiman insisting on bleeding her." She gave a small shudder, drawing her shawl round her shoulders one-handed. "He gives me the creeps, the Doctor. He looks like a little goblin or something, and he's got the clammiest hands I ever felt. And he smells terrible, speaking of stinking."

"I haven't had the pleasure yet," Roger said, amused. "Come on." He pushed aside the hanging veil of willow branches, alert lest he disturb some courting couple that had beaten them to the stone bench, but all was well. Everyone was up at the house, dancing, eating, drinking, and planning a later serenade of the wedding pair. Better Duncan and Jocasta than us, he thought, rolling his eyes inwardly at some of the things he'd heard suggested. Another time, he might have been interested to see a shivaree, and trace all the roots of it from French and Highland customs—but not bloody now.

It was suddenly quiet under the willows, most of the noise from the house drowned by the rushing of water and the monotonous chirping of frogs. It was also dark as midnight, and Brianna felt carefully for the bench, in order to set down her tray.

Roger shut his eyes hard and counted to thirty; when he opened them, he could at least make out her form, silhouetted against the dim light that filtered through the willows, and the horizontal line of the bench. He set down the glasses and poured out the wine, the neck of the bottle chinking faintly against the goblets as he felt his way.

He put out a hand and ran it down her arm, locating her hand in order to put the full goblet safely into it. He raised his own glass in salute.

"To beauty," he said, letting the smile show in his voice.

"To privacy," she said, returning the toast, and drank. "Oh, that's good," she said, a moment later, sounding slightly dreamy. "I haven't had wine in . . . a year? No, nearly two. Not since before Jemmy was born. In fact, not since . . ." Her voice stopped abruptly, then resumed, more slowly. "Not since our *first* wedding night. In Wilmington, remember."

"I remember." He reached out and cupped a hand round her cheek, tracing the bones of her face softly with his thumb. It was no wonder that she thought of that night now. They had begun it there, under the drooping branches of a huge horse-chestnut tree, that had sheltered them from the noise and light of a nearby tavern. Their present situation was oddly and movingly reminiscent of that dark and private secrecy, the two of them amid the smell of leaves and nearby water—the nearby racket of lust-crazed tree frogs replacing the tavern noises.

That had been a hot night, though, thick and humid enough that flesh melted to flesh. Now it was cold enough that his body yearned for the warmth of hers, and the scent that enclosed them was the spring smell of green leaves and running river, not the musty smell of leaf-litter and mudflats.

"Do you think they'll sleep together?" Brianna asked. She sounded slightly breathless; perhaps it was the wine.

"Who? Oh, Jocasta, ye mean, and Duncan? Why not? They'll be married." He drained his own glass and set it down, the glass chiming faintly on the stone.

"It was a beautiful wedding, wasn't it?" She didn't resist as he took the glass from her hand and set it down with his own. "Quiet, but awfully nice."

"Aye, very nice." He kissed her, softly, and held her close against him. He could feel the back lacing of her gown, criss-crossed under the thin knitted shawl.

"Mmm. You taste good."

"Oh, aye, like sausages and wine. So do you." His hand twitched up the edge of the shawl, getting beneath and fumbling for the end of the lace, somewhere down near the small of her back. She pressed against him, making it easier.

"Will we still want to make love, do you think, when we're as old as they are?" she murmured in his ear.

"I will," he assured her, getting hold of the small bow that secured the lace. "I hope you will, too; I shouldna like to have to do it alone."

She laughed, and took a deep breath, her back swelling suddenly as the tight lacing came loose. There were the stays underneath, too, though, damn it. He used both hands, looking for the inner lacings, and she arched her back helpfully, which made her breasts swell up into sight just below his chin. The sight made him take one hand off her back, to deal with this new and delightful development.

"I haven't got my . . . I mean, I didn't bring . . ." She pulled back a little, sounding dubious.

"Ye've taken the seeds today, though?" Away to hell with pizza and loo-paper, he thought; at the moment, he'd trade all prospects of indoor plumbing for a rubber condom.

"Yes." She still sounded doubtful, though, and he gritted his teeth, taking a firmer hold on her, as though she might bolt.

"It's all right," he whispered, nuzzling his way down the side of her neck toward that heartbreaking slope where the muscle of her shoulder joined it. She was smooth beneath his lips, her skin cool in the air, warm and scented beneath the fall of her hair. "We needn't . . . I mean . . . I won't . . . just let me . . ."

The neckline of her dress was fashionably low with her kerchief pulled off, still lower, with her gown unlaced, and her breast was heavy and soft in his hand. He felt the nipple big and round as a ripe cherry against his palm, and bent on impulse to put his mouth to it.

She stiffened, then relaxed with an odd little sigh, and he felt a warm sweet taste on his tongue, then a strange pulsing and a flooding of the . . . he swallowed by reflex, shocked. Shocked, and terribly aroused. He hadn't thought; he hadn't meant . . . but she pulled his head hard against her, holding him.

He went on, emboldened, and pushed her gently backward, easing her down onto the edge of the bench, so that he knelt before her. A sudden thought had come to him, prompted by the stinging memory of that entry in her dreambook.

"Don't worry," he whispered to her. "We won't . . . risk anything. Let me do this—just for you."

She hesitated, but let him run his hands under her skirt, up the silken curves of stockinged calf and round, bare thigh, under the flattened curve of her buttocks, cool and bare on the stone, beneath the froth of petticoats. One of Seamus's songs had described a gentleman's exploits "in the lists of Venus." The words drifted through his head with the rushing of the water, and he was determined to acquit himself with honor in those lists.

Maybe she couldn't describe it, but he meant to make sure she knew it had happened. She shivered between his hands, and he cupped one hand between her thighs.

"Miss Bree?"

Both of them jerked convulsively, Roger snatching his hands away as though burned. He could feel the thunder of blood in his ears—and his balls.

"Yes, what is it? Is that you, Phaedre? What's wrong—is it Jemmy?"

He was sitting back on his heels, trying to breathe, feeling dizzy. He caught the brief pale gleam of her breasts above him as she stood up and turned toward the voice, tucking her kerchief hastily back in, pulling the shawl up over her unfastened gown.

"Yes, ma'am." Phaedre's voice came out from under the willow nearest the house; nothing of the slave showed but the whiteness of her cap, floating dimly in the shadows. "Poor child, he woke up hot and fussin', wouldn't take neither mush nor milk, and then he started in to cough, sounded bad enough, Teresa said we best fetch Dr. Fentiman along to him, but I said . . ."

"Dr. Fentiman!"

Brianna disappeared with a ferocious rustling of willow branches, and he heard the hurrying thump of slippered feet on earth as she ran toward the house, Phaedre in her wake.

Roger got to his feet, and paused for a moment, hand on his fly-buttons. The temptation was strong; it wouldn't take more than a minute—less, probably, in his present condition. But no, Bree might need him to deal with Fentiman. The thought of the Doctor using his gory instruments on Jemmy's soft flesh was enough to send him crashing through the willows in hot pursuit. The lists of Venus would have to wait.

HE FOUND BREE and Jemmy in Jocasta's boudoir, the center of a small knot of women, all of whom looked surprised—even mildly scandalized—at his appearance. Disregarding the raised eyebrows and huffing noises, he forged his way through the skirts to Brianna's side.

The little fella did look bad, and Roger felt a clutch of fear in the pit of his stomach. Christ, how could it happen so fast? He'd seen Jem at the wedding only a few hours before, curled up pink and sweet in his makeshift cradle, and before that, being his usual raucously genial self at the party. Now he lay against Brianna's shoulder, flush-cheeked and heavy-eyed, whimpering a little, with a slick of clear mucus dribbling from his nose.

"How is he?" He reached out and touched a flushed cheek gently, with the back of his hand. God, he was hot!

"He's sick," Brianna said tersely. As though in confirmation, Jemmy began to cough, a dreadful noise, loud but half-choked, like a seal choking on its fish. The blood surged into his already flushed face, and his round blue eyes bulged with the effort of drawing breath between the spasms.

"Shit," Roger muttered. "What do we do?"

"Cold water," one of the women standing beside him said, authoritatively. "Put him altogether under a bath of cold water, then make him drink more of it."

"No! Heavens, Mary, you'll kill the child." Another young matron reached out to pat Jemmy's quivering back. "It's the croup; my lot have had it now and again. Sliced garlic, warmed and put to the soles of his feet," she told Brianna. "That works well, sometimes."

"And if it doesn't?" another woman said, skeptical. The first woman's nostrils pinched, and her friend butted in helpfully.

"Johanna Richards lost two babes to the croup. Gone like that!" She snapped her fingers, and Brianna flinched as though the sound were one of her own bones cracking.

"Why are we havering so, and a medico to hand? You, girl, go and fetch Dr. Fentiman! Did I not say so?" One of the women clapped her hands sharply at Phaedre, who stood pressed back against the wall, eyes fixed on Jemmy. Before she could move to obey, though, Brianna's head shot up.

"No! Not him, I won't have him." She glared round at the women, then shot Roger a look of urgent entreaty. "Find Mama for me. Quick!"

He turned and shoved past the women, fear momentarily assuaged by the ability to do something. Where was Claire likely to be? *Help*, he thought, *help me find her, help him be all right*, directing the incoherent prayer toward anyone who might be listening—God, the Reverend, Mrs. Graham, Saint Bride, Claire herself—he wasn't particular.

He thundered down the front stair to the foyer, only to meet Claire hurrying across it toward him. Someone had told her; she gave him one quick look, asked, "Jemmy?" with a lift of her chin, and at his breathless nod, was up the stairs in a flash, leaving a foyer full of people gaping after her.

He caught her up in the hall above and was in time to open the door for her—and to receive an undeserved but much appreciated look of gratitude from Bree.

He stood back out of the way, catching his breath and marveling. The moment Claire stepped into the room, the atmosphere of worry and near-panic changed at once. There was still an air of concern among the women, but they gave way without hesitation, standing back respectfully and murmuring to one another as Claire headed straight for Jemmy and Bree, ignoring everything else.

"Hallo, lovey. What is it, then, are we feeling miserable?" She was murmuring to Jem, turning his head to one side and feeling gently under his flushed chubby jowls and behind his ears. "Poor thing. It's all right, sweetheart, Mummy's here, Grannie's here, everything will be just fine. . . . How long has he been like this? Has he had anything to drink? Yes, darling, that's right. . . . Does it hurt him to swallow?"

She alternated between comforting remarks to the baby and questions to Brianna and Phaedre, all delivered in the same tone of calm reassurance as her hands touched here and there, exploring, soothing. Roger felt it working on him, too, and drew a deep breath, feeling the tightness in his own chest ease a bit.

Claire took a sheet of Jocasta's heavy notepaper from the secretary, rolled it into a tube, and used it to listen intently to Jemmy's back and chest as he made more of the choking-seal noises. Roger noticed dimly that her hair had fallen down somehow; she had to brush it out of the way to listen.

"Yes, of course it's croup," she said absently, in answer to a half-questioning diagnosis offered diffidently by one of the bystanders. "But that's only the cough and the difficult breathing. You can have croup by itself, so to speak, or as an early symptom of various other things."

"Such as?" Bree had a death grip on Jemmy, and her face was nearly as white as her knuckles.

"Oh. . . ." Claire seemed to be listening intently, but not to Bree. More to whatever was happening inside Jemmy, who had quit coughing and was lying exhausted against his mother's shoulder, breathing thickly in steam-engine gasps. "Um . . . coryza—that's only a common cold. Influenza. Asthma. Diphtheria. But it isn't that," she added hurriedly, looking up and catching a glimpse of Brianna's face.

"You're sure?"

"Yes," Claire replied firmly, straightening up and putting aside her makeshift stethoscope. "It doesn't feel at all like diphtheria to me. Besides, there isn't any of that about, or I'd have heard. And he's still being breast-fed; he'll have immunity—" She stopped speaking abruptly, suddenly aware of the women looking on. She cleared her own throat, bending down again, as though to encourage Jemmy by example. He made a small whimper and coughed again. Roger felt it, like a rock in his chest.

"It isn't serious," Claire announced firmly, straightening. "We must put him in a croup tent, though. Bring him down to the kitchen. Phaedre, will you find me a couple of old quilts, please?"

She moved toward the door, shooing the women before her like a flock of hens.

Obeying an impulse that he didn't stop to question, Roger reached for the baby, and after a instant's hesitation, Brianna let him take him. Jemmy didn't fuss, but hung listless and heavy, the limp slackness a terrible change from his normal India-rubber bounce. The baby's cheek burned through the cloth of Roger's shirt as he carried the little boy downstairs, Bree at his elbow.

The kitchen was in the brick-walled basement of the house, and Roger had a brief vision of Orpheus descending into the underworld, Eurydice close behind him, as they made their way down the dark back stair into the shadowy depths of the kitchen. Instead of a magic lyre, though, he bore a child who burned like coal and coughed as though his lungs would burst. If he didn't look back, he thought, the boy would be all right.

"Perhaps a little cold water wouldn't come amiss." Claire put her hand on Jemmy's forehead, judging his temperature. "Have you got an ear infection, sweetheart?" She blew gently into one of the baby's ears, then the other; he blinked, coughed hoarsely, and swiped a chubby hand across his face, but didn't flinch. The slaves were bustling round in a corner of the kitchen, bringing boiling water, pinning the quilts to a rafter to make the tent at her direction.

Claire took the baby out of Roger's arms to bathe him, and he stood bereft, wanting urgently to do something, anything, until Brianna took his hand and clutched it hard, her nails digging into his palm.

"He'll be all right," she whispered. "He will." He squeezed hard back, wordless.

Then the tent was ready, and Brianna ducked under the hanging quilt, turning to reach back for Jemmy, who was alternately coughing and crying, having not liked the cold water at all. Claire had sent a slave to fetch her medicine box, and now rummaged through it, coming up with a vial filled with a pale yellow oil, and a jar of dirty white crystals.

Before she could do anything with them, though, Joshua, one of the grooms, came thumping down the stairs, half-breathless with his hurry.

"Mrs. Claire, Mrs. Claire!"

Some of the gentlemen had been firing off their pistols in celebration of the happy event, it seemed, and one of them had suffered some kind of mishap, though Josh seemed uncertain as to exactly what had happened.

"He isna bad hurt," the groom assured Claire, in the Aberdonian Scots that came so peculiarly from his black face, "but he is bleedin' quite free, and Dr. Fentiman—well, he's maybe no quite sae steady as he might be the noo. Will ye come, Ma'am?"

"Yes, of course." In the blink of an eye, she had thrust vial and jar into Roger's hands. "I'll have to go. Here. Put some in the hot water; keep him breathing the steam until he stops coughing." Quick and neat, she'd closed up her box and handed it to Josh to carry, heading for the stair before Roger could ask her anything. Then she was gone.

Wisps of steam were escaping through the opening in the tent; seeing that, he paused long enough to shed coat and waistcoat, leaving them in a careless heap on the floor as he bent and ducked into the darkness, vial and jar in hand.

Bree was crouched on a stool, Jemmy on her lap, a big white pudding-basin full of steaming water at her feet. A swath of light from the hearth fell momentarily across her face, and Roger smiled at her, trying to look reassuring, before the quilt dropped back into place.

"Where's Mama? Did she leave?"

"Aye, there was some sort of emergency. It'll be fine, though," he said firmly. "She gave me the stuff to put in the water; said just to keep him in the steam until the coughing stops."

He sat down on the floor beside the basin of water. It was very dim in the tent, but not totally dark. As his eyes adjusted, he could see well enough. Bree still looked worried, but not nearly so frightened as she'd been upstairs. He felt better, too; at least he knew what to be doing, and Claire hadn't seemed too bothered about leaving her grandson; obviously she thought he wasn't going to choke on the spot.

The vial contained pine oil, sharp and reeking of resin. He wasn't sure how much to use, but poured a generous dollop into the water. Then he pried the cork out of the jar, and the pungent scent of camphor rose up like a genie from the bottle. Not really crystals, he saw; lumps of some sort of dried resin, grainy and slightly sticky. He poured some into the palm of his hand, then rubbed them hard between his hands before dropping them into the water, wondering even as he did so at the instinctive familiarity of the gesture.

"Oh, that's it," he said, realizing.

"What's it?"

"This." He waved a hand round the snug sanctuary, rapidly filling with pungent steam. "I remember being in my cot, with a blanket over my head. My mother put this stuff in hot water—smelled just like this. That's why it seemed familiar."

"Oh." The thought seemed to reassure her. "Did you have croup when you were little?"

"I suppose so, though I don't remember it. Just the smell." Steam had quite filled the little tent by now, moist and pungent. He drew a deep breath, pulling in a penetrating lungful, then patted Brianna's leg.

"Don't worry; this'll do the trick," he said.

Jemmy promptly started coughing his guts out with more seal noises, but they seemed less alarming now. Whether it was the darkness, the smell, or simply the homely racket of the renewed kitchen noises outside the tent, things seemed calmer. He heard Bree take in a deep breath, too, and let it out, and felt rather than saw the subtle shift of her body as she relaxed a little, patting Jemmy's back.

They sat quietly for a bit, listening to Jemmy cough, wheeze, gasp, cough, and finally catch his breath, hiccuping slightly. He'd stopped whimpering, seeming soothed by the proximity of his parents.

Roger had dropped the cork to the camphor jar; he patted round on the floor until he found it, then pushed it firmly back in.

"I wonder what your mother's done with her rings?" he said, looking for some easy subject of conversation to break the steam-filled silence.

"Why should she have done anything with them?" Brianna brushed back a lock of hair; she'd had it put up for the evening, but it was slipping out of its pins, clinging damply to her face.

"She wasn't wearing them when she gave me the stuff." He nodded at the camphor jar, set out of harm's way near the wall. He had a clear memory of her hands, the fingers long, white, and bare; they'd struck him, since he'd never seen her hands without the gold and silver rings.

"Are you sure? She never takes them off, except to do something really nasty." She giggled, a nervous, unexpected sound. "The last time I remember was when Jem dropped his bawbee in the chamber pot."

Roger gave a brief snort of amusement. A bawbee was any sort of small object, but that's what they'd taken to calling the iron ring—originally meant for leading cattle by the nose—that Jem liked to chew on. It was his favorite toy, and he didn't like to go to bed without it.

"Ba-ba?" Jem raised his head, eyes half-closed. He was still breathing thickly, but beginning to display an interest in something besides his own discomfort. "Ba-ba!"

"Oops, shouldn't have mentioned it." Bree joggled him gently on her knee, and began to sing softly, half under her breath, to distract him.

*"In a can-yon, in a cav-ern, exca-va-ting for a mine . . . Dwelt a min-er, forty-nin-er, and his daugh-ter, Clementine . . ."*

The dark privacy of the tent reminded Roger of something; he realized that it had something of the same feeling of peaceful enclosure that the bench beneath the willows had had, though the tent was a lot hotter. The linen of his shirt was already limp on his shoulders, and he could feel sweat trickling down his back from under the hair tied at his neck.

"Hey." He nudged Bree's leg. "D'ye maybe want to go up and take off your new dress? It'll be spoilt if ye stay in here for long."

"Oh. Well . . ." She hesitated, biting her lip. "No, I'll stay, it's okay."

He got up, stooping under the quilts, and gathered Jem up off her lap, hacking and gurgling.

"Go," he said firmly. "You can fetch his b—his you-know-what. And don't worry. Ye can tell it's helping, the steam. He'll be right in no time."

It took a bit more argument, but at last she consented, and Roger sat down on the vacated stool, Jemmy cuddled in the crook of his arm. The pressure of the wooden seat reminded him of a certain amount of residual congestion from the encounter under the willows, and he shifted slightly to ease the discomfort.

"Well, it doesn't do ye any lasting harm," he muttered to Jemmy. "Ask any girl; they'll tell ye."

Jemmy snorted, snuffled, said something unintelligible beginning with "Ba—?" and coughed again, but only briefly. Roger put the back of his hand against the soft round cheek. He *thought* it was cooler. Hard to tell, warm as it was in here. The sweat was running freely down his face, and he wiped it with a sleeve.

"Ba-ba?" asked a froggy little voice against his chest.

"Aye, in a bit. Hush, now."

"Ba-ba. Ba-ba!"

"Shhhh."

"Ba—"

*"Light she was, and like a fairy—"* He groped for the words to the song.

"BA—"

*"AND HER SHOES WERE NUMBER NINE!"* Roger abruptly raised the volume, causing startled silence both inside the tent and outside, in the kitchen. He cleared his throat and lowered his voice back to lullaby level.

"Erm . . . *Herring boxes without topses . . . Sandals were for Clementine. Oh, my darling, oh, my darling, oh, my darling Clementine . . . Thou art lost, and gone for-ev-er, oh, my dar-ling . . . Clementine."*

The singing seemed to be having an effect. Jemmy's eyelids had dropped to half-mast. He put a thumb in his mouth and began to suck, but plainly couldn't breathe through his clogged nose. Roger gently pulled the thumb away, and held the little fist enclosed in his own. It was wet and sticky, and very small, but felt reassuringly sturdy.

*"Fed she duck-lings, by the water, every mor-ning just at nine . . . Hit her foot a-gainst a splin-ter, fell into the foaming brine."*

The eyelids fluttered briefly, then gave up the struggle and closed. Jemmy sighed and went completely limp, the heat coming off his skin in waves. Tiny beads of moisture trembled on each lash—tears, sweat, steam, or all three.

*"Ruby lips a-bove the wa-ter, blowing bub-bles soft and fine . . . Alas for me, I was no swim-mer, so I lost my Clementine. Oh, my darling, oh, my darling . . ."*

He wiped his face again, bent and kissed the soft thatch of damp, silky hair. *Thank you*, he thought with heartfelt sincerity, addressing everyone from God on down the line.

*". . . Oh, my darling . . . Clementine."*

48

# STRANGERS IN THE NIGHT

IT WAS VERY LATE by the time I made my way to bed after a last check on the welfare of all my patients. DeWayne Buchanan had suffered a slight flesh wound in the upper arm when Ronnie Campbell neglected to raise his pistol high enough while carousing on the riverbank, but was in good spirits after having the wound cleaned and dressed. Having been liberally plied with further spirits by a remorseful Ronnie, he was quite literally feeling no pain at present.

One of Farquard Campbell's slaves, a man named Rastus, had been badly burned on the hand when taking grilled fowl off a skewer; all I could do there was to wrap the hand in clean cloth, set it in a bowl of cold water, and prescribe gin, to be taken internally. I had also treated several young men who were considerably the worse for drink, and sporting miscellaneous contusions, abrasions, and missing teeth as the result of a disagreement over dice. Six cases of indigestion, all treated with peppermint tea, and reporting improvement. Betty was in what looked like a deep but natural sleep, snoring loudly in bed. Jemmy was doing likewise, his fever abated.

Most of the loud revelry had died down by now; only the

most die-hard of the card players were still at it, peering red-eyed at their pasteboards through a cloud of tobacco smoke in the small drawing room. I glanced into the other rooms as well, as I made my way across the ground floor to the front stair. A few gentlemen lingered in low-voiced political conversation at one end of the dining room, the table long since cleared and empty brandy glasses forgotten by their elbows. Jamie wasn't one of them.

A heavy-eyed slave in livery bowed as I poked my head in, murmuring to ask whether I wanted food or drink. I hadn't eaten anything since supper, but I waved him away, too tired to think of food.

I paused at the first landing and glanced down the hall toward Jocasta's suite of rooms, but all was quiet there, the charivari and horseplay over. There was a large dent in the linenfold paneling, where a heavy body had struck, and glancing up, I could see several burned spots in the ceiling, where shots had been fired into it.

The butler Ulysses sat guard on a stool by the door, still dressed in wig and formal livery, head nodding over folded arms. A candle guttered and spat in the sconce above him. By its wavering light, I could see that his eyes were closed, but he wore a deep frown; he hunched in his sleep, and his lips moved briefly, as though he dreamed of evil things. I thought to waken him, but even as I moved toward him, the dream passed. He stretched, half-rousing, then fell asleep again, his face relaxing into calm. An instant later, the candle flickered out.

I listened, but heard no sound in the darkness save Ulysses's heavy breathing. Whether Duncan and Jocasta murmured understandings to each other behind the curtains of their bed, or lay silent, side by side and eternally separate, no one would ever know. I sent them a mental wish for happiness, and dragged myself upward, knees and back aching, wishing for my own bed—and my own husband's understanding.

Through an open casement on the second-floor landing, I heard distant whoops, laughter, and the occasional crack of recreational gunfire, borne on the night air. The younger, wilder gentlemen—and a few old enough to know better—

had gone down to the river landing in company with a dozen bottles of whisky and brandy to shoot frogs, or so I was informed.

The ladies, though, were all asleep. The second floor was quiet save for the buzz of muffled snoring. By contrast to the chilly corridor outside, the chamber itself was stifling, though the fire had burned down to a crimson coal bed that shed no more than an eerie red glow across the hearth.

With so many guests in the house, the only people with the luxury of a private bedroom were the bridal pair; everyone else was crammed into the few available rooms, willy-nilly. Two large tester beds and a trundle occupied the room, with straw-tick pallets spread over most of the remaining floor space. Each bed was packed like a sardine tin with shift-clad women lying side by side across the mattress, radiating as much moist heat as a greenhouse full of orchids.

I breathed shallowly—the air was filled with a cloying mixture of stale sweat, barbecue, and fried onions, French perfume, drink-sodden breath, and the sharp, sweet smell of vanilla beans—and shed my gown and shoes as quickly as I could, hoping not to break out into a drenching sweat before I could undress. I was still keyed up from the events of the day, but exhaustion was pulling like lead weights at my limbs, and I was glad enough to tiptoe through the sprawl of bodies and creep into my accustomed space near the foot of one of the big beds.

My mind was still buzzing with speculations of all sorts, and in spite of the hypnotic lull of so much slumber all around me, I lay stiff-limbed and sore, watching the silhouette of my bare toes against the hearth's dying light.

Betty had passed from her stupor into what looked like a normal deep sleep. When she woke in the morning, we would find out who had given her the cup, and—perhaps—what was in it. I hoped that Jemmy would sleep comfortably as well. But what was really on my mind, of course, was Jamie.

I hadn't seen him among the card players, nor yet among the men talking low-voiced of taxes and tobacco.

I hadn't seen Phillip Wylie anywhere on the first floor of the house, either. I could well believe he was out with the revelers by the river landing. That was his set and his style, wealthy young men who would seek diversion in drink and carouse in the dark, careless both of cold and danger, laughing and chasing each other by the light of random gunfire.

That was neither Jamie's set nor his style, but the thought of him among them was what made my feet curl with chill, despite the heat of the room.

*He wouldn't do anything stupid*, I assured myself, rolling onto my side, knees drawn up as much as possible in the cramped quarters. He wouldn't; but his notion of stupid wasn't always the same as mine, by any means.

Most of the male guests were bedded down in the outbuildings, or in the parlors; as I passed, I had seen anonymous sleeping figures sprawled on the floor of the front parlor, snoring loudly, wrapped in their cloaks before the fire. I had not gone to poke among them, but doubtless Jamie was there—he had had as long a day as I had, after all.

But it was not like him to retire without coming to wish me good night, no matter what the circumstances. Of course, he had been annoyed with me, and despite the promise of our interrupted conversation on the terrace, we had not quite made up the quarrel. Re-inflamed it, rather, with beastly Phillip Wylie's invitation. My hands curled, thumbs rubbing at the slight calluses that marked the spots where my rings normally sat. Effing Scot!

Next to me Jemima Hatfield stirred and murmured, disturbed by my restlessness. I eased myself slowly back onto my side, and stared sightlessly at the oaken footboard in front of me.

Yes, he was undoubtedly still angry about Phillip Wylie's advances. So was I—or I would be, were I not so tired. How dare he—I yawned, nearly dislocating my jaw, and decided that it really wasn't worth the bother of being annoyed, at least not now.

But it wasn't like Jamie to avoid me, angry or not. He wasn't the sort of man to sulk or brood. He would seek a confrontation or provoke a fight, without a moment's hesitation; but I didn't think he had ever let the sun go down on anger—at least not with regard to me.

Which left me to worry about where he was, and what in

bloody hell he was doing. And the necessity of worrying about him was making me *really* angry, if only because that was better than being worried.

But it *had* been a very long day, and as the moments passed, and the faint pops of gunfire from the river landing gradually ceased, languor stole over me, blunting my fears and scattering my thoughts like spilled sand. The gentle breathing of the women all around me lulled me like the sound of wind in the trees, and my grip on reality slackened and at last fell free.

I might have expected dreams of violence or nightmares of dread, but my subconscious had plainly had enough of that. In the contrary way of such things, it instead chose to dwell on another thread of the day's events. Perhaps it was the warmth of the room, or simply the closeness of so many bodies, but I dreamed vividly and erotically, the tides of arousal washing me now and then near to the shores of wakefulness, then once more carrying me out into the deeps of unconsciousness.

There were horses in my dreams; glowing black Friesians with flowing manes that rippled in the wind as the stallions ran beside me. I saw my own legs stretch and leap; I was a white mare, and the ground flew past in a blur of green beneath my hooves, until I stopped and turned, waiting for the one, a broad-chested stallion who came to me, his breath hot and moist against my neck, his white teeth closing on my nape . . .

*"I am the King of Ireland,"* he said, and I came slowly awake, tingling from head to foot, to find that someone was gently stroking the sole of said foot.

Still bemused by the carnal images of my dreams, I was not alarmed by this, but merely muzzily pleased to discover that I had feet after all, and not hooves. My toes curled and my foot flexed, reveling in the delicate touch of the thumb that traced its way from the ball of my foot down the high arch and up into the hollow below my anklebone, managing to stimulate an entire plexus of sensation. Then I came all the way awake, with a small jerk.

Whoever it was plainly sensed my return to consciousness, for the touch left my foot momentarily. Then it came back, this time more firmly, a large warm hand curling quite round my foot, the thumb executing a firm but languid massage at the base of my toes.

By this time, I was quite awake, and mildly startled, but not frightened. I wiggled my foot briefly, as though to throw off the hand, but it squeezed my foot lightly in response, and then its companion gently pinched my great toe.

*This little piggy went to market, this little piggy stayed home* . . . I could hear the rhyme as clearly as though it had been spoken aloud, as the fingers deftly pinched their way across my toes, one by one.

*And this little piggy went weee-weee-weee, all the way home!* The touch flicked tickling down the sole of my foot and I jerked, an involuntary giggle caught in my throat.

I lifted my head, but the hand seized my foot again and squeezed in admonition. The fire had gone out altogether and the room was black as velvet; even with eyes completely dark-adapted, I could gain nothing but the sense of a hunched figure near my feet, an amorphous blob that shifted like mercury, its edges blending with and disappearing into the dark of the air.

The hand slid gently up the calf of my leg. I twitched violently, and the woman next to me snorted, reared up with a bleary, "Hnh?" and collapsed again, in a whoosh.

My stomach muscles quivered with suppressed laughter. He must have felt the slight vibration—the fingers left my little toe with a gentle squeeze, and stroked the bottom of my foot, making all my toes curl tight.

The fingers curled into a fist, pressing along the length of my sole, then suddenly opened, cupping my heel. His thumb stroked my ankle, and paused, questioning. I didn't move.

His fingers were getting warmer; there was only a faint sensation of cold as they followed the curve of my calf and sought shelter in the soft place behind my knee. The fingers played a quick tattoo on the sensitive skin there, and I twitched in agitation. They slowed and stopped, settling surely on the artery where my pulse beat fast; I could feel it, blood rushing past where the skin was so thin the veins would show blue beneath it.

I heard a sigh as he shifted his weight; then one hand

cupped the round of my thigh, and slid slowly upward. The other followed, pressing my legs gently, inexorably apart.

My heart was thumping in my ears and my breasts felt swollen, nipples poking hard and round through the thin muslin of my shift. I took a deep breath, and smelled rice powder.

All at once, my heart gave a double-thump and nearly stopped, as the sudden thought sprang to life in my mind—what if it wasn't Jamie?

I lay quite still, trying not to breathe, concentrating on the hands, which were doing something delicate and quite unspeakable. Large hands, they *were* large hands; I could feel the knuckles pressing the soft inner flesh of my thigh. But Phillip Wylie had large hands, too; quite large for his size. I had seen him scoop up a handful of oats for his stallion, Lucas, and the horse bury its big black nose in the palm.

Calluses; the roving hands—oh, God!—were smoothly callused. But so were Wylie's; dandy he might be, but a horseman; his palms were quite as smooth and hard as Jamie's.

It had to be Jamie, I assured myself, lifting my head an inch or so and peering into the black velvet darkness. Ten little pigs . . . of course it was Jamie! Then one of the hands did something quite startling and I gasped out loud and jerked, limbs twitching. My elbow slammed into the ribs of the woman next to me, who snapped upright with a loud exclamation. The hands retreated abruptly, squeezing my ankles in a hasty farewell.

There was a shuffling noise as someone crawled hurriedly across the floor, then a flash of dim light and a breath of cold air from the corridor as the door opened and shut again immediately.

"Wha—?" said Jemima next to me, in woozy astonishment. "Whozat?"

Receiving no answer, she flounced, muttered, and at last lay down again, to fall promptly fast asleep.

I did not.

# 49

# IN VINO VERITAS

I LAY SLEEPLESS for quite a long time, listening to the peaceful snores and rustlings of my bedmates, and to the agitated thump of my own heart. Every nerve in my body felt as though it were sticking out through my skin, and when Jemima Hatfield rolled unconsciously into me, I jabbed her viciously in the ribs with my elbow, so that she uttered a startled "Whoof?" and sat halfway up, blinking and muttering, before collapsing slowly back into the communal sea of sleep.

As for me, my small bark of consciousness was adrift on the flood, spinning rudderless, but without the slightest chance of being pulled under.

I simply couldn't decide how to feel. On the one hand, I was aroused—unwillingly, to be sure, but still most definitely aroused. Whoever my nocturnal visitor had been, he knew his way around a woman's body.

That would argue for its being Jamie, I thought. Still, I had no idea how experienced Phillip Wylie might be in the arts of love—I had spurned his approaches in the stable so promptly that he had had no chance of demonstrating any skills he might possess in that direction.

But my midnight visitor had not used any caress that I could positively identify as being in Jamie's repertoire. Now, if he had used his mouth . . . I shied away from *that* line of thought like a spooked horse, and Jemima gave a muffled grunt as I convulsed slightly, my skin rippling in involuntary response to the images it evoked.

I didn't know whether to feel amused or outraged, seduced or violated. I *was* extremely angry; I was sure of that much, at least, and the surety gave me some small anchor in the maelstrom of emotion. Still, I had no idea as to the correct target of my anger, and with nowhere to aim that particularly destructive emotion, it was simply crashing round inside me, knocking things down and leaving dents.

"Oof," said Jemima, in a pointed—and quite conscious—tone of voice. Evidently I wasn't the only one being dented by my emotions.

"Mmmm?" I murmured, feigning half-sleep. "Glrgl. Bzg."

There was a small tinge of guilt in the mix, as well.

If I were sure it *had* been Jamie, would I be angry?

The worst of it was, I realized, that there was absolutely nothing I could do to find out who it had been. I could scarcely ask Jamie whether he had crept in and fondled me in the darkness—because if he *hadn't*, his immediate response would certainly be to assassinate Phillip Wylie bare-handed.

I felt as though tiny electric eels were squirming under my skin. I stretched as hard as I could, alternately tensed and relaxed every muscle—and still could find no way to keep still.

At last, I slid cautiously off the bed, and made my way to the door, with a glance at my erstwhile bedmates, who lay slumbering peacefully under the quilts like a row of perfumed sausages. Moving with great stealth, I eased the door open and peeked out into the hallway. It was either very late or very early; the tall window at the end of the corridor had gone to gray, but the last of the stars still showed, vanishing pinpoints on the charcoal satin of the sky.

It was cold in the hall, away from the contained body heat of the women, but I welcomed the chill; the blood was pulsing just under my skin, and I bloomed with heat and agitation. A nice cooldown was exactly what I wanted. I made my way quietly to the back stairs, meaning to go down and outside for a breath of air.

I stopped dead at the top of the staircase. A man stood at the foot of the stair, a silhouette tall and black against the panes of the double French doors. I didn't think I had made any sound, but he turned at once, face lifted toward me. Even in the poor light, I knew at once that it was Jamie.

He was still clad in the clothes he had worn the night before—coat and waistcoat, frilled shirt and belted plaid. The
shirt was open at the neck, though, coat and weskit unbut-
toned and askew. I could see the narrow line of white linen,
the flesh of his throat dark against it. His hair was loose; he
had been running his hands through it.

"Come down," he said softly.

I hesitated, looking back over my shoulder. A ladylike
medley of snores came from the room I had just left. Two
slaves were sleeping on the floor in the hall, curled under
blankets, but neither moved.

I looked back. He didn't speak again, but lifted two fingers, beckoning. The scent of smoke and whisky filled the
stairwell.

The blood was thrumming in my ears—and elsewhere.
My face was flushed, my hair damp at the temples and on my
neck; cool air rose up under my shift, touched the patch of
dampness at the base of my spine, the film of slickness where
my thighs brushed together.

I came down slowly, cautiously, trying not to let the stairs
creak under my bare feet. It occurred to me belatedly that
this was ridiculous; the slaves thundered up and down these
stairs hundreds of times a day. Even so, I felt the need for secrecy; the house was still asleep, and the stairwell was filled
with a gray light that seemed as fragile as smoked glass. A
sudden sound, a move too quick, and something might explode under my feet, with a flash like a lightbulb popping.

His eyes stayed fixed on me, dark triangles in the paler
dark of his face. He stared at me with a fierce intensity, as
though to drag me down the stairs by the force of his gaze
alone.

I stopped, one step from the bottom. There was no blood
on his clothes; thank God for that.

It wasn't that I'd never seen Jamie drunk before. No wonder he hadn't come up the stairs to me. I thought he was very
drunk now, and yet there was something quite different in
this. He stood rock-solid, legs set wide, betrayed only by a
certain deliberation in the way he moved his head to look
at me.

"What—" I began, whispering.

"Come here," he said. His voice was low, rough with sleeplessness and whisky.

I hadn't time either to reply or to acquiesce; he seized my arm and pulled me toward him, then swept me off the last step, crushed me to him, and kissed me. It was a most disconcerting kiss—as though his mouth knew mine all too well, and would compel my pleasure, regardless of my desires.

His hair smelled of a long night's smoke—tobacco and woodsmoke and the smoke of beeswax candles. He tasted so strongly of whisky that I felt light-headed, as though the alcohol in his blood were seeping into mine through our skins where they touched, through the sealed membranes of our mouths. Something else was seeping into me from him, as well—a sense of overpowering lust, as blind as it was dangerous.

I wanted to remonstrate with him, to push him away. Then I decided that I didn't, but it wouldn't have made any difference if I had. He didn't mean to let go.

One big hand was gripping the back of my neck, warm and hard on my skin, and I thought of a stallion's teeth closing on the neck of the mare he mounts, and shivered from scalp to sole. His thumb accidentally pressed the great artery under my jaw; darkness swam behind my eyes and my knees began to buckle. He felt it and let go, easing me back so that I was almost lying supine upon the stairs, his weight half on me and his hands seeking.

I was naked under my shift, and the thin muslin might as well not have been there.

The hard edge of a stair pressed into my back, and it occurred to me, in the dim way that things do when you're drunk, that he was just about to take me right there on the stairs, and devil take anyone who might see.

I got my mouth free of his long enough to gasp, "Not here!" in his ear. That seemed to bring him momentarily to his senses; he lifted his head, blinking like one roused from a nightmare, eyes wide and blind. Then he nodded once, jerkily, and rose, pulling me to my feet with him.

The maids' cloaks were hanging by the door; he seized one and wrapped it round me, then picked me up bodily and shouldered his way through the door, past a staring house-maid with a slop jar in her hands.

He set me down when he reached the brick path outside; the bricks were cold under my feet. Then we were moving together through the gray light across a landscape of shadow and wind, still entangled with each other, stumbling, jostling, and yet somehow almost flying, clothes fluttering round us and cold air brushing our skins with the rude touch of spring, bound for some vaguely sensed and yet inevitable destination.

The stables. He hit the door and pulled me through with him into the warm dark, thrust me hard against a wall.

"I must have ye now, or die," he said, breathless, and then his mouth was on mine again, his face cold from the air outside, and his breath steaming with mine.

Then he drew abruptly away, and I staggered, pressing my hands against the rough bricks of the wall to keep my balance.

"Hold up your hands," he said.

"What?" I said stupidly.

"Your hands. Put them up."

In complete bewilderment, I held them up, and felt him take hold of the left one, fumbling. Pressure and warmth, and the faint light from the open door shone on my gold wedding ring. Then he seized my right hand, shoved my silver ring onto my finger, the metal warm from the heat of his body. He raised my hand to his mouth, and bit my knuckles, hard.

Then his hand was on my breast, cold air brushed my thighs, and I felt the scratch of the bricks on my bare backside.

I made a noise, and he clapped a hand over my mouth. Speared as neatly as a landed trout, I was just as helpless, pinned flapping against the wall.

He took his hand away and replaced it with his mouth, engulfing mine. I could feel the small urgent growls he was making in his throat, and felt another one, much louder, rising in mine.

My shift was wadded high around my waist, and my bare buttocks smacked rhythmically against the roughened brick, but I felt no pain at all. I gripped him by the shoulders and held on.

His hand skimmed my thigh, pushing at the drifts of linen that threatened to come between us. I remembered, vividly, those hands in the darkness, and bucked convulsively.

"Look." His breath came hot in my ear. "Look down. Watch while I take ye. Watch, damn you!"

His hand pressed my neck, bending my head forward to look down in the dimness, past the folds of sheltering fabric to the naked fact of my possession.

I arched my back and then collapsed, biting the shoulder of his coat to make no noise. His mouth was on my neck, and fastened tight as he shuddered against me.

WE LAY TANGLED together in the straw, watching daylight creep through the half-open door across the red-brick floor of the stable. My heart was still thumping in my ears, blood tingling through skin and temples, thighs and fingers, but I felt somehow detached from such sensations, as though they were happening to someone else. I felt unreal—and slightly shocked.

My cheek lay flat against his chest. Moving my eyes slightly, I could see the fading red flush of his skin in the open neck of his shirt, and the coarse curly hairs, so deep an auburn that they looked nearly black in the shadowed light.

A pulse was throbbing in the hollow of his throat, no more than an inch from my hand. I wanted to lay my fingers on it, feel his heartbeat echo in my blood. I felt oddly shy, though, as though such a gesture were too intimate to contemplate. Which was completely ridiculous, in view of what we had just done with—and to—each another.

I did move my index finger, just a bit, so that my fingertip brushed the tiny three-cornered scar on his throat; a faded white knot, pale against his bronzed skin.

There was a slight catch in the rhythm of his breathing, but he didn't move. His arm was round me, his hand splayed on the small of my back. Two breaths, three . . . and then the faint pressure of a fingertip against my spine.

We lay silent, breathing lightly, both concentrated on the delicate acknowledgment of our connection, but didn't speak or move; slightly embarrassed, with the return of reason, at what we had just done.

The sound of voices coming toward the stable galvanized me into motion, though. I sat up abruptly, yanked my shift up over my shoulders, and began to brush straw from my hair. Jamie rolled up onto his knees, his back to me, and began hastily to tuck in his shirttail.

The voices outside stopped abruptly, and we both froze. There was a brief, charged silence, and then the sound of footsteps, delicately retreating. I let out the breath I had been holding, feeling my racing heart begin to slow. The stable was filled with the rustlings and whickers of the horses, who had heard the voices and footsteps, too. They were getting hungry.

"So you won," I said to Jamie's back. My voice sounded strange to me, as though I hadn't used it in a long time.

"I promised ye I would." He spoke softly, head bent as he rearranged the folds of his plaid.

I stood up, feeling mildly dizzy, and leaned against the wall to keep my balance as I brushed sand and straw from my feet. The rough feel of the bricks behind me was a vivid reminder, and I spread my hands out against them, bracing myself against the rush of recalled sensation.

"Are ye all right, Sassenach?" He turned his head sharply to look up at me, sensing my movement.

"Yes. Yes," I repeated. "Fine. Just . . . I'm fine. And you?"

He looked pale and scruffy, his face stubbled and hollow with strain, eyes smudged black from a long and sleepless night. He met my eyes for a moment, then glanced away. A hint of color showed on his cheekbones, and he swallowed audibly.

"I—" he began, then stopped. He got to his feet and stood before me. His formal queue had come undone, and the tails of his hair splayed over his shoulder, glimmering redly as the bar of light from the door lit him.

"Ye dinna hate me?" he asked abruptly. Taken by surprise, I laughed.

"No," I said. "Do you think I should?"

His mouth twitched a little, and he rubbed his knuckles across it, scraping on the stubble of his beard.

"Well, maybe so," he said, "but I'm glad if ye don't."

He took my hands gently in his own, his thumb rubbing lightly across the interlaced pattern of my silver ring. His hands were cold, chilled by the dawn.

"Whyever do you think I might hate you?" I asked. "Because of the rings, do you mean?" Granted, I would have been upset and furious with him, had he lost either one. Since he hadn't . . . Of course, he *had* caused me to worry all night about where he was and what he was doing, to say nothing of sneaking into my room and making improper advances to my feet. Perhaps I ought to be annoyed with him, after all.

"Well, starting wi' that," he said dryly. "I havena let my pride get the better of me in some time, but I couldna seem to stop myself, what with wee Phillip Wylie preenin' about, smirkin' at your breasts, and—"

"He was?" I hadn't noticed that part.

"He was," Jamie said, glowering momentarily at the thought. Then he dismissed Phillip Wylie, returning to the catalogue of his own sins.

"And then, draggin' ye out of the house in your shift and going after ye like a ravening beast—" He gently touched my neck, where I could still feel the tingling soreness of a bite mark.

"Oh. Well, I quite liked that part, actually."

"You did?" His eyes flicked wide and blue in momentary startlement.

"Yes. Though I rather think I have bruises on my bottom."

"Oh." He looked down, apparently abashed, though the corner of his mouth twitched slightly. "I'm sorry for that. When I'd finished—at the whist, I mean—I couldna think of anything but finding ye, Sassenach. I went up and down that stair a dozen times, going to your door, and back away again."

"Oh, you did?" I was pleased to hear this, as it seemed to increase the odds that he had in fact been my midnight visitor.

He picked up a hank of my rumpled hair and ran his fingers gently through it.

"I kent I couldna sleep, and thought, well, I shall go out and walk in the night for a time, and I would, but then I should find myself again outside your room, not knowing how I'd come there, but only trying to think how I might get to ye—trying to will ye to come out to me, I suppose."

Well, that explained my dreams of wild stallions, I thought. The place where he had bitten my neck throbbed slightly. And where had he brought me? A stable. King of Ireland, forsooth..

He squeezed my hands lightly.

"I thought the force of my wanting must wake ye, surely. And then ye *did* come. . . ." He stopped, looking at me with eyes gone soft and dark. "Christ, Claire, ye were so beautiful, there on the stair, wi' your hair down and the shadow of your body with the light behind ye. . . ." He shook his head slowly.

"I did think I should die, if I didna have ye," he said softly. "Just then."

I reached up to stroke his face, his beard a soft bristle on my palm.

"Wouldn't want you to die," I whispered, tucking back a lock of hair behind his ear.

We smiled at each other then, but whatever else we might have said was interrupted by a loud whinny from one of the horses, followed by stamping noises. We were interfering with their breakfast.

I dropped my hand and Jamie bent to pick up his coat, which lay half-buried in the straw. He didn't lose his balance as he bent, but I saw him wince as the blood went suddenly to his head.

"Did you have a terrible lot to drink last night?" I asked, recognizing the symptoms.

He straightened up with a small grunt of amusement.

"Aye, quarts," he said, ruefully. "Ye can tell?"

A person with much less experience than I had could have told at a distance of roughly half a mile; putting aside the more obvious indications of recent intoxication, he smelled like a distillery.

"It didn't impair your card playing, evidently," I said, being tactful. "Or was Phillip Wylie similarly affected?"

He looked surprised, and slightly affronted.

"Ye dinna think I'd get besotted whilst I was playing, do ye? And with your rings at stake? No, that was after—Mac-Donald fetched a bottle of champagne and another of whisky, and insisted that we must celebrate our winnings in proper style."

"MacDonald? Donald MacDonald? He was playing with you?"

"Aye, he and I were partnered against Wylie and Stanhope." He shook the coat, sending bits of straw flying. "I couldna say what sort of soldier he was, but the man's a fine hand at the whist, to be sure."

Mention of the words "fine hand" reminded me. He'd come to the door of my room, he said; he hadn't mentioned coming in. Had he, and been too far gone between liquor and longing to recall doing it? Had I, dazed with dreams of equine lust, imagined the whole thing? Surely not, I thought, but shook off the sense of vague disquiet engendered by the memory, in favor of another word from his remark.

"You said winnings?" In the stress of the moment, it had only seemed important that he had kept my rings, but it occurred to me belatedly that those were only his stake. "What did you take off Phillip Wylie?" I asked, laughing. "His embroidered coat buttons? Or his silver shoe buckles?"

His face had an odd expression as he glanced at me.

"Well, no," he said. "I took his horse."

HE SWUNG HIS COAT round my shoulders, put an arm round my waist, and led me down the main aisle of the stable block, past the loose-boxes and stalls.

Joshua had come in quietly, through the other door, and was working at the far end of the stable, silhouetted against the light from the open double-doors as he pitchforked hay into the end stall. As we reached him, he glanced at us and nodded in greeting, his face carefully neutral at the sight of us, bedraggled, barefoot, and prickled with straw. Even in a household with a blind mistress, a slave knew what not to see.

No business of his, his downcast countenance said clearly. He looked nearly as tired as I felt, eyes heavy and bloodshot.

"How is he?" Jamie asked, lifting his chin toward the stall. Josh perked up a bit at the inquiry, putting down his pitchfork.

"Oh, he's bonnie," he said, with an air of satisfaction. "A bonnie lad, Mr. Wylie's Lucas."

"Indeed he is," Jamie agreed. "Only he's mine now."

"He's what?" Josh goggled at him, openmouthed.

"He's mine." Jamie went to the railing and reached out a hand to scratch the ears of the big stallion, busily engaged in eating hay from his manger.

*"Seas,"* he murmured to the horse. *"Ciamar a tha thu, a ghille mhoir?"*

I followed him, peering over his arm at the horse, who lifted his head for a moment, regarded us with a genial eye, snorted, tossed his veil-like mane out of his face, and went back to his breakfast with single-minded intent.

"A lovely creature, is he no?" Jamie was admiring Lucas, a look of distant speculation in his eyes.

"Well, yes, he is, but—" My own admiration was substantially tinged with dismay. If Jamie had set out to avenge his own pride at the cost of Wylie's, he'd done it in spades. Despite my irritation with Wylie, I couldn't help a small pang at the thought of how he must be feeling at the loss of his magnificent Friesian.

"But what, Sassenach?"

"Well, just—" I fumbled awkwardly for words. I could scarcely say I felt sorry for Phillip Wylie, under the circumstances. "Just—well, what do you mean to do with him?"

Even I could see that Lucas was totally unsuited to life on Fraser's Ridge. The thought of plowing or hauling with him seemed sacrilegious, and while I supposed Jamie *could* use him only for riding . . . I frowned dubiously, envisioning the boggy bottoms and rocky trails that would threaten those well-turned legs and splinter the glossy hooves; the hanging boughs and undergrowth that would tangle in mane and tail. Gideon the Man-eater was a thousand times better suited to such rough environs.

"Oh, I dinna mean to keep him," Jamie assured me. He looked at the horse and sighed regretfully. "Though I should dearly love to. But ye're right; he wouldna do for the Ridge. No, I mean to sell him."

"Oh, good." I was relieved to hear this. Wylie would undoubtedly buy Lucas back, no matter what the cost. I found that a comforting thought. And we could certainly use the money.

Joshua had gone out while we were talking. At this point, he reappeared in the doorway, a sack of grain on his shoulder. His previous sluggish air had disappeared, though; his eyes were still bloodshot, but he looked alert, and mildly alarmed.

"Mrs. Claire?" he said. "Beggin' your pardon, ma'am, but I met Teresa by the barn just now; she's says as how there's summat gone amiss wi' Betty. I thought ye'd maybe want to know."

50

## BLOOD IN THE ATTIC

THE ATTIC ROOM looked like the scene of a murder, and a brutal one, at that. Betty was struggling on the floor beside her overturned bed, knees drawn up and fists doubled into her abdomen, the muslin of her shift torn and saturated with blood. Fentiman was on the floor with her, dwarfed by her bulk but vainly grappling with her spasming body, nearly as smeared with gore as she was.

The sun was fully up now, and pouring in through the tiny windows in brilliant shafts that spotlighted parts of the chaos, leaving the rest in shadowed confusion. Cots were pushed aside and upset, bedding tangled in mounds, worn shoes and bits of clothing scattered like debris among the splotches of fresh blood on the wooden floor.

I hurried across the attic, but before I could reach her, Betty gave a deep, gurgling cough, and more blood gushed from her mouth and nose. She curled forward, arched back, doubled hard again . . . and went limp.

I fell to my knees beside her, though it was apparent from a glance that her limbs had relaxed into that final stillness from which there could be no hope of revival. I lifted her head and pressed my fingers under her jaw; her eyes had rolled back, only the whites showing. No breath, no sign of a pulse in the clammy neck.

From the quantities of blood spread round the room, I thought there could be very little left in her body. Her lips were blue, and her skin had gone the color of ashes. Fentiman knelt behind her, wigless and white-faced, skinny arms still locked about her heavy torso, holding her slumped body half off the floor.

He was in his nightshirt, I saw, a pair of blue satin breeches hastily pulled on beneath it. The air reeked of blood, bile, and feces, and he was smeared with all those substances. He looked up at me, though he showed no sign of recognition, his eyes wide and blank with shock.

"Dr. Fentiman." I spoke softly; with the noise of struggle ceased, the attic was stricken with that absolute silence that often follows in the wake of death, and it seemed sacrilege to break it.

He blinked, and his mouth worked a little, but he seemed to have no notion how to reply. He didn't move, though the spreading pool of blood had soaked through the knees of his breeches. I put a hand on his shoulder; it was bird-boned, but rigid with denial. I knew the feeling; to lose a patient you have fought for is a terrible thing—and yet one all doctors know.

"You have done all you can," I said, still softly, and tightened my grip. "It is not your fault." What had happened the day before wasn't important. He was a colleague, and I owed him what absolution lay in my power to give.

He licked dry lips, and nodded once, then bent to lay the body gently down. A shaft of light skimmed the top of his head, glowing through the scanty bristles of cropped gray hair, and making the bones of his skull seem thin and fragile.

He seemed suddenly frail altogether, and let me help him to his feet without protest.

A low moan made me turn, still holding his arm. A knot of female slaves huddled in the shadowed corner of the room, faces stark and dark hands fluttering with distress against the pale muslin of their shifts. There were male voices on the stair outside, muted and anxious. I could hear Jamie, low-voiced and calm, explaining.

"Gussie?" I called toward the women in the corner with the first name that came to mind.

The knot of slaves clung together for a moment, then reluctantly unraveled, and Gussie stepped out, a pale brown moth of a girl from Jamaica, small under a turban of blue calico.

"Madam?" She kept her eyes on mine, steadfastly away from the still form on the floor.

"I'm taking Doctor Fentiman downstairs. I'll have some of the men come to . . . to take care of Betty. This . . ." I made a small gesture toward the mess on the floor, and she nodded, still shocked, but obviously relieved to have something to do.

"Yes, Madam. We do that, quick." She hesitated, eyes darting round the room, then looked back at me. "Madam?"

"Yes?"

"Someone must go—tell that girl name Phaedre what's gone with Betty. You tell her, please?"

Startled, I looked, and realized that Phaedre was not among the slaves in the corner. Of course; as Jocasta's body servant, she would sleep downstairs, near her mistress, even on her wedding night.

"Yes," I said, uncertainly. "Of course. But—"

"This Betty that girl's mama," Gussie said, seeing my incomprehension. She swallowed, tears swimming in her soft brown eyes. "Somebody—can I go, Madam? Can I go tell her?"

"Please," I said, and stepped back, motioning her to go. She tiptoed past the body, then darted for the door, callused bare feet thumping softly on the boards.

Dr. Fentiman had begun to emerge from his shock. He pulled away from me and stooped toward the floor, making vague groping gestures. I saw that his medical kit had been upset in the struggle; bottles and instruments were strewn across the floor in a litter of metal and broken glass.

Before he could retrieve his kit, though, there was a brief commotion on the stair, and Duncan came into the room, Jamie on his heels. I noticed with some interest that Duncan was still wearing his wedding clothes, though minus coat and waistcoat. Had he been to bed at all? I wondered.

He nodded to me, but his eyes went at once to Betty, now sprawled on the floor, bloody shift crumpled round her broad, splayed thighs. One breast spilled from the torn fabric, heavy and slack as a half-filled pouch of meal. Duncan blinked several times. Then he wiped the back of his hand across his mustache, and took a visible breath. He bent to pluck a quilt from the carnage and laid it gently over her.

"Help me with her, *Mac Dubh*," he said.

Seeing what he was about, Jamie knelt and gathered the dead woman up into his arms. Duncan drew himself upright, and turned his face toward the women in the corner.

"Dinna fash yourselves," he said quietly. "I shall see her taken care of." There was an unusual note of authority in his voice that made me realize that in spite of his natural modesty, he had accepted the fact that he was master here.

The men left with their burden, and I heard Dr. Fentiman give a deep sigh. It felt as though the whole attic sighed with him; the atmosphere was still thick with stench and sorrow, but the shock of violent death was dissipating.

"Leave it," I said to Fentiman, seeing him move again to pick up a bottle lying on the floor. "The women will take care of it." Not waiting for argument, I took him firmly by the elbow and marched him out the door and down the stair.

People were up; I caught the sounds of rattling dishes from the dining room, and the faint scent of sausages. I couldn't take him through the public rooms in his current state, nor up to the bedrooms; he was undoubtedly sharing a room with several other men, any of whom might still be abed. For lack of a better idea, I took him outside, pausing to snatch another of the maids' cloaks from the pegs by the door and wrap it round his shoulders.

So Betty was—or had been—Phaedre's mother. I hadn't

known Betty well, but I did know Phaedre, and felt grief for her tighten my throat. There was nothing I could do for her just now, though; but perhaps I could help the doctor.

Silent with shock, he followed me obediently as I led him down the side path by the lawns, shielded from view by Hector Cameron's white-marble mausoleum and its growth of ornamental yew bushes. There was a stone bench by the river, half-hidden under a weeping willow. I doubted anyone would be patronizing it at this hour of the morning.

No one was, though two wine goblets sat on the bench, stained red with beeswing, abandoned remnants of the night's festivities. I wondered briefly whether someone had been having a romantic rendezvous, and was reminded suddenly of my own midnight tryst. Damn it, I still didn't know for sure who the owner of those hands had been!

Pushing the nagging question away with the wineglasses, I sat down, gesturing to Doctor Fentiman to join me. It was chilly, but the bench was in full sun at this hour, and the heat was warm and comforting on my face. The Doctor was looking better for the fresh air; vestiges of color had come back into his cheeks, and his nose had resumed its normal roseate hue.

"Feeling a bit better, are you?"

He nodded, hunching the cloak around his narrow shoulders.

"I am, I thank you, Mrs. Fraser."

"Rather a shock, wasn't it?" I asked, employing my most sympathetic bedside manner.

He closed his eyes, and shook his head briefly.

"Shocked . . . yes, very shocked," he muttered. "I would never have . . ." He trailed off, and I let him sit quiet for a moment. He would need to talk about it, but best to let him take it at his own pace.

"It was good of you to come so quickly," I said, after a bit. "I see they called you from your bed. Had she grown suddenly worse, then?"

"Yes. I could have sworn she was on the mend last night, after I bled her." He rubbed his face with both hands, and emerged blinking, eyes very bloodshot. "The butler roused me just before dawn, and I found her once again complaining of griping in the guts. I bled her again, and then administered a clyster, but to no avail."

"A clyster?" I murmured. Clysters were enemas; a favorite remedy of the time. Some were fairly harmless; others were positively corrosive.

"A tincture of nicotiana," he explained, "which I find answers capitally in most cases of dyspepsia."

I made a noncommittal noise in response. Nicotiana was tobacco; I supposed a strong solution of that, administered rectally, would probably dispose promptly of a case of pinworms, but I didn't think it would do much for indigestion. Still, it wouldn't make anyone bleed like that, either.

"Extraordinary amount of bleeding," I said, putting my elbows on my knees and resting my chin in my hands. "I don't think I've ever seen anything like it." That was true. I was curious, turning over various possibilities in my mind, but no diagnosis quite fit.

"No." Doctor Fentiman's sallow cheeks began to show spots of red. "I—if I had thought . . ."

I leaned toward him, and laid a consoling hand on his arm.

"I'm sure you did all that anyone could possibly do," I said. "She wasn't bleeding at all from the mouth when you saw her last night, was she?"

He shook his head, hunching deeper into his cloak.

"No. Still, I blame myself, I really do."

"One does," I said ruefully. "There's always that sense that one should have been able to do *something* more."

He caught the depth of feeling in my voice and turned toward me, looking surprised. The tension in him relaxed a little, and the red color began to fade from his cheeks.

"You have . . . a most remarkably sympathetic understanding, Mrs. Fraser."

I smiled at him, not speaking. He might be a quack, he might be ignorant, arrogant, *and* intemperate—but he had come at once when called, and had fought for his patient to the best of his ability. That made him a physician, in my book, and deserving of sympathy.

After a moment, he put his hand over mine. We sat in silence, watching the river go by, dark brown and turbid with silt. The stone bench was cold under me, and the morning breeze kept sticking chilly fingers under my shift, but I was too preoccupied to take much note of such minor discomforts. I could smell the drying blood on his clothes, and saw again the scene in the attic. What on earth had the woman died of?

I prodded him gently, asking tactful questions, extracting what details he had gleaned, but they were not helpful. He was not an observant man at the best of times, and it had been very early and the attic dark. He grew easier with the talking, though, gradually purging himself of that sense of personal failure that is the frequent price of a physician's caring.

"I hope Mrs. Cameron—Mrs. Innes, I mean—will not feel that I have betrayed her hospitality," he said uneasily.

That seemed a rather odd way to put it. On the other hand . . . Betty *had* been Jocasta's property. I supposed that beyond any sense of personal failure, Dr. Fentiman was also contemplating the possibility that Jocasta might blame him for not preventing Betty's death, and try to claim recompense.

"I'm sure she'll realize that you did all you could," I said soothingly. "I'll tell her so, if you like."

"My dear lady." Doctor Fentiman squeezed my hand with gratitude. "You are as kind as you are lovely."

"Do you think so, Doctor?"

A male voice spoke coldly behind me, and I jumped, dropping Dr. Fentiman's hand as though it were a high-voltage wire. I whirled on the bench to find Phillip Wylie, leaning against the trunk of the willow tree with a most sardonic expression on his face.

" 'Kind' is not the word that springs most immediately to mind, I must say. 'Lewd,' perhaps. 'Wanton,' most certainly. But 'lovely,' yes—I'll give you that."

His eyes raked me from head to toe with an insolence that I would have found absolutely reprehensible—had it not suddenly dawned on me that Dr. Fentiman and I had been sitting hand in hand in what could only be called a compromising state of dishabille, both still in our nightclothes.

I stood up, drawing my cloak round me with great dignity.

His eyes were fixed on my breasts—with a knowing expression? I wondered. I folded my arms under my breasts, lifting my bosom defiantly.

"You forget yourself, Mr. Wylie," I said, as coldly as possible.

He laughed, but not as though he thought anything were funny.

"I forget myself? Have you not forgotten something, Mrs. Fraser? Such as your gown? Do you not find it a trifle cold, dressed like that? Or do the good doctor's embraces warm you sufficiently?"

Doctor Fentiman, as shocked as I was by Wylie's appearance, had got to his feet and now pushed his way in front of me, his thin cheeks mottled with fury.

"How dare you, sir! How do you have the infernal presumption to speak to a lady in such fashion? Were I armed, sir, I should call you out upon the instant, I swear it!"

Wylie had been staring boldly at me. At this, his gaze shifted to Fentiman, and he saw the blood staining the doctor's legs and breeches. His hot-eyed scowl grew less certain.

"I—has something happened, sir?"

"It is none of your concern, I assure you." Fentiman bristled like a banty rooster, drawing himself upright. Rather grandly, he presented me with his arm.

"Come, Mrs. Fraser. You need not be exposed to the insulting gibes of this puppy." He glared at Wylie, red-eyed. "Allow me to escort you back to your husband."

Wylie's face underwent an instant transformation at the word "puppy," turning a deep, ugly red. So early in the morning, he was wearing neither paint nor powder, and the blotches of fury stood out like a rash on his fair skin. He seemed to swell noticeably, like an enraged frog.

I had a sudden urge to laugh hysterically, but nobly suppressed it. Biting my lip instead, I accepted the doctor's proffered arm. He came up roughly to my shoulder, but pivoted on his bare heel and marched us away with all the dignity of a brigadier.

Looking back over my shoulder, I saw Wylie still standing under the willow tree, staring after us. I lifted my hand and gave him a small wave of farewell. The light sparked from my gold ring, and I saw him stiffen further.

"I do hope we'll be in time for breakfast," Doctor Fentiman said cheerfully. "I believe I have quite recovered my appetite."

## SUSPICION

THE GUESTS BEGAN TO DEPART after breakfast. Jocasta and Duncan stood together on the terrace, the very picture of a happily united couple, bidding everyone farewell, as a line of carriages and wagons made its slow way down the drive. Those folk from downriver waited on the quay, the women exchanging last-minute recipes and bits of gossip, while the gentlemen lit pipes and scratched themselves, relieved of their uncomfortable clothes and formal wigs. Their servants, all looking considerably the worse for wear, sat openmouthed and red-eyed on bundles of luggage.

"You look tired, Mama." Bree looked rather tired herself; she and Roger had both been up 'til all hours. A faint smell of camphor wafted from her clothes.

"Can't imagine why," I replied, stifling a yawn. "How's Jemmy this morning?"

"He's got a sniffle," she said, "but no fever. He ate some porridge for breakfast, and he's—"

I nodded, listened automatically, and went with her to examine Jemmy, who was cheerfully rambunctious, if runnynosed, all in a slight daze of exhaustion. It reminded me of nothing so much as the sensation I had had now and then when flying from America to England. Jet lag, they called it;

an odd feeling, of being conscious and lucid, and yet not quite solidly fixed within one's body.

The girl Gussie was watching Jemmy; she was as pale and bloodshot as everyone else on the premises, but I thought her air of dull suffering derived from emotional distress rather than hangover. All the slaves had been affected by Betty's death; they went about the chores of clearing up after the wedding festivities in near-silence, their faces shadowed.

"Are you feeling all right?" I asked her, when I had finished looking in Jemmy's ears and down his throat.

She looked startled, then confused; I wondered whether anyone had ever asked her that before.

"Oh. Oh, yes, Madam. Surely." She smoothed down her apron with both hands, clearly nervous at my scrutiny.

"All right. I'll just go and have a look at Phaedre, then."

I had come back to the house with Dr. Fentiman and turned him over to Ulysses, to be fed and tidied up. I had then gone directly to find Phaedre, taking time only to wash and change my clothes—not wanting to come to her so visibly smeared with her mother's blood.

I had found her in Ulysses's pantry, sitting numb and shocked on the stool where he sat to polish silver, a large glass of brandy by her side, undrunk. One of the other slaves, Teresa, was with her; she breathed a short sigh of relief at my appearance and came to greet me.

"She's none sae weel," Teresa muttered to me, shaking her head with a wary glance back at her charge. "She's no said a word, nor wept a drop."

Phaedre's beautiful face might have been carved of fruit-wood; normally a delicate cinnamon, her complexion had faded to a pale, ligneous brown, and her eyes stared fixedly through the open door of the pantry at the blank wall beyond.

I put a hand on her shoulder; it was warm, but so motionless that she might have been a stone in the sun.

"I am sorry," I said to her, softly. "Very sorry. Dr. Fentiman came to her; he did all that he could." That was true; no point in giving an opinion of Fentiman's skill—it was irrelevant now, in any case.

No response. She was breathing; I could see the slight rise and fall of her bosom, but that was all.

I bit the inside of my lower lip, trying to think of anything or anyone that might possibly give her comfort. Jocasta? Did Jocasta even know of Betty's death yet? Duncan knew, of course, but he might have chosen not to tell her until after the guests had left.

"The priest," I said, the idea occurring suddenly to me. "Would you like Father LeClerc to—to bless your mother's body?" I thought it rather too late for Last Rites—assuming that Phaedre knew what those were—but I was sure that the priest would not mind offering any comfort he could. He had not left yet; I had seen him in the dining room only a few moments since, polishing off a platter of pork-chops garnished with fried eggs and gravy.

A slight tremor went through the shoulder under my hand. The still, beautiful face turned toward me, dark eyes opaque.

"What good will that do?" she whispered.

"Ah . . . well . . ." Flustered, I groped for a reply, but she had already turned away, staring at a stain in the wood of the table.

What I had done in the end was to give her a small dose of laudanum—an irony I resolutely ignored—and tell Teresa to put her to bed on the cot where she normally slept, in the dressing room off Jocasta's boudoir.

I pushed open the door of the dressing room now, to see how she was. The small room was windowless and dark, smelling of starch and burnt hair and the faint flower fragrance of Jocasta's toilet water. A huge armoire and its matching chiffonier stood at one side, a dressing table at the other. A folding screen marked off the far corner, and behind this was Phaedre's narrow cot.

I could hear her breathing, slow and deep, and felt reassured by that. I moved quietly through the dark room, and pulled back the screen a little; she lay on her side, turned away, curled into a ball with her knees drawn up.

Bree had come into the dressing room behind me; she looked over my shoulder, her breath warm on my ear. I made a small gesture indicating that everything was all right, and pushed the screen back into place.

Just inside the door to the boudoir, Brianna paused. She turned to me suddenly, put her arms about me, and hugged me fiercely. In the lighted room beyond, Jemmy missed her and began to shriek.

"Mama! Ma! Ma-MA!"

I THOUGHT I ought to eat something, but with the smell of the attic and the scent of toilet water still lingering in the back of my sinuses, I had no appetite. A few guests still lingered in the dining room; particular friends of Jocasta's, they would be staying on for a day or two. I nodded and smiled as I passed, but ignored the invitations to come and join them, instead heading for the stairs to the second floor.

The bedroom was empty, the mattresses stripped and the windows opened to air the room. The hearth had been swept and the room was cold, but blessedly quiet.

My own cloak still hung in the wardrobe. I lay down on the bare ticking, pulled the cloak over me, and fell instantly asleep.

I WOKE JUST BEFORE sunset, starving, with an oddly mixed sense of reassurance and unease. The reassurance I understood at once; the scent of blood and flowers had been replaced by one of shaving soap and body-warmed linen, and the pale gold light streaming through the window shone on the pillow beside me, where a long red-gold hair glinted in the hollow left by someone's head. Jamie had come and slept beside me.

As though summoned by my thought, the door opened and he smiled in at me. Shaved, combed, freshly dressed, and clear-eyed, he seemed to have erased all traces of the night before—bar the expression on his face when he looked at me. Frowsy and ill-kempt as I was by contrast with his own neat appearance, the look of tenderness in his eyes warmed me, in spite of the lingering chill in the room.

"Awake at last. Did ye sleep well, Sassenach?"

"Like the dead," I replied automatically, and felt a small internal lurch as I said it.

He saw it reflected on my face, and came swiftly to sit down on the bed beside me.

"What is it? Have ye had an evil dream, Sassenach?"

"Not exactly," I said slowly. In fact, I had no memory of having dreamed at all. And yet, my mind appeared to have been ticking away in the shadows of unconsciousness, making notes and drawing its deductions. Prompted now by the word "dead," it had just presented me with its conclusions, which accounted for the feeling of unease with which I had awoken.

"That woman Betty. Have they buried her yet?"

"No. They've washed the body and put it in a shed, but Jocasta wished to wait until the morning for the burial, so as not to trouble her guests. Some are staying on for another night." He frowned slightly, watching me. "Why?"

I rubbed a hand over my face, less to rouse myself than to collect my words.

"There's something wrong. About her death, I mean."

"Wrong ... . how?" One eyebrow lifted. "It was a fearful way to die, to be sure, but that's not what ye mean, is it?"

"No." My hands were cold; I reached automatically for his, and he took them, engulfing my fingers with warmth. "I mean—I don't believe it was a natural death. I think someone killed her."

Blurted out that way, the words hung cold and stark in the air between us.

His brows drew together, and he pursed his lips slightly, thinking. I noticed, though, that he did not reject the idea out of hand, and that strengthened my conviction.

"Who?" he asked at last. "And are ye sure of it, Sassenach?"

"I have no idea. And I can't be totally sure," I admitted. "It's only—" I hesitated, but he squeezed one of my hands lightly in encouragement. I shook my head. "I've been a nurse, a doctor, a healer, for a long time, Jamie. I've seen a dreadful number of people die, and from all sorts of things. I can't quite put into words what it is here, but now that I've slept on it, I just know—I think—it's wrong," I ended, rather lamely.

The light was fading; shadows were coming down from the corners of the room, and I shivered suddenly, gripping his hands.

"I see," he said softly. "But there's no way ye can tell for sure, is there?"

The window was still half-open; the curtains billowed suddenly into the room with a gust of wind, and I felt the hairs rise on my arms with cold.

"There might be," I said.

# A HARD DAY'S NIGHT

THE OUTBUILDING where they had put the body was well away from the house—a small tool-shed outside the kitchen garden. The waning moon was low in the sky, but still shed light enough to see the brick path through the garden; the espaliered fruit trees spread black as spiderwebs against the walls. Someone had been digging; I could smell the cold damp of recently turned earth, and shivered involuntarily at the hint of worms and mold.

Jamie felt it, and put a light hand on my back.

"All right, Sassenach?" he whispered.

"Yes." I gripped his free hand for reassurance. They would hardly be burying Betty in the kitchen garden; the digging must be for something prosaic, like an onion bed or a trench for early peas. The thought was comforting, though my skin still felt cold and thin, prickling with apprehensions.

Jamie himself was far from easy, though he was outwardly composed, as usual. He was no stranger to death, and had no great fear of it. But he was both Catholic and Celt, with a strong conviction of another, unseen world that lay past the dissolution of the body. He believed implicitly in *tannasgeach*—in spirits—and had no desire to meet one. Still, if I was determined, he would brave the otherworld for my sake; he squeezed my hand hard, and didn't let go.

I squeezed back, deeply grateful for his presence. Beyond the debatable question of how Betty's ghost might feel about my proposed plan of action, I knew that the notion of deliberate mutilation disturbed him deeply, however much his own intelligence might be convinced that a soulless body was no more than clay.

"To see men hacked to death on a battlefield is one thing," he'd said earlier in the evening, still arguing with me. "That's war, and it's honorable, cruel as it may be. But to take a blade and carve up a poor innocent like yon woman in cold blood . . ." He looked at me, eyes dark with troubled thought. "Ye're sure ye must do it, Claire?"

"Yes, I am," I had said, eyes fixed on the contents of the bag I was assembling. A large roll of lint wadding, to soak up fluids, small jars for organ samples, my largest bone saw, a couple of scalpels, a wicked pair of heavy-bladed shears, a sharp knife borrowed from the kitchen . . . it was a sinister-looking collection, to be sure. I wrapped the shears in a towel to prevent them clanking against the other implements, and put them in the bag, carefully marshaling my words.

"Look," I said at last, raising my eyes to meet his. "There's something wrong, I know it. And if Betty was killed, then surely we owe it to her to find that out. If you were murdered, wouldn't you want someone to do whatever they could to prove it? To—to avenge you?"

He stood still for a long moment, eyes narrowed in thought as he looked down at me. Then his face relaxed, and he nodded.

"Aye, I would," he said quietly. He picked up the bone saw, and began wrapping it with cloth.

He hadn't protested further. He hadn't asked me again whether I was sure. He had merely said firmly that if I was going to do it, he was coming with me, and that was all about it.

As for being sure, I wasn't. I did have an abiding feeling that something was very wrong about this death, but I was less confident in my sense of what it was, with the cold moon sinking through an empty sky and wind brushing my cheeks with the touch of icy fingers.

Betty might have died only by accident, not malice. I could be wrong; perhaps it was a simple hemorrhage of an esophageal ulcer, the bursting of an aneurysm in the throat, or some other physiological oddity. Unusual, but natural. Was I doing this, in fact, only to try to vindicate my faith in my own powers of diagnosis?

The wind belled my cloak and I pulled it tighter around me, one-handed, stiffening my spine. No. It wasn't a natural death, I knew it. I couldn't have said *how* I knew it, but fortunately Jamie hadn't asked me that.

I had a brief flash of memory; Joe Abernathy, a jovial smile of challenge on his face, reaching into a cardboard box full of bones, saying, "I just want to see can you do it to a dead person, Lady Jane?"

I could; I had. He had handed me a skull, and the memory of Geillis Duncan shuddered through me like liquid ice.

"Ye needna do it, Claire." Jamie's hand tightened on mine. "I willna think ye a coward." His voice was soft and serious, barely audible above the wind.

"I would," I said, and felt him nod. That was the matter settled, then; he let go of my hand and went ahead of me, to open the gate.

He paused, and my dark-adapted eyes caught the clean sharp line of his profile as he turned his head, listening. The dark-lantern he carried smelled hot and oily, and a faint gleam escaping from its pierced-work panel sprinkled the cloth of his cloak with tiny flecks of dim light.

I glanced round myself, and looked back at the house. Late as it was, candles still burned in the back parlor, where the card games lingered on; I caught a faint murmur of voices as the wind changed, and a sudden laugh. The upper floors were mostly dark—save one window which I recognized as Jocasta's.

"Your aunt's awake late," I whispered to Jamie. He turned and looked up at the house.

"Nay, it's Duncan," he said softly. "My aunt doesna need the light, after all."

"Perhaps he's reading to her in bed," I suggested, trying to leaven the solemnity of our errand. A small derisive huff came from Jamie, but the oppressive atmosphere did lift just a bit. He unlatched the gate and pushed it open, showing a square of utter black beyond. I turned my back on the friendly lights of the house and stepped through, feeling just a bit like Persephone entering the Underworld.

Jamie swung the gate to, and handed me the lantern.

"What are you doing?" I whispered, hearing the rustle of his clothing. It was so dark by the gate that I couldn't see him as more than a dark blur, but the faint sound that came next told me what he was doing.

"Pissing on the gateposts," he whispered back, stepping back and rustling further as he did up his breeks. "If we must, then we will, but I dinna want anything to be following us back to the house."

I made my own small huffing noise at that, but made no demur when he insisted upon repeating this ritual at the door to the shed. Imagination or not, the night seemed somehow inhabited, as though invisible things moved through the darkness, murmuring under the voice of the wind.

It was almost a relief to go inside, where the air was still, even though the scents of death mingled thickly with the dankness of rust, rotted straw, and mildewed wood. There was a faint rasp of metal as the dark-lantern's panel slid back, and a dazzling shaft of light fell over the confines of the shed.

They had laid the dead slave on a board across two trestles, already washed and properly laid out, wrapped in a rough muslin shroud. Beside her stood a small loaf of bread and a cup of brandy. A small posy of dried herbs, carefully twisted into a knot, lay on the shroud, just above the heart. Who had left those? I wondered. One of the other slaves, surely. Jamie crossed himself at the sight, and looked at me, almost accusingly.

"It's ill luck to touch grave goods."

"I'm sure it's only ill luck to take them," I assured him, low-voiced, though I crossed myself before taking the objects and putting them on the ground in a corner of the shed. "I'll put them back when I've finished."

"Mmphm. Wait just a moment, Sassenach. Dinna touch her yet."

He dug in the recesses of his cloak, and emerged with a tiny bottle. He uncorked this, and putting his fingers to the opening, poured out a little liquid, which he flicked over the corpse, murmuring a quick Gaelic prayer that I recognized as an invocation to St. Michael to protect us from demons, ghouls, and things that go bump in the night. Very useful.

"Is that holy water?" I asked, incredulous.

"Aye, of course. I got it from Father LeClerc." He made the sign of the Cross over the body, and laid his hand briefly on the draped curve of the head, before nodding reluctant approval for me to proceed.

I extracted a scalpel from my bag and slit the stitching on the shroud carefully. I'd brought a stout needle and waxed thread, to sew up the body cavity; with luck, I could also repair the shroud sufficiently that no one would realize what I'd been doing.

Her face was almost unrecognizable, round cheeks gone slack and sunken, and the soft bloom of her black skin faded to an ashy gray, the lips and ears a livid purple. That made it easier; it was clear that this was indeed only a shell, and not the woman I had seen before. That woman, if she was still in the vicinity, would have no objections, I thought.

Jamie made the sign of the Cross again and said something soft in Gaelic, then stood still, the lantern held high so that I could work by its light. The light threw his shadow on the wall of the shed, gigantic and eerie in the wavering flicker. I looked away from it, down to my work.

The most formal and sanitary of modern autopsies is simple butchery; this was no better—and worse only in the lack of light, water, and specialized tools.

"You needn't watch, Jamie," I said, standing back for a moment to wipe a wrist across my brow. Cold as it was in the shed, I was sweating from the heavy work of splitting the breastbone, and the air was thick with the ripe smells of an open body. "There's a nail on the wall; you could hang up the lantern, if you want to go out for a bit."

"I'm all right, Sassenach. What is that?" He leaned forward, pointing carefully. The look of disquiet on his features had been replaced by one of interest.

"The trachea and bronchi," I replied, tracing the graceful rings of cartilage, "and a bit of a lung. If you're all right, then can I have the light a little closer here, please?"

Lacking spreaders, I couldn't wrench the rib cage far enough apart to expose the complete lung on either side, but thought I could see enough to eliminate some possibilities. The surfaces of both lungs were black and grainy; Betty was in her forties, and had lived all her life with open wood fires.

"Anything nasty that you breathe in and don't cough up again—tobacco smoke, soot, smog, what-have-you—gradually gets shoved out between the lung tissue and the pleura," I explained, lifting a bit of the thin, half-transparent pleural membrane with the tip of my scalpel. "But the body can't get rid of it altogether, so it just stays there. A child's lung would be a nice clean pink."

"Do mine look like that?" Jamie stifled a small, reflexive cough. "And what is smog?"

"The air in cities like Edinburgh, where you get smoke mixing with fog off the water." I spoke abstractedly, grunting slightly as I pulled the ribs back, peering into the shadowed cavity. "Yours likely aren't so bad, since you've lived out of doors or in unheated places so much. Clean lungs are one compensation to living without fire."

"That's good to know, if ye've got no choice about it," he said. "Given the choice, I expect most folk would rather be warm and cough."

I didn't look up, but smiled, slicing through the upper lobe of the right lung.

"They would, and they do." No indication of hemorrhage in either lung; no blood in the airway; no evidence of pulmonary embolism. No pooling of blood in the chest or abdominal cavity, either, though I was getting some seepage. Blood will clot soon after death, but then gradually reliquefies.

"Hand me a bit more of the wadding, will you, please?" A

little spotting of blood on the shroud likely wouldn't worry anyone, given the spectacular nature of Betty's demise, but I didn't want enough to make anyone sufficiently suspicious to check inside.

I leaned across to take the lint from his hand, inadvertently putting a hand on the corpse's side. The body emitted a low groan and Jamie leaped back with a startled exclamation, the light swinging wildly.

I had jumped, myself, but quickly recovered.

"It's all right," I said, though my heart was racing and the sweat on my face had gone suddenly cold. "It's only trapped gas. Dead bodies often make odd noises."

"Aye." Jamie swallowed and nodded, steadying the lantern. "Aye, I've seen it often. Takes ye a bit by surprise, though, doesn't it?" He smiled at me, lopsided, though a pale sheen of sweat gleamed on his forehead.

"It does that." It occurred to me that he had doubtless dealt with a good many dead bodies, all unembalmed, and was likely at least as familiar with the phenomena of death as I was. I set a cautious hand in the same place, but no further noises resulted, and I resumed my examination.

Another difference between this impromptu autopsy and the modern form was the lack of gloves. My hands were bloody to the wrist, and the organs and membranes had a faint but unpleasant feel of sliminess; cold though it was in the shed, the inexorable process of decomposition had started. I got a hand under the heart and lifted it toward the light, checking for gross discolorations of the surface, or visible ruptures of the great vessels.

"They move, too, now and then," Jamie said, after a minute. There was an odd tone to his voice, and I glanced up at him, surprised. His eyes were fixed on Betty's face, but with a remote look that made it plain he was seeing something else.

"Who moves?"

"Corpses."

Gooseflesh rippled up my forearms. He was right, though I thought he might have kept that particular observation to himself for the moment.

"Yes," I said, as casually as possible, looking back at my

work. "Common postmortem phenomena. Usually just the movement of gases."

"I saw a dead man sit up once," he said, his tone as casual as my own.

"What, at a wake? He wasn't really dead?"

"No, in a fire. And he was dead enough."

I glanced up sharply. His voice was flat and matter-of-fact, but his face bore an inward look of deep abstraction; whatever he'd seen, he was seeing it again.

"After Culloden, the English burned the Highland dead on the field. We smelled the fires, but I didna see one, save when they took me out and put me in the wagon, to send me home."

He had lain hidden under a layer of hay, nose pressed to a crack in the boards in order to breathe. The wagon driver had taken a circuitous route off the field, to avoid any questions from troops near the farmhouse, and at one point, had stopped for a moment to wait for a group of soldiers to move away.

"There was a fresh pyre burning, perhaps ten yards away; they'd set it alight no more than a short time before, for the clothes had only just begun to char. I saw Graham Gillespie lyin' on the heap near me, and he was surely dead, for there was the mark of a pistol shot on his temple."

The wagon had waited for what seemed a long time, though it was hard to tell, through the haze of pain and fever. But as he watched, he had seen Gillespie suddenly sit up amid the flames, and turn his head.

"He was lookin' straight at me," he said. "Had I been in my right mind, I expect I would ha' let out a rare skelloch. As it was, it only seemed . . . friendly of Graham." There was a hint of uneasy amusement in his voice. "I thought he was perhaps tellin' me it wasna so bad, being dead. That, or welcoming me to hell, maybe."

"Postmortem contracture," I said, absorbed in the excavation of the digestive system. "Fire makes the muscles contract, and the limbs often twist into very lifelike positions. Can you bring the light closer?"

I had the esophagus pulled free, and carefully slit the length of it, turning back the flabby tissue. There was some irritation toward the lower end, and there was blood in it, but no sign of rupture or hemorrhage. I bent, squinting up into the pharyngeal cavity, but it was too dark to see much there. I was in no way equipped for detailed exploration, so instead returned my examinations to the other end, slipping a hand under the stomach and lifting it up.

I felt a sharpening of the sense of wrongness that I had had through this whole affair. If there was something amiss, this was the most likely place to find evidence of it. Logic as well as sixth sense said as much.

There was no food in the stomach; after such vomiting that was hardly surprising. When I cut through the heavy muscular wall, though, the sharp scent of ipecac cut through the reek of the body.

"What?" Jamie leaned forward at my exclamation, frowning at the body.

"Ipecac. That quack dosed her with ipecac—and recently! Can you smell it?"

He grimaced with distaste, but took a cautious sniff, and nodded.

"Would that not be a proper thing to do, when you've a person wi' a curdled wame? Ye gave wee Beckie MacLeod ipecacuanha yourself, when she'd drunk your blue stuff."

"True enough." Five-year-old Beckie had drunk half a bottle of the arsenic decoction I made to poison rats, attracted by the pale blue color, and evidently not at all put off by the taste. Well, the rats liked it, too. "But I did that right away. There's no point in giving it hours afterward, when the poison or irritant has already passed out of the stomach."

Given Fentiman's state of medical knowledge, though, would he have known that? He might simply have administered ipecac again because he could think of nothing else to do. I frowned, turning back the heavy wall of the stomach. Yes, this was the source of the hemorrhage; the inner wall was raw-looking, dark red as ground meat. There was a small amount of liquid in the stomach; clear lymph that had begun to separate from the clotted blood left in the body.

"So you're thinking that it was maybe the ipecac that killed her?"

"I was . . . but now I'm not so sure," I murmured, probing

carefully. It had occurred to me that if Fentiman had given Betty a heavy dose of ipecac, the violent vomiting provoked by it might have caused an internal rupture and hemorrhage—but I wasn't finding any evidence of that. I used the scalpel to slit the stomach further open, pulling back the edges, and opening the duodenum.

"Can you hand me one of the small empty jars? And the wash bottle, please?"

Jamie hung the lantern on the nail and obligingly knelt to rummage through the bag, while I rummaged further through the stomach. There was some granular material forming a pale sludge in the furrows of the rugae. I scraped gingerly at it, finding that it came free easily, a thick, gritty paste between my fingertips. I wasn't sure what it was, but a suspicion was growing unpleasantly in the back of my mind. I meant to flush the stomach, collect the residue, and take it back to the house, where I could examine it in a decent light, come morning. If it was what I thought—

Without warning, the door of the shed swung open. A whoosh of cold air made the flame of the lantern burn suddenly high and bright—bright enough to show me Phillip Wylie's face, pale and shocked in the frame of the doorway.

He stared at me, his mouth hanging slightly open, then closed it and swallowed; I heard the sound of it clearly. His eyes traveled slowly over the scene, then returned to my face, wide pools of horror.

I was shocked, too. My heart had leapt into my throat, and my hands had frozen, but my brain was racing.

What would happen if he caused an outcry? It would be the most dreadful scandal, whether I was able to explain what I was doing, or not. If not—fear rippled over me in a chilly wave. I had come close to being burned for witchcraft once before; and that was one time too often.

I felt a slight movement of the air near my feet, and realized that Jamie was crouched in the deep shadow below the table. The light of the lantern was bright, but limited; I stood in a pool of darkness that reached to my waist. Wylie hadn't seen him. I reached out a toe and nudged him, as a signal to stay put.

I forced myself to smile at Phillip Wylie, though my heart

was stuck firmly in my throat, and beating wildly. I swallowed hard and said the first thing that came into my mind, which happened to be "Good evening."

He licked his lips. He was wearing neither patch nor powder at the moment, but was quite as pale as the muslin sheet.

"Mrs. . . . Fraser," he said, and swallowed again. "I—er—what *are* you doing?"

I should have thought that was reasonably obvious; presumably his question had to do with the reasons why I was doing it—and I had no intention of going into those.

"Never you mind that," I said crisply, recovering a bit of nerve. "What are *you* doing, skulking round the place at dead of night?"

Evidently that was a good question; his face shifted at once from open horror to wariness. His head twitched, as though to turn and look over his shoulder. He stopped the motion before it was completed, but my eyes followed the direction of it. There was a man standing in the darkness behind him; a tall man who now stepped forward, his face glimmering pale in the glow of the lantern, sardonic eyes the green of gooseberries. Stephen Bonnet.

"Jesus H. Roosevelt Christ," I said.

A number of things happened at that point: Jamie came out from under the table with a rush like a striking cobra, Phillip Wylie leaped back from the door with a startled cry, and the lantern crashed from its nail to the floor. There was a strong smell of splattered oil and brandy, a soft *whoosh* like a furnace lighting, and the crumpled shroud was burning at my feet.

Jamie was gone; there were shouts from the darkness outside, and the sound of running feet on brick. I kicked at the burning fabric, meaning to stamp it out.

Then I thought better, and instead lunged against the table, knocking it over and dumping its contents. I seized the blazing shroud with one hand and dragged it over corpse and upturned table. The floor of the shed was thick with sawdust, already burning in spots. I kicked the shattered lantern hard, knocking it into the dry boards of the wall, and spilling out the rest of its oil, which ignited at once.

There were shouts from the kitchen garden, voices calling

in alarm; I had to get out. I seized my bag and fled, red-handed, into the night, my fist still clenched tight about the evidence. It was the one point of certainty in the prevailing chaos. I had no notion what was going on, or what might happen next, but at least I knew for sure that I was right. Betty had indeed been murdered.

THERE WERE A PAIR of agitated servants in the kitchen garden, apparently wakened by the disturbance. They were casting round in a haphazard manner, calling out to each other, but with no light but that of the fading moon, it was an easy matter to keep to the shadows and slip past them.

No one had come out of the main house yet, but the shouts and flames were going to attract attention soon. I crouched against the wall, in the shadows of a huge raspberry cane, as the gate flung open and two more slaves came rushing through from the stable, half-dressed and incoherent, shouting something about the horses. The smell of burning was strong in the air; no doubt they thought the stable was on fire, or about to be.

My heart was pounding so hard against the inside of my chest that I could feel it, like a fist. I had an unpleasant vision of the flaccid heart I had just held in my hand, and of what my own must look like now—a dark red knob of slick muscle, pulsing and thumping, battering mindlessly away in its neatly socketed cave between the lungs.

The lungs weren't working nearly so well as the heart; my breath came short and hard, in gasps that I tried to stifle for fear of detection. What if they dragged Betty's desecrated body from the shed? They wouldn't know who had been responsible for the mutilation, but the discovery would cause the most fearful outcry, with resultant wild rumors and public hysteria.

A glow was visible now above the far wall of the kitchen garden; the roof of the shed was beginning to burn, fire-glow showing in brilliant thin lines as the pine shingles began to smoke and curl.

Sweat was prickling behind my ears, but my breath came a little easier when I saw the slaves standing by the far gate in a knot, bunched together in awed silhouette. Of course—they wouldn't try to put it out, well caught as it was. The nearest water was in the horse troughs; by the time buckets were fetched, the shed would be well on its way to ashes. There was nothing near it that would burn. Best to let it go.

Smoke purled up in quickening billows, high into the air. Knowing what was in the shed, it was much too easy to imagine spectral shapes in the transparent undulations. Then the fire broke through the roof, and tongues of flame lit the smoke from below in an eerie, beautiful glow.

A high-pitched wail broke from behind me, and I started back, banging my elbow against the brick wall. Phaedre had come through the gate, Gussie and another female slave behind her. She ran through the garden, screaming "Mama!" as her white shift caught the light of the flames that now burst through holes in the shed's roof, showering sparks.

The men by the gate caught her; the women hurried after, reaching for her, calling out in agitation. I tasted blood in my mouth, and realized that I had bitten my lower lip. I closed my eyes convulsively, trying not to hear Phaedre's frantic cries and the antiphonal babble of her comforters.

A frightful sense of guilt washed over me. Her voice was so like Bree's, and I could imagine so clearly what Bree might feel, were it my own body, burning in that shed. But there were worse things Phaedre might feel, had I not let loose the fire. My hands were shaking from cold and tension, but I groped for my bag, which I had dropped on the ground at my feet.

My hands felt stiff and dreadful, gummy with drying blood and lymph. I mustn't—*mustn't*—be found this way. I fumbled in the sack with my free hand, finally coming up by feel with a lidded jar, normally used to keep leeches, and the small wash bottle of dilute alcohol and water.

I couldn't see, but felt blood crack and flake away as I opened my cramped fingers and gingerly scraped the contents of my hand into the jar. I couldn't grip the cork of the bottle with my shaking fingers; finally I pulled it out with my teeth, and poured the alcohol over my open palm, washing the rest of the grainy residue into the jar.

The house had been roused now; I could hear voices coming from that direction. What was going on? Where was Jamie—and where were Bonnet and Phillip Wylie? Jamie had not been armed with anything save a bottle of holy water; were either of the others? I had heard no shots, at least—but blades made no noise.

I rinsed both hands hastily with the rest of the wash bottle, and dried them on the dark lining of my cloak, where the smears wouldn't show. People were running back and forth through the garden, shadows flitting along the walkways like phantoms, mere feet from my hiding place. Why did they make no noise? Were they truly people, or shades, somehow roused by my sacrilege?

Then one figure shouted; another replied. I realized dimly that the running people made no sound on the bricks because they were barefoot and because my ears were ringing. My face was tingling with cold sweat, my hands far more numb than chill would account for.

*You idiot, Beauchamp*, I thought to myself. *You're going to faint. Sit down!*

I must have managed to do so, for I came to myself a few moments later, sprawled in the dirt under the raspberry canes, half-leaning against the wall. The kitchen garden seemed full of people by now; jostling pale shapes of guests and servants, indistinguishable as ghosts in their shifts.

I waited for the space of a few breaths, to be sure I was recovered, then lurched awkwardly to my feet and stepped out onto the dark path, bag in hand.

The first person I saw was Major MacDonald, standing on the path watching the shed burn, his white wig gleaming in the light from the fire. I gripped him by the arm, startling him badly.

"What is happening?" I said, not bothering to apologize.

"Where is your husband?" he said in the same moment, peering round me in search of Jamie.

"I don't know," I said, all too truthfully. "I'm looking for him."

"Mrs. Fraser! Are you all right, dear lady?" Lloyd Stanhope popped up by my elbow, looking like a very animated boiled egg in his nightshirt, his polled head startlingly round and pale without his wig.

I assured him that I was quite all right, which I was, by now. It wasn't until I saw Stanhope and noticed that most of the other gentlemen present were in a similar state of dishabille that I realized the Major was fully clothed, from wig to buckled shoes. My face must have changed as I looked at him, for I saw his brows raise and his gaze run from my bound hair to my shod feet, as he quite obviously noticed the same thing about me.

"I heard shouts of 'Fire!' and thought someone might be hurt," I said coolly, lifting the bag. "I've brought my medical kit. Is everyone all right, do you know?"

"So far as I—" MacDonald began, but then sprang back in alarm, grasping my arm and dragging me back, too. The roof gave way with a deep sighing noise, and sparks plumed high, showering down among the crowd in the garden.

Everyone gasped and cried out, falling back. Then there came one of those brief, inexplicable pauses when everyone in a crowd falls suddenly silent at once. The fire was still burning, with a noise like crumpling paper, but over it I could hear a distant shouting. It was a woman's voice, high and cracked, but strong for all that, and full of fury.

"Mrs. Cameron!" Stanhope exclaimed, but the Major was already making for the house at a run.

# 53

# THE FRENCHMAN'S GOLD

WE FOUND JOCASTA CAMERON
Innes on the window seat in her room, clad in her
chemise, bound hand and foot with strips of bed
linen, and absolutely scarlet-faced with fury. I had no time to
take further note of her condition, for Duncan Innes, clad for
the night in nothing but his shirt, was lying sprawled on his
face on the floor near the hearth.

I rushed over and knelt by him at once, searching for a
pulse.

"Is he dead?" The Major peered over my shoulder, evidencing more curiosity than sympathy.

"No," I said briefly. "Get these people out of here, will
you?" The chamber was crammed with guests and servants,
all exclaiming over the newly freed Jocasta, expostulating,
speculating, and generally making bloody nuisances of
themselves. The Major blinked at my peremptory tone, but
retired without demur to deal with the situation.

Duncan was certainly alive, and a cursory examination
showed me no injury beyond a large lump behind one
ear; evidently, he had been clubbed with the heavy silver
candlestick which lay beside him on the floor. He had a nasty
color, but his pulse was fairly good, and he was breathing
evenly. I thumbed open his eyelids, one at a time, and
bent close to check his pupils. They stared back at me,
glazed, but the same size and not abnormally dilated. So far,
so good.

Behind me, the Major was making good use of his military experience, barking orders in a parade-ground voice.

Since most of those present were not soldiers, this was having a limited effect.

Jocasta Cameron was having a much greater one. Released from her bonds, she staggered across the room, leaning heavily on Ulysses's arm, parting the crowd like the waves of the Red Sea.

"Duncan! Where is my husband?" she demanded, turning her head from side to side, blind eyes fierce. People gave way before her, and she reached my side in seconds.

"Who is there?" Her hand swept in a flat arc before her, searching for position.

"It's me—Claire." I reached up to touch her hand, guiding her down beside me. Her own fingers were chilled and trembling, and there were deep red marks on her wrists from the bonds. "Don't worry; I think Duncan will be all right."

She put out a hand, seeking to see for herself, and I guided her fingers to his throat, setting them on the big vein I could see pulsing at the side of his neck. She uttered a small exclamation and leaned forward, putting both hands on his face, tracing his features with an anxious tenderness that quite moved me, so at odds as it was with her normal autocratic mien.

"They struck him . . . is he badly hurt?"

"I think not," I assured her. "Only a knock on the head."

"Are you quite sure?" Her face turned toward me, frowning, and her sensitive nostrils flared. "I smell blood."

With a small shock, I realized that while my hands were mostly clean, my fingernails were still heavily ringed with dark blood from the impromptu autopsy. I repressed the urge to curl my hands, instead murmuring discreetly, "That's me, I expect; my courses." Major MacDonald was glancing curiously in our direction; had he heard her?

There was a stir at the doorway, and I turned. To my immense relief, it was Jamie. He was disheveled, his coat was torn, and he sported what looked like the beginnings of a black eye, but otherwise appeared undamaged.

My relief must have shown on my face, for his grim look softened a little, and he nodded as he met my eye. Then it hardened again, as he saw Duncan. He dropped to one knee beside me.

"He's all right," I said, before he could ask. "Someone hit him on the head and tied up your aunt."

"Aye? Who?" He glanced up at Jocasta, and laid a hand on Duncan's chest, as though to reassure himself that Duncan was indeed still breathing.

"I havena the slightest notion," she replied crisply. "If I had, I should have sent men to hunt the ill-deedie shargs down by now." Her lips tightened into a thin line, and the high color surged back into her face at thought of the assailants. "Did no one see the rascals?"

"I think not, Aunt," Jamie replied calmly. "With such a boiling in the house, no one kens what to look for, aye?"

I raised one eyebrow at him in silent question. What did he mean by that? Had Bonnet got away? For surely it must have been Bonnet who had invaded Jocasta's chamber; boiling or no, there couldn't be multiple violent criminals at large on the same night in a place the size of River Run.

Jamie shook his head briefly. He glanced at my hands, saw the blood under my nails, and raised an eyebrow of his own. Had I discovered anything? Had there been time for me to be sure? I nodded, and a slight shudder went over me; yes, I knew.

*Murder*, I mouthed to him.

He squeezed my arm in quick reassurance, and glanced over his shoulder; the Major had at last succeeded in pushing most of the crowd out into the hallway, sending the servants for restoratives and refreshments, a groom for the Sheriff in Cross Creek, the men out to search the grounds for possible miscreants, and the ladies down to the salon in a flutter of excited puzzlement. The Major closed the door firmly behind them, then came briskly over to us.

"Shall we get him onto the bed, then?"

Duncan was beginning to stir and groan. He coughed and gagged a little, but fortunately didn't throw up. Jamie and Major MacDonald got him up and conveyed him to the big four-poster, where they laid him down with complete disregard for the quilted silk coverlet.

With a faint atavistic sense of housewifeliness, I tucked a soft green velvet pillow under his head. It was filled with bran, but crackled faintly under my hand and gave off a strong scent of lavender. Lavender was good for headache, all right, but I wasn't sure it was quite up to this.

"Where is Phaedre?"

Ulysses had guided Jocasta to her chair, and she sank back in its leather depths, looking suddenly exhausted and old. The color had left her face along with her rage, and her white hair was coming down in straggles round her shoulders.

"I sent Phaedre to bed, Auntie." Bree had come in, unnoticed in the scrum, and had resisted removal by the Major. She bent over Jocasta, touching her hand with solicitude. "Don't worry; I'll take care of you."

Jocasta put her own hand over Bree's in gratitude, but sat up straighter, looking puzzled.

"Sent her to bed? Why? And what in God's name is burning?" She jerked bolt upright, alarmed. "Are the stables afire?" The wind had changed, and the night air was streaming in through a broken pane above the window seat, heavy with the scent of smoke and a faint, dreadful smell of burned flesh.

"No, no! The stables are fine. Phaedre was upset," Bree explained, with some delicacy. "The shed by the kitchen garden seems to have burned down; her mother's body . . ."

Jocasta's face went quite blank for a moment. Then she drew herself up, and an extraordinary look came into her face, something almost like satisfaction, though with a tinge of puzzlement.

Jamie was standing behind me. He evidently saw it, too, for I heard him give a soft grunt.

"Are ye somewhat recovered, Aunt?" he asked.

She turned her face toward him, one eyebrow lifted in sardonic reply.

"I shall be the better for a dram," she said, accepting the cup that Ulysses set deftly into her hands. "But aye, nephew, I'm well enough. Duncan, though?"

I was sitting by Duncan on the bed, his wrist in my hand, and could feel him coming toward the surface of consciousness, eyelids fluttering and fingers twitching slightly against my palm.

"He's coming round," I assured her.

"Give him brandy, Ulysses," Jocasta commanded, but I stopped the butler with a shake of my head.

"Not quite yet. He'll choke."

"Do ye feel yourself equal to telling us what happened, Aunt?" Jamie asked, with a noticeable edge to his voice. "Or must we wait for Duncan to come to himself?"

Jocasta sighed, closing her eyes briefly. She was as good as all the MacKenzies at hiding what she thought, but in this case, it was evident at least that she *was* thinking, and furiously, at that. The tip of her tongue flicked out, touching a raw spot at the corner of her mouth, and I realized that she must have been gagged as well as bound.

I could feel Jamie behind me, seething with some strong feeling. Near as he was, I could hear his stiff fingers drumming softly on the bedpost. Much as I wanted to hear Jocasta's story, I wanted even more to be alone with Jamie, to tell him what I had discovered, and to find out what had happened in the darkness of the kitchen garden.

Outside, voices murmured in the hall; not all the guests had dispersed. I caught muffled phrases—"quite burnt up, nothing left but the bones," ". . . stolen? Don't know . . ." ". . . check the stables," "Yes, completely burned . . ." A deep shiver struck me, and I gripped Duncan's hand hard, fighting a panic that I did not understand. I must have looked odd, for Bree said softly, "Mama?" She was looking at me, brow creased with worry. I tried to smile at her, but my lips felt stiff.

Jamie's hands settled on my shoulders, large and warm. I had been holding my breath without realizing it; at his touch, I let it out in a small gasp, and breathed again. Major Mac-Donald glanced curiously at me, but his attention was at once deflected by Jocasta, who opened her eyes and turned her face in his direction.

"It is Major MacDonald, is it not?"

"At your service, Mum." The Major made an automatic bow, forgetting—as folk often did—that she could not see him.

"I thank ye for your gallant service, Major. My husband and I are most indebted to ye."

The Major made a politely dismissive sound.

"No, no," she insisted, straightening up and brushing back her hair with one hand. "Ye've been put to great trouble on our account, and we must not impose further on your kindness. Ulysses—take the Major down to the parlor and find him proper refreshment."

The butler bowed obsequiously—I noticed for the first time that he was dressed in a nightshirt over unbuckled breeches, though he had clapped his wig on his head—and ushered the Major firmly toward the door. MacDonald looked ludicrously surprised and not a little disgruntled at being given the push in this civilized fashion, he having quite obviously intended to stay and hear all the gory details. Still, there was no graceful way of resisting, and he made the best of it, bowing in a dignified manner as he took his leave.

The panic had begun to recede, as bafflingly as it had come. Jamie's hands radiated a warmth that seemed to spread through my body, and my breath came easily again. I was able to focus my attention on my patient, who had got his eyes open, though he seemed to be regretting it.

"Och, *mo cheann*!" Duncan squinted against the glow of the lamp, focusing with some difficulty on my face, then rising to Jamie's behind me. "*Mac Dubh*—what's come amiss?"

One of Jamie's hands left my shoulder, and reached down to tighten on Duncan's arm.

"Dinna fash yourself, *a charaid*." He glanced meaningfully at Jocasta. "Your wife is just about to tell us what has happened. Are ye not, Aunt?"

There was a slight but definite emphasis on the "not," and Jocasta, thus put on the spot, pursed her lips, but then sighed and sat straight, plainly resigned to the unpleasant necessity of confidence.

"There is no one here but family?"

Being assured that there was not, she nodded, and began.

She had sent away her maid, and been on the point of retiring, she said, when the door from the hall had suddenly opened to admit what she thought were two men.

"I am sure there was more than one—I heard their footsteps, and breathing," she said, frowning in concentration. "There *might* have been three, but I think not. Only one of them spoke, though. I think the other must have been someone I ken, for he stayed far away, quite at the end of the room, as though he were afraid I should recognize him by some means."

The man who had spoken to her was a stranger; she was positive that she had never heard his voice before.

"He was an Irishman," she said, and Jamie's hand tightened abruptly on my shoulder. "Well enough spoken, but not a gentleman, by any means." Her nostrils flared a little, with unconscious disdain.

"No, hardly that," Jamie said, under his breath. Bree had started slightly at the word "Irishman," though her face bore no more than a slight frown of concentration as she listened.

The Irishman had been polite, but blunt in his demands; he wanted the gold.

"Gold?" It was Duncan who spoke, but the question was plain on everyone's face. "What gold? We've no money in the house save a few pounds sterling and a bit of the Proclamation money."

Jocasta's lips pressed tight. There was no help for it, though; not now. She made a small growling noise in her throat, an inarticulate protest at being compelled to give up the secret she had kept for so long.

"The Frenchman's gold," she said, abruptly.

"What?" said Duncan in bewilderment. He touched the lump behind his ear, gingerly, as though convinced it had affected his hearing.

"The French gold," Jocasta repeated, rather irritably. "That was sent, just before Culloden."

"Before—" Bree began, wide-eyed, but Jamie interrupted her.

"Louis's gold," he said softly. "That's what ye mean, Aunt? The Stuarts' gold?"

Jocasta uttered a short laugh, quite without humor.

"Once it was."

She paused, listening. The voices had moved away from the door, though there were still noises in the hallway. She turned toward Bree, and motioned toward the door.

"Go and see that no one's got his lug to the keyhole, lass. I havena held my peace these twenty-five years only to spill it to the whole county."

Bree opened the door briefly, peered out, then closed it, reporting that no one was near.

"Good. Come ye here, lass. Sit by me. But no—first, fetch me the case I showed ye yesterday."

Looking more than puzzled, Bree vanished into the dressing room, returning with a slender case of worn black leather. She laid it in Jocasta's lap and settled onto a stool beside her aunt, giving me a look of faint concern.

I was feeling quite myself again, though a faint echo of that odd fear still rang in my bones. I nodded reassuringly to Bree, though, and bent to give Duncan a sip of watered brandy. I knew what it was now, that ancient distress. It was that phrase overheard, the words by chance the same that a small girl had once heard spoken, whispered in the next room by the strangers who had come to say her mother would not be coming back, that she had died. An accident; a crash; fire. *Burnt to bones,* the voice had said, filled with the awe of it. *Burnt to bones,* and the desolation of a daughter, forever abandoned. My hand trembled, and the cloudy liquid ran in a trickle down Duncan's chin.

*But that was long ago, and in another country,* I thought, steeling myself against the riptide of memory.

*And besides . . .*

Jocasta drained her own cup, set it down with a small thump, and opened the case in her lap. A gleam of gold and diamonds showed inside, and she lifted out a slender wooden rod that held three rings.

"I had three daughters, once," she said. "Three girls. Clementina, Seonag, and Morna." She touched one of the rings, a wide band, set with three large diamonds.

"This was for my girls; Hector gave it to me when Morna was born. She was his, Morna—you know it means 'beloved'?" Her other hand left the box and stretched out, groping. She touched Bree's cheek, and Bree took the hand, cradling it between her own.

"I had one living child of each marriage." Jocasta's long fingers probed delicately, touching each ring in turn. "Clementina belonged to John Cameron; him I wed when I myself was little more than a child; I bore her at sixteen. Seonag was the daughter of Black Hugh—she was dark, like her sire, but she had my brother Colum's eyes." She turned her own blind eyes toward Jamie, briefly, then bent her head back, touching the ring with three diamonds again.

"And then Morna, my last child. She was but sixteen when she died."

The old woman's face was bleak, but the line of her mouth softened, speaking the names of her vanished girls.

"I'm sorry, Aunt." Bree spoke softly. She bent her head to kiss the knuckles of the hand she cradled, knobbed with age. Jocasta tightened her hand a little in acknowledgment, but did not mean to be distracted from her story.

"Hector Cameron gave me this," Jocasta said, touching the ring. "And he killed them all. My children, my daughters. He killed them for the Frenchman's gold."

The shock of it took my breath and hollowed my stomach. I felt Jamie go still behind me, and saw Duncan's bloodshot eyes go wide. Brianna didn't change expression. She closed her eyes for a moment, but still held on to the long bony hand.

"What happened to them, Aunt?" she said quietly. "Tell me."

Jocasta was silent for a few moments. So was the room; there was no sound save the hiss of beeswax burning, and the faint asthmatic wheeze of her breath. To my surprise, when she spoke again, it wasn't to Brianna. Instead, she lifted her head and turned again toward Jamie.

"You know about the gold, then, *a mhic mo pheathar*?" she said. If he found this a strange question, he gave no sign of it, but answered calmly.

"I have heard something of it," he said. He moved, coming round the bed to sit beside me, closer to his aunt. "It has been a rumor in the Highlands, ever since Culloden. Louis would send gold, they said, to help his cousin in his holy fight. And then they said the gold had come, yet no man saw it."

"I saw it." Jocasta's wide mouth, so like her nephew's, widened further in a sudden grimace, then relaxed. "I saw it," she repeated.

"Thirty thousand pound, in gold bullion. I was with them the night it came ashore, rowed in from the French ship. It was in six small chests, each one so heavy that only two at a time could be brought, else the boat would sink. Each chest had the fleur-de-lis carved on the lid, each one bound with iron bands and a lock, each lock itself sealed with red wax, and the wax bore the print of King Louis's ring. The *fleur-de-lis*."

A sigh ran through us all at the words, a collective breath of awe. Jocasta nodded slowly, blind eyes open to the sights of that night long past.

"Where was it brought ashore, Aunt?" Jamie asked softly.

She nodded slowly, as though to herself, eyes fixed on the scene her memory painted.

"On Innismaraich," she said. "A tiny isle, just off Coigach."

I had been holding my breath. Now I let it out, slowly, and met Jamie's eyes. Innismaraich. Island of the Sea-people; the silkies' isle, it meant. We knew that place.

"There were the three men trusted with it," she said. "Hector was one, my brother Dougal was another—the third man was masked; they all were, but of course I kent Hector and Dougal. I didna ken the third man, nor did any of them speak his name. I knew his servant, though; a man named Duncan Kerr."

Jamie had stiffened slightly at Dougal's name; at the name of Duncan Kerr he froze.

"There were servants, too?" he asked.

"Two," she said, and a faint, bitter smile twisted her mouth. "The masked man brought Duncan Kerr, as I said, and my brother Dougal had a man with him from Leoch—I kent his face, but not his name. Hector had me to help him; I was a braw, strong woman—like you, *a leannan*, like you," she said softly, squeezing Brianna's hand. "I was strong, and Hector trusted me as he could trust no other. I trusted him, too—then."

The noises from outside had died away, but a breeze through the broken pane stirred the curtains, uneasy as a ghost that hears its name called from a distance.

"There were three boats. The chests were small, but heavy enough that it took two persons to carry one between them. We took two chests into our boat, Hector and I, and we rowed away, into the fog. I could hear the splash of the others' oars, growing fainter as they drew away, and then lost in the night."

"When was this, Aunt?" Jamie asked, his eyes intent on her. "When did the gold come from France?"

"Too late," she whispered. "Much too late. Damn Louis!" she exclaimed, with a sudden fierceness that brought her upright in her seat. "Damn the wicked Frenchman, and may his eyes rot as mine have! To think what might have been, had he been true to his blood and his word!"

Jamie's eyes met mine, sidelong. Too late. Had the gold come sooner—when Charles landed at Glenfinnan, perhaps, or when he took Edinburgh, and for a few brief weeks held the city as a king returned—what then?

The ghost of a smile touched Jamie's lips with ruefulness, and he glanced at Brianna, then back at me, the question asked and answered in his eyes. What, then?

"It was March," Jocasta said, recovering from her outburst. "A freezing night, but clear as ice. I stood upon the cliff and looked far out to sea, and the path of the moon lay like gold on the water. The ship came sailing in upon that golden path, like a king to his coronation, and I did think it a sign." Her head turned toward Jamie, and her mouth twisted abruptly.

"I did think I heard him laughing, then," she said. "Black Brian. Him who took my sister from me. It would have been like him. But he was not there; I suppose it was only the barking of the silkies."

I was watching Jamie as she spoke. He didn't move, but like magic, the reddish hairs on his forearm rose, glinting like wires in the candlelight.

"I didna ken ye knew my father," he said, a faint edge to his voice. "But let that be for now, Aunt. It was March, ye say?"

She nodded.

"Too late," she repeated. "It was meant to have come two months before, Hector said. There were delays . . ."

It *had* been too late. In January, after the victory at Falkirk, such a show of support from France might have been decisive. But in March, the Highland Army was already moving north, turned back at Derby from its invasion of

England. The last slim chance of victory had been lost, and Charles Stuart's men were marching then toward destruction at Culloden.

With the chests safe ashore, the new guardians of the gold had conferred over what to do with the treasure. The army was moving, and Stuart with it; Edinburgh was once more in the hands of the English. There was no safe place to take it, no trustworthy hands into which it could be delivered.

"They didna trust O'Sullivan or the others near the Prince," Jocasta explained. "Irishmen, Italians . . . Dougal said he hadna gone to so much trouble, only to have the gold squandered or stolen by foreigners." She smiled, a little grimly. "He meant he didna want to chance losing the credit for having got it."

The three keepers had been no more willing to trust one another than the Prince's advisers. Most of the night had been spent in argument in the bleak upper room of a desolate tavern, while Jocasta and the two servants slept on the floor, among the red-sealed chests. Finally, the gold had been divided; each man had taken two of the chests, swearing on his blood to keep the secret and hold the treasure faithfully, in trust for his rightful monarch, King James.

"They made the two servants swear as well," Jocasta said. "They cut each man, and the drops of blood shone redder in the candlelight than the wax seals on the chests."

"Did you swear, too?" Brianna spoke quietly, but her eyes were intent on the white-haired figure in the chair.

"No, I didna swear." Jocasta's lips, still finely shaped, curved slightly, as though amused. "I was Hector's wife; his oath bound me. Then."

Uneasy in possession of so much wealth, the conspirators had left the tavern before dawn, bundling the chests in blankets and rags to hide them.

"A pair of travelers rode in, as the last of the chests was brought down. It was their coming that saved the innkeeper's life, for it was a lonely spot, and he the only witness to our presence there that night. I think Dougal and Hector would not have thought to do such a thing—but the third man, he meant to dispose of the landlord; I saw it in his eyes, in the crouch of his body as he waited near the bottom of the stair, his hand on his dirk. He saw me watching—he smiled at me, beneath his mask."

"And did he never unmask, this third man?" Jamie asked. His ruddy brows drew together as though by sheer concentration he could recreate the scene she saw in her mind's eye, and identify the stranger.

She shook her head.

"No. I asked myself, now and then, when I thought of that night, would I know the man again, did I see him. I thought I would; he was dark, a slender man, but with a strength in him like knife steel. Could I see his eyes again, I would be sure of it. But now . . ." She shrugged. "Would I ken him by his voice alone? I canna say, so long ago it was."

"But he wasna by any means an Irishman, this man?" Duncan was still pale and clammy-looking, but had raised himself on one elbow, listening with deep absorption.

Jocasta started a little, as though she had forgotten his presence.

"Ah! No, *a dhuine*. A Scot by his speech—a Highland gentleman."

Duncan and Jamie exchanged glances.

"A MacKenzie or a Cameron?" Duncan asked softly, and Jamie nodded.

"Or perhaps one of the Grants."

I understood their half-voiced speculations. There were— had been—a staggeringly complex array of associations and feuds among the Highland clans, and there were many who would not—could not—have cooperated in an undertaking of such importance and secrecy.

Colum MacKenzie had negotiated a close alliance with the Camerons; in fact, Jocasta herself had been part of that alliance, her marriage to a Cameron chief the token of it. If Dougal MacKenzie was one of the men who had engineered the receipt of the French gold, and Hector Cameron another, it was odds-on that the third man had been someone from one of those clans, or from another trusted by both. MacKenzie, Cameron . . . or Grant. And if Jocasta had not known the man by sight, the odds on his being a Grant improved, for she would have known most high-ranking tacksmen of clans MacKenzie or Cameron.

But there was no time now to consider such things; the story was not finished.

The conspirators had separated then, each going by his own way, each with one-third of the French gold. Jocasta had no knowledge of what Dougal MacKenzie or the unknown man had done with their chests; Hector Cameron had put the two chests he brought away into a hole in the floor of his bedroom, an old hiding place made by his father to conceal valuables.

Hector meant to leave it there until the Prince had reached some place of safety, where he could receive the gold, and use it for the furtherance of his aims. But Charles Stuart was already in flight, and would not find a place to rest for many months. Before he reached his final refuge, disaster intervened.

"Hector left the gold—and me—at home, and went to join the Prince and the army. On the seventeenth of April, he rode back into the dooryard at sunset, his horse lathered to a froth. He swung down and left the poor beast to a groom, while he rushed into the house and bade me pack what valuables I could—the Cause was lost, he said, and we must flee, or die with the Stuarts."

Cameron was wealthy, even then, and canny enough to have kept his coach and horses, rather than giving them to the Stuart cause. Canny enough, too, not to carry two chests of French gold in his flight.

"He took three bars of the gold from one of the chests, and gave them to me. I hid them under the seat of the coach; he and the groom carried the chests awa to the wood—I didna see where they buried them."

It was midday of April 18, when Hector Cameron boarded his coach, with his wife, his groom, his daughter Morna, and three bars of French bullion, and headed hell-for-leather south toward Edinburgh.

"Seonag was married to the Master of Garth—he declared early for the Stuarts; he was killed at Culloden, though of course we didna know it then. Clementina was widowed already, and living with her sister at Rovo."

She took a deep breath, shuddering slightly, unwilling to relive the events she recounted, unable to resist them.

"I begged Hector to go to Rovo. It was only ten miles out of the way—it would have taken no but a few hours—but he wouldna stop. We could not, he said. Too big a risk, to take the time needed to fetch them. Clementina had two children, Seonag the one. Too many people for the coach, he said; it would slow us too much.

"Not to bring them away, then, I said. Only to warn them—only to see them once more."

She paused.

"I kent where we were bound—we had talked of it, though I didna ken he had things in such readiness."

Hector Cameron had been a Jacobite, but was also a keen judge of human affairs, and no man to throw his own life after a lost cause. Seeing how matters were falling out, and fearing some disaster, he had taken pains to engineer an escape. He had quietly put aside a few bags of clothing and necessities, turned what he could of his property into money, and secretly booked three open passages, from Edinburgh to the Colonies.

"Sometimes, I think I canna blame him," Jocasta said. She sat bolt upright, the light of the candles gleaming from her hair. "He thought Seonag wouldna go without her husband, and Clementina wouldna risk her bairns at sea. Perhaps he was right about that. And perhaps it would have made no difference to warn them. But I knew I shouldna see them again. . . ." Her mouth closed, and she swallowed.

In any case, Hector had refused to stop, fearing pursuit. Cumberland's troops had converged upon Culloden, but there were English soldiers on the Highland roads, and word of Charles Stuart's defeat was spreading like ripples near the edge of a whirlpool, moving faster and faster, in a vortex of danger.

As it was, the Camerons were discovered, two days later, near Ochtertyre.

"A wheel came off the coach," Jocasta said with a sigh. "Lord, I can see it now, spinning down the road by itself. The axletree was broke, and we'd no choice but to camp there by the road, while Hector and the groom made shift to mend it."

Repairs had taken the best part of a day, and Hector had

grown more and more edgy as the work went on, his anxiety infecting the rest of the party.

"I didna ken then what he'd seen at Culloden," Jocasta said. "He kent weel enough that if the English took him, it was all up wi' him. If they didna kill him on the spot, he'd be hangit as a traitor. He was sweating as he worked, and more wi' fear than with the heat of his labor. But even so . . ." Her lips pressed tight for a moment, before she went on.

"It was nearly dusk—it was spring, dusk came early—when they got the wheel back on the coach, and everyone got back aboard. The coach had been in a wee hollow when the wheel flew off; the groom urged the horses up a long slope, and just as we reached the crest of the hill, two men with muskets stepped out from the shadows into the road ahead."

It was a company of English soldiers, Cumberland's men. Arriving too late to join in the victory at Culloden, they were inflamed by news of it—but frustrated at not sharing in the battle, and only too ready to wreak what vengeance they could on fleeing Highlanders.

Always a quick thinker, Hector had sunk back in the corner of the coach at sight of them, his head bent and a shawl pulled over it, pretending to be an aged crone, sunk in sleep. Following his hissed instructions, Jocasta had leaned out of the window, prepared to pose as a respectable lady traveling with her daughter and mother.

The soldiers had not waited to hear her speech. One yanked open the door of the coach, and dragged her out. Morna, panicked, had leapt out after her, trying to pull her mother away from the soldier. Another man had grabbed the girl, and dragged her back, so that he stood between Jocasta and the coach.

"Another minute, and they meant to have 'Grannie' out on the ground as well—and then they would find the gold, and it would be all up wi' all of us."

A pistol shot startled all of them into momentary immobility. Leaning from the coach's open door, Hector had fired at the soldier holding Morna—but it was dusk and the light was poor; perhaps the horses had moved, jostling the coach. The shot struck Morna in the head.

"I ran to her," Jocasta said. Her voice was hoarse, her throat gone dry and thick. "I ran to her, but Hector jumped out and seized me. The soldiers were all standing, staring with the shock. He dragged me back, into the coach, and shouted to the groom to drive, drive on!"

She licked her lips and swallowed, once.

" 'She is dead,' he said to me. Over and over, 'She is dead, you cannot help,' he said, and held me tight when I would have thrown myself from the coach in my despair."

Slowly she pulled her hand away from Brianna; she had needed support to begin her story, but needed none to finish it. Her hands folded into fists, pressed hard against the white linen of her shift, as though to stanch the bleeding of a desecrated womb.

"It had gone dark by then," she said, and her voice was remote, detached. "I saw the glow of fires against the sky to the north."

Cumberland's troops were spreading outward, burning and pillaging. They reached Rovo, where Clementina and Seonag were with their families, and set the manor house afire. Jocasta never learned whether they had died in the fire, or later, starved and freezing in the cold Highland spring.

"So Hector saved his life—and mine, for what it was worth then," she said, still detached. "And of course, he saved the gold." Her fingers sought the ring again, and turned it slowly round upon its rod, so the stones caught the lamplight, glimmering.

"Indeed," Jamie murmured. His eyes were fixed on the blind face, watching her intently. It struck me suddenly as unfair that he should watch her so, almost judging, when she could not look back, or even know how he looked at her. I touched him, and he glanced aside at me, then took my hand, squeezing it hard.

Jocasta put aside the rings and rose, restless now that the worst part of the story was told. She moved toward the window seat, knelt there, and brushed back the curtains. It was hard to believe her blind, seeing her move with such purpose—and yet this was her room, her place, and every item in it was scrupulously placed so that she could find her way.

She pressed her hands against the icy glass and the night outside, and a white fog of condensation flared around her fingers like cold flames.

"Hector bought this place with the gold we brought," she
said. "The land, the mill, the slaves. To do him credit"—her
tone suggested that she was not inclined to do any such
thing—"the worth of it now is due in great part to his own
work. But it was the gold that bought it, to begin with."

"What of his oath?" Jamie asked softly.

"What of it?" she said, and uttered a short laugh. "Hector
was a practical man. The Stuarts were finished; what need
had they of gold, in Italy?"

"Practical," I repeated, surprising myself; I hadn't meant
to speak, but I thought I had heard something odd in the way
she spoke the word.

Evidently, I had. She turned around to face us, turning
toward my voice. She was smiling, but a chill ran down my
backbone at the sight of it.

"Aye, practical," she said, nodding. "My daughters were
dead; he saw no reason to waste tears upon them. He never
spoke of them, and would not let me speak, either. He had
been a man of worth once, he would be, again—not so easy
here, had anyone known." She breathed out, a heavy sound
of stifled anger. "I daresay there are none in this land who
even ken I was once a mother."

"You still are," said Brianna softly. "That much I know."
She glanced at me, and her blue eyes met mine, dark with
understanding. I felt the sting of tears behind the smile I gave
her back. Yes, that much she knew, as did I.

So did Jocasta; the lines of her face relaxed for a moment,
fury and remembered despair displaced for a moment by
longing. She walked slowly to where Brianna sat on her
stool, and laid her free hand on Bree's head. It rested there
for a moment, then slid down, the long, sensitive fingers
probing Brianna's strong cheekbones, her wide lips and long,
straight nose, tracing the small track of the wetness down her
cheek.

"Aye, *a leannan*," she said softly. "Ye ken what I mean.
And ye ken now, why I would leave this place to you—or to
your blood?"

Jamie coughed, breaking in before Bree could answer.

"Aye," he said, in a matter-of-fact tone. "So that is what ye told the Irishman tonight? Not all the story, to be sure—but that ye have no gold here?"

Jocasta's hands dropped from Brianna's face and she turned to face Jamie.

"Aye, I told them. Him. Told him that for all I kent, those chests were still buried in the wood in Scotland; he was welcome, I said, to go and dig there, and it suited him." One corner of her mouth curled up in a bitter smile.

"He wasna inclined to take your word for it?"

She shook her head, lips pressed together.

"He wasna a gentleman," she said again. "I canna say how it might have fallen out—for I sat near the bed, and I keep a wee knife beneath my pillow; I wouldna have suffered him to lay hands on me unscathed. Before I could reach for it, though, I heard footsteps in the dressing room."

She waved a hand toward the door near the fireplace; her dressing room lay beyond, joining her bedroom to another— the room that had once been Hector Cameron's, and was now presumably Duncan's.

The intruders had heard the footsteps, too; the Irishman hissed something to his friend, then moved away from Jocasta, toward the hearth. The other fellow had come close then, and seized her from behind, a hand across her mouth.

"All I could tell ye from that was that the fellow wore a cap pulled low over his head, and he stank of liquor, as though he'd poured it over himself instead of drinking it." She made a brief grimace of distaste.

The door had opened, Duncan had come in, and the Irishman had apparently leapt from behind the open door and clubbed him over the head.

"I dinna recall a thing," Duncan said ruefully. "I came to bid Miss—that is, my wife—good night. I recall settin' my hand upon the knob of the door, and next thing, I was lyin' here wi' my head split open." He touched the lump tenderly, then looked at Jocasta with an anxious concern.

"You are all right, yourself, *mo chridhe*? The bastards didna offer ye ill use?" He stretched out his hand to her, then, realizing that she could not see him, tried to sit up. He collapsed with a stifled groan, and she stood up at the sound, coming hurriedly to the bedside.

"Of course I am all right," she said, crossly, groping until she found his hand. "Save for the distress of thinking myself about to be a widow for the fourth time." She let out a sigh of exasperation and sat down beside him, smoothing back a swath of loosened hair from her face.

"I couldna tell what had happened; I only heard the thud, and a dreadful groan as ye fell. Then the Irishman came back toward me, and the creature holding me let go."

The Irishman had informed her pleasantly that he did not believe a word of her claim that there was no gold at River Run. He was convinced that the gold was here, and while he would not dream of offering harm to a lady, the same inhibitions did not obtain with respect to her husband.

"If I didna tell him where it was, he said, he and his companion would set in to cut wee bits off Duncan, beginning with his toes, and advancing to his ballocks," Jocasta said bluntly. Duncan hadn't much blood in his face to begin with, but what there was drained away at this. Jamie glanced at Duncan, then away, clearing his throat.

"Ye were convinced he meant it, I suppose."

"He'd a good sharp knife; he ran it across the palm of my hand to show me that he was in earnest." She opened her free hand; sure enough, a hair-thin red line ran across the heel of it.

She shrugged.

"Well, I supposed I couldna have that. So I made pretense of reluctance, until the Irishman went to pick up one of Duncan's feet—then I wept and carried on, in hopes that someone would hear, but the damned servants had gone to bed, and the guests were too busy drinking my whisky and fornicating in the grounds and stables to hear."

At this last remark, Bree's face flamed a sudden crimson. Jamie saw it and coughed, avoiding my eye.

"Aye. So then—"

"So then I told them at last that the gold was buried under the floor of the shed outside the kitchen garden." The look of satisfaction returned briefly to her face. "I thought they would come upon the body and 'twould put them off their stride for a bit. By the time they'd nerved themselves to dig, I hoped I should have found some way to escape or to give the alarm—and so I did."

They had bound and gagged her hastily and gone to the shed, threatening to return and resume operations where they had left off, should they discover she had been lying to them. They had made no great job of the gag, though, and she had soon succeeded in tearing it away and kicking out a window-pane, through which to shout for help.

"So I am thinking that when they opened the door to the shed and saw the corpse, they must have dropped their lantern in shock, and so set fire to the place." She nodded in grim satisfaction. "A small price. I could but wish I thought they had gone up with it!"

"Ye dinna suppose they set the fire on purpose?" Duncan asked. He was looking a little better, though still gray and ill. "To cover any marks of digging?"

Jocasta shrugged, dismissing the notion.

"To what end? There was nothing to be found there, and they dug themselves to China." She was beginning to relax a little, a normal color returning to her face, though her broad shoulders had begun to droop with exhaustion.

Silence fell among us, and I became aware that there had been rising noises downstairs for some minutes now; male voices and footsteps. The various search parties had returned, but it was apparent from the tired, disgruntled tones that no suspects had been apprehended.

The candle on the table had burned very low by now; the flame stretched high near my elbow as the wick reached its last inch. One of the candles on the mantelpiece guttered and went out in a fragrant wisp of beeswax smoke. Jamie glanced automatically at the window; it was still dark outside, but the character of the night had changed, as it does soon before dawn.

The curtains moved silently, a chilly, restless air breathing through the room. Another candle went out. A second sleepless night was telling on me; I felt cold all over, numb and disembodied, and the various horrors I had seen and heard had begun to fade into unreality in my mind, with nothing save a lingering strong scent of burning to bear witness to them.

There seemed no more to say or to do. Ulysses came back, sliding discreetly into the room with a fresh candlestick and a tray holding a bottle of brandy and several glasses. Major MacDonald reappeared briefly to report that indeed, they had found no sign of the miscreants. I checked both Duncan and Jocasta briefly, and then left Bree and Ulysses to put them to bed.

Jamie and I made our way downstairs in silence. At the bottom of the staircase, I turned to him. He was white with fatigue, his features drawn and set as though he had been carved of marble, his hair and beard stubble dark in the shadowed light.

"They'll come back, won't they?" I said quietly.

He nodded, and taking my elbow, led me toward the kitchen stair.

54

# TÊTE-À-TÊTE, WITH CRUMBCAKE

SO EARLY IN THE YEAR, the kitchen in the cellar of the house was still in use, with the summer cookhouse reserved for messier or malodorous preparations. Roused by the commotion, all the slaves were up and working, though a few looked as though they would collapse into the nearest corner and go back to sleep at the first opportunity. The chief cook, though, was wide-awake, and it was clear that no one was sleeping on *her* watch.

The kitchen was warm and welcoming, the windows still

dark, walls red with hearth-glow, and the air suffused with the comforting scents of broth, hot bread, and coffee. I thought this would be an excellent place to sit down and re- cuperate for a bit before toddling off to bed, but evidently Jamie had other ideas.

He paused in conversation with the cook, just long enough for politeness, acquiring in the process not only an entire fresh crumb cake, dusted with cinnamon and soaked with melted butter, but a large jug of freshly brewed coffee. Then he made his farewells, scooped me up off the stool onto which I had thankfully subsided, and we were off again, into the cool wind of the dying night.

I had a very odd sense of déjà vu as he turned down the brick path toward the stables. The light was just the same as it had been twenty-four hours earlier, with the same pinprick stars just fading from the same blue-gray sky. The same faint breath of spring passed by, and my skin shivered in memory.

But we were walking sedately side by side, not flying— and overlaid on my memories of the day before were the un- settling odors of blood and burning. With each step I felt as though I were about to reach out to push through the swing- ing doors of a hospital; that the hum of fluorescent light and the subdued reek of medicines and floor polish were about to engulf me.

"Lack of sleep," I murmured to myself.

"Time enough for sleep later, Sassenach," Jamie replied. He shook himself briefly, throwing off tiredness as a dog shakes off water. "There's a thing or two to be done, first." He shifted the paper-wrapped cake, though, and took hold of my elbow with his free hand, in case I was about to fall facefirst into the cabbage bed from fatigue.

I wasn't. I had meant only that it was the lack of sleep that was giving me the mildly hallucinatory feeling of being back in a hospital. For years, as an intern, resident, and mother, I had worked through long sleepless shifts, learning to func- tion—and function well—despite complete exhaustion.

It was that same feeling that was stealing over me now, as I passed through simple sleepiness and out again, into a state of artificially heightened alertness.

I felt cold and shrunken, as though I inhabited only the

innermost core of my body, insulated from the world around me by a thick layer of inert flesh. At the same time, every tiny detail of my surroundings seemed unnaturally vivid, from the delicious fragrance of the food Jamie carried and the rustle of his coat skirts, to the sound of someone singing in the distant slave quarters and the spikes of sprouting corn in the vegetable beds beside the path.

The sense of lucid detachment stayed with me, even as we followed the turn of the path toward the stables. A thing to be done, he'd said. I supposed that he did not mean he intended to repeat yesterday's performance. If he proposed a more sedate form of orgy, though, involving cake and coffee, it seemed peculiar to hold it in the stable, rather than the parlor.

The side door was unbarred; he pushed it open, and the warm scents of hay and sleeping animals rushed out.

"Who is it?" said a soft, deep voice from the shadows inside. Roger. Of course; he hadn't been among the mob in Jocasta's room.

"Fraser," Jamie replied, equally softly, and drew me inside, closing the door behind us.

Roger stood silhouetted against the dim glow of a lantern, near the end of the row of loose-boxes. He was wrapped in a cloak, and the light shone in a reddish nimbus round his dark hair as he turned toward us.

"How is it, *a Smeòraich*?" Jamie handed him the jug of coffee. Roger's cloak fell back as he reached for it, and I saw him thrust a pistol into the waist of his breeches with his other hand. Without comment, he pulled the cork and lifted the jug to his mouth, lowering it several moments later with an expression of sheer bliss. He sighed, breath steaming.

"Oh, God," he said fervently. "That's the best thing I've tasted in months."

"Not quite." Sounding faintly amused, Jamie took the jug back and handed him the wrapped crumb cake. "How is he, then?"

"Noisy at first, but he's been quiet for a bit. I think he may be asleep."

Already tearing at the butter-soaked wrappings, Roger nodded toward the loose-box. Jamie took down the lantern from its hook and held it high over the barred gate. Peering under his arm, I could see a huddled shape, half-buried in the straw at the back of the box.

"Mr. Wylie?" Jamie called, still softly. "Are ye asleep, sir?"

The shape stirred, with a rustling of hay.

"I am not, sir," came the reply, in tones of cold bitterness. The shape began slowly to unfold itself, and Phillip Wylie rose to his feet, shaking straw from his clothes.

I had certainly seen him appear to better advantage. Several buttons were missing from his coat, one shoulder seam was split, and both knees of his breeches hung loose, the buckles burst and his stockings drooping in unseemly fashion about his shins. Someone had evidently hit him in the nose; a trickle of blood had dried on his upper lip, and there was a splotch of crusty brown on the embroidered silk of his waistcoat.

Despite the deficiencies of his wardrobe, his manner was unimpaired, being one of icy outrage.

"You will answer for this, Fraser, by God you will!"

"Aye, I will," Jamie said, unperturbed. "At your pleasure, sir. But not before I've had answers from yourself, Mr. Wylie." He unlatched the gate of the loose-box and swung it open. "Come out."

Wylie hesitated, unwilling either to remain in the box, or to come out of it at Jamie's command. I saw his nostrils twitch, though; evidently he had caught scent of the coffee. That seemed to decide him, and he came out of the box, head held high. He brushed within a foot of me, but kept his eyes straight ahead, affecting not to see me.

Roger had collected two stools and an upturned bucket. I took the latter and shoved it modestly into the shadows, leaving Jamie and Wylie to seat themselves within easy strangling distance of each other. Roger himself retired discreetly into the shadows beside me with the crumb cake, looking interested.

Wylie accepted the jug of coffee stiffly, but a few deep swallows seemed to restore his composure to a noticeable degree. He lowered it at last and breathed audibly, his features a little more relaxed.

"I thank you, sir." He handed the jug back to Jamie with a

small bow and sat bolt upright on his stool, tenderly adjusting his wig, which had survived the evening's adventures, but was much the worse for its experiences. "Now, then. May I inquire the reason for this . . . this . . . unspeakable behavior?"

"Ye may, sir," Jamie replied, drawing himself up straight in turn. "I wish to discover the nature of your associations with a certain Stephen Bonnet, and your knowledge of his present whereabouts."

Wylie's face went almost comically blank.

"Who?"

"Stephen Bonnet."

Wylie began to turn toward me, to ask for clarification, then recalled that he was not acknowledging my presence. He glowered at Jamie, dark brows drawn down.

"I have no acquaintance with any gentleman of that name, Mr. Fraser, and thus no knowledge of his movements— though if I did, I greatly doubt that I should feel myself obliged to inform you of them."

"No?" Jamie took a thoughtful sip of coffee, then handed the jug to me. "What of the obligations of a guest toward his host, Mr. Wylie?"

The dark brows rose in astonishment.

"What do you mean, sir?"

"I take it that you are not aware, sir, that Mrs. Innes and her husband were assaulted last evening, and an attempt at robbery made upon them?"

Wylie's mouth fell open. Either he was a very good actor, or his surprise was genuine. Given my acquaintance with the young man to date, I thought he was no kind of actor.

"I was not. Who—" A thought struck him, and bewilderment vanished in renewed outrage. His eyes bulged slightly. "You think that I was concerned in this—this—"

"Dastardly enterprise?" Roger suggested. He seemed to be enjoying himself, relieved of the boredom of guard duty. "Aye, I expect we do. A bit of crumb cake with your coffee, sir?" He held out a chunk of cake; Wylie stared at it for a moment, then leaped to his feet, striking the cake out of Roger's hand.

"You blackguard!" He rounded on Jamie, fists clenched. "You dare to imply that I am a thief?"

Jamie rocked back a little on his stool, chin lifted.

"Aye, I do," he said coolly. "Ye tried to steal my wife from under my nose—why should ye scruple at my aunt's goods?"

Wylie's face flushed a deep and ugly crimson. Had it not been a wig, his hair would have stood on end.

"You . . . absolute . . . *cunt!*" he breathed. Then he launched himself at Jamie. Both of them went over with a crash, in a flurry of arms and legs.

I leaped back, clasping the coffee jug to my bosom. Roger lunged toward the fray, but I snatched at him, catching his cloak to hold him back.

Jamie had the advantage of size and skill, but Wylie was by no means a novice in the art of fisticuffs, and was in addition propelled by a berserk rage. Given a few moments more, Jamie would have him hammered into submission, but I was not inclined to wait.

Monstrously irritated with the pair of them, I stepped forward and upended the coffee jug. It wasn't boiling, but hot enough. There were simultaneous yelps of surprise, and the two men rolled apart, scrambling and shaking themselves. I thought I heard Roger laugh behind me, but when I whirled on him, he had assumed a look of straight-faced interest. He raised his eyebrows at me, and crammed another chunk of cake into his mouth.

I turned back to find Jamie already on his feet, and Wylie rising from his knees, both soaked with coffee, and both with expressions implying that they intended to resume proceedings at the point where I had interrupted them. I pushed my way between them and stamped my foot.

"I have bloody well had enough of this!"

"I haven't!" Wylie said hotly. "He has impugned my honor, and I demand—"

"Oh, to hell with your beastly honor—and yours, too!" I snarled, glaring from him to Jamie. Jamie, who had evidently been going to say something equally inflammatory, contented himself instead with a resounding snort.

I kicked one of the fallen stools, and pointed at it, still glaring at Jamie.

"Sit!"

Plucking the soaked fabric of his shirt away from his

chest, he righted the stool and sat on it, with immense dignity.

Wylie was less inclined to pay attention to me, and was carrying on with further remarks about his honor. I kicked him in the shin. This time, I was wearing stout boots. He yelped and hopped on one foot, holding his affronted leg. The horses, thoroughly roused by the commotion, were stamping and snorting in their boxes, and the air was full of floating chaff.

"Ye dinna want to trifle with her when she's in a temper," Jamie told Wylie, with a wary glance at me. "She's dangerous, aye?"

Wylie glowered at me, but his scowl altered to a look of uncertainty—whether because of the empty coffee jug, which I was now holding by the neck like a club, or because of his memories of the night before, when he had discovered me in the midst of Betty's autopsy. With an effort, he swallowed whatever he had been going to say, and sat slowly down upon the other stool. He pulled a kerchief from his stained waistcoat pocket, and blotted a trickle of blood that was running down the side of his face from a cut above the brow.

"I would like," he said, with exquisite politeness, "to know what is going on here, please."

He had lost his wig; it was lying on the floor in a puddle of coffee. Jamie bent and picked it up, holding it gingerly, like a dead animal. He wiped a smear of mud off the side of his jaw with his free hand, and held the wig out, dripping, to Wylie.

"We are in agreement, then, sir."

Wylie took the wig with a stiff nod of acknowledgment and laid it on his knee, disregarding the coffee soaking into his breeches. Both men looked at me, with identical expressions of skeptical impatience. Evidently, I had been appointed mistress of ceremonies.

"Robbery, murder, and heaven knows what else," I said firmly. "And we mean to get to the bottom of it."

"Murder?" Roger and Wylie spoke together, both sounding startled.

"Who has been murdered?" Wylie asked, looking wildly back and forth between me and Jamie.

"A slave woman," Jamie said, with a nod toward me. "My wife suspected ill doing in her death, and so we meant to discover the truth of the matter. Thus our presence in the shed when you came upon us last night."

"Presence," Wylie echoed. His face was already pale, but he looked slightly ill at the recollection of what he had seen me doing in the shed. "Yes. I . . . see." He darted a look at me from the corner of his eye.

"So she was killed?" Roger came into the circle of lantern light and set the bucket back in place, sitting down at my feet. He set the remains of the cake on the floor. "What killed her?"

"Someone fed her ground glass," I said. "I found quite a lot of it still in her stomach."

I paid particular attention to Phillip Wylie as I said this, but his face bore the same expression of blank astonishment as did Jamie's and Roger's.

"Glass." Jamie was the first to recover. He sat up on his stool, shoving a disordered hank of hair behind his ear. "How long might that take to kill a body, Sassenach?"

I rubbed two fingers between my brows; the numbness of the early hour was giving way to a throbbing headache, made worse by the rich smell of coffee and the fact that I hadn't gotten to drink any of it.

"I don't know," I said. "It would go into the stomach within minutes, but it might take quite a long time to do enough damage to cause major hemorrhage. Most of the damage would likely be to the small intestine; the glass particles would perforate the lining. And if the digestive system were somewhat impaired—by drink, say—and not moving well, then it might take even longer. Or if she'd taken a lot of food with it."

"Is this the woman that you and Bree found in the garden?" Roger turned to Jamie, inquiring.

"Aye." Jamie nodded, his eyes still fixed on me. "She was insensible wi' the drink then. And when ye saw her later, Sassenach—were there signs of it, then?"

I shook my head.

"The glass might have been working then—but she was out cold. One thing—Fentiman did say she woke in the middle of the night, complaining of griping in her guts. So she was certainly affected by that time. But I can't say for sure whether she'd been given the ground glass before you and Bree found her, or whether perhaps she roused from her stupor in the early evening, and someone gave it to her then."

"Griping in the guts," Roger murmured. He shook his head, mouth grim at the thought. "Christ, what a way to go."

"Aye, it's black wickedness," Jamie agreed, nodding. "But why? Who should wish the woman's death?"

"A good question," Wylie said shortly. "However, I can assure you that it wasn't I."

Jamie gave him a long stare of assessment.

"Aye, maybe," he said. "If not, though—how came ye to the shed last night? What business might ye have there, save perhaps to look upon the face of your victim?"

"*My* victim!" Wylie jerked bolt upright, stiff with renewed outrage. "It was not I in that shed, red to the elbow with the woman's gore and snatching bits of bone and offal!" He snapped his head to the side, glaring up at me.

"My victim, indeed! It is a capital crime to defile a body, Mrs. Fraser. And I have heard things—oh, yes, I have heard things about you! I put it to you that it is *you* who did the woman to death, for the purpose of obtaining—"

His words ended in a gurgle, as Jamie's hand jerked his shirtfront tight and twisted it hard about his neck. He punched Wylie in the stomach, hard, and the young man doubled up, coughed, and spewed coffee, bile, and a few more disagreeable substances all over the floor, his knees, and Jamie.

I sighed wearily. The briefly warming effects of the discussion had faded, and I was feeling cold and mildly disoriented again. The stench didn't help.

"That's not really helpful, you know," I said reprovingly to Jamie, who had released Wylie and was now hastily removing his own outer garments. "Not that I don't appreciate the vote of confidence."

"Oh, aye," he said, voice muffled in the shirt as he pulled

it over his head. He popped out, glaring at me, and dropped the shirt on the floor with a splat. "D'ye think I'm going to sit idle and let this popinjay insult ye?"

"I don't suppose he'll do it again," Roger said. He stood and bent over Wylie, who was still doubled up on his stool, rather green in the face. Roger glanced back over his shoulder at Jamie.

"Is he right, though? About it being a capital crime to tamper with a body?"

"I dinna ken," Jamie said, rather shortly. Stripped to the waist, stained with blood and vomit, and with his red hair wild in the lantern light, he looked a far cry from the polished gentleman who had gone off to play whist.

"It scarcely matters," he added, "as he isna going to tell anyone about it. Because if he does, I shall cut him like a stirk and feed both his ballocks and his lying tongue to the pigs." He touched the hilt of his dirk, as though assuring himself that it was handy if wanted.

"But I am sure ye dinna mean to make any such unfounded accusations regarding my wife, do ye . . . sir?" he said to Wylie, with excessive politeness.

I was not surprised to see Phillip Wylie shake his head, evidently still incapable of speech. Jamie made a noise of grim satisfaction and stooped to pick up the cloak he had dropped earlier.

Feeling rather weak-kneed after this latest exhibition of the male sense of honor, I sat down on the bucket.

"All right," I said, and pushed back a strand of hair. "Fine. If we've got all that settled, then . . . where were we?"

"Betty's murder," Roger prompted. "We don't know who, we don't know when, and we don't know why—though for the sake of argument, might I suggest we assume that no one amongst the present company had anything to do with it?"

"Verra well." Jamie dismissed murder with a brusque gesture and sat down. "What about Stephen Bonnet?"

Roger's expression, hitherto one of interest, darkened at that.

"Aye, what about him? Is he involved in this business?"

"Not in the murder, perhaps—but my aunt and her husband were assaulted in their chamber last evening by two villains. One of whom was an Irishman." Jamie wrapped his cloak about his bare shoulders, bending a sinister glance on Phillip Wylie, who had recovered sufficiently to sit up.

"I repeat," he said coldly, hands still pressed against his stomach, "that I have no acquaintance with a gentleman of that name, whether Irishman or Hottentot."

"Stephen Bonnet is not a gentleman," Roger said. The words were mild enough, but carried an undertone that made Wylie glance up at him.

"I do not know the fellow," he said firmly. He took a shallow breath by way of experiment, and finding it bearable, breathed deeper. "Why do you suppose that the Irishman who committed the outrage upon Mr. and Mrs. Innes should be this Bonnet? Did he leave his card, perchance?"

I laughed, surprising myself. In spite of everything, I had to admit to a certain amount of respect for Phillip Wylie. Held captive, battered, threatened, doused with coffee, and deprived of his wig, he retained a good deal more dignity than would most men in his situation.

Jamie glanced at me, then back at Wylie. I thought the corner of his mouth twitched, but it was impossible to tell in the dim light.

"No," he said. "I *do* claim some acquaintance with Stephen Bonnet, who is a felon, a degenerate, and a thief. And I saw the man with ye, sir, when ye happened upon my wife and myself at the shed."

"Yes," I said. "I saw him, too—standing right behind you. And what were you doing there, anyway?" I asked, this question suddenly occurring to me.

Wylie's eyes had widened at Jamie's accusation. At my statement, he blinked. He took another deep breath and looked down, rubbing his knuckles beneath his nose. Then he looked up at Jamie, the bluster gone.

"I do not know him," he said quietly. "I had some thought that I was followed, but, glancing behind me, I saw no one, and so paid it no great mind. When I . . . saw what lay within the shed"—his eyes flicked toward me, but would not quite meet my own—"I was too much shocked to give heed to aught but what lay before my eyes."

That, I could believe.

Wylie lifted his shoulders, and let them fall.

"If this Bonnet was indeed behind me, then I must take your word for it, sir. And yet I assure you that he was not there by my doing, nor with my recognition."

Jamie and Roger exchanged glances, but they could hear the ring of truth in Wylie's words, just as I could. There was a brief silence, in which I could hear the horses moving in their stalls. They were no longer agitated, but were getting restive, anticipating food. Dawn light was filtering through the cracks beneath the eaves, a soft, smoky radiance that leached the air inside the stable of all color, and yet revealed the dim outlines of harness hanging on the wall, pitchforks and shovels standing in the corner.

"The grooms will be coming soon." Jamie stirred and drew breath, drawing up his shoulders in a half-shrug. He glanced back at Wylie.

"Verra well, sir. I accept your word as a gentleman."

"Do you? I am flattered."

"Still," Jamie went on, pointedly ignoring the sarcasm, "I should like to know what it was that brought ye to the shed last night."

Wylie had half-risen from his seat. At this, he hesitated, then slowly sat again. He blinked once or twice, as though thinking, then sighed, giving up.

"Lucas," he said simply. He didn't look up, but kept his eyes fixed on his hands, hanging limp between his thighs. "I was there, the night he was foaled. I raised him, broke him to the saddle, trained him." He swallowed once; I saw the tremor move beneath the frill at his neck. "I came to the stable to have a few moments alone with him . . . to bid him farewell."

For the first time, Jamie's face lost the shadow of dislike that it bore whenever he looked at Wylie. He breathed deep, and nodded slightly.

"Aye, I see," he said quietly. "And then?"

Wylie straightened a little.

"When I left the stable, I thought I heard voices near the wall of the kitchen garden. And when I came nearer to see what might be afoot, I saw light shining through the cracks of the shed." He shrugged. "I opened the door. And you know better than I what happened then, Mr. Fraser."

Jamie rubbed a hand hard over his face, then shook his head hard.

"Aye," he said. "I do. I went for Bonnet, and ye got in my way."

"You attacked me," Wylie said coldly. He hitched the ruined coat higher up on his shoulders. "I defended myself, as I had every right to do. And then you and your son-in-law seized me between you, frog-marched me in there"—he jerked his chin at the box stall behind him—"and held me captive half the night!"

Roger cleared his throat. So did Jamie, though with more dour intent.

"Aye, well," he said. "We willna argue about it." He sighed and stood back, gesturing to Wylie that he might go. "I suppose ye didna see in which direction Bonnet fled?"

"Oh, yes. Though I did not know his name, of course. I expect he is well beyond reach by now," Wylie said. There was an odd note in his voice; something like satisfaction. Jamie turned sharply.

"What d'ye mean?"

"Lucas." Wylie nodded down the dim aisle of the stable, toward the shadows at the farther end. "His stall is at the far end. I know his voice well, the sound of his movement. And I have not heard him this morning. Bonnet—if that was who it was—fled toward the stable."

Before Wylie had finished talking, Jamie had seized the lantern and was striding down the stable. Horses thrust inquiring noses over their stall doors as he passed, snorting and whuffling in curiosity—but no black nose appeared at the end of the row, no black mane floated out in joyous greeting. The rest of us hastened after him, leaning to see past him as he held the lantern high.

The yellow light shone on empty straw.

We stood silent for a long moment, looking. Then Phillip Wylie sighed and drew himself up.

"If I no longer have him, Mr. Fraser—neither do you." His

eyes rested on me, then, darkly ironic. "But I wish you joy of your wife."

He turned and walked away, stockings sagging, the red heels of his shoes winking in the growing light.

OUTSIDE, DAWN WAS BREAKING, still and lovely. Only the river seemed to move, the spreading light flashing silver on its current beyond the trees.

Roger had gone off to the house, yawning, but Jamie and I lingered by the paddock. People would be stirring within minutes; there would be more questions, speculations, talk. Neither one of us wanted any more talk; not now.

At last, Jamie put his arm about my shoulders, and with an air of decision, turned away from the house. I didn't know where he was going, and didn't much care, though I did hope I could lie down when we got there.

We passed the smithy, where a small, sleepy-looking boy was blowing up the forge with a pair of bellows, making red sparks float and flash like fireflies in the shadows. Past the outbuildings, around a corner, and then we were in front of a nondescript shed with a large double door. Jamie lifted the latch and swung one door open a bit, beckoning me inside.

"I canna think why I never thought of this place," he said, "when I was looking for a spot to be private."

We were in the carriage shed. A wagon and a small buggy stood in the shadows, as did Jocasta's phaeton. An open carriage like a large sleigh on two wheels, it had a bench seat with blue velvet squabs, and a scroll-like front like the prow of a ship. Jamie picked me up by the waist and swung me in, then clambered up after me. There was a buffalo robe lying across the squabs; he pulled this off and spread it on the floor of the phaeton. There was just room for two people to curl up there, if they didn't mind lying close together.

"Come on, Sassenach," he said, sinking to his knees. "Whatever comes next . . . it can wait."

I quite agreed. Though on the verge of unconsciousness, I

couldn't help drowsily asking, "Your aunt . . . do you trust her? What she said, about the gold and all?"

"Oh, aye, of course I do," he mumbled in my ear. His arm was heavy where it lay over my waist. "At least as far as I could throw her."

## 55

## DEDUCTIONS

A T LAST FORCED FROM OUR REFUGE by thirst and hunger, we made our way out of the carriage shed and past the tactfully averted eyes of the yard slaves, still busy clearing up the debris from the wedding feast. At the edge of the lawn, I saw Phaedre, coming up from the mausoleum with her arms full of plates and cups that had been left in the shrubbery. Her face was swollen and blotched with grief, and her eyes were red, but she was not crying.

She saw us, and stopped.

"Oh," she said. "Miss Jo be lookin' for you, Master Jamie."

She spoke dully, as though the words had little meaning for her, and appeared to find nothing odd in our sudden appearance or disheveled dress.

"Oh? Aye." Jamie rubbed a hand over his face, nodding. "Aye, I'll go up to her."

She nodded, and was turning to go when Jamie reached out and touched her shoulder.

"I'm sorry for your trouble, lass," he said quietly.

Sudden tears welled in her eyes and spilled over, but she didn't speak. She dropped a brief curtsy, turned, and hurried away, moving so fast that a knife fell from the stack of crockery, bouncing on the grass behind her.

I stooped and picked it up, the feel of the knife's handle reminding me suddenly and vividly of the blade I had used to open her mother's body. For a disorienting moment, I was no longer on the lawn before the house, but in the dark confines of the shed, the scent of death heavy in the air and the proof of murder gritty in my hand.

Then reality readjusted itself, and the green lawn was covered with flocks of doves and sparrows, foraging peacefully for crumbs at the feet of a marble goddess, bright with sun.

Jamie was saying something.

". . . . go and wash and rest a bit, Sassenach?"

"What? Oh . . . no, I'll come with you." I was suddenly anxious to have this business done with, and go home. I had had enough society for the moment.

WE FOUND JOCASTA, Duncan, Roger, and Brianna all together in Jocasta's sitting room, digging into what looked like a substantial, if very late, breakfast. Brianna cast a sharp look at Jamie's ruined clothes, but said nothing, and went back to sipping tea, her eyebrows still raised. She and Jocasta both wore dressing gowns, and while Roger and Duncan were dressed, they looked pale and scruffy after the adventures of the night. Neither had shaved, and Duncan sported a large blue bruise on the side of his face where he had hit the hearthstone in falling, but he seemed otherwise all right.

I assumed that Roger had told everyone about our tête-à-tête with Phillip Wylie, and the disappearance of Lucas. At least no one asked questions. Duncan silently shoved a platter of bacon in Jamie's direction, and there was no sound for a bit save the musical tinkling of cutlery on plates and the sloshing noises of tea being drunk.

At last, replete and feeling somewhat restored, we sat back and began hesitantly to discuss the events of the day—and night—before. So much had happened that I thought perhaps it might be best to try to reconstruct events in a logical sort of way. I said as much, and while Jamie's mouth twitched in an annoying manner that suggested he found the notion of logic incompatible with me personally, I ignored this and firmly called the meeting to order.

"It begins with Betty, don't you think?"

"Whether it does or not, I suppose that's as good a starting point as any, Sassenach," Jamie agreed.

Brianna finished buttering a final slice of toast, looking amused.

"Carry on, Miss Marple," she said, waving it at me before taking a bite. Roger made a brief choking noise, but I ignored that, too, with dignity.

"Fine. Now, I thought Betty was likely drugged when I saw her, but since Dr. Fentiman stopped me examining her, I couldn't be positive. But we are reasonably sure that Betty did drink drugged punch, is that right?" I looked round the circle of faces, and both Bree and Jamie nodded, adopting solemn expressions.

"Aye, I tasted *something* in the cup that wasna liquor," Jamie said.

"And I talked to the house slaves after I left Da," Brianna added, leaning forward. "Two of the women admitted that Betty tipples—tippled—from the dregs of drinks at parties, but both of them insisted she was no more than what they called 'cheerful' when she helped serve rum punch in the drawing room."

"And I was in the drawing room then, with Seamus Hanlon and his musicians," Roger confirmed. He glanced at Bree and squeezed her knee gently. "I saw Ulysses make the punch himself—that was the first time during the day that you made it, Ulysses?"

All heads swiveled toward the butler, who stood closed-faced behind Jocasta's chair, his neat wig and pressed livery a silent reproach to the general air of exhausted dishevelment.

"No, the second," he said softly. "The first was all drunk at breakfast." His eyes were alert, if bloodshot, but the rest of his face might have been chiseled from gray granite. The household and its servants were his charge, and it was clear

that he felt recent events to be a mortifying personal reproach to his stewardship.

"Right." Roger turned back toward me, rubbing a hand
over his stubbled face. He might have snatched a nap since
the confrontation with Wylie in the stable, but he didn't
look it.

"I didn't take any notice of Betty myself, but the point is, I
think I *would* surely have noticed, if she were drunk and reeling at that point. So would Ulysses, I expect." He glanced
over his shoulder for confirmation, and the butler nodded, reluctantly.

"Lieutenant Wolff *was* drunk and reeling," Roger added.
"Everyone noticed that—they all remarked how early it was
for anyone to be in that condition."

Jocasta made a rude noise, and Duncan bent his head, hiding a smile.

"The point being," Jamie summed up neatly, "that the second lot of rum punch was served out just past midday, and I
found the woman flat on her back in the dung heap, steamin'
with drink and a punch cup beside her, nay more than an
hour later. I'll no say it couldna be done, but it would be
quick work to get mortal in that span of time, especially if it
was all done wi' dregs."

"So we assume that she was indeed drugged," I said. "The
most likely substance being laudanum. Was there some available in the stillroom here?"

Jocasta caught the lift of my voice and knew the question
was addressed to her; she straightened up in her chair, tucking a wisp of white hair back under her ribboned cap. She
seemed to have recovered nicely from the night before.

"Oh, aye. But that's naught to go by," she objected. "Anyone might ha' brought it; it's no sae hard to come by, and ye
have the price. I ken at least two women among the guests
who take the stuff regular. I daresay they'd have brought a bit
with them."

I would have loved to know which of Jocasta's acquaintances were opium addicts, and how she knew, but dismissed
that point, moving on to the next.

"Well, wherever the laudanum—for the sake of argument—came from, it apparently ended up inside Betty." I

turned to Jamie. "Now, you said that it occurred to you when you found her that she might have drunk something—drugged or poisonous—intended for someone else."

He nodded, following me closely.

"Aye, for why would someone seek to harm or kill a slave?"

"I don't know why, but someone *did* kill her," Brianna interrupted, a definite edge in her voice. "I can't see how she could have eaten ground glass meant for someone else, can you?"

"Don't rush me! I'm trying to be logical." I frowned at Bree, who made a rude noise akin to Jocasta's, but not as loud.

"No," I went on, "I don't think she can have taken the ground glass by accident, but I don't know when she *did* take it. Almost certainly, it was sometime after you and Jamie took her up to the attic, though, and after Dr. Fentiman saw her the first time."

Fentiman's emetics and purgatives would have caused extensive bleeding, had Betty already ingested the glass—as indeed they did, when he returned to treat her renewed complaints of internal distress toward dawn.

"I think you're right," I told Brianna, "but just to be tidy—when you went to look round, Roger, you didn't find any of the guests who looked as though they might be drugged?"

He shook his head, dark brows drawn together, as though the sunlight bothered him. I wasn't surprised if he had a headache; the cotton-wool feeling had turned into a throbbing inside my own skull.

"No," he said, and dug a knuckle hard between his brows. "There were at least twenty who were beginning to stagger a bit, but they all seemed just legitimately drunk."

"What about Lieutenant Wolff?" Duncan asked at this point, to everyone's surprise. He blushed slightly, seeing everyone's eyes on him, but doggedly pursued his point.

"*A Smeòraich* said the man was drunk and reeling in the drawing room. Might he have taken the laudanum, or whatever it was, drunk the half, and given the rest to the slave there?"

"I don't know," I said dubiously. "If ever I saw anyone who could have achieved intoxication within an hour, purely on the basis of straight alcohol . . ."

"When I went to check the guests, the Lieutenant was propped up against the wall of the mausoleum with a bottle in his fist," Roger said. "Mostly incoherent, but still conscious."

"Aye, he fell down in the shrubbery later," Jamie put in, looking dubious. "I saw him, in the afternoon. He didna look like yon slave woman, though, only drunk."

"The timing is about right, though," I said thoughtfully. "So it's possible, at least. Did anyone see the Lieutenant later in the day?"

"Yes," Ulysses said, causing everyone to swivel round to look at him again. "He came into the house during the supper, asked me to find him a boat at once, and left by water. Still very drunk," he added precisely, "but lucid."

Jocasta made a small puffing sound with her lips, and muttered, "Lucid, forbye," under her breath. She massaged her temples with both forefingers; evidently she had a headache, too.

"I suppose that puts the Lieutenant out as a suspect? Or is the fact that he left so suddenly suspicious by itself?" Brianna, the only person present who seemed *not* to have a headache, dropped several lumps of sugar into her tea and stirred it vigorously. Jamie shut his eyes, wincing at the noise.

"Are ye no overlooking something?" Jocasta had been following all the arguments intently, a slight frown of concentration on her face. Now she leaned forward, stretching out her hand toward the low table with its breakfast things. She tapped her fingers lightly here and there to locate what she wanted, then picked up a small silver cup.

"Ye showed me the cup from which Betty drank, Nephew," she said to Jamie, holding out the one in her hand. "It was like this, aye?"

The cup was sterling silver, and brand-new, the incised design barely showing. Later, when the metal began to acquire a patina, black tarnish would settle into the lines of the etching and cause it to stand out, but for the moment, the capital letter "I" and the small fish that swam around it were almost lost in the gleam of light off the metal.

"Aye, it was one like that, Aunt," Jamie replied, touching the hand that held the cup. "Brianna says it was one of a set?"

"It was. I gave them to Duncan in the morning of our wedding day, as a bride-gift." She set down the cup, but laid her long fingers across the top of it. "We drank from two of the cups, Duncan and I, with our breakfast, but the other four stayed up here." She waved a hand behind her, indicating the small sideboard against the wall, where the platters of bacon and fried eggs had been placed. Decorated plates were propped upright along the back of the sideboard, interspersed with a set of crystal sherry glasses. I counted; all six of the silver fish cups were on the table now, filled with port, which Jocasta appeared to like with breakfast. There was no indication which of them had held the drugged liquor, though.

"Ye didna take any of these cups down to the drawing room on the wedding day, Ulysses?" she asked.

"No, Madam." He looked shocked at the thought. "Of course not."

She nodded, and turned her blind eyes toward Jamie, then toward me.

"So ye see," she said simply. "It was Duncan's cup."

Duncan looked startled, then uneasy, as the implications of what she had said sank in.

"No," he said, shaking his head. "Ach, no. Couldna be." But tiny droplets of sweat had begun to form a dew across the weathered skin of his jaw.

"Did anyone offer ye a drink day before yesterday, *a charaid*?" Jamie asked, leaning forward intently.

Duncan shrugged helplessly.

"Aye, everyone did!"

And of course they had. He was, after all, the bridegroom. He had accepted none of the proffered refreshment, though, owing to the digestive upset occasioned by his nerves. Nor had he noticed particularly whether any of the drinks on offer had been served in a silver cup.

"I was that distracted, *Mac Dubh*, I shouldna have noticed

if anyone had been offering me a live snake in his hand." Ulysses plucked a linen napkin from the tray and offered it unobtrusively. Blindly, Duncan took it and wiped his face.

"So . . . you think that someone was trying to harm *Duncan*?" The astonishment in Roger's voice might not have been strictly flattering, but Duncan appeared not to take it amiss.

"But why?" he said, bewildered. "Who could hate *me*?"

Jamie chuckled under his breath, and the tension round the table relaxed slightly. It was true; while Duncan was intelligent and competent, he was of so modest a disposition that it was impossible to conceive of his having offended anyone, let alone driven them into a murderous frenzy.

"Well, *a charaid*," Jamie said tactfully, "it might not just be personal, ken?" He caught my eye, and made a wry grimace. More than one attempt had been made on his own life, for reasons having to do only with who he was, rather than anything he had done. Not that people hadn't tried to kill him occasionally for things he'd done, as well.

Jocasta appeared to have been thinking along the same lines.

"Indeed," she said. "I have been thinking, myself. Do ye not recall, nephew, what happened at the Gathering?"

Jamie lifted one eyebrow, and picked up a cup of tea.

"A good many things happened there, Aunt," he said. "But I take it ye mean what happened with Father Kenneth?"

"I do." She reached up a hand automatically, as Ulysses set a fresh cup into it. "Did ye not tell me that yon Lillywhite said something about the priest being prevented from performing ceremonials?"

Jamie nodded, closing his eyes briefly as he took a mouthful of tea.

"Aye, he did. So, ye think it was maybe your marriage with Duncan he meant? That was the 'ceremonial' to be prevented?"

My headache was growing worse. I pressed my fingers between my brows; they were warm from the teacup, and the heat felt good on my skin.

"Wait just one minute," I said. "Are you saying that someone wanted to prevent your aunt's marriage to Duncan, and succeeded in doing so at the Gathering, but then couldn't think of any way of preventing it now, and so tried to murder Duncan, in order to stop it?" My own voice echoed the astonishment on Duncan's features.

"I'm no saying so, myself," Jamie said, eyeing Jocasta with interest, "but I gather that my aunt is suggesting as much."

"I am," she said calmly. She drank off her tea, and set down the cup with a sigh. "I dinna wish to rate myself too high, nephew, but the fact is that I have been courted by this one and that one, ever since Hector died. River Run is a rich property, and I am an auld woman."

There was a moment's silence, as everyone absorbed that. Duncan's face reflected an uneasy horror.

"But—" he said, stuttering slightly, "but—but—if it was that, *Mac Dubh*, why wait?"

"Wait?"

"Aye." He looked around the table, seeking understanding. "See you, if someone meant to stop the marriage at the Gathering, well and good. But it's been four months since then, and no one's lifted a hand against me. I mostly ride alone; 'twould have been a simple matter, surely, to lay for me on the road as I went about my business, and put a bullet through my head." He spoke matter-of-factly, but I saw a small shiver pass through Jocasta at the notion.

"So why wait until almost the hour of the wedding itself, and in the presence of hundreds of people? Aye, well, it's a point, Duncan," Jamie admitted.

Roger had been following all this, elbows propped on his knees, chin resting in his hands. He straightened up at this.

"One reason I can think of," he said. "The priest."

Everyone stared at him, eyebrows raised.

"The priest was here," he explained. "See, if it's River Run that's behind all this, then it isn't only a matter of getting Duncan out of the way. Kill him, and our murderer is right back where he started—Jocasta's not married to Duncan, but she isn't married to *him*, either, and no way to force the issue.

"But," Roger raised a finger, "if the priest is here, and all set to perform a private ceremony . . . then it's simple. Kill Duncan—in a manner that might suggest suicide or accident—and then swoop up to Jocasta's suite, and force the priest to perform the marriage at gunpoint. The servants and guests are all occupied with Duncan, no one to make objections or interfere. There's the bed to hand—" He nodded at the big tester, visible through the doorway into the bedroom. "Take Jocasta straight there and consummate the marriage by force . . . and Bob's your uncle."

At this point, Roger caught sight of Jocasta's dropped jaw and Duncan's stunned look, and it occurred to him that this was not merely an interesting academic proposition. He blushed crimson, and cleared his throat.

"Ah . . . I mean . . . it's been done."

Jamie coughed, and cleared his own throat. It had been done. His own bloody-minded grandfather had begun his social rise by forcibly wedding—and promptly bedding—the elderly and wealthy dowager Lady Lovat.

*"What?"* Brianna swiveled round to stare at Roger, obviously appalled. "That's the most . . . but they couldn't get away with something like that!"

"I expect they could, really," Roger said, almost apologetically. "See, hen, possession is a lot more than nine-tenths of the law when it comes to women. Marry a woman and take her to bed, and she and all her property are yours, whether she likes it or not. Without another male relative to protest, it's not likely a court would do a thing."

"But she *does* have a male relative!" Brianna flipped a hand toward Jamie—who did have a protest to make, but probably not along the lines Brianna had expected.

"Aye, well, but. Witnesses," he objected. "Ye canna do something like that, without ye have a witness to say it was a valid marriage." He cleared his throat again, and Ulysses reached for the teapot.

Old Simon had had witnesses; two of his friends, plus the two attendants of the dowager. One of whom had later become Jamie's grandmother, though I did trust less force had been involved in that transaction.

"I can't see that that's a difficulty," I said, brushing crumbs off my bosom. "Obviously, this wasn't a one-man show. Whoever the intending bridegroom is—and mind, we don't even know there is one, but for the sake of argument—

anyway, whoever he is, if he exists, plainly he has accomplices. Randall Lillywhite, for one."

"Who wasna here," Jamie reminded me.

"Hm. That's true," I admitted. "But still, the principle holds."

"Yes," Roger said stubbornly, "and if he *does* exist, then the chief suspect is Lieutenant Wolff, isn't he? Everyone knows he's made more than one try to marry Jocasta. And he *was* here."

"But pie-eyed," Jamie added, dubiously.

"Or not. As I said, Seamus and his boys were surprised that anyone could be that drunk so early on, but what if it was a sham?" Roger glanced round the table, one eyebrow lifted.

"If he were only pretending to be reeling drunk, no one would pay attention to him or treat him later as a suspect, and yet he could manage to be in position to poison a cup of punch, give it to Betty with instructions to give it to Duncan, then slip away and hang about, ready to nip upstairs the moment word came that Duncan had collapsed. And if Betty then offered it to Duncan, who refused it—well, there she was, with a full cup of fresh rum punch in her hand."

He shrugged.

"Who could blame her for stealing away into the kitchen garden to enjoy it?"

Jocasta and Ulysses snorted simultaneously, making it reasonably clear what they thought of the blameworthiness of Betty's action. Roger coughed and hurried on with his analysis.

"Right. Well. But the dose didn't kill Betty. Either the murderer miscalculated or . . ." Another bright thought occurred to Roger. "Perhaps he didn't intend the drug to kill Duncan. Maybe he only meant to render him unconscious, and then tip him quietly into the river. That would have been even better. Ye can't swim, can you?" he asked, turning to Duncan, who shook his head in a dazed sort of way. His one hand rose, mechanically massaging the stump of his missing arm.

"Aye. So a nice drowning would have passed for accident, no worry." Roger rubbed his hands together, looking pleased. "But then it all went wrong, because the maid drank the drugged punch, not Duncan. And *that's* why she was killed!"

"Why?" Jocasta was looking quite as dazed as Duncan.

"Because she could identify the man who'd given her the cup," Jamie put in. He nodded, lounging thoughtfully back in his chair. "And she would have, the minute folk started in on her about it. Aye, that's sense. But of course he couldna make away with her by violent means; the risk of being seen coming or going to the attic was too great."

Roger nodded approval at this quick appreciation.

"Aye. But it would have been no great trick to get your hands on ground glass—how many goblets and tumblers were floating through this place during the day? Drop one on the bricks and grind the shards under your heel, and there ye are."

Even that might not have been necessary; there had been shattered glass all over the paths and the terrace, after the post-wedding celebrations. I had dropped one glass myself, when surprised by Phillip Wylie.

I turned to address Ulysses.

"There's still the problem of how the ground glass was administered. Do you know what Betty was given to eat or drink, Ulysses?"

A frown rippled over the butler's face, like a stone thrown into dark water.

"Dr. Fentiman ordered her a syllabub," he said slowly. "And a bit of porridge, if she were awake enough to swallow. I made up the syllabub myself, and gave it to Mariah to take up to her. I gave the order for porridge to the cook, but I do not know whether Betty ate it, or who might have carried it."

"Hmm." Jocasta pursed her lips, frowning. "The cookhouse would be madness. And with so many folk about . . . well, we can ask Mariah and the others, but I shouldna be surprised if they dinna recall even carrying the dishes, let alone someone tampering with them. It would take nay more than a moment, ken; distract the girl, whisk in the glass . . ." She waved a hand, indicating the scandalous ease with which murder could be committed.

"Or someone could have gone up to the attic under the pretext of seeing how she was, and given her something to drink, with the glass in it then," I suggested. "A syllabub would be perfect. People were coming and going, but Betty was alone up there for long stretches, between Dr. Fentiman's visit, and the time the other slaves came to bed. It would be quite possible for someone to go up there unseen."

"Very nice, Inspector Lestrade," Brianna said to Roger, *sotto voce*. "But there's no proof, is there?"

Jocasta and Duncan were sitting side by side, rigid as a pair of Toby jugs, carefully not facing each other. At this, Jocasta took a deep and audible breath, obviously forcing herself to relax.

"True," she said. "There's not. Ye dinna recall Betty offering you a cup of punch, *a dhuine*?"

Duncan gnawed fiercely on his moustache for a moment, concentrating, but then shook his head.

"She might have . . . *a bhean*. But she might not, too."

"Well, then."

Everyone fell silent for a moment, during which Ulysses moved silently round the table, clearing things away. At last Jamie gave a deep sigh and straightened up.

"Well, so. Then there's what happened last night. We are agreed that the Irishman who entered your chamber, Aunt, was Stephen Bonnet?"

Brianna's hand jerked, and the cup of tea crashed to the table.

"Who?" she said hoarsely. "Stephen Bonnet—here?"

Jamie glanced at me, frowning.

"I thought ye'd told her, Sassenach."

"When?" I said, with some irritation. "I thought *you'd* told her," I said, turning to Roger, who merely shrugged, stone-faced. Ulysses had swooped down with a cloth and was blotting up the tea. Bree was white-faced, but had regained her self-possession.

"Never mind," she said. "He was here? Last night?"

"Aye, he was," Jamie said reluctantly. "I saw him."

"So he was the thief who came after the gold—or one of them?" Brianna reached for one of the silver cups of port and drank it off as though it were water. Ulysses blinked, but hastened to refill the cup from the decanter.

"It would seem so." Roger reached for a fresh scone, carefully avoiding Brianna's eyes.

"How did he find out about the gold, Aunt?" Jamie leaned back in his chair, eyes half-closed in concentration.

Jocasta gave a small snort, and held out her hand. Ulysses, accustomed to her needs, put a piece of buttered toast into it.

"Hector Cameron told someone; my brother Dougal told someone; or the third man told someone. And knowing them as I did, I should lay odds it wasna either Hector nor Dougal." She shrugged and took a bite of toast.

"But I'll tell ye one thing," she added, swallowing. "The second man in my room, the one who reeked of drink. I said he didna speak, aye? Well, that's plain enough, no? He was someone I ken, whose voice I should have known, if he spoke."

"Lieutenant Wolff?" Roger suggested.

Jamie nodded, a crease forming between his brows.

"Who better than the navy, to find a pirate when one's wanted, aye?"

"*Would* one want a pirate?" Brianna murmured. The port had restored her composure, but she was still pale.

"Aye," Jamie said, paying little attention to her. "No small undertaking, ten thousand pound in gold. It would take more than one man to deal with such a sum—Louis of France and Charles Stuart kent that much; they sent six to deal with thirty thousand." Little wonder, then, if whoever learned of the gold had enlisted the help of Stephen Bonnet—a well-known smuggler and pirate, and one with not only the means of transport but the connections to dispose of the gold.

"A boat," I said slowly. "The Lieutenant left by boat, during the supper. Suppose that he went downriver, and met Stephen Bonnet. They came back together, and waited for the opportunity to sneak into the house and try to terrorize Jocasta into telling them where the gold was."

Jamie nodded.

"Aye, that could be. The Lieutenant has had dealings here for years. Is it possible, Aunt, that he saw something that made him suspect ye had the gold here? Ye said Hector had three bars; is any of it left?"

Jocasta's lips pressed tight, but after a moment's hesitation, she gave a grudging nod.

"He *would* keep a lump of it on his desk, to weight his papers. Aye, Wolff might have seen—but how would he have kent what it was?"

"Perhaps he didn't at the time," Brianna suggested, "but then later heard about the French gold, and put two and two together."

There was a nodding and murmuring at this. As a theory, it fitted well enough. I didn't see quite how one would go about proving it, though, and said so.

Jamie shrugged, and licked a smear of jam off his knuckle.

"I shouldna think proving what's happened is so important, Sassenach. It's maybe what comes next." He looked at Duncan, straight on.

"They'll come back, *a charaid*," he said quietly. "Ye ken that, aye?"

Duncan nodded. He looked unhappy, but determined.

"Aye, I ken." He reached out a hand and took Jocasta's— the first gesture of the sort I had ever seen him make toward her. "We shall be ready, *Mac Dubh*."

Jamie nodded, slowly.

"I must go, Duncan. The planting willna wait. But I shall send word to those I ken, to have a watch of some sort kept upon Lieutenant Wolff."

Jocasta had sat silent, her hand unmoving in Duncan's. She sat up taller in her chair at this.

"And the Irishman?" she said. Her other hand rubbed slowly across her knee, pressing lightly with the heel of her hand, where the knife blade had cut.

Jamie exchanged a glance with Duncan, then with me.

"He'll come back," he said, grim certainty in his voice.

I was looking at Brianna as he said it. Her face was calm, but I was her mother, and I saw the fear move in her eyes, like a snake through water. Stephen Bonnet, I thought, with a sinking heart, was already back.

WE LEFT NEXT DAY for the mountains. We were no more than five miles on our journey, when I caught the sound of hoofbeats on the road behind us, and saw a flash of scarlet, through the spring-green of the chestnut trees.

It was Major MacDonald, and the look of delight upon his face as he spurred toward us told me all I needed to know.

"Oh, bloody *hell*!" I said.

The note bore Tryon's scarlet seal, bloodred as the Major's coat.

"It came this morning to Greenoaks," the Major said, reining up to watch as Jamie broke the seal. "I offered to bring it, as I was bound this way, in any case." He knew already what the note contained; Farquard Campbell would already have opened his.

I watched Jamie's face as he read. His expression didn't change. He finished reading, and handed me the note.

> *19th March, 1771*
>
> *To the Commanding Officers of the Militia:*
>
> *Sirs:*
>
> *I Yesterday determined by Consent of His Majesty's Council to march with a Body of Forces taken from several Militia Regiments, into the Settlements of the Insurgents to reduce them to Obedience, who by their Rebellious Acts and Declarations have set the Government at defiance and interrupted the Course of Justice by obstructing, overturning and shutting up the Courts of Law. That some of your Regiment therefore may have a Share in the Honor of serving their Country in this important Service, I am to require you to make a choice of thirty men, who shall join the Body of my Force in this Endeavor.*
>
> *It is not intended to move the Troops before the twentieth of next Month before which time you shall be informed of the day you are to assemble your Men, the time of march and the Road you are to take.*

> It is recommended as a Christian Duty incumbent
> on every Planter that remains at Home, to take care
> of, and assist to the utmost of his Abilities the Families
> of those Men who go on this Service that neither their
> Families nor plantations may suffer while they are
> employed on a Service where the Interest of the whole
> is concerned.
>
> For the Expenditures ordered on this Expedition I
> shall give printed Warrants payable to the Bearers,
> These Warrants will become negotiable, until the Trea-
> sury can pay them out of the contingent Fund in case
> there is not a sufficiency of Money in the Treasury to
> answer the necessary Services of this Expedition.
>
> I am &c. &c.,
> William Tryon

Had Hermon Husband and James Hunter known, when
they left River Run? I thought they must. And the Major, of
course, was bound for New Bern now, to offer his services to
the Governor. His boots were filmed with the dust of his ride,
but the hilt of his sword gleamed in the sun.

"Bloody, bloody, fucking hell," I said softly, again, with
emphasis. Major MacDonald blinked. Jamie glanced at me,
and the corner of his mouth twitched up.

"Aye, well," he said. "Nearly a month. Just time to get the
barley in."

# PART SIX

*The War of the Regulation*

# 56

# ". . . AND FIGHT THEM, SAYING THEY HAD MEN ENOUGH TO KILL THEM, WE CAN KILL THEM"

*Deposition of Waightstill Avery, Witness*
*North Carolina*
*Mecklenburg County*

Waightstill Avery Testifieth and saith that on the sixth Day of March Instant about nine or Ten OClock in the Morning He this Deponent was at the now dwelling house of one Hudgins who lives at the lower end of the long Island.

And He this Deponent there saw Thirty or Forty of those People who style themselves Regulators, and was then and there arrested and forceably detained a prisoner by one of them (who said his Name was James McQuiston) in the Name of them all, and that soon after one James Graham (or Grimes) spoke to this Deponent these Words "You are now a Prisoner and You must not go any where without a Guard." immediately after adding that "You must keep with Your Guard and You shan't be hurt."

This Deponent was then conducted under Guard of two Men to the regulating Camp (as they termed it) about a Mile distant, where were many more persons of the same Denomination and others came there some Hours after, in the whole as this Deponent supposes and imagines about two hundred and Thirty.

That from themselves He this Deponent learned the

*Names of five of their Captains or leading Men then present (Viz., Thomas Hamilton and one other Hamilton, James Hunter, Joshua Teague one Gillespie and the aforesaid James Grimes (or Graham)). He this Deponent heard many of them whose Names are to Him unknown say approbrious Things against the Governor, the Judges of the Superior Court, against the House of Assembly and other persons in Office. While a surrounding Crowd were uttering Things still more approbrious the said Thomas Hamilton stood in the Midst and spoke Words of the following Tenor and purport (the Crowd still assenting to and affirming the Truth of what was said):*

*"What Business has Maurice Moore to be judge, He is no Judge, he was not appointed by the King He nor Henderson neither, They'll neither of them hold Court. The Assembly have gone and made a Riotous Act, and the people are more inraged than ever, it was the best thing that could be for the Country for now We shall be forced to kill all the Clerks and Lawyers, and We will kill them and I'll be damned if they are not put to Death. If they had not made that Act We might have suffered some of them to live. A Riotous Act! there never was any such Act in the Laws of England or any other Country but France, they brought it from France, and they'll bring the Inquisition."*

*Many of them said the Governor was a Friend to the Lawyers and the Assembly had worsted the Regulators in making Laws for Fees. They shut Husband up in Gaol that He might not see their roguish proceedings and then the Governor and the Assembly made just such Laws as the Lawyers wanted. The Governor is a Friend to the Lawyers, the Lawyers carry on every Thing, they appoint weak ignorant Justices of Peace for their own purposes.*

*There should be no Lawyers in the province, they damned themselves if there should. Fanning was outlawed as of the Twenty-Second of March and any Regulator that saw Him after that Time would kill him and some said they would not wait for that, wished they*

*could see him, and swore they would kill him before
they returned if they could find him at Salisbury—
Some wished they could see Judge Moore at Salisbury
that they might flog him, others that they might kill
him. One Robert Thomson said Maurise Moore was
purjured and called him by approbrious Names as
Rascal, Rogue, Villian, Scoundral, etc. others assented
to it.*

*When News was brought that Captain Rutherford
at the head of His Company was parading in the
Streets of Salisbury, this Deponent heard Sundry of
them urge very hard and strenuously that the whole
Body of the Regulators then present should March into
Salisbury with their Arms and fight them saying They
had Men enough to kill them, We can kill them We'll
teach them to oppose Us.*

*Taken sworn to & Subscribed this eighth
Day of March 1771 before Me*

*(signed) Waightstill Avery*

*(witnessed) Wm. Harris, Justice of the Peace*

> *William Tryon to General Thomas Gage*
> *North Carolina*
> *New Bern ye 19th March 1771*

*Sir,*

*It was Yesterday determined in His Majestys Coun-
cil of this Province to Raise a Body of Forces from the
Militia Regiments and Companies to March into the
Settlements of the Insurgents, who by their Rebellious
Acts and Declarations have set this Government at
defiance.*

*As we have few Military Engines or implements in
this Country, I am to request your assistance in*

*procuring me for this Service the Articles (cannon, shot, colours, drums, etc.) listed hereby.*

*I intend to begin My March from this Town about the Twentieth of next Month, and assemble the Militia as I march through the Counties. My Plan is to form fifteen Hundred Men, though from the Spirit that now appears on the Side of Government that Number may be considerably increased.*

*I am with much Respect and Esteem Sir Your Most Obedt. Servt., Wm. Tryon*

# NOW I LAY ME DOWN TO SLEEP . . .

*Fraser's Ridge*
*15 April, 1771*

ROGER LAY IN BED, listening for the intermittent whine of an invisible mosquito that had squeezed past the hide covering the cabin window. Jem's cradle was covered by gauze netting, but he and Brianna had no such shielding. If the damn thing would just light on him, he'd get it—but it seemed to circle tirelessly above their bed, occasionally swooping down to sing taunting little *neeeee* songs into his ear, before zooming off again into the dark.

He should have been tired enough to fall asleep in the face of an assault by airborne squadrons of mosquitoes, after the last few days of frantic activity. Two days of fast riding through the mountain coves and ridges, spreading the word to the nearer settlements, whose inhabitants would in turn alert those militia members farther away. The spring planting had been accomplished in record time, all the available men spending the hours from dawn to dusk in the fields. His system was still charged with adrenaline, and little jolts of it zapped through mind and muscle, as though he'd been taking coffee intravenously.

He'd spent all day today helping to ready the farm for their departure, and fragmented images of the round of chores scrolled behind his closed lids whenever he shut his eyes. Fence repair, hay hauling, a hasty excursion to the mill for the bags of flour needed to feed the regiment on the march. Fixing a split rim on the wagon's wheel, splicing a broken harness trace, helping to catch the white sow, who had made an abortive escape attempt from the stable, wood-chopping, and finally, a brisk hour's digging just before supper so Claire could plant her wee patch of yams and peanuts before they left.

In spite of the hurry and labor, that dusk-lit digging had been a welcome respite in the organized frenzy of the day; the thought of it made him pause now, reliving it in hopes of slowing his mind and calming himself enough to sleep.

It was April, warm for the season, and Claire's garden was rampant with growth: green spikes and sprouting leaves and small brilliant flowers, climbing vines that twisted up the palisades and opened silent white trumpets slowly above him as he worked in the gathering twilight.

The smells of the plants and the fresh-turned earth rose round him as the air cooled, strong as incense. The moths came to the trumpet flowers, soft things drifting out of the wood in mottled shades of white and gray and black. Clouds of midges and mosquitoes came too, drawn to his sweat, and after them, the mosquito-hawks, dark fierce creatures with narrow wings and furry bodies, who whirred through the hollyhocks with the aggressive attitude of football hooligans.

He stretched long toes out against the weight of the quilts, his leg just touching his wife's, and felt in memory the chunk of the spade, hard edge beneath his foot, and the satisfying feeling of cracking earth and snapping roots as another spadeful yielded, the black earth moist and veined with the blind white rhizomes of wild grass and the fugitive gleam of earthworms writhing frantically out of sight.

A huge cecropia moth had flown past his head, lured by the garden scents. Its pale brown wings were the size of his hand, and marked with staring eyespots, unearthly in their silent beauty.

*Who makes a garden works with God.* That had been written on the edge of the old copper sundial in the garden of the manse in Inverness where he had grown up. Ironic, in view of the fact that the Reverend had neither time nor talent for gardening, and the place was a jungle of unmown grass and ancient rosebushes run wild and leggy with neglect. He smiled at the thought, and made his mental good-night to the Reverend's shade.

*Good-night, Dad. God bless you.*

It had been a long time since he'd lost the habit of bidding good-night in this fashion to a brief list of family and friends; the hangover of a childhood of nightly prayers that ended with the usual list of, "God bless Nana, and Grandpa Guy in heaven, and my best friend Peter, and Lillian the dog, and the grocer's cat . . ."

He hadn't done it in years, but a memory of the peace of that small ritual made him draw up a new list, now. Better than counting sheep, he supposed—and he wanted the sense of peace he remembered, more than he wanted sleep.

*Good-night, Mrs. Graham,* he thought, and smiled to himself, summoning a brief, vivid image of the Reverend's old housekeeper, dipping her hand in a bowl and flicking water onto a hot griddle, to see if the drops would dance. *God bless.*

The Reverend, Mrs. Graham, her granddaughter Fiona and Fiona's husband Ernie . . . his parents, though that was a *pro forma* nod toward two faceless shapes. Claire, up at the big house, and, with a slight hesitation, Jamie. Then his own small family. He warmed at the thought of them.

*Good night, wee lad,* he thought, turning his head in the direction of the cradle where Jemmy slept. *God bless.* And Brianna.

He turned his head the other way, and opened his eyes, seeing the dark oval of her sleeping face turned toward his, no more than a foot away on the pillow. He eased himself as quietly as possible onto his side, and lay watching her. They had let the fire go out, since they would be leaving early in the morning; it was so dark in the room he could make out no more of her features than the faint markings of brows and lips.

Brianna never lay wakeful. She rolled onto her back, stretched and settled with a sigh of content, took three deep breaths and was out like a light. Maybe exhaustion, maybe just the blessings of good health and a clear conscience—but he sometimes thought it was eagerness to escape into that private dreamscape of hers, that place where she roamed free at the wheel of her car, hair snapping in the wind.

What was she dreaming now? he wondered. He could feel the faint warmth of her breath on his face.

*Last night, I dreamed I made love with Roger.* The memory of that particular entry still rankled, hard as he'd tried to dismiss it. He had been drifting toward sleep, lulled by his litany, but the memory of her dreambook pulled him back to wakefulness. She had damn well better not be dreaming such a thing now! Not after the time he'd just given her.

He closed his eyes again, concentrating on the regular pulse of her breathing. His forehead was mere inches from hers. Perhaps he could catch the echo of her dream, through the bones of her skull? What he felt, though, was the echo of her flesh, and the reverberations of their farewell, with all its doubts and pleasures.

She and the lad would leave in the morning, too; their things were packed and stood with his own bundle beside the door. Mr. Wemyss would drive them to Hillsborough, where she would presumably be safely—and gainfully—employed in painting Mrs. Sherston's portrait.

"You be bloody careful," he'd said to her, for the third time in an evening. Hillsborough was smack in the center of the Regulators' territory, and he had considerable reservations about her going at all. She had dismissed his concern, though, scoffing at the notion that she or Jem might be in any danger. She was likely right—and yet he wasn't so sure that she would act differently if there *was* danger. She was so excited at the prospect of her damn commission, he thought, she'd walk straight through armed mobs to get to Hills-borough.

She was singing softly to herself—"Loch Lomond," of all bloody things. "Oh, you'll take the high road, and I'll take the low road, and I'll be in Scotland aforrrrrrre ye . . ."

"Did ye hear me?" he'd asked, catching hold of her arm as she folded the last of Jemmy's dresses.

"Yes, dear," Bree had murmured, lashes fluttering in mocking submission. That had irritated him into grabbing her wrist and pulling her round to face him.

"I mean it," he said. He stared into her eyes, wide open now, but with a hint of mockery still glinting in dark blue tri-angles. He tightened his grip on her wrist; tall and well-built as she was, her bones felt delicate, almost frail in his grasp. He had a sudden vision of the bones beneath Brianna's skin—high, wide cheekbones, domed skull, and long white teeth; all too easy to imagine those teeth exposed to the root in a permanent rictus of bone.

He had pulled her to him then with sudden violence, kissed her hard enough to feel her teeth against his own, not caring if he bruised either of them.

She wore only a shift and he hadn't bothered to take it off, merely shoving her backward onto the bed and pushing it above her thighs. She'd lifted her hands toward him, but he hadn't let her touch him; he'd pinned her arms at first, then later, borne her into the hollow of the mattress with the weight of his body, grinding, grasping, seeking reassurance in the thin padding of flesh that kept her bones from his.

They had done it in silence, half-aware of the sleeping child nearby. And yet somewhere in the midst of it, her body had answered him, in some deep and startling way that went beyond words.

"I mean it," he'd repeated, moments later, speaking softly into the tangle of her hair. He lay on her, enclosing her with his arms, keeping her from moving. She twitched, and he tightened his grasp, holding her still. She sighed, and he felt her mouth move, her teeth sink gently into the flesh below his collarbone. She bit him. Not abruptly, but in a slow, suck-ing bite that made him gasp and lift up to break away.

"I know," she said, and wriggled her arms free, to come round his back and hold him close to her damp, warm softness. "I mean it, too."

"THAT WHAT YOU WANTED?" He whispered the words now, but softly, not to awaken her. The warmth of her body radiated through the bedclothes; she was deep asleep.

If it was what she'd wanted—what, exactly, was it? Was it the brutal nature of his lovemaking that she'd responded to? Or had she sensed the strength of what lay behind it, and acknowledged that—the desperation of his need to keep her safe?

And if it was the roughness . . . he swallowed, clenching a fist against the thought of Stephen Bonnet. She'd never told him what had passed between them, her and Bonnet—and it was unthinkable that he should ask. More unthinkable that he should suspect anything in that encounter might have shamefully stirred her. And yet she did stir visibly on those rare occasions when something led him to take her abruptly, without his usual gentleness.

He was a long way from praying now.

He felt as he had once before, trapped in a rhododendron hell, with the same maze of damp roots and hanging leaves always before him, no matter in which direction he turned. Dim tunnels seemed to offer hope of escape, and yet led only to further tangles.

*For me and my true love will never meet again, on the bonnie banks and braes of Loch Lomond . . .*

He was wound tight again, skin prickling and his legs twitching with restlessness. The mosquito whined by and he slapped at it—too late, of course. Unable to keep still, he slid quietly out of bed, and did a quick series of deep knee-bends to loosen the cramped muscles.

That brought some relief, and he dropped to the floor to do push-ups, counting silently as he dipped toward the floorboards. One. Two. Three. Four. Concentrating only on the increasing burn in chest and arms and shoulders, the soothing monotony of the count. Twenty-six, twenty-seven, twenty-eight . . .

At last, muscles quivering with temporary exhaustion, he stood up, untacked the hide from the window, and stood naked, letting the damp night air flood in upon him. He might let in more mosquitoes—but the one might go out, too.

The wood was silvered with moonlight, and a faint fire-glow in the darkened heart of it spoke of the militia encamped there. They had been coming in all day, on mules or ragged horses, muskets laid across the bundles of their blankets. He caught the sound of voices and casual laughter, a fragment borne on the breeze. At least he wasn't the only one wakeful; the notion comforted him.

A brighter light glowed at the side of the big house, at the farther side of the clearing. A lantern; two figures walking close together, one tall, one smaller.

The man said something, an interrogative rumble; he recognized Jamie's voice, but couldn't make out the words.

"No," Claire's voice answered, lighter, clear as they came closer. He saw her hands flutter, silhouetted in the lantern's glow. "I'm filthy from the planting. I'm going to wash before I come in. You go up to bed."

The larger figure hesitated, then handed her the lantern. Roger saw Claire's face in the light for a moment, turned upward, smiling. Jamie bent and kissed her briefly, then stepped back.

"Hurry, then," he said, and Roger could hear the answering smile in his voice. "I dinna sleep well without ye beside me, Sassenach."

"You're going to sleep right away, are you?" She paused, a bantering note in her voice.

"Not right away, no." Jamie's figure had melted into the darkness, but the breeze was toward the cabin, and his voice came out of the shadows, part of the night. "But I canna very well do the other unless ye're beside me, either, now can I?"

Claire laughed, though softly.

"Start without me," she said, turning away toward the well. "I'll catch you up."

Roger waited by the window until he saw her come back, the lantern swinging with the haste of her step, and go inside.

The breeze had turned, and he heard no more of the men in the wood, though their fire still burned.

He looked toward the wood, his skin cool now, and goose-flesh rose on his chest. He rubbed absently at it, and felt the tender spot where she had bitten him. It was dark in the moonlight, a faint blotch on his skin; would it still be there come morning? he wondered.

Reaching up to pull the hide back into place, he caught the gleam of moonlight on glass. Brianna's small collection of personal items lay on the shelf by the window: the pair of tortoiseshell combs Jocasta had given her, her silver bracelet. The small glass jar of tansy oil, two or three discreet slips of sponge beside it. And the larger gleam of the jarful of Dauco seeds. She hadn't had time for the tansy oil tonight, but he'd bet his life she'd taken the seeds sometime today.

He tacked down the hide, and made his way back to bed, pausing by the cradle to put down a hand and feel the baby's breath through the mosquito-netting, warm and reassuring on his skin.

Jem had kicked his covers off; Roger lifted the netting and pulled them up by feel, tucking them firmly in. There was something soft . . . oh, Jemmy's rag-doll; the baby was clutching it to his chest. Roger stood for a moment, hand on Jemmy's back, feeling the soothing rise and fall of his breathing.

"Good-night, laddie," he whispered at last, and touched the soft padded round of the little boy's bottom. "God bless you and keep you safe."

# HAPPY BIRTHDAY TO YOU

I WOKE UP JUST PAST DAWN, roused by an in-
sect of some sort walking up my leg. I twitched my foot
and whatever it was scuttled hastily away into the grass,
evidently alarmed to discover that I was alive. I wriggled my
toes suspiciously, but finding no more intruders in my blanket, drew a deep breath of sap-filled fresh air and relaxed
luxuriously.

I could hear faint stirrings nearby, but it was only the
stamp and blowing of the officers' horses, who woke long before the men did. The camp itself was still silent—or as silent
as a camp containing several hundred men was likely to be at
any hour. The sheet of canvas overhead glowed with soft
light and leaf-shadows, but the sun was not yet fully up. I
closed my eyes half-way, delighted at the thought that I
needn't get up for some time yet—and when I did, someone
else would have made breakfast.

We had come into camp the night before, after a winding
journey down from the mountains and across the piedmont,
to arrive at the place of rendezvous, at Colonel Bryan's plantation. We were in good time; Tryon had not yet arrived with
his troops from New Bern, nor had the Craven and Carteret
County detachments, who were bringing the artillery field
pieces and swivel guns. Tryon's troops were expected sometime today; or so Colonel Bryan had told us over supper the
night before.

A grasshopper landed on the canvas above with an audible thump. I eyed it narrowly, but it didn't seem disposed to come inside, thank goodness. Perhaps I should have accepted Mrs. Bryan's offer to find me a bed in the house, along with a few other officers' wives who had accompanied their husbands. Jamie had insisted upon sleeping in the field with his men, though, and I had gone with him, preferring a bed involving Jamie and bugs to one with neither.

I glanced sideways, careful not to move in case he was still asleep. He wasn't. He was lying quite still, though, utterly relaxed, save for his right hand. He had this raised, and appeared to be examining it closely, turning it to and fro and slowly curling and uncurling his fingers—as well as he could. The fourth finger had a fused joint, and was permanently stiff; the middle finger was slightly twisted, a deep white scar spiraling round the middle joint.

His hand was callused and battered by work, and the tiny stigma of a nail-wound still showed, pale-pink, in the middle of his palm. The skin of his hand was deeply bronzed and weathered, freckled with sun-blots and scattered with bleached gold hairs. I thought it remarkably beautiful.

"Happy Birthday," I said, softly. "Taking stock?"

He let the hand fall on his chest, and turned his head to look at me, smiling.

"Aye, something of the sort. Though I suppose I've a few hours left. I was born at half-six; I willna have lived a full half-century until suppertime."

I laughed and rolled onto my side, kicking the blanket off. The air was still delightfully cool, but it wouldn't last long.

"Do you expect to disintegrate much further before supper?" I asked, teasing.

"Oh, I dinna suppose anything is likely to fall off by then," he said, consideringly. "As to the workings . . . aye, well . . ." He arched his back, stretching, and sank back with a gratified groan as my hand settled on him.

"It all seems to be in perfect working order," I assured him. I gave a brief, experimental tug, making him yelp slightly. "Not loose at all."

"Good," he said, folding his hand firmly over mine to

prevent further unauthorized experiments. "How did ye ken what I was doing? Taking stock, as ye say?"

I let him keep hold of the hand, but shifted to set my chin in the center of his chest, where a small depression seemed made for the purpose.

"I always do that, when I have a birthday—though I generally do it the night before. More looking back, I think, reflecting a bit on the year that's just gone. But I do check things over; I think perhaps everyone does. Just to see if you're the same person as the day before."

"I'm reasonably certain that I am," he assured me. "Ye dinna see any marked changes, do ye?"

I lifted my chin from its resting place and looked him over carefully. It was in fact rather hard to look at him objectively; I was both so used to his features and so fond of them that I tended to notice tiny, dear things about him—the freckle on his earlobe, the lower incisor pushing eagerly forward, just slightly out of line with its fellows—and to respond to the slightest change of his expression—but not really to look at him as an integrated whole.

He bore my examination tranquilly, eyelids half-lowered against the growing light. His hair had come loose while he slept and feathered over his shoulders, its ruddy waves framing a face strongly marked by both humor and passion—but which possessed a paradoxical and most remarkable capacity for stillness.

"No," I said at last, and set my chin down again with a contented sigh. "It's still you."

He gave a small grunt of amusement, but lay still. I could hear one of the cooks stumbling round nearby, cursing as he tripped over a wagon-tongue. The camp was still in the process of assembling; a few of the companies—those with a high proportion of ex-soldiers among their officers and men—were tidy and organized. A good many were not, and tipsy tents and strewn equipment sprawled across the meadow in a quasi-military hodgepodge.

A drum began to beat, to no apparent effect. The army continued to snooze.

"Do you think the Governor is going to be able to do anything with these troops?" I asked dubiously.

The local avatar of the army appeared to have gone back to sleep as well. At my question, though, the long auburn lashes lifted in lazy response.

"Oh, aye. Tryon's a soldier. He kens well enough what to do—at least to start. It's no so verra difficult to make men march in column and dig latrines, ken. To make them fight is another thing."

"Can he do that?"

The chest under my chin lifted in a deep sigh.

"Maybe so. Maybe no. The question is—will he have to?"

That was the question, all right. Rumors had flown round us like autumn leaves in a gale, all the way from Fraser's Ridge. The Regulators had ten thousand men, who were marching in a body upon New Bern. General Gage was sailing from New York with a regiment of official troops to subdue the Colony. The Orange County militia had rioted and killed their officers. Half the Wake County men had deserted. Hermon Husband had been arrested and spirited onto a ship, to be taken to London for trial on charges of treason. Hillsborough had been taken by the Regulators, who were preparing to fire the town and put Edmund Fanning and all his associates to the sword. I did hope that one wasn't true—or if it was, that Hubert Sherston was not one of Fanning's intimates.

Sorting through the mass of hearsay, supposition, and sheer wild invention, the only fact of which we could be sure appeared to be that Governor Tryon was en route to join the militia. After which, we would just see, I supposed.

Jamie's free hand rested on my back, his thumb idly stroking the edge of my shoulder blade. With his usual capacity for mental discipline, he appeared to have dismissed the uncertainty of the military prospects completely from his mind, and was thinking of something else entirely.

"Do ye ever think—" he began, and then broke off.

"Think what?" I bent and kissed his chest, arching my back to encourage him to rub it, which he did.

"Well . . . I'm no so sure I can explain, but it's struck me that now I have lived longer than my father did—which is not something I expected to happen," he added, with faint wryness. "It's only . . . well, it seems odd, is all. I only wondered, did ye ever think of that, yourself—having lost your mother young, I mean?"

"Yes." My face was buried in his chest, my voice muffled in the folds of his shirt. "I used to—when I was younger. Like going on a journey without a map."

His hand on my back paused for a moment.

"Aye, that's it." He sounded a little surprised. "I kent more or less what it would be like to be a man of thirty, or of forty—but now what?" His chest moved briefly, with a small noise that might have been a mixture of amusement and puzzlement.

"You invent yourself," I said softly, to the shadows inside the hair that had fallen over my face. "You look at other women—or men; you try on their lives for size. You take what you can use, and you look inside yourself for what you can't find elsewhere. And always . . . always . . . you wonder if you're doing it right."

His hand was warm and heavy on my back. He felt the tears that ran unexpectedly from the corners of my eyes to dampen his shirt, and his other hand came up to touch my head and smooth my hair.

"Aye, that's it," he said again, very softly.

The camp was beginning to stir outside, with clangings and thumps, and the hoarse sound of sleep-rough voices. Overhead, the grasshopper began to chirp, the sound like someone scratching a nail on a copper pot.

"This is a morning my father never saw," Jamie said, still so softly that I heard it as much through the walls of his chest, as with my ears. "The world and each day in it is a gift, *mo chridhe*—no matter what tomorrow may be."

I sighed deeply and turned my head, to rest my cheek against his chest. He reached over gently and wiped my nose with a fold of his shirt.

"And as for taking stock," he added practically, "I've all my teeth, none of my parts are missing, and my cock still stands up by itself in the morning. It could be worse."

# MILITARY ENGINES

*Journal of the Expedition against the Insurgents*
*Kept by William Tryon, Governor*

**Thursday, May 2nd**
  The Craven and Carteret Detachments marched out
of New Bern with the two Field Pieces, Six Swivel
Guns mounted on Carriages, Sixteen Waggons, & four
Carts, loaded with Baggage, Ammunition and as much
provisions as would supply the several Detachments
that were to join them on their Route to Col. Bryan's,
the place of General Rendezvous.
  The Governor left New Bern the 27th of April, and
arrived at Col. Bryan's the 1st of May. Today the
Troops from the two Districts joined.

**Friday, 3d. of May, Union Camp**
  The Governor Reviewed at 12 O'Clock the Detachments in the Meadow at Smiths Ferry on the West Side
of Neuse River.

**Saturday, the 4th of May**
  The Whole marched to Johnston Court House. Nine
Miles.

**Sunday, 5th of May**

Marched to Major Theophilus Hunter's in Wake County. Thirteen Miles.

**Monday, 6th of May**

The Army halted, and the Governor reviewed the Wake Regiment at a Genl. Muster. Mr. Hinton Colonel of the Regiment acquainted the Governor that he had got but Twenty two Men of the Company he had received Orders to raise, owing to a Disaffection among the Inhabitants of the County.

The Governor observing a General Discontent in the Wake Regiment as he passed along the Front Rank of the Battalion, seeing that not more than one Man in five had Arms, & finding that upon his calling on them to turn out as Volunteers in the Service, they refused to obey, ordered the Army to surround the Battalion; which being effected he directed three of his Colonels to draft out Forty of the most Sightly & Most active Men, which Manouvre caused no small Panic in the Regiment, consisting at the Time of about four Hundred Men.

During the drafting the Officers of the Army were active in persuading the men to enlist, and in less than two Hours completed the Wake Company to Fifty Men. Night coming on the Wake Regiment was dismissed, much ashamed both of their Disgrace, & their own Conduct which occasioned it. The Army returned to Camp.

**Wednesday, the 8th of May**

Col. Hinton's Detachment was left behind, with a View to prevent the disaffected in that County from forming into a Body, and joining the Regulators in the adjacent Counties.

This Morning a Detachment marched to the dwelling House of Turner Tomlinson, a Notorious Regulator, and brought him prisoner to Camp, where he *was closely confined. He confess'd he was a Regulator, but would make no discoveries.*

*The Army marched, & incamped near Booth's, on New Hope Creek.*

**Friday, the 10th of May**

*Halted, ordered the Waggons to be refitted, Horses to be shod, and every thing put in Repair. Reviewed in Hillsborough two Companies of the Orange Militia.*

*The Prisoner Tomlinson made his escape this Evening, from the Quarter Guard. Detachments set after him, but without Success.*

**Sunday, the 12th of May**

*Marched, and forded Haw River, and encamped on the West Side of the Banks. It was expected the Regulators would have opposed the passages of the Royalists over this River, as it was their Intent, but not suspecting that the Army would move out of Hillsborough till after Monday, they were by this Sudden Movement of the Army defeated in that part of their plan.*

*Received this Day flying Reports that General Waddell was forced by the Regulators, with the Troops under his Command to repass the Yadkin River.*

*Divine Service, with Sermon, performed by the Revd. Mr. McCartny. Text: "If You have no Sword Sell your Garment & Buy One."*

*This Day Twenty Gentlemen Volunteers joined the Army, chiefly from Granville & Bute Counties. They were formed into a Troop of Light Horse under the Command of Major MacDonald. A Regulator taken by the flanking parties laying in ambush with his Gun. The Commissary took out of his House part of a Hogshead of Rum lodged there for the Use of the Regulators. Also some Hogs which were to be accounted to His Family.*

**Monday, the 13th of May**

 *Marched to O'Neal. At 12 O'Clock an Express rider arrived from General Waddell, with a Verbal Message, the Express not daring to take a Letter for fear of its being intercepted. The Purport of which Message was that on Thursday Evening the 9th Instant the Regulators to the Number of two Thousand surrounded his Camp, and in the most daring & insolent Manner required the General to retreat with the Troops over the Yadkin River, of which he was then within two Miles. He refused to comply, insisting he had the Governor's Orders to proceed. This made them more insolent, and with many Indian shouts they endeavoured to intimidate his Men.*

 *The General finding his Men not exceeding three Hundred, and generally unwilling to engage; and many of his Sentries going over to the Regulators, was reduced to comply with their requisition, & early the next Morning repassed the Yadkin River, with his Cannon and Baggage; the Regulators agreeing to disperse and return to their several Habitations.*

 *A Council of War was held immediately to deliberate on the Subject of the Intelligence brought by the Express, composed of the Honorable John Rutherford, Lewis DeRosset, Robert Palmer, & Sam Cornell, of His Majesty's Council, and the Colonels & Field Officers of the Army, Wherein it was resolved that the Army should change their Route, get into the Road at Captain Holt's that leads from Hillsborough to Salisbury, pass the little and great Alamance Rivers with all possible Expedition, & march without Loss of Time to join General Waddell; accordingly the Army got under March, and before Night encamped on the West Side of little Alamance, a strong Detachment being sent forward to take possession of the West Banks of Great Alamance, to prevent the Enemy's Parties from occupying that strong Post.*

 *This evening received Intelligence that the Regulators were sending Scouts through all their Settlements, and assembling on Sandy Creek, near Hunter's.*

Marched and joined the Detachment on the West Banks of Great Alamance where a strong Camp was chosen. Here the Army halted till more provisions could be brought from Hillsborough, for which purpose several Waggons now emptied and sent from Camp to Hillsborough.

Intelligence being brought this Evening into Camp that the Rebels intended to attack the camp in the Night, the Necessary preparations were made for an Engagement, and one third of the Army ordered to remain under Arms all Night, & the Remainder to lay down near their Arms. No Alarm given.

**Tuesday, the 14th of May**

Halted, the Men ordered to keep in Camp.

The Army lay on their Arms all Night, as in the preceeding. No alarm.

**Wednesday, the 15th of May**

About 6 O'Clock in the Evening, the Governor received a Letter from the Insurgents which he laid before the Council of War, wherein it was determined that the Army should march against the Rebels early the next Morning, that the Governor should send them a Letter offering them Terms, and in Case of Refusal, should attack them.

The Men remained all Night under Arms. No alarm, tho' the Rebels lay within five Miles of the Camp.

**From the Dreambook:**
**Hillsborough, May 15**

*"Last night I fell asleep early, and woke up before dawn inside a gray cloud. All day, I've felt like I was walking inside a mist; people talk to me and I don't*

*hear them; I can see their mouths move, and I nod and
smile, and then go away. The air is hot and muggy and
everything smells like hot metal. My head aches, and
the cook is clanging pans.*

*I've tried all day to remember what I dreamed of,
and I can't. There's only gray, and a feeling of fear.
I've never been near a battle, but I have the feeling
that what I'm dreaming of is cannon smoke."*

## 60

## COUNCIL OF WAR

JAMIE CAME BACK from the Council of War, well
after suppertime, and informed the men briefly of
Tryon's intent. The general response was approval, if not
outright enthusiasm.

"Ist gut we move now," said Ewald Mueller, stretching out
his long arms and cracking all his knuckles simultaneously.
"Longer we stay, we are growing moss!"

This sentiment was greeted by laughter and nods of
agreement. The mood of the company brightened noticeably
at the prospect of action in the morning; men settled down to
talk around the fires, the rays of the setting sun glinting off
tin cups and the polished barrels of the muskets laid carefully
by their feet.

Jamie made a quick round of inspection, answering questions and administering reassurances, then came to join me
at our smaller fire. I looked at him narrowly; in spite of the
stress of the immediate situation, there was a sense of suppressed satisfaction about him that at once excited my suspicions.

"What have you done?" I asked, handing him a large chunk of bread and a bowl of stew.

He didn't bother denying that he'd been doing something.

"Got Cornell alone long enough after the Council, to ask him about Stephen Bonnet." He ripped off a chunk of bread with his teeth and swallowed it with the minimum of chewing. "Christ, I'm starved. I've not eaten all day, what wi' creepin' through the brambles on my belly like a snake."

"Surely Samuel Cornell wasn't hanging about in the brambles." Cornell was one of the Governor's Royal Council, a stout and wealthy merchant from Edenton, and grossly unsuited by position, build, and temperament for snaking through brambles.

"No, that was later." He swabbed the bread through the stew, took another enormous bite, then waved a hand, momentarily speechless. I handed him a cup of cider, which he used to wash down the mess.

"We were searchin' out the Rebel lines," he explained, the obstruction cleared. "They're no far off, ken. Though 'lines' is giving them the benefit of considerable doubt," he added, scooping up more stew. "I've not seen such a rabble since I fought in France, and we took a village where a gang o' wine-smugglers were. Half of them whoring and all of them drunk; we had to pick them up off the ground to arrest them. This lot's little better, from what I could see. Not so many whores, though," he added, to be fair, and shoved the rest of his bread into his mouth.

At least half the Governor's army was slightly the worse for drink at the moment, but that was so usual a condition as not to call for comment. I gave him another piece of bread, concentrating on the important aspect of the conversation.

"So you've found out something about Bonnet, then?"

He nodded, chewed, and gulped.

"Cornell's not met him, but he's heard talk. It seems he works his way up and down the Outer Banks for a bit, and then disappears for three or four months. Then suddenly, one day he'll be there again, drinking in the taverns in Edenton or Roanoke, gold pieces spilling from his pockets."

"So he's bringing in goods from Europe and selling

them." Three or four months was the time it would take to sail a ship to England and back. "Contraband, I suppose?"

Jamie nodded.

"Cornell thinks so. And d'ye ken where he brings the stuff ashore?" He wiped the back of a hand across his mouth, seeming grimly amused. "Wylie's Landing. Or so rumor says."

"What—you don't mean Phillip Wylie is in cahoots with him?" I was shocked—and rather distressed—to hear this, but Jamie shook his head.

"As to that, I couldna say. But the Landing adjoins Phillip Wylie's plantation, to be sure. And the wee shite *was* wi' Bonnet the night he came to River Run, no matter what he may have said about it, later," he added. He flapped a hand, dismissing Phillip Wylie for the moment.

"But Cornell says that Bonnet's disappeared again; he's been gone, this past month. So my aunt and Duncan are likely safe enough, for the moment. That's one thing off my mind—and a good thing; there's enough to worry about without that."

He spoke without irony, glancing round at the encampment that sprawled around us. As the light failed, the fires began to glow through the dimness of twilight, like hundreds of fireflies along the banks of Great Alamance.

"Hermon Husband is here," he said.

I looked up from the fresh bowl of stew I was dishing out.

"Did you speak to him?"

He shook his head.

"I couldna go near. He's with the Regulators, aye? I was on a wee hill, lookin' down across the stream, and saw him in the distance; he was in a great mass of men, but I couldna mistake his dress."

"What will he do?" I handed him the full bowl. "Surely he won't fight—or allow them to fight." I was inclined to view Husband's presence as a hopeful sign. Hermon Husband was the closest thing the Regulators had to a real leader; they would listen to him, I was sure.

Jamie shook his head, looking troubled.

"I dinna ken, Sassenach. He willna take up arms himself, no—but as for the rest . . ." He trailed off, thinking. Then his face set in sudden decision. He handed me back the bowl, and turning on his heel, made his way across the camp.

I saw him touch Roger on the shoulder, and draw him aside a little. They spoke together for a few moments, then Jamie reached into his coat, drew out something white, and handed it to Roger. Roger looked at whatever it was for a moment, then nodded, and tucked it away in his own coat.

Jamie clapped him on the shoulder, left him, and came back across the camp, pausing to laugh and exchange rude remarks with the Lindsay brothers.

He came back smiling, and took the bowl from me, seeming relieved.

"I've told Roger Mac to go first thing in the morning, to find Husband," he said, setting about the stew with renewed appetite. "If he can, I've told him to bring Husband here—to speak face to face wi' Tryon. If he canna convince Tryon—which he can't—perhaps Tryon will convince Husband that he's in earnest. If Hermon sees that it will mean bloodshed, then perhaps he will prevail upon his men to stand down."

"Do you really think so?" It had rained lightly in the afternoon, and banks of cloud still covered the eastern sky. The edges of those clouds glowed faintly red—not from the slanting rays of sunset, but from the fires of the Regulators, camped invisibly on the opposite bank of the Alamance.

Jamie wiped his bowl and took a last bite of bread, shaking his head.

"I dinna ken," he said simply. "But there's nothing else to try, is there?"

I nodded, and stooped to put more wood on the fire. No one would sleep early tonight.

The campfires had burned all day, smoking and sputtering in a light rain. Now, though, the drizzle had ceased and the clouds had parted, shredding into long, wispy mare's-tails that glowed like fire across the whole arc of the western sky, eclipsing the puny efforts of the earthbound flames. Seeing it, I put a hand on Jamie's arm.

"Look," I said. He turned, wary lest someone had appeared at his heels with a fresh problem, but his face relaxed as I gestured upward.

Frank, urged to look at some wonder of nature whilst

preoccupied with a problem, would have paused just long enough not to seem discourteous, said, "Oh, yes, lovely, isn't it?" and returned at once to the maze of his thoughts. Jamie lifted his face to the glowing glory of the heavens and stood still.

*What is the matter with you?* I thought to myself. *Can't you let Frank Randall rest in peace?*

Jamie put an arm about my shoulders, and sighed.

"In Scotland," he said, "the sky would be like lead all day, and even at the twilight, ye'd see no more than the sun sinking into the sea like a red-hot cannonball. Never a sky like this one is."

"What makes you think of Scotland?" I asked, intrigued that his mind should run as mine did, on things of the past.

"Dawn and twilight, and the season of the year," he said, and his wide mouth curled slightly upward in reminiscence. "Whenever there is a change in the air around me, it makes me think of what has been, and what is now. I dinna always do it in a house, but when I'm living rough, I'll often wake dreaming of folk I once knew, and then sit quiet in the twilight, thinking of other times and places." He shrugged a little. "So now the sun is going down, and it is Scotland in my mind."

"Oh," I said, comforted at having such an explanation. "That must be it."

"Must be what?" The setting sun bathed his face in gold, softening the lines of strain as he looked down at me.

"I was thinking of other times and places, too," I said, and leaned my head against his shoulder. "Just now, though . . . I can't think of anything but this."

"Oh?" He hesitated for a moment, but then said, carefully, "I dinna much mention it, Sassenach, for if the answer's 'yes,' there's nay so much I can do to mend it—but do ye often long for . . . the other times?"

I waited for the space of three heartbeats to answer; I heard them, Jamie's heart beating slow under my ear, and I curled my left hand closed, feeling the smooth metal of the gold ring on my finger.

"No," I said, "but I remember them."

# 61

# ULTIMATUMS

*Great Alamance Camp*
*May 16th 1771*

*To the People now Assembled*
*in Arms, who Style themselves*
*Regulators*

*In Answer to your Petition, I am to acquaint you*
*that I have ever been attentive to the true Interest of*
*this Country, and to that of every Individual residing*
*within it. I lament the fatal Necessity to which you*
*have now reduced me, by withdrawing yourselves from*
*the Mercy of the Crown, and the Laws of your Coun-*
*try, to require you are assembled as Regulators, to lay*
*down your Arms, Surrender up the outlawed Ringlead-*
*ers, and Submit yourselves to the Laws of your Coun-*
*try, and then rest on the lenity and Mercy of*
*Government. By accepting these Terms in one Hour*
*from the delivery of this Dispatch, you will prevent an*
*effusion of Blood, as you are at this time in a state of*
*War and Rebellion against your King, your Country,*
*and your Laws.*

*Wm. Tryon*

JAMIE HAD GONE before I woke; his blanket lay neatly folded beside me, and Gideon was gone from the pin-oak to which Jamie had tethered him the night before.

"Colonel's gone to meet with the Governor's Council of War," Kenny Lindsay told me, yawning widely. He blinked, shaking himself like a wet dog. "Tea, ma'am, or coffee?"

"Tea, please." I supposed it was the tenor of current events that was causing me to think of the Boston Tea Party. I couldn't recall for sure when that brouhaha and its subsequent events were due to occur, but had an obscure feeling that I ought to seize every opportunity of drinking tea while it was still obtainable, in hopes of saturating my tissues—like a bear tucking into the grubs and berries in anticipation of winter.

The day had dawned still and clear, and while it was cool for the moment, there was already a hint of mugginess in the air from the rain the day before. I sipped my tea, feeling small tendrils of hair escape from bondage to curl round my face, sticking to my cheeks in the steam from my cup.

Tissues restored for the moment, I fetched a couple of buckets and set off for the stream. I hoped it wouldn't be needed, but it would be as well to have a quantity of boiled sterile water on hand, just in case. And if it wasn't needed for medical purposes, I could rinse my stockings, which were much in need of attention.

Despite its name the Great Alamance was not a particularly impressive river, being no more than fifteen or twenty feet across for most of its length. It was also shallow, mud-bottomed, and kinked like a wool-raveling, with multiple small arms and tributaries that wandered all over the landscape. I supposed it was a decent military demarcation, though; while a body of men could certainly ford the stream without much trouble, there was no chance of them doing so by stealth.

Dragonflies darted over the water, and over the heads of a couple of militia-men, chatting companionably as they relieved themselves into the murky waters of the stream. I paused tactfully behind a bush until they had left, reflecting as I made my way down the sloping bank with my buckets how fortunate it was that most of the troops would consider *drinking* water only if actually dying of dehydration.

When I came back into camp, I found it wide awake, every man alert, if red-eyed. The atmosphere was one of watchfulness, though, rather than immediate battle-readiness, and there was no more than a general stir of interest when Jamie returned, Gideon threading his way past the campfires with surprising delicacy.

"How is it, *Mac Dubh*?" Kenny asked, standing to greet him as Jamie reined up. "Anything ado?"

Jamie shook his head. He was dressed with a neatness approaching severity, hair clubbed back, dirk and pistols fixed on his belt, sword at his side. A yellow cockade fixed to his coat was the only touch of decoration. Battle-ready, and a small *frisson* crept up my spine at the thought.

"The Governor's sent across his wee letter to the Regulators. Four sheriffs each took a copy; they're to read it out to every group they come across. We must just wait, and see what happens."

I followed his glance toward the third campfire. Roger had likely left as soon as it was light, before the camp woke.

I had emptied the buckets into the kettle for boiling. I picked them up for another trip to the stream, when Gideon's ears pricked and he lifted his head suddenly, with a sharp whicker of greeting. Jamie instantly nudged the horse in front of me, and his hand dropped to his sword. My view was blocked by Gideon's enormous chest and withers; I couldn't see who was coming, but I did see Jamie's hand relax its grip on the sword-hilt as whoever it was came in sight. A friend, then.

Or if not precisely a friend, at least someone he didn't mean to run through or hack out of the saddle. I heard a familiar voice, raised in greeting, and peered out from under Gideon's chin to see Governor Tryon riding across the small meadow, accompanied by two aides.

Tryon sat his horse decently, if without great style, and was dressed as usual for campaigning, in a serviceable blue uniform coat and doeskin breeches, a yellow officer's cockade in his hat, and with one of the cavalry cutlasses called a hanger at his side—not for show; the hilt showed nicks and the scabbard was worn.

Tryon pulled up his horse and nodded, touching his hat to Jamie, who did likewise. Seeing me lurking in Gideon's shadow, the Governor politely removed his cocked hat altogether, bowing from the saddle.

"Mrs. Fraser, your servant." He glanced at the pails I held, then turned in his saddle, beckoning to one of the aides. "Mr. Vickers. Kindly help Mrs. Fraser, if you will."

I surrendered the pails gratefully to Mr. Vickers, a pink-cheeked young man of eighteen or so, but instead of going with him, I simply directed him where to take them. Tryon raised one eyebrow at me, but I returned his expression of mild displeasure with a bland smile, and stood my ground. I wasn't going anywhere.

He was wise enough to recognize that, and make no issue of my presence. Dismissing me instead from his cognizance, he nodded again to Jamie.

"Your troops are in order, Colonel Fraser?" He glanced pointedly around. The only troops visible at the moment were Kenny, who had his nose buried in his cup, and Murdo Lindsay and Geordie Chisholm, who were engaged in a vicious game of mumblety-peg in the shadows of the copse.

"Aye, sir."

The Governor raised both brows in patent skepticism.

"Call them, sir. I will inspect their readiness."

Jamie paused for a moment, gathering up his reins. He squinted against the rising sun, evaluating the Governor's mount. "A nice gelding ye have there, sir. Is he steady?"

"Of course." The Governor frowned. "Why?"

Jamie threw back his head and gave a ululating Highland cry, of the sort meant to be heard over several acres of mountainside. The Governor's horse jerked at the reins, eyes rolling back. Militiamen poured out of the thicket, shrieking like banshees, and a black cloud of crows exploded from the trees above them like a puff of cannon smoke, raucous in flight. The horse reared, decanting Tryon in an undignified heap on the grass, and bolted for the trees on the far side of the meadow.

I took several steps backward, out of the way.

The Governor sat up, purple-faced and gasping for breath, to find himself in the center of a ring of grinning militiamen, all pointing their weapons at him. The Governor glared into the barrel of the rifle poking into his face and batted it away with one hand, making small choking noises, like an angry squirrel. Jamie cleared his throat in a meaningful manner, and the men faded quietly back into the copse.

I thought that on the whole, it would be a mistake either to offer the Governor a hand to arise, or to let him get a look at my face. I tactfully turned my back and wandered a few steps away, affecting to have discovered an absorbing new plant springing from the ground near my feet.

Mr. Vickers reappeared from the wood, looking startled, a pail of water in each hand.

"What has happened?" He started toward the Governor, but I put a hand on his sleeve to detain him. Best if Mr. Tryon had a moment to recover both his breath and his dignity.

"Nothing important," I said, recovering my pails before he could spill them. "Er . . . how many militia troops are assembled here, do you know?"

"One thousand and sixty-eight, mum," he said, looking thoroughly bewildered. "That is not accounting for General Waddell's troops, of course. But what—"

"And you have cannon?"

"Oh, yes, several, mum. We have two detachments with artillery. Two six-pounders, ten swivel-guns, and two eight-pound mortars." Vickers stood a little straighter, important with the thought of so much potential destruction.

"There are two thousand men across the creek, sir—but the most of them barely armed. Many carry no more than a knife." Jamie's voice came from behind me, drawing Vickers's attention away. I turned round, to find that Jamie had dismounted, and was standing face to face with the Governor, holding the latter's hat. He slapped it casually against his thigh and offered it back to its owner, who accepted it with as much grace as might be managed under the circumstances.

"I have been told as much, Mr. Fraser," he said dryly, "though I am pleased to hear that your intelligence corroborates my own. Mr. Vickers, will you be so kind as to go and fetch my horse?" The purple hue had faded from Tryon's face, and while his manner still held a certain constraint, he seemed not to be holding a grudge. Tryon had both a sense of fairness, and—more importantly at present—a sense of humor, both of which seemed to have survived the recent demonstration of military readiness.

Jamie nodded.

"I suppose that your agents have also told you that the Regulators have no leader, as such?"

"On the contrary, Mr. Fraser. I am under the impression that Hermon Husband is and has been for some considerable time one of the chief agitators of this movement. James Hunter, too, is a name that I have often seen appended to letters of complaint and the endless petitions that reach me in New Bern. And there are others—Hamilton, Gillespie . . ."

Jamie made an impatient gesture, brushing a hovering cloud of gnats from his face.

"In some circumstances, sir, I should be willing to dispute with ye whether the pen is mightier than the sword—but not on the edge of a battlefield, and that is where we stand. A boldness in writing pamphlets does not fit a man to lead troops—and Husband is a Quaker gentleman."

"I have heard as much," Tryon agreed. He gestured toward the distant creek, one brow raised in challenge. "And yet he is here."

"He is here," Jamie agreed. He paused for a moment, gauging the governor's mood before proceeding. The Governor was tightly wound; there was no missing the tautness in his figure, or the brightness of his eyes. Still, battle was not yet imminent and the tension was well-leashed. He could still listen.

"I have fed the man at my own hearth, sir," Jamie said carefully. "I have eaten at his. He makes no secret either of his views or his character. If he has come here today, I am certain that he has done so in torment of mind." Jamie drew a deep breath. He was on dicey ground here.

"I have sent a man across the creek, sir, to find Husband, and beg him to meet with me. It may be that I can persuade him to use his considerable influence to cause these men— these citizens"—he gestured briefly toward the creek and the invisible myrmidons beyond—"to abandon this disastrous course of action, which cannot but end in tragedy." He met Tryon's eyes straight on.

"May I ask you, sir—may I beg of you—if Husband will come, will you not speak with him yourself?"

Tryon stood silent, oblivious of the dusty tricorne he turned around and around in his hands. The echoes of the recent commotion had faded; a vireo sang from the branches of the elm above us.

"They are citizens of this colony," he said at last, with a nod in the direction of the creek. "I should regret that harm should come to them. Their grievances are not without merit; I have acknowledged as much—publicly!—and taken steps toward redress." He glanced toward Jamie, as though to see whether this statement was accepted. Jamie stood silent, waiting.

Tryon took a deep breath, and slapped the hat against his leg.

"Yet I am Governor of this colony. I cannot see the peace disturbed, the law flouted, riot and bloodshed run rampant and unpunished!" He glanced bleakly at me. "I will not."

He turned his attention back to Jamie.

"I think he will not come, sir. Their course is set"—he nodded once more toward the trees that edged Alamance Creek—"and so is mine. Still . . ." He hesitated for a moment, then made up his mind, and shook his head.

"No. If he *does* come, then by all means reason with him, and if he will agree to send his men home peaceably—at that point, bring him to me and we shall arrange terms. But I cannot wait upon the possibility."

Mr. Vickers had retrieved the Governor's mount. The boy stood a little way apart, holding both horses by their reins, and I saw him nod slightly at this, as though affirming the Governor's words. His own hat shaded him from the sun, yet his face was flushed, and his eyes bright; he was eager for the fight.

Tryon was not; yet he was ready. Neither was Jamie—but he was ready, too. He held the Governor's gaze for a moment, and then nodded, accepting inevitability.

"How long?" he asked quietly.

Tryon glanced upward at the sun, which stood a little

short of mid-morning. Roger had been gone for nearly two hours; how long might it take him to find Hermon Husband and return?

"The companies are in battle order," Tryon said. He glanced at the copse, and the corner of his mouth twitched. Then he returned a dark gaze to Jamie's face. "Not long. Stand ready, Mr. Fraser."

He turned away, and clapping his hat on his head, seized the reins of his horse and swung into the saddle. He rode away without looking back, followed by his aides.

Jamie watched him go, expressionless.

I moved beside him, touching his hand. I didn't need to say that I hoped Roger would hurry.

# "STRAGLERS AND SUSPECTED PERSONS"

*Item #12 - No Officer or Soldier to go beyond the Limits of the Camp which is within the distance of the Grand Guard.*

*Item #63 - Commanding Officers of Corps are to examine all Straglers and suspected Persons, and those who cannot give a good account of themselves to be confined and Report thereof made to Head Quarters.*

*"Camp Duties and Regulations": Orders Given Out by His Excellency Governor Tryon to the Provincials of North Carolina.*

ROGER TOUCHED THE POCKET of his breeches, where he had tucked away his pewter militia badge. An inch-and-a-half-wide button of metal, pierced round the edges, stamped with a crude "FC" for "Fraser's Company" and meant to be sewn onto coat or hat, such badges—and the cloth cockades—were the sole items of uniform for most of the Governor's foot-troops, and the only means of distinguishing a member of the militia from one of the Regulators.

"And exactly how d'ye know whom to shoot?" he had inquired ironically, when Jamie had handed him the badge at supper, two days before. "If you get close enough to see the badge before ye fire, won't the other bugger get you first?"

Jamie had given him a glance of equal irony, but courteously forbore any observations on Roger's marksmanship and the likelihood—or otherwise—of his doing any damage with his musket.

"I wouldna wait to see, myself," he said. "If anyone runs toward ye with a gun, fire, and hope for the best."

A few men seated around the fire nearby sniggered at this, but Jamie ignored them. He reached for a stick and pulled three roasting yams out of the coals, so they lay side by side, black and steaming in the cool evening air. He kicked one gently, sending it rolling back into the ashes.

"That's us," he explained. He kicked the next yam. "That's Colonel Leech's company, and that"—he booted the third, which rolled erratically after its fellows—"is Colonel Ashe's. D'ye see?" He cocked an eyebrow at Roger.

"Each company will go forward in its own path, so ye're no likely to see any other militia, at least to begin with. Anyone coming toward us is most probably the enemy." Then his long mouth curled up a bit, as he gestured toward the men all round them, busy with their suppers.

"Ye ken every man here well enough? Well, dinna shoot any of them, and ye'll be fine, aye?"

Roger smiled ruefully to himself as he made his way carefully down a slope covered with tiny yellow-flowered plants. It was sound advice; he was much less concerned with the possibility of being shot than with the fear of accidentally harming someone himself—including the not-inconsiderable worry of blowing off a few of his own fingers.

Privately, he was resolved not to fire at anyone, regardless either of circumstance or of the possibility of his hitting them. He'd heard enough of the Regulators' stories—Abel MacLennan, Hermon Husband. Even allowing for the natural hyperbole of Husband's style, his pamphlets burned with a sense of injustice that was inescapable. How could Roger look to kill a man or maim him, only for protesting against abuses and corruption so blatant that they must offend any just-minded person?

A trained historian, he'd seen enough of present circumstances to understand just how widespread the problems were, how they'd come about—and he understood well enough the difficulties of correcting them. He sympathized with Tryon's position—to a point—but his sympathy stopped a good way short of rendering him a willing soldier in the cause of upholding the Crown's authority—still less, the cause of preserving William Tryon's reputation and personal fortune.

He stopped for a moment, hearing voices, and stepped softly behind the trunk of a large poplar.

Three men came in sight a moment later, talking casually amongst themselves. All three had guns and bullet-boxes, but the impression they gave was of three friends on their way to hunt rabbits, rather than grim troopers on the eve of battle.

In fact, this appeared to be exactly what they were—foragers. One had a cluster of furry bodies slung from his belt, and another carried a muslin bag stained with something that might have been fresh blood. As Roger watched from the shelter of the poplar, one man stopped, hand out to check his comrades, who both stiffened like hounds, noses pointing toward a clump of trees some sixty yards distant.

Even knowing something was there, it took a moment before Roger spotted the small deer, standing still against a grove of saplings, a veil of dappled light through the spring leaves overhead masking it almost perfectly from view.

The first man swung his gun stealthily down from his shoulder, reaching for rod and cartridge, but one of the others stopped him with a hand on his arm.

"Hold there, Abram," said the second man, speaking softly but clearly. "You don't want to be firing so close to the crick. You heard what the Colonel said—Regulators are drawn right up to the bank near that point." He nodded toward the heavy growth of alder and willow that marked the edge of the invisible creek, no more than a hundred yards distant. "You don't want to be provokin' them, not just now."

Abram nodded reluctantly, and put up his gun again.

"Aye, I suppose. Will it be today, do you think?"

Roger glanced back at the sapling grove, but the deer had vanished, silent as smoke.

"Can't see how it won't be." The third man pulled a yellow kerchief from his sleeve and wiped his face; the weather was warm and the air muggy. "Tryon's had his guns in place since dawn; he's not the man to let anybody get a jump on him. He might wait for Waddell's men—but he may think he's no need of them."

Abram snorted with mild contempt.

"To crush those rabble? Seen them, have you? A poorer set of soldiers you'd not see in a month of Sundays."

The man with the kerchief smiled cynically.

"Well, that's as may be, Abie. Seen some of the backcountry militia, have you? Speakin' of rabble. And speakin' of the Regulators, there's a lot of 'em, rabble or not. Two to one, Cap'n Neale says."

Abram grunted, casting a last reluctant glance toward the wood and the creek beyond.

"Rabble," he repeated, more confidently, and turned away. "Come along, then, let's have a look upslope."

The foragers were on the same side as himself; they wore no cockades, but he saw the militia badges on breast and hat, glinting silver in the morning sun. Still, Roger remained in the shadows until the men had vanished, talking casually amongst themselves. He was reasonably sure that Jamie had sent him on this mission with no authority beyond his own; best if he were not asked to explain himself.

The attitude amongst most of the militia toward the Regulation was at best scornful. At worst—at the upper levels of command—it was coldly vindictive.

"Crush them once and for all," Caswell had said, over a cup of coffee by the fire the night before. A plantation owner from the eastern part of the colony, Richard Caswell had no sympathy with the Regulators' grievances.

Roger patted his pocket again, considering. No, best leave it. He could produce the badge if he were challenged, and he didn't think anyone would shoot him in the back without at least a shout of warning. Still, he felt oddly exposed as he walked through the lush grass of the river-meadow, and sighed with involuntary relief, as the languishing branches of the creek-side willows enfolded him in cool shadow.

He had, with Jamie's approval, left his musket behind, and come unarmed, save for the knife at his belt that was a normal accoutrement for any man. His only other item of equipment was a large white kerchief, presently folded up inside his coat.

"If ye should be threatened—anywhere—wave it and cry 'Truce,' " Jamie had instructed him. "Then tell them to fetch me, and dinna say more until I come. If no one prevents you, bring me Husband under its protection."

The vision of himself leading Hermon Husband back across the creek, holding the flapping kerchief on a stick above his head like a guide leading tourists through an airport, made him want to hoot with laughter. Jamie hadn't laughed, though, or even smiled, and so he had accepted the cloth solemnly, tucking it away with care. He peered through the screen of drooping leaves, but the creek ran past sparkling in the new day's sun, silent save for the rush of water past stones and clay. No one was in sight, and the noise of the water drowned any sound that might have come from beyond the trees on the other side. While the militia might not shoot him in the back, he wasn't so sanguine about the possibilities of Regulators shooting him from the front, if they saw him crossing from the Government side.

Still, he couldn't skulk in the trees all day. He emerged onto the bank, and made his way downstream toward the point the foragers had indicated, watching the trees carefully for any signs of life. The crossing near the point was better, shallow water and a rocky bottom. Still, if the Regulators were "drawn up" anywhere nearby, they were being damned quiet about it.

A more peaceful scene could scarcely be imagined, and yet his heart was hammering suddenly in his ears. He had again the odd feeling of someone standing near him. He glanced around in all directions, but nothing moved save the rushing water and the trailing willow fronds.

"That you, Dad?" he said softly, under his breath, and at once felt foolish. Still, the feeling of someone near remained strong, though benign.

With a mental shrug, he bent and took off his shoes and stockings. It must be the circumstances, he thought. Not that one could quite compare wading a shallow creek in search of a Quaker rabble-rouser to flying a Spitfire across the night-time Channel on a bombing run to Germany. A mission was a mission, though, he supposed.

He looked round once again, but saw only tadpoles wriggling in the shallows. With a slightly crooked smile, he stepped into the water, sending the tadpoles into frenzied flight.

"Over the top, then," he said to a wood-duck. The bird ignored him, going on with its foraging among the dark-green rafts of floating cress.

No challenge came from the trees on either side; no sounds at all, bar the cheerful racket of nesting birds. It was as he sat on a sunwarmed rock, drying his feet before putting his shoes and stockings back on, that he finally heard some indication that the far side of the creek was populated by humans.

"So what do you want then, sweeting?"

The voice came from the shrubbery behind him, and he froze, blood thundering in his ears. It was a woman's voice. Before he could move or think to answer, though, he heard a laugh, deeper in pitch, and with a particular tone to it that made him relax.

Instinct informed him before his reason did that voices with that particular intonation were not a threat.

"Dunno, hinney, what will it cost me?"

"Ooh, hark at him! Not the time to count your pennies, is it?"

"Don't you worry, ladies, we'll take up a collection amongst us if we have to."

"Oh, is that the way of it? Well and good, sir, but be you aware, in this congregation, the collection comes *before* the singing!"

Listening to this amiable wrangling, Roger deduced that the voices in question belonged to three men and two women, all of whom seemed confident that whatever the financial arrangements, three would go into two quite evenly, with no awkward remainders.

Picking up his shoes, he stole quietly away, leaving the unseen sentries—if that's what they were—to their sums. Evidently, the army of the Regulation wasn't quite so organized as the government troops.

Less organized was putting it mildly, he thought, a little later. He had kept to the creek bank for some distance, unsure where the main body of the army might be. He had walked nearly a quarter-mile, with neither sight nor sound of a soul other than the two whores and their customers. Feeling increasingly surreal, he wandered through small pine groves, and across the edges of grassy meadows, with no company save courting birds and small gossamer butterflies in shades of orange and yellow.

"What the hell sort of way is this to run a war?" he muttered, shoving his way through a blackberry bramble. It was like one of those science fiction stories, in which everyone but the hero had suddenly vanished from the face of the earth. He was beginning to be anxious; what if he didn't manage to find the bloody Quaker—or even the army—before the shooting started?

Then he rounded a bend in the creek, and caught his first glimpse of the Regulators proper; a group of women, washing clothes in the rushing waters by a cluster of boulders.

He ducked back into the brush before they should see him, and turned away from the creek, heartened. If the women were here, the men weren't far away.

They weren't. Within a few more yards, he heard the sounds of camp—casual voices, laughter, the clank of spoons and tea-kettles and the clunk of splitting wood. Rounding a clump of hawthorn, he was nearly knocked over by a gang of young men who ran past, hooting and yelling, as they chased one of their number who brandished a fresh-cut racoon's tail overhead, floating in the breeze as he ran.

They charged past Roger without a second glance, and he went on, a bit less warily. He wasn't challenged; there were no sentries. In fact, a strange face appeared to be neither a novelty nor a threat. A few men glanced casually at him, but then turned back to their talk, seeing nothing odd in his appearance.

"I'm looking for Hermon Husband," he said bluntly to a man roasting a squirrel over the pale flames of a fire. The man looked blank for a moment.

"The Quaker?" Roger amplified.

"Oh, aye, him," the man said, features clearing. "He's a ways beyond—that way, I think." He gestured helpfully with his stick, the charred squirrel pointing the way with the stubs of its blackened forelegs.

"A ways beyond" was some way. Roger passed through three more scattered camps before reaching what looked to be the main body of the army—if one could dignify it by such a term. True, there did seem to be an increasing air of seriousness; there was less of the carefree frolicking he had seen near the creek. Still, it wasn't Strategic Command headquarters, by a long shot.

He began to feel mildly hopeful that violence could still be avoided, even with the armies drawn up face to face and the gun-crews standing by. There had been an air of excited readiness among the militia as he passed through their lines, but no atmosphere of hatred or blood-thirstiness.

Here, the situation was far different than it was among the orderly militia lines, but even less disposed to immediate hostilities. As he pressed on further, though, asking his way at each campfire he passed, he began to feel something different in the air—a sense of increasing urgency, almost of desperation. The horseplay he'd seen in the outer camps had vanished; men clustered talking in close groups, their heads together, or sat by themselves, grimly loading guns and sharpening knives.

As he got closer, the name of Hermon Husband was recognized by everyone, the pointing fingers surer of direction. The name seemed almost a magnet, pulling him farther and farther into the center of a thickening mass of men and boys, all excited—all armed. The noise grew greater all the time, voices beating on his ears like hammers on a forge.

He found Husband at last, standing on a rock like a large gray wolf at bay, surrounded by a knot of some thirty or forty men, all clamoring in angry agitation. Elbows jabbed and feet trampled, without regard to impact on their fellows. Clearly they were demanding an answer, but unable to pause long enough to hear one were it given.

Husband, stripped to his shirtsleeves and red in the face, was shouting at one or two of those closest to him, but Roger could hear nothing of what was said, above the general hubbub. He pushed through the outer ring of spectators, but was stopped nearer the center by the press of men. At least here, he could pick up a few words.

"We must! You know it, Hermon, there's no choice!" shouted a lanky man in a battered hat.

"There's *always* a choice!" Husband bellowed back. "Now is the time to choose, and God send we do it wisely!"

"Aye, with cannon pointed at us?"

"No, no, forward, we must go forward, or all is lost!" -

"Lost? We have lost everything so far! We must—"

"The Governor's taken choice from us, we must—"

"We must—"

"We must—!"

All single words were lost in a general roar of anger and frustration. Seeing that there was nothing to be gained by waiting for an audience, Roger shoved his way ruthlessly between two farmers and seized Husband by the sleeve of his shirt.

"Mr. Husband—I must speak with you!" he shouted in the Quaker's ear.

Husband gave him a glazed sort of look, and made to shake him off, but then stopped, blinking as he recognized him. The square face was flushed with color above the sprouting beard, and Husband's coarse gray hair, unbound, bristled out from his head like the quills of a porcupine. He shook his head and shut his eyes, then opened them again, staring at Roger like a man seeking to dispel some impossible vision, and failing.

He grabbed Roger's arm, and with a fierce gesture at the crowd, leaped down from his rock and made off toward the shelter of a ramshackle cabin that leaned drunkenly in the shade of a maple grove. Roger followed, glaring round at those nearest to discourage pursuit.

A few followed, nonetheless, waving arms and expostulating hotly, but Roger slammed the door in their faces, and dropped the bolt, placing his back against the door for good measure. It was cooler inside, though the air was stale and smelt of wood-ash and burnt food.

Husband stood panting in the middle of the floor, then picked up a dipper and drank deeply from a bucket that stood upon the hearth—the only object left in the cabin, Roger saw. Husband's coat and hat hung neatly on a hook by the door, but bits of rubbish were scattered across the packed-earth floor. Whoever owned the cabin had evidently decamped in haste, carrying their portable belongings.

Calmed by the moment's respite, Husband straightened his rumpled shirt and made shift to tidy his hair.

"What does thee here, friend MacKenzie?" he asked, with characteristic mildness. "Thee does not come to join the cause of Regulation, surely?"

"Indeed I do not," Roger assured him. He cast a wary eye at the window, lest the crowd try to gain access that way, but while the rumble of voices outside continued their argument, there was no immediate sound of assault upon the building. "I have come to ask if you will go across the creek with me—under a flag of truce, your safety is assured—to speak with Jamie Fraser."

Husband glanced at the window, too.

"I fear the time for speaking has long passed," he said, with a wry twist of the lips. Roger was inclined to think so, too, but pressed on, determined to fulfill his commission.

"Not so far as the Governor is concerned. He has no wish

to slaughter his own citizenry; if the mob could be convinced to disperse peaceably—"

"Does it seem to thee a likely prospect?" Husband waved at the window, giving him a cynical glance.

"No," Roger was forced to admit. "Still, if you would come—if they could see that there was still some possibility of—"

"If there were possibility of reconciliation and redress, it should have been offered long since," Husband said sharply. "Is this a token of the Governor's sincerity, to come with troops and cannon, to send a letter that—"

"Not redress," Roger said bluntly. "I meant the possibility of saving all your lives."

Husband stood quite still. The ruddy color faded from his cheeks, though he looked still composed.

"Has it come to that?" he asked quietly, his eyes on Roger's face. Roger took a deep breath and nodded.

"There is not much time. Mr. Fraser bid me tell you—if you could not come to speak with him yourself—there are two companies of artillery arrayed against you, and eight of militia, all well-armed. All lies in readiness—and the Governor will not wait past dawn of tomorrow, at the latest."

He was aware that it was treason to give such information to the enemy—but it was what Jamie Fraser would have said, could he have come himself.

"There are near two thousand men of the Regulation here," Husband said, as though to himself. "Two thousand! Would thee not think the sight of it would sway him? That so many would leave home and hearth and come in protest—"

"It is the Governor's opinion that they come in rebellion, therefore in a state of war," Roger interrupted. He glanced at the window, where the oiled parchment covering hung in tatters. "And having seen them, I must say that I think he has reasonable grounds for that opinion."

"It is no rebellion," Husband said stubbornly. He drew himself up, and pulled a worn black silk ribbon from his pocket, with which to tie back his hair. "But our legitimate complaints have been ignored, disregarded! We have no choice but to come as a physical body, to lay our grievances before Mr. Tryon and thus impress him with the rightness of our objection."

"I thought I heard you speak of choice a few moments past," Roger said dryly. "And if now is the time to choose, as you say, it would seem to me that most of the Regulators have chosen violence—judging from such remarks as I heard on my way here."

"Perhaps," Husband said reluctantly. "Yet we—they—are not an avenging army, not a mob . . ." And yet his unwilling glance toward the window suggested his awareness that a mob was indeed what was forming on the banks of the Alamance.

"Do they have a chosen leader, anyone who can speak officially for them?" Roger interrupted again, impatient to deliver his message and be gone. "Yourself, or perhaps Mr. Hunter?"

Husband paused for a long moment, wiping the back of his hand across his mouth as though to expunge some lingering rancid taste. He shook his head.

"They have no real leader," he said softly. "Jim Hunter is bold enough, but he has no gift of commanding men. I asked him—he said that each man must act for himself."

"You have the gift. You can lead them."

Husband looked scandalized, as though Roger had accused him of a talent for card-sharping.

"Not I."

"You have led them here—"

"They have *come* here! I asked none to—"

"You are here. They followed you."

Husband flinched slightly at this, his lips compressed. Seeing that his words had some effect, Roger pressed his case.

"You spoke for them before, and they listened. They came with you, after you. They'll still listen, surely!"

He could hear the noise outside the cabin growing; the crowd was impatient. If it wasn't yet a mob, it was damn close. And what would they do if they knew who he was, and what he had come to do? His palms were sweating; he pressed them down across the fabric of his coat, feeling the small lump of his militia badge in the pocket, and wished he had paused to bury it somewhere when he crossed the creek.

Husband looked at him a moment, then reached out and seized him by both hands.

"Pray with me, friend," he said quietly.

"I—"

"Thee need say nothing," Husband said. "I know thee is Papist, but it is not our way to pray aloud. If thee would but remain still with me, and ask in your heart that wisdom be granted—not only to me, but to all here . . ."

Roger bit his tongue to keep from correcting Husband; his own religious affiliation was scarcely important at the moment, though evidently Husband's was. Instead he nodded, suppressing his impatience, and squeezed the older man's hands, offering what support he might.

Husband stood quite still, his head slightly lowered. A fist hammered on the flimsy door of the cabin, voices calling out.

"Hermon! You all right in there?"

"Come on, Hermon! There's no time for this! Caldwell's come back from the Governor—"

"An hour, Hermon! He's given us an hour, no more!"

A trickle of sweat ran down Roger's back between his shoulder blades, but he ignored the tickle, unable to reach it.

He glanced from Husband's weathered fingers to his face, and found the other man's eyes seemingly fixed on his own—and yet distant, as though he listened to some far-off voice, disregarding the urgent shouts that came through the walls. Even Husband's eyes were Quaker gray, Roger thought—like pools of rainwater, shivering into stillness after a storm.

Surely they would break down the door. But no; the blows diminished to an impatient knocking, and then to random thumps. He could feel the beating of his own heart, slowing gradually to a quiet, even throb in his chest, anxiety fading in his blood.

He closed his own eyes, trying to fix his thoughts, to do as Husband asked. He groped in his mind for some suitable prayer, but nothing save confused fragments of the Book of Common Worship came to hand.

*Help us, O Lord . . .*

*Hear us . . .*

*Help us, O Lord*, his father's voice whispered. His other father, the Reverend, speaking somewhere in the back of his mind. *Help us, O Lord, to remember how often men do wrong through want of thought, rather than from lack of love; and how cunning are the snares that trip our feet.*

Each word flickered briefly in his mind like a burning leaf, rising from a bonfire's wind, and then disappeared away into ash before he could grasp it. He gave it up then and simply stood, clasping Husband's hands in his own, listening to the man's breathing, a low rasping note.

*Please*, he thought silently, though with no idea what he was asking for. That word too evaporated, leaving nothing in its place.

Nothing happened. The voices still called outside, but they seemed of no more importance now than the calling of birds. The air in the room was still, but cool and lively, as though a draft played somewhere in the corners, not touching them where they stood in the center of the floor. Roger felt his own breath ease, his heart slow its beat still more.

He didn't remember opening his eyes, and yet they were open. Husband's soft gray eyes had flecks of blue in them, and tiny splinters of black. His lashes were thick, and there was a small swelling at the base of one, a healing sty. The tiny dome was smooth and red, fading from a ruby dot at the center through such successions of crimson, pink, and rose red as might have graced the dawn sky on the day of Creation.

The face before him was sculpted with lines that drew rough arcs from nose to mouth, that curved above the heavy, grizzled brows whose every hair was long and arched with the grace of a bird's wing. The lips were broad and smooth, a dusky rose; the white edge of a tooth glistened, strangely hard by contrast with the pliable flesh that sheltered it.

Roger stood without moving, wondering at the beauty of what he saw. The notion of Husband as a stocky man of middle age and indeterminate feature had no meaning; what he saw now was a heartbreaking singularity, a thing unique and wonderful; irreplaceable.

It struck him that this was same feeling with which he had studied his infant son, marveling at the perfection of each small toe, the curve of cheek and ear that squeezed his heart, the radiance of the newborn skin that let the innocence within shine through. And here was the same creation, no longer new, perhaps less innocent, but no less marvelous.

He looked down and saw his own hands then, still gripping Husband's smaller ones. A sense of awe came on him, with the realization of the beauty of his own fingers, the curving bones of wrist and knuckle, the ravishing loveliness of a thin red scar that ran across the joint of his thumb.

Husband's breath left him in a deep sigh, and he pulled his hands away. Roger felt momentarily bereft, but then felt the peace of the room settle upon him once more, the astonishment of beauty succeeded by a sense of deep calm.

"I thank thee, Friend Roger," Husband said softly. "I had not hoped to receive such grace—but it is welcome."

Roger nodded, wordless. He watched as Husband took down his coat and put it on, his face settled now in lines of calm determination. Without hesitation, the Quaker lifted the bolt from the door and pushed it open.

The crowd of men outside fell back, the surprise on their faces giving way at once to eagerness and irritation. Husband ignored the storm of questions and exhortations, and walked directly to a horse that stood tethered to a sapling behind the cabin. He untied it and swung up into the saddle, and only then looked down into the faces of his fellow Regulators.

"Go home!" he said, in a loud voice. "We must leave this place; each man must return to his own home!"

This announcement was met with a moment of stunned silence, and then by cries of puzzlement and outrage.

"What home?" called a young man with a scraggly ginger beard. "Maybe you got a home to go to—I ain't!"

Husband sat solid in his saddle, unmoved by the outcry.

"Go home!" he shouted again. "I exhort you—nothing but violence remains to be done here!"

"Aye, and we'll bloody do it!" bellowed one thickset man, thrusting his musket overhead, to a ragged chorus of cheers.

Roger had followed Husband, and was largely ignored by the Regulators. He stood at a little distance, watching as the Quaker began slowly to ride away, bending down from his saddle as he did so, to shout and gesture to the men who ran and shoved beside him. One man grabbed Husband by the sleeve, and the Quaker drew up his rein, leaning down to listen to what was obviously an impassioned speech.

At the end of it, though, he straightened up, shaking his head, and clapped his hat on.

"I cannot stay and let blood be shed by my staying. If thee remain here, friends, there will be murder done. Leave! Thee can still go—I pray thee do so!"

He was no longer shouting, but the noise around him had ceased long enough for his words to carry. He raised a face creased with worry, and saw Roger standing in the shadow of a dogwood. The stillness of peace had left him, but Roger saw that the look of determination was still there in his eyes.

"I am going!" he called. "I beg thee all—go home!" He reined his horse round with sudden decision, and kicked it into a trot. A few men ran after him, but soon stopped. They turned back, looking puzzled and resentful, muttering in small groups and shaking their heads in confusion.

The noise was rising again, as everyone talked at once, arguing, insisting, denying. Roger turned away, walking quietly toward the cover of the maple grove. It seemed wiser to be gone as soon as possible, now that Husband had departed.

A hand seized him by the shoulder, and spun him round.

"Who the hell are you? What did you say to Hermon to make him go?" A grimy fellow in a ragged leather vest confronted him, fists clenched. The man looked angry, ready to take out his frustration on the nearest available object.

"I told him that the Governor doesn't want anyone to be harmed, if it can be avoided," Roger said, in what he hoped was a calming tone.

"Do you come from the Governor?" a black-bearded man asked skeptically, eyeing Roger's grubby homespun. "D'ye come to offer different terms than Caldwell has?"

"No." Roger had been still under the effects of the meeting with Husband, feeling sheltered from the currents of anger and incipient hysteria that swirled about the cabin, but the peace of it was fading fast. Others were coming to join his interrogators, attracted by the sound of confrontation.

"No," he said again, louder. "I came to warn Husband—to warn all of you. The Governor wants—"

He was interrupted by a chorus of rude shouts, indicating that what Tryon wanted was a matter of no concern to those present. He glanced around the circle of faces, but saw none that offered any expression of forbearance, let alone friendliness. He shrugged then, and stepped back.

"You'll suit yourselves, then," he said, as coolly as possible. "Mr. Husband gave you his best advice—I second it." He turned to leave, but was gripped by a pair of hands that descended on his shoulders, pulling him forcibly around to face the ring of questioners once more.

"Not so fast, chuck," said the man in the leather vest. He was still flushed with angry excitement, but his fists were no longer clenched. "You've spoke with Tryon, have you?"

"No," Roger admitted. "I was sent—" He hesitated; ought he to use Jamie Fraser's name? No, better not; it was as likely to cause trouble as to save it. "I came to ask Hermon Husband to come across the creek and discover for himself how matters stand. He chose instead to accept my account of the situation. You saw what his response was."

"So *you* say!" A burly man with ginger sidewhiskers raised his chin pugnaciously. "And why should anyone accept your account of the situation?" He mimicked Roger's clipped Scots in a burlesque that brought laughter from his comrades.

The calm he had carried from the cabin had not altogether left him; Roger gathered its remnants about him and spoke quietly.

"I cannot compel you to listen, sir. But for those who have ears—hear this." He looked from one face to another, and reluctantly, one by one, they left off making noise, until he stood as the center of a ring of unwilling attention.

"The Governor's troops stand ready and well-armed." His voice sounded odd to his own ears, calm but somehow muffled, as though someone else were speaking, some distance away. "I have not seen the Governor myself, but I have heard his stated purpose: he does not wish to see blood shed, but he is determined to take such actions as he perceives necessary to disperse this assembly. Yet if you will return peaceably to your homes, he is disposed to leniency."

A moment of silence greeted this, to be broken by a hawking noise. A glob of mucus, streaked brown with tobacco juice, landed with a splat in the mud near Roger's boot.

"That," observed the spitter concisely, "for the Governor's leniency."

"And that for you, fuckwit!" said one of his companions, swinging an open palm toward Roger's face.

He ducked the blow, and lowering his shoulder, charged the man, who staggered off-balance and gave way. There were more beyond him, though; Roger stopped, fists balled, ready to defend himself if need be.

"Don't hurt him, boys," called the man in the leather vest. "Not yet, anyways." He sidled round Roger, keeping well out of range of his fists, and eyed him warily.

"Whether you've seen Tryon's face or not, reckon you've seen his troops, haven't you?"

"I have." Roger's heart was beating fast, and the blood sang in his temples, but oddly enough, he wasn't afraid. The crowd was hostile, but not bloodthirsty—not yet.

"So how many men does Tryon have?" The man was watching him closely, with a glint in his eye. Best to answer honestly; the odds were good that the answer was already known; there was nothing whatever to hinder men of the Regulation from crossing the Alamance and assessing the situation for themselves.

"A few more than a thousand," Roger said, watching the man's face carefully. No surprise; he *had* known. "But they are trained militia," Roger added pointedly, with a glance at a number of the Regulators, who, having lost interest in Roger, had resumed a wrestling match nearby. "And they have artillery. I think you have none, sir?"

The man's face closed like a fist.

"Think what you like," he said shortly. "But you can tell Tryon that we boast twice his number. And be we *trained* or not—" his mouth twisted ironically, "we are all armed, each man with his musket." He tilted back his head, squinting against the light.

"An hour, is it?" he asked, more softly. "Sooner than that, I think." He lowered his gaze, looking Roger in the eye.

"Go you back across the creek, then, sir. Tell Governor Tryon that we mean to have our say, and have our way of it. If he will listen and do as we demand, well and good. If not . . ." He touched the hilt of the pistol in his belt, and nodded once, his face settling into grim lines.

Roger glanced around at the circle of silent faces. Some bore looks of uncertainty, but most were sullen or openly defiant. He turned without a word and walked away, the Reverend's words whispering among the spring leaves as he passed beneath the trees.

*Blessed are the peacemakers: for they shall be called the children of God.*

He hoped one got credit for trying.

# THE SURGEON'S BOOK I

*Item #28 - The Surgeons to keep a Book and enter each Man that comes under his care, Vixt. the Mans Name, the Company he belongs to, the Day he comes under his Hands, and the day he discharges him.*

—*"Camp Duties and Regulations"*

I FELT A COOL BREEZE touch my cheek, and shivered, though the day was very warm. I had the sudden absurd thought that it was the glancing touch of a wing-feather, as though the Angel of Death had silently passed by me, intent on his dark business.

"Nonsense," I said aloud. Evan Lindsay heard me; I saw his head turn momentarily, but then turn back. Like all the others, he kept glancing toward the east.

People who don't believe in telepathy have never set foot on a battlefield, nor served with an army. Something passes unseen from man to man when an army is about to move; the air itself is live with feeling. Half dread, half eagerness, it dances over the skin and bores the length of the spine with an urgency like sudden lust.

No messenger had come yet, but one would, I knew it. Something had happened, somewhere.

Everyone stood rooted, waiting. I felt an overwhelming urge to move, to break that spell, and turned abruptly, my hands flexing with the need to stir, to do something. The kettle had boiled, the water sat ready, covered with a piece of clean linen. I had set up my medicine chest on a stump; I put back the lid and began to go mindlessly through its contents yet again, though I knew all was in order.

I touched the gleaming bottles one by one, their names a soothing litany.

Atropine, Belladonna, Laudanum, Paregoric, Oil of Lavender, Oil of Juniper, Pennyroyal, Lady's-vetch, . . . and the squat brown-glass bottle of alcohol. Always alcohol. I had a keg of it, still on the wagon.

Movement caught my eye; it was Jamie, the sun sparking on his hair through the leaves as he moved quietly under the trees, bending here to speak a word in someone's ear, touching there a shoulder, like a magician bringing statues to life.

I stood still, hands twisted in the folds of my apron, not wanting to distract him, yet wanting very much to attract his attention. He moved easily, joking, touching casually—and yet I could see the tension in him. When had he last stood with an army, waiting the order to charge?

At Culloden, I thought, and the hairs rippled erect on my forearms, pale in the spring sun.

Hoofsteps sounded nearby, and the crashing sound of horses moving through brush. Everyone swung round in expectation, muskets held loose in their hands. There was a general gasp and murmur as the first rider came into view, ducking her bright red head beneath the maple boughs.

"Holy Christ," Jamie said, loudly enough to be heard across the clearing. "What in hell is *she* doing here?" There was a ripple of laughter from the men who knew her, fracturing the tension like cracks in ice. Jamie's shoulders relaxed, very slightly, but his face was rather grim as he strode to meet her.

By the time Brianna had pulled up her horse and swung down from her saddle next to him, I had reached them, too.

"What—" I began, but Jamie was already nose to nose with his daughter, his hand on her arm, eyes narrowed and speaking in a rapid torrent of low-voiced Gaelic.

"I'm that sorry, Mum, but she *would* come." A second horse ambled out of the trees, an apologetic-looking young black man on top. It was Joshua, Jocasta's groom. "I couldna prevent her, nor could Missus Sherston. We did try."

"So I see," I said.

Brianna's color had risen in response to whatever Jamie was saying to her, but she showed no sign of getting back on her horse and leaving. She said something to him, also in Gaelic, that I didn't catch, and he reared back as though stung on the nose by a wasp. She nodded sharply once, as though satisfied with the impact of her statement, and turned on her heel. Then she saw me, and a wide smile transformed her face.

"Mama!" She embraced me, her gown smelling faintly of fresh soap, beeswax, and turpentine. There was a small streak of cobalt-blue paint on her jaw.

"Hallo, darling. Wherever did you come from?" I kissed her cheek and stood back, cheered by the sight of her, in spite of everything. She was dressed very plainly, in the rough brown homespun she wore on the Ridge, but the clothes were fresh and clean. Her long red hair was tied back in a plait, and a broad straw hat hung from its strings down her back.

"Hillsborough," she said. "Someone who came to dinner at the Sherstons' last night told us that the militia was camped here—so I came. I brought some food"— she waved at the bulging saddlebags on her horse—"and some herbs from the Sherstons' garden I thought you might use."

"Oh? Oh, yes. Lovely." I was uneasily aware of Jamie's glowering presence somewhere behind me, but didn't look around. "Ah . . . I don't mean to sound as though I'm not pleased to see you, darling, but there is just possibly going to be a fight here before too long, and . . . ."

"I know that." Her color was still high, and it deepened somewhat at this. She raised her voice slightly.

"That's all right; I didn't come to fight. If I had, I would have worn my breeches." She darted a glance over my shoulder, and I heard a loud snort from that direction, followed by guffaws from the Lindsay brothers. She lowered her head to hide a grin, and I couldn't help smiling, too.

"I'll stay with you," she said, lowering her voice as well, and touching my arm. "If there's nursing to be done . . . afterward—I can help."

I hesitated, but there was no question that if things did come to a fight, there would be wounded to treat, and an extra pair of hands would be useful. Brianna wasn't skilled at nursing, but she did understand about germs and antisepsis, knowledge of much more value in its way than a grasp of anatomy or physiology.

Bree had straightened. Her glance flickered over the men who waited in the maples' shade, searching.

"Where's Roger?" she asked, her voice low but level.

"He's all right," I assured her, hoping it was true. "Jamie sent him across the creek this morning, with a flag of truce, to bring back Hermon Husband to talk with the Governor."

"He's over *there*?" Her voice rose involuntarily, and she lowered it, self-conscious. "With the enemy? If that's the right word for them."

"He'll be back." Jamie stood by my elbow, viewing his daughter with no great favor, but obviously resigned to her presence. "Dinna fash, lassie. No one will trouble him, under a flag of truce."

Bree raised her head, looking as far as she could into the distance toward the creek. Her face had drawn in upon itself, a pale knot of apprehension.

"Will a flag of truce help him if he's still over there when the shooting starts?"

The answer to that—which she obviously knew—was "Probably not." So did Jamie, who didn't bother saying it. He also didn't bother saying that perhaps it wouldn't come to shooting; the air was thick with anticipation, acrid with the scent of spilled black powder and nervous sweat.

"He'll be back," Jamie repeated, though in a gentler tone. He touched her face, smoothing back a random lock of hair. "I promise, lass. He'll be all right."

The look of apprehension faded a bit as she searched his face. She seemed to find some reassurance there, for a little of the tension left her, and she nodded, in mute acceptance. Jamie leaned forward and kissed her on the forehead, then turned away to speak to Rob Byrnes.

Bree stood looking after him for a moment, then untied the strings of her bonnet and came to sit down beside me on a rock. Her hands were trembling slightly; she took a deep breath, and clasped her knees to still them.

"Is there anything I can do to help now?" she asked, with a nod toward my open medicine box. "Do you need me to fetch anything?"

I shook my head.

"No, I have everything I need. There isn't anything to do but wait." I grimaced slightly. "That's the hardest part."

She made a small sound of reluctant agreement, and relaxed, with a visible effort. She assessed the waiting equipment, a slight frown between her brows: the fire, the boiling water, the folding table, the large instrument box, and the smaller pack that held my emergency kit.

"What's in there?" she asked, poking a boot-shod toe at the canvas sack.

"Alcohol and bandages, a scalpel, forceps, amputation saw, tourniquets. They'll bring the wounded here, if they can, or to one of the other surgeons. But if I have to go to a man wounded on the field—someone too bad to walk or be carried—I can snatch that up and go at once."

I heard her swallow, and when I glanced up at her, the freckles stood out on the bridge of her nose. She nodded, and drew a deep breath to speak. Her face changed suddenly, though, switching comically from seriousness to repugnance. She sniffed once, suspiciously, her long nose wrinkling like an anteater's.

I could smell it, too; the stink of fresh feces, coming from the grove directly behind us.

"That's rather common before a battle," I said, low-voiced, trying not to laugh at her expression. "They're caught short, poor things."

She cleared her throat and didn't say anything, but I saw her gaze roam round the clearing, resting now on one man, then another. I knew what she was thinking. How was it possible? How could one look at such an orderly, compact bundle as a man, head bent to catch a friend's words, arm stretched to take a canteen, face moving from smile to frown, eyes lighted and muscles taut—and envision rupture, abrasion, fracture . . . and death?

It couldn't be done. It was an act of the imagination that lay beyond the capability of one who hadn't ever seen that particular obscene transformation.

It could, however, be remembered. I coughed, and leaned forward, hoping to distract us both.

"Whatever did you say to your father?" I asked, out of the side of my mouth. "When you came, when you were speaking Gaelic."

"Oh, that." A slight flush of amusement momentarily relieved her paleness. "He was snarling at me, wanting to know what I thought I was playing at—did I mean to leave my child an orphan, he said, risking my life along with Roger's?" She wiped a strand of red hair away from her mouth, and gave me a small, edgy smile. "So I said to him, if it was so dangerous, where did he get off, risking making *me* an orphan by having you here, hm?"

I laughed, though keeping that, too, under my breath.

"It's not dangerous for you, is it?" she asked, surveying the militia encampment. "Back here, I mean?"

I shook my head.

"No. If the fighting comes anywhere close, we'll move, right away. But I don't think—"

I was interrupted by the sound of a horse, coming fast, and was on my feet, along with the rest of the camp, by the time the messenger appeared; one of Tryon's baby-faced aides, pale with bottled-up excitement.

"Stand ready," he said, hanging out of his saddle, half-breathless.

"And what d'ye think we've been doing since dawn?" Jamie demanded, impatient. "What in God's name is happening, man?"

Very little, apparently, but that little was important enough. A minister from the Regulators' side had come to parley with the Governor.

"A minister?" Jamie interrupted. "A Quaker, do you mean?"

"I do not, sir," said the aide, annoyed at being interrupted. "Quakers have no clergy, anyone knows as much. No, it was a minister named Caldwell, the Reverend David Caldwell."

Regardless of religious affiliation, Tryon had been unmoved by the ambassador's appeal. He could not, would not, deal with a mob, and there was an end to it. Let the Regulators disperse, and he would promise to consider any just complaints laid before him in a proper manner. But disperse they must, within an hour.

"Could you, would you, in a box?" I murmured under my breath, half unhinged by the waiting. "Could you, would you, with a fox?" Jamie had taken off his hat, and the sun shone bright on his ruddy hair. Bree gave a strangled giggle, as much shock as amusement.

"He could not, would not, with a mob," she murmured back. "Could not, would not . . . do the job?"

"He can, though," I said, sotto voce. "And I'm very much afraid he will." For the hundredth time that morning, I glanced toward the scrim of willows through which Roger had disappeared on his errand.

"An hour," Jamie repeated, in answer to the aide's message. He glanced in the same direction, toward the creek. "And how much time is left of that?"

"Perhaps half an hour." The aide looked suddenly much younger even than his years. He swallowed, and put on his hat. "I must go, sir. Listen for the cannon, sir, and luck to you!"

"And with you, sir." Jamie touched the aide's arm in

farewell, then slapped the horse's rump with his hat, sending it off.

As though it had been a signal, the camp sprang into a flurry of activity, even before the Governor's aide had disappeared through the trees. Weapons already primed and loaded were checked and rechecked, buckles unfastened and refastened, badges polished, hats beaten free of dust and cockades affixed, stockings pulled up and tightly gartered, filled canteens shaken for reassurance that their contents had not evaporated in the last quarter-hour.

It was catching. I found myself running my fingers over the rows of glass bottles in the chest yet again, the names murmuring and blurring in my mind like the words of someone telling rosary beads, sense lost in the fervor of petition. *Rosemary, atropine, lavender, oil of cloves . . .*

Bree was notable for her stillness among all this bustle. She sat on her rock, with no movement save the stir of a random breeze in her skirts, her eyes fixed on the distant trees. I heard her say something, under her breath, and turned.

"What did you say?"

"It's not in the books." She didn't take her eyes off the trees, and her hands were knotted in her lap, squeezing together as though she could will Roger to appear through the willows. She lifted her chin, gesturing toward the field, the trees, the men around us.

"This," she said. "It's not in the history books. I read about the Boston Massacre. I saw it *there*, in the history books, and I saw it *here*, in the newspaper. But I never saw this there. I never read a word about Governor Tryon, or North Carolina, or a place called Alamance. So nothing's going to happen." She spoke fiercely, willing it. "If there was a big battle here, someone would have written *something* about it. Nobody did—so nothing's going to happen. Nothing!"

"I hope you're right," I said, and felt a small warming of the chill in the small of my back. Perhaps she was. Surely it couldn't be a major battle, at least. We were no more than four years from the outbreak of the Revolution; even the minor skirmishes preceding that conflict were well-known.

The Boston Massacre had happened a little more than a year before—a street-fight, a clash between a mob and a platoon of nervous soldiers. Shouted insults, a few stones thrown. An unauthorized shot, a panicked volley, and five men dead. It had been reported, with a good deal of fierce editorializing, in one of the Boston newspapers; I had seen it, in Jocasta's parlor; one of her friends had sent her a copy.

And two hundred years later, that brief incident was immortalized in children's textbooks, evidence of the rising disaffection of the Colonists. I glanced at the men who stood around us, preparing to fight. Surely, if there was to be a major battle here, a Royal Governor putting down what was essentially a taxpayer's rebellion, that would have been worth noting!

Still, that was theory. And I was uneasily aware that neither warfare nor history took much account of what *should* happen.

Jamie was standing by Gideon, whom he had tethered to a tree. He would go into battle with his men, on foot. He was taking his pistols from the saddlebag, putting away the extra ammunition in the pouch at his belt. His head was bent, absorbed in the details of what he was doing.

I felt a sudden, dreadful urgency. I must touch him, must say something. I tried to tell myself that Bree was right; this was nothing; likely not even a shot would be fired—and yet there were three thousand armed men here on the banks of the Alamance, and the knowledge of bloodshed hummed and buzzed among them.

I left Brianna sitting on her rock, burning eyes fixed on the wood, and hurried to him.

"Jamie," I said, and put a hand on his arm.

It was like touching a high-voltage wire; power hummed inside the insulation of his flesh, ready to erupt in a burst of crackling light. They say one can't let go of such a line; a victim of electrocution simply freezes to the wire, helpless to move or save himself, as the current burns through brain and heart.

He put his hand on mine, looking down.

*"A nighean donn,"* he said, and smiled a little. "Have ye come to wish me luck, then?"

I smiled back as best I could, though the current sizzled through me, stiffening the muscles of my face as it burned.

"I couldn't let you go without saying ... something. I suppose 'Good luck' will do." I hesitated, words jamming in my throat with the sudden urge to say much more than there was time for. In the end, I said only the important things. "Jamie—I love you. Be careful!"

He didn't remember Culloden, he said. I wondered suddenly whether that loss of memory extended to the hours just before the battle, when he and I had said farewell. Then I looked into his eyes and knew it did not.

"'Good luck' will do," he said, and his hand tightened on mine, likewise frozen to the current that surged between us. "'I love ye' does much better."

He touched my hand, lifted his own and touched my hair, my face, looking into my eyes as though to capture my image in this moment—just in case it should be his last glimpse of me.

"There may come a day when you and I shall part again," he said softly, at last, and his fingers brushed my lips, light as the touch of a falling leaf. He smiled faintly. "But it willna be today."

The notes of a bugle came through the trees, far away, but piercing as a woodpecker's call. I turned, looking. Brianna sat still as a statue on her rock, looking toward the wood.

# SIGNAL FOR ACTION

*Note, when on the March the discharge of three Pieces of Cannon will be the signal to form the line of Battle, and five the signal for Action.*

—*Order of Battle, Wm. Tryon*

ROGER WALKED SLOWLY away from the Regulators' camp, willing himself neither to run nor to look back. A few shouted insults and half-meant threats were hurled in his direction, but by the time he was well into the trees, the crowd had lost interest in him, drawn back into its buzzing controversy. It was past noon, and a hot day for May, but he found his shirt sweat-soaked and clinging to him in a manner more befitting July.

He stopped as soon as he was out of sight. He was breathing fast, and felt dizzy, slightly sick with the aftereffects of adrenaline. In the center of that ring of hostile faces, he hadn't felt a thing—not a thing. Safely away, though, the muscles of his legs were trembling and his fists ached from clenching. He uncurled them, flexed his stiff fingers, and tried to slow his breathing.

Maybe a bit more like the night-time Channel and the anti-aircraft guns than he'd thought, after all.

He'd made it back, though; would be going home to his wife and son. The thought gave him a queer pang; bone-deep relief, and an even deeper grief, quite unexpected, for his father, who hadn't been so lucky.

A slight breeze played about him, lifting the damp hairs on his neck with a breath of welcome coolness. He'd sweated through shirt and coat together, and his damp stock felt suddenly as though it would strangle him. He shucked his coat and pawed at the neckband, jerking it off with shaking fingers, then stood with his eyes closed and the piece of cloth dangling from his hand, breathing great draughts of air, until the momentary sense of nausea subsided.

He called to mind his last sight of Brianna, framed in the doorway, Jemmy in her arms. He saw her lashes wet with tears and the baby's round solemn eyes, and felt a deep echo of the feeling he had experienced in the cabin with Husband; a vision of beauty, a conviction of joy that soothed his mind and eased his soul. He would go back to them; that was all that mattered.

After a moment, he opened his eyes, picked up his coat,

and set off, beginning to feel more settled in body, if not in mind, as he made his way slowly back toward the creek.

He hadn't brought back Husband to Jamie, but he had achieved as much as Jamie himself might have. It was possible that the mob—they were no army, whatever Tryon thought of them—would in fact fall apart, disperse now and go home, deprived of even the faint semblance of leadership Husband had provided. He hoped so.

Or they might not. Another man might rise out of that seething mob, one fit to take command. A thought struck him, with a phrase recalled from the confusion near the cabin.

*"D'ye come to offer different terms than Caldwell has?"* The man with the black beard had asked him that. And earlier, dimly heard through the pounding at the door of the cabin, as he stood in prayer with Husband—*"There's no time for this!"* someone had shouted. *"Caldwell's come back from the Governor—"* and someone else had added, in tones of desperation, *"An hour, Hermon! He's given us an hour, no more!"*

"Shit," he said, aloud. David Caldwell, the Presbyterian minister who had married him and Bree. It must be. Evidently the man had gone to speak with Tryon on the Regulators' behalf—and been rebuffed, with a warning.

*"An hour, no more."* An hour to disperse, to leave peaceably? Or an hour to reply to some ultimatum?

He glanced up; the sun stood overhead, just a bit past noon. He pulled on his coat and stuffed the discarded stock in his pocket, next to the unused flag of truce. Whatever it meant, that hour's grace, it was clearly time to be going.

The day was still bright and hot, the smell of grass and tree-leaves pungent with rising sap. Now, though, his sense of urgency and his memory of the Regulators, buzzing like hornets, deprived him of any appreciation of the beauties of nature. Even so, some trace of peace remained deep within him as he made his way quickly toward the creek; a faint echo of what he had felt in the cabin.

That odd sense of awe had stayed with him, hidden but accessible, like a smooth stone in his pocket. He turned it over in his mind as he made his way toward the creek, largely oblivious to clutching brambles and brush in his path.

How peculiar, he thought. Nothing whatever had *happened*, and in fact the entire experience had felt quite ordinary—nothing otherworldly or supernatural about it. And yet, having seen by that particular clear light, he could not forget it. Could he explain it to Brianna? he wondered.

A trailing branch brushed past his face and he reached to push it aside, feeling even as he did so a faint surprise at the cool green gloss of the leaves, the odd delicacy of their edges, jagged as knives but paper-light. An echo, faint but recognizable, of what he had seen before, that piercing beauty. Did Claire see that? he thought suddenly. Did she see the touch of beauty in the bodies beneath her hands? Was that perhaps how—and why—she was a healer?

Husband had seen it, too, he knew; had shared that perception. And seeing it, had been confirmed in his Quaker principles, and had left the field, unable either to do violence or to countenance it.

And what of his own principles? He supposed they were unchanged; if he hadn't meant to shoot anyone before, he could mean it still less, now.

The scents of spring still hung in the air, and a small blue butterfly floated past his knee with no apparent sense of care. It was still a fine spring day, but all illusion of tranquillity had vanished. The smell of sweat, of dirt and fear and anger, that seemed to hang in the air of the encampment, was still in his nostrils, mingling with the cleaner scents of trillium and water.

What about Jamie Fraser's principles? he wondered, turning past the thicket of willow that marked the ford. He often wondered what made Fraser tick, drawn both by a personal liking for the man, and by his colder historian's curiosity. Roger had made his own decision regarding this conflict—or had it made for him. He couldn't in conscience intend harm to anyone, though he supposed he could defend his own life, if needful. But Jamie?

He was fairly sure that Jamie's sympathies, as such, lay with the Regulators. He thought it likely also that his father-in-law had no sense of personal loyalty to the Crown; oath or no oath, surely no man could have lived through Culloden and its aftermath and emerged with any notion that he owed the King of England fealty, let alone anything more substantial. No, not to the Crown, but perhaps to William Tryon?

No loyalty of a personal nature there, either—but there was definitely an obligation felt. Tryon had summoned Jamie Fraser, and he had come. Given conditions as they stood, he had had little choice about that. Having come, though—would he fight?

How could he not? He must lead his men, and if it came to a battle—Roger glanced over his shoulder, as though the cloud of anger that hung over the Regulators' army might be now visible, swelling dark above the treetops—yes, he would have to fight, no matter what his private feelings on the matter might be.

Roger tried to envision himself aiming a musket at a man with whom he had no quarrel and pulling the trigger. Or worse, riding down a neighbor, sword in hand. Smashing in Kenny Lindsay's head, for instance? Imagination failed completely. No wonder that Jamie had sought to enlist Husband's help in ending the conflict before it began!

Still, Claire had told him once that Jamie had fought in France as a mercenary, as a young man. He *had* presumably killed men with whom he had no quarrel. How—

He pushed through the willows, and heard their voices before he saw them. A group of women were working on the near side of the stream; camp-followers. Some crouched bare-legged in the shallows, washing, others were carrying wet laundry up the bank, to be hung from trees and bushes. His eye passed casually beyond them, then jerked back, caught by . . . what? What was it?

There. He couldn't say why he had spotted her at all— there was nothing even faintly distinctive about her. And yet she stood out among the other women as though she had been outlined, drawn with black ink to stand out against the backdrop of stream and budding foliage.

"Morag," he whispered, and his heart thumped suddenly with a small shock of joy. She was alive.

He was halfway through the screen of willows before it occurred to him to wonder what he was doing, let alone why he was doing it. It was too late by then, though; he was already out on the bank, walking openly toward them.

Several of the women glanced at him; a few half-froze, watchful. But he was only one man, unarmed. There were more than twenty women by the river, their own men nearby. They watched him, curious, but not alarmed, as he splashed across the shallow creek.

She stood stock-still, knee-deep in the water, her skirts kirtled high, and watched him come. She knew him, he could see, but she gave him no sign of acknowledgment.

The other women fell back slightly, wary of him. She stood among the darting dragonflies, strands of brown hair poking out from her cap, a wet smock held forgotten in her hands. He stepped up out of the water and stood before her, wet to the knees.

"Mrs. MacKenzie," he said softly. "Well met."

A tiny smile touched the corner of her mouth. Her eyes were brown; he hadn't noticed that before.

"Mr. MacKenzie," she said, and gave him a small nod. His mind was working, thinking what to do. He must warn her, but how? Not before all the other women.

He stood helpless and awkward for a moment, not knowing what to do, then, inspired, he stooped and seized an armload of dripping laundry where it swirled in the water near her legs. He turned and clambered up the bank with it, Morag following in sudden haste.

"What are ye doing?" she demanded. "Here, come back wi' my clothes!"

He carried the wad of wet clothes a short way into the trees, then dropped them casually into a bush, mindful enough of the effort of washing not to let them drag in the dirt. Morag was right behind him, face flushed with indignation.

"What d'ye think you're about, ye thievin' clotheid?" she demanded heatedly. "Give those back!"

"I'm not stealing them," Roger assured her. "I only wanted to talk to you alone for a bit."

"Oh, aye?" She gave him a suspicious glance. "What about, then?"

He smiled at her; she was still thin, he saw, but her arms were brown and her small face a healthy color—she was clean, and she had lost the pallid, bruised look she had had on board the *Gloriana*.

"I wished to ask if you are well," he said softly. "And your child—Jemmy?" To speak the name gave him an odd frisson, and for a split second he saw the image of Brianna in the doorway, her son in her arms, laid over his memory of Morag, holding her baby in the dimness of the hold, ready to kill or die to keep him.

"Oh," she said, and the suspicion faded slightly, replaced by a reluctant acknowledgment of his right to ask. "We're well . . . the both of us. And my husband, too," she added pointedly.

"I'm pleased to hear it," he assured her. "Very pleased." He groped for something else to say, feeling awkward. "I—had thought of you now and then . . . wondered whether—whether everything was all right. When I saw you just now . . . well, I thought I'd ask, that's all."

"Oh, aye. Aye, I see. Well, I do thank ye, Mr. MacKenzie." She looked up and met his eyes directly as she said it, her own gaze brown and earnest. "I ken what ye did for us. I'll not forget; ye're in my prayers each night."

"Oh." Roger felt as though some soft weight had struck him in the breast. "Ahh . . . thank you." He had wondered, now and then, if she ever thought of him. Did she remember the kiss he had given her, there in the hold, seeking the spark of her warmth as some shield against the chill of loneliness? He cleared his throat, flushing at the memory.

"You—live nearby?"

She shook her head, and some thought, some memory, tightened her mouth.

"We did, but now—well, that's no matter." She turned, suddenly businesslike, and began to take her wet clothes from the bush, shaking each one before folding it. "I do thank ye for your concern, Mr. MacKenzie."

He was clearly dismissed. He wiped his hands down his breeks and shifted his feet, not wanting to leave. He must tell her—but having found her again, he was oddly reluctant simply to warn her and leave; curiosity bubbled in him—curiosity and a peculiar sense of connection.

Perhaps not so peculiar; this small brown woman was his

relative, his own family—the only person of his own blood he had known since the death of his parents. At the same time, it was *very* peculiar, he realized, even as his hand reached out and curved around her arm. She was his many-times great-grandmother, after all.

She stiffened, tried to pull away, but he kept hold of her forearm. Her skin was cold from the water, but he felt her pulse throb under his fingers.

"Wait," he said. "Please. Just a moment. I—I need to tell you . . . things."

"No, ye don't. I'd rather ye didn't." She pulled harder, and her hand slid through his, pulled free.

"Your husband. Where is he?" Belated realizations were forming in his brain. If she did not live nearby, then she was what he had first thought when he saw the women—a camp-follower. She was not a whore, he would stake his life on that; so she followed her husband, which meant—

"He is very nearby!" She backed up a step, eyeing the distance between herself and the remnants of her laundry. Roger stood between her and the bush; she would have to pass near him in order to retrieve her petticoats and stockings.

Realizing suddenly that she was slightly afraid of him, he turned hastily, grabbing a handful of things at random.

"I'm sorry. Your laundry . . . here." He thrust them at her, and she reached to take them by reflex. Something fell—a baby's gown—and both ducked to reach for it, cracking foreheads with a solid smack.

"Oh! Oh! Mary and Bride!" Morag clutched her head, though she still clasped the wet clothes against her bosom with one hand.

"Christ, are you all right? Morag—Mrs. MacKenzie—are you all right? I'm very sorry!" Roger touched her shoulder, squinting at her through eyes that watered with pain. He stooped to pick up the tiny gown that had fallen to the ground between them, and made a vain effort to wipe the smears of mud off the wet cloth. She blinked, eyes similarly watering, and laughed at his expression of dismay.

The collision had somehow broken the tension between them; she stepped back, but seemed not to feel threatened now.

"Aye, I'm fine." She sniffed and wiped her eyes, then touched the spot on her forehead gingerly. "I've got a thick skull, my Mam always said. Are you all right yourself, then?"

"Aye, fine." Roger touched his own forehead, suddenly and tinglingly aware that the curve of the browbone under his fingers was precisely echoed on the face before him. Hers was smaller, lighter—but just the same.

"I've a thick skull, too." He grinned at her, feeling ridiculously happy. "It runs in my family."

He handed her the mud-stained shirt, carefully.

"I *am* sorry," he said, apologizing again—and not only for the ruined laundry. "Your husband. I asked about him because—is he one of the Regulators, then?"

She looked at him curiously, one brow lifted.

"Of course. Are ye not with the Regulation yourself?"

Of course. Here on this side of Alamance, what else? Tryon's troops were drawn up in good military order on the field beyond the creek; over here, the Regulators swarmed like bees, without leadership or direction, an angry mass buzzing with random violence.

"No," he said. "I've come with the militia." He waved toward the distant smudge, where the smoke of Tryon's campfires hung, far beyond the creek. Her eyes grew wary again, but not frightened; he was only one man.

"That's the thing I wanted to tell you," he said. "To warn you, and your husband. The Governor is serious this time; he's brought organized troops, he's brought cannon. Lots of troops, all armed." He leaned toward her, holding out the rest of the wet stockings. She reached out a hand to take them, but kept her eyes on his, waiting.

"He means to put down this rebellion, by any means necessary. He has given orders to kill, if there is resistance. Do you understand? You must tell your husband, make him leave before—before anything happens."

She paled, and her hand went reflexively to her belly. The wet from the clothes had soaked through her muslin dress, and he saw the small swelling that had been hidden there, round and smooth as a melon under the damp cloth. He felt the jolt of her fear go through him, as though the wet stockings she held conducted electricity.

*"We did, but not now . . ."* she had said, when he asked whether they lived nearby. She might mean only that they had moved to some new place, but . . . there were baby's things in her wash; her son was with her here. Her husband was somewhere in this boiling of men.

A single man might pick up his gun and join a mob, for no reason beyond drink or boredom; a married man with a child would not. That spoke of serious disaffection, consequential grievance. And to bring both wife and child to war suggested that he had no safe place to leave them.

Roger thought it likely that Morag and her husband had no home at all now, and he understood her fear perfectly. If her husband should be maimed or killed, how was she to provide for Jemmy, for the new baby swelling under her skirt? She had no one, no family here to turn to.

Except that she did, though she did not know it. He gripped her hand hard, pulling her toward him, overcome with the need somehow to protect her and her children. He had saved them once; he could do it again.

"Morag," he said. "Hear me. If anything should happen— anything—come to me. If you are in need of anything at all. I'll take care of you."

She made no effort to pull away, but searched his face, her eyes brown and serious, a small frown between those curving brows. He had an irresistible urge to make some physical connection between them—this time for her sake, as much as his. He leaned forward and kissed her, very gently.

He opened his eyes then, and lifted his head, to find himself looking over her shoulder, into the disbelieving face of his many-times great-grandfather.

"GET AWAY FROM MY WIFE." William Buccleigh MacKenzie emerged from the shrubbery with a great rustling of leaves and a look of sinister intent upon his face. He was a tall man, close to Roger's own height, and burly through the shoulders. Further personal details seemed inconsequent, given that he also had a knife. It was still sheathed at his belt, but his hand rested on the hilt in a significant manner.

Roger resisted his original impulse, which had been to say, "It's not what you think." It wasn't, but there weren't any plausible alternatives to suggest.

"I meant her no disrespect," he said, instead, straightening up slowly. He felt it would be unwise to make any quick moves. "My apologies."

"No? And just what the hell d'ye mean by it, then?" MacKenzie put a possessive hand on his wife's shoulder, glowering at Roger. She flinched; her husband's fingers were digging into her flesh. Roger would have liked to knock the hand away, but that was likely to cause more trouble than he had already.

"I met your wife—and you—" he added, "on board the *Gloriana*, a year or two ago. When I recognized her here, I thought to inquire as to the family's welfare. That's all."

"He meant nay harm, William." Morag touched her husband's hand, and the painful grip lessened. "It's right, what he says. Do ye not ken the man? It was him that found me and Jemmy in the hold when we hid there—he brought us food and water."

"You asked me to care for them," Roger added pointedly. "During the fight, that night when the sailors threw the sick ones into the sea."

"Oh, aye?" MacKenzie's features relaxed a trifle. "It was you, was it? I didna see your face, in the dark."

"I didn't see yours, either." He could see it clearly now, and despite the awkwardness of the present circumstances, couldn't help studying it with interest.

So this was the son—unacknowledged—of Dougal MacKenzie, erstwhile war chief of the MacKenzies of Leoch. He looked it. His was a rougher, squarer, fairer version of the family face, but looking carefully, Roger could easily spot the broad cheekbones and high forehead that Jamie Fraser had inherited from his mother's clan. That and the family height; MacKenzie stood over six feet tall, nearly eye to eye with Roger himself.

The man turned slightly at a sound in the brush, and the

sun lit those eyes with a flash of bright moss-green. Roger had a sudden urge to shut his own eyes, lest MacKenzie feel the same bolt of recognition.

MacKenzie had other concerns, though. Two men emerged from the bushes, wary-eyed and grimy with long camping. One held a musket; the other was armed with nothing but a rough club cut from a fallen limb.

"Who's this, then, Buck?" the man with the gun asked, eyeing Roger with some suspicion.

"That's what I mean to be finding out." The momentary softening had disappeared, leaving MacKenzie's face grimly set. He turned his wife away from him and gave her a small push. "Go ye back to the women, Morag. I'll deal with this fellow."

"But, William—" Morag glanced from Roger to her husband, face drawn in distress. "He hasna done anything—"

"Oh, ye think it's nothing, do you, that a man should cheek up to ye in public, like a common radge?" William turned a black look on her, and she blushed suddenly crimson, evidently recalling the kiss, but stumbled on.

"I—no, I mean—that is—he was kind to us, we shouldna be—"

"I said go back!"

She opened her mouth as though to protest, then flinched as William made a sudden move in her direction, fist clenched. Without an instant of conscious decision, Roger swung from the waist, his own fist hitting MacKenzie's jaw with a crack that jarred his arm to the elbow.

Caught off-balance, William staggered and fell to one knee, shaking his head like a pole-axed ox. Morag's gasp was drowned by startled exclamations from the other men. Before he could turn to face them, Roger heard a sound behind him—quiet in itself, but loud enough to chill the blood; the small, cold snick of a hammer drawing back.

There was a brief *pst!* of igniting powder, and then a *phfoom!* as the gun went off with a roar and a puff of black smoke. Everyone jerked and stumbled with the noise, and Roger found himself struggling in a confused sort of way with one of the other men, both of them coughing and half-deafened. As he shoved his assailant off, he caught sight of

Morag, kneeling in the leaves, dabbing at her husband's face with a bit of wet laundry. William shoved her roughly away, scrambled to his feet, and headed for Roger, his eyes bulging, face blotched red with fury.

Roger spun on his heel, slipping in the leaves, and shook off the grip of the man with the gun, making for the shelter of the bushes. Then he was into the thicket, twigs and small branches splintering around him, raking face and arms as he thrust his way through. A heavy crashing and the huff of breath came just behind him, and a hand fastened on his shoulder with a grip of iron.

He seized the hand and twisted hard, hearing a crack of joint and bone. The hand's owner yelled and jerked back, and Roger flung himself headlong toward an opening in the scrub.

He hit the ground on one shoulder, half-curled, rolled, broke through a small bush, and tobogganed down a steep clay bank and into the water, where he landed with a splash.

Scrabbling to find a foothold, he plunged and coughed and flapped upright, shaking hair and water from his eyes, only to see William MacKenzie poised at the top of the bank above him. Seeing his enemy thus at a disadvantage, MacKenzie launched himself with a whoop.

Something like a cannonball crashed into Roger's chest and he fell back into the water in a mighty splash, hearing the distant shrieks of women. He couldn't breathe and couldn't see, but grappled with the twisting mess of clothes and limbs and roiling mud, churning the bottom as he strove vainly for footing, lungs bursting for air.

His head broke the surface. His mouth opened and closed like a fish's, gulping air, and he heard the wheeze of his breath, and MacKenzie's, too. MacKenzie broke away, floundering, and stood upright a few feet away, wheezing like an engine as water poured from his clothes. Roger bent, chest heaving, hands braced on his thighs and his arms quivering with effort. With a final gulp of air, he straightened, wiping away the wet hair plastered over his face.

"Look," he began, panting, "I—"

He got no further, for MacKenzie, still breathing heavily himself, was advancing on him through the waist-deep water.

The man's face had an odd, eager look, and the moss-green eyes were very bright.

Belatedly, Roger thought of something else. The man was the son of Dougal MacKenzie. But the son also of Geillis Duncan, witch.

Somewhere beyond the willows, there was a deep booming noise, and flocks of startled birds rose screeching from the trees. The battle had begun.

# ALAMANCE

*The Governor then sent Captain Malcolm, one of his Aides-de-Camp, and the Sherif of Orange, with his Letter, requiring the Rebels, to lay down their Arms, Surrender up their outlawed Ringleaders &c. About half past ten Capt. Malcolm and the Sherif returned with the Information that the Sherif had read the Letter four several Times, to different Divisions of the Rebels, who rejected the Terms offered, with disdain, said they wanted no time to consider of them, & with Rebellious Clamours called out for Battle.*

—*"A Journal of the Expedition against the Insurgents," Wm. Tryon*

"YE'LL WATCH FOR MACKENZIE." Jamie touched Geordie Chisholm's shoulder, and Geordie turned his head, acknowledging the message with a slight nod.

All of them knew. They were good lads, they'd be careful. They'd find him, surely, coming back toward them.

He told himself so for the dozenth time, but the reassurance rang as hollow this time as it had before. Christ, what had happened to the man?

He moved up into the lead, shoving aside the brush with as much violence as though it were a personal enemy. If they were watching out, they'd see MacKenzie in time, not shoot him by mistake. Or so he told himself, knowing perfectly well that in the midst of enemies and the heat of battle, one fired at whatever moved, and there was seldom time to check the features of a man who came at you out of the smoke.

Not that it would make so much difference who did for MacKenzie, if anyone did. Brianna and Claire would hold him responsible for the man's life, and rightly so.

Then, to his relief, there was no more time to think. They broke out into open ground and the men spread out and ran, bending low, zigzagging through the grass in threes and fours as he had taught them, one seasoned soldier to each group. Somewhere behind them, the first boom of cannon came like thunder from a sunny sky.

He spotted the first of the Regulators then, a group of men running, as they were, coming from the right across the open ground. They hadn't seen his men yet.

Before they could, he bellowed "Casteal an DUIN!" and charged them, musket raised overhead in signal to the men behind him. Roars and shrieks split the air, and the Regulators, startled and taken unawares, stumbled to an untidy halt, fumbling their weapons and interfering with each other.

*"Thugham! Thugham!"* To me, to me! Close enough, it was close enough. He dropped to one knee, crouched over the musket, brought it to bear, and fired just over the heads of the milling men.

Behind him, he heard the grunt of his men falling into firing order, the clink of flint and then the deafening noise of the volley.

One or two of the Regulators crouched, returning fire. The rest broke and ran for cover, toward a small rise of grassy ground.

*"A draigha!* Left! *Nach links!* Cut them off!" He heard

himself bellowing, but did it without thought, already running himself.

The small group of Regulators split, a few making off toward the creek, the rest bunching like sheep, galloping for the shelter of the rise.

They made it, disappearing around the curve of the hill, and Jamie called his troops back, with a piercing whistle that would carry over the rising thunder of the guns. He could hear firing now, a rattle of muskets, away to their left. He sheared off in that direction, trusting that they would follow.

A mistake; the land here was marshy, full of boggy holes and clinging mud. He shouted and waved again, back toward the higher ground. Fall back there, let the enemy come to them across the bog, if they would.

The high ground was heavy with brush, but dry, at least. He spread his fingers wide and waved, gesturing the men to spread out, take cover.

The blood was pumping through his veins, and his skin prickled and tingled with it. A puff of gray-white smoke drifted through the nearby trees, acrid with the scent of black powder. The boom of artillery was regular now, as the gun-crews fell into their rhythm, thumping like a huge, slow heart in the distance.

He made his way slowly toward the west, keeping an eye out. The brush here was mostly sumac and redbud, with waist-high tangles of bramble and clumps of pine that rose above his head. Visibility was poor, but he would hear anyone coming, long before he saw them—or they saw him.

None of his own men were in sight. He took cover in a stand of dogwood and gave a sharp call, like a bobwhite quail. Similar calls of "bob-WHITE!" came from behind him, none in front. Good, they knew roughly where one another were. Cautiously, he went forward, pressing through the brush. It was cooler here, with the shade of the trees, but the air was thick and sweat ran down his neck and back.

He heard the thump of feet and pressed back into the branches of a pinetree, letting the dark-needled fans swing over him, his musket raised to sight on an opening in the bushes. Whoever it was was coming fast. A crack of snapping twigs underfoot and the sound of labored breath, and a young man shoved through the shrubbery, panting. He had no gun, but a skinning-knife glinted in his hand.

The lad was familiar, the first glance gave him that, and Jamie's memory put a name to the young man's face before his finger had relaxed upon the trigger.

"Hugh!" he called, low-voiced but sharp. "Hugh Fowles!"

The young man let out a startled yelp, and swung round staring. He saw Jamie and his gun through the screen of needles, and froze like a rabbit.

Then a surge of panicked determination rose in his face, and he launched himself toward Jamie, screaming. Startled, Jamie barely got his musket up in time to catch the knife-blade on its barrel. He forced the knife up and back; it sheared down the barrel with a screech of metal, glancing off Jamie's knuckles. Young Hugh whipped back his arm for a stab, and he kicked the boy briskly in the knee, stepping back out of the way as the lad lost his balance and lurched to one side, knife swinging wildly.

Jamie kicked him again, and he fell down, the knife embedding itself in the ground.

"Will ye stop that?" Jamie said, rather crossly. "For Christ's sake, lad, do ye not know me?"

He couldn't tell whether Fowles knew him or not—nor even whether the boy had heard him. Face white and eyes staring, Fowles was thrashing in a panic, stumbling and gasping as he tried to get up, trying at the same time to wrench his knife free.

"Will you—" Jamie began, and then jerked back as Fowles abandoned the knife and threw himself forward with a grunt of effort.

The boy's weight knocked Jamie backward, and hands scrabbled at him, trying for a grip on his throat. He dropped the musket, turned a shoulder into Fowles's grip, and put a stop to this nonsense with a quick, brutal punch to the lad's midsection.

Hugh Fowles collapsed and lay curled into a ball on the ground, twitching like a wounded centipede, and making the shocked breathless faces of a man whose breakfast has just been knocked up into his lungs.

Jamie put his right hand to his mouth, sucking blood from

his grazed knuckles. The boy's knife had skinned all four, and the punch hadn't helped; they burned like fire, and the blood had the taste of hot silver in his mouth.

More feet, coming fast. He had barely time to seize his musket before the bushes burst open once more, this time to reveal Fowles's father-in-law, Joe Hobson, his own musket held at the ready.

"Stop right there." Jamie crouched behind his gun, training the muzzle on Hobson's chest. Hobson halted as though a puppet-master had jerked his strings.

"What have ye done to him?" Hobson's eyes flicked from Jamie to his son-in-law and back.

"Nothing permanent. Put your gun down, aye?"

Hobson didn't move. He was grimed with filth and sprouting a beard, but the eyes were live and watchful in his face.

"I mean ye nay harm. Set it down!"

"We'll not be taken," Hobson said. His finger rested on the trigger of his gun, but there was a dubious note in his voice.

"Ye already are, fool. Dinna fash yourself, nay harm will come to you or the lad. You're a deal safer in gaol than out here, man!"

A whistling crash punctuated his statement, as something flew through the trees a few feet overhead, shearing branches as it went. Chain shot, Jamie thought automatically, even as he ducked in reflex, bowels clenched.

Hobson jerked in terror, swinging the barrel of his musket toward Jamie. He jerked again, and his eyes went wide with surprise, as a red stain flowered slowly on his breast. He looked down at it in puzzlement, the muzzle of his gun drooping like a wilted stem. Then he dropped the gun, sat down quite suddenly, leaned back against a fallen tree, and died.

Jamie whirled on his heel, still squatting, and saw Geordie Chisholm behind him, face half-black with the smoke of his shot, looking at Hobson's body as though wondering just how *that* had happened.

The boom of artillery came again, and another missile crashed through the branches and landed nearby with a thud Jamie felt through the soles of his boots. He flung himself flat on his belly and writhed toward Hugh Fowles, who had got himself up on hands and knees now, retching.

He grabbed Fowles's arm, disregarding the pool of vomit, and jerked, hard.

"Come on!" He scrambled up, seizing Fowles by waist and shoulder, and dragged him toward the shelter of the copse behind them. "Geordie! Geordie, help me!"

Chisholm was there. Between them, they got Fowles onto his feet and half-dragged, half-carried him, running and stumbling as they went.

The air was filled with the pungent scent of tree-sap, oozing from the severed branches, and he thought fleetingly of Claire's garden, turned earth, churned earth beneath his boots, the fresh-turned earth of furrows and graves, and Hobson sitting in the sun by the log, the look of surprise not yet gone from his eyes.

Fowles stank of vomit and shit. He hoped it was Fowles.

He thought he would vomit himself from sheer nerves, but bit his tongue, tasting blood again, and clenched the muscles of his belly, willing his wame to go back down.

Someone rose from the shrubbery to his left. He held the gun in his left hand, raised it by reflex, fired one-handed. He stumbled through his own smoke, seeing whoever he had fired at turn and run, smashing heedless through the trees.

Fowles had his feet back under him now, and Jamie let go his arm, leaving Geordie to it. He fell to one knee, groping for powder and shot, ripped the cartridge with his teeth and tasted gunpowder tinged with blood, poured and rammed home, filled his priming pan, checked his flint—all the while noticing with a sense of bemusement that his hands were not shaking in the least, but went about their business with a deft calm, as though they knew just what to do.

He raised the barrel and bared his teeth, only half-conscious of doing it. There were men coming, three, and he raised the gun to bear on the first. With a last shred of conscious thought, he jerked it higher and fired above their heads, the musket jolting in his hands. They stopped, and he dropped the gun, ripped the dirk from his belt, and charged them, screaming.

The words seared his throat, raw from the smoke.

"Run!"

As though from a distance, he watched himself, thinking that it was just so that Hugh Fowles had done, and he had thought it foolish then.

"Run!"

The men scattered like fleeing quail. As a wolf might do, he turned at once after the slowest, bounding over the broken ground, a ferocious joy flooding his legs, blooming in his belly. He could run forever, the wind cold on his skin and shrill in his ears, the spring of the earth beneath him lifting his feet so he flew over grass and rock.

The man he pursued heard him coming, glanced back over his shoulder, and with a shriek of terror, ran full-tilt into a tree. He threw himself upon his prey, landing on the man's back and feeling the springy crack of ribs beneath his knee. He gripped a handful of hair, slick and hot with greasy sweat, and jerked back the man's head. He barely stopped himself cutting the naked throat that lay before him, stretched and defenseless. He could feel the shock of the blade on flesh, the hotness of the spurting blood, and wanted it.

He gulped air, panting.

Very slowly, he drew the knife away from the leaping pulse. The movement left him trembling with need, as though he had been dragged from his woman's body on the verge of spilling seed.

"You are my prisoner," he said.

The man stared up at him, uncomprehending. The man was weeping, tears making tracks through the dirt on his face, and trying to speak, sobbing, but unable to draw enough air to make words with his head wrenched back. Vaguely, it occurred to Jamie that he had spoken in Gaelic; the man did not understand.

Slowly, he loosened his grip, made himself release the man's head. He groped for the English words, buried somewhere under the bloodlust that pulsed through his brain.

"You are . . . my . . . prisoner," he managed at last, panting for air between words.

"Yes! Yes! Anything, don't kill me, please don't kill me!" The man huddled under him, sobbing, hands clasped to the back of his neck and shoulders hunched around his ears, as though he feared Jamie would seize his neck in his teeth and snap his spine.

At the thought, he felt a dim desire to do so, but the thrum of his blood was even now dying down. He could hear again, as his heartbeat faded in his ears. The wind no longer sang to him, but made its own way, heedless and alone, through the leaves above. There was a popping of distant gunshots, but the boom of the artillery had ceased.

Sweat dripped from chin and eyebrows, and his shirt was sodden with it, reeking.

He slid slowly off his prisoner, and knelt beside the prone body. The muscles of his thighs trembled and burned from the effort of the chase. He felt a sudden inexpressible tenderness for the man, and reached to touch him, but the feeling was succeeded by a sense of horror, quite as sudden, and as suddenly gone. He closed his eyes and swallowed, feeling sick, the place where he had bitten his tongue throbbing.

The energy the earth had lent him was draining from his body now, flowing out of his legs, going back to the earth. He reached out and patted the prisoner's shoulder, awkwardly, then struggled to his feet against the dead weight of his own exhaustion.

"Get up," he said. His hands were shaking; it took three tries to sheathe his dirk.

*"Ciamar a tha thu, Mac Dubh?"* Ronnie Sinclair was at his side, asking if he was all right. He nodded, and stood back as Sinclair pulled the man to his feet and made him turn his coat. The others were coming, in ones and twos: Geordie, the Lindsays, Gallegher, catching up and clustering round him like iron filings drawn to a bit of magnet steel.

The others had bagged prisoners, too; six in all, looking sullen, frightened, or simply exhausted, their coats turned lining-out to show their status. Fowles was among them, white and wretched.

His mind had cleared now, though his body felt limp and heavy. Henry Gallegher had a bloody graze across his forehead; one of the men from Brownsville—Lionel, was it?—carried one arm at an awkward angle, obviously broken. Bar that, no one seemed to be injured; that was good.

"Ask if they have seen MacKenzie," he said to Kenny Lindsay in Gaelic, with a small gesture toward the prisoners.

The gunshots had mostly ceased. There was only a random firing now, and a flock of doves passed overhead in a racket of wings, belatedly alarmed.

None had seen Roger MacKenzie, to know him. Jamie nodded, hearing, and wiped the last of the sweat from his face with his sleeve.

"Either he has come back safe, or he has not. But whatever's done is done now. Ye've done brawly, lads—let's go."

# A NECESSARY SACRIFICE

*This Evening the Dead were interred with military Honors; and three Outlaws taken in the Battle were hanged at the Head of the Army. This gave great Satisfaction to the Men & at this Time it was a necessary Sacrifice to appease the Murmurings of the Troops, who were importunate that public Justice should be immediately executed against some of the Outlaws that were taken in the Action and in opposing of whom they had braved so many Dangers, & suffered such Loss of lives and Blood.*

> —*"A Journal of the Expedition against the Insurgents," Wm. Tryon*

ROGER JERKED HARD at the rope round his wrists, but succeeded only in digging the rough hemp farther into his flesh. He could feel the burn of abraded skin and a damp feel that he thought was oozing blood, but his hands had gone so numb that he wasn't sure. His fingers felt the size of sausages, the skin stretched tight.

He was lying where Buccleigh and his friends had thrown him, after tying his wrists and ankles, in the shade of a fallen log. Soaked through from the river, he would have been shivering with cold, had he not been struggling so desperately to get loose. Instead, sweat ran down his neck, his cheeks burned, and he felt as though his head would burst from the influx of furious blood.

They'd gagged him with the flag of truce, stuffing the kerchief so deep into his throat that he was close to choking, and knotting his own stock round his mouth. Ancestor or no, he was going to mangle William Buccleigh MacKenzie, if it was the last thing he ever did.

Shots were still being fired nearby; not in volleys, but a ragged popcorn rattle. The air reeked with black powder smoke, and every so often, something came whistling through the trees like a jabberwock, with a tremendous ripping and snapping of branches and leaves. Chain-shot? Cannonballs?

A cannonball had thudded into the riverbank, earlier, burying itself in a small explosion of mud and momentarily interrupting the fight. One of Buccleigh's friends had uttered a cry and run, splashing, for the shelter of the trees, but the other had stayed, grappling and punching, heedless of the shooting and yelling, until he and Buccleigh had managed to press Roger's head beneath the water and overpower him. He could still feel the burn of the river-water in his sinuses.

He'd managed to get to his knees now, hunched like an inch-worm, but didn't dare to raise his head above the log, for fear of having it shot off. Fury was running so strong through his veins that he hadn't really been frightened, even at the realization that the battle was going on round him, but he hadn't lost his mind entirely.

He rubbed his face hard against the crumbling bark of the log, trying to snag the strip of linen tied round his head. It worked; the stub of a twig caught, and he jerked his head up, pulling the stock down below his chin. Grunting with the effort, he shoved the wadded kerchief out a little way, caught it on the same twig, and drew back, the soggy rag pulling out of his throat like a snake-swallower in reverse.

He gagged with reaction, feeling bile rise up the back of his throat. He gulped air, greedy for oxygen, and his stomach settled a bit.

Great, he could breathe, now what? The firing was still going on, and he could hear crashing off to his left, as several men plowed through the bushes, heedless of obstruction.

Running feet were coming toward him; he ducked behind the shelter of the log, just in time to avoid being flattened as a body catapulted over it. His new companion scrambled up onto hands and knees, pressing tight against the log, only then becoming aware of his presence.

"You!" It was Black-beard, from Husband's encampment. He stared at Roger, face suffusing slowly with blood. He could smell the man, a rank, penetrating reek of fear and anger.

Black-beard grabbed him by the shirt-front, jerking him close.

"This is your fault! Bastard!"

With his hands and feet still tied, he had no means of fighting back, but jerked back, trying to free himself.

"Let go, fool!"

Only then did the man realize that he was tied, and in his astonishment, did let go. Off-balance, Roger fell to the side, scraping his face painfully on the rough bark of the log. Black-beard's eyes bulged with amazement, then narrowed in glee.

"By Dad, you been captured! If that ain't luck! Who's got you, fool?"

"He's mine." A low Scottish voice behind him announced the return of William Buccleigh MacKenzie. "What d'ye mean it's his fault? What is?"

"This!" Black-beard flung out an arm, indicating the field around them, and the dying battle. The artillery had ceased, and there were no more than scattered rifle-shots in the distance.

"This damn smooth-talker come unto the camp this morning, asking for Hermon Husband, and took him away for a private word. I don't know what in desolation's name he said, but when he finished it, Husband come out, got straight onto his horse, told us all to go home, and rode off!"

Black-beard glared at Roger, and drawing back his hand, slapped him hard across the face. "What did you say to him, arse-bite?"

Without waiting for an answer, he turned back to Buccleigh, who was glancing back and forth between his captive and his visitor, a look of deep interest furrowing the thick, fair brows. "If Hermon had stuck with us, we might ha' stood," Black-beard raged. "But with him goin' off like that, it cut the ground right from under us—wasn't no one knew quite what to do, and the next thing you know, here's Tryon a-bawling surrender at us—and a course we wasn't goin' to do that, but we wasn't what you'd call prepared to fight neither . . ." He trailed off at this, catching Roger's eye on him, and uncomfortably aware that Roger had seen him fleeing in panic.

There was nothing but silence on the far side of the log; all firing had stopped. It was dawning on Roger that the battle was not only over, but well and truly lost. Which meant in turn that the militia were likely to be swarming over this place in short order. His eyes were still watering from the slap, but he blinked them clear, glaring at Black-beard.

"I said to Husband what I say to you," he said, with as much authority as he could muster, lying trussed on the ground like a Christmas goose. "The Governor is serious. He means to put down this rebellion, and by the looks of things, he's done just that. If you have a care for your skin—and I'd say you do—"

With an inarticulate growl of rage, Black-beard seized Roger by the shoulders and tried to smash his head into the log.

Roger twisted like an eel. He reared back, breaking the man's grip, then threw himself forward, and butted the man squarely, smashing Black-beard's nose with his forehead. He felt the satisfying crunch of bone and cartilage, and the spurt of blood hot and wet against his face, and fell back onto one elbow, panting.

He'd not given anyone a Glasgow kiss before, but it seemed to come natural. The jar of it hurt his wrist badly, but he was beyond caring. Just let Buccleigh come close enough to get the same, that's all he wanted.

Buccleigh eyed him with a mixture of amusement and wary respect.

"Oh, a man of talent, aye? A traitor, a wife-stealer, *and* a bonnie brawler, all in the same wee bundle, is it?"

Black-beard threw up, choking on the blood from his crushed nose, but Roger paid no attention. His vision clear now, he kept his eyes square on Buccleigh. He knew which man of the two was the greater threat.

"A man who's sure of his wife needn't worry that someone else might steal her," he said, anger only slightly tempered with wariness. "I'm sure of my own wife, and have no need of yours, *amadain*."

Buccleigh was sunburned and deeply flushed from fighting, but at this, a darker red crept into his cheeks. Still, he kept his composure, smiling lightly.

"Marrit, are ye? Your wife must be ill-favored, surely, for ye to be sniffing after mine. Or is it only that she's put ye out of her bed, because ye couldna serve her decently?"

The rasp of the rope on his wrists reminded Roger that he was in no position to bandy words. With an effort, he bit back the retort that sat at the tip of his tongue, and swallowed it. It tasted foul, going down.

"Unless ye mean your wife to be a widow, I think it's time ye were going, aye?" he said. He jerked his head toward the far side of the log, where the brief silence had been succeeded by the distant sound of voices.

"The battle's over, your cause is lost. I don't know if they mean to take prisoners—"

"They've taken several." Buccleigh frowned at him, clearly undecided. There weren't that many options, Roger thought; Buccleigh must let him go, leave him tied, or kill him. Either of the first two was acceptable. As for the third, surely if Buccleigh meant to kill him, he'd be already dead.

"You'd best go while ye can," Roger suggested. "Your wife will be worried."

It was a mistake to have mentioned Morag again. Buccleigh's face grew darker, but before he could say anything, he was interrupted by the appearance of the woman herself, in company with the man who had helped Buccleigh tie him earlier.

"Will! Oh, Willie! Thank Christ you're safe! Are ye hurt at all?" She was pale and anxious, and had a small child in her arms, clinging monkeylike to her neck. Despite the burden, she reached out a hand to touch her husband, to assure herself that he was indeed unharmed.

"Dinna fash yourself, Morag," Buccleigh said gruffly. "I've taken no harm." Still, he patted her hand, and kissed her self-consciously on the forehead.

Ignoring this tender reunion, Buccleigh's companion prodded Roger interestedly in the side with the toe of his boot.

"What shall we do with this, then, Buck?"

Buccleigh hesitated, his attention drawn momentarily from his wife. Morag, spotting Roger on the ground, uttered a muffled scream and clapped her hand across her mouth.

"What have ye done, Willie?" she cried. "Let him go, for Bride's sake!"

"I shan't. He's a damned traitor." Buccleigh's mouth set in a grim line, obviously displeased at his wife's taking notice of Roger.

"He's not, he can't be!" Clutching her son tightly to her, Morag stooped to peer at Roger, an anxious crease between her brows. Seeing the state of his hands, she gasped and turned indignantly to her husband.

"Will! How can ye treat this man so, and after he's done such service to your own wife and bairn!"

*For God's sake, Morag, back off!* Roger thought, seeing Buccleigh's fist clench suddenly. Buccleigh was plainly a jealous bastard to start with, and being on the losing side of the battle just past was doing his temper no good at all.

"Bugger off, Morag," said Buccleigh, echoing Roger's sentiment in less-gallant language. "This is no place for you or the bairn; take him and go."

Black-beard had recovered slightly by this time, and loomed up alongside Buccleigh. He glared down at Roger, hands pressed tenderly to his swollen nose.

"Slit his throat, I say, and good riddance." He emphasized this opinion with a kick in the ribs that curled Roger up like a shrimp.

Morag uttered a fierce cry and kicked Black-beard in the shin.

"Let him alone!"

Black-beard, taken off-guard, let out a yelp and hopped backward. Buccleigh's other companion appeared to find this more than funny, but stifled his hilarity when Buccleigh turned an awful glare on him.

Morag was on her knees, her small belt-knife in her hand, trying one-handed to cut the bonds about Roger's wrists. Much as he appreciated her intent, Roger wished she wouldn't try to help him. It was all too apparent that the original green-eyed monster had firm possession of the soul of William Buccleigh MacKenzie, and was glaring out of his eye-sockets in an emerald fury.

Buccleigh seized his wife by the arm and jerked her to her feet. The baby, startled, began to shriek.

"Leave, Morag!" Buccleigh snarled. "Go, and go now!"

"Yes, go!" Black-beard put in, glowering. "We've no need of your help, you interfering little bizzom!"

"Don't you speak to my wife that way!" Turning on his heel, Buccleigh punched Black-beard swiftly in the stomach. The man sat down hard, his mouth opening and closing in comical astonishment. Roger could almost feel a certain sympathy for Black-beard, who appeared to be faring no better between the two MacKenzies than he was himself.

Buccleigh's other friend, who had been observing the exchange with the fascination of someone watching a close tennis match, seized the opportunity to join the conversation, butting in as Morag tried to soothe her baby's crying.

"Whatever ye mean to do, Buck, best we do it and be gone." He nodded toward the creek, uneasy. There were a number of men coming in their direction, judging from the rumble of voices. Not fleeing Regulators; it was a purposeful sound. Militia, coming in search of prisoners? Roger sincerely hoped so.

"Aye." Buccleigh glanced in the direction of the noises, then turned to his wife. He took her by the shoulders, but gently.

"Go, Morag. I'd have ye safe."

She heard the note of pleading in his voice, and her face softened. Still, she looked from her husband to Roger, who was now trying mental telepathy, beaming thoughts at her in increasing desperation.

*Leave, for God's sake, woman, before you get me killed!*

Morag turned back to her husband, small jaw set in determination.

"I'll go. But you swear to me, William Buccleigh, that ye willna harm one hair of this man's head!"

Buccleigh's eyes bulged slightly, and his hands curled into fists, but Morag stood her ground, small and fierce.

"Swear it!" she said. "For by the name of Bride, I'll not share the bed of a murderer!"

Clearly torn, Buccleigh glanced from the sullen Blackbeard to his other friend, who was shuffling from one foot to the other like a man in urgent need of a privy. The party of militia was getting closer. Then he looked down into his wife's face.

"All right, Morag," he said gruffly. He gave her a small push. "Go, now!"

"No." She reached out and took her husband's hand, pulling it toward her breast. Little Jemmy had got over his alarm, and was curled into his mother's shoulder, noisily sucking his thumb. Morag placed his father's hand on the little boy's head.

"Swear on your son's head, Will, that ye'll not hurt this man nor see him killed."

Roger mentally applauded the gesture, but was afraid she'd gone too far; Buccleigh stiffened for a moment, and the blood rose in his face again. After a tense moment, though, he nodded, once.

"I swear," he said quietly, and let his hand fall. Morag's face eased, and without a word, she turned then and hurried away, the baby held close to her bosom.

Roger let out the breath he'd been holding. God, what a woman! He hoped passionately that she and her baby *would* be safe—though if her fat-headed husband chose to step in a gopher hole and break his neck . . .

William Buccleigh was looking down at him, green eyes narrowed in contemplation, ignoring the increasing agitation of his friend.

"Come on, Buck!" The man glanced over his shoulder toward the creek, where loud calls to and fro indicated searchers combing the ground. "There's no time to be lost. They did say Tryon means to hang prisoners, and I've no mind to be one!"

"Does he," Buccleigh said softly. He held Roger's eyes with his, and Roger thought for a moment that something familiar stirred in those depths. A chill of unease ran down his spine.

"He's right," he said to Buccleigh, with a jerk of the head toward the other man. "Go. I'll not speak against you—for your wife's sake."

Buccleigh pursed his lips slightly, thinking.

"No," he said at last, "I dinna think ye will. Speak against me, that is." He stooped and picked up the sodden, dirt-smeared ex-flag of truce from the ground. "Go along with ye, Johnny. See to Morag. I'll meet ye later."

"But, Buck . . . "

"Go! I'm safe enough." With a faint smile, his eyes still on Roger, Buccleigh put his hand in his pouch and drew out a small bit of dull silver metal. With a small shock, Roger recognized his own militia badge, the crudely lettered "FC" burned black in the pewter disc.

Tossing the badge lightly in his palm, Buccleigh turned to Black-beard, who was taking a suddenly renewed interest in the proceedings.

"I've a thought, sir, regarding our mutual friend." He nodded toward Roger. "If you're with me?"

Black-beard looked at Roger, back at MacKenzie, and a slow smile began to grow beneath his bulbous, reddened nose. The ripple of unease down Roger's back blossomed suddenly into a full-blown jolt of fear.

"Help!" he roared. "Help, militia! Help!" He rolled, twisting to avoid them, but Black-beard seized him by the shoulders, pulling him back. Calls came from beyond the trees, and the sound of feet, beginning to run.

"No, sir," said William Buccleigh, kneeling down in front of him. He seized Roger's jaw in a grip of iron, strangling his yells and squeezing his cheeks to force open his mouth. "I do not think you'll speak, indeed." With a slight smile, he rammed the sodden cloth down Roger's throat again, and tied the tattered neckcloth fast around it.

He stood up, then, the militia badge held tight in his hand. As the bushes opened, he turned toward them and waved an arm in hearty greeting.

# 67

# AFTERMATH

*It being now half past two O'Clock the Enemy entirely dispersed, and the Army five Miles from Camp, it was thought adviseable to lose no Time, but to return immediately to the Camp at Alamance. Empty Waggons were ordered from Camp which took both the killed and wounded of the Loyalists, and even several of the wounded Rebels, who acknowledged had they gained the day no Quarters would have been given but to such as would have turned Regulators, these were nevertheless, taken good Care of, and had their wounds dressed.*

—*"A Journal of the Expedition against the Insurgents," Wm. Tryon*

A MUSKET-BALL had shattered David Wingate's elbow. Bad luck; had it struck an inch higher, it would have broken the bone, but healed cleanly. I'd opened the joint with a semi-circular incision across the outer aspect, and dug out both the flattened ball and several bone chips, but the cartilage was badly damaged, and the biceps tendon had been sheared through completely; I could see the silvery gleam of one end, hiding deep in the dark-red meat of the muscle.

I gnawed my lower lip, considering. If I left matters as they were, the arm would be permanently—and badly—crippled. If I could reattach the severed tendon and bring the bone-ends in the joint capsule into good alignment, he might just possibly regain some use of it.

I glanced round the campsite, which now resembled an ambulance depot, littered with bodies, equipment, and blood-stained bandages. Most of the bodies were moving, thank God, if only to curse or moan. One man had been dead when his friends brought him in; he lay quiet in the shade of a tree, wrapped in his blanket.

Most of the injuries I saw had been slight, though there were two men shot through the body; I could do nothing for them but keep them warm and hope for the best. Brianna was checking them every few minutes for signs of shock and fever, in between rounds of administering honeyed water to those suffering more superficial wounds. Best she kept busy, I thought, and she did keep moving, though her face looked like one of the wild morning glories on the vine that climbed the bush behind me—white and puckered, pinched tight closed against the terrors of the day.

I had had to amputate a leg, soon after the battle ended. It was a man from Mercer's Company—camped near to us, and lacking a surgeon of their own—struck by a rebounding chunk of a mortar round that had torn off most of his foot and left the flesh of the lower leg hanging in ribbons from the shattered bone. I'd thought she would faint when the heavy limb thumped into the dirt at her feet, and she'd thought so, too, but had by some miracle stayed upright, supporting the patient—who really *had* fainted, thank the Lord for small mercies—while I cauterized the bleeding vessels and bound the stump with brutal speed.

Jamie was gone; he had brought back his men, hugged me hard and kissed me once, fiercely, then left with the Lindsays to take the prisoners to the Governor—and inquire along the way for any news of Roger.

Relief at Jamie's return buoyed my heart, but fear for Roger was a small heavy counterweight below my breast-bone. I could ignore it while I worked, though. No news was good news for a short time yet, and I welcomed the immediate realities of triage and treatment as a refuge from imagination.

Nothing else looked exigent. Men were still straggling in, but Bree looked up at each one, her heart in her eyes. If any of them needed me, she would call. All right, I decided. There was time; I'd try it. There was little to lose, bar a bit more suffering for Mr. Wingate, and I would ask if he were willing.

He was wax-pale and sweating, but still upright. He nodded his permission and I gave him the whisky bottle again; he applied it to his mouth with his sound hand as though it contained the elixir of life. I called one of the other men to hold his arm steady while I worked, and swiftly incised the skin just above the bend of the elbow in an inverted "T," exposing the lower head of the biceps and making the site more accessible. I began to probe with my longest forceps, teasing out the tough silver strand of the sheared tendon, pulling it down as far as I could, until I had a sound spot where I could pierce it with a suture, and set about the delicate work of rejoining the severed ends.

I lost touch then with everything around me, all my attention focused on the problem before me. I was dimly conscious of the *pit! pit! pit!* of drops striking the ground at my feet, but didn't know whether it was the sweat that ran down my arms and face, the patient's oozing blood, or both. I could have used the hands of a trained surgical nurse to help, but didn't have them, so made do with my own. I had a fine surgeon's needle, though, and thin boiled-silk sutures; the stitches showed small and neat, a stark black zigzag that marked a sturdy hold on the slippery, gleaming tissue. I would normally have used the cat-gut sutures for internal work like this, as those would gradually dissolve and be absorbed by the body. Tendons healed so slowly, though—if at all—that I couldn't risk that. The silk stitches would simply stay permanently in place, and I prayed would cause no problems of their own.

Then the hard part was done, and time started again. I was able to talk soothingly to David, who had come through it gallantly; he nodded and made a feeble attempt to smile when I told him it was done, though his teeth were clenched and his cheeks wet with tears. He screamed when I washed the wounds with diluted alcohol—they always did; they couldn't help it, poor things—but then sagged back, trembling, while I stitched the surgical incisions and bandaged the wounds.

That took no great skill, though; I had attention to spare now, and gradually became aware that some of the men behind me were discussing the recent battle, full of praise for Governor Tryon.

"Did you see it, then?" one was asking eagerly. "Did he really do as they said?"

"Hope I may be gutted and fried for breakfast if it ain't so," his companion replied sententiously. "Saw him with my own eyes, didn't I? He rode up within a hundred yards of the swine, and ordered 'em face-to-face to surrender. They wasn't much answer for a minute, only them kind of lookin' to and fro amongst themselves to see who might speak, and then somebody shouts out that no, damn it all, they ain't a-going to surrender nohow. So the Governor, he's a-scowlin' fit to fright a thundercloud, and he rears up and lifts his sword high, then brings it down and shouts, 'Fire on them!' "

"And did they do so straight off?"

"No, we didn't," put in another voice, more educated, and rather dry in tone. "Do you blame us? A forty-shilling bounty for joining the militia is one thing, but to fire in cold blood on folk you know is something else. I looked across and who should I see on the other side but my wife's own cousin, grinning back at me! Now, I'm not saying that the rascal is any great favorite with me or the family, but how am I to go home and tell my Sally as I've just shot her cousin Millard full of holes?"

"Better than Cousin Millard doin' the same service by

you," said the first voice, with an audible grin, and the third man laughed.

"True enough," he said. "But we didn't wait to see if it might come to that. The Governor, he went red as a turkey-cock when the men there with him hesitated. He stood up in his stirrups with his sword held on high, glared round at us all, and he hollered out, 'Fire, Goddamn you! Fire on them, or on me!'"

The narrator put a good deal of enthusiasm into this re-enactment, and there was a murmur of admiration from his hearers.

"Now there's a soldier for ye!" said one voice, followed by a general rumble of agreement.

"So we fired," said the narrator, a faint shrug in his voice. "Didn't take so long, once it started. Cousin Millard is right fast, it seems, once he's started running. Bastard got clean away."

More laughter at this, and I smiled, patting David's shoulder. He was listening, too, the conversation a welcome distraction.

"No sir," another agreed. "I reckon Tryon means to make sure of his victory this time. Heard he's gone to hang the leaders of the Regulation on the field."

"He what?" I whirled round at this, bandage still in hand. The small group of men blinked up at me, surprised.

"Yes, ma'am," said one man, with an awkward tug at the brim of his hat. "A fellow from Lillington's brigade told me so; he was off to see the fun."

"Fun," muttered another of the men, and crossed himself.

"Shame if he hangs the Quaker," another opined, face shadowed. "Old Husband's a right terror in print, but he ain't a ruffian. Nor are James Hunter or Ninian Hamilton."

"Perhaps he'll hang Cousin Millard," another suggested, nudging his neighbor with a grin. "Then you'll be rid of him and your wife can blame the Governor!"

There was a chorus of laughter at this, but the tone was subdued. I turned back to my work, concentrating fiercely to blot out the picture of what was now happening on the field of war.

War was bad enough, even when it was necessary. Cold-blooded revenge by the victor was one degree beyond. And yet from Tryon's point of view, that might be necessary, too. As battles went, this one had been both quick, and relatively minor in terms of casualty. I had only twenty or so wounded in my keeping, and had seen only one fatality. There would be more elsewhere, of course, yet from the comments of those nearby, it had been a rout, but not a slaughter, the militiamen being largely unenthusiastic about butchering their fellow citizens, cousins or not.

That meant that most of the men of the Regulation survived unharmed. I supposed that the Governor might feel that a drastic gesture was required, to seal his victory, intimidate the survivors, and stamp once and for all on the long-smoldering wick of that dangerous movement.

There was a stir, and the sound of a horse's hooves. I looked up—next to me, Bree's head jerked up, her body tense—to see Jamie returning, riding double with Murdo Lindsay. Both men slid off, and he sent Murdo away with a word to care for Gideon, then came at once to me.

I could see from the anxious look of his face that he had no word of Roger; he glanced at my face and saw the answer to his own question there. His shoulders dropped slightly in discouragement, then straightened, stiffening.

"I will go to search the field," he said to me, low-voiced. "I have sent word already, through the companies. If he is brought in anywhere, someone will bring us word."

"I'm going with you." Brianna was already taking off her grubby apron, wadding it into a ball.

Jamie glanced at her, then nodded.

"Aye, lass, of course. Just a moment, then—I'll fetch wee Josh to help your mother."

"I'll get—get the horses ready." Her movements were quick and jerky, without her usual athletic grace, and she dropped the water bottle she was holding, fumbling several times before she succeeded in retrieving it. I took it from her before she could drop it again, and squeezed her hand, hard.

The corner of her mouth trembled as she looked at me; I thought she meant it for a smile.

"He'll be all right," she said. "We'll find him."

"Yes," I said, and let go her hand. "I know you will."

I watched her hurry across the clearing, hands clenched in her raised skirts, and felt the counterweight of fear come loose, plunging like a stone into my belly.

68

## EXECUTION OF ORDERS

ROGER WOKE SLOWLY, to throbbing pain and a sense of dreadful urgency. He had no idea where he was, or how he came to be there, but there were voices, lots of voices, some talking just beyond the range of comprehension, some singing like harpies, in shrill discord. For a moment, he felt the voices were inside his head. He could see them, little brown things with leather wings and sharp teeth, banging into each other in paroxysms of interruption that set off small bombs of light behind his eyes.

He could feel the seam along which his head must surely split under the pressure, a burning streak across the top of his skull. He wanted someone to come and unzip it, to let out all the flying voices and their racket, to leave his skull an empty bowl of shining bone.

He had no real sense of opening his eyes, and stared numbly for some minutes, thinking that the scene on which he looked was still part of the confusion inside his skull. Men swarmed before him in a sea of colors, swirling blues and reds and yellows, mixed with blobs of green and brown.

A defect in his vision deprived him of perspective and caused him to see them in fragments—a distant cluster of heads floating like a bobble of hairy balloons, a waving arm that held a crimson banner, seemingly severed from its body.

Several pairs of legs that must be close by . . . was he sitting on the ground? He was. A fly droned past his ear and landed, buzzing, on his upper lip, and he moved by reflex to swat it, only then realizing that he was indeed awake—and still bound.

His hands had gone numb beyond any sense of pain, but the ache now throbbed through the straining muscles of his arms and shoulders. He shook his head to clear it, a terrible mistake. Blinding pain shot through his head, bringing water to his eyes.

He blinked hard and breathed deep, willing himself to grasp some shred of reality, to come to himself. *Focus*, he thought. *Hold on.* The singing voices had faded away, leaving only a faint ringing in his ears. The others were still talking, though, and now he knew that the sound was real, he was able to seize on a word here and there, and pin it down, flapping, to examine for meaning.

"Example."

"Governor."

"Rope."

"Piss."

"Regulators."

"Stew."

"Foot."

"Hang."

"Hillsborough."

"Water."

"Water." That one made sense. He knew water. He *wanted* water; wanted it badly. His throat was dry, his mouth felt as though it was stuffed with . . . it was stuffed with something; he gagged as his tongue moved in an unconscious attempt at swallowing.

"Governor." The repeated word, spoken just above him, made him look up. He fixed his floating vision on a face. Lean, dark, frowning with a fierce intent.

"You are sure?" the face said, and he wondered dimly, *Sure of what?* He was sure of nothing, save that he was in a bad way.

"Yessir," said another voice, and he saw another face swim into view alongside the first. This one seemed familiar, fringed with thick black beard. "I saw him in Hermon Husband's camp, palavering with Husband. You ask amongst the prisoners, sir—they'll say so."

The first head nodded. It turned to the side, and up, addressing someone taller. Roger's eyes drifted up, seeking, and he jerked upright with a muffled exclamation, as he saw the green eyes looking down on him, dispassionate.

"He's James MacQuiston," said the green-eyed man, nodding confirmation. "From Hudgin's Ferry."

"You saw him in the battle?" The first man was coming into complete focus, a soldierly-looking fellow in his late thirties, dressed in uniform. Something else was coming into focus—James MacQuiston. He'd heard of MacQuiston . . . what . . . ?

"He killed a man in my company," Green-eyes said, his voice rough with anger. "Shot him in cold blood as he lay wounded on the ground."

The Governor—that was who it must be, Governor . . . Tryon! That was the name! The Governor was nodding, the frown etched deep on his face.

"Take him, too, then," he said, and turned away. "Three are enough for now."

Hands gripped Roger's arms and jerked him upright, supporting him for a moment, then pulling him so that he stumbled, off-balance, and found himself half-walking, his weight supported by two men dressed in uniform. He pulled against them, wanting to turn and find Green-eyes—damn, what was the man's name?—but they yanked him round, compelling him to stumble toward a small rise, topped with a huge white oak.

The rise was surrounded by a sea of men, but they fell back, making way for Roger and his escorts. The sense of urgency was back, a feeling like ants beneath the surface of his brain.

*MacQuiston*, he thought, the name suddenly clear in his memory. *James MacQuiston.* MacQuiston was a minor leader of the Regulation, a rabble-rouser from Hudgin's Ferry whose fiery speech of threat and denunciation had been published in the *Gazette*; Roger had seen it.

Why in hell had Green-eyes—Buccleigh! It was

Buccleigh. His sense of relief at remembering the name was succeeded instantly by shock as he realized that Buccleigh had told them he was MacQuiston. Why—

He had not even time to form the question when the last ranks broke before him, and he saw the horses beneath the tree, the looped nooses hanging above the empty saddles from its branches.

THEY HELD THE horses by the heads, while the men were put upon them. Leaves brushed his cheek; twigs caught in his hair, and he ducked, turning his head by instinct to save his eyes being put out.

Some way across the clearing, he saw a woman's figure, half-hidden in the crowd; indistinct but with the unmistakable curve of a child in her arm, a small brown Madonna. The sight brought him upright with a jolt through chest and belly, the memory of Bree with Jemmy in her arms searing through his mind.

He threw himself to the side, back arched, felt himself slide and had no hands to save himself. Other hands caught him, pushed him back, one struck him hard across the face. He shook his head, eyes watering, and through the blur of tears saw the brown Madonna thrust her burden into someone's hands, pick up her skirts, and run as though the devil chased her.

Something dropped upon his breast with the heavy slither of a serpent. Prickly hemp touched his neck, drew tight about his throat, and he screamed behind the gag.

He struggled without thought for consequence or possibility, impelled by the desperation of the instinct to survive. Heedless of bleeding wrists and wrenching muscle, thighs clenched so hard about the horse's body that it jerked under him in protest, he strained at his bonds with a strength beyond what he had ever imagined he possessed.

Across the clearing, the child had begun to shriek for his mother. The crowd had fallen silent and the baby's cries rang loud. The dark soldier sat on his horse, arm lifted, sword upraised. He seemed to speak, but Roger heard nothing for the roar of blood in his ears.

The bones of his hands popped and a line of liquid heat ran down one arm as a muscle tore. The sword fell, a flash of sunlight from its blade. His buttocks slid back over the horse's rump, legs trailing helpless, and his weight fell free in an empty-bellied plunge.

A wrenching jerk . . .

And he was spinning, choking, fighting for air, and his fingers scrabbled, nails tearing at the rope sunk deep in his flesh. His hands had come loose, but it was too late, he couldn't feel them, couldn't manage. His fingers slipped and slid on the twisted strands, futile, numb, and unresponsive as wood.

He dangled, kicking, and heard a far-off rumble from the crowd. He kicked and bucked, feet pawing empty air, hands clawing at his throat. Chest strained, back arched, and his sight had gone black, small lightnings flickering in the corners of his eyes. He reached for God and heard no plea for mercy deep within himself but only a shriek of *no!* that echoed in his bones.

And then the stubborn impulse left him and he felt his body stretch and loosen, reaching, reaching for the earth. A cool wind embraced him and he felt the soothing warmth of his body's voidings. A brilliant light blazed up behind his eyes, and he heard nothing more but the bursting of his heart and the distant cries of an orphaned child.

**69**

# HIDEOUS EMERGENCY

JAMIE AND BREE were nearly ready to leave. Smoke-stained and weary as they were, a number of the men had offered to join the search-party, an offer that made Bree bite her lip and nod thanks. She was grateful for the offer of help, I knew—but it takes time to move a larger group, and I could see the impatience flare up in red blotches under her skin as weapons were cleaned, canteens refilled, cast-off shoes located.

"Wee Josh" had been mildly apprehensive regarding his new position as surgeon's assistant, but he was a groom, after all, and thus accustomed to tending the ills of horseflesh. The only difference, as I told him—making him grin—was that human patients could tell you where it hurt.

I had paused to wash my hands before stitching a lacerated scalp, when I became aware of some disturbance taking place at the edge of the meadow behind me. Jamie, hearing it too, turned his head—and then came swiftly back across the clearing, eyebrows raised.

"What is it?" I turned to look, and saw a young woman, evidently in a dreadful state, heading toward us at a lopsided trot. She was slight of build and limping badly—she had lost a shoe somewhere—but still half-running, supported on one side by Murdo Lindsay, who seemed to be expostulating with her even as he helped her along.

"Fraser," I heard her gasp. "Fraser!" She let go of Murdo and pushed her way through the waiting men, her eyes raking the faces as she passed, searching. Her brown hair was tangled and full of leaves, her face scratched and bloody.

"James . . . Fraser . . . I must . . . are you . . . ?" She was panting for breath, her chest heaving and her face so red it looked as though she might have an apoplexy on the spot.

Jamie stepped forward and took her by the arm.

"I'm Jamie Fraser, lass," he said. "Is it me ye want?"

She nodded, gasping, but had no breath for words. I hastily poured a cup of water and offered it to her, but she shook her head violently, instead waving her arms in agitation, gesturing wildly toward the creek.

"Rog . . . er," she got out, gulping air like a landed fish. "Roger. MacKen . . . zie." Before the final syllable left her mouth, Brianna was at the young woman's side.

"Where is he? Is he hurt?" She seized the young woman's arm, as much to compel answers as to provide support.

The girl's head bobbed up and down, shook back and forth, and she gasped out, "Hang . . . they . . . they are . . . hanging him! Gov—ner!"

Brianna let go of her and ran for the horses. Jamie was already there, untying reins with the same swift intensity he had shown when the fighting began. Without a word, he stooped, hands cupped; Brianna stepped up and swung into the saddle, kicking the horse into motion before Jamie had reached his own. Gideon caught the mare up within moments, though, and both horses disappeared into the willows, as though swallowed up.

I said something under my breath, with no consciousness of whether I'd uttered a curse or a prayer. I thrust needle and suture into Josh's startled hands, caught up the sack with my emergency kit, and ran for my own horse, leaving the brown-haired woman collapsed on the grass, vomiting from her effort.

I CAUGHT THEM UP within a few moments. We didn't know precisely where Tryon was holding his drumhead court, and valuable time was lost as Jamie was compelled to stop, time and again, and lean from his horse to ask directions—these often muddled and contradictory. Bree was gathered into herself, quivering like a nocked arrow, ready for flight, but lacking direction.

I tried to ready myself for anything, including the worst. I had no idea what preliminaries Tryon might have engaged in, or how much time might elapse between condemnation and execution. Not bloody long, I thought. I'd known Tryon long enough to see that he acted with thought, but also with dispatch—and he would know that if such things were done, 'twas best they were done quickly.

As to the why of it . . . imagination failed completely. I could only hope that the woman was wrong; that she had mistaken someone else for Roger. And yet I didn't think so; neither did Brianna, urging her horse through a boggy patch ahead with an intensity that suggested she would be better pleased to leap off the horse and drag it bodily through the mud.

The afternoon was fading, and clouds of small gnats surrounded us, but Jamie made no move to brush them away. His shoulders were set like stone, braced to bear the burden of knowledge. It was that as much as my own fears that told me Roger was likely dead.

The thought beat against me like a small, sharp hammer, the sort meant for breaking rocks. So far, I felt only brief, recurrent shocks of imagined loss, each time I glanced at Brianna's white face, thought of tiny Jemmy orphaned, heard the echo of Roger's soft, deep voice, laughing in the distance, singing through my heart. I did not try to push the hammering thoughts aside; it would do no good. And I would not truly break, I knew, until I saw his body.

Even then, the break would be internal. Brianna would need me. Jamie would stand like a rock for her, would do what must be done—but he, too, would need me, later. No one could absolve him of the guilt I knew he felt, but I could at least be confessor for him, and his intercessor with Brianna. My own mourning could wait—a long time, I hoped.

The ground opened, flattening into the edge of a wide meadow, and Jamie kicked Gideon into a gallop, the other horses streaming after him. Our shadows flew like bats across the grass, the sound of our hoofbeats lost in the sounds of a crowd of men who filled the field.

On a rise at the far end of the meadow stood a huge white oak, its spring leaves bright in the slanting sun. My horse moved suddenly, dodging past a group of men, and I saw them, three stick-figures, dangling broken in the tree's deep shadow. The hammer struck one final blow, and my heart shattered like ice.

Too late.

IT WAS A BAD HANGING. Without benefit of official troops, Tryon had had no one to hand with a hangsman's gruesome—and necessary—skills. The three condemned men had been sat on horses, the ropes round their necks thrown over tree branches above, and at the signal, the horses had been led out from under them, leaving them dangling.

Only one had been fortunate enough to die of a snapped neck. I could see the sharp angle of his head, the limpness of his limbs in their bonds. It wasn't Roger.

The others had strangled, slowly. The bodies were twisted, held by their bonds in the final postures of their struggle. One man—one body—was cut down as I rode up, and carried past me in the arms of his brother. There was not much to choose between their faces, each contorted, each darkened in its separate agony. They had used what rope was to hand; it was new, unstretched. Roger's toes trailed in the dust; he had been taller than the rest. His hands had come free; he had managed to hook the fingers of one hand beneath the rope. The fingers were nearly black, all circulation cut off. I couldn't look at his face at once. I looked at Brianna's, instead; white and utterly still, each bone and tendon set like death.

Jamie's face was the same, but where Brianna's eyes were blank with shock, Jamie's burned, holes charred black in the bone of his skull. He stood for a moment before Roger, then crossed himself, and said something very quietly in Gaelic. He drew the dirk from his side.

"I'll hold him. Cut him down, lass." Jamie handed the knife to Brianna, not looking at her, and stepping forward, took hold of the body round the middle, lifting slightly to take the strain off the rope.

Roger moaned. Jamie froze, arms wrapped tight, and his eyes flicked to me, huge with shock. It was the faintest of sounds; it was only Jamie's response that convinced me I had indeed heard it—but I had, and so had Brianna. She leapt at the rope, and sawed at it in silent frenzy, and I—stunned into temporary immobility—began to think, as fast as possible.

Maybe not; maybe it was only the sound of the body's residual air escaping with the movement—but it wasn't; I could see Jamie's face, holding him, and I knew it wasn't.

I darted forward, reaching upward as Roger's body fell, to catch and cradle the head in my hands, to steady him as Jamie lowered him to the ground. He was cold, but firm. Of course, if he were alive, he must be, but I had prepared myself for the flaccid-meat touch of dead flesh, and the shock of feeling life under my hands was considerable.

"A board," I said, breathless as though someone had just punched me in the stomach. "A plank, a door, something to put him on. We mustn't move his head; his neck may be broken."

Jamie swallowed once, hard, then jerked his head in an awkward nod, and set off, walking stiffly at first, then faster and faster, past the knots of sorrowing kin and eager gawkers, whose curious gaze was turning now in our direction.

Brianna had the dirk still in her hand. As people began to come toward us, she moved past me, and I caught a glimpse of her face. It was still white, still set—but the eyes burned now with a black light that would sear any soul so reckless as to come too near.

I had no attention to spare for interference—or anything else. I pulled the gag from his mouth but he wasn't breathing visibly; no obvious movement of the chest, no twitch of lips or nostrils. I felt vainly for a pulse in his free wrist—pointless to poke at the mass of swollen tissue in his neck—finally found an abdominal pulse, beating faintly just below the breastbone.

The noose was sunk deep in his flesh; I groped frantically in my pocket for my penknife. It was a new rope, raw hemp. The fibers were hairy, stained brown with dried blood. I registered the fact faintly, in the remote part of my mind that had time for such things while my hands were busy. New ropes stretch. A real hangsman has his own ropes, already stretched and oiled, well-tested for ease of use. The raw hemp jabbed my fingers, stabbed painfully under my nails as I clawed and pried and ripped at it.

The last strand popped and I yanked it free, heedless of laceration—that hardly mattered. I daren't risk tilting his head back; if the cervical vertebrae were fractured, I could cripple or kill him. And if he couldn't breathe, that wouldn't matter, either.

I gripped his jaw, tried to sweep my fingers through his mouth, to clear mucus and obstructions. No good, his tongue was swollen, not sticking out, but in the way. Air takes less room than fingers do, though. I pinched his nose tight, breathed two or three times, as deeply as I could, then sealed my mouth on his and blew.

Had I seen his face as he hung, I would have realized at once that he wasn't dead; his features had gone slack with loss of consciousness and his lips and eyelids were blue—but his face wasn't black with congested blood, and his eyes were closed, not bulging. He'd lost his bowels, but his spinal cord wasn't snapped, and he hadn't strangled—yet.

He was, however, in the process of doing so before my eyes. His chest wasn't moving. I took another breath, and blew, free hand on his breast. Nothing. Blow. No movement. Blow. Something. Not enough. Blow. Air leaking all around the edges of my mouth. Blow. Like blowing up a rock, not a balloon. Blow again.

Confused voices over my head, Brianna shouting, then Jamie at my elbow.

"Here's the board," he said calmly. "What must we do?"

I gasped for breath, and wiped my mouth.

"Take his hips, Bree his shoulders. Move when I tell you, not before."

We shifted him quickly, my hands holding his head like the Holy Grail. There were people all around us now, but I had no time to look or listen; I had eyes only for what must be done.

I ripped off my petticoat, rolled it and used it to brace his neck; I hadn't felt any grinding or crackling in the neck when we lifted him, but I needed all the luck I had for other things.

By stubbornness or sheer miracle, he wasn't dead. But he had hung by the neck for the best part of an hour, and the swelling of the tissues in his throat was very shortly going to accomplish what the rope itself hadn't.

I didn't know whether I had a few minutes or an hour, but the process was inevitable, and there was only one thing to do about it. No more than a few molecules of air were seeping through that mass of crushed and mangled tissue; a bit more swelling would seal it off altogether. If no air could reach his lungs by means of nose or mouth, another channel must be provided.

I turned to look for Jamie, but it was Brianna who knelt beside me. A certain amount of racket in the background indicated that Jamie was dealing with the spectators.

A cricothrotomy? Fast, and requiring no great skill, but difficult to keep open—and it might not be sufficient to relieve the obstruction. I had one hand on Roger's sternum, the soft bump of his heart secure under my fingers. Strong enough . . . maybe.

"Right," I said to Brianna, hoping I sounded quite calm. "I'll need a bit of help."

"Yes," she said—and thank God, *she* sounded calm. "What shall I do?"

In essence, nothing all that difficult; simply hold Roger's head pulled well back, and keep it steady while I slit his throat. Of course, hyperextending the neck could easily sever the spinal cord if there were a fracture, or compress it irreversibly. But Brianna needn't worry about that—or know about it, either.

She knelt by his head and did as I told her, and the mediastinum of the trachea bulged into view as the skin and fascia over it tightened. There it was, neatly lined up—I hoped—between the great vessels on either side. If it wasn't, I could easily lacerate the common carotid or the internal jugular, and he'd bleed to death right under my hands.

The only virtue to hideous emergency is that it gives one license to attempt things that could never be done in cold blood.

I fumbled for the small bottle of alcohol that I carried in my pocket. I nearly dropped it, but by the time I had poured the contents over my fingers and wiped both my scalpel and Roger's neck, the surgeon's trance had come over me, and my hands were once more steady.

I took a moment, hands on his neck, eyes closed, feeling for the faint throb of the artery, the slightly softer mass of the thyroid. I pressed upward; yes, it moved. I massaged the isthmus of the thyroid, pushing it out of the way, hard toward his head, and with my other hand, pressed the knife blade down into the fourth tracheal cartilage.

The cartilage here was U-shaped, the esophagus behind it soft and vulnerable; I must not stab too deeply. I felt the fibrous parting of skin and fascia, resistance, then the soft pop as the blade went in. There was a sudden loud gurgle, and a wet kind of whistling noise; the sound of air being sucked through blood. Roger's chest moved. I felt it, and it was only then that I realized my eyes were still shut.

# 70

# ALL IS WELL

THE BLACKNESS CRADLED HIM, comforting in its warm completeness. He felt some faint stirring of something outside it, a painful, intrusive presence, and shrank back into the shelter of the dark. It was melting away around him, though, slowly exposing parts of him to light and harshness.

He opened his eyes. He couldn't tell what he was looking at, and struggled to understand. His head throbbed and so did a dozen smaller pulses, each one a brilliant, tender burst of pain. He felt the points of pain like pins that nailed him like a butterfly to a board. If he could but pry them free, he might fly away . . .

He closed his eyes again, seeking the comfort of the darkness. He felt a dim recollection of terrible effort, his ribmuscles tearing with the struggle for air. There was water somewhere in his memory, filling his nose, wetness ballooning the hollows of his clothes . . . was he drowning? The idea sent a faint flicker of alarm through his mind. They said it was an easy death, drowning, like falling asleep. Was he sinking, falling into a treacherous and final ease, even as he sought the beguiling dark?

He jerked, flailing with his arms, trying to turn and reach the surface. Pain burst through his chest and burned in his throat; he tried to cough and could not, tried to gulp air and found none, struck something hard—

Something seized him, held him still. A face appeared above him, a blur of skin, a blaze of reddish hair. Brianna? The name floated into his mind like a bright balloon. Then his eyes focused a little, bringing a harsher, fiercer face into view. Jamie. The name hung in front of him, floating, but seeming somehow reassuring.

Pressure, warmth . . . a hand was clasping his arm, another on his shoulder, pressing hard. He blinked, his vision swimming, gradually clearing. He felt no air moving in mouth or nose, his throat was closed and his chest still burned, but he *was* breathing; he felt the soreness of the tiny muscles between his ribs as they moved. He hadn't drowned then; it hurt too much.

"You are alive," Jamie said. Blue eyes stared intently into his, so close he felt warm breath on his face. "You are alive. You are whole. All is well."

He examined the words with a sense of detachment, turning them over like a handful of pebbles, feeling the weight of them in the palm of his mind.

*You are alive. You are whole. All is well.*

A vague feeling of comfort came over him. That seemed to be all he needed to know just then. Anything else could wait. The waiting black rose up again, with the inviting aspect of a soft couch, and he sank gratefully upon it, still hearing the words like plucked harpstrings.

*You are alive. You are whole. All is well.*

# 71

# A FEEBLE SPARK

MRS. CLAIRE?"
It was Robin McGillivray hovering in the doorway of the tent, his dark wiry hair standing up on end like a bottle-brush. He looked like a harried raccoon, the skin round his eyes wiped free of sweat and soot, the rest still blackened with the smoke of battle.

At sight of him, Claire rose at once.

"Coming." She was on her feet, kit in hand and already moving toward the door before Brianna could speak.

"Mother!" It was no more than a whisper, but the tone of panic brought Claire round as though she had stepped on a turntable. The amber eyes fastened on Brianna's face for a moment, flicked to Roger, then back to her daughter.

"Watch his breathing," she said. "Keep the tube clear. Give him honey-water, if he's conscious enough to swallow a bit. And touch him. He can't turn his head to see you; he needs to know you're there."

"But—" Brianna stopped dead, her mouth too dry to speak. *Don't go!* she wanted to cry. *Don't leave me alone! I can't keep him alive, I don't know what to do!*

"They need me," Claire said, very gently. She turned, skirts whispering, to the impatiently waiting Robin, and vanished into the twilight.

"And I don't?" Brianna's lips moved, but she didn't know whether she had spoken aloud or not. It didn't matter; Claire was gone, and she was alone.

She felt light-headed, and realized that she had been holding her breath. She breathed out, and in, deeply, slowly. The fear was a poisonous snake, writhing round her spine, slithering through her mind. Ready to sink its fangs in her heart. She took one more breath through gritted teeth, seized the snake by the head, mentally stuffed it wriggling into a basket, and slammed down the lid. So much for panic, then.

Her mother would not have left, were there any immediate danger, she told herself firmly, nor if there were anything more that could be done medically. So there wasn't. Was there anything *she* could do? She breathed, deep enough to make the boning of her stays creak.

*Touch him. Speak to him. Let him know you're with him.* That was what Claire had said, speaking urgently but somehow absentmindedly, during the messy proceedings following the impromptu tracheotomy.

Brianna turned back to Roger, looking in vain for something safe to touch. His hands were swollen like inflated gloves, stained purple-red with bruising, the crushed fingers nearly black, raw rope-weals sunk so deep in the flesh of his wrists that she was queasily sure she could see white bone. They looked unreal, badly-done makeup for a horror play.

Grotesque as they were, they were better than his face. That was bruised and swollen, too, with a ghastly ruff of leeches attached beneath his jaw, but it was more subtly deformed, like some sinister stranger pretending to be Roger.

His hands were lavishly decorated with leeches, too. He must be wearing every leech available, she thought. Claire had sent Josh rushing to the other surgeons, to beg their supplies, and then sent him and the two Findlay boys splashing down the creek banks in hasty search of more.

*Watch his breathing.* That, she could do. She sat down, moving as quietly as she could, from some obscure urge not to wake him. She laid a hand lightly over his heart, so relieved to find him warm to the touch that she gave a great sigh. He grimaced slightly at the feel of her breath on his face, tensed, then relaxed again.

His own breath came so shallowly that she took her hand away, feeling that the pressure of her palm on his chest might be enough to stop its labored rise. He *was* breathing, though; she could hear the faint whistle of air through the tube in his throat. Claire had commandeered Mr. Caswell's imported English pipe, ruthlessly breaking off the amber stem. Rinsed hastily with alcohol, it was still stained with tobacco tar, but seemed to be functioning well enough.

Two fingers of Roger's right hand were broken, all his nails clawed bloody, torn, or missing. Her own throat tightened at this evidence of just how ferociously he had fought to live. His state seemed so precarious that she hesitated to touch him, as though she might startle him over some invisible edge between death and life. And yet she could see what her mother meant; the same touch might hold him back, keep him from stumbling over just such an edge, lost in the dark.

She squeezed his thigh firmly, reassured by the solid feel of the long, curving muscle under the blanket that covered his lower body. He made a small sound, tensed, and relaxed again. She wondered for a surreal moment whether to cup his genitals.

"That would let him know I'm here, all right," she murmured, swallowing a hysterical desire to laugh. His leg quivered slightly at the sound of her voice.

"Can you hear me?" she asked softly, leaning forward. "I'm here, Roger. It's me—Bree. Don't worry, you aren't alone."

Her own voice sounded strange; too loud, stiff and awkward.

*"Bi socair, mo chridhe,"* she said, and relaxed a little. *"Bi samnach, tha mi seo."*

It was easier, somehow, in Gaelic, its formality a thin dam against the intensity of feelings that might swamp her, were they ever set free. Love and fear and anger, swirled together in a mix so strong her hand trembled with it.

She realized suddenly that her breasts were turgid, aching with milk; there had been no time in the last several hours even to think of it, let alone take the time to relieve the pressure. Her nipples stung and tingled at the thought, and she gritted her teeth against the small gush of milk that leaked into her bodice, mingling with her sweat. She yearned toward Roger, wanting suddenly to suckle him, wanting to cradle him against her breast and let life flow into him from her.

*Touch him.* She was forgetting to touch him. She stroked his arm, squeezed his forearm gently, hoping to distract herself from discomfort.

He seemed to feel her hand on his arm; one eye opened a little, and she thought she saw a consciousness of her flicker in its depths.

"You look like the male version of Medusa," she said, the first thing that popped into her head. One dark eyebrow twitched slightly upward.

"The leeches," she said. She touched one of those on his neck, and it contracted sluggishly, already half-full. "A beard of snakes. Can you feel them? Do they bother you?" she asked before remembering what her mother had said. His lips moved, though, forming a soundless "no," with obvious effort.

"Don't talk." She glanced at the other bed, feeling self-conscious, but the wounded man in it was quiet, eyes closed. She turned back, bent, and quickly kissed Roger, the merest touch of lips. His mouth twitched; she thought he meant to smile.

She wanted to shout at him. *What happened? What in hell did you DO?* But he couldn't answer.

Suddenly, fury overwhelmed her. Mindful of the people passing to and fro nearby, she didn't shout, but instead leaned down and gripped his shoulder—that seeming one of the reasonably undamaged spots—and hissed, "How in God's name did you *do* this?" in his ear.

His eyes rolled slowly toward her, fixing on her face. He made a slight grimace which she couldn't interpret at all, and then the shoulder under her hand began to vibrate. She stared at him in complete perplexity for a few seconds, before she realized that he was laughing. Laughing!

The tube in his throat jiggled, and made a soft wheezing noise, which aggravated her beyond bearing. She stood up, hands pressed against her aching breasts.

"I'll be right back," she said. "Don't you bloody go anywhere, damn you!"

# 72

# TINDER AND CHAR

GERALD FORBES WAS A SUCCESSFUL lawyer, and normally looked the part. Even dressed in his campaigning gear, and with the soot of gunpowder staining his face, he still had an air of solid assurance that served him well as a captain of militia. This air had not quite deserted him, but he seemed visibly uneasy, curling and uncurling the brim of his hat as he stood in the doorway of the tent.

At first I assumed that it was merely the discomfort that afflicts many people in the presence of illness—or perhaps awkwardness over the circumstances of Roger's injury. But evidently it was something else; he barely nodded toward Brianna, who sat by Roger's bed.

"My sympathies for your misfortune, ma'am," he said, then turned at once to Jamie. "Mr. Fraser. If I might—a word? And Mrs. Fraser, too," he added, with a grave bow in my direction.

I glanced at Jamie, and at his nod, got up, reaching by reflex for my medical kit.

There was not a great deal I could do; that much was obvious. Isaiah Morton lay on his side in Forbes's tent, his face dead-white and sheened with sweat. He still breathed, but slowly, and with a horrible gurgling effect that reminded me unpleasantly of the sound when I had pierced Roger's throat. He wasn't conscious, which was a small mercy. I made a cursory examination, and sat back on my heels, wiping sweat from my face with the hem of my apron; the evening had not cooled much, and it was close and hot in the tent.

"Shot through the lung," I said, and both men nodded, though they both clearly knew as much already.

"Shot in the back," Jamie said, a grim tone to his voice. He glanced at Forbes, who nodded, not taking his eyes from the stricken man.

"No," he said quietly, answering an unspoken question. "He wasn't a coward. And it was a clean advance—no other companies in the line behind us."

"No Regulators behind you? No sharpshooters? No ambush?" Jamie asked, but Forbes was shaking his head before the questions were finished.

"We chased a few Regulators as far as the creek, but we stopped there and let them go." Forbes still held the hat between his fingers, and he mechanically rolled and unrolled the brim, over and over. "I had no stomach for killing."

Jamie nodded, silent.

I cleared my throat, and drew the bloody remnants of Morton's shirt gently over him.

"He was shot *twice* in the back," I said. The second bullet had only grazed his upper arm, but I could plainly see the direction of the furrow it had left.

Jamie closed his eyes briefly, then opened them.

"The Browns," he said, in grim resignation.

Gerald Forbes glanced at him, surprised.

"Brown? That's what he said."

"He spoke?" Jamie squatted beside the injured man, a frown drawing his ruddy brows together. He glanced at me, and I shook my head mutely. I was holding Isaiah Morton's wrist, and could feel the flutter and stumble in his pulse. He would not likely speak again.

"When they brought him in." Forbes squatted by Jamie, at last setting down the maltreated hat. "He asked for you, Fraser. And then he said, 'Tell Ally. Tell Ally Brown.' He said that several times, before he—" He gestured mutely at Morton, whose half-closed lids showed slices of white, his eyes rolled up in agony.

Jamie said something obscene, very softly, under his breath in Gaelic.

"Do you really think they did this?" I asked, equally softly. The pulse thumped and shuddered under my thumb, struggling.

He nodded, looking down at Morton.

"I shouldna have let them go," he said, as though to himself. Morton and Alicia Brown, he meant.

"You couldn't have stopped them." I reached my free hand toward him, to touch him in reassurance, but couldn't quite reach him, tethered as I was to Morton's pulse.

Gerald Forbes was looking at me in puzzlement.

"Mr. Morton . . . eloped with the daughter of a man named Brown," I explained delicately. "The Browns weren't happy about it."

"Oh, I see." Forbes nodded understandingly. He glanced down at Morton's body and clicked his tongue, a sound mingling reproof with sympathy. "The Browns—do you know which company they belong to, Fraser?"

"Mine," Jamie said shortly. "Or they did. I havena seen either of them, since the end of the battle." He turned to me. "Is there aught to do for him, Sassenach?"

I shook my head, but didn't let go of his wrist. The pulse hadn't improved, but it hadn't gotten worse, either.

"No. I thought he might be gone already, but he isn't sinking yet. The ball must not have struck a major vessel. Even so . . ." I shook my head again.

Jamie sighed deeply and nodded.

"Aye. Will ye stay with him, then, until . . . ?"

"Yes, of course. Will you go back to our tent, though, and make sure everything's under control there? If Roger—I mean, come and fetch me if I'm needed."

He nodded once more and left. Gerald Forbes came near, and put a tentative hand on Morton's shoulder.

"His wife—I shall see that she has help. If he should come round again, will you tell him that?"

"Yes, of course," I said again, but my hesitation made him look up, brows raised.

"It's just that he . . . um . . . has *two* wives," I explained. "He was already married when he eloped with Alicia Brown. Hence the difficulty with her family, you see."

Forbes's face went comically blank.

"I see," he said, and blinked. "The . . . ah . . . first Mrs. Morton. Do you know her name?"

"No, I'm afraid I—"

"Jessie."

The word was barely more than a whisper, but it might have been a gunshot, for its effect in stopping the conversation.

"What?" My grip on Morton's wrist must have tightened, for he flinched slightly, and I loosened it.

His face was still dead white, but his eyes were open, fogged with pain but definitely conscious.

"Jessie . . ." he whispered again. "Jeze . . . bel. Jessie Hatfield. Water?"

"Wat—oh, yes!" I let go of his wrist and reached at once for the water jug. He would have glugged it, but I let him have only small sips, for the present.

"Jezebel Hatfield, and Alicia Brown," Forbes said carefully, evidently noting the names in his neatly-docketed lawyer's mind. "That is correct? And where do these women live?"

Morton took a breath, coughed, and interrupted the cough abruptly with a gasp of pain. He struggled for a moment, then found speech.

"Jessie—in Granite Falls. Ally's—in Guildford." He breathed very shallowly, gasping between words. And yet I heard no gurgling of blood in his throat, saw none oozing from nose or mouth. I could still hear the sucking sound from the wound in his back, and moved by inspiration, I pulled him slightly forward and jerked back the pieces of his shirt.

"Mr. Forbes, have you a sheet of paper?"

"Why . . . yes. I . . . that is . . ." Forbes had thrust his hand into his coat in automatic response, and come out with a folded sheet of paper. I snatched this from him, unfolded it, poured water over it, and plastered it flat against the small hole beneath Morton's shoulder blade. The ink mixed with blood and ran in little dark runnels over the pasty skin, but the sucking noise abruptly stopped.

Holding the paper in place with my hand, I could feel the

beating of his heart. It was still faint, but steadier—yes, it was steadier.

"I'll be damned," I said, leaning to the side to look at his face. "You aren't going to die, are you?"

Sweat poured from his face, and the rags of his shirt hung dark and sodden against his chest, but the edge of his mouth trembled in an attempt at a smile.

"No, ma'am," he said. "I ain't." He was still breathing in short gasps, but the breaths were deeper. "Ally. Baby's . . . next . . . month. Told her . . . I be there."

I picked up the edge of the blanket with my free hand, and wiped some of the sweat from his face.

"We'll do our best to see that you are," I assured him, then glanced up at the lawyer, who had been watching these proceedings with his mouth hanging slightly open.

"Mr. Forbes. I think perhaps we had better take Mr. Morton back to my tent. Will you find a couple of men to carry him?"

He closed his mouth abruptly.

"Oh. Yes. Of course, Mrs. Fraser. At once." He didn't move right away, though, and I saw his eyes dart toward the wet sheet of paper plastered over Morton's back. I glanced down at it. I could read only a few indistinct words between my fingers, but those were enough to tell me that Jamie's casually insulting references to Forbes as a sodomite were likely inaccurate. "My darling Valencia," the letter began. I knew only one woman named Valencia in the vicinity of Cross Creek—in the colony of North Carolina, for that matter. Farquard Campbell's wife.

"I'm terribly sorry about your paper," I said, looking up at Forbes. Holding his gaze with my own, I carefully rubbed the palm of my hand over the sheet of paper, irrevocably smearing every word on it into a mess of blood and ink. "I'm afraid it's quite ruined."

He took a deep breath, and clapped his hat back on his head.

"That is quite all right, Mrs. Fraser. Perfectly all right. I'll—go and fetch some men."

EVENING BROUGHT RELIEF from the flies, as well as the heat. Drawn by sweat, blood, and manure, they swarmed over the encampment, biting, stinging, crawling, and buzzing in maddening fashion. Even after they had gone, I kept slapping absentmindedly at arms and neck, imagining I felt the tickle of feet.

But they were gone, at last. I glanced round my small kingdom, saw that everyone was breathing—if with an astounding variety of sound effects—and ducked out of the tent for a breath of cool air, myself.

A highly undervalued activity, breathing. I stood for a moment, eyes closed, appreciating the easy rise and fall of my bosom, the soft inrush, the cleansing flux. Having spent the last several hours in keeping air out of Isaiah Morton's chest, and getting it into Roger's, I was inclined to cherish the privilege. Neither of them would draw a single breath without pain for some time—but they *were* both breathing.

They were my only remaining patients; the other seriously wounded had all been claimed by the surgeons of their own companies, or taken to the Governor's tent to be tended by his personal physician. Those with minor injuries had gone back to their fellows, to boast of their scars or nurse their pains with beer.

I heard a ruffle of drums in the distance, and stood still, listening. A solemn cadence played, and stopped abruptly. There was a moment's silence, in which all motion seemed suspended, and then the boom of a cannon.

The Lindsay brothers were nearby, sprawled on the ground by their fire. They too had looked up at the sound of drums.

"What is it?" I called to them. "What's happening?"

"They're bringin' up the dead, Mrs. Fraser," Evan called back. "Ye'll no be worrit, aye?"

I waved to them in reassurance, and began to walk toward the creek. The frogs were singing, a descant to the distant drums. Full military honors for the battle dead. I wondered whether the two hanged ringleaders would be buried in the same place, or whether some separate and less honorable grave would be set aside for them, if their families didn't claim them. Tryon wasn't the sort to leave even an enemy to the flies.

He would know by now, surely. Would he come, to apologize for his mistake? What apology was possible, after all? It was only by the fluke of fortune and a new rope that Roger was alive.

And he might still die.

When I set my hand on Isaiah Morton, I could feel the burning of the bullet lodged in his lung—but I could feel the stronger burning of his ferocious will to live in spite of it, too. When I set my hand on Roger, I felt that same burning . . . but it was a feeble spark. I listened to the whistle of his breath and in my mind I saw charred wood, with a tiny patch of white-hot ember still alight, but trembling on the verge of abrupt extinction.

*Tinder*, I thought, absurdly. That's what you did with a fire that threatened to go out. You blew on the spark—but then there must be char; something for the spark to catch, to feed on and grow.

A creaking of wagon wheels made me look up from my contemplation of a patch of reeds. It was a small wagon, with a single horse, and a single driver.

"Mrs. Fraser? Is that you?"

It took a moment for me to recognize the voice.

"Mr. MacLennan?" I asked, astonished.

He pulled up alongside me, and touched a hand to his hat. By starlight, his face was dim and grave in its shadow.

"What are you doing here?" I asked, drawing close and lowering my voice, though there was no one anywhere near to hear me.

"I came to find Joe," he replied, with a slight motion of his head toward the wagonbed. It should have been no great shock; I had been seeing death and destruction all day, and I was no more than slightly acquainted with Joe Hobson. I hadn't known he was dead, though, and the hairs rippled on my forearms.

Without speaking further, I went round to the back of the wagon. I felt the small jerk and vibration through the wood as Abel put on the wagon-brake, and got down to join me.

The body wasn't shrouded, though someone had laid a large half-clean kerchief over the face. Three huge black flies rested on it, still and bloated. It made no difference, but I dashed them away with the back of my hand. They drifted up buzzing, and settled again, out of my reach.

"Were you in the fighting?" I asked, not looking at Abel MacLennan. He must have been with the Regulators, but there was no smell of gunpowder on him.

"No," he said softly behind my shoulder. "I'd no wish to fight. I came wi' Joe Hobson, Mr. Hamilton, and the others—but when it looked as though there would be fighting, I came awa'. I walked away, as far as the mill on the other side of the town. And then, when the sun went down, and no sign of Joe . . . I came back," he finished simply.

"What now?" I asked. We both spoke softly, as though we might disturb the dead man's slumber. "Shall we give you help to bury him? My husband—"

"Och, no," he interrupted, still softly. "I'll be takin' him home, Mrs. Fraser. Though I thank ye for the kindness. If ye might spare a bit o' water, though, or food for the way . . ."

"Of course. Wait here—I'll get it."

I hurried back toward our tent, thinking as I went of the distance to Drunkard's Spring from Alamance. Four days, five, six? And the sun so hot, and the flies . . . but I knew the sound of a Scot whose mind was made up, and went without argument.

I took a moment to check the two men; both breathing. Noisily, painfully—but breathing. I had replaced the wet paper on Morton's wound with a bit of oiled linen, stuck down round the edges with honey, which made an excellent seal. No leakage; very good.

Brianna still sat by Roger. She had found a wooden comb, and was combing out his tumbled hair, gently removing burs and twigs, working at the tangles, slowly and patiently. She was singing something under her breath—*"Frère Jacques."* The bodice of her dress showed wet circles. She had gone out once or twice during the day to relieve the growing pressure of milk, but obviously it was time again. The sight made my own breasts ache with remembered strain.

She looked up and I caught her eye. I touched my breast briefly and nodded toward the tent-flap, eyebrow raised. She gave me a nod and a tiny smile, meant to be bravely reassuring, but I could see the bleakness in her eyes. I supposed it had occurred to her that while Roger might live, he would likely never sing—or perhaps even talk—again.

I couldn't speak past the lump in my own throat; only nodded to her and hurried out again, the parcel under my arm.

A figure stepped out of the darkness in front of me, and I nearly ran bang into it. I stopped short with an exclamation, clutching the parcel to my chest.

"My apologies, Mrs. Fraser. I did not realize that you didn't see me." It was the Governor. He took another step, into the glow of light from the tent.

He was alone, and looked very tired, the flesh of his face furrowed and loose. He smelt of drink; his Council and the militia officers would have been toasting his victory, I supposed. His eyes were clear, though, and his step firm.

"Your son-in-law," he said, and glanced toward the tent behind me. "Is he—"

"He is alive," said a soft, deep voice behind the Governor. He whirled round with a smothered exclamation, and my head jerked up.

I saw a shadow move and take shape, and Jamie rose up slowly out of the night; he had been sitting at the base of a hickory tree, invisible in the dark. How long had he been there? I wondered.

"Mr. Fraser." The Governor had been startled, but he firmed his jaw, hands folded into fists at his sides. He was obliged to tilt his head back to look up at Jamie, and I could see that he didn't like it. Jamie could see it, too, and plainly didn't care. He stood close to Tryon, looming over him, with an expression on his face that would have rattled most people.

It appeared to rattle Tryon, too, but he lifted his chin, determined to say whatever he had come to say.

"I have come to make my apologies for the injury done to your son-in-law," he said. "It was a most regrettable error."

"Most regrettable," Jamie repeated, with an ironic intonation. "And would ye care to say, sir, how this . . . error . . . came about?" He took a step forward, and Tryon automatically took a step back. I could see the heat rise in the Governor's face, and his jaw clench.

"It was a mistake," he said, through his teeth. "He was wrongly identified as one of the outlawed ringleaders of the Regulation."

"By whom?" Jamie's voice was polite.

Small hectic spots burned in the Governor's cheeks.

"I do not know. By several people. I had no reason to doubt the identification."

"Indeed. And did Roger MacKenzie say nothing in his own defense? Did he not say who he was?"

Tryon's lower teeth fastened briefly in the flesh of his upper lip, then let go.

"He . . . did not."

"Because he was bloody bound and gagged!" I said. I had pulled the gag from his mouth myself, when Jamie had cut him down from the hanging tree. "You didn't *let* him speak, did you, you—you—"

The lamplight from the tent-flap gleamed off Tryon's gorget, a crescent of silver that hung round his throat. Jamie's hand rose slowly—so slowly that Tryon plainly perceived no threat—and very gently fitted itself around the Governor's throat, just above the gorget.

"Leave us, Claire," he said. There was no particular threat in his voice; he sounded merely matter-of-fact. A flash of panic lit Tryon's eyes, and he jerked backward, gorget flashing in the light.

"You dare to lay hands on me, sir!" The panic subsided at once, replaced by fury.

"Oh, I do, aye. As ye laid hands on my son."

I didn't *think* Jamie actually intended to harm the Governor. On the other hand, this was by no means merely an act of intimidation; I could feel the core of cold rage inside him, and see it like an ice-burn in his eyes. So could Tryon.

"It was a mistake! And one I have come to rectify, so far as I may!" Tryon was standing his ground, jaw tight as he glared upward.

Jamie made a sound of contempt, low in his throat.

"A mistake. And is the loss of an innocent man's life no more than that to ye? You will kill and maim, for the sake of your glory, and pay no heed to the destruction ye leave—save only that the record of your exploits may be enlarged. How will it look in the dispatches ye send to England—sir? That ye brought cannon to bear on your own citizens, armed with no more than knives and clubs? Or will it say that ye put down rebellion and preserved order? Will it say that in your haste to vengeance, ye hanged an innocent man? Will it say there that ye made 'a mistake'? Or will it say that ye punished wickedness, and did justice in the King's name?"

Tryon's jaw muscles bulged, and his limbs trembled, but he kept his temper in check. He breathed deeply through his nose, in and out, before he spoke.

"Mr. Fraser. I will tell you something that is known to a few, but is not yet public knowledge."

Jamie didn't reply, but raised one brow, glinting red in the light. His eyes were cold, dark and unblinking.

"I am made Governor of the colony of New York," Tryon said. "The letter of appointment arrived more than a month past. I shall leave by July to take up the new appointment; Josiah Martin is made Governor here in my room." He glanced from Jamie to me, and back. "So you see. I had no personal stake in this; no need to glorify my exploits, as you put it." His throat moved as he swallowed, but fear had been replaced now by a coldness equal to Jamie's own.

"I have done what I have done as a matter of duty. I would not leave this colony in a state of disorder and rebellion, for my successor to deal with—though I might rightfully have done so."

He took a deep breath, and stepped back, forcing his hands to relax from the fists into which they had been clenched.

"You have experience of war, Mr. Fraser, and of duty. And if you are an honest man, you will know that mistakes are made—and made often—in both realms. It cannot be otherwise."

He met Jamie's eyes straight on, and they stood in silence, looking at each other.

My attention was jerked away from this confrontation quite suddenly, by the distant sound of a baby crying. I turned, head up, just as Brianna emerged from the tent-flap behind me, in a rustle of agitated skirts.

"Jem," she said. "That's Jemmy!"

It was, too. A disturbance of voices at the far side of the camp came closer, resolving itself into the round, flounced shape of Phoebe Sherston, looking frightened but determined, followed by two slaves: a man carrying two huge baskets, and a woman, with a wrapped and squirming bundle in her arms that was making a terrible racket.

Brianna made for the bundle like a compass needle swinging north, and the racket ceased as Jemmy emerged from his blankets, hair sticking up in red tufts and feet churning in paroxysms of joyous relief. Mother and child disappeared promptly into the shadows under the trees, and a certain amount of confusion ensued, with Mrs. Sherston explaining disjointedly to a gathering crowd of interested onlookers that she had just become *so* distraught, hearing reports of the battle, so terrible, and she feared . . . but Mr. Rutherford's slave had come to say all was well . . . and she thought perhaps . . . and so . . . and the child would *not* give over shrieking . . . so . . .

Jamie and the Governor, shaken out of their nose to nose confrontation, had also retired to the shadows; I could see them, two stiff shadows, one tall and one shorter, standing close together. The element of danger had gone out of their *tête-à-tête*, though; I could see Jamie's head bent slightly toward Tryon's shadow, listening.

". . . brought food," Phoebe Sherston was telling me, her round face pink with excited self-importance. "Fresh bread, and butter, and some blackberry jam and cold chicken and . . ."

"Food!" I said, abruptly reminded of the parcel I held under my arm. "Do pardon me!" I gave her a quick, bright smile, and ducked away, leaving her open-mouthed in front of the tent.

Abel MacLennan was where I had left him, waiting patiently under the stars. He brushed aside my apologies, thanking me for the food and jug of beer.

"Is there anything—?" I began, then broke off. What else could I possibly do for him?

And yet it seemed there was something.

"Young Hugh Fowles," he said, tidily tucking the parcel beneath the wagon's seat. "They said he was taken prisoner.

Would—would your husband maybe speak for him, d'ye think? As he did for me?"

"I expect he would. I'll ask him."

It was quiet here, far enough from the camp that the sounds of conversation didn't carry above the song of frogs and crickets, and the rushing of the creek.

"Mr. MacLennan," I said, moved by impulse, "where will you go? After you've taken Joe Hobson back, I mean."

He took off his hat and scratched his balding head, quite unself-consciously, though the gesture was not one of puzzlement, but merely of one preparing to state something already settled in his mind.

"Och," he said. "I dinna mean to go anywhere. There are the women there, aye? And the weans. They've no man, with Joe dead and Hugh prisoner. I shall stay."

He bowed to me then, and put on his hat. I shook his hand—surprising him—and then he climbed aboard his wagon and clicked his tongue to the horse. He lifted his hand to me in farewell, and I waved back, realizing the difference in him as I did so.

There was still grief in his voice, and sorrow on his shoulders; and yet he sat upright on his errand, the starlight shining on his dusty hat. His voice was firm, and his hand likewise. If Joe Hobson had left for the land of the dead, Abel MacLennan had come back from there.

Things had settled somewhat by the time I came back to the tent. The Governor and Mrs. Sherston were gone, with her slaves. Isaiah Morton slept, moaning now and then, but without fever. Roger lay still as a tomb-figure, face and hands black with bruises, the faint whistle of his breathing tube a counterpoint to Brianna's murmured song as she rocked Jemmy.

The little boy's face was slack, mouth pinkly open in the utter abandonment of sleep. With sudden inspiration, I held out my arms, and Bree, looking surprised, let me take him. Very carefully, I laid the limp, heavy little body on Roger's chest. Bree made a small movement, as though to catch the baby and stop him sliding off—but Roger's arm moved up, stiff and slow, and folded across the sleeping child. *Tinder*, I thought, satisfied.

Jamie was outside the tent, leaning against the hickory tree. When I had made sure of things inside, I came out to join him in the shadows. He raised his arms without speaking, and I came inside them.

We stood together in the shadows, listening to the crackle of campfires and the crickets' songs.

Breathing.

*Great Alamance Camp*
*Friday 17th May 1771*
*Parole - Granville*
*Countersign - Oxford*

*The Governor impressed with the most affectionate sense of Gratitude gives Thanks to both Officers and Soldiers of the Army for the Vigorous and Generous support they afforded Him Yesterday in the Battle near Alamance, it was to their Valour and steady Conduct that he owed under the Providence of Almighty God, the signal Victory obtained over obstinate and infatuated Rebels,—His Excellency simpathises with the Loyalists for the brave Men that fell and suffered in the Action, but when he reflects that the fate of Constitution depended on the success of the Day, and the important Services thereby rendered to their King and Country, He considers this Loss (though at present the Cause of Affliction to their Relations and Friends) as a Monument of lasting Glory and Honor to themselves and Families.*

*The Dead to be interred at five OClock this Evening in the Front of the Park of Artillery, Funeral Service to be performed with Military Honors to the deceased—after the Ceremony, Prayers and Thanksgiving for the signal Victory it has pleased Divine Providence Yesterday to Grant the Army over the Insurgents.*

# PART SEVEN

*Alarms of Struggle and Flight*

# 73

# A WHITER SHADE OF PALE

**M**RS. SHERSTON, with an unexpected generosity, offered us her hospitality. I moved to the Sherstons' large house in Hillsborough with Brianna, Jemmy, and my two patients; Jamie divided his time between Hillsborough and the militia camp, which remained in place at Alamance Creek while Tryon satisfied himself that the Regulation had indeed been decisively crushed.

While I couldn't reach the bullet lodged in Morton's lung with my forceps, it didn't appear to be troubling him greatly, and the wound had begun to seal itself in a satisfactory fashion. There was no telling exactly where the bullet was, but plainly it hadn't pierced any major vessels; as long as it didn't move further, it was quite possible for him simply to live with the bullet embedded in his body; I had known a good many war veterans who had—Archie Hayes among them.

I was not at all sure how stable my small stock of penicillin might prove to be, but it seemed to work; there was a little redness and seepage at the wound site, but no infection, and very little fever. Beyond penicillin, the appearance a few days after the battle of Alicia Brown, now enormously pregnant, was the most important boost to Morton's recovery. Within an hour of her arrival, he was sitting up in his cot, pale but jubilant, hair sticking up on end and his hand lovingly pressed against the writhing bulges of his unborn child.

Roger was another matter. He was not badly injured, beyond the crushing of his throat—though that was bad enough. The fractures to his fingers were simple; I had set them with splints and they should heal with no trouble. The bruising faded fairly quickly from livid reds and blues into a spectacular array of purple, green, and yellow that made him look as though he had just been exhumed after having been dead for a week or so. His vital signs were excellent. His vitality was not.

He slept a great deal, which should have been good. His slumber wasn't restful, though; it had about it something unsettling, as though he sought unconsciousness with a fierce desire, and once achieved, clung to it with a stubbornness that bothered me more than I wanted to admit.

Brianna, who possessed her own brand of stubbornness, had the job of forcing him back to wakefulness every few hours, to take some nourishment and have the tube and its incision cleansed and tended. During these procedures, he would fix his eyes on the middle distance, and stare darkly at nothing, making the barest acknowledgment of remarks addressed to him. Once finished, his eyes would close again, and he would lie back on his pillow, bandaged hands folded across his chest like a tomb-figure, with no sound save the soft, breathy whistle from the tube in his neck.

Two days after the battle of Alamance, Jamie arrived at the Sherstons' house in Hillsborough just before supper, tired from long riding, and covered with reddish dust.

"I had a wee talk wi' the Governor today," he said, taking the cup of water I had brought out to him in the yard. He drained it in a gulp and sighed, wiping sweat from his face with a coat-sleeve. "He was fashed about wi' all the to-do, and of no mind to think about what happened after the battle—but *I* was of no mind to let it be."

"I don't imagine it was much of a contest," I murmured, helping him to peel off the dusty coat. "William Tryon's not even Scots, let alone a Fraser."

That got me a reluctant half-smile. "Stubborn as rocks," was the succinct description of the Fraser clan I had been given years before—and nothing in the intervening time period had given me cause to think it inaccurate in any way.

"Aye, well." He shrugged and stretched luxuriously, his vertebrae cracking from the long ride. "Oh, Christ. I'm starved; is there food?" He relaxed and lifted his long nose, sniffing the air hopefully.

"Baked ham and sweet potato pie," I told him, unnecessarily, since the honey-soaked fragrances of both were thick on the humid air. "So what did the Governor say, once you'd got him properly browbeaten?"

His teeth showed briefly at that description of his interview with Tryon, but I gathered from his faint air of satisfaction that it wasn't totally incorrect.

"Oh, a number of things. But to begin with, I insisted he recall to me the circumstances when Roger Mac was taken; who gave him up, and what was said. I mean to get to the bottom of it." He pulled the thong from his hair and shook out the damp locks, dark with sweat.

"Did he remember anything when you pressed him?"

"Aye, a bit more. Tryon says there were three men who had Roger Mac captive; one of them had a badge for Fraser's Company, so of course he thought the man was one of mine. He says," he added, with irony.

That would have been a reasonable assumption for the Governor to make, I thought—but Jamie was plainly in no mood to be reasonable.

"It must have been Roger's badge that the man had," I said. "The rest of your company came back with you—all except the Browns, and it wouldn't have been them." The two Browns had vanished, seizing the opportunity of the confusion of battle to take their vengeance on Isaiah Morton and then to escape before anyone discovered the crime. They wouldn't have hung about to frame Roger, even had they some motive for doing so.

He nodded, dismissing the conclusion with a brief gesture.

"Aye. But why? He said Roger Mac was bound and gagged—a dishonorable way to treat a prisoner of war, as I said to him."

"And what did he say to that?" Tryon might be slightly less stubborn than Jamie; he wasn't any more amenable to insult.

"He said it wasna war; it was treasonable insurrection,

and he was justified in taking summary measures. But to seize and hang a man, without allowing him to speak a word in his own behalf—" The color was rising dangerously in his face. "I swear to ye, Claire, if Roger Mac had died at the end of yon rope, I would have snapped Tryon's neck and left him for the crows!"

I hadn't the slightest doubt that he meant it; I could still see his hand, fitting itself so slowly, so gently, about the Governor's neck above the silver gorget. I wondered whether William Tryon had had the slightest notion of the danger in which he had stood, that night after the battle.

"He didn't die, and he isn't going to." I hoped I was right, but spoke as firmly as I could, laying a hand on his arm. The muscles in his forearm bulged and shifted with the restrained desire to hit someone, but stilled under my touch, as he looked down at me. He took a deep breath, then another, drummed his stiff fingers twice against his thigh, then got his anger under control once more.

"Well, so. He said the man identified Roger Mac as James MacQuiston, one of the ring-leaders of the Regulation. I have been asking after MacQuiston," he added, with another glance at me. He was growing slightly calmer, talking. "Would it surprise ye, Sassenach, to discover that no one kens MacQuiston, by his face?"

It would, and I said so. He nodded, the high color receding slightly from his cheeks.

"So it did me. But it's so; the man's words are there in the papers for all to see—but no one has ever seen the man. Not auld Ninian, not Hermon Husband—no one of the Regulators that I could find to speak to—though the most of them are lying low, to be sure," he added.

"I even found the printer who set one of MacQuiston's speeches in type; he said the script of it was left upon his doorstep one morning, with a brick of cheese and two certificates of proclamation money to pay for the printing."

"Well, that *is* interesting," I said. I took my hand gingerly off his arm, but he seemed under control now. "So you think 'James MacQuiston' is likely an assumed name."

"Verra likely indeed."

Pursuing the implications of that line of thought, I had a sudden idea.

"Do you think that perhaps the man who identified Roger to the Governor as MacQuiston might have been MacQuiston himself?"

Jamie's brows went up, and he nodded slowly.

"And he sought to shield himself, by having Roger Mac hanged in his place? Being dead is an excellent protection against arrest. Aye, that's a bonnie idea—if a trifle vicious," he added judiciously.

"Oh, just a trifle."

He seemed less angry with the vicious and fictitious Mac-Quiston than with the Governor—but then, there was no doubt as to what Tryon had done.

We had moved across the yard to the well. There was a half-filled bucket sitting on the coping, warm and brackish from the day's heat. He rolled up his sleeves, cupped his hands, and dashed water from the bucket up into his face, then shook his head violently, spattering droplets into Mrs. Sherston's hydrangeas.

"Did the Governor recall what any of these men who had Roger looked like?" I asked, handing him a crumpled linen towel from the well-coping. He took it and wiped his face, shaking his head.

"Only the one. The one who had the badge, who did most of the talking. He said it was a fair-haired fellow, verra tall and well set up. Green-eyed, he thought. Tryon wasna taking careful note of his appearance, of course, bein' exercised in his mind at the time. But he recalled that much."

"Jesus H. Roosevelt Christ," I said, struck by a thought. "Tall, fair-haired, and green-eyed. Do you think it could have been Stephen Bonnet?"

His eyes opened wide and he stared at me over the towel for a moment, face blank with astonishment.

"Jesus," he said, and set the towel down absentmindedly. "I never thought of such a thing."

Neither had I. What I knew of Bonnet didn't seem to fit the picture of a Regulator; most of them were poor and desperate men, like Joe Hobson, Hugh Fowles, and Abel

MacLennan. A few were outraged idealists, like Husband and Hamilton. Stephen Bonnet might occasionally have been poor and desperate—but I was reasonably sure that the notion of seeking redress from the government by protest wasn't one that would have occurred to him. Take it by force, certainly. Kill a judge or sheriff in vengeance for some offense, quite possibly. But—no, it was ridiculous. If I was certain of anything regarding Stephen Bonnet, it was that he didn't pay taxes.

"No." Jamie shook his head, having evidently come to the same conclusions. He wiped a lingering droplet off the end of his nose. "There's nay money anywhere in this affair. Even Tryon had to appeal to the Earl of Hillsborough for funds to pay his militia. And the Regulators—" He waved a hand, dismissing the thought of the Regulators paying anyone for anything. "I dinna ken everything about Stephen Bonnet, but from what I've seen of the man, I think that only gold or the promise of it would bring him to a battlefield."

"True." The clink of china and chime of silver came faintly through the open window, accompanying the soft voices of slaves; the table was being set for dinner. "I don't suppose there's any way Bonnet could be James MacQuiston, is there?"

He laughed at that, his face relaxing for the first time.

"No, Sassenach. That I *can* be sure of. Stephen Bonnet canna read, nor write much more than his name."

I stared at him.

"How do you know that?"

"Samuel Cornell told me so. He hasna met Bonnet himself, but he said that Walter Priestly came to him once, to borrow money urgently. He was surprised, for Priestly's a wealthy man—but Priestly told him that he had a shipment coming that must be paid for in gold—for the man bringing it would not take warehouse receipts, proclamation money, or even bank-drafts. He didna trust words on paper that he couldna read himself, nor would he trust anyone to read them to him. Only gold would do."

"Yes, that does sound like Bonnet." I had been holding his coat, folded over one arm. Now I shook it out, and began to beat the red dust from its skirts, averting my face from the resultant clouds. "What you said about gold . . . do you think Bonnet could have been at Alamance by accident? On his way to River Run, perhaps?"

He considered that one for a moment, but then shook his head, rolling down the cuffs of his shirt.

"It wasna a great war, Sassenach—not the sort of thing where a man might be caught up unawares and carried along. The armies faced each other for more than two days, and the sentry lines had holes like a fishing seine; anyone could have left Alamance, or ridden round it. And Alamance is nowhere near River Run. No, whoever it was that tried to kill wee Roger, it was someone who was there on his own account."

"So we're back to the mysterious Mr. MacQuiston—whoever he might be."

"Perhaps," he said dubiously.

"But who else could it be?" I protested. "Surely no one among the Regulators could have had anything personal against Roger!"

"Ye wouldna think so," Jamie admitted. "But we're no going to know until the lad can tell us, aye?"

AFTER SUPPER—during which there was naturally no mention of MacQuiston, Stephen Bonnet, or anything else of an upsetting nature—I went up to check on Roger. Jamie came with me, and quietly dismissed the slave woman who sat by the window, mending. Someone had to stay with Roger at all times, to make sure the tube in his throat didn't become clogged or dislodged, as it was still his only means of breathing. It would be several days yet before the swelling of the mangled tissues in his throat subsided enough for me to risk removing it.

Jamie waited until I had checked Roger's pulse and breathing, then at my nod, sat down by his bedside.

"Do ye ken the names of the men who denounced ye?" he asked without preliminaries. Roger looked up at him, frowning, dark brows drawn together. Then he nodded slowly, and held up one finger.

"One of them. How many were there?"

Three fingers. That agreed with Tryon's recollection, then. "They were Regulators?"

A nod.

Jamie glanced at me, then back at Roger.

"It wasna Stephen Bonnet?"

Roger sat up bolt upright, mouth open. He clutched at the tube in his throat, struggling vainly to speak, and shaking his head violently.

I grabbed for his shoulder, one hand reaching for the tube; the violence of his movement had jerked it nearly out of the incision, and a trickle of blood ran down his neck where the wound had reopened. Roger himself seemed oblivious; his eyes were fixed on Jamie's and his mouth was working urgently, asking silent questions.

"No, no. If ye didna see him, then he wasna there." Jamie took him firmly by the other shoulder, helping me to ease him back on the pillow. "It was only that Tryon described the man who betrayed ye as a tall, fair-haired fellow. Green-eyed, maybe. We thought perhaps . . ."

Roger's face relaxed at that. He shook his head again and sank back, mouth twisted a little. Jamie pressed on.

"Ye kent the man, though; ye'd met him before?" Roger glanced away, nodded, then shrugged. He looked both irritated and helpless; I could hear his breathing quicken, whistling through the amber tube. I cleared my throat significantly, frowning at Jamie. Roger was out of immediate danger; that didn't mean he was well, or anywhere near it.

Jamie ignored me. He'd picked up Bree's sketching-box on his way upstairs; laying a sheet of paper on it, he put it on Roger's lap, then extended one of the sticks of hardened charcoal to him.

"Will ye try again?" He had been trying to get Roger to communicate on paper ever since he had regained full consciousness, but Roger's hands had been too swollen even to close around a pen. They were still puffed and bruised, but repeated leeching and gentle massage had improved them to the point that they did at least *look* vaguely like hands again.

Roger's lips pressed together momentarily, but he wrapped his hand clumsily around the charcoal. The first two fingers on that hand were broken; the splints stuck out in a crude "V" sign—which I thought rather appropriate, under the circumstances.

Roger frowned in concentration, and began to scrawl something slowly. Jamie watched intently, holding the paper flat with both hands to keep it from sliding.

The stick of charcoal snapped in two, the fragments flying off across the floor. I went to pick them up, while Jamie leaned frowning over the smeared sheet of paper. There was a sprawling "W" and an "M," then a space, and an awkward "MAC."

"William?" He looked up at Roger for verification. Sweat shone on Roger's cheekbones, but he nodded, very briefly.

"William Mac," I said, peering over Jamie's shoulder. "A Scotsman, then—or a Scottish name, at least?" Not that that narrowed down the possibilities a great deal: MacLeod, MacPherson, MacDonald, MacDonnel, Mac . . . Quiston?

Roger raised his hand and thumped it against his chest. He thumped it again, and mouthed a word. Recalling television shows based on charades, I was for once quicker than Jamie.

"MacKenzie?" I asked, and was rewarded with a quick flash of green eyes, and a nod.

"MacKenzie. William MacKenzie." Jamie was frowning, obviously running through his mental roster of names and faces, but not turning up a match.

I was watching Roger's face. Still heavily bruised, it too was beginning to look more normal, despite the livid weal under his jaw, and I thought there was something odd about his expression. I could see physical pain in his eyes, helplessness, and frustration at his immediate inability to tell Jamie what he wanted to know, but I thought there was something else there, too. Anger, certainly, but something like bafflement, as well.

"Do you know any William MacKenzies?" I asked Jamie, who was tapping his fingers lightly on the table as he thought.

"Aye, four or five," he replied, brows still knotted in concentration. "In Scotland. But none here, and none that—"

Roger's hand lifted abruptly at the word "Scotland," and Jamie stopped, fixed on Roger's face like a pointing bird dog.

"Scotland," he said. "Something about Scotland? The man is a new immigrant?"

Roger shook his head violently, then stopped abruptly, grimacing in pain. He squeezed his eyes shut for a moment, then opened them, and waved urgently at the bits of charcoal I still held in my hand.

It took several tries, and at the end of it Roger lay back exhausted on the pillow, the neck of his nightshirt damp with sweat and spotted with blood from his throat. The result of his effort was smeared and straggling, but I could read the word clearly.

*Dougal*, it said. Jamie's look of interest sharpened into something like wariness.

"Dougal," he repeated carefully. He knew several Dougals as well; a few of them resident in North Carolina. "Dougal Chisholm? Dougal O'Neill?"

Roger shook his head and the tube in his throat wheezed with his exhalation. He lifted his hand and pointed emphatically at Jamie, the splinted fingers jabbing. Getting only a blank look in response, he fumbled for the bit of charcoal again, but it rolled off the sketch-box and shattered on the floor.

His fingers were smeared with charcoal dust. Grimacing, he pressed the tip of his ring finger against the page, and by dint of using all the fingers in turn, produced a faint and ghostly scrawl that sent a small electric shock shooting up from the base of my spine.

*Geilie*, it said.

Jamie stared at the name for a moment. Then I saw a small shiver move over him, and he crossed himself.

*"A Dhia,"* he said softly, and looked at me. Awareness thickened between us; Roger saw it and fell back on his pillow, exhaling loudly through his breathing-tube.

"Dougal's son by Geillis Duncan," Jamie said, turning to Roger with incredulity writ large on his face. "He was named William, I think. Ye mean it? Ye're sure of it?"

A brief nod, and Roger's eyes closed. Then they opened again; one splinted finger rose wavering, and pointed to his own eye—a deep, clear green, the color of moss. He was white as the linen he lay on, and his charcoal-smeared fingers were trembling. His mouth was twitching; he wanted badly to talk, to explain—but further explanations were going to have to wait, for a little while, at least.

His hand dropped, and his eyes closed again.

THE REVELATION OF William Buccleigh MacKenzie's identity didn't alter Jamie's urgent desire to find the man, but it did change his intention of murdering him immediately, once found. On the whole, I was grateful for small favors.

Brianna, summoned from her painting to consult, arrived in my room in her smock, smelling strongly of turpentine and linseed oil, with a smear of cobalt blue on one earlobe.

"Yes," she said, bewildered by Jamie's abrupt questions. "I've heard of him. William Buccleigh MacKenzie. The changeling."

"The what?" Jamie's brows shot up toward his hairline.

"That's what I called him," I said. "When I saw Roger's family tree, and realized who William Buccleigh MacKenzie must be. Dougal gave the child to William and Sarah MacKenzie, remember? And they gave him the name of the child they'd lost two months before."

"Roger mentioned that he'd seen William MacKenzie and his wife, on board the *Gloriana*, when he sailed from Scotland to North Carolina," Bree put in. "But he said he didn't realize who the man was until later, and didn't have a chance to talk to him. So he is here—William, I mean—but why on earth would he try to kill Roger—and why that way?" She shuddered briefly, though the room was very warm. It was early summer, and even with the windows open, the air was hot and liquid with humidity.

"He's the witch's get," Jamie said shortly, as though that was sufficient answer—as perhaps it was.

"They thought I was a witch, too," I reminded him, a little tartly. That got me a sideways blue glance, and a curve of the mouth.

"So they did," he said. He cleared his throat, and wiped a sleeve across his sweating brow. "Aye, well. I suppose we must just wait and find out. And having a name helps. I shall send to Duncan and Farquard; have them put out word." He drew a deep breath of exasperation, and blew it out again.

"What am I to do when I find him, though? Witch-son or no, he's my own blood; I canna kill him. Not after Dougal—" He caught himself in time, and coughed. "I mean, he's Dougal's son. He's my own cousin, for God's sake."

I knew what he really meant. Four people knew what had happened in that attic room at Culloden House, the day before that distant battle. One of those was dead, the other disappeared and almost certainly dead too, in the tumult of the Rising. Only I was left as the witness to Dougal's blood and the hand that had spilled it. No matter what crime William Buccleigh MacKenzie had committed, Jamie would not kill him, for his father's sake.

"You were going to kill him? Before you found out who he was?" Bree didn't look shocked at the thought. She had a stained paint-rag in her hands, and was twisting it slowly.

Jamie turned to look at her.

"Roger Mac is your man, the son of my house," he said, very seriously. "Of course I would avenge him."

Brianna flicked a glance at me, then looked away. She looked thoughtful, with a certain intentness that gave me a slight chill to see.

"Good," she said, very softly. "When you find William Buccleigh MacKenzie, I want to know about it." She folded up the rag, thrust it into the pocket of her smock, and went back to her work.

BRIANNA SCRAPED a tiny blob of viridian onto the edge of her palette, and feathered a touch of it into the big smear of pale gray she had created. She hesitated a moment, tilting the palette back and forth in the light from the window to judge the color, then added the faintest dab of cobalt to the other side of the smear, producing a range of subtle tones that ran from blue-gray to green-gray, all so faint as scarcely to be distinguishable from white by the uneducated eye.

She took one of the short, thick brushes, and worked the

gray tones along the curve of the jaw on her canvas with tiny overlapping strokes. Yes, that was just about right; pale as fired porcelain, but with a vivid shadow under it—something both delicate and earthy.

She painted with a deep absorption that shut out her surroundings, engrossed in an artist's double vision, comparing the evolving image on the canvas with the one so immutably etched in her memory. It wasn't that she had never seen a dead person before. Her father—Frank—had had an open-casket funeral, and she had been to the obsequies of older family friends in her own time, as well. But the colors of the embalmer's art were crude, almost coarse by comparison with those of a fresh corpse. She had been staggered by the contrast.

It was the blood, she thought, taking a fine two-haired brush to add a dot of pure viridian in the deep curve of the eye socket. Blood and bone—but death didn't alter the curves of the bones, nor the shadows they cast. Blood, though, colored those shadows. In life, you got the blues and reds and pinks and lavenders of moving blood beneath the skin; in death, the blood stilled and pooled and darkened . . . clay-blue, violet, indigo, purple-brown . . . and something new: that delicate, transient green, barely there, that her artist's mind classified with brutal clarity as "early rot."

Unfamiliar voices came from the hall, and she looked up, wary. Phoebe Sherston was fond of bringing in visitors to admire the painting in progress. Normally, Brianna didn't mind being watched, or talking about what she was doing, but this was a tricky job, and one with limited time; she couldn't work with such subtle colors save for a short period just before sunset, when the light was clear but diffuse.

The voices passed on to the parlor, though, and she relaxed, taking up the thicker brush again.

She resummoned the vision in her mind; the dead man they had laid under a tree at Alamance, near her mother's makeshift field hospital. She had expected to be shocked by battle-wounds and death—and was instead shocked by her own fascination. She had seen terrible things, but it wasn't like attending at her mother's normal surgeries, where there was time to empathize with the patients, to take note of all the small indignities and nastinesses of weak flesh. Things happened too fast on a battlefield; there was too much to be done for squeamishness to take hold.

And in spite of the haste and urgency, each time she had passed near that tree, she had paused for an instant. Bent to turn back the blanket over the corpse and look at the man's face; appalled at her own fascination but making no effort to resist it—committing to memory the amazing, inexorable change of color and shadow, the stiffening of muscle and shifting of shape, as skin settled and clung to bone, and the processes of death and decay began to work their awful magic.

She hadn't thought to ask the dead man's name. Was that unfeeling? she wondered. Probably; the fact was that all her feelings had been otherwise engaged at the time—and still were. Still, she closed her eyes for a moment and said a quick prayer for the repose of the soul of her unknown sitter.

She opened her eyes to see that the light was fading. She scraped the palette and began to clean her brushes and hands, returning slowly and reluctantly to the world outside her work.

Jem would have been fed his supper and bathed already, but he refused to go to bed without being nursed and rocked to sleep. Her breasts tingled slightly at the thought; they were pleasantly full, though they seldom became excruciatingly engorged since he had taken to eating solid food and thus decreased his voracious demands on her flesh.

She'd nurse Jem and put him down, and then go have her own belated supper in the kitchen. She had not eaten with the others, wanting to take advantage of the evening light, and her stomach was growling softly, as the lingering smells of food in the air replaced the astringent scents of turps and linseed oil.

And then . . . then she would go upstairs to Roger. Her lips tightened at the thought; she realized it, and forced her mouth to relax, blowing air out so that her lips vibrated with a flatulent noise like a motorboat.

At this unfortunate moment, Phoebe Sherston's capped head popped through the door. She blinked slightly, but had sufficiently good manners to pretend that she hadn't seen anything.

"Oh, my dear, there you are! Do come into the parlor for a moment, won't you? Mr. and Mrs. Wilbur are *so* eager to make your acquaintance."

"Oh—well, yes, of course," Brianna said, with what graciousness she could summon. She gestured at her paint-stained smock. "Let me just go and change—"

Mrs. Sherston waved away the smock, obviously wanting to show off her tame artist in costume.

"No, no, don't trouble about that. We are quite simple this evening. No one will mind."

Brianna moved reluctantly toward the drawing room.

"All right. Only for a minute, though; I need to put Jem to bed."

Mrs. Sherston's rosebud mouth primmed slightly at that; she saw no reason why her slaves could not take care of the child altogether—but she had heard Brianna's opinions on the subject before, and was wise enough not to press the issue.

Brianna's parents were in the parlor with the Wilburs, who turned out to be a nice, elderly couple—what her mother would call a Darby and Joan. They fussed appropriately over her appearance, insisted politely on seeing the portrait, expressed profound admiration for both subject and painter—though blinking slightly at the former—and generally behaved with such kindness that she felt herself relaxing.

She was just on the verge of making her excuses, when Mr. Wilbur took advantage of a lull in the conversation to turn to her, smiling benevolently.

"I understand that congratulations upon your good fortune are in order, Mrs. MacKenzie."

"Oh? Ah . . . thank you," she said, uncertain what she was being congratulated for. She glanced at her mother for some clue; Claire grimaced slightly, and glanced at Jamie, who coughed.

"Governor Tryon has granted your husband five thousand acres of land, in the back-country," he said. His voice was even, almost colorless.

"He has?" She felt momentarily bewildered. "What—why?"

There was a brief stir of embarrassment among the party, with small throat-clearings and marital glances between the Sherstons and the Wilburs.

"Compensation," her mother said tersely, darting a marital glance of her own at Jamie.

Brianna understood then; no one would be so uncouth as to mention Roger's accidental hanging openly, but it was much too sensational a story not to have made the rounds of Hillsborough society. She realized suddenly that Mrs. Sherston's invitation to her parents and Roger had perhaps not been motivated purely by kindness, either. The notoriety of having the hanged man as house-guest would focus the attention of Hillsborough on the Sherstons in a most gratifying way—better, even, than having an unconventional portrait painted.

"I do hope that your husband is much improved, my dear?" Mrs. Wilbur tactfully bridged the conversational gap. "We were so sorry to hear of his injury."

Injury. That was as circumspect a description of the situation as could well be imagined.

"Yes, he's much better, thank you," she said, smiling as briefly as politeness allowed before turning back to her father.

"Does Roger know about this? The land grant?"

He glanced at her, then away, clearing his throat.

"No. I thought perhaps ye might wish to tell him of it yourself."

Her first response was gratitude; she would have something to say to Roger. It was an awkward business, talking to someone who couldn't talk back. She stored up conversational fodder during the day; tiny thoughts or events that she could turn into stories, to tell him when she saw him. Her stock of stories ran out all too soon, though, and left her sitting by his bed, groping for inanities.

Her second response was a feeling of annoyance. Why had her father not told her privately, rather than exposing her family's business to total strangers? Then she caught the subtle interplay of glances between her parents, and realized that her mother had just asked him that, silently—and he had replied, with the briefest flick of the eyes toward Mr. Wilbur, then toward Mrs. Sherston, before the long auburn lashes swept down to hide his gaze.

*Better to speak the truth before a reputable witness*, his expression said, *than to let gossip spread of its own accord.*

She had no great regard for her own reputation—"notorious" did not begin to encompass it—but she had grasped enough of the social realities to realize that real damage could be done to her father by scandal. If a false report were to get around, for instance, that Roger had really been a Regulation ring-leader, then Jamie's own loyalties would be suspect.

She had begun to realize, listening to the talk in the Sherstons' parlor over the last few weeks, that the Colony was a vast spiderweb. There were innumerable strands of commerce along which a few large spiders—and a number of smaller ones—made their delicate way, always listening for the faint hum of distress made by a fly that had blundered in, always testing for a thinning strand, a broken link.

The smaller entities glided warily along the margins of the web, with an eye out always for the movements of the bigger ones—for spiders were cannibals—and so, she thought, were ambitious men.

Her father's position was prominent—but by no means so secure as to resist the undermining effects of gossip and suspicion. She and Roger had talked about it before, privately, speculating; the fracture-lines were already there, plain enough to someone who knew what was coming; the strains and tensions that would deepen into sudden chasm—one deep enough to sunder the colonies from England.

Let the strain grow too great, too quickly, let the strands between Fraser's Ridge and the rest of the Colony fray too far . . . and they might snap, wrapping sticky ends in a thick cocoon round her family and leaving them suspended by a thread—alone, and prey to those who would suck their blood.

*You* are *morbid tonight*, she thought to herself, sourly amused at her mind's choice of imagery. She supposed that painting death would do that.

Neither the Wilburs nor the Sherstons appeared to have noticed her mood; her mother had, and gave her a long, thoughtful look—but said nothing. She exchanged a few more pleasantries, then excused herself to the company.

Her mood was not lightened by the discovery that Jemmy had grown tired of waiting for her to come, and fallen asleep, tear-tracks on his cheeks. She knelt by his crib for a minute, one hand laid lightly on his back, hoping that he might sense her nearness and wake up. His small back rose and fell in the warm rhythm of utter peace, but he didn't stir. Perspiration glimmered wetly in the creases of his neck.

The heat of the day rose upward, and the second floor of the house was always stifling by evening. The window, of course, was firmly closed, lest the dangerous night airs get in and do the baby harm. Mrs. Sherston had no children of her own, but she knew what precautions must be taken.

In the mountains, Brianna would not have hesitated to open the window. In a heavily-populated town like Hillsborough, full of strangers from the coast, and rife with stagnant horse troughs and dank wells . . .

Weighing the relative danger of malaria-bearing mosquitoes versus that of suffocation, Brianna finally settled for pulling the light quilt off her son and gently removing his gown, leaving him comfortably sprawled on the sheet in nothing but a clout, his soft skin damp and rosy in the dim light.

Sighing, she put out the candle and left, leaving the door ajar so that she could hear if he woke. It was nearly dark now; light welled up through the bannisters from the floor below, but the upstairs hall lay in deep shadow. Mrs. Sherston's gilded tables and the portraits of Mr. Sherston's ancestors were no more than spectral shapes in the darkness.

There was a light in Roger's room; the door was shut, but a fan of soft candle-glow spread across the polished boards beneath it, just catching the edge of the blue hall-runner. She moved toward the door, thoughts of food subsumed in a greater hunger for touch. Her breasts had begun to ache.

A slave was nodding in the corner, hands slack on the knitting that had fallen to her lap. She jerked, startled, as the door opened, and blinked guiltily at Brianna.

Bree looked at once toward the bed, but it was all right;

she could hear the hiss and sigh of his breath. She frowned a little at the woman, but made a small gesture of dismissal. The woman clumsily gathered up her half-finished stocking and blundered out, avoiding Brianna's eye.

Roger lay on his back, eyes closed, a sheet drawn tidily over the sharp angles of his body. *He's so thin*, she thought, *how did he get so thin, so fast*? He could swallow no more than a few spoonsful of soup and Claire's penicillin broth, but surely two or three days was not enough to leave his bones showing so prominently?

Then she realized that he had likely been thin already, from the stress of campaigning—both her parents were thinner than usual. The prominence of his bones had been disguised by the dreadful swelling of his features; now that that had subsided, his cheekbones were high and gaunt, the hard, graceful line of his jaw once more visible, stark above the white linen of the bandage wrapped around his lacerated throat.

She realized that she was staring at his jaw, appraising the color of the fading bruises. The yellow-green of a healing bruise was different than the delicate gray-green of new death; just as sickly, but withal, a color of life. She took a deep breath, suddenly aware that the window in this room was closed, too, and sweat was trickling down the small of her back, seeping unpleasantly into the crack of her buttocks.

The sound of the sash rising wakened him—he turned his head on the pillow, and smiled faintly when he saw her.

"How are you?" She spoke in a hushed voice, as though in a church. Her own voice always seemed too loud, talking to herself.

He lifted one shoulder in a slight shrug, but mouthed a silent "Okay." He looked wilted and damp, the dark hair at his temples sweat-soaked.

"It's awfully hot, isn't it?" She waved at the window, where warm air—but moving air—came in. He nodded, poking at the collar of his shirt with one bandaged hand. She took the hint and untied it, spreading the slit open as far as it would go, to expose his chest to the breeze.

His nipples were small and neat, the aureoles pinkish-brown under the dark curly hairs. The sight reminded her of her own milk-full breasts, and she had a moment's insane urge to lift his head, pull down her shift, and put his mouth to her breast. She had an instant's vivid recall of the moment when he had done that, under the willows at River Run, and a warm rush spread through her, tingling from breasts to womb. Blood rising in her cheeks, she turned to look over the nourishment available on the bedside table.

There was cold meat-broth—spiked with penicillin—in a covered bowl, and a flask of honey-sweetened tea alongside. She took up the spoon and raised a brow inquiringly, her hand hovering over the table.

He grimaced slightly, but nodded at the broth. She picked up the cup and sat down on the stool beside him.

"Open up the stable-door," she said cheerily, circling the spoon toward his mouth as though he were Jem. "Heeeeere comes the horsie!" He rolled his eyes upward in exasperation.

"When I was little," she said, ignoring his scowl, "my parents said things like, 'Here comes the tugboat, open the drawbridge!' 'Open the garage, here comes the car!'—but I can't use those with Jem. Did your mother do cars and airplanes?"

His lips twisted, but finally settled on a reluctant smile. He shook his head and lifted one hand, pointing toward the ceiling. She turned to see a dark spot on the plaster—looking closer, she could see that it was a vagrant bee, blundered in from the garden during the day, somnolent now in the shadows.

"Yeah? Okay, here comes the honeybee," she said, more softly, slipping the spoon into his mouth. "Bzzz, bzzz, bzzz."

She couldn't keep up the attempted air of playfulness, but the atmosphere had relaxed a little. She talked about Jem, who had a new favorite word—"Wagga"—but no one yet had figured out what he meant by it.

"I thought maybe it meant 'cat,' but he calls the cat 'Mowmow.'" She brushed a drop of sweat from her forehead with the back of her hand, then dipped the spoon again.

"Mrs. Sherston says he should be walking by now," she said, eyes fixed on his mouth. "Her sister's children were both walking at a year old, naturally! I asked Mama, though;

she says he's fine. She says kids walk when they're ready, and it can be any time between ten months and as much as eighteen, but fifteen months is about the usual."

She had to watch his mouth in order to guide the spoon, but was aware of his eyes, watching her. She wanted to look into them, but was halfway afraid of what she might see in those dark green depths; would it be the Roger she knew, or the silent stranger—the hanged man?

"Oh—I almost forgot." She interrupted herself in the middle of an account of the Wilburs. She hadn't forgotten, but hadn't wanted to blurt the news out right away. "Da spoke to the Governor this afternoon. He—the Governor, I mean—is giving you a land grant. Five thousand acres." Even as she said it, she realized the absurdity of it. Five thousand acres of wilderness, in exchange for a life almost destroyed. *Cancel the "almost,"* she thought suddenly, looking at Roger.

He frowned at her in what looked like puzzlement, then shook his head and lay back on the pillow, eyes closing. He lifted his hands and let them fall, as though this was simply too much to be asked to contemplate. Maybe it was.

She stood watching him in silence, but he didn't open his eyes. There were deep creases where his brows drew together.

Moved by the need to touch him, to bridge the barrier of silence, she traced the shadow of the bruise that lay over his cheekbone, her fingers drifting, barely touching his skin.

She could see the oddly blurred edges of the bruise, could almost see the dark clotted blood beneath the skin, where the capillaries had ruptured. It was beginning to yellow; her mother had told her that the body's leukocytes would come to the site of an injury, where they gradually broke down the injured cells, thriftily recycling the spilled blood; the changing colors were the result of this cellular housekeeping.

His eyes opened, fixed on her face, his own expression impassive. She knew she looked worried, and tried to smile.

"You don't look dead," she said. That broke the impassive facade; his eyebrows twitched upward, and a faint gleam of humor came into his eyes.

"Roger—" At a loss for words, she moved impulsively toward him. He stiffened slightly, hunching instinctively to protect the fragile tube in his throat, but she put her arms around his shoulders, careful, but needing desperately to feel the substance of his flesh.

"I love you," she whispered, and her hand tightened on the muscle of his arm, urging him to believe it.

She kissed him. His lips were warm and dry, familiar—and yet a feeling of shock ran through her. No air moved against her cheek, no warm breath touched her from his nose or mouth. It was like kissing a mask. Air, damp from the secret depths of his lungs, hissed cool from the amber tube against her neck, like the exhalation from a cave. Gooseflesh ran down her arms and she stepped back, hoping that neither shock nor revulsion showed on her face.

His eyes were closed, squeezed tight shut. The muscle of his jaw bulged; she saw the shift of the shadow there.

"You . . . rest," she managed, her voice shaky. "I'll—I'll see you in the morning."

She made her way downstairs, barely noticing that the candlestick in the hall was lit now, or that the waiting slave slid silently from the shadows back into the room.

Her hunger had come back, but she didn't go downstairs in search of food. She had to do something about the unused milk, first. She turned toward her parents' room, feeling a faint draft move through the stifling shadows. In spite of the warm, muggy air, her fingers felt cold, as though turpentine was still evaporating from her skin.

*Last night I dreamed about my friend Deborah. She used to make money doing Tarot readings in the Student Union; she'd always offer to do one for me, for free, but I wouldn't let her.*

*Sister Marie Romaine told us in the fifth grade that Catholics aren't allowed to do divination—we weren't to touch Ouija boards or Tarot cards or crystal balls, because things like that are seductions of the D-E-V-I-L—she always spelled it out like that, she'd never say the word.*

*I'm not sure where the Devil came into it, but*

somehow I couldn't bring myself to let Deb do readings for me. She was, last night, though, in my dream.

I used to watch her do it for other people; the Tarot cards fascinated me—maybe just because they seemed forbidden. But the names were so cool—the Major Arcana, the Minor Arcana; Knight of Pentacles, Page of Cups, Queen of Wands, King of Swords. The Empress, the Magician. And the Hanged Man.

Well, what else would I dream about? I mean, this was not a subtle dream, no doubt about it. There it was, right in the middle of the spread of cards, and Deb was telling me about it.

"A man is suspended by one foot from a pole laid across two trees. His arms, folded behind his back, together with his head, form a triangle with the point downward; his legs form a cross. To an extent, the Hanged Man is still earthbound, for his foot is attached to the pole."

I could see the man on the card, suspended permanently halfway between heaven and earth. That card always looked odd to me—the man didn't seem to be at all concerned, in spite of being upside-down and blind-folded.

Deb kept scooping up the cards and laying them out again, and that one kept coming up in every spread.

"The Hanged Man represents the necessary process of surrender and sacrifice," she said. "This card has profound significance," she said, and she looked at me and tapped her finger on it. "But much of it is veiled; you have to figure out the meaning for yourself. Self-surrender leads to transformation of the personality, but the person has to accomplish his own regeneration."

Transformation of the personality. That's what I'm afraid of, all right. I liked Roger's personality just fine the way it was!

Well . . . rats. I don't know how much the D-E-V-I-L has to do with it, but I am sure that trying to look too far into the future is a mistake. At least right now.

# 74

# THE SOUNDS OF SILENCE

IT WAS TEN DAYS before Penelope Sherston's portrait was completed to her satisfaction. By that point, both Isaiah Morton and Roger had recovered sufficiently for travel. Given the imminence of Morton's offspring and the danger to him in coming anywhere near either Granite Falls or Brownsville, Jamie had arranged for him and Alicia to lodge with the brewmaster of Mr. Sherston's brewery; Isaiah would undertake employment as a wagoner for the brewery, as soon as his strength permitted.

"I canna imagine why," Jamie had said to me privately, "but I've grown a bit fond of the immoral wee loon. I shouldna like to see him murdered in cold blood."

Isaiah's spirits had revived spectacularly upon the arrival of Alicia, and within a week, he had made his way downstairs, to sit watching Alicia like a devoted dog as she worked in the kitchen—and to pause on his way back to bed to offer comments on the progress of Mrs. Sherston's portrait.

"Don't it look just like her?" he'd said admiringly, standing in his nightshirt in the door of the drawing-room where the sitting was in progress. "Why, if you was to see that picture, you'd know just who it was."

Given the fact that Mrs. Sherston had chosen to be painted as Salome, I was not positive that this would be considered a compliment, but she flushed prettily and thanked him, evidently recognizing the sincerity in his tone.

Bree *had* done a marvelous job, contriving to portray Mrs. Sherston both realistically and flatteringly, but without overt irony—difficult as that must have been. The only point where she had given in to temptation was in a minor detail; the severed head of John the Baptist bore a striking resemblance to Governor Tryon's saturnine features, but I doubted that anyone would notice, what with all the blood.

We were ready to go home, and the house was filled with a spirit of restless excitement and relief—except for Roger.

Roger was indisputably better, in purely physical terms. His hands were mobile again, bar the broken fingers, and most of the bruising over his face and body had faded. Best of all, the swelling in his throat had subsided enough that he could move air through his nose and mouth again. I was able to remove the tube from his throat, and stitch up the incision—a small but painful operation that he had borne with body stiff and eyes wide open, staring up at the ceiling while I worked.

In mental terms, I was not so sure of his recovery. After stitching his throat, I had helped him sit up, wiped his face, and given him a little water mixed with brandy as a restorative. I had watched carefully as he swallowed, then put my fingers lightly on his throat, felt carefully, and asked him to swallow again. I closed my eyes, feeling the movement of his larynx, the rings of his trachea as he swallowed, assessing as best I could the degree of damage.

At last I opened my eyes, to find his eyes two inches from my own and still wide open, the question in them cold and stark as glacier ice.

"I don't know," I said at last, my own voice no more than a whisper. My fingers still rested on his throat; I could feel the thrum of blood through the carotid under my palm, his life flowing just below the skin. But the angular hardness of his larynx lay still under my fingers, queerly misshapen; I felt no pulsing there, no vibration of air across the vocal cords.

"I don't know," I said again, and drew my fingers slowly away. "Do you—want to try now?"

He had shaken his head then, and risen from the bed, going to the window, facing away from me. His arms were braced against the frame as he looked down into the street, and a faint, uneasy memory stirred in my mind.

It had been a moonlit night, then, not broad day—in Paris. I had waked from sleep to see Jamie standing naked in the window frame, the scars on his back pale silver, arms braced and body gleaming with cold sweat. Roger was sweating, too, from the heat; the linen of his shirt stuck to his body— and the lines of his body were just the same; the look of a man braced to meet fear; one who chose to face his demons alone.

I could hear voices in the street below; Jamie, coming back from the camp, with Jemmy held before him on his saddle. He had formed the habit of taking Jem with him on his daily errands, so that Bree could work without distraction. In consequence, Jemmy had learned four new words—only two of them obscene—and Jamie's good coat sported jam stains and smelled like a soiled diaper, but both of them seemed generally pleased with the arrangement.

Bree's voice floated up from below, laughing as she went out to retrieve her son. Roger stood as though he'd been carved out of wood. He couldn't call to them, but he might have knocked on the window frame, or made some other noise, waved to them. But he didn't move.

After a moment, I rose quietly and left the room, feeling a lump in my throat, hard and unswallowable.

When Bree had carried Jemmy off for his bath, Jamie told me that Tryon had released most of the men captured during the battle. "Hugh Fowles among them." He put aside his coat and loosened the collar of his shirt, raising his face to the slight breeze from the window. "I spoke for him—and Tryon listened."

"As well he might," I said, with an edge to my voice. He glanced at me, and made a noise deep in his throat. It reminded me of Roger, whose larynx was no longer capable of that peculiarly Scottish form of expression.

I must have looked distressed at the thought, for Jamie raised his brows and touched my arm. It was too hot to embrace, but I pressed my cheek against his shoulder briefly, taking comfort from the solidness of his body under the thin, damp linen.

"I sewed up Roger's throat," I said. "He can breathe—but I don't know whether he'll ever be able to talk again." *Let alone sing.* The unvoiced thought floated in the muggy air.

Jamie made another noise, this one deep and angry.

"I spoke to Tryon regarding his promise to Roger Mac, as well. He's given me the document of the land grant—five thousand acres, adjoining my own. His last official act as Governor—almost."

"What do you mean by that?"

"I said he's released most of the prisoners?" He moved away, restless. "All but twelve. He has a dozen men still gaoled, outlawed ringleaders of the Regulation. Or so he says." The irony in his voice was as thick as the dusty air. "He'll hold them for trial in a month, on charges of rebellion."

"And if they're found guilty—"

"At least they'll be able to speak before they hang."

He had stopped in front of the portrait, frowning, though I wasn't sure whether he was actually seeing it or not.

"I willna stay to see it. I told Tryon that we must go, to tend our crops and farms. He has released the militia company from service, on those grounds."

I felt a lightening of the weight on my heart. It would be cool in the mountains, the air green and fresh. It was a good place to heal.

"When will we go?"

"Tomorrow." He *had* noticed the portrait; he nodded at the gape-jawed head on the platter in grim approval. "There's only the one thing to stay for, and I think there's little point to it, now."

"What's that?"

"Dougal's son," he said, turning away from the portrait. "I have been seeking William Buccleigh MacKenzie from one end of the county to the other for the past ten days. I found some who kent him, but none who has seen him since Alamance. Some said perhaps he had left the Colony altogether. A good many of the Regulators have fled; Husband's gone—taken his family to Maryland, they say. But as for William MacKenzie, the man's disappeared like a snake down a rat-hole; him, and his family with him."

*Last night I dreamed that we were lying under a big rowan tree, Roger and I. It was a beautiful summer day, and we were having one of those conversations we used to have all the time, about things we missed. Only the things we were talking about were there on the grass between us.*

*I said I'd sell my soul for a Hershey bar with almonds, and there it was. I slipped the outer wrapper off, and I could smell the chocolate. I unfolded the white paper wrapper inside and started eating the chocolate, but it was the paper we were talking about, then—the wrapper.*

*Roger picked it up and said what he missed most was loo-paper; this was too slick to wipe your arse with. I laughed and said there wasn't anything complicated about toilet paper—people could make it now, if they wanted to. There was a roll of toilet paper on the ground; I pointed at it, and a big bumblebee flew down and grabbed the end of it and flew off, unfurling the toilet paper in its wake. It flew in and out, weaving it through the branches overhead.*

*Then Roger said it was blasphemy to think about wiping yourself with paper—it is, here. Mama writes in tiny letters when she does her case-notes, and when Da writes to Scotland he writes on both sides of the page, and then he turns it sideways and writes across the lines, so it looks like latticework.*

*Then I could see Da, sitting on the ground, writing a letter to Aunt Jenny on the toilet paper, and it was getting longer and longer and the bee was carrying it up into the air, flying off toward Scotland with it.*

*I use more paper than anyone. Aunt Jocasta gave me some of her old sketchbooks to use, and a whole quire of watercolor paper—but I feel guilty when I use them, because I know how expensive it is. I have to draw, though. A nice thing about doing this portrait for Mrs. Sherston—since I'm earning money, I feel like I can use a little paper.*

*Then the dream changed and I was drawing pictures of Jemmy, with a #2B yellow pencil. It said*

"Ticonderoga" on it in black letters, like the ones we used to use in school. I was drawing on toilet paper, though, and the pencil kept ripping through it, and I was so frustrated that I wadded up a bunch in my hand.

Then it went into one of those boring, uncomfortable dreams where you're wandering around looking for a place to go to the bathroom and can't find one— and finally you wake up enough to realize that you do have to go to the bathroom.

I can't decide whether I'd rather have the Hershey bar, the toilet paper, or the pencil. I think the pencil. I could smell the freshly-sharpened wood on the point, and feel it between my fingers, and my teeth. I used to chew my pencils, when I was little. I still remember what it felt like to bite down hard and feel the paint and wood give, just a little, and munch my way up and down the length of the pencil, until it looked like a beaver had been gnawing on it.

I was thinking about that, this afternoon. It made me feel sad that Jem won't have a new yellow pencil, or a lunchbox with Batman on it, when he goes to school—if he ever does go to school.

Roger's hands are still too bad to hold a pen.

And now I know that I don't want pencils or chocolate, or even toilet paper. I want Roger to talk to me again.

# 75

## SPEAK MY NAME

OUR JOURNEY BACK to Fraser's Ridge was much quicker than the one to Alamance, for all that the return was uphill. It was late May, and the cornstalks stood already high and green in the fields around Hillsborough, shedding golden pollen on the wind. The grain would just be up, in the mountains, and the newborn stock appearing, calves and foals and lambs needing protection from wolf and fox and bear. The militia company had disbanded at once upon receiving the Governor's dismissal, its members scattering in haste to return to their homesteads and fields.

We were in consequence a much smaller party going back; only two wagons. A few of the men who lived near the Ridge had chosen to travel with us, as had the two Findlay boys, since we would pass by their mother's homestead on our way.

I cast a covert glance at the Findlays, who were helping to unload the wagon and set up our nightly camp. Nice boys, though quiet. They were respectful of—and rather awed by—Jamie, but had developed a peculiar sense of allegiance to Roger over the course of the short-lived campaign, and this odd fidelity had continued, even after the militia's disbanding.

They had come, the two of them, to see him in Hillsborough, wriggling their bare toes in embarrassment on Phoebe Sherston's Turkish carpets. Scarlet-faced and nearly speechless themselves, they had presented Roger with three early apples, lopsided green nubbins obviously stolen from someone's orchard on the way.

He had smiled broadly at them in thanks, picked up one of the apples, and taken a heroic bite from it before I could stop him. He hadn't swallowed anything but soup for a week, and nearly choked to death. Still, he got it down, strangling and gasping, and all three of them had sat there grinning wordlessly at each other, tears standing in their eyes.

The Findlays were usually to be found somewhere near Roger as we traveled, always watchful, leaping to help with anything he couldn't quite manage with his injured hands. Jamie had told me about their uncle, Iain Mhor; plainly they had a good deal of experience in anticipating unspoken needs.

Young and strong, Roger had healed quickly, and the fractures weren't bad ones—but two weeks was not a long time for broken bones to knit. I would have preferred to keep him bandaged for another week, but he was all too plainly chafing at the restraint. I had reluctantly taken the splints off his fingers the day before, warning him to take things easy.

"Don't you *dare*," I said now, seizing his arm as he reached into the wagon for one of the heavy rucksacks of supplies. He looked down at me, one eyebrow raised, then shrugged good-naturedly and stood back, letting Hugh Findlay pull out the sack and carry it away. Roger pointed at the ring of fire-stones Iain Findlay was assembling, then at the woods nearby. Could he gather firewood?

"Certainly not," I said firmly. He pantomimed drinking, and raised his brows. Fetch water?

"No," I said. "All it needs is for a bucket to slip, and . . ."

I looked around, trying to think of something he could safely do, but all camp-making chores involved rough work. At the same time, I knew how galling he found it to stand by, feeling useless. He was bloody tired of being treated like an invalid, and I could see the gleam of incipient rebellion in his eye. One more "no" and he would probably try to pick up the wagon, just to spite me.

"Can he write, Sassenach?" Jamie had paused by the wagon, and noticed the impasse in progress.

"Write? Write what?" I asked in surprise, but he was already reaching past me, digging out the battered portable writing-desk he carried when traveling.

"Love letters?" Jamie suggested, grinning down at me. "Or sonnets, maybe?" He tossed the lap-desk to Roger, who caught it neatly in his arms, even as I yelped in protest. "But perhaps before ye compose an epic in William Tryon's honor, Roger Mac, ye might oblige me wi' the tale of how our mutual kinsman came to try and murder ye, aye?"

Roger stood stock-still for a moment, clutching the desk, but then gave Jamie a lopsided smile, and nodded slowly.

He had begun while the camp was set up, paused to eat supper, and then taken up the task again. It was tiresome work, and very slow; the fractures were mostly healed, but his hands were very stiff, sore, and awkward. He had dropped the quill a dozen times. It made my own finger-joints ache just to watch him.

"Ow! Will you *stop* that?" I looked up from scouring out a pan with a handful of rushes and sand, to find Brianna locked in mortal combat with her son, who was arched backward like a bow over her arm, kicking, squirming, and making the sort of nerve-wracking fuss that makes even devoted parents momentarily contemplate infanticide. I saw Roger's shoulders draw up toward his ears at the racket, but he went doggedly on with his writing.

"What is the *matter* with you?" Bree demanded crossly. She knelt and wrestled Jemmy into a semi-sitting position, evidently trying to make him lie down so she could change his clout for the night.

The diaper in question was much in need of attention, being wet, grimy, and hanging halfway down the little boy's legs. Jem, having slept most of the afternoon in the wagon, had wakened sun-dazed, cranky, and in no mood to be trifled with, let alone changed and put to bed.

"Perhaps he isn't tired yet," I suggested. "He's eaten, though, hasn't he?" This was a rhetorical question; Jemmy's face was smeared with hasty pudding, and he had bits of eggy toast in his hair.

"Yes." Bree ran a hand through her own hair, which was cleaner, but no less disheveled. Jem wasn't the only cranky one in the MacKenzie family. "Maybe *he's* not tired, but *I* am." She was; she had walked beside the wagon most of the day, to spare the horses on the steepening slopes. So had I.

"Leave him here and go have a wash, why don't you?" I said, nobly suppressing a yawn. I picked up a large wooden spoon and waggled it alluringly toward Jem, who was oscillating backward and forward on his hands and knees, emitting horrible whining noises. Spotting the spoon, he stopped making the noise, but crouched in place, glaring suspiciously.

I added an empty tin cup to the lure, setting it on the ground near him. That was enough; he rolled onto his bottom with a squish, picked up the spoon with both hands and began trying to pound the cup into the dirt with it.

Bree cast me a look of profound gratitude, scrambled to her feet, and disappeared into the woods, heading down the slope to the small creek. A quick rinse in cold water, surrounded by dark forest, wasn't quite the sybaritic escape that a fragrant bubble-bath by candlelight might be—but "escape" was the important word here. A little solitude worked wonders for a mother, as I knew from experience. And if cleanliness was not quite next to godliness, having clean feet, face, and hands definitely improved one's outlook on the universe, particularly after a day of sweat, grime, and dirty diapers.

I examined my own hands critically; between horse-leading, fire-starting, cooking, and pot-scouring, my own outlook on the universe could stand a bit of improvement, too.

Still, water was not the only liquid capable of lifting one's spirits. Jamie reached over my shoulder, put a cup of something into my hands, and sat down beside me, his own cup in hand.

*"Slàinte, mo nighean donn,"* he said softly, smiling at me as he lifted his cup in salute.

"Mmm." I closed my eyes, inhaling the fragrant fumes. "Is it proper to say '*Slàinte*,' if it isn't whisky you're drinking?" The liquid in the cup was wine—and a nice one, too, rough but with a good round flavor, redolent of sun and grape leaves.

"I canna see why not," Jamie said logically. "It's only to wish ye good health, after all."

"True, but I think 'Good Health' may be more a practical wish than a figurative one, at least with some whiskies—that you hope the person you're toasting survives the experience of drinking it, I mean."

He laughed, eyes creasing in amusement.

"I havena killed anyone wi' my distilling yet, Sassenach."

"I didn't mean yours," I assured him, pausing for another sip. "Oh, that's nice. I was thinking of those three militiamen from Colonel Ashe's regiment." The three in question had been found blind-drunk—in one case, literally blind—by a sentry, after having indulged in a bottle of so-called whisky, obtained from God knew where.

As Ashe's Company had no surgeon, and we were camped next to them, I had been summoned in the middle of the night to deal with the matter, as best I could. All three men had survived, but one had lost the sight in one eye and another plainly had minor brain-damage—though privately, I had my doubts as to how intelligent he could have been to start with.

Jamie shrugged. Drunkenness was a simple fact of life, and bad brewing was another.

*"Thig a seo, a chuisle!"* he called, seeing Jemmy, who had lost interest in spoon and cup, making off on hands and knees toward the coffeepot, which had been left to keep hot between the stones of the fire-ring. Jemmy ignored the summons, but was snatched away from danger by Hugh Findlay, who snagged him neatly round the waist and delivered him, kicking, to Jamie.

"Sit," Jamie said firmly to him, and without waiting for a response, parked the child on the ground and handed him his ball of rags. Jemmy clutched this, looking craftily from his grandfather to the fire.

"Throw that in the fire, *a chuisle*, and I'll smack your bum," Jamie informed him pleasantly. Jemmy's brow contorted and his lower lip protruded, quivering dramatically. He didn't throw the ball into the fire, though.

*"A chuisle?"* I said, trying out the pronunciation. "That's a new one. What's it mean?"

"Oh." Jamie rubbed a finger across the bridge of his nose, considering. "It means 'my blood.' "

"I thought that was *mo fuil.*"

"Aye, it is, but that's blood like what comes out when ye

wound yourself. *A chuisle* is more like . . . 'O, thou in whose veins runs my very blood.' Ye only say it to a wee bairn, mostly—one ye're related to, of course."

"That's lovely." I set my empty wine-cup on the ground and leaned against Jamie's shoulder. I still felt tired, but the magic of the wine had smoothed the rough edges of exhaustion, leaving me pleasantly muzzy.

"Would you call Germain that, do you think, or Joan? Or is it meant very literally, *a chuisle*?"

"I should be more inclined to call Germain *un petit emmerdeur*," he said, with a faint snort of amusement. "But Joan—aye, I would call wee Joanie *a chuisle*. It's blood of the heart, ken, not only the body."

Jemmy had let his rag-ball fall to the ground and was staring in openmouthed enchantment at the fireflies, which had begun to blink in the grass as darkness fell. With our stomachs full and cool rest at hand, everyone was beginning to feel the soothing effects of the gathering night.

The men were sprawled in the grassy dark under a sycamore tree, passing the wine bottle from hand to hand and exchanging talk in the easy, half-connected fashion of men who know each other well. The Findlay boys were on the wagon-track, that being the only really clear space, throwing something back and forth, missing half their catches as darkness fell, and exchanging genial shouted insults.

There was a loud rustling of bushes beyond the fire, and Brianna emerged, looking damp, but much more cheerful. She paused by Roger, a hand light on his back, and looked over his shoulder at what he was writing. He glanced up at her, then, with a shrug of resignation, withdrew the finished pages of his opus and handed them to her. She knelt down beside him and began to read, brushing back wet strands of hair and frowning to make out the letters by firelight.

A firefly landed on Jamie's shirt, glowing cool green in the shadowed folds of cloth. I moved a finger toward it, and it flew away, spiraling above the fire like a runaway spark.

"It was a good idea, making Roger write," I said, looking across the fire with approval. "I can't wait to find out what actually happened to him."

"Nor I," Jamie agreed. "Though wi' William Buccleigh vanished, what's happened to Roger Mac is maybe no so important as what *will* happen to him."

I didn't have to ask what he meant by that. More than anyone, he knew what it meant, to have a life kicked out from under one—and what strength was required to rebuild it. I reached for his right hand, and he let me take it. Under cover of darkness, I stroked his crippled fingers, tracing the thickened ridges of the scars.

"So it doesn't matter to you, to find out whether your cousin is a cold-blooded murderer or not?" I asked lightly, to cover the more serious conversation going on silently between our hands.

He made a small, gruff sound that might have been a laugh. His fingers curled over mine, smooth with callus, pressing in acknowledgment.

"He's a MacKenzie, Sassenach. A MacKenzie of Leoch."

"Hm." The Frasers were stubborn as rocks, I'd been told. And Jamie himself had described the MacKenzies of Leoch—*charming as larks in the field—and sly as foxes, with it.* That had certainly been true of his uncles, Colum and Dougal. I hadn't heard anything to indicate that his mother, Ellen, had shared that particular family characteristic—but then, Jamie had been only eight when she died. His aunt Jocasta? No one's fool, certainly, but with a good deal less scope for plotting and scheming than her brothers had had, I thought.

"You *what*?" Brianna's exclamation drew my attention back to the other side of the fire. She was looking at Roger, the pages in her hand, an expression of mingled amusement and dismay on her face. I couldn't see Roger's face; he was turned toward her. One hand rose in a shushing gesture, though, and he turned his head toward the tree where the men sat drinking, to be sure no one had heard her exclamation.

I caught a glimpse of firelight shining on the bones of his face, and then his expression changed in an instant, from wariness to horror. He lunged to his feet, mouth open.

"STOKH!" he roared.

It was a terrible cry, loud and harsh, but with a ghastly

strangled quality to it, like a shout forced out around a fist shoved down his throat. It froze everyone in earshot—including Jemmy, who had abandoned the fireflies and stealthily returned to an investigation of the coffeepot. He stared up at his father, his hand six inches from the hot metal. Then his face crumpled, and he began to wail in fright.

Roger reached across the fire and snatched him up; the little boy screamed, kicking and squirming to get away from this terrifying stranger. Bree hastily took him, clutching him to her bosom and burying his face in her shoulder. Her own face had gone pale with shock.

Roger looked shocked, too. He put a hand to his throat, gingerly, as though unsure he was really touching his own flesh. The ridge of the rope-scar was still dark under his jaw; I could see it, even in the flicker of the firelight, along with the smaller, neater line of my own incision.

The initial shock of his shout had worn off, and the men came scrambling out from under the tree, the Findlays rushing in from the road, to gather round Roger, exclaiming in astonishment and congratulation. Roger nodded, submitting to having his hand shaken and his back pounded, all the while looking as though he would strongly prefer to be elsewhere.

"Say somethin' else," Hugh Findlay coaxed him.

"Yes, sir, you can do it," Iain joined in, round face beaming. "Say . . . say 'She sells sea shells, by the sea-shore'!"

This suggestion was howled down, to be replaced by a rain of other excited proposals. Roger was beginning to look rather desperate, his jaw set tight. Jamie and I had got to our feet; I could feel Jamie setting himself to intervene in some way.

Then Brianna pushed her way through the excited throng, with Jemmy perched on one hip, regarding the proceedings with intense distrust. She took Roger's hand with her free one, and smiled at him, the smile trembling only a little round the edges.

"Can you say my name?" she asked.

Roger's smile matched hers. I could hear the air rasp in his throat as he took a breath.

This time he spoke softly; very softly, but everyone held silence, leaning forward to listen. It was a ragged whisper, thick and painful, the first syllable punched hard to force it through his scarred vocal cords, the last of it barely audible. But,

"BRREEah . . . nah," he said, and she burst into tears.

# 76

# BLOOD MONEY

*Fraser's Ridge*
*June, 1771*

I SAT IN THE VISITOR'S CHAIR in Jamie's study, companionably grating bloodroots while he wrestled with the quarterly accounts. Both were slow and tedious businesses, but we could share the light of a single candle and enjoy each other's company—and I found enjoyable distraction in listening to the highly inventive remarks he addressed to the paper under his quill.

"Egg-sucking son of a porcupine!" he muttered. "Look at this, Sassenach—the man's nay more than a common thief! Two shillings, threepence for two loaves of sugar and a brick of indigo!"

I clicked my tongue sympathetically, forbearing to note that two shillings seemed a modest enough price for substances produced in the West Indies, transported by ship to Charleston, and thence carried by wagon, pirogue, horseback, and foot another several hundred miles overland, to be finally brought to our door by an itinerant peddler who did not expect payment for the three or four months until his next visit—and who would in any case likely not get cash, but rather six pots of gooseberry jam or a haunch of smoked venison.

"Look at that!" Jamie said rhetorically, scratching his way down a column of figures and arriving with a vicious stab at the bottom. "A cask of brandywine at twelve shillings, two bolts of muslin at three and ten each, ironmongery—what in the name of buggery is wee Roger wanting wi' an ironmonger, has he thought of a way to play tunes on a hoe?—ironmongery, ten and six!"

"I believe that was a ploughshare," I said pacifically. "It's not ours; Roger brought it for Geordie Chisholm." Ploughshares were in fact rather expensive. Having to be imported from England, they were rare amongst colonial small farmers, many of whom made do with nothing more than wooden dibbles and spades, with an ax and perhaps an iron hoe for ground-clearing.

Jamie squinted balefully at his figures, rumpling a hand through his hair.

"Aye," he said. "Only Geordie hasna got a spare penny to bless himself with, not until next year's crops are sold. So it's me that's paying the ten and six now, isn't it?" Without waiting for an answer, he plunged back into his calculations, muttering "Turd-eating son of a flying tortoise" under his breath, with no indication whether this applied to Roger, Geordie, or the ploughshare.

I finished grating a root and dropped the stub into a jar on the desk. Bloodroot is aptly named; the scientific name is *Sanguinaria*, and the juice is red, acrid, and sticky. The bowl in my lap was full of oozy, moist shavings, and my hands looked as though I had been disemboweling small animals.

"I have six dozen bottles of cherry cordial made," I offered, picking up another root. As though he didn't know that; the whole house had smelled like cough syrup for a week. "Fergus can take those over to Salem and sell them."

Jamie nodded absently.

"Aye, I'm counting on that to buy seedcorn. Have we anything else that can go to Salem? Candles? Honey?"

I gave him a sharp glance, but encountered only the whorled cowlicks on top of his head, bent studiously over his figures. The candles and honey were a sensitive subject.

"I think I can spare ten gallons of honey," I said guardedly. "Perhaps ten—well, all right, twelve dozen candles."

He scratched the tip of his nose with the end of the quill, leaving a blot of ink.

"I thought ye'd had a good year wi' the hives," he said mildly.

I had; my original single hive had expanded, and I now had nine bee-gums bordering my garden. I had taken nearly fifty gallons of honey from them, and enough beeswax for a good thirty dozen candles. On the other hand, I had uses in mind for those things.

"I need some of the honey for the surgery," I said. "It makes a good antibacterial dressing over wounds."

One eyebrow went up, though he kept his eyes on the hen-scratches he was making.

"I should think it would draw flies," he said, "if not bears." He flicked the end of his quill, dismissing the thought. "How much d'ye need then? I shouldna think you've so many wounded coming through your surgery as to require forty gallons of honey—unless you're plastering them with it, head to toe."

I laughed, despite my wariness.

"No, two or three gallons should be enough for dressings—say five, allowing extra to make up electrolytic fluids."

He glanced up at me, both brows raised.

"Electric?" He looked at the candle, its flame wavering in the draft from the window, then back at me. "Did Brianna not say that was something to do wi' lights? Or lightning, at least?"

"No, electrolyte," I amplified. "Sugar-water. You know, when a person is feeling shocked, or is too ill to eat, or has the flux—an electrolytic fluid is one that supports the body by putting back the essential ions they've lost from bleeding or diarrhea—the bits of salt and sugar and other things—which in turn draws water into the blood and restores blood pressure. You've seen me use it before."

"Oh, is that how it works?" His face lighted with interest, and he seemed about to ask for an explanation. Then he caught sight of the stack of receipts and correspondence still waiting on his desk, sighed, and picked up his quill again.

"Verra well, then," he conceded. "Keep the honey. Can I sell the soap?"

I nodded, pleased. I had, with a good deal of cautious experimentation, succeeded at last in producing a soap that did not smell like a dead pig soaked in lye, and that did not remove the upper layer of the epidermis. It required sunflower oil or olive oil in lieu of suet, though; both very expensive.

I had it in mind to trade my spare honey to the Cherokee ladies for sunflower oil with which to make both more soap and shampoo. Those, in turn, would fetch excellent prices almost anywhere—Cross Creek, Wilmington, New Bern— even Charleston, should we ever venture that far. Or so I thought. I was unsure whether Jamie would agree to gamble on that enterprise, though; it would take months to come to fruition, while he could dispose of the honey at an immediate profit. If he saw for sure that the soap would bring much more than the raw honey, though, there would be no difficulty in getting my way.

Before I could expound on the prospects, we heard the sound of light footsteps in the hall, and a soft rap at the door.

"Come," Jamie called, pulling himself up straight. Mr. Wemyss poked his head into the room, but hesitated, looking mildly alarmed at the sight of the sanguinary splotches on my hands. Jamie beckoned him companionably in with a flick of his quill.

"Aye, Joseph?"

"If I might speak a word in your ear, sir?" Mr. Wemyss was dressed casually, in shirt and breeks, but had slicked down his fine, pale hair with water, indicating some formality about the situation.

I pushed back my chair, reaching to gather up my leavings, but Mr. Wemyss stopped me with a brief gesture.

"Oh, no, Ma'am. If ye wouldna mind, I should like ye to stay. It's about Lizzie, and I should value a woman's opinion on the matter."

"Of course." I sat back, brows raised in curiosity.

"Lizzie? Have ye found our wee lass a husband, then, Joseph?" Jamie dropped his quill into the jar on his desk and sat forward, interested, gesturing toward an empty stool.

Mr. Wemyss nodded, the candlelight throwing the bones of his thin face into prominence. He took the proffered seat with a certain air of dignity, quite at odds with his usual attitude of mild discombobulation.

"I am thinking so, Mr. Fraser. Robin McGillivray came to call upon me this morning, to speir for my Elizabeth, to be pledged to his lad, Manfred."

My eyebrows went a little higher. To the best of my knowledge, Manfred McGillivray had seen Lizzie less than half a dozen times, and had not spoken more than the briefest of courtesies to her. It wasn't impossible that he should have been attracted; Lizzie had grown into a delicately pretty girl, and if still very shy, was possessed of nice manners. It scarcely seemed the basis for a proposal of marriage, though.

As Mr. Wemyss laid out the matter, it became a little clearer. Jamie had promised Lizzie a dowry, consisting of a section of prime land, and Mr. Wemyss, freed from his indenture, had a freeman's homestead claim of fifty acres as well—to which Lizzie was heir. The Wemyss land adjoined the McGillivrays' section, and the two together would make a very respectable farm. Evidently, with her three girls now married or suitably engaged, Manfred's marriage was the next step in Ute McGillivray's master plan. Reviewing all of the available girls within a twenty-mile radius of the Ridge, she had settled upon Lizzie as the best prospect, and sent Robin round to open negotiations.

"Well, the McGillivrays are a decent family," Jamie said judiciously. He dipped a finger into my bowl of bloodroot shavings and dotted it thoughtfully on his blotter, leaving a chain of red fingerprints. "They've not much land, but Robin does well enough for himself, and wee Manfred's a hard worker, from all I hear." Robin was a gunsmith, with a small shop in Cross Creek. Manfred had been apprenticed to another gun-maker in Hillsborough, but was now a journeyman himself.

"Would he take her to live in Hillsborough?" I asked. That might weigh heavily with Joseph Wemyss. While he would do anything to insure his daughter's future, he loved Lizzie dearly, and I knew that the loss of her would strike him to the heart.

He shook his head. His hair had dried, and was beginning to rise in its usual fair wisps.

"Robin says not. He says the lad plans to ply his trade in Woolam's Creek—providing he can manage a wee shop. They'd live at the farm." He darted a sideways glance at Jamie, then looked away, blood rising under his fair skin.

Jamie bent his head, and I saw the corner of his mouth tuck in. So this was where he entered the negotiation, then. Woolam's Creek was a small but growing settlement at the base of Fraser's Ridge. While the Woolams, a local Quaker family, owned the mill there, and the land on the far side of the creek, Jamie owned all of the land on the Ridge side.

He had so far provided land, tools, and supplies to Ronnie Sinclair, Theo Frye, and Bob O'Neill, for the building of a cooper's shop, a smithy—still under construction—and a small general store, all on terms that provided us with an eventual share of any profit, but no immediate income.

If Jamie and I had plans for the future, so did Ute McGillivray. She knew, of course, that Lizzie and her father held a place of special esteem with Jamie, and that he would in all likelihood be moved to do what he could for her. And that—of course—was what Joseph Wemyss was very delicately asking now; might Jamie provide premises for Manfred at Woolam's Creek as part of the agreement?

Jamie glanced at me out of the corner of his eye. I lifted one shoulder in the faintest of shrugs, wondering whether Lizzie's physical delicacy had entered into Ute McGillivray's calculations. There were a good many girls sturdier than Lizzie, and better prospects for motherhood. Still, if Lizzie should die in childbirth, then the McGillivrays would be the richer both for her dower-land, and the Woolam's Creek property—and new wives were not so difficult to come by.

"I expect something might be done," Jamie said cautiously. I saw his gaze drift to the open ledger, with its depressing columns of figures, then speculatively to me. Land was not a problem; with no cash and precious little credit, tools and materials would be. I firmed my lips and returned his stare; no, he was not getting his hands on my honey!

He sighed, and sat back, tapping his red-tinged fingers lightly on the blotter.

"I'll manage," he said. "What does the lass say, then? Will she have Manfred?"

Mr. Wemyss looked faintly dubious.

"She says she will. He's a 'nice enough lad, though his mother . . . a fine woman," he added hurriedly, "verra fine. If just a trifle . . . erhm. But . . ." he turned to me, narrow forehead furrowed. "I am not sure Elizabeth knows her mind, ma'am, to say truly. She kens 'twould be a good match, and that it would keep her near me . . ." His expression softened at the thought, then firmed again. "But I wouldna have her make the match only because she thinks I favor it." He glanced shyly at Jamie, then at me.

"I did love her mother so," he said, the words coming out in a rush, as though confessing some shameful secret. He blushed bright pink, and looked down at the thin hands he had twisted together in his lap.

"I see," I said, tactfully averting my own gaze, and brushing a few bits of stray bloodroot off the desk. "Would you like me to talk to her?"

"Oh, I should be most grateful, Mum!" Lightened by relief, he nearly sprang to his feet. He wrang Jamie's hand fervently, bowed repeatedly to me, and at last made his way out, with much bobbing and murmuring of thanks.

The door closed behind him, and Jamie sighed, shaking his head.

"Christ knows it's trouble enough to get daughters married when they *do* ken their own minds," he said darkly, plainly thinking of Brianna and Marsali. "Maybe it's easier if they don't."

THE SINGLE CANDLE was guttering, casting flickering shadows over the room. I got up and went to the shelf where a few fresh ones lay. To my surprise, Jamie got up and came to join me. He reached past the assortment of half-burned tapers and fresh candles, pulling out the squat clock-candle that sat behind them, hidden in the shadows.

He set it on the desk, and used one of the tapers to light it. The wick was already blackened; the candle had been used before, though it wasn't burned down very far. He looked at me, and I went quietly to shut the door.

"Do you think it's time?" I asked softly, moving back to stand beside him.

He shook his head, but didn't answer. He sat back a little in his chair, hands folded in his lap, watching the flame of the clock-candle take hold and swell into a wavering light.

Jamie sighed and put out a hand to turn his account-book toward me. I could see the state of our affairs laid out there in black and white—dismal, so far as cash went.

Very little business in the Colony was done on a cash basis—virtually none, west of Cross Creek. The mountain homesteaders all dealt in barter, and so far as that went, we managed fairly well. We had milk, butter, and cheese to trade; potatoes and grain, pork and venison, fresh vegetables and dried fruit, a little wine made from the scuppernong grapes of the autumn past. We had hay and timber—though so did everyone else—and my honey and beeswax. And above everything else, we had Jamie's whisky.

That was a limited resource, though. We had fifteen acres in new barley, which—bar hailstones, forest fires, and other Acts of God—would eventually be made into nearly a hundred kegs of whisky, which could be sold or traded for quite a lot, even completely raw and unaged. The barley was still green in the field, though, and the whisky no more than a profitable phantom.

In the meantime, we had used or sold almost all the spirit on hand. True, there were fourteen small kegs of spirit remaining—buried in a small cave above the whisky-spring— but that couldn't be used. From each distilling, Jamie put aside two kegs, to be religiously kept for aging. The eldest barrel in this cache was only two years old; it would stay there for ten more, God willing, to emerge as liquid gold— and almost as valuable as the solid kind.

The immediate financial demands were not going to wait ten years, though. Beyond the possibility of a gunsmith's shop for Manfred McGillivray and a modest dowry for Lizzie, there were the normal expenses of farming, livestock maintenance, and an ambitious plan to provide plough- shares to every tenant—many of whom were still tilling by hand.

And beyond our own expenses, there was one very

burdensome obligation. Bloody Laoghaire MacKenzie damn-her-eyes Fraser.

She wasn't precisely an ex-wife—but she wasn't precisely not an ex-wife, either. Thinking me permanently gone, if not actually dead, Jamie had married her, under the prodding of his sister Jenny. The marriage had rather quickly proved to be a mistake, and upon my reappearance, an annulment had been sought, to the relief—more or less—of all parties.

Generous to a fault, though, Jamie had agreed to pay a large sum to her in annual maintenance, plus a dowry to each of her daughters. Marsali's dowry was being paid gradually, in land and whisky, and there was no news of Joan's impending marriage. But the money to keep Laoghaire in whatever style she kept in Scotland was falling due—and we didn't have it.

I glanced at Jamie, who was brooding, eyes half-closed over his long, straight nose. I didn't bother suggesting that we allow Laoghaire to put in for a gaberlunzie badge and go begging through the parish. No matter what he thought of the woman personally, he considered her his responsibility, and that was that.

I supposed that paying the debt in casks of salt fish and lye-soap was not a suitable option, either. That left us three alternatives: We could sell the whisky from the cache, though that would be a great loss in the long term. We could borrow money from Jocasta; possible, but highly distasteful. Or we could sell something else. Several horses, for instance. A large number of pigs. Or a jewel.

The candle was burning strongly, and the wax around the wick had melted. Looking down into the clear puddle of molten wax, I could see them: three gemstones, dark against the pale gray-gold of the candle, their vivid hues subdued but still visible in the wax. An emerald, a topaz, and a black diamond.

Jamie didn't touch them, but stared at them, thick ruddy brows drawn together in concentration.

Selling a gemstone in colonial North Carolina would not be easy; it would likely require a trip to Charleston or Richmond. It could be done, though, and would result in enough money to pay Laoghaire her blood-money, as well as to meet the other mounting expenses. The gemstones had a value, though, that went beyond money—they were the currency of travel through the stones; protection for the life of a traveler.

What few things we knew about that perilous journey were based largely on the things that Geillis Duncan had written or had told me; it was her contention that gems gave a traveler not only protection from the chaos in that unspeakable space between the layers of time, but some ability to navigate, as it were—to choose the time in which one might emerge.

Moved by impulse, I went back to the shelf, and standing on tiptoe, groped for the hide-wrapped bundle hidden in the shadows there. It was heavy in my hand, and I unwrapped it carefully, laying the oval stone on the desk beside the candle. It was a large opal, its fiery heart revealed within a matrix of dull stone by the carving that covered the surface—a spiral; a primitive drawing of the snake that eats its tail.

The opal was the property of another traveler—the mysterious Indian called Otter-Tooth. An Indian whose skull showed silver fillings in the teeth; an Indian who seemed at one time to have spoken English. He had called this stone his "ticket back"—so it seemed that Geilie Duncan was not the only one who believed that gemstones had some power in that dreadful place . . . between.

"Five, the witch said," Jamie said thoughtfully. "She said ye needed five stones?"

"She thought so." It was a warm evening, but the down hairs on my jaw prickled at the thought of Geilie Duncan, of the stones—and of the Indian I had met on a dark hillside, his face painted black for death, just before I had found the opal, and the skull buried with it. Was it his skull we had buried, silver fillings and all?

"Was it needful for the stones to be polished, or cut?"

"I don't know. I think she said cut ones were better—but I don't know why she thought so—or if she was right." That was always the rub; we knew so little for sure.

He made a little *hmf* noise, and rubbed the bridge of his nose slowly with one knuckle.

"Well, we've these three, and my father's ruby. Those are cut and polished stones, and that makes four. Then that wee bawbee"—he glanced at the opal—"and the stone in your amulet, which are not." The point here being that the cut or polished stones would fetch a great deal more in cash than would the rough opal or the raw sapphire in my medicine bag. And yet—could we risk losing a stone that might be needed, that might someday spell the difference between life and death for Bree or Roger?

"It's not likely," I said, answering his thought, rather than his words. "Bree will stay, certainly until Jemmy's grown; perhaps for good." After all, how could one abandon a child, the possibility of grandchildren? And yet, I had done it. I rubbed a finger absently over the smooth metal of my gold ring.

"Aye. But the lad?" He looked up at me, one eyebrow raised, the candlelight clear in his eyes, blue as sapphires cut and polished.

"He wouldn't," I said. "He wouldn't leave Bree and Jemmy." I spoke stoutly, but there was a thread of doubt in my heart, and it was reflected in my voice.

"Not yet," Jamie said quietly.

I took a deep breath, but did not reply. I knew very well what he meant. Wrapped in silence, Roger seemed to withdraw further day by day.

His fingers had healed; I had suggested to Brianna that perhaps he would find solace in his bodhran. She had nodded, doubtfully. I didn't know whether she had mentioned it to him or not—but the bodhran hung on the wall of their cabin, silent as its owner.

He did still smile and play with Jemmy, and was unfailingly attentive to Brianna—but the shadow in his eyes never lessened, and when he was not required for some chore, he would disappear for hours, sometimes all day, to walk the mountains, returning after dark, exhausted, dirt-stained—and silent.

"He hasna slept with her, has he? Since it happened?"

I sighed, brushing a strand of hair off my forehead.

"A few times. I asked. My guess would be that it hasn't happened lately, though."

Bree was doing her best to keep him close, to draw him out of the depths of his gathering depression—but it was clear to me, as well as to Jamie, that she was losing the battle, and knew it. She too was growing silent, and had shadows in her eyes.

"If he went . . . back . . . might there be a cure for his voice? There in your own time?" Jamie ran a finger over the opal as he spoke, eyes following the spiral as his finger traced it.

I sighed again, and sat down.

"I don't know. There would be help—perhaps surgery, certainly speech therapy. I can't say how *much* it would help; no one can. The thing is . . . he might recover a good deal of his voice naturally, if he'd only work at it. But he isn't going to do that. And of course," honesty compelled me to add, "he might *not* get it back, no matter how hard he worked."

Jamie nodded, silent. Regardless of the possibilities of medical help, the fact was that if the marriage between Roger and Brianna failed, there was nothing whatever to keep him here. Whether he would choose to go back then . . .

Jamie sat up in his chair, and blew the candle out.

"Not yet," he said in the darkness, his voice firm. "We've a few weeks yet before I must send money to Scotland; I'll see what else we might contrive. For now, we'll keep the stones."

*Last night I dreamed that I was making bread. Or at least I was trying to make bread. I'd be mixing dough and suddenly realize that I didn't have any flour. Then I'd put the bread in pans and put it in the oven and realize that it hadn't risen, and take it back out. I'd knead it and knead it and then I'd be carrying it around in a bowl under a cloth, looking for a warm place to put it, because you have to keep it warm or the yeast dies, and I was getting frantic because I couldn't find a warm place; there was a cold wind blowing and the bowl was heavy and slippery and I thought I was going to drop it; my hands and feet were freezing and going numb.*

*Then I woke up and I really was cold. Roger had*

*pulled all the covers off and rolled himself up in them, and there was a terrible draft blowing in under the door. I nudged him and yanked on the blankets, but I couldn't get them loose and I didn't want to make a lot of noise and wake Jemmy up. Finally, I got up and got my cloak off the peg and went back to sleep under that.*

*Roger got up before me this morning and went out; I don't think he noticed that he'd left me in the cold.*

# A PACKAGE FROM LONDON

THE PACKAGE ARRIVED in August, by the good offices of Jethro Wainwright, one of the few itinerant peddlers with sufficient enterprise to ascend the steep and winding paths that led to the Ridge. Red-faced and wheezing from the climb and the work of unloading his donkey's pack-frame, Mr. Wainwright handed me the package with a nod, and staggered gratefully off toward the kitchen at my invitation, leaving his donkey to crop grass in the yard.

It was a small parcel, a box of some sort, sewn up carefully in oilskin and tied with twine for good measure. It was heavy. I shook it, but the only sound was a soft clunking, as though whatever lay within was padded. The label read simply "To Mr. James Fraser, Esq., Fraser's Ridge, the Carolinas."

"Well, what do you suppose this is?" I asked the donkey. It was a rhetorical question, but the donkey, an amiable creature, looked up from her meal and hee-hawed in reply, stems of fescue hanging from the corner of her mouth.

The sound set off answering cries of curiosity and welcome from Clarence and the horses, and within seconds, Jamie and Roger appeared from the direction of the barn, Brianna came out of the springhouse, and Mr. Bug rose up from behind the manure pile in his shirtsleeves like a vulture rising from a carcass, all drawn by the noise.

"Thanks," I said to the donkey, who flicked a modest ear at me and went back to the grass.

"What is it?" Brianna stood on her toes to peer over Jamie's shoulder as he took the package from me. "It's not from Lallybroch, is it?"

"No, it's neither Ian's hand . . . nor my sister's," Jamie replied with no more than a brief hesitation, though I saw him glance twice to make sure. "It's come a good way, though—by ship?" He held the parcel under my nose inquiringly. I sniffed and nodded.

"Yes; there's a whiff of tar about it. No documents, though?"

He turned the package over, then shook his head.

"It had a seal, but that's gone." Grayish fragments of wax clung to the twine, but the seal that might have provided a clue to the sender had long since succumbed to the vicissitudes of travel and Mr. Wainwright's pack.

"Ump." Mr. Bug shook his head, squinting dubiously at the package. "Not a mattock."

"No, it's nay a mattock-head," Jamie agreed, hefting the little parcel appraisingly. "Nor yet a book, let alone a quire of paper. I havena ordered anything else that I can think of. D'ye think it might be seeds, Sassenach? Mr. Stanhope did promise to send ye bits from his friend's garden, aye?"

"Oh, it might be!" That was an exciting possibility; Mr. Stanhope's friend Mr. Crossley had an extensive ornamental garden, with a large number of exotic and imported species, and Stanhope had offered to see whether Crossley might be amenable to an exchange; seeds and cuttings of some of the rarer European and Asian herbs from his collection, for bulbs and seeds from what Stanhope described as my "mountain fastness."

Roger and Brianna exchanged a brief look. Seeds were a good deal less intriguing to them than either paper or books would be. Still, the novelty of any letter or package was sufficient that no one suggested opening it until the full measure of enjoyment should have been extracted from speculation about its contents.

In the event, the package was not opened until after supper, when everyone had had a chance to weigh the parcel, poke and sniff at it, and offer an opinion regarding its contents. Pushing his empty plate aside, Jamie finally took up the parcel with all due ceremony, shook it once more, and then handed it to me.

"That knot's a job for a surgeon's hands, Sassenach," he said with a grin. It was; whoever had tied it was no sailor, but had substituted thoroughness for knowledge. It took me several minutes of picking, but I got the knot undone at last, and rolled the twine up tidily for future use.

Jamie then slit the stitching carefully with the point of his dirk, and drew out a small wooden box, to gasps of astonishment. It was plain in design, but elegant in execution, made of a polished dark wood, equipped with brass hinges and hasp, and with a matching small brass plate set into the lid.

"From the Workshop of Messrs. Halliburton and Halliburton, 14 Portman Square, London." Brianna read it out, leaning across the table and craning her neck. "Who on earth are Halliburton and Halliburton?"

"I havena the slightest idea," Jamie replied. He lifted the hasp with one finger, and delicately put back the lid. Inside was a small bag of dark red velvet. He pulled this out, opened its drawstring, and slowly drew out a . . . thing.

It was a flat golden disk, about four inches across. Goggling in astonishment, I could see that the rim was slightly raised, like that of a plate, and printed with tiny symbols of some kind. Set into the central part of the disk was an odd pierced-work arrangement, made of some silvery metal. This consisted of a small open dial, rather like a clock-face, but with three arms connecting its outer rim to the center of the bigger, golden disk.

The small silver circle was also adorned with printed arcana, almost too fine to see, and attached to a lyre-shape which itself rested in the belly of a long, flat silver eel, whose back curved snugly round the inner rim of the golden disk. Surmounting the whole was a gold bar, tapered at the ends like a very thick compass needle, and affixed with a pin that passed through the center of the disk and allowed the bar to revolve. Engraved in flowing script down the center of the bar was the name "James Fraser."

"Why, whatever in the name of Bride will *that* be?" Mrs. Bug, naturally, recovered first from her surprise.

"It's a planispheric astrolabe," Jamie answered, recovered from his surprise, and sounding now almost matter-of-fact.

"Oh, of *course*," I murmured. "Naturally!"

He turned the thing over, displaying a flat surface etched with several concentric circles, these in turn subdivided by hundreds of tiny markings and symbols. This side had a revolving bit like the compass-needle thing on the other side, but rectangular in shape, and with the ends bent upward, flattened and notched so that the notches formed a pair of sights.

Bree reached out a finger and touched the gleaming surface reverently.

"My God," she said. "Is that really *gold*?"

"It is." Jamie placed the object gingerly into her outstretched palm. "And what I should like to know is why?"

"Why gold, or why an astrolabe?" I asked.

"Why gold," he replied, frowning at the thing. "I'd been wanting such an instrument for some time, and couldna find one anywhere between Albany and Charleston. Lord John Grey had promised to have one sent me from London, and I suppose this is it. But why in Christ's name . . ."

Everyone's attention was still riveted by the astrolabe itself, but Jamie glanced away, reaching instead for the box it had come in. Sure enough, at the bottom of the box lay a note, crisply folded and sealed with blue wax. The insignia, though, was not Lord John's customary smiling half-moon-and-stars, but an unfamiliar crest, showing a fish with a ring in its mouth.

Jamie glanced at this, frowning, then broke the seal and opened the note.

*Mr. James Fraser, Esq.*
*at Fraser's Ridge*
*Royal Colony of North Carolina*

*My dear sir,*

    *I have the honor to send the enclosed, with the*
*compliments of my father, Lord John Grey. Upon my*
*departure for London, he gave me instructions to*
*obtain the finest instrument possible, and with knowl-*
*edge of the high esteem in which he holds your friend-*
*ship, I have taken pains to do so. I hope it will meet*
*with your approval.*

                *Your obdt. servant,*
                *William Ransome, Lord Ellesmere,*
                *Captain, 9th Regiment*

"William Ransome?" Brianna had stood up in order to
read over Jamie's shoulder. She glanced at me, frowning.
"He says his father's Lord John—but isn't Lord John's son
still a little boy?"

"He's fifteen." Jamie's voice held an odd note, and I saw
Roger glance up abruptly from the astrolabe in his hands,
green eyes suddenly intent. His gaze shifted to me, with that
odd look he had developed of late, of listening to something
no one else could hear. I looked away.

". . . not Grey," Brianna was saying.

"No." Jamie was still looking at the note in his hand, and
sounded a little abstracted. He shook his head briefly, as
though dispelling some thought, and returned to the matter at
hand.

"No," he repeated more firmly, laying down the note.
"The lad is John's stepson—his father was the Earl of
Ellesmere; the boy's the ninth of that title. Ransome is
Ellesmere's family name."

I kept my eyes fixed sedulously on the table and the empty
box, afraid to look up for fear that my transparent face might
reveal something—if only the fact that there was something
to be revealed.

William Ransome's father had not, in fact, been the eighth Earl of Ellesmere. His father had been James Fraser, and I could feel the tension in Jamie's leg where it touched mine beneath the table, though his face now wore an expression of mild exasperation.

"Evidently the lad's been bought a commission," he said, folding the letter neatly and tucking it back in the box. "So he's gone off to London, and purchased the thing there at John's instruction. But I suppose that to a lad of his background, 'fine' must necessarily mean plated wi' gold!"

He stretched out a hand and Mr. Wainwright, who had been admiring his reflection in the polished golden surface, reluctantly surrendered the astrolabe.

Jamie examined it critically, rotating the inset silver eel with an index finger.

"Aye, well," he said, almost reluctantly. "It *is* verra fine, as to the workmanship of the thing."

"Pretty." Mr. Bug nodded his approval, reaching for one of the hot stovies his wife was offering round. "Survey?"

"Aye, that's right."

"Survey?" Brianna took two of the little potato dumplings and sat down beside Roger, automatically passing him one. "It's for surveying?"

"Among other things." Jamie turned the astrolabe over and gently pushed the flat bar, making the notched sights revolve. "This bit—it's used as a transit. Ye'll ken what that is?"

Brianna nodded, looking interested.

"Sure. I know how to do different sorts of surveying, but we generally used . . ."

I saw Roger grimace as he swallowed, the roughness of the stovie catching at his throat. I lifted my hand toward the water pitcher, but he caught my eye and shook his head, almost imperceptibly. He swallowed again, more easily this time, and coughed.

"I recall ye said ye could survey." Jamie regarded his daughter with approval. "That's why I wanted this"—he hefted the object in his hand—"though I did have something a wee bit less gaudy in mind. Pewter would ha' been more serviceable. Still, so long as I havena got to pay for it . . ."

"Let me see." Brianna extended a hand and took the thing, frowning in absorption as she moved the inner dial.

"Do you know how to use an astrolabe?" I asked her dubiously.

"I do," Jamie said, with a certain degree of smugness. "I was taught, in France." He stood up, and jerked his chin toward the door.

"Bring it outside, lass. I'll show ye how to tell the time."

"... AYE, JUST THERE." Jamie leaned intently over Bree's shoulder, pointing at a spot on the outer dial. She moved the inner dial carefully to match, looked up at the sun, and twitched the pointer a fraction of an inch.

"Five-thirty!" she exclaimed, flushed with delight.

"Five thirty-five," Jamie corrected, grinning broadly. "See there?" He pointed at one of the tiny symbols on the rim, which at this distance, appeared to be no more than a flyspeck to me.

"Five thirty-five," Mrs. Bug said, in tones of awe. "Think of that, Arch! Why—I havena kent the time for sure, since . . . since . . ."

"Edinburgh," her husband said, nodding.

"Aye, that's right! My cousin Jane had a case-clock, a lovely thing, 'twould chime like a church bell, and its face wi' brass numbers, and a pair of wee cherubs flying right across, so—"

"This is the first time I've known what time it was, since I left the Sherstons' house." Bree was ignoring both Mrs. Bug's raptures and the instrument in her hands. I saw her meet Roger's eyes, and smile—and after a moment, his own lopsided smile in return. How long had it been for him?

Everyone was squinting up at the setting sun, waving clouds of gnats from their eyes and discussing when they had last known the time. How very odd, I thought, with some amusement. Why this preoccupation with measuring time? And yet I had it, too.

I tried to think when the last time had been for me. At Jocasta's wedding? No—on the field near Alamance Creek, just before the battle. Colonel Ashe had had a pocket watch, and—I stopped, remembering. No. It was after the battle. And that was very likely the last time Roger had known what time it was—if he had been sufficiently conscious to hear one of the Army surgeons announce that it was then four o'clock—and to give his considered opinion that Roger would not live to see the hour of five.

"What else can you do with it, Da?"

Bree handed the astrolabe carefully back to Jamie, who took it and at once began polishing away the fingermarks with the tail of his shirt.

"Oh, a great number of things. Ye can find your position, whether on land or at sea, tell the time, find a particular star in the sky . . ."

"Very useful," I observed. "Though perhaps not quite so convenient as a clock. But I suppose telling time wasn't your chief intent?"

"No." He shook his head, stowing the astrolabe tenderly away in its velvet bag. "I must have the land of the two grants properly surveyed—and soon."

"Why soon?" Bree had been turning to go, but turned back at this, one brow raised.

"Because time grows short." Jamie looked up at her, the pleasure of his acquisition subsiding into seriousness. He glanced over his shoulder, but there was no one left on the porch save himself and me, Brianna and Roger.

Mr. Wainwright, uninterested in scientific marvels, had gone down to the yard and was lugging his packs into the house, aided by Mr. Bug, and hindered by Mrs. Bug's running commentary. Everyone on the Ridge would know he was here by tomorrow, and would come to the house to buy, sell, and hear the latest news.

"Ye ken what's coming, the two of ye." Jamie glanced from Bree to Roger. "The King may fall, but the land will stay. And if we are to hold this land through it all, we must have it properly surveyed and registered. When there is trouble, when folk must leave their land or maybe have it seized—it's the devil and all to get back, but it's maybe possible, forbye—and ye have a proper deed to say what was once yours."

The sun sparked gold and fire from the curve of his head as he looked up. He nodded toward the dark line of the mountains, silhouetted by a glorious spray of pink and gold cloud, but I could see from the look of distance in his eyes that he saw something far beyond.

"Lallybroch—we saved it by means of a deed of sasine. And Young Simon, Lovat's son—he fought for his land, after Culloden, and got most of it back at last. But only because he had the papers to prove what had been his. So."

He put back the lid of the box he had brought out, and laid the velvet bag gently in it. "I will have papers. And whether it is one George or the other who rules in time—this land will be ours. And yours," he added softly, raising his eyes to Brianna's. "And your children's after you."

I laid my hand on his, where it rested on the box. His skin was warm with work and the heat of the day, and he smelt of clean sweat. The hairs on his forearm shone red and gold in the sun, and I understood very well just then, why it is that men measure time. They wish to fix a moment, in the vain hope that so doing will keep it from departing.

# 78

# NO SMALL THING

BRIANNA HAD COME UP to the big house to borrow a book. She left Jemmy in the kitchen with Mrs. Bug, and went down the hall to her father's study. He was gone, the room empty, though it smelled faintly of him—some indefinable masculine scent, composed of leather, sawdust, sweat, whisky, manure—and ink.

She rubbed a finger under her nose, nostrils twitching,

and smiled at the thought. Roger smelled of those things, too—and yet he had his own scent, underneath. What was it? she wondered. His hands used to smell slightly of varnish and metal, when he owned a guitar. But that was long ago and far away.

Pushing away the thought, she bent her attention to the books on the shelf. Fergus had brought back three new books from his latest trip to Wilmington: a set of essays by Michel de Montaigne—those were in French, no good—a tattered copy of Daniel Defoe's *Moll Flanders*, and a very thin, paper-covered book by B. Franklin, *The Means and Manner of Obtaining Virtue*.

No contest, she thought, plucking out *Moll Flanders*. The book had seen hard use; the spine was cracked and the pages loose. She hoped they were all there; nothing worse than reaching a good part of the story and discovering that the next twenty pages were missing. She flipped carefully through, checking, but the pages seemed to be complete, if occasionally crumpled or stained with food. The book had a rather peculiar smell, as though it had been dipped in tallow.

A sudden crash from her mother's surgery jerked her from her contemplation of the books. She looked instinctively for Jem—but of course he wasn't there. Shoving the book hastily back into place, she rushed out of the study, only to meet her mother hurrying down the hall from the kitchen.

She beat Claire to the door of the surgery by a scant moment.

"Jem!"

The door of the big standing cupboard stood ajar, and the smell of honey was strong in the air. A broken stoneware bottle lay on the floor in a sticky golden puddle, and Jemmy sat in the middle of it, liberally smeared, his blue eyes absolutely round, mouth open in guilty shock.

Blood surged into her face. Ignoring the stickiness, she grabbed him by the arm and stood him on his feet.

"Jeremiah Alexander MacKenzie," Brianna said, in awful tones, "you are a Bad Boy!" She checked him hastily for blood or injury, found none, and fetched him a smack on the bottom, hard enough to make the palm of her hand sting.

The resulting screech gave her an instant qualm of guilt. Then she saw the rest of the carnage in the surgery, and quelled the impulse to spank him again.

"Jeremiah!"

Bunches of dried rosemary, yarrow, and thyme had been pulled out of the drying rack and shredded. One of the gauze shelves of the rack itself had been pulled loose, the fabric ripped and hanging. Bottles and jars from the cupboards lay tipped and rolling; some of the corks had fallen out, spilling multicolored powders and liquids. A big linen bag of coarse ground salt had been rifled, handsful of the crystals tossed around with abandon.

Worst of all, her mother's amulet lay on the floor, the little leather pouch torn open, flat and empty. Scattered bits of dried plants, a few tiny bones, and other debris lay strewn round it.

"Mama, I'm so sorry—he got away. I wasn't looking—I should have kept a better eye on—" She had nearly to shout her apologies, to be heard above Jemmy's bawling.

Claire, flinching slightly at the noise, looked round the surgery, taking hasty inventory. Then she stooped and picked Jemmy up, disregarding the honey.

"Shhhh," she said, putting a hand lightly over his mouth. This proving ineffective, she patted the hand over the gaping orifice, producing a "wa-wa-wa-wa" sound that made Jemmy stop bellowing at once. He stuck a thumb in his mouth, snuffling loudly round it, and pressed a filthy cheek to Claire's shoulder.

"Well, they do get into things," she said to Bree, looking more amused than upset. "Don't worry, darling, it's only a bit of a mess. He couldn't reach the knives, thank goodness, and I keep the poisons up high, too."

Brianna felt her heart begin to slow down. Her hand felt hot, pulsing with blood.

"But your amulet . . ." She pointed, and saw a shadow cross her mother's face when she saw the desecration.

"Oh." Claire took a deep breath, patted Jemmy's back, and put him down. Her teeth set in her lower lip, she stooped and gingerly picked up the limp pouch with its draggled feathers.

"I'm sorry," Brianna repeated, helplessly.

She could see the effort it cost, but her mother made a small dismissive gesture, before crouching to pick up the bits and pieces from the floor. Her curly hair was untied, and swung forward, hiding her face.

"I always did wonder what was in this thing," Claire said. She gingerly began to pick up the tiny bones, collecting them carefully in the palm of one hand. "What do you think these are from—a shrew?"

"I don't know." Keeping a wary eye on Jemmy, Brianna squatted and began to pick things up. "I thought maybe they were from a mouse or a bat."

Her mother glanced up at her, surprised. "Aren't you clever—look." She plucked a small, papery brown object from the floor and held it out. Bending to look closer, Brianna could see that the thing that looked like a crumpled dried leaf was in fact a fragment of a tiny bat's wing, the fragile leather dried to translucence, a bone slender as a needle curving through it like the central rib of a leaf.

"Eye of newt, and toe of frog / Wool of bat, and tongue of dog," Claire quoted. She spilled the handful of bones onto the counter, looking at them with fascination. "I wonder what she meant by that?"

"She?"

"Nayawenne—the woman who gave me the pouch." Crouching, Claire swept up the crumbled bits of leaf—at least Brianna hoped they were real leaves—into her hand, and sniffed them. There were so many odors in the air of the surgery that she herself couldn't distinguish anything beyond the overwhelming sweetness of honey, but evidently her mother's sensitive nose had no trouble in making out individual scents.

"Bayberry, balsam fir, wild ginger, and Arsesmart," she said, sniffing like a truffle-hound. "Bit of sage, too, I think."

"Arsesmart? Is that a comment on what she thought of you?" In spite of her distress, Brianna laughed.

"Ha bloody ha," he mother replied tartly, dusting the little heap of dried plant matter onto the table with the bones. "Otherwise known as water-pepper. It's a rather irritating little thing that grows near brooks—gives you blisters and smarts the eyes—or other things, I imagine, if you happen to carelessly sit on it."

Jemmy, rebukes forgotten, had got hold of a surgical clamp and was turning it to and fro, evidently trying to decide whether it was edible. Brianna debated taking it away from him, but given that her mother always sterilized her metal implements by boiling, decided to let him keep it for the moment, since it had no sharp edges.

Leaving him with Claire, she went back to the kitchen to fetch hot water and some cloths with which to deal with the honey. Mrs. Bug was there but was sound asleep, snoring gently on the settle, hands folded on her rounded stomach, her kerch comfortably askew over one ear.

Tiptoeing back with the bucket of water and a handful of cloths, she found most of the debris already swept up, and her mother crawling round on hands and knees, peering under things.

"Have you lost something?" She glanced at the bottom shelf of the cupboard, but didn't see anything missing, bar the honey-jar. The other bottles had been neatly stoppered and replaced, and everything looked much as usual.

"Yes." Claire crouched lower, frowning as she peered under the cupboard itself. "A stone. About so big"—she held out a hand, thumb and index finger circled, describing a sphere about the diameter of a small coin—"and a sort of grayish-blue. Translucent in spots. It's a raw sapphire."

"Was it in the cupboard? Maybe Mrs. Bug moved it."

Claire sat back on her heels, shaking her head.

"No, she doesn't touch anything in here. Besides, it wasn't in the cupboard—it was in there." She nodded at the table, where the amulet's empty pouch lay beside the bones and plant debris.

A quick search—and then a slower one—of the surgery revealed no sign of the stone.

"You know," Claire said, running a hand through her hair as she looked thoughtfully at Jemmy, "I hate to suggest this, but do you think . . . ?"

"Shi—I mean rats," Brianna said, concern escalating to mild alarm. She stooped to look at Jemmy, who loftily ignored her, concentrating on the job of inserting the surgical clamp into his left nostril. There *were* crumbs of dried plant matter stuck to the honey around his mouth, but surely that was just rosemary or thyme . . .

Offended at the close scrutiny, he tried to whack her with the clamp, but she seized his wrist in a grip of iron, removing the clamp from his grasp with her other hand.

"Don't hit Mummy," she said automatically, "it's not nice. Jem—did you swallow Grannie's rock?"

"No," he said, just as automatically, grabbing at the clamp. "Mine!"

She sniffed at his face, causing him to lean back at an alarming angle, but couldn't be sure. She didn't think it was rosemary, though.

"Come smell him," she said to her mother, standing up. "I can't tell."

Claire stooped to oblige, and Jemmy shrieked in giggling alarm, preparing for an enjoyable game of "Eat me up." He was disappointed, though; his grandmother merely inhaled deeply, said definitely, "wild ginger," then leaned in for a closer look, seizing a damp cloth to rub away the honey smears, in spite of increasing howls of protest.

"Look." Claire pointed at the soft skin around his mouth. Freshly cleansed, Brianna could see them clearly—two or three tiny blisters, like seed pearls.

"Jeremiah," she said sternly, attempting to look him in the eye. "Tell Mummy. Did you eat Grannie's rock?"

Jeremiah avoided her gaze and wriggled away, putting both hands protectively behind him.

"No hit," he said. "Nod nice!"

"I'm not going to spank you," she assured him, grabbing an escaping foot. "I just want to know. Did you swallow a rock about this big?" She held up thumb and forefinger. Jemmy giggled.

"Hot," he said. That was his new favorite word, applied without distinction to any object he liked.

Brianna closed her eyes, sighing in exasperation, then opened them to look at her mother.

"I'm afraid so. Will it hurt him?"

"Shouldn't think so." Claire regarded her grandson thoughtfully, tapping a finger against her lips. Then she crossed the room, opening one of the high cupboards and withdrawing a large brown-glass bottle.

"Castor-bean oil," she explained, rummaging in a drawer for a spoon. "Not *quite* as tasty as honey," she added, fixing Jemmy with a gimlet eye, "but *very* effective."

CASTOR OIL MIGHT BE effective, but it took a while. Keeping a close eye on Jemmy, who was set down to play with his basket of wooden blocks after being dosed, Brianna and Claire used the waiting time to tidy the surgery, and then turned to the peaceful, but time-consuming, job of compounding medicines. It was some time since Claire had had time to do this, and there was a staggering profusion of leaves and roots and seeds to be shredded, grated, pounded, boiled in water, steeped in oil, extracted with alcohol, strained through gauze, stirred into melted beeswax or bear grease, mixed with ground talc or rolled into pills, then jarred or bottled or bagged for preservation.

It was a pleasantly warm day, and they left the windows open for the breeze, even though this meant constantly swatting flies, shooing gnats, and picking the occasional enthusiastic bumblebee out of some bubbling solution.

"Be careful, sweetie!" Brianna reached hastily to brush away a honeybee that had lighted on one of Jemmy's blocks, just before Jem could grab it. "Bad bug. Ouchie!"

"They smell their honey," Claire said, waving away another. "I'd better give them some of it back." She set a bowl of honey-water on the windowsill, and within moments, bees were thick about the rim of it, drinking greedily.

"Single-minded, aren't they?" Brianna observed, blotting a trickle of sweat that ran between her breasts.

"Well, single-mindedness will get you a long way," Claire murmured absently, frowning slightly as she stirred a solution warming over an alcohol lamp. "Does this look done to you?"

"You know a lot better than I do." Still, she bent obligingly and sniffed. "I think so; it smells pretty strong."

Claire dipped a quick finger into the bowl, then tasted it.

"Mm, yes, I think so." Taking the bowl off the flame, she poured the dark greenish liquid carefully through a gauze strainer into a bottle. Several other tall glass bottles stood in a row on the counter, the sunlight glowing through their contents like red and green and yellow gems.

"Did you always know you were meant to be a doctor?" Brianna asked curiously. Her mother shook her head, skillfully shredding a handful of dogwood bark with a sharp knife.

"Never thought of it when I was young. Girls mostly didn't, then, of course. Growing up, I always assumed that I'd marry, have children, make a home . . . does Lizzie look all right to you? I thought she was looking a bit yellow round the edges last night, but it might only have been the candlelight."

"I think she's all right. Do you think she's really in love with Manfred?" They had celebrated Lizzie's betrothal to Manfred McGillivray the night before, with the entire McGillivray family traveling from their homestead for a lavish supper. Mrs. Bug, who was fond of Lizzie, had given of her best; no wonder she was asleep today.

"No," Claire said frankly. "But as long as she isn't in love with anyone else, it's probably all right. He's a good lad, and quite good-looking. And Lizzie likes his mother, which is also a good thing, under the circumstances." She smiled at the thought of Ute McGillivray, who had taken Lizzie at once under her capacious maternal wing, picking out particularly delicious tidbits and poking them assiduously down Lizzie's gullet, like a robin feeding a puny nestling.

"I think she may like Mrs. McGillivray more than she likes Manfred. She was really young when her own mother died; it's nice for her to sort of have one again." Brianna glanced at her mother from the corner of her eye. She could remember all too well the feeling of being motherless—and the sheer bliss of being mothered once more. By reflex, she glanced at Jemmy, who was holding an animated if mostly unintelligible conversation with Adso the cat.

Claire nodded, rubbing the shredded bark between her hands into a small round jar full of alcohol.

"Yes. Still, I think it's as well they wait a bit—Lizzie and

Manfred, I mean—and get used to each other." It had been agreed that the marriage would take place the next summer, after Manfred had finished setting up his shop in Woolam's Creek. "I hope this will work."

"What?"

"The dogwood bark." Claire stoppered the bottle and put it in the cupboard. "Dr. Rawlings' casebook says it can be used as a substitute for cinchona bark—for quinine, you know. And it's certainly easier to get, to say nothing of less expensive."

"Great—I hope it does work." Lizzie's malaria had stayed in abeyance for several months—but there was always the threat of recurrence, and cinchona bark *was* hideously expensive.

The subject of their earlier conversation lingered in her mind, and she returned to it, as she took a fresh handful of sage leaves for her mortar, bruising them carefully before putting them to steep.

"You didn't plan to be a doctor when you were young, you said. But you seemed pretty single-minded about it, later on." She had scattered, but vivid, memories of Claire's medical training; she could still smell the hospital smells caught in her mother's hair and clothing, and feel the soft cool touch of the green scrubs her mother sometimes wore, coming in to kiss her goodnight when she came in late from work.

Claire didn't answer at once, concentrating on the dried corn silk she was cleaning, plucking out rotted bits and flicking them through the open window.

"Well," she said at last, not taking her eyes off her work. "People—and it's not just women, not by any means—people who know who they are, and what they're meant to be . . . they'll find a way. Your father—Frank, I mean—" She scooped up the cleaned silk and transferred it to a small woven basket, small fragments scattering across the counter as she did so. "He was a very good historian. He liked the subject, and he had the gift of discipline and concentration that made him a success, but it wasn't really a . . . a *calling* for him. He told me himself—he could have done other things just as well, and it wouldn't have mattered a great deal. For some people, one thing *does* matter a

great deal, though. And when it does . . . well, medicine
mattered a great deal to me. I didn't know, early on, but
then I realized that it was simply what I was meant to do.
And once I knew that . . ." She shrugged, dusting her hands,
and covered the basket with a bit of linen, securing it with
twine.

"Yes, but . . . you can't always do what you're meant to,
can you?" she said, thinking of the ragged scar on Roger's
throat.

"Well, life certainly forces some things on one," her
mother murmured. She glanced up, meeting Brianna's eyes,
and her mouth quirked in a small, wry smile. "And for the
common man—or woman—life as they find it is often the
life they lead. Marsali, for instance. I shouldn't think it's ever
entered her mind that she might do other than she does. Her
mother kept a house and raised children; she sees no reason
why she should do anything else. And yet—" Claire lifted
one shoulder in a shrug, and reached across the table for the
other mortar. "She had one great passion—for Fergus. And
that was enough to jar her out of the rut her life would have
been—"

"And into another just like it?"

Claire bent her head in a half-nod, not looking up.

"Just like it—except that she's in America, rather than
Scotland. And she's got Fergus."

"Like you have Jamie?" She seldom used his given name,
and Claire glanced up in surprise.

"Yes," she said. "Jamie's part of me. So are you." She
touched Bree's face, quick and light, then turned half away,
reaching to take down a tied bundle of marjoram from the array of hanging herbs on the beam above the hearth. "But
neither of you is all of me," she said softly, back turned. "I
am . . . what I am. Doctor, nurse, healer, witch—whatever
folk call it, the name doesn't matter. I was born to be that; I
will be that 'til I die. If I should lose you—or Jamie—I
wouldn't be quite a whole person any longer, but I would still
have that left. For a little time," she went on, so softly that
Brianna had to strain to hear her, "after I went . . . back . . .
before you came . . . that was all I had. Just the knowing."

Claire crumbled the dried marjoram into the mortar, and

took up the pestle to grind it. The sound of clumping boots came from outside, and then Jamie's voice, a friendly remark to a chicken that crossed his path.

And was loving Roger, loving Jemmy, not enough for her? Surely it should be. She had a dreadful, hollow feeling that perhaps it was not, and spoke quickly, before the thought should find words.

"What about Da?"

"What about him?"

"Does he—is he one who knows what he is, do you think?"

Claire's hands stilled, the clanking pestle falling silent.

"Oh, yes," she said. "He knows."

"A laird? Is that what you'd call it?"

Her mother hesitated, thinking.

"No," she said at last. She took up the pestle and began to grind again. The fragrance of dried marjoram filled the room like incense. "He's a man," she said, "and that's no small thing to be."

# 79

# LONESOME ME

**B**RIANNA CLOSED THE BOOK, with a mingled sense of relief and foreboding. She hadn't objected to Jamie's notion that she teach a few of the little girls on the Ridge their ABC's. It filled the cabin with cheerful noise for a couple of hours, and Jemmy loved the cosseting of a half-dozen miniature mothers.

Still, she was not a natural teacher, and always felt relieved at the end of a lesson. The foreboding came on its heels, though. Most of the girls came alone, or under the care of an older sister. Anne and Kate Henderson, who lived two miles away, were escorted by their older brother, Obadiah.

She wasn't sure when or how it had started. Perhaps from the first day, when he had looked her in the eye, smiling faintly, and held the glance for a moment too long before patting his sisters' heads and leaving them to her care. But there had been nothing she could reasonably object to. Not then, not in the days since. And yet . . .

Stated bluntly to herself, Obadiah Henderson gave her the creeps. He was a tall lad of twenty or so, heavily muscled and not bad-looking, brown-haired and blue-eyed. But there was something about him that was somehow not right; a sense of something brutal about the mouth, something feral in the deepset eyes. And something very unsettling in the way he looked at her.

She hated going to the door at the end of a lesson. The little girls would scatter in a flutter of dresses and giggles—and Obadiah would be waiting, leaning against a tree, sitting on the well-coping, once even lounging on the bench outside her door.

The constant uncertainty, never knowing where he would be—but knowing that he was there, somewhere, got on her nerves nearly as much as that half-smiling look of his, and the silent smirk as he left her, almost winking, as though he knew some dirty little secret about her, but chose to keep it to himself—for now.

It occurred to her, with a certain sense of irony, that her discomfort near Obadiah was at least partly because of Roger. She had grown accustomed to hearing things that weren't spoken aloud.

And Obadiah didn't speak aloud. He didn't say anything to her, made no improper motions toward her. Could she tell him not to look at her? That was ridiculous. Ridiculous, too, that something so simple could cause her heart to jump into her throat when she opened the door, and make sweat prick beneath her arms when she saw him.

Bracing herself, she opened the door for the girls and called goodbye as they scattered, then stood and looked around. He wasn't there. Not by the well, the tree, the bench . . . nowhere.

Anne and Kate weren't looking; they were already halfway across the clearing with Janie Cameron, all three hand in hand.

"Annie!" she called. "Where's your brother?"

Annie half-turned, pigtails bouncing.

"He's gone to Salem, Miss," she called back. "We're going home to sup with Jane today!" Not waiting for acknowledgment, the girls all skipped away, like a trio of bouncing balls.

The tension melted slowly from her neck and shoulders as she drew a long, deep breath. She felt blank for a moment, as though she weren't quite sure what to do. Then she drew herself up and brushed down her rumpled apron. Jemmy was asleep, lulled by the girls' nasal singing of the alphabet song. She could take advantage of his nap to go and fetch some buttermilk from the springhouse. Roger liked buttermilk biscuits; she'd make them for supper, with a little ham.

The springhouse was cool and dark, and restful with the sound of water running through the stone-lined channel in the floor. She loved going in there, and waiting for her eyes to adjust to the darkness, so she could admire the trailing fronds of dark-green algae that clung to the stone, drifting in the current. Jamie had mentioned that a family of bats had taken up residence in the springhouse, too—yes, there they were, four tiny bundles hung up in the darkest corner, each one barely two inches long, as neat and tidy as a Greek dolmade wrapped in grape leaves. She smiled at the thought, though it was followed by a pang.

She had eaten dolmades with Roger, at a Greek restaurant in Boston. She didn't care all that much for Greek food, but it would have been a memory of their own time to share with him, when she told him about the bats. If she told him now, she thought, he would smile in response—but the smile wouldn't quite reach his eyes, and she would remember alone.

She left the springhouse, walking slowly, the bucket of buttermilk in one hand balanced by a wedge of cheese in the other. A cheese omelette would be good for lunch; quick to cook, and Jemmy loved it. He preferred to use his spoon to kill his prey, then devour it messily with both hands, but he *would* feed himself, and that was progress.

She was still smiling when she looked up from the path to see Obadiah Henderson sitting on her bench.

"What are you doing here?" Her voice was sharp, but higher than she'd intended it to be. "The girls said you'd gone to Salem."

"So I had." He rose to his feet and stepped forward, that knowing half-smile on his lips. "I came back."

She suppressed the urge to take a step back. This was her house; damned if he'd make her back away from her own door.

"Well, the girls have gone," she said, as coolly as she could manage. "They're at the Camerons'." Her heart was thumping heavily, but she moved past him, meaning to put the bucket down on the porch.

She bent, and he put his hand on the small of her back. She froze momentarily. He didn't move his hand, didn't try to stroke or squeeze—but the weight of it lay on her spine like a dead snake. She jerked upright and whirled around, taking a step back, and to hell with not letting him intimidate her. He'd already done that.

"I brought ye something," he said. "From Salem." The smile was still on his lips, but it seemed completely disconnected from the look in his eyes.

"I don't want it," she said. "I mean—thank you. But no. It isn't right for you to—my husband wouldn't like it."

"No need for him to know." He took a step toward her; she took one back, and the smile grew wider.

"I hear your husband's not home much, these days," he said softly. "That sounds lonesome."

He put out a large hand, reaching toward her face. Then there was an odd, small sound, a sort of meaty *tnk!*, and his face went blank, his eyes shocked wide.

She stared at him for a moment, completely unable to grasp what had happened. Then he turned those staring eyes to his outstretched hand, and she saw the small knife stuck in the flesh of his forearm, and the growing stain of red on the shirt around it.

"Leave this place." Jamie's voice was low, but distinct. He stepped out of the trees, eyes fixed on Henderson in a most unfriendly manner. He reached them in three strides, put out his hand, and pulled the knife from Henderson's arm. Obadiah made a small sound, deep in his throat, like a wounded animal might make, baffled and pitiable.

"Go," Jamie said. "Never come here again."

The blood was flowing down Obadiah's arm, dripping from his fingers. A few drops fell into the buttermilk, floating crimson on the rich yellow surface. In a dazed sort of way, she recognized the horrid beauty of it—like rubies set in gold.

Then the boy was going, free hand clamped to his wounded arm, shambling, then running for the trail. He disappeared into the trees, and the dooryard was very still.

"Did you have to do that?" was the first thing she managed to say. She felt stunned, as though she herself had been struck with something. The blood drops were beginning to blur, their edges dissolving into the buttermilk, and she thought she might throw up.

"Should I have waited?" Her father caught her by the arm, pulled her down to sit on the porch.

"No. But you—couldn't you just . . . have *said* something to him?" Her lips felt numb and there were small flashing lights in the periphery of her vision. Remotely, she realized that she was going to faint, and leaned forward, her head between her knees, face buried in the sanctuary of her apron.

"I did. I told him to go." The porch creaked as Jamie sat down beside her.

"You know what I mean." Her voice sounded odd to her own ears, muffled in the folds of cloth. She sat up slowly; the red spruce by the big house wavered slightly in her vision, but then steadied. "What were you *doing*? Showing off? How could you count on sticking somebody with a knife at that distance? And what was that, anyway—a *pen*knife?"

"Aye. It was all I had in my pocket. And in fact, I didna mean to stick him," Jamie admitted. "I meant to throw into the wall o' the cabin, and when he looked to see what made the noise, hit him from behind. He moved, though."

She closed her eyes and breathed deeply through her nose, willing her stomach to settle.

"Ye're all right, *a muirninn*?" he asked quietly. He laid a hand gently on her back—somewhat higher than Obadiah had. It felt good; large, warm and comforting.

"I'm fine," she said, opening her eyes. He looked worried, and she made an effort, smiling at him. "Fine."

He relaxed a bit, then, and his eyes grew less troubled, though they stayed intent on hers.

"Well, then," he said. "It's no the first time, aye? How long has yon gomerel been tryin' it on wi' you?"

She took another breath, and forced her fists to uncurl. She wanted to minimize the situation, moved by a sense of guilt—for surely she should have found some way to stop it? Faced with that steady blue gaze, though, she couldn't lie.

"Since the first week," she said.

His eyes widened.

"So long? And why did ye not tell your man about it?" he demanded, incredulous.

She was startled, and fumbled for a reply.

"I—well—I didn't think . . . I mean, it wasn't his problem." She heard the sudden intake of his breath, no doubt the precursor to some biting remark about Roger, and hurried to defend him.

"It—he—he didn't actually *do* anything. Just looks. And . . . smiles. How could I tell Roger he was *looking* at me? I didn't want to look weak, or helpless." Though she had been both, and knew it. The knowledge burned under her skin like ant bites.

"I didn't want to . . . to have to ask him to defend me."

He stared at her, his face blank with incomprehension. He shook his head slowly, not taking his eyes away from her.

"What in God's name d'ye think a man is *for*?" he asked at last. He spoke quietly, but in tones of complete bewilderment. "Ye want to keep him as a pet, is it? A lapdog? Or a caged bird?"

"You don't understand!"

"Oh. Do I not?" He blew out a short breath, in what might have been a sardonic laugh. "I have been marrit near thirty years, and you less than two. What is it that ye think I dinna understand, lass?"

"It isn't—it isn't the same for you and Mama as it is for me and Roger!" she burst out.

"No, it's not," he agreed, his voice level. "Your mother has regard for my pride, and I for hers. Or do ye maybe think her a coward, who canna fight her own battles?"

"I . . . no." She swallowed, feeling perilously close to tears, but determined not to let them escape. "But, Da—it *is* different. We're from another place, another time."

"I ken that fine," he said, and she saw the edge of his mouth curl up in a wry half-smile. His voice grew more gentle. "But I canna think that men and women are so different, then."

"Maybe not." She swallowed, forcing her voice to steady. "But maybe Roger's different. Since Alamance."

He drew breath as though to speak, but then let it out again slowly, saying nothing. He had taken his hand away; she felt the lack of it. He leaned back a little, looking out over the dooryard, and his fingers tapped lightly on the boards of the porch between them.

"Aye," he said at last, quietly. "Maybe so."

She heard a muffled thump in the cabin behind them, then another. Jem was awake, throwing his toys out of his cradle. In a moment, he would start calling for her to come and pick them up. She stood up suddenly, straightening her dress.

"Jem's up; I have to go in."

Jamie stood up, too, and picking up the bucket, flung the buttermilk in a thick yellow splash across the grass.

"I'll fetch ye more," he said, and was gone before she could tell him not to bother.

Jem was standing up, clinging to the side of his cradle, eager for escape, and launched himself into her arms when she bent to pick him up. He was getting heavy, but she clutched him tightly to her, pressing her cheek against his head, damp with sweaty sleep. Her heart was beating heavily, feeling bruised inside her chest.

*"That sounds lonesome,"* Obadiah Henderson had said. He was right.

# 80

# CREAMED CRUD

JAMIE LEANED BACK from the table, sighing in repletion. As he started to get up, though, Mrs. Bug popped up from her place, wagging an admonitory finger at him.

"Now, sir, now, sir, ye'll be going nowhere, and me left wi' gingerbread and fresh crud to go to waste!"

Brianna clapped a hand to her mouth, with the muffled noise characteristic of one who has just shot milk up one's nose. Jamie and Mr. Bug, to whom "crud" was the familiar Scottish usage for "curds," both looked at her curiously, but made no comment.

"Well, I'll surely burst, Mrs. Bug, but I expect I'll die a happy man," Jamie informed her. "Bring it on, then—but I've a wee thing to fetch whilst ye serve it out." With amazing agility for a man who had just consumed a pound or two of spiced sausage with fried apples and potatoes, he slid out of his chair and disappeared down the hall toward his study.

I took a deep breath, pleased that I had smelled the gingerbread cooking earlier in the afternoon, and had had the foresight to remove my stays before sitting down to supper.

"Wan' crud!" Jemmy crowed, picking up infallibly on the word most calculated to cause maternal consternation. He pounded his hands on the table in ecstasy, chanting, "Crud-crud-crud-crud!" at the top of his lungs.

Roger glanced at Bree with a half-smile, and I was pleased to see that she caught it, smiling back even as she captured Jemmy's hands and started the job of wiping the remains of dinner off his face.

Jamie returned just as the gingerbread and curds—these being sugared and whipped into creamy blobs—made their appearance. He reached over Roger's shoulder as he passed, and deposited a cloth-bound ledger on the table in front of him, topped with the small wooden box containing the astrolabe.

"The weather's good for another two months, maybe," he said casually, sitting down and sticking a finger into the huge dollop of creamed crud on his plate. He stuck the finger in his mouth, closing his eyes in bliss.

"Aye?" The word came out choked and barely audible, but enough to make Jemmy quit babbling and stare at his father open-mouthed. I wondered whether it was the first time Roger had spoken today.

Jamie had opened his eyes and picked up his spoon, eyeing his dessert with the determination of a man who means to die trying.

"Aye, well, Fergus will be going down to the coast just before snowfall—if he can take the surveying reports to be filed in New Bern then, that will be good, no?" He dug into the gingerbread in a businesslike way, not looking up.

There was a silence, filled only with heavy breathing and the clack of spoons on wooden plates. Then Roger, who had not picked up his spoon, spoke.

"I can . . . do that." It might have been no more than the effort it took to force air through his scarred throat, but there was an emphasis on the last word, that made Brianna wince. Only slightly, but I saw it—and so did Roger. He glanced at her, then looked down at his plate, lashes dark against his cheek. His jaw tightened, and he picked up his spoon.

"Good, then," Jamie said, even more casually. "I'll show ye how. Ye can go in a week."

*Last night I dreamed that Roger was leaving. I've been dreaming about his going for a week, ever since Da suggested it. Suggested—ha. Like Moses brought down the Ten Suggestions from Mount Sinai.*

*In the dream, Roger was packing things in a big*

*sack, and I was busy mopping the floor. He kept get-*
*ting in my way, and I kept pushing the sack aside to*
*get at another part of the floor. It was filthy, with all*
*sorts of stains and sticky glop. There were little bones*
*scattered around, like Adso had eaten some little ani-*
*mal there, and the bones kept getting caught up in*
*my mop.*

*I don't want him to go, but I do, too. I hear all the*
*things he isn't saying; they echo in my head. I keep*
*thinking that when he's gone, it will be quiet.*

SHE PASSED ABRUPTLY from sleep to instant wakefulness. It was just past dawn, and she was alone. There were
birds singing in the wood. One was caroling near the cabin,
its notes sharp and musical. Was it a thrush? she wondered.

She knew he was gone, but lifted her head to check. The
rucksack was gone from beside the door, as was the bundle
of food and bottle of cider she had prepared for him the night
before. The bodhran still hung in its place on the wall, seeming to float suspended in the unearthly light.

She had tried to get him to play again, after the hanging,
feeling that at least he could still have music, if not his voice.
He had resisted, though, and finally she could see that she
was angering him with her insistence, and had stopped. He
would do things his way—or not at all.

She glanced toward the cradle, but all was quiet, Jemmy
still sound asleep. She lay back on her pillow, hands lifting to
her breasts. She was naked, and they were smooth, round,
and full as gourds. She squeezed one nipple gently, and tiny
pearls of milk popped out. One swelled bigger, overflowed,
and ran in a tiny, tickling droplet down the side of her breast.

They had made love before sleeping, the night before. At
first, she hadn't thought he would, but when she came up to
him and put her arms around him, he had clasped her hard
against himself, kissed her slowly for a long, long time, and
finally carried her to bed.

She had been so anxious for him, wanting to assure him
of her love with mouth and hands and body, to give him

something of herself to take away, that she had forgotten herself completely, and been surprised when the climax overtook her. She slid one hand down, between her legs, remembering the sense of being caught up suddenly by a great wave, swept helplessly toward shore. She hoped that Roger had noticed; he hadn't said anything, nor opened his eyes.

He had kissed her goodbye in the dark before dawn, still silent. Or had he? She put a hand to her mouth, suddenly unsure, but there was no clue in the smooth, cool flesh of her lips.

*Had* he kissed her goodbye? Or had she only dreamed it?

# 81

# BEAR-KILLER

*August, 1771*

THE HORSES NEIGHING from the direction of the paddock announced company. Curious, I abandoned my latest experiment and went to peer out of the window. Neither horse nor man was in evidence in the dooryard, but the horses were still snorting and carrying on as they did when they saw someone new. The company must be afoot, then, and have gone round to the kitchen door—which most people did, this being mannerly.

This supposition was almost instantly borne out by a high-pitched shriek from the back of the house. I poked my head out into the hall just in time to see Mrs. Bug race out of the kitchen as though discharged from a cannon, screaming in panic.

Not noticing me, she shot past and out of the front door,

which she left hanging open, thus enabling me to see her cross the dooryard and vanish into the woods, still in full cry. It came as something of an anticlimax, when I glanced the other way and saw an Indian standing in the kitchen doorway, looking surprised.

We eyed each other warily, but as I appeared indisposed to screaming and running, he relaxed slightly. As he appeared unarmed and lacking paint or any other evidence of malevolent intent, I relaxed slightly.

"*Osiyo*," I said cautiously, having observed that he was a Cherokee, and dressed for visiting. He wore three calico shirts, one atop the other, homespun breeches, and the odd drooping cap, rather like a half-wound turban, that men favored for formal occasions, plus long silver earrings and a handsome brooch in the shape of the rising sun.

He smiled brilliantly in response to my greeting, and said something I didn't understand at all. I shrugged helplessly, but smiled in return, and we stood there nodding at one another and smiling back and forth for several moments, until the gentleman, struck by inspiration, reached into the neck of his innermost shirt—a dressy number printed with small yellow diamonds on a blue background,—and withdrew a leather thong, on which were strung the curved black claws of one or more bears.

He held these up, rattled them gently, and raised his eyebrows, glancing to and fro as though searching for someone under the table or on the cabinet.

"Oh," I said, comprehending immediately. "You want my husband." I mimed someone aiming a rifle. "The Bear-Killer?"

A flash of good teeth in a beaming smile rewarded my intelligence.

"I expect he'll be along any minute," I said, waving first at the window, indicating the path taken by the exiting Mrs. Bug—who had undoubtedly gone to inform Himself that there were red savages in the house, bent on murder, mayhem, and the desecration of her clean floor—and then in the direction of the kitchen. "Come back, won't you, and have a drink of something?"

He followed me willingly, and we were seated at the table,

companionably sipping tea and exchanging further nods and smiles, when Jamie came in, accompanied not only by Mrs. Bug, who stuck close to his coattails, casting suspicious looks at our guest, but by Peter Bewlie.

Our guest was promptly introduced as Tsatsa'wi, the brother of Peter's Indian wife. He lived in a small town some thirty miles past the Treaty Line, but had come to visit his sister, and was staying with the Bewlies for a time.

"We were havin' a wee pipe after our supper last night," Peter explained, "and Tsatsa'wi was a-telling of my wife about a difficulty in their village—and she tellin' it to me, ye see, him havin' no English and me not speakin' so verra much of their tongue, no but the names of things and the odd politeness here and there—but as I say, he was telling of a wicked bear, what's been a-plaguing of them for months past."

"I should think Tsatsa'wi well-equipped to deal wi' such a creature, by the looks of it," Jamie said, nodding at the Indian's necklace of claws, and touching his own chest in indication. He smiled at Tsatsa'wi, who evidently gathered the meaning of the compliment and smiled broadly back. Both men bowed slightly to each other over the cups of tea, in token of mutual respect.

"Aye," Peter agreed, licking droplets of liquid from the corners of his mouth, and smacking his lips in approval. "He's a bonnie hunter, is Tsatsa'wi, and in the usual course o' things, I expect he and his cousins might manage well enough. But it seems as how this particular bear is just that wee bit above the odds. So I says to him as perhaps we'll come and tell *Mac Dubh* about it, and maybe as Himself would spare the time to go and sort the creature for them."

Peter lifted his chin to his brother-in-law, and nodded toward Jamie, with a proprietorial air of pride. *See*, said the gesture. *I told you. He can do it.*

I suppressed a smile at this. Jamie caught my eye, coughed modestly and set down his cup.

"Aye, well. I canna come just yet awhile, but perhaps when the hay is in. D'ye ken what's the nature of this problematical bear, Peter?"

"Oh, aye," Peter said cheerfully. "It's a ghost."

I choked momentarily on my own tea. Jamie didn't seem too shocked, but rubbed his chin dubiously.

"Mmphm. Well, what's it done, then?"

The bear had first made its presence known nearly a year before, though no one had seen it for some time. There had been the usual incidents of depredation—the carrying away of racks of drying fish or strings of corn hung outside houses, the stealing of meat from lean-tos—but at first the townspeople had regarded this merely as the work of a bear slightly more clever than the usual—the usual bear being completely unconcerned as to whether he was observed in the act.

"It would only come at night, ye see," Peter explained. "And it didna make a great deal o' noise. Folk would just come out in the morning and find their stores broken into, and not a sound made to rouse them."

Brianna, who had seen Mrs. Bug's unceremonious exit and come up to investigate the cause, began humming softly under her breath—a song to which memory promptly supplied the words, *"Oh, he'll sleep 'til noon, but before it's dark . . . he'll have every picnic basket that's in Jellystone Park . . ."* I pressed a napkin to my mouth, ostensibly to blot the remains of the tea.

"They kent it was a bear from the first, aye?" Peter explained. "Footprints."

Tsatsa'wi knew that word; he spread his two hands out on the table, thumb to thumb, demonstrating the span of the footprint, then touched the longest of the claws hung round his neck, nodding significantly.

The townspeople, thoroughly accustomed to bears, had taken the usual precautions, moving supplies into more protected areas, and putting out their dogs in the evening. The result of this was that a number of dogs had disappeared—again without sound.

Evidently the dogs had grown warier, or the bear hungrier. The first victim was a man, killed in the forest. Then, six months ago, a child had been taken. Brianna stopped humming abruptly.

The victim was a baby, snatched cradle-board and all from the bank of the river where its mother was washing clothes toward sunset. There had been no sound, and no clue left save a large clawed footprint in the mud.

Four more of the townspeople had been killed in the months since. Two children, picking wild strawberries by themselves in late afternoon. One body had been found, the neck broken, but otherwise untouched. The other had disappeared; marks showed where it had been dragged into the woods. A woman had been killed in her own cornfield, again toward sunset, and partially eaten where she fell. The last victim, a man, had in fact been hunting the bear.

"They didna find anything of *him*, save his bow and a few bits o' bloodied clothes," Peter said. I heard a small thump behind me, as Mrs. Bug sat down abruptly on the settle.

"So they have hunted it themselves?" I asked. "Or tried to, I should say?"

Peter took his eyes off Jamie and looked at me, nodding seriously.

"Oh, aye, Mrs. Claire. That's how they kent what it was, finally."

A small party of hunters had gone out loaded—literally—for bear, armed with bows, spears, and the two muskets the village boasted. They had circled the village in a widening gyre, convinced that since the bear's attentions focused on the town, it would not wander far away. They had searched for four days, now and then finding old spoor, but no trace of the bear itself.

"Tsatsa'wi was wi' them," Peter said, lifting a finger toward his brother-in-law. "He and one of his friends were sittin' up at night, keepin' watch whilst the others slept. 'Twas just past moonrise, he said, when he got up to make water. He turned back to the fire—just in time to see his friend bein' dragged off, stone-dead, wi' his neck crushed in the jaws of the thing itself!"

Tsatsa'wi had been following the tale intently. At this juncture, he nodded, and made a gesture that appeared to be the Cherokee equivalent of the Sign of the Cross—some quick and formal gesture to repel evil. He began to talk himself, then, hands flying as he pantomimed the subsequent events.

He had of course shouted, rousing his remaining com-

rades, and had rushed at the bear, hoping to frighten it into
dropping his friend—though he could see that the man was
already dead. He tilted his head sharply to indicate a broken
neck, letting his tongue loll in an expression that would have
been quite funny under different circumstances.

The hunters were accompanied by two dogs, which had
also flown at the bear, barking. The bear had in fact dropped
its prey, but instead of fleeing, had charged toward him. He
had thrown himself to one side, and the bear had paused long
enough to swipe one of the dogs off its feet, and then disappeared into the darkness of the wood, pursued by the other
dog, a hail of arrows, and a couple of musket balls—none of
which had touched it.

They had chased the bear into the wood with torches, but
been unable to discover it. The second dog had returned,
looking ashamed of itself—Brianna made a small fizzing
noise at Tsatsa'wi's pantomime of the dog—and the hunters,
thoroughly unnerved, had gone back to their fire, and spent
the rest of the night awake, before returning to their village
in the morning. From whence, Tsatsa'wi indicated with a
graceful gesture, he had now come to solicit the assistance of
the Bear-Killer.

"But why do they think it's a ghost?" Brianna leaned forward, interest displacing her initial horror at the tale.

Peter glanced at her, one eyebrow raised.

"Oh, aye, he didna say—or rather I expect he did, but not
so as ye'd understand it. The thing was much bigger than the
usual bear, he says—and pure white. He says when it turned
to look at him, the beast's eyes glowed red as flame. They
kent at once it must be a ghost, and so they werena really surprised that their arrows didna touch it."

Tsatsa'wi broke in again, pointing first at Jamie, then tapping his bear-claw necklace, and then—to my surprise—
pointing at me.

"Me?" I said. "What have I got to do with it?"

The Cherokee heard my tone of surprise, for he leaned
across the table, took my hand in his own, and stroked it—
not in any affectionate manner, but merely as an indication of
my skin. Jamie made a small sound of amusement.

"You're verra white, Sassenach. Perhaps the bear will

think ye're a kindred spirit." He grinned at me, but Tsatsa'wi evidently gathered the sense of this, for he nodded seriously. He dropped my hand, and made a brief cawing noise—a raven's call.

"Oh," I said, distinctly uneasy. I didn't know the words in Cherokee, but evidently the people of Tsatsa'wi's town had heard of White Raven as well as the Bear-Killer. Any white animal was regarded as being significant—and often sinister. I didn't know whether the implication here was that I might exert some power over the ghost-bear—or merely serve as bait—but evidently I was indeed included in the invitation.

And so it was that a week later, the hay safely in and four sides of venison peacefully hanging in the smokehouse, we set off toward the Treaty Line, bent on exorcism.

BESIDES JAMIE AND MYSELF, the party consisted of Brianna and Jemmy, the two Beardsley twins, and Peter Bewlie, who was to guide us to the village, his wife having gone ahead with Tsatsa'wi. Brianna had not wanted to come, more for fear of taking Jemmy into the wilderness than from disinclination to join the hunt, I thought. Jamie had insisted that she come, though, claiming that her marksmanship would be invaluable. Unwilling to wean Jemmy yet, she had been obliged to bring him—though he seemed to be thoroughly enjoying the trip, hunched bright-eyed on the saddle in front of his mother, alternately gabbling happily to himself about everything he saw, or sucking his thumb in dreamy content.

As for the Beardsleys, it was Josiah that Jamie wanted.

"The lad's killed two bears, at least," he told me. "I saw the skins, at the Gathering. And if his brother likes to come along, I canna see the harm in it."

"Neither do I," I agreed. "But why are you making Bree come? Can't you and Josiah handle the bear between you?"

"Perhaps," he said, running an oily rag over the barrel of his gun. "But if two heids are better than one, then a third should be better still, no? Especially if it shoots like yon lass can."

"Yes?" I said skeptically. "And what else?"

He glanced up at me and grinned.

"What, ye dinna think I have ulterior motives, do ye, Sassenach?"

"No, I don't think so—I know so."

He laughed and bent his head over his gun. After a few moments' swabbing and cleaning, though, he said, not looking up, "Aye, well. I thought it no bad idea for the lass to have friends among the Cherokee. In case she should need a place to go, sometime."

The casual tone of voice didn't fool me.

"Sometime. When the Revolution comes, you mean?"

"Aye. Or . . . when we die. Whenever that might be," he added precisely, picking the gun up and squinting down the barrel to check the sight.

It was bright Indian summer still, but I felt shards of ice crackle down my back. Most days, I managed to forget that newspaper clipping—the one that reported the death by fire of one James Fraser and his wife, on Fraser's Ridge. Other days, I remembered it, but shoved the possibility to the back of my mind, refusing to dwell on it. But every now and then, I would wake up at night, with bright flames leaping in the corners of my mind, shivering and terrified.

"The clipping said, 'no living children,'" I said, determined to face down the fear. "Do you suppose that means that Bree and Roger will have gone . . . somewhere . . . before then?" To the Cherokee, perhaps. Or to the stones.

"It might." His face was sober, eyes on his work. Neither one of us was willing to admit the other possibility—no need, in any case.

Reluctant though she had been to come, Brianna too seemed to be enjoying the trip. Without Roger, and relieved of the chores of cabin housekeeping, she seemed much more relaxed, laughing and joking with the Beardsley twins, teasing Jamie, and nursing Jemmy by the fire at night, before curling herself around him and falling peacefully asleep.

The Beardsleys were having a good time, too. The removal of his infected adenoids and tonsils had not cured Keziah's deafness, but had improved it markedly. He could understand fairly loud speech now, particularly if you faced him and spoke clearly, though he seemed to make out anything his twin said with ease, no matter how softly voiced. Seeing him look round wide-eyed as we rode through the thick, insect-buzzing forest, fording streams and finding faint deer paths through the thickets, I realized that he had never been anywhere in his life, save the area near the Beardsley farm, and Fraser's Ridge.

I wondered what he would make of the Cherokee—and they of him and his brother. Peter had told Jamie that the Cherokee regarded twins as particularly blessed and lucky; the news that the Beardsleys would be joining the hunt had delighted Tsatsa'wi.

Josiah seemed to be having fun, too—insofar as I could tell, he being a very contained sort of person. As we drew closer to the village, though, I thought that he was becoming slightly nervous.

I could see that Jamie was a trifle uneasy, too, though in his case, I suspected the reason for it. He didn't mind at all going to help with a hunt, and was pleased to have the opportunity to visit the Cherokee. But I rather thought that having his reputation as the Bear-Killer trumpeted before him, so to speak, was making him uncomfortable.

This supposition was borne out when we camped on the third night of our journey. We were no more than ten miles from the village, and would easily make it by mid-day next day.

I could see him making up his mind to something as we rode, and as we all sat down to supper round a roaring fire, I saw him suddenly set his shoulders and stand up. He walked up to Peter Bewlie, who sat staring dreamily into the fire, and faced him with decision.

"There's a wee thing I have to be sayin', Peter. About this ghost-bear we're off to find."

Peter looked up, startled out of his trance. He smiled, though, and slid over to make room for Jamie to sit down.

"Oh, aye, *Mac Dubh?*"

Jamie did so, and cleared his throat.

"Well, ye see—the fact is that I dinna actually ken a great deal about bears, as there havena been any in Scotland for quite some years now."

Peter's eyebrows went up.

"But they say ye killed a great bear wi' naught but a dirk!"

Jamie rubbed his nose with something approaching annoyance.

"Aye, well . . . so I did, then. But I didna hunt the creature down. It came after me, so I hadna got a choice about it, after all. I'm none so sure that I shall be of any great help in discovering this ghost-bear. It must be a particularly clever bear, no? To have been walking in and out of their village for months, I mean, and no one with more than a single glimpse of it?"

"Smarter than the average bear," Brianna agreed, her mouth twitching slightly. Jamie gave her a narrow look, which he switched to me as I choked on a swallow of beer.

"What?" he demanded testily.

"Nothing," I gasped. "Nothing at all."

Turning his back on us in disgust, Jamie suddenly caught sight of Josiah Beardsley, who, while not guffawing, was doing a little mouth-twitching of his own.

"What?" Jamie barked at him. "They're no but loons"— he jerked a thumb over his finger at Brianna and me—"but what's to do wi' *you*, eh?"

Josiah immediately erased the grin from his face and tried to look grave, but the corner of his mouth kept on twitching, and a hot flush was rising in his narrow cheeks, visible even by firelight. Jamie narrowed his eyes and a stifled noise that might have been a giggle escaped Josiah. He clapped a hand across his mouth, staring up at Jamie.

"What, then?" Jamie inquired politely.

Keziah, obviously gathering that something was up, hunched closer to his twin, squaring up beside him in support. Josiah made a brief, unconscious movement toward Kezzie, but didn't look away from Jamie. His face was still red, but he seemed to have got himself under control.

"Well, I suppose I best say, sir."

"I suppose ye had." Jamie gave him a quizzical look.

Josiah drew a deep breath, resigning himself.

" 'Twasn't a bear, always. Sometimes it was me."

Jamie stared at him for a moment. Then the corners of his mouth began to twitch.

"Oh, aye?"

"Not all the time," Josiah explained. But when his wanderings through the wilderness brought him within reach of one of the Indian villages—"Only if I was hungry, though, sir"—he hastened to add—he would lurk cautiously in the forest nearby, stealing into the place after dark and absconding with any easily-reached edibles. He would remain in the area for a few days, eating from the village stores until his strength and his pack were replenished, then move on to hunt, eventually returning with his hides to the cave where he had made a cache.

Kezzie's expression throughout this recital hadn't changed; I wasn't sure how much of it he had heard, but he didn't appear surprised. His hand rested on his twin's arm for a moment, then slid off, reaching for a skewer of meat.

Brianna's laughter had subsided, and she had been listening to Josiah's confession with a furrowed brow.

"But you didn't—I mean, I'm *sure* you didn't take the baby in its cradleboard. And you didn't kill the woman who was partly eaten . . . did you?"

Josiah blinked, though he seemed more baffled than shocked by the question.

"Oh, no. Why'd I do that? You don't think *I* ate 'em, do ye?" He smiled at that, an incongruous dimple appearing in one cheek. "Mind, I been hungry enough now and then as I might consider it, if I happened on somebody dead—providin' it was fairly recent," he added judiciously. "But not hungry enough as I'd kill someone a-purpose."

Brianna cleared her throat, with something startlingly like one of Jamie's Scottish noises.

"No, I didn't think you ate them," she said dryly. "I just thought that if *someone* happened to have killed them—for some other reason—the bear could have come along and gnawed on the bodies."

Peter nodded thoughtfully, seeming interested but unfazed by the assorted confessions.

"Aye, a bear'll do that," he said. "They're no picky eaters, bears. Carrion is fine by them."

Jamie nodded in response, but his attention was still fixed on Josiah.

"Aye, I've heard that, forbye. But Tsatsa'wi said he did see the bear take his friend—so it *does* kill people, no?"

"Well, it killed that one," Josiah agreed. There was an odd tone to his voice, though, and Jamie's look sharpened. He lifted a brow at Josiah, who worked his lips slowly in and out, deciding something. He glanced at Kezzie, who smiled at him. Kezzie, I saw, had a dimple in his left cheek, while Josiah's was in the right.

Josiah sighed and turned back to face Jamie.

"I wasn't a-goin' to say about this part," he said frankly. "But you been straight with us, sir, and I see it ain't right I let you go after that bear not knowin' what else might be there."

I felt the hairs rise on the back of my neck, and resisted the sudden impulse to turn round and look into the shadows behind me. The urge to laugh had left me.

"What else?" Jamie slowly lowered the chunk of bread he had been about to bite into. "And just . . . what else *might* be there, then?"

"Well, 'twas only the once I saw for sure, mind," Josiah warned him. "And 'twas a moonless night, too. But I'd been out all the night, and my eyes was well-accustomed to the starlight—you'll know the way of it, sir."

Jamie nodded, looking bemused.

"Aye, well enough. And ye were where, at the time?"

Near the village we were headed toward. Josiah had been there before, and was familiar with the layout of the place. A house at the end of the village was his goal; there were strings of corn hung to dry beneath the eaves, and he thought he could get away with one easily enough, provided he didn't rouse the village dogs.

"Rouse one, ye've got 'em all a-yowling on your tail," he said, shaking his head. "And it wasn't but a couple of hours before the dawn. So I crept along slow-like, looking to see was one of the rascals curled up asleep by the house I had my eye on." Lurking in the wood, he had seen a figure come out of the house. As no dogs took exception to this, it was a reasonable conclusion that the person belonged to the house. The man had paused to make water, and then, to Josiah's alarm, had shouldered a bow and quiver, and marched directly toward the woods where he lay hidden.

"I didn't think as he could be after me, but I went up a tree quick as a bob-tail cat, and not makin' no more noise than one, neither," he said, not bragging.

The man had most likely been a hunter, making an early start for a distant stream where raccoon and deer would come to drink at dawn. Not seeing any need of caution so near his own village, the man had not displayed any, walking through the forest quietly, but with no attempt at concealment.

Josiah had crouched in his tree, no more than a few feet above the man's head, holding his breath. The man had gone on, disappearing at once into the heavy undergrowth. Josiah had been just about to descend from his perch when he had heard a sudden exclamation of surprise, followed by the sounds of a brief scuffle that concluded with a sickening *thunk!*

"Just like a ripe squash when you chunk it with a rock to break it open," he assured Jamie. "Made my arse-hole draw up like a purse-string, hearin' that noise, there in the dark."

Alarm was no bar to curiosity, though, and he had eased through the wood in the direction of the sound. He could hear a rustling noise, and as he peered cautiously through a screen of cedar branches, he made out a human form stretched upon the ground, and another bending over it, evidently struggling to pull some kind of garment off the prone man's body.

"He was dead," Josiah explained, matter-of-factly. "I could smell the blood, and a shit-smell, too. Reckon the little fella caved in his head with a rock or maybe a club."

"Little fella?" Peter had been following the story with close attention. "How little d'ye mean? Did ye see his face?"

Josiah shook his head.

"No, I saw naught but the shadow of him, movin' about. It was full dark, still; the sky hadn't started to go light yet." He squinted, making a mental estimate. "Reckon he'd be shorter than me; maybe so high." He held out a hand in illustration, measuring a distance some four and a half feet from the ground.

The murderer had been interrupted in his work of plundering the body, though. Josiah, intent on watching, had noticed nothing, until there came a sudden crack from a breaking stick, and the inquiring *whuff* of a questing bear.

"You best believe the little fella run when he heard that," he assured Jamie. "He dashed right past, no further from me than you are now. That was when I got the only good look I had at him."

"Well, don't keep us in suspense," I said, as he paused to take a gulp of his beer. "What *did* he look like?"

He wiped a line of foam from the sparse whiskers on his upper lip, looking thoughtful.

"Well, ma'am, I was pretty near sure he was the devil. Only I did think the devil would be bigger," he added, taking another drink.

This statement naturally caused some confusion. Upon further elucidation, it appeared that Josiah merely meant that the mysterious "little fella" had been black.

"Wasn't 'til I went along to that Gathering of yours that it come to me that some regular folks just *are* black," he explained. "I hadn't never seen anybody who was, nor heard tell of it, neither."

Kezzie nodded soberly at this.

"Devil in the Book," he said, in his odd, gruff voice.

"The Book," it seemed, was an old Bible that Aaron Beardsley had taken somewhere in trade and never found a buyer for. Neither of the boys had ever been taught to read, but they were most entertained by the pictures in the Book, which included several drawings of the devil, depicted as a crouching black creature, going about his sly business of tempting and seduction.

"I didn't see no forked tail," Josiah said, shaking his head, "but then, he went by so fast, stood to reason I might have missed it in the dark and all."

Not wanting to draw the attention of such a person to himself, Josiah had stood still, and thus been in a position to hear the bear giving its attention to the unfortunate inhabitant of the village.

"It's like Mr. Peter says," he said, nodding at Peter Bewlie in acknowledgment. "Bears ain't particular. I never did see this 'un, so I can't say was it the white one or no—but it surely did eat on that Indian. I heard it, chawin' and slobberin' like anything." He seemed untroubled by this recollection, but I saw Brianna's nostrils pinch at the thought.

Jamie exchanged looks with Peter, then glanced back at Josiah. He rubbed a forefinger slowly down the bridge of his nose, thinking.

"Well, then," he said at last. "It seems that not all the evil doings in your brother-in-law's village can be laid at the ghost-bear's door, aye? What wi' Josiah stealin' food, and wee black devils killing folk. What d'ye ken, Peter? Might a bear take a taste for human flesh, once he'd had it, and then maybe go to hunting humans on his own?"

Peter nodded slowly, face creased in concentration.

"That might be, *Mac Dubh*," he allowed. "And if there's a wee black bastard hangin' about in the wood—who's to say how many the bear's killed, and how many the wee black devil's done for, and the bear takin' the blame?"

"But who *is* this wee black devil?" Bree asked. The men looked from one to another, and shrugged, more or less in unison.

"It must be an escaped slave, surely?" I said, lifting my brows at Jamie. "I can't see why a free black in his right mind would off go into the wilderness alone like that."

"Maybe he isn't in his right mind," Bree suggested. "Slave *or* free. If he's going around killing people, I mean." She cast an uneasy look at the wood around us, and put a hand on Jemmy, who was curled in a blanket on the ground beside her, sound asleep.

The men looked automatically to their weapons, and even I reached under my apron to touch the knife I wore at my belt for digging and chopping.

The forest seemed suddenly both sinister and claustrophobic. It was much too easy to imagine lurking eyes in the shadows, ascribe the constant soft rustle of leaves to stealthy footsteps or the brush of passing fur.

Jamie cleared his throat.

"Your wife's not mentioned black devils, I suppose, Peter?"

Bewlie shook his head. The concern with which he had greeted Josiah's tale was still stamped upon his grizzled face, but a small touch of amusement gleamed in his eyes.

"No. I can't say as she has, *Mac Dubh*. The only thing I recall in that regard is the Black Man o' the West."

"And who is that?" Josiah asked, interested.

Peter shrugged and scratched at his beard.

"Aye, well, I shouldna say it's anyone, so to speak. Only that the shamans say there is a spirit who lives in each o' the four directions, and each spirit has a color to him—so when they go to singin' their prayers and the like, they'll maybe call the Red Man o' the East to help the person they're singing for, because Red is the color of triumph and success. North, that's blue—the Blue Man, to give the spirit of the North his right name—that's defeat and trouble. So ye'd call on *him* to come and give your enemy a bit of grief, aye? To the South, that's the White Man, and he's peace and happiness; they sing to him for the women with child, and the like."

Jamie looked both startled and interested to hear this.

"That's verra like the four airts, Peter, is it no?"

"Well, it is, then," Peter agreed, nodding. "Odd, no? That the Cherokee should get hold of the same notions as we Hielanders have?"

"Oh, not so much." Jamie gestured to the dark wood, beyond the small circle of our fire. "They live as we do, aye? Hunters, and dwellers in the mountains. Why should they not see what we have seen?"

Peter nodded slowly, but Josiah was impatient with this philosophizing.

"Well, what's the Black Man o' the West, then?" he demanded. Both Jamie and Peter turned their heads as one to look at him. The two men looked nothing alike—Peter was short, squat, and genially bearded, Jamie tall and elegant, even in his hunting clothes—and yet there was something identical in their eyes, that made little mouse-feet run skittering down my spine. "What we have seen," indeed! I thought.

"The West is the home of the dead," Jamie said softly, and Peter nodded, soberly.

"And the Black Man o' the West is death himself," he added. "Or so say the Cherokee."

Josiah was heard to mutter that he didn't think so very much of *that* idea, but Brianna thought even less of it.

"I do *not* believe that the spirit of the West was out in the woods conking people on the head," she declared firmly. "It was a person Josiah saw. And it was a black person. Ergo, it was either a free black or an escaped slave. And given the odds, I vote for escaped slave."

I wasn't sure it was a matter for democratic process, but I was inclined to agree with her.

"Here's another thought," she said, looking round. "What if it's this little black man who's responsible for some of the half-eaten people? Aren't some of the African slaves cannibals?"

Peter Bewlie's eyes popped at that; so did the Beardsleys'. Kezzie cast an uneasy look over his shoulder and edged closer to Josiah.

Jamie appeared amused at this suggestion, though.

"Well, I suppose ye might get the odd cannibal here and there in Africa," he agreed. "Though I canna say I've heard of one amongst the slaves. I shouldna think they'd be verra desirable as house-servants, aye? Ye'd be afraid to turn your back, for fear of being bitten in the backside."

This remark made everyone laugh, and relieved the tension somewhat. People began to stir and make preparations for going to bed.

We took especial care in putting the food into two of the saddlebags, which Jamie hung up in a tree, a good distance from the camp. Even if the ghost-bear had been revealed to be less powerful than previously supposed, there was an unspoken agreement that there was no sense taking chances.

For the most part, I managed to put aside the knowledge that we lived in a wilderness. Now and then some tangible evidence would shove the fact under my nose: nocturnal visits by foxes, possums, and raccoons, or the occasional unnerving screams of panthers, with their uncanny resemblance to the crying of women or the shrieks of small children. It was quiet now, where we were. But there was no way of standing in the center of those mountains at night, submerged in the absolute black at their feet, listening to the secret murmurs of the great trees overhead, and pretending that one was anywhere but in the grip of the forest primeval—or of doubting that the wilderness could swallow us in one gulp, if it cared to, leaving not a clue behind of our existence.

For all her logic, Brianna was by no means immune to the whispers of the forest—not with a small and tender child to guard. She didn't help with the readying of camp for the night, but instead sat close to Jemmy, loading her rifle.

Jamie, after a quick look at Brianna, announced that he and she would take the first watch; Josiah and I the next, and Peter and Kezzie the last watch of the night. Heretofore, we hadn't kept a watch, but no one complained at this suggestion.

A long day in the saddle is one of the best soporifics, and I lay down beside Jamie with that utter gratitude for being horizontal that compensates for the hardest of beds. Jamie's hand rested gently on my head; I turned my face and kissed his palm, feeling safe and protected.

Peter and the Beardsley twins fell asleep within seconds; I could hear them snoring on the other side of the fire. I was nearly asleep myself, lulled by the quiet, half-heard talk between Jamie and Bree, when I became aware that the tenor of their conversation had changed.

"Are ye worrit for your man, *a nighean*?" he asked softly.

She gave a small, unhappy laugh.

"I've been worrit since they hanged him," she said. "Now I'm scared, too—or should that be 'scairt'?" she asked, trying to make a joke of it.

Jamie made a low noise in his throat, which I think he meant to be soothing.

"He's in no more danger tonight than he was last night, lass—nor any night since he set out."

"True," she answered dryly. "But just because I didn't know about ghost-bears and black murderers last week doesn't mean they weren't out there."

"My point precisely," he replied. "He'll be no safer for your fear, will he?"

"No. You think that's going to stop me worrying?"

There was a low, rueful chuckle in reply.

"I shouldna think so, no."

There was a brief silence, before Brianna spoke again.

"I just—keep thinking. What will I do, if something does happen—if he . . . doesn't come back? I'm all right during the day, but at night, I can't help thinking . . ."

"Och, well," he said softly. I saw him tilt up his head to the stars, blazing overhead. "How many nights in twenty years, *a nighean*? How many hours? For I spent that long in wondering whether my wife still lived, and how she fared. She and my child."

His hand ran smoothly over my head, gently stroking my hair. Brianna said nothing in reply, but made a small, inarticulate sound in her throat.

"That is what God is for. Worry doesna help—prayer does. Sometimes," he added honestly.

"Yes," she said, sounding uncertain. "But if—"

"And if she had not come back to me"—he interrupted firmly—"if you had not come—if I had never known—or if I had known for sure that both of you were dead . . ." He turned his head to look at her, and I felt the shift of his body as he lifted his hand from my hair and reached out his other hand to touch her. "Then I would still have lived, *a nighean*, and done what must be done. So will you."

# A DARKENING SKY

ROGER PUSHED HIS WAY through a thick growth of sweet gum and pin oak, sweating. He was close to water; he couldn't hear it yet, but could smell the sweet, resinous scent of some plant that grew on streambanks. He didn't know what it was called, or even for sure which plant it was, but he recognized the scent.

The strap of his pack caught on a twig, and he jerked it

free, setting loose a flutter of yellow leaves like a small flight of butterflies. He would be glad to reach the stream, and not only for the sake of water, though he needed that. The nights were growing cold, but the days were still warm, and he had emptied his canteen before noon.

More urgently than water, though, he needed open air. Down here in the bottomland, the stands of dogwood and sweet bay grew so thickly that he could barely see the sky, and where the sun poked through, thick grass sprang up knee-high and the prickly leaves of dahoon caught at him as he passed.

He had brought Clarence the mule, as being better suited than the horses to the rough going in the wilderness, but some places were too rough even for a mule. He had left Clarence hobbled on the higher ground, with his bedroll and saddlebags, while he thrashed his way through the brush to reach the next point for a survey reading.

A wood-duck burst from the brush at his feet, nearly stopping his heart with the drumming of its wings. He stood still, heart thumping in his ears, and a horde of vivid little parakeets came chattering through the trees, swooping down to look at him, friendly and curious. Then something unseen gave them alarm and they rose up in a bright shriek of flight, arrowing away through the trees.

It was hot; he took off his coat and tied the sleeves round his waist, then wiped his face with a shirtsleeve and resumed his shoving, the weight of the astrolabe swinging on a thong round his neck. From the top of a mountain, he could look down on the misty hollows and wooded ridges, and take a certain awed pleasure in the thought that he owned such a place. Down here, come to grips with wild vines, burrowing fox-tails, and thickets of bamboolike cane higher than his head, the thought of ownership was ridiculous—how could something like this—this fucking swamp primeval—possibly be *owned*?

Ownership aside, he wanted to finish with this jungle and get back to higher ground. Even dwarfed by the gigantic trees of the virgin forest, a man could breathe in the space beneath. The limbs of the giant tulip trees and chestnuts stretched in a canopy overhead that shaded the ground beneath, so that only small things grew beneath—mats of delicate wildflowers, lady's slippers, trilliums—and the trees' dead leaves rained down in such profusion that one's feet sank inches into the springy mat.

Incomprehensible that such a place should ever alter— and yet it did, it would. He knew that fine; *knew* it—better than knew it, he'd bloody *seen* it! He'd driven a car down a paved highway, straight through the heart of a place once like this. He knew it could be changed. And yet as he struggled through the growth of sumac and partridgeberry, he knew even better that this place could swallow him without a second's hesitation.

Still, there was something about the sheer awful scale of the wilderness that soothed him. Among the gigantic trees and teeming wildlife, he found some peace; peace from the dammed-up words inside his head, from the unspoken worry in Brianna's eyes, the judgment in Jamie's—judgment withheld, but hanging there like the sword of Damocles. Peace from the glances of pity or curiosity, from the constant slow, aching effort of speech—peace from the memory of singing.

He missed them all, especially Bree and Jem. He seldom dreamed with any coherence; not like Bree—what was she writing now in her book?—but he had wakened this morning from a vivid impression of Jem, crawling over him as he liked to do, poking and prodding inquisitively, then softly patting Roger's face, exploring eyes and ears, nose and mouth, as though searching for the missing words.

He hadn't spoken at all for the first few days of surveying, terribly relieved not to have to. Now he was beginning to talk again, though—disliking the hoarse, mangled sound of the words, but not so bothered, since there was no one else to hear.

He heard the gurgle then of water over stones, and burst through a screen of willow saplings to find the stream at his feet, sun sparking off the water. He knelt and drank and splashed his face, then chose the spots along the bank from which to take his sightings. He dug the ledger book, ink, and quill from the leather bag over his shoulder, and fished the astrolabe out of his shirt.

He had a song in his head—again. They sneaked in when he wasn't looking, melodies singing in his inner ear like sirens from the rocks, ready to dash him in pieces.

Not this one, though. He smiled to himself, as he nudged the bar of the astrolabe and sighted on a tree on the opposite bank. It was a children's song, one of the counting songs Bree sang to Jemmy. One of those terrible songs that got into one's head and wouldn't get out again. As he took his sightings and made the notations in his book, he chanted under his breath, ignoring the cracked distortion of the sounds.

"The . . . ants go . . . mar-shing . . . one . . . by one."

Five thousand acres. What in hell was he to do with it? What in hell was he to do, period?

"Down . . . to . . . the gr-grround . . . to ggetout . . . atha RAIN . . . bum, bum, bum . . ."

I DISCOVERED QUICKLY why my name had appeared to have significance to Tsatsa'wi; the name of the village was Kalanun'yi—Raventown. I didn't see any ravens as we rode in, but did hear one, calling hoarsely from the trees.

The village lay in a charming location; a narrow river valley at the foot of a smallish mountain. The town itself was surrounded by a small spread of fields and orchards. A middling stream ran past it, dropping down a small cataract and flowing off down the valley into what looked from a distance like a huge thicket of bamboo—a canebrake, it was called, the leafy giant canes glowing dusty gold in the sun of early afternoon.

We were greeted with cordial enthusiasm by the residents of the town, lavishly fed and entertained for a day and a night. In the afternoon of the second day, we were invited to join in what I gathered was a petition to whichever Cherokee deity was in charge of hunting, to invoke favor and protection for the expedition against the ghost-bear that was to take place next day.

It had not occurred to me, prior to meeting Jackson Jolly, that there might be as much variance in talent among Indian shamans as there was among the Christian clergy. I had by this time encountered several of both species, but buffered by the mysteries of language, had not previously realized that a calling as shaman did not necessarily guarantee a person the possession of personal magnetism, spiritual power, or a gift for preaching.

Watching a slow glaze spread across the features of the people packed into Peter Bewlie's wife's father's house, I realized now that whatever his personal charm or connections with the spirit world, Jackson Jolly was sadly lacking in the last of these talents.

I had noticed a certain look of resignation on the faces of some of the congregation as the shaman took his place before the hearth, clad in a shawl-like blanket of red flannel, and wearing a mask carved in the semblance of a bird's face. As he began to speak, in a loud, droning voice, the woman next to me shifted her weight heavily from one leg to the other and sighed.

The sighing was contagious, but it wasn't as bad as the yawning. Within minutes, half the people around me were gaping, eyes watering like fountains. My own jaw muscles ached from being clenched, and I saw Jamie blinking like an owl.

Jolly was undoubtedly a sincere shaman; he also appeared to be a boring one. The only person who appeared riveted by his petitions was Jemmy, who perched in Brianna's arms, mouth hanging open in awe.

The chant for bear-hunting was a fairly monotonous one, featuring endless repetitions of *"He! Hayuya'haniwa, hayuya'haniwa, hayuya'haniwa . . ."* Then slight variations on the theme, each verse ending up with a rousing—and rather startling—*"Yoho!"*, as though we were all about to set sail on the Spanish main with a bottle of rum.

The congregation exhibited more enthusiasm during this song, though, and it finally dawned on me that what was wrong was probably not with the shaman himself. The ghost-bear had been plaguing the village for months; they must have gone through this particular ceremony several times, already, with no success. No, it wasn't that Jackson Jolly was a poor preacher; only that his congregation was suffering a lack of faith.

After the conclusion of the song, Jolly stamped fiercely on the hearth as punctuation to something he was saying, then took a sage-wand from his pouch, thrust it into the fire, and began to march round the room, waving the smoke over the congregation. The crowd parted politely as he marched up to Jamie and circled him and the Beardsley twins several times, chanting and perfuming them with wafts of fragrant smoke.

Jemmy thought this intensely funny. So did his mother, who was standing on my other side, vibrating with suppressed giggling. Jamie stood tall and straight, looking extremely dignified, as Jolly—who was quite short—hopped around him like a toad, lifting the tail of his coat to perfume his backside. I didn't dare catch Brianna's eye.

This phase of the ceremony complete, Jolly regained his position by the fire and began to sing again. The woman next to me shut her eyes and grimaced slightly.

My back was beginning to ache. At long last, the shaman concluded his proceedings with a shout. He then retired into the offing and took off his mask, wiping the sweat of righteous labor from his brow and looking pleased with himself. The headman of the village then stepped up to speak, and people began to shift and stir.

I stretched, as unobtrusively as possible, wondering what there might be for supper. Distracted by these musings, I didn't at first notice that the shiftings and stirrings were becoming more pronounced. Then the woman beside me straightened up abruptly and said something loud, in a tone of command. She cocked her head to one side, listening.

The headman stopped talking at once, and all around me people began to look upward. Bodies grew rigid and eyes grew wide. I heard it, too, and a sudden shiver raised gooseflesh on my forearms. The air was filled with a rush of wings.

"What on earth is that?" Brianna whispered to me, looking upward like everyone else. "The descent of the Holy Ghost?"

I had no idea, but it was getting louder—much louder. The air was beginning to vibrate, and the noise was like a long, continuous roll of thunder.

*"Tsiskwa!"* shouted a man in the crowd, and all of a sudden there was a stampede for the door.

Rushing out of the house, I thought at first that a storm had come suddenly upon us. The sky was dark, the air filled with thunder, and a strange, dim light flickered over everything. But there was no moisture in the air, and a peculiar smell filled my nose—not rain. Definitely not rain.

"Birds, my god, it's birds!" I barely heard Brianna behind me, among the chorus of amazement all around. Everyone stood in the street, looking up. Several children, frightened by the noise and darkness, started to cry.

It *was* unnerving. I had never seen anything like it—nor had most of the Cherokee, judging from their reaction. It felt as though the ground was shaking; the air was certainly shaking, vibrating to the clap of wings like a drum being slapped with frantic hands. I could feel the pulse of it on my skin, and the cloth of my kerchief tugged, wanting to rise on the wind.

The paralysis of the crowd didn't last long. There were shouts here and there, and all of a sudden, people were rushing up and down the street, charging into their houses and racing out again, with bows. Within seconds, a perfect hail of arrows was zipping up into the cloud of birds, and feathered bodies plopped out of the sky to land in limp, blood-soaked blobs, pierced with arrows.

Bodies weren't the only thing plopping out of the sky. A juicy dropping struck my shoulder, and I could see a rain of falling particles, a noxious precipitation from the thundering flock overhead, raising tiny puffs of dust from the street as the droppings struck. Down feathers shed from the passing birds floated in the air like dandelion seeds, and here and there, larger feathers knocked from tails and wings spiraled down like miniature lances, bobbing in the wind. I hastily backed up, taking shelter under the eaves of a house with Brianna and Jemmy.

We watched from our refuge in awe, as the villagers jostled each other in the street, archers shooting as fast as they could, one arrow following on the heels of another. Jamie, Peter Bewlie, and Josiah had all run for their guns, and were among the crowd, blasting away, not even troubling to aim. It wasn't necessary; no one could miss. Children, streaked with bird droppings, dodged and darted through the crowd, picking up the fallen birds, piling them in heaps by the doorsteps of the houses.

It must have lasted for nearly half an hour. We crouched under the eaves, half-deafened by the noise, hypnotized by the unceasing rush overhead. After the first fright, Jemmy stopped crying, but huddled close in his mother's arms, head buried under the drape of her kerchief.

It was impossible to make out individual birds in that violent cascade; it was no more than a river of feathers that filled the sky from one side to the other. Above the thunder of the wings, I could hear the birds calling to each other, a constant susurrus of sound, like a wind storm rushing through the forest.

At last—at long last—the great flock passed, stray birds trailing from the ragged fringe of it as it crossed the mountain and disappeared.

The village sighed as one. I saw people rubbing at their ears, trying to get rid of the clap and echo of the flight. In the midst of the crowd, Jackson Jolly stood beaming, liberally plastered with down feathers and bird droppings, eyes glowing. He spread out his arms and said something, and the people nearby murmured in response.

"We are blessed," Tsatsa'wi's sister translated for me, looking deeply impressed. She nodded at Jamie and the Beardsley twins. "The Ancient White has sent us a great sign. They will find the evil bear, surely."

I nodded, still feeling slightly stunned. Beside me, Brianna stooped and picked up a dead bird, holding it by the slender arrow that pierced it through. It was a plump thing, and very pretty, with a delicate, smoky-blue head and buff-colored breast feathers, the wing plumage a soft reddish-brown. The head lolled limp, the eyes covered by fragile, wrinkled gray-blue lids.

"It is, isn't it?" she said, softly.

"I think it must be," I answered, just as softly. Gingerly, I put out a finger and touched the smooth plumage. As signs and portents went, I was unsure whether this one was a good omen, or not. I had never seen one before, but I was quite sure that the bird I touched was a passenger pigeon.

THE HUNTERS SET FORTH before dawn the next day. Brianna parted reluctantly from Jemmy, but swung up into her saddle with a lightness that made me think she wouldn't pine for him while hunting. As for Jemmy himself, he was much too absorbed in rifling the baskets under the bed platform to take much notice of his mother's leaving.

The women spent the day in plucking, roasting, smoking, and preserving the pigeons with wood-ash; the air was filled with drifting down and the scent of grilled pigeon livers was thick in the air, as the whole village gorged on this delicacy. For my part, I helped with the pigeons, interspersing this work with entertaining conversation and profitable barter, only pausing now and then to look toward the mountain where the hunters had gone, and say a brief silent prayer for their well-being—and Roger's.

I had brought twenty-five gallons of honey with me, as well as some of the imported European herbs and seeds from Wilmington. Trade was brisk, and by the evening, I had exchanged my stocks for quantities of wild ginseng, cohosh, and—a real rarity—a chaga. This item, a huge warty fungus that grows from ancient birch trees, had a reputation—or so I was told—for the cure of cancer, tuberculosis, and ulcers. A useful item for any physician to have on hand, I thought.

As for the honey, I had traded that straight across, for twenty-five gallons of sunflower oil. This was provided in bulging skin bags, which were piled up under the eaves of the house where we were staying, like a small heap of cannon balls. I paused to look at them with satisfaction whenever I went outside, envisioning the soft, fragrant soap to be made from the oil—no more hands reeking of dead pig fat! And with luck, I could sell the bulk of it for a high enough price to make up the next chunk of Laoghaire's blood money, damn her eyes.

The next day was spent in the orchards with my hostess, another of Tsatsa'wi's sisters, named Sungi. A tall, sweet-faced woman of thirty or so, she had a few words of English, but some of her friends had slightly more—and a good thing, my own Cherokee being so far limited to "Hello," "Good," and "More."

In spite of the Indian ladies' increased fluency, I had some difficulty in making out exactly what "Sungi" meant—depending upon whom I was talking to, it seemed to mean either "onion," "mint," or—confusingly—"mink." After a certain amount of cross talk and sorting out, I got it established that the word seemed to mean none of these things precisely, but rather to indicate a strong scent of some kind.

The apple trees in the orchard were young, still slender, but bearing decently, providing a small yellowish-green fruit that wouldn't have impressed Luther Burbank, but which did have a nice crunchy texture and a tart flavor—an excellent antidote to the greasy taste of pigeon livers. It was a dry year, Sungi said, frowning critically at the trees; not so much fruit as the year before, and the corn was not so good, either.

Sungi put her two young daughters in charge of Jemmy, obviously warning them to be careful, with much pointing toward the wood.

"Is good the Bear-Killer come," she said, turning back to me, apple basket on her hip. "This bear not-bear; is not speak us."

"Oh, ah," I said, nodding intelligently. One of the other ladies helpfully amplified this idea, explaining that a reasonable bear would pay attention to the shaman's invocation, which called upon the bear-spirit, so that hunters and bears would meet appropriately. Given the color of this bear, as well as its stubborn and malicious behavior, it was apparent that it was not a real bear, but rather some malign spirit that had decided to manifest itself as a bear.

"Ah," I said, somewhat more intelligently. "Jackson mentioned 'the Ancient White'—was it the bear he meant?" Surely Peter had said that white was one of the favorable colors, though.

Another lady—who had given me her English name of
Anna, rather than try to explain what her Cherokee name
meant—laughed in shock at that.

"No, no! Ancient White, he the fire." Other ladies chip-
ping in here, I finally gathered that the fire, while obviously
powerful and to be treated with deep respect, was a beneficial
entity. Thus the atrociousness of the bear's conduct; white
animals normally were accorded respect and considered to
be carriers of messages from the otherworld—here one or
two of the ladies glanced sideways at me—but this bear was
not behaving in any manner they understood.

Knowing what I did about the bear's assistance from
Josiah Beardsley and the "wee black devil," I could well understand this. I didn't want to implicate Josiah, but I mentioned that I had heard stories—carefully not saying where I
had heard them—of a black man in the forest, who did evil
things. Had they heard of this?

Oh, yes, they assured me—but I should not be troubled.
There was a small group of the black men, who lived "over
there"—nodding toward the far side of the village, and the
invisible canebrake and bottomlands beyond the river. It was
possible that these persons were demons, particularly since
they came from the west.

It was possible that they were not. Some of the village
hunters had found them, and followed them carefully for several days, watching to see what they did. The hunters reported that the black men lived wretchedly, having barely
scraps of clothing and without decent houses. This seemed
not how self-respecting demons should live.

However, they were too few and too poor to be worth raiding—and the hunters said there were only three women, and
those very ugly—and they might be demons, after all. So the
villagers were content to leave them alone for now. The black
men never came near the village, one lady added, wrinkling
her nose; the dogs would smell them. Conversation lapsed
then, as we spread out through the orchard, gathering ripe
fruit from the trees, while the younger girls gathered the
windfalls from the ground.

We went home in mid-afternoon, tired, sunburnt, and
smelling of apples, to find that the hunters had come back.

"Four possums, eighteen rabbits, and nine squirrels," Jamie reported, sponging his face and hands with a damp cloth. "We found a great many birds, too, but what wi' the pigeons, we didna bother, save for a nice hawk that George Gist wanted for the feathers." He was windblown, the bridge of his nose burned red, but very cheerful. "And Brianna, bless her, killed a fine elk, just the other side of the river. A chest shot, but she brought it down—and cut the throat herself, though that's a dicey thing to do, and the beast's still thrashing."

"Oh, good," I said, rather faintly, envisioning a flurry of sharp hooves and lethal antlers in the close vicinity of my daughter.

"Dinna fash yourself, Sassenach," he said, seeing my expression. "I taught her the proper way of it. She came from behind."

"Oh, good," I said, a little more tartly. "I imagine the hunters were impressed?"

"Verra much," he said cheerfully. "Did ye ken, Sassenach, that the Cherokee let their women make war, as well as hunt? Not that they do it so often," he added, "but now and again, one will take it into her head, and go out as what they call a War Woman. The men will follow her, in fact."

"Very interesting," I said, trying to ignore the vision this summoned up, of Brianna being invited to head up a Cherokee raiding party. "Blood will out, I suppose."

"What?"

"Never mind. Did you happen to see any bears, or were you too busy exchanging interesting tidbits of anthropological lore?"

He narrowed one eye at me over the towel with which he was wiping his face, but answered equably enough.

"We found a deal of bear-sign. Josiah's an eye for it. Not only the droppings; he spotted a scratching-tree—one wi' bits of hair caught in the bark. He says that a bear has a favorite tree or two, and will come back to the same one again and again, so if ye're set to kill a particular bear, ye could do worse than camp nearby and wait."

"I gather that strategy didn't answer at present?"

"I daresay it would," he answered, grinning, "save it was

the wrong bear. The hair on the tree was dark brown, not white."

The expedition had not, however, been a failure. The hunters had completed a great semi-circle round the village, casting far out into the wood, then ranging down as far as the river. And in the soft earth of the bottomland near the canebrake, they had found footprints.

"Josiah said they were different than the prints of the bear whose hair we found—and Tsatsa'wi thought they were the same as the prints he'd seen when the white bear killed his friend."

The logical conclusion, agreed upon by all the bear-experts present, was that the ghost-bear had in all probability made its den in the canebrake. Such places were dense, dark, and cool in the heat of summer, and teeming with birds and small game. Even deer would hide there in hot weather.

"You can't get into such a place on horseback, can you?" I asked. He shook his head, combing leaves out of his hair with his fingers.

"No, nor can ye make much headway on foot, either, dense as it is. But we dinna mean to go in after the bear."

Instead, the plan was to set fire to the canebrake, driving the bear—and any other game present—out onto the flat bottomland on the other side, where it could be easily killed. Evidently, this was common practice in hunting, particularly in the fall, when the canebrakes grew dry and flammable. However, the burning would likely drive out a good deal more game than only the bear. That being so, an invitation had been sent to another village, some twenty miles distant, for their hunters to come and join with those of Ravenstown. With luck, enough game would be taken to supply both villages for the winter, *and* the extra hunters would insure that the evil ghost-bear did not escape.

"Very efficient," I said, amused. "I hope they don't smoke out the slaves, too."

"What?" He paused in his tidying.

"Black devils," I said, "or something along those lines." I told him what I had learned about the settlement—if that's what it was—of escaped slaves—if that's what they were.

"Well, I dinna suppose they're demons," he said dryly, sitting down in front of me so that I could braid his hair up neatly into a queue. "But I shouldna think they'll be in danger. They must live on the far side of the canebrake, on the opposite bank o' the river. I'll ask, though. There's time; it will be three or four days before the hunters come from Kanu'gala'yi."

"Oh, good," I said, tying the thong neatly in a bow. "That will give you just about time enough to eat all the leftover pigeon livers."

THE NEXT FEW DAYS PASSED pleasantly, though with a sense of rising anticipation that culminated with the arrival of the hunters from Kanu'gala'yi—Briertown, or so I was told. I wondered whether they had been invited because of a particular expertise in dealing with thorny territory, but forbore asking. Jamie, with his usual spongelike facility, was picking up Cherokee words like headlice, but I didn't want to tax his ability with trying to translate puns, just yet.

Jemmy appeared to have inherited his grandfather's touch with languages, and in the week since our arrival, had roughly doubled his vocabulary, with half his words being now in English and the other half in Cherokee, which rendered him unintelligible to everyone except his mother. My own vocabulary had expanded by the addition of the words for "water," "fire," "food," and "Help!"—for the rest, I depended on the kindness of the English-speaking Cherokee.

After the proper ceremonies and a large welcoming feast—featuring smoked pigeon livers with fried apples—the large party of hunters set off at dawn, equipped with pine torches and firepots, in addition to bows, muskets, and rifles. Having seen them off with a suitable breakfast—cornmeal mush mixed with pigeon livers and fresh apples—those of us not in the hunting party repaired to the houses, to pass the time in basketry, sewing, and talk.

The day was hot, muggy, and still. Not a breeze stirred in the fields, where the dry stalks of harvested corn and sunflowers lay like scattered pick-up sticks. No breath of air moved the dust in the village street. If one was going to set something on fire, I thought, it was a good day for the job. For myself, I was pleased to take refuge in the cool, shadowy interior of Sungi's cabin.

In the course of the day's conversation, I thought to ask about the components of the amulet that Nayawenne had made for me. Granted, she had been a Tuscaroran medicine-woman, so the underlying beliefs might not be the same— but I *was* curious about the bat.

"There is a story about bats," Sungi began, and I hid a smile. The Cherokee were in fact a great deal like the Scottish Highlanders, particularly in terms of liking stories. I had heard several already, in the few days we had spent in the village.

"The animals and the birds decided to play a ball game," Anna said, translating smoothly as Sungi talked. "At this time, bats walked on four feet, like the other animals. But when they came to play in the ball game, the other animals said no, they couldn't play; they were too small, and would surely be crushed. The bats didn't like this." Sungi frowned, with a grimace indicating a displeased bat.

"So the bats went to the birds, and offered to play on their side, instead. The birds accepted this offer, and so they took leaves and sticks, and they made wings for the bats. The birds won the ball game, and the bats liked their wings so much that—"

Sungi stopped talking abruptly. Her head lifted, and she sniffed the air. All around us, the women stopped talking. Sungi rose swiftly and went to the door, hand braced on the doorframe as she looked out.

I could smell the smoke—had been smelling it for the last hour as it came floating in on the wind—but I realized that the reek of burning had indeed gotten much stronger now. Sungi stepped outside; I got up and followed her with the other women, small prickles of unease beginning to nip at the backs of my knees.

The sky was beginning to darken with rain clouds, but the cloud of smoke was darker still, a roiling black smudge that rose above the distant trees. A wind had come up, riding on the edge of the approaching storm, and flurries of dry leaves rolled past us with a sound like small, skittering feet.

Most languages have a few monosyllables suitable for use in situations of sudden dismay, and so does Cherokee. Sungi said something I didn't catch, but the meaning was clear. One of the younger women licked a finger and held it up, but the gesture was unnecessary—I could feel the wind on my face, strong enough to lift the hair from my shoulders, cool on my neck. It was blowing straight toward the village.

Anna drew a long, deep breath; I could see her inflate herself, shoulders squaring to deal with the situation. Then all at once, the women were in motion, hurrying down the street toward their houses, calling for children, stopping to sweep the contents of a rack of drying jerky into a skirt or snatch a string of onions or squash from the eaves in passing.

I wasn't sure where Jemmy was; one of the older Indian girls had taken him to play with, but in the flurry, I couldn't be sure which one it was. I picked up my skirts and hurried down the street, ducking into each house without invitation, looking for him. There was a strong feeling of urgency in the air, but not panic. The sound of the dry leaves seemed constant, though, a faint rustling that followed at my heels.

I found him in the fifth house, sound asleep with several other children of different ages, all nestled like puppies in the folds of a buffalo robe. I would never have spotted him, save for his bright hair, shining like a beacon in the midst of the soft darkness. I woke them as gently as possible, and extricated Jemmy. He came awake at once, though, and was looking round, blinking in confusion.

"Come with Grannie, sweetheart," I said. "We're going to go now."

"Go horsie?" he asked, brightening at once.

"An excellent idea," I replied, hoisting him onto one hip. "Let's go find the horsie, shall we?"

The smell of smoke was much stronger when we emerged into the street. Jemmy coughed, and I could taste something acrid and bitter at the back of my mouth as I breathed. The evacuation was in full progress; people—mostly women—were hurrying in and out of the houses, pushing children before them, carrying hastily wrapped bundles of belongings. Still, there was no sense of panic or alarm in the exodus; everyone seemed concerned, but fairly matter-of-fact about it all. It occurred to me that a wooden village located in a deep forest must now and then be exposed to the risk of fire. No doubt the inhabitants had faced at least the possibility of a forest fire before, and were prepared to deal with it.

That realization calmed me a little—though the further realization that the constant dry-leaf rustling that I was hearing was in fact the crackle of the approaching fire wasn't calming at all.

Most of the horses had gone with the hunters. When I reached the brush pen, there were only three left. One of the older men of the village was mounted on one, and had Judas and the other horse on tethers, ready to lead away. Judas was saddled, and wore his saddlebags, and a rope halter. When the old man saw me, he grinned and called something, gesturing to Judas.

"Thank you!" I called back. The man leaned down and scooped Jemmy deftly from my arms, allowing me to mount Judas and get proper hold of the reins before handing Jemmy carefully back.

The horses were all restless, stamping and shifting. They knew as well as we did what fire was—and liked it even less. I took a firm hold on the halter with one hand, and a firmer hold on Jemmy with the other.

"Right, beast," I said to Judas, with an assumption of authority. "We're going now."

Judas was all in favor of this suggestion; he headed for the open gap in the brush fence as though it were the finish line of a race, snagging my skirts on the thorns of the fence as we passed. I managed to hold him back a little, long enough for the old man and his two horses to emerge from the brushy paddock and catch us up.

The man shouted something to me, and pointed toward the mountain, away from the fire. The wind had picked up; it blew his long gray hair across his face, muffling his words. He shook it away, but didn't bother to repeat himself, instead merely wheeling his mount in the direction he had pointed.

I kneed Judas in the side, turning him to follow, but kept a close rein, hesitating. I looked back over my shoulder toward the village, to see small streams of people trickling out from between the houses, all heading in the general direction the old man had indicated. No one was running, though they were all walking with great purpose.

Bree would be coming for Jemmy, as soon as she realized that the village was in danger. I knew she trusted me to see him safe, but no mother in such circumstances would rest until reunited with her child. We were not in any immediate peril, so I held back, waiting, in spite of Judas's increasing agitation.

The wind was lashing through the trees now, ripping loose billows of green and red and yellow leaves that pelted past us, plastering my skirt and Judas's hide in autumn patchwork. The whole sky had gone a violet-black, and I heard the first grumbles of thunder under the whistle of wind and rustle of fire. I could smell the tang of coming rain, even through the smoke, and felt a sudden hope. A good hard drench seemed just what the situation called for, and the sooner the better.

Jemmy was wildly excited by the atmospherics, and beat his fat little hands on the pommel, shouting a personal war chant toward the heavens that sounded something like "Oogie-oogie-oogie!"

Judas didn't care for this sort of behavior at all. I was having an increasingly hard time keeping him under any sort of control; he kept jerking at the halter while executing a sort of corkscrew maneuver that carried us in erratic circles. The wrapped rope was cutting hard into my hand, and Jemmy's bare heels were drumming a tattoo against my thighs.

I had just decided to give up and let the horse have his head, when he suddenly swung round and flung the head in question up, neighing loudly toward the village.

Sure enough, there were riders coming; I saw several horses coming out of the forest on the far side of the village at a trot. Judas, overjoyed to see other horses, was more than willing to go back into the village, even though it was in the direction of the fire.

I met Brianna and Jamie in the middle of the village, both looking anxiously round as they rode down the street. Jemmy shrieked with delight at sight of his mother, and lunged across into her arms, narrowly missing being dropped under the horses' nervous hooves.

"Did you get the bear?" I called to Jamie.

"No!" he shouted back, over the rising wind. "Come away, Sassenach!"

Bree was already off, heading for the forest, where the last of the villagers were disappearing into the trees. Relieved of my responsibility for Jemmy, though, I had thought of something else.

"Just a minute!" I shouted. I pulled up, and slid off Judas's back, throwing the reins toward Jamie. He leaned out to catch them, and yelled something after me, but I didn't catch it.

We were outside Sungi's house, and I had caught sight of the skins of sunflower oil, piled under the eaves. I risked a glance back in the direction of the canebrake. The fire was definitely coming closer; there were visible wisps of smoke swirling past me, and I *thought* I could see the glimmer of distant flame among the lashing trees. Still, I was fairly sure that we could outrun the fire on horseback—and that was a year's honey-profit lying about on the ground; I wasn't leaving it for the fire to take.

I dashed into the house, ignoring Jamie's infuriated bellows, and scrabbled madly through the scattered baskets, hoping against hope that Sungi hadn't taken . . . she hadn't. I seized a handful of rawhide strips and ran back outside.

Kneeling amid the swirling dust and smoke, I whipped strips of hide around the necks of two of the skin bags, and knotted the long ends of the two strips together, pulling the leather as tight as I could. Gathering the unwieldy pair up into my arms, I staggered back to the horses.

Jamie, seeing what I was about, gathered both sets of reins up one-handed, leaned out, and grabbed the makeshift handle that joined the skins, heaving the contraption over Gideon's withers so that the bags hung on either side.

"Come on!" he shouted.

"One more!" I called back, already running back to the house. From the corner of my eye, I could see him fighting the horses, who were plunging and snorting, anxious to be away. He was yelling uncomplimentary things about me in

Gaelic, but I sensed a certain resignation in his tone, and couldn't help smiling to myself, in spite of the anxiety that tightened my chest and made me fumble with the slippery hide strips.

Judas was snorting and rolling his eyes, baring his teeth intermittently with fear, but Jamie pulled him up close, holding his head tightly while I managed to fling the second pair of oil-filled bags across his saddle, and then mount myself.

The moment Jamie's iron grip on his halter relaxed, Judas was off. The rope was in my hands, but realizing its uselessness, I merely clung to the saddle for dear life, the oil bags bouncing madly against my legs as we hightailed it for the safety of the rising ground.

The storm was a lot closer now; the wind had dropped, but the thunder sounded in a loud clap overhead, which made Judas dig in his heels and bound over the open ground like a jackrabbit. Judas hated thunder. Remembering what had happened the last time I'd ridden him in a rainstorm, I flattened myself along his back and clung like a cocklebur, grimly determined not to be thrown or scraped off in his mad career.

Then we were into the wood, and leafless branches lashed at me like whips. I pressed myself lower against the horse's neck, closing my eyes to avoid having one poked out. Judas was moving more slowly now, by necessity, but was clearly still panicked; I could feel the churn of his hindquarters, driving us upward, and hear the breath whistling through his nostrils.

The thunder came again, and he lost his footing on the slippery leaves, slewing sideways and smashing into a stand of saplings. The springy wood saved us major damage, though, and we stumbled and staggered back upright, still moving upward. Opening one eye cautiously, I could tell that Judas had somehow found a trail—I could see the faint line of it, zigging through the dense growth in front of us.

Then the trees closed in again, and I could see nothing but a claustrophobic array of interwoven trunks and branches, twined with the yellowing remnants of wild honeysuckle and the flash of scarlet creepers. The thick growth slowed the horse still further, and I was at last able to draw a deep breath and wonder where Jamie was.

The thunder cracked again, and in its wake, I heard a high-pitched neigh, not far behind me. Of course—Judas hated thunder, but Gideon hated to follow another horse. He would be close behind, pushing to catch up.

A heavy drop of rain struck me between the shoulder blades, and I heard the rustle of the beginning rain, striking drop by drop by drop on leaves and wood and ground around me. The scent of ozone was sharp in my nostrils, and the whole wood seemed to give a green sigh, opening itself to the rain.

I gave a deep sigh, too, of relief.

Judas took a few steps further, and lurched to a halt, panting and blowing. Not waiting for another clap of thunder to set him off again, I hastily slid to the ground, and seizing his halter-rope, tied him to a small tree—no easy task, with my hands stiff and shaking.

Just in time. The thunder crashed again, a clap so loud that I could feel it on my skin. Judas screamed and reared, jerking at his rope, but I had wrapped it round the tree trunk. I stumbled back to get away from his panic, and Jamie caught me from behind. He started to say something, but the thunder boomed again, drowning him out.

I turned and clung to him, shaking with the adrenaline of delayed shock. The rain began to fall in good earnest now, drops cool on my face. He kissed my forehead, then let go and led me under the overhang of a big hemlock, whose fans of needles broke the rain, providing a fragrant, almost-dry cave beneath.

As the adrenaline surging through my body began to die down, I had a moment to look around, and realized that we were not the first inhabitants of this refuge.

"Look," I said, pointing into the shadows. The traces were slight, but obvious; someone had eaten here, discarding a tidy pile of small bones. Animals were not so tidy. Animals didn't scrape up dead needles into a comfy pillow, either.

Jamie winced at another bang of thunder, but nodded.

"Aye, it's a mankiller's spot, though I dinna think it's been used lately."

"A *what*?"

"Mankiller," he repeated. The lightning flashed behind

him, a vivid sheet that left his silhouette imprinted on my retina. "It's what they call the sentries; the warriors who stay outside the village, to keep watch and stop anyone coming in unaware. D'ye see?"

"I can't see a thing, just yet." I put out a hand, groping, and touched his coatsleeve, moving blindly into the shelter of his arm. I closed my eyes, in hopes of restoring my vision, but even against my sealed lids, I could see the flash and burst of lightning.

The thunder seemed to be moving off a little, or at least growing less frequent. I blinked, and found that I could see again. Jamie moved aside, gesturing, and I saw that we were standing on a sort of ledge, with the face of the mountain rising steeply behind us. Screened from view from below by a row of conifers, there was a narrow clearing—obviously man-made, as that was the only sort of clearing that occurred in these mountains. Looking out through the conifer branches, though, I had a breathtaking view over the small valley where Ravenstown lay.

The rain had slackened. Looking out from this high vantage point, though, I could see that the clouds were not one storm, but several; patches of dark rain hung randomly from the clouds like veils of gray velvet, and silent, jagged forks of lightning lanced suddenly across the black sky above the distant peaks, thunder grumbling in their wake.

Smoke still bloomed from the canebrake, a low flat crown of pale gray, almost white against the darkened sky. Even as high as we were, the smell of burning stung the nose, mingling oddly with the scent of rain. Here and there I could see flame-licks, still burning in the cane, but it was apparent that the fire was mostly out; the next shower of rain would quench it entirely. I could see, too, the people returning to the village, small groups making their way from the wood, bundles and children in tow.

I looked for riders, but saw none, let alone any with red hair. Surely Brianna and Jemmy were safe, though? I shivered suddenly; with the changeableness of mountain weather, the air had gone from smothering blanket to chill within less than an hour.

"All right, Sassenach?" Jamie's hand settled warmly on

my neck, fingers rubbing gently along the tense ridge of my shoulders. I took a deep breath and let them relax, as much as I could.

"Yes. Do you think it's safe to ride down?" My only impression of the trail was that it was both narrow and steep; it would be muddy now, and slippery with wet, dead leaves.

"No," he said, "but I dinna think—" He stopped abruptly, frowning in thought as he gauged the sky. He glanced behind us; I could barely make out the outline of the horses, standing close together under the shelter of the tree where I had tied Judas.

"I was going to say I didna think it particularly safe to stay here," he said at last. His fingers tapped gently on my shoulder as he thought, pattering like raindrops.

"But yon storm is moving fast; ye can see the lightning come across the mountain, and the thunder . . ." With melodramatic timing, a sharp boom of thunder rolled across the valley. I heard a shrill whinny of protest from one of the horses, and the rattle of foliage as he tugged at his halter. Jamie glanced over his shoulder, expression bleak.

"Your mount's got a strong mislike of thunder, Sassenach."

"Yes, I noticed that," I said, huddling closer to him for warmth. The wind was picking up again, as the next storm rolled in.

"Aye, he'll likely break his neck, and yours, too, if ye're so misfortunate as to be on that trail when it—" Another boom of thunder drowned his words, but I took his meaning.

"We'll wait," he said, positively.

He pulled me in front of him, and put his arms round me, sighing as he rested his chin on the top of my head. We stood together in the shelter of the hemlock, waiting for the storm to come.

Far below, the canebrake seethed and hissed, the smoke of the burning beginning to rise and fly with the wind. Away from the village, this time, toward the river. I wondered suddenly where Roger was—somewhere under that murky sky. Had he found safe refuge from the storm?

"I wonder where that bear is, too," I said, voicing half my thoughts. Jamie's chest moved in a rueful laugh, but the thunder drowned his voice.

# WILDFIRE

ROGER HALF-WOKE with the smell of smoke burning in his throat. He coughed and sank back into sleep, fragmented images of a sooty hearth and burnt sausages fading into mist. Tired from a morning of shoving his way through impenetrable thickets of brush and cane, he had eaten a sparse lunch and lain down for an hour's rest in the shade of a black willow on the river bank.

Lulled by the rushing water, he might have sunk back into solid slumber, but a distant shriek pulled him upright, blinking. The shriek was repeated, far off but loud. The mule!

He was on his feet, stumbling toward the sound, before he remembered the leather bag that held his ink and quills, the half-chain, and the precious surveying records. He lunged back to snatch it, then splashed across the shallows toward Clarence's hysterical braying, the weight of the astrolabe swinging on its thong against his chest. He crammed it inside his shirt to stop it catching on branches, looking desperately for the way by which he had come.

Smoke—he *did* smell smoke. He coughed, half choking as he tried to stifle it. Coughing hurt his throat, with a searing pain as the scar tissue inside seemed to tear.

"Coming," he breathed, in Clarence's direction. It wouldn't have mattered if he could have shouted; even when he'd had a voice, it hadn't the carrying quality of Clarence's. He'd left the mule hobbled in a grassy patch on the edge of the canebrake, but he hadn't come in very far.

"Again," he muttered, throwing his weight against a stand of young cane to force his way through. "Yell . . . again . . .

dammit." The sky was dark. Springing from sleep and blundering off as he had, he had no sense of where he was, save for Clarence.

Shit, what was happening? The smell of smoke was noticeably stronger; as his mind cleared from the muddle of sleep and panic, he realized that something was drastically wrong. The birds, normally somnolent in mid-day, were agitated, fluttering and calling with loud, disjointed screeches past his head. Air moved restless through the canes, fluttering their ragged leaves, and he caught a touch of warmth on his face—not the moist, clinging, all-embracing warmth of the muggy canebrake, but a dry, hot touch that brushed his cheek and sent a paradoxical chill right down his back. Holy Christ, the place was on fire.

He took a deep breath, calming himself deliberately. The canebrake was alive around him; a hot wind was moving, rattling dry canes, driving flocks of songbirds and parakeets before it, flung like handsful of bright confetti through the leaves. The smoke crept into his chest and gripped his lungs, burning, keeping him from drawing a full breath.

"Clarence," he rasped, as loudly as he could. No good; he could scarcely hear himself above the rising agitation of the canebrake. He couldn't hear the mule at all. Surely the fatheaded animal hadn't been burned to a crisp already? No, more likely, he'd broken his rag hobbles and galloped off to safety.

Something brushed his leg and he looked down in time to see the naked, scaly tail of a possum, scampering into the brush. That was as good a direction as any, he thought, and plunged into the growth of buttonbush after it.

There was a grunting somewhere near; a small pig burst out of a patch of yaupon and crossed his path, heading to the left. Pig, possum—was either known to have a good sense of direction? He hesitated for a moment, then followed the pig; it was big enough to help break a path.

A path there seemed to be; small patches of bare earth showed here and there, trampled between the tussocks of grass. Wild orchids winked among them, vivid as small jewels, and he wondered at the delicacy of them—how could he notice such things, at such a time?

The smoke was thicker; he had to stop and cough, bending nearly double and clutching at his throat, as though he could keep the tissue intact, keep it from tearing with his hands. Eyes streaming, he straightened up to find that the trail had disappeared. A thrill of panic squeezed his insides as he saw a wisp of drifting smoke, nosing its way slowly through the undergrowth, delicately questing.

He clenched his fists hard enough to feel the short nails bite into his palms, using the pain to focus his mind. He turned slowly round, eyes closed to concentrate, listening, turning his face from side to side, searching for a draft of fresh air, a sense of heat—anything that would tell him which way to go, away from the fire.

Nothing. Or rather, everything. Smoke was everywhere now, in thickening clouds that crept low across the ground, rolled black out of thickets, choking. He could *hear* the fire now, a chuckling noise, like someone laughing, low down in a scar-choked throat.

Willows. His mind clung to the notion of willows; he could see a growth of them in the distance, barely visible above the waving canes. Willows grow near water; that was where the river was.

A small red and black snake slid across his foot as he reached the water, but he scarcely noticed. There was no time for any fear but the fear of fire. He splashed into the center of the stream and dropped to his knees, bending to get his face as close to the water as he could.

There was moving air, there, cool from the water, and he gulped it, deep enough to make him cough again, shaking his body with a series of racking, tearing spasms. Which way, which way? The stream wound to and fro through acres of cane and river thicket. To follow it one way would lead him toward the bottomland—perhaps, out of the fire, or at least to open country—a place where he could see again to run. To go the other way might take him straight to the heart of the fire. But there was nothing overhead but cloudy darkness, and no way of knowing.

He pressed his arms tight against his body, trying to stifle the coughing, and felt the bulge of his leather bag. The records. Goddamn it, he could countenance the possibility of his own death, but not the loss of those records, made over so many laborious days. Floundering and stumbling, he made his way to the river's edge. He dug frantically with his hands, scrabbling in the soft mud, ripping out handsful of the long, tough grass, yanking horsetails up by the roots. They came apart in his hands and he flung the segments heedless over his shoulder, breath sobbing in his chest as he gasped and dug.

The air was hot all round him, searing in his lungs. He crammed the leather bag into the damp hole he had made, reached out his arms and grasped the dirt, pulling it to him, the mud a comfort on his skin as he scooped it in.

He stopped, panting. He should be sweating, but the sweat dried before it reached the surface of his skin. The fire was close. Rocks, he needed rocks to mark the place—they wouldn't burn. He splashed back into the creek, groped beneath the surface, oh God it was cold, it was wet, thank God, grasped a boulder slick with green slime and threw it toward the bank. Another, a handful of smaller rocks, grasped in desperation, another big one, a flat one, another—enough, it would have to be enough, the fire was coming.

He piled his rocks into a hasty cairn, and commending his soul to the mercy of God, plunged back into the river and fled, stumbling and choking, rocks rolling and sliding under his feet, fled for as long as his trembling legs would carry him, before the smoke seized him by the throat, filled head and nose and chest, and choked him, the band of scarring a hand that squeezed out air and life, and left only blackness behind his eyes, lit by the flickering redness of fire.

HE WAS FIGHTING. Fighting the noose, fighting the bonds on his wrists, fighting most of all the black void that crushed his chest and sealed his throat, fighting for one final sip of precious air. He bucked, straining with every ounce of force, and then was rolling on the ground, arms flying free.

He struck something with one flailing hand. It was soft, and yelped in surprise.

Then there were hands on his shoulders, his legs, and he

was sitting up, vision fractured and chest heaving in the effort to breathe. Something struck him hard in the middle of the back. He choked, coughed, gulped enough air to cough down deep in the charred center of himself, and a huge gobbet of black phlegm rolled up out of his chest, warm and slimy as a rotten oyster on his tongue.

He spat it out, choked and heaved as the bile rose up burning through the raw squeezed channel of his throat. Then spat again, gulped, and sat up, gasping.

He had no attention to spare for anything, lost in the miracle of air and breath. There were voices around him, and vague faces in the dark; everything smelled of burning. Nothing mattered but the oxygen flooding through his chest, plumping up his shriveled cells like raisins soaked in water.

Water touched his mouth, and he looked up, eyes blinking and watering in the effort to see. His eyeballs felt seared; light and shadow smeared together, and he blinked hard, warm tears a balm to the rawness of his eyes, cooling his skin as they ran down his cheeks. Someone held a cup to his lips; a woman, face blackened with soot. No, not soot. He blinked, squinted, blinked. She was black of herself. Slave?

He took a brief gulp of water, unwilling to interrupt his breathing even for the pleasure of the coolness on his ravaged throat. It was good, though—very good. His hands rose and wrapped around the cup, surprising him. He had expected the pain of broken fingers, long-numbed flesh . . . but his hands were whole and serviceable. He reached automatically for the hollow of his neck, expecting pain and the whistle of amber—and prodded unbelievingly at the solid flesh there. He breathed, and the air whistled through his nose and down the back of his throat. The world shifted around him, and realigned itself.

He was sitting in a ramshackle hut of some sort. There were several people in the hut, and more peering in at the door. Most of them were black, all were in rags, and none of the faces looked even faintly friendly.

The woman who had given him water looked scared. He tried a smile at her, and coughed again. She looked up at him under the ragged cloth tied round her brows, and he saw that the whites of her eyes were scarlet, the lids red-rimmed and swollen. His must look the same, from the feel of them. The air was still thick with smoke, and he could hear the distant cracks and pops of heat-split cane, the dying rumble of the fire. Somewhere nearby, a bird called once in alarm, then fell abruptly silent.

There was a conversation going on near the door, conducted in sibilant whispers. The men who were talking—no, arguing—glanced at him now and then, their faces masks of fear and distrust. It had begun to rain outside; he couldn't smell it, but cool air struck his face, and he heard the patter of drops on the roof, on the trees outside.

He drained the rest of the water, then offered the woman back the cup. She shrank back, as though he might be contaminated. He set the cup on the ground, nodding to her, and swiped at his eyes with the back of his wrist. The hair on his arm was singed; it crumbled to dust at a touch.

He strained to pick out words, but heard nothing but gabble. The men weren't speaking English, nor yet French or Gaelic. He had heard some of the fresh blackbirds brought up from Charleston for sale in the Wilmington market, talking among themselves in just that sort of husky, secretive murmur. Some African tongue—or more than one.

His skin was blistered, hot and painful in several places, and the air in the hut was so thickly warm that sweat ran down his face with the water from his eyes, but a chill touched the base of his spine at the realization. He was not on a plantation—there were none, so far into the mountains. Such isolated homesteads as there were up here would be too poor to have slaves, let alone such a number. Some of the Indians kept slaves—but not black ones.

Only one answer possible, one confirmed by their behavior. They were maroons, then, his captors—his saviors? Escaped slaves, living here in secrecy.

Their freedom—and perhaps their lives—depended on that secrecy. And here he sat, a living threat to it. His insides gelled as he realized just how tenuous his position was. *Had* they saved him from the fire? If so, they must now be regretting it, judging from the looks of the men by the door.

One of the arguants broke away from the group, came and squatted down before him, pushing the woman out of the way. Narrow black eyes darted over him, from face to chest, then back. "Who you?"

He didn't think the pugnacious questioner wanted his name. Rather, he wanted to know Roger's purpose. Possibilities flickered through Roger's mind—what would be most likely to keep him alive?

Not "hunter"—if they thought him English and alone, they'd kill him for sure. Could he pretend to be French? A Frenchman wouldn't seem so dangerous to them. Perhaps.

He blinked hard to clear his vision, and was opening his mouth to say, *"Je suis Français—un voyageur,"* when he felt a sharp pain in the center of his chest that made him suck breath.

The metal of the astrolabe had seared him in the fire, and quick blisters had risen and burst beneath it, gluing the thing to him with their sticky fluid. As he moved now, the weight of it had torn free, ripping the ragged shreds of skin away, and leaving a throbbing raw patch in the center of his chest.

He dipped two fingers into the neck of his shirt, and carefully pulled up the leather thong.

"Sur . . . vey . . . or," he croaked, forcing the syllables past the knot of soot and scar in his throat.

*"Hau!"*

His questioner stared at the golden disk, eyes bulging. The men by the door pushed and shoved each other, trying to get close enough to see.

One reached out and snatched the astrolabe, dragging it off over his head. He made no attempt to keep it, but sat back, taking advantage of their preoccupation with the gaudy thing to gather his feet slowly under him. He strained to keep his eyes open, against the nearly irresistible urge to squeeze them shut; even the soft daylight from the door was painful.

One of the men glanced at him, and said something sharp. Two of them moved at once between him and the door, bloodshot eyes fixed on him like basilisks. The man holding the astrolabe called out something, a name, he thought, and there was a movement at the door, someone pushing through the bodies there.

The woman who came in looked much like the others; dressed in a ragged shift, damp with rain, with a square of cloth tied round her head, hiding her hair. One major difference, though; the thin arms and legs protruding from the shift were the weathered, freckled brown of a white person. She stared at Roger, keeping her eyes fixed on him as she moved into the center of the hut. Only the weight of the astrolabe in her hand pulled her gaze away from him.

A tall, rawboned man with one eye shoved forward. He moved close to the woman, poked a finger at the astrolabe, and said something that sounded like a question. She shook her head slowly, tracing the markings round the edge of the disk with puzzled fascination. Then she turned it over.

Roger saw her shoulders stiffen when she saw the engraved letters, and a flicker of hope sprang up in his chest; she knew it. She recognized the name.

He had been gambling that they might know what a surveyor was, might realize that the word implied that there were people awaiting his results—people who would come looking for him, if he did not return. From their point of view, there could be no gain in killing him, if others would come searching. But if the woman knew the name "James Fraser" . . .

The woman shot Roger a sudden, hard look, quite at odds with her earlier hesitation. She approached him, slowly, but without apparent fear.

"You are not Jameth Frather," she said, and he jerked, startled at the sound of her voice, clear but lisping. He blinked and squinted, then rose slowly to his feet, shading his eyes to see her against the glare of light from the door.

She might have been any age between twenty and sixty, though the light brown hair that showed at her temples was unmarked with gray. Her face was lined, but with struggle and hunger, he thought, not age. He smiled at her, deliberately, and her mouth drew back in reflex, a hesitant grimace, but nonetheless enough for him to catch a glimpse of her front teeth, broken off at an angle. Squinting, he made out the thin slash of a scar through one eyebrow. She was much thinner than Claire's description of her, but that was hardly surprising.

"I am not . . . James Fraser," he agreed hoarsely, and had to stop to cough. He cleared his throat, hawking up more soot and slime. He spat, turning politely aside, then turned back to her. "But you are . . . Fanny Beardsley . . . aren't you?"

He hadn't been sure, in spite of the teeth, but the look of shock that crossed her face at his words was solid confirmation. The men knew that name, too. The one-eyed man took a quick step forward and seized the woman by the shoulder; the others moved menacingly closer.

"James Fraser is . . . my wife's father," he said, as quickly as he could, before they could lay hands on him. "Do you want to know—about the child?"

The look of suspicion faded from her face. She didn't move, but a look of such hunger rose in her eyes that he had to steel himself not to step back from it.

"Fahnee?" The tall man still had a hand on her shoulder. He drew closer to her, his one eye flicking back and forth in suspicion, from the woman to Roger.

She said something, almost under her breath, and put up her hand, to cover the man's where it rested on her shoulder. His face went suddenly blank, as though wiped with a slate eraser. She turned to him, looking up into his face, talking in a low tone, quick and urgent.

The atmosphere in the hut had changed. It was still charged, but an air of confusion now mingled with the general mood of menace. There was thunder overhead, much louder than the sound of the rain, but no one took note of it. The men near the door looked at each other, then, frowning, at the couple arguing in whispers. Lightning flashed, silent, framing the people in the door with darkness. There were murmuring voices outside, sounds of puzzlement. Another boom of thunder.

Roger stood motionless, gathering his strength. His legs felt like rubber, and while breathing was still a joy, each breath burned and tickled in his lungs. He wouldn't go fast or far, if he had to run.

The argument stopped abruptly. The tall man turned and made a sharp gesture toward the door, saying something that made the other men grunt with surprise and disapproval. Still, they went, slowly, and with much muttered grumbling. One short fellow with his hair in knots glared back at Roger, bared his teeth, and drew the edge of a hand across his throat with a hiss. With a small shock, Roger saw that the man's teeth were jagged, filed to points.

The ramshackle door had barely closed behind them when the woman clutched his sleeve.

"Tell me," she said.

"Not so . . . fast." He coughed again, wiping spittle from his mouth with the back of his hand. His throat was seared; the words felt like cinders, forced burning from his chest. "You get . . . me . . . out of here. Then . . . I'll tell you. All I know."

"Tell me!"

Her fingers dug hard into his arm. Her eyes were bloodshot from the smoke, and the brown irises glowed like coals. He shook his head, coughing.

The tall man brushed the woman aside, grabbing Roger by a handful of shirt. Something gleamed dully, too close to Roger's eye to see clearly, and amid the stench of burning, he caught the reek of rotting teeth.

"You tell her, man, or I rip you guts!"

Roger brought a forearm up between them, and with an effort, shoved the man back, stumbling.

"No," he said doggedly. "You get . . . me out. Then I tell."

The man hesitated, crouched, the knife blade wavering in a small arc of uncertainty. His one eye flicked to the woman.

"You sure he know?"

The woman had not taken her eyes off Roger's face. She nodded slowly, not looking away.

"He knows."

"It was . . . a girl." Roger looked at her steadily, fighting the urge to blink. "You'll know . . . that much . . . yourself."

"Does she live?"

"Get me . . . out."

She was not a tall woman, nor a large one, but her urgency seemed to fill the hut. She fairly quivered with it, hands clenched into fists at her sides. She glared at Roger for a long minute more, than whirled on her heel, saying something violent to the man in the odd African tongue.

He tried to argue, but it was fruitless; the stream of her words struck him like water from a fire hose. He flung up his hands in frustrated surrender, then reached out and snatched the rag from the woman's head. He undid the knots with quick, long fingers, and whipped it into the shape of a blindfold, muttering under his breath.

The last thing Roger saw before the man fastened the cloth round his eyes was Fanny Beardsley, hair in a number of small greasy plaits round her shoulders, her eyes still on him, burning like embers. Her broken teeth were bared, and he thought she would bite him, if she could.

THEY DIDN'T GET OUT without some argument; a chorus of angry voices surrounded them for some way, and hands plucked at his clothes and limbs. But the one-eyed man still had the knife. Roger heard a shout, a scuffling of feet and bodies close by, and a sharp cry. The voices dropped, and the hands no longer snatched at him.

They walked on, his hand on Fanny Beardsley's shoulder for guidance. He thought it was a small settlement; at least, it took very little time before he felt the trees close around him. Leaves brushed his face, and the resin smell of sap was heightened by the hot, smoky air. It was still raining fairly hard, but the smell of smoke was everywhere. The ground was lumpy, layers of leaf-mold punctuated by upthrusting rocks, studded with stumps and fallen branches.

The man and woman exchanged occasional remarks, but soon fell silent. His clothes grew wet and clung to him, the seams of his breeches chafing as he walked. The blindfold was too tight to allow him to see anything, but light leaked under the edge, and from that, he could judge the changing time of day. He thought it was just past mid-afternoon when they left the hut; when they stopped at last, the light had faded almost completely.

He blinked when the blindfold was taken off, the sudden flood of light compensating for its dimness. It was late twilight. They stood in a hollow, already halfway filled with darkness. Looking up, he saw the sky above the mountains blazing with orange and crimson, the smoky haze lit up as though the world itself were still burning. Overhead, the clouds had broken; a slice of pure blue sky shone through, soft, and bright with twilight stars.

Fanny Beardsley faced him, looking smaller beneath the canopy of a towering chestnut tree, but every bit as intent as she had in the hut.

He had had plenty of time to think about it. Ought he to tell her where the child was, or should he claim not to know? If she knew, would she make an attempt to reclaim the little girl? And if so, what might be the fallout—for the child, the escaped slaves—or even for Jamie and Claire Fraser?

Neither of them had said anything about the events that had transpired at the Beardsley farmhouse, beyond the simple fact that Beardsley had died of an apoplexy. Roger was sufficiently familiar with them both, though, to draw silent deductions from Claire's troubled face and Jamie's impassive one. He didn't know what had happened, but Fanny Beardsley did—and it might well be something the Frasers would prefer remain undiscovered. If Mrs. Beardsley reappeared in Brownsville, seeking to reclaim her daughter, questions would certainly be asked—and perhaps it was to no one's benefit that they be answered.

The blazing sky washed her face with fire, though, and faced with the hunger in those burning eyes, he could speak nothing but the truth.

"Your daughter . . . is well," he began firmly, and she made a small strangled noise, deep in her throat. By the time he had finished telling what he knew, the tears were running down her face, making tracks in the soot and dust that covered her, but her eyes stayed wide, fixed on him as though to blink would be to miss some vital word.

The man hung back a little, wary, keeping watch. His attention was mostly on the woman, but he stole occasional glances at Roger as he spoke, and at the end, stood beside the woman, his one eye bright as hers.

"She have de money?" he asked. He had the lilt of the Indies in his speech, and a skin like dark honey. He would have been handsome, save for whatever accident had deprived him of his eye, leaving a pocket of livid flesh beneath a twisted, drooping lid.

"Yes, she's . . . inherited . . . all of Aaron . . . Beardsley's property," Roger assured him, breath rasping in his throat from so much talking. "Mr. Fraser saw . . . to it." He and Jamie had both gone to the hearing of the Orphan's Court, for Jamie to bear witness to the girl's identity. Richard Brown and his wife had been given the guardianship of the child—and her property. They had named the little girl—from what depths of sentiment or outrage, he had no idea—"Alicia."

"No matta she black?" He saw the slave's one eye flick sideways toward Fanny Beardsley, then slide away. Mrs. Beardsley heard the note of uncertainty in the man's voice, and turned on him like a viper striking.

"She is yourss!" she said. "She could not be histh, could not!"

"Yah, you say so," he replied, his face cast down in sullenness. "Dey give money to black girl?"

She stamped her foot, noiseless on the ground, and slapped at him. He straightened up and turned his face aside, but made no other attempt to escape her fury.

"Do you think I would have left her, *ever* left her, if she had been white, if she could posthibly have been white?" she shouted. She punched at him, pummelling his arms and chest with blows. "It wath your fault I had to leave her, yourss! You and that damned black hide, God damn you—"

It was Roger who seized her flailing wrists and held them tight against her straining, letting her shriek herself to hoarseness before she collapsed at last in tears.

The slave, who had watched all this with an expression between shame and anger, lifted his hands a little toward her. It was the slightest of movements, but enough; she turned at once from Roger and flung herself into her lover's arms, sobbing against his chest. He wrapped his arms awkwardly around her and held her close, rocking back and forth on his bare heels. He looked sheepish, but no longer angry.

Roger cleared his throat, grimacing at the soreness. The slave looked up at him, and nodded.

"You go, man," he said softly. Then, before Roger could turn to go, he said, "Wait . . . true, man, de child fix good?"

Roger nodded, feeling unutterably tired. Whatever adrena-

line or sense of self-preservation had been keeping him going was all used up. The blazing sky had gone to ashes, and
everything in the hollow was fading, blurring into dark.

"She's all . . . right. They'll take . . . good care of her." He
groped, wanting to offer something else. "She's . . . pretty,"
he said at last. His voice was nearly gone, no more than a
whisper. "A pretty . . . girl."

The man's face shifted, caught between embarrassment,
dismay, and pleasure.

"Oh," he said. "Dat be from de mama, sure." He patted
Fanny Beardsley's back, very gently. She had stopped sobbing, but stood with her face pressed against his chest, still
and silent. It was nearly full dark; in the deep dusk, all color
was leached away; her skin seemed the same color as his.

The man wore nothing but a tattered shirt, wet through, so
that his dark skin showed in patches through it. He had a
rope belt, though, with a rough cloth bag strung on it. He
groped one-handed in this, and drew out the astrolabe, which
he extended toward Roger.

"You don't mean . . . to keep that?" Roger asked. He felt
as though he was standing inside a cloud; everything was beginning to feel far away and hazy, and words reached him as
though filtered through cotton wool.

The ex-slave shook his head.

"No, man, what I do wid dat? Beside," he added, with a
wry lift of the mouth, "maybe no one come look you, man,
but de masta what own dat ting—he come look, maybe."

Roger took the heavy disk, and put the thong over his
neck. It took two tries; his arms felt like lead.

"Nobody . . . will come looking," he said. He turned and
walked away, with no idea where he was, or where he might
be going. After a few steps, he turned and looked back, but
the night had already swallowed them.

# 84

## BURNT TO BONES

THE HORSES SETTLED SLIGHTLY, but were still uneasy, pawing, stamping, and jerking at their tethers, as the thunder rumbled hollowly in the distance. Jamie sighed, kissed the top of my head, and pushed his way back through the conifers to the tiny clearing where they stood.

"Well, if ye dinna like it up here," I heard him say to them, "why did ye come?" He spoke tolerantly, though, and I heard Gideon whinny briefly in pleasure at seeing him. I was turning to go and help with the reassuring, when a flicker of movement caught my eye below.

I leaned out to see it, keeping a tight grip on one of the hemlock's branches for safety, but it had moved. A horse, I thought, but coming from a different direction than that in which the refugees had come. I wove my way down the line of conifers, peeking through the branches, and reached a spot near the end of the narrow ledge where I had a clear view of the river valley below.

Not a horse, quite—it was—

"It's Clarence!" I shouted.

"Who?" Jamie's voice came back from the far end of the ledge, half-drowned by the rustle of the branches overhead. The wind was still rising, damp with returning rain.

"Clarence! Roger's mule!" Not waiting for a reply, I ducked beneath an overhanging branch and balanced myself precariously on the lip of the ledge, clinging to a rocky outcrop that jutted from the cliff where it met the ledge. There were serried ranks of trees below, marching down the slope, their tops no more than a few inches below the level of my feet, but I didn't want to risk falling down into them.

It *was* Clarence, I was sure of it. I was by no means expert enough to recognize any quadruped by its distinctive gait, but Clarence had suffered some form of mange or other skin disease in his youth, and the hair had grown in white over the healed patches, leaving him peculiarly piebald over the rump.

He was lolloping over the stubbled corn fields, ears pointed forward and obviously happy to be rejoining society. He was also saddled and riderless, and I said a very bad word under my breath when I saw it.

"He's broken his hobbles and run." Jamie had appeared at my shoulder, peering down at the small figure of the mule. He pointed. "See?" I hadn't noticed, in my alarm, but there was a small rag of cloth tied round one of his forelegs, flapping as he ran.

"I suppose that's better," I said. My hands had gone sweaty, and I wiped my palms on the elbows of my sleeves, unable to look away. "I mean—if he was hobbled, then Roger wasn't on him. Roger wasn't thrown, or knocked off and hurt."

"Ah, no." Jamie seemed concerned, but not alarmed. "He'll have a long walk back, is all." Still, I saw his gaze shift out, over the narrow river valley, now nearly filled with smoke. He shook his head slightly, and said something under his breath—no doubt a cousin to my own bad word.

"I wonder if this is how the Lord feels," he said aloud, and gave me a wry glance. "Able to see what foolishness men are up to, but canna do a bloody thing about it."

Before I could answer him, lightning flashed, and the thunder cracked on its heels with a clap so loud and sudden that I jumped, nearly losing my grip. Jamie seized my arm to stop me falling, and pulled me back from the edge. The horses were throwing fits again, at the far end of the ledge, and he turned toward them, but stopped suddenly, his hand still on my arm.

"What?" I looked where he was looking, and saw nothing but the wall of the cliff, some ten feet away, festooned with small rock plants.

He let go my arm, and without answering, walked toward the cliff. And, I saw, toward an old fire-blasted snag that stood near it. Very delicately, he reached out and tweaked something from the dead tree's bark. I reached his side and peered into the palm of his hand, where he cradled several long, coarse hairs. White hairs.

Rain began to fall again, settling down in a businesslike way to the job of soaking everything in sight. A piercing pair of whinnies came from the horses, who didn't like being abandoned one bit.

I looked at the trunk of the tree; there were white hairs all over it, caught in the cracks of the ragged bark. *A bear has special scratching trees*, I could hear Josiah saying. *He'll come back to one, again and again.* I swallowed, hard.

"Perhaps," Jamie said very thoughtfully, "it's no just the thunder that troubles the horses."

Perhaps not, but it wasn't helping. Lightning flashed into the trees far down the slope and the thunder sounded with it. Another flash-bang following on its heels, and another, as though an ack-ack gun were going off beneath our feet. The horses were having hysterics, and I felt rather like joining them.

I had put on my hooded cloak when I left the village, but both hood and hair were matted to my skull, the rain pounding down on my head like a shower of nails. Jamie's hair was plastered to his head as well, and he grimaced through the rain.

He made a "stay here" gesture, but I shook my head and followed him. The horses were in a complete state, saturated manes dangling over rolling eyes. Judas had succeeded in half-uprooting the small tree I had tied him to, and Gideon had his ears laid flat, flexing his lip repeatedly over his big yellow teeth, looking for someone or something to bite.

Seeing this, Jamie's lips tightened. He glanced back toward the place where we had found the scratching-tree, invisible from our present position. The lightning flashed, the thunder shuddered through the rock, and the horses both screamed and lunged. Jamie shook his head, making the decision, and grabbed Judas's reins, holding him steady. Evidently we were getting off the mountain, slippery trail or not.

I got into the saddle in a swash of wet skirts, and took a firm grip, trying to shout soothing words into Judas's ear as he skittered and danced, eager to be gone. We were dangerously close to the conifers at the edge, and I leaned hard inward, trying to get him toward the cliff side of the ledge.

An extraordinary prickling sensation ran over my body, as though I were being bitten from head to toe by thousands of tiny ants. I looked at my hands and saw them glowing, limned in blue light. The hairs on my forearms stood straight out, each one glowing blue. My hood had fallen back, and I felt the hair on my head rise all at once, as though a giant hand had gently lifted it.

The air smelled suddenly of brimstone, and I looked about in alarm. Trees, rocks, the ground itself was bathed in blue light. Tiny snakes of brilliant white electricity hissed across the surface of the cliff, a few yards away.

I turned, calling for Jamie, and saw him on Gideon, turning toward me, his mouth open as he shouted, all words lost in the reverberation of the air around us.

Gideon's mane began to rise, as though by magic. Jamie's hair floated up from his shoulders, shot with wires of crackling blue. Horse and rider glowed with hell-light, each muscle of face and limb outlined. I felt a rush of air over my skin, and then Jamie flung himself from his saddle and into me, hurling us both into emptiness.

The lightning struck before we hit the ground.

I came to, smelling burned flesh and the throat-searing sting of ozone. I felt as though I had been turned inside out; all of my organs seemed to be exposed.

It was still raining. I lay still for a while, letting the rain run over my face and soak my hair, while the neurons of my nervous system slowly began to work again. My finger twitched, by itself. I tried to do it on purpose, and succeeded. I flexed my fingers—not so good. A few more minutes, though, and enough circuits were working to allow me to sit up.

Jamie was lying near me, sprawled on his back like a rag doll amid a patch of sumac. I crawled over to him, and found that his eyes were open. He blinked at me, and a muscle twitched at the side of his mouth in an attempt at a smile.

I couldn't see any blood, and while his limbs were thrown awry, they were all straight. The rain pooled in his eye sockets, running into his eyes. He blinked violently, then turned his head to let the water drain off his face. I put a hand on his stomach, and felt the big abdominal pulse beneath my fingers, very slow, but steady.

I didn't know how long we had been unconscious, but this storm too had moved away. Sheet lightning flashed beyond the distant mountains, throwing the peaks into sharp relief.

"Thunder is good," I quoted, watching it in a sort of dreamy stupor, "thunder is impressive; but it is the lightning that does the work."

"It's done a job of work on me. Are ye all right, Sassenach?"

"Splendid," I said, still feeling pleasantly remote. "And you?"

He glanced at me curiously, but seemed to conclude that it was all right. He grasped a sumac bush and dragged himself laboriously to his feet.

"I canna feel my toes just yet," he told me, "but the rest is all right. The horses, though—" He glanced upward, and I saw his throat move as he swallowed.

The horses were silent.

We were some twenty feet below the ledge, among the firs and balsams. I *could* move, but didn't seem able to summon the will to do so. I sat still, taking stock, while Jamie shook himself, then began the climb back up to the mankiller's ledge.

It seemed very quiet; I wondered whether I had been deafened by the blast. My foot was cold. I looked down and discovered that my left shoe was gone—whether knocked off by the lightning or lost in the fall, I had no idea, but I didn't see it anywhere nearby. The stocking was gone, too; there was a small dark starburst of veins, just below the anklebone—a legacy of my second pregnancy. I sat staring at it as though it were the key to the secrets of the universe.

The horses must be dead; I knew that. Why weren't we? I breathed in the stink of burning flesh, and a tiny shudder arose, somewhere deep inside me. Were we alive now, only because we were doomed to die in four years? When it came our turn, would we lie in the burnt ruins of our house, shells of charred and reeking flesh?

*Burnt to bones*, whispered the voice of my memory. Tears ran down my face with the rain, but they were distant tears—for the horses, for my mother—not for myself. Not yet.

There were blue veins beneath the surface of my skin, more prominent than before. On the backs of my hands, they traced a roadmap . . . in the tender flesh behind my knee, they showed in webs and traceries; along my shin, one large vein swelled snakelike, distended. I pressed a finger on it; it was soft and disappeared, but came back the instant I removed the finger.

The inner workings of my body were becoming slowly more visible, the taut skin thinning, leaving me vulnerable, with everything outside, exposed to the elements, that once was safely sheltered in the snug casing of the body. Bone and blood push through . . . there was an oozing graze on the top of my foot.

Jamie was back, drenched to the skin and breathless from the climb. Both his shoes were gone, I saw.

"Judas is dead," he said, sitting down beside me. He took my cold hand in his own cold hand and pressed it hard.

"Poor thing," I said, and the tears ran faster, warm streams mingling with cold rain. "He knew, didn't he? He always hated thunder and lightning, always."

Jamie put an arm round my shoulders and pressed my head against his chest, making little soothing noises.

"And Gideon?" I asked at last, raising my head and making an effort to wipe my nose on a fold of sodden cloak. Jamie shook his head, with a small, incredulous smile.

"He's alive," he said. "He's burnt down the side of his right shoulder and foreleg and his mane's singed off entirely." He picked up a fold of his own tattered cloak and tried to wipe my face, with no better results than I had had myself. "I expect it will do wonders for his temper," he said, trying to make a joke of it.

"I suppose so." I was too worn out and shaken to laugh, but I managed a small smile, and it felt good. "Can you lead him down, do you think? I—I have some ointment. It's good for burns."

"Aye, I think so." He gave me a hand and helped me stand up. I turned to brush down my crumpled skirts, and as I did so, caught sight of something.

"Look," I said, my voice no more than a whisper. "Jamie—look."

Ten feet away, up the slope from us, stood a big balsam fir, its top sheared cleanly away and half its remaining branches charred and smoking. Wedged between one branch and the stump of the trunk was a huge, rounded mass. It was half black, the tissues turned to carbon—but the hair on the other half lay in sodden white spikes, the cream-white color of trilliums.

Jamie stood looking up at the corpse of the bear, his mouth half open. Slowly he closed it, and shook his head. He turned to me, then, and looked past me, toward the distant mountains, where the retreating lightning flashed silently.

"They do say," he said softly, "that a great storm portends the death of a king."

He touched my face, very gently.

"Wait here, Sassenach, while I fetch the horse. We'll go home."

# HEARTHFIRE

*Fraser's Ridge*
*October, 1771*

THE SEASON CHANGED, from one hour to the next. She had gone to sleep in the cool balm of an Indian summer evening, and wakened in the middle of the night to the sharp bite of autumn, her feet freezing under the single quilt. Still drowsy, she couldn't fall sleep again, not without more covers.

She dragged slit-eyed out of bed, padded over the icy floor to check Jemmy. He was warm enough, sunk deep into his tiny featherbed, the quilt drawn up around his small pink ears. She laid a gentle hand on his back, waiting for the reassurance of the rise and fall of his breath. Once, twice, once more.

She rummaged for an extra quilt and spread it on the bed, reached for a cup of water to ease her dry throat, and realized with a grunt of annoyance that it was empty. She thought with longing of crawling back into bed, sinking into deep, warm slumber—but not dying of thirst.

There was a bucket of well water by the stoop. Yawning and grimacing, she slid the bolt from its brackets and set it gently down—though Jem slept so soundly at night, there wasn't much danger of waking him.

Still, she opened the door with care and stepped out, shivering slightly as the cold air twitched the shift about her legs. She bent and groped in the darkness. No bucket. Where—

She saw a flicker of movement from the corner of her eye and whirled. For an instant, she thought it was Obadiah Henderson, sitting on the bench beside her door, and her heart clenched like a fist as he stood up. Then she realized, and was in Roger's arms before her mind could consciously sort out the details of him.

Pressed against him, speechless, she had time to notice things: the arch of his collarbone against her face, the smell of clothes gone so long worn, so long unwashed that they didn't smell even of sweat any longer, but of the wood he walked through and the earth he slept upon, and mostly of the bitter smoke he breathed. The strength of his arm about her and the rasp of his beard on her skin. The cracked cold leather of his shoes beneath her bare toes, and the shape of the bones of his feet within them.

"It's you," she said, and was crying. "You're home!"

"Aye, I'm home," he whispered in her ear. "You're well? Jem's well?"

She relaxed her hold on his ribs and he smiled at her, so

strange to see his smile through a growth of thick black beard, the curve of his lips familiar in the moonlight.

"We're fine. You're all right?" She sniffed, eyes overflowing as she looked at him. "What are you doing out here, for heaven's sake? Why didn't you knock?"

"Aye. I'm fine. I didn't want to scare ye. Thought I'd sleep out here, knock in the morning. Why are ye crying?"

She realized then that he wasn't whispering from any desire to avoid waking Jem; what voice he had was a ragged husk, warped and breathless. And yet he spoke clearly, the words unforced, without the painful hesitation he had had.

"You can talk," she said, wiping hastily at her eyes with the back of a wrist. "I mean—better." Once, she would have hesitated to touch his throat, fearful of his feelings, but instinct knew better than to waste the sudden intimacy of shock. The strain might come again, and they be strangers, but for a moment, for *this* moment in the dark, she could say anything, do anything, and she put her fingers on the warm ragged scar, touched the incision that had saved his life, a clean white line through the whiskers.

"Does it still hurt to talk?"

"It hurts," he said, in the faint croaking rasp, and his eyes met hers, dark and soft in the moonlight. "But I can. I will— Brianna."

She stepped back, one hand on his arm, unwilling to let go.

"Come in," she said. "It's cold out here."

I HAD ANY NUMBER of objections to hearthfire, ranging from splinters under the fingernails and pitch on the hands to blisters, burns, and the sheer infuriating contrariness of the element. I would, however, say two things in its favor: it was undeniably warm, and it cast the act of love in a light of such dim beauty that all the hesitations of nakedness could safely be forgotten.

Our mingled shadows flowed together on the wall, here a limb, there the curve of back or haunch showed clean, some part of an undulating beast. Jamie's head rose clear, a great maned creature looming over me, back arched in his extremity.

I reached up across the stretch of glowing skin and trembling muscle, brushed the sparking hairs of arms and chest, to bury my hands in the warmth of his hair and pull him down gasping to the dark hollow of my breasts.

I kept my eyes half-closed, my legs as well, unwilling to surrender his body, to give up the illusion of oneness—if illusion it was. How many more times might I hold him so, even in the enchantment of firelight?

I clung with all my might to him, and to the dying pulse of my own flesh. But joy grasped is joy vanished, and within moments I was no more than myself. The dark starburst on my ankle showed clearly, even in firelight.

I slackened my grip on his shoulders and touched the rough whorls of his hair with tenderness. He turned his head and kissed my breast, then stirred and sighed and slid sideways.

"And they say hen's teeth are rare," he said, gingerly touching a deep bite-mark on one shoulder.

I laughed, in spite of myself.

"As rare as a rooster's cock, I suppose." I raised myself on one elbow and peered toward the hearth.

"What is it, wee hen?"

"Just making sure my clothes won't catch fire." What with one thing and another, I hadn't much noticed where he'd thrown my garments, but they seemed to be a safe distance from the flames; the skirt was in a small heap by the bed, the bodice and shift somehow had ended up in separate corners of the room. My brassiere-strip was nowhere to be seen.

Light flickered on the whitewashed walls, and the bed was full of shadows.

"You are beautiful," he whispered to me.

"If you say so."

"Do ye not believe me? Have I ever lied to you?"

"That's not what I mean. I mean—if you say it, then it's true. You make it true."

He sighed and shifted, easing us into comfort. A log cracked suddenly in the hearth, sending up a spray of gold sparks, and subsided, hissing as the heat struck a hidden seam of damp. I watched the new wood turn black, then red, blazing into white-hot light.

"Do ye say it of me, Sassenach?" he asked suddenly. He sounded shy, and I turned my head to look up at him in surprise.

"Do I say what? That you're beautiful?" My mouth curved involuntarily, and he smiled in return.

"Well . . . not that. But that ye can bear my looks, at least."

I traced the faint white line of the scar across his ribs, left by a sword, long ago. The longer, thicker scar of the bayonet that had ripped the length of one thigh. The arm that held me, browned and roughened, the hairs of it bleached white-gold with long days of sun and work. Near my hand, his cock curled between his thighs, gone soft and small and tender now, in its nest of auburn hair.

"You're beautiful to me, Jamie," I said softly, at last. "So beautiful, you break my heart."

His hand traced the knobs of my backbone, one at a time.

"But I am an auld man," he said, smiling. "Or should be. I've white hairs in my head; my beard's gone gray."

"Silver," I said, brushing the soft stubble on his chin, parti-colored as a quilt. "In bits."

"Gray," he said firmly. "And scabbit-looking with it. And yet . . ." His eyes softened as he looked at me. "Yet I burn when I come to ye, Sassenach—and will, I think, 'til we two be burned to ashes."

"Is that poetry?" I asked cautiously. "Or do you mean it literally?"

"Oh," he said. "No. I hadna meant . . . no." He tightened his arm around me and bent his head to mine.

"I dinna ken about that. If it should be—"

"It won't."

A breath of laughter stirred my hair.

"Ye sound verra sure of it, Sassenach."

"The future can be changed; I do it all the time."

"Oh, aye?"

I rolled away a bit, to look at him.

"I do. Look at Mairi MacNeill. If I hadn't been there last

week, she would have died, and her twins with her. But I *was* there, and they didn't."

I put a hand behind my head, watching the reflection of the flames ripple like water across the ceiling beams.

"I do wonder—there are lots I can't save, but some I do. If someone lives because of me, and later has children, and *they* have children, and so on . . . well, by the time you reach my time, say, there are probably thirty or forty people in the world who wouldn't otherwise have been there, hm? And they've all been doing things meanwhile, living their lives—don't you think that's changing the future?" For the first time, it occurred to me to wonder just how much I was single-handedly contributing to the population explosion of the twentieth century.

"Aye," he said slowly. He picked up my free hand and traced the lines of my palm with one long finger.

"Aye, but it's *their* future ye change, Sassenach, and perhaps you're meant to." He took my hand in his and pulled gently on the fingers. One knuckle popped, making a small sound like a log spitting in the hearth. "Physicians have saved a good many folk over the years, surely."

"Of course they do. And not just physicians, either." I sat up, impelled by the force of my argument. "But it doesn't matter—don't you see? You—" I pointed one finger at him, "—you've saved a life now and then. Fergus? Ian? And here they are, both going about the world doing things and procreating and what-not. You changed the future for them, didn't you?"

"Aye, well . . . perhaps. I couldna do otherwise, though, could I?"

That simple statement stopped me, and we lay in silence for a bit, watching the flicker of light on the white-plastered wall. At last he stirred beside me, and spoke again.

"I dinna say it for pity," he said. "But ye ken . . . now and then my bones ache a bit." He didn't look at me, but spread his crippled hand, turning it in the light, so the shadow of the crooked fingers made a spider on the wall.

Now and then. I kent, all right. I knew the limits of the body—and its miracles. I'd seen him sit down at the end of a day's labor, exhaustion written in every line of his body. Seen him move slowly, stubborn against the protests of flesh and bone when he rose on cold mornings. I would be willing to bet that he had not lived a day since Culloden without pain, the physical damages of war aggravated by damp and harsh living. And I would also be willing to bet that he had never mentioned it to anyone. Until now.

"I know that," I said softly, and touched the hand. The twisting scar that runneled his leg. The small depression in the flesh of his arm, legacy of a bullet.

"But not with you," he said, and covered my hand where it lay on his arm. "D'ye ken that the only time I am without pain is in your bed, Sassenach? When I take ye, when I lie in your arms—my wounds are healed, then, my scars forgotten."

I sighed and laid my head in the curve of his shoulder. My thigh pressed his, the softness of my flesh a mold to his harder form.

"Mine, too."

He was silent for a time, stroking my hair with his good hand. It was wild and bushy, freed from its moorings by our earlier struggles, and he smoothed one curly strand at a time, combing down each lock between his fingers.

"Your hair's like a great storm cloud, Sassenach," he murmured, sounding half-asleep. "All dark and light together. No two hairs are the same color."

He was right; the lock between his fingers bore strands of pure white, of silver and blond, dark streaks, nearly sable, and several bits still of my young light brown.

His fingers went under the mass of hair, and I felt his hand cup the base of my skull, holding my head like a chalice.

"I saw my mother in her coffin," he said at last. His thumb touched my ear, drew down the curve of helix and lobule, and I shivered at his touch.

"The women had plaited her hair, to be seemly, but my father wouldna have it. I heard him. He didna shout, though, he was verra quiet. He would have his last sight of her as she was to him, he said. He was half-crazed wi' grief, they said, he should let well alone, be still. He didna trouble to say more to them, but went to the coffin himself. He undid her plaits and he spread out her hair in his two hands across the pillow. They were afraid to stop him."

He paused, his thumb stilled.

"I was there, keepin' quiet in the corner. When they all went out to meet the priest, I crept up close. I hadna seen a dead person before."

I let my fingers curl over the ridge of his forearm, quietly. My mother had left me one morning, kissed my forehead, and slid in the clip that fell out of my curly hair. I had never seen her again. Her coffin had been closed.

"Was it—her?"

"No," he said softly. His eyes were half-lidded as he looked into the fire. "Not quite. The face had the look of her, but no more. Like as if someone had set out to carve her from birch wood. But her hair—that was still alive. That was still . . . her."

I heard him swallow, and half-clear his throat.

"The hair lay down across her breast, so it covered the child who lay with her. I thought perhaps he wouldna like it; to be smothered so. So I lifted up the locks of red to let him out. I could see him—my wee brother, curled up in her arms, wi' his head on her breast, all shadowed and snug under the curtain of her hair.

"So then I thought no, he'd be happier if I left him so—so I smoothed her hair down again, to cover his head." He drew a deep breath, and I felt his chest rise under my cheek. His fingers ran slowly down through my hair.

"She hadna one white hair, Sassenach. Not one."

Ellen Fraser had died in childbirth, aged thirty-eight. My own mother had been thirty-two. And I . . . I had the richness of all those long years lost to them. And more.

"To see the years touch ye gives me joy, Sassenach," he whispered, "—for it means that ye live."

He lifted his hand and let my hair fall slowly from his fingers, brushing my face, skimming my lips, floating soft and heavy on my neck and shoulders, lying like feathers at the tops of my breasts.

*"Mo nighean donn,"* he whispered, *"mo chridhe.* My brown lass, my heart.

"Come to me. Cover me. Shelter me, *a bhean*, heal me. Burn with me, as I burn for you."

I lay on him, covered him, my skin, his bone, and still—still!—that fierce bright core of flesh to join us. I let my hair fall down around us both, and in the fire-shot cavern of its darkness, whispered back.

"Until we two be burned to ashes."

# 86

# THERE'S A HOLE IN THE BOTTOM OF THE SEA

*Fraser's Ridge*
*October, 1771*

ROGER WAS INSTANTLY AWAKE, in that way that allowed no transition through drowsiness; body inert, but mind alert, ears tuned to the echo of what had wakened him. He had no conscious recollection of Jemmy's cry, but it echoed in his inner ear, with that combination of hope and resignation that is the lot of the more-easily wakened parent.

Sleep dragged at him, pulling him back under the waves of slumber like a ten-ton boulder chained to his foot. A tiny rustling noise kept his head momentarily above the surface.

*"Go back to sleep,"* he thought fiercely, in the direction of the cradle. *"Shhhhh. Hush. Quiet. Go . . . to . . . sleeeeeep."* This telepathic hypnosis seldom worked, but it delayed for a few precious seconds the necessity of moving. And now and then the miracle happened, and his son actually *did* go back to sleep, relaxing into the warm sogginess of wet diaper and crumb-caked dreams.

Roger held his breath, clinging to the fading edge of sleep, hoarding the cherished seconds of immobility. Then another small sound came, and he was on his feet at once.

"Bree? Bree, what is it?" The "r" in her name fluttered in his throat, not quite there, but he didn't take the time to be troubled by it. All his attention was for her.

She was standing by the cradle, a ghostly column in the dark. He touched her, took her by the shoulders. Her arms were wrapped tight around the little boy, and she was shuddering with cold and fear.

He pulled her close by instinct; her cold infected him at once. He felt the chill on his heart and forced himself to hold tighter, not to look at the empty cradle.

"What is it?" he whispered. "Is it Jemmy? What's . . . happened?"

A shiver rose up the length of her body, and he felt the goosebumps rise under the thin cloth of her shift. Despite the warmth of the room, he felt the hair on his own arms rising.

"Nothing," she said. "He's all right." Her voice was thick, but she was right; Jem, waking to find himself uncomfortably squashed between his parents, let out a sudden yelp of surprised indignation, and began to churn his arms and legs like an eggbeater.

This sturdy battering filled Roger with a flood of warm relief, drowning the cold imaginings that had seized his mind at the sight of her. With a little difficulty, he pried Jemmy from his mother's arms and hoisted him high against his own shoulder.

He patted the solid little back in reassurance—reassurance of himself, as much as Jemmy—and made soft hissing noises through his teeth. Jemmy, finding this accustomed procedure soothing, yawned widely, relaxed into his normal hamlike state, and began to hum drowsily in Roger's ear, with the rising and falling note of a distant siren.

"DadeeDadeeDadee . . ."

Brianna was still standing by the cradle, empty arms wrapped now around herself. Roger reached out with his free hand and stroked her hair, her hard-boned shoulder, and drew her close against him.

"Shhh," he said to them both. "Shhh, shhh. It's all right now, shhh."

Her arms went around him, and he could feel the wetness on her face through the linen shirt. His other shoulder was already damp with Jemmy's sleepy, sweaty warmth.

"Come to bed," he said softly. "Come under the quilt, it's . . . cold out here." It wasn't; the air in the cabin was warm. She came, nonetheless.

Brianna reached for the child, taking him to her breast even before she lay down. Never one to refuse nourishment at any hour, Jemmy accepted the offer with alacrity, curling up into an apostrophe of content against his mother's stomach as she settled on one side.

Roger slid into bed behind her, and echoed his son's posture, bringing up his knees behind Brianna's, curling his body in a protective comma around her. Thus securely punctuated, Brianna began slowly to relax, though Roger could still feel the tension in her body.

"All right now?" he asked softly. Her skin was still clammy to the touch, but warming.

"Yeah." She took in a deep breath and let it out in a shuddering sigh. "Had a bad dream. I'm sorry I woke you."

"It's OK." He stroked the swell of her hip, over and over, like one gentling a horse. "Want to tell me?" He hoped she did, though the sound of Jemmy's suckling was rhythmic and soothing, and he felt sleep stealing over him as the three of them warmed, melting together like candle wax.

"I was cold," she said softly. "I think the quilt must have fallen off. But in the dream, I was cold because the window was open."

"Here? One of these windows?" Roger lifted a hand, indicating the faint oblong of the window in the far wall. Even in the middle of the darkest night, the oiled hide covering the window was very slightly lighter than the surrounding blackness.

"No." She took a deep breath. "It was in the house in Boston; where I grew up. I was in bed, but I was cold, and the cold woke me—in the dream. I got up to see where the draft was coming from."

There were French windows in her father's study. The cold wind came from there, bellying the long white curtains into the room. The cradle stood by the antique desk, the end of a thin white blanket flickering in the draft.

"He was gone." Her voice had steadied, but had a momentary catch in it at the memory of terror. "Jemmy was gone. The cradle was empty, and I knew something came through the window and took him."

She pressed back against him, unconsciously seeking reassurance. "I was afraid of it—whatever it was—but it didn't matter—I had to find Jemmy."

One hand was curled up tight under her chin. He folded it in his, and squeezed lightly, embracing her.

"I threw open the curtains and ran out, and—and there was nothing there. Only water." She was shaking at the memory.

"Water?" He stroked her clenched fist with a thumb, trying to calm her.

"Ocean. The sea. Just—water, lapping up against the edge of the terrace. It was dark, and I knew it went down forever, and that Jemmy was down there, he'd drowned, and I was too late—" She choked, but got her voice back and went on, more steadily. "But I dived in anyway, I had to. It was dark, and there were things in the water with me—I couldn't see them, but they brushed by me; big things. I kept looking and looking but I couldn't see anything, and then the water suddenly got lighter and I—I saw him."

"Jemmy?"

"No. Bonnet—Stephen Bonnet."

Roger forced himself not to move, not to stiffen. She dreamed often; he always imagined that the dreams she would not tell him were of Bonnet.

"He was holding Jemmy, and laughing. I went to take him, and Bonnet held him up away from me. He kept doing that, and I tried to hit him, and he just caught my hand and laughed. Then he looked up and his face changed."

She took a deep breath, and took hold of Roger's fingers, holding on for comfort.

"I never saw a look like that, Roger, never. There was something behind me that he could see, something coming—

and it scared him more than I've ever seen anyone scared. He was holding me; I couldn't turn around to look, and I couldn't get away—I couldn't leave Jemmy. It was coming—and . . . then I woke up."

She gave a small, shaky laugh.

"My friend Gayle's grandmother always said that when you fall off a cliff in a dream, if you hit the bottom, you'll die. Really die, I mean. You figure the same thing goes for getting eaten by a sea monster?"

"No. Besides, you always wake up in time from dreams like that."

"I have so far." She sounded a little dubious. Still, dream told, she was eased of its terror; her body let go its last resistance and she breathed deep and easy against him; he could feel the swell of her rib cage under his arm.

"You always will. Don't be troubled now; Jemmy's safe. I'm here; I'll keep you both safe." He put his arm gently round her, and cupped his hand around Jemmy's fat bottom, warm in its linen clout. Jemmy, all his bodily needs met, had relapsed into a peaceful torpor, contagious in its abandon. Brianna sighed and put her hand over Roger's, squeezing lightly.

"There were books on the desk," she said, beginning to sound drowsy. "On Dad's desk. He'd been working, I could tell—there were open books and scattered papers everywhere. There was a paper lying in the middle of the desk, with writing on it; I wanted to read it, to see what he'd been doing—but I couldn't stop."

"Mm-hm."

Brianna shivered slightly, and the movement rustled the corn shucks in the mattress, a tiny seismic disturbance of their small, warm universe. She tensed, fighting sleep, and then relaxed, as his hand cupped her breast.

Roger lay awake, watching the square of the window grow slowly lighter, holding his family safe in his arms.

IT WAS OVERCAST and morning-cool, but very humid; Roger could feel the sweat film his body like the skin on boiled milk. It was no more than an hour past dawn, they weren't yet out of sight of the house, and his scalp was prickling already, slow droplets gathering under the plait at the base of his skull.

He flexed his shoulders with resignation, and the first trickle crawled tickling down his backbone. At least sweating helped to ease the soreness; his arms and shoulders had been so stiff this morning that Brianna had had to help him dress, pulling his shirt over his head and buttoning his flies with deft fingers.

He smiled inwardly, remembering what else those long fingers had done. It had taken his mind temporarily off the stiffness of his body, and banished the troubling memory of dreams. He stretched, groaning, feeling the pull of muscle on tender joints. The clean linen was already sticking to chest and back.

Jamie was ahead of him on the trail, a damp patch growing visibly between his shoulder blades where the strap of the canteen crossed his back. Roger noted with some consolation that his father-in-law was moving with a good bit less than his usual pantherlike grace this morning, too. He knew the Great Scot was only human, but it was reassuring to have that fact confimed now and then.

"Think the weather will hold?" Roger said it as much for the sake of speaking as for anything else; Jamie was by no means garrulous, but he seemed abnormally quiet this morning, barely speaking beyond a murmured "Aye, morning," in reply to Roger's earlier greeting. Perhaps it was the grayness of the day, with its threat—or promise—of rain.

The sky overhead curved low and dull as the inside of a pewter bowl. An afternoon indoors, with rain beating on the oiled hides of the windows, and wee Jemmy curled up peaceful as a dormouse for a nap, while his mother shed her shift and came to bed in the soft gray light . . . aye, well, some ways of breaking a sweat were better than others.

Jamie stopped and glanced up at the lowering sky. He flexed his right hand, closing it to an awkward fist, then opening it slowly. The stiff fourth finger made delicate chores such as writing difficult, but did provide one dubious benefit in compensation; the swollen joints signaled rain as reliably as a barometer.

Jamie wiggled the fingers experimentally, and gave Roger a faint smile.

"No but a wee twinge," he said. "Nay rain before nightfall." He stretched, easing his back in anticipation, and sighed. "Let's get to it, aye?"

Roger glanced back; the house and cabin had disappeared. He frowned at Jamie's retreating back, debating. It was nearly half a mile to the new field; ample time for conversation. Not the right time, though, not yet. It was a matter to be addressed face-to-face, and at leisure—later, then, when they paused to eat.

The woods were hushed, the air still and heavy. Even the birds were quiet, only the occasional machine-gun burst of a woodpecker startling the silence. They threaded their way through the forest, silent as Indians on the layer of rotted leaves, and emerged from the scrub-oak thicket with a suddenness that sent a flock of crows shrieking out of the torn earth of the new-cleared field like demons escaping from the netherworld.

"Jesus!" Jamie murmured, and crossed himself involuntarily. Roger's throat closed tight, and his stomach clenched. The crows had been feeding on something lying in the hollow left by an uprooted tree; all he could see above the ragged clods of earth was a pale curve that looked unsettlingly like the round of a naked shoulder.

It *was* a naked shoulder—of a pig. Jamie squatted by the boar's carcass, frowning at the livid weals that marred the thick, pale skin. He touched the deep gouges on the flank with distaste; Roger could see the busy movement of flies inside the black-red cavities.

"Bear?" he asked, squatting beside Jamie. His father-in-law shook his head.

"Cat." He brushed aside the stiff, sparse hairs behind the ear and pointed to the bluish puncture wounds in the folded lard. "Broke the neck wi' one bite. And see the claw marks?" Roger had, but lacked the knowledge to differentiate the marks of a bear's claws from those of a panther's. He looked closely, committing the pattern to memory.

Jamie stood, and wiped a sleeve across his face.

"A bear would ha' taken more of the carcass. This is barely touched. Cats will do that, though—make a kill and leave it, then come back to nibble at it, day after day."

Muggy as it was, the hair pricked with chill on Roger's neck. It was much too easy to imagine yellow eyes in the shadow of the thicket behind him, fixed with cool appraisal on the spot where skull met fragile spine.

"Think it's still close by?" He glanced about, trying to seem casual. The forest was just as it had been, but now the silence seemed unnatural and sinister.

Jamie waved away a couple of questing flies, frowning.

"Aye, maybe. This is a fresh kill; no maggots yet." He nodded at the gaping wound in the pig's flank, then stooped to grasp the stiff trotters. "Come, let's hang it. It's too much meat to waste."

They dragged the carcass to a tree with a low, sturdy limb. Jamie reached into his sleeve and pulled out a grubby kerchief, to tie round his head to keep the sweat from burning into his eyes. Roger groped for his own kerchief—carefully washed, neatly ironed—and did likewise. Mindful of the laundering, they stripped their clean shirts and hung them over an alder bush.

There was rope in the field, left from the stump-pulling of earlier days' work; Jamie whipped a length several times around the pig's forelimbs, then flung the free end over the branch above. It was a full-grown boar, some two-hundred-weight of solid flesh. Jamie set his feet and hauled back on the rope, grunting with the sudden effort.

Roger held his breath as he bent to help hoist the stiffened corpse, but Jamie had been right; it was fresh. There was the usual fleshy pig-scent, gone faint with death, and the sharper tang of blood—nothing worse.

Rough hair scraped the skin of his belly as he wrapped his arms around the carcass, and he set his teeth against a grimace of distaste. There are few things deader than a large, dead pig. Then a word from Jamie, and the carcass was secure. He let go, and the pig swung gently to and fro, a meaty pendulum.

Roger was wringing wet; more than the effort of lifting

accounted for. There was a big smudge of brownish blood over his chest and stomach. He rubbed the heel of his hand over the knot in his belly, smearing the blood with sweat. He glanced casually round once more. Nothing moved among the trees.

"The women will be pleased," he said.

Jamie laughed, taking the dirk from his belt.

"I shouldna think so. They'll be up half the night, butchering and salting." He nodded in the direction of Roger's glance.

"Even if it's near, it willna trouble us. Cats dinna hunt large prey unless they're hungry." He looked wryly at the torn flank of the dangling pig. "A half-stone of prime bacon will ha' satisfied it for the moment, I should think. Though if not—" He glanced at his long rifle, leaning loaded against the trunk of a nearby hickory.

He held the pig while Jamie gutted it, then wrapped the stinking mass of intestines in the cloth from their lunch, while Jamie patiently worked at kindling a fire of green sticks that would keep the flies away from the hanging carcass. Streaked and reeking with blood, waste, and sweat, Roger walked across the field to the small stream that ran by the woods.

He knelt and splashed, arms and face and torso, trying to rid himself of the feeling of being watched. More than once, he had crossed an empty moor in Scotland, only to have a full-grown stag erupt from nowhere in front of him, springing by apparent magic from the heather at his feet. Despite Jamie's words, he was all too aware that some piece of quiet landscape could abruptly detach itself and take life in a thunder of hooves or a snarl of sudden teeth.

He rinsed his mouth, spat, and drank deep, forcing water past the lingering tightness in his throat. He could still feel the stiff coldness of the pig's carcass, see the caked dirt in the nostrils, the raw sockets where crows had pecked out the eyes. Gooseflesh prickled over his shoulders, chilled as much by his thoughts as by the cold stream-water.

No great difference between a pig and a man. Flesh to flesh, dust to dust. One stroke, that's all it took. Slowly, he stretched, savoring the last soreness in his muscles.

There was a raucous croaking from the chestnut overhead. The crows, black blotches in the yellow leaves, voicing their displeasure at the robbery of their feast.

*"Whaur . . . shall we gang and . . . dine the day?"* he murmured under his breath, looking up at them. "Not here . . . you bastards. Get along!" Seized by revulsion, he scooped a stone from the bank and hurled it into the tree with all his might. The crows erupted into shrieking flight, and he turned back to the field, grimly satisfied.

But his belly was still knotted, and the words of the corbies' mocking song echoed in his ears: *"Ye'll sit on his white hause-bane/and I'll pick oot his bonny blue e'en. Wi' ae lock o' his golden hair/we'll theek oor nest when it grows bare."*

Jamie glanced at his face when he came back, but said nothing. Beyond the field, the pig's carcass hung above the fire, its outlines hidden in wreaths of smoke.

They had cut the fencerails already, made from pine saplings they'd uprooted; the rough-barked logs lay ready by the edge of the forest. The fence would have drystone pillars to join the wooden rails, though; not one of the simple rick-rack fences meant to keep out deer or mark boundaries, but one solid enough to withstand the jostling of three- and four-hundred-pound hogs.

Within the month, it would be time to drive in the pigs that had been turned out to live wild in the forest, fattening themselves on the chestnut mast that lay thick on the ground. Some would have fallen prey to wild animals or accident, but there would likely be fifty or sixty left to slaughter or sell.

They worked well together, he and Jamie. Much of a size, each had an instinct for the other's moves. When a hand was needed, it was there. No need for it just now, though—this part of the job was the worst, for there was no interest to soften the tedium, no skill to ease the labor. Only rocks, hundreds of rocks, to be hoisted from the loamy soil and carried, dragged, wrestled to the field, to be piled and fitted into place.

Often they talked as they worked, but not this morning. Each man worked alone with his thoughts, tramping to and fro with the endless load. The morning passed in silence, broken only by the far-off calling of the disgruntled crows, and by the thunk and grate of stones, dropped on the growing pile.

It had to be done. There was no choice. He'd known that for a long time, but now that the dim prospect had hardened into reality . . . Roger eyed his father-in-law covertly. Would Jamie agree to it, though?

From a distance, the scars on his back were barely visible, masked by the gleam of sweat. Constant hard work kept a man trim and taut, and no one seeing Fraser in outline—or close enough to see the deep groove of his backbone, the flat belly and long clean lines of arm and thigh—would have taken him for a man in middle age.

Jamie had showed him the scars, though, the first day they went out to work together, after he had come back from the surveying. Standing by the half-built dairy-shed, Jamie had pulled the shirt off and turned his back, saying casually, "Have a keek, then."

Up close, the scars were old and well-healed, thin white crescents and lines for the most part, with here and there a silvery net or a shiny lump, where a whipstroke had flayed the skin in too wide a patch for the edges of the wound to draw cleanly together. There was some skin untouched, showing fair and smooth among the weals—but not much.

And what was he to say? Roger had wondered. I'm sorry for it? Thanks for the viewing privileges?

In the event, he had said nothing. Jamie had merely turned around, handed Roger an ax with complete matter-of-factness, and they had begun their work, bare-chested. But he had noticed that Jamie never stripped to work, if the other men were with them.

All right. Of all men, Jamie would understand the need, the necessity—the burden of Brianna's dreaming, that lay in Roger's belly like a stone. Certainly he would help. But would he consent to allow Roger to finish it alone? Jamie, after all, had some stake in the matter, too.

The crows were still calling, but farther off, their cries thin and desperate, like those of lost souls. Perhaps he was foolish even to think of acting alone. He flung an armload of stones onto the pile; small rocks clacked and rolled away.

"Preacher's lad." That's what the other lads at school had

called him, and that's what he was, with all the ambiguity the term implied. The initial urge to prove himself manly by means of force, the later awareness of the ultimate moral weakness of violence. But that was in another country—

He choked off the rest of the quotation, grimly bending to lever a chunk of rock free of moss and dirt. Orphaned by war, raised by a man of peace—how was he to set his mind to murder? He trundled the stone down toward the field, rolling it slowly end over end.

"You've never killed anything but fish," he muttered to himself. "What makes you think . . ." But he knew all too well what made him think.

BY MID-MORNING, there were enough rocks collected to begin the first pillar; with a nod and a murmur, they set to work, dragging and heaving, stacking and fitting, with now and then a muffled exclamation at a smashed finger or bruised toes.

Jamie heaved a big stone into place, then straightened up, gasping for breath.

Roger drew his own deep breath. It might as well be now; no better opportunity was likely to come.

"I've a favor to ask," he said abruptly.

Jamie glanced up, breathing heavily, one eyebrow raised. He nodded, waiting for the request.

"Teach me to fight."

Jamie wiped an arm across his streaming face, and blew out a deep breath.

"Ye ken well enough how to fight," he said. One corner of his mouth quirked up. "D'ye mean will I teach ye to handle a sword without cutting off your foot?"

Roger kicked a stone back into the pile.

"That will do, to start."

Jamie stood for a moment, looking him over. It was a thoroughly dispassionate examination, much as he would have given a bullock he thought to buy. Roger stood still, feeling the sweat stream down the groove of his back, and thought that once more, he was being compared—to his disadvantage—with the absent Ian Murray.

"You're auld for it, mind," Jamie said at last. "Most swordsmen start when they're boys." He paused. "I had my first sword at five."

Roger had had a train when he was five. With a red engine that tooted its whistle when you pulled the cord. He met Jamie's eye, and smiled pleasantly.

"Old for it, maybe," he said. "But not dead."

"Ye could be," Fraser answered. "A little learning is a dangerous thing—a fool wi' a blade by his side in a scabbard is safer than a fool who thinks he kens what to do with it."

*"A little learning is a dangerous thing,"* Roger quoted. *"Drink deep, or taste not the Pierian spring.* Do you think me a fool?"

Jamie laughed, surprised into amusement.

*"There shallow draughts intoxicate the brain,"* he replied, finishing the verse. *"And drinking largely sobers us again.* As for foolish—ye'll no just be drunk on the thought of it, I suppose?"

Roger smiled slightly in reply; he had given up being surprised by the breadth of Jamie's reading.

"I'll drink deep enough to stay sober," he said. "Will ye teach me?"

Jamie squinted, then lifted one shoulder slightly. "Ye've size to your credit, and a good reach, forbye." He looked Roger head to toe once more and nodded. "Aye, ye'll maybe do."

He turned and walked away, toward the next heap of stones. Roger followed, feeling oddly gratified, as though he had passed some small but important test.

The test hadn't yet begun, though. It was only partway through the building of the new pillar that Jamie spoke again.

"Why?" he asked, eyes on the huge stone he was slowly heaving into place. It was too heavy to lift, the size of a whisky keg. Knotted clumps of grass roots stuck out from under it, ripped out of the earth by the stone's slow and brutal passage across the ground.

Roger bent to lend his own weight to the task. The lichens

on the rock's surface were rough under his palms, green and scabby with age.

"I've a family to protect," he said. The rock moved grudgingly, sliding a few inches across the uneven ground. Jamie nodded, once, twice; on the silent "three," they shoved together, with an echoed grunt of effort. The monster half-rose, paused, rose altogether and overbalanced, chunking down into place with a *thunk!* that quivered through the ground at their feet.

"Protect from what?" Jamie stood and wiped a wrist across his jaw. He glanced up and away, gesturing with his chin at the hanging pig. "I shouldna care to take on a panther wi' a sword, myself."

"Oh, aye?" Roger bent his knees and maneuvered another large rock into his arms. "I hear you've killed two bears— one with a dirk."

"Aye, well," Jamie said dryly. "A dirk's what I had. As for the other—if it was a sword, it was Saint Michael's, not mine."

"Aye, and if ye'd known ahead of time that you might— ugh—meet it—would you not have armed yourself—better?" Roger bent his knees, lowering the stone carefully into place. He let it drop the last few inches, and wiped stinging hands on his breeks.

"If I'd *known* I should meet a damn bear," Jamie said, grunting as he lifted another stone into place, "I would have taken another path."

Roger snorted and wiggled the new stone, easing its fit against the others. There was a small gap at one side that left it loose; Jamie eyed it, walked to the stone pile, and picked up a small chunk of granite, tapered at one end. It fit the gap exactly, and the two men smiled involuntarily at each other.

"D'ye think there's another path to take, then?" Roger asked.

Fraser rubbed a hand across his mouth, considering.

"If it's the war ye mean—then, aye, I do." He gave Roger a stare. "Maybe I'll find it and maybe I won't—but aye, there's another path."

"Maybe so." He hadn't meant the oncoming war, and he didn't think Jamie had, either.

"As to bears, though . . ." Jamie stood still, eyes steady. "There's a deal of difference, ye ken, between meeting a bear unawares—and hunting one."

THE SUN STILL WASN'T VISIBLE, but it wasn't necessary, either. Noon came as a rumbling in the belly, a soreness of the hands; a sudden awareness of the weariness of back and legs as timely as the chiming of a grandfather's clock. The last large rock fell into place, and Jamie straightened up, gasping for breath.

By unspoken but mutual consent, they sat down with the packet of food, clean shirts draped across bare shoulders, against the chill of drying sweat.

Jamie chewed industriously, washing down a large bite with a gulp of ale. He made an involuntary face, pursed his lips to spit, then changed his mind and swallowed.

"Ach! Mrs. Lizzie's been at the mash again." He grimaced and took a remedial bite of biscuit, to erase the taste.

Roger grinned at his father-in-law's face.

"What's she put in it this time?" Lizzie had been trying her hand at flavored ales—with indifferent success.

Jamie sniffed warily at the mouth of the stone bottle.

"Anise?" he suggested, passing the bottle to Roger.

Roger smelt it, wrinkling up his nose involuntarily at the alcoholic whiff.

"Anise *and* ginger," he said. Nevertheless, he took a cautious sip. He made the same face Jamie had, and emptied the bottle over a compliant blackberry vine.

"Waste not, want not, but . . ."

"It's nay waste to keep from poisoning ourselves." Jamie heaved himself up, took the emptied bottle, and set off toward the small stream on the far side of the field.

He came back, sat down, and handed Roger the bottle of water. "I've had word of Stephen Bonnet."

It was said so casually that Roger didn't register the meaning of the words at first.

"Have you?" he said at last. Piccalilli relish was oozing over his hand. Roger wiped the relish from his wrist with a finger, and put it into his mouth, but didn't take another bite of sandwich; his appetite had vanished.

"Aye. I dinna ken where he is now—but I ken where he'll be come next April—or rather, where I can cause him to be. Six months, and then we kill him. Do ye think that will give ye time?"

He was looking at Roger, calm as though he had suggested an appointment with a banker, rather than an appointment with death.

Roger could believe in netherworlds—and demons, too. He hadn't dreamed last night, but the demon's face floated always at the edge of his mind, just out of sight. Time to summon him, perhaps, and bring him into view. You had to call a demon up, didn't you, before you could exorcise him?

There were preparations to make, though, before that could happen. He flexed his shoulders and his arms once more, this time in anticipation. The soreness had mostly gone.

> *"There's mony an ane for him maks mane*
> *but nane shall ken where he is gane.*
> *O'er his white banes when they are bare,*
> *The wind shall blaw forever mair, O—*
> *The wind shall blaw forever mair."*

"Aye," he said. "That'll do."

# 87

# EN GARDE

FOR A MOMENT, he didn't think he was going to be able to lift his hand to the latch-string. Both arms hung as though weighted with lead, and the small muscles of his forearm jumped and trembled with exhaustion. It took two tries, and even then, he could do no more than catch the string clumsily between two middle fingers; his thumb wouldn't close.

Brianna heard him fumbling; the door opened suddenly and his hand fell nerveless from the latch. He had no more than a glimpse of tumbled hair and a beaming face with a smear of soot down one cheek, and then she had her arms around him, her mouth on his, and he was home.

"You're back!" she said, letting go.

"I am." And glad of it, too. The cabin smelt of hot food and lye soap, with a clean, faint tang of juniper overlaying the smoke of reed candles and the muskier scents of human occupation. He smiled at her, suddenly a little less tired.

"Dadee, Dadee!" Jemmy was bouncing up and down in excitement, clinging to a low stool for balance. "Da—deeee!"

"Hallo, hallo," Roger said, reaching down to pat the boy's fluffy head. "Who's a good lad, then?" He missed his mark and his hand brushed a soft cheek instead, but Jemmy didn't care.

"Me! Me!" he shouted, and grinned with a huge expanse of pink gum, showing off all his small white teeth. Brianna echoed the grin, with substantially more enamel but no less delight.

"We have a surprise for you. Watch this!" She went swiftly toward the table, and sank to one knee, a pace from Jemmy. She stretched out her arms, her hands no more than a few inches from his. "Come to Mama, sweetie. Come here, baby, come to Mama."

Jemmy swayed precariously, loosed one hand, reached for his mother, then let go and took one drunken step, then two, and fell shrieking into her arms. She clutched him, giggling in delight, then turned him toward Roger.

"Go to Daddy," Brianna encouraged. "Go on, go to Daddy."

Jemmy screwed up his face in doubtful concentration, looking like a first-time parachutist at the open door of a circling plane. He swayed dangerously to and fro.

Roger squatted, hands held out, tiredness forgotten for the moment.

"Come on, mate, come on, you can do it!"

Jemmy clung a moment, leaning, leaning, then let go his mother's hand and staggered drunkenly toward Roger, faster and faster and faster through three steps, falling headlong into Roger's saving grasp.

He hugged Jemmy tight against him, the little boy wriggling and crowing in triumph.

"Good lad! Be into everything now, won't you?"

"Like he's not already!" Brianna said, rolling her eyes in resignation. As though in illustration, Jemmy wriggled loose from Roger's grasp, dropped to hands and knees, and crawled off at a high rate of speed, heading for his basket of toys.

"And what else have ye been doing today?" Roger asked, sitting down at the table.

"What *else*?" Her eyes went wide, then narrowed. "You don't think learning to walk is enough for one day?"

"Of course; it's wonderful, it's marvelous!" he assured her hastily. "I was only making conversation."

She relaxed, appeased.

"Well, then. We scrubbed the floor—not that anybody could tell the difference—" She glanced down with some distaste at the rough, discolored boards underfoot, "—and we made bread and set it to rise, only it didn't, so that's why you're having flat-bread with your dinner."

"Love flat-bread," he assured her hastily, catching the gimlet gleam in her eye.

"Sure you do," she said, lifting one thick red brow. "Or at least you know which side it's buttered on."

He laughed. Here in the warm, the chill was wearing off, and his hands were starting to throb, but he felt good, nonetheless. Tired enough to fall off his stool, but good. Good and hungry. His stomach growled in anticipation.

"Flat-bread and butter is a start," he said. "What else? I smell something good." He looked at the bubbling cauldron and sniffed hopefully. "Stew?"

"No, laundry." Bree glowered at the kettle. "The third bloody batch today. I can't fit much in that dinky thing, but I couldn't take the wash up to the big kettle at the house, because of washing the floor and spinning. When you do wash outside, you have to stay there, to tend the fire and stir it, so you can't do much else at the same time." Her lips clamped and thinned. "Very inefficient."

"Shame." Roger passed lightly over the logistics of laundry, in favor of more pressing issues. He lifted his chin toward the hearth.

"I do smell meat. You don't think a mouse has fallen into the pot?"

Jemmy, catching this, let go his hold on a rag-ball and crawled eagerly toward the fire. "Mouzee? See mouzee?"

Brianna grabbed the collar of Jemmy's smock and turned the glower on Roger.

"Certainly not. No, baby, no mousie. Daddy's being silly. Here, Jemmy, come eat." Letting go the collar, she seized the little boy by the waist and lifted him—kicking and struggling—into his high chair. "Eat, I said! You stay put." Jemmy arched his back, grunting and squealing in protest, then suddenly relaxed, sliding down out of the chair and disappearing into the folds of his mother's skirt.

Brianna grappled for him, going red in the face with laughter and exasperation.

"All *right*!" she said, hauling him upright. "Don't eat,

then. See if I care." She reached for the litter of toys, spilled out of their basket, and plucked a battered corn-husk doll from the rubble. "Here, see dolly? Nice dolly."

Jemmy clasped the doll to his bosom, sat down abruptly on his bottom, and began to address the doll in earnest tones, shaking it now and then for emphasis.

"Eat!" he said sternly, poking it in the stomach. He laid the doll on the floor, picked up the basket, and carefully turned it over on top of the dolly. "Say put!"

Brianna rubbed a hand down her face, and sighed. She gave Roger a glance. "And you want to know what I do all day."

The glance sharpened, as she truly looked at him for the first time.

"And what have *you* been doing, Mr. MacKenzie? You look like you've been in the wars." She touched his face gently; there was a knot forming on his forehead; he could feel the skin tightening there, and the tiny stab of pain when she touched it.

"Something like. Jamie's been showing me the rudiments of swordsmanship."

Her brows went up, and he laughed self-consciously, keeping his hands in his lap.

"Wooden swords, aye?"

Several wooden swords. They'd broken three so far, though the makeshift weapons were stout lengths of wood; not twigs, by any means.

"He stabbed you in the *head*?" Brianna's voice had a slight edge, though Roger couldn't tell whether it was meant for him or for her father.

"Ah . . . no. Not exactly."

With hazy memories of swashbuckling films and university fencing matches, he'd been unprepared for the sheer brutal force involved in hand-to-hand combat with swords. Jamie's first blow had knocked Roger's sword from his hand and sent it flying; a later one had split the wood and sent a large chunk of it rocketing past his ear.

"What does 'not exactly' mean?"

"Well, he was showing me something called *corps à corps*—which appears to be French for 'Get your opponent's sword wrapped round your own, then knee him in the balls and punch his head while he's trying to get loose.' "

Brianna gave a brief, shocked laugh.

"You mean he—"

"No, but it was a near thing," he said, wincing at the memory. "I've a bruise on my thigh the size of my hand."

"Are you hurt anywhere else?" Brianna was frowning at him, worried.

"No." He smiled up at her, keeping his hands in his lap. "Tired. Sore. Starving."

The frown eased and her smile flickered back, though a small line stayed between her brows. She reached for the wooden platter on the sideboard, turned, and squatted by the hearth.

"Quail," she said with satisfaction, raking a number of blackened bundles out of the ashes with the poker. "Da brought them this morning. He said not to pluck them; just wrap them in mud and bake them. I hope he knows what he's talking about." She jerked her head toward the boiling cauldron. "Jemmy helped me with the mud; that's why we had to do another pot of laundry. Ouch!" She snatched away her hand and sucked a burned finger, then picked up the platter and brought it to the table.

"Let them cool a little," she instructed him. "I'll get some of those pickles you like."

The quail looked like nothing so much as charred rocks. Still, a tantalizing steam drifted up through cracks in a few of the blackened lumps. Roger felt like picking one up and eating it on the spot, burned mud and all. Instead, he fumbled at the cloth-covered plate on the table, discovering the maligned flat-bread underneath. Stiff-fingered, he managed to tear off a good chunk, and stuffed it silently into his mouth.

Jemmy had abandoned his ball of rags under the bed, and come to see what his father was doing. Pulling himself upright by the table leg, he spotted the bread and reached up, making urgent noises of demand. Roger carefully tore off another bit of bread and handed it to his offspring, nearly dropping it in the process. His hands were cut and battered; the knuckles of his right hand blood-grazed, swollen, and black with fresh bruising. Half his right thumbnail had been knocked away, and the bit of raw nail bed showed red and oozing.

"Ow-ee." Clutching his bread, Jemmy looked at Roger's hands, then up at his face. "Daddy owee?"

"Dad's all right," Roger assured him. "Just tired."

Jemmy stared at the injured thumb, then slowly raised his hand to his mouth and inserted his own thumb, sucking loudly.

It actually looked like a good idea. His thumb stung and ached, where the nail had gone, and all his fingers were cold and stiff. With a quick glance at Brianna's back, he lifted his hand and stuck his thumb in his mouth.

It felt alien, thick and hard and tasting of silvery blood and cold grime. Then suddenly it fit, and tongue and palate closed round the injured digit in a warm and soothing pressure.

Jemmy butted him in the thigh, his usual signal for "up," and he grasped the back of the little boy's clout with his free hand, boosting him up onto his knee. Jemmy made himself at home, rooting and squirming, then relaxed in sudden peace, bread squashed in one hand, sucking quietly on his thumb.

Roger slowly relaxed, one elbow propped on the table, the other arm round his son. Jemmy's heavy warmth and heavy breathing against his ribs were a soothing accompaniment to the homely noises Brianna was making as she dished the supper. To his surprise, his thumb stopped hurting, but he left it where it was, too tired to question the odd sense of comfort.

His muscles were gradually relaxing, too, coming off the state of tensed readiness in which he'd held them for hours.

His inner ear still rang with brisk instruction. *Use your forearm, man—the wrist, the wrist! Dinna move your hand out like that, keep it near the body. It's a sword, aye? Not a bloody club. Use the tip!*

He'd thrown Jamie heavily against a tree, at one point. And Fraser had tripped over a rock and gone down once, Roger on top. As for any actual damage inflicted with a sword, he might as well have been fighting a cloud.

*Dirty fighting is the only kind there is*, Fraser had told

him, panting, as they knelt at the stream and splashed cold water over sweating faces. *Anything else is no but exhibition.*

His head jerked on his neck and he blinked, coming back abruptly from the grate and crash of wooden swords to the dim warmth of the cabin. The platter was gone; Brianna was cursing softly under her breath at the sideboard, banging the hilt of his dirk against the blackened lumps of clay-baked quail to crack them open.

*Watch your footing. Back, back—aye, now, come back at me! No, dinna reach so far . . . keep your guard up!*

And the stinging *whap!* of the springy "blade" across arms and thighs and shoulders, the solid thunk of it driven bruising home between his ribs, sunk deep and breathless in his belly. Had it been cold steel, he would have been dead in minutes, cut to bleeding ribbons.

*Don't catch the blade on yours—throw it off. Beat, beat it off! Come at me, thrust! Keep it close, keep it close . . . aye, good . . . ha!*

His elbow slipped and his hand fell. He jerked upright, barely keeping hold of the sleeping child, and blinked, vision swimming with firelight.

Brianna started guiltily and shut her notebook. Getting to her feet, she thrust it out of sight behind a pewter plate, resting upright on its edge at the back of the sideboard.

"It's ready," she said hurriedly. "I just—I'll get the milk." She disappeared into the pantry in a rustle of skirts.

Roger shifted Jemmy, got a grip, and lifted the small, solid body up to his shoulder, though his arms felt like cooked noodles. The little boy was sound asleep, but kept his thumb plugged firmly into his mouth.

Roger's own thumb was wet with spittle, and he felt a flush of embarrassment. Christ, had she been drawing him that way? No doubt; she must have caught sight of him sucking his thumb and thought it "cute"; it wouldn't be the first time she'd drawn him in what he considered a compromising position. Or was she writing dreams again?

He laid Jemmy gently in his cradle, brushed damp bread crumbs off the coverlet, and stood rubbing his bruised knuckles with the fingers of his other hand. Sloshing noises came from the pantry. Moving quietly, he stepped to the sideboard and extracted the book from its hiding place. Sketches, not dreams.

It was no more than a few quick lines, the essence of a sketch. A man tired to death, still watchful; head on one hand, neck bowed with exhaustion—free arm clamped tight around a treasured, helpless thing.

She'd titled it. *En garde*, it said, in her slanted, spiky script.

He closed the book and slid it back behind the plate. She was standing in the pantry doorway, the milk jug in her hand.

"Come and eat," she said softly, eyes on his. "You need your strength."

## 88

## ROGER BUYS A SWORD

*Cross Creek*
*November, 1771*

HE'D HANDLED EIGHTEENTH-CENtury broadswords before; neither the weight nor the length surprised him. The basket around the hilt was slightly bent, but not enough to interfere with fitting his hand inside the grip. He'd done that before, too. There was a considerable difference, though, beyond reverently placing an antique artifact into a museum display, and picking up a length of sharpened metal with the conscious intent of driving it through a human body.

"It's a bit battered," Fraser had told him, squinting critically down the length of the sword before handing it to him, "but the blade's well-balanced. Try the feel of it, to see if it suits."

Feeling a total fool, he slipped his hand into the basket and struck a fencing pose, based on memories of Errol Flynn films. They were standing in the busy lane outside the smithy in Cross Creek, and a few passersby paused to watch and offer helpful comment.

"What's Moore asking for that bit of pot tin?" someone asked disparagingly. "Anything more than two shillings, and it's highway robbery."

"That's a fine sword," said Moore, leaning over the half-door of his forge and glowering. "I had it from my uncle, who saw service at Fort Stanwyck. Why, that blade's killed a-many Frenchmen, and no but the one wee nick to be seen in it."

"One nick!" cried the disparager. "Why, the thing's bent so, if you went to stick a man, you'd end up cutting off his ear!"

There was a laugh from the gathering crowd that drowned the smith's response. Roger lowered the point of the sword, raised it slowly. How the hell did one road-test a sword? Ought he to wave it to and fro? Stick something with it? There was a cart standing a little way down the lane, loaded with burlap bags of something—raw wool, from the smell.

He looked for the proprietor of the bags, but couldn't pick him out from the growing crowd; the huge draft horse hitched to the cart was unattended, ears twitching sleepily over his dropped reins.

"Ah, if it's a sword the young man's wanting, sure and Malachy McCabe has a better one than that, left from his service. I think he'd part with it for nay more than three shillings." The cobbler from across the lane pursed his lips, nodding shrewdly at the sword.

" 'Tisn't an elegant piece," one middle-aged ex-soldier agreed, head tilted on one side. "Serviceable, though, I grant you that."

Roger extended his arm, lunged toward the door of the smithy, and narrowly missed Moore, coming out to defend the quality of his wares. The smith leaped aside with a startled cry, and the crowd roared.

Roger's apology was interrupted by a loud, nasal voice behind him.

"Here, sir! Let me offer a foe more worthy of your steel than an unarmed smith!"

Whirling round, Roger found himself confronting Dr. Fentiman, who was pulling a long, thin blade from the head of his ornamental cane. The doctor, who was roughly half Roger's size, brandished his rapier with a genial ferocity. Obviously fueled by a liberal luncheon, the tip of his nose glowed like a Christmas bulb.

"A test of skill, sir?" The doctor whipped his sword to and fro, so the narrow blade sang as it cut the air. "First to pink his man, first to draw blood is the victor, what say you?"

"Oh, an unfair advantage to the doctor! And isn't drawing blood your business, then?"

"Ha ha! And if ye run him through instead of pinking him, will ye patch the hole for no charge?" yelled another onlooker. "Or are ye out to drum up business, leech?"

"Watch yourself, young man! Turn your back on him and he's like to give ye a clyster!"

"Better a clyster than a blade up the arse!"

The doctor ignored these and similar vulgar observations, holding his blade upright in readiness. Roger shot a glance at Jamie, who was leaning against the wall, looking amused. Jamie raised one eyebrow and shrugged slightly.

"Try the feel of it," Jamie'd said. Well, and he supposed a duel with a drunken midget was as good a test as any.

Roger raised his blade and fixed the doctor with a menacing look.

*"En garde,"* he said, and the knot of onlookers roared approval.

*"Gardez-vous,"* replied the doctor promptly, and lunged. Roger spun on one heel and the doctor shot past, rapier pointed like a lance. Moore the smith leaped aside just in time to avoid being skewered for the second time, cursing fluently.

"What am I, a friggin' target?" he shouted, shaking a fist.

Disregarding the near miss, the doctor regained his balance and charged back toward Roger, uttering shrill cries of self-encouragement.

It was rather like being attacked by a wasp, Roger thought. If you didn't panic, you found it possible to follow the thing and bat it away. Perhaps the doctor was a decent swordsman when sober; in his current state, his frenzied thrusts and mad flurries were easily fended off—as long as Roger paid attention.

It occurred to him early on that he could end the contest at any time, merely by meeting the doctor's slender rapier edge-on with his own much heavier weapon. He was beginning to enjoy himself, though, and was careful to parry with the flat of the broadsword.

Gradually everything disappeared from Roger's view but the flashing point of the rapier; the shouts of the crowd faded to a bee-buzz, the dirt of the lane and the wall of the smithy were scarcely visible. He grazed his elbow on the wall, moved back, moved in a circle to gain more room, all without conscious thought.

The rapier beat on his wider blade, engaged, and screeched loose with a *whinggg!* of metal. Clang and click and the whish of empty air and the ringing beat that vibrated in his wristbones with every blow of the doctor's sword.

Watch the stroke, follow it, bat it away. He had no idea what he was doing, but did it anyway. The sweat was running in his eyes; he shook his head to fling it away, nearly missed a low lunge toward his thigh, stopped it close, and flung the rapier back.

The doctor staggered, thrown off balance, and feral shouts of *"Now! Take him! Stick him now!"* rang in the dust-filled air. He saw the expanse of the doctor's embroidered waist-coat, unguarded, filled with silken butterflies, and choked back the visceral urge to lunge for it.

Shaken by the intensity of the urge, he took a step back. The doctor, sensing weakness, leapt forward, bellowing, blade pointed. Roger took a half-step sideways, and the doctor shot past, grazing the hock of the draft horse in his path.

The horse emitted an outraged scream, and promptly sent swordsman and sword flying through the air, to crash against the front of the cobbler's shop. The doctor fell to ground like a crushed fly, surrounded by lasts and scattered shoes.

Roger stood still, panting. His whole body was pulsing

with every heartbeat, hot with the fighting. He wanted to go on, he wanted to laugh, he wanted to hit something. He wanted to get Brianna up against the nearest wall, and *now*.

Jamie gently lifted his hand and pried his fingers from the hilt of the sword. He hadn't remembered he was holding it. His arm felt too light without it, as though it might fly up toward the sky, all by itself. His fingers were stiff from gripping so hard, and he flexed them automatically, feeling the tingle as the blood came back.

The blood was tingling everywhere. He hardly heard the laughter, the offers of drinks, or felt the blows of congratulation rained on his back.

"A clyster, a clyster, give him a clyster!" a gang of apprentices was chanting, following along as the doctor was borne off for first-aid in the nearest tavern. The horse's owner was fussing solicitously over the big bay, who looked more bemused than injured.

"I suppose he's won. After all, he drew first blood."

Roger didn't realize that he'd spoken until he heard his own voice, strangely calm in his ears.

"Will it do?" Jamie was looking at him in question, the sword held lightly on the palms of his hands.

Roger nodded. The lane was bright and filled with white dust; it gritted under his eyelids, between his teeth when he closed his mouth.

"Aye," he said. "It will do."

"Good," said Jamie. "So will you," he added casually, turning away to pay the smith.

# PART EIGHT

## *A-Hunting We Will Go*

# 89

# THE MOONS OF JUPITER

***Late November, 1771***

FOR THE FOURTH TIME in as many minutes, Roger assured himself that it was not medically possible to die of sexual frustration. He doubted that it would even cause lasting damage. On the other hand, it wasn't doing him any great good, either, in spite of his efforts to consider it as an exercise in building character.

He eased himself onto his back, careful of the rustling mattress, and stared at the ceiling. No good; from a crack at the edge of the oiled hide covering the window, early morning sun was streaming in across the bed, and from the corner of his eye, he could still see the pure golden haunches of his wife, lit as though spotlighted.

She was lying on her stomach, face buried in the pillow, and the linen sheet had slipped down past the swell of her buttocks, leaving her bare from her nape to the crack of her arse. She lay so close in the narrow bed that his leg touched hers, and the warmth of her breathing brushed his bare shoulder. His mouth was dry.

He closed his eyes. That didn't help; he promptly started seeing images of the night before: Brianna by the dim light of a smothered fire, the flames of her hair sparking in the shadows, light gleaming sudden across the curve of a naked breast as she slipped the butter-soft linen from her shoulders.

Late as it was, tired as he was, he'd wanted her desperately. Someone else had wanted her more, though. He cracked an eyelid and raised himself just slightly, enough to see over Brianna's tumbled red locks, to where the cradle stood against the wall, still in shadow. No sign of movement.

They had a long-standing agreement. He woke instantly when disturbed, she was groggy and maladroit. So when a siren shriek from the cradle jerked him into heart-pounding alertness, it was Roger who would rise, pick up the soggy, yowling bundle, and deal with the immediate necessities of hygiene. By the time he brought Jemmy to his mother, bucking and squirming in the search for sustenance, Brianna would have roused herself far enough to wriggle free of her gown, and would reach up for the child, drawing him down in warm dark to the murmuring, milky refuge of her body.

Now that Jem was older, he seldom woke at night, but when he did, with bellyache or nightmare, it took a lot longer to settle him back to sleep than it had when he was tiny. Roger had fallen back to sleep while Bree was still administering comfort, but woke when she turned in the narrow bed, her buttocks sliding past his thigh. The corn shucks under them crackled loudly with a noise like a thousand distant firecrackers, all going off down the length of his spine, waking him to full awareness of an urgent, nearly painful arousal.

He'd felt the pressure of her arse against him and narrowly restrained himself from rolling over and assaulting her from the rear. Small suckling noises from the other side of her body stopped him. Jem was still in their bed.

He'd lain still, listening, praying that she'd stay awake long enough to return the little bugger to his cradle; sometimes they fell asleep together, mother and child, and Roger would wake in the morning to the confusingly mingled scents of a beddable woman and baby pee. And then in the end, he'd fallen asleep himself, in spite of his discomfort, worn out from a day of felling logs on the mountainside.

He inhaled gently. No, she'd put him back. No scent in his bed now save Brianna's, the earthy smell of woman-flesh, a faint, sweet cloud of sweat and slippery willingness.

She sighed in her sleep, murmured something incomprehensible, and turned her head on the pillow. There were blue smudges under her eyes; she'd been up late making jelly, up again twice more with the little bas—with the baby. How could he wake her, only to gratify his own base urges?

How could he *not*?

He gritted his teeth, torn between temptation, compassion, and the sure conviction that if he yielded to his inclinations, he would get precisely as far as the worst possible moment before an interruption from the vicinity of the cradle compelled him to stop.

Experience had been a harsh teacher, but the urgings of the flesh were louder than the voice of reason. He put out a stealthy hand and gently grasped the buttock nearest. It was cool and smooth and round as a gourd.

She made a small noise deep in her throat and stretched luxuriously. She arched her back, pushing her backside up in a way that convinced Roger that the course of wisdom was to fling back the quilt, roll on top of her, and achieve his goal in the ten seconds flat it was likely to take.

He got as far as flinging back the quilt. As he raised his head from the pillow, a round, pale object rose slowly into view over the rim of the cradle, like one of the moons of Jupiter. A pair of blue eyes regarded him with clinical dispassion.

"Oh, *shit*!" he said.

"Oh, *chit*!" Jemmy said, in happy mimicry. He clambered to his feet and stood, bouncing up and down as he gripped the edge of the cradle he was rapidly outgrowing, chanting *"Chit-chit-chit-chit"* in what he evidently thought was a song.

Brianna jerked into wakefulness, blinking through tangled locks.

"What? What's wrong?"

"Ah . . . something stung me." Roger flipped the edge of the quilt discreetly back in place. "Must be a wasp in here."

She stretched on her pillow, groaning and smoothing her hair out of her face with one hand, then picked up the cup from the table and took a drink; she always woke up thirsty.

Her eyes traveled over him, and a slow smile spread across her wide, soft mouth. "Yeah? Nasty sting you got there. Want me to rub it?" She put down the cup, rolled gracefully up onto an elbow, and reached out a hand.

"Ye're a sadist," Roger said, gritting his teeth. "No doubt about it. Ye must get it from your father."

She laughed, took her hand off the quilt, and stood up, pulling her shift on over her head.

"MAMA! Chit, Mama!" Jemmy informed her, beaming, as she swung him up out of his cradle with a grunt of effort.

"You rat," she said, affectionately. "You aren't very popular with Daddy this morning. Your timing stinks." She wrinkled her nose. "And not only your timing."

"Depends on your perspective, I suppose." Roger rolled onto his side, watching. "I imagine from *his* point of view, the timing was perfect."

"Yeah." Brianna gave him a raised brow. "Hence the new word, huh?"

"He's heard it before," Roger said dryly. "Many times." He sat up, swinging his legs out of bed, and rubbed a hand through his hair and over his face.

"Well, all we have to do now is figure out how to get from the abstract to the concrete, huh?" She put Jemmy on his feet and knelt in front of him, kissing him on the nose, then unpinning his diaper. "Oh, yag. Is eighteen months too soon for toilet-training, do you think?"

"Are ye asking me, or him?"

"Pew. I don't care; whichever one of you has an opinion."

Jemmy plainly didn't; cheerfully stoic, he was ignoring his mother's determined assault on his private parts with a cold, wet cloth, absorbed in a new song of his own composition, which went along the lines of "Pew, pew, chit, chit, PEW, PEW . . ."

Brianna put a stop to this by swinging him up in her arms and sitting down with him in the nursing chair by the hearth.

"Want snackies?" she said, pulling down the neck of her shift invitingly.

"God, yes," Roger said, with feeling. Bree laughed, not without sympathy, as she settled Jemmy on her lap, where he settled happily to suckling.

"Your turn next," she assured Roger. "You want oatmeal porridge, or fried mush for breakfast?"

"Anything else on the menu?" Damn, he'd been nearly ready to stand up. Back to square one.

"Oh, sure. Toast with strawberry jam. Cheese. Eggs, but

you'll have to go get them from the coop; I don't have any in the pantry."

Roger found it hard to concentrate on the discussion, faced with the sight of Brianna in the dim smoky light of the cabin, long thighs spread under her shift, her heels tucked under the chair. She seemed to detect his lack of interest in matters dietary, for she looked up and smiled at him, her eyes taking in his own nakedness.

"You look nice, Roger," she said softly. Her free hand drifted down, resting lightly on the inner curve of one thigh. The long, blunt-nailed fingers made slow circles, barely moving.

"So do you." His voice was husky. "Better than nice."

Her hand rose and patted Jemmy softly on the back.

"Want to go see Auntie Lizzie after breakfast, sweetie?" she asked, not looking at him. Her eyes were fixed on Roger's, and her wide mouth curved in a slow smile.

He didn't think he could wait until after breakfast to touch her, at least. Her shawl was thrown across the foot of the bed; he grabbed it and wrapped it round his hips for the sake of decency as he got out of bed and crossed to kneel beside her chair.

Her hair stirred and lifted in a draft from the window, and he saw the stipple of gooseflesh break out suddenly on her arms. He put his arms around them both. The draft was cold on his bare back, but he didn't care.

"I love you," he whispered in her ear. His hand lay over hers, resting on her thigh.

She turned her head and kissed him, a glancing contact of soft lips.

"I love you, too," she said.

She had rinsed her mouth with water and wine, and tasted of autumn grapes and cold streams. He was just settling down to more serious business when a loud hammering shivered the timbers of the door, accompanied by his father-in-law's voice.

"Roger! Are ye in there, man? Up wi' ye this minute!"

"What does he mean am I in here?" Roger hissed to Brianna. "Where the hell else would I be?"

"Shh." She nipped his neck and reluctantly let go, her eyes traveling over him with deep appreciation.

"He's already up, Da!" she called.

"Aye, it's likely to be a permanent condition, too," Roger muttered. "Coming!" he bellowed. "Where the hell are my clothes?"

"Under the bed where you left them last night." Brianna set down Jemmy, who shrieked ecstatically at the sound of his grandfather's voice and ran to pound on the bolted door. Having finally ventured to walk, he had lost no time with the next stage, moving on to rapid—and perpetual—locomotion within a matter of days.

"Hurry!" Sunlight flooded into the cabin as the hide over the window was thrust aside, revealing Jamie Fraser's broad-boned face, flushed with excitement and morning sun. He lifted an eyebrow at the view of Roger thus revealed, crouched on the floor with a shirt clutched protectively to his midsection.

"Move yourself, man," he said, mildly. "It's no time to be hangin' about bare-arsed; MacLeod says there are beasts just over the ridge." He blew a kiss to Jemmy. *"A ghille ruaidh, a charaid! Ciamar a tha thu?"*

Roger forgot both sex and self-consciousness. He jerked the shirt over his head and stood up.

"What kind? Deer, elk?"

"I dinna ken, but they're meat!" The hide dropped suddenly, leaving the room half in shadow.

The intrusion had let in a blast of cold air, breaking the warm, smoke-laden atmosphere and bringing with it the breath of hunting weather, of crisp wind and crimson leaves, of mud and fresh droppings, of wet wool and sleek hide, all spiced with the imaginary reek of gunpowder.

With a final, longing look at his wife's body, Roger grabbed his stockings.

# 90

# DANGER IN THE GRASS

GRUNTING AND PUFFING, the men pushed into the dark-green zone of the conifers by noon. High on the upper ridges, clusters of balsam fir and hemlock huddled with spruce and pine, over the tumbled rock. Here they stood secure in seasonal immortality, needles murmuring lament for the bright fragility of the fallen leaves below.

Roger shivered in the cold shadow of the conifers, and was glad of the thick wool hunting shirt he wore over the linen one. There was no conversation; even when they paused briefly to draw breath, there was a stillness in the wood here that forbade unnecessary speech.

The wilderness around them felt calm—and empty. Perhaps they were too late, and the game had moved on; perhaps MacLeod had been wrong. Roger had not yet mastered the killing skills, but he had spent a good deal of time alone in sun and wind and silence; he had acquired some of the instincts of a hunter.

The men came out into full sun as they emerged on the far side of the ridge. The air was thin and cold, but Roger felt heat strike through his chilled body, and closed his eyes in momentary pleasure. The men paused together in unspoken appreciation, basking in a sheltered spot, momentarily safe from the wind.

Jamie stepped to the edge of a rocky shelf, sun glinting off his tailed copper hair. He turned to and fro, squinting downward through the trees. Roger saw his nostrils flare, and smiled to himself. Well, then, perhaps he did smell the game.

He wouldn't be surprised. Roger sniffed experimentally, but got nothing but the must of decaying leaves and a strong whiff of well-aged perspiration from the body of Kenny Lindsay.

Fraser shook his head, then turned to Fergus, and with a quiet word, climbed over the edge of the shelf and disappeared.

"We wait," Fergus said laconically to the others, and sat down. He produced a pair of carved stone balls from his bag, and sat rolling them to and fro in his palm, concentrating intently, rolling a sphere out and back along the length of each dexterous finger.

A brilliant fall sun poked long fingers through the empty branches, administering the last rites of seasonal consolation, blessing the dying earth with a final touch of warmth. The men sat talking quietly, reeking in the sun. He hadn't noticed in the colder wood, but here in the sun, the tang of fresh sweat was apparent, overlying the deeper layers of grime and body odors.

Roger reflected that perhaps it was not extraordinary olfactory acuteness on the part of animals, but merely the extreme smelliness of human beings that made it so difficult to get near game on foot. He had sometimes seen the Mohawk rub themselves with herbs, to disguise their natural odor when hunting, but even oil of peppermint wouldn't make a dent in Kenny Lindsay's stench.

He didn't reek like that himself, did he? Curious, he bent his head toward the open neck of his shirt and breathed in. He felt a trickle of sweat run down the back of his neck, under his hair. He blotted it with his collar and resolved to bathe before going back to the cabin, no matter if the creek was crusted with ice.

Showers and deodorants were of more than aesthetic importance, he reflected. One got used to almost any habitual stink in short order, after all. What he'd not realized, secure in his relatively odorless modern environment, were the more intimate implications of smell. Sometimes he felt like a bloody baboon, his most primitive responses unleashed without warning, by some random assault of odor.

He remembered what had happened just the week before, and felt a hot blush creep over him at the memory.

He had walked into the dairy shed, looking for Claire. He'd found her—and Jamie, too. They were both fully clothed, standing well apart—and the air was so filled with the musk of desire and the sharp scent of male completion that Roger had felt the blood burn in his face, the hair on his body prickling erect.

His first instinct had been to turn and leave, but there was no excuse for that. He had given his message to Claire, conscious of Fraser's eyes on him, bland and quizzical. Conscious, too, of the unspoken communication between the two of them, an unseen thrum in the air, as though they were two beads strung on a wire stretched tight.

Jamie had waited until Roger left, before leaving himself. From the corner of his eye, Roger had caught a slight movement, seen the light touch of the hand with which he left her, and even now, felt a queer clutch of his insides at the memory.

He blew out his breath to ease the tightness in his chest, then stretched out in the leaves, letting the sun beat down on his closed eyelids. He heard a muffled groan from Fergus, then the rustle of footsteps as the Frenchman made another hasty withdrawal. Fergus had eaten half-cured sauerkraut the night before—a fact made clear to anyone who sat near him for long.

His thoughts drifted back to that awkward moment in the dairy shed.

It was not prurience, nor even simple curiosity, and yet he often found himself watching them. He saw them from the cabin window, walking together in the evening, Jamie's head bent toward her, hands clasped behind his back. Claire's hands moved when she talked, rising long and white in the air, as though she would catch the future between them and give it shape, would hand Jamie her thoughts as she spoke them, smooth and polished objects, bits of sculptured air.

Once aware of what he was doing, Roger watched them purposefully, and brushed aside any feelings of shame at such intrusion, minor as it was. He had a compelling reason for his curiosity; there was something he needed to know, badly enough to excuse any lack of manners.

How was it done, this business of marriage?

He had been brought up in a bachelor's house. Given all he needed as a boy in terms of affection by his great-uncle and the Reverend's elderly housekeeper, he found himself lacking something as an adult, ignorant of the threads of touch and word that bound a married couple. Instinct would do, for a start.

But if love like that could be learned . . .

A touch on his elbow startled him and he jerked round, flinging out an arm in quick defense. Jamie ducked neatly, eluding the blow, and grinned at him.

Fraser jerked his head toward the edge of the shelf.

"I've found them," he said.

JAMIE RAISED A HAND, and Fergus went at once to his side. The Frenchman came barely to the big Scot's shoulder, but didn't look ridiculous. He shaded his eyes with his one hand, peering down where Fraser pointed.

Roger came up behind them, looking down the slope. A flicker shot through a clearing below, marked by the swooping dip and rise of its flight. Its mate called deep in the wood, a sound like a high-pitched laugh. He could see nothing else remarkable below; it was the same dense tangle of mountain laurel, hickory, and oak that existed on the side of the ridge from which they had come; far below, a thick line of tall leafless trees marked the course of a stream.

Fraser saw him, and gestured downward with a twist of the head, pointing with his chin.

"By the stream; d'ye see?" he said.

At first, Roger saw nothing. The stream itself wasn't visible, but he could chart its course by the growth of bare-limbed sycamore and willows. Then he saw it; a bush far down the slope moved, in a way that wasn't like the wind-blown tossings of the branches near it. A sudden jerk that shook the bush as something pulled at it, feeding.

"Jesus, what's that?"

His glimpse of a sudden dark bulk had been enough only to tell him that the thing was big—very big.

"I dinna ken. Bigger than a deer. Wapiti, maybe." Fraser's eyes were intent, narrowed against the wind. He stood easy, musket in one hand, but Roger could see his excitement.

"A moose, perhaps?" Fergus frowned under his shading hand. "I have not seen one, but they are very large, no?"

"No." Roger shook his head. "I mean yes, but that's not what it is. I've hunted moose—with the Mohawk. They don't move like that at all." Too late, he saw Fraser's mouth tighten briefly, then relax; by unspoken consent, they avoided mention of Roger's captivity among the Mohawk. Fraser said nothing, though, only nodded at the tangle of woodland below.

"Aye, it's not deer or moose, either—but there's more than one. D'ye see?"

Roger squinted harder, then saw what Fraser was doing, and did likewise—swaying from foot to foot, deliberately letting his eyes drift casually across the landscape.

With no attempt to focus on a single spot in the panorama below, he could instead see the whole slope as a blurred patchwork of color and motion—like a Van Gogh painting, he thought, and smiled at the thought. Then he saw what Jamie had seen, and stiffened, all thought of modern art forgotten.

Here and there among the faded grays and browns and the patches of evergreen was a disjunction, a knot in the pattern of nature's weft—strange movements, not caused by the rushing wind. Each beast was invisible itself, but made its presence known, nonetheless, by the twitchings of the bushes nearby. God, how big must they be? There . . . and there . . . he let his eyes drift to and fro, and felt a tightening of excitement through chest and belly. Christ, there were half a dozen, at least!

"I was right! I was right, was I no, *Mac Dubh*?" MacLeod exulted. His round face beamed from one to another, flushed with triumph. "I did say as I'd seen beasts, aye?"

"Jesus, there's a whole herd of them," Evan Lindsay breathed, echoing his thought. The Highlander's face was bright, fierce with anticipation. He glanced at Jamie.

"How will it be, *Mac Dubh*?"

Jamie lifted one shoulder slightly, still peering into the valley. "Hard to say; they're in the open. We canna corner them anywhere." He licked a finger and held it to the breeze, then pointed.

"The wind's from the west; let us come down the runnel there to the foot of the slope. Then wee Roger and I will pass to the side, near that great outcrop; ye see the one?"

Lindsay nodded slowly, a crooked front tooth worrying the thin flesh of his lip.

"They're near the stream. Do you circle about—keep well clear until ye're near to the big cedar tree; ye see it? Aye, then spread yourselves, two to each bank of the stream. Evan's the best marksman; have him stand ready. Roger Mac and I will come behind the herd, to drive them toward ye."

Fergus nodded, surveying the land below.

"I see. And if they shall see us, they will turn into that small defile, and so be trapped. Very good. *Allons-y!*"

He gestured imperiously to the others, his hook gleaming in the sun. Then he grimaced slightly, hand to his belly, as a long, rumbling fart despoiled the silence of the wood. Jamie gave him a thoughtful look.

"Keep downwind, aye?" he said.

IT WAS IMPOSSIBLE to walk silently through the drifts of dry leaves, but Roger stepped as lightly as possible. Seeing Jamie load and prime his own gun, Roger had done likewise, feeling mingled excitement and misgiving at the acrid scent of powder. From his impressions of the size of the beasts they followed, even he might have a chance at hitting one.

Putting aside his doubts, he paused for a moment, turning his head from side to side to listen. Nothing but the faint rush of wind through the bare branches overhead, and the far-off murmur of water. A small *crack* sounded in the underbrush ahead, and he caught a glimpse of red hair. He cupped the gunstock in his hand, the wood warm and solid in his palm, barrel aimed upward over his shoulder, and followed.

Stealing carefully round a sumac bush, Roger felt something give suddenly under his foot, and jerked back to keep his balance. He looked at what he'd stepped on, and in spite of his instant disappointment, felt a strong urge to laugh.

"Jamie!" he called, not bothering any longer about stealth or silence.

Fraser's bright hair appeared through a screen of laurel, followed by the man himself. He didn't speak, but lifted one thick brow in inquiry.

"I'm no great tracker," Roger said, nodding downward, "but I've stepped in enough of these to know one when I see one." He scraped the side of his shoe on a fallen log, and pointed with his toe. "What d'ye think we've been creeping up on, all this time?"

Jamie stopped short, squinting, then walked forward and squatted next to the corrugated brown splotch. He prodded it with a forefinger, then looked up at Roger with an expression of mingled amusement and dismay.

"I will be damned," he said. Still squatting, he turned his head, frowning as he surveyed the wilderness around them. "But what are they doing here?" he murmured.

He stood up, shading his eyes as he looked toward the creek, where the lowering sun dazzled through the branches.

"It doesna make a bit of sense," he said, squinting into the shadows. "There are only three kine on the Ridge, and I saw two of them bein' milked this morning. The third belongs to Bobby MacLeod, and I should think he'd ken if it was his own cow he'd seen. Besides . . ." He turned slowly on his heel, looking up the steep slope they'd just descended.

He didn't have to speak; no cow not equipped with a parachute could have come down that way.

"There's more than one—a lot more," Roger said. "You saw."

"Aye, there are. But where did they come from?" Jamie glanced at him, frowning in puzzlement. "The Indians dinna keep kine, especially not at this season—they'd slaughter any beasts they had, and smoke the meat. And there's no farm in thirty miles where they might have come from."

"Maybe a wild herd?" Roger suggested. "Escaped a long time ago, and wandering?" Speculation sprang up in Jamie's eyes, echoing the hopeful gurgle of Roger's stomach.

"If so, they'll be easy hunting," Jamie said. Skepticism tempered his voice, even as he smiled. He stooped and broke off a small piece of the cow-pat, crushed it with a thumb, then tossed it away.

"Verra fresh," he said. "They're close; let's go."

Within a half-hour's walking, they emerged onto the bank of the stream they had glimpsed from above. It was wide and shallow here, with willows trailing leafless branches in the water. Nothing moved save a sparkle of sun on the riffles, but it was plain that the cows had been there; the mud of the bank was cut and churned with drying hoofprints, and in one place, the dying plants had been pawed away in a long, messy trough where something large had wallowed.

"Why did I not think to bring rope?" Jamie muttered, pushing through the willow saplings on the bank as they skirted the wallow. "Meat's one thing, but milk and cheese would be—" The muttering died away, as he turned from the stream, following a trail of broken foliage back into the wood.

Without speaking, the two men spread out, walking softly. Roger listened with all his might to the quiet of the forest. They had to be nearby; even such an inexperienced eye as Roger's had picked up the freshness of the signs. And yet the wood was autumn-still, the silence broken only by a raven, calling in the distance. The sun was hanging low in the sky, filling the air in the wood with a golden haze. It was getting noticeably colder; Roger passed through a patch of shadow, and shivered, in spite of his coat. They'd have to find the others and make camp soon; twilight was short. A fire would be good. Better, of course, if there were something to cook over it.

They were going down, now, into a small hollow where wisps of autumn mist rose from the cooling earth. Jamie was some distance ahead, walking with as much purpose as the broken ground allowed; evidently the trail was still plain to him, in spite of the thick vegetation.

A herd of cows couldn't just vanish, he thought, even in mist as heavy as this . . . not unless they were faery kine. And that, he wasn't quite prepared to believe, in spite of the unearthly quiet of the woods just here.

"Roger." Jamie spoke very quietly, but Roger had been listening so intently that he located his father-in-law at once, some distance to his right. Jamie jerked his head at something nearby. "Look."

He held aside a large, brambly bush, exposing the trunk of a substantial sycamore tree. Part of the bark had been rubbed away, leaving an oozing whitish patch on the gray bark.

"Do cows rub themselves like that?" Roger peered dubiously at the patch, then picked out a swatch of woolly dark hair, snagged by the roughened bark.

"Aye, sometimes," Jamie replied. He leaned close, shaking his head as he peered at the dark-brown tangle in Roger's hand. "But damned if I've ever seen a cow wi' a coat like that. Why ye'd think it was . . ."

Something moved at Roger's elbow and he turned, to find a monstrous dark head peering over his shoulder. A tiny, blood-dark eye met his own, and he let out a yell and jerked backward. There was a loud bang as his gun went off, and then a rush and a thud, and he was lying wrapped round a tree trunk, the breath knocked out of him, left with no more than a fleeting notion of a hairy dark bulk and a power that had sent him flying like a leaf.

He sat up, fighting for breath, and found Jamie on his knees in the leaves, scrabbling frantically for Roger's gun.

"Up!" he said. "Up, wee Roger! My God, it's buffalo!"

Then he was up, following Jamie. Still half-winded, but running, his gun in his hand with no clear memory of how it got there, powder-horn bumping against his hip.

Jamie was bounding like a deer through bushes, bundled cloak bouncing against his back. The wood wasn't silent any longer; ahead there were crashings and splinterings, and low snorting bellows.

He caught up Jamie on the upward slope; they labored up it, feet sliding on damp leaves, lungs burning from the effort, then topped a rise and came out onto a long downward slope, scattered with spindly pine and hickory saplings.

There they were; eight or nine of the huge, shaggy beasts, clustering together as they thundered down the hill, splitting to go around thickets and trees. Jamie dropped to one knee, sighted, and fired, to no apparent effect.

There was no time to stop and reload; they must keep the herd in sight. A bend of the stream glinted between the trees, below and to the right. Roger charged down the slope in a rush of excitement, canteen and bullet-box flying, heart thundering like the hooves of the buffalo herd. He could hear Jamie bellowing behind him, shouting Gaelic exhortations.

An exclamation in a different tone made Roger glance back. Jamie had stopped, his face frozen in shock. Before Roger could call to him, shock shifted to a look of fury. Teeth bared, he seized his gun by the barrel, and brought down the stock with a vicious *tchunk!* Barely pausing, he lifted the gun and clubbed it down again—and again, shoulders rolling with the effort.

Reluctantly abandoning the chase, Roger turned and bounded up the slope toward him.

"What the hell—?" Then he saw, and felt the hair on his body rise in a surge of revulsion. Brown coils squirmed between the tussocks, thick and scaly. One end of the snake had been battered to pulp, and its blood stained the butt of Fraser's musket, but the body writhed on, wormlike and headless.

"Stop! It's dead. D'ye hear me? Stop, I say!" He grasped Fraser's arm, but his father-in-law jerked free of his hold and brought the gun-butt down once more. Then he did stop, and stood shuddering violently, half-leaning on his gun.

"Christ! What happened? Did it get you?"

"Aye, in the leg. I stepped on it." Jamie's face was white to the lips. He looked at the still-writhing corpse and a deep shudder ran through him again.

Roger repressed his own shudder and grabbed Fraser's arm.

"Come away. Sit down, we'll have a look."

Jamie came, half-stumbling, and collapsed onto a fallen log. He fumbled at his stocking top, fingers shaking. Roger pushed Jamie's hand away and stripped buskin and stocking off the right foot. The fang marks were clear, a double dark-red puncture in the flesh of Fraser's calf. The flesh around the small holes had a bluish tinge, visible even in the late gold light.

"It's poisonous. I've got to cut it." Roger felt dry-mouthed,

· but oddly calm, with no sense of panic. He pulled the knife from his belt, thought briefly of sterilization, and dismissed the notion. It would take precious minutes to light a fire, and there was no time at all to waste.

"Wait." Fraser was still white, but had stopped shaking. He took the small flask from his belt and trickled whisky over the blade, then poured a few drops on his fingers and rubbed the liquid over the wound. He gave Roger a brief twitch of the mouth, meant as a smile.

"Claire does that, when she sets herself to cut someone." He leaned back, hands braced on the mossy trunk, and nodded. "Go on, then."

Biting his lip in concentration, Roger pressed the tip of the knife into the skin just above one of the puncture marks. The skin was surprisingly tough and springy; the knife dented it, but didn't penetrate. Fraser reached down and clasped his hand around Roger's; he shoved, with a deep, vicious grunt, and the knife sank suddenly in, an inch or more. Blood welled up around the blade; the gripping hand fell away.

"Again. Hard—and quick, man, for God's sake." Jamie's voice was steady, but Roger felt clear droplets of sweat fall onto his hand from Fraser's face, warm and then cold on his skin.

He braced himself to the necessary force, stabbed hard and cut quick—two X marks over the punctures, just as the first-aid guides said. The wounds were bleeding a lot, blood pouring down in thick streams. That was good, though, he thought. He had to go deep; deep enough to get beyond the poison. He dropped the knife and bent, mouth to the wounds.

There was no panic, but his sense of urgency was rising. How fast did venom spread? He had no more than minutes, maybe less. Roger sucked as hard as he could, blood filling his mouth with the taste of hot metal. He sucked and spat in quiet frenzy, blood spattering on the yellow leaves, Fraser's leg hairs scratchy against his lips. With the peculiar diffusion of mind that attends emergency, he thought of a dozen fleeting things at once, even as he bent his whole concentration to the task at hand.

Was the bloody snake really dead?

How poisonous was it?

Had the bison got away?

Christ, was he doing this right?

Brianna would kill him if he let her father die. So would Claire.

He had the devil of a cramp in his right thigh.

Where in hell were the others? Fraser should call for them—no, he *was* calling, was bellowing somewhere outside Roger's ken. The flesh of the leg Roger held had gone rock-hard, muscles rigid under his pressing fingers.

Something grasped the hair on the back of his head and twisted, forcing him to stop. He glanced up, breathing hard.

"That's enough, aye?" Jamie said mildly. "You'll drain me dry." He gingerly wiggled his bared foot, grimacing at his leg. The slashmarks were vivid, still oozing blood, and the flesh around them was swollen from the sucking, blotched and bruised.

Roger sat back on his heels, gulping air.

"I've made more—of a mess—than the snake did."

His mouth filled with saliva; he coughed and spat. Fraser silently offered him the whisky flask; he swirled a mouthful round and spat once more, then drank deep.

"All right?" He wiped his chin with the back of a hand, still tasting iron, and nodded at the lacerated leg.

"I'll do." Jamie was still pale, but one corner of his mouth turned up. "Go and see are the others in sight."

They weren't; the view from the top of the outcrop showed nothing but a sea of bare branches, tossing to and fro. The wind had come up. If the bison still moved along the river, there was no trace visible, either of them or of their hunters.

Hoarse from hallooing into the wind, Roger made his way back down the slope. Jamie had moved a little, finding a sheltered spot among rocks at the foot of a big balsam fir. He was sitting, back against a rock and legs outstretched, a handkerchief bound round his wounded leg.

"No sign of anyone. Can ye walk?" Roger bent over his father-in-law, and was alarmed to see him flushed and sweating heavily, despite the gathering chill of the air.

Jamie shook his head and gestured toward his leg.

"I can—but not for long." The leg was noticeably swollen near the bite, and the blue tinge had spread; it showed like a faint fresh bruise on either side of the encircling handkerchief.

Roger felt the first stab of uneasiness. He had done everything he knew to do; first-aid guides always had as the next step in the treatment of snakebite, "Immobilize limb and get patient to hospital as soon as possible." The cutting and sucking were meant to pull poison from the wound—but clearly there was plenty still left, spreading slowly through Jamie Fraser's body. He hadn't been in time to get it all—if he'd gotten any. And the nearest thing to a hospital—Claire and her herbs—a day's walk away.

Roger sank slowly down onto his haunches, wondering what the hell to do next. Immobilize the limb—well, that was effectively taken care of, for what good it might do.

"Hurt much?" he asked awkwardly.

"Yes."

With this unhelpful response, Jamie leaned back against the rock and closed his eyes. Roger eased himself down onto a sheaf of dry needles, trying to think.

It was getting dark fast; the brief warmth of the day had faded, and the shadows under the trees had taken on the deep blue look of evening, though it couldn't be more than four or so. Plainly they weren't going anywhere tonight; navigation in the mountains was nearly impossible in the dark, even if Fraser could walk. If the others were here, they could make shift to carry him—but would that be any better than leaving him where he was? While he urgently wished Claire were here, sense told him there was little even she could do—except, perhaps, comfort Jamie if he were to die . . .

The thought knotted his belly. Shoving it firmly aside, he reached into his pouch, checking supplies. He had a small quantity of johnny-cake still in his bag; water was never a difficulty in these mountains—through the sound of the trees, he could hear the gurgle of a stream somewhere below, not far off. He'd better be gathering wood while it was still light, though.

"We'd best make a fire." Jamie spoke suddenly, startling Roger with this echo of his thought. Jamie opened his eyes and looked down at one hand, turning it over and back as though he'd never seen it before.

"I've pins and needles in my fingers," he remarked with interest. He touched his face with one hand. "Here, too. My lips have gone numb. Is that usual, d'ye ken?"

"I don't know. I suppose it is, if you've been drinking the whisky." It was a feeble joke, but he was relieved to have it greeted with a faint laugh.

"Nay." Jamie touched the flask beside him. "I thought I might need it more, later."

Roger took a deep breath and stood up.

"Right. Stay there; you shouldn't move. I'll fetch along some wood. The others will likely see the light of the fire." The other men would be of no particular help, at least not until morning—but it would be a comfort not to be alone.

"Fetch the snake, too," Jamie called after him. "Fair's fair; we'll hae a bite of *him* for our supper!"

Grinning in spite of present worry, Roger gave a reassuring wave and turned down the slope.

What were the chances? he asked himself, stooping to wrest a thick pine knot from the soft wood of a rotted log. Fraser was a big man, and in robust health. Surely he would survive.

Yet folk did die of snakebite, and not infrequently; he'd heard only last week of a German woman near High Point; bent to pick up a stick of wood from her woodpile, struck full in the throat by a snake lying hidden there, dead in minutes. Reaching under a bush for a dry branch just as this recollection came to him, he hastily withdrew his bare hand, gooseflesh running up his arm. Berating himself for stupidity, he got a stick and thoroughly stirred the drift of dry leaves before reaching once more cautiously into it.

He couldn't help glancing up the slope every few minutes, feeling a small stab of alarm whenever Fraser was out of sight. What if he should collapse before Roger returned?

Then he relaxed a little as he remembered. No, it was all right. Jamie wasn't going to die tonight, either of snakebite or cold. He couldn't; he was meant to die some years hence, by fire. For once, future doom meant present reassurance. He took a deep breath and let it out in relief, then steeled himself to approach the snake.

It was motionless now, quite obviously dead. Still, it took some effort of will to pick the thing up. It was as thick around as his wrist and nearly four feet long. It had begun to stiffen; in the end, he was obliged to lay it across the armload of firewood, like a scaly branch. Seeing it so, he had no trouble imagining how the snake that had bitten the German woman had escaped notice; the subtle browns and grays of its patterns made it nearly invisible against its background.

Jamie skinned the thing while Roger built the fire. Watching from the corner of his eye, he could see that his father-in-law was making an unusually clumsy job of it; the numbness in his hands must be getting worse. Still, he went on doggedly, hacking at the corpse, stringing chunks of pale raw flesh onto a half-peeled twig with trembling fingers.

The job complete, Jamie extended the stick toward the budding fire and nearly dropped it. Roger grabbed for it, and felt through the stick the tremor that shook Jamie's hand and arm.

"You all right?" he said, and reached automatically to feel Jamie's forehead. Fraser jerked back, surprised and mildly affronted.

"Aye," he said, but then paused. "Aye, well . . . I do feel a bit queer," he admitted.

It was hard to tell in the uncertain light, but Roger thought he looked a good bit more than queer.

"Lie down for a bit, why don't you?" he suggested, trying to sound casual. "Sleep if ye can; I'll wake ye when the food's ready."

Jamie didn't argue, which alarmed Roger more than anything else so far. He curled himself into a drift of leaves, moving his wounded leg with a care that told Roger just how painful it was.

The snakemeat dripped and sizzled, and in spite of a slight distaste at the notion of eating snake, Roger felt his stomach rumble in anticipation; damned if it didn't smell like roasting chicken! Not for the first time, he reflected on the thin line that separated appetite from starvation; give the most finicky gourmand a day or two without food, and he'd be eating slugs and lizards without the least hesitation; Roger had, on the journey back from his surveying trip.

He kept an eye on Jamie; he didn't move, but Roger could see him shiver now and then, in spite of the now-leaping flames. His eyes were closed. His face looked red, but that might be only firelight—no telling his real color.

By the time the meat had cooked through, it was full dark. Roger fetched water, then heaped armloads of dried grass and wood on the fire, making the flames dance and crackle, higher than his head; if the other men were anywhere within a mile, they should see it.

Fraser roused himself with difficulty to eat. It was clear that he had no appetite, but he forced himself to chew and swallow, each bite a dogged effort. What was it? Roger wondered. Simple stubbornness? A notion of vengeance against the snake? Or perhaps some Highland superstition, the idea that consuming the reptile's flesh might be a cure for its bite?

"Did the Indians ken aught to do for snakebite?" Jamie asked abruptly, lending some credence to the last guess.

"Yes," Roger answered cautiously. "They had roots and herbs that they mixed with dung or hot cornmeal, to make a poultice."

"Did it work?" Fraser held a bit of meat in his hand, wrist drooping as though too tired to raise it to his mouth.

"I only saw it done twice. Once, it seemed to work perfectly—no swelling, no pain; the little girl was quite all right by evening of the same day. The other time—it didn't work." He had only seen the hide-wrapped body taken from the longhouse, not witnessed the grisly details of the death. Evidently he was going to get another chance to see the effects of snakebite up close, though.

Fraser grunted.

"And what would they do in your time?"

"Give you an injection of something called antivenin."

"An injection, aye?" Jamie looked unenthusiastic. "Claire did that to me, once. I didna like it a bit."

"Did it work?"

Jamie merely grunted in reply, and tore off another small morsel of meat between his teeth.

In spite of his worry, Roger wolfed his share of the meat, and the uneaten part of Jamie's meal as well. The sky spread black and starry overhead, and a cold wind moved through the trees, chilling hands and face.

He buried the remnants of the snake—all they needed now was for some large carnivore to show up, drawn by the smell of blood—and tended the fire, all the time listening for a shout from the darkness. No sound came but the moaning of wind and cracking of branches; they were alone.

Fraser had pulled off his hunting shirt in spite of the chill, and was sitting with his eyes closed, swaying slightly. Roger squatted next to him and touched his arm. Jesus! The man was blazing hot to the touch.

He opened his eyes, though, and smiled faintly. Roger held up a cup of water; Jamie nodded and took the cup, fumbling. The leg was grotesquely swollen below the knee, nearly twice its normal size. The skin showed irregular dark red blotches, as though some succubus had come to place its hungry mouth upon the flesh, then left unsatisfied.

Roger wondered uneasily whether he might, perhaps, be wrong. He'd been convinced that the past couldn't be changed; ergo, the time and manner of Fraser's death was set—some four years in the future. If it weren't for that certainty, though, he thought, he'd be bloody worried by the look of the man. Just how certain *was* he, after all?

"Ye could be wrong." Jamie had put down the cup and was regarding him with a steady blue gaze.

"About what?" he asked, startled to hear his thought spoken aloud. Had he been muttering to himself, not realizing it?

"About the changing. Ye thought it wasna possible to change history, ye said. But what if ye're wrong?"

Roger bent to poke the fire.

"I'm not wrong," he said firmly, as much to himself as to Fraser. "Think, man. You and Claire—you tried to stop Charles Stuart—change what he did—and ye couldn't. It can't be done."

"That's no quite right," Fraser objected. He leaned back, eyes half-hooded against the fire's brightness.

"What's not right?"

"It's true we failed to keep him from the Rising—but that didna depend only on us and on him; there were a good many other folk had to do wi' that. The chiefs who followed him, the damn Irishmen who flattered him—even Louis; him and his gold."

He waved a hand, dismissing it. "But that's neither here nor there. Ye said Claire and I couldna stop him—and it's true, we couldna stop the beginning. But we might have stopped the end."

"Culloden, you mean?" Roger stared into the fire, remembering dimly that long-ago day when Claire had first told him and Brianna the story of the stones—and Jamie Fraser. Yes, she had spoken of a last opportunity—the chance to prevent that final slaughter of the clans . . .

He glanced up at Fraser.

"By killing Charles Stuart?"

"Aye. If we had done so—but neither she nor I could bring ourselves to it." His eyes were nearly closed, but he turned his head restlessly, clearly uncomfortable. "I have wondered many times since, if that was decency—or cowardice."

"Or maybe something else," Roger said abruptly. "You don't know. If Claire had tried to poison him, I'm betting something would have happened; the dish would have spilled, a dog would have eaten it, someone else would have died—it wouldn't have made a difference!"

Fraser's eyes opened slowly.

"So ye think it's all destined, do ye? A man has no free choice at all?" He rubbed at his mouth with the back of his hand. "And when ye chose to come back, for Brianna, and then again, for her and the wean—it wasna your choice at all, aye? Ye were meant to do it?"

"I—" Roger stopped, hands clenched on his thighs. The smell of the *Gloriana*'s bilges seemed suddenly to rise above the scent of burning wood. Then he relaxed, and gave a short laugh. "Hell of a time to get philosophical, isn't it?"

"Aye, well," Fraser spoke quite mildly. "It's only that I may not have another time." Before Roger could expostulate, he went on. "If there is nay free choice . . . then there is neither sin nor redemption, aye?"

"Jesus," Roger muttered, shoving the hair back from his

forehead. "Come out with Hawkeye and end up under a tree with bloody Augustine of Hippo!"

Jamie ignored him, intent on his point.

"We chose—Claire and I. We wouldna do murder. We wouldna shed the blood of one man; but does the blood of Culloden then rest on us? We wouldna commit the sin—but does the sin find us, still?"

"Of course not." Roger rose to his feet, restless, and stood poking the fire. "What happened at Culloden—it wasn't your fault, how could it be? All the men who took part in that— Murray, Cumberland, all the chiefs . . . it was not any one man's doing!"

"So ye think it is all meant? We're doomed or saved from the moment of birth, and not a thing can change it? And you a minister's son!" Fraser gave a dry sort of chuckle.

"Yes," Roger said, feeling at once awkward and unaccountably angry. "I mean no, I don't think that. It's only . . . well, if something's already happened one way, how can it happen another way?"

"It's only you that thinks it's happened," Fraser pointed out.

"I don't think it, I know!"

"Mmphm. Aye, because ye've come from the other side of it; it's behind you. So perhaps *you* couldna change something—but I could, because it's still ahead of me?"

Roger rubbed a hand hard over his face.

"That makes—" he began, and then stopped. How could he say it made no sense? Sometimes he thought nothing in the world made sense anymore.

"Maybe," he said wearily. "God knows; I don't."

"Aye. Well, I suppose we'll find out soon enough."

Roger glanced sharply at him, hearing a strange note in his voice.

"What d'ye mean by that?"

"Ye think ye ken that I died three years from now," Fraser said calmly. "If I die tonight, then you're wrong, aye? What ye think happened won't have happened—so the past *can* be changed, aye?"

"You're not going to die!" Roger snapped. He glowered at Fraser, daring him to contradict.

"I'm pleased to hear it," Fraser said. "But I think I'll take a bit o' the whisky now. Draw the cork for me, aye? My fingers willna grasp it."

Roger's own hands were far from steady. Perhaps it was only the heat of Fraser's fever that made his own skin feel cold as he held the flask for his father-in-law to drink. He doubted that whisky was recommended for snakebite, but it didn't seem likely to make much difference now.

"Lie down," he said gruffly, when Jamie had finished. "I'll fetch a bit more wood."

He was unable to keep still; there was plenty of wood to hand, yet still he prowled the darkness, keeping just within sight of the blazing fire.

He had had a lot of nights like this; alone under a sweep of sky so vast that it made him dizzy to look up, chilled to the bone, moving to keep warm. The nights when he had wrestled with choice, too restless to lie in a comforting burrow of leaves, too tormented to sleep.

The choice had been clear then, but far from easy to make: Brianna on the one hand, and all that came with her; love and danger, doubt and fear. And on the other, surety. The knowledge of who and what he was—a certainty he had forsaken, for the sake of the woman who was his . . . and the child who might be.

He had chosen. Dammit, he *had* chosen! Nothing had forced him, he had made the choice himself. And if it meant remaking himself from the ground up, then he'd bloody well chosen that, too! And he'd chosen to kiss Morag, too. His mouth twisted at the thought; he'd had even less notion of the consequences of *that* small act.

Some small echo stirred in his mind, a soft voice far back in the shadows of his memory.

"*. . . what I was born does not matter, only what I will make of myself, only what I will become.*"

Who'd written that? he wondered. Montaigne? Locke? One of the bloody Enlightenment lads, them and their notions of destiny and the individual? He'd like to see what they had to say about time traveling! Then he remembered where he'd read it, and the marrow of his spine went cold.

"*This is the grimoire of the witch, Geillis. It is a witch's name, and I take it for my own; what I was born does not matter, only what I will make of myself, only what I will become."*

"Right!" he said aloud, defiant. "Right, and you couldn't change things either, could you, Grandma?"

A sound came from the forest behind him, and the hair rose on the back of his neck before he recognized it; it wasn't laughter, as he'd thought at first—only a panther's distant cry.

She had, though, he thought suddenly. True, she'd not managed to make a king of Charles Stuart—but she'd done a good number of other things. And now he came to think on the matter . . . She and Claire had both done something guaranteed to change things; they'd borne children, to men of another time. Brianna . . . William Buccleigh—and when he thought of the effect those two births had had on his own life, let alone anything else . . .

That *had* to change things, didn't it? He sat down slowly on a fallen log, feeling the bark cold and damp under him. Yes, it did. To name one minor effect, his own bloody existence was the result of Geilie Duncan's taking charge of her destiny. If Geilie hadn't borne a child to Dougal MacKenzie . . . of course, she hadn't *chosen* to do that.

Did intention make any difference, though? Or was that exactly the point he'd been arguing with Jamie Fraser?

He got up and circled the fire quietly, peering into the shadows. Fraser was lying down, a humped shape in the darkness, very still.

He walked lightly, but his feet crunched on the needles. Fraser didn't twitch. His eyes were closed. The blotchiness had spread to his face. Roger thought his features had a thick, congested look, lips and eyelids slightly swollen. In the wavering light, it was impossible to tell whether he was still breathing.

Roger knelt and shook him, hard.

"Hey! Are ye still alive?" He'd meant to say it jokingly, but the fear in his voice was apparent to his own ears.

Fraser didn't move. Then one eye cracked open.

"Aye," he muttered. "But I'm no enjoying it."

Roger didn't leave again. He wiped Jamie's face with a wet cloth, offered more whisky—which was refused—then sat beside the recumbent form, listening for each rasping breath.

Much against his will, he found himself making plans, proceeding from one unwelcome assumption to the next. What if the worst happened? Against his will, he thought it possible; he had seen several people die who didn't look nearly as bad as Fraser did just now.

If the worst *should* happen, and the others not have returned, he would have to bury Jamie. He could neither carry the body nor leave it exposed; not with panthers or other animals nearby.

His eye roamed uneasily over the surroundings. Rocks, trees, brush—everything looked alien, the shapes half-masked by darkness, outlines seeming to waver and change in the flickering glow, the wind moaning past like a prowling beast.

There, maybe; the end of a half-fallen tree loomed jagged in the darkness, leaning at an angle. He could scrape a shallow trench, perhaps, then lever the tree and let it fall to cover the temporary grave . . .

He pressed his head hard against his knees.

*"No!"* he whispered. "Please, no!"

The thought of telling Bree, telling Claire, was a physical pain, stabbing him in chest and throat. It wasn't only them, either—what about Jem? What about Fergus and Marsali, Lizzie and her father, the Bugs, the Lindsays, the other families on the Ridge? They all looked to Fraser for confidence and direction; what would they do without him?

Fraser shifted, and groaned with the movement. Roger laid a hand on his shoulder, and he stilled.

*Don't go,* he thought, the unspoken words balled tight in his throat. *Stay with us. Stay with me.*

He sat for a long time, his hand resting on Fraser's shoulder. He had the absurd thought that he was somehow holding Fraser, keeping him anchored to the earth. If he held on 'til the sunrise, all would be well; if he lifted his hand, that would be the end.

The fire was burning low now, but he put off from moment to moment the necessity of tending it, unwilling to let go.

"MacKenzie?" It was no more than a murmur, but he bent at once.

"Aye, I'm here. Ye want water? A drop of whisky?" He was reaching for the cup even as he spoke, spilling water in his anxiety. Fraser took two swallows, then waved the cup away with a twitch of his hand.

"I dinna ken yet if ye're right or you're wrong," Fraser said. His voice was soft and hoarse, but distinct. "But if you're wrong, wee Roger, and I'm dying, there are things I must say to ye. I dinna want to leave it too late."

"I'm here," Roger repeated, not knowing what else to say.

Fraser closed his eyes, gathering strength, then brought his hands beneath him and rolled halfway over, ponderous and clumsy. He grimaced, and took a moment to catch his breath.

"Bonnet. I must tell ye what I've put in train."

"Aye?" For the first time, Roger felt something other than simple worry for Fraser's welfare.

"There is a man named Lyon—Duncan Innes will ken best how to find him. He works on the coast, buying from the smugglers who run the Outer Banks. He sought me out at the wedding, to see would I deal with him, over the whisky."

The plan in outline was simple enough; Jamie meant to send word—by what route, Roger had no notion—to this Lyon, indicating that he was willing to enter into business, provided that Lyon would bring Stephen Bonnet to a meeting, to prove that he had a man of the necessary reputation and skill to manage the transport up and down the coast.

"Necessary reputation," Roger echoed under his breath. "Aye, he's got that."

Fraser made a sound that might have been a laugh.

"He'll not agree that easily—he'll bargain and set terms— but he'll agree. Tell him ye've got enough whisky to make it worth his while—give him a barrel of the two-year-old to try, if ye must. When he sees what folk will pay for it, he'll be eager enough. The place—" He stopped, frowning, and breathed for a moment before going on.

"I'd thought to make it Wylie's Landing—but if it's you, ye should choose a place to your liking. Take the Lindsays with ye to guard your back, if they'll go. If not, find someone else; dinna go alone. And go ready to kill him at the first shot."

Roger nodded, swallowing heavily. Jamie's eyelids were swollen, but he looked up under them, his eyes glinting sharp in the firelight.

"Dinna let him get close enough to take ye with a sword," he said. "Ye've done well—but ye're not good enough to meet a man like Bonnet."

"And you are?" Roger couldn't stop himself from saying. He thought Fraser was smiling, but it was difficult to tell.

"Oh, aye," he said softly. "If I live." He coughed then, and lifted a hand, dismissing Bonnet for the moment.

"For the rest . . . watch Sinclair. He's a man to be used— he kens everything that passes in the district—but no a man to turn your back on, ever."

He paused, brow furrowed in thought.

"Ye can trust Duncan Innes and Farquard Campbell," he said. "And Fergus—Fergus will help ye, if he can. For the rest—" He shifted again and winced. "Go wary of Obadiah Henderson; he'll try ye. A-many of them will, and ye let them—but dinna let Henderson. Take him at the first chance—ye willna get another."

Slowly, with frequent pauses to rest, he went down the list of the names of the men on the Ridge, the inhabitants of Cross Creek, the prominent men of the Cape Fear valley. Characters, leanings, secrets, obligations.

Roger fought down panic, struggling to listen carefully, commit it all to memory, wanting to reassure Fraser, tell him to stop, to rest, that none of this was necessary—at the same time knowing it was more than necessary. There was war coming; it didn't take a time traveler to know it. If the welfare of the Ridge—of Brianna and Jemmy, of Claire—were to be left in Roger's inexperienced hands, he must take heed of every scrap of information that Fraser could give him.

Fraser's voice trailed off in hoarseness. Had he lost consciousness? The shoulder under Roger's hand was slack, inert. He sat quietly, not daring to move.

It wouldn't be enough, he thought, and a dull fear settled in the pit of his stomach, an aching dread that underlay the sharper pangs of grief. He couldn't do it. Christ, he couldn't even shoot a thing the size of a house! And now he was meant to step into Jamie Fraser's shoes? Keep order with fists and brain, feed a family with gun and knife, tread the tightrope of politics over a lighted powderkeg, tenants and family all balanced on his shoulders? Replace the man they called Himself? Not fucking likely, he thought bleakly.

Fraser's hand twitched suddenly. The fingers were swollen like sausages, the skin stretched red and shiny. Roger laid his free hand over it, and felt the fingers move, trying to curl around his own.

"Tell Brianna I'm glad of her," Fraser whispered. "Give my sword to the bairn."

Roger nodded, unable to speak. Then, realizing that Fraser couldn't see him, cleared his throat.

"Aye," he said gruffly. "I'll tell her." He waited, but Fraser said no more. The fire had burned very low, but the hand in his burned hot as embers. A gust of wind knifed past, whipping strands of his hair against his cheek, sending up a spray of sudden sparks from the fire.

He waited as long as he thought he dared, the cold night creeping past in lonely minutes. Then leaned close, so Fraser could hear him.

"Claire?" he asked quietly. "Is there anything ye'd have me tell her?"

He thought he'd waited too long; Fraser lay motionless for several minutes. Then the big hand stirred, half-closing swollen fingers; the ghost of a motion, grasping after time that slipped away.

"Tell her . . . I meant it."

# 91

# DOMESTIC MANAGEMENT

I'VE NEVER SEEN ANYTHING like that in my entire life." I leaned closer, peering. "That is absolutely *bizarre*."

"And you a healer half your life," Jamie muttered crossly. "Ye canna tell me they've no got snakes in your time."

"They haven't got many in downtown Boston. Besides, they wouldn't call out a surgeon to deal with a case of snakebite. Closest I came was when a keeper at the zoo was bitten by a king cobra—a friend of mine did the autopsy, and invited me to come and watch."

I refrained from saying that Jamie looked a lot worse at present than the subject of the autopsy had.

I set a hand gingerly on his ankle. The skin was puffy, hot and dry under my hand. It was also red. Bright red. The brilliant color extended from his feet up nearly to his rib cage; he looked as though he'd been dipped in boiling water.

His face, ears, and neck were also flushed the color of a plum tomato; only the pale skin of his chest had escaped, and even that was dotted with pinpricks of red. Beyond the lobsterlike coloration, the skin was peeling from his feet and hands, hanging in wispy shreds like Spanish moss.

I peered closely at his hip. Here, I could see that the redness was caused by a denser version of the rash on his chest; the stipple of tiny dots showed up clearly on the stretched skin over the ilial crest.

"You look like you've been roasted over a slow fire," I said, rubbing a finger over the rash in fascination. "I've never seen anything so red in my life." Not raised; I couldn't feel the individual spots, though I could see them at close range. Not a rash as such; I thought it must be petechiae, pinpoint hemorrhages under the skin. But so many of them . . .

"I shouldna say ye've much room to criticize, Sassenach," he said. Too weak to nod, he cut his eyes at my fingers—stained with huge blotches of yellow and blue.

"Oh, *damn*!" I leaped to my feet, threw the quilts hastily on top of him, and ran for the door. Distracted by Jamie's dramatic arrival, I had left a vat full of dyeing to mind itself in the side yard—and the water had been low. Christ, if it boiled dry and burned the clothes . . .

The hot reek of urine and indigo hit me in the face as I shot out the door. In spite of that, I drew a deep breath of relief, as I saw Marsali, red in the face with the effort of levering a dripping mass from the pot with the big wooden clothes-fork. I went hastily to help her, snatching the steaming garments one by one from the sopping pile and flinging them onto the blackberry bushes to dry.

"Thank goodness," I said, waving my scalded fingers in the air to cool them. "I was afraid I'd ruined the lot."

"Weel, they'll be a bit dark, maybe." Marsali wiped a hand across her face, plastering back the fine blond strands that escaped from her kerch. "If the weather keeps fine, though, ye can leave them in the sun to fade. Here, let's move the pot before it scorches!"

Crusts of indigo had already started to crackle and blacken in the bottom of the pot as we tipped it off the fire, and clouds of acrid smoke rose up around us.

"It's all right," Marsali said, coughing and fanning smoke from her face. "Leave it, Mother Claire; I'll fetch up water so it can soak. Ye'll need to see to Da, aye? I came down at once when I heard; is he verra poorly?"

"Oh, thank you, dear." I was overwhelmed with gratitude; the last thing I had time to do just now was to haul several buckets of water from the spring to soak the pot. I blew on my scalded fingers to cool them; the skin under the splotches of dye was nearly as red as Jamie's.

"I think he'll be all right," I assured her, suppressing my own fears. "He feels dreadful, and looks worse—I've never seen anyone look like that in all my born days—but if the wound doesn't get infected . . ." I crossed my sore fingers in superstitious prophylaxis.

"Ah, he'll do," Marsali said confidently. "Fergus said as they thought he was dead when they found him and Roger Mac, but by the time they crossed the second ridge, he was makin' terrible jokes about the snake, so they didna worry anymore."

I wasn't quite so sanguine myself, having seen the state of his injured leg, but I smiled reassuringly.

"Yes, I think he'll be fine. I'm just going to make an onion poultice and clean out the wound a bit. Go and see him, why don't you, while I fetch the onions?"

Luckily there were plenty of onions; I had pulled them two weeks before, when the first frost came, and dozens of knobbly braided strings hung in the pantry, fragrant and crackling when I brushed against them. I broke off six large onions and brought them into the kitchen to slice. My fingers were tingling, half-burned and stiff from handling the boiling clothes, and I worked slowly, not wanting to slice off a finger accidentally.

"Here, I'll do that, *a leannan*." Mrs. Bug took the knife out of my hand and dealt briskly with the onions. "Is it a poultice? Aye, that'll be the thing. A good onion poultice will mend anything." Still, a worried frown puckered her forehead as she glanced toward the surgery.

"Can I help, Mama?" Bree came in from the hallway, also looking worried. "Da looks awful; is he all right?"

"Ganda full?" Jem popped into the kitchen after his mother, less worried about his grandfather than interested in the knife Mrs. Bug was using. He dragged his little stool toward her, face purposeful under his coppery fringe. "Me do!"

I brushed the hair out of my face with the back of my hand, eyes watering fiercely from the onions.

"I think so." I sniffed and blotted my eyes. "How's Roger?"

"Roger's good." I could hear the small note of pride in her voice; Jamie had told her Roger had saved his life. Possibly he had. I just hoped it *stayed* saved.

"He's asleep," she added. Her mouth curved slightly as

she met my eyes, with complete understanding. If a man was in bed, at least you knew where he was. And that he was safe, for the moment.

"Jem! You leave Mrs. Bug alone!" She scooped him off his stool and whirled him away from the chopping board, feet kicking in protest. "Do you need anything, Mama?"

I rubbed a finger between my brows, considering.

"Yes, can you try to find me some maggots? I'll need them for Jamie's leg." I frowned, glancing out the window at the bright autumn day. "I'm afraid the frost has killed all the flies; I haven't seen one in days. Try the paddock, though; they'll lay eggs in the warm dung."

She made a brief face of distaste, but nodded, setting Jemmy down on the floor.

"Come on, pal, let's go find ickies for Grannie."

"Icky-icky-icky-icky!" Jemmy scampered after her, enchanted at the prospect.

I dropped the sliced onions into a bowl made from a hollowed gourd and scooped a little of the hot water from the cauldron into it. Then I left the onions to stew, and went back to the surgery. In the center of the room was a sturdy pine table, serving as examination table, dentist's chair, drug preparation surface, or auxiliary dining table, depending on medical exigencies and the number of dinner guests. At the moment, it was supporting the supine form of Jamie, scarcely visible under his heap of quilts and blankets. Marsali stood close to the table, head bent toward him as she held a cup of water for him to sip.

"You're sure you're all right, Da?" she said. One hand stole toward him, but she stopped, clearly afraid to touch him in his present condition.

"Oh, aye, I'll do." I could hear the deep fatigue in his voice, but a big hand rose slowly out from under the quilts to touch her cheek.

"Fergus did braw work," he said. "Kept the men together through the night, found me and Roger Mac in the morning, brought everyone home safe across the mountain. He's a fine sense of direction."

Marsali's head was still bent, but I saw her cheek curve in a smile.

"I did tell him so. He'll no give over berating himself for lettin' the beasts get away, though. Just one would ha' fed the whole Ridge for the winter, he said."

Jamie gave a small grunt of dismissal.

"Och, we'll manage."

It was plainly an effort for him to speak, but I didn't try to send Marsali away. Roger told me Jamie had been vomiting blood as they brought him back; I couldn't give him brandy or whisky to ease the pain, and I hadn't any laudanum. Marsali's presence might help to distract him from his wretchedness.

I opened the cupboard quietly and brought out the big lidded bowl where I kept my leeches. The pottery was cold, soothing to my scalded hands. I had a dozen or so big ones; somnolent black blobs, half-floating in their murky brew of water and cattail roots. I scooped three into a smaller bowl full of clear water, and set it by the brazier to warm.

"Wake up, lads," I said. "Time to earn your keep."

I laid out the other things I would need, listening to the murmured conversation behind me—Germain, baby Joan, a porcupine in the trees near Marsali and Fergus's cabin.

Coarse gauze for the onion poultice, the corked bottle with its mixture of alcohol and sterile water, the stoneware jars of dried goldenseal, coneflower, and comfrey. And the bottle of penicillin broth. I cursed silently, looking at the label on it. It was nearly a month old; caught up in the bear hunt and the autumn chores upon our return, I had not made a fresh batch for weeks.

It would have to do. Pressing my lips together, I rubbed the herbs between my hands, into the beechwood brewing cup, and with no more than a faint sense of self-consciousness, silently said the blessing of Bride over it. I'd take all the help I could get.

"Are the cut pine-fans ye find on the ground verra fresh?" Jamie asked, sounding slightly more interested in the porcupine than in Joan's new tooth.

"Aye, green and fresh. I ken weel enough he's up there, the wicked creature, but it's a great huge tree, and I canna spot him from the ground, let alone fire on him." Marsali was no more than a middling shot, but since Fergus couldn't fire a musket at all with his one hand, she did the family's hunting.

"Mmphm." Jamie cleared his throat with an effort, and she hastily gave him more water. "Take a bit o' salted pork rind from the pantry and rub it ower a stick of wood. Set it on the ground, not too far from the trunk of the tree, and let Fergus sit up to watch. Porcupines are gey fond o' the salt, and of grease; they'll smell it and venture down after dark. Once it's on the ground, ye needna waste shot; just bat it ower the head. Fergus can do that fine."

I opened the medical chest and frowned into the tray that held saws and scalpels. I took out the small, curve-bladed scalpel, its handle cool under my fingers. I would have to de-bride the wound—clean away the dead tissue, the shreds of skin and bits of leaf and cloth and dirt; the men had plastered his leg with mud and wrapped it with a filthy neckerchief. Then I could sprinkle the penicillin solution over the exposed surfaces; I hoped that would help.

"That would be grand," Marsali said, a little wistfully. "I've no had such a beast before, but Ian did tell me they were fine; verra fat, and the quills good for sewing and all manner o' things."

I bit my lip, looking at the other blades. The biggest was a folding saw, meant for field amputation, with a blade nearly eight inches long; I hadn't used it since Alamance. The thought of using it now made cold sweat spring out under my arms and inch down my sides—but I'd seen his leg.

"The meat's greasy," Jamie said, "but that's good—" He stopped abruptly as he shifted his weight, with a muffled groan as he moved his leg.

I could feel the steps of the process of amputation, echoing in the muscles of my hands and forearms; the tensile severing of skin and muscle, the grate of bone, the snap of tendon, and the slippery, rubbery, blood-squirting vessels, sliding away into the severed flesh like . . . snakes.

I swallowed. No. It wouldn't come to that. Surely not.

"Ye need fat meat. You're verra thin, *a muirninn*," Jamie said softly, behind me. "Too thin, for a woman breeding."

I turned round, swearing silently to myself once more. I'd

thought so, but had hoped I was wrong. Three babies in four years! And a one-handed husband, who couldn't manage the man's work of a homestead and wouldn't do the "women's work" of baby-minding and mash-brewing that he could handle.

Marsali made a small sound, half-snort, half-sob.

"How did you know? I havena even told Fergus yet."

"Ye should—though he kens it already."

"He told you?"

"No—but I didna think it only the indigestion that troubled him, whilst we were hunting. Now I see ye, I ken what it is that's weighin' on him."

I was biting my tongue hard enough to taste blood. Did the tansy oil and vinegar mixture I'd given her not work? Or the *dauco* seeds? Or, as I strongly suspected, had she just not bothered to use either one regularly? Well, too late for questions or reproaches. I caught her eye as she glanced up, and managed—I hoped—to look encouraging.

"Och," she said with a feeble smile. "We'll manage."

The leeches were stirring, bodies stretching slowly like animated rubber bands. I turned back the quilt over Jamie's leg, and pressed the leeches gently onto the swollen flesh near the wound.

"It looks nastier than it is," I said reassuringly, hearing Marsali's unguarded gasp at the sight. That was true, but the reality was nasty enough. The slashmarks were crusted black at the edges, but still gaped. Instead of the sealing and granulation of normal healing, they were beginning to erode, the exposed tissues oozing pus. The flesh around the wounds was hugely swollen, black and mottled with sinister reddish streaks.

I bit my lip, frowning as I considered the situation. I didn't know what kind of snake had bitten him—not that it made much difference, with no antivenin for treatment—but it had plainly had a powerful hemolytic toxin. Tiny blood vessels had ruptured and bled all over his body—internally, as well as externally—and larger ones, near the site of the wound.

The foot and ankle on the injured side were still warm and pink—or rather, red. That was a good sign, insofar as it meant the deeper circulation was intact. The problem was to improve circulation near the wound, enough to prevent a massive die-off and sloughing of tissue. The red streaks bothered me very much indeed, though; they *could* be only part of the hemorrhagic process, but it was more likely that they were the early signs of septicemia—blood poisoning.

Roger hadn't told me much of their night on the mountain, but he hadn't had to; I'd seen men before who'd sat through the dark with death beside them. If Jamie had lived a night and a day since then, chances were he would go on surviving—if I could control the infection. But in what condition?

I hadn't treated snakebite injuries before, but I'd seen sufficient textbook illustrations. The poisoned tissue would die and rot; Jamie could easily lose most of the muscle of his calf, which would cripple him permanently—or worse, the wound could turn gangrenous.

I stole a look at him under my lashes. He was covered with quilts and so ill he could barely move—and yet the lines of his body were drawn with grace and the promise of strength. I couldn't bear the thought of mutilating him—and yet I would do it if I must. To cripple Jamie . . . to leave him halt and half-limbed . . . the thought made my stomach clench and sweat break out on my blue-blotched palms.

Would he wish that himself?

I reached for the cup of water by Jamie's head and drained it myself. I wouldn't ask him. The choice was his by right—but he was mine, and I had made my choice. I wouldn't give him up, no matter what I had to do to keep him.

"You're sure you're all right, Da?" Marsali had been watching my face. Her eyes darted from me to Jamie and back, looking scared. I hastily tried to rearrange my features into a look of competent assurance.

Jamie had been watching me, too. One corner of his mouth turned up.

"Aye, well, I did think so. Now I'm none so sure, though."

"What's the matter? Do you feel worse?" I asked anxiously.

"No, I feel fine," he assured me—lying through his teeth. "It's only, when I've hurt myself, but it's all right, ye always scold like a magpie—but if I'm desperate bad, ye're tender as milk. Now, ye havena called me wicked names or uttered a word of reproach since I came home, Sassenach. Does that mean ye think I'm dyin'?"

One eyebrow rose in irony, but I could see a true hint of worry in his eyes. There were no vipers in Scotland; he couldn't know what was happening to his leg.

I took a deep breath and laid my hands lightly on his shoulders.

"Bloody man. Stepping on a snake! Couldn't you have looked where you were going?"

"Not whilst chasing a thousand-weight of meat downhill," he said, smiling. I felt a tiny relaxation in the muscles under my hands, and repressed the urge to smile back. I glared down at him instead.

"You scared bloody hell out of me!" That at least was sincere.

The eyebrow went up again.

"Maybe ye think I wasna frightened, too?"

"You're not allowed," I said firmly. "Only one of us can be scared at a time, and it's my turn."

That made him laugh, though the laughter was quickly succeeded by coughing and a shaking chill.

"Fetch me a hot stone for his feet," I said to Marsali, quickly tucking in the quilts around him. "And fill the teapot with boiling water and bring that, too."

She darted hastily toward the kitchen. I glanced toward the window, wondering whether Brianna was having any luck in finding maggots. They had no equal in cleaning pustulant wounds without damage to the healthy flesh nearby. If I was to save his leg as well as his life, I needed more help than Saint Bride's.

Wondering vaguely if there were a patron saint of maggots, I lifted the edge of the quilt and stole a quick look at my other invertebrate assistants. Good; I let out a small sigh of relief. The leeches worked fast; they were already swelling into plumpness, sucking away the blood that was flooding the tissues of his leg from ruptured capillaries. Without that pressure, healthy circulation *might* be restored in time to keep skin and muscle alive.

I could see his hand clenched on the edge of the table, and could feel the shuddering of his chill through my thighs, pressed against the wood.

I took his head between my hands; the skin of his cheeks was burning hot.

"You are *not* going to die!" I hissed. "You're not! I won't let you!"

"People keep sayin' that to me," he muttered, eyes closed and sunken with exhaustion. "Am I not allowed my own opinion?"

"No," I said. "You're not. Here, drink this."

I held the cup of penicillin broth to his lips, steadying it while he drank. He made faces, squinching his eyes shut, but swallowed it obediently enough.

Marsali had brought the teapot, brimful of boiling water. I poured most of it over the waiting herbs, and left them to steep, while I poured him a cup of cold water to wash away the taste of the penicillin.

He swallowed the water, eyes still shut, then lay back on the pillow.

"What is that?" he asked. "It tastes of iron."

"Water," I replied. "Everything tastes of iron; your gums are bleeding." I handed the empty water jug to Marsali and asked her to bring more. "Put honey in it," I said. "About one part honey to four parts water."

"Beef tea is what he needs," she said, pausing to look at him, brow furrowed with concern. "That's what my Mam did swear by, and her Mam before her. When a body's lost a deal o' blood, there's naught like beef tea."

I thought Marsali must be seriously worried; she seldom mentioned her mother in my hearing, out of a natural sense of tact. For once, though, bloody Laoghaire was right; beef tea would be an excellent thing—if we happened to have any fresh beef, which we didn't.

"Honey water," I said briefly, shooing her out of the room. I went to fetch reinforcements from the leech department, pausing to check on Brianna's progress through the front window.

She was out by the paddock, barefoot, skirts kilted up above the knee, shaking bits of horse dung from one foot. No luck so far, then. She saw me at the window and waved, then motioned to the ax that stood nearby, then to the edge of the wood. I nodded and waved back; a rotted log might be a possibility.

Jemmy was on the ground nearby, his leading-strings securely tied to the paddock fence. He certainly didn't need them to help him stay upright, but they did keep him from escaping while his mother was busy. He was industriously engaged in pulling down the remains of a dried gourd-vine that had grown up over the fence, crowing with delight as bits of crumbled leaf and the dried remains of frostbitten gourds showered over his flaming hair. His round face bore a look of determined intent, as he set about the task of getting a gourd the size of his head into his mouth.

A movement caught the corner of my eye; Marsali, bringing up water from the spring, to fill the crusted cauldron. No, she wasn't showing at all yet—Jamie was right, she was much too thin—but now that I knew, I could see the pallor in her face, and the shadows under her eyes.

Damn. Another glimpse of movement; Bree's long pale legs, flashing under her kilted skirts in the shadow of the big red spruce. And was *she* using the tansy oil? She was still nursing Jemmy, but that was no guarantee, not at his age . . .

I swung around at a sound behind me, to find Jamie climbing slowly back into his nest of quilts, looking like a great crimson sloth, my amputation saw in one hand.

"What the hell are you doing?"

He eased himself down, grimacing, and lay back on the pillow, breathing in long, deep gasps. The folded saw was clasped to his chest.

"I repeat," I said, standing menacingly over him, hands on my hips, "what the hell . . ."

He opened his eyes and lifted the saw an inch or so.

"No," he said positively. "I ken what ye're thinking, Sassenach, and I willna have it."

I took a deep breath, to keep my voice from quivering.

"You know I wouldn't, not unless I absolutely had to."

"No," he said again, and gave me a familiar look of obstinacy. No surprise at all that *he* never wondered who Jemmy looked like, I thought with sour amusement.

"You don't know what may happen—"

"I ken what's happening to my leg better than you do, Sassenach," he interrupted, then paused to breathe some more. "I dinna care."

"Maybe you don't, but *I* do!"

"I'm no going to die," he said firmly, "and I dinna wish to live with half a leg. I've a horror of it."

"Well, I'm not very keen on it myself. But if it's a choice between your leg and your life?"

"It's not."

"It damn well may be!"

"It won't." Age made not the slightest difference, I thought. Two years or fifty, a Fraser was a Fraser, and no rock was more stubborn. I rubbed a hand through my hair.

"All. Right," I said, between clenched teeth. "Give me the bloody thing and I'll put it away."

"Your word."

"My what?" I stared at him.

"Your word," he repeated, giving me back the stare, with interest. "I may be fevered and lose my wits. I dinna want ye to take my leg if I'm in no state to stop it."

"If you're in that sort of state, I'll have no choice!"

"Perhaps ye don't," he said evenly, "but I do. I've made it. Your word, Sassenach."

"You bloody, unspeakable, *infuriating*—"

His smile was startling, a white grin in the ruddy face. "If ye call me a Scot, Sassenach, then I *know* I'm going to live."

A shriek from outside kept me from answering. I swung round to the window, in time to see Marsali drop two pails of water on the ground. The water geysered over her skirt and shoes, but she paid no attention. I glanced hastily in the direction she was looking, and gasped.

It had walked casually through the paddock fence, snapping the rails as though they were matchsticks, and stood now in the midst of the pumpkin patch by the house, vines jerking in its mouth as it chewed. It stood huge and dark and wooly, ten feet away from Jemmy, who stared up at it with round, round eyes and open mouth, his gourd forgotten in his hands.

Marsali let out another screech, and Jemmy, catching her

terror, began to scream for his mother. I turned, and—feeling as though I were moving in slow motion, though I was surely not—snatched the saw neatly from Jamie's hand, went out the door, and headed for the yard, thinking as I did so that buffalo looked so much smaller in zoos.

As I cleared the stoop—I must have leaped; I had no memory of the steps—Brianna came out of the woods. She was running silently, ax in her hand, and her face was set, inward and intent. I had no time to call out before she reached it.

She had drawn back the ax, still running, swung it in an arc as she took the last step, and brought it down with all her strength, just behind the huge beast's ears. A thin spray of blood flew up and spattered on the pumpkins. It bellowed and lowered its head, as though to charge forward.

Bree dodged to one side, dived for Jemmy, was on her knees, tugging at the strings that bound him to the fence. From the corner of my eye, I could see Marsali, yelling Gaelic prayers and imprecations as she seized a newly dyed petticoat from the blackberry bushes.

I had somehow unfolded the saw as I ran; I cut Jemmy's strings with two swipes, then was on my feet and running back across the dooryard. Marsali had thrown the petticoat over the buffalo's head; it stood bewildered, shaking its head and swaying to and fro, blood showing black on the yellow-green of the fresh-dyed indigo.

It stood as tall as I at the shoulder, and it smelt strange; dusty and warm, gamey but oddly familiar, with a barn-smell, like a cow. It took a step, another, and I dug my fingers into its wool, holding on. I could feel the tremors running through it; they shook me like an earthquake.

I had never done it, but felt as though I had, a thousand times. Dreamlike and sure, I ran a hand under slobbering lips, felt warm breath blow down my sleeve. The great pulse throbbed in the angle of the jaw; I could see it in my mind, the big meaty heart and its pumping blood, warm in my hand, cold against my cheek where it pressed the sodden petticoat.

I drew the saw across the throat, cut hard, and felt in hands and forearms the tensile severing of skin and muscle, the grate of bone, the snap of tendon, and the slippery, rubbery, blood-squirting vessels, sliding away.

The world shook. It shifted and slid, and landed with a thud. When I came to myself, I was sitting in the middle of my dooryard, one hand still twisted in its hair, one leg gone numb beneath the weight of the buffalo's head, my skirts plastered to my thighs, hot and stinking, sodden with its blood.

Someone said something and I looked up. Jamie was on his hands and knees on the stoop—mouth open, stark naked. Marsali sat on the ground, legs splayed out in front of her, soundlessly opening and closing her mouth.

Brianna stood over me, Jemmy held against her shoulder. Terror forgotten, he leaned far over, looking down in curiosity at the buffalo.

"Ooo!" he said.

"Yes," I said. "Very well put."

"You're all right, Mama?" Bree asked, and I realized she had asked several times before. She put down a hand and rested it gently on my head.

"I don't know," I said. "I think so."

I took her hand and laboriously worked my leg free, leaning on her as I stood up. The same tremors that had gone through the buffalo were going through her—and me—but they were fading. She took a deep breath, looking down at the massive body. Lying on its side, it rose nearly as high as her waist. Marsali came to stand beside us, shaking her head in awe at its size.

"Mother of God, how on earth are we going to butcher *that*?" she said.

"Oh," I said, and dragged a trembling hand through my hair. "I suppose we'll manage."

# 92

# I GET BY WITH A LITTLE
# HELP FROM MY FRIENDS

I LEANED MY FOREHEAD against the cool glass of my surgery window, blinking at the scene outside. Exhaustion lent the scene in the dooryard an extra tinge of surrealism—not that it needed much extra.

The sun had all but set, flaming gold in the last ragged leaves of the chestnut trees. The spruces stood black against the dying glow, as did the gibbet in the center of the yard, and the grisly remains that swung from it. A bonfire had been lit near the blackberry bushes, and silhouetted figures darted everywhere, disappearing in and out of flames and shadow. Some attacked the hanging carcass, armed with knives and hatchets; others plodded laden away, carrying slabs of flesh and buckets of fat. Near the fire, the skirted bell-shapes of women showed, bending and reaching in silent ballet.

Dark as it was, I could pick Brianna's tall, pale figure out of the horde of demons hacking at the buffalo—keeping order, I thought. Before being forcibly returned to the surgery, Jamie had estimated the buffalo's weight at something between eighteen hundred and two thousand pounds. Brianna had nodded at this, handed Jemmy to Lizzie, then walked slowly around the carcass, squinting in deep thought.

"Right," she'd said, and as soon as the men began to appear from their homesteads, half-dressed, unshaven, and wild-eyed with excitement, had issued cool directions for the cutting of logs and the building of a pulley-frame capable of hoisting and supporting a ton of meat.

The men, disgruntled at not being in on the kill, hadn't

been inclined to pay attention to her at first. Brianna, however, was large, vivid, strongly-spoken—and stubborn.

"Whose stroke is that?" she'd demanded, staring down Geordie Chisholm and his sons as they started toward the carcass, knives in hand. She pointed at the deep gash across the neck, then wiped her hand slowly down her sleeve, drawing attention to the splashed blood there. "Or that?" One long bare foot pointed delicately at the severed throat, and the pool of blood that soaked the dooryard. My stockings lay at the edge of the congealing puddle where I had stripped them off, limp red rags, but recognizably feminine.

Watching from the window, I had seen more than one face glance toward the house, frowning with the realization that Brianna was Himself's daughter—a fact the wise kept well in mind.

It was Roger who had turned the tide for her, though, with a cool stare that brought the Lindsay brothers to heel behind him, axes in hand.

"It's her kill," he said, in his husking croak. "Do what she says." He squared his shoulders and gave the other men a look that strongly suggested there should be no further controversy.

Seeing this, Fergus had shrugged and bent to seize the beast—one-handed—by its spindly tail.

"Where will you have us put it, Madame?" he asked politely. The men had all laughed, and then with sheepish glances and shrugs of resignation, reluctantly pitched in as well, following her directions.

Brianna had given Roger a look of surprise, then gratitude, and then—the bit firmly between her teeth—had taken charge of the whole enterprise, with remarkable results. It was barely nightfall, and the butchery was almost done, the meat distributed to all the households on the Ridge. She knew everyone, knew the number of mouths in each cabin, and parceled out the meat and sweetbreads as they were cut. Not even Jamie could have managed it better, I thought, feeling a warm swell of pride in her.

I glanced across at the table, where Jamie lay swaddled in blankets. I had wanted to move him upstairs to his bed, but he had insisted on staying downstairs, where he could hear—if not see—what was going on.

"They're nearly finished with the butchering," I said, coming to lay a hand on his head. Still flushed and blazing. "Brianna's done a wonderful job of it," I added, to distract both of us.

"Has she?" His eyes were half-open, but fixed in a fever-stare; that dream-soaked daze where shadows writhe in the wavering hot air over a fire. As I spoke, though, he came slowly back from wherever he had been, and his eyes met mine, heavy-lidded but clear, and he smiled faintly. "That's good."

The hide had been pegged out to dry, the enormous liver sliced for quick searing, intestines taken to soak for cleaning, haunches to the shed for smoking, strips of meat taken off for drying into jerky, fat for rendering into suet and soap. Once stripped bare, the bones would be boiled for soup, salvaged for buttons.

The prized hooves and horns sat bloodily discreet on my counter, brought in by Murdo Lindsay. Tacit trophies, I supposed; the eighteenth-century equivalent of two ears and a tail. I had got the gallbladder, too, though that was simply by default; no one wanted it, but it was popularly assumed that I must have some medicinal use for almost any natural object. A greenish thing the size of my fist, it sat oozing in a dish, looking rather sinister next to the set of detached and muddy hooves.

Everyone on the Ridge had come at the news—even Ronnie Sinclair, from his cooper's shop at the foot of the slope—and little remained of the buffalo now, save a rack of scavenged bones. I caught the faint odor of roasting meat, of burning hickory wood and coffee, and pushed up the window all the way to let in the appetizing smells.

Laughter and the crackle of fire came in on a gust of cold wind. It was warm in the surgery now, and the cold air from the window felt good against my flushed cheeks.

"Are you hungry, Jamie?" I asked. I was starving myself; though I hadn't realized it 'til I smelled food. I closed my eyes and inhaled, buoyed up by the hearty scent of liver and onions.

"No," he said, sounding drowsy. "I dinna fancy anything."

"You should eat a bit of soup, if you can, before you fall asleep." I turned and smoothed the hair off his face, frowning a little as I looked at him. The flush had faded a bit, I thought—hard to tell for sure in the uncertain light of fire and candle. We had got enough honey-water and herb tea into him so that his eyes were no longer sunken with dehydration, but the bones of cheek and jaw were still prominent; he hadn't eaten in more than forty-eight hours, and the fever was consuming an immense amount of energy, consuming his tissues.

"D'ye need more hot water, ma'am?" Lizzie appeared in the doorway, looking more disheveled than usual, Jemmy clutched in her arms. She had lost her kerch and her fine, fair hair had escaped from its bun; Jemmy had a good handful of it in his chubby fist, and was yanking fretfully at it, making her squint with each yank.

"Mama-mama-mama," he said, in an escalating whine that made it obvious that he'd been saying the same thing for quite some time. "Mama-mama-MAMA!"

"No, I have enough; thank you, Lizzie. Stop that, young man," I said, getting hold of Jemmy's hand and forcibly unpeeling his fat little fingers. "We don't pull hair." There was a small chuckle from the nest of blankets on the table behind me.

"Ye'd never ken it to look at ye, Sassenach."

"Mm?" I turned my head and stared blankly at him for a moment, then followed the direction of his glance with my hand. Sure enough, my own cap had somehow disappeared, and my hair was standing out like a bramblebush. Attracted by the word "hair," Jemmy abandoned Lizzie's fine locks, leaned over, and grabbed a fistful of mine.

"Mama-mama-mama-mama . . ."

"Foo," I said, crossly, reaching to disentangle him. "Let go, you little fiend. And why aren't you in bed, anyway?"

"MAMA-MAMA-MAMA . . ."

"He wants his mother," Lizzie explained, rather redundantly. "I've put him in his cot a dozen times, but he'll be climbin' out again, the instant my back's turned. I couldna keep him—"

The outer door opened, letting in a strong draft that made the embers in the brazier glow and smoke, and I heard the pad of bare feet on the oak boards in the hall.

I'd heard the expression, "blood to the eyebrows" before, but I hadn't seen it all that often, at least not outside the confines of a battlefield. Brianna's eyebrows were invisible, being red enough to have blended into the mask of gore over her face. Jemmy took a good look at her, and turned down his mouth in an expression of doubtful distress, just this side of outright wails.

"It's me, baby," she reassured him. She reached a hand toward him, but stopped short of touching him. He didn't cry, but burrowed his face into Lizzie's shoulder, rejecting the notion that this apocalyptic vision had anything at all to do with the mother he'd been fussing for a few minutes earlier.

Brianna ignored both her son's rejection and the fact that she was leaving footprints composed in equal parts of mud and blood all over the floor.

"Look," she said, holding out a closed fist to me. Her hands were caked with dried blood, her fingernails crescents of black. She reverently uncurled her fingers to show me her treasure; a handful of tiny, wriggling white worms that made my heart give a quick bump of excitement.

"Are they the right kind?" she asked anxiously.

"I think so; let me check." I hastily dumped the wet leaves from the herb tea onto a small plate, to give the worms a temporary refuge. Brianna gently deposited them on the mangled foliage and carried the plate to the counter where my microscope stood, as though the plate bore specks of gold dust, rather than maggots.

I picked up one of the worms with the edge of a fingernail, and deposited it on a glass slide, where it writhed unhappily in a futile search for nourishment. I beckoned to Bree to bring me another candle.

"Nothing but a mouth and a gut," I muttered, tilting the mirror to catch the light. It was much too dim for microscopic work, but might just be sufficient for this. "Voracious little buggers."

I held my breath, peering through the fragile eyepiece, straining to see. Ordinary blow-fly and flesh-fly larvae had one line visible on the body; screw-worm larvae had two. The lines were faint, invisible to the naked eye, but very important. Blow-fly maggots ate carrion, and only carrion—dead, decaying flesh. Screw-worm larvae burrowed into the living flesh, and consumed the live muscle and blood of their host. Nothing I wanted to insert into a fresh wound!

I closed one eye, to let the other adapt to the moving shadows in the eyepiece. The dark cylinder of the maggot's body writhed, twisting in all directions at once. One line was clearly visible. Was that another? I squinted until my eye began to water, but could see no more. Letting out the breath I'd been holding, I relaxed.

"Congratulations, Da," Brianna said, moving to Jamie's side. He opened one eye, which passed with a marked lack of enthusiasm down Brianna's figure. Stripped to a knee-length shift for butchering, she was splotched from head to toe with gouts of dark blood, and the muslin had stuck to her in random patches.

"Oh, aye?" he said. "For what?"

"The maggots. You did it," she explained. She opened her other hand, revealing a misshapen blob of metal—a squashed rifle-ball. "The maggots were in a wound in the hind-quarters—I dug this out of the hole behind them."

I laughed, as much from relief as from amusement.

"Jamie! You shot it in the arse?"

Jamie's mouth twitched a little.

"I didna think I'd hit it at all," he said. "I was only trying to turn the herd toward Fergus." He reached up a slow hand and took the ball, rolling it gently between his fingers.

"Maybe you should keep it for good luck," Brianna said. She spoke lightly, but I could see the furrow between her invisible brows. "Or to bite on while Mama's working on your leg."

"Too late," he said, with a very faint smile.

It was then she caught sight of the small leather strip that lay on the table near his head, marked with overlapping crescents—the deep imprints of Jamie's teeth. She glanced at me, appalled. I lifted one shoulder slightly. I had spent more than an hour cleaning the wound in his leg, and it hadn't been easy on either of us.

I cleared my throat, and turned back to the maggots. From the corner of my eye, I saw Bree lay the back of her hand gently against Jamie's cheek. He turned his head and kissed her knuckles, blood notwithstanding.

"Dinna fash, lassie," he said. His voice was faint, but steady. "I'm fine."

I opened my mouth to say something, but caught sight of Bree's face and bit my tongue instead. She'd been working hard, and still had Jemmy and Roger to care for; she needn't worry for Jamie, too—not yet.

I dropped the maggots into a small bowl of sterile water and swished them rapidly round, then dumped them back on the bed of wet leaves.

"It won't hurt," I said to Jamie, trying to reassure myself as much as him.

"Oh, aye," he said, with an unbecoming cynicism. "I've heard *that* one before."

"Actually, she's right," said a soft, rasping voice behind me. Roger had already had a quick wash; his dark hair lay damp against his collar, and his clothes were clean. Jemmy, half asleep, lay against his father's shoulder, dreamily sucking his thumb. Roger came over to the table to look down at Jamie.

"How is it, man?" he said quietly.

Jamie moved his head on the pillow, dismissive of discomfort.

"I'll do."

"That's good." To my surprise, Roger grasped Jamie's shoulder in a brief gesture of comfort. I'd never seen him do that before, and once more I wondered just what had passed between them on the mountain.

"Marsali's bringing up some beef tea—or rather, buffalo tea—for him," Roger said, frowning slightly as he looked at me. "Maybe you'd best be having some, too."

"Good idea," I said. I closed my eyes briefly and took a deep breath.

Only when I sat down did I realize that I had been on my feet since the early morning. Pain outlined every bone in my feet and legs, and I could feel the ache where I had broken my left tibia, a few years before. Duty called, though.

"Well, time and tide wait for no maggot," I said, struggling back to my feet. "Best get on with it."

Jamie gave a small snort and stretched, then relaxed, his long body reluctantly readying itself. He watched with resignation while I fetched the plate of maggots and my forceps, then reached for the leather strip by his head.

"You'll not need that," Roger said. He pulled up another stool and sat down. "It's true what she said, the wee beasts don't hurt."

Jamie snorted again, and Roger grinned at him.

"Mind," he said, "they tickle something fierce. That's only if ye think about it, though. If ye can keep all thought of them out of your mind, why, there's nothing to it."

Jamie eyed him.

"Ye're a great comfort, MacKenzie," he said.

"Thanks," said Roger, with a husk of a laugh. "Here, I brought ye something." He leaned forward and deposited a drowsy Jemmy into Jamie's arms. The little boy uttered a small squawk of surprise, then relaxed as Jamie's arms tightened about him in reflex. One chubby hand swung free, seeking anchorage, then found it.

"Hot," he murmured, smiling beatifically. Fist twined in Jamie's ruddy hair, he sighed deeply and went soundly to sleep on his grandfather's fever-warm chest.

Jamie narrowed his eyes at me as I picked up the forceps. Then he gave a slight shrug, laid his stubbled cheek gently against Jemmy's silk-bright hair, and closed his own eyes, though the tenseness in his features was a marked contrast to the rounded peace of Jemmy's.

It couldn't have been easier; I simply lifted away the fresh onion poultice, and tucked the maggots one by one into the ulcerated slashmarks on Jamie's calf. Roger circled behind me to watch.

"It looks almost like a leg again," he said, sounding surprised. "I never thought it would."

I smiled, though I didn't look round at him, too intent on my delicate work. "Leeches are very effective," I said. "Though your rather crude knifework may have been useful, too—you left big enough holes that the pus and fluid were able to drain; that helped."

It was true; while the limb was still hot and grossly discolored, the swelling had subsided markedly. The long stretch of shinbone and the delicate arch of foot and ankle were once more visible. I was under no illusion about the dangers still remaining—infection, gangrene, sloughing—but nonetheless, my heart grew lighter. It was recognizably Jamie's leg.

I pinched another maggot just behind the head with my forceps, careful not to crush it. I lifted the edge of the skin with the slender probe I held in my other hand, and deftly inserted the tiny, wiggling thing into the small pocket thus provided—trying to ignore the nastily spongy feel of the flesh under my fingers, and my memory of Aaron Beardsley's foot.

"Done," I said, a moment later, and gently replaced the poultice. Stewed onion and garlic wrapped in muslin and soaked with penicillin broth would keep the wounds moist and draining. Renewed every hour or so, I hoped that the warmth of the poultices would also encourage circulation in the leg. And then a dressing of honey, to prevent any further bacterial invasions.

Concentration alone had kept my hands steady. Now it was done, and there was nothing more to do but wait. The saucer of wet leaves rattled against the counter as I set it down.

I didn't think I had ever been so tired before.

# 93

# CHOICES

**B**ETWEEN THEM, Roger and Mr. Bug got Jamie up to our bedroom. I hadn't wanted to disturb his leg by moving him from the surgery, but he insisted.

"I dinna want ye to be sleeping on the floor down here,

Sassenach," he said, when I protested. He smiled at me. "Ye should be in your bed—but I ken ye willna leave me alone, and so that means I must go and be in it, too, aye?"

I would have argued further, but in all truth, I was so tired that I wouldn't have complained much if he had insisted we both sleep in the barn.

Once he was settled, though, my doubts returned.

"I'll joggle your leg," I said, hanging up my gown on one of the pegs. "I'll just make up a pallet by the fire here, and—"

"You will not," he said definitely. "Ye'll sleep wi' me." He lay back on the pillows, eyes closed, his hair an auburn tumble against the linen. His skin had begun to fade; it wasn't quite so red. It was, however, alarmingly pale where the tiny hemorrhages didn't stain it.

"You would argue on your deathbed," I said crossly. "You don't *have* to be constantly in charge, you know. You *could* lie still and let other people take care of things, for once. What do you think would happen, if—"

He opened his eyes and gave me a dark blue look.

"Sassenach," he said softly.

"What?"

"I would like ye to touch me . . . without hurting me. Just once before I sleep. Would ye mind much?"

I stopped and drew breath, terribly disconcerted at the realization that he was right. Caught up in the emergency and worry of his condition, everything I had done to him during the day had been painful, intrusive, or both. Marsali, Brianna, Roger, Jemmy—all of them had touched him in gentleness, offering sympathy and comfort.

And I—I had been so terrified at the possibility of what might happen, of what I might be forced to do, that I had taken no time, allowed no room for gentleness. I looked away for a moment, blinking until the tears retreated. Then I stood and walked over to the bed, bent, and kissed him, very softly.

I stroked the hair back from his forehead, smoothed his brows with my thumb. Arch Bug had shaved him; the skin of his cheek was smooth, hot against the side of my hand. His bones were hard under his skin, framing his strength—and yet he seemed suddenly fragile. I felt fragile, too.

"I want ye to sleep beside me, Sassenach," he whispered.

"All right." I smiled at him, my lips trembling only a little. "Let me brush out my hair."

I sat down in my shift, shook out my hair, and took up the brush. He watched me, not speaking, but with a faint smile on his lips, as I worked. He liked to watch me brush my hair; I hoped it was as soothing to him as it was to me.

There were noises downstairs, but they were muffled, safely distant. The shutters were ajar; firelight flickered against the glass of the window from the dying bonfire in the yard. I glanced at the window, wondering if I ought to close the shutters.

"Leave them, Sassenach," he murmured from the bed. "I like to hear the talk." The sound of voices from outside *was* comforting, rising and falling, with small bursts of laughter.

The sound of the brush was soft and regular, like surf on sand, and I felt the stress of the day lessen slowly, as though I could brush all the anxieties and dreads out of my hair as easily as tangles and bits of pumpkin vine. When at last I put down the brush and rose, Jamie's eyes were closed.

I knelt to smoor the fire, rose to blow out the candle, and went at last to bed.

I eased myself gently into the bed beside him, not to jostle. He lay turned away from me, on his side, and I turned toward him, echoing the curve of his body with my own, careful not to touch him.

I lay very quietly, listening. All the house sounds had settled to their night-time rhythm; the hiss of the fire and the rumble of wind in the flue, the sudden startling *crack!* of the stairs, as though some unwary foot had stepped upon a riser. Mr. Wemyss's adenoidal snoring reached me, reduced to a soothing buzz by the thickness of the intervening doors.

There were still voices outside, muffled by distance, disjointed with drink and the lateness of the hour. All jovial, though; no sound of hostility or incipient violence. I didn't really care, though. The inhabitants of the Ridge could hammer each other senseless and dance on the remains, for all I cared. All my attention was focused on Jamie.

His breathing was shallow but even, his shoulders relaxed. I didn't want to disturb him; he needed rest above all things. At the same time, I ached to touch him. I wanted to reassure myself that he was here, alive beside me—but I also needed badly to know how things went with him.

Was he feverish? Had the incipient infection in his leg blossomed in spite of the penicillin, spreading poison through his blood?

I moved my head cautiously, bringing my face within an inch of his shirt-covered back, and breathed in, slow and deep. I could feel the warmth of him on my face, but couldn't tell through the linen nightshirt just how hot he really was.

He smelt faintly of the woods, more strongly of blood. The onions in the dressing gave off a bitter tang; so did his sweat.

I inhaled again, testing the air. No scent of pus. Too early for the smell of gangrene, even if the rot was beginning, invisible under the bandages. I thought there was a strange scent about his skin, though; something I hadn't smelled before. Necrosis of the tissue? Some breakdown product of the snake's venom? I blew a short breath through my nose and took in a fresh one, deeper.

"Do I stink verra badly?" he inquired.

"Uk!" I said, startled into biting my tongue, and he quivered slightly, in what I took to be suppressed amusement.

"Ye sound like a wee truffle-pig, Sassenach, snortling away back there."

"Oh, indeed," I said, a bit crossly. I touched the tender spot on my tongue. "Well, at least you're awake. How do you feel?"

"Like a pile of moldy tripes."

"Very picturesque," I said. "Can you be a trifle more specific?" I put a hand lightly on his side, and he let his breath out in a sound like a small moan.

"Like a pile of moldy tripes . . ." he said, and pausing to breathe heavily, added, " . . . .with *maggots*."

"You'd joke on your deathbed, wouldn't you?" Even as I said it, I felt a tremor of unease. He *would*, and I hoped this wasn't it.

"Well, I'll try, Sassenach," he murmured, sounding drowsy. "But I'm no really at my best under the circumstances."

"Do you hurt much?"

"No. I'm just . . . tired." He sounded as though he were in fact too exhausted to search for the proper word, and had settled for that one by default.

"Little wonder if you are. I'll go and sleep somewhere else, so you can rest." I made to throw back the covers and rise, but he stopped me, raising one hand slightly.

"No. No, dinna leave me." His shoulder fell back toward me, and he tried to lift his head from the pillow. I felt still more uneasy when I realized that he was too weak even to turn over by himself.

"I won't leave you. Maybe I should sleep in the chair, though. I don't want to—"

"I'm cold," he said softly. "I'm verra cold."

I pressed my fingers lightly just under his breastbone, seeking the big abdominal pulse. His heartbeat was rapid, shallower than it should have been. He wasn't feverish. He didn't just feel cold, he *was* cold to the touch, his skin chilled and his fingers icy. I found that very alarming.

No longer shy, I cuddled close against him, my breasts squashing softly against his back, cheek resting on his shoulder blade. I concentrated as hard as I could on generating body heat, trying to radiate warmth through my skin and into his. So often he had enfolded me in the curve of his body, sheltering me, giving me the warmth of his big body. I wished passionately that I were larger, and could do the same for him now; as it was, I could do no more than cling to him like a small, fierce mustard plaster, and hope I had the same effect.

Very gently, I found the hem of his shirt and pulled it up, then cupped my hands to fit the rounds of his buttocks. They tightened slightly in surprise, then relaxed.

It occurred to me to wonder just why I felt I must lay hands on him, but I didn't trouble my mind with it; I had had the feeling many times before, and had long since given up worrying that it wasn't scientific.

I could feel the faintly pebbled texture of the rash upon his skin, and the thought came unbidden of the lamia. A creature smooth and cool to the touch, a shape-shifter, passionately venomous, its nature infectious. A swift bite and the snake's poison spreading, slowing his heart, chilling his warm blood; I could imagine tiny scales rising under his skin in the dark.

I forcibly repressed the thought, but not the shudder that went with it.

"Claire," he said softly. "Touch me."

I couldn't hear his heartbeat. I could hear mine; a thick, muffled sound in the ear pressed to the pillow.

I slid my hand over the slope of his belly, and more slowly down, fingers parting the coarse curly tangle, dipping low to cup the rounded shapes of him. What heat he had was here.

I stroked him with a thumb and felt him stir. The breath went out of him in a long sigh, and his body seemed to grow heavier, sinking into the mattress as he relaxed. His flesh was like candle wax in my hand, smooth and silky as it warmed.

I felt very odd; no longer frightened, but with all my senses at once preternaturally acute and yet . . . peaceful. I was no longer conscious of any sounds save Jamie's breathing and the beating of his heart; the darkness was filled with them. I had no conscious thought, but seemed to act purely by instinct, reaching down and under, seeking the heart of his heat in the center of his being.

Then I was moving—or we were moving together. One hand reached down between us, up between his legs, my fingertips on the spot just behind his testicles. My other hand reached over, around, moving with the same rhythm that flexed my thighs and lifted my hips, thrusting against him from behind.

I could have done it forever, and felt that perhaps I did. I had no sense of time passing, only of a dreamy peace, and that slow, steady rhythm as we moved together in the dark. Somewhere, sometime, I felt a steady pulsing, first in the one hand, then in both. It melded with the beat of his heart.

He sighed, long and deep, and I felt the air rush from my own lungs. We lay silent and passed gently into unconsciousness, together.

I WOKE FEELING utterly peaceful. I lay still, without thought, listening to the thrum of blood through my veins, watching the drift of sunlit particles in the beam of light that fell through the half-opened shutters. Then I remembered, and flung myself over in bed, staring.

His eyes were closed, and his skin was the color of old ivory. His head was turned slightly away from me, so that the cords of his neck stood out, but I couldn't see any pulse in his throat. He was still warm, or at least the bedclothes were still warm. I sniffed the air, urgently. The room was fetid with the scent of onions and honey and fever-sweat, but no stink of sudden death.

I clapped a hand on the center of his chest, and he jerked, startled, and opened his eyes.

"You *bastard*," I said, so relieved to feel the rise of his chest as he drew breath that my voice trembled. "You tried to die on me, didn't you?"

His chest rose and fell, rose and fell, under my hand, and my own heart jerked and shuddered, as though I had been pulled back at the last moment from an unexpected precipice.

He blinked at me. His eyes were heavy, still clouded with fever.

"It didna take much effort, Sassenach," he said, his voice soft and husky from sleep. "Not dying was harder."

He made no pretense of not understanding me. In the light of day, I saw clearly what exhaustion and the aftereffects of shock had stopped me seeing the night before. His insistence on his own bed. The open shutters, so he could hear the voices of his family below, his tenants outside. And me beside him. He had, very carefully, and without saying a word to me, decided how and where he wanted to die.

"You thought you were dying when we brought you up here, didn't you?" I asked. My voice sounded more bewildered than accusing.

It took him a moment to answer, though he didn't look hesitant. It was more as though he was looking for the proper words.

"Well, I didna ken for sure, no," he said slowly. "Though I did feel verra ill." His eyes closed, slowly, as though he were too tired to keep them open. "I still do," he added, in a detached sort of voice. "Ye needna worry, though—I've made my choice."

"What on earth do you mean by that?"

I groped beneath the covers, and found his wrist. He *was* warm; hot again, in fact, and with a pulse that was too fast, too shallow. Still, it was so different from the deathly chill I had felt in him the night before that my first reaction was relief.

He took a couple of deep breaths, then turned his head and opened his eyes to look at me.

"I mean I could have died last night."

He could, certainly—and yet that wasn't what he meant. He made it sound like a conscious—

"What do you mean you've made your choice? You've decided not to die, after all?" I tried to speak lightly, but it wasn't working very well. I remembered all too well that odd sense of timeless stillness that had surrounded us.

"It was verra strange," he said. "And yet it wasna strange at all." He sounded faintly surprised.

"I think," I said carefully, keeping a thumb on his pulse, "you'd better tell me just what happened."

He actually smiled at that, though the smile was more in his eyes than his lips. Those were dry, and painfully cracked in the corners. I touched his lips with a finger, wanting to go and fetch some soothing ointment for him, some water, some tea—but I put aside the impulse, steeling myself to stay and hear.

"I dinna really know, Sassenach—or rather, I do, but I canna think quite how to say it." He still looked tired, but his eyes stayed open. They lingered on my face, a vivid blue in the morning light, with an expression almost of curiosity, as though he hadn't seen me before.

"You are so beautiful," he said, softly. "So verra beautiful, *mo chridhe*."

My hands were covered with fading blue blotches and overlooked smears of buffalo blood, I could feel my hair clinging in unwashed tangles to my neck, and I could smell everything from the stale-urine odor of dye to the reek of fear-sweat on my body. And yet whatever he saw lit his face as though he were looking at the full moon on a summer night, pure and lovely.

His eyes stayed fixed on my face as he talked, absorbed, moving slightly as they seemed to trace my features.

"I felt verra badly indeed when Arch and Roger Mac brought me up," he said. "Terribly sick, and my leg and my head both throbbing with each heartbeat, so much that I began to dread the next. And so I would listen to the spaces between. Ye wouldna think it," he said, sounded vaguely surprised, "but there is a great deal of time between the beats of a heart."

He had, he said, begun to hope, in those spaces, that the next beat would not come. And slowly, he realized that his heart was indeed slowing—and that the pain was growing remote, something separate from himself.

His skin had grown colder, the fever fading from both body and mind, leaving the latter oddly clear.

"And this is where I canna really say, Sassenach." He pulled his wrist from my grip in the intensity of his story, and curled his fingers over mine. "But I . . . saw."

"Saw what?" And yet I already knew that he couldn't tell me. Like any doctor, I had seen sick people make up their minds to die—and I knew that look they sometimes had; eyes wide-fixed on *something* in the distance.

He hesitated, struggling to find words. I thought of something, and jumped in to try to help.

"There was an elderly woman," I said. "She died in the hospital where I was on staff—all her grown children with her, it was very peaceful." I looked down, my own eyes fixed on his fingers, still red and slightly swollen, interlaced with my own stained and bloody digits.

"She died—she was *dead*, I could see her pulse had stopped, she wasn't breathing. All her children were by her bedside, weeping. And then, quite suddenly, her eyes opened. She wasn't looking at any of them, but she was seeing *something*. And she said, quite clearly, 'Oooh!' Just like that—thrilled, like a little girl who's just seen something wonderful. And then she closed her eyes again." I looked up at him, blinking back tears. "Was it—like that?"

He nodded, speechless, and his hand tightened on mine.

"Something like," he said, very softly.

He had felt oddly suspended, in a place he could by no means describe, feeling completely at peace—and seeing very clearly.

"It was as if there was a—it wasna a door, exactly, but a passageway of some kind—before me. And I could go through it, if I wanted. And I did want to," he said, giving me a sideways glance and a shy smile.

He had known what lay behind him, too, and realized that for that moment, he could choose. Go forward—or turn back.

"And that's when you asked me to touch you?"

"I knew ye were the only thing that could bring me back," he said simply. "I didna have the strength, myself."

There was a huge lump in my throat; I couldn't speak, but squeezed his hand very tight.

"Why?" I asked at last. "Why did you . . . choose to stay?" My throat was still tight, and my voice was hoarse. He heard it, and his hand tightened on mine; a ghost of his usual firm grip, and yet with the memory of strength within it.

"Because ye need me," he said, very softly.

"Not because you love me?"

He looked up then, with a shadow of a smile.

"Sassenach . . . I love ye now, and I will love ye always. Whether I am dead—or you—whether we are together or apart. You know it is true," he said quietly, and touched my face. "I know it of you, and ye know it of me as well."

He bent his head then, the bright hair swinging down across his cheek.

"I didna mean only you, Sassenach. I have work still to do. I thought—for a bit—that perhaps it wasna so; that ye all might manage, with Roger Mac and auld Arch, Joseph and the Beardsleys. But there is war coming, and—for my sins—" he grimaced slightly, "I am a chief."

He shook his head slightly, in resignation.

"God has made me what I am. He has given me the duty—and I must do it, whatever the cost."

"The cost," I echoed uneasily, hearing something harsher than resignation in his voice. He looked at me, then glanced, almost off-handed, toward the foot of the bed.

"My leg's no much worse," he said, matter-of-factly, "but it's no better. I think ye'll have to take it off."

I SAT IN MY SURGERY, staring out the window, trying to think of another way. There had to be something else I could do. Had to.

He was right; the red streaks were still there. They hadn't advanced any further, but they were still there, ugly and threatening. The oral and topical penicillin had evidently had some effect on the infection, but not enough. The maggots were dealing nicely with the small abscesses, but they couldn't affect the underlying bacteremia that was poisoning his blood.

I glanced up at the brown glass bottle; only about a third full. It might help him hold his ground for a little longer, but there wasn't enough—and it wasn't likely to have sufficient effect, administered by mouth—to eradicate whatever deadly bacterium was multiplying in his blood.

"Ten thousand to ten million milligrams," I murmured to myself. Recommended dosage of penicillin for bacteremia or sepsis, according to the *Merck Manual*, the physician's basic desk reference. I glanced at Daniel Rawlings' casebook, then back at the bottle. With no way of telling what concentration of penicillin I had, administration was likely still more efficacious than the combination of snakeroot and garlic Rawlings advised—but not enough to matter, I was afraid.

The amputation saw was still lying on the counter, where he had left it the day before. I'd given him my word—and he'd given it back.

I clenched my hands, a feeling of unutterable frustration washing over me, so strongly as almost to overwhelm my sense of despair. Why, why, *why* hadn't I started more penicillin brewing at once? How could I have been so feckless, so careless—so bloody fucking *stupid*?

Why had I not insisted on going to Charleston, or at least Wilmington, in hopes of finding a glassblower who could make me the barrel and plunger for a hypodermic syringe? Surely I could have improvised *something* for a needle. All that difficulty, all that experimentation, to get the precious substance in the first place—and now that I desperately needed it . . .

A tentative movement at the open door made me turn round, struggling to get my face under control. I'd have to tell the household what was happening, and soon. But it would be better to choose my time, and tell them all together.

It was one of the Beardsleys. With their hair grown out and neatly trimmed to the same length by Lizzie, it was increasingly difficult to tell them apart—unless one was close enough to see their thumbs. Once they spoke, of course, it was simple.

"Ma'am?" It was Kezzie.

"Yes?" No doubt I sounded short, but it didn't matter; Kezzie couldn't distinguish nuances of speech.

He was carrying a cloth bag. As he came into the room, I saw the bag twitch and change shape, and a small shudder of revulsion came over me. He saw that, and smiled a little.

"This for Himself," he said, in his loud, slightly flat voice, holding up the bag. "Him—old Aaron—said this works good. A big snake bite you, get you a little 'un, cut his head off, drink his blood." He thrust out the bag, which I very gingerly accepted, holding it as far away from me as I could. The contents of the sack shifted again, making my skin crawl, and a faint buzzing noise issued through the cloth.

"Thank you," I said faintly. "I'll . . . ah . . . do something with it. Thank you."

Keziah beamed and bowed his way out, leaving me in personal custody of a sack containing what appeared to be a small but highly annoyed rattlesnake. I looked round frantically for some place to put it. I didn't dare throw it out of the window; Jemmy often played in the dooryard near the house.

Finally, I pulled the big clear glass jar of salt over to the edge of the counter, and—holding the bag at arm's length—used my other hand to dump the salt out on the counter. I dropped the bag into the jar and slammed the lid on it, then rushed to the other side of the room and collapsed on a stool, the backs of my knees sweaty with dread.

I didn't really mind snakes in theory; in practice, though . . .

Brianna poked her head through the door.

"Mama? How's Da this morning?"

"Not all that well." My face evidently told her just how serious it was, for she came into the room and stood beside me, frowning.

"Really bad?" she asked softly, and I nodded, unable to speak. She let her breath out in a deep sigh.

"Can I help?"

I let out an identical sigh, and made a helpless gesture. I had one vague glimmering of an idea—or rather, the return of an idea I'd had in the back of my mind for some time.

"The only thing I can think of doing is to open the leg—cut down deep through the muscle—and pour what penicillin I have left directly into the wounds. It's much more effective against bacterial infections if you can inject it, rather than give it orally. Raw penicillin like this"—I nodded at the bottle—"is very unstable in the presence of acid. It's not likely enough would make it through the stomach to do any good."

"That's more or less what Aunt Jenny did, isn't it? That's what made that huge scar on his thigh."

I nodded, wiping my palms unobtrusively over my knees. I didn't normally suffer from sweaty hands, but the feel of the amputation saw was much too clear in my memory.

"I'd have to do two or three deep cuts. It would likely cripple him permanently—but it might work." I tried to give her a smile. "I don't suppose MIT taught you how to engineer a hypodermic syringe, did they?"

"Why didn't you say so before?" she said calmly. "I don't know if I can make a syringe, but I'd be really surprised if I can't figure out something that does the same thing. How long have we got?"

I stared at her, my mouth half open, then shut it with a snap.

"A few hours, at least. I thought if we didn't get any improvement with the hot poultices, I'd have to either cut or amputate by this evening."

"Amputate!" All the blood drained out of her face. "You can't do that!"

"I can—but my God, I don't want to." My hands curled hard, denying their skill.

"Let me think, then." Her face was still pale, but the shock was passing as her mind began to focus. "Oh—where's Mrs. Bug? I was going to leave Jemmy with her, but—"

"She's gone? Are you sure she isn't just out in the hencoop?"

"No, I stopped there when I came up to the house. I didn't see her anywhere—and the kitchen fire is smoored."

That was more than odd; Mrs. Bug had come to the house as usual to make breakfast—what could have induced her to leave again? I hoped Arch hadn't suddenly been taken ill; that would just about put the cocked hat on things.

"Where's Jemmy, then?" I asked, looking round for him. He didn't normally go far away from his mother, though he was beginning to wander a bit, as small boys did.

"Lizzie took him upstairs to see Da. I'll ask her to look after him for a while."

"Fine. Oh!"

My exclamation made her turn back at the door, eyebrows raised in question.

"Do you think you could take that"—I gestured distastefully at the big glass jar—"outside, darling? Dispose of it somewhere?"

"Sure. What is it?" Curious, she walked over to the jar. The little rattlesnake had crawled out of its bag and was coiled up in a suspicious dark knot; as she extended a hand toward the jar, it lunged, striking at the glass, and Brianna jumped back with a yelp.

*"Ifrinn!"* she said, and I laughed, in spite of the general stress and worry.

"Where did you get him, and what is he for?" she asked. Recovering from the initial shock, she leaned forward cautiously and tapped lightly on the glass. The snake, who appeared irascible in the extreme, struck the side of the jar with an audible thump, and she jerked her hand away again.

"Kezzie brought him in; Jamie is meant to drink his blood as a cure," I explained.

She reached out a cautious forefinger, and traced the path of a small droplet of yellowish liquid, sliding down the glass. Two droplets, in fact.

"Look at that! He tried to bite me right through the glass!

That's a really mad snake; I guess he doesn't think much of the idea."

He didn't. He—if it was a he—was coiled again, tiny rattles vibrating in an absolute frenzy of animosity.

"Well, that's all right," I said, coming to stand beside her. "I'm sure Jamie wouldn't think much of the idea, either. He's rather strongly anti-snake at the moment."

"Mmphm." She was still staring at the little snake, a slight frown drawing down her thick red brows. "Did Kezzie say where he got it?"

"I didn't think to ask. Why?"

"It's getting cold out—snakes hibernate, don't they? In dens?"

"Well, Dr. Brickell says they do," I replied, rather dubiously. The good doctor's *Natural History of North Carolina* made entertaining reading, but I took leave to doubt some of his observations, particularly those pertaining to snakes and crocodiles, of whose prowess he appeared to have a rather exaggerated opinion.

She nodded, not taking her eyes off the snake.

"See, the thing is," she said, sounding rather dreamy, "pit-vipers have beautiful engineering. Their jaws are disarticulated, so they can swallow prey bigger than they are—and their fangs fold back against the roof of their mouth when they aren't using them."

"Yes?" I said, giving her a slightly fishy look, which she ignored.

"The fangs are hollow," she said, and touched a finger to the glass, marking the spot where the venom had soaked into the linen cloth, leaving a small yellowish stain. "They're connected to a venom sac in the snake's cheek, and so when they bite down, the cheek muscles squeeze venom out of the sac . . . and down through the fang into the prey. Just like a—"

"Jesus H. Roosevelt Christ," I said.

She nodded, finally taking her eyes off the snake in order to look at me.

"I was thinking of trying to do something with a sharpened quill, but this would work lots better—it's already designed for the job."

"I see," I said, feeling a small surge of hope. "But you'll need a reservoir of some kind . . ."

"First I need a bigger snake," she said practically, turning toward the door. "Let me go find Jo or Kezzie, and see if that one *did* come from a den—and if so, if there are more of them there."

She set off promptly on this mission, taking the glass jar with her, and leaving me to return to a contemplation of the antibiotic situation with renewed hope. If I was going to be able to inject the solution, it needed to be strained and purified as much as possible.

I would have liked to boil the solution, but didn't dare to; I didn't know whether high temperatures would destroy or in-activate raw penicillin—if, in fact, there still *was* active penicillin in there. The surge of hope I had experienced at Brianna's idea dimmed somewhat. Having a hypodermic apparatus wouldn't help, if I had nothing useful to inject.

Restlessly, I moved around the surgery, picking things up and putting them down again.

Steeling myself, I put my hand on the saw again, and closed my eyes, deliberately reliving the movements and sensations, trying also to recapture the sense of otherworldly detachment with which I had killed the buffalo.

Of course, it was Jamie who'd been talking to the otherworld this time. *Nice of you to give him the choice*, I thought sardonically. *I see you aren't going to make it easy on him, though.*

But he wouldn't have asked for that. I opened my eyes, startled. I didn't know whether that answer came from my own subconscious, or elsewhere—but there it was in my mind, and I recognized the truth of it.

Jamie was accustomed to make his choice and abide by it, no matter what the cost. He saw that living would likely mean the loss of his leg and all that that implied—and had accepted that as the natural price of his decision.

"Well, I don't bloody accept it!" I said out loud, chin up-lifted toward the window. A cedar waxwing swinging on the end of a tree limb gave me a sharp look through his black robber's mask, decided I was mad but harmless, and went about his business.

I pulled open the cupboard door, threw open the top of my medicine chest, and fetched a sheet of paper, quill, and ink from Jamie's study.

A jar of dried red wintergreen berries. Extract of pipsissewa. Slippery elm bark. Willow bark, cherry bark, fleabane, yarrow. Penicillin was by far the most effective of the antibiotics available, but it wasn't the only one. People had been waging war on germs for thousands of years, without any notion what they were fighting. I knew; that was some slight advantage.

I began to make a list of the herbs I had on hand, and under each name, all the uses that I knew for that herb—whether I had ever made such use of it or not. Any herb used to treat a septic condition was a possibility—cleansing lacerations, treating mouth sores, treatment of diarrhea and dysentery . . . I heard footsteps in the kitchen, and called to Mrs. Bug, wanting her to bring me a kettle of boiling water, so I could set things to steeping at once.

She appeared in the doorway, her cheeks bright pink from the cold and her hair coming down in untidy wisps from under her kerch, a large basket clutched in her arms. Before I could say anything, she came and plunked the basket down on the counter in front of me. Just behind her came her husband, with another basket, and a small open keg, from which came a pungent alcoholic scent. The air around them held a faint ripe smell, like the distant reek of a garbage dump.

"I did hear ye say as how ye'd not enough mold on hand," she started in, anxious but bright-eyed, "so I said to Arch, I said, we must go round to the houses nearabouts, and see what we can fetch back wi' us for Mrs. Fraser, for after all, bread does go bad so quick when it's damp, and the good Lord kens that Mrs. Chisholm is a slattern, for all I'm sure she's a good heart, and what goings-on there may be at her hearth I'm sure I shouldna like even to *think* about, but we—"

I wasn't paying attention, but was staring at the results of the Bugs' morning raid on the pantries and middens of the Ridge. Crusts of bread, spoilt biscuit, half-rotted squash, bits of pie with the marks of teeth still visible in the pastry . . . a hodgepodge of gluey orts and decaying fragments—all sprouting molds in patches of velvet-blue and lichen-green, interspersed with warty blobs of pink and yellow and dustings of splotchy white. The keg was half-filled with decaying corn, the resultant murky liquid rimmed with floating islands of blue mold.

"Evan Lindsay's pigs," Mr. Bug explained, in a rare burst of loquacity. Both Bugs beamed at me, begrimed with their efforts.

"Thank you," I said, feeling choked, and not only from the smell. I blinked, eyes watering slightly from the miasma of the corn liquor. "Oh, thank you."

IT WAS JUST AFTER DARK when I made my way upstairs, carrying my tray of potions and implements, feeling a mixture of excitement and trepidation.

Jamie was propped on his pillows, surrounded by visitors. People had been coming by the house all day to see him and wish him well; a good many of them had simply stayed, and a host of anxious faces turned toward me as I came in, glimmering in the light of the candles.

He looked very ill, flushed and drawn, and I wondered whether I ought to have chased the visitors away. I saw Murdo Lindsay take his hand, though, and squeeze it tight, and realized that the distraction and support of his company through the day was probably much more helpful to him than the rest that he wouldn't have taken in any case.

"Well, then," Jamie said, with a good assumption of casualness, "we're ready, I suppose." He stretched his legs, flexing his toes hard under the blanket. Given the state of his leg, it must have hurt dreadfully, but I recognized that he was taking what he thought would be the last opportunity to move the limb, and bit the inside of my lip.

"Well, we're ready to have a go at something," I said, smiling at him with an attempt at confident reassurance. "And anyone who would like to pray about it, please do."

A rustle of surprise replaced the air of dread that had been sprung up at my appearance, and I saw Marsali, who was holding a sleeping Joan with one hand, grope hastily in her pocket with the other to pull out her rosary.

There was a rush to clear the bedside table, which was littered with books, papers, candle-stubs, various treats brought up to tempt Jamie's appetite—all untouched—and, for some unfathomable reason, the fret-board of a dulcimer and a half-tanned groundhog hide. I set down the tray, and Brianna, who had come up with me, stepped forward, her invention carefully held in both hands, like an acolyte presenting bread to a priest.

"What in the name of Christ is that?" Jamie frowned at the object, then up at me.

"It's sort of a do-it-yourself rattlesnake," Brianna told him.

Everyone murmured with interest, craning their necks to see—though the interest was diverted almost at once as I turned back the quilt and began to unwrap his leg, to a chorus of shocked murmurs and sympathetic exclamations at sight of it.

Lizzie and Marsali had been faithfully applying fresh, hot onion and flaxseed poultices to it all day, and wisps of steam rose from the wrappings as I put them aside. The flesh of his leg was bright red to the knee, at least in those parts that weren't black or seeping with pus. We had removed the maggots temporarily, afraid the heat would kill them; they were presently downstairs on a plate in my surgery, happily occupied with some of the nastier bits of the Bugs' gleanings. If I succeeded in saving the leg, they could help with the tidying-up, later.

I had carefully gone through the detritus bit by bit, examining the blue molds with my microscope, and putting aside everything that could be identified as bearing *Penicillium* into a large bowl. Over this miscellaneous collection I had poured the fermented corn liquor, allowing the whole to steep during the day—and with luck, to dissolve any actual raw penicillin from the garbage into the alcoholic liquid.

Meanwhile, I had made a selection of those herbs with a reputation for the internal treatment of suppurative conditions, and made a stiff decoction of them, steeped in boiling water for several hours. I poured a cup of this highly aromatic solution, and handed it to Roger, carefully averting my nose.

"Make him drink it," I said. "All of it," I added pointedly, fixing Jamie with a look.

Jamie sniffed the proffered cup, and gave me the look back—but obediently sipped, making exaggerated faces for the entertainment of his company, who giggled appreciatively. The mood thus lightened, I proceeded to the main event, turning to take the makeshift hypodermic from Bree.

The Beardsley twins, standing shoulder-to-shoulder in the corner, pressed forward to see, swelling with pride. They had gone out at once at Bree's request, coming back in mid-afternoon with a fine rattlesnake, nearly three feet long—and fortunately dead, having been cut nearly in half with an ax, so as to preserve the valuable head.

I had dissected out the poison sacs with great caution, detaching the fangs, and then had put Mrs. Bug to the task of rinsing the fangs repeatedly with alcohol, to eradicate any lingering traces of venom.

Bree had taken the oiled silk that had been used to wrap the astrolabe, and stitched part of it into a small tube, gathering one end of this with a draw-stitch, like a purse-string. She had cut a thick segment from a turkey's wing-quill, softened with hot water, and used this to join the gathered end of the silk tube to the fang. Melted beeswax had sealed the joints of tube, quill, and fang, and been spread carefully along the line of the stitching, to prevent leakage. It was a nice, neat job—but it *did* look quite like a small, fat snake with one enormous curved fang, and occasioned no little comment from the spectators.

Murdo Lindsay was still holding one of Jamie's hands. As I motioned to Fergus to hold the candle for me, I saw Jamie reach out the other toward Roger. Roger looked momentarily startled, but grabbed the hand and knelt down by the bed, holding on tight.

I ran my fingers lightly over the leg, selected a good spot, clear of major blood vessels, swabbed it with pure alcohol, and jabbed the fang in, as deeply as I could. There was a gasp from the spectators, and a sharp intake of breath from Jamie, but he didn't move.

"All right." I nodded at Brianna, who was standing by with the bottle of strained corn-alcohol. Teeth sunk in her lower lip, she poured carefully, filling the silk tube as I supported it. I folded the open top tightly over, and with thumb and forefinger, firmly pressed downward, forcing the liquid out through the fang and into the tissues of the leg.

Jamie made a small, breathless noise, and both Murdo and Roger leaned inward instinctively, their shoulders pressing against his, holding on.

I didn't dare go too fast, for fear of cracking the wax seals by exerting too much pressure, though we had a second syringe, made with the other fang, just in case. I worked my way up and down the leg, with Bree refilling the syringe with each injection, and blood rose glistening from the holes as I withdrew the fang, rolling in tiny rivulets down the side of his leg. Without being asked, Lizzie picked up a cloth and blotted it clean, eyes intent on the job.

The room was silent, but I felt everyone's breath held as I chose a new spot, let out in a sigh as the stab was made—and then the unconscious leaning toward the bed as I squeezed the stinging alcohol deep into the infected tissues. The muscles stood out in knots on Jamie's forearms, and sweat ran down his face like rain, but neither he, nor Murdo, nor Roger made a sound or moved.

From the corner of my eye, I saw Joseph Wemyss stroke back the hair from Jamie's forehead, and wipe away the sweat from his face and neck with a towel.

*"Because ye need me,"* he'd said. And I realized then that it wasn't only me that he'd meant.

It didn't take a long time. When it was done, I spread honey carefully over all the open wounds, and rubbed oil of wintergreen into the skin of foot and calf.

"That's a nice job of basting, Sassenach. D'ye reckon it's ready for the oven yet?" Jamie asked, and wiggled his toes, causing the tension in the room to relax into laughter.

Everyone did leave, then, patting Jamie's shoulder or kissing his cheek in farewell, with gruff wishes of good luck. He smiled and nodded, lifting his hand in farewell, exchanging goodbyes, making small jokes.

When the door closed behind the last of them, he lay back on the pillow and closed his eyes, letting all his breath out in a long, deep sigh. I set about tidying my tray, setting the syringe to soak in alcohol, corking bottles, folding bandages. Then I sat down beside him, and he reached out a hand to me, not opening his eyes.

His skin was warm and dry, the hand reddened from Murdo's fierce grip. I traced his knuckles gently with my thumb, listening to the rumble and clatter of the house below, subdued but lively.

"It will work," I said softly, after a minute. "I know it will."

"I know," he said. He took a deep breath, and at last, began to weep.

# 94

# NEW BLOOD

ROGER WOKE ABRUPTLY, out of a black and dreamless sleep. He felt like a landed fish, jerked gasping into an alien and unimagined element. He saw but did not grasp his surroundings; strange light and flattened surfaces. Then his mind made sense of Brianna's touch on his arm, and he was once more inside his skin, and in a bed.

"Hwh?" He sat up suddenly, making a hoarse noise of inquiry.

"I'm sorry to wake you." Brianna smiled, but a line of concern drew her brows together as her eyes searched his face. She smoothed the tangled hair back from his brow, and he reached for her by reflex, falling back against the pillow with her heavy in his arms.

"Hwm." Holding her was an anchor to reality—solid flesh and warm skin, her hair soft as dreams against his face.

"Okay?" she asked softly. Long fingers touched his chest and his nipple puckered, curly hairs around it rising.

"Okay," he said, and sighed deeply. He kissed her fore-head briefly, and relaxed, blinking. His throat was dry as sand, and his mouth felt sticky, but he was beginning to think coherently again. "Whatime ist?" He was in his own bed, and it was dim enough in the room to be evening, but that was because the door was closed and the windows covered. Something felt wrong about the light, the air.

She pushed herself up off him, sweeping back the fall of red hair with one hand.

"It's a little past noon. I wouldn't have waked you up, but there's a man, and I don't know what to do about him." She glanced in the direction of the big house, and lowered her voice, though surely no one was near enough to hear her.

"Da's sound asleep, and Mama, too," she said, confirming this impression. "I don't want to wake them—even if I could." She smiled briefly, one corner of her long mouth curling up with her father's irony. "It would take gunpowder, I think. They're dead to the world."

She turned away and reached for the pitcher on the table. The sound of water pouring fell on Roger's ears like rain on parched land, and he drained the offered cup in three gulps and held it out again.

"More. Please. Man?" That was an improvement; he was making complete words again, and his capacity to think co-herently was coming back.

"He says his name is Thomas Christie. He's come to see Da; he says he was at Ardsmuir."

"Yeah?" Roger drank the second cup more slowly, assem-bling his thoughts. Then he put down the cup and swung his legs out of bed, reaching for the discarded shirt that hung from the peg. "Okay. Tell him I'll be there in a minute."

She kissed him briefly and left, pausing long enough to untack the hide over the window and let in a brilliant shaft of light and chilly air.

He dressed slowly, his mind still pleasantly torpid. As he bent to dredge his stockings out from under the bed, though, something in the tumbled bedclothes caught his eye, just un-der the edge of the pillow. He reached out slowly and picked it up. The "auld wifie"—the tiny fertility charm, its ancient pink stone smooth in the sun, surprisingly heavy in his hand.

"I will be damned," he said, aloud. He stood staring at it for a moment, then bent and tucked it gently back beneath the pillow.

BRIANNA HAD PUT the visitor in Jamie's study—what most of the tenants still called the speak-a-word room. Roger stopped for a moment in the corridor, checking to be sure all his bodily parts were present and attached. There hadn't been time to shave, but he'd combed his hair; there was a limit to what this Christie might expect, under the circumstances.

Three faces turned toward the door as he came in, surprising him. Bree hadn't thought to warn him that Christie had outriders. Still, the elder man, a square-set gentleman with trimly cut black hair streaked with gray, was obviously Thomas Christie; the dark-haired younger man was no more than twenty, and just as obviously Christie's son.

"Mr. Christie?" He offered the older man his hand. "I'm Roger MacKenzie; I'm married to Jamie Fraser's daughter—you've met my wife, I think."

Christie looked mildly surprised, and looked over Roger's shoulder, as though expecting Jamie to materialize behind him. Roger cleared his throat; his voice was still thick from sleep, and thus even more hoarse than it usually was.

"I'm afraid my father-in-law is . . . not available at present. Could I be of service to you?"

Christie frowned at him, assessing his potential, then nodded slowly. He took Roger's hand, and shook it firmly. To his astonishment, Roger felt something both familiar and grossly unexpected; the distinctive pressure against his knuckle of a Masonic greeting. He had not experienced that in years, and it was more reflex than reason that caused him to respond with what he hoped was the proper countersign. Evidently it was satisfactory; Christie's severe expression eased slightly, and he let go.

"Perhaps ye may, Mr. MacKenzie, perhaps ye may," Christie said. He fixed a piercing gaze on Roger. "I wish to find land on which to settle with my family—and I was told that Mr. Fraser might feel himself in a position to put something suitable in my way."

"That might be possible," Roger replied cautiously. *What the hell?* he thought. Had Christie just been trying it on at a venture, or had he reason to expect that sign would be recognized? If he did—that presumably meant that he knew Jamie Fraser would recognize it, and thought his son-in-law might, as well. Jamie Fraser, a Freemason? The thought had never so much as crossed Roger's mind, and Jamie himself had certainly never spoken of it.

"Please—do sit down," he said abruptly, motioning to the visitors. Christie's family—the son and a girl who might be either Christie's daughter or the son's wife—had risen as well when Roger came in, standing behind the paterfamilias like attendants behind some visiting potentate.

Feeling more than slightly self-conscious, Roger waved them back to their stools, and sat down himself behind Jamie's desk. He plucked one of the quills from the blue salt-glazed jar, hoping this would make him seem more businesslike. Christ, what questions ought he to ask a potential tenant?

"Now, then, Mr. Christie." He smiled at them, conscious of his unshaven jaws. "My wife says that you were acquainted with my father-in-law, in Scotland?"

"In Ardsmuir prison," Christie answered, darting Roger a sharp look, as though daring him to make something of this.

Roger cleared his throat again; healed as it was, it tended still to be clogged and rasping for some time after rising. Christie appeared to take it as an adverse comment, however, and bristled slightly. He had thick brows and prominent eyes of a light yellowish-brown color, and this, coupled with feathery, close-clipped dark hair and the lack of any visible neck, gave him the aspect of a large, irascible owl.

"Jamie Fraser was a prisoner there as well," he said. "Surely ye knew as much?"

"Why, yes," Roger said mildly. "I understand that several of the men who are settled here on the Ridge came from Ardsmuir."

"Who?" Christie demanded, increasing the owlish impression.

"Ah . . . the Lindsays—that's Kenny, Murdo, and Evan," Roger said, rubbing a hand over his brow to assist thought. "Geordie Chisholm and Robert MacLeod. I think—yes, I'm fairly sure Alex MacNeill was from Ardsmuir, too."

Christie had been following this list with close attention, like a barn owl keeping track of a rustling in the hay. Now he relaxed, settling his feathers, as Roger thought.

"I know them," he said, with an air of satisfaction. "Mac-Neill will vouch for my character, if that's needful." His tone strongly suggested that it shouldn't be.

Roger had never seen Jamie interview a potential tenant, but he had heard Fraser talk to Claire about the ones he chose. Accordingly, he posed a few questions regarding Christie's more recent past, trying to balance courtesy with an attitude of authority, and—he thought—managing it none too badly.

Christie had been transported with the other prisoners, he said, but had been fortunate in having his indenture purchased by a plantation owner in South Carolina, who upon finding that Christie possessed some learning, had made him school-master to his own six children, taking fees from the nearby families for the privilege of sending their children also to be tutored by Christie. Once Christie's term of indenture had expired, he had agreed to remain, working for wages.

"Really?" Roger said, his interest in Christie increasing markedly. A schoolmaster, eh? It would please Bree no end, to be able to resign her involuntary position as what she disparagingly termed Bo-Peep. And Christie looked more than capable of dealing with intransigent scholars. "What brings you here, then, Mr. Christie? It's some way from South Carolina."

The man shrugged broad shoulders. He was road-worn and quite dusty, but his coat was of decent cloth, and he had sound shoes.

"My wife died," he said gruffly. "Of the influenza. So did Mr. Everett, the owner. His heir did not require my services, and I did not wish to remain there without employment." He shot Roger a piercing look under shaggy brows. "You said Mr. Fraser is not available. How long will it be until his return?"

"I couldn't say." Roger tapped the end of the quill against his teeth, hesitating. In fact, he couldn't say how long Jamie might be incapacitated; when seen last night, he'd looked barely alive. Even if he recovered uneventfully, he could be ill for some time. And he hated to send Christie away, or make him wait; it was late in the year, and not much time to spare, if the man and his family were to be settled for the winter.

He glanced from Christie to his son. Both sizable men, and strong, from the looks of them. Neither had the look of a drunkard or a lout, and both had the callused palms that bespoke at least familiarity with manual labor. They had a woman to look after their domestic requirements. And after all, Masonic brotherhood quite aside, Christie had been one of Jamie's Ardsmuir men. He knew that Jamie always made a special effort to find such men a place.

Making a decision, Roger pulled out a clean sheet of paper and uncapped the inkwell. He cleared his throat once more.

"Very well, Mr. Christie. I think we can reach some . . . accommodation."

To his pleased surprise, the study door opened, and Brianna came in, carrying a tray of biscuits and beer. She cast down her eyes modestly as she set it on the desk, but he caught the flash of amusement she sent him under her lashes. He bent his head, smiling, and touched her wrist lightly in acknowledgment as she set out the mugs in front of him. The gesture reminded him of Christie's handshake, and he wondered whether Brianna knew anything about Jamie's history in that direction. He rather thought not; surely she would have mentioned it.

"Brianna, say hello to our new tenants," he said, with a nod at the Christies. "Mr. Thomas Christie, and . . ."

"My son, Allan," Christie said, with a jerk of the head, "and my daughter, Malva."

The son had none of his father's owlish look, being much fairer in aspect, with a broad, square, clean-shaven face, though he had the same feathery, tufted dark hair. He nodded in silent acknowledgment of the introduction, eyes fixed on the refreshment.

The girl—Malva?—barely looked up, her hands folded modestly in her lap. Roger had the vague impression of a tallish girl, perhaps seventeen or eighteen, neat in a dark blue dress and white kerch, with a soft frill of black curls just visible around the pale oval of her face. Another point in Christie's favor, Roger thought absently; girls of marriageable age were rare, pretty ones still rarer. Malva Christie would likely have several offers before the spring planting.

Bree nodded to each of them, looking at the girl with particular interest. Then a loud shriek came from the kitchen, and she fled with a murmured excuse.

"My son," Roger said, in apology. He lifted a mug of beer, offering it. "Will you take a bit of refreshment, Mr. Christie?"

The tenant contracts were all kept in the left-hand drawer of the desk; he'd seen them, and knew the general outlines. Fifty acres would be granted outright, more land rented as needed, with provision for payment made according to individual situations. A little discussion over the beer and biscuits, and they had reached what seemed an adequate agreement.

Completing the contract with a flourish, Roger signed his own name, as agent for James Fraser, and pushed the paper across the desk for Christie to sign. He felt a deep, pleasant glow of accomplishment. A sound tenant, and willing to pay half his quitrent by serving as schoolmaster for five months of the year. Jamie himself, Roger thought complacently, would not have done better.

Then he caught himself. No, Jamie would have taken one more step, and seen the Christies offered not only hospitality but lodging, a place to stay until they could achieve some shelter of their own. Not here, though; not with Jamie ill and Claire occupied in nursing him. He thought for a moment, then stepped to the door and called for Lizzie.

"We've a new tenant come, and his family, *a muirninn*," he said, smiling at her anxious, willing mouse-face. "This is Mr. Thomas Christie, and his son and daughter. Can ye ask your Da will he take them up to Evan Lindsay's cabin? It's near where they'll have their own land, and I'm thinking perhaps Evan and his wife have room for them to stay for a bit, until they can get a start on a place of their own."

"Oh, aye, Mister Roger." Lizzie bobbed a quick curtsy toward Christie, who acknowledged her with a small bow. Then she glanced at Roger, thin brows lifted. "Will Himself know about it, then?"

Roger felt a slight flush rise in his cheeks, but gave no sign of discomposure.

"That's all right," he said. "I'll be telling him, so soon as he's feeling better."

"Mr. Fraser is ill? I am sorry to hear it." The unfamiliar soft voice came from behind, startling him, and he turned to find Malva Christie looking up at him in question. He hadn't taken much notice of her, but was now struck by the beauty of her eyes—an odd light gray, almond-shaped and luminous, and thickly fringed with long black lashes. Perhaps sooner than the spring planting, he thought, and coughed.

"Bitten by a snake," he said abruptly. "Not to worry, though; he's mending."

He thrust out a hand to Christie, ready this time for the secret grip.

"Welcome to Fraser's Ridge," he said. "I hope you and your family will be happy here."

JAMIE WAS SITTING UP in bed, attended hand and foot by devoted women, and looking desperate in consequence. His face relaxed a little at sight of a fellow man, and he waved away his handmaidens. Lizzie, Marsali, and Mrs. Bug left reluctantly, but Claire remained, busy with her bottles and blades.

Roger moved to sit down on the bed-foot, only to be shooed off by Claire, who motioned him firmly to a stool before lifting the sheet to check matters beneath and be sure that his ill-advised gesture had caused no damage.

"All right," she said at last, poking at the white cheese-cloth dressing with an air of satisfaction. The maggots were back, evidently earning their keep. She straightened up and nodded to Roger—like the Grand Vizier granting an audience with the Caliph of Baghdad, Roger thought, amused. He glanced at Jamie, who rolled his eyes upward, then gave Roger a small, wry smile of greeting.

"How is it?" both of them said at once. Roger smiled, and the corner of Jamie's mouth turned up. He gave a brief shrug.

"I'm alive," he said. "Mind, that doesna prove ye were right. Ye're not."

"Right about what?" Claire asked, glancing up with curiosity from the bowl in her hands.

"Oh, a wee point of philosophy," Jamie told her. "Regarding choice, and chance."

She snorted.

"I don't want to hear a word about it."

"Just as well. I'm no inclined to discuss such matters on nothing but bread and milk." Jamie glanced with mild distaste at a bowl of that nourishing but squashy substance, sitting half-finished on the table at his side. "So, have ye seen to the ulcer on the mule's leg, then, Roger Mac?"

"I did," Claire told him. "It's healing very well. Roger's been busy, interviewing new tenants."

"Oh, aye?" Fraser's brows went up in interest.

"Aye, a man named Tom Christie and his family. He said he was at Ardsmuir with you."

For a split second, Roger felt as though all the air in the room had been removed by a vacuum, freezing everything. Fraser stared at him, expressionless. Then he nodded, his expression of pleasant interest restored as though by magic, and normal time resumed.

"Aye, I mind Tom Christie fine. Where has he been in the last twenty years?"

Roger explained both Tom Christie's account of his wanderings, and what accommodations had been reached for his tenancy.

"That will do verra well," Jamie said approvingly, hearing of Christie's willingness to be schoolmaster. "Tell him he may use any of the books here—and ask him to make up a list of others he might need. I'll tell Fergus to look about, next time he's in Cross Creek or Wilmington."

The conversation moved on to more mundane affairs, and after a few minutes, Roger got up to take his leave.

Everything seemed perfectly all right, and yet he felt obscurely uneasy. Surely he hadn't imagined that instant? Turning to close the door behind him, he saw that Jamie had folded his hands neatly on his chest and closed his eyes; if not yet asleep, effectively forbidding conversation. Claire was looking at her husband, her yellow hawk-eyes narrowed in speculation. No, she'd seen it, too.

So he hadn't imagined it. What on earth was the matter with Tom Christie?

## 95

## THE SUMMER DIM

THE NEXT DAY Roger closed the door behind him and stood on the porch for a moment, breathing the cold bright air of the late morning—late, Christ, it couldn't be more than half seven, but it was a good deal later than he was accustomed to start the day. The sun had already drifted into the chestnut trees on the highest ridge, the curve of its flaming disk visible in silhouette through the last of the yellow leaves.

The air still held the tang of blood, but there was no trace of the buffalo left, beyond a dark patch in the flattened pumpkin vines. He glanced around, taking stock as he mentally made his list of chores for the day. Chickens scratched in the fall-shabby yard, and he could hear a small group of hogs rooting for mast in the chestnut grove.

He had the odd feeling that he had left his work months, or even years, before, not days. The feeling of dislocation—so strong at first—had left him for quite a long time, but now it had come back again, stronger than before. If he closed his eyes for a moment, then opened them again, surely he would find himself on the Broad Street in Oxford, the smell of auto exhaust in his nostrils and the prospect of a peaceful morning's work among the dusty books of the Bodleian ahead.

He smacked a hand against one thigh, to dispel the feeling. Not today. This was the Ridge, not Oxford, and the work might be peaceful, but it would be done with hands, not head. There were trees to be girdled and hay to be gathered; not the field hay, but the small wild patches scattered through the hills that would yield an armload here, an armload there—enough to allow the keeping of an extra cow through the winter.

A hole in the roof of the smoke-shed, made by a falling tree branch. The roof to be mended and re-shingled and the branch itself to be chopped for wood. A fresh privy-hole to be dug, before the ground froze or turned to mud. Flax to be chopped. Fence rails to split. Lizzie's spinning wheel to mend . . .

He felt groggy and stupid, incapable of simple choice, let alone complex thought. He had slept enough—more than enough—to be physically recovered from the exhaustion of the last few days, but Thomas Christie and his family, coming on the heels of the desperate business of getting Jamie safely home, had taken all the mental energy he had.

He glanced at the sky; a low sweep of mare's tails, sketched against the sky. No rain for a bit, the roof could wait. He shrugged and scratched his scalp. Hay, then, and tree-girdling. He stuffed a stone jar of ale and the packet of sandwiches Bree had made for him into his bag, and went to fetch the hand-scythe and hatchet.

Walking began to rouse him. It was cold in the shadows under the pines, but the sun was now high enough to make itself felt whenever he walked through the bright patches. His muscles warmed and loosened with the exercise, and by the time he had climbed to the first of the high meadows, he had begun to feel himself again, solidly embedded in the physical world of mountain and forest. The future had gone back to the world of dreams and memory, and he was once more present and accounted for.

"Good thing, too," he muttered to himself. "Don't want to be cutting off your foot." He dropped the ax under a tree, and bent to cut hay.

It wasn't the soothingly monotonous labor of regular haying, where the big two-handed scythe laid the dry, rich grass in pleasing swathes across a field. This was at once rougher but easier work, that involved grasping a clump of sprouting muhly or blue-stem with one hand, slicing the stalks near the root, and stuffing the handful of wild hay into the burlap sack he had brought.

It took no great strength, but required attention, rather than the mindless muscular effort of field-haying. The grass clumps grew thickly all over this small break in the trees, but were interspersed with outcrops of granite, small bushes, decaying snags, and brambles.

It was soothing labor, and while it did require some watchfulness, soon enough his mind began to stray to other things. The things Jamie had told him, out on the black mountainside, under the stars.

Some he had known; that there was bad feeling between Alex MacNeill and Nelson McIver, and the cause of it; that one of Patrick Neary's sons was likely a thief, and what should be done about it. Which land to sell, when, and to whom. Others, he had had no inkling of. He pressed his lips tight together, thinking of Stephen Bonnet.

And what should be done about Claire.

"If I am dead, she must leave," Jamie had said, rousing suddenly from a feverish stupor. He had gripped Roger's arm with surprising strength, his eyes burning dark. "Send her. Make her go. Ye should all go, if the bairn can pass. But she must go. Make her go to the stones."

"Why?" Roger had asked quietly. "Why should she go?" It was possible that Jamie was deranged by fever, not thinking clearly. "It's a dangerous thing, to go through the stones."

"It is dangerous for her here, without me." Fraser's eyes had momentarily lost their sharp focus; the lines of his face relaxed in exhaustion. His eyes half-closed and he sagged back. Then, suddenly, his eyes opened again.

"She is an Old One," he said. "They will kill her, if they

know." Then his eyes had closed again, and he had not spoken again until the others had found them at daylight.

Viewed now in the clear light of an autumn morning, safely removed from the whining wind and dancing flames of that lost night on the mountain, Roger was reasonably sure that Fraser had only been wandering in the mists of his fever, concern for his wife muddled by phantoms that sprang from the poison in his blood. Still, Roger couldn't help but take notice.

*"She is an Old One."* Fraser had been speaking in English, which was too bad. Had it been Gaelic, his meaning would have been clearer. Had he said *"She is ban-sidhe,"* Roger would have known whether Jamie truly thought his wife was one of the faery-folk, or only a thoroughly human wisewoman.

Surely he couldn't . . . but he might. Even in Roger's own time, the belief in "the others" ran strongly, if less widely admitted, in the blood of the Highlands. Now? Fraser believed quite openly in ghosts—to say nothing of saints and angels. To Roger's cynical Presbyterian mind, there wasn't a great deal of difference between lighting candles to St. Genevieve and putting out a pan of milk for the faeries.

On the other hand, he was uneasily aware that he would himself never have disturbed milk meant for the Others, nor touched a charm hung over cow-byre or door lintel—and not only from respect for the person who had placed it there.

The work had warmed him thoroughly; his shirt was beginning to stick to his shoulders, and sweat trickled down his neck. He paused for a moment, to drink from his water gourd and tie a rag round his brow as a sweatband.

Fraser might just have a point, he thought. While the notion of himself or Brianna—even of Claire—as being *sidheanach* was laughable on the face of it . . . there was more than one face to it, wasn't there? They *were* different; not everyone could travel through the stones, let alone did.

And there were others. Geillis Duncan. The unknown traveler she had mentioned to Claire. The gentleman whose severed head Claire had found in the wilderness, silver fillings intact. The thought of that one made the hairs prickle on his forearms, sweat or no.

Jamie had buried the head, with due respect and a brief prayer, on a hill near the house—the first inhabitant of the small, sun-filled clearing intended as the future cemetery of Fraser's Ridge. At Claire's insistence, he had marked the small grave with a rough chunk of granite, unlabeled—for what was there to say?—but marbled with veins of green serpentine.

Was Fraser right? *Ye should all go back, if the bairn can pass.*

And if they didn't go back . . . then someday they might all lie there in the sunny clearing together: himself, Brianna, Jemmy, each under a chunk of granite. The only difference was that each would bear a name. What on earth would they carve for dates? he wondered suddenly, and wiped sweat from his jaw. Jemmy's would be no problem, but for the rest of them . . .

There was the rub, of course—or one of them. *If the bairn can pass.* If Claire's theory was right, and the ability to pass through the stones was a genetic trait, like eye color or blood-type—then fifty/fifty, if Jemmy were Bonnet's child; three chances out of four, or perhaps certainty, if he were Roger's.

He hacked savagely at a clump of grass, not bothering to grasp it, and grain heads flew like shrapnel. Then he remembered the small pink figure underneath his pillow, and breathed deep. And if it worked, if there were to be another child, one that was his for sure, by blood? Odds three out of four—or perhaps another stone, one day, in the family graveyard.

The bag was almost full, and there was no more hay worth the cutting here. Fetching the hatchet, he slung the bag across his shoulder and made his way downhill, to the edge of the highest cornfield.

It bore no more resemblance to the British cornfields he had been used to than did the high meadows to a hayfield. Once a patch of virgin forest, the trees still stood, black and dead against the pale blue sky. They had been girdled and left to die, the corn planted in the open spaces between them.

It was the quickest way to clear land sufficiently for crops.

With the trees dead, enough sunlight came through the leafless branches for the corn below. One or two or three years later, the dead tree roots would have rotted sufficiently to make it possible to push the trunks over, to be gradually cut for wood and hauled away. For now, though, they stood, an eerie band of black scarecrows, spreading empty arms across the corn.

The corn itself had been gathered; flocks of mourning doves foraged for bugs among the litter of dry stalks, and a covey of bobwhite took fright at Roger's approach, scattering like a handful of marbles thrown across the ground. A ladder-backed woodpecker, secure above his head, uttered a brief shriek of startlement and paused in its hammering to inspect him before returning to its noisy excavations.

"You should be pleased," he said to the bird, setting down the bag and unlimbering the hatchet from his belt. "More bugs for you, aye?" The dead trees were infested by myriad insects; several woodpeckers could be found in any field of girdled trees, heads cocked to hear the subterranean scratchings of their burrowing prey.

"Sorry," he murmured under his breath to the tree he had selected. It was ridiculous to feel pity for a tree; the more so in this sprawling wilderness, where saplings sprang out of the thawing earth with such spring vigor as to crack solid rock and the mountains were so thickly blanketed with trees that the air itself was a smoky blue with their exhalations. For that matter, the emotion wouldn't last longer than it took to begin the job; by the time he reached the third tree, he would be sweating freely and cursing the awkwardness of the work.

Still, he always approached the job with a faint reluctance, disliking the manner of it more than the result. Chopping down a tree for timber was straight-forward; girdling it seemed somehow mean-spirited, if practical, leaving the tree to die slowly, unable to bring water from its roots above the ring of bare, exposed wood. It was not so unpleasant in the fall, at least, when the trees were dormant and leafless already; it must be rather like dying in their sleep, he thought. Or hoped.

Chips of aromatic wood flew past his head, as he chopped his way briskly around the big trunk, and went on without pause to the next victim.

Needless to say, he took care never to let anyone hear him apologize to a tree. Jamie always said a prayer for the animals he killed, but Roger doubted that he would regard a tree as anything other than fuel, building material, or sheer bloody obstruction. The woodpecker screeched suddenly overhead. Roger swung round to see what had caused the alarm, but relaxed at once, seeing the small, wiry figure of Kenny Lindsay approaching through the trees. It appeared that Lindsay had come on the same business; he flourished his own girdling knife in cordial greeting.

*"Madain mhath, a Smeòraich!"* he shouted. "And what's this I hear, that we've a newcomer?"

No longer even faintly surprised at the speed with which news passed over the mountain, Roger offered his ale-jug to Lindsay, and gave him the details of the new family.

"Christie is their name, is it?" Kenny asked.

"Yes. Thomas Christie, and his son and daughter. You'll know him—he was at Ardsmuir."

"Aye? Oh."

There it was again, that faint tremor of reaction at Christie's name.

"Christie," Kenny Lindsay repeated. The tip of his tongue showed briefly, tasting the name. "Mm. Aye, well."

"What's the matter with Christie?" Roger demanded, feeling more uneasy by the minute.

"Matter?" Kenny looked startled. "Nothing's the matter with him—is there?"

"No. I mean—you seemed a bit taken aback to hear his name. I wondered whether perhaps he was a known thief, or a drunkard, or the like."

Enlightenment spread across Kenny's stubbled face like sun on a morning meadow.

"Oh, aye, I take your meaning now. No, no, Christie's a decent enough sort, so far as I ken the man."

"So far as ye ken? Were ye not at Ardsmuir together, then? He said so."

"Och, aye, he was there right enough," Kenny agreed, but

seemed still vaguely hesitant. Additional prodding by Roger elicited nothing, though, save a shrug, and after a few moments, they returned to the cutting, pausing only for the occasional swig of ale or water. The weather was cool, thank God, but working like that made the sweat run free, and at the end of the job, Roger took a last drink, and then poured the rest of his water over his head, gasping with the welcome chill on his heated skin.

"You'll come ben for a bit, *a Smeòraich*?" Kenny laid down his ax and eased his back with a groan. He jerked his head toward the pines on the far side of the meadow. "My wee house is just there. The wife's awa' to sell her pork, but there's fresh buttermilk in the spring."

Roger nodded, smiling.

"I will then, Kenny, thanks."

He went with Kenny to tend his beasts; Lindsay had two milch-goats and a penned sow. Kenny fetched them water from a small nearby creek, while Roger stacked the hay and threw a forkful into the goats' manger.

"Nice pig," Roger said politely, waiting while Kenny poured cracked corn into the trough for the sow, a big mottled creature with one ragged ear and a nasty look in her eye.

"Mean as a viper, and nearly as fast," Kenny said, giving the pig a narrow look. "Near as Godalmighty took my hand off at the wrist yesterday. I meant to take her to *Mac Dubh*'s boar for breeding, but she wasna inclined to go."

"Not much ye can do with a female who's not in the mood," Roger agreed.

Kenny wobbled his head from one side to the other, considering.

"Och, well, that's as may be. There are ways to sweeten them, aye? That's a trick my brother Evan taught me." He gave Roger a gap-toothed grin, and nodded toward a barrel in the corner of the shed, that gave off the sweet pungency of fermenting corn.

"Aye?" Roger said, laughing. "Well, I hope it works, then." He had an involuntary vision of Kenny and his imposing wife, Rosamund, in bed together, and wondered in passing whether alcohol played much part in their unlikely marriage.

"Oh, it'll work," Kenny said with confidence. "She's a terror for the sour-mash, is that one. Trouble is, if ye give her enough to improve her disposition, she canna walk just so verra well. We'll need to bring the boar to her, instead, when *Mac Dubh*'s on his feet."

"Is she in season? I'll bring the boar tomorrow," Roger said, feeling reckless. Kenny looked startled, but then nodded, pleased.

"Aye, that's kind, *a Smeòraich*." He paused a moment, then added casually, "I hope *Mac Dubh* is on his feet soon, then. Will he be well enough to have met Tom Christie?"

"He hasn't met him, no—but I told him."

"Oh? Oh. Well, that's fine, isn't it?"

Roger narrowed his eyes, but Kenny looked away.

His sense of unease about Christie persisted, and seized by a sudden impulse, Roger leaned across the hay and grasped Kenny by the hand, startling the older man considerably. He gave the squeeze, the tap on the knuckle, and then let go.

Kenny gawked at him, blinking in the beam of sunlight from the door. Finally, he set down the empty pail, carefully wiped his hand on his ragged kilt, and offered it formally to Roger.

When he let go, they were still friendly, but the situation between them had altered, very subtly.

"Christie, too," Roger observed, and Kenny nodded.

"Oh, aye. All of us."

"All of you at Ardsmuir? And—Jamie?" He felt a sense of astonishment at the thought.

Kenny nodded again, bending to pick up his bucket.

"Oh, aye, it was *Mac Dubh* started it. Ye didna ken?"

No point in prevarication. He shook his head, dismissing the matter. He'd mention it to Jamie when he saw him—assuming Jamie was in any shape to be questioned then. He fixed Kenny with a direct look.

"So, then. About Christie. Is there anything wrong about the man?"

Lindsay's earlier constraint had disappeared, now that it was no longer a matter of discussing a Masonic brother with an outsider. He shook his head.

"Och, no. It's only I was a bit surprised to see him here. He didna quite get on sae well wi' *Mac Dubh*, is all. If he had another place to go, I wouldna have thought he'd seek out Fraser's Ridge."

Roger was momentarily surprised by the revelation that there was someone from Ardsmuir who didn't think the sun shone out of Jamie Fraser's arse, though on consideration, there was no reason why this shouldn't be so; God knew the man was quite as capable of making enemies as friends.

"Why?"

What he was asking was plain. Kenny looked about the goat-shed, as though seeking escape, but Roger stood between him and the door.

"No great matter," he said, finally, shoulders slumping in capitulation. "Only Christie's a Protestant, see?"

"Aye, I see," Roger said, very dryly. "But he was put in with the Jacobite prisoners. So, was there trouble in Ardsmuir over it, is that what you're telling me?"

Likely enough, he reflected. In his own time, there was no love lost between the Catholics and the stern Scottish sons of John Knox and his ilk. Nothing Scots liked better than a wee spot of religious warfare—and if you got right down to it, that's what the entire Jacobite cause had been.

Take a few staunch Calvinists, convinced that if they didn't tuck their blankets tight, the Pope would nip down the chimney and bite their toes, and bang them up in a prison cheek-by-jowl with men who prayed out loud to the Virgin Mary . . . aye, he could see it. Football riots would be nothing to it, numbers being equal.

"How did he come to be in Ardsmuir, then—Christie, I mean?"

Kenny looked surprised.

"Och, he was a Jacobite—arrested wi' the rest after Culloden, tried and imprisoned."

"A Protestant Jacobite?" It wasn't impossible, or even far-fetched—politics made stranger bedfellows than that, and always had. It was unusual, though.

Kenny heaved a sigh, glancing toward the horizon, where the sun was slowly sinking into the pines.

"Come along inside then, MacKenzie. If Tom Christie's

come to the Ridge, I suppose it's best someone tells ye all about it. If I hurry myself, ye'll be in time for your supper."

Rosamund was not at home, but the buttermilk was cool in the well, as advertised. Stools fetched and the buttermilk poured, Kenny Lindsay was good as his word, and started in in businesslike fashion. Christie was a Lowlander, Kenny said; MacKenzie would have gathered as much. From Edinburgh. At the time of the Rising, Christie had been a merchant in the city, with a good business, newly inherited from a hard-working father. Tom Christie was far from lazy, himself, and determined to set up for a gentleman.

With this in mind, and Prince *Tearlach*'s army occupying the city, Christie had put on his best suit of clothes and gone calling on O'Sullivan, the Irishman who had charge of the army commissary. "Naebody kens what passed between them, other than words—but when Christie came out, he had a contract to victual the Highland Army, and an invitation to dance at Holyrood that night." Kenny took a long drink of sweet buttermilk and set down the cup, his mustache thickly coated with white. He nodded wisely at Roger.

"We heard what they were like, those balls at the Palace. *Mac Dubh* told us of them, time and again. The Great Gallery, wi' the portraits of all the kings o' Scotland, and the hearths of blue Dutch tile, big enough to roast an ox. The Prince, and all the great folk who'd come to see him, dressed in silks and laces. And the food! Sweet Jesus, such food as he'd tell about." Kenny's eyes grew round and dreamy, remembering descriptions heard on an empty stomach. His tongue came out and absently licked the buttermilk from his upper lip.

Then he shook himself back to the present.

"Well, so," he said, matter-of-factly. "When the Army left Edinburgh, Christie cam' along. Whether it was to mind his investment, or that he meant to keep himself in the Prince's eye, I canna say."

Roger noted privately that the notion of Christie having acted from patriotic motives wasn't on Kenny Lindsay's list of possibilities. Whether from prudence or ambition, whatever his reasons, Christie had stayed—and stayed too long. He had left the Army at Nairn, the day before Culloden, and started back toward Edinburgh, driving one of the commissary wagons.

"If he'd left the wagon and ridden one o' the horses, he might ha' made it," Kenny said cynically. "But no; he ran smack into a sackful o' Campbells. Government troops, aye?"

Roger nodded.

"I heard tell as he tried to pass himself off as a peddler, but he'd taken a load of corn from a farmhouse on that road, and the farmer swore himself purple that Christie'd been in his yard no more than three days before, wi' a white cockade on his breast. So they took him, and that was that."

Christie had gone first to Berwick Prison, and then—for reasons known only to the Crown—to Ardsmuir, where he had arrived a year before Jamie Fraser.

"I came at the same time." Kenny peered into his empty mug, then reached for the pitcher. "It was an old prison— half-falling down—but they'd not used it for some years. When the Crown decided to reopen it, they brought men from here and from there; maybe a hundred and fifty men, all told. Mostly convicted Jacobites—the odd thief, and a murderer or two." Kenny grinned suddenly, and Roger couldn't help smiling in response.

Kenny was no great storyteller, but he spoke with such simple vividness that Roger had no trouble seeing the scene he described: the soot-streaked stones and the ragged men. Men from all over Scotland, ripped from home, deprived of kin and companions, thrown like bits of rubbish into a heap of compost, where filth, starvation, and close quarters generated a heat of rot that broke down both sensibility and civilness.

Small groups had formed, for protection or for the comfort of society, and there was constant conflict between one group and another. They banged to and fro like pebbles in the surf, bruising each other and now and then crushing some hapless individual who got in between.

"It's food and warmth, aye?" Kenny said dispassionately. "There's naught else to care for, in a place like that."

Among the groups had been a small obdurate knot of Calvinists, headed by Thomas Christie. Mindful of their own, they shared food and blankets, defended each other—and behaved with a dour self-righteousness that roused the Catholics to fury.

"If one of us was to catch afire—and now and then, some-one would, bein' pushed into the hearth whilst sleepin'—they wouldna piss on him to put it out," Kenny said, shaking his head. "They wouldna be stealing food, to be sure, but they *would* stand in the corner and pray out loud, rattlin' on and on about whore-mongers and usurers and idolaters and the lot—and makin' damn sure we kent who was meant by it!"

"And then came *Mac Dubh*." The late autumn sun was sinking; Kenny's stubbled face was blurred with shadow, but Roger could see the slight softening that came across it, re-laxing the grimness of expression that accompanied Lind-say's reminiscence.

"Something like the Second Coming, was it?" Roger said. He spoke half under his breath, and was surprised when Kenny laughed.

"Only if ye mean some of us kent *Sheumais ruaidh* al-ready. No, man, they'd brought him by boat. Ye'll ken Jamie Roy doesna take to boats, aye?"

"I'd heard something of the sort," Roger answered dryly.

"Whatever ye heard, it's true," Kenny assured him, grin-ning. "He staggered into the cell green as a lass, vomited in the corner, then crawled under a bench and stayed there for the next day or two."

Upon his emergence, Fraser had kept quiet for a time, watching to see who was who and what was what. But he was a gentleman born, and had been both a laird and a fierce warrior; a man much respected among the Highlanders. The men deferred to him naturally, seeking his opinion, asking his judgment, and the weaker sheltering in his presence.

"And that griped Tom Christie's arse like a saddle-gall," Kenny said, nodding wisely. "See, he'd got to thinking as how he was the biggest frog in the pond, aye?" Kenny ducked his chin and puffed his throat, popping his eyes in illustra-tion, and Roger burst out laughing.

"Aye, I see. And he didn't care for the competition, was that it?"

Kenny nodded, off-hand.

"It wouldna have been so bad, maybe, save that half his wee band of salvationers started creepin' off from their prayers to hear *Mac Dubh* tell stories. But the main thing was the new governor."

Bogle, the prison's original governor, had left, replaced by Colonel Harry Quarry. Quarry was a relatively young man, but an experienced soldier, who had fought at Falkirk and at Culloden. Unlike his predecessor, he viewed the prisoners under his command with a certain respect—and he knew Jamie Fraser by repute, regarding him as an honorable, if defeated, foe.

"Quarry had *Mac Dubh* brought up to see him, soon after he took command at Ardsmuir. I couldna say what happened between them, but soon it was a matter of course; once a week, the guards would come and take *Mac Dubh* off to shave and wash himself, and he would go take a bit of supper with Quarry, and speak to him of whatever was needed."

"And Tom Christie didn't like that, either," Roger guessed. He was forming a comprehensive picture of Christie; ambitious, intelligent—and envious. Competent himself, but lacking Fraser's fortunate birth and skill at warfare—advantages that a self-made merchant with social aspirations might well have resented, even before the catastrophe of Culloden. Roger felt a certain sneaking sympathy for Christie; Jamie Fraser was stiff competition for the merely mortal.

Kenny shook his head, and tilted back to drain his cup. He set it down with a sigh of repletion, raising his brows with a gesture toward the jug. Roger waved a hand, dismissing it.

"No, no more, thanks. But the Freemasons . . . how did that happen? You said it was to do with Christie?" The light was nearly gone. He would have to walk home in the dark— but that was no matter; his curiosity wouldn't let him leave without learning what had happened.

Kenny grunted, rearranging his kilt over his thighs. Hospitality was all very well, but he had chores to do as well. Still, courtesy was courtesy, and he liked the Thrush for himself, not only that he was *Mac Dubh*'s good-son.

"Aye, well." He shrugged, resigning himself. "No,

Christie didna like it a bit, that *Mac Dubh* should be the great one, when he felt it his own place by right." He cast a shrewd glance at Roger, assessing. "I dinna think he kent what it might cost to be chief in a place like that—not 'til later. But that's naught to do with it." He flapped a hand, waving off irrelevancy.

"The thing was, Christie *was* a chief himself; only not just so good at it as was *Mac Dubh*. But there were those who listened to him, and not only the God-naggers."

If Roger was a trifle taken aback at hearing this characterization of his co-religionists, he disregarded it in his eagerness to hear more.

"Aye, so?"

"There was trouble again." Kenny shrugged again. "Small things, aye, but ye could see it happening."

Shifts and schisms, the small faults and fractures that result when two land masses come together, straining and shoving until either mountains rise between them or one is subsumed by the other, in a breaking of earth and a shattering of stone.

"We could see *Mac Dubh* thinking," Kenny said. "But he's no the man to be telling anyone what's in his mind, aye?"

*Almost no one*, Roger thought suddenly, with the memory of Fraser's voice, so low as barely to be heard beneath the whining autumn wind. *He told me*. The thought was a small sudden warmth in his chest, but he pushed it aside, not to be distracted.

"So one evening *Mac Dubh* came back to us, quite late," Kenny said. "But instead of lying down to his rest, he came and summoned us—me and my brothers, Gavin Hayes, Ronnie Sinclair . . . and Tom Christie."

Fraser had roused the six men quietly from their sleep, and brought them to one of the cell's few windows, where the light of the night sky might shine upon his face. The men had gathered round him, heavy-eyed and aching from the day's labors, wondering what this might mean. Since the last small clash—a fight between two men over a meaningless insult—Christie and Fraser had not exchanged a word, but had kept each man to himself.

It was a soft spring night, the air still crisp, but smelling of fresh green things from the sprouting moor and the salt scent of the distant sea; a night to make a man yearn to run free upon the earth and feel the blood humming dark in his veins. Tired or not, the men roused to it, alive and alert.

Christie was alert; wary-eyed and watchful. Here he was, called face-to-face with Fraser and five of his closest allies— what might they intend? True, they stood in a cell with fifty men sleeping round them, and some of those would come to Christie's aid if he called; but a man could be beaten or killed before anyone knew he was threatened.

Fraser had spoken not a word to start, but smiled and put out his hand to Tom Christie. The other man had hesitated for a moment, suspicious—but there was no choice, after all.

"Ye would have thought *Mac Dubh* held a bolt of lightning in his hand, the way the shock of it went through Christie." Kenny's own hand lay open on the table between them, the palm hard as horn with calluses. The short, thick fingers curled slowly closed, and Kenny shook his head, a broad grin creasing his face.

"I dinna ken how it was *Mac Dubh* found out that Christie was a Freemason, but he knew it. Ye should have seen the look on Tom's face when he realized that Jamie Roy was one besides!

"It was Quarry did it," Kenny explained, seeing the question still on Roger's face. "He was a Master himself, see."

A Master Mason, that was, and head of a small military lodge, composed of the officers of the garrison. One of their members had died recently, though, leaving them one man short of the required seven. Quarry had considered the situation, and after some cautiously exploratory conversation on the matter, invited Fraser to join them. A gentleman was a gentleman, after all, Jacobite or no.

Not precisely an orthodox situation, Roger thought, but this Quarry sounded the type to adjust regulations to suit himself. For that matter, so was Fraser.

"So Quarry made him, and he moved from Apprentice to Fellow Craft in a month's time, and was a Master himself a month after that—and that was when he chose to tell us of it. And so we founded a new lodge that night, the seven of us— Ardsmuir Lodge Number Two."

Roger snorted in wry amusement, seeing it.

"Aye. You six—and Christie." Tom Christie the Protestant. And Christie, stiff-necked but honorable, sworn to the Mason's oaths, would have had no choice, but been obliged to accept Fraser and his Catholics as brethren.

"To start with. Within three months, though, every man in the cells was made Apprentice. And there wasna so much trouble after that."

There wouldn't have been. Freemasons held as basic principles the notions of equality—gentleman, crofter, fisherman, laird; such distinctions were not taken account of in a lodge—and tolerance. No discussion of politics or religion among the brothers, that was the rule.

"I can't think it did Jamie any harm to belong to the officers' lodge, either," Roger said.

"Oh," said Kenny, rather vaguely. "No, I dinna suppose it did." He pushed back his stool and made to rise; the story was done; the dark had come and it was time to light a candle. He made no move toward the clay candlestick that stood on the hearth, but Roger glanced toward the glow of the banked fire, and noticed for the first time that there was no smell of cooking food.

"It's time I was away home for supper," he said, rising himself. "Come with me, aye?"

Kenny brightened noticeably.

"I will, then, *a Smeòraich*, and thanks. Give me a moment to milk the goats, and I'll be right along."

WHEN I CAME BACK upstairs next morning after a delicious breakfast featuring omelettes made with minced buffalo meat, sweet onions, and mushrooms, I found Jamie awake, though not noticeably bright-eyed.

"How are you this morning?" I asked, setting down the tray I had brought him and putting a hand on his forehead. Still warm, but no longer blazing; the fever was nearly gone.

"I wish I were deid, if only so folk would stop asking how am I?" he replied grumpily. I took his mood as an indicator of returning health, and took my hand away.

"Have you used the chamberpot yet this morning?"

He raised one eyebrow, glowering.

"Have you?"

"You know, you are perfectly impossible when you don't feel well," I remarked, rising to peer into the crudely glazed pot for myself. Nothing.

"Does it not occur to ye, Sassenach, that perhaps it's yourself that's impossible when I'm ill? If ye're not feeding me some disgusting substance made of ground beetles and hoof-shavings, you're pokin' my belly and making intimate inquiries into the state of my bowels. Ahh!"

I had in fact pulled down the sheet and prodded him in the lower abdomen. No distention from a swollen bladder; his exclamation appeared to be due entirely to ticklishness. I quickly palpated the liver, but found no hardness—that was a relief.

"Have you a pain in your back?"

"I've a marked pain in my backside," he said, narrowing one eye at me and folding his arms protectively across his middle. "And it's getting worse by the moment."

"I am trying to determine whether the snake venom has affected your kidneys," I explained patiently, deciding to overlook this last remark. "If you can't piss—"

"I can do that fine," he assured me, pulling the sheet up to his chest, lest I demand proof. "Now, just leave me to my breakfast, and I'll—"

"How do you know? You haven't—"

"I have." Seeing my skeptical glance at the chamberpot, he glowered under his brows, and muttered something ending in ". . . window." I swung round to the open window, shutters open and sash raised in spite of the chilly morning air.

"You did what?"

"Well," he defended himself, "I was standing up, and I just thought I would, that's all."

"Why were you standing up?"

"Oh, I thought I would." He blinked at me, innocent as a day-old child. I left the question, going on to more important matters.

"Was there blood in—"

"What have ye brought for my breakfast?" Ignoring my

clinical inquiries, he rolled to one side, and lifted the napkin draped over the tray. He looked at the bowl of bread and milk thus revealed, then turned his head, giving me a look of the most profound betrayal.

Before he could start in on further grievances, I forestalled him by sitting down on the stool beside him and demanding bluntly, "What's wrong with Tom Christie?"

He blinked, taken by surprise.

"Is something amiss wi' the man?"

"I wouldn't know; I haven't seen him."

"Well, I havena seen him in more than twenty years myself," he said, picking up the spoon and prodding the bread and milk suspiciously. "If he's grown a spare head in that time, it's news to me."

"Ho," I said tolerantly. "You may—and I say *may*—possibly have fooled Roger, but I know you."

He looked up at that, and gave me a sidelong smile.

"Oh, aye? D'ye know I dinna care much for bread and milk?"

My heart fluttered at sight of that smile, but I maintained my dignity.

"If you're thinking of blackmailing me into bringing you a steak, you can forget it," I advised him. "I can wait to find out about Tom Christie, if I have to." I stood up, shaking out my skirts as though to leave, and turned toward the door.

"Make it parritch with honey, and I'll tell ye."

I turned round to find him grinning at me.

"Done," I said, and came back to the stool.

He considered for a moment, but I could see that he was only deciding how and where to begin.

"Roger told me about the Masonic lodge at Ardsmuir," I said, to help out. "Last night."

Jamie shot me a startled look.

"And where did wee Roger Mac find that out? Did Christie tell him?"

"No, Kenny Lindsay did. But evidently Christie gave Roger a Masonic sign of some sort when he arrived. I thought Catholics weren't allowed to be Masons, actually."

He raised one eyebrow.

"Aye, well. The Pope wasna in Ardsmuir prison, and I was. Though I havena heard that it's forbidden, forbye. So wee Roger's a Freemason, too, is he?"

"Apparently. And perhaps it isn't forbidden, now. It will be, later." I flapped a hand, dismissing it. "There's something else about Christie, though, isn't there?"

He nodded, and glanced away.

"Aye, there is," he said quietly. "D'ye recall a Sergeant Murchison, Sassenach?"

"Vividly." I had met the Sergeant only once, more than two years previously, in Cross Creek. The name seemed familiar in some other, more recent context, though. Then I recalled where I had heard it.

"Archie Hayes mentioned him—or them. That was it; there were two of them, twins. One of them was the man who shot Archie at Culloden, wasn't he?"

Jamie nodded. His eyes were hooded, and I could see that he was looking back into the time he had spent in Ardsmuir.

"Aye. And to shoot a lad in cold blood was nay more than one could expect from either of them. A crueler pair I hope never to meet." The corner of his mouth turned up, but without humor. "The only thing I ken to Stephen Bonnet's credit is that he killed one o' yon lurdans."

"And the other?" I asked.

"I killed the other."

The room seemed suddenly very quiet, as though the two of us were far removed from Fraser's Ridge, alone together, that bald statement floating in the air between us. He was looking straight at me, blue eyes guarded, waiting to see what I would say. I swallowed.

"Why?" I asked, vaguely surprised at the calmness of my own voice.

He did look away then, shaking his head.

"A hundred reasons," he said softly, "and none." He rubbed absently at his wrist, as though feeling the weight of iron fetters.

"I could tell ye stories of their viciousness, Sassenach, and they would be true. They preyed upon the weak, robbing and beating—and they were the sort who took delight in cruelty for its own sake. There's no recourse against such men, not in a prison. But I dinna say so as an excuse—for there is none."

The prisoners at Ardsmuir were used for labor, cutting peats, quarrying and hauling stone. They worked in small groups, each group guarded by an English soldier, armed with musket and club. The musket, to prevent escape—the club, to enforce orders and ensure submission.

"It was summer. Ye'll ken the summer in the Highlands, Sassenach—the summer dim?"

I nodded. The summer dim was the light of the Highland night, early in summer. So far to the north, the sun barely set on Midsummer's Eve; it would disappear below the horizon, but even at midnight, the sky was pale and milky white, and the air was not dark, but seemed filled with unearthly mist.

The prison governor took advantage of the light, now and then, to work the prisoners into the late hours of the evening.

"We didna mind so much," Jamie said. His eyes were open, but fixed on whatever he was seeing in the summer dim of memory. "It was better to be outside than in. And yet, by the evening, we would be so droukit wi' fatigue that we could barely set one foot before the other. It was like walking in a dream."

Both guards and men were numb with exhaustion, by the time the work of the day was done. The groups of prisoners were collected, formed up into a column, and marched back toward the prison, shuffling across the moorland, stumbling and nodding, drunk with the need to fall down and sleep.

"We were still by the quarry, when they set off; we were to load the wagon wi' the stone-cutting tools and the last of the blocks, and follow. I remember—I heaved a great block up into the wagon bed, and stood back, panting wi' the effort. There was a sound behind me, and I turned to see Sergeant Murchison—Billy, it was, though I didna find that out 'til later."

The Sergeant was no more than a squat black shape in the dim, face invisible against a sky the color of an oyster's shell.

"I wondered, now and then, if I wouldna have done it, had

I seen his face." The fingers of Jamie's left hand stroked his wrist absently, and I realized that he still felt the weight of the irons he had worn.

The Sergeant had raised his club, poked Jamie hard in the ribs, then used it to point to a maul left lying on the ground. Then the Sergeant turned away.

"I didna think about it for a moment," Jamie said softly. "I was on him in two steps, wi' the chain of my fetters hard against his throat. He hadna time to make a sound."

The wagon stood no more than ten feet from the lip of the quarry pool; there was a drop of forty feet straight down, and the water below, a hundred feet deep, black and waveless under that hollow white sky.

"I tied him to one of the blocks and threw him over, and then I went back to the wagon. The two men from my group were there, standing like statues in the dim, watching. They said nothing, nor did I. I stepped up and took the reins, they got into the back of the wagon, and I drove toward the prison. We caught up to the column before too long, and all went back together, without a word. No one missed Sergeant Murchison until the next evening, for they thought he was down in the village, off-duty. I dinna think they ever found him."

He seemed to notice what he was doing, then, and took his hand away from his wrist.

"And the two men?" I asked softly. He nodded.

"Tom Christie and Duncan Innes."

He sighed deeply, and stretched his arms, shifting his shoulders as though to ease the fit of his shirt—though he wore a loose nightshirt. Then he raised one hand and turned it to and fro, frowning at his wrist in the light.

"That's odd," he said, sounding faintly surprised.

"What is?"

"The marks—they're gone."

"Marks . . . from the irons?" He nodded, examining both his wrists in bemusement. The skin was fair, weathered to a pale gold, but otherwise unblemished.

"I had them for years—from the chafing, aye? I never noticed that they'd gone."

I set a hand on his wrist, rubbing my thumb gently over the pulse where his radial artery crossed the bone.

"You didn't have them when I found you in Edinburgh, Jamie. They've been gone a long time."

He looked down at his arms, and shook his head, as though unable to believe it.

"Aye," he said softly. "Well, so has Tom Christie."

# PART NINE

*A Dangerous Business*

# 96

# AURUM

IT WAS QUIET IN THE HOUSE; Mr. Wemyss had gone to the gristmill, taking Lizzie and Mrs. Bug with him, and it was too late in the day for anyone on the Ridge to come visiting—everyone would be at their chores, seeing that the beasts were fed and bedded down, wood and water fetched, the fires built up for supper.

My own beast was already fed and bedded; Adso perched in a somnolent ball in a patch of late sun on the window ledge, feet tucked up and eyes closed in an ecstasy of reple-tion. My contribution to the supper—a dish Fergus referred to elegantly as *lapin aux chanterelles* (known as rabbit stew to the vulgar among us)—had been burbling cheerfully away in the cauldron since early morning, and needed no attention from me. As for sweeping the floor, polishing the windows, dusting, and general drudgery of that sort . . . well, if women's work was never done, why trouble about how much of it wasn't being accomplished at any given moment?

I fetched down ink and pen from the cupboard, and the big black clothbound casebook, then settled myself to share Adso's sun. I wrote up a careful description of the growth on little Geordie Chisholm's ear, which would bear watching, and added the most recent measurements I had taken of Tom Christie's left hand.

Christie *did* suffer from arthritis in both hands, and had a slight degree of clawing in the fingers. Having observed him closely at dinner, though, I was nearly sure that what I was seeing in the left hand was not arthritis, but Dupuytren's con-tracture—an odd, hooklike drawing-in of the ring and little fingers toward the palm of the hand, caused by shortening of the palmar aponeurosis.

Ordinarily, I should have been in no doubt, but Christie's hands were so heavily callused from years of labor that I couldn't feel the characteristic nodule at the base of the ring finger. The finger had felt *wrong* to me, though, when I'd first looked at the hand—in the course of stitching a gash across the heel of it—and I'd been checking it, whenever I caught sight of Tom Christie and could persuade him to let me look at it—which wasn't often.

In spite of Jamie's apprehensions, the Christies had been ideal tenants so far, living quietly and keeping largely to themselves, aside from Thomas Christie's schoolmastering, at which he appeared to be strict but effective.

I became aware of a looming presence just behind my head. The sunbeam had moved, and Adso with it.

"Don't even think of it, cat," I said. A rumbling purr of anticipation started up in the vicinity of my left ear, and a large paw reached out and delicately patted the top of my head.

"Oh, all right," I said, resigned. No choice, really, unless I wanted to get up and go write somewhere else. "Have it your way."

Adso could not resist hair. Anyone's hair, whether attached to a head or not. Fortunately, Major MacDonald had been the only person reckless enough to sit down within Adso's reach while wearing a wig, and after all, I *had* got it back, though it meant crawling under the house where Adso had retired with his prey; no one else dared snatch it from his jaws. The Major had been rather austere about the incident, and while it hadn't stopped him coming round to see Jamie now and then, he no longer removed his hat on such visits, but sat drinking chicory coffee at the kitchen table, his tricorne fixed firmly on his head and both eyes fixed firmly upon Adso, monitoring the cat's whereabouts.

I relaxed a bit, not quite purring myself, but feeling quite mellow. It was rather soothing to have the cat knead and comb with his half-sheathed claws, pausing now and then in his delicate grooming to rub his face lovingly against my head. He was only really dangerous if he'd been in the catnip, but that was safely locked up. Eyes half-closed, I contemplated the minor complication of describing Depuytren's contracture without calling it that, Baron Depuytren not having been born yet.

Well, a picture was worth a thousand words, and I thought I could produce a competent line drawing, at least. I did my best, meanwhile wondering how I was to induce Thomas Christie to let me operate on the hand.

It was a fairly quick and simple procedure, but given the lack of anesthesia and the fact that Christie was a strict Presbyterian and a teetotaller . . . perhaps Jamie could sit on his chest, Roger on his legs. If Brianna held his wrist tightly . . .

I gave up the problem for the moment, yawning drowsily. The drowsiness disappeared abruptly, as a three-inch yellow dragonfly came whirring in through the open window with a noise like a small helicopter. Adso sailed through the air after it, leaving my hair in wild disarray and my ribbon—which he appeared to have been quietly chewing—hanging wet and mangled behind my left ear. I removed this object with mild distaste, laid it on the sill to dry, and flipped back a few pages, admiring the neat drawing I had done of Jamie's snakebite, and of Brianna's rattlesnake hypodermic.

The leg, to my amazement, had healed cleanly and well, and while there had been a good bit of tissue sloughing, the maggots had dealt with that so effectively that the only permanent traces were two small depressions in the skin where the original fang marks had been, and a thin, straight scar across the calf where I had made an incision for debridement and maggot-placement. Jamie had a slight limp still, but I thought this would cure itself in time.

Humming in a satisfied sort of way, I flipped back farther, idly browsing through the last few pages of Daniel Rawlings' notes.

> *Josephus Howard . . . chief complaint being a fistula of the rectum, this of so long a standing as to have become badly abscessed, together with an advanced case of Piles. Treated with a decoction of Ale Hoof, mixed with Burnt Alum and small amount of Honey, this boiled together with juice of Marigold.*

A later note on the same page, dated a month later, referred to the efficacy of this compound, with illustrations of the condition of the patient before and after administration. I raised a brow at the drawings; Rawlings was no more an artist than I was, but had succeeded in capturing, to a remarkable degree, the intrinsic discomfort of the condition.

I tapped the quill against my mouth, thinking, then added a careful note in the margin, to the effect that a diet rich in fibrous vegetables should be recommended as an adjunct to this treatment, useful also in preventing both constipation and the more serious complications thereof—nothing like a little object lesson!

I wiped the quill, laid it down, and turned the page, wondering whether Ale Hoof was a plant—and if so, which one—or a suppurative condition of horses' feet. I could hear Jamie rustling about in his study; I'd go ask him in a moment.

I nearly missed it. It had been jotted on the back of the page containing the drawing of Mr. Howard's fistula, evidently added as a casual afterthought on the day's activities.

> *Have spoke with Mr. Hector Cameron of River*
> *Run, who begs me come examine his wife's eyes, her*
> *sight being sadly affected. It is a far distance to his*
> *plantation, but he will send a horse.*

That bit overcame the soporific atmosphere of the afternoon at once. Fascinated, I sat up and turned the page, looking to see whether the doctor had in fact examined Jocasta. I had—with some difficulty—persuaded her to allow me to examine her eyes once, and I was curious as to Rawlings' conclusions. Without an ophthalmoscope, there was no way of making sure of the cause of her blindness, but I had strong suspicions—and I could at least rule out such things as cataracts and diabetes with a fair amount of certainty. I wondered whether Rawlings had seen anything I had missed, or whether her condition had changed noticeably since he had seen her.

> *Bled the smith of a pint, purged his wife with senna oil (10 minims), and administered 3 minims of same to the cat (gratis), I having observed a swarming of worms in the animal's stool.*

I smiled at that; however crude his methods, Daniel Rawlings was a good doctor. I wondered once again what had happened to him, and whether I should ever get the chance to meet him. I had the rather sad feeling that I should not; I couldn't imagine a doctor not returning somehow to claim such beautiful instruments as his, if he was in any condition to do so.

Under the prodding of my curiosity, Jamie had obligingly made inquiries, but with no results. Daniel Rawlings had set out for Virginia—leaving his box of instruments behind—and had promptly vanished into thin air.

Another page, another patient; bleeding, purging, lancing of boils, removal of an infected nail, drawing of an abscessed tooth, cautery of a persistent sore on a woman's leg . . . Rawlings had found plenty of business in Cross Creek. Had he ever made it as far as River Run, though?

Yes, there it was, a week later and several pages on.

> *Reached River Run after a dire journey, wind and rain fit to sink a ship, and the road washed away entirely in places, so was obliged to ride cross-country, lashed by hail, mud to the eyebrows. Had set out at dawn with Mr. Cameron's black servant, who brought a horse for me—did not reach sanctuary 'til well past dark, exhausted and starving. Made welcome by Mr. Cameron, who gave me brandy.*

Having gone to the expense of procuring a doctor, Hector Cameron had evidently decided to make the most of the opportunity, and had had Rawlings examine all the slaves and servants, as well as the master of the house himself.

> *Aged Seventy-three, of middling height, broad-shouldered, but somewhat bowed in Stature,* Rawlings

had written of Hector, *with hands so gnarled by
rheumatism as to make the handling of any implement
more subtle than a spoon impossible. Otherwise, is
well-preserved, very Vigorous in his age. Complains of
rising in the night, painful Micturition. I am inclined
to suspect a prurient Distemper of the Bladder, rather
than Stone or chronic Disease of the inward male
parts, as the complaint is recurrent, but not of long
standing on any occasion of its evidence—two weeks
being the average duration of each attack and accompanied by Burning in the male Organ. A low fever, tenderness upon palpation of the lower abdomen and a
Black Urine, smelling strongly, incline me further to
this belief.*

*The household being possessed of a good quantity
of dried cranberries, have prescribed a decoction, the
inspissated juice to be drunk thrice daily, a cupful at a
time. Also recommend infusion of Cleavers, drunk
morning and evening, for its cooling Effect, and in
case of there being Gravel present in the Bladder,
which may aggravate this Condition.*

I found myself nodding approvingly. I didn't always agree
with Rawlings, either in terms of diagnosis or treatment, but
I thought he was likely spot-on on this occasion. What about
Jocasta, though?

There she was, on the next page.

*Jocasta Cameron, Sixty-four years in age, tri-
gravida, well-nourished and in good Health generally,
very youthful in Aspect.*

*Tri-gravida?* I paused for a moment at that matter-of-fact
remark. So plain, so stark a term, to stand for the bearing—
let alone the loss—of three children. To have raised three
children past the dangers of infancy, only to lose them all at
once, and in such cruel fashion. The sun was warm, but I felt
a chill on my heart, thinking of it.

If it was Brianna? Or little Jemmy? How did a woman
bear such loss? I had done it, myself, and still had no idea. It

had been a long time, and yet still, now and then, I would wake in the night, feeling a child's warm weight sleeping on my breast, her breath warm on my neck. My hand rose and touched my shoulder, curved as though the child's head lay there.

I supposed that it might be easier to have lost a daughter at birth, without the years of acquaintance that would leave ragged holes in the fabric of daily life. And yet I knew Faith to the last atom of her being; there was a hole in my heart that fit her shape exactly. Perhaps it was that that had been a natural death, at least; it gave me the feeling that she was still with me in some way, was taken care of, and not alone. But to have children slain in blood, butchered in war?

So many things could happen to children in this time. I returned to my perusal of her case history with a troubled mind.

*No sign of organic Illness, nor external Damage to the Eyes. The White of the Eye is clear, the lashes free of any Matter, no Tumor visible. The Pupils respond normally to a Light passed before them, and to shading of the Light. A candle held close to one side illuminates the vitreous Humor of the Eye, but shows no Defect therein. I note a slight Clouding, indicating incipient Cataract in the lens of the right eye, but this is insufficient to explain the gradual loss of Sight.*

"Hum," I said aloud. Both Rawlings' observations and his conclusions matched mine. He briefly noted the length of time over which sight had failed—roughly two years—and the process of its failure—nothing abrupt, but a gradual shrinking of the field of vision.

I thought it likely had taken longer; sometimes the loss was so gradual that people didn't notice the tiny decrements at all, until the sight was seriously threatened.

*. . . bits of the vision whittled away like cheese parings. Even the small remnant of sight remaining is of use only in dim light, as patient exhibits great irritation and pain when the eye is exposed to strong sunlight.*

> *I have seen this condition twice before, always in*
> *persons of some age, though not so far advanced.*
> *Gave it as my opinion that sight would soon be com-*
> *pletely obliterated, with no amelioration possible. For-*
> *tunately, Mr. Cameron has a black servant capable of*
> *reading, whom he has given to his wife to accompany*
> *her and warn her of obstacles, likewise to read to her*
> *and apprise her of her surroundings.*

It had gone further than that now; the light had gone, and
Jocasta was entirely blind. So, a progressive condition—that
didn't tell me much, most of them were. When had Rawlings
seen her?

It could be any number of conditions—macular degenera-
tion, tumor of the optic nerve, parasitic damage, retinitis pig-
mentosa, temporal arteritis—probably not retinal detachment,
that would have happened abruptly—but my own preliminary
suspicion was of glaucoma. I remembered Phaedre, Jocasta's
body servant, wringing out cloths in cold tea, observing that
her mistress was suffering from headache *"again,"* in a tone
of voice that suggested this was a frequent occurrence—and
Duncan asking me to make up a lavender pillow, to ease his
wife's "megrims."

The headaches might have nothing to do with Jocasta's
eyesight, though—and I had not inquired at the time as to the
nature of the headaches; they might be simple tension
headaches or migraines, rather than the pressure-band type
that might—or might not—attend glaucoma. Arteritis would
cause frequent headache, too, after all. The frustrating thing
about it was that glaucoma by itself had absolutely no predictable symptoms—save eventual blindness. It was caused
by a failure of proper drainage of the fluid inside the eyeball,
so that pressure inside the eye increased to the point of damage, with no warning at all to the patient or her physician.
But other kinds of blindness were largely symptomless as
well . . .

I was still contemplating the possibilities, when I became
aware that Rawlings had continued his notes onto the back of
the page—in Latin.

I blinked at that, a little surprised. I could tell that he had written it as a continuation of the earlier passage; quill-writing shows a characteristic darkening and fading of words, as the ink is renewed with each dip of the pen, and the shading of each passage tended to be different, as different inks were used. No, this had been written at the same time as the passage on the preceding page.

But why drop suddenly into Latin? Rawlings knew some Latin, plainly—which argued some degree of formal education, even if not formal medical education—but he didn't normally use it in his clinical notes, beyond the occasional word or phrase required for the formal description of some condition. Here was a page and a half of Latin, though, and written in scrupulous letters, smaller than his usual writing, as though he had thought carefully about the contents of the passage—or perhaps as though he felt secretive about it, as the Latin itself seemed to argue.

I flipped back through the casebook, checking to verify my impression. No, he had written in Latin here and there—but not often, and always as he did here; as the continuation of a passage begun in English. How odd. I turned back to the passage concerning River Run and began to try to puzzle it out.

Within a sentence or two, I abandoned the effort and went to find Jamie. He was in his own study, across the hall, writing letters. Or not.

The inkstand—made of a small gourd with a cork to keep the ink from drying—stood at hand, freshly filled; I could smell the woody reek of oak galls brewed with iron filings. A new turkey quill lay on the desk, trimmed to a point of such sharpness that it looked more suitable for stabbing than writing, and a fresh sheet of paper lay on the blotter, three words black and lonely at its head. It took no more than a glance at his face to know what they said.

*My dear Sister.*

He looked up at me, smiled wryly, and shrugged.

"What shall I say?"

"I don't know." At sight of him, I had shut the casebook, clasping it under one arm. I came in and stood behind him, laying a hand on his shoulder. I squeezed gently, and he laid his own hand over mine for a moment, then reached to pick up the quill.

"I canna go on saying that I'm sorry." He rolled the quill slowly to and fro between his thumb and middle finger. "I've said it in each letter. If she was disposed to forgive me . . ."

If she was, Jenny would have replied by now to at least one of the letters that he sent faithfully to Lallybroch each month.

"Ian's forgiven you. And the children." Missives from Jamie's brother-in-law arrived sporadically—but they did come, along with occasional notes from his namesake, Young Jamie, and now and then a line from Maggie, Kitty, Michael, or Janet. But the silence from Jenny was so deafening as to drown out all other communications.

"Aye, it would be worse if . . ." he trailed off, staring at the blank paper. In fact, nothing could be worse than this estrangement. Jenny was closer to him, more important to him, than anyone in the world—with the possible exception of myself.

I shared his bed, his life, his love, his thoughts. She had shared his heart and soul since the day he was born—until the day when he had lost her youngest son. Or so she plainly saw it.

It pained me to see him go on carrying the guilt of Ian's disappearance—and I felt some small resentment toward Jenny. I understood the depth of her loss, and sympathized with her grief, but still, Ian wasn't dead—so far as we knew. She alone could absolve Jamie, and surely she must know it.

I pulled up a stool and sat down by him, laying the book aside. A small stack of papers lay to one side, covered with his labored writing. It cost him dearly to write, wrong-handed, and that hand crippled—and yet he wrote stubbornly, almost every evening, recording the small events of the day. Visitors to the Ridge, the health of the animals, progress in building, new settlers, news from the Eastern counties . . . He wrote it down, one word at a time, to be sent off when some visitor arrived who would take the accumulated pages away, on the first stage of their precarious journey to Scotland. All the letters might not arrive at their destination, but some would. Likewise, most letters from Scotland would reach us, too—if they were sent.

For a time, I had hoped that Jenny's letter had simply been mis-sent, misplaced, lost somewhere in transit. But it had been too long, and I had stopped hoping. Jamie hadn't.

"I thought perhaps I should send her this." He shuffled through the stack of papers at the side of the desk, and withdrew a small sheet, stained and grubby, ragged along one edge where it had been torn from a book.

It was a message from Ian; the only concrete evidence we had that the boy was still alive and well. It had reached us at the Gathering in November, through the agency of John Quincy Myers, a mountain man who roamed the wilderness, as much at home with Indian as with settler, and more at home with deer and possum than with anyone who lived in a house.

Written in clumsy Latin as a joke, the note assured us that Ian was well, and happy. Married to a girl "in the Mohawk fashion" (meaning, I thought, that he had decided to share her house, bed, and hearth, and she had decided to let him), he expected to become a father himself "in the spring." And that was all. Spring had come and gone, with no further word. Ian wasn't dead, but the next thing to it. The chances of us ever seeing him again were remote, and Jamie knew it; the wilderness had swallowed him.

Jamie touched the ratty paper gently, tracing the round, still-childish letters. He'd told Jenny what the note said, I knew—but I also knew why he hadn't sent the original before. It was the only physical link with Ian; to give it up was in some final way to relinquish him to the Mohawk.

*"Ave!"* said the note, in Ian's half-formed writing. *"Ian salutat avunculus Jacobus."* Ian salutes his uncle James.

Ian was more to Jamie than one of his nephews. Much as he loved all of Jenny's children, Ian was special—a foster-son, like Fergus; but unlike Fergus, a son of Jamie's blood, replacement in a way for the son he had lost. That son wasn't dead, either, but could not ever be claimed. The world seemed suddenly full of lost children.

"Yes," I said, my throat tight. "I think you should send it. Jenny should have it, even if . . ." I coughed, reminded suddenly by the note of the casebook. I reached for it, hoping it would distract him.

"Um. Speaking of Latin . . . there's an odd bit in here. Could you have a look at it, perhaps?"

"Aye, of course." He set Ian's note aside and took the book from me, moving it so the last of the afternoon sun fell across the page. He frowned slightly, a finger tracing the lines of writing.

"Christ, the man's no more grasp of Latin grammar than ye have yourself, Sassenach."

"Oh, thanks. We can't all be scholars now, can we?" I moved closer, peering over his shoulder as he read. I'd been right, then; Rawlings didn't drop casually into Latin for the fun of it, or merely to show off his erudition.

"An oddity . . ." Jamie said, translating slowly as his finger moved across the page. "I am awake—no, he means 'I was wakened,' I think—by sounds in the chamber adjoining that where I lay. I am thinking—'I thought'—that my patient went to make water, and am risen to follow . . . Why should he do that, I wonder?"

"The patient—it's Hector Cameron, by the way—had a problem with his bladder. Rawlings would have wanted to watch him urinate, to see what sort of difficulty he had, whether he had pain, or blood in the urine, that sort of thing."

Jamie gave me a side-long glance, one brow raised, then shook his head and returned to the casebook, murmuring something about the peculiar tastes of physicians.

"*Homo procediente* . . . the man proceeds . . . Why does he call him 'the man,' rather than his name?"

"He was writing in Latin to be secret," I said, impatient to hear what came next. "If Cameron saw his name in the book, he'd be curious, I expect. What happened?"

"The man goes out—outdoors, does he mean, or only out of his chamber?—outdoors, it must be . . . goes out, and I follow. He walks steadily, quickly . . . Why should he not? Oh, here—I am puzzled. I give—have given—the man twelve grains of laudanum . . ."

"Twelve *grains*? Are you sure that's what he says?" I leaned over Jamie's arm, peering, but sure enough—he pointed to the entry, inscribed in clear black and white. "But that's enough laudanum to fell a horse!"

"Aye, 'twelve grains of laudanum to assist sleep,' he says.

No wonder the doctor was puzzled, then, to see Cameron scampering about the lawn in the middle of the night."

I nudged him with an elbow.

"Get on!"

"Mmphm. Well, he says he went to the necessary house—no doubt thinking to find Cameron—but no one was there, and there wasna any smell of . . . er . . . he didna think anyone had been there recently."

"You needn't be delicate on my account," I said.

"I know," he said, grinning. "But my own sensibilities are no quite coarsened yet, in spite of my long association with you, Sassenach. Ow!" He jerked away, rubbing his arm where I had pinched him. I lowered my brows and gave him a stare, though inwardly pleased to have lightened the mood for both of us.

"Less about your sensibilities, *if* you please," I said, tapping my foot. "Besides, you haven't got any in the first place, or you'd never have married me. Where was Cameron, then?"

He scanned the page, lips silently forming words.

"He doesna ken. He prowled about the place until the butler popped out of his wee hole, thinking him a marauder of some sort, and threatened him wi' a bottle of whisky."

"A formidable weapon, that," I observed, smiling at the thought of a nightcapped Ulysses, brandishing his implement of destruction. "How do you say 'bottle of whisky' in Latin?"

Jamie gave the page a glance.

"*He* says '*aqua vitae*,' which is doubtless as close as he could manage. It must have been whisky, though; he says the butler gave him a dram to cure the shock."

"So he never found Cameron?"

"Aye, he did, after he left Ulysses. Tucked up in his wee white bed, snoring. Next morning, he asked, but Cameron didna recall getting up in the night." He flipped the page over with one finger and glanced at me. "Would the laudanum keep him from remembering?"

"It could do," I said, frowning. "Easily. But it's simply incredible that anyone with that much laudanum in him could have been up marching round in the first place . . . unless . . ." I cocked a brow at him, recalling Jocasta's remarks during our discussion at River Run. "Any chance your Uncle Hector was an opium-eater or the like? Someone who took a great deal of laudanum by habit would have a tolerance for it, and might not be really affected by Rawlings' dose."

Never one to be shocked by any intimation of depravity among his relatives, Jamie considered the suggestion, but finally shook his head.

"If so, I've heard naught of it. But then," he added logically, "there's no reason anyone would tell me so."

That was true enough. If Hector Cameron had had the means to indulge in imported narcotics—and he certainly had, River Run being one of the most prosperous plantations in the area—then it would have been no one's business save his own. Still, I did think someone might have mentioned it.

Jamie's mind was running on other lines.

"Why would a man leave his house in dead of night to piss, Sassenach?" he asked. "I *know* Hector Cameron had a chamber pot; I've used it myself. It had his name and the Cameron badge painted on the bottom."

"Excellent question." I stared down at the page of cryptic scratchings. "If Hector Cameron was having great pain or difficulty—passing a kidney stone, for example—I suppose he might have gone out, to avoid waking the house."

"I havena heard my uncle was an opium-eater, but I havena heard he was ower-mindful of his wife or servants' convenience, either," Jamie observed, rather cynically. "From all accounts, Hector Cameron was a bit of a bastard."

I laughed.

"No doubt that's why your aunt finds Duncan so congenial."

Adso wandered in, the remains of the dragonfly in his mouth, and sat down at my feet so I could admire his prize.

"Fine," I told him, with a cursory pat. "Don't spoil your appetite, though; there are a lot of cockroaches in the pantry that I want you to deal with."

"*Ecce homo,*" Jamie murmured thoughtfully, tapping a finger on the casebook. "A French homo, do you think?"

"A what?" I stared at him.

"Does it not occur to ye, Sassenach, that perhaps it wasna Cameron that the doctor followed outside?"

"Not 'til this minute, no." I leaned forward and peered at the page. "Why ought it to be anyone else, though, let alone a Frenchman?"

Jamie pointed to the edge of the page, where there were a few small drawings; doodles, I'd thought. The one under his finger was a fleur-de-lis.

*"Ecce homo,"* he said again, tapping it. "The doctor wasna easy in his mind about the man he followed—that's why he didna call him by name. If Cameron were drugged, then it was someone else who left the house that night—yet he doesna speak of anyone else who was present."

"But he might not mention it, unless he'd examined whoever it was," I argued. "He does put in personal notes, but most of this is strictly his case histories; his observations of his patients and the treatments he was administering. But still . . ." I frowned at the page. "A fleur-de-lis scribbled in the margin doesn't necessarily mean anything at all, let alone that there was a Frenchman there." Save Fergus, Frenchmen were not at all common in North Carolina. There were some French settlements south of Savannah, I knew—but that was hundreds of miles away.

The fleur-de-lis *could* be nothing more than a random doodle—and yet, Rawlings hadn't made such scribbles anywhere else in his book that I recalled. When he added drawings, they were careful and to the point, intended as a reminder to himself, or as a guide to any physician who should come after him.

Above the fleur-de-lis was a figure that looked rather like a triangle with a small circle at the apex and a curved base; below it was a sequence of letters. *Au et Aq.*

"A . . . u," I said slowly, looking at that. "Aurum."

"Gold?" Jamie glanced up at me, surprised. I nodded.

"It's the scientific abbreviation for gold, yes. 'Aurum et aqua.' Gold and water—I suppose he means *goldwasser*, bits of gold flake suspended in an aqueous solution. It's a remedy for arthritis—oddly enough, it often works, though no one knows why."

"Expensive," Jamie observed. "Though I suppose Cameron could afford it—perhaps he saved an ounce or two of his gold bars, eh?"

"He did say Cameron suffered from arthritis." I frowned at the page and its cryptic marginalia. "Maybe he meant to advise the use of *goldwasser* for the condition. But I don't know about the fleur-de-lis or that other thing—" I pointed at it. "It's not the symbol for any medical treatment *I* know of."

To my surprise, Jamie laughed.

"I shouldna think so, Sassenach. It's a Freemason's compass."

"It is?" I blinked at it, then glanced at Jamie. "Was Cameron a Mason?"

He shrugged, running a hand through his hair. Jamie never spoke of his own association with the Freemasons. He had been "made," as the saying went, in Ardsmuir, and beyond any secrecy imposed by membership in the society, he seldom spoke of anything that had happened between those dank stone walls.

"Rawlings must have been one as well," he said, clearly reluctant to talk about Freemasonry, but unable to keep from making logical connections. "Else he'd not have kent what that is." One long finger tapped the sign of the compass.

I didn't know quite what to say next, but was saved from indecision by Adso, who spit out a pair of amber wings, and sprang up onto the desk in search of more hors d'oeuvres. Jamie made a grab for the inkwell with one hand, and seized his new quill protectively in the other. Deprived of prey, Adso strolled to the edge of the desk and sat on the stack of Jamie's letters, tail waving gently as he pretended to admire the view.

Jamie's eyes narrowed at this insolence.

"Take your furry wee arse off of my correspondence, beast," he said, poking at Adso with the sharp end of his quill. Adso's big green eyes widened as they fixed on the tip of the moving feather, and his shoulder blades tensed in anticipation. Jamie twiddled the quill tantalizingly, and Adso made an abortive swipe at it with one paw.

I seized the cat hastily before mayhem could ensue, lifting him off the papers with a surprised and indignant *mirp!* of protest.

"No, that's *his* toy," I said to the cat, and gave Jamie a reproving look. "Come along now; there are cockroaches to attend to."

I reached for the casebook with my free hand, but to my surprise, Jamie stopped me.

"Let me keep it a bit longer, Sassenach," he said. "There's something verra odd about the notion of a French Freemason wandering River Run by night. I should like to see what else Dr. Rawlings might have to say when he's speaking Latin."

"All right." I hoisted Adso, who had begun to purr loudly in anticipation of cockroaches, to my shoulder, and glanced out the window. The sun had set to a burning glow beyond the chestnut trees, and I could hear the noise of women and children in the kitchen; Mrs. Bug was starting to lay the supper, helped by Brianna and Marsali.

"Dinner soon," I said, and bent to kiss the top of Jamie's head, where the last of the light touched his crown with fire. He smiled and touched his fingers to his lips and then to me, but he had already gone back to a perusal of the close-written pages by the time I reached the door. The single sheet with its three black words lay at the edge of the desk, forgotten—for the moment.

# CONDITIONS OF THE BLOOD

I CAUGHT A FLASH OF BROWN outside the door, and Adso shot off the counter as though someone had shouted "Fish!" The next best thing, evidently; it was Lizzie, on her way back from the dairy shed, a bowl of clotted cream in one hand, a butter dish in the other, and a large jug of milk pressed to her bosom, precariously held in place by her crossed wrists. Adso was twining round her ankles like a furry rope, in obvious hopes of tripping her up and making her drop the booty.

"Think again, cat," I told him, reaching to rescue the milk jug.

"Oh, thank ye, ma'am." Lizzie relaxed, easing her shoulders with a little sigh. "It's only as I didna want to be making two trips." She sniffed and tried to wipe her nose with a forearm, imperiling the butter.

I snatched a handkerchief from my pocket and applied it, repressing the maternal impulse to say, "Now, blow."

"Thank ye, ma'am," she repeated, bobbing.

"Are you quite well, Lizzie?" Without waiting for an answer, I took her by the arm and towed her into my surgery, where the large windows gave me light enough to see by.

"I'm well enough, ma'am. Truly, I'm fine!" she protested, clutching the cream and butter to her as though for protection.

She was pale—but Lizzie was always pale, looking as though she had not a corpuscle to spare. There was an odd pallid look to her skin, though, that gave me an uneasy feeling. It had been nearly a year since her last attack of malarial fever, and she did seem generally well, but . . .

"Come here," I said, drawing her toward a pair of high stools. "Have a seat, just for a moment."

Clearly unwilling, but not daring to protest, she sat down, balancing the dishes on her knees. I took them from her and—after a glance at Adso's unblinkingly predatory green gaze—put them in the cupboard for safekeeping.

Pulse normal—normal for Lizzie, that is; she tended always to be a trifle fast and shallow. Breathing . . . all right, no catch or wheezing. The lymph glands under the jaw were palpable, but that was not unusual; the malaria had left them permanently enlarged, like the curve of a quail's egg under the tender skin. Those in the neck were enlarged now, too, though—and those I generally could *not* feel.

I thumbed an eyelid up, peering closely at the pale gray orb that looked anxiously back. Superficially fine, though slightly bloodshot. Again, though—there was something not quite . . . right . . . about her eyes, though I couldn't put my finger on what that something might be. Could there possibly be a tinge of yellow to the white? I frowned, turning her head to the side with a hand under her unresisting chin.

"Hullo, there. Everything all right?" Roger paused in the doorway, a very large, very dead bird held nonchalantly in one hand.

"A turkey!" I exclaimed, summoning a warm note of admiration. I liked turkeys, all right, but Jamie and Bree had killed five of the enormous birds the week before, introducing a certain note of monotony into dinner of late. Three of the things were hanging in the smoking shed at the moment. On the other hand, wild turkeys were wily and difficult to kill, and so far as I knew, Roger had never managed to bag one before.

"Did you shoot it yourself?" I asked, coming dutifully to admire the thing. He held it by the feet, and the big cupped wings flapped halfway open, the breast-feathers catching sunlight in iridescent patterns of blackish green.

"No." Roger's face was flushed, from sun, excitement, or both, a warm hue spreading under the tanned skin. "I ran it down," he said proudly. "Hit it in the wing with a stone, then chased it and broke its neck."

"Wonderful," I said, with somewhat more genuine enthusiasm. We wouldn't have to pick buckshot out of the flesh while cleaning it, or risk breaking a tooth in the eating.

"It's a lovely bird, Mr. Mac." Lizzie had slid off her stool and come to admire it, too. "Such a fat one as it is! Will I take it and clean it for ye, then?"

"What? Oh, thanks, Lizzie, no—I'll, um, take care of it." The color rose a little higher under his skin, and I suppressed a smile. He meant he wanted to show off his catch to Brianna, in all its glory. He shifted the bird to his left hand, and held out the right to me, wrapped in a bloodstained cloth.

"I had a bit of an accident, wrestling the bird. Do you think perhaps . . . ?"

I unwrapped the cloth, pursing my lips at what lay underneath. The turkey, fighting for its life, had ripped three jagged gashes across the back of his hand with its claws. The blood had mostly clotted, but fresh drops welled up from the deepest puncture, rolling down his finger to drip on the floor.

"Oh, just a bit," I said, glancing up at him with eyebrows raised. "Yes, I do think perhaps. Come over here and sit down. I'll clean it, and—Lizzie! Wait a moment!"

Lizzie, seizing the distraction as an opportunity to escape, was sidling toward the door. She stopped as though shot in the back.

"Really, ma'am, I'm quite all right," she pleaded. "Nothing's wrong, really there isn't."

In fact, I had stopped her only to remind her to retrieve the butter and cream from the cupboard. Too late for the milk; Adso stood on his hind legs, head and shoulders stuck completely into the mouth of the jug, from which came small lapping noises. The sound of it echoed the small splat of Roger's blood dripping on the floor, though, and gave me a sudden thought.

"I've had an idea," I said. "Sit down again, Lizzie—I want just a tiny bit of your blood."

Lizzie looked like a field mouse that has suddenly looked up from its crumb to discover itself in the midst of a meeting of barn owls, but she wasn't the sort to defy an order from anyone. Very reluctantly, she climbed back onto the stool beside Roger, who had laid his turkey on the floor beside him.

"Why do you want blood?" he asked, interested. "You can have all ye want of mine, for free." Grinning, he lifted the injured hand.

"A generous offer," I said, laying out a linen cloth and a handful of clean glass rectangles. "But you haven't had malaria, have you?" I plucked Adso out of the milk jug by the scruff of the neck and dropped him on the floor, before reaching into the cupboard above.

"Not so far as I know." Roger was watching my preparations, deeply interested.

Lizzie gave a small, forlorn sound of mirth.

"Ye'd ken it well enough if ye had, sir."

"I suppose I would." He gave her a look of sympathy. "Very nasty, from all I hear."

"It is that. Your bones ache so ye think they've all broken inside ye, and your eyes flame like a demon's. Then the sweat pours off your skin in rivers, and the chills come on, fit to crack your teeth with the chatterin' . . ." She hunched into herself, shuddering at the memory. "I did think it was gone, though," she said, glancing uneasily at the lancet I was sterilizing in the flame of my alcohol lamp.

"I hope it is," I said, frowning at the tiny blade. I picked up a small cloth and the blue glass bottle that held my distilled alcohol, and thoroughly cleaned the tip of her middle finger. "Some people never have another attack after the first, and I do hope you're one of them, Lizzie. But for most people, it does come back now and then. I'm trying to find out whether yours might be coming back. Ready?"

Without waiting for her nod, I jabbed the lancet swiftly through the skin, then set it down and snatched up a glass slide. I squeezed the fingertip, dotting generous blood drops on each of three slides, then wrapped the cloth round her finger and let go.

Working swiftly, I took up a clean slide and laid it over a blood-drop, then drew it quickly away, smearing the blood thinly across the original slide. Again, and a third, and I laid them down to dry.

"That's all, then, Lizzie," I told her with a smile. "It will take a bit of preparation before these are ready to look at. When they are, I'll call you, shall I?"

"Oh . . . no, that's quite all right, ma'am," she murmured, sliding off the high stool with a fearful look at the blood-smeared slides. "I dinna need to see." She set down the discarded cloth, brushed at her apron, and scampered out of the room—forgetting the butter and cream, after all.

"Sorry to keep you waiting," I apologized to Roger. "I just thought . . ." I reached into the cupboard, withdrew three small earthenware pots, and uncorked them.

"Not a problem," he assured me. He watched with fascination as I checked each slide to be sure the blood-smear was dry, then slid a bit of glass into each of the pots.

"All right, then." Now I could turn my attention to cleaning and dressing his hand—a straightforward-enough process. "Not so bad as I thought," I murmured, wiping caked blood off his knuckles. "It bled quite a bit, which is good."

"Aye, if you say so." He didn't flinch at all, but carefully kept his face turned away from what I was doing, his attention focused out the window.

"Washes out the wounds," I explained, dabbing with alcohol. "I needn't swab so deeply to clean them."

He drew in his breath with a sharp hiss, then, to distract himself, nodded at the pots where the slides were soaking.

"Speaking of blood, what are you doing with Mistress Mousie's?"

"Trying something. I don't know whether it will work or not, but I've made up some experimental stains, using extracts from some of the dyeing-plants. If any of them work on blood, I'll be able to see the red cells clearly under the microscope—and what's in them." I spoke with a mixture of hope and tentative excitement.

Trying to duplicate cellular stains with the materials I had at hand was a long shot—but not totally unfeasible. I had the ordinary solvents—alcohol, water, turpentine and its distillates—and I had a great range of plant pigments to try, from indigo to rosehips, along with a good working knowledge of their dyeing properties.

I hadn't any crystal violet or carbofuchsin, but I had been able to produce a reddish stain that made epithelial cells highly visible, if only temporarily. It remained to be seen whether the same stain would work on red blood cells and their inclusions, or whether I should need to try differential staining.

"What *is* in them?" Roger turned to look at me, interested.

*"Plasmodium vivax,"* I said. "The protozoan that causes malaria."

"You can *see* it? I thought germs were much too small to see, even under a microscope!"

"You're as bad as Jamie," I said tolerantly. "Though I do love to hear a Scotsman say 'gerrrms.' Such a sinister word, spoken in a deep voice with that rolling 'r,' you know."

Roger laughed. The hanging had destroyed much of the power of his voice, but the lower, harsher registers remained.

"Nearly as good as murrrrderr," he said, rumbling like a cement mixer.

"Oh, nothing's as good as 'murrrderr' to a Scot," I assured him. "Bloody-minded blokes that you all are."

"What, all of us?" He grinned, plainly not minding this gross generalization in the least.

"To a man," I assured him. "Mild enough to look at, but insult a Scot or trouble his family, and it's up wi' the bonnets of bonnie Dundee. All the blue bonnets are over the border, and next thing you know, it's lances and swords all over the Haughs of Cromdale."

"Remarkable," he murmured, eyeing me. "And you've been married to one for . . ."

"Quite long enough." I finished my sponging and rinsing and blotted the back of his hand, small red patches soaking into the fresh gauze. "Speaking of bloody men," I added casually, "do you happen to know your own blood type?"

One dark brow went up at that. Well, I didn't mean to slip it by him, after all; I'd only wanted a way to broach the question.

"Yes," he said slowly, "I do. It's O-positive."

The dark green eyes were fixed on mine, steady with interest.

"Very interesting," I said. I replaced the gauze square with a fresh one, and started winding a bandage around it.

"Just *how* interesting is it?" he asked. I glanced at him, and met his eyes.

"Moderately." I drew out the slides, dripping pink and blue dyes. One slide I propped against the milk jug to dry, the other two I exchanged, putting the pink slide into the blue stain, and vice-versa.

"There are three main blood groups," I said, blowing gently on the propped-up slide. "More really, but those three are the ones everyone knows about. It's called the ABO grouping, and everyone is said to have type A, type B, or type O blood. The thing is, like all your other traits, it's determined genetically, and—human beings being heterosexual, generally speaking—you have one half your genes for any trait from one parent, the other half from the other."

"I dimly recall that bit from school," Roger said dryly. "All those bloody charts—excuse me—about hemophilia in the Royal Family, and the like. I assume it has a certain amount of personal significance now, though?"

"I don't know," I said. "It might have." The pink slide

looked dry; I laid it gently on the stage of the microscope and bent to adjust the mirror.

"The thing is," I said, squinting through the eyepiece as I twiddled the focusing knob, "those blood groups are to do with antibodies—little odd-shaped things on the surfaces of blood cells. That is, people who are type A have one sort of antibody on their cells, people with type B have a different sort, and people with type O don't have any at all."

The red blood cells showed up suddenly, faintly stained, like round pink ghosts. Here and there a blotch of darker pink indicated what might be a bit of cellular debris, or perhaps one of the larger white blood cells. Not much else, though.

"So," I went on, lifting the other two slides from their baths, "if one of his parents gave a child the gene for type O blood, and the other gave him one for type A, the child's blood will show up as type A, because it's the antibodies that are tested for. The child does still *have* the gene for type O, though."

I waved one of the slides gently in the air, drying it.

"My blood type is A. Now, I happen to know that my father's blood was type O. In order to show up with type O blood, that means that both his genes must have been for O. So whichever of those genes he gave me, it has to have been for O. The A gene therefore came from my mother."

Seeing a familiar glaze come over his features, I sighed and set the slide down. Bree had been drawing pictures of penicillin spores for me, and had left her pad and graphite pencil by the microscope. I took it and flipped to a fresh page.

"Look," I said, and drew a quick chart.

| Henry | Julia |
|---|---|
| OO=Type O | A?=A or AB |

| Claire |
|---|
| OA=Type A |

"Do you see?" I pointed with the stick of graphite. "I don't know my mother's type for sure, but it doesn't matter;

for me to have type A blood, she must have given me her gene for it, because my father hadn't one."

The next slide was nearly dry; I laid down the pencil, put the slide in place, and bent to look through the eyepiece.

"Can you see blood types—these antibodies—through a microscope?" Roger was quite close behind me.

"No," I said, not looking up. "The resolution's nowhere near good enough. But you can see other things—I hope." I moved the knob a fraction of an inch, and the cells sprang into focus. I let out the breath I had been holding, and a small thrill went through me. There they were; the disc-shaped pinkish blobs of the red blood cells—and here and there, inside a few of the cells, a darkish blob, some rounded, some looking like miniature nine-pins. My heart thumped with excitement, and I made a small exclamation of delight.

"Come look," I said, and stood aside. Roger bent, looking quizzical.

"What am I looking at?" he asked, squinting.

"*Plasmodium vivax*," I said proudly. "Malaria. The small dark blobs inside the cells." The rounded blobs were the protozoans, the single-celled creatures transferred to the blood in a mosquito's bite. The few that looked like bowling pins—those were protozoa in the act of budding, getting ready to reproduce themselves.

"When they bud," I explained, bending for another look myself, "they multiply until they burst the blood cell, and then they move into new blood cells, multiply, and burst those, too—that's when the patient suffers a malarial attack, with the fever and chills. When the *Plasmodium* are dormant—not multiplying—the patient is all right."

"And what makes them multiply?" Roger was fascinated.

"No one knows, exactly." I drew a deep breath, and corked up my bottles of stain again. "But you can check, to see what's happening, if they *are* multiplying. No one can live on quinine, or even take it for a long period—Jesuit bark is too expensive, and I don't know what the long-term effects on the body might be. And you can't touch most protozoans with penicillin, unfortunately.

"But I'll check Lizzie's blood every few days; if I see the

*Plasmodium* increasing sharply, then I'll start giving her the quinine at once. With luck, that might prevent an outbreak. Worth a try, certainly."

He nodded, looking at the microscope and the pink-and-blue-splotched slide.

"Well worth it," he said quietly.

He watched me move about, tidying up the small debris of my operations. As I bent to retrieve the bloody cloth in which he'd wrapped his hand, he asked, "And you know Bree's blood type, of course?"

"Type B," I said, eyes on the box of bandages. "Quite rare, particularly for a white person. You see it mostly in small, rather isolated populations—some Indian tribes in the American Southwest, certain black populations; probably they came from a specific area of Africa, but of course by the time blood groups were discovered, that connection had been long lost."

"Small, isolated populations. Scottish Highlanders, perhaps?"

I lifted my eyes.

"Perhaps."

He nodded silently, clearly thinking to himself. Then he picked up the pencil, and slowly drew a small chart of his own on the pad.

| Claire | Jamie |
|---|---|
| AO=Type A | B?=B or AB |

| Brianna |
|---|
| OB=Type B |

"That's right," I said, nodding as he looked up at me in question. "Exactly right."

He gave me a small, wry smile in response, then dropped his eyes, studying the charts.

"Can you tell, then?" he asked finally, not looking up. "For sure?"

"No," I said, and dropped the cloth into the laundry basket with a small sigh. "Or rather—I can't tell for sure whether Jemmy is yours. I *might* be able to tell for sure if he's not."

The flush had faded from his skin.

"How's that?"

"Bree is type B, but I'm type A. That means she'll have a gene for B *and* my gene for O, either of which she might have given Jemmy. You could only have given him a gene for type O, because that's all you have."

I nodded at a small rack of tubes near the window, the serum in them glowing brownish-gold in the late afternoon sun.

"So. If Bree gave him an O gene, and you—his father— gave him an O gene, he'd show up as type O—his blood won't have any antibodies, and won't react with serum from my blood or from Jamie's or Bree's. If Bree gave him her B gene, and you gave him an O, he'd show up as type B—his blood would react with my serum, but not Bree's. In either case, you might be the father—but so might anyone with type-O blood. IF, however—"

I took a deep breath, and picked up the pencil from the spot where Roger had laid it down. I drew slowly as I talked, illustrating the possibilities.

| Brianna | Roger |
|---|---|
| OB=Type B | OO=Type O |

Jemmy

OB or OO=Type B or Type O

*"But"*—I tapped the pencil on the paper—"if Jemmy were to show as type A or type AB—then his father was not homozygous for type O—homozygous means both genes are the same—and you are." I wrote in the alternatives, to the left of my previous entry.

| X | Brianna | Roger |
|---|---------|-------|
| AO/AA/AB/BB/BO/OO | BO=Type B | OO=Type O |

| Jemmy | Jemmy |
|-------|-------|
| AB=Type AB | BO=Type B |
| AO=Type A | OO=Type O |
| OB/BO=Type B | |
| BB=Type B | |
| OO=Type O | |

I saw Roger's eyes flick toward that "X," and wondered what had made me write it that way. It wasn't as though the contender for Jemmy's paternity could be just anyone, after all. Still, I could not bring myself to write "Bonnet"—perhaps it was simple superstition; perhaps just a desire to keep the thought of the man at a safe distance.

"Bear in mind," I said, a little apologetically, "that type O is very common, in the population at large."

Roger grunted, and sat regarding the chart, eyes hooded in thought.

"So," he said at last. "If he's type O or type B, he may be mine, but not for sure. If he's type A or type AB, he's not mine—for sure."

One finger rubbed slowly back and forth over the fresh bandage on his hand.

"It's a very crude test," I said, swallowing. "I can't—I mean, there's always the possibility of a mistake in the test itself."

He nodded, not looking up.

"You told Bree this?" he asked softly.

"Of course. She said she doesn't want to know—but that if you did, I was to make the test."

I saw him swallow, once, and his hand lifted momentarily to the scar across his throat. His eyes were fixed on the scrubbed planks of the floor, hardly blinking.

I turned away, to give him a moment's privacy, and bent over the microscope. I would have to make a grid, I thought—a counting grid that I could lay across a slide, to help me estimate the relative density of the *Plasmodium*-infected cells. For the moment, though, a crude eyeball count would have to do.

It occurred to me that now that I had a workable stain, I ought to test the blood of others on the Ridge—those in the household, for starters. Mosquitoes were much rarer in the mountains than near the coast, but there were still plenty, and while Lizzie might be well herself, she was still a sink of potential infection.

". . . four, five, six . . ." I was counting infected cells under my breath, trying to ignore both Roger on his stool behind me, and the sudden memory that had popped up, unbidden, when I told him Brianna's blood type.

She had had her tonsils removed at the age of seven. I still recalled the sight of the doctor, frowning at the chart he held—the chart that listed her blood type, and those of both her parents. Frank had been type A, like me. And two type-A parents could not, under any circumstances, produce a type B child.

The doctor had looked up, glancing from me to Frank and back, his face twisted with embarrassment—and his eyes filled with a kind of cold speculation as he looked at me. I might as well have worn a scarlet "A" embroidered on my bosom, I thought—or in this case, a scarlet "B."

Frank, bless him, had seen the look, and said easily, "My wife was a widow; I adopted Bree as a baby." The doctor's face had thawed at once into apologetic reassurance, and Frank had gripped my hand, hard, behind the folds of my skirt. My hand tightened in remembered acknowledgment, squeezing back—and the slide tilted suddenly, leaving me staring into blank and blurry glass.

There was a sound behind me, as Roger stood up. I turned round, and he smiled at me, eyes dark and soft as moss.

"The blood doesn't matter," he said quietly. "He's my son."

"Yes," I said, and my own throat felt tight. "I know."

A loud crack broke the momentary silence, and I looked down, startled. A puff of turkey-feathers drifted past my foot, and Adso, discovered in the act, rushed out of the surgery, the huge fan of a severed wing-joint clutched in his mouth.

"You *bloody* cat!" I said.

# 98

# CLEVER LAD

A COLD WIND BLEW from the east tonight; Roger could hear the steady whine of it past the mud-chinked wall near his head, and the lash and creak of the wind-tossed trees beyond the house. A sudden gust struck the oiled hide tacked over the window; it bellied in with a *crack!* and popped loose at one side, the whooshing draft sending papers scudding off the table and bending the candle flame sideways at an alarming angle.

Roger moved the candle hastily out of harm's way, and pressed the hide flat with the palm of his hand, glancing over his shoulder to see if his wife and son had been awakened by the noise. A kitchen-rag stirred on its nail by the hearth, and the skin of his bodhran thrummed faintly as the draft passed by. A sudden tongue of fire sprang up from the banked hearth, and he saw Brianna stir as the cold air brushed her cheek.

She merely snuggled deeper into the quilts, though, a few loose red hairs glimmering as they lifted in the draft. The trundle where Jemmy now slept was sheltered by the big bed; there was no sound from that corner of the room.

Roger let out the breath he had been holding, and rummaged briefly in the horn dish that held bits of useful rubbish, coming up with a spare tack. He hammered it home with the heel of his hand, muffling the draft to a small, cold seep, then bent to retrieve his fallen papers.

> *"O will ye let Telfer's kye gae back?*
> *Or will ye do aught for regard o' me?"*

He repeated the words in his mind as he wiped the half-dried ink from his quill, hearing the words in Kimmie Clellan's cracked old voice.

It was a song called "Jamie Telfer of the Fair Dodhead"—one of the ancient reiving ballads that went on for dozens of verses, and had dozens of regional variations, all involving the attempts of Telfer, a Borderer, to revenge an attack upon his home by calling upon the help of friends and kin. Roger knew three of the variations, but Clellan had had another—with a completely new subplot involving Telfer's cousin Willie.

> *"Or by the faith of my body, quo' Willie Scott.*
> *I'se ware my dame's calfskin on thee!"*

Kimmie sang to pass the time of an evening by himself, he had told Roger, or to entertain the hosts whose fire he shared. He remembered all the songs of his Scottish youth, and was pleased to sing them as many times as anyone cared to listen, so long as his throat was kept wet enough to float a tune.

The rest of the company at the big house had enjoyed two or three renditions of Clellan's repertoire, began to yawn and blink through the fourth, and finally had mumbled excuses and staggered glazen-eyed off to bed—*en masse*—leaving Roger to ply the old man with more whisky and urge him to another repetition, until the words were safely committed to memory.

Memory was a chancy thing, though, subject to random losses and unconscious conjectures that took the place of fact. Much safer to commit important things to paper.

> *"I winna let the kye gae back,*
> *Neither for thy love, nor yet thy fear . . ."*

The quill scratched gently, capturing the words one by one, pinned like fireflies to the page. It was very late, and Roger's muscles were cramped with chill and long sitting, but he was determined to get all the new verses down, while they were fresh in his mind. Clellan might go off in the morning to be eaten by a bear or killed by falling rocks, but Telfer's cousin Willie would live on.

> *"But I will drive Jamie Telfer's kye,*
> *In spite of every Scot that's . . ."*

The candle made a brief sputtering noise as the flame struck a fault in the wick. The light that fell across the paper shook and wavered, and the letters faded abruptly into shadow as the candle flame shrank from a finger of light to a glowing blue dwarf, like the sudden death of a miniature sun.

Roger dropped his quill, and seized the pottery candlestick with a muffled curse. He blew on the wick, puffing gently, in hopes of reviving the flame.

*"But Willie was stricken owre the head,"* he murmured to himself, repeating the words between puffs, to keep them fresh. *"But Willie was stricken owre the head/And through the knapscap the sword has gane/And Harden grat for very rage/When Willie on the grund lay slain . . . When Willie on the grund lay slain . . ."*

A ragged corona of orange rose briefly, feeding on his breath, but then dwindled steadily away despite continued puffing, winking out into a dot of incandescent red that glowed mockingly for a second or two before disappearing altogether, leaving no more than a wisp of white smoke in the half-dark room, and the scent of hot beeswax in his nose.

He repeated the curse, somewhat louder. Brianna stirred in the bed, and he heard the corn shucks squeak as she lifted her head with a noise of groggy inquiry.

"It's all right," he said in a hoarse whisper, with an uneasy glance at the trundle in the corner. "The candle's gone out. Go back to sleep."

*But Willie was stricken owre the head . . .*

"Ngm." A plop and sigh, as her head struck the goose-down pillow again.

Like clockwork, Jemmy's head rose from his own nest of blankets, his nimbus of fiery fluff silhouetted against the hearth's dull glow. He made a sound of confused urgency, not quite a cry, and before Roger could stir, Brianna had shot out of bed like a guided missile, snatching the boy from his quilt and fumbling one-handed with his clothing.

"Pot!" she snapped at Roger, poking blindly backward with one bare foot as she grappled with Jemmy's clothes. "Find the chamber pot! Just a minute, sweetie," she cooed to Jemmy, in an abrupt change of tone. "Wait juuuuust a minute, now . . ."

Impelled to instant obedience by her tone of urgency, Roger dropped to his knees, sweeping an arm in search through the black hole under the bed.

*Willie was stricken owre the head . . . And through the . . . kneecap? nobskull?* Overwhelmed by the situation, some remote bastion of memory clung stubbornly to the song, singing in his inner ear. Only the melody, though—the words were fading fast.

"Here!" He found the earthenware pot, accidentally struck the leg of the bed with it—thank Christ, it didn't break!—and bowled it across the floor to Bree.

She clapped the now-naked Jemmy down onto it with an exclamation of satisfaction, and Roger was left to grope about in the semi-dark for his fallen candle while she murmured encouragements.

"OK, sweetie, yes, that's right . . ."

*Willie was struck about . . . no, stricken . . .*

He found the candle, luckily uncracked, and sidled carefully round the drama in progress to kneel and relight the charred wick from the embers of the fire. While he was at it, he poked up the embers and added a fresh stick of wood. The fire revived, illuminating Jemmy, who was making what looked like a very successful effort to go back to sleep, in spite of his position and his mother's urging.

"Don't you need to go potty?" she was saying, shaking his shoulder gently.

"Go potty?" Roger said, this curious locution pushing the remnants of the verse from his mind. "What do you mean, *go* potty?" It was his personal opinion, based on current experience as a father, that small children were *born* potty, and improved very slowly thereafter. He said as much, causing Brianna to give him a remarkably dirty look.

*"What?"* she said, in an edgy tone. "What do you mean, they're *born potty*?" She had one hand on Jemmy's shoulder, balancing him, while the other cupped his round little belly, an index finger disappearing into the shadows below to direct his aim.

"Potty," Roger explained, with a brief circular gesture at his temple in illustration. "You know, barmy. Daft."

She opened her mouth to say something in reply to this, but Jemmy swayed alarmingly, his head sagging forward.

"No, no!" she said, taking a fresh grip. "Wake up, honey! Wake up and go potty!"

The insidious term had somehow taken up residence in Roger's mind, and was merrily replacing half the fading words of the verse he had been trying to recapture.

*Willie sat upon his pot/The sword to potty gane . . .*

He shook his head, as though to dislodge it, but it was too late—the real words had fled. Resigned, he gave it up as a bad job and crouched down next to Brianna to help.

"Wake up, chum. There's work to be done." He drew a finger gently under Jemmy's chin, then blew in his ear, ruffling the silky red tendrils that clung to the child's temple, still damp with sleep-sweat.

Jemmy's eyelids cracked in a slit-eyed glower. He looked like a small pink mole, cruelly excavated from its cozy burrow and peering balefully at an inhospitable upper world.

Brianna yawned widely, and shook her head, blinking and scowling in the candlelight.

"Well, if you don't like 'go potty,' what do you say in Scotland, then?" she demanded crabbily.

Roger moved the tickling finger to Jem's navel.

"Ah . . . I seem to recall a friend asking his wee son if he needed to do a poo," he offered. Brianna made a rude noise, but Jemmy's eyelids flickered.

"Poo," he said dreamily, liking the sound.

"Right, that's the idea," Roger said encouragingly. His finger twiddled gently in the slight depression, and Jemmy gave the ghost of a giggle, beginning to wake up.

"Pooooooo," he said. "Poopoo."

"Whatever works," Brianna said, still cross, but resigned.

"Go potty, go poo—just get it over with, all right? Mummy wants to go to sleep."

"Perhaps you should take your finger off of his . . . mmphm?" Roger nodded toward the object in question. "You'll give the poor lad a complex or something."

"Fine." Bree took her hand away with alacrity, and the stubby object sprang back up, pointing directly at Roger over the rim of the pot.

"Hey! Now, just a min—" he began, and got his hand up as a shield just in time.

"Poo," Jemmy said, beaming in drowsy pleasure.

"Shit!"

"Chit!" Jemmy echoed obligingly.

"Well, that's not quite—would you stop laughing?" Roger said testily, wiping his hand gingerly on a kitchen rag.

Brianna snorted and gurgled, shaking her head so the straggling locks of hair that had escaped her plait fell down around her face.

"*Good* boy, Jemmy!" she managed.

Thus encouraged, Jemmy took on an air of inner absorption, scrunched his chin down into his chest, and without further ado, proceeded to Act Two of the evening's drama.

"Clever lad!" Roger said sincerely.

Brianna glanced at him, momentary surprise interrupting her own applause.

He was surprised himself. He had spoken by reflex, and hearing the words, just for a moment, his voice hadn't sounded like his own. Very familiar—but not his own. It was like writing the words of Clellan's song, hearing the old man's voice, even as his own lips formed the words.

"Aye, that's clever," he said, more softly, and patted the little boy gently on his silky head.

He took the pot outside to empty it while Brianna put Jemmy back to bed with kisses and murmurs of admiration. Basic sanitation accomplished, he went to the well to wash his hands before coming back inside to bed.

"Are you through working?" Bree asked drowsily, as he slid into bed beside her. She rolled over and thrust her bottom unceremoniously into his stomach, which he took as a gesture of affection, given the fact that she was about thirty degrees warmer than he was after the sortie outside.

"Aye, for tonight." He put his arms round her and kissed the back of her ear, the warmth of her body a comfort and delight. She took his chilly hand in hers without comment, folded it, and tucked it snugly beneath her chin, with a small kiss on the knuckle. He stretched slightly, then relaxed, letting his muscles go slack and feeling the tiny movements as their bodies adjusted, shaping to each other. A faint buzzing snore rose from the trundle, where Jemmy slept the sleep of the righteously dry.

Brianna had freshly smoored the fire; it burned with a low, even heat and the sweet scent of hickory, making small occasional pops as the buried flame reached a pocket of resin or a spot of damp. Warmth crept over him, and sleep tiptoed in its wake, drawing a blanket of drowsiness up round his ears, unlocking the tidy cupboards of his mind, and letting all the thoughts and impressions of the day spill out in brightly colored heaps.

Resisting unconsciousness for a last few moments, he poked desultorily among the scattered riches thus revealed, in the faint hope of finding a corner of the Telfer song poking out; some scrap of word or music that would allow him to seize the vanished verses and drag them back into the light of consciousness. It wasn't the story of the ill-fated Willie that emerged from the rubble, though, but rather a voice. Not his own, and not that of old Kimmie Clellan, either.

*Clever lad!* it said, in a clear warm contralto, tinged with laughter. Roger jerked.

"Whaju say?" Brianna mumbled, disturbed by the movement.

"Go on—be clever," he said slowly, echoing the words as they formed in his memory. "That's what she said."

"Who?" Brianna turned her head, with a rustle of hair on the pillow.

"My mother." He put his free hand round her waist, resettling them both. "You asked what they said in Scotland. I'd forgotten, but that's what she used to say to me. 'Go on—be clever!' or 'Do ye need to be clever?' "

Bree gave a small grunt of sleepy amusement.

"Well, it's better than poo," she said.

They lay quiet for a bit. Then she said, still speaking softly, but with all traces of sleep gone from her voice, "You talk about your dad now and then—but I've never heard you mention your mother before."

He gave a one-shouldered shrug, bringing his knees up against the yielding backs of her thighs.

"I don't remember a lot about her."

"How old were you when she died?" Brianna's hand floated up to rest over his.

"Oh, four, I think, nearly five."

"Mmm." She made a small sound of sympathy, and squeezed his hand. She was quiet for a moment, alone in private thought, but he heard her swallow audibly, and felt the slight tension in her shoulders.

"What?"

"Oh . . . nothing."

"Aye?" He disengaged his hand, used it to lift the heavy plait aside, and gently massaged the nape of her neck. She turned her head away to make it easier, burying her face in the pillow.

"Just—I was just thinking—if I died now, Jemmy's so young—he wouldn't remember me at all," she whispered, words half-muffled.

"Yes, he would." He spoke in automatic contradiction, wanting to give her reassurance, even knowing that she was likely right.

"You don't remember, and you were lots older when you lost your mother."

"Oh . . . I do remember her," he said slowly, digging the ball of his thumb into the place where her neck joined her shoulder. "Only, it's just in bits and pieces. Sometimes, when I'm dreaming, or thinking of something else, I get a quick glimpse of her, or some echo of her voice. A few things I recall clearly—like the locket she used to wear round her neck, with her initials on it in wee red stones. Garnets, they were."

That locket had perhaps saved his life, during his first ill-fated attempt to pass through the stones. He felt the loss of it now and then, like a small thorn buried beneath the surface of the skin, but pushed the feeling aside, telling himself that after all, it was nothing more than a bit of metal.

At the same time, he missed it.

"That's a *thing*, Roger." Her voice held a hint of sharpness. "Do you remember *her*? I mean—what would Jemmy know about me—about you, for that matter—if all he had left of us was"—she cast about for some suitable object—"was your bodhran and my pocket knife?"

"He'd know his dad was musical, and his mum was bloodthirsty," Roger said dryly. "Ouch!" He recoiled slightly as her fist came down on his thigh, then set his hands placatingly on her shoulders. "No, really. He'd know a lot about us, and not just from the bits and bobs we'd left behind, though those would help."

"How?"

"Well . . ." Her shoulders had relaxed again; he could feel the slender edge of her shoulder blade, hard against the skin—she was too thin, he thought. "You studied history for a time, didn't you? You know how much one can tell from homely objects like dishes and toys."

"Mmm." She sounded dubious, but he thought that she simply wanted to be convinced.

"And Jem would know a lot more than that about you, from your drawings," he pointed out. *And a hell of a lot more than a son ought, if he ever read your dream-book,* he thought. The sudden impulse to say so, to confess that he himself had read it, trembled on his tongue, but he swallowed it. Beyond simple fear of how she might respond if she discovered his intrusion, was the greater fear that she would cease to write in it, and those small secret glimpses of her mind would be lost to him.

"I guess that's true," she said slowly. "I wonder if Jem will draw—or be musical."

*If Stephen Bonnet plays the flute,* Roger thought cynically, but choked off that subversive notion, refusing to contemplate it.

"That's how he'll know the most of us," he said instead, resuming his gentle kneading. "He'll look at himself, aye?"

"Mmm?"

"Well, look at you," he pointed out. "Everyone who sees

you says, 'You must be Jamie Fraser's lass!' And the red hair isn't the only thing—what about the shooting? And the way you and your mother are about tomatoes . . ."

She smacked her lips reflexively, and giggled when he laughed.

"Yeah, all right, I see," she said. "Mmm. Why did you have to mention tomatoes? I used the last of the dried ones last week, and it'll be six months before they're on again."

"Sorry," he said, and kissed the back of her neck in apology.

"I did wonder," he said, a moment later. "When you found out about Jamie—when we began to look for him—you must have wondered what he was like." He knew she had; *he* certainly had. "When you found him—how did he compare? Was he at all like you thought he'd be, from what you knew about him already? Or—from what you knew about yourself?"

That made her laugh again, a little wryly.

"I don't know," she said. "I didn't know then, and I still don't know."

"What d'ye mean by that?"

"Well, when you hear things about somebody before you meet them, of course the real person isn't just like what you heard, or what you imagined. But you don't forget what you imagined, either; that stays in your mind, and sort of merges with what you find out when you meet them. And then—" She bent her head forward, thinking. "Even if you know somebody *first*, and then hear things about them later—that kind of affects how you see them, doesn't it?"

"Aye? Mmm, I suppose so. Do ye mean . . . your other dad? Frank?"

"I suppose I do." She shifted under his hands, shrugging it away. She didn't want to talk about Frank Randall, not just now.

"What about your parents, Roger? Do you figure that's why the Reverend saved all their old stuff in those boxes? So later you could look through it, learn more about them, and sort of add that to your real memories of them?"

"I—yes, I suppose so," he said uncertainly. "Not that I have any memories of my real dad in any case; he only saw me the once, and I was less than a year old then."

"But you do remember your mother, don't you? At least a little bit?"

She sounded slightly anxious; she wanted him to remember. He hesitated, and a thought struck him with a small shock. The truth of it was, he realized, that he never consciously *tried* to remember his mother. The realization gave him a sudden and unaccustomed feeling of shame.

"She died in the War, didn't she?" Bree's hand had taken up his suspended massage, reaching back to gently knead the tightened muscle of his thigh.

"Yes. She—in the Blitz. A bomb."

"In Scotland? But I thought—"

"No. In London."

He didn't want to speak of it. He never *had* spoken of it. On the rare occasions when memory led in that direction, he veered away. That territory lay behind a closed door, with a large "No Entry" sign that he had never sought to pass. And yet tonight . . . he felt the echo of Bree's brief anguish at the thought that her son might not recall her. And he felt the same echo, like a faint voice calling, from the woman locked behind that door in his mind. But was it locked, after all?

With a hollow feeling behind his breastbone that might have been dread, he reached out and put his hand on the knob of that closed door. How much *did* he recall?

"My Gran, my mother's mum, was English," he said slowly. "A widow. We went south to live with her in London, when my dad was killed."

He had not thought of Gran, any more than his mum, in years. But with his speaking, he could smell the rosewater and glycerine lotion his grandmother had used on her hands, the faintly musty smell of her upstairs flat in Tottenham Court Road, crammed with horsehair furniture too large for it, remnants of a previous life that had held a house, a husband, and children.

He took a deep breath. Bree felt it, and pressed her broad firm back encouragingly against his chest. He kissed the back of her neck. So the door *did* open—just a crack, maybe, but the light of a wintry London afternoon shone through it, lighting up a stack of battered wooden blocks on a threadbare carpet. A woman's hand was building a tower with them, the faint sun scattering rainbows from a diamond on her hand. His own fingers curled in reflex, seeing that slim hand.

"Mum—my mother—she was small, like Gran. That is, they both seemed big, to me, but I remember . . . I remember seeing her stand on her tiptoes to reach things down from the shelf."

Things. The tea-caddy, with its cut-glass sugar bowl. The battered kettle, three mismatched mugs. His had had a panda bear on it. A package of biscuits—bright red, with a picture of a parrot . . . My God, he hadn't seen those kind ever again—did they still make them? No, of course not, not now . . .

He pulled his veering mind firmly back from such distractions.

"I know what she looked like, but mostly from pictures, not from my own memories." And yet he did *have* memories, he realized, with a disturbing sensation in the pit of his stomach. He thought "Mum," and suddenly he didn't see the photos anymore; he saw the chain of her spectacles, a string of tiny metal beads against the soft curve of a breast, and a pleasant warm smoothness, smelling of soap against his cheek; the cotton fabric of a flowered housedress. Blue flowers. Shaped like trumpets, with curling vines; he could see them clearly.

"What did she look like? Do you look like her at all?"

He shrugged, and Bree shifted, rolling over to face him, her head propped upon her outstretched arm. Her eyes shone in the half-dark, sleepiness overcome by interest.

"A little," he said slowly. "Her hair was dark, like mine." *Shiny, curly. Lifting in the wind, sprinkled with white grains of sand. He'd sprinkled sand on her head, and she brushed it from her hair, laughing. A beach somewhere?*

"The Reverend kept some pictures of her, in his study. One showed her holding me on her lap. I don't know what we were looking at—but both of us look as though we're trying hard to keep from laughing. We look a lot alike in that one. I have her mouth, I think—and . . . maybe . . . the shape of her brows."

For a long time he had felt a tightness in his chest

whenever he saw the pictures of his mother. But then it had passed, the pictures lost their meaning and became no more than objects in the casual clutter of the Reverend's house. Now he saw them clearly once again, and the tightness in his chest was back. He cleared his throat hard, hoping to ease it.

"Need water?" She made to rise, reaching for the jug and cup she kept for him on the stool by the bed, but he shook his head, a hand on her shoulder to stop her.

"It's all right," he said, a little gruffly, and cleared his throat again. It felt as tight and painful as it had in the weeks just past the hanging, and his hand involuntarily sought the scar, smoothing the ragged line beneath his jaw with the tip of a finger.

"You know," he said, seeking at least a momentary diversion, "you should do a self-portrait, next time you go to see your aunt at River Run."

"What, me?" She sounded startled, though, he thought—perhaps a bit pleased at the idea.

"Sure. You could, I know. And then there'd be . . . well, a permanent record, I mean." *For Jem to remember, in case anything should happen to you.* The words floated above them in the dark, striking them both momentarily silent. Damn, and he'd been trying to reassure her.

"I'd like a portrait of you," he said softly, and reached out a finger to trace the curve of cheek and temple. "So we can look at it when we're very old, and I can tell ye that you haven't changed a bit."

She gave a small snort, but turned her head and kissed his fingers briefly, before rolling onto her back. She stretched, pointing her toes until her joints cracked, then relaxed with a sigh.

"I'll think about it," she said.

The room was quiet, save for the murmur of the fire and the gentle creak of settling timber. The night was cold, but still; the morning would be foggy—he had felt the damp gathering in the ground when he'd gone outside, breathing from the trees. But it was warm and dry within. Brianna sighed again; he could feel her sinking back toward sleep beside him, could feel it coming for him, too.

The temptation to give in and let it carry him painlessly

away was great. But while Brianna's fears were eased for the moment, he still heard that whisper—"He wouldn't remember me at all." But it came now from the other side of the door in his mind.

*Yes, I do, Mum,* he thought, and shoved it open all the way.

"I was with her," he said softly. He was on his back, staring up at the pine-beamed ceiling, the joins of the rafters barely visible to his dark-adapted eyes.

"What? With who?" He could hear the lull of sleep in her voice, but curiosity roused her briefly.

"With my mother. And my grandmother. When . . . the bomb."

He heard her head turn sharply toward him, hearing the strain in his voice, but he looked straight upward into the dark roof-beams, not blinking.

"Do you want to tell me?" Brianna's hand found his, curled round it, squeezing. He wasn't sure at all that he did, but he nodded a little, squeezing back.

"Aye. I suppose I must," he said softly. He sighed deeply, smelling the lingering scents of fried corn-mush and onions that hung in the corners of the cabin. Somewhere in the back of his nose, the imagined scents of hot-air registers and breakfast porridge, wet woolens, and the petrol fumes of lorries woke silent guides through the labyrinth of memory.

"It was at night. The air-raid sirens went. I knew what it was, but it scared the shit out of me every time. There wasn't time to dress; Mum pulled me out of bed and put my coat on over my pajamas, then we rushed out and down the stairs— there were thirty-six steps, I'd counted them all that day, coming home from the shops—and we hurried to the nearest shelter."

The nearest shelter for them was the Tube station across the street; grubby white tiles and the flicker of fluorescent lights, the thrilling rush of air somewhere deep below, like the breathing of dragons in nearby caves.

"It was exciting." He could see the crush of people, hear the shouting of the wardens over the noise of the crowd. "Everything was vibrating; the floors, the walls, the air itself."

Feet thundered on the wooden treads as streams of

refugees poured into the bowels of the earth, down one level to a platform, down another, yet another, burrowing toward safety. It was panic—but an orderly panic.

"The bombs could go through fifty feet of earth—but the lower levels were safe."

They had reached the bottom of the first stairway, run jostling with a mass of others through a short, white-tiled tunnel to the head of the next. There was a wide space at the head of the stairway, and the crowd pooled in a swirling eddy into it, swelling with the pressure of refugees pouring from the tunnel behind, draining only slowly as a thin stream crowded onto the stair leading down.

"There was a wall round the head of the stair; I could hear Gran worrying that I'd be crushed against it—people were pouring down from the street, pressing from behind."

He could just see over the wall, standing on his toes, chest pressed against the concrete. Down below, emergency lights shone in interrupted streaks along the walls, striping the milling crowd below. It was late night; most of the people were dressed in whatever they had been able to seize when the siren went, and the light glowed on unexpected flashes of bare flesh and extraordinary garments. One woman sported an extravagant hat, decorated with feathers and fruit, worn atop an ancient overcoat.

He had been watching the crowd below in fascination, trying to see if it was really a whole pheasant on the hat. There was shouting; an air-raid warden in a white helmet with a big black "W," beckoning madly, trying to hasten the already rushing crowd toward the far end of the platform, making room for those coming off the stair.

"There were children crying, but not me. I wasn't really afraid at all." He hadn't been afraid, because Mum was holding his hand. *If she was there, nothing bad could happen.*

"There was a big thump nearby. I could see the lights shake. Then there was a noise like something tearing overhead. Everyone looked up and began to scream."

The crack through the slanted ceiling hadn't looked particularly frightening; just a thin black line that zigzagged back and forth like a jigsaw snake, following the lines of the tiles. But then it widened suddenly, a gaping maw like a dragon's mouth, and dirt and tiles began to pour down.

He had long since thawed, and yet every hair on his body rippled now with gooseflesh. His heart pounded against the inside of his chest, and he felt as though the noose had drawn tight about his neck again.

"She let go," he said, in a strangled whisper. "She let go my hand."

Brianna's hand gripped his in both of hers, hard, trying to save the child he'd been.

"She had to," she said, in an urgent whisper. "Roger, she wouldn't have let go unless she had to."

"No." He shook his head violently. "That's not what—I mean—wait. Wait a minute, OK?"

He blinked hard, trying to slow his breathing, fitting back the shattered pieces of that night. Confusion, frenzy, pain . . . but what had actually *happened*? He had kept nothing save an impression of bedlam. But he had lived through it; he must know what had happened—if he could bring himself to live through it again.

Brianna's hand clutched his, her fingers still squeezing tight enough to stop the blood. He patted her hand, gently, and her grip relaxed a little.

He closed his eyes, and let it happen.

"I didn't remember at first," he said at last, quietly. "Or rather, I did—but I remembered what people told me had happened." He had had no memory of being carried unconscious through the tunnel, and once rescued, he had spent several weeks being shuttled round Aid shelters and foster homes with other orphans, mute with terrified bewilderment.

"I knew my name, of course, and my address, but that didn't help much under the circumstances. My dad had already gone down—anyway, by the time the Aid people located Gran's brother—that was the Reverend—and he came to fetch me, they'd pieced together the story of what happened in the shelter.

"It was a miracle that I hadn't been killed with everyone else on that stair, they told me. They said my mother must somehow have lost hold of me in the panic—I must have been separated from her and carried down the stair by the crowd; that's how I ended on the lower level, where the roof hadn't given way."

Brianna's hand was still curled over his, protective, but no longer squeezing.

"But now you remember what happened?" she asked quietly.

"I did remember her letting go my hand," he said. "And so I thought the rest of it was right, too. But it wasn't.

"She let go my hand," he said. The words came more easily now; the tightness in his throat and chest was gone. "She let go my hand . . . and then she picked me up. That small woman—she picked me up, and threw me over the wall. Down into the crowd of people on the platform below. I was knocked mostly out by the fall, I think—but I remember the roar as the roof went. No one on the stair survived."

She pressed her face against his chest, and he felt her take a deep, shuddering breath. He stroked her hair, and his pounding heart began to slow at last.

"It's all right," he whispered to her, though his voice was thick and cracked, and the firelight burst in starry blurs through the moisture in his eyes. "We won't forget. Not Jem, not me. No matter what. We won't forget."

He could see his mother's face, shining clear among the stars.

*Clever lad,* she said, and smiled.

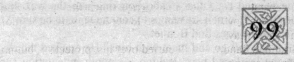

# 99

# BROTHER

THE SNOW BEGAN TO MELT. I was torn between pleasure at the thawing of the world and the throb of spring in the ground—and disturbance at the loss of the frozen barrier that shielded us, however temporarily, from the world outside.

Jamie had not changed his mind. He spent an evening in composing a carefully worded letter to Milford Lyon. He was now ready, he wrote, to contemplate the sale of his goods—for which, read illegal whisky—as Mr. Lyon had suggested, and was pleased to say that a substantial quantity was now available. He was, however, concerned lest his goods suffer some misfortune in delivery—i.e., interception by customs authorities or pilferage en route—and wished some assurance that his goods would be handled by a gentleman of known ability in such matters—in other words, a smuggler who knew his way up and down the coast.

He had received assurances from his good friend Mr. Priestly of Edenton (whom he did not, of course, know from a hole in the ground), he wrote, and from Mr. Samuel Cornell, with whom he had had the honor to serve upon the Governor's Council of War, that one Stephen Bonnet was by far the most able in such endeavors, with a reputation for ability unsurpassed by others. If Mr. Lyon would arrange a meeting with Mr. Bonnet, so that Jamie might form his own impressions and assure himself of the safety of the arrangement contemplated, why then . . .

"Do you think he'll do it?" I asked.

"If he knows Stephen Bonnet or can find him, aye, he will."

Jamie pressed his father's cabochon ring into the wax seal. "Priestly and Cornell are names to conjure with, to be sure."

"And if he does find Bonnet—"

"Then I will go and meet with him." He cracked the ring from the hardened wax, leaving a smooth indentation surrounded by the tiny strawberry leaves of the Fraser crest. Constancy, they stood for. In some moods, I was sure this was merely another word for stubbornness.

The letter to Lyon was dispatched with Fergus, and I tried to dismiss it from my mind. It was still winter; with only a little luck, Bonnet's ship might meet with a storm and sink, saving us all a good deal of trouble.

Still, the matter lurked in the recesses of my mind, and when I returned to the house after attending a childbirth to find a pile of letters on the desk in Jamie's study, my heart leaped into my throat.

There was—thank God!—no answer among them from Milford Lyon. Even had such an answer come, though, it would have been promptly eclipsed and forgotten—for among the sheaf of correspondence was a letter bearing Jamie's name, written in his sister's strong black hand.

I could scarcely keep myself from tearing it open at once—and if it were some searing reproach, sticking it directly into the fire before Jamie could see it. Honor prevailed, though, and I managed to contain myself until Jamie arrived from an errand to Salem, plastered with mud from the impassable trails. Informed of the waiting missive, he splashed hands and face hastily with water, and came to the study, carefully shutting the door before breaking the seal of the letter.

His face showed nothing, but I saw him take a deep breath before opening it, as though bracing for the worst. I moved quietly round behind him, and put a hand on his shoulder in encouragement.

He unfolded the pages carefully, and I saw him frown slightly. There was a flattened mass of dried flowers pressed between the pages; a sprig of yellow roses, still faintly fragrant. He separated these carefully from the paper, laid them on the desk, then turned to the letter itself.

Jenny Fraser Murray wrote in a well-schooled hand, the letters round and graceful, the lines straight and easily readable on the page.

*September 16, 1771*

*Brother,*

*Well. Having taken up my pen and written the single word above, I have now sat here staring at it 'til the candle has burned almost an inch, and me having not one thought what I shall say. It would be a wicked waste of good beeswax to continue so, and yet if I were to put the candle out and go to bed, I should have spoilt a sheet of paper to no purpose—so I see I must go on, in the name of thrift.*

*I could berate you. That would occupy some space upon the page, and preserve what my husband is pleased to compliment as the most foul and hideous curses he has been privileged to hear in a long life. That seems thrifty, as I was at great pains in the composition of them at the time, and should not like to see the effort wasted. Still, I think I have not so much paper as would contain them all.*

*I think also that perhaps, after all, I do not wish to rail or condemn you, for you might take this as a just punishment, and so ease your conscience in perceived expiation, so that you leave off your chastising of yourself. That is too simple a penance; I would that if you have wove a hairshirt for yourself, you wear it still, and may it chafe your soul as the loss of my son chafes mine.*

*In spite of this, I suppose that I am writing to forgive you—I had some purpose in taking up my pen, I know, and while forgiveness seems a doubtful enterprise to me at present, I expect the notion will grow more comfortable with practice.*

Jamie's brows rose nearly to his hairline at this, but he continued to read aloud with fascination.

*You will be curious to know what has led me to this action, I suppose, so I will tell you.*

*I rode to visit Maggie early Monday last; she has a new babe, so you are once more an uncle; a bonnie wee lassie called Angelica, which is a foolish name, I think, but she is very fair and born with a strawberry mark on her chest, which is a charm for good. I left them in the evening, and had made some way towards home when my mule chanced to step into a mole's hole and fell. Both mule and I rose up somewhat lamed from this accident, and it was clear that I could not ride the creature nor yet make shift to travel far by foot myself.*

*I found myself on the road to Auldearn just over the hill from Balriggan. I should not normally seek the society of Laoghaire MacKenzie—for she has resumed that name, I having made plain in the district my dislike of her use of "Fraser," she having no proper claim to that style—but it was the only place where I might obtain food and shelter, for night was coming on, with the threat of rain.*

*So I unsaddled the mule and left him to find his supper by the road, while I limped off in search of mine.*

*I came down behind the house, past the kailyard, and so came upon the arbor that you built. The vines are well grown on it now, so I could see nothing, but I could hear that there were folk inside, for I heard voices.*

*The rain had begun by then. It was not but a smizzle, yet the patter on the leaves must have drowned my voice, for no one answered when I called. I came closer—creeping like a spavined snail, to be sure, for I was gromished from the fall and my right ankle gruppit—and was just about to call once more, when I heard sounds of a rare hochmagandy from inside the arbor.*

"Hochmagandy?" I glanced at Jamie, brows raised in question.

"Fornication," he said tersely.

"Oh," I said, and moved to look over his shoulder at the letter.

> *I stood still, of course, thinking what was best to do. I could hear that it was Laoghaire shedding her shanks, but I had no hint who her partner might be. My ankle was blown up like a bladder, so I could not walk much farther, and so I was obliged to stand about in the wet, listening to all this inhonesté.*
>
> *I should have known, had she been courted by a man of the district, and I had heard nothing of her paying heed to any—though several have tried; she has Balriggan, after all, and lives like a laird on the money you pay her.*
>
> *I was filled with outrage at the hearing, but somewhat more filled with amazement to discover the cause. That being a sense of fury on your behalf— irrational as such fury might be, in the circumstances. Still, having discovered such an emotion springing full-blown in my breast, I was reluctantly compelled to the realization that my feelings for you must not in fact have perished altogether.*

Here the text broke off, as Jenny had apparently been called away upon some domestic errand. It resumed, freshly dated, on the next page.

> *September 18, 1771*
> *I dream of young Ian now and then. . . .*

"What?" I exclaimed. "To hell with Young Ian—who was with Laoghaire?"

"I should like to know that myself," Jamie muttered. The tips of his ears were dark with blood, but he didn't look up from the page.

> *I dream of Ian now and then. These dreams most often take the shape of daily life, and I see him here at Lallybroch, but now and again I dream of him in his*

*life among the savages—if indeed he still lives (and I persuade myself that my heart would by some means know if he did not).*

*So I see that what it comes to in the end is only the same thing with which I began—that one word, "Brother." You are my brother, as young Ian is my son, the both of you my flesh and my spirit and always shall be. If the loss of Ian haunts my dreams, the loss of you haunts my days, Jamie.*

He stopped reading for a moment, swallowing, then went on, his voice steady.

*I have been writing letters all the morning, debating with myself whether to finish this one, or to put it into the fire instead. But now the accounts are done, I have written to everyone I can think of, and the clouds have gone away, so the sun shines through the window by my desk, and the shadows of Mother's roses are falling over me.*

*I have thought to myself often and often that I heard my mother speak to me, through all these years. I do not need to hear her now, though, to ken well enough what she would say. And so I shall not put this in the fire.*

*You remember, do you, the day I broke the good cream-pitcher, flinging it at your head because you deviled me? I know you recall the occasion, for you once spoke to Claire of it. I hesitated to admit the crime, and you took the blame upon yourself, but Father kent the truth of it, and punished us both.*

*So now I am a grandmother ten times over, with my hair gone grey, and still I feel my cheeks go hot with shame and my wame shrink like a fist, thinking of Father bidding us kneel down side by side and bend over the bench to be whipped.*

*You yelped and grunted like a puppy when he tawsed you, and I could scarce breathe and did not dare to look at you. Then it was my turn, but I was so wrought with emotion that I think I barely felt the*

*strokes. No doubt you are reading this and saying
indignantly that it was only Father was softer with me
because I was a lass. Well, maybe so, and maybe no; I
will say Ian is gentle with his daughters.*

Jamie snorted at this.

"Aye, ye've got that right," he muttered. He rubbed his
nose with one finger and resumed, drumming his fingers on
the desk as he read.

*But then Father said you would have another whip-
ping, this one for lying—for the truth was the truth,
after all. I would have got up and fled away then, but
he bade me stay as I was, and he said to me, quiet,
that while you would pay the price of my cowardice,
he did not think it right for me to escape it altogether.*

*Do you know that you did not make a sound, the
second time? I hope you did not feel the strokes of the
tawse on your backside, because I felt each one.*

*I swore that day that I should not ever be a coward
again.*

*And I see that it is cowardice indeed, that I should
go on blaming you for Young Ian. I have always kent
what it is to love a man—be he husband or brother,
lover or son. A dangerous business; that's what it is.*

*Men go where they will, they do as they must; it is
not a woman's part to bid them stay, nor yet to
reproach them for being what they are—or for not
coming back.*

*I knew it when I sent Ian to France with a cross of
birchwood and a lock of my hair made into a love
knot, praying that he might come home to me, body
and soul. I knew it when I gave you a rosary and saw
you off to Leoch, hoping you would not forget Lallybroch or me. I knew it when Young Jamie swam to the
seal's island, when Michael took ship for Paris, and I
should have known it, too, when wee Ian went
with you.*

*But I have been blessed in my life; my men have
always come back to me. Maimed, perhaps; a bit*

*singed round the edges now and then; crippled, crumpled, tattered, and torn—but I have always got them back. I grew to expect that as my right, and I was wrong to do so.*

*I have seen so many widows since the Rising. I cannot say why I thought I should be exempt from their suffering, why I alone should lose none of my men, and only one of my babes, my wee girl-child. And since I had lost Caitlin, I treasured Ian, for I knew he was the last babe I should bear.*

*I thought him my babe still; I should have kent him for the man he was. And that being so, I know well enough that whether you might have stopped him or no, you would not—for you are one of the damnable creatures, too.*

*Now I have nearly reached the end of this sheet, and I think it profligate to begin another.*

*Mother loved you always, Jamie, and when she kent she was dying, she called for me, and bade me care for you. As though I could ever stop.*

*Your most Affectionate and Loving Sister,*
*Janet Flora Arabella Fraser Murray*

Jamie held the paper for a moment, then set it down, very gently. He sat with his head bent, propped on his hand so that I couldn't see his face. His fingers were splayed through his hair, and kept moving, massaging his forehead as he slowly shook his head, back and forth. I could hear him breathing, with a slight catch in his breath now and then.

Finally he dropped his hand and looked up at me, blinking. His face was deeply flushed, there were tears in his eyes, and he wore the most remarkable expression, in which bewilderment, fury, and laughter were all mingled, laughter being only slightly uppermost.

"Oh, God," he said. He sniffed, and wiped his eyes on the back of his hand. "Oh, Christ. How in *hell* does she do that?"

"Do what?" I pulled a clean handkerchief from my bodice and handed it to him.

"Make me feel as though I am eight years old," he said ruefully. "And an idiot, to boot."

He wiped his nose, then reached out a hand to touch the flattened roses, gently.

I WAS THRILLED with Jenny's letter, and knew that Jamie's heart was substantially lightened by its receipt. At the same time, I remained extremely curious about the incident she had begun to describe—and knew that Jamie was even more interested, though he carefully refrained from saying so.

A letter arrived a week or so later, sent by his brother-in-law Ian, but while this contained the usual news of Lallybroch and Broch Mordha, it made no mention whatever of Jenny's adventure near Balriggan, nor her subsequent discovery in the grape arbor.

"I don't suppose you could ask either of them?" I suggested delicately, perched on the fence as I watched him preparing to castrate a litter of piglets. "Ian or Jenny?"

"I could not," Jamie replied firmly. "And after all, it's no my business, is it? If yon woman was ever my wife, she surely is not now. If she chooses to take a lover, it's her own affair. Surely." He stamped on the foot-bellows, fanning up the small fire in which the cautery iron was heating, and pulled the castrating shears from his belt. "Which end of the business d'ye want, Sassenach?"

It was a choice between the strong possibility of being bitten while clipping the teeth and the certainty of being shitten while assaulting the other end. The unfortunate truth was that Jamie was far stronger than I, and while he could certainly castrate an animal with no difficulty at all, I did have some professional expertise. It was therefore practicality rather than heroism that dictated my choice, and I had prepared for this activity by donning my heavy canvas apron, wooden clogs, and a ragged ex-shirt that had once belonged to Fergus, and was bound from the pigpen straight into the fire.

"You hold; I'll snip." I slid off the fence and took the shears.

There ensued a brief but noisy interlude, after which the five piglets were sent off to a consolatory meal of kitchen scraps, their rear aspects heavily daubed with a tar and turpentine mixture to prevent infection.

"What do you think?" I asked, seeing them settle down to their feeding in an apparent state of content. "If you were a pig, I mean. Would you rather root for your food, but keep your balls, or give them up and wallow in luxurious swill?" These would be kept penned, raised carefully on slops for tender meat, while most of the pigs were routinely turned out into the wood to manage for themselves.

Jamie shook his head.

"I suppose they canna miss what they've never had," he said. "And they've had food, after all." He leaned on the fence for a few moments, watching the curly tails begin to wag and twirl with pleasure, the tiny wounds beneath apparently forgotten.

"Besides," he added cynically, "a pair of ballocks may bring a man more sorrow than joy—though I havena met many who'd wish them gone, for all that."

"Well, priests might find them a burden, I suppose." I pulled the stained shirt gingerly away from my body before lifting it over my head. "Phew. Nothing smells worse than pig excrement—nothing."

"What—not a blackbirder's hold, or a rotting corpse?" he asked, laughing. "Festering wounds? A billy goat?"

"Pig shit," I said firmly. "Hands down."

Jamie took the wadded shirt from me and ripped it into strips, reserving the cleanest ones for jobs like wiping tools and wedging cracks. The rest he consigned to the fire, stepping back as a random breeze blew a plume of reeking smoke in our direction.

"Aye, well, there was Narses. He was a great general, or so they say, in spite of being a eunuch."

"Perhaps a man's mind works better without the distraction," I suggested, laughing.

He gave no more than a brief snort in reply to this, though it was tinged with amusement. He shoveled dirt onto the cinders of the fire, while I retrieved my cautery iron and tar-pot, and we went back to the house, talking of other things.

My mind lingered on that one remark, though—"a pair of ballocks may bring a man more sorrow than joy." Had he been speaking only generally? I wondered. Or had there been some personal allusion lurking in it?

In everything he had ever said to me regarding his brief marriage to Laoghaire MacKenzie—little as that was, by our common consent—there had been no hint that he had felt physically drawn to her. He had wed her from loneliness and a sense of duty, wanting some small anchor in the emptiness his life had been after his return from England. Or so he had said.

And I believed what he'd said. He was a man of honor and duty, and I knew what his loneliness had been—for I had had my own. On the other hand, I knew his body, nearly as well as my own. If it had a great capacity to endure hardship, it had an equal capacity to experience great joy. Jamie could be ascetic from necessity—never from natural temperament.

Most of the time I succeeded in forgetting that he had shared Laoghaire's bed, however briefly and—he said—unsatisfactorily. I did not forget that she had been, and was still, quite an attractive woman.

Which left me rather wishing that Jenny Murray had found some other inspiration for the conversion of her feelings toward her brother.

JAMIE WAS QUIET and abstracted through the rest of the day, though he roused himself to be sociable when Fergus and Marsali arrived with their children for a visit after supper. He taught Germain to play draughts, while Fergus recalled for Roger the words of a ballad he had picked up in the alleys of Paris as a juvenile pickpocket. The women retired to the hearth to stitch baby gowns, knit booties, and—in honor of Marsali's advancing pregnancy and Lizzie's engagement—entertain each other with hair-raising anecdotes of labor and birth.

"Laid sideways, the babe was, and the size of a six-month shoat . . ."

"Ha, Germain had a head like a cannonball, the midwife said, and he was facing *backward*, the wee rattan—"

"Jemmy had a huge head, but it was his shoulders that were the problem. . . ."

". . . *la bourse* . . . the lady's 'purse,' of course, is her—"

"Her means of making a living, aye, I see. Then the next bit, where her customer puts his fingers *in* her purse—"

"No, ye dinna get to move yet, it's still my turn, for I've jumped your man *there*, and so I can go *here*—"

*"Merde!"*

"Germain!" Marsali bellowed. She glared at her offspring, who hunched his shoulders, scowling at the draughtboard, lower lip thrust out.

"Dinna fash yourself, man, for see? Now it's your turn, ye can go *there*, and *there*, and *there*—"

". . . *Avez-vous été à la selle aujourd'hui?* . . . and what he is asking the whore, of course—"

" 'Have you—been in the saddle today?' Or would it be, 'Have you had a ride today?' "

Fergus laughed, the end of his aristocratic nose pinkening with amusement.

"Well, that is one translation, surely."

Roger lifted a brow at him, half-smiling.

"Aye?"

"That particular expression is also what a French doctor says," I put in, seeing his incomprehension. "Colloquially speaking, it means, 'Have you had a bowel movement today?' "

"The lady in question being perhaps *une spécialiste*," Fergus explained cheerfully. "I used to know one who—"

*"Fergus!"* Marsali's whole face was pink, though she seemed more amused than outraged.

"I see," Roger murmured, eyebrows still raised as he struggled with the nuances of this bit of sophisticated translation. I did wonder how one would set it to music.

*"Comment sont vos selles, Grand-père?"* Germain inquired chummily, evidently familiar with this line of social inquiry. And how are your stools, Grandfather?

"Free and easy," his grandfather assured him. "Eat up your parritch every morning, and ye'll never have piles."

"Da!"

"Well, it's true," Jamie protested.

Brianna was bright red, and emitting small fizzing noises. Jemmy stirred in her lap.

"*Le petit rouge* eats parritch," Germain observed, frowning narrowly at Jemmy, who was nursing contentedly at his mother's breast, eyes closed. "He shits stones."

"*Germain!*" all the women shouted in unison.

"Well, it's true," he said, in perfect imitation of his grandfather. Looking dignified, he turned his back on the women and began building towers with the draughts-men.

"He doesna seem to want to give up the teat," Marsali observed, nodding at Jemmy. "Neither did Germain, but he'd no choice—nor did poor wee Joanie." She glanced ruefully down at her stomach, which was barely beginning to swell with Number Three.

I caught the barest flicker of a glance between Roger and Bree, followed by a Mona Lisa smile on Brianna's face. She settled herself more comfortably, and stroked Jemmy's head. *Enjoy it while you can, sweetheart,* her actions said, more vividly than words.

I felt my own eyebrows rise, and glanced toward Jamie. He'd seen that little byplay, too, and gave me the male equivalent of Brianna's smile, before turning back to the draughts-board.

"I like parritch," Lizzie put in shyly, in a minor attempt to change the subject. "Specially with honey and milk."

"Ah," said Fergus, reminded of his original task. He turned back to Roger, lifting a finger. "Honeypots. The refrain, you see, where *les abeilles* come buzzing—"

"Aye, aye, that's so," Mrs. Bug neatly recaptured the conversation, when he paused to draw breath, "parritch wi' honey is the best thing for the bowels, though sometimes even that fails. Why, I kent a man once, who couldna move his bowels for more than a month!"

"Indeed. Did he try a pellet of wax rolled in goosegrease? Or a tisane of grape leaves?" Fergus was instantly diverted. French to the core, he was a great connoisseur of purges, laxatives, and suppositories.

"Everything," Mrs. Bug assured him. "Parritch, dried ap-

ples, wine mixed wi' an ox's gall, water drunk at the dark o'
the moon at midnight . . . nothing at all would shift him.
'Twas the talk of the village, wi' folk placing wagers, and the
poor man gone quite gray in the face. Nervous spasms, it
was, and his bowels tied up like garter strings, so that—"

"Did he explode?" Germain asked, interested.

Mrs. Bug shook briefly with laughter.

"No, that he didna, laddie. Though I did hear as how it
was a near thing."

"What was it finally shifted him, then?" Jamie asked.

"She finally said she'd marry me, and not the other fellow." Mr. Bug, who had been dozing in the corner of the settle through the evening, stood up and stretched himself, then
put a hand on his wife's shoulder, smiling tenderly down at
her upturned face. " 'Twas a great relief, to be sure."

IT WAS LATE when we went to bed, after a convivial
evening that ended with Fergus singing the prostitute's ballad
in its lengthy entirety to general applause, Jamie and Germain beating time on the table with their hands.

Jamie lay back against the pillow, hands crossed behind
his head, chuckling to himself now and then as bits of the
song came back to him. It was cold enough that the window-
panes were misted with our breath, but he wore no nightshirt,
and I admired the sight of him as I sat brushing my hair.

He had recovered well from the snakebite, but was still
thinner than usual, so that the graceful arch of his collarbone
was visible, and the long muscles of his arms roped from
bone to bone, distinct beneath his skin. The skin of his chest
was bronze where his shirt usually lay open, but the tender
skin on the underside of his arms was white as milk, a trac-
ery of blue veins showing. The light shadowed the prominent
bones of his face and glimmered from his hair, cinnamon and
amber where it lay across his shoulders, dark auburn and red-
gold where it dusted his bared body.

"The candlelight becomes ye, Sassenach," he said, smiling, and I saw that he was watching me, blue eyes the color
of bottomless ocean.

"I was just thinking the same of you," I said, standing up and putting aside my brush. My hair floated in a cloud round my shoulders, clean, soft, and shining. It smelled of marigolds and sunflowers and so did my skin. Bathing and shampooing in winter was a major undertaking, but I had been determined not to go to bed smelling of pig shit.

"Let it burn, then," he said, reaching out to stop me as I bent to blow the candle out. His hand curled round my wrist, urging me toward him.

"Come to bed, and let me watch ye. I like the way the light moves in your eyes; like whisky, when ye pour it on a haggis, and then set it on fire."

"How poetic," I murmured, but made no demur as he made room for me, pulled loose the drawstring of my shift, and slipped it off me. The air of the room was cold enough to make my nipples draw up tight, but the skin of his chest was delightfully warm on my breasts as he gathered me into him, sighing with pleasure.

"It's Fergus's song inspiring me, I expect," he said, cupping one of my breasts in his hand and weighing it with a nice balance between admiration and appraisal. "God, ye've the loveliest breasts. Ye recall that one verse, where he says the lady's tits were so enormous, she could wrap them round his ears? Yours aren't so big as that, of course, but d'ye think ye maybe could wrap them round—"

"I don't think they need to be enormous to do *that*," I assured him. "Move up. Besides, I don't believe it's actually wrapping round, so much as it is squashing together, and they're certainly large enough for . . . see?"

"Oh," he said, sounding deeply gratified and a little breathless. "Aye, ye're right. That's . . . oh, that looks verra beautiful, Sassenach—at least from here."

"It looks very interesting from here, too," I assured him, trying neither to laugh nor go cross-eyed. "Which one of us moves, do you think?"

"Me, for now. I'm no chafing ye, Sassenach?" he inquired.

"Well, just a bit. Wait, though—" I reached out a hand, feeling blindly over the table by the bed. I got hold of the little pot of creamy almond ointment I used for hand lotion, flicked the lid off, and dug a finger into it.

"Yes, that's much better," I said. "Isn't it?"

"Oh. Oh. Aye."

"And then there's that other verse, isn't there?" I said thoughtfully, letting go for a moment, and drawing a slippery finger slowly round the curve of his buttock. "About what the prostitute did to the choirboy?"

"Oh, Christ!"

"Yes, that's what he said. According to the song."

MUCH LATER, in the dark, I roused from sleep to feel his hands on me again. Still pleasantly adrift in dreams, I didn't move, but lay inert, letting him do what he would.

My mind was loosely tethered to reality, and it took some time for me to come to the slow realization that something wasn't quite right. It took even longer to focus my mind and struggle toward the surface of wakefulness, but at last I got my eyes open, blinking away clouds of sleep.

He was crouched half over me, his face half-lit by the dim glow from the smoored hearth. His eyes were closed, and he was frowning a little, his breath coming through half-opened lips. He moved almost mechanically, and I wondered, muzzily astonished, whether he could possibly be doing it in his sleep?

A thin film of sweat gleamed on the high cheekbones, the long straight bridge of his nose, on the slopes and curves of his naked body.

He was stroking me in an odd, monotonous sort of way, like a man working at some repetitive task. The touch was more than intimate, but weirdly impersonal; I might have been anybody—or anything—I thought.

Then he moved, and eyes still closed, flipped back the quilt covering me and moved between my legs, spreading them apart in a brusque fashion that was quite unlike him. His brows were drawn together, knotted in a frown of concentration. I moved instinctively to close my legs, squirming away. His hands clamped down on my shoulders then, his knee thrust my thighs apart, and he entered me roughly.

I made a high-pitched sound of startled protest, and his

eyes popped open. He stared at me, his eyes no more than an inch from mine, unfocused, then sharpening into abrupt awareness. He froze.

"Who the *bloody* hell do you think I am?" I said, low-voiced and furious.

He wrenched himself away and flung himself off the bed, leaving the covers hanging to the floor in disarray. He seized his clothes from the peg, reached the door in two strides, opened it, and disappeared, slamming it behind him.

I sat up, feeling thoroughly rattled. I scrabbled the quilts back up around myself, feeling dazed, angry—and halfway disbelieving. I rubbed my hands over my face, trying to wake up all the way. Surely *I* hadn't been dreaming?

No. He was. He'd been half-asleep—or wholly so—and he'd bloody thought I was bloody Laoghaire! Nothing else could account for the way he had been touching me, with a sense of painful impatience tinged with anger; he had never touched me like that in his life.

I lay back down, but it was patently impossible to go back to sleep. I stared at the shadowy rafters for a few minutes, then rose with decision, and got dressed.

The dooryard was bleak and cold under a high, bright moon. I stepped out, closing the kitchen door softly behind me, and clutched my cloak round me, listening. Nothing stirred in the cold, and the wind was no more than a sigh through the pines. At some distance, though, I heard a faint, regular noise, and turned toward it, making my way carefully through the dark.

The door of the haybarn was open.

I leaned against the doorjamb, and crossed my arms, watching as he stamped to and fro, pitching hay in the moonlight, working off his temper. Mine was still pulsing in my temples, but began to subside as I watched him.

The difficulty was that I did understand, and all too well. I had not met many of Frank's women—he was discreet. But now and then, I would catch a glance exchanged at a faculty party or the local supermarket—and a feeling of black rage would well up in me, only to be followed by bafflement as to what, precisely, I was to do with it.

Jealousy had nothing to do with logic.

Laoghaire MacKenzie was four thousand miles away; likely neither of us would ever see her again. Frank was even farther away, and it was certain neither of us would ever see him again, this side the grave.

No, jealousy had nothing at all to do with logic.

I began to be cold, but went on standing there. He knew I was there; I could see it in the way he kept his head turned toward his work. He was sweating, in spite of the cold; the thin cloth of his shirt stuck to him, making a dark spot on his back. At last, he stabbed the pitchfork into the stack, left it, and sat down on a bench made from half a log. He put his head in his hands, fingers rubbing violently through his hair.

Finally, he looked up at me, with an expression halfway between dismay and reluctant amusement.

"I dinna understand it."

"What?" I moved toward him, and sat down near him, curling my feet under me. I could smell the sweat on his skin, along with almond cream and the ghost of his earlier lust.

He gave me a sidelong glance, and answered dryly, "Anything, Sassenach."

"Can't be that bad, can it?" I reached tentatively for him, and ran a hand lightly down the curve of his back.

He heaved a deep sigh, blowing air through pursed lips.

"When I was three-and-twenty, I didna understand how it was that to look at a woman could turn my bones to water, yet make me feel I could bend steel in my hands. When I was five-and-twenty, I didna understand how I could want both to cherish a woman and ravish her, all at once."

"*A* woman?" I asked, and got what I wanted—the curl of his mouth and a glance that went through my heart.

"One woman," he said. He took the hand I laid on his knee, and held it tightly, as though afraid I might snatch it back. "Just one," he repeated, his voice husky.

It was quiet in the barn, but the boards creaked and settled in the cold. I moved a little on the bench, scooting toward him. Just a little. Moonlight streamed through the wide-open door, glowing dimly off the piled hay.

"And that," he said, squeezing my fingers tighter, "is what I dinna ken now. I love *you, a nighean donn*. I have loved ye from the moment I saw ye, I will love ye 'til time itself is done, and so long as you are by my side, I am well pleased wi' the world."

A flush of warmth went through me, but before I could do more than squeeze his hand in reply, he went on, turning to look at me with an expression of bewilderment so desperate as to be almost comical.

"And that bein' so, Claire—why, in the name of Christ and all his saints—*why* do I want to take ship to Scotland, hunt down a man whose name and face I dinna ken at all, and kill him, for swiving a woman to whom I have nay claim, and who I couldna stand to be in the same room with for more than three minutes at the most?"

He brought his free hand down in a fist, striking the log with a thump that vibrated through the wood under my buttocks.

"I do *not* understand!"

I suppressed the urge to say, "And you think *I* do?" Instead, I merely sat quietly, and after a moment, stroked his knuckles very lightly with my thumb. It was less a caress than a simple reassurance, and he took it so.

After a moment, he sighed deeply, squeezed my hand, and stood up.

"I am a fool," he said.

I sat still for a moment, but he seemed to expect some sort of confirmation, so I nodded obligingly.

"Well, perhaps," I said. "But you aren't going to Scotland, are you?"

Instead of replying, he got to his feet and walked moodily to and fro, kicking clumps of dried mud, which burst like small bombs. Surely he wasn't contemplating . . . he couldn't be. With some difficulty, I kept my mouth shut, and waited patiently, until he came back to stand in front of me.

"All right," he said, in the tone of one stating a declaration of principle. "I dinna ken why it galls me that Laoghaire should seek another man's company—no, that's no the truth, is it? I ken well enough. And it isna jealousy. Or . . . well, it is, then, but that's no the main thing." He shot me a look, as though daring me to contradict this assertion, but I kept my mouth shut. He exhaled strongly through his nose, and took a deep breath, looking down.

"Well, then. If I'm honest about it." His lips pressed tight together for a moment. "Why?" he burst out, looking up at me. "What is it about him?"

"What is what about who? The man she—"

"She hated it, the bedding!" he interrupted me, stamping a clod into powder. "Perhaps I flatter myself, or you flatter me . . ." He gave me a look that wanted to be a glare, but ended in bewilderment. "Am I . . . am I . . . ?"

I wasn't sure whether he wanted me to say, "Yes, you are!" or "No, you're not!" but satisfied myself with a smile that said both.

"Aye. Well," he said reluctantly. "I didna *think* it was me. And before we were wed, even Laoghaire liked me well enough." I must have made a small snort at that, for he glanced at me, but I shook my head, dismissing it.

"I thought it must be a mislike for men in general, or only for the act. And if it was so . . . well, it wasna quite so bad, if it wasna my fault, though I did feel somehow I should be able to mend it. . . ." He trailed off into this thoughts, brow furrowed, then resumed with a sigh.

"But maybe I was wrong about that. Perhaps it *was* me. And that's a thought that sticks in my craw."

I had no real idea what to say to him, but clearly I had to say something.

"I think it was her," I said, firmly. "Not you. Though of course I may be prejudiced. She did try to kill me, after all."

"She what?" He swung round, looking blank.

"You didn't know that? Oh." I tried to think; had I not told him? No, I supposed not. What with one thing and another, it hadn't seemed important at the time; I had never expected to see her again. And later . . . well, it really *wasn't* important then. I explained briefly about Laoghaire's having sent me to join Geillie Duncan that day in Cranesmuir, fully aware that Geillie was about to be arrested for witchcraft, and hoping that I would be taken with her—as indeed I was.

"The wicked wee bitch!" he said, sounding more astonished than anything else. "No, I didna ken that at all—Christ, Sassenach, ye canna think I would have marrit the woman, knowing she'd done such a thing to you!"

"Well, she was only sixteen at the time," I said, able under the circumstances to be tolerantly forgiving. "And she might not have realized that we'd be tried or that the witch-court would try to burn us. She might only have meant mischief— thinking that if I were accused as a witch, it would make you lose interest in me." The revelation of her chicanery seemed at least to have distracted Jamie's mind, which was all to the good.

His only response to this was a snort. He paced restlessly to and fro for a bit, his feet rustling in the spilled straw. He hadn't taken his shoes or stockings, and was barefoot, though the cold seemed not to trouble him.

At last he stopped, heaved a massive sigh, and bent forward, resting a hand on the bench, his head on my shoulder.

"I'm sorry," he whispered.

I put my arms round his shoulders and pulled him close, holding him hard until at last he sighed again, and the knotted strain in his shoulders relaxed. I let go, and he stood up, giving me a hand to rise.

We closed the barn door and walked back to the house in silence, hand in hand.

"Claire," he said suddenly, sounding a little shy.

"Yes?"

"I dinna mean to excuse myself—not at all. It's only I was wondering . . . do ye ever . . . think of Frank? When we . . ." He stopped and cleared his throat. "Does the shadow of the Englishman perhaps cross my face—now and then?"

And what on earth could I say to that? I couldn't lie, surely, but how could I say the truth, either, in a way he would understand, that wouldn't hurt him?

I drew a deep breath and let it out, watching the mist of it purl softly away.

"I don't want to make love to a ghost," I said at last, firmly. "And I don't think you do, either. But I suppose every now and then a ghost might have other ideas."

He made a small sound that was mostly a laugh.

"Aye," he said. "I suppose they might. I wonder if Laoghaire would like the Englishman's bed better than mine?"

"Serve her right if she did," I said. "But if you like mine, I suggest you come and get back into it. It's *bloody* cold out here."

## 100

# DEAD WHALE

B Y LATE MARCH, the trails down the mountain were passable. No word had come yet from Milford Lyon, and after some debate on the matter, it was decided that Jamie and I, with Brianna, Roger, and Marsali, would travel to Wilmington, while Fergus took the survey reports to New Bern to be formally filed and registered.

The girls and I would buy supplies depleted over the winter, such as salt, sugar, coffee, tea, and opium, while Roger and Jamie would make discreet inquiries after Milford Lyon—and Stephen Bonnet. Fergus would come to join us, so soon as the surveying reports were taken care of, making his own inquiries along the coast as chance offered.

After which, presumably, Jamie and Roger, having located Mr. Bonnet, would drop round to his place of business and take turns either shooting him dead or running him through with a sword, before riding back into the mountains, congratulating themselves on a job well done. Or so I understood the plan to be.

"The best-laid plans of mice and men gang aft agley," I quoted to Jamie, in the midst of one discussion on the matter. He raised one brow and gave me a look.

"What sorts of plans have mice got?"

"Well, there you have me," I admitted. "The principle holds, though; you haven't any idea what may happen."

"That's true," he agreed. "But whatever *does* happen, I

shall be ready for it." He patted the dirk that lay on the corner of his desk, and went back to making lists of farm supplies.

The weather warmed markedly as we descended from the mountains, and as we drew nearer to the coast, flocks of seagulls and crows wheeled and swarmed over the fresh-plowed fields, shrieking ecstatically in the bright spring sunshine.

The trees in the mountains were barely beginning to leaf out, but in Wilmington, flowers were already glowing in the gardens, spikes of yellow columbine and blue larkspur nodding over the tidy fences on Beaufort Street. We found lodgings in a small, clean inn a little way from the quay. It was relatively cheap and reasonably comfortable, if a trifle crowded and dark.

"Why don't they have more windows?" Brianna grumbled, nursing a stubbed toe after stumbling over Germain in the darkness on the landing. "Somebody's going to burn the place down, lighting candles to see where they're going. Glass can't be *that* expensive."

"Window tax," Roger informed her, picking Germain up and dangling him head-down over the bannister, to Germain's intense delight.

"What? The Crown taxes *windows*?"

"It does. Ye'd think people would care more about that than stamps or tea, but apparently they're used to the window tax."

"No wonder they're about to have a revolu— Oh, good morning, Mrs. Burns! The breakfast smells wonderful."

The girls, the children, and I spent several days in careful shopping, while Roger and Jamie mixed business with pleasure in assorted taprooms and taverns. Most of their errands were completed, and Jamie produced a small but useful subsidiary income from card-playing and betting on horses, but all he was able to hear of Stephen Bonnet was that he had not been seen in Wilmington for some months. I was privately relieved to hear this.

It rained later in the week, hard enough to keep everyone indoors for two days. More than simple rain; it was a substantial storm, with winds high enough to bend the palmetto trees half over and plaster the muddy streets with torn leaves and fallen branches. Marsali sat up late into the night, listening to the wind, alternating between saying the rosary and playing cards with Jamie for distraction.

"Fergus did say it was a large ship he would be coming on from New Bern? The *Octopus*? That sounds good-sized, doesn't it, Da?"

"Oh, aye. Though I believe the packet boats are verra safe, too. No, dinna discard that, lass—throw away the trey of spades instead."

"How do ye know I have the trey of spades?" she demanded, frowning suspiciously at him. "And it's no true about the packet boats. Ye ken that as well as I do; we saw the wreckage of one at the bottom of Elm Street, day before yesterday."

"I know ye've got the trey of spades because I haven't," Jamie told her, tucking his hand of cards neatly against his chest, "and all the other spades have already turned up on the table. Besides, Fergus might come overland from New Bern; he may not be on a boat at all."

A gust of wind struck the house, rattling the shutters.

"Another reason not to have windows," Roger observed, looking over Marsali's shoulder at her hand. "No, he's right, discard the trey of spades."

"Here, you do it. I've got to go and see to Joanie." She rose suddenly, and thrusting the cards into Roger's hand, rustled off to the small room next door that she shared with her children. I hadn't heard Joanie cry.

There was a loud thump and scrape overhead, as a detached tree limb sailed across the roof. Everyone looked up. Below the high-pitched keen of the wind, we could hear the hollow rumble of the surf, boiling across the submerged mudflats, pounding on the shore.

"They that go down to the sea in ships," Roger quoted softly, "that do business in great waters; these see the works of the Lord, and his wonders in the deep. For he commandeth, and raiseth the stormy wind, which lifteth up the waves thereof."

"Oh, you're a big help," Brianna said crossly. Already edgy, her temper had not been improved by the enforced seclusion. Jemmy, terrified by all the racket, had been wrapped around her like a poultice for the better part of two days; both of them were hot, damp, and exceedingly cranky.

Roger appeared not to be put off by her mood. He smiled, and bending down, peeled Jemmy away from her, with some difficulty. He put the little boy on the floor, holding him by the hands.

"They reel to and fro," he said theatrically, pulling Jem's hands so that he lurched, off-balance. "And stagger like a drunken man, and are at their wit's end."

Jemmy was giggling, and even Brianna was beginning to smile, reluctantly.

"Then they cry unto the Lord in their trouble, and he *bringeth* them out of their distresses—" On *"bringeth,"* he swung Jemmy suddenly up in the air, caught him under the arms and whirled him round, making him shriek in delight.

"He maketh the storm a calm, so that the waves thereof are still. Then are they glad because they be quiet—" He pulled Jemmy in close, and kissed him on the head, "—so he bringeth them unto their desired haven."

Bree applauded the performance sarcastically, but smiled nonetheless. Jamie had retrieved the cards, shuffling the deck neatly back together. He stopped, looking up. Caught by his sudden stillness, I turned my head to look at him. He glanced at me and smiled.

"The wind has dropped," he said. "Hear it? Tomorrow, we'll go out."

THE WEATHER HAD CLEARED by morning, and a fresh breeze came in from the sea, bearing with it a tang of the shore, smelling of sea-lavender, pines, and a strong reek of something maritime rotting in the sun. The quay still exhibited a depressing lack of masts; no large ships lay at anchor, not even a ketch or packet boat, though the water in Wilmington harbor swarmed with dinghies, rafts, canoes, and pirettas, the little four-oared boats that flitted across the water like dragonflies, droplets sparkling from their flying oars.

One of these spotted our small party standing disconsolately on the wharf, and darted toward us, its oarsmen calling out to know whether we required transport? As Roger leaned out to shout a polite refusal, the breeze off the harbor whipped away his hat, which whirled giddily out over the brownish waters and lighted on the foam, spinning like a leaf.

The craft sculled at once toward the floating hat, and one of the oarsmen speared it deftly, raising it dripping in triumph on the end of his oar. As the piretta drew up beside the quay, though, the boatman's look of jubilation changed to one of astonishment.

"MacKenzie!" he cried. "Bugger me wi' a silver toothpick if it isn't!"

"Duff! Duff, me auld lad!" Roger leaned down and grabbed his hat, then reached back to give his erstwhile acquaintance a hand up. Duff, a small, grizzled Scot with a very long nose, sparse jowls, and a fine sprout of graying whiskers that made him look as though he'd been thickly dusted in icing sugar, leaped nimbly up onto the quay and proceeded to clasp Roger in a manly embrace, punctuated by fierce thumpings on the back and ejaculations of amazement, all heartily returned by Roger. The rest of us stood politely watching this reunion, while Marsali prevented Germain from jumping off the quay into the water.

"Do you know him?" I asked Brianna, who was dubiously examining her husband's old friend.

"I *think* he might have been on a ship with Roger once," she replied, renewing her grip on Jemmy, who was wildly excited by the sight of seagulls, finding these much more entertaining than Mr. Duff.

"Why, look at him!" Duff exclaimed, finally standing back and wiping a sleeve happily under his nose. "A coat like a lairdie's and buttons to match. And the hat! Christ, lad, ye're so slick these days as shit wouldna stick to ye, would it?"

Roger laughed, and bent to pick up his soggy hat. He slapped it against his thigh to dislodge a strand of bladderwrack, and handed it absently to Bree, who was still viewing Mr. Duff with a rather narrow eye.

"My wife," Roger introduced her, and waved a hand at the

rest of us. "And her family. Mr. James Fraser, Mrs. Fraser . . . and my wife's good-sister, also Mrs. Fraser."

"Your servant, sir—ladies." Duff bowed to Jamie, and put a finger to the disreputable object on his head in brief token of respect. He glanced at Brianna, and a broad grin stretched his lips.

"Oh, so ye married her. Got her out o' the breeks, I see." He nudged Roger familiarly in the ribs, lowering his voice to a hoarse whisper. "Did ye pay her faither for her, or did he pay you to take her?" He emitted a creaking noise, which I took to be laughter.

Jamie and Bree gave Mr. Duff identical cold looks down the bridges of their long, straight noses, but before Roger could reply, the other oarsman shouted something incomprehensible from the boat below.

"Oh, aye, aye, hold your water, man." Mr. Duff waved a quelling hand at his partner. "That's by way of a jest," he explained to me confidentially. "What with us bein' sailors, ken. 'Hold your water,' aye? Forbye ye *don't* hold water, then ye'll be at the bottom o' the harbor, aye?" He quivered with merriment, making the creaking noise again.

"Most amusing," I assured him. "Did he say something about a whale?"

"Oh, to be sure! Was that not why ye've come down to the shore this morning?"

Everyone looked blank.

"No," Marsali said, too bent upon her errand to pay much attention to anything else, including whales. "Germain, come back here! No, sir, we've come to see if there's any word of the *Octopus*. Ye'll not have heard anything, yourself?"

Duff shook his head.

"No, Missus. But the weather's been that treacherous off the Banks for a month past . . ." He saw Marsali's face go pale, and hastened to add, "A good many ships will ha' sheered off, see? Gone to another port, maybe, or lyin' to just off the coast, in hopes of fair skies to make the run in. Ye recall, MacKenzie—we did that ourselves, when we came in wi' the *Gloriana*."

"Aye, that's true." Roger nodded, though his eyes grew

wary at mention of the *Gloriana*. He glanced briefly at Brianna, then back at Duff, and lowered his voice slightly. "You've parted company with Captain Bonnet, I see."

A small jolt shot through the soles of my feet, as though the dock had been electrified. Jamie and Bree both reacted, too, though in different fashion. He took an immediate step toward Duff, she took one back.

"Stephen Bonnet?" Jamie said, eyeing Duff with interest. "Ye'll be acquainted with that gentleman, will ye?"

"I have been, sir," Duff said, and crossed himself.

Jamie nodded slowly, seeing this.

"Aye, I see. And will ye ken somewhat about Mr. Bonnet's present whereabouts, perhaps?"

"Och, well, as to that . . ."

Duff looked up at him speculatively, taking in the details of his clothing and appearance, and obviously wondering exactly how much the answer to that question might be worth. His partner below was growing increasingly restive, though, and shouted impatiently.

Marsali was restive, too.

"Where might they go, then? If they've gone to another port? Germain, stop! Ye'll fall in, next thing!" She bent to retrieve her offspring, who had been hanging over the edge of the wharf, peacefully exploring its underside, and hoicked him up onto one hip.

"Bonnet?" Jamie raised his brows, contriving to look simultaneously encouraging and menacing.

"They gone see da whale or don't they?" yelled the gentleman in the boat, impatient to be off on more profitable ventures.

Duff seemed somewhat at a loss as to whom to reply to first. His small eyes blinked, shifting to and fro between Jamie, Marsali, and his increasingly vociferous partner below. I stepped in to break the impasse.

"What's all this about a whale?"

Compelled to focus on this straightforward question, Duff looked relieved.

"Why, the dead whale, Missus. A big 'un, gone aground on the Island. I thought sure as ye'd all come down to see."

I looked out across the water, and for the first time realized that the boat traffic was not entirely random. While a few large canoes and barges were headed toward the mouth of Cape Fear, most of the smaller craft were plying to and fro, disappearing into the distant haze, or returning from it, bearing small groups of passengers. Linen parasols sprouted like pastel mushrooms from the boats, and there was a sprinkling of what were obviously townspeople on the dock, standing as we were, looking expectantly across the harbor.

"Two shillin's the boatload," Duff suggested ingratiatingly. "Over and back."

Roger, Brianna, and Marsali looked interested. Jamie looked uneasy.

"In *that*?" he asked, with a skeptical glance at the piretta, bobbing gently below. Duff's partner—a gentleman of indeterminate race and language—seemed inclined to take offense at this implied criticism of his craft, but Duff was reassuring.

"Oh, it's dead calm today, sir, dead calm. Why, 'twould be like sittin' on a tavern bench. Congenial, aye? Verra suitable to conversation." He blinked, innocently affable.

Jamie drew a deep breath in through his nose, and I saw him glance once more at the piretta. Jamie hated boats. On the other hand, he would do far more desperate things than get into a boat in pursuit of Stephen Bonnet. The only question was whether Mr. Duff actually had information to that end, or was only inveigling passengers. Jamie swallowed hard and braced his shoulders, steeling himself to it.

Not waiting, Duff reinforced his position by turning craftily to Marsali.

"There's a lighthouse on the Island, ma'am. Ye can see a good ways out to sea from the top o' that. See if any ships should be lyin' off."

Marsali's hand dropped at once to her pocket, fumbling for the strings. I observed Germain solicitously poking a dead mussel over her shoulder toward Jemmy's eagerly open mouth, like a mother bird feeding her offspring a nice juicy worm, and tactfully intervened, taking Jemmy into my own arms.

"No, sweetheart," I said, dropping the mussel off the dock. "You don't want that nasty thing. Wouldn't you like to go see a nice dead whale, instead?"

Jamie sighed in resignation, and reached for his sporran. "Ye'd best call for another boat, then, so as we'll not all drown together."

IT WAS LOVELY out on the water, with the sun covered by a hazy layer of cloud, and a cool breeze that made me take my hat off for the pleasure of feeling the wind in my hair. While not quite flat calm, the rise and fall of the surf was peacefully lulling—to those of us not afflicted by seasickness.

I glanced at Jamie's back, but his head was bent, shoulders moving in an easy, powerful rhythm as he rowed.

Resigned to the inevitable, he had taken brisk charge of the situation, summoning a second boat and herding Bree, Marsali, and the boys into it. Thereupon Jamie had unfastened his brooch and announced that he and Roger would row the remaining piretta, in order that Duff might put himself at ease and thus improve his chances of recollecting interesting facts regarding Stephen Bonnet.

"Less chance of me puking if I've something to do," he muttered to me, stripping off his coat and plaid.

Roger gave a small snort of amusement, but nodded agreeably and shed his own coat and shirt. With Duff and Peter installed at one end of the craft in a state of high hilarity over the turnabout of being paid to be rowed in their own boat, I was told off to sit in the other end, facing them.

"Just to keep a bit of an eye on things, Sassenach." Under cover of the wadded clothes, Jamie wrapped my hand around the stock of his pistol, and squeezed gently. He handed me down into the boat, then climbed down gingerly himself, going only slightly pale as the craft swayed and shifted under his weight.

It *was* a calm day, fortunately. A faint haze hung over the water, obscuring the dim shape of Smith Island in the distance. Kittiwakes and terns wheeled in gyres far above, and a heavy-bodied gull seemed to hang immobile in the air nearby, riding the wind as we sculled slowly out into the harbor mouth.

Seated just before me, Roger rowed easily, broad bare shoulders flexing rhythmically, obviously accustomed to the exercise. Jamie, on the seat in front of Roger, handled the oars with a fair amount of grace, but somewhat less assurance. He was no sailor, and never would be. Still, the distraction of rowing did seem to be keeping his mind off his stomach. For the moment.

"Oh, I could find myself accustomed to this, what d'ye say, Peter?" Duff lifted a long nose into the breeze, half-closing his eyes as he savored the novelty of being rowed.

Peter, who appeared to be some exotic blend of Indian and African, grunted in reply, but lounged on the seat beside Duff, equally pleased. He wore nothing but a pair of stained homespun breeches, tied at the waist with a length of tarred rope, and was burned so dark by the sun that he might have been a Negro, save for the spill of long black hair that fell over one shoulder, decorated with bits of shell and tiny dried starfish tied into it.

"Stephen Bonnet?" Jamie inquired pleasantly, drawing strongly on the oars.

"Oh, him." Duff looked as though he would have preferred to put off this subject of discussion indefinitely, but a glance at Jamie's face resigned him to the inevitable.

"What d'ye want to know, then?" The little man hunched his shoulders warily.

"To begin with, where he is," Jamie said, grunting slightly as he hauled on the oars.

"No idea," Duff said promptly, looking happier.

"Well, where did ye last see the bugger?" Jamie asked patiently.

Duff and Peter exchanged glances.

"Well, noo," Duff began cautiously, "d'ye mean by 'see,' where it was I last clapped een on the captain?"

"What else would he mean, clotheid?" Roger said, grunting with a backward stroke.

Peter nodded thoughtfully, evidently awarding a point to our side, and elbowed Duff in the ribs.

"He was in a pot-house on Roanoke, eatin' fish pie," Duff said, capitulating. "Baked wi' oysters and breadcrumbs on the top, and a pint of dark ale to wash it down. Molasses pudding, too."

"Ye've a keen sense of observation, Mr. Duff," Jamie said. "How's your sense of time, then?"

"Eh? Oh, aye, I tak' your meanin', man. When was it . . . twa month past, aboot."

"And if ye were close enough to see what the man was eating," Jamie observed mildly, "then I expect ye were at table with him, no? What did he speak of?"

Duff looked mildly embarrassed. He glanced at me, then up at one of the circling gulls.

"Aye, well. The shape of the arse on the barmaid, mostly."

"I shouldna think that a topic of conversation to occupy the course of a meal, even if the lassie was particularly shapely," Roger put in.

"Ah, ye'd be surprised how much there is to say about a woman's bum, lad," Duff assured him. "This one was round as an apple, and heavy as a steamed puddin'. 'Twas cold as charity in the place, and the thought of havin' such a plump, hot, wee bridie in your hands—meanin' no offense to ye, ma'am, I'm sure," he added hurriedly, tipping his hat in my direction.

"None taken," I assured him cordially.

"Can you swim, Mr. Duff?" Jamie asked, his tone still one of mild curiosity.

"What?" Duff blinked, taken back. "I . . . ah . . . well . . ."

"No, he can't," Roger said cheerfully. "He told me."

Duff gave him a look of outraged betrayal over Jamie's head.

"Well, there's loyalty!" he said, scandalized. "A fine shipmate *you* are! Givin' me away so—ye should be ashamed of yersel', so ye should!"

Jamie raised his oars, dripping, out of the water, and Roger followed suit. We were perhaps a quarter-mile from shore, and the water beneath our hull was a deep, soft green, portending a bottom several fathoms deep. The boat rocked gently, lifting on the bosom of a long, slow swell.

"Bonnet," Jamie said, still politely, but with a definite edge. Peter folded his arms and closed his eyes, making it clear that the subject had nothing to do with *him*. Duff sighed and eyed Jamie narrowly.

"Aye, well. It's true, I've no notion where the man is. When I saw him on Roanoke, he was makin' arrangements to have some . . . goods . . . brought in. For what that might be worth to ye," he added, rather ungraciously.

"What goods? Brought in where? And going where?" Jamie was leaning on his shipped oars, apparently casual. I could see a certain tension in the line of his body, though, and it occurred to me that while his attention might be fixed on Duff's face, he was of necessity also watching the horizon behind Duff—which was rising and falling hypnotically as the swell lifted the piretta and let it drop. Over and over and . . .

"Tea-chests was what I took in for him," Duff answered warily. "Couldna say, for the rest."

"The rest?"

"Christ, man, every boat on this water brings in the odd bit of jiggery-pokery here and there—surely ye ken that much?"

Peter's eyes had opened to half-slits; I saw them rest on Jamie's face with a certain expression of interest. The wind had shifted a few points, and the smell of dead whale was decidedly stronger. Jamie took a slow, deep breath, and let it out again, rather faster.

"Ye brought in tea, then. Where from? A ship?"

"Aye." Duff was watching Jamie, too, in growing fascination. I shifted uneasily on the narrow seat. I couldn't tell from the back of his neck, but I thought it more than likely that he was beginning to turn green.

"The *Sparrow*," Duff went on, eyes fixed on Jamie. "She anchored off the Banks, and the boats went out to her. We loaded the cargo and came in through Joad's Inlet. Cam' ashore at Wylie's Landing, and handed over to a fellow there."

"What . . . fellow?" The wind was cool, but I could see sweat trickling down the back of Jamie's neck, dampening his collar and plastering the linen between his shoulders.

Duff didn't answer immediately. A look of speculation flickered in his small, deep-set eyes.

"Don't think about it, Duff," Roger said, softly, but with great assurance. "I can reach ye from here with an oar, ken?"

"Aye?" Duff glanced thoughtfully from Jamie, to Roger, and then to me. "Aye, reckon ye might. But allowin' for the sake for argyment as how you can swim, MacKenzie—and even that Mr. Fraser might keep afloat—I dinna think that's true of the lady, is it? Skirts and petticoats . . ." He shook his head, pursing thin lips in speculation as he looked at me. "Go to the bottom like a stone, she would."

Peter shifted ever so slightly, bringing his feet under him.

"Claire?" Jamie said. I saw his fingers curl tight round the oars, and heard the note of strain in his voice. I sighed and drew the pistol out from under the coat across my lap.

"Right," I said. "Which one shall I shoot?"

Peter's eyes snapped open, wide enough that I saw a rim of white show all round his black pupils. He looked at the pistol, then at Duff, then directly at Jamie.

"Give tea to a man name Butlah," he said. "Work for Mist' Lyon." He pointed at me, then at Duff. "Shoot him," he suggested.

The ice thus broken, it took very little time for our two passengers to confide the rest of what they knew, pausing only momentarily for Jamie to be sick over the side between questions.

Smuggling was, as Duff had suggested, so common in the area as to constitute general business practice; most of the merchants—and all of the small boatmen—in Wilmington engaged in it, as did most others on the Carolina coast, in order to avoid the crippling duties on officially imported goods. Stephen Bonnet, however, was not only one of the more successful smugglers, but also rather a specialist.

"Brings in goods to order, like," Duff said, twisting his neck in order to scratch more effectively between his shoulder blades. "And in what ye might call quantity."

"How much quantity?" Jamie's elbows rested on his knees, his head sunk onto his hands. It seemed to be helping; his voice was steady.

Duff pursed his lips and squinted, calculating.

"There was six of us at the tavern on Roanoke. Six wi' small boats, I mean, as could run the inlets. If we were each to be fetchin' along as much as we could manage . . . say, fifty chests of tea all told, then."

"And he brings in such a load how often—every two months?" Roger had relaxed a little, leaning on his oars. I hadn't, and gave Duff a hard eye over the pistol to indicate as much.

"Oh, more often than that," Duff answered, eyeing me warily. "Couldn't say exactly, but you hear talk, aye? From what the other boats say, I reckon he's got a load comin' every two weeks in the season, somewhere on the coast betwixt Virginia and Charleston." Roger gave a brief grunt of surprise at that, and Jamie looked up briefly from his cupped hands.

"What about the Navy?" he asked. "Who's he paying?" That was a good question. While small boats might escape the Navy's eye, Bonnet's operation evidently involved large quantities of contraband, coming in on large ships. It would be hard to hide something on that scale—and the obvious answer was that he wasn't bothering to hide it.

Duff shook his head and shrugged.

"Can't say, man."

"But you haven't worked for Bonnet since February?" I asked. "Why not?"

Duff and Peter exchanged a glance.

"You eat scorpion-fish, you hungry," Peter said to me. "You don' eat dem, iffen you got sumpin' bettah."

"What?"

"The man's dangerous, Sassenach," Jamie translated dryly. "They dinna like to deal with him, save for need."

"Well, see him, Bonnet," Duff said, warming to the topic. "He's no bad at all to deal with—sae long as your interest runs wi' his. Only, if it might be as all of a sudden it *doesna* quite run with his . . ."

Peter solemnly drew a finger across his stringy neck, nodding in affirmation.

"And it's no as if there's warnin' about it, either," Duff added, nodding too. "One minute, it's whisky and segars, the next, ye're on your back in the sawdust, breathin' blood, and happy still to be breathin' at that."

"A temper, has he?" Jamie drew a hand down over his face, then wiped his sweaty palm on his shirt. The linen clung damply to his shoulders, but I knew he wouldn't take it off.

Duff, Peter, and Roger all shook their heads simultaneously at the question.

"Cold as ice," Roger said, and I heard the small note of strain in his voice.

"Kill ye without the turn of an arse-hair," Duff assured Jamie.

"Rip you like dem whale," Peter put in helpfully, with a wave toward the island. The current had carried us a good deal closer to the land, and I could see the whale as well as smell it. Seabirds whirled and screamed in a great cloud over the carcass, swooping down to tear away gobbets of flesh, and a small crowd of people clustered nearby, hands to their noses, clearly clutching handkerchiefs and sachets.

Just then, the wind changed, and a fetid gust of decay washed over us like a breaking wave. I clapped Roger's shirt to my own face, and even Peter appeared to pale.

"Mother of God, have mercy on me," Jamie said, under his breath. "I—oh, Christ!" He leaned to the side and threw up, repeatedly.

I nudged Roger in the buttock with my toe.

"Row," I suggested.

Roger obeyed with alacrity, putting his back into it, and within a few minutes, the keel of the piretta touched sand. Duff and Peter leaped out to run the hull up onto the beach, then gallantly assisted me out of the boat, evidently not holding the pistol against me.

Jamie paid them, then staggered a short distance up the beach and sat down, quite suddenly, in the sand beneath a loblolly pine. He was roughly the same shade as the dead whale, a dirty gray with white blotches.

"Will we wait for ye, sir, and row ye back?" Duff, his purse now bulging healthily, hovered helpfully over Jamie.

"No," Jamie said. "Take them." He waved feebly at me and Roger, then closed his eyes and swallowed heavily. "As for me, I believe . . . I shall just . . . swim back."

# 101

# MONSTERS AND HEROES

THE LITTLE BOYS WERE mad to see the whale, and tugged their reluctant mothers along like kites. I came along, keeping a somewhat more discreet distance from the towering carcass, leaving Jamie on the beach to recover. Roger took Duff aside for a bit of private conversation, while Peter subsided into somnolence in the bottom of the boat.

The carcass was newly washed up on the beach, though it must have been dead for some time before its landing; such an impressive state of decomposition must have taken days to develop. The stench notwithstanding, a number of the more intrepid visitors were standing on the carcass, waving cheerily to their companions on the beach below, and a gentleman armed with a hatchet was employed in hacking chunks of flesh from the side of the animal, dropping these into a pair of large buckets. I recognized him as the proprietor of an ordinary on Hawthorn Street, and made a mental note to strike that establishment from our list of potential eating-places.

Numbers of small crustaceans, not nearly so fastidious in their habits, swarmed merrily over the carcass, and I saw several people, also armed with buckets, picking the larger crabs and crayfish off like ripe fruit. Ten million sand fleas had joined the circus, too, and I retreated to a safe distance, rubbing my ankles.

I glanced back down the beach, seeing that Jamie had risen now and joined the conversation—Duff was looking increasingly restive, glancing back and forth from the whale to his boat. Clearly, he was anxious to return to business, before the attraction should disappear altogether.

At last he succeeded in escaping, and scampered away toward his piretta, looking hunted. Jamie and Roger came toward me, but the little boys were clearly not ready yet to leave the whale. Brianna nobly volunteered to watch them both, so that Marsali could climb the nearby lighthouse tower, to see whether there might be any sign of the *Octopus*.

"What have you been saying to poor Mr. Duff?" I asked Jamie. "He looked rather worried."

"Aye? No need of worry," he said, glancing toward the water, where Duff's piretta was rapidly pulling back to the quay. "I've only put a wee bit of business in his way."

"He knows where Lyon is," Roger put in. He looked disturbed, but excited.

"And Mr. Lyon knows where Bonnet is—or if not where, precisely, at least how to get word to him. Let us go a bit higher, aye?" Jamie was still pale; he gestured toward the stair of the tower with his chin, wiping sweat from the side of his neck.

The air *was* fresher at the top of the tower, but I had little attention to spare for the view out over the ocean.

"And so . . . ?" I said, not sure I wanted to hear the answer.

"So I have commissioned Duff to carry a message to Mr. Lyon. All being agreeable, we will meet with Mr. Bonnet at Wylie's Landing, in a week's time."

I swallowed, feeling a wave of dizziness that had nothing to do with the height. I closed my eyes, clutching the wooden rail that surrounded the tiny platform we stood on. The wind was blowing hard, and the boards of the tower creaked and groaned, feeling frighteningly insubstantial.

I heard Jamie shift his weight, moving toward Roger.

"He is a man, ken?" he said quietly. "Not a monster."

Was he? It was a monster, I thought, who haunted Brianna—and perhaps her father. Would killing him reduce him, make him no more than a man again?

"I know." Roger's voice was steady, but lacked conviction.

I opened my eyes, to see the ocean falling away before me into a bank of floating mist. It was vast and beautiful—and empty. One might well fall off the end of the world, I thought.

"YE SAILED WI' our Stephen, aye? For what, two months, three?"

"Near on three," Roger answered.

*Our Stephen*, was it? And what did Jamie mean by that homely usage, then?

Jamie nodded, not turning his head. He looked out over the rolling wash of the sea, the breeze whipping strands of hair loose from their binding to dance like flames, pale in daylight.

"Ye'll have kent the man well enough, then."

Roger leaned his weight against the rail. It was solid, but wet and sticky with half-dried spray, where spume from the rocks below had reached it.

"Well enough," he echoed. "Aye. Well enough for what?"

Jamie turned then, to look him in the face. His eyes were narrowed against the wind, but straight and bright as razors.

"Well enough to ken he *is* a man—and no more."

"What else would he be?" Roger felt the edge in his own voice.

Jamie turned back toward the sea, shading his eyes with his hand as he looked toward the sinking sun.

"A monster," he said softly. "Something less than a man—or more."

Roger opened his mouth to reply, but found he could not. For it was a monster that shadowed his own heart with fear.

"How did the sailors see him?" Claire's voice came from Jamie's other side; she leaned over the rail to look around him, and the wind seized her hair and shook it out in a flying cloud, stormy as the distant sky.

"On the *Gloriana*?" Roger took a deep breath, a whiff of dead whale mingling with the fecund scent of the salt marsh behind. "They . . . respected him. Some of them were afraid of him." *Like me.* "He had the reputation of a hard captain, but a good one. Competent. Men were willing to ship with him, because he always came safe into port, his voyages were always profitable."

"Was he cruel?" Claire asked. A faint line showed between her brows.

"All captains are cruel sometimes, Sassenach," Jamie said, with a slight tinge of impatience. "They need to be."

She glanced up at him, and Roger saw her expression change, memory softening her eyes, a wry thought tightening the corner of her mouth. She laid a hand on Jamie's arm, and he saw her knuckles whiten as she squeezed.

"You've never done other than you had to," she said, so quietly that Roger could scarcely hear her. No matter; the words were plainly not meant for him. She raised her voice then, slightly. "There's a difference between cruelty and necessity."

"Aye," Jamie said, half under his breath. "And a thin line, maybe, between a monster and a hero."

# 102

# THE BATTLE OF WYLIE'S LANDING

THE SOUND WAS CALM and flat, the surface barely ruffled by tiny wind-driven waves. And a bloody good thing, too, Roger thought, looking at his father-in-law. Jamie had his eyes open, at least, fixed on the shore with a sort of desperate intensity, as though the sight of solid land, however unreachable, might yet impart some comfort. Droplets of sweat gleamed on his upper lip, and his face was the same nacreous color as the dawn sky, but he hadn't vomited yet.

Roger wasn't seasick, but he felt nearly as ill as Jamie looked. Neither of them had eaten any breakfast, but he felt as though he'd swallowed a large mass of parritch, liberally garnished with carpet-tacks.

"That's it." Duff sat back on his oars, nodding toward the wharf ahead. It was cool on the water—almost cold at this hour—but the air was thick with moisture, and sweat ran down his face from his efforts. Peter sat silent on his own oars, dark face set in an expression indicating that he wanted nothing to do with this enterprise, and the sooner their unwelcome cargo disembarked, the better.

Wylie's Landing seemed like a mirage, floating in a layer of mist above the water amid a thick growth of needlerush and cord grass. Marshland, clumps of stunted coastal forest, and broad stretches of open water surrounded it, under an overwhelming arch of pale gray sky. By comparison to the green enclosures of the mountains, it seemed uncomfortably exposed. At the same time, it was completely isolated, evidently miles from any other sign of human habitation.

That was in part illusion; Roger knew that the plantation house was no more than a mile from the landing, but it was hidden by a dense growth of scraggy-looking forest that sprang from the marshy ground like some misshapen, dwarfish Sherwood, thick with vines and brush.

The landing itself consisted of a short wooden dock on pilings, and a collection of ramshackle sheds adjoining it, weathered to a silver-gray that seemed about to disappear into the lowering sky. A small open boat was drawn up on the shore, hull upturned. A zigzag split-rail fence enclosed a small pen beyond the sheds; Wylie must ship livestock by water now and then.

Jamie touched the cartridge box that hung at his belt, either for reassurance, or perhaps only to insure that it was still dry. His eyes went to the sky, assessing, and Roger realized with a sudden qualm that if it rained, the guns might not be dependable. Black powder clumped in the damp; more than a trace of moisture and it wouldn't fire at all. And the last thing he wanted was to find himself facing Stephen Bonnet with a useless gun.

*He is a man, no more,* he repeated silently to himself. Let

Bonnet swell to supernatural proportions in his mind, and he was doomed. He groped for some reassuring image, and fastened on a memory of Stephen Bonnet, seated in the head of the *Gloriana*, breeches puddled round his bare feet, blond-stubbled jaw slack in the morning light, his eyes half-closed in the pleasure of taking a peaceful crap.

*Shit,* he thought. Think of Bonnet as a monster, and it became impossible; think of him as a man, and it was worse. And yet, it had to be done.

His palms were sweating; he rubbed them on his breeks, not even bothering to try to hide it. There was a dirk on his belt, along with the pair of pistols; the sword lay in the bottom of the boat, solid in its scabbard. He thought of John Grey's letter, and Captain Marsden's eyes, and tasted something bitter and metallic at the back of his throat.

At Jamie's direction, the piretta drew slowly nearer the landing, everyone on board alert for any sign of life.

"No one lives here?" Jamie asked, low-voiced, leaning over Duff's shoulder to scan the buildings. "No slaves?"

"No," Duff said, grunting as he pulled. "Wylie doesna use the landing sae often these days, for he's built a new road from his house—goes inland and joins wi' the main road toward Edenton."

Jamie gave Duff a cynical glance.

"And if Wylie doesna use it, there are others who do, aye?"

Roger could see that the landing was well situated for casual smuggling; out of sight from the landward side, but easily accessible from the Sound. What he had at first taken for an island to their right was in fact a maze of sandbars, separating the channel that led to Wylie's Landing from the main sound. He could see at least four smaller channels leading into the sandbanks, two of them wide enough to accommodate a good-sized ketch.

Duff chuckled under his breath.

"There's a wee shell-road as leads to the house, man," he said. "If anyone should come that way, ye'll have fair warnin'."

Peter stirred restively, jerking his head toward the sandbars.

"Tide," he muttered.

"Oh, aye. Ye'll no have long to wait—or ye will, depending." Duff grinned, evidently thinking this funny.

"Why?" Jamie said gruffly, not sharing the amusement. He was looking somewhat better, now that escape was at hand, but was obviously in no mood yet for jocularity.

"The tide's comin' in." Duff stopped rowing and leaned on his oars long enough to remove his disreputable cap and wipe his balding brow. He waved the cap at the sandbars, where a crowd of small shorebirds were running up and down in evident dementia.

"When the tide's out, the channel's too shallow to float a ketch. In two hours"—he squinted at the glow in the east that marked the sun's rising, and nodded to himself—"or a bit more, they can come in. If they're waitin' out there now, they'll come in at once, so as to finish the job and get off again before the tide turns. But if they've not come yet, they'll maybe need to wait for the evening surge. It's a chancy job, to risk the channels by night—but Bonnet's no the lad to be put off by a bit o' darkness. Still, if he's in nay rush, he might well delay 'til next morning. Aye, ye might have a bit of a wait."

Roger realized he had been holding his breath. He let it out and drew a deep, slow breath, smelling of salt and pines, with a faint stink of dead shellfish. So it would be soon—or perhaps not until after nightfall, or not until the next day's dawn. He hoped it would be soon—and hoped at the same time that it wouldn't.

The piretta slid in close to the wharf, and Duff thrust out an oar against one of the barnacle-crusted pilings, swinging the tiny boat deftly alongside. Jamie hoisted himself up onto the dock with alacrity, eager to reach dry land. Roger handed up the swords and the small bundle that contained their canteens and spare powder, then followed. He knelt on the dock, all his senses alert for the slightest sound of human movement, but heard nothing but the liquid singing of blackbirds in the marsh and the cry of gulls on the Sound.

Jamie rummaged in his pouch and pulled out a small purse, which he tossed down to Duff, with a nod. No more need be said; this was a token payment. The rest would be paid when Duff returned for them, in two days.

Jamie had waited to the last possible moment to make the arrangements, ensuring that Bonnet at least would be unreachable until after the meeting—the ambush—had taken place. If it was successful, Jamie would pay the rest of the money agreed; if it was not—Claire would pay.

He had a vision of Claire's face, pale and drawn, nodding in stiff-lipped agreement as Jamie explained the arrangements to Duff. Her eyes had flicked to Duff, then, with the fierce yellow ruthlessness of a hawk about to eviscerate a rat, and he had seen Duff flinch at the implicit threat. He hid a smile at the memory. If friendship and money were insufficient to keep Duff's mouth shut, perhaps fear of the White Lady would suffice.

They stood silently together on the dock, watching the piretta pull slowly away. The knot in Roger's stomach tightened. He would have prayed, but could not. He couldn't ask help for such a thing as he meant now to do—not from God or Michael the archangel; not from the Reverend or his parents. Only from Jamie Fraser.

He wondered now and then how many men Fraser had killed—if he counted. If he knew. It was a different thing, of course, to kill a man in battle or in self-defense, than to lie in ambush for him, planning murder in cold blood. Still, surely it would be easier for Fraser, what they meant to do.

He glanced at Fraser, and saw him watching the boat pull away. He stood still as stone, and Roger saw that his eyes were fixed somewhere far beyond the boat, beyond the sky and water—looking on some evil thing, not blinking. Fraser took a deep breath and swallowed hard. No, it wouldn't be easier for him.

Somehow, that seemed a comfort.

THEY EXPLORED ALL the sheds briefly, finding nothing but scattered rubbish: broken packing crates, heaps of moldy straw, a few gnawed bones left by dogs or slaves. One or two of the sheds had evidently once been used as living quarters, but not recently. Some animal had built a large, untidy nest against the wall of one shed; when Jamie prodded it with a stick, a plump gray rodent-like thing shot out, ran between Roger's feet, and sailed off the dock into the water with an unnerving splash.

They took up quarters in the largest shed, which was built on the wharf itself, and settled down to wait. More or less.

The plan was simplicity itself; shoot Bonnet the instant he appeared. Unless it rained, in which case it would be necessary to employ swords or knives. Stated like that, the procedure sounded altogether straightforward. Roger's imagination, though, was unable to leave it at that.

"Walk about if ye like," Jamie said, after a quarter-hour of watching Roger fidget. "We'll hear him come." He himself sat tranquil as a frog on a lily pad, methodically checking the assortment of weapons laid out before him.

"Mmphm. What if he doesna come alone?"

Jamie shrugged, eyes fixed on the flint of the pistol in his hand. He wiggled it to be sure it was firmly seated, then set the gun down.

"Then he does not. If there are men with him, we must separate him from them. I shall take him into one of the small sheds, on pretext of private conversation, and dispatch him there. You keep anyone from following; I shallna require more than a minute."

"Oh, aye? And then ye come strolling out and inform his men ye've just done for their captain, and then what?" Roger demanded.

Jamie rubbed a hand down the bridge of his nose, and shrugged again.

"He'll be dead. D'ye think he's the man to inspire such loyalty as would make his men seek vengeance for him?"

"Well . . . no," Roger said slowly. "Perhaps not." Bonnet was the type to inspire hard work from his men, but it was labor based on fear and the hope of profit, not love.

"I have discovered a good deal regarding Mr. Bonnet," Jamie observed, laying down the pistol. "He has regular associates, aye, but he doesna have particular friends. He doesna sail always with the same mate, the same crew—which sea captains often do when they find a few men who suit them well. Bonnet picks his crews as chance provides, and he chooses them for strength or skill—not for liking. That being so, I wouldna expect to find any great liking for him among them."

Roger nodded, acknowledging the truth of this observation. Bonnet had run a tight ship on the *Gloriana*, but there had been no sense of camaraderie, even with his mate and bosun. And it was true, what Jamie said; everything they had learned suggested that Bonnet picked up assistants as he required them; if he brought men with him to this rendezvous, they were unlikely to be a devoted lieutenant and crew—more likely sailors picked at random off the docks.

"All right. But if—when—we kill him, any men with him—"

"Will be in need of new employment," Jamie interrupted. "Nay, so long as we take care not to fire upon them, or give them reason to think we threaten them, I dinna think they'll trouble owermuch about Bonnet's fate. Still—" He picked up his sword, frowning slightly, and slid it in and out of the scabbard, to be sure it moved easily.

"I think if that should be the situation, then I will take Bonnet aside, as I said. Give me a minute to deal with him, then make some excuse and come as though to fetch me. Dinna stop, though; go straight through the sheds, and head for the trees. I'll come and meet ye there."

Roger eyed Jamie skeptically. Christ, the man made it sound like a Sunday outing—a turn by the river, and we'll meet in the park, I'll bring ham sandwiches and you fetch the tea.

He cleared his throat, cleared it again, and picked up one of his own pistols. The feel of it was cool and solid in his hand, a reassuring weight.

"Aye, then. Just the one thing. I'll take Bonnet."

Fraser glanced sharply at him. He kept his own eyes steady, listening to the pulse that had begun to hammer hard inside his ears.

He saw Fraser start to speak, then stop. The man stared thoughtfully at him, and he could hear the arguments, hammering on his inner ear with his pulse, as plainly as if they'd been spoken aloud.

*You have never killed a man, nor even fought in battle. You are no marksman, and only half-decent with a sword. Worse, you are afraid of the man. And if you try and fail . . .*

"I know," he said aloud, to Fraser's deep blue stare. "He's mine. I'll take him. Brianna's your daughter, aye—but she's my wife."

Fraser blinked and looked away. He drummed his fingers on his knee for a moment, then stopped, drawing breath in a deep sigh. He drew himself slowly upright and turned toward Roger once again, eyes straight.

"It is your right," he said, formally. "So, then. Dinna hesitate; dinna challenge him. Kill him the instant ye have the chance." He paused for a moment, then spoke again, eyes steady on Roger's. "If ye fall, though—know I will avenge you."

The nail-studded mass in his belly seemed to have moved upward, sticking in his throat. He coughed to shift it, and swallowed.

"Great," he said. "And if you fall, I'll avenge *you*. A bargain, is it?"

Fraser didn't laugh, and in that moment, Roger understood why men would follow him anywhere, to do anything. He only looked at Roger for a long moment, and then nodded.

"A rare bargain," he said softly. "Thank you." Taking the dirk from his belt, he began to polish it.

THEY HAD NO TIMEPIECE, but they didn't need one. Even with the sky shrouded in low-lying clouds and the sun invisible, it was possible to feel the creep of minutes, the gradual shift of the earth as the rhythms of the day changed. Birds that had sung at dawn ceased singing, and the ones who hunted in morning began. The sound of water lapping against the pilings changed in tone, as the rising tide echoed in the space beneath the wharf.

The time of high tide came and passed; the echo beneath the wharf began to grow hollow, as the water started to drop. The pulse in Roger's ears began to slacken, along with the knots in his gut.

Then something struck the dock, and the vibration juddered through the floor of the shed.

Jamie was up in an instant, two pistols through his belt, another in his hand. He cocked his head at Roger, then disappeared through the door.

Roger jammed his own pistols securely in his belt, touched the hilt of his dirk for reassurance, and followed. He caught a quick glimpse of the boat, the dark wood of its rail just showing above the edge of the wharf, and then was inside the smaller shed to the right. Jamie was nowhere in sight; he'd got to his own post, then, to the left.

He pressed himself against the wall, peering out through the slit afforded between hinge and door. The boat was drifting slowly along the edge of the dock, not yet secured. He could see just a bit of the stern; the rest was out of sight. No matter; he couldn't fire until Bonnet appeared on the wharf.

He wiped his palm on his breeks and drew the better of his two pistols, checking for the thousandth time that priming and flint were in order. The metal of the gun smelled sharp and oily in his hand.

The air was damp; his clothes stuck to him. Would the powder fire? He touched the dirk, for the ten-thousandth time, running through Fraser's instructions on killing with a knife. *Hand on his shoulder, drive it up beneath the breastbone, hard. From behind, the kidney, up from under.* God, could he do it face to face? Yes. He hoped it would be face to face. He wanted to see—

A coil of rope hit the dock; he heard the heavy thump, and then the scramble and thud of someone springing over the rail to tie up. A rustle and a grunt of effort, a pause . . . He closed his eyes, trying to hear through the thunder of his heart. Steps. Slow, but not furtive. Coming toward him.

The door stood half-ajar. He stepped silently to the edge of it, listening. Waiting. A shadow, dim in the cloudy light, fell through the door. The man stepped in.

He lunged out from behind the door and flung himself bodily at the man, knocking him back into the wall with a hollow thud. The man whooped in surprise at the impact, and the sound of the cry stopped him just as he got his hands round a distinctly unmasculine throat.

"Shit!" he said. "I mean, I—I—I beg your pardon, ma'am."

She was pressed against the wall, all his weight on her, and he was well aware that the rest of her was unmasculine, too. Blood hot in his cheeks, he released her and stepped back, breathing heavily.

She shook herself like a dog, straightening her garments, and tenderly touching the back of her head where it had struck the wall.

"I'm sorry," he said, feeling both shocked and a complete prat. "I didn't mean— Are you hurt?"

The girl was as tall as Brianna, but more solidly built, with dark brown hair and a handsome face, broad-boned and deep-eyed. She grinned at Roger and said something incomprehensible, strongly scented with onions. She looked him up and down in a bold sort of way, then, evidently approving, put her hands under her breasts in a gesture of unmistakable invitation, jerking her head toward a corner of the shed, where mounds of damp straw gave off a fecund scent of notunpleasant decay.

"Ahhh . . ." Roger said. "No. I'm afraid you're mistaken—no, don't touch that. No. *Non! Nein!*" He fumbled with her hands, which seemed determined to unfasten his belt. She said something else in the unfamiliar tongue. He didn't understand a word, but he got the sense of it well enough.

"No, I'm a married man. Would ye stop!"

She laughed, gave him a flashing glance from under long black lashes, and renewed her assault on his person.

He would have been convinced he was hallucinating, were it not for the smell. Engaged at close quarters, he realized that onions were the least of it. She wasn't filthy to look at, but had the deep-seated reek of someone just off a long sea voyage; he recognized that smell at once. Beyond that, though, the unmistakable scent of pigs wafted from her skirts.

"*Excusez-moi, Mademoiselle.*" Jamie's voice came from somewhere behind him, sounding rather startled. The girl was startled, too, though not frightened. She let go of his balls, though, allowing him to step back.

Jamie had a pistol drawn, though he held it by his side. He raised one eyebrow at Roger.

"Who's this, then?"

"How in hell should I know?" Struggling for composure, Roger shook himself back into some kind of order. "I thought she was Bonnet or one of his men, but evidently not."

"Evidently." Fraser seemed disposed to find something humorous in the situation; a muscle near his mouth was twitching fiercely. *"Qui êtes-vous, Mademoiselle?"* he asked the girl.

She frowned at him, clearly not understanding, and said something in the odd language again. Both Jamie's brows rose at that.

"What's she speaking?" Roger asked.

"I've no idea." His look of amusement tinged with wariness, Jamie turned toward the door, raising his pistol. "Watch her, aye? She'll no be alone."

This was clear; there were voices on the wharf. A man's voice, and another woman. Roger exchanged baffled glances with Jamie. No, the voice was neither Bonnet's nor Lyon's— and what in God's name were all these women doing here?

The voices were coming closer, though, and the girl suddenly called out something in her own language. It didn't sound like a warning, but Jamie quickly flattened himself beside the door, pistol at the ready and his other hand on his dirk.

The narrow door darkened almost completely, and a dark, shaggy head thrust into the shed. Jamie stepped forward and shoved his pistol up under the chin of a very large, very surprised-looking man. Seizing the man by the collar, Jamie stepped backward, drawing him into the shed.

The man was followed almost at once by a woman whose tall, solid build and handsome face identified her at once as the girl's mother. The woman was blond, though, while the man—the girl's father?—was as dark as the bear he strongly resembled. He was nearly as tall as Jamie, but almost twice as broad, massive through the chest and shoulders, and heavily bearded.

None of them appeared to be at all alarmed. The man

looked surprised, the woman affronted. The girl laughed heartily, pointing at Jamie, then at Roger.

"I begin to feel rather foolish," Jamie said to Roger. Removing the pistol, he stepped back warily. *"Wer seid Ihr?"* he said.

"I don't think they're German," Roger said. "She"—he jerked a thumb at the girl, who was now eyeing Jamie in an appraising sort of way, as though sizing up his potential for sport in the straw—"didna seem to understand either French or German, though perhaps she was pretending."

The man had been frowning, glancing from Jamie to Roger in an attempt to make out what they were saying. At the word "French," though, he seemed to brighten.

*"Comment allez-vous?"* he said, in the most execrable accent Roger had ever heard.

*"Parlez-vous français?"* Jamie said, still eyeing the man cautiously.

The giant smiled and put a callused thumb and forefinger an inch apart.

*"Un peu."*

A very little *peu*, as they shortly discovered. The man had roughly a dozen words of French, just about enough to introduce himself as one Mikhail Chemodurow, his wife Iva, and his daughter, Karina.

"Rooshki," Chemodurow said, slapping a hand across his beefy chest.

"Russians?" Roger stared at them, flabbergasted, though Jamie seemed fascinated.

"I've never met a Russian before," he said. "What in Christ's name are they doing here, though?"

With some difficulty, this question was conveyed to Mr. Chemodurow, who beamed and flung a massive arm out, pointing toward the wharf.

*"Les cochons,"* he said. *"Pour le Monsieur Wylie."* He looked expectantly at Jamie. *"Monsieur Wylie?"*

Given the eye-watering aroma rising off all three of the Russians, the mention of pigs came as no great surprise. The connection between Russian swineherds and Phillip Wylie was somewhat less obvious. Before the question could be gone into, though, there was a loud thump outside, and a grinding noise, as though some large wooden object had struck the dock. This was succeeded immediately by a piercing chorus of bellows and squeals—mostly porcine, but some of them human—and female.

Chemodurow moved with amazing speed for his size, though Jamie and Roger were on his heels as he shot through the door of the shed.

Roger had barely time to see that there were two boats now tied up at the wharf; the Russian's small bark, and a smaller open boat. Several men, bristling with knives and pistols, were swarming out of the smaller boat onto the dock.

Seeing this, Jamie dived to one side, disappearing out of sight round the edge of a smaller shed. Roger grabbed his pistol, but hesitated, not sure whether to fire or run. Hesitated a moment too long. A musket jammed up under his ribs, knocking out his breath, and hands snatched at his belt, taking pistols and dirk.

"Don't move, mate," the man holding the musket said. "Twitch, and I'll blow your liver out through your backbone."

He spoke with no particular animus, but sufficient sincerity that Roger wasn't inclined to test it. He stood still, hands half-raised, watching.

Chemodurow had waded into the invaders without hesitation, laying about him with hands like hams. One man was in the water, evidently having been knocked off the wharf, and the Russian had another in his grip, throttling him with brutal efficiency. He ignored all shouts, threats, and blows, his concentration fixed on the man he was killing.

Screams rent the air; Iva and Karina had rushed toward their boat, where two of the invaders had appeared on deck, each clutching a slightly smaller version of Karina. One of the men pointed a pistol at the Russian women. He appeared to pull the trigger; Roger saw a spark, and a small puff of smoke, but the gun failed to fire. The women didn't hesitate, but charged him, shrieking. Panicking, he dropped the gun and the girl he was holding, and jumped into the water.

A sickening thud wrenched Roger's attention from this byplay. One of the men, a short, squat figure, had clubbed Chemodurow over the head with the butt of a gun. The Russian blinked, nodded, and his grip on his victim loosened slightly. His assailant grimaced, took a tighter hold on the gun, and smashed him again. The Russian's eyes rolled up into his head and he dropped to the dock, shaking the boards with the impact.

Roger had been looking from man to man, searching urgently amid the melee for Stephen Bonnet. Look as he might, though, there was no trace of the *Gloriana*'s erstwhile captain.

What was wrong? Bonnet was no coward, and he was a natural fighter. It wasn't thinkable that he would send men in, and hang back himself. Roger looked again, counting heads, trying to keep track of men, but the conclusion became stronger, as the chaos quickly died down. Stephen Bonnet wasn't there.

Roger hadn't time to decide whether he was disappointed or relieved by this discovery. The man who had clubbed Chemodurow turned toward him at this point, and he recognized David Anstruther, the sheriff of Orange County. Anstruther recognized him, too—he saw the man's eyes narrow—but didn't seem surprised to see him.

The fight—such as it was—was wrapping up quickly. The four Russian women had all been rounded up and pushed into the largest shed, amid much screaming and shouting of curses, and the fallen Chemodurow was dragged in as well, leaving a disquieting smear of blood along the boards in his wake.

At this point, a pair of well-kept hands appeared on the edge of the dock, and a tall, elegantly lean man pulled himself up from the boat. Roger had no difficulty in recognizing Mr. Lillywhite, one of the Orange County magistrates, even without his wig and bottle-green coat.

Lillywhite had dressed for the occasion in plain black broadcloth, though his linen was as fine as ever and he had a gentleman's sword at his side. He made his way across the dock, in no great hurry, observing the disposition of matters as he went. Roger saw his mouth tighten fastidiously at sight of the trail of blood.

Lillywhite gestured to the man holding Roger, and at last, the bruising pressure of the gun-muzzle eased, allowing him to draw a deep breath.

"Mr. MacKenzie, is it not?" Lillywhite asked pleasantly. "And where is Mr. Fraser?"

He'd been expecting that question, and had had time to contemplate the answer.

"In Wilmington," he said, matching Lillywhite's pleasant tone. "You're rather far afield yourself, are ye not, sir?"

Lillywhite's nostrils pinched momentarily, as though smelling something bad—which he certainly was, though Roger doubted the reek of pigs was causing his disedification.

"Do not trifle with me, sir," the magistrate said curtly.

"Wouldn't dream of it," Roger assured him, keeping an eye on the fellow with the musket, who seemed disposed to resume jabbing. "Though if we're asking that sort of question—where's Stephen Bonnet?"

Lillywhite gave a brief laugh, a sort of wintry amusement coming into his pale gray eyes.

"In Wilmington."

Anstruther appeared at the magistrate's elbow, squat and sweaty. He gave Roger a nod and an ugly grin.

"MacKenzie. Nice to see you again. Where's your father-in-law, and more important—where's the whisky?"

Lillywhite frowned at the sheriff.

"You haven't found it? Have you searched the sheds?"

"Aye, we looked. Nothing there but bits of rubbish." He rocked up onto his toes, menacing. "So, MacKenzie, where'd you hide it?"

"I haven't hidden anything," Roger replied equably. "There isn't any whisky." He was beginning to relax a little. Wherever Stephen Bonnet was, he wasn't here. He didn't expect them to be pleased at discovering that the whisky was a ruse, but—

The Sheriff hit him in the pit of the stomach. He doubled up, his vision went dark, and he struggled vainly to breathe, fighting a flash of panic as he relived his hanging, the black, the lack of air . . .

Bright floating spots appeared at the edges of his vision, and he drew breath, gasping. He was sitting on the dock, legs splayed out before him, the Sheriff clutching a handful of his hair.

"Try again," Anstruther advised him, shaking him roughly by the hair. The pain was irritating, rather than discomfiting, and he swiped a fist at the Sheriff, catching him a solid blow on the thigh. The man yelped and let go, hopping backward.

"Did you look on the other boat?" Lillywhite demanded, ignoring the Sheriff's discomfort. Anstruther glowered at Roger, rubbing his thigh, but shook his head in answer.

"Nothing there but pigs and girls. And where in fuck's name did *they* come from?" he demanded.

"Russia." Roger coughed, clenched his teeth against the resulting burst of pain, and got slowly to his feet, holding an arm across his middle to keep his guts from spilling out. The Sheriff doubled a fist in anticipation, but Lillywhite made a quelling gesture toward him. He looked incredulously at Roger.

"Russia? What have they to do with this business?"

"Nothing, so far as I know. They arrived soon after I did."

The magistrate grunted, looking displeased. He frowned for a moment, thinking, then decided to try another tack.

"Fraser had an arrangement with Milford Lyon. I have now assumed Mr. Lyon's part of the agreement. It is altogether proper for you to deliver the whisky to me," he said, attempting to infuse a note of businesslike politeness into his voice.

"Mr. Fraser has made other arrangements," Roger said, with equal politeness. "He sent me to say as much to Mr. Lyon."

That seemed to take Lillywhite aback. He pursed his lips, and worked them in and out, staring hard at Roger, as though to estimate his truthfulness. Roger stared blandly back, hoping that Jamie wouldn't reappear inopportunely and put paid to his story.

"How did you get here?" Lillywhite demanded abruptly. "If you did not travel on that boat?"

"I came overland from Edenton." Blessing Duff for the information, he waved casually over his shoulder. "There's a shell road back there."

The two of them stared at him, but he stared back, undaunted.

"Something smells fishy, and it isn't the marsh."

Anstruther sniffed loudly in illustration, then coughed and snorted. "Phew! What a stink."

Lillywhite disregarded this, but went on looking at Roger with a narrowed eye.

"I think perhaps I must inconvenience you for a little longer, Mr. MacKenzie," he said, and turned to the Sheriff. "Put him in with the Russians—if that's what they are."

Anstruther accepted this commission with alacrity, prodding Roger in the buttocks with the muzzle of his musket as he forced him toward the shed where the Russians were imprisoned. Roger gritted his teeth and ignored it, wondering how high the Sheriff might bounce, if picked up and slammed down on the boards of the dock.

The Russians were all clustered in the corner of the shed, the women tending solicitously to their wounded husband and father, but they all looked up at Roger's entrance, with a babble of incomprehensible greetings and questions. He gave them as much of a smile as he could manage, and waved them back, pressing his ear to the wall of the shed in order to hear what Lillywhite and company were up to now.

He had hoped they would simply accept his story and depart—and they might still do that, once they satisfied themselves that there really was no whisky hidden anywhere near the landing. Another possibility had occurred to him, though; one that was making him increasingly uneasy.

It was clear enough from the behavior of the men that they had intended to take the whisky by force—if there had been any. And the way Lillywhite had held back, concealing himself . . . it wouldn't do, obviously, for a county magistrate to be revealed as having connections with smugglers and pirates.

As it was, since there was no whisky, Roger could report no actual wrongdoing on Lillywhite's part—it was illegal to deal in contraband, of course, but such arrangements were so common on the coast that the mere rumor of it wasn't likely to damage Lillywhite's reputation in his own inland county. On the other hand, Roger was alone—or Lillywhite thought he was.

There was clearly some connection between Lillywhite and Stephen Bonnet—and if Roger and Jamie Fraser began to ask questions, chances were good that it would come to light. Was whatever Lillywhite was engaged in sufficiently dangerous that he might think it worth killing Roger to prevent his talking? He had the uneasy feeling that Lillywhite and Anstruther might well come to that conclusion.

They could simply take him into the marsh, kill him and sink his body, then return to their companions, announcing that he had gone back to Edenton. Even if someone eventually traced the members of Lillywhite's gang, *and* if they could be persuaded to talk—both matters of low probability—nothing could be proved.

There was a lot of thumping and banging outside, gradually succeeded by more distant calling, as the sheds were re-searched, and the search then spread to the nearby marsh.

It occurred to Roger that Lillywhite and Anstruther might well have intended to kill him and Jamie after taking the whisky. In which case, there was still less to prevent them doing it now; they would be already prepared for it. As for the Russians—would they harm them? He hoped not, but there was no telling.

A light pattering rang on the tin roof of the shed; it was beginning to rain. Fine, if their powder got wet, they wouldn't shoot him; they'd have to cut his throat. He went from hoping that Jamie wouldn't show up too soon, to hoping fervently that he wouldn't show up too late. As to what he might do if and when he *did* show up . . .

The swords. Were the swords still where they had left them, in the corner of the shed? The rain had grown too loud for him to hear anything outside, anyway; he abandoned his listening post and went to look.

The Russians all looked up at him with mingled expressions of wariness and concern. He smiled and nodded, making little shooing gestures to get them out of the way. Yes, the swords were still there—that was something, and he felt a small surge of hope.

Chemodurow was conscious; he said something in a slurred voice, and Karina got up at once and came to stand by Roger. She patted him gently on the arm, then took one of the swords from him. She drew it from its scabbard with a ringing whoosh that made them all jump, then laugh nervously. She wrapped her hands round the hilt and held it over her shoulder, like a baseball bat. She marched over to the door and took up her station beside it, scowling fiercely.

"Great," Roger said, and gave her a broad smile of approval. "Anyone pokes his head in, take it off, aye?" He mimed a chopping motion with the side of his hand, and the Russians all made loud growling sounds of enthusiastic support. One of the younger girls reached for the other sword, but he smiled and indicated that he would keep it, thanks anyway.

To his surprise, she shook her head, saying something in Russian. He raised his eyebrows and shook his head helplessly. She tugged on his arm, and made him come with her, back toward the corner.

They had been busy during the brief period of their captivity. They had moved aside the rubbish, made a comfortable pallet for the injured man—and uncovered the large trapdoor installed in the floor, meant to be used by boats coming under the wharf at low tide, so that cargo could be handed directly up into the shed, rather than unloaded onto the dock.

The tide was going out now; it was a drop of more than six feet to the water's dark surface. He stripped to his breeks and hung by his hands from the edge of the trapdoor before dropping in feetfirst, not wanting to risk a dive into what might be dangerous shallows.

The water was higher than his head, though; he sank in a shower of silver bubbles, then his feet touched the sandy bottom and he launched himself upward, breaking the surface with a whoosh of air. He waved reassuringly at the circle of Russian faces peering down at him through the trapdoor, then struck out for the far end of the wharf.

FROM HIS PERCH on the roof of the shed, Jamie assessed the magistrate's way of moving, and the manner in which he fondled the weapon. Lillywhite turned away, his hand nervously caressing the hilt of his sword. A long reach, and a good bearing; quick, too, if a little jerky. To wear a sword under these circumstances suggested both a habit of familiarity with the weapon and a fondness for it.

He couldn't see Anstruther, who had pressed himself back against the wall of the shed, under the overhang of the roof, but he was less concerned with the Sheriff. A brawler, that one, and short in the arm.

"I say we kill them all. Only way to be safe."

There was a grunt of dubious assent from Lillywhite.

"That may be—but the men? We do not wish to put our fate in the hands of witnesses who may talk. We could have dealt with Fraser and MacKenzie safely out of sight—but so many . . . perhaps we may leave these Russians; they are foreigners and seem not to speak any English. . . ."

"Aye, and how did they come here, I'd like to know? I'll warrant they wasn't caught up in a waterspout and set down here by accident. Someone knows about 'em, someone will come looking for 'em—and whoever that someone is, he's got some means to talk to 'em, I'll be bound. They've seen too much already—and if you mean to go on using this place . . ."

The rain was still light, but coming down steadily. Jamie turned his head to wipe the moisture out of his eyes against his shoulder. He was lying flat, arms and legs outspread like a frog's to keep from sliding down the pitch of the tin roof. He didn't dare to move, just yet. The rain was whispering out on the Sound, though, puckering the water like drawn silk, and making a faint ringing noise on the metal around him. Let it rain just that wee bit harder, and it would cover any noise he made.

He shifted his weight a little, feeling the press of the dirk, hard under his hipbone. The pistols lay beside him on the roof, likely useless in the rain. The dirk was his only real weapon at the moment, and one much better suited to surprise than to a frontal attack.

". . . send the men back with the boat. We can go by the road, after . . ."

They were still talking, low-voiced, but he could tell that the decision had been made; Lillywhite only needed to convince himself that it was a matter of necessity, and that wouldn't take long. They'd send the men away first, though; the magistrate was right to be afraid of witnesses.

He blinked water out of his eyes and glanced toward the larger shed, where Roger Mac and the Russians were. The sheds were close together; the gaps between the staggered tin roofs no more than three or four feet. There was one shed between him and the larger one. Well, then.

He would take advantage of the men leaving to move across the roofs, and trust to luck and the rain to prevent Lillywhite or Anstruther from looking up. Crouch above the door to the shed, and when they came to do the deed, wait just until they'd got the door open, then drop on the magistrate from above and hope to break his neck or at least disable him at once. Roger Mac could be depended on to rush out and help deal with the Sheriff, then.

It was the best plan he could contrive under the circumstances, and not a bad one, he thought. If he didn't slip and break his own neck, of course. Or a leg. He flexed his left leg, feeling the slight stiffness of the muscles in his calf. It was healed, but there was no denying the slight weakness remaining. He could manage well enough, walking, but jumping across rooftops . . .

"Aye, well, needs must when the Devil drives," he muttered. If it came to smash and he ruined the leg again, he'd better hope the Sheriff killed him, because Claire surely would.

The thought made him smile, but he couldn't think about her now. Later, when it was finished. His shirt was soaked through, stuck to his shoulders, and the rain was chiming off the tin roofs like a chorus of fairy-bells. Squirming cautiously backward, he got his knees under him and rose to a crouch, ready to drop flat again if anyone was looking up.

No one was on the dock. There were four men besides Lillywhite and the Sheriff; all of them were out in the soft ground to the south of the landing, poking through the waist-high grass in a desultory fashion. He took a deep breath and got his feet slowly under him. As he swiveled round, though, he caught a flicker of movement from the corner of his eye, and froze.

Holy Christ, there were men coming out of the wood. For an instant, he thought it was more of Lillywhite's doing, and then he realized that the men were black. All but one.

*Les Cochons,* the Russian had said. *Pour le Monsieur Wylie.* And here was Monsieur Wylie, coming with his slaves to collect his pigs!

He lay down on his belly again and squirmed over the wet metal, eeling toward the back of the shed roof. It was open to question, he thought, whether Wylie would be better disposed to help him or to run him through himself—but he did suppose the man had some stake in preserving his Russians.

THE WATER WAS COLD, but not numbing, and the pull of the tidal current wasn't great yet. Still, the injury to his throat and the searing of the canebrake fire had left him much shorter of breath than he used to be, and Roger found himself obliged to bob to the surface and gasp for air with every three or four strokes.

*Ruby lips, above the water,* he sang ironically to himself, *blowing bubb-les soft and fine . . ..* He drew in a gulp of air, and trod water, listening. He had headed toward the south side of the landing first, but had heard voices above, and so reversed direction. He was just under the north edge of the wharf now, hidden in the deep shadow by the Russians' boat.

The smell of pigs was overwhelming, and he could hear muffled thumps and grunts from the hold, coming through the wood beside him. Christ, had they sailed that tiny craft all the way from Russia? It looked it; the wood was battered and dented.

No sound of voices nearby. It was raining hard, shushing into the Sound; that would help cover any racket he made. Ready, steady, go, then. He took a great lungful of air and launched himself into the rainy light beyond the landing.

He swam desperately, trying not to splash, expecting a musket ball between the shoulder blades every moment. He blundered into the weeds, felt the grasp and slash of sawgrass on arm and leg, rolled half-over, gasping, salt burning in the cuts, and then was on his hands and knees, crawling through the growth of marsh plants, black needlerushes waving over his head, rain pounding on his back, the water lapping just below his chin.

He stopped at last, chest heaving with the need for air, and wondered what in hell to do next. It was good to be out of the shed, but he hadn't a plan for what happened now. Find Jamie, he supposed—if he could, without being caught again.

As though the thought had drawn attention to him, he heard the slosh and swish of someone walking slowly through the marsh nearby. Searching. He froze, hoping the rain would cover the sound of his breath, loud and rasping in his ears.

Closer. Damn, they were coming closer. He fumbled at his belt, but he had lost the dirk, somewhere in his swimming. He got one knee up under his chin, braced himself to spring and run.

The grass above him swept suddenly away, and he leaped to his feet, just in time to avoid the spear that sliced into the water where he'd lain.

The spear quivered in front of him, six inches from his face. On the other side of it, a black man gaped at him, eyes saucered in amazement. The Negro closed his mouth, blinked at him, and spoke in tones of deepest accusation.

"You ain't no possum!"

"No," said Roger, mildly. "I'm not." He brushed a trembling hand down his chest, assuring himself that his heart was still inside it. "Sorry."

PHILLIP WYLIE LOOKED a great deal different at home, Roger thought, than he did in society. Attired for pig-catching in loose breeks and a farmer's smock, damp with rain, and minus any trace of wig, paint, powder, or patches, he was still elegantly slender, but looked quite normal, and reasonably competent. He also looked somewhat more intelligent, though his mouth did tend to keep dropping open, and he did insist on breaking into Jamie's account with questions and expostulations.

"Lillywhite? Randall Lillywhite? But what can he—"

"Concentrate, man," Jamie said impatiently. "I'm telling ye now, and I'll tell ye more later, but he and yon sheriff are like to be carving up your Russians like a set of Christmas hams, and we dinna go and tend to the matter this minute."

Wylie glared at Jamie, then looked suspiciously at Roger, who was standing under the cover of the forest, half-naked, soaking wet, and covered with blood-streaked mud.

"He's right," Roger croaked, then coughed, cleared his throat, and repeated it, more firmly. "He's right; there's not much time."

Wylie's lips compressed into a thin line, and he exhaled strongly through his nose. He looked round at his slaves, as though counting them; a half-dozen men, all carrying stout sticks. One or two had cane-knives at their belts. Wylie nodded, making up his mind.

"Come on, then."

Avoiding the telltale crunching of the shell-road, they made slow but steady progress through the marsh.

"Why pigs?" He heard Jamie ask curiously, as he and Wylie forged ahead of the group.

"Not pigs," Wylie replied. "Russian boars. For sport." He spoke rather proudly, swishing his own stick through the thick grass. "Everyone says that of all game, the Russian boar is the fiercest and most wily opponent. I propose to release them in the woods on my property and allow them to breed."

"Ye mean to hunt them?" Jamie sounded mildly incredulous. "Have ye ever hunted a boar?"

Roger saw Wylie's shoulders stiffen under his damp smock at the question. The rain had slackened, but was still coming down.

"No," he said. "Not yet. Have you?"

"Yes," Jamie said, but wisely didn't amplify the answer.

As they drew near the landing, Roger caught a glimpse of movement beyond. The smaller boat was pulling away.

"They've given up looking for me or the whisky, and sent their men away." Jamie wiped a hand down his face, slicking the rain off. "What say ye, Wylie? There's no time to lose. The Russians are in the main shed, on the wharf."

Once decided, Wylie was no ditherer.

"Storm the place," he said shortly.

He waved a hand, beckoning his slaves to follow, and headed for the landing at a trot. The whole party swerved onto the shell-road, thundering toward the wharf with a noise like an avalanche. That ought to give Lillywhite and Anstruther pause in their murdering, Roger thought. They sounded like an approaching army.

Barefoot, Roger kept to the marshy ground, and was in consequence slower than the rest. He saw a startled face peer out between the sheds, and quickly withdraw.

Jamie saw it too, and gave one of his wild Highland cries. Wylie jerked, startled, but then joined in, bellowing "Get out of it, you bastards!" Thus encouraged, the Negroes all began shouting and bellowing, waving their sticks with enthusiasm as they charged the landing.

It was something of an anticlimax to arrive on the wharf and find no one there save the captive Russians, who narrowly missed beheading Phillip Wylie when he imprudently shoved open the door to their prison without announcing himself.

A brief search of the Russian boat and the surrounding marsh turned up no trace of Lillywhite and Anstruther.

"Most like they swim for it," one of the Negroes said, returning from the search. He nodded across the channel, toward the tangle of the sandbars, and fingered his spear. "We go hunt them?" It was the man who had discovered Roger, evidently still eager to try his luck.

"They didn't swim," Wylie said shortly. He gestured at the tiny beach near the landing, an empty stretch of oyster shells. "They've taken my boat, blast them."

He turned away, disgusted, and began to give orders for unloading and penning the Russian boars. Chemodurow and his family had already been taken off to the plantation house, with the girls alternating between amazement at the black slaves and coy looks at Roger, who had retrieved his shirt and shoes, but whose breeches were still plastered to his body.

One of the slaves appeared from the shed with an armful of discarded weaponry, recalling Wylie temporarily to the duties of a host.

"I am obliged to you for your help in preserving my property, sir," he said to Jamie. He bowed, rather stiffly. "Will you not allow me to offer you and Mr. MacKenzie my hospitality?" He didn't sound thrilled about it, Roger noted, but still, he'd offered.

"I am obliged to you, sir, for your help in preserving our lives," Jamie said with equal stiffness, returning the bow. "And I thank ye, but—"

"We'd be delighted," Roger interrupted. "Thanks." He gave Wylie a firm handshake, surprising him very much, and grabbed Jamie by the arm, steering him toward the shell-road before he could protest. There were times and places to be on your high horse, he supposed, but this wasn't one of them.

"Look, ye havena got to kiss the man's bum," he said, in response to Jamie's mutterings, as they slogged toward the forest. "Let his butler give us a dry towel and a bit of lunch, and we'll be off while he's still busy with his boars. I've had no breakfast, and neither have you. And if we've got to walk to Edenton, I'm no doing it on an empty belly."

The mention of food seemed to go some way toward restoring Jamie's equanimity, and as they reached the semi-shelter of the wood, a mood of almost giddy cheerfulness had sprung up between them. Roger wondered if this was the sort of way you felt after a battle; the sheer relief of finding yourself alive and unwounded made you want to laugh and arse about, just to prove you still could.

By unspoken consent, they left discussion of recent events—and speculation as to the present whereabouts of Stephen Bonnet—for later.

"Russian boars, for Christ's sake," Jamie said, shaking himself like a dog as they paused under the shelter of the wood. "And I doubt the man's ever seen a boar in his life! Ye'd think he could manage to kill himself without going to such expense about it."

"Aye, what d'ye think it must have cost? More money than we'll see in ten years, likely, just to haul a lot of pigs . . . what, six thousand miles?" He shook his head, staggered at the thought.

"Well, to be fair about it, they're more than only pigs," Jamie said tolerantly. "Did ye not see them?"

Roger had, though only briefly. The slaves had been herding one of the animals across the dock as he'd emerged from the shed with his clothes. It was tall and hairy, with long yellow tushes that looked nasty enough.

It was emaciated from the long sea-voyage, though, its ribs showing and half its bristly pelt rubbed bald. It had obviously not got its landlegs yet, staggering and careening drunkenly on its ridiculous small hooves, eyes rolling, grunting in panic as the slaves shouted and poked at it with their poles. Roger had felt quite sorry for it.

"Oh, they're big enough, aye," he said. "And I suppose once they're filled out a bit, they'd be something to see. I wonder how they'll like this, though, after Russia?" He waved a hand at the damp, scrubby wood around them. The air was moist with rain, but the trees blocked most of the downfall, leaving it dark and resin-smelling under the low canopy of scrub oak and scraggy pines. Twigs and acorn caps crunched pleasantly under their boots on the sandy earth.

"Well, there are acorns and roots aplenty," Jamie observed, "and the odd Negro now and then, for a treat. I expect they'll do well enough."

Roger laughed, and Jamie grunted in amusement.

"Ye think I'm jesting, aye? Ye'll not have hunted boar, either, I suppose."

"Mmphm. Well, perhaps Mr. Wylie will invite us to come and—"

The back of his head exploded, and everything disappeared.

AT SOME POINT, he became aware again. Aware mostly of a pain so great that unconsciousness seemed immensely preferable. But aware too of pebbles and leaves pressing into his face, and of noises nearby. The clash and thud and grunt of men fighting in earnest.

He forced himself toward consciousness, and raised his head, though the effort made colored fireworks go off inside his eyes and made him want very badly to throw up. He braced himself on his folded arms, teeth gritted, and after a moment, his vision cleared, though things were still blurred.

It took a moment to make out what was happening; they were ten feet or so beyond the spot where he lay, with bits of tree and brush obscuring the fight. He caught a muttered "*A Dhia!*" though, among the panting and grunting, and felt a sharp pang of relief. Jamie was alive, then.

He got to his knees, swaying, and stayed there for a moment, his vision winking in and out of blackness. When it steadied, his head had fallen forward and he was staring at the ground. His sword lay a few feet away, half-covered with scuffed sand and leaves. One of his pistols was with it, but he didn't bother with that; he couldn't hold it steady, even if the powder were still dry enough to fire.

He scrabbled and fumbled, but once he'd got his hand wedged into the basket of the sword's hilt, he felt a little better; he wouldn't drop it, now. Something wet was running down his neck—blood, rain? It didn't matter. He staggered, clutched a tree with his free hand, blinked away the blackness, took another step.

He felt like the boar, unfamiliar ground shifting and treacherous under his feet. He trod on something that rolled and gave way, and he fell, landing hard on one elbow.

He turned awkwardly over, hampered by the sword, and found that he had stepped on Anstruther's leg. The Sheriff was lying on his back, mouth open, looking surprised. There was a large rip in his neck, and a lot of blood had soaked into the sand around him, rusty and stinking.

He recoiled, and the shock of it got him on his feet, with no memory of having stood up. Lillywhite's back was to him, the linen of his shirt wet and sticking to his flesh. He lunged, grunting, then flung back, beat, riposted . . .

Roger shook his head, trying to clear it of the idiotic terms of swordsmanship, then stopped, gasping with pain. Jamie's face was set in a maniac half-grin, teeth bared with effort as he followed his opponent's weapon. He'd seen Roger, though.

"Roger!" he shouted, breathless with the fight. "Roger, *a charaid!*"

Lillywhite didn't turn, but flung himself forward, feinting, beating away, lunging back in tierce.

"Not . . . stupid . . ." he gasped.

Roger realized dimly that Lillywhite thought Jamie was bluffing, trying to make him turn around. His vision was flickering round the edges again, and he grabbed for a tree, gripping hard to stay upright. The foliage was wet; his grip was slipping.

"Hey . . ." he called hoarsely, unable to think of any words. He raised his sword, the tip trembling. "Hey!"

Lillywhite stepped back and whirled around, eyes wide with shock. Roger lunged blindly, with no aim, but with all the power left in his body behind it.

The sword went into Lillywhite's eye, and a slithering crunch ran up Roger's arm, as metal scraped bone and went through to something softer, where it stuck. He tried to let go, but his hand was trapped in the basket-hilt. Lillywhite went stiff, and Roger could feel the man's life run straight down the sword, through his hand, and up his arm, swift and shocking as an electric current.

Panicked, he jerked and twisted, trying to get the sword free. Lillywhite spasmed, went limp, and fell toward him, flopping like a huge dead fish as Roger wrenched and yanked, vainly trying to free himself from the sword.

Then Jamie seized him by the wrist and got him loose, got an arm around him, and led him away, stumbling and blind with panic and pain. Held his head and rubbed his back, murmuring nonsense in Gaelic while he puked and heaved. Wiped his face and neck with handsful of wet leaves, wiped the snot from his nose with the wet sleeve of his shirt.

"You okay?" Roger mumbled, somewhere in the midst of this.

"Aye, fine," Jamie said, and patted him again. "You're fine, too, all right?"

At length he was on his feet again. His head had gone past the point of pain; it still hurt, but the pain seemed a separate thing from himself, hovering somewhere nearby, but not actually touching him.

Lillywhite lay face-up in the leaves. Roger closed his eyes and swallowed. He heard Jamie mutter something under his breath, and then a grunt, a rustling of leaves, and a small thud. When Roger opened his eyes, Lillywhite was lying facedown, the back of his shirt smeared with sand and acorn hulls.

"Come on." Jamie got him under the arm, pulled the arm over his shoulder. Roger lifted his free hand, waved it vaguely toward the bodies.

"Them. What should we do with . . . them?"

"Leave them for the pigs."

Roger could walk by himself by the time they left the wood, though he had a tendency to drift to one side or the other, unable to steer quite straight as yet. Wylie's house lay before them, a handsome construction in red brick. They picked their way across the lawn, ignoring the stares of several house-servants, who clustered at the upstairs windows, pointing down at them and murmuring to one another.

"Why?" Roger asked, stopping for a moment to shake some of the leaves from his shirt. "Did they say?"

"No." Jamie pulled a soggy wad of cloth that had once been a handkerchief from his sleeve and swished it in the ornamental fountain. He used it to mop his face, looked critically at the resultant streaks of filth, and soused it in the fountain again.

"The first I knew was the thud when Anstruther clubbed ye—here, your head's still bleedin'. I turned round to see ye lyin' on the ground, and the next instant, a sword came at me out o' nowhere, right across my ribs. Look at that, will ye?" He poked his fingers through a large rent in his shirt, wiggling them. "I ducked behind a tree, and barely got my own blade out in time. But neither of them said a word at all."

Roger pressed the proffered handkerchief gingerly to the back of his head. He sucked air through his teeth with a hiss as the cold water touched the wound.

"Shit. Is it only that my head's cracked, or does that make no sense? Why in Christ's name try so hard to kill us?"

"Because they wanted us dead," Jamie said logically, turning up his sleeves to wash his hands in the fountain. "Or someone else does."

The pain had decided to take up residence in Roger's head again. He was feeling sick again.

"Stephen Bonnet?"

"If I were a gambling man, I'd put good odds on it."

Roger closed one eye in order to correct a tendency for there to be two of Jamie.

"You *are* a gambling man. I've seen ye do it."

"Well, there ye are, then."

Jamie ran a hand absently through his matted hair, and turned toward the house. Karina and her sisters had appeared at the window, and were waving ecstatically.

"What I want verra much to know just now is, where *is* Stephen Bonnet?"

"Wilmington."

Jamie swung round, frowning at him.

"What?"

"Wilmington," Roger repeated. He cautiously opened the other eye, but it seemed all right. Only one Jamie. "That's what Lillywhite said—but I thought he was joking."

Jamie stared at him for a moment.

"I hope to Christ he was," he said.

## AMONG THE MYRTLES

*Wilmington*

BY CONTRAST WITH FRASER'S RIDGE, Wilmington was a giddy metropolis, and under normal circumstances, the girls and I should have fully enjoyed its delights. Given the absence of Roger and Jamie, and the nature of the errand they were bound upon, though, we were able to find little distraction.

Not that we didn't try. We lived through the creeping minutes of nights broken by crying children and haunted by imaginations worse than nightmare might be. I was sorry that Brianna had seen as much as she had, after the battle at Alamance; vague imaginings based on fear were bad enough; those based on close acquaintance with the look of ruined flesh, of smashed bone and staring eyes, were a good deal worse.

Rising heavy-eyed amid a crumple of discarded clothes and stale linen, we fed and dressed the children and went out to seek what mental respite might be found during the day in the distractions of horse-racing, shopping, or the competing musicales hosted once a week—on successive evenings—by Mrs. Crawford and Mrs. Dunning, the two most prominent hostesses in town.

Mrs. Dunning's evening had taken place the day after Roger and Jamie left. Performances upon the harp, violin, harpsichord, and flute were interspersed with recitations of poetry—at least it was referred to as poetry—and "Songs, both Comick and Tragick," sung by Mr. Angus McCaskill, the popular and courteous proprietor of the largest ordinary in Wilmington.

The Tragick songs were actually much funnier than the Comick ones, owing to Mr. McCaskill's habit of rolling his eyes up into his head during the more lugubrious passages, as though he had the lyrics written on the inside of his skull. I adopted a suitably solemn expression of appreciation, though, biting the inside of my cheek throughout.

Brianna required no such aid to courtesy. She sat staring at all the performances with a countenance of such brooding intensity that it seemed to disconcert a few of the musicians, who eyed her nervously, and edged toward the other side of the room, getting the harpsichord safely between her and them. Her attitude had nothing to do with the performance, I knew, but rather with a reliving of the arguments that had preceded the men's departure.

These had been prolonged, vigorous, and conducted in low voices, as the four of us walked up and down the quay at sunset. Brianna had been impassioned, eloquent, and ferocious. Jamie had been patient, cool, and immovable. I had kept my mouth shut, for once more stubborn than either of them. I could not in conscience side with Bree; I knew what Stephen Bonnet was. I would not side with Jamie; I knew what Stephen Bonnet was.

I knew what Jamie was, too, and while the thought of his going to deal with Stephen Bonnet was enough to make me feel as though I were hanging from a fraying rope over a bottomless pit, I did know that there were few men better equipped for such a task. For beyond the question of deadly skill, which he certainly had, there was the question of conscience.

Jamie was a Highlander. While the Lord might insist that vengeance was His, no male Highlander of my acquaintance had ever thought it right that the Lord should be left to handle such things without assistance. God had made man for a reason, and high on the list of those reasons was the protection of a family and the defense of its honor—whatever the cost.

What Bonnet had done to Brianna was not a crime that Jamie would ever forgive, let alone forget. And beyond simple vengeance, and the continuing threat that Bonnet might pose to Bree or Jemmy, there was the fact that Jamie felt himself responsible, at least in part, for such harm as Bonnet might do in the world—to our family, or to others. He had helped Bonnet to escape the gallows once; he would not be at peace until he had amended that mistake—and said so.

"Fine!" Brianna had hissed at him, fists clenched at her sides. "So you'll be at peace. Just fine! And how peaceful do you think Mama and I will be, if you or Roger is dead?"

"Ye'd prefer me to be a coward? Or your husband?"

"Yes!"

"No, ye wouldn't," he said with certainty. "Ye only think so now, because ye're afraid."

"Of course I'm afraid! So is Mama, only she won't say so, because she thinks you'll go anyway!"

"If she does think so, she's right," Jamie said, giving me a sidelong look, with a hint of a smile. "She's known me a long time, aye?"

I glanced at him, but shook my head and turned away, sealing my lips and staring out at the masts of the ships anchored in the harbor while the argument raged on.

Roger had finally put a stop to it.

"Brianna," he said softly, when she paused for breath. She turned toward him, face anguished, and he touched her shoulder. "I willna have this man in the same world as my children," he said, still softly, "or my wife. Do we go then with your blessing—or without it?"

She had sucked in her breath, bitten her lip, and turned away. I saw the tears brimming in her eyes, and the working of her throat as she swallowed them. She said no more.

Whatever word of blessing she had given him had been spoken in the night, in the quiet of their bed. I had given Jamie blessing and farewell in that same darkness—still without speaking a word. I couldn't. He *would* go, no matter what I said.

Neither of us slept that night; we lay in each other's arms, silently aware of each breath and shift of body, and when the shutters began to show cracks of gray light, we rose—he to make his preparations, I because I could not lie still and watch him go.

As he left, I stood on tiptoe to kiss him, and whispered the only important thing.

"Come back," I'd said. He'd smiled at me, smoothing a curl behind my ear.

"Ye ken what I said at Alamance? Well, it's no today, either, Sassenach. We'll both be back."

MRS. CRAWFORD'S ASSEMBLY, held the next evening, boasted the same performers, for the most part, as had Mrs. Dunning's, but had one novelty; it was there that I smelled myrtle candles for the first time.

"What is that lovely scent?" I asked Mrs. Crawford during the interval, sniffing at the candelabra that decorated her harpsichord. The candles were beeswax, but the scent was something both delicate and spicy—rather like bayberry, but lighter.

"Wax-myrtle," she replied, gratified. "I don't use them for the candles themselves, though one *can*—but it does take such a tremendous quantity of the berries, near eight pound to get only a pound of the wax, imagine! It took my bond-maid a week of picking, and she brought me barely enough as would make a dozen candles. So I rendered the wax, but then I mixed it in with the regular beeswax when I dipped the candles, and I will say I am pleased. It does give such a pleasant aroma, does it not?"

She leaned closer to me, lowering her voice to a confidential whisper.

"*Someone* said to me that Mrs. Dunning's home smelt last night as though the cook had scorched the potatoes at supper!"

And so, on the third day, faced with the alternatives of a day spent cooped up with three small children in our cramped lodgings, or a repeat visit to the much-diminished remains of the dead whale, I borrowed several buckets from our landlady, Mrs. Burns, commissioned a picnic basket, and marshalled my troops for a foraging expedition.

Brianna and Marsali consented to the notion with alacrity, if not enthusiasm.

"Anything is better than sitting around worrying," Brianna said. "Anything!"

"Aye, and anything is better than the stink of filthy clouts and sour milk, too," Marsali added. She fanned herself with a book, looking pale. "I could do wi' a bit of air."

I worried a little about Marsali's ability to walk so far, given her expanding girth—she was in her seventh month—but she insisted that the exercise would benefit her, and Brianna and I could help to carry Joanie.

As is usual in cases of travel with small children, our departure was somewhat prolonged. Joanie spit up mashed sweet potato down the front of her gown, Jemmy committed a sanitary indiscretion of major proportions, and Germain disappeared during the confusion occasioned by these mishaps. He was discovered, at the conclusion of a half-hour search involving everyone in the street, behind the public livery stable, happily engaged in throwing horse dung at passing carriages and wagons.

Everyone forcibly cleaned, redressed, and—in Germain's case—threatened with death and dismemberment, we descended the stairs again, to find that the landlord, Mr. Burns, had helpfully dug out an old goat-cart, with which he kindly presented us. The goat, however, was employed in eating nettles in the next-door garden, and declined to be caught. After a quarter of an hour's heated pursuit, Brianna declared that she would prefer to pull the cart herself, rather than spend any longer playing ring-around-the-rosy with a goat.

"Mrs. Fraser, Mrs. Fraser!" We were halfway down the street, the children, buckets, and picnic basket in the goat-cart, when Mrs. Burns came hurrying out of the inn after us, a jug of small beer in one hand, and an ancient flintlock pistol in the other.

"Snakes," she explained, handing me the latter. "My Annie says she saw at least a dozen adders, last time she walked that way."

"Snakes," I said, accepting the object and its attendant paraphernalia with reluctance. "Quite."

Given that "adder" could mean anything from a water moccasin to the most harmless grass snake, and also given that Annie Burns had a marked talent for melodrama, I was not unduly concerned. I thought of dropping the gun into the picnic basket, but a glance at Germain and Jemmy, pictures of cherubic innocence, decided me of the unwisdom of leaving even an unloaded firearm anywhere near them. I dropped the pistol into my berry-bucket, instead, and put it over my arm.

The day was overcast and cool, with a light breeze off the ocean. The air was damp, and I thought there was a good chance of rain before long, but for the moment, it was very pleasant out, with the sandy earth packed down sufficiently from earlier rains to make the walking easy.

Following Mrs. Crawford's directions, we made our way a mile or so down the beach, and found ourselves at the edge of a thick growth of coastal forest, where scanty-needled pines mingled with mangroves and palmetto in a dense, sun-splintered tangle, twined with vines. I closed my eyes and breathed in, nostrils flaring at the intoxicating mixture of scents: mudflats and wet sand, pine resins and sea air, the last faint whiffs of dead whale, and what I had been looking for—the fresh, tangy scent of wax-myrtles.

"That way," I said, pointing into the tangle of vegetation.

The going was too heavy for the cart now, so we left it, allowing the little boys to run wild, chasing tiny crabs and
bright birds, as we made our way slowly into the scrubby forest. Marsali carried Joan, who curled up like a dormouse in
her mother's arms and went to sleep, lulled by the sound of
ocean and wind.

In spite of the heavy growth, the walking was more pleasant here than on the open beach; the wind-stunted trees were
tall enough to give a pleasing sense of secrecy and refuge,
and the footing was better, with a thin layer of decaying
leaves and needles underfoot.

Jemmy grew tired of walking, and tugged on my skirt,
raising both arms to be picked up.

"All right." I hung a berry-bucket from one wrist, and
swung him up, with a crackle and pop of vertebrae; he was a
very solid little boy. He twined his sandy feet comfortably
round my waist and rested his face on my shoulder with a
sigh of relief.

"All very well for you," I said, gently patting his back.
"Who's going to give Grannie a ride, hey?"

"Grand-da," he said, and giggled. He lifted his head, looking round. "W'ere Grand-da?"

"Grand-da's busy," I told him, taking care to keep my
voice light and cheerful. "We'll see Grand-da and Daddy
soon."

"Want Daddy!"

"Yes, so does Mummy," I murmured. "Here, sweetie. See
that? See the little berries? We're going to pick some, won't
that be fun? No, don't eat them! Jemmy, I said *no*, do *not* put
them in your mouth, they'll make you sick!"

We had found a luxuriant patch of wax-myrtles, and soon
spread out, losing sight of each other amid the bushes as we
picked, but calling out every few minutes, in order not to lose
each other entirely.

I had put Jemmy down again, and was idly contemplating
whether there might be any use for the berry-pulp, once the
myrtle berries were boiled to render the wax, when I heard
the soft crunch of footsteps on the other side of the bush I
was picking from.

"Is that you, darling?" I called, thinking it was Brianna. "Perhaps we ought to have our lunch soon; I think it's maybe coming on to rain."

"Well, it's a kind invitation, sure," said a male voice, sounding amused. "I thank ye, ma'am, but I've made a decent breakfast not long since."

He stepped out from behind the bush, and I stood paralyzed, completely unable to speak. My mind, oddly enough, was not paralyzed in the slightest; my thoughts were running at the speed of light.

*If Stephen Bonnet's here, Jamie and Roger are safe, thank God.*

*Where are the children?*

*Where is Bree?*

*Where's that gun, goddamnit?*

"Who's that, *Grand-mère*?" Germain, appearing from behind a bush with what appeared to be a dead rat dangling from one hand, approached me warily, blue eyes narrowed at the intruder.

"Germain," I said in a croak, not taking my eyes off Bonnet. "Go find your mother, and stay with her."

"*Grand-mère*, is it? And who will his mother be, then?" Bonnet glanced from me to Germain and back, interested. He tilted back the hat he wore, and scratched at the side of his jaw.

"Never mind that," I said, as firmly as I could. "Germain, go!" I stole a look downward, but the pistol was not in my bucket. There were six buckets, and we had left three on the goat-cart; undoubtedly the gun was in one of those, worse luck.

"Oh, don't be goin' just yet, young sir." Bonnet made a move toward Germain, but the little boy took alarm at the gesture and skittered back, throwing the rat at Bonnet. It hit him in the knee, surprising him and making him hesitate for the split second necessary for Germain to vanish into the myrtles. I could hear his feet chuffing the sand as he ran, and hoped he knew where Marsali was. The last thing we needed was for him to lose himself.

Well, possibly not the very last thing, I amended. The very

last thing we needed was for Stephen·Bonnet to lay eyes on Jemmy, which he promptly did, when the latter wandered out of the bushes an instant later, his short gown smeared with mud, more mud oozing through the fingers of his clenched fists.

There was no sun, but Jemmy's hair seemed to blaze with the brilliance of a striking match. Paralysis disappearing in a heartbeat, I grabbed him up, and backed away several steps, knocking over the half-filled bucket of myrtle berries.

Bonnet's eyes were the pale green of a cat's, and they brightened now with the intentness of a cat that spots a creeping mouse.

"And who will this sweet manneen be?" he asked, taking a step toward me.

"My son," I said instantly, and pulled Jem tight against my shoulder, ignoring his struggles. With the natural perversity of small children, he seemed to be fascinated by Bonnet's Irish lilt, and kept turning his head to stare at the stranger.

"Favors his father, I see." Drops of sweat glistened in the heavy blond brows. He smoothed first one, then the other, with the tip of his finger, so the sweat ran in trickles down the sides of his face, but the pale green eyes never wavered in their regard. "As does his . . . sister. And is your lovely daughter anyplace nearby, dear one? I should enjoy to renew our acquaintaince—such a charmin' girl, Brianna." He smiled.

"No doubt you would," I said, making no particular effort to disguise the edge in my voice. "No, she isn't. She's at home—with her husband." I leaned heavily on the word *husband*, hoping that Brianna was near enough to hear me and take warning, but he paid it no mind.

"At home, now. And where do ye call home then, Mum?" He took off the hat and wiped his face with his sleeve.

"Oh . . . in the backcountry. A homestead." I waved vaguely in the direction I thought roughly west. What was this—social conversation? And yet the choices seemed distinctly limited. I could turn and flee—at which point he would catch me handily, burdened as I was with Jemmy. Or I could stand here until he revealed what he wanted. I didn't think he was out for a picnic among the myrtles.

"A homestead," he repeated, a muscle twitching in his

cheek. "What business brings ye so far from home, and I might ask?"

"You might not," I said. "Or rather—you might ask my husband. He'll be along shortly."

I took another step backward as I said this, and he took a step toward me at the same time. A flicker of panic must have crossed my face, for he looked amused, and took another step.

"Oh, I doubt that, Mrs. Fraser dear. For see, the man's dead by now."

I squeezed Jemmy so hard that he let out a strangled squawk.

"What do you mean?" I demanded hoarsely. The blood was draining from my head, coagulating in an icy ball round my heart.

"Well, d'ye see, it was a bargain," he said, the look of amusement growing. "A division of duties, ye might say. My friend Lillywhite and the good Sheriff were to attend to Mr. Fraser and Mr. MacKenzie, and Lieutenant Wolff was to manage Mrs. Cameron's end of the business. That left me with the pleasant task of makin' myself reacquainted with my son and his mother." His eyes sharpened, focusing on Jemmy.

"I don't know what you are talking about," I said, through stiff lips, taking a better grip on Jemmy, who was watching Bonnet, owl-eyed.

He gave a short laugh at that.

"Sure, and ye're no hand at lyin', ma'am; you'll forgive the observation. Ye'd never make a card player. Ye know well enough what I mean—ye saw me there, at River Run. Though I confess as how I should be obliged to hear exactly what you and Mr. Fraser was engaged in, a-butchering that Negro woman that Wolff killed. I did hear as how the picture of a murderer shows in the victim's eyes—but ye didn't seem to be looking at her eyes, from what I could see. Was it magic of a sort ye were after doing?"

"Wolff—it *was* him, then?" Just at the moment, I didn't really care whether Lieutenant Wolff had murdered scores of women, but I was willing to engage in any line of conversation that offered the possibility of distracting him.

"Aye. He's a bungler, Wolff," he said, dispassionately. "But 'twas him that found out about the gold to begin with, so he claimed a part in the doings."

How far away were Marsali and Brianna? Had Germain found them? I could hear nothing over the whine of insects and the distant wash of surf. Surely they must hear us talking, though.

"Gold," I said, raising my voice a little. "Whatever do you mean, gold? There isn't any gold at River Run; Jocasta Cameron told you as much."

He puffed air through his lips in genial disbelief.

"I will say as Mrs. Cameron is a better liar than yourself, dear one, but sure, I didn't believe her, either. The doctor saw the gold, see."

"What doctor?" A baby's high-pitched cry came faintly through the bushes—Joan. I coughed, hoping to drown it out, and repeated, more loudly, "What doctor do you mean?"

"Rawls, I think was his name, or Rawlings." Bonnet was frowning slightly, head turned toward the sound. "I'd not the pleasure of his acquaintance, though; I might be mistaken."

"I'm sorry—I still have no idea what you're talking about." I was trying simultaneously to hold his gaze and to scan the ground nearby for anything that might be used as a weapon. Bonnet had a pistol in his belt, and a knife, but showed no disposition to draw either one. Why should he? A woman with an armload of two-year-old was not any sort of threat.

One thick blond brow flicked up, but he seemed in no great hurry, whatever he was about.

"No? Well, 'twas Wolff, as I was sayin'. It was a tooth to be drawn or somesuch; he met with this sawbones in Cross Creek. Bought the fellow a drink in reward, and spent the evening inside a wine-skin with him, in the end. Ye'll know the Lieutenant's weakness for the drink—the doctor was another sot, I hear, and the two of them thick as thieves before the dawn. Rawlings let out that he'd seen a great quantity of gold at River Run, for he'd just come from there, see?"

Rawlings had either passed out or sobered up enough to say no more, but the revelation had been enough to renew the

Lieutenant's determination to gain the hand—and property—of Jocasta Cameron.

"The lady would be havin' none of him, though, and then she ups and declares as she'll be takin' the one-armed fella instead. 'Twas a cruel blow to the Lieutenant's pride, alas." He grinned at that, showing a missing molar on one side.

Lieutenant Wolff, furious and baffled, appealed to his particular friend, Randall Lillywhite, for advice.

"Why, that—so that's why he arrested the priest at the Gathering? To prevent him marrying Mrs. Cameron to Duncan Innes?"

Bonnet nodded.

"That would be the way of it. A matter of delay, ye might say, so as to be havin' the opportunity of lookin' further into the matter."

Said opportunity had occurred at the wedding. As we had theorized, someone—Lieutenant Wolff—had in fact attempted to drug Duncan Innes with a cup of punch spiked with laudanum. The plan had been to render him insensible and pitch him into the river. During the uproar occasioned by Duncan's disappearance and presumedly accidental death, Wolff would have the chance to search the premises thoroughly for the gold—and eventually, to renew his addresses to Jocasta.

"But the black bitch drank the stuff herself," he said dispassionately. "Didn't die of it, worse luck—but she could have said who gave the cup to her, of course, and so Wolff slipped round and mixed ground glass into the gruel they were after feedin' her."

"What I want to know," I said, "is just how *you* got involved in this. Why were you there at River Run?"

"And isn't the Lieutenant the friend of my bosom these many years past, dear one? He came to me for help in disposing of the one-armed lad, so as he could take care to be seen in the midst of the party, enjoyin' himself in all innocence whilst accident was befallin' his rival." He frowned slightly, tapping a finger on the hilt of his pistol.

"I would have done better to bash the Innes fella on the head and toss him in, once I saw the laudanum had gone astray. Couldn't get at him, though—he spent half the day in the jakes, and someone always in there with him, bad cess to them."

There was nothing on the ground near me that could possibly be used as a weapon. Twigs, leaves, scattered fragments of shell, a dead rat—well, that had worked for Germain, but I didn't think Bonnet could be surprised twice in that fashion. Jemmy was losing his fear of the stranger as we talked, and was beginning to squirm to get down.

I edged backward a little; Bonnet saw it, and smiled. He wasn't bothered. Obviously he didn't think I could escape, and just as obviously, he was waiting for something. Of course—he had told me, himself. He was waiting for Brianna. I realized belatedly that he had clearly followed us out here from town; he knew that Marsali and Brianna were somewhere nearby—much easier simply to wait until they revealed themselves.

My best hope was that someone else would happen along; the weather was muggy and damp, but not raining yet, and this was a well-known spot for picnicking, according to Mrs. Burns. If someone did come along, how could I take advantage of it? I knew that Bonnet would not have the slightest compunction in simply shooting anyone who got in his way—he was boasting about the rest of his bloodthirsty plans.

"Mrs. Cameron—Mrs. Innes, she'll be now—seemed willin' enough to talk, when I suggested that her husband might soon be lackin' a few of his treasured parts, though as it happens, she was lyin', then, too, deceitful old trout. But it came to me, ponderin' the matter afterward, that she might be more obligin', were it a matter of her heir." He nodded toward Jemmy, and clicked his tongue at the boy. "So, lad, will we be goin' to see your great-auntie, then?"

Jemmy looked suspiciously at Bonnet, cuddling back against me.

"Whozat?" he asked.

"Oh, it's a wise child that knows its father, isn't it? I'm your Da, lad—was your mother not after telling you so?"

"Daddy?" Jemmy looked at Bonnet, then at me. "At's not Daddy!"

"No, he isn't your daddy," I assured Jemmy, shifting my hold. My arms were beginning to ache under the strain of holding him. "He's a bad man; we don't like him."

Bonnet laughed.

"Is there no shame with you at all, dear one? Of course he's mine—it's your daughter has said so, to my face."

"Nonsense," I said. I had maneuvered my way into a narrow gap between two of the evergreen wax-myrtle bushes. I'd try to distract him back into conversation, then seize a moment to whirl round, set Jemmy down, and urge him to run. With luck, I could block the gap long enough to prevent Bonnet grabbing him before he could get away—if he *would* run.

"Lillywhite," I said, taking hold of the conversation. "What did you mean, Lillywhite and the Sheriff were going to—to attend to my husband and Mr. MacKenzie?" Merely mentioning the possibility made me feel sick; sweat was running down my sides, but my face felt cold and clammy.

"Oh, that? What I said, Mrs. Fraser. Your husband is dead." He had started looking past me, pale green eyes flicking through the shrubbery. He was clearly expecting Brianna to show up at any moment.

"What happened at the wedding showed us clear enough that it wouldn't do, to leave Mrs. Cameron with so much protection. No, if we meant to try again, the thing to do was to see that she's no manfolks to call upon, either for help, or vengeance. So when your husband suggested to Mr. Lyon that he fetch me along to a private meeting, I thought that might be a suitable opportunity to dispose of him and Mr. MacKenzie—two birds with one whisky keg, as ye might be sayin'—but then I thought best if Lillywhite were the lad to handle that end of things, him and his tame sheriff." He smiled. "I thought best I come to be fetchin' my son and his mother along, so as not to risk anything goin' amiss, ye see. We'll—"

I shifted weight, spun on my heel, and plunked Jemmy on the ground on the far side of the bushes.

"Run!" I said urgently to him. "Run, Jem! Go!" There was a flash of red as he scampered away, whimpering with fear, and then Bonnet crashed into me.

He tried to shove me aside, but I was ready for that, and

grabbed for the pistol at his belt. He felt me snatch, and jerked back, but I had my fingers on the butt. I got it free and flung it behind me, as I fell to the ground with him on top of me.

He rolled off me and up on to his knees, where he froze.

"Stay there, or by the Holy Virgin, I'll blow your head off!"

Gasping from the fall, I sat up slowly, to see Marsali, pale as a sheet, aiming the ancient flintlock at him over the swell of her belly.

"Shoot him, *Maman*!" Germain was behind her, small face alight with eagerness. "Shoot him like a porcupine!"

Joan was somewhere back in the bushes; she began to wail at the sound of her mother's voice, but Marsali didn't take her eyes off Bonnet. Christ, had she loaded and primed the gun? I thought she must have; I could smell a whiff of black powder.

"Well, now," Bonnet said slowly. I could see his eyes trace the distance between him and Marsali—fifteen feet or more, too much to reach her with a dive. He put one foot on the ground, beginning to rise. He could reach her in three strides.

"Don't let him stand up!" I scrabbled up onto my own feet, shoving at his shoulder. He fell to the side, catching himself on one hand, then heaved back, faster than I could have imagined, seizing me round the waist and pulling me back down, this time on top of him.

There were screams from behind me, but I had no attention to spare. I stabbed my fingers at his eye, narrowly missing as he jerked me sideways; my nails slid off his cheekbone, raking furrows in his skin. We rolled in a flurry of petticoats and Irish oaths, me grabbing for his privates, him trying at once to throttle me and protect himself.

Then he squirmed and flipped over like a fish, and we ended with his arm locked tight around my neck, holding me against his chest. There was a whisper of metal on leather, and something cold against my neck. I stopped struggling, and took a deep breath.

Marsali's eyes were the size of saucers, her mouth clamped tight. Her gaze, thank heaven, was still trained on Bonnet, and so was the gun.

"Marsali," I said, very calmly, "shoot him. Right now."

"Be putting the gun down, colleen," Bonnet said, with equal calmness, "or I'll cut her throat on the count of three. One—"

"Shoot him!" I said, with all my force, and took my last deep gulp of air.

"Two."

"Wait!"

The pressure of the blade across my throat lessened, and I felt the sting of blood as I took a breath I had not expected to be given. I hadn't time to enjoy the sensation, though; Brianna stood amid the myrtles, Jemmy clinging to her skirts.

"Let her go," she said.

Marsali had been holding her breath; she let it out with a gasp and sucked air deep.

"He isn't about to let me go, and it doesn't matter," I said fiercely to them both. "Marsali, shoot him. *Now!*"

Her hand tightened on the gun, but she couldn't quite do it. She glanced at Brianna, white-faced, then back, her hand trembling.

"Shoot him, *Maman*," Germain whispered, but the eagerness had gone from his face. He was pale, too, and stood close to his mother.

"You'll come along with me, darlin', you and the lad." I could feel the vibration through Bonnet's chest as he spoke, and sensed the half-smile on his face, though I couldn't see it. "The others can go."

"Don't," I said, trying to make Bree look at me. "He won't let us go, you know he won't. He'll kill me and Marsali, no matter what he says. The only thing to do is shoot him. If Marsali can't do it, Bree, you'll have to."

That got her attention. Her eyes jerked to me, shocked, and Bonnet grunted, half in annoyance, half in amusement.

"Condemn her mother? She's not the girl to be doing such a thing, Mrs. Fraser."

"Marsali—he'll kill you, and the babe with you," I said, straining every muscle to make her understand, to force her to fire. "Germain and Joan will die out here, alone. What happens to me doesn't matter, believe me—for God's sake, *shoot him now!*"

She fired.

There was a spark and puff of white smoke, and Bonnet jerked. Then her hand sagged, the muzzle of the gun tilted down—and the wad and ball fell out on the sand with a tiny plop. Misfire.

Marsali moaned in horror, and Brianna moved like lightning, seizing the fallen bucket and hurling it at Bonnet's head. He yelped and threw himself aside, letting go his grip on me. The bucket struck me in the chest and I caught it, stupidly staring down into it. It was damp inside, with a scattering of the blue-white waxy berries stuck to the wood.

Then Germain and Jemmy were both crying, Joan was shrieking her head off in the wood, and I dropped the bucket and crawled madly for shelter behind a yaupon bush.

Bonnet was back on his feet, face flushed, the knife in his hand. He was clearly furious, but made an effort to smile at Brianna.

"Ah, now, darlin'," he said, having to raise his voice to be heard above the racket. "It's only yourself and my son I'm wanting. I'll not be harming either of you."

"He's not your son," Brianna said, low-voiced and vicious. "He'll never be yours."

He grunted contemptuously.

"Oh, aye? That's not how I heard it, in that dungeon in Cross Creek, sweetheart. And now I see him . . ." He looked at Jemmy again, nodding slowly. "He's mine, darlin' girl. He's the look of me—haven't ye, boyo?"

Jemmy buried his face in Brianna's skirts, howling.

Bonnet sighed, shrugged, and gave up any pretense of cajolement.

"Come on, then," he said, and started forward, obviously intending to scoop Jemmy up.

Brianna's hand rose out of her skirts, and aimed the pistol I had yanked out of his belt back at the place it had come from. Bonnet stopped in mid-step, mouth open.

"What about it?" she whispered, and her eyes were fixed, unblinking. "Do you keep your powder dry, Stephen?"

She braced the pistol with both hands, drew aim at his crotch, and fired.

He was fast, I'd give him that. He hadn't time to turn and run, but was reaching to cover his threatened balls with both hands, even as she pulled the trigger. Blood exploded in a thick spray through his fingers, but I couldn't tell what she'd hit.

He staggered back, clutching himself. He stared wildly round, as though unable to believe it, then sank to one knee. I could hear him breathing, hard and fast.

We all stood paralyzed, watching. One hand scrabbled at the sand, leaving bloody furrows. Then he rose, slowly, doubled over, the other hand pressed into his middle. His face was dead white, green eyes like dull water.

He stumbled round, gasping, and made off like a bug that's been stepped on, leaking and hitching. There was a crashing noise as he blundered through the bushes, and then he was gone. Beyond a palmetto tree, I could see a line of pelicans flying, ungainly and impossibly graceful against the lowering sky.

I was still crouched on the ground, chilled with shock. I felt something warm slide down my cheek, and realized it was a raindrop.

"Is he right?" Brianna was crouching beside me, helping me sit up. "Do you think he's right? Are they dead?" She was white to the lips, but not hysterical. She had Jemmy in the crook of her arm, clinging to her neck.

"No," I said. Everything seemed remote, as though it were happening in slow motion. I stood up slowly, balancing precariously, as though not sure quite how to do it.

"No," I said again, and felt no fear, no panic at the memory of what Bonnet had said; nothing but a certainty in my chest, like a small, comforting weight. "No, they're not." Jamie had told me; this was not the day when he and I would part.

Marsali had vanished into the wood to retrieve Joanie. Germain was bent over the splotches of blood on the sand, studying them with fascination. It occurred to me dimly to wonder what type they were, but then I dismissed the thought from my mind.

*"He'll never be yours,"* she had said.

"Let's go," I said, patting Jemmy gently. "I think we'll make do with unscented candles, for now."

ROGER AND JAMIE appeared at dawn two days later, rousing everyone in the inn by pounding at the door, and causing people in the neighboring houses to throw open their shutters and put their nightcapped heads out in alarm, owing to the resultant whooping and yelling. I was reasonably sure that Roger had a minor concussion, but he refused to be put to bed—though he did allow Bree to hold his head in her lap and make noises of shocked sympathy about the impressive lump on it, while Jamie gave us a terse account of the battle of Wylie's Landing, and we gave a somewhat confused explanation of our adventures in the myrtle groves.

"So Bonnet's not dead?" Roger asked, opening one eye.

"Well, we don't know," I explained. "He got away, but I don't know how badly he was hurt. There wasn't a dreadful lot of blood, but if he was hit in the lower abdomen, that would be a terrible wound, and almost certainly fatal. Peritonitis is a very slow and nasty way to die."

"Good," Marsali said, vindictively.

"Good!" Germain echoed, looking proudly up at her. "*Maman* shot the bad man, *Grand-père*," he told Jamie. "So did Auntie. He was *full* of holes—there was blood everywhere!"

"Holes," Jemmy said happily. "Holes, holes, lotsa holes!"

"Well, maybe one hole," Brianna murmured. She didn't look up from the damp cloth with which she was gently sponging dried blood from Roger's scalp and hair.

"Oh, aye? Well, if ye only took off a finger or one of his balls, lass, he might survive," Jamie observed, grinning at her. "Wouldna improve his temper, though, I dinna suppose."

Fergus arrived on the noon packet boat, triumphantly bearing the registered, stamped, and officially sealed deeds for the two land grants, thus putting the cocked hat on the day's rejoicing. The celebrations were limited, though, owing to the sobering knowledge that one rather major loose end remained.

After a vigorous discussion, it was decided—meaning that Jamie made up his mind and pigheadedly refused to entertain dissenting views—that he and I would ride west at once to River Run. The young families would remain in Wilmington for a few days, to complete business, and to keep an ear out for any report of a wounded or dying man. They would then proceed back to Fraser's Ridge, keeping strictly clear of Cross Creek and River Run.

"Lieutenant Wolff canna be using threats to you or the lad to influence my aunt, if ye're nowhere near him," Jamie pointed out to Brianna.

"And as for you, *mo charadean*," he said to Roger and Fergus, "ye canna be leaving the women and weans to look out for themselves—God kens who they might shoot next!"

It was only as he closed the door on the resulting laughter that he turned to me, ran a fingertip over the scratch on my throat, and then pulled me so hard against himself that I thought my ribs would break. I clung tight to him on the landing, not caring that I couldn't breathe, nor whether anyone might see; happy only to be touching him—and to have him there to touch.

"Ye did right, Claire," he muttered at last, mouth against my hair. "But for God's sake, never do it again!"

So it was that he and I left at dawn next day, alone.

## 104

# SLY AS FOXES

WE ARRIVED AT RIVER RUN near sundown three days later, horses lathered and filthy, and ourselves in no better case. The place seemed peaceful enough, the last of the spring light glowing on green lawns and spotlighting the white marble statues and the stone of Hector's mausoleum among its dark yews.

"What do you think?" I asked Jamie. We had reined up at the foot of the lawn, looking the situation over cautiously before approaching the house.

"Well, no one's burned the place down," he replied, standing in his stirrups to survey the prospect. "And I dinna see rivers of blood cascading down the front stair. Still . . ." He sat down, reached into his saddlebag, and withdrew a pistol, which he loaded and primed as a precaution. With this tucked into the waistband of his breeks and concealed by the skirts of his coat, we rode slowly up the drive to the front door.

By the time we had reached it, I knew something was wrong. There was a sinister air of stillness about the house; no sound of scurrying servants, no music from the parlor, no scents of supper being fetched in from the cookhouse. Most peculiar of all, Ulysses was not there to greet us; our knocking went unanswered for several minutes, and when the door was at last opened, it was Phaedre, Jocasta's body-servant, who appeared.

She had looked dreadful when I had last seen her, nearly a year before, after her mother's death. She didn't look much better now; there were circles under her eyes, and her skin looked bruised and drawn, like a fruit beginning to go bad.

When she saw us, though, her eyes lighted and her mouth relaxed in visible relief.

"Oh, Mr. Jamie!" she cried. "I been prayin' for somebody to come help, ever since yesterday, but I thought for sure it would be Mr. Farquard, and then we maybe be in worse trouble, he such a man for the law and all, even if he is your auntie's friend."

Jamie raised an eyebrow at this rather confused declaration, but nodded reassuringly and squeezed her hand.

"Aye, lass. I dinna believe I've been an answer to prayer before, but I've no objection. Is my aunt . . . well?"

"Oh, yes, sir—*she's* well enough."

Withdrawing before we could ask further questions, she beckoned us toward the stair.

Jocasta was in her boudoir, knitting. She raised her head

at the sound of feet, alert, and before anyone could say anything, asked "Jamie?" in a quavering voice, and stood up. Even at a distance, I could see that there were mistakes in the knitting, missed stitches and open runs; most unlike her usual fastidious needlework.

"Aye, it's me, Aunt. And Claire. What's amiss, then?" Crossing the room in two strides, he reached her side and took her arm, patting her hand in reassurance.

Her face underwent the same transformation of relief that we had seen in Phaedre, and I thought she might give way at the knees. She stiffened her spine, though, and turned toward me.

"Claire? Thank Blessed Bride ye've come, though how—well, never mind it for now. Will ye come? Duncan's hurt."

Duncan lay in bed in the next room, inert under a stack of comforters. At first, I was afraid he might be dead, but he stirred at once at the sound of Jocasta's voice.

*"Mac Dubh?"* he said, puzzled. He poked his head up from the mound of covers, squinting to see in the dimness of the room. "What in God's name brings you here?"

"Lieutenant Wolff," Jamie said, a little caustically. "Is the name perhaps familiar to ye?"

"Aye, ye might say so." There was a slightly odd tone to Duncan's voice, but I paid it no mind, engaged in lighting candles and in excavating him sufficiently from the bedclothes to find out what the matter was.

I was expecting to find a knife or gunshot wound. At first examination, there was nothing whatever of the sort visible, and it took a few moments' mental regrouping to discover that what he was suffering from was a broken leg. It was a simple fracture of the lower tibia, fortunately, and while undoubtedly painful, it seemed to be no great threat to his health.

I sent Phaedre to find some splinting materials, while Jamie, informed that Duncan stood in no great danger, sat down to get to the bottom of things.

"He has been here? Lieutenant Wolff?" he asked.

"Aye, he has." Again the slight hesitation.

"Has he gone, then?"

"Oh, aye." Duncan shuddered a little, involuntarily.

"Am I hurting you?" I asked.

"Oh, no, Mrs. Claire," he assured me. "I was only—well . . ."

"Ye may as well tell me straight out, Duncan," Jamie said, in a tone of mild exasperation. "I think it'll no be a tale that improves wi' keeping, aye? And if it's the sort of tale I think, then I have a bittie story to tell to you, as well."

Duncan eyed him narrowly, but then sighed, capitulating, and lay back on the pillow.

The Lieutenant had arrived at River Run two days before, but unlike his usual habit, had not come to the front door to be announced. Instead, he had left his horse hobbled in a field a mile from the house, and approached stealthily on foot.

"We only realized as much, because of finding the horse later, ye see," Duncan explained to me, as I bound his leg. "I didna ken he was here at all, until I went out to the necessary after supper, and he leaped at me, out o' the dark. I near died o' fright, and then I near died of being shot, for he fired at me, and if I had had an arm on that side, I daresay he would have struck it. Only I hadna got one, so he didn't."

In spite of his disability, Duncan had fought back ferociously, butting the Lieutenant in the face, charging him, and knocking him backward.

"He staggered and tripped himself on the brick walk, and fell backward so as he hit his head a dreadful smackit." He shuddered again at memory of the sound. "Like a melon hit wi' an ax, it was."

"Och, aye. So, was he killed at once, then?" Jamie asked, interested.

"Well, no." Duncan had grown easier in his manner, telling the tale, but now began to look uneasy again. "Now, see, *Mac Dubh*, here's the pinch of the matter. For I'd gone staggering, too, when I knocked him ower, and I stepped into the stone channel from the necessary and snapped my leg, and there I lay, groaning by the walk. Ulysses heard me callin' at last, and came down, and Jo after him."

Duncan had told Jocasta what had happened, as Ulysses had gone to fetch a couple of grooms to help carry Duncan into the house. And then, between the pain of his broken leg and his habit of leaving difficulties to the butler to be re-solved, had likewise left the Lieutenant.

"It was my fault, *Mac Dubh*, and I ken it well," he said, his face drawn and pale. "I ought to have given orders of some kind; though in fact I canna think even now what I ought to have said, and I've had time and plenty enough to think."

The rest of the story, pried out of him with some reluc-tance, was that Jocasta and Ulysses had evidently conferred on the matter, and concluded that the Lieutenant had gone beyond being a nuisance, and become an outright threat. And that being so . . .

"Ulysses killed him," Duncan said baldly, then stopped, as though appalled afresh. He swallowed, looking deeply un-happy. "Jo says as how she ordered him to do it—and Christ knows, *Mac Dubh*, she might have done so. She's no the woman to be trifled with, let alone to have her servants mur-dered, herself threatened, and her husband set upon."

I gathered from his hesitance, though, that some small doubt about Jocasta's part in this still lingered in his mind.

Jamie had grasped the main point troubling him, though.

"Christ," he said. "The man Ulysses will be hangit on the spot, or worse, if anyone hears of it. Whether my aunt or-dered it, or no."

Duncan looked a little calmer, now that the truth was out. He nodded.

"Aye, that's it," he agreed. "I canna let him go to the gal-lows—but what am I to do about the Lieutenant? There's the Navy to be considered, to say nothing of sheriffs and magis-trates." That was a definite point. A good deal of the prosper-ity of River Run depended upon its naval contracts for timber and tar; Lieutenant Wolff had in fact been the naval liaison responsible for such contracts. I could see that His Majesty's Navy might just possibly be inclined to look squiggle-eyed at a proprietor who had killed his local naval representative, no matter what the excuse. I imagined that the law, in the person of Sheriff and magistrates, might take a more lenient view of the situation—save for the person of the perpetrator.

A slave who shed the blood of a white person was auto-matically condemned, regardless of provocation. It would make no difference what had happened—even with a dozen witnesses to testify to Wolff's attack on Duncan, Ulysses would be doomed. If anyone found out about it. I began to understand the air of desperation that hung over River Run; the other slaves were well aware of what might happen.

Jamie rubbed a knuckle over his chin.

"Ah . . . just how did . . . I mean, would it not be possible to say that ye'd done it yourself, Duncan? It was self-defense, after all—and I've evidence that the man did come in order to murder ye, wi' the notion of marrying my aunt then by force, or at least holding her hostage so as she might be threatened into telling about the gold."

"Gold?" Duncan looked blank. "But there isna any gold here. I thought we'd got that straight last year."

"The Lieutenant and his associates thought there was," I told him. "But Jamie can tell you all about that, in a bit. What *did* happen to the Lieutenant, exactly?"

"Ulysses cut his throat," Duncan said, and swallowed, Adam's apple bobbing in his own throat. "I should be pleased enough to say I'd done it, aye, only . . ."

Beyond the simple difficulty of cutting someone's throat with only one hand, it was evidently all too apparent that the Lieutenant's throat had been cut by a left-handed person—and Duncan, of course, lacked a left hand altogether.

I happened to know that Jocasta Cameron—like her nephew—was left-handed, but it seemed more tactful not to mention that at the moment. I glanced at Jamie, who raised both brows at me.

*Would she?* I asked silently.

*A MacKenzie of Leoch?* his cynical look said back.

"Where *is* Ulysses?" I asked.

"In the stable, most like, if he hasna already headed west." Knowing that if anyone learned the truth of the Lieutenant's death, Ulysses would be condemned at once, Jocasta had sent her butler to saddle a horse, with instructions to flee into the mountains, should anyone come.

Jamie drew a deep breath and rubbed a hand over his head, thinking.

"Well, then. I should say the best thing, perhaps, is for the Lieutenant to disappear. Where have ye put him for the moment, Duncan?"

A muscle near Duncan's mouth twitched, in an uneasy attempt at a smile.

"I believe he's in the barbecue pit, *Mac Dubh*. Covered over wi' burlap, and piled with hickory wood, disguised as a pork carcass."

Jamie's brows went up again, but he merely nodded.

"Aye, then. Leave it to me, Duncan."

I left instructions for Duncan to be given honeyed water and tea brewed with boneset and cherry bark, and went outside with Jamie to contemplate methods of disappearance.

"The simplest thing would be just to bury him somewhere, I suppose," I said.

"Mmphm," Jamie said. He lifted the pine torch he was carrying, frowning thoughtfully at the humped mound of burlap in the pit. I hadn't liked the Lieutenant in the least, but it looked rather pitiful.

"Maybe. I'm thinkin', though—the slaves all ken what's happened. If we bury him on the place, they'll ken that, too. They wouldna tell anyone, of course—but he'll haunt the place, aye?"

A shiver ran up my spine, engendered as much by the matter-of-factness of his tone as by his words, and I pulled my shawl closer round me.

"Haunt the place?"

"Aye, of course. A murder victim, done to death here, and hidden, unavenged?"

"You mean . . . really haunt the place?" I asked, carefully, "or do you only mean the slaves would think so?"

He shrugged, twitching his shoulders uneasily.

"I dinna think it matters so much, does it? They'll avoid the spot where he's buried, one of the women will see the ghost at night, rumors will get round, as they do—and next thing, a slave at Greenoaks will say something, someone in Farquard's family will hear of it, and before ye know it, someone will be over here, asking questions. Given that the Navy is like to be looking for the Lieutenant before too long anyway . . . what d'ye say to weighting the body and putting it in the river? That's what he had in mind for Duncan, after all."

"Not a bad notion," I said, considering it. "But he meant

Duncan to be found. There's a lot of boat traffic on the river, and it isn't very deep up this far. Even if we weighted the body well, it's possible it would rise, or someone snag it with a pole. Would it matter if someone found it, though, do you think? The body wouldn't be connected with River Run."

He nodded slowly, moving the torch aside to keep the sparks from showering over his sleeve. There was a light wind, and the elms near the barbecue pit whispered restlessly overhead.

"Aye, that's so. Only, if someone does find him, there'll be an inquiry. The Navy will send someone to try to find out the truth of the matter—and they'll come here, asking questions. What d'ye think will happen, if they were to badger the slaves, askin' had they seen the Lieutenant, and so on?"

"Mm, yes." Given the slaves' present acute state of nerves, I imagined that any inquiry would send one or more of them into a state of panic, in which anything might be blurted out.

Jamie was standing quite still, staring at the burlap-draped shape with an expression of deep abstraction. I drew a deep breath, caught a faint scent of decaying blood, and let it out again, quick.

"I suppose . . . we could burn him," I said, and swallowed a sudden taste of bile. "He *is* already in the pit, after all."

"It's a thought," Jamie said, and one corner of his mouth quirked in a faint smile. "But I think I've a better one, Sassenach." He turned to look thoughtfully at the house. A few windows were dimly alight, but everyone was inside, cowering.

"Come on, then," he said, with sudden decision. "There'll be a sledgehammer in the stable, I expect."

THE FRONT OF THE MAUSOLEUM was covered by an ornamental grille of black wrought iron, with an enormous lock, its metal decorated by sixteen-petalled Jacobite roses. I had always considered this to be merely one of Jocasta Cameron's affectations, since I doubted that grave-robbers were a great threat in such a rural setting. The hinges scarcely creaked when Jamie unlocked the grille and swung it open; like everything else at River Run, it was maintained in impeccable condition.

"You really think this is better than burying or burning him?" I asked. There was no one nearby, but I spoke in a near whisper.

"Oh, aye. Auld Hector will take care of him, and prevent him doin' harm," Jamie replied matter-of-factly. "And it's blessed ground, in a manner of speaking. No a matter of leaving his soul to wander about, makin' trouble, aye?"

I nodded, a little uncertainly. He was probably right; in terms of belief, Jamie understood the slaves much better than I did. For that matter, I wasn't sure whether he was speaking only of what the psychological effect on them might be—or whether he was himself convinced that Hector Cameron ought to be capable of dealing with this *ex post facto* threat to his wife and plantation.

I lifted the torch so Jamie could see what he was doing, and set my teeth in my lower lip.

He had wrapped the sledgehammer in rags, so as not to chip the marble blocks. The small blocks of the front wall, inside the grille, had been expertly cut to fit and lightly mortared in place. The first blow knocked two of the blocks a few inches out of place. A few more blows, and a dark space showed, where the blocks had given way enough to show the blackness inside the mausoleum.

Jamie stopped to wipe sweat from his forehead, and muttered something under his breath.

"What did you say?"

"I said, it stinks," he replied, sounding puzzled.

"This is surprising, is it?" I asked, a little testily. "How long has Hector Cameron been dead, four years?"

"Well, aye, but it's no—"

*"What are you doing?"* Jocasta Cameron's voice rang out behind me, sharp with agitation, and I jumped, dropping the torch.

It flickered, but didn't go out, and I snatched it up again, waving it to encourage the flame. The flame rose and steadied, shedding a ruddy glow on Jocasta, who stood on the path behind us, ghostly in her white nightgown. Phaedre huddled behind her mistress, no more of her face visible than the brief shine of eyes in the darkness. The eyes looked scared, flicking from Jamie and me to the dark hole in the facade of the mausoleum.

"What am I doing? Disposing of Lieutenant Wolff, what else?" Jamie, who had been as startled as I had by his aunt's sudden appearance, sounded a little cross. "Leave it to me, Aunt. Ye needna concern yourself."

"You are not—no, ye mustn't open Hector's tomb!" Jocasta's long nose twitched, obviously picking up the scent of decay—which was faint, but distinct.

"Dinna fash yourself, Aunt," Jamie said. "Go back to the house. I'll manage. It will all be well."

She ignored his soothing words, advancing blindly over the walk, hands groping in the empty air.

"No, Jamie! Ye mustn't. Close it up again. Close it, for God's sake!"

The panic in her voice was unmistakable, and I saw Jamie frown in confusion. He looked uncertainly from his aunt to the hole in the mausoleum. The wind had dropped, but now rose in a small gust, wafting a much stronger scent of death around us. Jamie's face changed, and ignoring his aunt's cries of protest, he knocked loose more blocks with several quick blows of the padded hammer.

"Bring the torch, Sassenach," he said, setting down the hammer, and with a sense of creeping horror, I did so.

We stood shoulder to shoulder, peering through the narrow gap in the blocks. Two coffins of polished wood stood inside, each on a pedestal of marble. And on the floor between them . . .

"Who is he, Aunt?" Jamie's voice was quiet as he turned to speak to her.

She stood as if paralyzed, the muslin of her gown flapping round her legs in the wind, pulling strands of white hair from beneath her cap. Her face was frozen, but the blind eyes darted to and fro, seeking an impossible escape.

Jamie stepped forward and grabbed her fiercely by the arm, making her start from her frozen trance.

*"Co a th'ann?"* he growled. "Who is he? Who?"

Her mouth worked, trying to form words. She stopped,

swallowed, tried again, eyes still flickering to and fro over his shoulder, looking at God knew what. Had she still been able to see when they put him in there? I wondered. Did she see it now, in memory?

"His name—his name was Rawlings," she said faintly, and something inside my chest fell like an iron weight.

I must have moved or made some sound, for Jamie's eyes went to me. He reached out a hand for mine, and held on tightly, though his eyes went back to Jocasta.

"How?" he asked, calmly, but with a tone that warned that he would brook no evasion.

She closed her eyes then, and sighed, broad shoulders slumping suddenly.

"Hector killed him," she said.

"Oh, aye?" Jamie cast a cynical glance at the coffins inside the mausoleum, and the huddled mass that lay on the floor between them. "A good trick, that. I hadna realized my uncle was so capable."

"Before." Her eyes opened again, but she spoke dully, as though nothing mattered any longer. "He was a doctor, Rawlings. He'd come to look at my eyes, once before. When Hector took ill, he called the man back. I canna say quite what happened, but Hector caught him nosing round where he should not, and smashed his head in. He was a hot-tempered man, Hector."

"I should say so," Jamie said, with another glance at the body of Dr. Rawlings. "How did he get in here?"

"We—he—hid the corpse, meaning to carry it off and leave it in the wood. But then . . . Hector got worse, and couldna leave his bed. Within a day, he was dead, too. And so . . ." She lifted a long white hand, gesturing toward the draft of dank chill that floated from the open tomb.

"Great minds think alike," I murmured, and Jamie gave me a dirty look, letting go my hand. He stood contemplating the stillness inside the violated mausoleum, thick brows drawn down in a frown of concentration.

"Oh, aye?" he said again. "Whose is the second coffin?"

"Mine." Jocasta was recovering her nerve; her shoulders straightened and her chin lifted.

Jamie made a small puffing noise and glanced at me. I

could believe that Jocasta would callously leave a dead man to lie exposed, rather than put him in her own pristine coffin . . . and yet. To do so drastically increased the odds of discovery, slim as those might be.

No one would have opened Jocasta's coffin until it was time to receive her own body; Dr. Rawlings' corpse could have lain there in complete safety, even were the mausoleum to be opened for some reason. Jocasta Cameron was selfish—but by no means stupid.

"Put Wolff in, then, if you must," she said. "He can lie on the floor with the other one."

"Why not put him in your coffin, Aunt?" Jamie asked, and I saw that he was looking at her intently.

"No!" She had begun to turn away, but at this whipped back, her blind face fierce in the torchlight. "He is dung. Let him lie and rot in the open!"

Jamie narrowed his eyes at her response, but didn't reply. Instead, he turned to the tomb and began to shift the loosened blocks.

"What are you doing?" Jocasta could hear the grating noise of the shifting marble, and became agitated anew. She turned round on the walk, but became disoriented, staring off toward the river. I realized that she must now be completely blind, unable even to see the light from the torch.

I had no attention to pay her just then, though. Jamie wedged himself through the gap in the blocks, and stepped inside.

"Light me, Sassenach," he said softly, and his voice echoed slightly in the small stone chamber.

Breathing very shallowly, I followed him. Phaedre had begun to moan in the darkness outside; she sounded like the *ban-sidhe* that howls for approaching death—but this death had come long since.

The coffins were equipped with brass plates, gone slightly green with damp, but still easily readable. "Hector Alexander Robert Cameron," read one, and "Jocasta Isobeail MacKenzie Cameron," the other. Without hesitation, Jamie seized the edges of the lid of Jocasta's coffin and pulled up.

It wasn't nailed; the lid was heavy, but shifted at once.

"Oh," Jamie said softly, looking down.

Gold will never tarnish, no matter how damp or dank its surroundings. It will lie at the bottom of the sea for centuries, to emerge one day in some random fisherman's net, bright as the day it was smelted. It glimmers from a rocky matrix, a siren's song that has called to men for thousands of years.

The ingots lay in a shallow layer over the bottom of the coffin. Enough to fill two small chests, each chest heavy enough to require two men—or a man and a strong woman—to carry it. Each ingot stamped with a fleur-de-lis. One third of the Frenchman's gold.

I blinked at the shimmer, and looked aside, my eyes blurring with fractured light. It was dark on the floor, but I could still make out the huddled form against the pale marble. "Nosing where he should not." And what had he seen, Daniel Rawlings, that had made him draw the fleur-de-lis in the margin of his casebook, with that discreet notation, "Aurum"?

Hector Cameron was still alive, then. The mausoleum had not yet been sealed. Perhaps when Dr. Rawlings rose to follow his wandering patient, Hector had led him here unwitting, going down in the night to view his hoard? Perhaps. Neither Hector Cameron nor Daniel Rawlings could say, now, how it had been, or what had happened.

I felt a thickening in my throat, for the man whose bones lay now at my feet, the friend and colleague whose instruments I had inherited, whose shade had stood at my elbow, lending me both courage and comfort, when I laid hands on the sick and sought to heal them.

"Such a waste," I said softly, looking down.

Jamie lowered the coffin lid, gently, as though the coffin held an occupant whose rest had been disturbed.

Outside, Jocasta stood still on the path. She had an arm round Phaedre, who had stopped whimpering, but it was not clear which of them was supporting the other. Jocasta must know now from the noise where we were, but she faced the river still, eyes fixed, unblinking in the torchlight.

I cleared my throat, hugging the shawl tighter with my free hand.

"What shall we do, then?" I asked Jamie.

He turned and looked back into the tomb for a moment, then shrugged a little.

"We'll leave the Lieutenant to Hector, as we planned. As for the doctor . . ." He drew breath slowly, troubled gaze fixed on the slender bones that lay in a graceful fan, pale and still in the light. A surgeon's hand—once.

"I think," he said, "we will take him home with us—to the Ridge. Let him lie among friends."

He brushed past the two women without acknowledgment or pardon, and went to fetch Lieutenant Wolff.

# A THRUSH'S DREAM

*Fraser's Ridge
May, 1772*

THE NIGHT AIR WAS COOL and fresh. So early in the year, the bloodthirsty flies and mosquitoes hadn't started yet; only random moths came in through the open window now and then, to flutter round the smoored hearth like bits of burning paper, brushing past their outflung limbs in brief caress.

She lay as she had fallen, half on top of him, heart thumping loud and slow in her ears. From here, she could see out through the window; the jagged black line of trees on the far side of the dooryard, and beyond them a section of sky, lit with stars, so near and bright that it should be possible to step out among them and walk from one to another, higher and higher, to the hook of the crescent moon.

"You're not mad at me?" he whispered. He spoke more easily now, but lying with her ear on his chest, she could hear the faint catch in his voice, the point where he forced air hard through his scarred throat to form the words.

"No." His hand was on her hair, stroking. "I didn't ever tell you not to read it."

His fingers touched her shoulder, lightly, and her toes curled with pleasure at the feeling. Did she mind? No. She supposed she ought to feel exposed in some way, the privacy of her thoughts and dreams laid bare to him—but she trusted him with them. He would never use those things against her.

Besides, once set down on paper, the dreams became a separate thing from her, herself. Much like the drawings that she made; a reflection of one facet of her mind, a brief glimpse of something once seen, once thought, once felt—but not the same thing as the mind or heart that made them. Not quite.

"Fair's fair, though." Her chin rested in the hollow of his shoulder. He smelled good, bitter and musky with the scent of satisfied desire. "Tell me one of your dreams, then."

A laugh vibrated through his chest, nearly soundless, but she felt it.

"Only one?"

"Yes, but it has to be an important one. Not the flying ones, or the ones where you're being chased by a monster, or the ones where you go to school without your clothes on. Not the ones that everybody has—one that only *you* have."

One of her hands was on his chest, scratching gently to make the dark curly hairs twitch and rise. The other was under the pillow; if she moved her fingers slightly, she could feel the smooth little shape of the ancient wifie, as she called it. She could imagine her own womb swelling, round and hard. She could feel the clutch and soft spasm in her lower belly; aftershocks of their lovemaking. Would it be this time?

He turned his head on the pillow, thinking. Long lashes lay against his cheek, black as the lines of the trees outside. He turned back then, lifting them, and his eyes were the color of moss, soft and vivid in the shadowed light.

"I could be romantic," he whispered, and his fingers

drifted down her back, so that she felt gooseflesh rise in their wake. "I could say this is my dream—you and me, here alone . . . us and our children." He turned his head a little, checking the trundle in the corner, but Jemmy was sound asleep, invisible.

"You could," she echoed, and ducked her head so her forehead pressed against his shoulder. "But that's a waking dream—not a real dream. You know what I mean."

"Aye, I do."

He was quiet for a minute, his hand lying still, broad and warm across the base of her spine.

"Sometimes," he whispered at last, "sometimes, I dream I am singing, and I wake from it with my throat aching."

He couldn't see her face, or the tears that prickled at the corners of her eyes.

"What do you sing?" she whispered back. She heard the *shush* of the linen pillow as he shook his head.

"No song I've ever heard, or know," he said softly. "But I know I'm singing it for you."

# 106

# THE SURGEON'S BOOK II

*July 27, 1772*

*"Was called from churning to attend Rosamund Lindsay, who arrived in late afternoon with a severe laceration to the left hand, sustained with an axe while girdling trees. Wound was extensive, having nearly severed the left thumb; laceration extended from base of index finger to two inches above the styloid process*

*of the radius, which was superficially damaged. Injury
had been sustained approximately three days prior,
treated with rough binding and bacon grease.
Extensive sepsis apparent, with suppuration, gross
swelling of hand and forearm. Thumb blackened; gangrene apparent; characteristic pungent odor. Subcuta-
neous red streaks, indicative of blood poisoning,
extended from site of injury nearly to antecubital
fossa.*

*Patient presented with high fever (est. 104 degrees
F., by hand), symptoms of dehydration, mild disorientation. Tachycardia evident.*

*In view of the seriousness of patient's condition,
recommended immediate amputation of limb at elbow.
Patient refused to consider this, insisting instead upon
application of pigeon poultice, consisting of the split
body of a freshly-killed pigeon, applied to wound
(patient's husband had brought pigeon, neck freshly
wrung). Removed thumb at base of metacarpal, li-
gated remains of radial artery (crushed in original
injury) and superficialis volae. Debrided and drained
wound, applied approximately 1/2 oz. crude penicillin
powder (source: rotted casaba rind, batch #23, prep.
15/6/72) topically, followed by application of mashed
raw garlic (three cloves), barberry salve—and pigeon
poultice, at insistence of husband applied over dressing. Administered fluids by mouth; febrifuge mixture of
red centaury, bloodroot, and hops; water ad lib.
Injected liquid penicillin mixture (batch # 23), IV,
dosage 1/4 oz in suspension in sterile water.*

*Patient's condition deteriorated rapidly, with
increasing symptoms of disorientation and delirium,
high fever. Extensive urticaria appeared on arm and
upper torso. Attempted to relieve fever by repeated
applications of cold water, to no avail. Patient being
incoherent, requested permission to amputate from
husband; permission denied on grounds that death
appeared imminent, and patient "would not want to be
buried in pieces."*

> *Repeated penicillin injection. Patient lapsed into unconsciousness shortly thereafter, and expired just before dawn.*

I DIPPED MY QUILL, again, but then hesitated, letting the drops of ink slide off the sharpened point. How much more should I say?

The deeply-ingrained disposition for scientific thoroughness warred with caution. It was important to describe what had happened, as fully as possible. At the same time, I hesitated to put down in writing what might amount to an admission of manslaughter—it wasn't murder, I assured myself, though my guilty feelings made no such distinctions.

"Feelings aren't truth," I murmured. Across the room, Brianna looked up from the bread she was slicing, but I bent my head over the page, and she returned to her whispered conversation with Marsali by the fire. It was no more than mid-afternoon, but dark and rainy outside. I had lit a candle by which to write, but the girls' hands flickered over the dim table like moths, lighting here and there among the plates and platters.

The truth was that I didn't think Rosamund Lindsay had died of septicemia. I was fairly sure that she had died of an acute reaction to an unpurified penicillin mixture—of the medicine I gave her, in short. Of course, the truth also was that the blood poisoning would certainly have killed her, left untreated.

The truth also was that I had had no way of knowing what the effects of the penicillin would be—but that was rather the point, wasn't it? To make sure someone else *might* know?

I twiddled the quill, rolling it between thumb and forefinger. I had kept a faithful account of my experiments with penicillin—the growing of cultures on media ranging from bread to chewed pawpaw and rotted melon rind, painstaking descriptions of the microscopic and gross identification of the *Penicillium* molds, the effects of—to this point—very limited applications.

Yes, certainly I must include a description of the effects. The real question, though, was—for whom was I keeping this careful record?

I bit my lip, thinking. If it was only for my own reference, it would be a simple matter; I could simply record the symptoms, timing, and effects, without explicitly noting the cause of death; I was unlikely to forget the circumstances, after all. But if this record were ever to be useful to someone else . . . someone who had no notion of the benefits and dangers of an antibiotic . . .

The ink was drying on the quill. I lowered the point to the page.

*Age—44,* I wrote slowly. In this day, casebook accounts like this often ended with a pious description of the deceased's last moments, marked—presumably—by Christian resignation on the part of the holy, repentance by the sinful. Neither attitude had marked the passage of Rosamund Lindsay.

I glanced at the coffin, sitting on its trestles under the rain-smeared window. The Lindsays' cabin was very small, not suited for a funeral in the pouring rain, where a large number of mourners were expected. The coffin was open, awaiting the evening wake, but the muslin shroud had been drawn up over her face.

Rosamund had been a whore in Boston; growing too stout and too old to ply her trade with much profit, she had drifted south, looking for a husband. "I couldn't bide another of them winters," she had confided to me, soon after her arrival on the Ridge. "Nor yet another of them stinkin' fishermen."

She had found the necessary refuge in Kenneth Lindsay, who was looking for a wife to share the work of home-steading. Not a match born of physical attraction—the Lindsays had had perhaps six sound teeth between them—or emotional compatibility, still it had seemed an amicable relationship.

Shocked rather than grief-stricken, Kenny had been taken off by Jamie for medication with whisky—a somewhat more effective treatment than my own. At least I didn't think it would be lethal.

*Immediate cause of death*—I wrote, and paused again. I doubted that Rosamund's response to approaching death would have found outlet in either prayer or philosophy, but she had had opportunity for neither. She had died blue-faced, congested, and bulging-eyed, unable to force word or breath past the swollen tissues of her throat.

My own throat felt tight at the memory, as though I were being choked. I picked up the cooling cup of catmint tea and took a sip, feeling the pungent liquid slide soothingly down. It was little comfort that the septicemia would have killed her more lingeringly. Suffocation was quicker, but not much more pleasant.

I tapped the quill point on the blotter, leaving inky pinpoints that spread through the rough fibers of the paper, forming a galaxy of tiny stars. As to that—there was another possibility. Death might conceivably have been due to a pulmonary embolism—a clot in the lung. That would be a not-impossible complication of the septicemia, and could have accounted for the symptoms.

It was a hopeful thought, but not one I placed much credence in. It was the voice of experience, as much as the voice of conscience, that bade me dip the quill and write down "anaphylaxis," before I could think again.

Was anaphylaxis a known medical term yet? I hadn't seen it in any of Rawlings' notes—but then, I hadn't read them all. Still, while death from the shock of allergic reaction was not unknown in any time, it wasn't common, and might not be known by name. Better describe it in detail, for whoever might read this.

And that was the rub, of course. Who *would* read it? I thought it unlikely, but what if a stranger should read this and take my account for a confession of murder? That was far-fetched—but it could happen. I had come perilously close to being executed as a witch, in part because of my healing activities. Once almost burned, twice shy, I thought wryly.

*Extensive swelling in affected limb*, I wrote, and lifted the quill, the last word fading as the pen ran dry. I dipped it again and scratched doggedly on. *Swelling extended to upper torso, face, and neck. Skin pale, marked with reddish blotches. Respiration increasingly rapid and shallow, heartbeat very fast and light, tending to inaudibility. Palpitations evident. Lips and ears cyanotic. Pronounced exophthalmia.*

I swallowed again, at the thought of Rosamund's eyes, bulging under the lids, rolling to and fro in uncomprehending terror. We had tried to shut them, when we cleansed the body and laid it out for burial. It was customary to uncover the corpse's face for the wake; I thought it unwise in this case.

I didn't want to look at the coffin again, but did, with a small nod of acknowledgment and apology. Brianna's head turned toward me, then sharply away. The smell of the food laid out for the wake was filling the room, mingling with the scents of oak-wood fire and oak-gall ink—and the fresh-planed oak of the coffin's boards. I took another hasty gulp of tea, to stop my gorge rising.

I knew damn well why the first line of Hippocrates' oath was, "First, do no harm." It was too bloody easy to do harm. What hubris it took to lay hands on a person, to interfere. How delicate and complex were bodies, how crude a physician's intrusions.

I could have sought seclusion in surgery or study, to write these notes. I knew why I hadn't. The coarse muslin shroud glowed soft white in the rainy light from the window. I pinched the quill hard between thumb and forefinger, trying to forget the *pop* of the cricoid cartilage, when I had jabbed a penknife into Rosamund's throat in a final, futile attempt to let air into her straining lungs.

And yet . . . there was not one practicing physician, I thought, who had never faced this. I had had it happen a few times before—even in a modern hospital, equipped with every life-saving device known to man—then.

Some future physician here would face the same dilemma; to undertake a possibly dangerous treatment, or to allow a patient to die who *might* have been saved. And that was my own dilemma—to balance the unlikely possibility of prosecution for manslaughter against the unknown value of my records to someone who might seek knowledge in them.

Who might that be? I wiped the pen, thinking. There were as yet few medical schools, and those few, mostly in Europe.

Most physicians gained their knowledge from apprenticeship and experience. I slipped a finger into the casebook, feeling blind between the early pages, kept by the book's original owner.

Rawlings had not gone to a medical school. Though if he had, many of his techniques would still have been shocking by my standards. My mouth twisted at the thought of some of the treatments I had seen described in those closely written pages—infusions of liquid mercury to cure syphilis, cupping and blistering for epileptic fits, lancing and bleeding for every disorder from indigestion to impotence.

And still, Daniel Rawlings had been a doctor. Reading his case notes, I could feel his care for his patients, his curiosity regarding the mysteries of the body.

Moved by impulse, I turned back to the pages containing Rawlings' notes. Perhaps I was only delaying to let my subconscious reach a decision—or perhaps I felt the need of communication, no matter how remote, with another physician, someone like me.

Someone like me. I stared at the page, with its neat, small writing, its careful illustration, seeing none of the details. Who was there, like me?

No one. I had thought of it before, but only vaguely, in the way of a problem acknowledged, but so distant as not to require any urgency. In the colony of North Carolina, so far as I knew, there was only one formally designated "doctor"— Fentiman. I snorted, and took another sip of tea. Better Murray MacLeod and his nostrums—most of those were harmless, at least.

I sipped my tea, regarding Rosamund. The simple truth was that I wouldn't last forever, either. With luck, a good long time yet—but still, not forever. I needed to find someone to whom I could pass on at least the rudiments of what I knew.

A stifled giggle from the table, the girls whispering over the pots of head-cheese, the bowls of sauerkraut and boiled potatoes. No, I thought, with some regret. Not Brianna.

She would be the logical choice; she knew what modern medicine was, at least. There would be no overcoming of ignorance and superstition, no need to convince of the virtues of asepsis, the dangers of germs. But she had no natural inclination, no instinct for healing. She was not squeamish or afraid of blood—she had helped me with any number of childbirths and minor surgical procedures—and yet she lacked that peculiar mixture of empathy and ruthlessness a doctor needs.

She was perhaps Jamie's child more than mine, I reflected, watching the firelight ripple in the falls of her hair as she moved. She had his courage, his great tenderness—but it was the courage of a warrior, the tenderness of a strength that could crush if it chose. I had not managed to give her my gift; the knowledge of blood and bone, the secret ways of the chambers of the heart.

Brianna's head lifted sharply, turning toward the door. Marsali, slower, turned too, listening.

It was barely audible through the thrumming of the rain, but knowing it was there, I could pick it out—a male voice, raised high, chanting. A pause, and then a faint answering rumble that might have been distant thunder, but wasn't. The men were coming down from the shelter on the mountain.

Kenny Lindsay had asked Roger to chant the *caithris* for Rosamund; the formal Gaelic lament for the dead. "She wasna Scots," Kenny had said, wiping eyes bleared from tears and a long night's watching. "Nor even God-fearin'. But she was that fond o' singin', and she fair admired your way o' it, MacKenzie."

Roger had never done a *caithris* before; I knew he had never heard one. "Dinna fash," Jamie had murmured to him, hand on his arm, "all ye need to be is loud." Roger had bent his head gravely in acquiescence, and went with Jamie and Kenneth, to drink whisky by the malting floor and learn what he could of Rosamund's life, the better to lament her passing.

The hoarse chant vanished; the wind had shifted. It was a freak of the storm that we had heard them so soon—they would be headed down the Ridge now, to collect mourners from the outlying cabins, and then to lead them all in procession back up to the house, for the feasting and singing and storytelling that would go on all night.

I yawned involuntarily, my jaw cracking at the thought of it. I'd never last, I thought in dismay. I had had a few hours' sleep in the morning, but not enough to sustain me through a full-blown Gaelic wake and funeral. The floors would be thick with bodies by dawn, all of them smelling of whisky and wet clothes.

I yawned again, then blinked, my eyes swimming as I shook my head to clear it. Every bone in my body ached with fatigue, and I wanted nothing more than to go to bed for several days.

Deep in thought, I hadn't noticed Brianna coming to stand behind me. Her hands came down on my shoulders, and she moved closer, so I felt the warmth of her touching me. Marsali had gone; we were alone. She began to massage my shoulders, long thumbs moving slowly up the cords of my neck.

"Tired?" she asked.

"Mm. I'll do," I said. I closed the book, and leaned back, relaxing momentarily in the sheer relief of her touch. I hadn't realized I was strung so tightly.

THE BIG ROOM was quiet and orderly, ready for the wake. Mrs. Bug was tending the barbecue. The girls had lit a pair of candles, one at each end of the laden table, and shadows flickered over the whitewashed walls, the quiet coffin, as the candle flames bent in a sudden draft.

"I think I killed her," I said suddenly, not meaning to say it at all. "It was the penicillin that killed her."

The long fingers didn't stop their soothing movement.

"Was it?" she murmured. "You couldn't have done any differently, though, could you?"

"No."

A small shudder of relief went over me, as much from the bald confession as from the gradual release of the painful tightness in my neck and shoulders.

"It's okay," she said softly, rubbing, stroking. "She would have died anyway, wouldn't she? It's sad, but you didn't do wrong. You know that."

"I know that." To my surprise, a single tear slid down my cheek and dropped on the page, puckering the paper. I blinked hard, struggling for control. I didn't want to distress Brianna.

She wasn't distressed. Her hands left my shoulders, and I heard the scraping of stool legs. Then her arms came around me, and I let her draw me back, my head resting just under her chin. She simply held me, letting the rise and fall of her breathing calm me.

"I went to dinner with Uncle Joe once, just after he'd lost a patient," she said finally. "He told me about it."

"Did he?" I was a little surprised; I wouldn't have thought Joe would talk about such things with her.

"He didn't mean to. I could see something was bothering him, though, so I asked. And—he needed to talk, and I was there. Afterward, he said it was almost like having you there. I didn't know he called you Lady Jane."

"Yes," I said. "Because of the way I talk, he said." I felt a breath of laughter against my ear, and smiled slightly in response. I closed my eyes, and could see my friend, gesturing in passionate conversation, face alight with the desire to tease.

"He said—that when something like that happened, sometimes there would be a sort of formal inquiry, at the hospital. Not like a trial, not that—but a gathering of the other doctors, to hear exactly what happened, what went wrong. He said it was sort of like confession, to tell it to other doctors, who could understand—and it helped."

"Mm-hm." She was swaying slightly, rocking me as she moved, as she rocked Jemmy, soothing.

"Is that what's bothering you?" she asked quietly. "Not just Rosamund—but that you're alone? You don't have anybody who can really understand?"

Her arms wrapped around my shoulders, her hands crossed, resting lightly on my chest. Young, broad, capable hands, the skin fresh and fair, smelling of fresh-baked bread and strawberry jam. I lifted one, and laid the warm palm against my cheek.

"Apparently I do," I said.

The hand curved, stroked my cheek, and dropped away. The big young hand moved slowly, smoothing the hair behind my ear with soft affection.

"It will be all right," she said. "Everything will be all right."

"Yes," I said, and smiled, despite the tears blurring my eyes.

I couldn't teach her to be a doctor. But evidently I had, without meaning to, somehow taught her to be a mother.

"You should go lie down," she said, taking her hands away reluctantly. "It will be an hour at least, before they get here."

I let my breath go out in a sigh, feeling the peace of the house around me. If Fraser's Ridge had been a short-lived haven for Rosamund Lindsay, still it had been a true home. We would see her safe, and honored in death.

"In a minute," I said, wiping my nose. "I need to finish something, first."

I sat up straight and opened my book. I dipped my pen, and began to write the lines that must be there, for the sake of the unknown physician who would follow me.

# 107

# ZUGUNRUHE

*September, 1772*

I WOKE DRENCHED in sweat. The thin chemise in which I slept clung to me, transparent with wet; the darkness of my flesh showed in patches through the cloth, even in the dim light from the unshuttered window. I had kicked away sheet and quilt in my disordered sleep, and lay sprawled with the linen shift rucked up above my thighs— but still my skin pulsed with heat, waves of smothering warmth that flowed over me like melted candle wax.

I swung my legs over the side of the bed, and stood up, feeling dizzy and disembodied. My hair was soaked and my neck was slick with perspiration; a trickle of sweat ran down between my breasts and disappeared.

Jamie was still asleep; I could see the humped mound of his upturned shoulder, and the spill of his hair, dark across the pillow. He shifted slightly and mumbled something, but then lapsed into the regular deep breaths of sleep. I needed air, but didn't want to wake him. I pushed away the gauze netting, stepped softly across to the door, and into the small box-room across the hall.

It was a small room, but it had a large window, in order to balance the one in our bedroom. This one had no glass as yet; it was covered only by wooden shutters, and I could feel drafts of night air drifting through the slats, swirling across the floor, caressing my bare legs. Urgent for the coolness of it, I stripped off my wet shift and sighed in relief as the draft skimmed upward over hips and breasts and arms.

The heat was still there, though, hot waves pulsing over my skin with each heartbeat. Fumbling in the dark, I unfastened the shutters and pushed them open, gasping for the great draughts of cool night that flooded in upon me.

From here, I could see above the trees that screened the house, down the slope of the ridge, almost to the faint black line of the river far away. The wind stirred in the treetops, murmuring, and wafted over me with blessed coolness and the pungent green smell of leaves and summer sap. I closed my eyes and stood still; within a minute or two, the heat was gone, vanished like a quenched coal, leaving me damp but peaceful.

I didn't want to go back to bed yet; my hair was damp, and the sheets where I had lain would still be clammy. I leaned naked on the sill, the down-hairs of my body prickling pleasantly as my skin cooled. The peaceful whooshing of the trees was interrupted by the thin sound of a child's wail, and I glanced toward the cabin.

It was a hundred yards from the house; the wind must be toward me, to have carried the sound. Sure enough, the wind changed as I leaned out of the window, and the crying was lost in the flutter of leaves. The breeze passed on, though, and I could hear the screeching, louder now, in the silence.

It was louder because it was getting closer. There was a creak and the groan of wood as the cabin door opened, and someone stepped out. There was no lamp or candle lit in the cabin, and the quick glimpse I had of the emerging figure showed me nothing but a tall form silhouetted against the dim glow of the banked hearth inside. It seemed to have long hair—but both Roger and Brianna slept with their hair untied and capless. It was pleasant to imagine Roger's glossy black locks mingling with the fire of Brianna's on the pillow—did they share a pillow? I wondered suddenly.

The screeching hadn't abated. Fretful and cranky, but not agonized. Not belly-ache. A bad dream? I waited a moment, watching, to see whether whoever it was would bring the child to the house, in search of me, and put out a hand to my crumpled shift, just in case. No—the tall figure had vanished into the spruce grove; I could hear the receding wails. Not fever, then.

I realized that my breasts had begun to tingle and stiffen in response to the crying, and smiled, a little ruefully. Strange, that instinct went so deep and lasted so long— would I come one day to a point when nothing in me stirred to the sound of a crying baby, to the scent of a man aroused, to the brush of my own long hair against the skin of my naked back? And if I did come to such a point—would I mourn the loss, I wondered, or find myself peaceful, left to contemplate existence without the intrusion of such animal sensations?

It wasn't only the glories of the flesh that were the gifts of the world, after all; a doctor sees the plentiful miseries flesh is heir to, as well—and yet . . . standing cool in the flood of late summer's air from the window, the boards smooth under my bare feet and the touch of wind on bare skin . . . I could not wish to be a pure spirit—not yet.

The crying grew louder, and I heard the low murmur of an adult's voice below it, trying unsuccessfully to soothe it. Roger, then.

I cupped my breasts gently, liking the soft, full weight of them. I remembered what they'd been like when I was very young; small hard swellings, so sensitive that the touch of a boy's hand made me weak in the knees. The touch of my own hand, come to that. They were different now—and yet peculiarly the same.

This was not the discovery of a new and unimagined

thing, but rather only a new awareness, the acknowledgment of something that had risen while my back was turned, like a shadow cast upon the wall, its presence unsuspected, seen only when I turned to look at it—but there all the time.

*Oh, I have a little shadow that goes in and out with me,*
*And what can be the use of him, is more than I can see.*

And if I turned my back again, the shadow would not leave me. It was irrevocably attached to me, whether I chose to notice it or not, crouched always insubstantial, intangible but *present*, small to vanishing under my feet when the light of other preoccupations shone upon me, blown up to gigantic proportions in the glare of some sudden urge.

Resident demon, or guardian angel? Or only the shadow of the beast, constant reminder of the inescapability of the body and its hungers?

Another noise mingled with the whinging below; coughing, I thought, but it didn't stop, and the rhythm sounded wrong. I put my head out, cautious as a snail after a thunderstorm, and made out a few words in the rasping gurgle.

" . . . *excavating for a mine . . . forty-niner . . . da-aughter, Clementine.*"

Roger was singing.

I felt the tears sting my eyes, and drew my head in hastily, lest I be seen. There was no tune to it—the pitch varied no more than the hooting of wind across the mouth of an empty bottle—and yet it was music. A dogged, ragged gasp of a song, and yet Jemmy's wailing quieted to sniffling sobs, as though he was trying to make out the words, so painfully forced through his father's scarred throat.

"*Fed she duck-lings . . . by the wa-ter . . .*" He was having to gasp for breath after each whispered phrase, the sound of it like tearing linen. I curled my fingers into fists, as though by sheer force of will I could help him get the words out.

"*Herring box-es . . . without top-ses . . . san-dals were for . . . Clementine.*" The breeze was rising again, stirring in the tops of the trees. The next line was lost in their rustle, and I heard no more for a minute or two, strain my ears as I would.

Then I saw Jamie, standing still.

He made no noise, but I felt him at once; a warmth, a thickening, in the cool air of the room.

"Are ye well, Sassenach?" he asked softly from the doorway.

"Yes, fine." I spoke in a whisper, not to wake Lizzie and her father, who slept in the back bedroom. "Just needed a breath of air; I didn't mean to wake you."

He came closer, a tall naked ghost, smelling of sleep.

"I always wake when you do, Sassenach; I sleep ill without ye by my side." He touched my forehead briefly. "I thought ye were maybe fevered; the bed was damp where ye'd lain. You're sure you're all right?"

"I was hot; I couldn't sleep. But yes, I'm all right. And you?" I touched his face; his skin was warm with sleep.

He came to stand beside me at the window, looking out into the late summer night. The moon was full, and the birds were restless; from near at hand, I heard the faint chirp of a late-nesting warbler, and farther off, the squeak of a hunting saw-whet owl.

"You recall Laurence Sterne?" Jamie asked, evidently reminded of the naturalist by the sounds.

"I doubt anyone who's met him would forget him," I said dryly. "The bag of dried spiders makes rather an impression. To say nothing of the smell." Sterne carried with him a distinctive aroma, composed in equal parts of natural body odor, an expensive cologne that he favored—which was sufficiently strong to compete with—though not to conquer— the pungencies of various preservatives such as camphor and alcohol—and a faint reek of decay from the specimens he collected.

He chuckled softly.

"That's true. He stinks worse than you do."

"I do not stink!" I said indignantly.

"Mmphm." He took my hand and lifted it to his nose, sniffing delicately. "Onions," he said, "and garlic. Something hot . . . peppercorns. Aye, and clove. Squirrel-blood and meat-juice." His tongue flicked out like a snake's, touching my knuckles. "Starch—potatoes—and something woody. Toadstools."

"Not fair at all," I said, trying to get my hand back. "You

know perfectly well what we had for dinner. And they weren't toadstools, they were woodears."

"Mm?" He turned my hand over and sniffed at my palm, then my wrist and up my forearm. "Vinegar and dill; ye've been making cucumber pickles, aye? Good, I like those. Mm, oh, and soured milk here in the fine hairs on your arm—were ye splashed churning butter, or skimming cream?"

"You guess, since you're so good at it."

"Butter."

"Damn." I was still trying to pull away, but only because the stubble on his face tickled the sensitive skin of my upper arm. He smelled his way up my arm into the hollow of my shoulder, making me squeak as the strands of his hair drifted across my skin.

He lifted my arm a bit, touched the damp silky hair there, and ran his fingers under his nose. *"Eau de femme,"* he murmured, and I heard the laughter in his voice. *"Ma petite fleur."*

"And I *bathed*, too," I said ruefully.

"Aye, with the sunflower soap," he said, a slight tone of surprise in his voice as he sniffed at the hollow of my collarbone. I gave a small, high-pitched yelp, and he reached up to lay a large, warm hand across my mouth. *He* smelt of gunpowder, hay, and manure, but I couldn't say so, what with him muffling me.

He straightened a little, and leaned close, so the roughness of his whiskers brushed my cheek. His hand fell away, and I felt the softness of his lips against my temple, the butterfly touch of his tongue on my skin.

"And salt," he said, very softly, his breath warm on my face. "There is salt on your face, and your lashes are wet. D'ye weep, Sassenach?"

"No," I said, though I had a sudden, irrational urge to do just that. "No, I sweat. I was . . . hot."

I wasn't any longer; my skin was cool; cold where the night-draft from the window chilled my backside.

"Ah, but here . . . mm." He was on his knees now, one arm about my waist to hold me still, his nose buried in the hollow between my breasts. "Oh," he said, and his voice had changed again.

I didn't normally wear perfume, but I had a special oil,

sent from the Indies, made with orange flowers, jasmine, vanilla beans, and cinnamon. I had only a tiny vial, and wore a small dab infrequently—for occasions that I thought might perhaps be special.

"Ye wanted me," he said ruefully. "And I fell asleep without even touching you. I'm sorry, Sassenach. Ye should have said."

"You were tired." His hand had left my mouth; I stroked his hair, smoothing the long dark strands behind his ear. He laughed, and I felt the warmth of his breath on my bare stomach.

"Ye could raise me from the dead for that, Sassenach, and I wouldna mind it."

He stood up then, facing me, and even in the dim light I could see that no such desperate measures on my part would be required.

"It's hot," I said. "I'm sweating."

"Ye think I'm not?"

His hands closed on my waist and he lifted me suddenly, setting me down on the broad windowsill. I gasped at contact with the cool wood, reflexively grasping the window frame on either side.

"What on earth are you doing?"

He didn't bother answering; it was an entirely rhetorical question, in any case.

"*Eau de femme,*" he murmured, his soft hair brushing across my thighs as he knelt. The floorboards creaked under his weight. "*Parfum d'amour*, mm?"

The cool breeze lifted my hair, drew it tickling across my back like the lightest of lover's touches. Jamie's hands were firm on the curve of my hips; I was in no danger of falling, and yet I felt the dizzy drop behind me, the clear and endless night, with its star-strewn empty sky into which I might fall and go on falling, a tiny speck, blazing hotter and hotter with the friction of my passage, bursting finally into the incandescence of a shooting . . . star.

"Ssh," Jamie murmured, far off. He was standing now, his hands on my waist, and the moaning noise might have been the wind, or me. His fingers brushed my lips. They might have been matches, striking flames against my skin. Heat danced over me, belly and breast, neck and face, burning in front, cool behind, like St. Lawrence on his gridiron.

I wrapped my legs around him, one heel settled in the cleft of his buttocks, the solid strength of his hips between my legs my only anchor.

"Let go," he said in my ear. "I'll hold you." I did let go, and leaned back on the air, safe in his hands.

"YOU DID START OUT to tell me something about Laurence Sterne," I murmured drowsily, much later.

"So I did." Jamie stretched and settled himself, a hand curved proprietorially over my buttock. My knuckles brushed the hairs on his thigh. It was too hot to lie pressed together, but we didn't want to separate entirely.

"We were talking of birds; he bein' uncommon fond of them. I asked him why it was that in the late summer, the birds sing at night—the nights are shorter then, ye'd think they'd want their rest, but no. There's rustling and twittering and all manner o' carryings-on, all the night long in the hedges and the trees."

"Are there? I hadn't noticed."

"Ye're no in the habit of sleeping in the forest, Sassenach," he said tolerantly. "I have been, and so had Sterne. He'd noticed the same thing, he said, and wondered why."

"And did he have an answer?"

"Not an answer—but a theory, at least."

"Oh, even better," I said, in sleepy amusement.

He gave a soft grunt of agreement and rolled slightly to one side, admitting a little welcome air between our salty skins. I could see the gleam of moisture over the slope of his shoulder, and the prickle of sweat among the dark curly hairs of his chest. He scratched gently at it, with a softly agreeable rasping sound.

"What he did was to capture a number of the birds, and shut them up in cages lined with blotting paper."

"What?" That waked me up a bit, if only to laugh. "Whatever for?"

"Well, not lined entirely, only on the floor," he explained.

"He put out a wee plate on the floor filled with ink and a cup of seed in the middle, so that they couldna feed without getting the ink on their feet. Then as they hopped to and fro, their footprints would show on the blotting paper."

"Umm. And what, precisely, did that show—other than black footprints?"

The insects were beginning to find us, drawn by the musk of our heated flesh. A tiny *zeeeeee* by my ear prompted me to slap at the invisible mosquito, then reach for the gauze-cloth that Jamie had pushed back when he rose to find me. This was fastened to an ingenious mechanism—Brianna's invention—fixed to the beam above the bed, so that when unrolled, the cloth fell down on all sides, shielding us from the blood-thirsty hordes of the summer nights.

I pulled it into place with some regret, for while it excluded mosquitoes, gnats, and the unnervingly large mosquito-hawk moths, it also unavoidably shut out some of the air and all sight of the luminous night sky beyond the window. I lay down again at a little distance on the bed; while Jamie's natural furnace was a great boon on winter nights, it had its drawbacks in the summer. I didn't mind melting in an inferno of blazing desire, if it came to that, but I had no more clean shifts.

"There were a great many footprints, Sassenach—but most of them were on one side of the cage. In all the cages."

"Oh, really? And what did Sterne think that signified?"

"Well, he had the bright thought of putting down a compass by the cages. And it seems that all the night through, the birds were hopping and striving toward the southeast—which is the direction in which they migrate, come the fall."

"That's very interesting." I pulled my hair back into a tail, lifting it off my neck for coolness. "But it's not quite the time to migrate, is it, in late summer? And they don't fly at night, do they, even when they migrate?"

"No. It was as though they felt the imminence of flight, and the pull of it—and that disturbed their rest. The stranger it was, because most of the birds that he had were young ones, who had never yet made the journey; they hadna seen the place where they were bound, and yet they felt it there—calling to them, perhaps, rousing them from sleep."

I moved slightly, and Jamie lifted his hand from my leg.

"Zugunruhe," he said softly, tracing with a fingertip the damp mark he had left on my skin.

"What's that?"

"It's what Sterne called it—the wakefulness of the wee birds, getting ready to leave on their long flight."

"Does it mean something in particular?"

"Aye. 'Ruhe' is stillness, rest. And 'zug' is a journey of some sort. So 'zugunruhe' is a restlessness—the uneasiness before a long journey."

I rolled toward him, butting my forehead affectionately against his shoulder. I inhaled, in the style of one savoring the delicate aroma of a fine cigar.

*"Eau d'homme?"*

He raised his head and sniffed dubiously, wrinkling up his nose.

*"Eau de chèvre,* I think," he said. "Though it might be something worse. Is there a French word for skunk, I wonder?"

*"Le Pew."* I suggested, giggling.

The birds sang all night.

## 108

## TULACH ARD

*October, 1772*

JAMIE NODDED at something behind him, smiling.

"I see we've help today."

Roger looked back to see Jemmy stumping along behind them, his small fair brow furrowed in fierce concentration, a fist-sized rock clutched to his chest with both hands. Roger wanted to laugh at the sight, but instead turned and squatted down, waiting for the boy to catch them up.

"Is that for the new hogpen, *a ghille ruaidh*?" he said.

Jemmy nodded solemnly. The morning was still cool, but the little boy's cheeks glowed with effort.

"Thank you," Roger said gravely. He held out his hand. "Shall I take it, then?"

Jemmy shook his head violently, heavy fringe flying.

"Me do!"

"It's a long walk, *a ghille ruaidh*," Jamie said. "And your mother will miss ye, no?"

"No!"

"Grand-da's right, *a bhalaich*, Mummy needs you," Roger said, reaching for the rock. "Here, let me take . . ."

"No!" Jemmy clutched the rock protectively against his smock, mouth set in a stubborn line.

"But ye can't . . ." Jamie began.

"Come!"

"No, I said ye must . . ." Roger began.

"COME!"

"Now, look, lad—" both men began together, then stopped, looked at each other, and laughed.

"Where's Mummy, then?" Roger said, trying another tack. "Mummy will be worried about you, aye?"

The small red head shook in vehement negation.

"Claire said the women meant to be quilting today," Jamie said to Roger. "Marsali's brought a pattern; they'll maybe have started the stitching of it." He squatted down beside Roger, eye to eye with his grandson.

"Have ye got away from your mother, then?"

The soft pink mouth, hitherto clamped tight, twitched, allowing a small giggle to escape.

"Thought so," Roger said in resignation. "Come on, then. Back to the house." He stood up and swung the little boy up into his arms, rock and all.

"No, no! NO!" Jemmy stiffened in resistance, his feet digging painfully into Roger's belly as his body arched backward like a bow. "Me help! Me HELP!"

Trying to make his own arguments heard through Jemmy's roars without shouting, while at the same time keeping the boy from falling backward onto his head, Roger didn't at first hear the cries from the direction of the house. When he finally resorted to clapping a hand over his offspring's wide-open mouth, though, feminine calls of "Jeeeeemmmeeeeeeee!" were clearly audible through the trees.

"See, Mrs. Lizzie's looking for ye," Jamie said to his grandson, jerking a thumb toward the sound.

"Not only Lizzie," Roger said. More women's voices were echoing the chorus, with increasing notes of annoyance. "Mum and Grannie Claire and Grannie Bug and Auntie Marsali, too, from the sounds of it. They don't sound very pleased with you, lad."

"We'd best take him, back, then," Jamie said. He looked at his grandson, not without sympathy. "Mind, you're like to get your bum smacked, laddie. Women dinna like it when ye run off on them."

This threatening prospect caused Jemmy to drop his rock and wrap his arms and legs tightly round Roger.

"Go with YOU, Daddy," he said coaxingly.

"But Mummy—"

"NO MUMMY! Want Daddy!"

Roger patted Jemmy's back, small but solid under his grubby smock. He was torn; this was the first time Jem had so definitely wanted *him* in preference to Bree, and he had to admit to a sneaking feeling of flattery. Even if his son's present partiality sprang as much from an urge to avoid punishment as from a desire for his company, Jem *had* wanted to come with him.

"I suppose we could take him," he said to Jamie, over Jem's head, now nestled trustingly against his collarbone. "Just for the morning; I could fetch him back at noon."

"Oh, aye," Jamie said. He smiled at his grandson, picked up the fallen stone, and handed it back to him. "Building hogpens is proper man's work, aye? None of this prinking and yaffling the ladies are so fond of."

"Speaking of yaffling . . ." Roger lifted his chin in the

direction of the house, where the cries of "JEEMEEEEE!" were now taking on a distinctly irritated tone, tinged with panic. "We'd best tell them we have him."

"I'll go." Jamie dropped the rucksack off his shoulder with a sigh, and raised one eyebrow at his grandson. "Mind, lad, ye owe me. When women are in a fret, they'll take it out on the first man they see, whether he's to blame or not. Like enough I'll get *my* bum smacked." He rolled his eyes, but grinned at Jemmy, then turned and set off for the house at a trot.

Jemmy giggled.

"Smack, Grand-da!" he called.

"Hush, wee rascal." Roger gave him a soft slap on the bottom, and realized that Jem was wearing short breeks under his smock, but no clout under them. He swung the boy down onto his feet.

"D'ye need to go potty?" he asked automatically, falling into Brianna's peculiar idiom.

"No," Jem said, just as automatically, but with a reflexive kneading of his crotch that made his father take him by the arm, firmly steering him off the path and behind a convenient bush.

"Come on. Let's have a try, while we wait for Grand-da."

IT SEEMED RATHER a long time before Jamie reappeared, though the indignant cries of the searchers had been quickly stilled. If Jamie had got his bum smacked, Roger thought cynically, he appeared to have enjoyed it. A slight flush showed on the high cheekbones, and he wore a faint but definite air of satisfaction.

This was explained at once, though, when Jamie produced a small bundle from inside his shirt and unwrapped a linen towel, revealing half a dozen fresh biscuits, still warm, and dripping with melted butter and honey.

"I think perhaps Mrs. Bug meant them for the quilting circle," he said, distributing the booty. "But there was plenty of batter left in the bowl; I doubt they'll be missed."

"If they are, I'll blame it on you," Roger assured him, catching a dribble of warm honey that ran down his wrist. He wiped it off and sucked his finger, eyes closing momentarily in ecstasy.

"What now, ye'd give me up to the Inquisition?" Jamie's eyes creased into blue triangles of amusement as he wiped crumbs from his mouth. "And after I shared my plunder with ye, too—there's gratitude!"

"Your reputation will stand it," Roger said wryly. "Jem and I are *persona non grata* after what happened to her spice cake last week, but Himself can do no wrong, as far as Grannie Bug is concerned. She wouldn't mind if you ate the entire contents of the pantry single-handed."

Jamie licked a smear of honey from the corner of his mouth, with the smug complacency of a man permanently in Mrs. Bug's good books.

"Well, that's as may be," he admitted. "Still, if ye expect to blame it on me, we'd best wipe a bit of the evidence off the laddie before we go home."

Jemmy had been addressing himself to his treat with single-minded concentration, with the result that his entire face gleamed with butter, daubs of honey ran in amber trails down his smock, and what appeared to be several small globs of half-chewed biscuit were stuck in his hair.

"How in hell did you do that so fast?" Roger demanded in amazement. "Look what ye've done to your shirt! Your mother will kill us both." He took the towel and made an abortive attempt to wipe some of the mess off, but succeeded only in spreading it farther.

"Dinna fash," Jamie said tolerantly. "He'll be so covered wi' filth by the end of the day, his mother will never notice a few crumbs extra. Watch out, lad!" A quick grab saved half a biscuit that had broken off as the boy made an attempt to cram the last pastry into his mouth in a single gulp.

"Still," Jamie said, biting thoughtfully into the rescued biscuit-half as he looked at his grandson, "perhaps we'll souse him in the creek a bit. We dinna want the pigs to smell the honey on him."

A faint qualm of unease went over Roger, as he realized that Jamie was in fact not joking about the pigs. It was common to see or hear pigs in the wood nearby, rooting through the leaf-mold under oaks and poplars, or grunting blissfully over a trove of chestnut mast. Food was plentiful at this season, and the pigs were no threat to grown men. A small boy, though, smelling of sweetness ... you thought of pigs as only eating roots and nuts, but Roger had a vivid memory of the big white sow, seen a few days before, with the naked, blood-smeared tail of a possum dangling from her maw as she champed placidly away.

A chunk of biscuit seemed to be stuck in his throat. He picked Jemmy up, despite the stickiness, and tucked him giggling under one arm, so the little boy's arms and legs dangled in the air.

"Come on, then," Roger said, resigned. "Mummy won't like it a bit, if you get eaten by a pig."

FENCE POLES LAY piled near the stone pillar. Roger dug about until he found a splintered piece short enough for convenience, and used it to lever a big chunk of granite up far enough to get both hands under it. Squatting, he got it onto his thighs, and very slowly stood up, his back straightening one vertebra at a time, fingers digging into the lichen-splotched surface with the effort of lifting. The rag tied round his head was drenched, and perspiration was running down his face. He shook his head to flick the stinging sweat out of his eyes.

"Daddy, Daddy!"

Roger felt a sudden tug at his breeches, blinked sweat out of his eye, and planted his feet well apart to keep his balance without dropping the heavy rock. He tightened his grip and glanced down, annoyed.

"What, lad?"

Jemmy had tight hold of the cloth with both hands. He was looking toward the wood.

"Pig, Daddy," he whispered. "*Big* pig."

Roger glanced in the direction of the little boy's gaze and froze.

It was a huge black boar, perhaps eight feet away. The thing stood more than three feet at the shoulder, and must weigh two hundred pounds or more, with curving yellow tushes the length of Jemmy's forearm. It stood with lifted head, piggy snout moistly working as it snuffed the air for food or threat.

"Shit," Roger said involuntarily.

Jemmy, who would normally have seized on any inadvertent vulgarity and trumpeted it gleefully, now merely clung tighter to his father's leg.

Thoughts raced through Roger's mind like colliding freight cars. Would it attack if he moved? He had to move; the muscles of his arms were trembling under the strain. He'd splashed Jem with water; did the boy still smell—or look—like something on the pig's menu?

He picked one coherent thought out of the wreckage.

"Jem," he said, his voice very calm, "get behind me. Do it *now*," he added with emphasis, as the boar turned its head in their direction.

It saw them; he could see the small dark eyes change focus. It took a few steps forward, its hooves absurdly small and dainty under its menacing bulk.

"Do you see Grand-da, Jem?" he asked, keeping his voice calm. Streaks of fire were burning through his arms, and his elbows felt as though they'd been crushed in a vise.

"No," Jemmy whispered. Roger could feel the little boy crowding close behind him, pressed against his legs.

"Well, look round. He went to the stream; he'll be coming back from that direction. Turn round and look."

The boar was cautious, but not afraid. That was what came of not hunting the things sufficiently, he thought. They ought to be gutting a few in the wood once a week, as an object lesson to the rest.

"Grand-da!" Jemmy's voice rang out from behind him, shrill with fear.

At the sound, the pig's hackles sprang suddenly erect in a ridge of coarse hair down its spine and it lowered its head, muscles bunching.

"Run, Jem!" Roger cried. "Run to Grand-da!" A surge of adrenaline shot through him and suddenly the rock weighed nothing. He flung it at the charging pig, catching it on the shoulder. It gave a *whuff!* of surprise, faltered, then opened its mouth with a roar and came at him, tushes slashing as it swung its head.

He couldn't duck aside and let it go past; Jem was still close behind him. He kicked it in the jaw with all his strength, then flung himself on it, grasping for a hold round its neck.

His fingers slipped and slid, unable to get a firm grip on the wiry hair, stubbing and sliding off the hard rolls of tight-packed flesh. Christ, it was like wrestling an animated sack of concrete! He felt something warm and wet on his hand and jerked it back; had it slashed him? He felt no pain. Maybe only saliva from the gnashing jaws—maybe blood from a gash too deep to feel. No time to look. He thrust the hand back down, flailing blindly, got his fingers round a hairy leg, and pulled hard.

The pig fell sideways with a squeal of surprise, throwing him off its back. He hit the ground on hands and one knee, and his knee struck stone. A bolt of pain shot from ankle to groin, and he curled up involuntarily, momentarily paralyzed from the shock.

The boar was up, shaking itself with a grunt and a rattle of bristles, but facing away from him. Dust rose from its coat and he could see the corkscrew tail, coiled up tight against its rump. A second more, and the pig would turn, rip him from gut to gullet, and stamp on the pieces. He grabbed for a rock, but it burst in his hand, nothing but a clod of dirt.

The gasp and thud of a running man came from his left, and he heard a breathless shout.

*"Tulach Ard! Tulach Ard!"*

The boar heard Jamie's cry and swung snorting round to meet this new enemy, mouth agape and eyes gone red with rage.

Jamie had his dirk in his hand; Roger saw the gleam of metal as Jamie dropped low and swung it wide, slashing at the boar, then danced aside as it charged. A knife. Fight that thing with a *knife*?

*You are out of your fucking mind*, Roger thought quite clearly.

"No, I'm not," Jamie said, panting, and Roger realized

that he must have spoken aloud. Jamie crouched, balanced on the balls of his feet, and reached his free hand toward Roger, his eyes still fastened on the pig, which had paused, kneading the ground with its hooves and clashing its teeth, swinging its head back and forth between the two men, estimating its chances.

*"Bioran!"* Jamie said, beckoning urgently. "Stick, spear—gie it to me!"

Spear . . . the splintered fence-pole. His numbed leg still wouldn't work, but he could move. He threw himself to the side, grabbed the ragged shaft of wood, and fell back on his haunches, bracing it before him like a boar-spear, sharp end pointed toward the foe.

*"Tulach Ard!"* he bellowed. "Come here, you fat fucker!"

Distracted for an instant, the boar swung toward him. Jamie lunged at it, stabbing down, aiming between the shoulder blades. There was a piercing squeal and the boar wheeled, blood flying from a deep gash in its shoulder. Jamie threw himself sideways, tripped on something, fell, and skidded hard across the mud and grass, the knife spinning from his outflung hand.

Lunging forward, Roger jabbed his makeshift spear as hard as he could just below the boar's tail. The animal uttered a piercing squeal and appeared to rise straight into the air. The spear jerked through his hands, rough bark ripping skin off his palms. He grabbed it hard and managed to keep hold of it as the boar crashed onto its side in a blur of writhing fury, gnashing, roaring, and spraying blood and black mud in all directions.

Jamie was up, mud-streaked and bellowing. He'd got hold of another fence-pole, with which he took a mighty swing at the rising pig, the wood meeting its head with a crack like a well-hit baseball just as the animal achieved its feet. The boar, mildly stunned, gave a grunt and sat down.

A shrill cry from behind made Roger whirl on his haunches. Jemmy, his grandfather's dirk held over his head with both hands and wobbling precariously, was staggering toward the boar, his face beet-red with ferocious intent.

"Jem!" he shouted. "Get back!"

The boar grunted loudly behind him, and Jamie shouted

something. Roger had no attention to spare; he lunged toward his son, but caught a flicker of movement from the wood beyond Jemmy that made him glance up. A streak of gray, low to the ground and moving so fast that he had no more than an impression of its nature.

That was enough.

"Wolves!" he shouted to Jamie, and with a feeling that wolves on top of pigs was patently unfair, reached Jemmy, grabbed the knife, and threw himself on top of the boy.

He pressed himself to the ground, feeling Jemmy squirm frantically under him, and waited, feeling strangely calm. Would it be tusk or tooth? he wondered.

"It's all right, Jem. Be still. It's all right, Daddy's got you." His forehead was pressed against the earth, Jem's head tucked in the hollow of his shoulder. He had one arm sheltering the little boy, the knife gripped in his other hand. He hunched his shoulders, feeling the back of his neck bare and vulnerable, but couldn't move to protect it.

He could hear the wolf now, howling and yipping to its companions. The boar was making an ungodly noise, a sort of long, continuous scream, and Jamie, too short of breath to go on shouting, seemed to be calling it names in brief, incoherent bursts of Gaelic.

There was an odd whirr overhead and a peculiar, hollow-sounding *thump!*, succeeded by sudden and utter silence.

Startled, Roger raised his head a few inches, and saw the pig standing a few feet before him, its jaw hanging open in what looked like sheer astonishment. Jamie was standing behind it, smeared from forehead to knee with blood-streaked mud, and wearing an identical expression.

Then the boar's front legs gave way and it fell to its knees. It wobbled, eyes glazing, and collapsed onto its side, the shaft of an arrow poking up, looking frail and inconsequential by comparison to the animal's bulk.

Jemmy was squirming and crying underneath him. He sat up slowly, and gathered the little boy up into his arms. He noticed, remotely, that his hands were shaking, but he felt curiously blank. The torn skin on his palms stung, and his knee was throbbing. Patting Jemmy's back in automatic comfort, he turned his head toward the wood and saw the Indian standing at the edge of the trees, bow in hand.

It occurred to him, dimly, to look for the wolf. It was nosing at the pig's carcass, no more than a few feet from Jamie, but his father-in-law was paying it no mind at all. He too was staring at the Indian.

"Ian," he said softly, and a look of incredulous joy blossomed slowly through the smears of mud, grass, and blood. "Oh, Christ. It's Ian."

# 109

# THE VOICE OF TIME

AS LIZZIE HAD NO MOTHER to see to her proper "fitting out" for marriage, the women on the Ridge had grouped together to provide things like petticoats, nightgowns, and knitted stockings, with a few of the more talented ladies piecing quilt blocks. When a quilt-top was completed, everyone would come up to the "Big House" to see to the actual quilting—the laborious stitching together of quilt-top and backing, with whatever might be available in the way of batting—worn-out blankets, stitched-together rags, or wool-combings—laid in between quilt-top and backing for warmth.

I had neither great talent nor great patience for sewing generally, but I did have the manual dexterity for small, fine stitches. More importantly, I had a large kitchen with good light and enough room for a quilting-frame, plus the services of Mrs. Bug, who kept the quilters well supplied with mugs of tea and endless plates of apple scones.

We were in the midst of quilting a block pattern Mrs.

Evan Lindsay had pieced out in creams and blues, when Jamie appeared suddenly in the door to the hallway. Caught up in an absorbing conversation about the snoring of husbands in general and theirs in particular, most of the women didn't notice him, but I was facing the door. He seemed not to want to interrupt, or to attract attention, for he didn't come into the room—but once he'd caught my eye, he jerked his head urgently, and disappeared toward his study.

I glanced at Bree, who was sitting next to me. She'd seen him; she raised an eyebrow and shrugged. I popped the knot—jerking the knotted end of my thread up between the layers of fabric, so it wouldn't show—stabbed my needle through the quilt-top, and got up, murmuring an excuse.

"Give him beer to his supper," Mrs. Chisholm was advising Mrs. Aberfeldy. "A great deal of it, and well-watered. That way, he'll have to wake to piss every half-hour, and can't get started wi' the sort of rumption that shakes the shingles loose."

"Oh, aye," Mrs. Aberfeldy objected. "I tried that. But then when he comes back to bed, he's wantin' to . . . mmphm." She flushed red as the ladies all cackled. "I get less sleep than I do with the snorin'!"

Jamie was waiting in the hall. The moment I appeared, he grabbed me by the arm and hustled me out of the front door.

"What—" I began, bewildered. Then I saw the tall Indian sitting on the edge of the stoop.

"What—" I said again, and then he stood up, turned, and smiled at me.

"Ian!" I shrieked, and flung myself into his arms.

He was thin and hard as a piece of sun-dried rawhide, and his clothes smelled of wood-damp and earth, with a faint echo of the smoke and body-smells of a long-house. I stood back, wiping my eyes, to look at him, and a cold nose nudged my hand, making me utter another small shriek.

"You!" I said to Rollo. "I thought I'd never see you again!" Overcome with emotion, I rubbed his ears madly. He uttered a short bark and dropped to his forepaws, wagging equally madly.

"Dog! Dog-dog! Here, dog!" Jemmy burst from the door of his own cabin, running as fast as his short legs would carry him, wet hair standing on end and face beaming. Rollo shot toward him, hitting him amidships and bowling him over in a flurry of squeals.

I had at first feared that Rollo—who was, after all, half-wolf—saw Jemmy as prey, but it was immediately apparent that the two were merely engaged in mutually ecstatic play. Brianna's maternal sonar had picked up the squealing, though, and she came rushing to the door.

"What—" she began, eyes going to the melee taking place on the grass. Then Ian stepped forward, took her in his arms, and kissed her. Her shriek in turn brought the quilting circle boiling out onto the porch, in an eruption of questions, exclamations, and small subsidiary shrieks in acknowledgment of the general excitement.

In the midst of the resulting pandemonium, I suddenly noticed that Roger, who had appeared from somewhere, was sporting a fresh raw graze across his forehead, a black eye, and a clean shirt. I glanced at Jamie, who was standing next to me watching the goings-on, his face wreathed in a permanent grin. His shirt, by contrast, was not only filthy but ripped down the front, and with an enormous rent in one sleeve. There were huge smears of mud and dried blood on the linen, too, though I didn't see any fresh blood showing. Given Jemmy's wet hair and clean shirt—not that it was, anymore—this was all highly suspicious.

"What on earth have you lot been doing?" I demanded.

He shook his head, still grinning.

"It doesna signify, Sassenach. Though I have got a fresh hog for ye to butcher—when ye've the time."

I pushed back a lock of hair in exasperation.

"Is this the local equivalent of killing the fatted calf in honor of the prodigal's return?" I asked, nodding at Ian, who was by now completely submerged in a tide of women. Lizzie, I saw, was clinging to one of his arms, her pale face absolutely ablaze with excitement. I felt a slight qualm, seeing it, but pushed it away for the moment.

"Has Ian brought friends? Or—his family, perhaps?" He had said his wife was expecting, and that was nearly two years back. The child—if all had gone well—must be nearly old enough to walk.

Jamie's smile dimmed a little at that.

"No," he said. "He's alone. Save for the dog, of course," he added, with a nod at Rollo, who was lying on his back, paws in the air, squirming happily under Jemmy's onslaught.

"Oh. Well." I smoothed down my hair and re-tied the ribbon, beginning to think what ought to be done regarding the quilters, the fresh hog, and some sort of celebratory supper—though I supposed Mrs. Bug would deal with that.

"How long is he staying, did he say?"

Jamie took a deep breath, putting a hand on my back.

"For good," he said, and his voice was full of joy—but with an odd tinge of sadness that made me look up at him in puzzlement. "He's come home."

IT WAS VERY LATE indeed before the butchering, the quilting, and the supper were all finished, and the visitors finally left, charged with gossip. Though not so much gossip as all that; Ian had been friendly to everyone, but reticent, saying very little about his journey from the north—and nothing at all about the reasons behind it.

"Did Ian tell you anything?" I asked Jamie, finding him temporarily alone in his study before dinner. He shook his head.

"Verra little. Only that he had come back to stay."

"Do you suppose something dreadful happened to his wife? And the baby?" I felt a deep pang of distress, both for Ian, and for the slight, pretty Mohawk girl called Wakyo'teyehsnonhsa—Works With Her Hands. Ian had called her Emily. Death in childbirth was not uncommon, even among the Indians.

Jamie shook his head again, looking sober.

"I dinna ken, but I think it must be something of the kind. He hasna spoken of them at all—and the lad's eyes are a great deal older than he is."

Lizzie had appeared at the door then, with an urgent message from Mrs. Bug regarding dispositions for supper, and I had to go. Following Lizzie toward the kitchen, though, I couldn't help wondering just what Ian's return might mean to her—particularly if we were right in our suppositions about Ian's Mohawk wife.

Lizzie had been half in love with Ian, before he had left, and had pined for months following his decision to stay with the Kahnyen'kehaka. But that was more than two years ago, and two years can be a very long time, especially in a young person's life.

I knew what Jamie meant about Ian's eyes, and knew for certain that he wasn't the same impulsive, cheerful lad we had left with the Mohawk. Lizzie wasn't quite the timidly adoring girl-mouse she had been, either.

What she *was*, though, was Manfred McGillivray's betrothed. I could only be thankful that neither Ute McGillivray nor any of her daughters had been present at this afternoon's quilting circle. With luck, the glamor of Ian's return would be short-lived.

"Will you be all right down here?" I asked Ian, dubiously. I had put several quilts and a goose-down pillow on the surgery table for him, he having politely rejected Mr. Wemyss's offer of his own bed and Mrs. Bug's desire to make him a comfortable pallet before the kitchen hearth.

"Oh, aye, Auntie," he said, and grinned at me. "Ye wouldna credit the places Rollo and I have been sleeping." He stretched, yawning and blinking. "Christ—I've no been up past sunset anytime this month or more."

"And up at dawn, too, I expect. That's why I thought you might be better in here; no one will disturb you, if you'd like to sleep late in the morning."

He laughed at that.

"Only if I leave the window open, so Rollo can come and go as he likes. Though he seems to think the huntin' might be good enough inside."

Rollo was seated in the middle of the floor, muzzle lifted in anticipation, his yellow wolf-eyes fixed unwaveringly on the upper cupboard door. A low rumbling noise, like water bumping in a kettle, issued from behind the door.

"I'll gie ye odds on the cat, Ian," Jamie observed, coming into the surgery. "He's a verra high opinion of himself, has wee Adso. I saw him chase a fox, last week."

"The fact that you were behind him with a gun had nothing to do with the fox's running away, of course," I said.

"Well, not so far as yon cheetie's concerned," Jamie agreed, grinning.

"Cheetie," Ian repeated softly. "It feels . . . verra good to speak Scots again, Uncle Jamie."

Jamie's hand brushed Ian's arm lightly.

"I suppose it does, *a mhic a pheathar*," he said, just as softly. "Will ye have forgot all your Gaelic, then?"

"*'S beag 'tha fhios aig fear a bhaile mar 'tha fear na mara bèo*," Ian replied, without hesitation. It was a well-known saying: "Little does the landsman know how the seaman lives."

Jamie laughed in gratified surprise, and Ian grinned broadly back. His face was weathered to a deep brown, and the dotted lines of his Mohawk tattoos ran in fierce crescents from nose to cheekbones—but for a moment, I saw his hazel eyes dance with mischief, and saw again the lad we had known.

"I used to say things over in my mind," he said, the grin fading a little. "I'd look at things, and say the words in my mind—'*Avbhar*,' '*Coire*,' '*Skirlie*'—so as not to forget." He glanced shyly at Jamie. "Ye did tell me to remember, Uncle."

Jamie blinked, and cleared his throat.

"So I did, Ian," he murmured. "I'm glad of it." He squeezed Ian's shoulder hard—and then they were embracing fiercely, thumping each other's backs with wordless emotion.

By the time I had wiped my own eyes and blown my nose, they had separated and resumed an air of elaborate casualness, affecting to ignore my descent into female sentiment.

"I kept hold of the Scots and the Gaelic, Uncle," Ian said, clearing his own throat. "The Latin was a bit beyond me, though."

"I canna think ye'd have much occasion to practice your Latin," Jamie said. He wiped his shirtsleeve under his nose, smiling. "Unless a wandering Jesuit happened by."

Ian looked a little queer at that. He glanced from Jamie to me, then at the door to the surgery, to be sure no one was coming.

"Well, it wasna exactly that, Uncle," he said.

He walked quietly to the door, peeked out into the hall-way, then closed the door softly, and came back to the table. He had worn a small leather bag tied at his waist, which—aside from knife, bow, and quiver—appeared to contain the whole of his worldly possessions. He had put this aside earlier, but now picked it up and rummaged briefly in it, withdrawing a small book, bound in black leather. He handed this to Jamie, who took it, looking puzzled.

"When I—that is, just before I left Snaketown—the old lady, Tewaktenyonh, gave me that wee book. I'd seen it before; Emily"—he stopped, clearing his throat hard, then went on steadily—"Emily begged a page of it for me, to send ye a note to say all was well. Did ye get that?"

"Yes, we did," I assured him. "Jamie sent it to your mother, later."

"Oh, aye?" Ian's expression lightened at thought of his mother. "That's good. She'll be pleased to hear I've come back, I hope."

"I'll lay ye any odds ye like on that one," Jamie assured him. "But what's this?" He lifted the book, raising a brow in question. "It looks like a priest's breviary."

"So it does." Ian nodded, scratching at a mosquito bite on his neck. "That's not what it is, though. Look at it, aye?"

I moved close to Jamie, looking over his elbow as he opened the book. There was a ragged edge of paper, where the flyleaf had been torn out. There was no title page, though, nor printing. The book appeared to be a journal of some sort; the pages were filled with writing in black ink.

Two words stood alone at the top of the first page, scrawled in large, shaky letters.

*Ego sum*, they said. *I am.*

"Are you, then?" said Jamie, half under his breath. "Aye, and who will ye be?" Half down the page, the writing continued. Here the writing was smaller, more controlled, though something seemed odd-looking about it.

*"Prima cogitatio est . . ."*

"This is the first thing that comes into my head," Jamie read softly, translating aloud.

*"I am; I still exist. Did I, in that place between? I must have, for I remember it. I will try later to describe it. Now I have no words. I feel very ill."*

The letters were small and rounded, each printed singly. The work of a neat and careful writer, but they staggered drunkenly, words slanting up the page. He did feel ill, if the writing were any indication.

When the tidy printing resumed on the next page, it had steadied, along with the writer's nerve.

*"Ibi denum locus . . .*
*It is the place. Of course it would be. But it is the proper time as well, I know it. The trees, the bushes are different. There was a clearing to the west and now it is completely filled with laurels. I was looking at a big magnolia tree when I stepped into the circle, and now it is gone; there is an oak sapling there. The sound is different. There is no noise of highway and vehicles in the distance. Only birds, singing very loudly. Wind.*
*I am still dizzy. My legs are weak. I cannot stand yet. I woke under the wall where the snake eats its tail, but some distance from the cavity where we laid the circle. I must have crawled, there are dirt and scratches on my hands and clothes. I lay for some time after waking, too ill to rise. I am better now. Still weak and sick, but I am exultant nonetheless. It worked. We have succeeded."*

*"We?"* I said, looking at Jamie with both eyebrows raised. He shrugged and turned the page.

*"The stone is gone. Only a smear of soot in my pocket. Raymond was right, then. It was a small unpolished sapphire. I must remember to put down everything, for the sake of others who may come after me."*

A small, cold shudder of premonition flowed up my back and over me, making my scalp tingle as the hair on my head began to stand. Others who may come after me. Not meaning to, I reached out and touched the book; an irresistible impulse. I needed to touch him somehow, make some contact with the vanished writer of these words.

Jamie glanced curiously at me. With some effort, I took my hand away, curling my fingers into a fist. He hesitated for a moment, but then looked back at the book, as though the neat black writing compelled his gaze as it did my own.

I knew now what had struck me about that writing. It had not been written with a quill. Quill-writing, even the best, was uneven in color, dark where the quill was freshly dipped, fading slowly through a line of writing. Every word of this was the same—written in a thin, hard line of black ink that slightly dented the fibers of the page. Quills never did that.

"Ball point," I said. "He wrote it with a ball-point pen. My God."

Jamie glanced back at me. I must have looked pale, for he moved as though to close the book, but I shook my head, motioning to him to go on reading. He frowned dubiously, but with one eye still on me, looked back. Then his attention shifted wholly to the book, and his brows rose as he looked at the writing on the next page.

"Look," he said softly, turning the book toward me and pointing to one line. Written in Latin like the others, but there were unfamiliar words mixed into the text—long, strange-looking words.

"Mohawk?" Jamie said. He looked up, into Ian's face. "That is a word in an Indian tongue, surely. One of the Algonquian tongues, no?"

"Rains Hard," said Ian, quietly. "It is the Kahnyen'kehaka—the Mohawk tongue, Uncle. Rains Hard is someone's name. And the others written there, too—Strong Walker, Six Turtles, and Talks With Spirits."

"I thought the Mohawk have no written language," Jamie said, one ruddy eyebrow lifted. Ian shook his head.

"Nor they do, Uncle Jamie. But someone wrote that"—he nodded at the page,—"and if ye work out the sound of the words . . ." He shrugged. "They are Mohawk names. I'm sure of it."

Jamie looked at him for a long moment, then without comment bent his head and resumed his translation.

*"I had one of the sapphires, Rains Hard the other. Talks With Spirits had a ruby, Strong Walker took the diamond, and Six Turtles had the emerald. We were not sure of the diagram—whether it should be four points, for the directions of the compass, or five, in a pentacle. But there were the five of us, sworn by blood to this deed, so we laid the circle with five points."*

There was a small gap between this sentence and the next, and the writing changed, becoming now firm and even, as though the writer had paused, then taken up his story at a later point.

*"I have gone back to look. There is no sign of the circle—but I see no reason why there should be, after all. I think I must have been unconscious for some time; we laid the circle just inside the mouth of the crevice, but there are no marks in the earth there to show how I crawled or rolled to the spot where I woke, and yet there are marks in the dust, made by rain. My clothes are damp, but I cannot tell if this is from rain, from morning dew, or sweat from lying in the sun; it was near midday when I woke, for the sun was over-head, and it was hot. I am thirsty. Did I crawl away from the crevice, and then collapse? Or was I thrown some distance by the force of the transition?"*

I had the most curious sense, hearing this, that the words were echoing, somewhere inside my head. It wasn't that I had heard it before, and yet the words had a dreadful famil-iarity. I shook my head, to clear it, and looked up to find Ian's eyes on me, soft brown and full of speculation.

"Yes," I said baldly, in answer to his look. "I am. Brianna and Roger, too." Jamie, who had paused to disentangle a phrase, looked up. He saw Ian's face, and mine, and reached to put his hand on mine.

"How much could ye read, lad?" he asked quietly.

"Quite a lot, Uncle," Ian answered, but his eyes didn't leave my face. "Not everything"—a brief smile touched his lips—"and I'm sure I havena got the grammar right—but I think I understand it. Do you?"

It wasn't clear whether he addressed the question to me or Jamie; both of us hesitated, exchanged a glance—then I turned back to Ian and nodded, and so did Jamie. Jamie's hand tightened on mine.

"Mmphm," Ian said, and his face lighted with an expression of profound satisfaction. "I *knew* ye weren't a fairy, Auntie Claire!"

UNABLE TO STAY AWAKE much longer, Ian had finally retired, yawning, though pausing in his flight toward bed to seize Rollo by the scruff of the neck and immobilize him while I removed Adso from the cupboard, fluffed to twice his normal size and hissing like a snake. Holding the cat by his own scruff to avoid being disemboweled, I had carried him out of harm's way, up to our bedroom, where I dumped him unceremoniously on the bed, turning at once to Jamie.

"What happened next?" I demanded.

He was already lighting a fresh candle. Unfastening his shirt with one hand and thumbing the book open with the other, he sank down onto the bed, still absorbed in the reading.

"He couldna find any of his friends. He searched the countryside nearby for two days, calling, but there was no trace. He was verra much distraught, but at last he thought he must go on; he was in need of food, and had nothing but a knife and a bit of salt with him. He must hunt, or find people."

Ian said that Tewaktenyonh had given him the book, enjoining him to bring it to me. It had belonged to a man named Otter-Tooth, she said—a member of my family.

An icy finger had touched my spine at that—and hadn't gone away. Little ripples of unease kept tickling over my skin like the touch of ghostly fingers. My family, indeed.

I *had* told her that Otter-Tooth was perhaps one of "my family," unable to describe the peculiar kinship of time-travelers in any other way. I had never met Otter-Tooth—at least not in the flesh—but if he was the man I thought he was, then his was the head buried in our small burying-ground—complete with silver fillings.

Perhaps I was at last going to learn who he had really been—and how on earth he had come to meet such a startling end.

"He wasna much of a hunter," Jamie said critically, frowning at the page. "Couldna catch so much as a ground-squirrel with a snare, and in the middle of summer, forbye!"

Fortunately for Otter-Tooth—if it was indeed he—he had been familiar with a number of edible plants, and seemed extremely pleased with himself for recognizing pawpaw and persimmon.

"Recognizing a persimmon is no great feat, for God's sake," I said. "They look like orange baseballs!"

"And they taste like the bottom of a chamber pot," Jamie added, he not caring at all for persimmons. "Still, he was hungry by that time, and if ye're hungry enough . . ." He trailed off, lips moving silently as he continued his translation.

The man had wandered through the wilderness for some time—though "wandering" seemed not quite right; he had chosen a specific direction, guided by the sun and stars. That seemed odd—what had he been looking for?

Whatever it was, he had eventually found a village. He didn't speak the language of the inhabitants—"Why ought he to think he should?" Jamie wondered aloud—but had become extraordinarily distraught, according to his writing, at the discovery that the women were using iron kettles to cook with.

"Tewaktenyonh said that!" I interrupted. "When she was telling me about him—if it's the same man," I added, *pro forma*, "she said he carried on all the time about the cooking pots, and the knives and guns. He said the Indians were . . . How did she put it?—they needed to 'return to the ways of their ancestors,' or the white man would eat them alive."

"A verra excitable fellow," Jamie muttered, still riveted to the book. "And with a taste for rhetoric, too."

Within a page or two, though, the source of Otter-Tooth's strange preoccupation with cooking pots became somewhat clearer.

"I have failed," Jamie read. "I am too late." He straightened his back, and glanced at me, then went on.

> *I do not know exactly when I am, nor can I find out—these people will not reckon years by any scale I know, even had I enough of their tongue to ask. But I know I am too late.*
>
> *Had I arrived when I meant to, before 1650, there would be no iron in a village so far inland. To find it here in such casual use means that I am at least fifty years too late—perhaps more!"*

Otter-Tooth was cast into great gloom by this discovery, and spent several days in utmost despair. But then he pulled himself together, determining that there was nothing to be done but to go on. And so he had set out alone, though with the gift of some food from the villagers—heading north.

"I've no idea what the man thought he was doing," Jamie observed. "But I will say he shows courage. His friends are dead or gone, and he's nothing with him, no notion where he is—and yet he goes on."

"Yes—though in all honesty, I don't suppose he could think of anything else to do," I said. I touched the book again, gently, remembering the first few days after my own passage through the stones.

The difference, of course, was that this man had chosen to come through the stones on purpose. Exactly *why* he had done it—and how—was not revealed just yet.

Traveling alone through the wilderness, with nothing but this small book for company, Otter-Tooth had—he said—decided that he would occupy his mind with setting down an account of his journey, with its motives and intents.

> *Perhaps I will not succeed in my attempt—our attempt. In fact, it seems likely at the moment that I will simply perish here in the wilderness. But if that is so, then the thought that some record of our noble*

*endeavor remains will be some consolation—and it is all the memorial I can provide for those who were my brothers; my companions in this adventure."*

Jamie stopped and rubbed his eyes. The candle had burned far down; my own eyes were watering so much from yawning that I could scarcely see the page in the flickering light, and I felt light-headed from fatigue.

"Let's stop," I said, and laid my head on Jamie's shoulder, taking comfort from its warm solidness. "I can't stay awake any longer, I really can't—and it doesn't seem right to rush through his story. Besides"—I stopped, interrupted by a jaw-cracking yawn that left me swaying and blinking—"perhaps Bree and Roger should hear this, too."

Jamie caught my yawn and gaped hugely, then shook his head violently, blinking like a large red owl shaken rudely out of its tree.

"Aye, ye're right, Sassenach." He closed the book, and laid it gently on the table by the bed.

I didn't bother with any sort of bedtime toilette, merely removing my outer clothes, brushing my teeth, and crawling into bed in my shift. Adso, who had been snoozing happily on the pillow, was disgruntled at our appropriation of his space, but grumpily moved at Jamie's insistence, making his way to the foot of the bed, where he collapsed on my feet like a large, furry rug.

After a few moments, though, he abandoned his pique, kneaded the bedclothes—and my feet—gently with his claws, and began to purr in a somnolent fashion.

I found his presence almost as soothing as Jamie's soft, regular snoring. For the most part, I felt at home, secure in the place I had made for myself in this world, happy to be with Jamie, whatever the circumstances. But now and then, I saw suddenly and clearly the magnitude of the gulf I had crossed—the dizzying loss of the world I had been born to—and felt very much alone. And afraid.

Hearing this man's words, his panic and desperation, had brought back to me the memory of all the terror and doubts of my journeys through the stones.

I cuddled close to my sleeping husband, warmed and anchored, and heard Otter-Tooth's words, as though they were spoken in my inner ear—a cry of desolation that echoed through the barriers of time and language.

Toward the foot of that one page, the tiny Latin writing had grown increasingly hasty, some of the letters no more than dots of ink, the endings of words swallowed in a frantic spider's dance. And then the last lines, done in English, the writer's Latin dissolved in desperation.

> *Oh God, oh God. . . .*
> *Where are they?*

IT WAS AFTERNOON of the next day before we managed to collect Brianna, Roger, and Ian and retire privately to Jamie's study without attracting unwanted attention. The night before, the haze of fatigue, following on the heels of Ian's sudden appearance, had combined to make almost anything seem reasonable. But going about my chores in the bright light of morning, I found it increasingly difficult to believe that the journal really existed, and was not merely something I had dreamed.

There it was, though, small, but black and solid on Jamie's desk-table. He and Ian had spent the morning in his study, immersed in translation; when I joined him, I could tell by the way Jamie's hair was sticking up that he had found the journal's account either deeply absorbing, terribly upsetting—or possibly both.

"I've told them what it is," he said without preamble, nodding toward Roger and Bree. The two of them sat close together on stools, looking solemn. Jemmy, having refused to be parted from his mother, was under the table, playing with a string of carved wooden beads.

"Have you read through the whole thing?" I asked, subsiding into the extra chair.

Jamie nodded, with a glance at Young Ian, who stood by the window, too restless to sit. His hair was cropped short, but nearly as disordered as Jamie's.

"Aye, we have. I'm no going to read the whole thing

aloud, but I thought I'd best start wi' the bit where he's made up his mind to put it all down from the beginning."

He had marked the spot with the scrap of tanned leather he customarily used as a bookmark. Opening the journal, he found his spot and began to read.

> *"The name I was given at birth is Robert Springer.*
> *I reject this name, and all that goes with it, because it*
> *is the bitter fruit of centuries of murder and injustice,*
> *a symbol of theft, slavery, and oppression—"*

Jamie looked up over the edge of the book, remarking, "Ye see why I dinna want to read every word; the man's gey tedious about it." Running a finger across the page, he resumed:

"In the year of Our Lord—their lord, that Christ in whose name they rape and pillage and—well, more of the same, but when he gets down to it, it was the year nineteen-hundred-and-sixty-eight. So I suppose ye'll be familiar wi' all this murder and pillage he's talking about?" He raised his eyebrows at Bree and Roger.

Bree sat up abruptly, clutching Roger's arm.

"I know that name," she said, sounding breathless. "Robert Springer. I know it!"

"You knew *him?*" I asked, feeling a thrill of something—excitement, dread, or simple curiosity—run through me.

She shook her head.

"No, I didn't know *him*, but I know the name—I saw it in the newspapers. Did you—?" She turned toward Roger, but he shook his head, frowning.

"Well, maybe you wouldn't, in the UK, but it was a big deal in Boston. I *think* Robert Springer was one of the Montauk Five."

Jamie pinched the bridge of his nose.

"The five what?"

"It was just a—a thing people did to call attention to themselves." Brianna flapped a hand in dismissal. "It's not important. They were AIM activists, or at least they started out that way, only they were even too nuts for AIM, and so—"

"Nuts? W'ere nuts?" Jemmy, picking the only word of

personal interest out of this account, emerged from under the table.

"Not that kind of nuts, baby, sorry." Looking around for some object of interest to distract him, Bree slipped off her silver bracelet and gave it to him. Seeing the puzzled looks on the faces of father and cousin, she took a deep breath and started over, trying—with occasional clarifications from Roger and me—to define things, and give a short, if confused, account of the sad state of the American Indian in the twentieth century.

"So this Robert Springer is—or was—an Indian, of sorts, in your own time?" Jamie tapped his fingers in a brief tattoo on the table, frowning in concentration. "Well, that corresponds wi' his own account; he and his friends apparently took no little exception to the behavior of what they called 'whites.' I would suppose those to be Englishmen? Or Europeans, at least?"

"Well, yes—except that by nineteen sixty-eight, of course they weren't Europeans anymore, they were Americans, only the Indians were Americans first—and so that's when they started calling themselves *native* Americans, and—"

Roger patted her knee, stopping her in mid-flow.

"Perhaps we can do the history a bit later," he suggested. "What was it ye read about Robert Springer in the papers?"

"Oh." Taken aback, she furrowed her brow in concentration. "He disappeared. They disappeared—the Montauk Five, I mean. They were all wanted by the government, for blowing things up or threatening to or something, I forget—and they were arrested, but then they got out on bail, and the next thing you know, they'd all disappeared."

"Evidently so," Young Ian murmured, glancing toward the journal.

"It was a big deal in the papers for a week or so," Brianna went on. "The other activist types were all accusing the government of having done away with them, so that stuff coming out of the trial wouldn't embarrass the government, and of course the government was denying it. So there was a big search on, and I think I remember reading that they found the body of one of the missing men—out in the woods somewhere in New Hampshire or Vermont or someplace—but they couldn't tell how he died—and nobody turned up any trace of the others."

*"Where are they?"* I quoted softly, the hair rippling on the back of my neck. *"My God, where are they?"*

Jamie nodded soberly.

"Aye, then; I think this Springer may well be your man." He touched the page before him, with something like respect.

"He and his four companions all renounced any association with the white world, taking new names from their real heritage—or so he says."

"That would be the proper thing to do," Ian said softly. He had a new, strange stillness to him, and I was forcibly reminded that he had been a Mohawk for the last two years—washed free of his white blood, renamed Wolf's Brother—one of the Kahnyen'kehaka, the Guardians of the Western Gate.

I thought Jamie was aware of this stillness, too, but he kept his eyes on the journal, flipping pages slowly as he summarized their content.

Robert Springer—or Ta'wineonawira—"Otter-Tooth," as he chose henceforth to call himself, had numerous associations in the shadow world of extremist politics and the deeper shadows of what he called Native American shamanism—I had no notion how much resemblance there was between what he was doing, and the original beliefs of the Iroquois, but Otter-Tooth believed that he was descended from the Mohawk, and embraced such remnants of tradition as he could find—or invent.

*It was at a naming ceremony that I first met Raymond.* I sat up abruptly, hearing that. He had mentioned Raymond in the beginning, but I had taken no particular note of the name, then.

"Does he describe this Raymond?" I asked urgently.

Jamie shook his head.

"Not in terms of appearance, no. He says only that Raymond was a great shaman, who could transform himself into birds or animals—and who could walk through time," he added delicately. He glanced at me, one eyebrow raised.

"I don't know," I said. "I thought so, once—but now, I don't know."

"What?" Ian was looking back and forth between us, puzzled. I shook my head, smoothing back my hair.

"Never mind. Someone I knew in Paris was named Raymond, and I thought—but what in the name of *anything* would he be doing in America in nineteen sixty-eight?" I burst out.

"Well, you were there, aye?" Jamie pointed out. "But putting that aside for the moment—" He returned to the text, laying it all out in the oddly stilted English of the translation: Intrigued by Raymond, Otter-Tooth had met with the man repeatedly, and brought several of his closest friends to him as well. Gradually, the scheme—*a great, audacious plan, stunning in conception*—"Modest, isn't he?" Roger muttered—*had been conceived.*

> *"There was a test. Many failed, but I did not. There were five of us who passed the test, who heard the voice of time, five of us who swore in our blood and by our blood that we would undertake this great venture, to rescue our people from catastrophe. To rewrite their history and redress their wrongs, to—"*

Roger gave a faint groan.

"Oh, God," he said. "What did they mean to do—assassinate Christopher Columbus?"

"Not quite," I said. "He meant to arrive before 1600, he said. What happened then, do you know?"

"I dinna ken what happened then," Jamie told me, rubbing a hand through his hair, "but I ken well enough what he thought he was doing. His plan was to go to the Iroquois League, and rouse them against the white settlers. He thought that there were few enough settlers then, that the Indians could easily wipe them out, if the Iroquois led the way."

"Perhaps he was right," Ian said softly. "I've heard the old people tell the stories. When the first of the O'seronni came, how they were welcomed, how they brought trade goods. A hundred years ago, the O'seronni were few—and the Kahnyen'kehaka were masters, leaders of the Nations. Aye, they could have done it—had they wished to."

"Well, but he couldn't possibly have stopped the Europeans," Brianna objected. "There were just way too many. He didn't mean to get the Mohawk to invade Europe, did he?"

A broad grin crossed Jamie's face at the thought.

"I should have liked to see that," he said. "The Mohawk would have given the Sassenachs something to think about. But no, alas"—he gave me a sardonic look—"our friend Robert Springer wasna *quite* so ambitious."

What Otter-Tooth and his companions had had in mind was sufficiently ambitious, though—and perhaps . . . just perhaps . . . possible. Their intention was not to prevent white settlement altogether—they were, just barely, sane enough to realize the impossibility of that. What they intended was to put the Indians on their guard against the whites, to establish trade on *their* terms, to deal from a position of power.

Instead of allowing them to settle in great numbers, they might keep the whites bottled up in small towns. Instead of allowing them to build fortifications, demand weapons from the start. Establish trade on their own terms. Keep them outnumbered, and outgunned—and force the Europeans to teach them the ways of metal.

"Prometheus redux," I said, and Jamie snorted.

Roger shook his head, half-admiringly.

"It's a crack-brained scheme," he said, "but ye do have to admire their nerve. It might just possibly have worked—*if* he could convince the Iroquois League, and *if* they acted at the right time, before the balance of power shifted to the Europeans. It all went wrong, though, didn't it? First he comes to the wrong time—much too late—and then he realizes none of his friends have made it with him."

I saw goosebumps rise suddenly on Brianna's arms, and caught the look she sent me—one of sudden understanding. She had abruptly imagined just how it might be, to arrive suddenly out of one's own time . . . alone.

I gave her a small smile, and put my hand on Jamie's arm. Absentmindedly, he put his own hand over mine, and squeezed it gently.

"Aye. He nearly despaired, as he says, when he realized that it had all gone wrong. He thought of going back—but he didna have a gemstone anymore, and this Raymond had said ye must have one, for protection."

"He did find one eventually, though," I said. Getting up, I reached to the top shelf and brought down the big raw opal, its inner fire flickering through the carved spiral on its surface.

"That is—I'm assuming there can't have been multiple Indians named Otter-Tooth, associated with Snaketown." I had found the opal buried with the skull with silver fillings. Tewaktenyonh, leader of the Council of Mothers in Snaketown, had recognized it, and had told me the story of Otter-Tooth, and how he met his death. I shivered, though it was warm in the room.

The big smooth stone felt warm in my hand, too; I rubbed a thumb gingerly over the spiral. *The snake that eats its tail,* he'd said.

"Aye. He doesna mention that, though." Jamie sat back, running both hands through his loosened hair, then rubbing a hand over his face. "The story ends with him deciding that there's no help for it; whatever year it may be—and he had no notion—and whether he was alone or not, he would carry out his plan."

Everyone was silent for a moment, regarding the enormity—and the futility—of such a plan.

"He can't have thought it would work," Roger said, the rasping husk of his voice giving the words a sense of finality.

Jamie shook his head, looking down at the book, though his eyes were clearly looking through it, dark blue and remote.

"Nor he did," he said softly. "What he said, here at the last"—his fingers touched the page, very gently—"was that thousands of his people had died for their freedom, thousands more would die in years to come. He would walk the path they walked, for the honor of his blood, and to die fighting was no more than a warrior of the Mohawk should ask."

I heard Ian draw breath behind me in a sigh, and Brianna bent her head, so the bright hair hid her face. Roger's own face was turned toward her, grave in profile—but it was none of them I saw. I saw a man with his face painted black for death, walking through a dripping forest at night, holding a torch that burned with cold fire.

A yank on my skirt pulled me away from this vision, and I glanced down to find Jemmy standing beside me, pulling on my hand.

"Watsat?"

"What—oh! It's a rock, sweetheart; a pretty rock, see?" I held out the opal, and he seized it with both hands, plumping down on his bottom to look at it.

Brianna wiped a hand underneath her nose, and Roger cleared his throat with a noise like ripping cloth.

"What I want to know," he said gruffly, gesturing toward the journal, "is why in hell did he write that in Latin?"

"Oh. He says that. He'd learnt Latin in school—perhaps that was what turned him against Europeans"—Jamie grinned at Young Ian, who grimaced—"and he thought if he wrote in Latin, anyone who happened to see it would think it only a priest's book of prayers, and pay it no heed."

"They did think that—the Kahnyen'kehaka," Ian put in. "Old Tewaktenyonh kept the book, though. And when I—left, she gave me the wee book, and said as I must bring it back wi' me, and give it to you, Auntie Claire."

"To me?" I felt a sense of hesitation at touching the book, but nonetheless reached out a hand and touched the open pages. The ink, I saw, had begun to run dry toward the end—the letters skipped and stuttered, and some words were no more than indentations on the paper. Had he thrown the empty pen away, I wondered, or kept it, a useless reminder of his vanished future?

"Do you think she knew what was in the book?" I asked. Ian's face was impassive, but his soft hazel eyes held a hint of trouble. When he had been a Scot, he hadn't been one to hide his feelings.

"I dinna ken," he said. "She kent *something*, but I couldna say what. She didna tell me—only that I must bring ye the book." He hesitated, glancing from me to Brianna and Roger, then back. "Is it true?" he asked. "What ye said, cousin—about what will happen to the Indians?"

She looked up, meeting his eyes squarely, and nodded.

"I'm afraid so," she said softly. "I'm sorry, Ian."

He only nodded, rubbing a knuckle down the bridge of his nose, but I wondered.

He hadn't forsaken his own people, I knew, but the Kahnyen'kehaka were his as well. No matter what had happened to cause him to leave.

I was opening my mouth to ask Ian about his wife, when I heard Jemmy. He had retired back under the table with his prize, and had been talking to it in a genially conversational—if unintelligible—manner for several minutes. His voice had suddenly changed, though, to a tone of alarm.

"Hot," he said, "Mummy, HOT!"

Brianna was already rising from her stool, a look of concern on her face, when I heard the noise. It was a high-pitched ringing sound, like the weird singing of a crystal goblet when you run a wet finger round and round the rim. Roger sat up straight, looking startled.

Brianna bent and snatched Jemmy out from under the table, and as she straightened with him, there was a sudden *pow!* like a gunshot, and the ringing noise abruptly stopped.

"Holy God," said Jamie, rather mildly under the circumstances.

Splinters of glimmering fire protruded from the bookshelf, the books, the walls, and the thick folds of Brianna's skirts. One had whizzed past Roger's head, barely nicking his ear; a thin trickle of blood was running down his neck, though he didn't seem to have noticed yet.

A stipple of brilliant pinpoints glinted on the table—a shower of the sharp needles had been thrust upward through the inch-thick wood. I heard Ian exclaim sharply, and bend to pull a tiny shaft from the flesh of his calf. Jemmy began to cry. Outside, Rollo the dog was barking furiously.

The opal had exploded.

IT WAS STILL broad daylight; the candleflame was nearly invisible, no more than a waver of heat in the late afternoon light from the window. Jamie blew out the taper he had used to light it, and sat down behind his desk.

"Ye didna sense anything odd about yon stone when ye gave it to the lad, Sassenach?"

"No." I still felt shaken by the explosion, the echoes of that eerie noise still chiming in my inner ear. "It felt warm—but everything in the room is warm. And it certainly wasn't making that noise."

"Noise?" He looked at me queerly. "When it went bang, d'ye mean?"

Now it was my turn to look askance.

"No—before that. Didn't you hear it?" He shook his head, a small frown between his brows, and I glanced round at the others. Bree and Roger nodded—both of them looked pale and ill—but Ian shook his head, looking interested, but puzzled.

"I didna hear a thing," he said. "What did it sound like?"

Brianna opened her mouth to answer, but Jamie raised a hand to stop her.

"A moment, *a nighean*. Jem, *a ruaidh*—did ye hear a noise before the bang?"

Jemmy had settled down from his fright, but was still crouching in his mother's lap, thumb in his mouth. He looked at his grandfather out of wide blue eyes that had already begun to show a definite slant, and slowly nodded, not removing the thumb.

"And the stone Grannie gave ye—it was hot?"

Jemmy cast a glare of intense accusation in my direction and nodded again. I felt a small surge of guilt—followed by a much larger one, when I thought of what might have happened, had Bree not snatched him up at once.

We had picked most of the splinters out of the woodwork; they lay on the desk in a small heap of brittle fire. One had sliced a tiny flap of skin from my knuckle; I put it in my mouth, tasting silver blood.

"My God, those things are sharp as broken glass."

"They *are* broken glass." Brianna clutched Jem a little closer.

"Glass? You mean it wasn't a real opal?" Roger raised his brows, leaning forward to pick up one of the needlelike shards.

"Sure it is—but opals are glass. Really hard volcanic

glass. Gemstones are gemstones because they have a crystalline structure that makes them pretty; opals just have a really brittle structure, compared to most." The color was beginning to come back into Brianna's face, though she kept her arms wrapped tightly round her son.

"I knew you could break one if you hit with a hammer or something, but I never heard of one doing *that*." She nodded at the pile of glimmering fragments.

Jamie picked a large shard out of the pile with finger and thumb and held it out to me.

"Put it in your hand, Sassenach. Does it feel warm to you?"

I accepted the jagged piece of stone gingerly. It was thin, nearly weightless, and translucent, sparkling with vivid blues and oranges.

"Yes," I said, tilting my palm cautiously to and fro. "Not remarkably hot—just about skin temperature."

"It felt cool to me," Jamie said. "Give it to Ian."

I transferred the bit of opal to Ian, who put it in the palm of his hand and stroked it cautiously with a fingertip, as though it were some small animal that might bite him if annoyed.

"It feels cool," he reported. "Like a bit of glass, like Cousin Brianna says."

A bit more experimentation established that the stone felt warm—though not strikingly so—to Brianna, Roger, and me—but not to Jamie or Ian. By this time, the wax had melted in the top of the big clock candle, allowing Jamie to extract the gemstones hidden there. He fished them out, rubbed the last of the hot wax off on his handkerchief, and laid them out in a row along the edge of the desk to cool.

Jemmy watched this with great interest, his misadventure apparently forgotten.

"D'ye like these, *a ghille ruaidh*?" Jamie asked him, and he nodded eagerly, leaning out of his mother's lap, reaching toward the stones.

"Hot," he said, then, remembering, shrank back a little, a look of doubt crossing his small, blunt features. "Hot?"

"Well, I do hope not," his grandfather said. He took a deep breath and picked up the emerald, a crudely faceted stone the size of his thumbnail. "Put out your hand, *a bhalaich.*"

Brianna looked as though she wanted to protest, but bit her lower lip, and encouraged Jemmy to do as his grandfather asked. He took the stone, still looking suspicious, but then the look of wariness faded into a smile as he looked down at the stone.

"Pretty rock!"

"Is it hot?" Brianna asked, poised to snatch it out of his hand.

"Yes, hot," he said, with satisfaction, holding it against his stomach.

"Let Mama see." With a little difficulty, Brianna succeeded in getting her fingers onto the rock, though Jemmy wouldn't surrender it. "It's warm," she said, looking up. "Like the piece of opal—but not way hot. If it gets way hot, you drop it *fast,* OK?" she said to Jemmy.

Roger had been watching this with fascination.

"He's got it, hasn't he?" he said softly. "Fifty/fifty, you said, or three chances in four, depending—but he's got it, doesn't he?"

"What?" Jamie glanced at Roger, then me, one red brow raised in question.

"I think he can . . . travel," I said, feeling a tightening of my chest at the thought. "You know what Otter-Tooth said—" I nodded at the journal, which lay discarded on the desk. "He said they had to take a test—to see if they could hear 'the voice of time.' We know that not everyone can . . . do this." I felt unaccountably shy, talking of it before Ian. "But some can. From what Otter-Tooth said, there was a way of finding out who could and couldn't, ahead of time, without having actually to try."

Jemmy was paying no attention to the grown-up conversation, instead rocking back and forth, humming to the stone clutched in his pudgy hand.

"Do you suppose the 'voice of time' is—Jem, can you *hear* the rock?" Roger leaned forward, taking hold of Jemmy's arm to compel his attention away from the emerald. "Jem, is the rock singing to you?"

Jemmy looked up, surprised.

"No," he said uncertainly. Then, "Yes." He held the rock up to his ear, frowning, then thrust it at Roger. "You sing, Daddy!"

Roger accepted the emerald gingerly, smiling at Jemmy.

"I don't know any rock songs," he said, in his husky rasp of a voice. "Unless ye count the Beatles." He lifted the rock to his own ear, looking self-conscious. He listened intently, frowning, then lowered his hand, shaking his head.

"It's not—I can't—I couldna really say I *hear* anything. And yet—here, you try." He passed the stone to Brianna, and she in turn to me. Neither of us heard anything in particular, and yet I thought I could perceive something, if I listened very hard. Not exactly a sound, more a sense of very, very faint vibration.

"What is it?" Ian asked. He had been following the proceedings with rapt interest. "Ye're no *sìdheanach*, the three of ye—but why is it you can do . . . what ye do, and Uncle Jamie and I canna? Ye can't, can ye, Uncle Jamie?" he asked dubiously.

"No, thank God," his uncle replied.

"It's genetic, isn't it?" Brianna asked, looking up. "It has to be."

Jamie and Ian looked wary at the unfamiliar term.

"Genetic?" Ian asked. His feathery brows drew together in puzzlement.

"Why shouldn't it be?" I said. "Everything else is—blood type, eye color."

"But everyone has eyes and blood, Sassenach," Jamie objected. "Whatever color his eyes may be, everyone can see. This—" He waved at the small collection of stones.

I sighed with impatience.

"Yes, but there are other things that are genetic—everything, if you come right down to it! Look—" I turned to him and stuck out my tongue. Jamie blinked, and Brianna giggled at his expression.

Disregarding this, I pulled in my tongue and put it out again, this time with the edges rolled up into a cylinder.

"What about that?" I asked, popping it back in. "Can you do that?"

Jamie looked amused.

"Of course I can." He stuck out a rolled tongue and wiggled it, demonstrating, then pulled it back. "Everyone can do that, surely? Ian?"

"Oh, aye, of course." Ian obligingly demonstrated. "Anyone can."

"I can't," said Brianna. Jamie stared at her, taken aback.

"What d'ye mean ye can't?"

"Bleah." She stuck out a flat tongue and waggled it from side to side. "I can't."

"Of course ye can." Jamie frowned. "Here, it's simple, lass—anyone can do it!" He stuck out his own tongue again, rolling and unrolling it like a paternal anteater, anxiously encouraging its offspring toward an appetizing mass of insects. He glanced at Roger, brows lifted.

"You'd think so, wouldn't you?" Roger said ruefully. He stuck out his own tongue, flat. "Bleah."

"See?" I said triumphantly. "Some people can roll their tongues, and some simply can't. It can't be learned. You're born with it, or you're not."

Jamie looked from Bree to Roger and back, frowning, then turned to me.

"Allowing for the moment that ye may be right—why can the lass not do it, if you and I both can? Ye did assure me she's my daughter, aye?"

"She is most assuredly your daughter," I said. "As anyone with eyes in their head could tell you." He glanced at Brianna, taking in her lean height and mass of ruddy hair. She smiled at him, blue eyes creasing into triangles. He smiled back and turned to me, shrugging in good-natured capitulation.

"Well, I shall take your word for it, Sassenach, as an honorable woman. But the tongue, then?" He rolled his own again, in doubtful fashion, still not quite believing that anyone couldn't do it if they put their mind to it.

"Well, you do know where babies come from," I began. "The egg and the . . ."

"I do," he said, with a noticeable edge to his voice. The tips of his ears turned slightly pink.

"I mean, it takes something from the mother and something from the father." I could feel my own cheeks pinken slightly, but carried on gamely. "Sometimes the father's influence is more visible than the mother's; sometimes the other way round—but both . . . er . . . influences are still there. We call them genes—the things babies get from their two parents that affect the child's appearance and abilities."

Jamie glanced at Jemmy, who was humming again, engaged in trying to balance one gemstone on top of another, the sunlight glinting off his coppery hair. Looking back, he caught Roger's eye, and quickly turned his attention to me.

"Aye, so?"

"Well, genes affect more than simply hair or eye-color. Now," I warmed to my lecture, "each person has two genes for every trait—one from the father, one from the mother. And when the . . er . . gametes are formed in the ovaries and testes—"

"Perhaps ye should tell me all about it later, Sassenach," Jamie interrupted, with a sidelong glance at Brianna. Evidently he didn't think the word "testes" suitable for his daughter's ears; his own were blazing.

"It's all right, Da. I know where babies come from," Bree assured him, grinning.

"Well, then," I said, taking back command of the conversation. "You have a pair of genes for each trait, one gene from your mother and one gene from your father—but when the time comes to pass these on to your own offspring, you can only pass *one* of the pair. Because the child will get another gene from his other parent, you see?" I raised an eyebrow at Jamie and Roger, who nodded in unison, as though hypnotized.

"Right. Well, then. Some genes are said to be dominant, and others recessive. If a person has a dominant gene, then that's the one that will be expressed—will be visible. They may have another gene that's recessive and so you don't see it—but it can still be passed to the offspring."

My collective audience looked wary.

"Surely you learned this in school, Roger?" Bree asked, amused.

"Well, I did," he muttered, "but I think perhaps I wasna paying proper attention at the time. After all, I wasn't expecting it actually to *matter*."

"Right," I said dryly. "Well, then. You and I, Jamie, evidently each have one of the dominant genes that allows us to roll our tongues. *But*—" I continued, raising a finger, "we must also each have a recessive gene, that *doesn't* allow tongue-rolling. And evidently, each of us gave the recessive gene to Bree. Therefore, she can't roll her tongue. Likewise, Roger must have two copies of the non-rolling recessive gene, since if he had even one of the dominant genes, he could do it—and he can't. Q.E.D." I bowed.

"Wat's tes-tees?" inquired a small voice. Jemmy had abandoned his rocks and was looking up at me in profound interest.

"Er . . ." I said. I glanced round the room in search of aid.

"That's Latin for your balls, lad," Roger said gravely, suppressing a grin.

Jemmy looked quite interested at that.

"I gots balls? W'ere I gots balls?"

"Er . . ." said Roger, and glanced at Jamie.

"Mmphm," said Jamie, and looked at the ceiling.

"Well, ye do have a kilt on, Uncle Jamie," Ian said, grinning. Jamie gave his nephew a look of gross betrayal, but before he could move, Roger had leaned forward and cupped Jemmy gently between the legs.

"Just there, *a bhalaich*," he said.

Jemmy kneaded his crotch briefly, then looked at Roger, small strawberry brows knitted into a puzzled frown.

"Nots a ball. 'Sa willy!"

Jamie sighed deeply and got up. He jerked his head at Roger, then reached down and took Jemmy's hand.

"Aye, all right. Come outside with me and your Da, we'll show ye."

Bree's face was the exact shade of her hair, and her shoulders shook briefly. Roger, also suspiciously pink about the cheeks, had opened the door and stood aside for Jamie and Jem to go through.

I didn't think Jamie paused to think about it; seized by impulse, he turned to Jemmy, rolling up his tongue into a cylinder and sticking it out.

"Can you do that, *a ruaidh*?" he asked, pulling it back in again.

Brianna drew in her breath with a sound like a startled duck, and froze. Roger froze, too, his eyes resting on Jemmy as though the little boy were an explosive device, primed to go off like the opal.

A second too late, Jamie realized, and his cheeks went pale. "Damn," he said, very quietly under his breath.

Jemmy's eyes grew round with reproach.

"Bad, Granda! At'sa bad word. Mama?"

"Yes," Brianna said, narrowed eyes on Jamie. "We'll have to wash Grand-da's mouth out with soap, won't we?"

He looked very much as though he had already swallowed a good mouthful of soap, and lye-soap, at that.

"Aye," he said, and cleared his throat. The flush had faded entirely from his face. "Aye, that was verra wicked of me, Jeremiah. I must beg pardon o' the ladies." He bowed, very formally, to me and Brianna. *"Je suis navré, Mesdames. Et Monsieur,"* he added softly to Roger. Roger nodded very slightly. His eyes were still on Jemmy, but his lids were lowered and his face carefully blank.

Jemmy's own round face assumed the expression of beatific delight that he wore whenever French was spoken near him, and—as Jamie had clearly intended—broke immediately into his own pet contribution to that language of art and chivalry.

*"Frère Jacques, Frère Jacques. . . ."*

Roger looked up at Bree, and something seemed to pass through the air between them. He reached down and took hold of Jem's other hand, momentarily interrupting his song.

"So, *a bhalaich*, can ye do it, then?"

*"FRÈRE* . . . do whats?"

"Look at Grand-da." Roger nodded at Jamie, who took a deep breath and quickly put out his tongue, rolled into a cylinder.

"Can ye do that?" Roger asked.

"Chure." Jemmy beamed and put out his tongue. Flat. "Bleah!"

A collective sigh gusted through the room. Jemmy, oblivious, swung his legs up, his weight suspended momentarily from Roger's and Jamie's hands, then stomped his feet down on the floor again, recalling his original question.

"Grand-da gots balls?" he asked, pulling on the men's hands and tilting his head far back to look up at Jamie.

"Aye, lad, I have," Jamie said dryly. "But your Da's are bigger. Come on, then."

And to the sound of Jemmy's tuneless chanting, the men trundled him outside, hanging like a gibbon between them, his knees drawn up to his chin.

## 110

## MAN OF BLOOD

I CRUMBLED DRY SAGE LEAVES in my hands, letting the gray-green flakes fall into the burning coals. The sun hung low in the sky above the chestnut trees, but the small burying-ground lay already in shadow, and the fire was bright.

The five of us stood in a circle around the chunk of granite with which Jamie had marked the stranger's grave. *There were five of us, and so we laid the circle with five points.* By common consent, this was not only for the man with the silver fillings, but for his four unknown companions—and for Daniel Rawlings, whose fresh and final grave lay under a mountain-ash, nearby.

The smoke rose up from the small iron fire-pot, pale and fragrant. I had brought other herbs as well, but I knew that for the Tuscarora, for the Cherokee, and for the Mohawk, sage was holy, the smoke of it cleansing.

I rubbed juniper needles between my hands into the fire, and followed them with rue, called herb-of-grace, and rosemary—that's for remembrance, after all.

The leaves of the trees nearby rustled gently in the evening breeze, and the twilight lit the drifting smoke, turning it from gray to gold as it rose up and up into heaven's vault, where the faint stars waited.

Jamie lifted his head, touched with fire as bright as the blaze by his feet, and looked toward the west, where the souls of the dead fly away. He spoke softly, in Gaelic, but all of us knew enough by now to follow.

> *"Thou goest home this night to thy home of winter,*
> *To thy home of autumn, of spring, and of summer;*
> *Thou goest home this night to thy perpetual home,*
> *To thine eternal bed, to thine eternal slumber.*
>
> *The sleep of the seven lights be thine, O brother,*
> *The sleep of the seven joys be thine, O brother,*
> *The sleep of the seven slumbers be thine, O brother,*
> *On the arm of the Jesus of blessings, the Christ of*
> *     grace.*
>
> *The shade of death lies upon thy face, beloved,*
> *But the Jesus of Grace has His hand round about thee;*
> *In nearness to the Trinity farewell to thy pains,*
> *Christ stands before thee and peace is in His mind."*

Ian stood by him, close, but not touching. The fading light touched his face, fierce upon his scars. He said it first in the Mohawk tongue, but then in English, for the rest of us.

> *"Be the hunt successful,*
> *Be your enemies destroyed before your eyes,*
> *Be your heart ever joyful in the lodge of your brothers."*

"Ye're meant to say it over and over again, a good many times," he added, ducking his head apologetically. "Wi' the drums, aye? But I thought once would do, for now."

"That will do fine, Ian," Jamie assured him, and looked then toward Roger.

Roger coughed and cleared his throat, then spoke, the husk of his voice as transparent and as penetrating as the smoke.

> *"Lord, make me to know mine end,*
> *And the measure of my days, what it is;*
> *That I may know how frail I am.*
> *Behold, Thou has made my days as an hand-breadth;*
> *And mine age is as nothing before Thee.*
> *Hear my prayer, O Lord, and give ear unto my cry;*
> *Hold not Thy peace at my tears:*
> *For I am a stranger with Thee,*
> *And a sojourner, as all my fathers were."*

We stood in silence then, as the darkness came quietly around us. As the last of the light faded and the leaves overhead lost their brilliance, Brianna picked up the pitcher of water, and poured it over the pot of coals. Smoke and steam rose up in a ghostly cloud, and the scent of remembrance drifted through the trees.

IT WAS NEARLY DARK as we came down the narrow trail back to the house. I could see Brianna in front of me, though, leading the way; the men were a little behind us. The fireflies were out in great profusion, drifting through the trees, and lighting the grass near my feet. One of the little bugs lighted briefly in Brianna's hair and clung there for a moment, blinking.

A wood at twilight holds a deep hush, that bids the heart be still, the foot step lightly on the earth.

"Have ye thought, then, a *cliamhuinn*?" Jamie said, behind me. His voice was low, the tone of it friendly enough—but the formal address made it clear that the question was seriously meant.

"Of what?" Roger's voice was calm, hushed from the service, the rasp of it barely audible.

"Of what ye shall do—you and your family. Now that ye ken both that the wee lad can travel—and what it might mean, if ye stay."

What it might mean to them all. I drew breath, uneasy. War. Battle. Uncertainty, save for the certainty of danger. The danger of illness or accident, for Brianna and Jem. The danger of death in the toils of childbirth, if she was again with child. And for Roger—danger both of body and soul. His head had healed, but I saw the stillness at the back of his eyes, when he thought of Randall Lillywhite.

"Oh, aye," Roger said, softly, invisible behind me. "I have thought—and am still thinking . . . *m'athair-cèile*."

I smiled a little, to hear him call Jamie "father-in-law," but the tone of his voice was altogether serious.

"Shall I tell ye what I think? And you will tell me?"

"Aye, do that. There is time still, for thinking."

"I have been thinking, lately, of Hermon Husband."

"The Quaker?" Jamie sounded surprised. Husband had left the colony with his family, after the battle of Alamance. I thought I heard that they had gone to Maryland.

"Aye, him. What d'ye think might have happened, had he not been a Quaker? Had he gone ahead, and led the Regulators to their war?"

Jamie grunted slightly, thinking.

"I dinna ken," he said, though he sounded interested. "Ye mean they might have succeeded, with a proper leader?"

"Aye. Or maybe not—they'd no weapons, after all—but they would have done better than they did. And if so—"

We had come within sight of the house, now. Light was glowing in the back windows as the hearth-fire was stoked up for the evening, the candles lit for supper.

"What's going to happen here—I am thinking, had the Regulation been properly led, perhaps it would have started here and then; not three years from now, in Massachusetts."

"Aye? And if so, what then?"

Roger gave a brief snort, the verbal equivalent of a shrug.

"Who knows? I know what's going on in England now—they are not ready, they've no notion of what they're risking here. If war were to break out suddenly, with little warning—if it *had* broken out, at Alamance—it might spread quickly. It might be over before the English had a clue what was happening. It might have saved years of warfare, thousands of lives."

"Or not," Jamie said dryly, and Roger laughed.

"Or not," he agreed. "But the point there is this; I think there are times for men of peace—and a time for men of blood, as well."

Brianna had reached the house, but turned and waited for the rest of us. She had been listening to the conversation, too.

Roger stopped beside her, looking up. Bright sparks flew from the chimney in a firework shower, lighting his face by their glow.

"Ye called me," he said at last, still looking up into the blazing dark. "At the Gathering, at the fire."

*"Seas ri mo lâmh, Roger an t'oranaiche, mac Jeremiah mac Choinneich,"* Jamie said quietly. "Aye, I did. Stand by my side, Roger the singer, son of Jeremiah."

*"Seas ri mo lâmh, a mhic mo thaighe,"* Roger said. "Stand by my side—son of my house. Did ye mean that?"

"Ye know that I did."

"Then I mean it, too." He reached out and rested his hand on Jamie's shoulder, and I saw the knuckles whiten as he squeezed.

"I will stand by you. We will stay."

Beside me, Brianna let out the breath she had been holding, in a sigh like the twilight wind.

111

# AND YET GO OUT
# TO MEET IT

THE BIG CLOCK CANDLE had burned down a little, but there were still a good many of the black rings that marked the hours. Jamie dropped the stones back into the pool of melted wax around the flame: one, two, three—and blew it out. The fourth stone, the big topaz, was ensconced in a small wooden box, which I had sewn up in oiled cloth. It was bound for Edinburgh, consigned to Mrs. Bug's cousin's husband, who, with his banking connections, would manage the sale of the stone, and—with the deduction of a suitable commission for his help—would see the funds transmitted to Ned Gowan.

The accompanying letter, lying sealed in the box with the stone, charged Ned to determine whether one Laoghaire MacKenzie was living with a man in a state tantamount to marriage—and if so, further charged him to declare the contract between one Laoghaire MacKenzie and one James Fraser to be fulfilled, whereupon the funds from the sale of the stone were to be placed on deposit in a bank, to be used for the dowry of one Joan MacKenzie Fraser, daughter of the aforesaid Laoghaire, when she should marry.

"You're sure you don't want to ask Ned particularly to tell you who the man is?" I asked.

He shook his head firmly.

"If he chooses to tell me, that's fine. And if he doesna, that's fine, as well." He looked up at me with a faint, wry look. Unsatisfied curiosity was to be his penance, evidently.

Down the hall, I could hear Brianna simultaneously talking to Mrs. Bug and admonishing Jemmy, then Roger's voice, interrupting, and Jemmy's excited squeal as Roger swept him up into the air.

"Do you think Roger chose well?" I asked quietly. I was very glad of Roger's decision—and knew that Jamie was, as well. But in spite of the peculiar perspective that Brianna, Roger, and I had on coming events, I knew that Jamie had far better an idea of what was truly coming. And if the stone passage had its dangers, so did war.

He paused, thinking, then leaned past me, reaching for a small volume at the end of the bookcase. It was bound cheaply in cloth, and much used; an edition of Thucydides he had acquired in the wildly optimistic hope that Germain and Jemmy might eventually learn sufficient Greek to read it.

He opened the book gently, to keep the pages from falling out. Greek lettering looked to me like the conniptions of an ink-soaked worm, but he found the bit he was looking for with no difficulty.

*"The bravest are surely those who have the clearest
vision of what is before them, glory and danger alike,
and yet notwithstanding go out to meet it."*

The words were before him, and yet I thought he was not
reading them from the paper, but from the pages of his memory, from the open book of his heart.

The door slammed, and I heard Roger shouting outside
now, cracked voice raised in warning, calling out to Jemmy,
and then his laugh, deep and half-choked, as Bree said something to him, a lighter sound too far away to hear in words.

Then they moved away, and there was silence, save for the
sough of the wind in the trees.

"The bravest are those who have the clearest vision. Well,
you'd know about that, wouldn't you?" I said softly. I laid a
hand on his shoulder, just where it joined his neck. I traced
the powerful cords of his neck with my thumb, looking at the
worm-writhings on the page. He would, and so would I; for
the vision he had was the one I had shown him.

He kept hold of the book, but tilted his head to one side,
so that his cheek brushed my hand, and the thickness of his
hair touched my wrist, soft and warm.

"Ah, no," he said. "Not me. It's only brave if there's a
choice about it, aye?"

I laughed, sniffed, and wiped the wrist of my free hand
across my eyes.

"And you think you haven't a choice?"

He paused for a moment, then shut the book, though he
continued to hold it in his hands.

"No," he said at last, with a queer tone in his voice. "Not
now."

He turned in his chair, looking through the window. Nothing was visible but the big red spruce at the side of the clearing, and the deep shade of the oak grove behind it, tangled
with the brambles of wild blackberry, escaped from the yard.
The blackened spot where the fiery cross had stood was over-
grown now, covered with thick wild barley.

The air moved and I realized that it was not silent, after
all. The sounds of the mountain were all around us, birds
calling, water rushing in the distance—and there were

voices, too, speaking in the murmured traffic of daily rounds, a word by the pigpen, a call from the privy. And under and over everything, the sound of children, faint shrieks and giggles borne on the restless air.

"I suppose you're right," I said, after a moment. He was; there *was* no choice about it now, and the knowledge gave me a sort of peace. What was coming, would come. We would meet it as best we might, and hope to survive; that was all. If we didn't—perhaps they would. I gathered the tail of his hair in my hand and twined my fingers through it, holding tight, like an anchor's rope.

"What about the other choices, though?" I asked him, looking out with him over the empty dooryard, and into the shades of the forest beyond. "All the ones you made that brought you here? Those were real—and bloody well brave, if you ask me."

Beneath the tip of my index finger, I could feel the hairthin line of his ancient scar, buried deep beneath the ruddy waves. He leaned back against the pull of my hand, and swiveled round to look up at me, so my hand now cupped the bone of his jaw.

"Oh. Well," he said, smiling slightly. His hand touched mine, and drew my fingers into his. "Ye'd know about that, now, wouldn't ye, Sassenach?"

I sat down beside him, close, my hand on his leg, and his hand on mine. We sat thus for a bit, side by side, watching the rain clouds roll in over the river, like a threat of distant war. And I thought that whether it was choice or no choice, it might be that it came to the same thing in the end.

Jamie's hand still lay on mine. It tightened a little, and I glanced at him, but his eyes were still fixed somewhere past the dooryard; past the mountains, and the distant clouds. His grip tightened further, and I felt the edges of my ring press into my flesh.

"When the day shall come, that we do part," he said softly, and turned to look at me, "if my last words are not 'I love you'—ye'll ken it was because I didna have time."